THE BEACH CLUB

ELIN HILDERBRAND

THE BEACH CLUB

St. Martin's Press 🌊 *New York*

Book design by Victoria Kuskowski

ISBN 0-312-26125-X

First Edition: June 2000

10   9   8   7   6   5   4   3   2   1

FOR CHIP,

WHO GAVE ME ENOUGH LOVE EACH DAY

TO LAST LIFETIMES,

AND WHO NEVER ONCE STOPPED BELIEVING

Acknowledgments

My warmest and most sincere thanks to the following people:

Michael Carlisle, my agent and fellow Nantucketer, for making this dream come true.

My entire family.

My "Nantucket family," whose essence is in this book: Rob, Nickie, Eric, Margie, Ginny, John, Jeff, Richard and Amanda, Jeffrey and Sue, Suki, Justin and Forest, the "G" and the "D", Vanessa, Keith, Misha, Sally, Brooks and Parker, John and Kelly, Martha, Glenn, J.L.N., and the great Mary Baker.

For their enormous kindnesses and friendship, thanks to John and Nancy, Paul, Rita and Palmer, Tal, Jonnie, Pat and Doris, Fred, Irene, Jim, Barbie and the rest of the "porch night" crew, and Tim and Mary.

Thanks to Richard and Teena for giving me the best part-time job on the island.

Special thanks to Heather, whose insight and criticism were invaluable.

My love for Nantucket Island is powerful and unlimited, but in the end, there is only one reason why I stayed. His name is Chip Cunningham, he is my husband and my hero, and this book is for him.

THE BEACH CLUB

1

The Opening

May 1

Dear Bill,

Another summer season is about to begin on beautiful Nantucket Island. I have just returned from my winter retreat—Nevis, Vail, Saipan—it's your guess where I've been. The important thing is that I'm back, and I am prepared to sweeten my offer to buy the hotel. I know you have some crazy idea about family loyalty and passing the business on to your daughter, but things don't always work out the way we want them to. Alas, I have learned this the hard way. So as you start this season of sun and sand, consider my offer: twenty-two million. That's a pretty good deal, and if you don't mind my saying so, you're not getting any younger.

Feel free to write to me at the usual P.O. box downtown. I'll be waiting to hear from you.

As ever,

S.B.T.

ON THE FIRST OF May, Mack Petersen swung his Jeep into the parking lot of the Nantucket Beach Club and Hotel for the start of his twelfth summer season as manager, the Almost Head Honcho. Twelve was an important number, Mack decided, with its own name. A dozen. Mack's dozen years of working at the hotel were like eggs, all in one basket, like the Boston cream doughnuts served at the hotel's Continental breakfast, one practically indistinguishable from the next. There were twelve months in a year, twelve signs in the Zodiac, twelve hours of A.M. and P.M. Twelve was a full cycle, a cycle completed.

Maybe Maribel was right, then. Maybe this was the year things would change.

Mack walked across the parking lot to look at Nantucket's most picturesque beach. Over the winter, northeasterly winds blew the sand into smooth, rounded dunes, in some places six and eight feet high. Mack trudged to the top of one of the dunes and gazed out over the water. The Beach Club sat on the north shore of the island, on Nantucket Sound, where the water was as flat and placid as a fishing pond. The white sand was clean and wide, although they lost beach to erosion, some years as much as twenty-five feet. Last year they had gained beach and the owner of the hotel, Bill Elliott, was so happy that he had thrown his arm around Mack's shoulder, and said, "See there? We're not going to lose her after all." As though the Beach Club and Hotel belonged to them both. Which, of course, was not the case.

Mack had stayed on Nantucket through the winter with his girl-friend Maribel, but he hadn't checked on the hotel even once. It was a rule he'd created over the years: *I won't think about the hotel in winter.* Were the shingles falling off? Was the paint peeling? Were they losing beach? Those were questions for Bill and his wife, Therese, but they spent their winters skiing in Aspen, and if anyone were going to check on the place, it would be Mack. But he never did. He knew that if he let it, the hotel would obsess him, drive him crazy.

The most photographed part of the hotel was the pavilion—a covered deck with five blue Adirondack chairs facing the water. All summer, guests sat in the low, wide chairs with their feet up on the railing, drinking coffee, reading the paper. This picture of summer bliss made it into the Nantucket chamber of commerce guide year after year.

The lobby of the hotel was its own freestanding building with a row of windows that looked over the pavilion and the beach. The hotel rooms began outside the back door of the lobby: twenty single-story, cedar-shingled rooms formed a giant L. Ten rooms ran down toward the water and ten rooms faced the water. All the rooms had small decks, and thus the rooms were distinguished by the names, "side deck" and "front deck." Therese had further nicknamed the front deck rooms the "Gold Coast," because they were so expensive.

Twenty rooms might not seem like a lot at first, but the beach also hosted a private Beach Club: One hundred members paid annual dues to sit under umbrellas for the ten weeks of summer. They could have saved themselves the money and gone to Steps Beach to the west, or Jetties Beach to the east, but year after year membership of the Beach Club was full. Mack's primary job was to treat the guests and the Beach Club members like royalty. He arranged dinner reservations and the delivery of flowers, wine, steamed lobsters, birthday cakes. He had a key to every door, and knew the location of every extension cord, vacuum cleaner bag, feather pillow. He hired and fired the staff and created the weekly work schedule. He knew every Beach Club member's name by heart and the names of all the children. Mack ran the place. Bill and Therese had owned the Beach Club and Hotel for twenty years but Mack understood its ins and outs, its cracks, sore spots, and hideaways better than anyone. It had been his course of study now for twelve years.

A thousand guests would walk into the lobby over the next six months. Some had been coming to the hotel as long as Mack had worked there. The baseball managers (in July, over the all-star break), Leo Hearn, a lawyer from Chicago (Memorial Day), Mrs. Ford, a widow who came for the month of September and smoked a pack of cigarettes in her room each day.

Then there would be Andrea Krane, a woman Mack thought he might be in love with. Andrea arrived in June and stayed for three weeks with her autistic son, James. Mack imagined her long, honey-colored hair twisted into a bun or a braid. Smiling a rare smile, because when she arrived at the Beach Club she was happy. She had three weeks stretched in front of her, twenty-one days sparkling like diamonds on a tennis bracelet.

Mack watched the ferry approach in the distance. It was full of people coming to work for the season—waiters and waitresses, ice cream scoopers, lifeguards, landscapers, nannies, chambermaids, bellmen. Twelve years ago it had been Mack on that boat—his first time on the ocean—and when he stepped off at Steamship Wharf his life changed. Nantucket had saved him.

• • •

TWELVE YEARS AGO, MACK was eighteen, a farm boy. Born and raised in Swisher, Iowa, where his father owned a 530-acre farm—corn and soybeans, hogs and chickens. The farm had originally belonged to Mack's grandfather, then his father, and Mack grew up understanding that it would one day be his. School felt like a waste of time, except that it was a place to socialize. Mack loved to talk—the bonus for spending hours on a combine by himself was that his father took him to The Alibi for a greasy ham-and-egg breakfast, or to the feed store— and there was always lots of talk.

Mack's mother worked part-time at an antique store in Swisher—a quiet job of crystal figurines and classical music. Mack's parents belonged to Swisher Presbyterian, but they weren't strict about going to church, nor were they prescriptive about what Mack should believe. In fact, his mother once told him she didn't believe in heaven.

"I just don't believe in it," she said as she scrubbed potatoes at the sink and Mack puzzled over his trigonometry homework at the long oak harvest table. "I believe that when you die, you die, and you're back to where you were before you were born. Oblivion, I guess you'd call it."

Two months before Mack's high school graduation, his parents went out for their Saturday night dinner date. On their way home on Route 380, a tractor trailer sideswiped their car and they crashed into the guardrail and died. There hadn't been foul weather—no rain, no ice. Only carelessness on the part of the truck driver, and possibly, on the part of Mack's father, who should have hit the brakes harder when the truck pulled in front of him. (Had his father been drinking? A cocktail before dinner, wine?) It didn't matter to Mack; it didn't change the fact that two good people were dead. Mack was left orphaned, although *orphaned* wasn't a word anyone used, and neither was it a word Mack thought of often. He was, after all, eighteen. An adult.

Mack left the farm to his father's lawyer, David Pringle, and his father's sidekick Wendell, and the farmhands who worked there. He picked up his high school diploma, caught a bus east and took it as far as it would go, a romantic idea, one his mother would have liked. When the bus stopped in Hyannis, Massachusetts, Mack thought he would find a small apartment and a job, but then he caught his first glimpse of the ocean and he learned there was a boat that would take him even farther east, to an island. Nantucket Island.

Mack found his job at the Beach Club by accident. When the ferry pulled in to Steamship Wharf, Bill Elliott stood waiting on the dock, and when Mack stepped off the boat, Bill tapped his shoulder.

"Are you here for the job at the Beach Club?" Bill asked.

Mack didn't even think about it. "Yes, sir, I am."

He followed Bill to an olive-colored Jeep. Bill hoisted Mack's duffel into the back and they drove off the wharf and down North Beach Road without another word. When they pulled into the parking lot of the hotel, Mack saw the view of the water—he was still not used to so much water—and then he heard a hum. *Hum. Hum.*

"What's that noise?" Mack asked.

"The seagulls?" Bill said. "They can be pretty loud. Where did you come from?"

"Iowa," Mack said.

Bill's forehead wrinkled. "I thought you were coming from New Jersey."

It confirmed Mack's fear: there was some kid from New Jersey standing on the wharf, waiting for Bill to pick him up.

"No, sir, I came from Swisher, Iowa." He heard the noise again. *Hum. Hum.* Home—it sounded like a voice saying "*Home.*" "You don't hear that?" Mack asked.

Bill smiled. "I guess you didn't have too many gulls out in Iowa. I guess this is all brand-new."

"Yes, sir," Mack said. A voice was saying "*Home, home.*" Mack could hear it as plain as day. He extended his hand. "I'm Mack Petersen."

Bill frowned. "Mack Petersen wasn't who I was picking up."

"I know," Mack said. "But you asked if I was here for a job, and I am."

"Do you know anything about hotels?" Bill asked.

"I will soon, I guess," Mack said. And he heard it again; it was the funniest thing. *Home.*

Mack didn't believe in spiritual guides, past lives, fortune-tellers, tarot cards, or crystal balls. He believed in God and in a heaven, despite what his mother told him. But what Mack heard wasn't the voice of God. The voice wasn't coming from the sky, it was coming from the land beneath his feet.

Mack had heard the voice at other times over the past twelve years, too many now to count. He read about phenomena like this—the Taos Hum, the Whisper of Carmel—but never on Nantucket. Mack once found the courage to ask Maribel, "Do you ever hear things on this island? *From* this island? Do you ever hear a voice?" Maribel blinked her blue eyes, and said, "I do think the island has a voice. It's the waves, the birds, the whisper of the dune grass."

Mack never mentioned the voice to anyone again.

MACK LISTENED FOR THE voice now as he lingered on the dune. Just four days earlier, he'd received a phone call from David Pringle, the lawyer who'd supervised the farm in Iowa for all the years since Mack left. David called every now and then urging Mack to rent out the farm-house, or to apprise him of profits and loss, taxes, weather. But he had never sounded as serious as he did four days ago.

"Wendell gave his notice," David said. "He's retiring after harvest."

"Yeah?" Mack said. Wendell, Mack's father's right-hand man, had been in charge since Mack left.

"I told you this was in the future, Mack. I told you to do some thinking."

"You did," Mack said. "You surely did."

"But you haven't done the thinking."

"No," Mack said. "Not really." When had Mack last talked to David? Last November after harvest? A Christmas card? Mack couldn't remember. He only vaguely recalled a conversation about Wendell getting ready to leave.

"We need someone to run things," David said.

"Hire one of the other hands to do it," Mack said. "I trust your judgment, David."

David sighed into the phone. He was a good person, and less like a lawyer than anybody Mack had met on the East Coast, where even men who weren't lawyers acted like lawyers. "Since the Oral B plant opened, we've lost a lot of help," David said. "We haven't had a hand here longer than six months. You want me to put a transient like that in charge of your father's farm?"

"Are they all transients? Aren't there a couple of hardworking kids, looking for a chance?"

"Wendell and I don't think so," David said. "We've talked about it. If your little love affair with that island isn't over, Mack, I mean, if you're going to stick it out in the East, then Wendell and I agree it's time to put the farm up."

"For sale, you mean?"

David hummed into the phone. "Mmmm-hmm."

"I don't think I can do that," Mack said.

"You have the summer to think it over," David said. "If you're not going to sell it, then you ought to come home and do the job yourself. You've been out there a long time."

"Twelve years," Mack said.

"Twelve years." Mack could practically see David shaking his head in disbelief. "Your decision, but this is what your father left you. I'd rather see you sell it than let it fall to pieces."

"Okay," Mack said. "So I'll talk to you in a couple of months, then?"

"I'll be in touch," David said.

MACK COULDN'T IMAGINE SELLING his family's farm but neither could he imagine leaving Nantucket. The farm was the last place he'd kissed his mother's cheek, he was born and raised there, and worked side by side

with his father. Sell the farm? Leave Nantucket? An impossible decision. Twelve years later, Mack didn't know where his home was. And
so, as he stood on top of the dune, he listened; he wanted the voice to
tell him what to do.

MAY FIRST WAS BILL Elliott's least favorite day of the year; it was one of
the few mornings that he didn't make love to his wife, Therese. May
first was Therese's day to sleep in undisturbed while Bill tried not to
panic. The doctor told him panic was bad for his heart; stress of any
kind could take months off his life. (Bill noted the use of that word,
"months," and it terrified him. His life had been pared down to incre-
ments of thirty days.)

At dawn, he left his house for a walk along Hulbert Avenue. The
summer homes on Hulbert were boarded up, Bill was relieved to see;
it looked as if the houses were sleeping. So there was still plenty of
time to whip the hotel into shape. The reservation book filled up by
the Ides of March, but taking reservations was the easy part. The hard
part was now, this morning, thinking about all the work that had to be
done. The enormous, rounded dunes of the beach. Twenty rooms
with furniture piled on top of the beds, draped with white sheets.
Dusty, disorganized.

Bill reached home, wheezing. He was sixty years old and because
of his weak heart, already an old man. This past winter in Aspen, he
hadn't been able to ski the black diamonds, nor the blues; he had been
embarrassingly limited to the gentle green slopes of Buttermilk Mountain. His hair was the color of nickels and dimes, his knees ached in
the evenings, and he needed good light for reading. Last week on the
flight back from Aspen, he used the lavatory four times. But the kicker
was this: Just after the New Year, he and Therese were out at Guido's
with another couple, a doctor (though not Bill's doctor) and his wife,
eating cheese fondue when Bill felt pressure in his chest, a squeezing,
as though his heart were a balloon ready to pop. The doctor at the
table took charge of calling an ambulance. There was talk of chopper-
ing Bill to Denver, but thankfully, that wasn't necessary, and in the

end, Bill was okay. It hadn't been a heart attack, just angina, heart muscle pain, a warning. The doctor recommended retirement. A few years ago, last year even, this would have been unthinkable, but now it sounded tempting. Bill's daughter, Cecily, would be graduating from high school in a couple of weeks and she'd already passed her eighteenth birthday. So it was only a matter of time before he could leave the running of the hotel to Cecily.

As Bill opened his front door, a white envelope fluttered to his feet. The letters had begun! Bill tore the envelope open and read the letter—as ever, from the mysterious S.B.T., an offer to buy the hotel out from under Bill's feet. Good old S.B.T. had been writing letters for several years now trying to convince Bill to sell. Twenty-two million? *Don't tempt me today, S.B.T.,* Bill thought. Bill occasionally wrote back to the post office box—he'd never met the man (or woman) and they wouldn't offer a name at the post office when Bill inquired. There weren't any S. B. T's in the phone book; for all Bill knew, the initials were fabricated. The mysteriousness of it was both frustrating and intriguing, like having a secret suitor. A suitor, at his age! Bill crumpled the letter and deposited it into the trash can at the side of his house. *Are you watching, S.B.T.? Are you watching?*

When Bill reached the kitchen and poured his first cup of decaf, he heard a car pull into the parking lot, and the tightness in his chest alleviated a bit. *Mack.* Bill was so happy that he wanted to shout to Therese, *Honey, Mack's here!* He interrupted more than a few of her May first slumbers this way. But this time Bill was quiet. He closed his eyes and recited "Stopping by Woods on a Snowy Evening" to himself, like a prayer. *And miles to go before I sleep.* It was amazing the way the words came to him. After the episode at the restaurant, Bill had retreated into poetry, into the words of an old man, a New Englander. Never mind that Frost's Vermont was a far cry from this island (there wasn't a single tree on Bill's whole property). Never mind that. For reasons unexplainable, Frost's poetry helped; it was a balm, a salve. It eased Bill's aging soul.

Mack looked exactly the same: the ruddy, smiling face and that bushy head of light brown hair. Bill knew Mack as well as he might have known a son. Bill shook Mack's hand and he couldn't stop himself from hugging him too.

"So," Bill said, "you decided to come back." This was their long-standing joke. Mack never said he would return in May, and Bill never asked. But every May first Mack appeared in the parking lot and each time, Bill greeted him this way. Bill wanted to say something else; he wanted to say "Thank you for coming back," but he didn't. It would embarrass Mack, and it might be better if Mack didn't know how much Bill needed him. "How was your winter?"

"Not bad. I worked for Casey Miller on a huge project in Cisco. It snowed twice and both times I got the day off and went sledding."

"How's Maribel?" Bill asked.

"The same," Mack said. "They love her at the library. And at the post office and the bank, and Stop & Shop. She knows everyone. It's like walking around with the mayor."

"She's hankering to get married?" Bill asked.

"I can hardly blame her," Mack said. "We've been together a long time."

"So is this it, then? Is this the year Mack gets married?"

Mack shrugged. Bill could see he was embarrassed now, by just this. Bill clapped him on the shoulder. "How about we give this place the once-over, for starters?"

Mack looked relieved. "Okay," he said.

THERE WAS NO WAY Bill Elliott could look at his hotel objectively; it was as familiar to him and well loved as the face of his wife. Always on May first the hotel looked formidable and tough, boarded up like an old western ghost town, and today was no exception. The hotel had gray cedar shingles like nearly every building on Nantucket. Plywood had been fastened over her doors and windows, paint peeled from her frames. Bill pictured the hotel at the height of summer; it was the only way he could keep his blood pressure from skyrocketing. Her trim would be as white as fresh eggs, her windows sparkling, Therese's

geraniums and impatiens in full bloom—red, white, pink. The water
temperature at sixty-eight degrees, the skies clear with a light south-
westerly wind that would barely flutter the scalloped edges of the
beach umbrellas. Who could complain then? Still, even today, Bill
was in love with what he saw. Despite the shutters and the peeling
paint and the undulating beach, she was the most beautiful hotel in the
world. He would no sooner sell it than cut out his own heart.

Bill and Mack walked along the side deck rooms and took a left by
the front deck rooms. Room 21 through room 1, skipping a room 13,
of course. All present and accounted for, although Bill had nightmares
during the winter of the rooms flying away in a northeaster like something from *The Wizard of Oz*. Bill stepped up onto each deck and
stamped his feet to check for rotting boards. Mack perused the roof for
missing shingles and inspected the shutters for leaks. "She's tight,"
Mack said. They headed back across the beach to the parking lot and
Bill took keys out of his pocket. He unlocked the doors to the lobby
and they stepped in.

"Home, sweet home," Bill said.

"Oh, brother," Mack said.

"Are you ready?" Bill said. He wished Mack looked more confident, more eager. Maybe this winter had taken a toll. "I'm going to
shower and change," he said. "And you can get started. We have a
hotel to run."

THE BEACH CLUB WAS Therese Elliott's canvas, her block of clay. Every
May presented the same challenge—to make the hotel look more glorious than the year before. Therese had embarked on the quest for
beauty when she was a girl growing up on Long Island—in Bilbo, perhaps the most unattractive town in all of America. Therese's family
lived in one of the first subdivisions, on a cul-de-sac where the houses
were built in three styles: ranch, split-level, and bastardized saltbox.
Her parents' house (from the age of ten she referred to it as her parents' house, never her own) was a ranch with plasterboard walls, white
Formica countertops threaded with gold, and veneered kitchen cabi-

nets. The house had a swatch of green lawn and a chain-link fence that marked the property line along the sides and the back.

Now that Therese was in the hotel business, she compared the neighborhood where she grew up to a Holiday Inn—every living space alike in its absolute sterility, in its absence of charm. As an adolescent she felt bewildered walking home from school past the identical houses and identical yards, realizing that for some reason people *chose* to live like this—without distinction, without beauty. Her neighborhood couldn't even be called *ugly*, because ugly might at least have been interesting. The best word to describe the neighborhood of Therese's childhood was *unliterary*. She couldn't imagine anything noteworthy or romantic happening among the white-and-black, gold-threaded Formica-ness of the place.

And so, at eighteen, she left.

For Manhattan, with its color and confusion, beauty and ugliness side by side. She flunked out of Hunter College after two semesters, because instead of studying she spent hours walking through China-town, Chelsea, Clinton, Sutton Place, the Upper West Side, Harlem. When her parents received her poor grades, they insisted she return to Bilbo and enroll at Katie Gibbs, but she refused. She found a job waitressing at a German restaurant on Eighty-sixth and York, where fat old men admired the color of her hair and gave her generous tips. She saved enough money to leave the city for the summer with a girlfriend whose family had a beach house on Nantucket.

Nantucket cornered the market on beauty—the tumbling south shore waves, blue herons standing one-legged in Coskata Pond, Great Point Lighthouse at sunset. Therese took a job as a chambermaid at the Jared Coffin House in town, and when summer turned into fall and her girlfriend returned to the city, Therese stayed. More than thirty years later, she loved it still. She had married a local boy, given birth to two children, one who died and one who lived, and she and Bill transformed the Beach Club into a hotel. A beautiful place where love flourished.

Bill and Therese lived on one edge of the hotel property, in an upside-down house. The first floor had two spacious bedrooms—one for their daughter, Cecily, and one for the baby that died. The second floor had a rounded bay window that overlooked the hotel, the beach, and the sound. Therese stood at the window on this first day of May, but all she could see was a reflection of herself. It was a bad, vain habit, catching glances of herself in mirrors and windows, in the glass of picture frames, but she couldn't keep from looking. What did she see? At the age of fifty-eight, she still fit into a silk skirt she bought before Cecily was born. Her hair was the color of ripe peaches, with one streak of pure white in front that appeared after she gave birth to her dead baby. Her mark of strength and wisdom, of Motherhood.

Above anything, Therese was a Wife and a Mother. But now her family was in danger of falling apart. Her husband suffered from heart problems and her daughter was graduating from high school and headed for college. Suddenly, Therese pictured herself abandoned, alone. Bill dying, Cecily going away, until there would be nothing in her life except her own reflection.

She had to force herself away from the window and down into the hotel lobby. When she flung open the doors, her spirits lifted. Mack crawled around on the exposed beams of the lobby, wiping them down with a damp rag. Mack in the rafters: it was a sure sign of spring.

"You got to work before I could hug and kiss you," she said. "You got to work before I could tell you what to do."

Mack swung around and sat with his legs dangling. "I already know what to do," he said. "I'm not exactly new here."

Therese flopped onto a sofa that was covered with one of the hotel's sheets and put her feet on a dusty sea captain's chest. "You could run this place alone, I suppose. The rest of us are only getting in your way." She had known Mack for twelve years and he was closer to her than anyone except for Bill and Cecily. She could tell him just about anything.

"You sound so melancholy," Mack said. "Where's the uptight woman I know and love? What happened to the never-ending pursuit of cleanliness?"

"I'm worried about Bill," she said. "He had heart problems this winter. Did he tell you?"

"No," Mack said. "What kind of problems?"

It was comforting to hear a voice from above. "Problems that happen when people get older," Therese said. "His doctor told him he could only ski the baby slopes. It wasn't a good winter for Bill."

"He looks okay," Mack said. "A little pale, maybe, but okay. And his spirit's up."

"You think so?" Therese was concerned about Bill's preoccupation with Robert Frost—he'd taken it up the way a dying person might take up religion—although the reading and reciting seemed to help him.

"How's Cecily doing?" Mack asked.

"She doesn't know about her father's heart," Therese said. "That's one nice thing about having her away at school. She doesn't have to worry. And since she's not worrying, she's doing quite well."

"She wrote a letter at Christmas telling me about some Brazilian guy she met and I haven't heard from her since," Mack said. "Is she going to graduate or did she run away to Rio?"

The Brazilian boyfriend, Gabriel, another stumbling block. But Cecily had barely mentioned him the last two times she called home, and Therese hoped that with the end of the school year in sight, her infatuation was petering out. "Believe it or not, she's going to graduate."

"And college?" Mack asked.

"The University of Virginia. Hard enough to get into that she impressed her friends, and reasonably priced enough to impress her father. We're thrilled."

"She'll be on the front desk this summer? She's *more* than capable, Therese. If she's going to run the hotel someday she needs to learn it."

"Not the desk," Therese said firmly. Mack rolled his eyes. He could think what he wanted, that Therese babied her daughter, but Cecily was still a child. She didn't need a job that could drive even a mature, well-adjusted adult insane. "Bill hired a woman to work the day desk, someone he met at the gym in Aspen. Her name is Love."

"Love?"

"Yes," said Therese. "We need more love around here. Speaking of which, you noticed I haven't asked about your girlfriend."

"I didn't expect you to," Mack said.

"I can't resist. How are things? Are you still together? Still happy?"

"Yes."

"Still happy, but you're not going to marry her?"

"We have no plans to get married, no," he said.

"Wait until you see Cecily," Therese said. "All grown up. A woman. And so gorgeous. Vibrant. Irresistible." And headstrong, opinionated, difficult, her Cecily. Therese lifted her feet from the dusty chest and stood up. "If you marry Cecily this will all be yours. Bill would be so relieved. He loves you like a son, you know. He really does."

"You make it sound like we're living in a fairy tale," Mack said. "If I marry the fair daughter, I get the whole kingdom."

"You could rule the Beach Club kingdom."

"I'm not marrying Cecily, Therese."

"Well, you're not marrying Maribel." Therese and Mack had this same conversation every year, and she knew it irked Mack, but Therese couldn't help herself. To her, only one course of events made any sense—Mack marrying Cecily and the two of them taking over where Bill and Therese left off. She also knew that people rarely did what made sense.

"I haven't decided about marriage at all yet," Mack said. "But I can tell you, if and when I do get married, it won't be to Cecily. And if you don't believe me, ask her. She'd rather eat glass, direct quote."

"I won't give up," Therese said. She caught her reflection in a tarnished mirror, and then she pulled out her artist's tools from the utility closet—vacuum, bucket, cleanser, and her feather duster—and started to work.

MARIBEL COX KNEW SHE was the subject of gossip—among her mother's friends at the Christian Calendar Factory, among her colleagues at the library, among Mack's co-workers and Bill and Therese down at the Beach Club. She knew they were all whispering, "When are Mack and Maribel going to do the *right thing*? When are they going to get *married*?"

The truth of the matter was this: Maribel wanted to get married with a raging, fiery passion, but the only person who knew it was Maribel's mother, Tina. Every Wednesday night, Maribel called Tina and every Wednesday night, Tina said, "Well?" Meaning: well, did Mack finally say those five little words, *"Maribel, will you marry me?"* Every Wednesday night, Maribel said, "Well, nothing." And her mother said, "Keep the faith."

Maribel and Mack had been dating for six years, living together for three. Maribel had found a man Afraid to Commit.

"Like mother, like daughter," Tina said. Maribel pictured her mother: twenty pounds overweight, permed hair, smoking a cigarette as she talked on the phone. Tina herself had never been married. She met Maribel's father at an outdoor concert, and Maribel was conceived in the woods nearby, up against a tree. Her mother never saw the man again; she'd only known him for one day.

"If he's anything like you," Tina was fond of saying, "he must be a great guy."

Maribel loved her mother dearly, although this love was tinged with shame and pity. Tina worked as a supervisor at the Christian calendar factory in Unadilla, New York. Her mother didn't belong to a church, and yet spending all day around Christian calendars, she picked up certain phrases: "Keep the faith," and "Godspeed," and "We are all His little lambs." It had always been just Tina and Maribel; there was never anyone to help them out, no man in Maribel's life growing up. Mack lost his parents in a car accident and Maribel tried to believe this was the same thing as her not having a father, but in fact, it was vastly different. When Maribel thought of her father, there was no one to picture. She was left with an empty spot inside, a part of her missing. A hole.

When Maribel was thirteen, she begged Tina to describe her father.

"Remember, Mama, remember everything you can." Tina sucked on her cigarette and closed her eyes: *His name was Stephen, he had sweet, chocolaty breath and a pencil-line scar above his eyebrow. I remember the scratch of bark against my back. It was getting dark, the sky turning pink and lavender through the trees. I didn't know your father real well. But when I was with him, I had a feeling something good would come of it.*

Maribel wanted to get married for two people—herself and her mother. She wanted Mack to take care of them, the way Stephen might have. Mack made just as many comments about the future as Maribel did, if not more. There was no doubt in Maribel's mind that Mack wanted to spend the rest of his life with her. He loved her.

So what, then, was the problem?

After years of taking self-help books off the shelves at the library, Maribel drew a conclusion: Mack was afraid to grow up. The phone call he received from David Pringle last week proved it. Mack owned a huge farm in Iowa, but he didn't want to go back and run it and he didn't want to sell it. Both options involved too much commitment, too much responsibility. It was as though he wanted the farm to exist on its own, magically, a farm from a dream, while he stayed on Nantucket and ran the stupid hotel. At any minute, Bill Elliott could drop dead and the hotel would go to Cecily, and Mack would be out of luck. But Mack loved his job at the hotel—six months on, six months off, never telling Bill if he were coming back or not—because it gave him freedom. Because he didn't have to take it—or anything else—too seriously.

In Maribel's opinion, Mack needed to ask Bill Elliott to profit-share. Thirty percent of the hotel's profit should go to Mack each year. Many of the guests who took Mack and Maribel out to dinner admitted (after a few cocktails) that should Mack ever leave his job, they would stop coming. The hotel was lovely, they said (but expensive, and the rates went up every year); it was the *service* that kept them coming back. It was walking into the lobby and having Mack there with his cheerful, booming voice, "*Hel-lo*, Mr. Page! Welcome back. How was your winter?" It was Mack who picked up the Page children and swung them around while he complimented Mrs. Page on her new haircut. And that was what people paid for. They wanted to be coddled; they wanted to be courted.

Maribel was convinced profit sharing was the answer. If Mack profit-shared, he would take his job seriously. He would take his life seriously. He could afford to hire someone really qualified to run the farm. His house would be in order. He would propose. And the empty spot inside of Maribel would shrivel, shrink, disappear.

ON MAY FIRST, MARIBEL and Mack had just moved into their "summer place"—a basement apartment in the middle of the island. It was the only housing they could afford in the summer, when island rents doubled and tripled. In winter, things were different; in the winter, they lived on Sunset Hill, next to Nantucket's Oldest House. The house on Sunset Hill was just a cottage, but Maribel and Mack called it the Palace. They loved the Palace—its low doorways and slanted ceilings and floors. In the quiet, cold, gray mornings of January, they lit a fire in the kitchen and Maribel made Mack cinnamon toast and oatmeal before he went out to bang nails. In the evenings, they walked into town through the deserted streets, past houses closed for the winter, sometimes not seeing another soul. They loved the Palace and it was sad every year to pack up their belongings and move to mid-island.

Maribel waited to broach the topic of profit sharing until Mack had worked at the Beach Club for three days. By then he'd gotten a taste of all the work the hotel needed and he'd had a chance to reflect on the crazy summer ahead of him. Then, on the fourth morning, Maribel made Mack scrambled eggs with fresh herbs. They sat at the dining table surrounded by stacks of unpacked boxes and duffel bags. Moving in went slowly.

"I've been thinking about money," she said. "And the housing."

"I know you hate this place," Mack said. "But every year you get used to it."

"I had an idea, Mack." She curled her bare toes into the fibers of the shag carpet. "I think you should ask Bill to profit-share."

There was a long silence, Mack eating. "You've been talking to your mother?" Mack said. "You've been reading one of those Men Live on Mars books?"

"You need to secure yourself a future at the club. It's been twelve years. It's time to ask Bill to profit-share." She spread her painted-pink fingernails out on the dining table and counted off twelve years, then she counted off six years of Mack and her together.

"I can't," he said.

"Why not?"

"Because I can be replaced. If I ask to profit-share, Bill can say no, and fire me. He can hire someone else."

Maribel clasped her hands and leaned forward. She wasn't eating. Too nervous. "He would never fire you. He loves you. And you say he's not doing well. Don't you think he wants to know that you'll be there to take care of the hotel after he's gone?"

"The hotel will be Cecily's," Mack said, his mouth full.

"She's a child."

"She's eighteen. She'll figure it out."

"What about you, then?" Maribel said. "Us? What do we do when Bill dies? I know it's not something you want to think about. . . ."

"You're right, it's not. He's not on death's door, Maribel. He's just a little frail."

"He's never been well. Now he's just one year closer."

Mack finished his eggs and buttered a piece of toast. Maribel brought him a jar of Concord grape jam. Then he said, "I don't want to ask."

"Why not?" Maribel said. She dipped a finger into the jam and tasted it.

"Because it's his business to pass on to Cecily. My father left me a business. I understand how it works. I'm not going to put Bill in the awkward position of having to relinquish part of his profits to keep me happy."

"You could use the money to hire someone to run the farm," Maribel said. Mack slathered the jam over his toast. Maribel watched his every move; he was a mystery to her. "And it's not as though you're asking him to hand over the business. You'd simply be asking for part of the profits. Don't you think you influence those profits?"

"Of course," Mack said. "But I'm not going to ask him. I've worked for Bill for a long time. It would embarrass us both."

"Okay, then," Maribel said. "If you don't want to ask Bill, let's move to Iowa. Let's run the farm ourselves."

"You don't want to move to Iowa," Mack said.

"Yes, I do," Maribel said. This wasn't a lie, exactly. If it would take moving to Iowa to get Mack to marry her, she would do it. She thought of her mother's life—twenty-eight Christian calendar years of being alone. That would not be Maribel's life.

"But I love Nantucket," Mack said. "I'm happy here."

"So you're going to sell the farm then?" Maribel said. "You've decided?"

"No," Mack said. Maribel felt a twinge of guilt, because he did look completely at a loss. He wiped his plate with the crust of his toast. "Why do I have to decide now?"

"Because you're thirty years old, Mack. Because you want more money, more respect. Don't you want things to change?"

"I guess," he said.

Maribel reached across the table and touched his hand. He trusted her; he knew that her thinking was for both of them. "Ask Bill to profit-share. If he says no we can leave for Iowa."

Mack took his empty plate to the sink. He turned the faucet on, then off, then on, and he poured a glass of water and drank it slowly and deliberately, in a way that made Maribel want to scream. He was always making her wait!

"Let me think about it," he said.

"Don't you think it's time we took the next step? Don't you think it's time you got what you deserved?"

"Yes?" Mack said.

"Okay, then," Maribel said.

Maribel watched from the living room window as Mack walked out to the Jeep and drove away. *I want you to feel good about yourself,* she thought. *I want you to ask me to marry you!*

THE FIRST THING JEM Crandall thought when he arrived at the Beach Club to interview for the bellman's position was that it was like a scene from a movie—the ocean, the sand, and then the leading man—strong handshake, sailing-instructor suntan, who called himself Mack, and said Why don't we interview on the pavilion? The pavilion! Nantucket was the fanciest place Jem had ever been, and he'd certainly never been interviewed on a pavilion before.

The pavilion turned out to be a covered deck with blue Adirondack chairs that faced the ocean.

"This is like a little porch," Jem said, taking one of the chairs.

"What do you think?" Mack said. He half sat, half leaned on the railing with his back to the water, so he could look at Jem. Jem stared at Mack's ankle, swinging back and forth like a pendulum. He was wearing deck shoes without any socks.

"It's fucking gorgeous," Jem said. He shut his eyes. What had he just said? *Fucking?* Swearing, in a job interview! "Excuse my French," he said. "I just meant . . ."

"I know what you meant," Mack said. He scribbled something down on his clipboard, probably, *Low-class, not right at all for the job.* Jem sat up straighter in the chair, but it was hard to achieve really perfect posture because of the way the back of the chair was slung.

"Sorry," Jem said.

Mack checked his Ironman sportswatch. He was dressed like a J. Crew model—navy cotton sweater, khakis, a Helly Hansen Gore-Tex vest lined with fleece. Jem tried to keep from fixating on Mack's swinging ankle.

"So you want to be a bellman," Mack said. "I have two questions. How long can you stay and do you have a place to live?"

Jem arranged his thoughts. In career counseling at William and Mary, he learned that the key to a good job interview was to tell the truth, and not what he thought the interviewer wanted to hear. "I can stay until closing," Jem said. "I graduated from college, like, last week."

"Where'd you go to college?" Mack asked.

"The College of William and Mary."

"Okay, so you graduated. And you don't have another job to start in the fall?"

"Not lined up, no."

"What are you planning to do?"

Jem tried to sit up. "I'm going to California. I want to be an agent." An agent: that was the first time he'd said the words out loud. It sounded okay. *I want to be an agent.* Jem was afraid to tell his parents about his plans because they would reject the words "Los Angeles" right away. They would argue it was too far from home. Jem's parents lived in Falls Church, Virginia; they were small-town people. They had to pull out the atlas to locate Nantucket.

"An agent?" Mack said.

"Yeah," Jem said. His feet itched and he wondered if he'd gotten sand in his socks. He stared at Mack's bare ankle, then tore his eyes away. "An agent for actors."

"Do you act?"

"I'm not very good. I modeled a little in college, though. I was Mr. November in the college calendar." Mr. November: It was a good, handsome picture—Jem in jeans, sitting on a split-rail fence in historic Williamsburg. But now Mr. November sounded ridiculous. Things that seemed okay in college didn't always translate to the real world. Jem should have kept his mouth shut. From now on, he was just going to answer the questions.

Mack pinched his lips together in a line, as if he were trying not to laugh. "What about a place to live?"

"I have a place to live," Jem said. Jem rented a room through a college friend's aunt who had a house on North Liberty Street. The room was fine, but it didn't have kitchen privileges. When Jem asked the friend's aunt how he was going to eat, she said, "I usually rent to people in the restaurant business." Jem's father owned a bar in Falls

Church—an English-style pub called the Locked Tower; if he'd wanted to wait tables, he would have stayed at home. "The room's decent," he told Mack. "But it doesn't have a kitchen. And I need to save money to go to California." He straightened his spine. "I'm on the lookout for free food in a big way. What I really need is a girlfriend who likes to cook."

"My girlfriend likes to cook," Mack said. "And look what it got me." He patted his gut. "Love handles."

Jem smiled politely.

"Are you handy?" Mack asked. "Can you change a lightbulb? Set an alarm clock? Do you know what a circuit breaker is? If a guest calls the front desk and says his electricity is out, could you fix it?"

"Probably. I can change a lightbulb and set an alarm clock. I know my way around a fuse box."

"You'd be surprised how many people can't set an alarm clock," Mack said.

"Well, I can," Jem said. "Like I said, I just graduated from college." He laughed. Mack scribbled down something else.

"Hopefully, you'll remember to set your own," Mack said. "The day bellman needs to be here at eight A.M."

"Do I have the job, then?"

"I need someone for three day shifts and three night shifts, one day off. There isn't a lot of sitting around. If you're not stripping the rooms for the chambermaids or helping a guest with bags, then you'll be doing projects, assigned by me. Small maintenance jobs, watering the plants, cleaning the exercise room, sweeping up shells in the parking lot. And part of the deal is helping to open the place, from now until Memorial Day. That's eight to four every day but Sunday. I can offer you ten bucks an hour, plus tips. Do you *want* the job?"

Tips. A world-class beach resort. Contacts waiting to be made. Jem could have kissed the guy. "Yes, I do. Absolutely."

Mack offered his hand and Jem tried for a nice, firm handshake that showed he meant what he said.

"You have the job," Mack said. "Welcome to the Nantucket Beach Club and Hotel. You'll work with a bellman named Vance Robbins who's been here twelve years, just as long as I have. Vance will show you the ropes. Come tomorrow at eight, ready to shovel."

Jem jumped to his feet. "I'll be here," he said. He probably sounded way too eager, but it was exciting—getting a job, spending the summer on this island. He couldn't wait to write to his parents and tell them. But first he had to find a grocery store and buy some bread and a jar of peanut butter and hope it didn't draw ants.

Mack led him to the front porch of the lobby. "We'll see you tomorrow," Mack said.

"Do you own this place?" Jem asked. A seagull dropped a shell onto the asphalt of the parking lot and then swooped down to eat whatever was inside.

"No," Mack said. He tugged at his vest defensively.

"Oh," Jem said. "Well, it is gorgeous."

"Fucking gorgeous," Mack said. "You're right. It is."

VANCE ROBBINS STOOD SIX feet and one half inch tall, which was the same height as Mack Petersen. He turned thirty years old on March 22, and so did Mack Petersen. They were exactly the same height and exactly the same age.

"Like twins," Maribel once made the mistake of saying. Vance and Mack were not twins. First of all, Vance was black and Mack was white. Secondly, Vance was a bellman and Mack was the manager.

Vance had hated Mack for twelve years. Twelve years ago, Vance was a high school graduate on his way to Fairleigh Dickinson in the fall, and he lined up a summer managerial position at the Beach Club with Bill Elliott over the phone. Bill was supposed to be waiting when Vance got off the ferry, but Mack cut in and replaced him. It was pure dumb luck—Mack got off the boat first and he was the right age, he had the right look, and Bill took him to the hotel instead of Vance. It wasn't until an hour later that Bill returned to the wharf to get Vance— and by then Mack had infiltrated the joint. Bill claimed Mack had bet- ter experience because he'd worked on a farm—a *farm*, for God's sake—and he wasn't leaving for school in September, and so Mack got the manager's job. Vance was Mack's equal in height and age, but returning to the Beach Club in the spring and seeing Mack made Vance only too aware of how they weren't equal. Vance was a black sheep, an evil twin, a kid who got off the boat thirty seconds too late. A bellman.

"Hey, Vance! Good to see you, man! How was your winter?" Here was Mack now, clapping Vance on the back, pumping his hand. Mack ran his palm over Vance's smooth skull. "You shaved your head . . . it looks great. You look, I don't know, intimidating."

"Thanks," Vance said. He couldn't help smiling. He expected Mack to say shaved heads weren't acceptable at the Beach Club. Vance caught himself and tried to scowl. This was how it happened every year. He spent all winter despising Mack and then when he showed up in the spring, Mack was disarmingly nice, *cool* even, and Vance was forced to abandon his hatred. But not this year. This year Vance was going to hang on to his hatred with both hands.

"Man, how was your winter?" Mack asked. "How was Thailand? Did you get laid?"

"Of course," Vance said, and again, he couldn't help smiling. When he pictured himself on the beach at Koh Samui or under the capable massaging hands of Pan, a nineteen-year-old Thai girl with long, shiny black hair, he wanted to give up every detail. Mack, he knew, had spent all winter on this gloomy rock. "Thailand kicked ass. I rented a bungalow on the beach for six bucks a night." He nodded toward the hotel. "Closer to the water than room eleven and a hundredth the price. I got massages that lasted well into the night. I ate banana pancakes and grilled fish every day."

A young guy with dark curly hair holding a shovel approached them. "That sounds like paradise," he said. "Where were you, California?"

"Thailand," Mack and Vance said at the same time. Their voices were indistinguishable. Vance shook his head.

"Thailand," Vance said again, on his own. The familiar acidity of hatred filled his chest, and he popped two Rolaids. In the summer, when Mack was around, Vance ate hundreds of them.

"Vance, this is Jem. I hired Jem yesterday. Jem, Vance Robbins, the head bellman."

Vance took another look at the kid as he ground the chalk between his molars. He was too handsome but probably impressionable. Easy to boss around.

"Jem, like in *To Kill a Mockingbird?*" Vance asked.

Jem nodded. "Not many people get the reference."

Vance stuck out his hand. "Pleasure," he said.

Mack ran his palms over Vance's noggin again. "I missed you, man. How come you didn't send me a postcard?"

Vance shrugged. Why the hell did Mack like him so much? Why couldn't he take a hint?

VANCE AND JEM STARTED digging out the snow fence. The sun was shining and it was actually kind of warm. By noon they would probably be able to work without shirts. Vance liked opening and closing work best because it was quiet work, and honest. He'd started jogging in Thailand, and doing sit-ups and push-ups. He'd swum every afternoon. He was bigger now in the arms and across the shoulders. Sometime this summer he was going to beat up Mack—beat him to a pulp, just once, so that Mack would know Vance hadn't forgiven him for horning in, for stealing away the job that should rightfully have been his.

Vance and Jem worked side by side peacefully with Jem only looking up once to ask, "Hey, do they buy you lunch around here? I'm starving."

Vance checked his watch; it was ten-thirty.

"Sometimes the boss will spring for subs," Vance said. "Bill Elliott, the owner. Have you met him yet?"

"No."

"It's always good to remember that Mack isn't *really* the boss. Bill is."

"So Bill buys us subs?" Jem asked.

"If we put in a hard morning he sometimes will," Vance said. "But not every day."

"Does this place serve breakfast?" Jem asked.

"Continental breakfast, eight-thirty to ten. You'll be in charge of setting it up and taking it down when you work the day shift. Didn't Mack tell you that?" Vance was annoyed; Mack was lax about explaining duties to new workers. It always fell to Vance to explain the whole truth and sometimes the new bellman got bristly, thinking Vance was creating more work for him. But this kid, Jem, just beamed.

"No," Jem said, "he didn't say anything about breakfast. That's great!"

Vance heard his name being called, and Maribel jogged onto the beach. She was wearing shorts and a red sports bra, and she had a windbreaker tied around her waist. Blond hair in a ponytail. She threw her arms around Vance's neck and kissed him on the cheek. As much as Vance hated Mack, he couldn't bring himself to feel anything but dumbstruck infatuation for Maribel.

"You look divine!" she said. "Positively exotic. I love men without hair. You look like Michael Jordan. How was Thailand?"

"Good." he said. He couldn't figure out what Maribel saw in him either. Every time she spoke to him he had trouble stringing together a sentence.

"You've got this incredible bod. This is the year you get a girl then, huh?"

Vance clenched the handle of his shovel, hoping she would see his forearm muscles ripple. He was glad he'd removed his shirt. Before Vance could answer, Jem said, "We haven't met. I'm Jem Crandall."

"Jem?" Maribel said. She shook Jem's hand and Vance felt a familiar sense of dread. Jem had his shirt off as well, and he was using some lady-killer smile that showed all his teeth. "Jem, like in *To Kill a Mockingbird*?"

"Exactly," Jem said. "Not many people get the reference. Vance did, though."

Maribel turned to Vance. "Well, of course. Vance is our literary lion."

Vance shrugged. Maribel called him that because he graduated from FDU with a degree in American lit, and he once had a story entitled "The Downward Spiral" published in a small magazine.

"I'm Maribel Cox. Mack is my boyfriend." She paused to let this information sink in. It was as though she were telling Jem, *I'm important, I'm with Mack.*

"Maribel works at the library," Vance said.

"Explains why you know about books," Jem said.

"Are you just starting here today?" Maribel asked.

"Yeah," Jem said. He leaned on his shovel with crossed arms. "They've got me digging ditches already."

Maribel turned back to Vance. "You guys should come over for dinner tonight. I'll roast a chicken, do those real French *pomme frites* that you like."

"I can't," Vance said. One of the rules he had set for himself was No More Socializing with Mack.

"I can," Jem said eagerly, but Maribel ignored him.

"Maybe next week then," she said. "Is Mack around?"

"Look out back," Vance said. "Or in the office. He might be in the office with Bill."

"Okay," Maribel said. She touched Vance's flexing forearm. "Hey, you, good to see you." She jogged toward the hotel. "And nice meeting you, Jem!"

When she was out of earshot, Jem said, "That girl is a knockout. And she cooks!"

"Taken," Vance said. He spoke in a way that might be construed as protecting Mack. But Vance just wanted Jem Mockingbird to realize that if Vance couldn't have Maribel, no one else could either.

LOVE O'DONNELL ARRIVED ON the island by high-speed ferry. Even though it was mid-May, the weather was gray and drizzly. And cold. Love stood on the bow of the boat, her Polar Fleece wrapped tightly around her. She wanted to watch the ferry approach Nantucket. She wanted to feel sea mist on her face. As it was, she wasn't sure if the moisture she felt on her face was sea mist or rain, and through the dense blanket of fog she couldn't see Nantucket at all until just before they reached the harbor. Then she caught a glimpse of the red beam of Brant Point Lighthouse and behind, the gray-shingled buildings of town, and the white steeple of the Congregational church she'd seen in pictures. The Beach Club, where she would be working, was to the west someplace and the cottage she had rented for the season was mid-island, where the locals lived.

Love wasn't a person who went places on impulse. This trip qualified as the most impulsive thing she'd ever done. She'd lived in Aspen for the past seven years working at a popular outdoor magazine. But then she met Bill Elliott at the gym. They were lying side by side on the mats, using the Abdominizers. Love sneaked a look at Bill in the mirror, because that was what one did at gyms in Aspen—inspected the opposite sex. Especially Love. Ever since her fortieth birthday, Love had been looking for a man to father her baby.

She smiled at Bill in the mirror. "Sometimes I wonder if these things actually work," she said, indicating the Abdominizer.

Bill laughed. "I figure everyone using them looks pretty good."

Love crunched twice more, then said, "Do you live here in Aspen?"

"Just for the winter," Bill said. "How about you?"

"Local," Love said. "Where do you live in the summer?"

"Nantucket," Bill said. He finished with his Abdominizer and stood up. Love stood as well and followed Bill to the StairMasters. An out-of-towner was a requirement in Love's search for a father for her baby, because she wanted a baby but absolutely did not want a husband.

"What do you do in Nantucket?" Love asked. She punched her weight, one hundred pounds even, into the console of the StairMaster.

"My wife and I own a hotel," he said.

"Oh, you're married," Love said. This was not necessarily an obstacle; after seven years in Aspen, Love knew he could still be thinking of an affair.

"Yes, and I have an eighteen-year-old daughter at boarding school.

Finishing up." Love pumped up and down on the stairs. She was so delighted to hear that Bill already had a child that she felt almost guilty. Out of town, previous reproductive success, a business owner—Love ran down her mental checklist, and glanced around the gym. There were two noticeably pregnant women using free weights, and who knew how many others not yet showing. Many of Love's friends, co-workers, and acquaintances were now, in their late thirties and early forties, starting families. In the past eighteen months, Love had taken a crash course on new millennium parenthood: seven-grain zwieback crackers, strollers with all-terrain mountain bike tires. She saw women in the gym and on the cross-country paths with healthy, swollen bellies. Love's desire to be a mother was a physical, painful hunger. Since her fortieth birthday, she could think of nothing else. Love wanted a baby, flesh and blood that would be connected to her for the rest of her life, and she wanted to raise her child alone. There was a group in Aspen called Single Mothers by Choice; Love saw their flyer posted in the health food store. When she finally got pregnant, she would join.

At the end of the workout she smiled at Bill, and said, "You're in good shape."

Bill winked. "Just doing what the doctor says: I get plenty of exercise, and I make love to my wife. Good for the spirit!"

Love's hopes fell down around her feet like a couple of sagging ankle weights. It was okay with her if a man wanted to admit he was married, but talking about his sex life was taboo. She hoped her disappointment didn't show. But then, on their way out of the gym, Bill offered to buy Love something from the juice bar. While Love sipped a carrot-raspberry juice, Bill told her about the hotel on Nantucket.

"She started out as a Beach Club in 1924. Men wore silk suits and top hats, and women carried parasols. There were over four hundred wooden changing rooms, rented twice a day to meet the demand. My father bought the place in 1952 and I built hotel rooms on the property when he retired twenty years ago."

"It sounds wonderful," Love said. "I've always wanted to see New England."

"Well, then, I'd like to make a proposition," Bill said.

Love's thighs tensed. "What's that?" she said.

"Why don't you come work for me this summer? We need a full-time person on the front desk. She's a beautiful hotel, I promise." Love was familiar with his tone of voice; she heard it all the time. He was setting her up on a blind date. Still, it might be the perfect plan. Leave Aspen for the summer and return in the fall, pregnant.

She finished the last of her juice, licking her teeth clean of raspberry seeds. "I already have a job," she said. "But it's a thought."

BILL OFFERED LOVE THE job every time he saw her at the gym. "What would you miss in six months?" he asked her. "Would you be leaving someone behind?"

This question offended her. She was certain Bill knew the answer was no. No one and nothing to leave behind. Not even a dog, like so many other athletic, unmarried Aspen women. Dogs made her sneeze.

"No," she said.

"Listen," Bill said, "I'm going to be retiring soon, whether I like it or not. I'd like to have a good summer. If you think you want to be part of it, I'd love to have you work for us."

His liver-spotted hands trembled at his sides, and despite all his exercise, his skin had a grayish tint. But his eyes sought her eagerly, as though he believed there really was a talented front-desk person somewhere inside of her. And so, at the beginning of April, with the closing of the ski slopes imminent, Love agreed to take the job. A summer at the beach, then, on Nantucket.

The ferry sounded its foghorn. Here she was.

LOVE O'DONNELL WAS ORGANIZED. She had three maps, and a book called *Vintage Nantucket* which she had read cover to cover. She disembarked onto Straight Wharf and picked up her luggage: a North Face duffel bag and her Cannondale M1000. (She never went anywhere without her mountain bike.) She inhaled the ocean air. It smelled of salt and fish, as she expected. What she did not expect was how rich it was, how luxurious; it was air pregnant with oxygen. If nothing else, she would be happy to live here all summer and breathe this air.

Love's taxi driver was a tall, thin girl with dyed-black hair, a nose ring, and seven or eight earrings in each ear.

"Where you headed?" the girl asked. Her T-shirt said Piping Plovers Taste Like Chicken.

"Hooper Farm Road. But I'd like to see a little first, if you don't mind. What's your name?"

"Tracey," the girl said. "And I'm no tour guide."

"Do you live on the island?" Love asked.

The girl glanced behind her at the line of cabs. She threw Love's bike in the back of her station wagon, got into the driver's seat and waited for Love to climb in, then she pulled away. "I'm here for the summer," she said.

"Your first summer?" Love asked.

Tracey nodded. They drove slowly up the cobblestones of Main Street.

"Mine, too," Love said. Her voice jumbled and bounced with the tires. "Did you know these cobblestones were brought here by the early settlers as ballast on their ships?"

Tracey didn't respond. Love looked out the window at the names of the shops and restaurants: Murray's Liquors, Espresso Café, Congdon's Pharmacy, Mitchell's Book Corner. Then they reached a brick building with stately white columns: Pacific National Bank.

Love tapped on the glass. "They call this the *Pacific* Bank because the Nantucket whaling ships had to sail to the Pacific Ocean to hunt whales. They went all the way down around Cape Horn. Sometimes ships were gone for five years. But that's where the money came from, the Pacific Ocean."

"You're a regular encyclopedia," Tracey said.

Love ignored the sarcasm. She didn't want her first interaction on Nantucket to be a negative one. She studied her map. "Let's keep going to the top of Main Street."

They crept up on the Greek Revival Hadwen House, which Love intended to tour in the next few days. "This big white place on the left has an upstairs ballroom," Love said. "The ballroom was built with a retractable roof, so people could dance under the stars."

"Really?" Tracey said. She slowed down. "You mean, the roof rolls back?"

"It's such a romantic idea, dancing under the stars," Love said. She leaned back in her seat. "I've got something to confess, Tracey. I came to this island to get pregnant."

"Whoa, lady, that's more information than I need to know," Tracey said. "If you want to tell me stuff about the history that's fine, that's stuff I might use again on somebody else, but don't tell me personal stuff, please. They don't pay me enough."

Love laughed. "Everybody comes to Nantucket for a reason. Some people came to hunt whales and the Quakers came to escape religious persecution. And I came to get pregnant. It feels good to tell you that I came here to have a baby. Now that someone knows, I feel like I'm responsible for it."

"You're not responsible to me," Tracey said. "Believe me, you're not."

"Would you look at me?" Love asked.

"What?" Tracey said.

"Would you turn around and look at me?"

Slowly, Tracey turned. Her brow twisted in extreme discomfort.

"I came to the island to get pregnant," Love said. "I will get pregnant."

"Okay, so now what do you want me to do? Say 'Amen'?"

"No, just watching me say it is enough." Love checked her map. "Let's go to the Old Mill," she said. "I know the way."

The next day, Love skated to the Beach Club. A pleasant-looking, sandy-haired man was standing on a stepladder, fiddling with the lamppost. Love swung in a half-circle near the ladder and came to an easy stop.

"I'm Love O'Donnell," she said. "You Mack?"

"Yep." He screwed the glass bulb back into the lamppost and patted it. "Hope this works." He stepped down from the ladder and shook Love's hand. "It's nice to meet you."

"Likewise," she said. He had nice blue eyes, and Love judged him to be in his early thirties. Too young.

"I need to wash my hands and then we'll get started," Mack said. "Feel free to look around. Those are the doors to the lobby." He pointed across the parking lot. "I'll meet you there in a few minutes."

Love skated across the parking lot. Bill had explained the hotel as an L, and that's what Love saw: plain, gray-shingled rooms, some running down toward the water and some facing the water. Nothing special about them from the outside except that they were all built in the sand and looked out over the ocean, which today was slate gray. Love felt a wave of disappointment. She was expecting world-class, something grandiose. What had Bill said he charged? Six hundred dollars a night?

Love skated over to the steps that led into the lobby. She removed her Rollerblades thinking she would go in and talk to this guy Mack, but if it didn't work out she could probably get a job in town. At the Jared Coffin House maybe, or another place with a bit more character.

The lobby, however, was a pleasant surprise. In fact, Love decided after about thirty seconds that it was the most attractive room she'd ever seen. The first thing she noticed were six quilts that hung from the exposed beams so that they resembled sheets billowing on a clothesline. The floors were polished wood and hunter green carpet that sank under Love's stocking feet. There was a brick fireplace against one wall and the opposite wall had giant windows that faced the beach. The room was decorated with white wicker furniture, plants and trees, a black grand piano, and toys: miniature bicycles, tiny Adirondack chairs, a rocking horse. Love approached the front desk, which was made of the same shiny, honey-colored wood as the floor. She picked up a tiny brass bell and gave it a tentative swing. Mack appeared from the back.

"Come around," he said.

He showed Love the door that led to the office. The office was a cramped, cluttered room with a stereo, a fax, and a horribly messy desk, although it had the same million-dollar view of the water. Then Love saw a cracked door and noticed there was another office behind it. Bill's office? Love knocked timidly and pushed the door a bit. Bill sat at a huge, lovely desk, reading.

"Hi, Bill," Love said.

Bill looked up. He fumbled with his book and it fell to his feet.

"Oh, hi," he said. "Hello. You're here. You came."

"Yes, of course," she said. Would it be presumptuous to imagine that her presence flustered him? "I told you I'd be here."

Bill picked the book up from underneath his desk.

"Well, okay," he said. "Good. What do you think?"

"The lobby's pretty," she said. "I haven't seen the rooms."

"They're not quite ready yet," Bill said. He flipped through the pages of his book and they made a ruffling noise, like a bird's wings flapping. "Mack will show you the ropes. But it's good to see you here. I guess I'll see a lot more of you."

"Yes," Love said. "I guess you will."

"THE KEY TO YOUR job as a front desk person is to dot your i's and cross your t's," Mack said. "Write everything down. A guest wants dinner reservations: write it down. A guest receives a fax: log it into the fax log book. A guest needs a cab to the airport at six A.M.: write it down for Tiny. Tiny works the night desk. She'll call the cab the night before, and make sure the guest has paid his bill. Never fails, once a summer a guest walks out of here without paying his bill because some desk person forgot to write it down. Not a good thing."

Love produced a notebook from the front pocket of her anorak, and scribbled things as Mack spoke. "Tiny," Love said.

"Tiny doesn't answer personal questions, so don't ask her any. She's probably the smartest one of us all. She doesn't air her dirty laundry. The rest of us, well, we work together so much, sometimes we can't help it. We're kind of like a family."

"Family," Love wrote.

"You brought a notebook," Mack said. "I like that. I've trained at least fifteen desk people over the years. There've been good ones and bad ones. Good desk people are detail oriented. They pay attention. They listen. They use discretion."

"Discretion." Big letters. Underlined.

"A lot of our clientele are very wealthy," Mack said. "They're used to having certain things done for them. For example, some people won't want to take a cab into town. They'll expect a ride."

"What do I tell them?" Love asked.

"Explain that it's not our policy to give rides but that you'd be more than happy to call them a cab."

"Common sense," Love said.

"There will be guests who say they don't like the fruit at breakfast. They'll want peaches instead of bananas. If someone asks for peaches, write it down. I buy the breakfast and I've been known to honor requests for peaches. We don't offer room service so we try to do the best we can on the breakfast."

"No room service," Love repeated. She wrote it down.

"You'll be working every day from eight to five, except Tuesday, your day off. That's a lot of time on the desk. In July and August it can get pretty hectic. You'll be bombarded with requests, questions, people checking out, people checking in. If it gets to be too much, let me know. Let Therese know, let Bill know. Don't try to tackle everyone's problems at once. It won't work."

"I took a magazine to deadline each month," Love said. "I can handle the pressure of twenty hotel rooms."

"Mid-June, of course, the Beach Club starts," Mack said. "We have a hundred members who pay dues to use the beach. They each have a locker. They each have a key. They all need chairs and towels. The kids want buckets and shovels. On a hot day in August when you have thirteen check-outs and twelve check-ins and twenty-five kids running through the lobby with sandy feet and a guest in room twelve telling you his toilet is overflowing and old Mrs. Stanford has lost the key to her Beach Club locker, *then* you will know the meaning of pressure."

Clearly he was trying to scare her. "I guess so," Love said.

Mack lowered his voice. "I did want to say a little more about the guests. What I've learned in twelve years is that it's common to experience feelings of . . . resentment." He looked around the lobby as though there might be a guest or two hiding behind the wicker sofas. "The people who stay here, the people who use the beach, all have a lot of money. And they look to you not as an equal but as someone who works for them. Listen, a guy comes from New York, he has two weeks off a year and he's spending that precious time and a boatload of money here at the hotel. He wants things perfect. You see what I mean? It gets tricky, dealing with egos. There's a lot of financial muscle flexing going on here."

Love smiled. Didn't he know she had come from *Aspen?* "I get your point."

"But what I've learned is that wealthy people are frequently sad people," Mack said.

"I've found that to be true as well," Love said. "Money can only get you so much. It can't cure your cancer or get you love. It can't make you fertile."

Mack smiled. "Fertile?"

Love blushed. Her personal life was slipping already, showing like a bra strap. "Yeah, you know, money can't get you a child. Your own child."

"Exactly," he said. "You're going to do a fantastic job. I can tell."

AFTER LOVE FINISHED HER lesson about the phones and the fax and the credit card machine, and after she impressed Mack with her knowledge of the island, he left to take care of a lock in one of the rooms. Love drummed her fingers on the polished wood of the desk, stared down at the phone console, gazed out at the lobby, and thought, *This is where I'm going to meet the father of my child.*

She heard a voice in the back office. She tiptoed through Mack's messy office and listened at Bill's door, which was still ajar.

Love held her breath and knocked. Bill cleared his throat, then said, "Come in!"

He was the only one in the office. "I heard you talking," she said. She smiled at him. "Do you always talk to yourself? I do."

"I was reciting Robert Frost," he said. " 'One could do worse than be a swinger of birches' and all that. I didn't realize anyone was still here."

"Sorry I startled you," Love said. "The poem you were reciting, is that a favorite of yours?"

"They're all favorites," Bill said, thumping the cover of his book. "This one is called 'Devotion.' I just stumbled across it."

Love moved farther into the office. There were two wicker chairs by the windows. Love sat down. "Read it to me," she said. "I don't read nearly enough poetry."

Bill closed his eyes and leaned back in his creamy leather chair. He was so thin his wrist bones protruded like knobs. " 'The heart can think of no devotion, greater than being shore to the ocean, holding the curve of one position, counting endless repetition.' " He opened his eyes. "You know what that means, don't you?"

My first day of work, a man reads poetry aloud to me. "What does it mean?" she asked.

"He's talking about love," Bill said. "He's saying the greatest demonstration of love is devotion, being there with your beloved day in and day out. Have you ever been married?"

"No," Love said.

"I've been married thirty years, and I love my wife more now than ever. It's like all those days, even the really boring, awful days, have added up. Each day I love her yet more." He closed the book. "So I guess I'm what Frost would call devoted."

"Sounds like it," Love said. Her feelings a bit crushed.

"How about you? Are you devoted to anything?" Bill asked. "Anyone?"

"I'm devoted to having a baby," Love said. "I'm devoted to finding someone to father my baby."

Bill's eyebrows arched, his mouth formed a silent O. Love's personal life was a woman popping out of a cake, *Surprise!*

"A baby is certainly a noble devotion," he said.

Love put her hands on her thighs and stood up. "Too bad *you* can't help me," she said.

Bill laughed nervously. "Endless devotion." As Love walked by his desk to leave, he held out his hand. It was a frail hand, but warm and sincere. "Someone is going to be very lucky," he said.

MACK HAD BEEN RUNNING the Beach Club for twelve years, Bill had owned it outright for twenty, but it was Lacey Gardner, the Grande Dame of Beacon Hill and Nantucket, who had true bragging rights. She had joined the Beach Club in the summer of 1945—fifty-three years ago—did she need to say it? Seven years before Bill's father, Big Bill Elliott, even bought the place. Lacey had been around longer than anybody.

At eighty-eight, she was the oldest living graduate of Radcliffe College and that earned her a permanent seat in the front row at Harvard's commencement. Every year on the day following commencement she drove from her apartment in Boston to Hyannis and put her car on the 9:45 ferry to Nantucket.

Lacey's tenure on Nantucket seemed to her like many different lifetimes. Her parents had brought her over to the island in 1920, when she was ten years old. She remembered the ferry docking and the hoteliers standing on the wharf calling out the names of their establishments: Sea Cliff Inn, Beach House, Point Breeze. Years later, she came to Nantucket for weekends with her chums from Radcliffe. On summer evenings they danced on the open porch at the Moby Dick in 'Sconset. Back then, 'Sconset was a refuge for actors and actresses when Broadway closed for the summer; Lacey still remembered productions of *Our Town, Candida*, and *The Bride the Sun Shines On* out at the 'Sconset Casino. Dancing on the porch, lobster and chicken dinners for a dollar fifty a plate, cabaret fashion shows—this was the lively, carefree summertime Nantucket of Lacey's youth. And she was the only one left to remember it.

In 1941, her gentleman friend Maximilian Gardner proposed to her on the beach in Madaket. Lacey was thirty-one years old and still not married. She worked for the Massachusetts Board of Health. Men called her feisty and independent, and women called her a career girl and a snob. But she loved Maximilian Gardner. At first he was just one of the young men in her fun-loving crowd, but then she noticed the way he looked at her. It was when Maximilian Gardner looked at her that Lacey felt most like a woman.

Lacey and Max were married by a justice of the peace on Madaket Beach, in November 1941, a month before the bomb fell on Pearl Harbor, a week before Max left for basic training. When he came home from the war three years later, they had a church wedding, but by then Lacey was thirty-four, and too old to start having children.

Lacey and Maximilian became permanent fixtures in Nantucket in the summer. They joined the Beach Club—and the Yacht Club and Sankaty Golf Club—and Lacey opened a hat shop on Main Street, called simply Lacey's. She and Max bought a house on Cliff Road, and they split time between this house and their town house on Beacon Hill. They were married for forty-five years, and they held hands every night as they fell asleep. Lacey was holding Max's hand on February 14, 1986, the night he died. She had never been a sentimental woman, and yet her heart was broken on Valentine's Day.

This was how her life on Nantucket seemed like a life divided: her life before Max, her life with Max, her life after Max. After Max, she sold the house on the Cliff and the town house in Boston. She rented an apartment in Boston, and asked Big Bill Elliott for a permanent room at the hotel.

"Don't forget," she told him, "I've been here longer than you have."

Big Bill didn't forget. He gave Lacey her own cottage, behind the lobby of the hotel. The view wasn't great—it looked out at the laundry room and the back of the parking lot—but it had three bedrooms and most importantly, it was her own place—Lacey Gardner's—bought and paid for with pure longevity. In Big Bill's last will and testament, he left the cottage to Lacey; it was hers to pass on when she died.

Well, she wasn't dead yet. She was alive enough to drive her new Buick off the ferry. Always, this thrilled her. She loved shooting down the ramp and feeling her tires hit Steamship Wharf. From the wharf, it was one mile exactly to the Beach Club.

When she pulled into the parking lot, she saw Mack standing on the tiny deck of her cottage, waiting for her with the same smile he wore in the photograph she kept on her refrigerator all winter. The first summer Mack worked at the Beach Club he had knocked on Lacey's door to introduce himself. This was the summer after Maximilian had passed away, a mere four months later. When the boy said his name, "Hi, I'm Mack," Lacey nearly tumbled out of her chair. Because of course, what she heard was "Hi, I'm Max," as though her husband had returned to her in the form of this boy. Now she knew better, but she believed in divine intervention; she believed that somehow, Maximilian had sent her Mack.

Lacey beeped the horn with abandon. She reached for the power window switch and suddenly Lacey and Mack were face to face. He kissed her through the open window before she could even pull into her parking space.

"Hey, Gardner," he said. "Welcome home."

Tears rose and she shooed Mack's face away. Pulled the car into her spot and put up the window and took a deep breath. Mack opened the door, gave her his gentleman's hand.

"You look wonderful, Lacey. I swear you're getting younger."

"Nonsense," she said. But she took Mack's face in her hands and gave him a kiss for saying so. Truth was she felt as alive and vital as ever. "Eighty-eight and still kicking."

"New car?" Mack asked, as he lifted her suitcases out of the trunk.

Lacey nodded. "They were hesitant to give me a loan down at the bank. I told them I'd pay it off in two years. That did the trick. So I'll be out of debt by age ninety."

Mack laughed and walked with Lacey toward the cottage. "Everyone's back. We have a new woman at the front desk and a new bellman. The bellman is very handsome, Lacey, so watch out. He's on his way to California."

"Don't tell me there's been another Gold Rush? See there, if you live long enough, everything will start to repeat itself."

"Vance is back. He went to Thailand and shaved his head. I'm warning you in advance so you don't make some kind of comment. You know Vance is sensitive."

"Goodness, yes," Lacey said.

"Bill and Therese are fine," Mack said. "Cecily got into the University of Virginia, but she has a Brazilian boyfriend, so who knows." Mack swung the door to her cottage open.

"Here we are," Lacey said. The place had a familiar smell, a mingling of Pine Sol and her scented talcum powder. She put down her pocketbook and looked around—her Spode on the kitchen shelves, her Maggie Meredith prints. The original sign from her hat shop hanging jauntily over the leather sofa seemed to announce her arrival: Lacey's. "Pour us a drink. Oh, wait, I forgot—there's a case of Dewar's in the trunk of the car."

"Be right back," Mack said.

Lacey wobbled down the hall to her bedroom. She touched her pillowcase, crisp and white. It was disturbing to look at the bed, however. She couldn't look at it without thinking, *This could be the bed I die in.* She supposed this was true for everyone; her odds were just greater.

MACK MIXED A DEWAR'S and water and poured himself a Coke while Lacey took a seat in her armchair.

"The cottage looks marvelous, dear," Lacey said.

"The new chambermaids tried to clean the place, but they didn't know that in Therese's vocabulary, *clean* is an absolute—like truth, or peace. I had to go in behind them and finish the job myself."

"That makes me feel all the better," Lacey said. She tried to straighten her dress hem around her knees. That was the darnedest thing about sitting down as an old woman—getting comfortable and looking good were nearly impossible. "You've given me an earful about everybody else, but I haven't heard about you. How, Mack Petersen, are *you* doing?"

Mack handed her the drink and settled himself on the sofa. There

2

Memorial Day

May 25

Dear S.B.T.,

So, we're at it once again this year! While it's true I'm not getting any younger, I still have no interest in selling the hotel. My staff is in place, Mack is back running the show, and my wife, Therese, is sitting next to me at the helm. The hotel has been buffed and polished and we look forward to a stellar season. As ever, you are invited to reveal your identity to me and come sit in my office, take in the view and talk. I feel we would have a great deal in common, and maybe after an hour or two of face time you will understand why my response to your offer has to be no, thank you. We're doing fine.

Cordially,

Bill Elliott

THERESE ELLIOTT WAS ONLY interested in the unhappy people who stayed at her hotel. She, like Tolstoy, found happy people all alike; they were boring, dullards, plukes. And so, Mack dealt with the happy guests (except for Andrea, the woman with the autistic son, but Therese sensed this was a different matter altogether) and he left Therese with the damaged and wounded, the guests who suffered despite their money. They had lost a wife, or a child, or their leg or their breasts to cancer. They assumed responsibility for a parent with Alzheimer's. They were divorced, widowed, married but alone. They had been abused. They fought suicide, depression, alcoholism.

Therese worked the reservation phone over the winter in Aspen and she heard all kinds of stories as she booked the rooms. She vividly remembered the day she spoke to Leo Hearn—February 6—it snowed eleven inches the night before, fresh powder, and Bill left the house at nine-thirty for Buttermilk Mountain. Therese's daughter, Cecily, called at ten—noon on the East Coast where she went to boarding school—to say she had the flu and was puking her guts up. Therese felt both upset and angry—upset that Cecily was sick and so far away, and angry that Bill wasn't home to worry with Therese because he was too busy skiing the green slopes. It was horribly sad to think of Bill, who had once raced down Jackpot with the best of them, limited to skiing with awkward beginners. *Why don't you stay home with me?* Therese had asked. *We'll play cards, go shopping.* But Bill got a thrill out of feeling his skis cut through the snow, just a few sweet turns. Therese imagined Bill falling, his body shattering like a teacup. She would be a widow, left to raise a headstrong teenage daughter and run the hotel all alone. Tragic possibilities always lurked near the front of Therese's mind, just behind her common sense.

At one o'clock, Leo Hearn called.

Leo Hearn wasn't a new client. He'd been coming to the hotel for four or five years and he'd always been Mack's domain—he was hale, robust, a Man's Man. He had started a second family in his late fifties: a young wife, two small children. He was a lawyer. In other words, someone who held very little interest for Therese, until this phone call.

She noticed something new in his voice right away. A softening, a surprising deference.

"Hello, I'd like to make a reservation for Memorial Day weekend, please," he said. "I might be too late, but, oh, heck, I hope not. This is Leo Hearn calling from Chicago."

"Leo *Hearn?*" Therese said. The man whose voice boomed through the lobby, making the staff cringe? The man who broke one of Mack's fingers with his crushing handshake? "Leo, this is Therese Elliott." She flipped through the reservation book to May, Memorial

Day. "I'm looking at Memorial Day right now and it's wide open. What do you need?"

"I need a better shrink and a better nanny," he said. "In fact, I think what I really need is to start over. You know, with my life."

Therese looked out her floor-to-ceiling window at the back of Aspen Mountain. "I see."

"My wife is gone," Leo said. "You remember Kelly? She left me. And I mean *left*. She left without any money and she left without the kids."

"The babies?" Therese asked.

"Whitney is ten months and Cole is almost four," he said. "She left them."

Therese's throat soured as she thought of Cecily, puking into a plastic bucket in some awful dorm room two thousand miles away. That was bad enough. She couldn't imagine a mother abandoning her children, her babies, forever.

"My doctor said I should keep everything as normal as possible. So that's why I'm calling. I want to bring the kids to the island. All my kids. I have two older boys too, did you know that? Boys, ha!" Leo said. "They're grown men. Of course I fouled everything up with them in the eighties when I divorced their mother. But they say they'll come to Nantucket. Humoring me, probably. I think my oldest son is gay. He's an attorney and he works on gay rights and the kid's never had a girlfriend that I've known about. My other son, Fred, is a third-year at Harvard Law, but Fred is tricky, see, because Fred's still angry with me from what happened with his mother. I was hoping if the kids spent time with their older brothers maybe they would stop crying." He paused, and Therese wondered if Leo Hearn weren't so boring after all. "I just want my children to stop crying."

Therese gazed out at the mountain, thinking, *Please, Bill, come home.* "I understand."

Leo cleared his throat. "Do you have three rooms available?"

• • •

THERESE WAS PUTTERING AROUND the lobby on the Friday of Memorial Day, perfecting it for opening weekend, when Leo Hearn and his children arrived.

"Leo," she said, walking over. "I'm glad you got here safely."

"Therese," Leo said. He hugged her and kissed her cheek awkwardly. He turned to his family. "Meet the gang. You know Cole and the baby. This is our nanny, Chantal, and my sons Bart and Fred. We're quite the entourage."

Entourage indeed. An attractive blonde held the baby girl. Then the sons: the one named Bart, tall and thin, dressed in a suit, and the one named Fred a younger replica of Leo Hearn himself—broad shouldered and stocky. Weaving between everyone's legs was the little boy, Cole. Therese crouched down, and said, "Hello, Cole. Welcome back."

Cole stopped a second and looked at her, his brown eyes suspicious. Then he went back to his aimless weaving. An unhappy child was the sign of an unhappy family; no one could convince Therese differently.

"Come here, Cole," Leo said. Cole ran and hid under the piano. Leo shrugged. He looked at his other two sons and rubbed his hands together. "So, what do you say, guys, should we play some tennis this afternoon?"

"I don't know," Fred, the young Leo, said. "We just got here. Maybe we could relax."

"Maybe," Leo said. "Or maybe we could play tennis like I suggested. You want to play, don't you, Bart?" he asked the son in the suit.

Bart loosened his tie. "Sure, Dad, I'll play."

"Well, then, we need a fourth," Leo said.

Slow down, Leo, stop trying so hard. Therese's mother instincts kicked in like adrenaline. She went back to watering her plants.

"We need a fourth," Leo repeated. His eyes scanned the lobby as though someone might magically materialize.

"I don't have to play," Fred said. "I'd really rather relax. You can play with Bart."

"This is a family weekend," Leo said. "I'd like to play tennis with both of you. We just need a fourth."

"I was third seed singles at Bilbo High School in 1958," Therese said. "But you probably don't want to play with an old woman."

Leo smiled. "No, that's great, that's perfect. We'd love to have you join us, Therese. Wouldn't we, guys?"

Fred and Bart rustled around and made gestures that looked sort of like nods.

"Shall we say four o'clock?" Leo asked.

"That gives you time to relax," Therese said. "Why don't you check in and Vance can show you to your rooms." She set her watering can down on the piano. Cole was stretched out on the carpet underneath, pretending to be asleep. Therese whispered to him, "When you wake up I have some beach toys you might like." She waited a few seconds and Cole raised his head.

"What kind of toys?" he asked.

"Toys for building castles," she said. "Want to see?"

"I want my mom back," Cole said. "She's not coming back." He had thick black eyelashes, the kind grown women envied.

"I know you want to see your mom," Therese said. "But what I have are beach toys. Do you want to see the beach toys?"

Cole nodded.

Therese held out her hand. "Come with me."

AFTER THERESE GAVE COLE a bucket, shovel, and a large inflatable lobster, and delivered him safely to his room, she went into Bill's office and collapsed in one of the wicker chairs by the window. Bill typed at his computer.

"The Hearns are here," she said. "Remember I told you the wife vanished and left mister with those two tiny children? Plus a couple of grown sons from the first marriage?" Out the window, she was glad to see both Bart and Fred spreading beach towels under an umbrella. "Remember I told you? Well, I'm playing tennis with them this afternoon."

Bill stopped typing. "Call me crazy, but it sounds like you're meddling, Therese. Or getting ready to meddle."

Cole and the nanny trudged onto the beach. Cole ran for the edge of the water with his pail and shovel. Just a normal little boy. Therese's mother instincts whistled like a tea kettle. She looked at Bill, and at the volume of Robert Frost poems on his desk. The two of them had known so much pain. Therese's way of dealing with it was to sniff out other people's sore spots, wanting to make them better. Bill's way was to read his poetry.

"I am meddling," she said. "But they needed a fourth."

"Be careful," Bill said. "These are people's lives you're dealing with. Not lab animals set up for one of your psychology experiments."

Therese stood up, smoothed the folds of her silk skirt. "I take great offense at that."

"I know you do," he said. "But will you please be careful?"

"I'm always careful," she said.

"When have you been careful?" Bill asked. "I have never met anyone more willing to get involved in the jumble of other people's lives. It's your insatiable need to clean everything up, to create order, to make things lovely again. You can't stand to see a mess."

"I want to help," Therese said. "I've never done anything except try to help."

"What about Mrs. Ling leaving her husband last year at the end of her stay? Are you going to tell me that wasn't any of your doing? What about convincing the Avermans that they should send their son to military school? What about arranging the wedding in the lobby for the woman who was dying of lupus?"

"She wanted to get married!" Therese said. "I helped make that woman's life complete. And Mrs. Ling is happier without her husband—you read the card she sent during the holidays."

Bill held up his palms. "Therese, I'm only asking you to think about pulling back a little this year. To begin with, think about letting Leo Hearn deal with his family problems on his own. What do you say to that?"

Therese put her hands on her hips. She and Bill were opposites: Bill liked numbers, and the cool, lofty images he found in poetry—

and not just any poetry but the poetry of Robert Frost, who wrote about the woods, lakes, paths, leaves. Frost: the man's very name dripped icicles. Bill wasn't equipped to deal with the guests—happy or miserable.

"Tennis is at four," she said. "So if anyone's looking for me, that's where I'll be."

"Be careful!" Bill said.

NANTUCKET IN MAY WAS funny as far as the weather was concerned. It had been fair and breezy all day but at four o'clock fog rolled in. Therese changed into her whites and she was standing on the front porch of the lobby when Fred popped out of the gray mist.

"Dad and Bart are going to be a minute," he said. "They were the ones who wanted to play and now they're not even ready."

Therese bounced her racket off her knee; she still used a wooden racket, with a frame. "So, have you been to Nantucket before?" she asked.

"No," Fred said. "Nantucket was a place where Dad brought his new family. We only got invited this year because the crisis hit."

"The crisis?"

"Dad's wife, Kelly, left him and the kids high and dry. I hate to say it but that's what you get for marrying someone twenty-five years younger than yourself. Dad deserved it. What goes around comes around and all that." Anger lifted off Fred like a bad smell.

"What do you do, Fred?" Therese asked.

"Me? I just finished law school. I'm studying for the bar."

"So you're going to be a lawyer," Therese said.

Fred shoved his hands in the pockets of his white shorts and bowed his head. "I don't know," he said. He looked at her. "Have you ever met a lawyer you liked?"

Therese laughed. "What a question. If I didn't like lawyers, I'd be out of business."

"I don't like lawyers," Fred said. "Actually, my brother's okay and he's a lawyer. But he's different." He swung around to look at the lobby. "Hey, do you own this place?"

"My husband and I do."

"Man, it must be a gold mine."

"It is," Therese said. Fred smiled as she hoped he would. And then Leo and Bart came around the corner with Chantal, Cole, and the baby.

"The kids are going to come with us," Leo said. "I thought I'd make this a real family affair. Cole can chase the balls."

Cole started to cry. "I was having fun on the beach," he said.

Fred kicked a hermit crab shell across the parking lot. "Great," he said. "Just great."

THEY REACHED THE COURTS at four-fifteen. The fog was thickening.

"Is this even worth it?" Fred asked. "In a few minutes we won't be able to see the ball."

Leo opened a can of balls and whacked one across the net at Fred's feet. "You need to change your attitude, Buster."

Chantal sat in the grass near the net while the baby toddled around her. Cole was crying.

"This is spectacular," Fred said. He turned to Therese. "Have you ever seen such a happy family?"

"Would you like to be on my team?" she asked.

"Okay," he said. He yelled across the net. "Hey, Dad, we're going to play mixed doubles. Me and Therese against you and Bart."

"Fuck you, Fred," Bart said.

"Watch your language," Leo said.

"That was uncalled for, Fred," Bart said.

"I was only kidding," Fred said. "I was only trying to add some levity to this little affair, this pathetic attempt at family bonding. Sorry if I offended you."

"Dad's right," Bart said. "You need to lighten up."

"Why are you kissing Dad's ass, Bart?" Fred said.

Leo raised his voice. "I *said* watch your language. We have the children here."

Then Bart turned to his father. "Why do you call *them* 'the children'? Fred and I are also your children."

"It's an age thing," Leo said.

"So now that I'm twenty-eight years old I'm no longer your child? I've become, what, your colleague?"

Chantal stood up. "I can't take this," she said. Therese hadn't even realized the girl spoke English. Chantal, wasn't that a French name? The girl had a flat, Midwestern accent. "This low-level ground fire is driving me nuts. You people don't need to be playing tennis. You need to be dealing with your issues. I'm going back to the hotel." She picked up Whitney and took Cole by the arm. He protested, and Chantal said, "Fine, you want to stay, stay." She marched off.

Therese watched her go. She should probably leave as well. Bill believed that the only people who could fix family problems were the family members themselves. But Therese worried about Cole. The skin around his eyes was red and mottled from so much crying. He wore a little white polo shirt and little tennis shoes. He sat in the grass with his feet out in front of him, his arms crossed.

"I should go, too," Therese said. "I don't belong here."

"Please stay, Therese." This from Fred. "I don't think any of us can handle it if another woman walks out."

"Yes," Leo echoed. "Please stay. We'll behave, won't we, guys?"

"Okay," Therese said. "I'll stay." She winked at Cole. He hiccuped.

THERESE CONCENTRATED ON HER tennis—the green ball and her old-fashioned racket—but she couldn't help noticing the silence that settled over them like the fog. The men barely grunted out the score. Was this their idea of good behavior? If you have nothing nice to say, say nothing at all? Didn't they know it was unhealthy to hold feelings in?

A little before five o'clock, they were tied at six games apiece.

"Shall we have a tiebreaker to see who gets the set?" Leo asked.

"I agree under one condition," Therese said. "You men have to talk to one another."

"Talk?" Fred said.

"Yes, you know, talk to one another, like normal people," Therese said. "Chantal was right. You need to communicate."

Fred got ready to serve. "Okay," he said. "I have something I'd like to talk about. I've decided I don't want to be a lawyer." He slammed the ball and it whizzed past Leo.

"What?" Leo said. "What did you say?"

Fred and Therese switched sides and Fred took another ball from his pocket. He tossed it up and caught it, and looked at his father. "I don't want to be a lawyer."

"You just graduated from Harvard Law School and now you don't want to be a lawyer? Ninety thousand dollars later and you've suddenly had a change of heart?"

"It's about more than ninety thousand dollars," Fred said. "It's about my life."

"Well, I'm gay," Bart said.

"Wait a minute," Leo said, wiping his forehead with the sleeve of his shirt. "One bombshell at a time. You don't want to be a lawyer?"

"Don't ignore what I said, Dad," Bart said. "Don't pretend like the fact that I'm gay doesn't exist."

"No," Fred said, "I don't want to be a lawyer."

The fog was so thick Therese could barely make out Cole at the edge of the court. But he sat there, listening.

Leo looked at Bart. "You're gay. I don't know what I'm supposed to do with that. Say great? That's wonderful? I'm so happy for you? What's appropriate?"

"How about, 'Thank you for telling me'?"

"Okay," Leo said. "Thank you for telling me. And, Fred, if you don't want to be a lawyer, then what *do* you want to be?"

"I don't know," Fred said. "A motorcycle cop. An independent filmmaker. A house husband."

Bart looked at his watch. "Our time's up," he said. "We have to be off the court."

"And nobody won," Fred said.

The fog made it look as though the afternoon were going up in smoke. Therese's fault, for meddling. As they walked back to the hotel, Cole took her hand.

"I want my mom," he whispered.

Therese squeezed him to her side. "I know," she said. "I know."

THE NEXT MORNING, THERESE followed behind the chambermaids with her checklist, inspecting their cleaning jobs. Was the toilet working? Was the temperature of the water in the toilet bowl correct? Did the tile floor in the entryway need scrubbing? Were the lightbulbs working? Therese had twenty-four items on her checklist. In all the years that the hotel had been open, no one had ever complained of a dirty room. Not once.

Therese watched one of her new chambermaids—a girl from Darien named Elizabeth—as she started on the bathroom in room 7.

"Check under the mirror for grime," Therese said. "Dirt has favorite hiding places and that's one of them."

Elizabeth wiped her forehead with the back of her rubber-gloved hand. "Okay," she said. She went back to scouring the top of the toilet, then she turned to Therese. "But do I really have to check the temperature of the water in the toilet bowl?"

"We need to make sure the mixing valves are working correctly. If the water's too hot the toilet will whistle, and the guests will be up all night listening to it. If the water's too cold . . . well, have you ever sat on a toilet filled with ice cold water?"

Elizabeth shook her head.

"It's no fun," Therese said. "Just take your gloves off and stick your finger in the water. See if it feels comfortable."

Elizabeth got two very distinct worry lines in her forehead. "But people *poop* in that water."

"By now the poop is hundreds of yards away. It's clean water, I assure you." Therese watched Elizabeth pull at her rubber glove one finger at a time and gingerly dip the end of her pinky into the water.

"It's comfortable," Elizabeth said.

"For goodness' sake." She nudged Elizabeth aside and dragged her own hand through the water. "You're right," Therese said.

Therese moved on to room 8, knowing that Elizabeth was rolling her eyes in frustration and would no doubt write a letter home to her mother complaining about her boss who made her test the toilet bowl water. Half the chambermaids Therese hired quit, but the ones who stayed became the world's best housekeepers.

In room 8, sitting on the unmade queen-sized bed, was Leo Hearn. Therese checked her clipboard.

"This isn't your room," she said. "What are you doing in here? You don't belong in here."

"I was waiting for you," he said.

"I'm working," Therese said. "Why aren't you with your children?"

"My children hate me," Leo said. "I can't get anything right. The nanny hates me and she's not even related to me. No wonder my wife left."

"Your kids don't hate you," Therese said. "You're just having a difficult time."

"I'll say it's difficult. One kid is a lawyer in a good practice but he's gay. He likes men. The other kid is straight but he doesn't want to be a lawyer. He wants to be a *house husband*. I told them if I took the lawyer part of Bart and joined it with the heterosexual part of Fred, they'd make the perfect son."

"Oh, Leo," Therese said.

"I let that pearl slip after four Stoli tonics at dinner last night. Now neither one of them is speaking to me. It's like I don't exist."

"You hurt them," Therese said. "You need to apologize."

"At the time, I thought maybe they'd take it as a compliment. They each got it half right."

"No," Therese said. "Because you're telling them that they only equal half a person in your eyes. You're not accepting their choices."

"I don't know what to do," Leo said, his broad shoulders slumping.

Therese sat next to him. "You want a piece of advice from an old woman?"

"You're no older than me," he said. "But you're right. I feel old."

Therese caught her reflection in the mirror over the dresser. If Bill were watching her now, he'd cringe. He'd tell her to pat Leo Hearn on the hand and wish him good luck. But Therese wanted to help. "Twenty-eight years ago, I lost a child. A son. Born dead." Therese felt Leo shift slightly away from her on the mattress. "And I would give anything to have just one of your three sons. They are strong, healthy, smart, good people and it's your responsibility to love them. That's all, Leo, just love them."

"I'm sorry you lost your son," Leo said.

"I'm sorry, too," she said. "But I'm even sorrier to see someone like you with four beautiful children acting like an ass."

"I am an ass," Leo said. "I am just a really big ass. No wonder my wife left me."

"Stop thinking about yourself, Leo. Parents aren't allowed to think about themselves."

"Do you have some kind of instruction manual that I don't have?" he asked.

"My instruction manual has been twenty-eight years of pain for my son. And it makes me grateful for what I do have, my husband, my daughter Cecily." Therese misted up. She waved her hand. "Go find your kids," she said.

Leo left the room and Therese watched him go. Then she eyed her checklist. At that moment it seemed so silly she wanted to pitch it out the window. Therese let a couple of tears drip down her cheeks, then she heard a knock on the door. It was Elizabeth.

"Are you okay?" Elizabeth asked.

Therese wiped her face and looked in the mirror. The white streak in her orange hair stood out like a scream in a nursery, something wrong, something amiss. Her baby boy dead. How shocked she'd been to look at herself in the mirror after thirteen grueling hours of labor and find that she'd turned into an old woman, with white hair. White hair that couldn't be dyed, that wouldn't hold color. So she wouldn't couldn't forget.

ON SUNDAY, LEO APPROACHED Therese during breakfast. He lowered his voice. "Things are better," he said. "I took your suggestion and recanted the statement about the perfect son."

"Good for you," Therese said.

Leo checked his watch. "Cole hasn't cried in twenty hours. A new record. But I still feel like I'm balancing a tray of expensive china on my head."

"That's known in the parents' manual as the balancing-expensive-china feeling," Therese said. "All parents feel that way sometimes."

"I'm taking Bart and Fred out alone tonight," Leo said. "A men's night out, you know, big, juicy steaks, red wine, cigars, the whole bit."

"Just love them, Leo," Therese said.

"I'm leaving Chantal with the kids and ordering them take-out shrimp and fried clams. But would you check on them? In case Cole starts to cry. I know he likes you."

"I'd be happy to check on them if it makes you feel better."

Leo spun his coffee cup in his hands. "You know, I've been thinking about what you said and I really am sorry about your son."

"I didn't tell you that story to get your sympathy, Leo," Therese said.

"I know." Leo turned red and looked down at the carpet. "I just wanted you to know it made me think."

"Good." It made him think, but he would never know what it felt like to hold a dead baby. Lucky, lucky man. "I'll keep an eye on your kids," she said. "Don't worry about a thing."

LATER, THERESE WOULD RECALL certain images: the Hearn men dressed in navy blazers and white shirts and bright summer ties standing on the front porch of the lobby while Chantal snapped their picture, their arms wound around each other, looking not so much like father and sons as like fraternity brothers, team members, friends. Then, another picture with Leo holding Cole, and Bart and Fred holding the baby girl. Therese watched all this from the bay window of her house, and she felt pride at that moment. Pride! She had helped! Therese noted the arrival of the young delivery man from Meals on Keels who showed up with Styrofoam cartons of food. She thought, "I'll check on them after they eat." Therese searched her empty kitchen cabinets for something that might qualify as dinner. She was a great housekeeper but a terrible cook and she thought guiltily of all the times Cecily had complained growing up, "There's nothing to eat in this house!" Therese fixed two cucumber and cream cheese sandwiches and a handful of pretzels. She poured herself a glass of Chardonnay and a cranberry juice for Bill. She took the glasses first and then the plates to the bedroom where Bill was lying in the near dark with a washcloth over his eyes, snoring. It was seven o'clock.

Then the phone rang and Therese left the plates of food on the bed next to Bill's sleeping body as she went to answer the phone. She remembered hoping it was Cecily.

But it was Tiny, her normally serene voice high-pitched, like the very top of a guitar string. "We have a situation down here. I've called an ambulance."

Therese flew down the stairs, out of her house, and across the parking lot, her long skirt billowing behind her. There had been no sense asking what or who. Her mother instinct shrieked like a siren. It was the Hearn children.

Chantal stood in the lobby holding Cole. His arms and legs were pink and swollen, his face a red, angry balloon.

Chantal was shaking. "He's not choking, I checked. I know how to do the Heimlich but he's not choking. I don't know what's happening."

Therese took Cole from her; he was heavier than she expected. "Go get the baby."

Therese put her ear to Cole's mouth. Cole's breathing was hoarse and wheezy. His eyes were swollen shut. "Can you hear me?" Therese asked him. "Are you awake?" Then Therese heard sirens. "Call a cab for the girl," Therese said to Tiny. "And call Leo Hearn at the Club Car. I'll go with the boy to the hospital."

Therese hurried out the front of the lobby to meet the ambulance. Cole's body went limp in her arms. The paramedic jumped out and took Cole from her.

"He fainted," Therese said. Cole's skin was turning scarlet; he looked like a boiled lobster. "Is he going to die?"

The ambulance driver flung the doors of the ambulance open, put Cole on a stretcher and loaded him in. "You coming with us?" he asked Therese. "You the boy's grandmother?"

"No," she said. Heart breaking at the word "grandmother" though she was certainly old enough. *Mother. Mother.* "But I am going with you." Therese hiked her skirt and climbed into the back of the ambulance. The siren sounded and they sped off down North Beach Road.

The paramedic lifted Cole's eyelids. "The kid's in shock," he said. He put a blanket over Cole, then took his blood pressure. He produced a needle from his bag and stuck it into Cole's arm.

"What are you doing?" Therese asked. "I said I'm not the boy's mother, or grandmother. Don't you have to ask permission or something?"

"We have a little anaphylactic reaction here," the paramedic said. "A severe allergic swelling accompanied by hives, low blood pressure, fainting. And the kid's having problems breathing because his throat is swelling shut. Has he been eating nuts maybe? Or shellfish?"

"Clams, I think," Therese said. She wondered if saying "a little anaphylactic reaction" was like saying "a little cancer" or "a little heart attack." Low blood pressure, shock, fainting—all that sounded so serious. "He's allergic, then?"

"Look at him," the paramedic said. "This is more than indigestion."

"Is he going to die?" Therese asked again. She might fend off the worst kind of news if she faced it head on. *Was the child going to die?* Less than six months before, she rode in another ambulance, when it was Bill on the stretcher, his face pale and shiny with sweat. The paramedics then talked about flying Bill to Denver in a helicopter that Therese suspected they saved for dying people. She had been too afraid then even to speak the words. But now she saw it was easier to start with the worst possibility; she might outsmart death by pretending she wasn't afraid.

The paramedic had red hair like Cecily and he was young, perhaps only a few years older than Cecily. He smiled and patted Therese's shoulder.

"No," he said, "he's not going to die."

AT THE HOSPITAL, THEY took Cole away on a gurney and the nurse tried to hand Therese forms to fill out, but she said, "I'm not his mother, I'm not his grandmother. I'm not related at all. I don't know his date of birth or anything. His father will be here soon."

A minute later, Chantal ran into the waiting room. She held the baby, who was asleep.

"I'm sure to get fired now," she said.

Therese took the baby from Chantal and nodded for her to sit down. Therese kissed the sweet, fragrant top of the baby's head. She remembered Cecily at this age: the tiny, solid weight of her. The smell of a baby, the softness of a baby. *Baby, baby.*

She whispered to Chantal, "It's not your fault, dear. Cole was allergic to what you ate. Did you have clams?"

Chantal sniffled. "Clams and shrimp. And then he swelled up like a piece of bubble gum. This whole trip has been a nightmare."

Leo stormed into the waiting room with Bart and Fred behind him. Tie loose, eyes bloodshot, smelling like smoke.

"What happened?" he said. "Where's Cole? I want to see my son."

Therese put a finger to her lips. "Cole had an allergic reaction to the clams. You need to speak to the nurse. She wants you to fill out some forms."

"I don't want to fill out any goddamned forms! I want to see my son! I get a call at the goddamned restaurant telling me my child has been rushed to the emergency room, and I'd like to see him." Leo glared at Therese, as though she were responsible. How could she blame him? She had given Leo permission to love his children, without warning him that as soon as you allowed yourself to love them fully, you left yourself open to this kind of hurt, this kind of incredible fear. Leo started in on the nurse at the desk.

"What happened?" Fred asked.

"It was an allergic reaction to the clams, they think," Therese said. She uneasily recalled that emergencies were like this: you repeated what little information you had again and again until finally you received more information. "He turned bright pink and puffy, and right before the ambulance arrived he fainted in my arms. The paramedic gave him a shot. The paramedic seemed to think Cole was going to be fine."

Leo returned from the desk with a clipboard. "They won't let me see him yet," he said. "They said the doctor will be out shortly, whatever that means. Cole had an allergic reaction to the shellfish." Leo looked at Fred. "Did you know he was allergic to shellfish?"

Fred shook his head.

"Bart, did you know Cole was allergic to shellfish?"

"No, Dad, I didn't."

"I didn't know either," Chantal offered up. "Otherwise I wouldn't have let him eat the clams. But he said he *wanted* some. I just gave them to him without thinking."

"I didn't know he was allergic," Leo said. "I'm the boy's father and I did not know he was allergic to shellfish." He collapsed into a molded plastic chair.

Bart patted him on the back. "It's okay, Dad."

"It's not okay," Leo said. "Because I'm sure his mother knew he was allergic, and his mother's not here. She took that important piece of information with her, just like she took all of the other important pieces of information. I didn't know Cole was allergic, I don't know how to make Cole stop crying, and I certainly don't know how to care for a baby girl. I only had boys, and I don't know much about them either."

They were all quiet for a while and then Fred cleared his throat. "Is it possible that this is the first time Cole's ever eaten shellfish and that nobody knew he was allergic because he'd never tried it before?"

"It's possible," Chantal said. "I've never seen Cole eat anything but hot dogs and pasta."

Fred tousled his father's gray hair. "So that means if Kelly were here, she wouldn't have known Cole was allergic either."

"Thinking like a lawyer," Bart said. "Harvard isn't wasted after all."

A bald man in a blue jogging suit came out into the waiting room. "Mr. Hearn? Mrs. Hearn?"

"Are you the doctor?" Leo asked.

"Dr. Maniscalco," he said, offering his hand. "Nice to meet you. Cole is going to be fine. He had an allergic reaction to some clams he ate but we gave him a shot of epinephrine, and some corticosteroids to reduce the swelling. That should take care of it. He can never eat any kind of shellfish again. He shouldn't be in a room where clams are steaming, he shouldn't even pick up a clam on the beach. If you hadn't gotten him here in time, there could have been some serious complications."

"But he's okay, right, Doctor?" Leo asked. "Can we take him home?"

The doctor nodded and Leo followed after him down the hall. He returned several minutes later holding Cole, whose brown eyes were wide open, thick lashes blinking; he was sucking his thumb. Therese felt the cool wind of relief. She watched her reflection in the sliding glass doors as she swayed the baby back and forth. It seemed so natural, holding a baby.

• • •

BILL WAS WAITING UP when she got home.

"What I want to know is," he said, "are we going to get sued?"

"No," Therese said.

"Good," Bill said. "It's the family of lawyers we're dealing with so I was nervous. I woke up and found the sandwiches and I wondered why I was eating alone, and so I called Tiny. I guess I slept through the sirens." He took Therese's hand and she sat on the floor in front of his chair so he could rub her shoulders. "Was it awful?" he asked.

"I've seen worse," Therese said. "But I was scared there for a while. In the end, though, the little boy's okay, and I think the family is going to make it as well."

"They survived the meddling of Therese Elliott," Bill said.

What Therese wanted more than anything else at that moment was for Cecily to come home. She wanted to look at her own child and know that she was safe. And she wanted a good night's sleep.

"We have fourteen check-outs tomorrow," Therese said. "And only three chambermaids. And if that's not bad enough, tomorrow is Memorial Day."

BILL ELLIOTT NEVER FORGOT Memorial Day. In the morning, he made love to Therese as sweetly and tenderly as he knew how. He kissed her eyelids and they leaked tears. Therese clung to him, and when Bill entered her, her sobs quieted. Therese had been his wife for thirty years and still, Bill could not believe the love that overcame him. This Memorial Day morning, the love and sadness mixed together.

"I love you," Bill said.

"I know."

One hour in bed and they relived the full weight of a pain that had assaulted them so long ago. Though perhaps Bill was the only one who felt the full brunt of the pain; perhaps for Therese, the pain had faded over the years. He hoped for her sake that it had.

Twenty-eight years ago, Therese was thirty and Bill was thirty-two. Therese was eight months pregnant with their first child, and Bill worked for his father at the Beach Club. The hotel rooms had not yet been built, although Bill and Therese planned to see an architect and approach Big Bill with the idea—a Beach Club and a *hotel*. Rooms facing the water. It was thrilling to think of handing something so concrete to their new child. Thrilling to think about passing the hotel on to a son.

No one was ever able to explain what went wrong. Therese had sharp pains one day while shopping in town. She called the doctor from the lunch counter at Congdon's Pharmacy and he jokingly told her not to drive the Jeep over the cobblestones. That night Therese asked Bill to feel her belly. Was the baby kicking? *Tell me you feel the baby kicking.* Bill spread both hands over Therese's naked belly, his fingers splayed, and rubbed it as though it were a crystal ball. He thought he felt a distant pounding, but then he realized it was Therese's frantic heartbeat. No, he felt nothing.

Therese called the doctor in the middle of the night, and he agreed to meet them at the hospital. Bill remembered the ride to the hospital—no ambulance, no sirens—just the quiet, dark minutes in the Jeep with Bill imagining how he would apologize to Dr. Stevenson for dragging him out of bed for no reason. *It's our first time,* he'd say. *We're just a little nervous.*

But an apology wasn't necessary: The baby was dead. Dr. Stevenson induced labor and for thirteen hours Therese pushed—Bill at her side—both of them crying, Therese screaming out, *It isn't fair!* Bill was thinking and maybe Therese too (Bill would never know), *What if the doctor is mistaken? What if the baby is alive?* Therese flung her arms against the metal rails of the bed, trying to hurt herself. *It isn't fair,* she screamed, and no one—not Bill, not the nurses, not Dr. Stevenson—told her she was wrong.

The baby was a boy. A perfectly shaped, normal-seeming little boy, except his skin was gray and when Bill held him he was cool to the touch, like a baby made of porcelain. The nurse left them alone in the room with the baby; she told Bill they should hold the baby for as long as they wanted. "It makes the grieving easier," she said. "Most couples who miscarry never get a chance to hold their baby." Bill and Therese both held the baby. They held him separately; they held him together—for a few minutes, a complete family.

Bill found it impossible to believe that holding his son made his grieving easier. Even now, twenty-eight years later with his wife in his arms, in their warm bed, he could remember what it felt like to hold his dead son. They named him W.T. Elliott—William Therese Elliott—and buried him in a plot in the cemetery on Somerset Road, even though everyone in Bill's family had always been cremated. But cremating the baby was unthinkable. What would he amount to? A handful of ashes that they would fling out into the sea? It would be too horrible to watch the ashes float away; it would be too much as if he never existed.

After they buried the baby, Bill vowed to make love to Therese in the mornings. At first he had to make himself go through the motions. He was afraid of getting Therese pregnant again—and he was afraid of not getting her pregnant. But making love to Therese was the best way he knew to show his devotion, and it became as natural for him as waking up, opening his eyes.

Ten years later when Therese was forty and Bill was forty-two, and Bill, at least, had given up hope of a child, Therese got pregnant again. It was impossible to feel joyful about this pregnancy—it was, Bill remembered, nine months of unspoken fear. But in the end, they had Cecily, who came out of the womb with red hair like her mother. She was kicking and screaming, undeniably alive.

AFTER THEIR LOVEMAKING, THERESE rose from the bed, blew her nose into a Kleenex and said, "I love him. This is Memorial Day. I remember him."

. Bill said, "I know. Me too."

He lay in bed a few minutes longer, listening to the sound of his wife in the shower, and he said, in a whisper,

" 'They cannot scare me with their empty spaces
Between stars—on stars where no human race is
I have it in me so much nearer home
To scare myself with my own desert places.' "

"My own desert places." Bill loved his wife and daughter until his heart and lungs and liver and brain stretched and ached and pressed at their boundaries. But he had one desert place: he wanted a son. Sometimes Bill heard Mack's voice or saw Mack throw his head back and laugh, and he thought, *My son would be almost this age. This could be my son fixing the lamppost, driving the Jeep. This could be my son. Why couldn't this be my son?*

MACK DIDN'T HAVE AN hour or even fifteen minutes on Memorial Day to meditate about his parents, but he thought of them more than usual. Maribel had asked him late one night, "If you could have your parents back for an hour, would you do it?" The question upset him so much, he turned away from her in the dark. Mack wanted to pluck his parents out of Oblivion and tell them, face to face, *I miss you, every day I miss you, and I love you.* Who wouldn't want that? But even if it were possible, he would never do it. To have his parents back for an hour meant giving them up after an hour, and that was a loss from which he would never recover. He couldn't stand the thought of losing them again.

Maribel was the only one to ever ask questions about the night of the accident. Mack had been out with friends, seeing a movie. When his friend Josh Pavel pulled down the long dirt road that led through cornfields to the Petersens' farmhouse, Mack saw the sheriff's car in his driveway. There were no flashing lights, nothing like you saw on TV, only the sheriff, a man Mack knew from school assemblies, sitting on the front porch steps, his hat resting on his knees. The sheriff stood up, put his hands on Mack's shoulders, and said, "Your mother and dad are gone. They've been killed."

"And how did you feel at that moment?" Maribel asked him.

Mack stared at her blankly. "What moment?"

"The moment you learned they were gone."

He swallowed. "I don't know. I can't remember the exact moment. It's nothing I think about. It was the worst moment of my life. I don't want to reexamine it."

"You've blocked it out," she said.

"I remember I threw up, he said. I vomited into my mother's rhododendrons. I remember being embarrassed about that, in front of the sheriff."

"Did you cry?" Maribel asked.

"I don't know."

"You must have cried."

"I don't know if I cried right then. I'm telling you, I can't remember much. I remember the sheriff waiting for me on the porch, his hat on his knees."

Ever since David Pringle's phone call, Mack found himself thinking about the farm—the smell of the soil, the barn, the hog pen. The rough, hairy skin of a sow's back, and the way the pigs squealed like children. To this day, Mack's house had been left just as it was— Mack's bedroom with his Iowa Hawkeyes pennants and his 1985 *Sports Illustrated* swimsuit calendar hanging on the wall. A valentine from Michele Waikowski thumbtacked to his bulletin board.

His parents' room too had been left as it was—his father's Carhartt overalls in the closet, and his mother's dresses. His mother's pale hair still in her hairbrush. The food in the kitchen had been cleaned out, except for Mack's mother's refrigerator pickles. "Leave the refrigerator pickles," Mack told David Pringle. His mother used to say they would last forever.

Mack knew it was odd to keep things as they were, crazy even. He supposed the farm hands gossiped about the house, along with the people in Swisher, along with people simply passing through Swisher; by now, it was legend. *The farmhouse, untouched since the couple was killed in a car crash twelve years ago. Haunted? The woman's hair still in her hairbrush.* For years, David Pringle had been urging Mack to clean out the house and rent it, but Mack refused. Mack's life with his parents was, in fact, frozen. The house was a museum of sorts, a museum Mack could visit if he ever found the desire, or the courage, to return.

Because it was Memorial Day, Mack let Love go home early—she'd been swamped all weekend—and he took over behind the front desk and imagined his parents standing there with him. *Here is the lobby*, the quilts Mack hung every year. *Look out at the ocean,* the ferry taking a crowd of people back to the mainland. *Listen to this couple here checking out.* They were sunburned across their cheeks, bike helmets tucked into their duffel bags.

"We had a great time," the man said, handing over his American Express card. (Mack would *not* want his parents to know how much the room cost.) "Thank you very much."

"Yes, and thank you for recommending the bike ride to Altar Rock," the woman chimed in. "It was spectacular."

The couple went to meet their cab, touching a few of Therese's wooden toys on the way out, as if for luck.

See? I made them happy. I made them smile. But when Mack turned around, of course, no one was there.

MEMORIAL DAY: A DAY for remembering. Still, Lacey Gardner had better days for remembering Maximilian—his birthday, August 18, or their wedding anniversary, November 11, even Valentine's Day, because that, sadly, was the day Maximilian had died. Besides, Memorial Day was for veterans, wasn't it? Or was Veterans' Day for veterans and Memorial Day for the rest of God's people? Darn it, Lacey couldn't remember and didn't much care except that she had invited the new bellman in for a drink and he was asking her all kinds of questions about Maximilian, practically forcing Lacey to remember him.

"What did your husband do for a living?" Jeremy asked. (He introduced himself as Jem, but Jem wasn't a real name in Lacey's opinion and she told him so. She would call him Jeremy.)

"Banker," Lacey said. The boy agreed to a scotch, a point in his favor. Lacey poured two drinks and brought them over to the coffee table. Jeremy sat on the sofa looking at a photograph of Maximilian taken the summer before he died. He was tan and healthy-looking in that picture, standing on the deck of their house on Cliff Road.

"Is this him here?" Jeremy asked.

"Indeed," Lacey answered. "That's Maximilian Percy Gardner." She walked back to the kitchen—although in this tiny cottage, living room, dining room, and kitchen were one and the same—and fished through her refrigerator for cheese. She put some brie on a plate with a few Carr's water crackers. Then there was a knock at the screen door. It was Vance with her bucket of ice. Goodness gracious, she forgot to put ice in the cocktails and hadn't even noticed.

"The iceman cometh," Lacey said. Vance didn't smile—his face remained clenched in the same tight scowl he always wore. It would do the young man a world of good to smile every now and again, but she'd been telling him that for years, and to no avail. Now Vance had shaved his head. What on earth for? Lacey asked him. Some kind of gang? For freedom, Vance told her. He liked to feel the cool breeze against his scalp.

Vance peered into the living room, took in Jeremy sitting on the sofa.

"I'd ask you to join us," Lacey said quickly, "but I know you're on duty. There's nothing like work to ruin a cocktail hour."

"That's okay," Vance said. He set the bucket of ice down on the counter. "See ya."

"Thank you, Vance!" Lacey called. She took the cheese and crackers to the table and went back for the ice. Having company meant a lot of dashing about. If she'd kept her mouth shut, she would be sitting in her chair, watching Dan Rather.

By the time Lacey reached the coffee table with the bucket of ice, Jeremy had dug into the cheese. Lacey was able to drop into her chair and relax just a minute while he finished chewing. She noticed he left the picture of Maximilian facedown on the sofa. This was quite definitely a strike against him.

"Let's hear about you," Lacey said. "Where do you come from? Your family?"

"I grew up in Falls Church, Virginia," he said. "My father owns a bar."

"A bar, really?" Lacey said. "Do you have siblings?"

Jem fixed himself another cracker. "A younger sister," he said. "She's bulimic. My parents go with her to counseling. You know what bulimia is, right? She stuffs her face with food and then she pukes it all up." Jeremy popped the cracker into his mouth.

Lacey sipped her drink. The photograph snagged Jeremy's interest again. "So this is your husband. He looks like Douglas Fairbanks, the old actor. How long were you married?"

"Forty-five years," Lacey said. "I married late in life. I was thirty-one years old. I had a career, you see, and many people, my father included, thought that was like hammering the final pegs into the coffin of my spinsterhood. But Maximilian married me anyway."

"So you were married for forty-five years," Jeremy said. "How many children do you have?"

Lacey wondered if there were a formula for determining how many questions a person would ask before finding the exact wrong question, the question that brought a second too long of silence, the question that caused the voice of heartache to answer. Jeremy had found it early on; Lacey hated to answer this question.

"No children," she said. "As I told you, we married late."

Jeremy fixed himself another cracker. "You said you were thirty-one. That's not too old to have children."

"It was for us," Lacey said. She had always blamed her barrenness on her advanced age—thirty-four by the time Maximilian returned from the war—although now she saw programs on TV about childless couples and she realized it could have been the result of any number of complications. The fact was, she hadn't gotten pregnant and she'd wanted to adopt. But Maximilian refused—it was the only time in forty-five years they had argued. They would not adopt! He was so stubborn about this, Lacey could hardly believe he was the same man she had married. By way of explanation, Maximilian told her he once had a chum who adopted a baby, and it turned out the baby was one-quarter Japanese. Who cared if the baby were one-quarter Japanese—or full-blooded Japanese for that matter? Lacey asked. She hadn't been in the war, Maximilian said. True, this was true; Lacey hadn't been in the war. But that had little to do with the matter at hand. Lacey had simply wanted a baby.

She looked at the photograph of Maximilian, which Jeremy returned to its upright position. She and Maximilian had a good life—a rich and varied life filled with work, travel, erudite people. But Maximilian didn't stick it out with her the way he promised. He died in his sleep. He wasn't even sick; it was as though he were just too tired to keep on living. Too tired! They fell asleep together, holding hands, but Lacey woke up alone. Clearly, when Maximilian made his decision about adoption he hadn't realized how alone she would be.

"Would you like another drink?" Lacey asked.

"I can fix them," Jeremy said.

"Good," she said, settling into her chair. "Because I'm getting comfortable."

Jeremy made the drinks and when he handed Lacey hers, she tasted it. "Very nice. Now tell me, Jeremy, about your career plans. I hear Nantucket is merely a resting stop for you, on your way to Hollywood."

Jeremy nodded. "That's right. I'm headed west in the fall. I want to be an agent."

Agent, Lacey thought, like the FBI? No, that couldn't be right. There was that old term, agency man; what had that meant? Or maybe not agent but aged, like herself.

"Agent?" she said.

"I used to think I wanted to act," Jem said. "I tried in college and it didn't work out so well. But I like business, so I figure I'll go out to L.A. and help people who can act. Represent them. Make them money. Be their friend."

The world had surely deteriorated if one now got paid for being a friend. "That sounds lovely," Lacey said.

Jeremy fixed himself yet another cracker. Well, he'd worked all day—it was understandable the boy would be hungry. Lacey was going to heat up a swordfish potpie for her dinner. She contemplated asking Jeremy to stay, but that seemed like too much.

"What do your parents think of all this?" Lacey asked.

A piece of cracker stuck in Jeremy's throat and he coughed. Perhaps she had stumbled upon Jeremy's sore spot. Perhaps the bulimic sister was a much safer topic than his parents.

"They don't know about California," he said. "My parents want me close to home, especially with my sister all messed up. They want me to find an internship in D.C. or something. So they don't know about California yet. Do you think that's bad?"

"To be honest, I've never understood why children feel they need their parents' approval," Lacey said. "I believe the earlier you stop hoping for that, the happier you'll be. Look at me—my father went to all kinds of trouble to send me to Radcliffe, but then he sniffed when I pursued a career. But I didn't let that stop me. I had a career that I adored and a husband, too."

Jeremy's face brightened. "Yeah, I figure they might not like the idea at first but once I make it, they'll be fine with the whole thing."

"You might be better off not worrying what your parents think at all. Ever."

"They *are* my parents," Jeremy said. "They did raise me."

"All a parent can do is hope for the best," Lacey said. This was the philosophy she always believed she would have followed with a child. Raise them as well as you can and then let them go. Jeremy looked at her strangely. Maybe he didn't understand how much eighty-eight years of life could teach a person. She was relieved when he stood up.

"I should be going," he said. He leaned over and kissed Lacey's cheek, another point in his favor. "Thanks for the drink and the cheese and stuff."

"You're welcome, my dear," she said. "Come again."

Jeremy left the cottage, closing the screen door quietly behind him. Lacey stayed in her chair. She could reach for the remote control and turn on Dan Rather, or she could stand up and retrieve the swordfish potpie from the freezer. But for a moment she did neither. She was paralyzed with loneliness, and anger about that loneliness. She kicked the coffee table and the picture of Maximilian fell over with a clatter. This pleased her for an instant and then she felt irritated. Surely there were better days to get angrier than hell at her dear, departed Maximilian than this, Memorial Day.

3

The Gold Coast

June 5

Dear Bill,

*I don't know why you insist on torturing yourself by continuing to
run the hotel. Just imagine—with the money I'm offering you, you
could buy a huge home here on Nantucket—right next door!—and a
house in Aspen as well—and enjoy life for a change. I have no evil
intentions in buying the hotel; I am only trying to right the wrongs
I've done in my life.*

*I've caught a glimpse or two of you over the past three weeks and
I must say, you look harried. Carrying that heavy book with you
everywhere! What is that book, anyway, Bill, the Bible? Don't turn
to religion, Bill—turn to me. My offer stands.*

S.B.T.

LOVE COULDN'T BE CERTAIN, but she thought Mr. Beebe, in room 8, was
interested in her. He and his wife arrived on Nantucket in their own
plane. This wasn't a big deal—Love knew people in Aspen who
owned jets, and some of them were just regular people that she saw in
line at all-you-can-eat taco night at La Cocina. But Mr. Beebe *called*
from his jet. To Love, this indicated a blatant disregard for the value of
money. She felt the same way about people who used the phones on
regular planes. It seemed ludicrous to pay so much money for something so transient. So while Love didn't begrudge Mr. Beebe his jet, a
part of her was annoyed by the phone call.

Mr. Beebe's question: Would there be a car at the airport to pick
him up?

"I'm sorry, sir," she said, loudly (the reception was poor.) "You'll have to take a taxi. There's a taxi stand in front of the terminal, and always plenty of taxis waiting."

"I'm arriving in my own plane," Mr. Beebe said.

Love agreed with the Beach Club's policy. All of the guests were important, but no one was important enough to get picked up at the airport. Not Michael Jackson, not George Bush, and not this man, Mr. Beebe.

"Yes, sir, I understand," she said. "We look forward to your arrival."

Mr. Beebe was a very handsome man. He stood well over six feet tall and had wonderfully broad shoulders, and his dark hair was going gray in the front. He wore white slacks, a crisp blue Façonnable shirt, a navy blazer, Gucci loafers. Mrs. Beebe was frosted blond and already deeply tanned. She wore a hot pink linen dress and about thirty gold bangle bracelets that jingled as she walked. They were a stunning couple.

Mr. Beebe smiled broadly as he approached the desk.

"Are you the young lady I spoke to on the phone?" he asked.

Love fought off the desire to snarl at him. She was *hardly* a young lady. The wealthy often assumed that anyone not as rich as they were was also inferior in other ways—younger, shorter, less intelligent. It drove Love nuts. "Yes, I am," she said. "My name is Love O'Donnell."

"Love," Mr. Beebe said. "What a beautiful name. Love."

"You're the Beebes?" Love asked. She pronounced the name like the gun. "You're in room eight, on the Gold Coast."

"The Gold Coast," Mr. Beebe said. "That's us."

Mrs. Beebe gave a shrill laugh. Love looked at her, startled.

"My wife's nervous," Mr. Beebe said. "In general, but now specifically. New place and everything."

Love called the laundry room, where she knew Vance would be sitting on one of the dryers, reading. "Check-in," she said.

Mrs. Beebe laughed again. Her laugh was almost inhuman; it sounded like the mating call of some exotic bird. Then she spoke. "That plane really did me in."

"Will you be needing dinner reservations?" Love asked.

"Yes," Mr. Beebe said. "I'll come back a little later and we'll talk. Right now I need to get my wife to the beach."

Vance appeared and took the Beebes' bags. When Mrs. Beebe saw Vance, she erupted again in laughter, and it sent shivers through Love. Was Mrs. Beebe laughing at Vance because he was black? Because of his shaved head? Oh, she hoped not.

A few minutes later, Vance returned to the desk, and said, "That lady was drunk in case you were wondering. Well, drunk or high. Rich people have access to drugs we can only dream about. Anyway, mister gave me a fifty and he said he'll talk with you in an hour or so."

Exactly an hour later, Mr. Beebe appeared again at the desk. He'd shed his blazer, and rolled up the sleeves of his shirt. He came into the lobby without shoes. His feet were pale and vulnerable looking.

He leaned on the desk with his arms crossed in a surprisingly casual and intimate way. "My wife is happily ensconced on the beach," he said.

"Good," Love said. In the hour he was gone, she'd looked through the files for a copy of his confirmation letter. There was no address on the letter, only a fax number in area code 212: Manhattan. A copy of Mr. Beebe's personal check was stapled to the letter, but that showed no address either, only the name—Arthur Beebe. Arthur. Love wondered if he went by Art or Artie. "Did you want to discuss dinner reservations?" she asked.

"Yes," he said. "We're here for six nights."

"Twenty-one Federal is a must. And American Seasons. You'll want to eat out in 'Sconset one night, perhaps at the Chanticleer. Do you like classic French?"

"No," he said, "I don't." He leaned forward. "How trustworthy are you, Love?"

"Oh, I don't know," Love said quickly. How trustworthy was she? She hoped to God he wasn't about to confide something in her. Mr. Beebe's eyes were an intense green, and she wondered if maybe he were drunk or high also. Maybe he and his wife had indulged in a little cocaine on the plane. And who cared if they did? It certainly wasn't Love's place to judge, just as long as Mr. Beebe didn't disclose where he got the drugs—or worse, tell her some private information about his wife. "I'd say I'm pretty trustworthy."

Mr. Beebe let his eyes drift down the length of Love's body at the speed that a feather floats through the air. "You look like you're in good shape," he said. "Will you go jogging with me tomorrow morning?"

"Jogging?" Love said. She should turn him down, of course. Mack said there was to be No Dating the Guests, although surely going running with a married man wouldn't qualify as a date. It sounded like a date to Love, however, because she always met the important men in her life while exercising.

"I need a jogging partner," Mr. Beebe said. "We could go before you start work, maybe?"

Tomorrow before work. Love's mind zipped around in a crazy pattern, like a balloon losing air. She had to be on the desk by eight-thirty. She could conceivably bring a change of clothes and shower in the bathhouses. If she got here by seven, that would all be possible. But what if someone saw her? Mack? Bill? Another guest? Could jogging with someone be considered a special service? If she jogged with Mr. Beebe tomorrow would she then be required to jog with any guest who asked? What would Mrs. Beebe think? Would it seem like just another concierge duty, this jogging? And what was all that about Love being trustworthy? If such a simple request brought up so many questions, then maybe the request wasn't so simple after all. What could *not* enter Love's decision making was the fact that she *wanted* to go jogging with Mr. Beebe. She wanted to spend an hour with him alone, their heart rates accelerating, their legs pumping. Love's own desire worried her. Her answer should definitely be no.

"Thanks for the offer but I don't think I can," Love said. "With work and everything, it would be too much, I'm afraid."

"Oh, come on," Mr. Beebe said. "Come on, Love. What about after work then?"

Love wished someone else would come into the lobby. Mack was at lunch. Bill was in his office with the door closed. Love felt both flattered and uncomfortable. Who was this man to insist Love go out of her way *on personal time* for him?

"I'm sorry," Love said, in what she hoped was a definitive way. "Now, what about the dinner reservations? Did you want to try American Seasons, or—"

Mr. Beebe straightened up and sliced his hand through the air. "You make them," he snapped. "Surprise me. But no classic French. Say, do you ever get a day off?"

"Tuesday," Love said. "My day off is Tuesday. But—"

"On Monday I'll come in and we'll make plans for Tuesday. How does that sound?"

"I'll have to see," Love said. "I mean, I'll check. Maybe. I don't know."

"I'm beginning to think you don't like me," he said. "I'm starting to take offense here."

"Please don't take offense," Love said. She liked his green eyes and his salt-and-pepper hair. She had an urge to use his name, Arthur, Art, but enough! She lowered her eyes. "I'll start on those dinner reservations." She picked up the phone to show Mr. Beebe that she was serious, and to get him to go away, which he did—Love heard the whisper of his bare feet sauntering off down the hall. When the reservationist at 21 Federal answered, Love's throat was dry, and it took her a second to think of what it was she had wanted to say.

LOVE THOUGHT ABOUT ARTHUR Beebe all afternoon and into the evening. There was no denying her attraction to him. He was sexy. She couldn't say what made him sexy—maybe his green eyes, maybe his friendly, almost cozy manner with her at the desk. Maybe his airplane. Or maybe, Love thought, she was simply impatient. Finding a father for her child made Love feel like a sniper, an assassin. Centering her crosshairs on every man she saw. But she'd been working the desk for two weeks now and not a single eligible gentleman her age had wandered into the lobby. Of course, Arthur Beebe wasn't an eligible gentleman. He only acted like one.

After work, Love skated home to her rented house on Hooper Farm Road. She lived with two other people. Randy and Alison were a couple in their twenties and they both worked at 21 Federal. Alison worked the reservation book and so it'd been easy for Love to get the Beebes a table there for tonight, even though it was last-minute. Alison always encouraged Love to stop by the restaurant for a drink. *You can't meet people if you don't go out!* she said.

Love enjoyed having the house to herself, although she was lonely at times. Their house was small, but it had a nice grassy yard with a picnic table out back. After Love got home from work, she tried to nap, but today she couldn't sleep. She was thinking of Arthur Beebe. Ridiculous, pathetic even, but true. She made herself lie still for twenty minutes, then she put on exercise tights and rode her Cannondale out to Madaket. She liked to exercise right around dusk, and then come home and fix herself dinner and eat outside if it was nice, read her book and fall asleep. It was a pleasant routine, if unexciting. But tonight when Love returned from her bike ride, she was antsy. She felt as though she might jump out of her skin. She showered, put on her short black skirt and called a taxi, which delivered her to 21 Federal.

Alison greeted her at the door.

"Love!" she said. "Good for you. Are you here for a cocktail or dinner?"

"Cocktail," Love said. She was afraid to turn her head and look around the restaurant. "Can you join me?"

Alison checked her watch. "I can join you in half an hour," she said. "Have a seat at the bar. I'll meet you there."

The bar at 21 was clubby, with a lot of brass and dark wood. Love chose a seat that faced the dining room. She ordered Champagne from the bartender. As Love brought the flute to her lips, she caught Mr. Beebe looking at her from his table in the dining room. Love pretended not to see him. She crossed her legs, wishing that she smoked cigarettes so that she'd have something to do with her hands other than idly twirl her Champagne flute. Usually when she went to restaurants alone, she took along a book or *Time* magazine. But really, wasn't that frumpy of her? Wasn't that shutting other people out? Love watched the bartender dunk highball glasses into soapy water, and she sneaked looks at the Beebes' table. Mrs. Beebe had her back to Love. She appeared to be doing most of the talking; Arthur Beebe said very little. He nodded every once in a while and ate his food. Love recrossed her legs. She felt Arthur staring at her. She flagged down the bartender.

"I'd like to see a menu," she said.

Love felt a tap on her shoulder and turned around, expecting to find Alison, but instead she saw Vance.

"Vance!" she said. "What are you doing here?" He was wearing jeans, a tweed sportscoat, and aviator sunglasses. His bald head gleamed like polished wood.

Vance took the stool next to her. "I come here all the time," he said. "Are you going to order something?"

Why was he wearing sunglasses inside? At night? Obviously he had emotional and possibly even psychological baggage. Love didn't want him to stay and eat with her. Arthur Beebe had seen her and Vance together at the Beach Club. If he saw them eating together tonight, he might think they were dating.

"I don't know," she said, putting the menu down. "I'm not that hungry."

"Get the portobello mushroom," Vance said. "It's outstanding. In fact, let me treat you to your first Twenty-one portobello. I promise you will never forget it."

"That's not necessary," she said. It was funny, though—she did love portobellos, almost better than anything in the world.

"I insist," Vance said. He waved at the bartender. "I'll have a Dewar's straight up, and we'd like two portobellos."

"And I guess I'll have another champagne," Love said. She peeked over at the Beebes, and accidentally locked eyes with Arthur. Love raised her eyebrows and Arthur winked. The wink nearly knocked her off her barstool.

Vance turned around. "I see the druggies are here," he said.

"Who?" Love said.

"You know, the people who checked into room eight this afternoon. The woman with the horrible laugh."

Love sipped her Champagne. "My roommate works here," she said. She swung around on her stool, still reeling from the wink, and searched for Alison. Alison was standing at the hostess station; she pointed to Vance and gave the thumbs-up.

Love rolled her eyes. Even Alison thought Vance was her date! How was it she only knew a handful of people on this island and they all converged here?

Vance leaned in close, and said, "There's something I want to know."

Love backed up. "Me too. Why are you wearing those sunglasses?"

"Traveling incognito," Vance said, pushing them up his nose. "Guests are crawling all over this place. I don't want them to recognize me."

The first thing someone would notice about Vance was that he was a large African American man with a shaved head, and no pair of sunglasses could hide that. "Why not?" she asked.

"Mixing business and pleasure makes me uneasy," he said.

"Oh," Love said. "Well, what did you want to know?"

"I want to know what you think of Mack."

"If you don't like mixing work and pleasure, then why are you asking about Mack?"

"Forget about work," Vance said. "What do you think about Mack as a person?"

"I don't really know him as a person," Love said. "He seems fine. He has that great Midwestern, apple-pie personality. He's a good boss. He has a pretty girlfriend. I guess you could say I like him as a person."

Vance shook his head. "So you've been taken in too."

"Taken in by what?"

"By the facade that is Mack," Vance said. "No one in the world is that happy all the time. That fucking pleasant. His whole attitude of not having an attitude. I'm surprised you don't see past that."

"I'm sorry," Love said. "I don't." Across the room, the Beebes got their check, and then a few minutes later, they stood up. Arthur Beebe took his wife's arm and left the restaurant. He didn't look her way once. Love experienced familiar pain. Really, this was absurd! How could Arthur Beebe, whom she had just met that day, matter to her enough to cause this crazy longing?

The portobellos arrived and thankfully, Vance seemed less interested in talking and more interested in eating. Love took a bite of her mushroom. It was delicious. At least there was that.

THE BREAKFAST HOUR WAS the busiest part of Love's day. By the time she reached work, Jem had set up the buffet table: the coffee and hot water thermoses, the carafes of orange and cranberry juice sitting in a tub of ice, the glass canisters of granola, Cheerios and All-Bran, the milk, sugar, butter, cream cheese, silverware, plates, bowls, napkins. Then at eight-thirty, Mack entered with the day's doughnuts, the bagels, the muffins and five loaves of Something Natural bread. A few people loitered while Jem set up; these were the people who needed their coffee. Mack's arrival indicated the Official Start of Breakfast, and the lobby filled with guests pretending to wait patiently for their choice of doughnut. It never ceased to amaze Love what waiting to eat did to people. They became completely irrational.

Arthur Beebe balanced three doughnuts on his plate and poured himself a glass of orange juice. Mrs. Beebe only drank coffee. They moved with their food to one of the wicker sofas. Some guests liked to take their food out onto the pavilion, and some liked to eat in their rooms. But thankfully, Arthur Beebe was a lobby eater. He set his plate and glass down on the carpet and then went in search of a desirable section of the newspaper.

The newspaper frenzy followed directly after the doughnut frenzy. The hotel provided complimentary editions of *The New York Times,* the *Boston Globe,* the *Wall Street Journal,* and *USA Today.* But everyone wanted *The New York Times,* and of course, being from Manhattan, Arthur Beebe was a *Times* reader. Love watched him as he read. She wanted him to look at her! She'd worn her sexiest dress—a short, flowered sundress with spaghetti straps. Then, finally, she got her wish. Mrs. Beebe finished her third cup of coffee, said in her shrill voice, "I'm going to *bathe*, Arthur," and left the lobby. A few seconds later, Arthur Beebe put down the paper and cha-chaed his way to the desk.

"The funniest thing just happened," he said.

Love surveyed the lobby. There were still a few stragglers refilling their coffee cups, but for the most part the guests had returned to their rooms.

"What's that?" she said.

"This morning I wanted a coconut doughnut. And I noticed only one coconut doughnut on the buffet table. So I reached for it. But another man snapped it up first."

"That's been known to happen," Love said.

"So I give this guy a dirty look to let him know he's taken my doughnut. Then I pick up the *Times* and who do you think is on the front page of the business section? The very same guy." Arthur Beebe held up the paper. Love squinted at the picture. The grainy photograph was of Mr. Songttha, room 17.

"You're right," Love said. "Well, if it makes you feel any better, that man's not even staying on the Gold Coast. He's only in a side deck room."

As soon as she said this, a human noise came from the back office: Mack clearing his throat. Love hadn't realized he was sitting back there. Giving out information about other guests was prohibited. Especially when Love was insinuating that Mr. Songttha hadn't paid as much for his room as Mr. Beebe. Love bounced on the balls of her feet nervously. What kind of effect was Arthur Beebe having on her? Her good judgment had totally vanished. She was so busy chastising herself that she didn't catch what Arthur Beebe said next.

"I'm sorry?"

"I asked if you had a good time last night at the restaurant."

"I stopped by for a drink and I bumped into a co-worker," Love said. This was her rehearsed line—getting across that she and Vance were *co-workers*, and that they hadn't *planned* to meet—but it didn't exactly answer his question. "How about you and Mrs. Beebe? Did you like your meal?"

"It was marvelous," he said. He put his hand over Love's. For an instant they were holding hands. Then Mr. Beebe gave her the wink. "Keep up the good work."

Love watched him leave the lobby. She took a few deep breaths, scribbled a note on a piece of paper, and wandered back into the office where Mack sat at his messy desk.

"I made a mistake out there," Love said. "I'm sorry."

"At least you recognized it yourself," Mack said. "It's important to be discreet. Don't discuss the guests at all, especially not with other guests."

Love thought of what Vance had said the night before. Was Mack a phony? Now that Love thought about it, it was a bit disconcerting to have him behind her, listening in like Big Brother.

"I need to make a request," she said.

"What's that?" Mack asked.

"More coconut doughnuts," she said. She handed him the slip of paper; it was amazing how doing this one small thing for Arthur Beebe delighted her. "Here, I've written it down."

ARTHUR BEEBE WALKED INTO the lobby that afternoon, wearing swimming trunks and a crisp white polo shirt. Love was perched on her high stool, reading *The Prince of Tides.*

He leaned on the desk, arms crossed, the face of his Tag Heuer flashing. "Hello there, Love. How are you?"

Love slipped a hotel brochure into her book to mark her page, and smiled. Arthur stared at her, and Love stared back, unembarrassed. Then the phone rang, catching them both off guard.

It was Mario Cuomo, calling for Mr. Songttha. Love tightened her grip on the receiver and said in her most professional voice, "Let me put you through to his room." She patched the call and laid the receiver down quietly. Arthur was smiling at her. She wished she could tell him that she'd just spoken to Mario Cuomo, but she'd learned her lesson that morning. She was attracted to Arthur Beebe but she wasn't prepared to lose her job for him.

"Did you need something special?" Love asked. "Beach towels or something?"

"No, no, nothing like that," Arthur Beebe said. "My wife is busy sitting in the sun. I can only take it for an hour or so before I get bored. I came in here to talk."

To talk. To her. He sought her out. The phone rang again. Love looked at the console and saw it was the same call—Mario Cuomo—bouncing back to her.

"I'm sorry, sir, Mr. Songttha's not in his room. Would you like to leave a message?" She wrote down Mario Cuomo's name and number, shielding the notepad with her body. She hung up and put the message in the slot for room 17.

"Songttha? That's the guy from the newspaper, right?" Arthur asked. "Who called for him, Alan Greenspan?"

Love laughed as though she found this preposterous. "No, no, not Alan Greenspan." She had to change the subject away from Mr. Songttha! She climbed back onto her stool. "So, Mr. Beebe, what do you do for a living?"

"Oh, a little of this and a little of that. I wish I could say I worked the front desk at this hotel. I'd probably be much happier."

"It has its ups and downs," Love said. "Did you go running this morning?"

"I did," Arthur said. "I ran through town."

"You should try the bike path," Love said. "Less traffic, and prettier."

"You can show me the way yourself when we go on Tuesday," Arthur said. "You promised, remember? Your day off, Tuesday."

Love knew she very specifically had *not* promised to run on Tuesday. She couldn't remember her exact words, but she was pretty sure she hadn't even agreed. It was just like the wealthy to assume everything would go just as they wanted. And what if Arthur Beebe didn't even work for his money? What if he were an example of the idle rich, flying his plane, sitting on beaches? Love knew this should make him far less attractive in her mind. But it didn't.

"Okay," she said. "Tuesday."

"It's a date," Arthur said. "So, where are we eating tonight?"

Love checked her notebook, although she already knew the answer. "Ships Inn," she said. "Eight o'clock."

"And will we see you there?" Arthur asked.

Love hesitated a second. Did Arthur Beebe think Love had intentionally followed him to 21 Federal the night before?

"No," she said. "Tonight is a stay-at-home night."

Arthur Beebe straightened up. "That's too bad," he said.

BUT, IN FACT, LOVE couldn't keep herself away from Ships Inn. After a fish burrito at home, Love told herself she would go for a walk through town, window shop, get an ice cream cone. She did just this. She spent half an hour in Mitchell's Book Corner before purchasing *What to Expect When You're Expecting*. She spent forty-five minutes in Top Drawer looking at lingerie, and bought a lacy white bra and panty set after realizing that all the underwear she owned was athletic and functional. She went to the Juice Bar and ordered a kiddy cup of Almond Joy ice cream, because she too loved coconut.

And at ten o'clock, she found herself walking home via Fair Street, where she lingered outside Ships Inn. She crossed the street to St. Paul's Episcopal Church and read last week's program, even though she was a nonpracticing Roman Catholic. Then she heard the freakish, high-pitched warble laugh. Mrs. Beebe. Love saw the Beebes standing in front of the restaurant waiting for a cab. It was unlikely that they would be able to pick Love out in the dark, and so she sat on the steps of the church and watched. She watched Arthur standing with his hands in his pockets while Mrs. Beebe did a tap dance around him. She was drunk, and happy.

Love watched them until the cab came. Arthur helped Mrs. Beebe into the cab. He hesitated before he got in himself. It seemed to Love he was looking at her. Love sat clutching her package in her lap as Arthur Beebe blew her a kiss.

• • •

THE NEXT MORNING, ARTHUR Beebe said, "That was you last night? In front of the church?"

Love had debated all night about how to answer this question. "Yes," she said.

"Good," Arthur said. He lowered his voice. "I didn't want to blow a kiss to a stranger."

"Don't worry, you didn't," she said.

"That's right," he said. "I blew one to you."

Love blushed. She was glad Mack was outside washing his Jeep.

"Well, thank you," Love said.

"I thought you said last night was a stay-at-home night."

"I went shopping," Love said. "I bought a book." She hesitated. "And some lingerie."

Arthur narrowed his eyes. "You know what I've always wanted to do?"

"What?" Love said.

"Fly my plane to Antarctica. What do you think of that? My wife thinks it would be too cold. Do you think it would be too cold?"

"Depends who you're with," she said. Desire shot through her. Her thighs ached. "I'd like to go to Antarctica."

"Yes, I thought so," Arthur said. "I thought you seemed like a woman in search of some adventure. So maybe Tuesday, then? A little adventure?"

"Adventure," Love said.

That night, the Beebes were eating at the Summer House out in 'Sconset, and thankfully Love managed to stay away. Instead, she rode her Cannondale to the airport. She inspected the private jets, wondering which one belonged to Arthur Beebe. She decided on a gray plane with a red racing stripe. The body of the plane was long and phallic. Love imagined herself boarding this plane for Antarctica, or places unknown.

Love's conversations with Arthur Beebe worked on her like aphrodisiacs. Arthur Beebe putting his hand over hers, and saying, "Keep up the good work!" Arthur Beebe asking to see her book so he would have an excuse to touch her fingers or the inside of her arm, Arthur

Beebe asking if she'd bought any more lingerie. Arthur Beebe reminding Love about Tuesday. Their running date Tuesday. Their date Tuesday. Tuesday, her day off. It became the world's biggest euphemism. Tuesday, to Love, meant only one thing: she was going to have sex with Arthur Beebe.

And how did Love feel about this? At certain times—the few heady moments after Arthur left the lobby, for example—it thrilled her. She envisioned herself and Arthur jogging along Cliff Road, Love inhaling deep breaths of the oxygen-rich air. At home, she could offer Arthur lemonade, a mimosa, a refreshing shower. Randy and Alison announced they would be off-island on Tuesday, which only convinced Love further that sex with Arthur was destined to happen. They would have the house to themselves. It would be fervent, Love supposed, maybe even rushed. He would have to get back to the hotel. Charged, delicious, secret—these were words Love associated with sex with Arthur Beebe.

But sometimes, other words popped into Love's mind. Foolish, irresponsible, not to mention *immoral*. How could she sleep with Arthur Beebe? He was a married man, and a hotel guest. She might ruin his marriage, jeopardize her job. The Beebes were leaving on Wednesday, paying their bill, boarding the jet plane, and flying back to Manhattan. Checking out. Would Arthur leave her a *tip*? It was too horrible to imagine.

On Monday afternoon, Love and Arthur confirmed their plans. They would meet in front of the lobby at 7:45 the following morning and start their run.

"We'll go where the day takes us," Arthur said with a wink.

Go where the day takes us. That seemed like a good way of looking at it. Love always operated with a plan, but why? Why not go with the flow, follow their noses, fly by the seats of their pants? No reason why Love had to decide in advance about having sex with Arthur Beebe. She needed to take it easy. Relax. At five o'clock, after work, Love walked home past the Hadwen House. The Hadwen House with its ballroom under the stars. Its dreams of romance.

•   •   •

TUESDAY MORNING, A TAXI dropped Love off at the Beach Club at 7:35. She liked being early. It gave her a few minutes to stretch her legs and look at the ocean. The 6:30 ferry was a white speck on the horizon. Love watched the seagulls drop hermit crab shells onto the parking lot. She glanced at Bill and Therese's house and figured they were probably in bed making love, but today Love didn't feel jealous. Today she would just be one of many lovers on Nantucket. That was all she wanted—to be another person's focus, if only for a day, if only for a few hours. Love was honest enough with herself to realize that unless a baby was conceived, this would be the best part of the whole affair: the sweet, exquisite anticipation.

But after another ten, twelve minutes, her anticipation became tinged with nerves. Her multipurpose sports watch said 7:48. Then 7:50, and then 7:53. Love jogged back and forth in front of the hotel; she peeked in the windows of the lobby, thinking perhaps Arthur was waiting for her inside. But the inside of the lobby was dark, deserted.

At 8:00, Mack pulled into the parking lot. He was early! She hid around the corner of the lobby and waited until he unloaded the cartons of that day's breakfast and carried them into the lobby. Then she sneaked behind the pavilion, and down the side deck rooms to the water. She jogged past the Gold Coast. A few of the guests were out on their decks reading, a woman sat on a mat doing yoga. Love ran by room 10, room 9, room 8. The door to room 8 was closed, the deck uninhabited. Love ran all the way down to room 1 and then cut behind the Gold Coast rooms. The back door to room 8 was also closed. Love returned to the front of the lobby in case she had missed Arthur somehow. She consulted her watch. It was 8:06. She shielded her eyes and peered into the lobby. Jem and Mack set up the breakfast, the coffee loiterers loitered. Tiny stood behind the front desk. But no Arthur Beebe.

A minute later, the front doors of the lobby opened. Mack lugged Therese's plants out onto the front porch. There was no time to hide again; Mack saw her.

"Hey, Love, what are you doing here?" he said.

"I was just . . . running," she said. Although she wanted to, there was no way she could ask Mack if he'd seen Arthur Beebe.

"Nice day for it," Mack said. He was in client mode: chipper, chatty, ready to skate across any topic of conversation. She could be in tears and he wouldn't notice.

"I'm off," she said.

Love ran home as fast as she could. She pushed herself to go faster, faster, faster than her fastest mile split (a 5:49 in the Boulder 10k, 1988). She arrived at home winded and sweaty, her heart pounding in her throat and her face. At first she was glad Randy and Alison were away, because she certainly didn't want anyone to witness her humiliation. But the empty house was awful too—the way the wind blew right through it—and she wished for some company.

Love waited until ten o'clock, the usual time for her first conversation with Arthur Beebe, and then she called the front desk.

Tiny answered. "Good morning, Nantucket Beach Club."

Love cleared her throat. "Yes, is Arthur Beebe in, please?"

"I'm sorry," Tiny said. "The Beebes are no longer staying with us."

"No, no," Love said. "Tiny, it's me, Love. I think you've got the wrong room. The Beebes are in room eight. They're not checking out until tomorrow."

"Oh, Love," Tiny said. "The chambermaids went in to clean about forty minutes ago and noticed all the Beebes' stuff was gone. So I called the airport. The Beebes' jet left at five o'clock this morning. They skipped out on their bill—two grand." She gave an amused little laugh. "Happens every year. I'm always suspicious of people who don't use a credit card, but you figure someone with his own plane is going to be able to foot the bill. But not these folks—they snuck out of here in the middle of the night, like they were on the lam or something. What's the deal? Did you know these people? What did you want with them anyway?"

Antarctica, Love thought. Would he have been so cruel as to dash his wife off to Antarctica? She hoped not, despite the fact that right now she wanted Arthur Beebe as far away from her as possible. At five o'clock this morning, Love had been lying in bed, listening to the birds, thinking about Arthur Beebe. Had she heard a plane flying overhead? No, just the birds.

"Oh, nothing," Love said. "I didn't want them for anything."

BY THE NEXT MORNING, Love had convinced herself that she was the reason Arthur Beebe had left the hotel in the predawn hours. Perhaps his feelings for her escalated, perhaps he was frightened by their intensity. Perhaps last night at dinner (Straight Wharf), he told Mrs. Beebe about his running date with Love—and maybe she was the one responsible for their early departure. There were many excuses Love could make for the man, but it didn't change the fact that Arthur had disappeared, literally, into thin air, taking her hopes for a child with him.

Love was folding hotel brochures, thinking of how she might surprise Arthur Beebe someday in New York when Vance poked his head out from Mack's office.

"Come here," he said. "I want to show you something."

The lobby was empty and so she slipped back into Mack's office. Mack was in the laundry room fixing a dryer.

"What?" she said.

"You know the people in room eight, the druggies? The ones who skipped their bill?" Vance said.

"The Beebes?" Love said. The name tasted funny on her tongue.

"I stripped their room yesterday and look what I found," he said. "This ain't no BB." He brought his hands out from behind his back and showed Love a gun.

"You found it in their room?" Love asked. It was a handgun, shiny and silver. She tried to picture it in Arthur Beebe's hand; she tried to picture him pointing it at someone.

"I told you they were drug dealers. Their own plane? Taking off in the middle of the night? And then I find this baby tucked in between the mattress and box spring? Come on, Love, we're not stupid here."

A little of this, a little of that. "What should we do?" Love asked. "Should we call them?" A part of Love wanted to speak to Arthur

Beebe again. He'd left her feeling empty. Angry and humiliated, yes, but mostly empty.

"They never left a *phone number*. Tiny searched for it yesterday, but when Bill made the reservation, all he wrote down was a fax," Vance said. "And guess what? We can't fax a gun."

"We could send a fax telling them we have the gun," Love suggested. She wanted to fax herself to Arthur Beebe.

"Tiny faxed them about their bill, and we haven't heard back. If we had the address, we could send the gun through the mail, although you can't send the clip and the gun together," Vance said. Love didn't ask how he knew this. Vance pointed the gun out the window. "Pow," he said softly. "Listen, I'll take care of the gun. Let me know if Beebe calls asking for it."

"Okay," she said. It was scary watching Vance point the gun. *Pow!*

Love went back to the desk. The gun created possibilities Love hadn't even considered. If Arthur Beebe were a drug dealer, if he did use his plane to fly back and forth between countries transporting illegal substances, then she should be glad nothing had happened between them. She should be *relieved* Arthur left. But she wasn't.

JEM CRANDALL WAS MAKING mistakes. He supposed his mistakes were standard, run-of-the-mill mistakes that any freshman on the job would make. What he couldn't figure out was how to stop them from happening before he got fired. If he got fired, he might not be able to find another job. It was June already and the college students had arrived in force. If Jem couldn't find another job, he would have to return to Virginia and work at his father's bar, the Locked Tower, and deal with his nutty sister, Gwennie, and her bulimia. He wrote himself a note—soap on the bathroom mirror—No More Mistakes! When he shaved, it was tattooed across his forehead.

Jem's first mistake was also the most embarrassing: Mrs. Worley. The Worleys were a heavy-set couple from Atlanta. He noticed them each morning hovering around the breakfast buffet while he tried to clear it. Once, mister followed Jem into the galley kitchen when Jem left with the platter of muffins. Mr. Worley selected the last two mixed-berry muffins, and Jem, who understood unreasonable hunger, said, "Yeah, those are my favorite, too."

Several days later, when mister was paying his bill, Love said, "Jem, room ten is ready to be stripped. The Worleys are checking out."

Jem licked his fingers clean of powdered sugar (he was allowed to eat the leftovers from breakfast), and said, "Okay, I'm going."

Stripping the rooms was Jem's least favorite part of the job. The chambermaids cracked jokes about "love stains" when they made the beds, and although Jem laughed at the term, it didn't make him feel any better about having to gather the sheets up in his arms. And love stains weren't as offensive as some of the things people left in the sheets. He'd seen blood, urine, used condoms, and food—globs of guacamole, a lobster claw. He was responsible for taking out the trash, and he tried not to look at what the guests threw away. One horrifying day, he found a Styrofoam head covered with a stringy brown toupee sitting on a dresser. He also collected the soiled towels, bathmat, and bathrobes from the bathroom. Another lovely task, but at least it was better than swabbing nests of hair out of the bottom of the shower.

Jem went to work on the Worleys' room. The TV was on—ESPN SportsCenter—and Jem watched the highlights, waiting for a score on the Orioles' game as he did his work. He threw the quilt and the blanket off the bed and stripped the sheets, trying not to think of the rotund Worleys rolling around in them. He removed the plastic bag from the trash can, twisted it and tied it. The TV announcer finally showed a clip of the Orioles' game—and Jem thought of his father, who had a collection of Orioles memorabilia hanging behind the bar at the Tower.

Jem checked the closets for items left behind. He checked the drawers. He'd heard Vance whispering about some great thing he found in one of the rooms. Jem guessed it was lingerie, or a dirty magazine. These closets and drawers were empty, thank God.

Jem swung open the door to the bathroom and heard a loud gasp. Mrs. Worley was sitting on the toilet, reading the TV Guide. She looked at him with wide brown eyes, her mouth agape. All Jem could think at that moment was *Please don't stand up.* But it was too late. Mrs. Worley stood, and Jem couldn't help but look. His eyes were drawn to her lower half: her shorts drooping around her ankles, her stomach hanging like so much bread dough over her . . .

"Get . . . get!" Mrs. Worley stuttered. Her face was bright pink.

"I'm sorry, ma'am," Jem said. "They said you were checking—"

Mrs. Worley lunged, slammed the door in his face. A second later, he heard Mrs. Worley crying. Jem hurried out the door, leaving the trash and the pile of dirty sheets behind. He stumbled into the sunshine, feeling exposed and ashamed. He wanted to run for the safety of his rented room, lock the door, jump into his bed and hide under the covers. Instead, he sought refuge in the coolness of the laundry room, which had the soothing, clean smell of detergent. He stayed there for nearly half an hour, wondering if Mrs. Worley would report him. Jem buried his face in a pile of green fluffy towels and tried to think of other things, pleasant things—going to the Muse and drinking a cold beer, talking to a pretty girl in a sundress—but he couldn't shake the image of Mrs. Worley, her thighs, white and dimpled like cottage cheese. It was far, far worse than even the Styrofoam head and toupee. Jem felt sick to his stomach. Then the phone rang in the laundry room. It was Mack.

When Jem walked into Mack's office, he was still shaking. "Are they gone?" he asked.

Mack nodded, his face grim. "You're lucky she wasn't thinking sexual harassment, or attempted rape."

The picture of Mrs. Worley standing up from the toilet presented itself again in Jem's mind, as he feared it would for the rest of his life. "No way," he said, "not in a million years."

"A smart thing to do when you see a closed door is to *knock,*" Mack said. "Otherwise we leave ourselves open to those kinds of allegations. You don't want that, do you?"

Jem shook his head. Mack's face twisted, and then he burst out laughing. "You poor kid," Mack said. "You should see yourself."

"It was so embarrassing," Jem said. He watched Mack laugh, and wished for some laughter from himself, a warm release, but none came. It *was* funny, in a way, wasn't it? Jem waltzed into the bathroom with every intention of collecting the towels until—whammo! Mrs. Worley, front and center. Of course, Mack hadn't heard Mrs. Worley scream, and he hadn't heard her crying.

Mack sobered up and wiped his eyes. "I'm not angry," he said. "But I am serious. Always knock before you strip the rooms. Do you hear me?"

"I hear you," Jem said.

"You'll have to write Mrs. Worley a note of apology. It was your mistake."

Jem wondered what he could possibly say to Mrs. Worley—*I'm sorry for the very awkward moment? I'm sorry to have barged in on you in the john?* He almost smiled until he heard Mack use the word "mistake." It was then the train of thought first materialized: getting fired, working at the Locked Tower, his sister, Gwennie.

"Okay," Jem said. "I will."

Three days later, a very famous man checked into room 6. The man was so famous that when Jem saw him at the front desk he had a hard time keeping a straight face. Why didn't Mack warn them people like this were coming? Jem might have worn a cleaner shirt. But the Beach Club showed no one favoritism, and so Jem led this famous man, a major player, a mogul (for if anyone in the world could be called a mogul this man was it) to room 6, as though he were anyone else. Jem could only think of the man as Mr. G. This was what he was called in the media, the same way that Donald Trump was called "the Donald." Mr. G had brought a briefcase, and a small black Samsonite suitcase. Jem took the Samsonite. It was so light that Jem wondered if it were empty. He walked just in front of Mr. G, reciting his spiel about the chambermaids, the ice machine, the Continental breakfast from eight-thirty to ten.

"I won't be here for breakfast," Mr. G said. "I'm only staying overnight. I have an extremely important meeting tomorrow in Washington."

"Just overnight?" Jem said. "At least you have a nice day for it." It was true: the sun was shining, the ocean a glorious blue. Jem walked along the boardwalk, then up the three steps to the deck of room 6, and paused for a minute, searching his pocket for the key. He couldn't believe he was about to unlock a door for Mr. G.

Mr. G cleared his throat and Jem fumbled with the keys. *Get the door open, you idiot!* he thought. *This is Mr. G!* Jem opened the door. "Here you go," he said. He waited until Mr. G stepped in and put down his briefcase. "My name is Jeremy Crandall. Just let me know if you need anything."

"I'd like a wake-up call for six-fifteen." Mr. G said. "And I need you to show me how this phone works."

Jem picked up the receiver of the phone. "The phone works just like a regular phone, sir," Jem said. Did this sound snide? He needed to get a grip. "Except you have to dial nine to get an outside line. If you want the front desk, you dial zero." He set the receiver down, then moved quickly to the alarm clock. "Is there anything else?"

Mr. G smiled. Jem smiled back. He and Mr. G were smiling at each other.

"No," Mr. G said. "Thanks for your help." He reached into his pocket but all he brought out were a few pennies and a dime. "I'll get you later."

Jem waved his hand. "Don't worry about it. It's a pleasure to help and meeting you. I mean it was nice meeting you. Exciting." Jem backed out of the room onto the deck. He waved to Mr. G. "Let me know if you need anything."

Mack wasn't in the office, but through the crack in the door, Jem saw Bill reading at his desk. Bill was a poetry buff, and half the time he sat in his office he wasn't even working; he was reading poems, then closing his eyes and trying to recite them from memory. It amazed Jem that Bill didn't seem at all flustered by Mr. G's arrival. Perhaps he didn't even know.

Jem tapped on Bill's door. "Bill? I just wanted to let you know Mr. G—is here and I've shown him to his room."

Bill knit his eyebrows. "Okay," he said. "Thanks for the update."

Love came into the office. "He's been on the phone since he got

here," she whispered. Her cheeks were pink. Love was always talking
about the big shots she saw in Aspen—Ed Bradley, Sean Connery,
Elle McPherson. But even Love was impressed by Mr. G. She put her
hands on her hips. "This doesn't seem like much of a vacation," she
said. "He's here for the afternoon, dinner with friends, and then he
leaves first thing tomorrow, poor thing." Love was returning to her
normal self, acting like everybody's aunt. "I wonder if he brought his
bathing suit. That's something I'd like to see. Mr. G—in a pair of
trunks."

The fax machine beeped and churned out a few pages. Love
checked it. "For Mr. G, naturally," she said. She wrote the fax information in her notebook then handed the pages to Jem. "Care to do the
honors?"

Jem walked to room 6, the fax pages fluttering in his hands. He
wondered what would happen if he let the pages go. What if he were
responsible for tossing Mr. G's fax to the wind? It was torturous to
consider. He wanted to read the fax, but it was good discipline to
respect the man's privacy, to resist peeking at the masthead.

Jem knocked on the door. "Jeremy Crandall here," he said in a
strong voice.

The door opened. Mr. G had the phone to his ear; he was still in
his suit. He looked at Jem quizzically, and Jem held out the fax pages.
Mr. G took the fax, glanced at it, and reached into his pants pocket.
He pulled out the same few coins then shook his head, and handed the
coins to Jem.

"Thanks," Jem said. When he returned to the lobby, he checked in
his pocket. Mr. G had given him thirteen cents.

THAT NIGHT, JEM ATE three peanut butter sandwiches and drank two
cans of warm Sprite, and he wrote his first letter home to his parents.
Jem's father was a famous man in Falls Church. The owner of the
Locked Tower, a member of Rotary, and Kiwanis. A model citizen.
Jem could have this kind of fame too. But, he was ashamed to say, he
wanted something bigger. He was cursed with aspirations.

"My job is going well," Jem wrote, "and guess who checked into the hotel today? Mr. G!" Jem wanted to show his parents that he could live away from home, hold a job, use good judgment. "He tipped me thirteen cents." If Jem gave his father news to share at the Tower—and surely Mr. G was news—maybe his parents wouldn't object quite so much when he brought up California. Lacey Gardner told Jem to disregard what his parents thought, and though he found this extreme, one thing was true: he was going to California whether his parents liked it or not.

Then Jem thought of his sister, Gwennie. She ate his mother's baked chicken, grilled steaks, chocolate cake, and then after dinner she disappeared into the upstairs bathroom or outside—no matter how closely Jem's parents watched her—and she puked it all up. And Gwennie had reinvented the laws of perpetual motion. When she was on the phone with her girlfriends, she paced the house. She went jogging in the middle of the night while their parents slept. She ate standing up, and if she had to eat sitting down, she scissored her legs back and forth under the table. Just thinking about it made Jem exhausted, and sad.

"All in all, I'm doing well," he wrote. "I think this summer is going to be quite a learning experience." His mother would appreciate that. "I miss you! Love, Jem."

JEM MAILED THE LETTER on his way to work the next morning. He still had the thirteen cents in his pocket. He might just carry that thirteen cents all summer, for luck. As Jem approached the Club, he saw Mr. G standing on the front steps of the lobby. Jem checked his watch. It was five of eight. Mack stood next to Mr. G, holding a carton of doughnuts.

"Jem!" Mack called out.

Jem ran to the front porch of the lobby. But something wasn't right. Both Mack and Mr. G looked upset.

"Did you set the alarm clock for Mr. G—yesterday afternoon?" Mack asked.

Jem's mind swam through murky water to yesterday afternoon. He had set it, hadn't he? Oh, God, his life was over. But he distinctly remembered sitting on the side of the bed and pressing the plastic buttons. Setting the alarm for six-fifteen. Mr. G had said six-fifteen, hadn't he?

"It didn't go off," Mr. G said quietly. He looked up into the sky. "Needless to say I had to call and cancel with the president."

The president? Of the United States? Jem clenched his stomach. "Oh, sir," Jem said. "I'm sorry."

"Sorry, of course, doesn't put me on my plane an hour ago," Mr. G said. "Sorry doesn't make it up to the president."

A cab pulled up to the front of the hotel. Jem reached for Mr. G's Samsonite, but Mack snapped it up first. "I've got it," Mack said. "Go wait for me in my office."

A FEW MINUTES LATER, Jem shuffled through the sand, following Mack to room 6.

"I asked you in the interview if you could set an alarm clock," Mack said. "And you assured me that you could. Do you remember?"

"Yes," Jem said glumly. He thought of the letter to his parents and wished he hadn't sent it. Jem imagined his mother at the Giant, pushing her cart through the produce section, telling everyone she knew that Jem had met Mr. G. What she wouldn't know was that Jem had screwed up royally, that Jem had single-handedly fouled up Mr. G's meeting with the president of the United States.

In room 6, Mack checked the alarm clock.

"It's set for six-fifteen," Mack said, and for a second Jem felt the sweet wash of vindication. Then Mack said, "Six-fifteen in the evening. See this P.M. thing here, P.M. means—"

"I know what it means," Jem said.

"The alarm must have gone off while Mr. G—was at dinner."

"I'll write a letter of apology," Jem said. "I'll sit down and write it now."

"Don't write a letter," Mack said. "I don't want you to waste any more of that man's time. Okay, Jem? But see if you can use your head.

See if you can make me feel like less an idiot for hiring you. Now, go
do your job."

JEM SAT ON A bench outside the Stop & Shop eating half a roasted
chicken. It was Monday, his day off, and he'd had another miserable
weekend. The incident with Mr. G depressed him so much that he
didn't feel like going out. It was the fifteenth of June and Jem hadn't
seen the inside of a bar since he and Vance had shot pool at the
Chicken Box back in May, before the hotel opened. He supposed if he
went out he would meet some girls at least, but he was shy about going
to the bars alone. His father always said that a person who goes into a
bar alone goes to drink, *and you know what that means.*

Was that any different from sitting outside the grocery store alone,
eating chicken alone, or going to the beach alone, which was where
Jem was headed next? He felt like a loser—he kept messing up at his
simple job, and after five weeks on the island, he still had no friends. If
this was what happened to him on Nantucket, what the hell would
California be like?

The Stop & Shop parking lot was jam-packed: cars lined up at the
entrance, snaking onto Pleasant Street. These were the Summer People, Jem supposed, coming to refill their cupboards with watermelons,
hamburger buns, Popsicles.

Jem gnawed on a chicken leg and watched a woman roll a shopping
cart with about fifty shopping bags and a baby girl up to her Isuzu
Trooper. She loaded in her groceries, which probably cost as much
money as Jem made in a week. The shopping cart with the baby rolled
backward just as a couple of college chicks in a red Cherokee rounded
the corner. Jem ran out in front of the Cherokee. The car jerked to a
stop. Jem pushed the shopping cart closer to the Isuzu, although he
was chagrined to see the cart hadn't really been in the way.

"Watch where you're going," he said to the girls. "And slow
down."

The girl driving said, "For your information, I was watching where
I was going. I wasn't even close to hitting it."

The baby's mother turned and saw Jem holding the cart.

"I'm sorry?" she said. Her eyes locked on Jem's fingers gripping the handle of the cart. Jem started to sweat. It was about a hundred degrees out and his face and hands were shiny with chicken grease. He pictured a scenario where he grabbed the shopping cart and it slipped from his greasy grasp and rolled right in front of the Cherokee, making him not a baby snatcher but a baby murderer. He needed to be more aware. Awareness, how did one acquire it?

"I'm sorry," he said. "Those girls almost hit your cart. Your baby."

The woman looked at him blankly and Jem experienced the uncomfortable feeling he got when he was waiting for a tip from one of the hotel guests. He walked away.

Jem returned to his bench and found Maribel sitting next to his messy pile of napkins and chicken bones.

"Busy saving the world?" she asked.

"Wait a minute," Jem said. This was exactly what he meant about being more aware. Where had Maribel come from? "You saw that?"

"Brave and valiant. This damsel's impressed." She shifted a backpack at her feet. "So, what are you doing here?"

"It's my day off," Jem said. "I'm headed for the beach."

"Me too," Maribel said. "The library is closed on Mondays."

Maribel was in a pair of jeans shorts and a yellow flowered bikini top. Her blond hair was in a bun. Jem saw faint yellow hairs on the tops of her thighs.

"Do you act?" he asked. "Sing? Dance? Juggle?"

Maribel laughed. "No, why? Do you only sit on benches with people if they have special talent?"

"I just thought you could be my first client," Jem said. "You know, I thought maybe you needed an agent."

"I'm a librarian," Maribel said. "In fact, I'm not even a librarian. I'm not brainy or organized enough to be a librarian. I'm a fund-raiser. I ask people for money, and when I get the money I think of ways to spend it. Now, do I need an agent? Yes, I do. A beach agent."

"I'm actually a very good beach agent," Jem said.

"Meaning you can guarantee me a fun time while I'm there?" Maribel asked. "What's your cut?"

"Fifty percent," Jem said. "Of the fun time."

"Okay," Maribel said, slinging her backpack over her shoulder. "Let's go."

MARIBEL DROVE A JEEP Wrangler just like Mack's, but newer. It was black and the inside was roasting hot. Jem's legs stuck to the vinyl seats.

Maribel pulled out of the parking lot, and said, "So, do I dare ask? How's work?"

"It's great," Jem said, trying to sound upbeat. Usually Jem felt comfortable with women, but with Maribel he was going to have to watch what he said. Talking to her was as good as talking to Mack.

"You like Bill and Therese?" Maribel asked.

"I almost never see them," Jem said. "Bill sits in his office reading and Therese is busy chasing the chambermaids around. She rides those girls hard."

"Therese is a renowned slave driver," Maribel said. "I suppose you've heard she hates me."

"No," Jem said, "I hadn't heard."

"Things used to be okay between us, but ever since Cecily got to high school—Cecily's their daughter, you know—Therese has been dead set on pushing Cecily and Mack together. An he's twelve years older than she is! It's ridiculous."

"Do you ever think maybe Mack will give in? You know, to get a piece of the Beach Club and all?"

"No," Maribel said sharply, "I don't."

"Sorry," Jem said. He should just keep his mouth shut! "I didn't mean I thought he should. Hell, no. You two make a great couple. How long have you been together?"

"Six years," Maribel said.

"Are you planning on getting married?"

"No," Maribel said. "We have no plans to get married." She paused. "You know what the funny thing is about Cecily? She and I are good friends. Everything would be so nice if Therese just backed off."

"Oh," Jem said.

"Never mind," Maribel said. "It's just politics. You're smart to stay out of it." They turned left by the high school. "So tell me, do you have a girlfriend?"

"Me?" Jem said. "No, not right now."

"Haven't met anyone on the island, a handsome guy like you? Mr. November?"

He'd opened his mouth during his job interview, and it would haunt him forever. "I haven't been out much," he said.

"Cecily's coming home next week," Maribel said. "Maybe you'll like her."

"I don't know," Jem said. "I hate being set up."

Maribel patted his knee. Jem felt a sort of thrill when she touched him, and instantly he began to worry. What was he doing with his boss's girlfriend? Maribel turned onto a sand road. The Jeep started bouncing up and down in whoop-dee-dos.

"Where are we going?" he asked.

"Miacomet," she said. "The pond's coming up on the left."

Jem looked out Maribel's window. Cattails and dune grass bordered the pond, and there were a few wild irises. A red-winged blackbird.

"This is one of my favorite spots," she said. "And the beach is terrific too—very peaceful. It's a nude beach."

Jem took a deep breath. *Nude beach?* "Wait a minute, I'm the beach agent here. I don't know if that's in the contract."

"Does it make you uncomfortable?" Maribel asked. "Because we can go someplace else." But she made no move to slow down the car.

"Well . . ."

"You can keep your suit on," she said. "I sometimes do. Tell you what, I will today, how about that?"

Now Jem felt like a child. What was wrong with a nude beach, really?

"Whatever you want," he said.

Maribel shrugged. "Okay."

Maribel drove the Jeep over the dunes onto the beach. She was right—it was peaceful. The beach was a long stretch of practically deserted sand—way down to the left Jem saw the mob of folks at Surfside, where he usually went. The waves here were giant and rolling, and the water bottle green. Behind them, all Jem could see was blue sky and dune grass. This was the real Gold Coast. He started to relax.

"This is nice," he said.

Maribel spread out a blanket, stripped off her shorts, and sat down. She waved Jem over. "Join me," she said. "I brought lunch."

Jem sat tentatively on the edge of her blanket. He removed his shirt and looked down at his abs. He did a hundred sit-ups before he went to bed each night and it was paying off. "Thanks, but I already ate some chicken."

"I packed enough for about sixty people," Maribel said. "And I'm a good cook in case you haven't heard." She unwrapped a sandwich and handed Jem half. "Here, this is Saga, prosciutto, and fig."

The sandwich was delicious, the kind of delicious Jem had never tasted before.

"You like it?" Maribel asked.

He finished chewing. "It's the best sandwich I've ever eaten."

"You can be my sandwich agent."

"Definitely," Jem said. "Definitely your sandwich agent." An old woman walked by, naked. She smiled at Maribel and Jem and wandered off down the beach.

"See, it's no big deal. This is a free and easy place." Maribel pulled more food out of her backpack: homemade potato chips, clusters of tiny purple grapes, thick chocolate brownies.

"Nothing at all like the chicken at Stop and Shop," he said. "And no exhaust. Where did you learn to cook like this?"

"I taught myself," Maribel said. She threw a scrap of bread to the seagulls. "My mother worked full-time and when she got home she was too tired to do much of anything. I liked having dinner ready for her. I cleaned the house and did the laundry, too. My mother called me her housewife. And I thought of it as practical training."

"Training?"

"For when I get married myself," Maribel said.

"So you do want to get married," Jem said.

"What's that supposed to mean?" she asked.

Jem had stepped in mud and he hadn't even seen it. "Nothing. It meant nothing. I'm sorry." Where was safe ground? He finished his sandwich and licked his fingers, and then, before he could stop, he thought about being married to Maribel himself, and how awesome that would be, awesome beyond his wildest dreams.

"You know when you asked me about work before?" Jem said. "I was just wondering, does Mack ever say how I'm doing?"

"Not really. He did tell me about Mr. G."

"He did?"

"Yeah, and I don't see what the big deal is. So the guy was an hour late. So he had to cancel with the president. Shit happens. I'll bet by noon he'd forgotten all about it."

"There was this other thing that happened, too," Jem said. "This woman Mrs. Worley. I walked in on her in the bathroom and she started to cry."

Jem was expecting Maribel to laugh the way Mack had, but she didn't.

"When I was a little girl, I walked into the men's room at a restaurant and I saw the men standing next to urinals. I didn't know men peed standing up. I don't have any brothers and my father wasn't around, and I just didn't know. Now, *that* was a shocker."

"So it was just you and your mother then?" Jem asked.

"My mom was only nineteen when she had me. It's just the two of us." Maribel fell back onto the blanket. "Nap time." She rolled onto her side and propped her head up with one arm. "I'm going to take my top off, if that's okay with you."

"Wait a second. You said—"

She put her hand on his arm, and again he felt a thrill.

"We don't have to tell Mack we met up," she said.

"We don't?" He didn't like where this was headed: lying, secrecy, a secret from his boss. But Jem was happy sitting next to Maribel—so astonishingly happy whereas just an hour before he'd been so miserable—that he didn't care. "Go ahead then," he said.

Maribel untied her bikini and slipped it over her head. Jem looked at her breasts; he knew she wanted him to look at them, and admire them the way he'd admired the food. They were just like the rest of Maribel—sunny, perky, gorgeous. They were the size of teacups with a pale pink nipple. She took a bottle of Coppertone from her bag and rubbed herself with lotion. In a minute, Jem had an aching erection pushing through his swim trunks. He flipped onto his stomach.

"Nap time," he said.

He closed his eyes and tried to think about other things, things that were not Maribel related, things that were not Maribel's breasts and their impossibly pink softness. He surprised himself by falling asleep. When he woke up, it felt as though he were emerging from a hot, dark tunnel. He raised his head. Maribel was lying on her stomach, reading. She still had her top off.

"What are you reading?" Jem asked.

She flashed him the cover. "*The Collected Stories of John Cheever*," she said. "And there's a whole lot of cheating going on."

"Really?" Jem said. What was *that* supposed to mean? "Hey, want to go for a swim?"

"Sure," she said. He was thankful that she put her top on, tying the strings tightly. When Jem felt ready, he dashed to the water. Maribel chased after him. The water was freezing but that was okay. He needed to cool down. Maribel went under and when she popped back up, she shrieked.

"This is great," Jem called out. A wave rolled over him.

"Next stop, Portugal," Maribel said. She went under again and surfaced right next to him. "The rip current is bad here," she said. "I don't want to get too far away from you."

"I don't want you too far away," Jem said. He touched Maribel's forehead. Her hair was sleek. God, she was pretty. If she were any-body else, he might playfully untie her bikini. He might go under and pop up with her on his back. He might simply hold her and let her rock in his arms as the waves passed over them. But it wasn't anybody else. It was Maribel.

"Would you like to come over for dinner some Sunday?" Maribel asked.

Here was the dinner invitation Jem had been waiting for, and yet now he felt uncomfortable. "Sunday is the day Mack eats with Lacey," he said.

Maribel squinted her eyes toward shore. "Yep."

"So it would just be us?" Jem asked.

"You're more than welcome to bring a date," Maribel said.

"I couldn't find a date," he said. "Would you tell Mack I was com-ing for dinner?"

"Would you want me to?"

He took a mouthful of salty green water and spouted it through his teeth. "I don't know."

"What do you say we call this a friendship," Maribel said. "Unless you're still determined to be my agent, in which case it's a business arrangement. Would that make you feel better?"

"Yeah," Jem said, "it would."

"So you'll come for dinner sometime?" she asked.

"Okay," Jem said.

"Great," she said. She rode the next wave all the way to shore, where she washed up on her hands and knees. Jem watched as she picked herself up, cleaned the sand from her legs, and headed back to the blanket. At that moment, Jem hoped she didn't tell Mack about their day together. It had been Jem's best day on Nantucket by leaps and bounds—good enough to wipe away all the nonsense that had preceded it, and Jem wanted the memory of it all to himself.

4

Summer Solstice

June 20

Dear S.B.T.,

*At the risk of sounding ridiculously proud, I will tell you that on
June 18, Therese and I traveled to Concord, Mass., where we
watched our daughter, Cecily, graduate from Middlesex. She
strolled across the manicured lawn like her other classmates, but
she stood out, a shining star, a flashing beacon. Cecily is already a
young woman, far more mature and sophisticated than her peers.
She is our pride and joy and I know you will understand that it is
for her sake that I will never sell the Beach Club.*

*Do you have children, S. B. T? You have never mentioned any.
I would be interested to know the answer to that question, if you are
willing to disclose it.*

Cordially,

Bill Elliott

ON THE TWENTY-FIRST OF June, summer officially arrived. The sun stayed
out longer, the restaurants opened seven nights a week, and the bars
were full of college girls who, Vance noticed, favored blue toenail polish and tattoos this year. The weekly edition of the *Inquirer and Mirror* printed its first five-section paper of the season. The Stop & Shop
was such a madhouse that management kept the store open twenty-
four hours, which meant Vance could pick up his Cheerios and lunch
meat at 3:00 A.M. if he wanted. The cobblestone streets of town were
clogged with cars coming off the ferry, bicyclists, and pedestrians,
people holding their maps, crossing the street without looking. Who

were all these people? The island became inundated with Range
Rovers from Connecticut (that sounded like a stereotype, but Vance
swore it was true; that morning on Main Street he counted no less
than three Range Rovers, all with the telltale blue license plate). The
Steamship Authority ran six boats a day in each direction and the
Nantucket airport was busier than Logan in Boston. The climbing
roses and hydrangeas bloomed, causing more slowdowns; through
his open window, Vance heard women cooing, "Look at the pretty
flowers!"

It was popular to complain about the tourists and so Vance decided
to take the opposite approach. He embraced the tourists. He waved to
people in the long lines outside the Juice Bar and the Brotherhood, he
gave directions to a family on bicycles—the man turning his map every
which way, while the mother, with a baby jammed in a booster seat on
the back of her Schwinn and three kids behind her, said, "Honey, why
don't you just ask someone if we're headed toward a beach? Here, ask
this nice man." Tourists, to Vance, meant one thing: money. Vance
had been raking in sweet tips from the hotel guests, especially since
Jem was constantly screwing up, making Vance look good.

June 21, summer solstice, was also the day the Beach Club opened.
This meant that a hundred Beach Club members would now be crawling over the property like ants on a picnic. The members wanted *their*
specific umbrella in *their* specific spot on the beach. Some members
had been sitting in the same spot for forty or fifty years. (Vance did the
math: if a person came to the Beach Club four times a week and stayed
for six hours a day during the ten weeks of summer over fifty years that
meant they had spent *twelve thousand hours* sitting in the same place.)

One of the good things about the Beach Club opening was that
Vance had two more lackeys to boss around. Mack hired beach boys
named Kevin and Bruce who looked just like all the other beach boys
Vance had seen over the years—pimply, sarcastic prep school kids
who somehow lucked into the cushiest job on the island. That morning, Vance wanted to scare the kids so they would not only respect
him but shudder a little when they saw him coming. They waited in
front of the lobby at eight o'clock sharp, a good sign. Vance parked his

Datsun 300ZX, and the two boys looked it over appreciatively, another good sign. As he stepped out of the car, they nervously eyed his shaved head. Excellent. Vance bit his tongue to keep himself from grinning.

"You the beach boys?" he asked.

"Man, could you call us something else?" the taller, skinnier kid asked. "I don't want to be associated with some washed-up sixties band." This kid wore a South Carolina Cocks hat, another popular item at the bars this summer. With a lightning-quick motion, Vance hit the bill of the cap and flipped it off the boy's head. The boy flinched and stepped back; his hair was matted as though he hadn't even run a comb through it that morning.

"Are you Kevin or Bruce?" Vance asked.

"Bruce."

"Bruce, let me tell you something. Beach boys have been called beach boys since the Club opened in 1924. And guess what, buddy? We're not changing it for you. Got that?"

Bruce bent down to pick up his hat while Kevin, who was chubbier with more pimples, stared wide-eyed at Vance. They were off to a good start.

VANCE TOOK THE BOYS past Lacey Gardner's cottage to the umbrella room.

"These are the beach umbrellas," he said. "They cost a hundred sixteen dollars apiece. If you break an umbrella because you're negligent, you get docked that much plus the amount it costs to ship these babies back to the south of France where they were made." This wasn't true but Vance found that saying this led to fewer broken umbrellas. "The umbrellas come in kelly green, royal blue, and canary yellow. Sometimes members want a certain color. You're going to have to memorize who those people are and their umbrella color. I'm not taking any crap from a pissed-off member because they got royal instead of canary. *Capiche?*"

Kevin picked at his chin. "How will we know which ones?"

"I'll teach you," Vance said. He hefted seven umbrellas onto his shoulder. "Follow me."

THE SUN WAS OUT and already hot. Vance raised his face. He'd picked up some kind of crazy sun addiction in Thailand; he couldn't get enough of it. But practically speaking, a warm, sunny summer solstice was bad news. The Beach Club would be packed, and because the beach boys were brand-new that meant Vance would have to set up all one-hundred umbrellas by himself.

"Now," Vance said, "this is how you set up an umbrella. Watch carefully." He held up the spike, as long as a Louisville Slugger. "This is the bottom of the umbrella, the part that gets driven into the sand. It's sharp, as you can see, and for this reason you have to make sure you drive it deep. I don't want to tell you about umbrellas I've seen that got loose in the wind because some beach boy did a half-ass plant job. Can you imagine catching this spike in the face?" He lowered his voice. "Or the balls?"

Bruce curled his lip, Kevin looked like he was about to lose his breakfast. Vance bit his tongue again. Then he raised the spike in his arms and blasted it into the sand.

"Pretend the sand is your ex-girlfriend," he said. "Or hell, pretend it's me." Plenty of times, Vance imagined the sand was Mack. "Then wag the spike back and forth until it goes even deeper. When you feel there's no possibility of it getting loose even in gale force winds, pack sand around it like this. Then you're ready to put up an umbrella." Vance slid the umbrella pole over the spike and locked it in. He opened the umbrella triumphantly; it bloomed like a big royal blue flower. "There," Vance said. "That's how it's done."

"Not bad for a bellman," a voice said.

Mack walked toward them through the sand. *Not bad for a bellman?* What the hell kind of comment was that? All of Vance's good work at getting these Romper Roomers to respect him was down the drain with that remark.

Mack shook hands with the two kids and then he put his arm

around Vance's shoulders. Vance tensed, like Mack's arm was one of the cobras he'd seen at the Snake Farm in Bangkok.

"Vance was a beach boy himself once upon a time," Mack said. "So maybe someday you too will be a bellman."

Bruce scoffed. Vance wanted to flip the kid's hat off again and make him eat it. Vance had half a mind to quit right then and there, and as long as he was at it, he might as well beat Mack to a pulp in front of these two clowns. If the money weren't so damn good, he would do it.

Vance picked up another spike. He threw it to Bruce, point first. "Here," Vance said. "You try."

Bruce lifted the spike the way Vance had done and brought it down with an "Ooomph!" The spike grazed the sand and shot between Bruce's legs, like he was hiking a football. Kevin giggled.

"Unbelievable," Vance said.

Mack clapped Vance on the back. "Keep up the good work, Professor," he said. "By the way, there's a twelve-knot west-southwest wind."

Vance thought briefly about how sweet it would be to set all the umbrellas facing east northeast just so he could watch them pop out of the ground and fly down the beach. He thought of the Beach Club members lying impaled and bloody in the sand. But why should he punish the members when the person he was after was Mack? Vance crunched two Rolaids between his teeth. Then he picked up the spike and tossed it to Bruce.

"Try again," he said.

BY NINE-THIRTY ALL THE umbrellas were up and Vance's arms ached. Bruce was the crappiest umbrella planter Vance had ever seen, although Kevin wasn't bad, just a little shallow. Vance showed the boys where the Sleepy Hollow chairs were kept and instructed them on how to properly open and close the chair without snapping their fingers off. He left them out on the beach, practicing opening and closing the chairs like the amateurs they were.

When Vance got back to the office, Mack was in the lobby schmoozing with the guests. Vance went into the utility closet and shoved past the stand of vacuum cleaners. There, in the back of the closet, sat Vance's locked toolbox. Vance found the key on his ring and opened the box. Inside was his hammer, various nails and screws, a set of adjustable wrenches, a ratty, torn-up copy of "The Downward Spiral," Vance's published short story, and Mr. Beebe's handgun. It was a .38. Vance held it straight out in his arms. Mack was lucky Vance didn't have the gun when he made his cutesy remark. Mack was lucky Vance didn't feel like going to jail, otherwise he would be Vance's first target, no question about it.

"Not bad for a bellman," Vance said softly. "Pow."

WITHIN TWENTY-FOUR HOURS of summer solstice, two important women in Mack's life arrived on the island: Andrea Krane and Cecily Elliott. Cecily arrived first, at ten o'clock on Sunday night. Mack was watching TV with Maribel asleep in his lap when the phone rang.

"I'm home. Mom and Dad said I should call. Hope I didn't wake you up."

"Cecily?" Mack said. Maribel blinked her eyes. "How are you, kid?"

"Butt tired. I partied until seven o'clock this morning, then spent the day trying to get my dorm room clean enough so they would give Dad his security deposit back."

"Are you happy to be home? We missed you, kid."

"I'm not a kid. I'm eighteen years old, Mack."

"I know. How was graduation?"

"Boring. Hot. I was hungover for that, too."

"How's the boyfriend?"

"I'll fill you in tomorrow," Cecily said. "Can I please talk to Maribel?"

Mack covered the receiver. "It's Cecily. She wants to talk to you."

"Of course," Maribel said. She took the phone from Mack. "Cecily? Hey, girlfriend, how are you? No, you didn't hurt his feelings. He understands there are some things that can only pass between the lips of women. Now, tell me everything." Maribel disappeared into the bedroom.

Mack listened to Maribel's muffled laughter through the wall. The friendship between Maribel and Cecily surprised him. For the past several years, Therese had been trying to light a fire between him and Cecily, insisting that if they got married, the Beach Club would go to them both. Mack loved Cecily like a sister and he supposed Cecily reciprocated, although she was frequently sarcastic with him, and sullen. She'd had a crush on him when she was eleven or twelve, but as soon as the crush faded it seemed as if he'd disappointed her, fallen short of her expectations. This made him feel like doing a better job, so he tried to stay updated about her boyfriends and school, but everything she told him sounded suspiciously like old news, or a lie.

Cecily adored Maribel, and for good reason: Maribel was beautiful, friendly, intelligent, genuine, and all despite the fact that she'd been raised by a single working mother in rural New York. Mack had met Maribel during her first summer on the island, when North Beach Road was part of her daily running route. Mack found himself waiting for her to show up, the blond runner. He volunteered to sweep the parking lot around ten o'clock, hoping she would take off her headphones and talk to him, but she never stopped, except for a brief moment, to drink in the sight of the ocean. One day Mack waited in the middle of the road with a bottle of Evian. She waved him away, but her eyes lingered on the bottle; it was, thankfully, a very hot day, and she gave in. She poured half the bottle down her front and inhaled the other half sloppily, letting it drip down her chin. She gasped, "Thanks," and was about to run off when he said, "Can I call you?" She readjusted her headphones, and said, "Library, in the afternoons." Mack remembered his first time walking into the Atheneum, its intimidating white columns, its intimidating quietness. He found Maribel in the stacks, reading a paperback romance, licking her finger as she turned each page. He tapped her on the shoulder and she whipped her head around, narrowed her blue eyes. She couldn't place him. He said, "I manage the Beach Club. I see you running." She reddened and quickly replaced the book on the shelf. "You like romances?" he said. "No," she answered sternly. "I don't."

But she did. Her job at the library was a summer position, and when the fall came, she stayed. And stayed, for six years.

This past Christmas Eve, Maribel had the stomach flu and yet she insisted on going to the midnight service at the Unitarian church. No sooner had the choir filed in singing "Oh, Come All Ye Faithful," then she had to be sick. Mack escorted her out and she threw up all over Orange Street. They sat on the steps in the cold still night, with the clock tower above them as they listened to the faint singing from inside. "The most beautiful night of the year," Maribel said. "And I ruined it." Mack almost proposed right then, and what a story it would have been, but no, he didn't have the courage, if courage was what he was missing. In the end he just held Maribel's hand, and when she felt well enough, they walked home. After six years, Maribel didn't pester him about marriage, but he wasn't stupid. He knew he had to make a decision soon. First, he had to decide about the farm and the Beach Club, and then he had to decide about Maribel.

An hour later, Mack went into bed. He found Maribel fast asleep in her clothes, holding the receiver of the phone to her chest. Her lips parted and she gave a sudden kick.

"Jump-starting your motorcycle," Mack said softly. He kissed her forehead. "Sweet dreams."

Maribel's eyes flew open. "What am I doing?" she asked.

"Running in place," he said. He wasn't sure if she was awake or not. "What did you and Cecily talk about?"

"Nothing," Maribel said. Her eyes fell closed again. "Love."

MACK SAW CECILY THE next morning after breakfast. He was standing on the front porch of the lobby when she popped out of her house. She was in bare feet, wearing baggy Umbro shorts and a Middlesex Field Hockey T-shirt. Cecily was tall and lanky and had long red curls, two shades darker than her mother. She walked toward Mack gingerly, over the asphalt and the broken hermit crab shells.

"You need to toughen your feet," Mack said.

"I liked being in a place that had grass, you know. Don't you ever miss grass, Mack?"

"If we had grass, I'd be mowing it," he said. He met Cecily on the first step and hugged her. "I missed you, though. And hey, congrats on getting into UVA. We have a bellman here from Virginia."

Cecily lifted her leg to inspect the sole of her foot. "I know. Mom told me."

"So when do you leave for college?"

"Geez, Mack. I just got here. Can't you let a person relax for a minute? College isn't exactly an exciting prospect for me. I just spent four years in a dorm, okay? We're talking about more of the same."

"Sorry," Mack said. "I thought college was pretty cool and I was only on the Cape."

"College is college," Cecily said. She squinted at him. "I can't believe you haven't proposed yet."

"How rude of me." He dropped to one knee. "Cecily, will you marry me?"

Cecily slouched, hip thrown out. "I don't know how Maribel puts up with you."

"That makes two of us," Mack said. "I'm impossible."

"Not an excuse," Cecily said. "When are you going to ask her?"

"I don't know," Mack said. "Maybe around the time you graduate from college."

"You are impossible," Cecily said.

"So," Mack said, "tell me about the boyfriend."

"He's smarter than you and much better looking," Cecily said. "But you're changing the subject. When are you going to ask Maribel to marry you?"

"Did Maribel send you out as her scout?" Mack said.

"No." Cecily avoided his eyes by inspecting her other foot. "We just want to know."

"Who's 'we'?" Mack asked.

"The world," Cecily said. "When are you going to marry her, Mack?"

"I don't know," Mack said. "One of the things you'll learn as you grow up is that sometimes 'I don't know' is the only answer you're going to get."

"Please spare me the growing-up bullshit," Cecily said. She looked past him into the lobby. "Can you believe Mom and Dad won't let me work the front desk? Dad's putting me on the beach. At least I'll get a tan. Who's that working?"

"Love O'Donnell," Mack said. "She's nice. You'll like her."

"I'll have to like her later. I'm going back to bed."

"The Beach Club opens today, Cecily. That makes this your first day of work."

She waved at him and headed back through the minefield of shells to her house. "I'm the owner's daughter," she said. "I do what I want."

ANDREA KRANE AND HER fifteen-year-old son, James, arrived on the late ferry, which docked at 10:30 P.M. Mack was working the desk, giving Tiny the night off, and he let Jem go home early. The lobby was quiet. From the front porch, Mack watched the lights of the ferry approach the island. Andrea was on that boat, standing on the upper deck trying to pick out the lights of the hotel from off the dark coast.

I'm right here where you left me. Last July he watched her boat leave from this very spot. It was morning then and Mack waved his arms, although he knew she couldn't see him.

When the ferry headed around Brant Point and Mack heard the long, low horn announcing the boat's arrival, he went back inside and sat behind the desk. Twenty minutes later, Andrea walked in the door. She was in sweatpants and a navy blue windbreaker, her hair pulled back in a ponytail. She carried a huge duffel across her back and a suitcase in each hand. Mack scrambled to help her.

"I got it," she said irritably when he reached for her bags. "If you help, you'll throw me off balance." She made it to the front desk and let everything drop. "Here I am." She took a deep breath and looked at the quilts, the wicker chairs, the fireplace, the plants. "God, I love this place. I'd like to buy this place. Do you think Bill and Therese would sell it to me? No, don't say anything. Just let me take this all in. In a minute, it's going to feel like I never left."

Mack hadn't seen Andrea in eleven months, he hadn't heard her voice or smelled her scent, and yet here she was in front of him, exactly as she had been when he last kissed her.

"Okay," she said. "I'm ready."

Mack kissed her.

"Do that again," she said.

Mack kissed her with more intensity, although still not the way he wanted to kiss her. If it weren't in violation of her rules, he would carry her back to room 18 and make love to her right then and there. Instead, he stepped back.

"How was your trip?" he asked. "And where's James?"

"He's in the truck, rocking," she said. "That should give you some indication of how the trip went. As soon as he gets out of his routine, he starts to panic. I bought him a book about airplanes to keep him occupied. His new thing is planes. We've been getting up at six o'clock each morning and driving to BWI to watch them take off."

"Let's go get him," Mack said. "I have his room all set up with the bedspread. That might make him feel better."

"You're a doll," she said. "And remember, don't let him upset you."

Mack had known James since he was five years old when he was afraid of toilet seats and he held his hands over his ears and screamed in a strangled voice. Every year Mack hoped James would become cured of his autism. Dealing with James was frustrating and even a little scary. Mack felt a familiar dread as he followed Andrea out to her truck.

James sat in the passenger side of Andrea's green Ford Explorer with his head bent, rocking back and forth. Andrea opened the door, but the rocking continued. James's rocking blocked out all other stimuli; it was his way of keeping himself under control.

"Climb out of the truck, James," Andrea said. She waited a few seconds. "Climb out."

James stopped rocking and got out of the truck like an automaton. He was such a handsome kid, with Andrea's honey-colored hair and gray-green eyes. Puberty had come to James this year—he was taller, with faint whiskers above his lip.

"Say hi to Mack," Andrea prompted.

"Hi, Mack," James said.

"Hi, James. I'm glad you got here safely." Mack looked at Andrea. "Are there other bags?"

"I'll get them," she said. "You take James to his room."

"Follow me, James," Mack said. He took the boy's arm but James pulled away. James opened the door to the truck and Mack thought he was going to climb back in and start rocking again but all he did was pick up a book.

"*Understanding Aeronautics,*" James said. "Three hundred twenty-five pages, illustrated, heavy stock laminate paper. Copyright 1990. Reprinted 1992, 1994. This copy belongs to James Christopher Krane." He tucked the book under his arm and followed Mack through the lobby, out the back door and along the boardwalk to room 17.

Mack stepped into the room and James followed. "This is your room, James."

James sat immediately down on the bed and started stroking the bedspread. "James's blanket," he said.

"That's your blanket," Mack said. "Nobody uses it but you." It was a green chenille bedspread, the kind the hotel rooms had ten years ago. Now all the rooms had hand-stitched quilts, but Mack stored one chenille bedspread in the utility closet for James.

Andrea opened the door that connected with room 18. "Mom's room is right here, remember, James?"

James turned on the TV.

"James, please put your clothes in the dresser," Andrea said. "We're going to be here for three weeks."

"Twenty-one days," James said.

"That's right. Twenty-one days just like always. Let me show you where the bathroom is." Andrea turned on the bathroom light. "It's right here. And Mack took off the toilet seat. There's no toilet seat in here, okay, buddy?"

James stared at the TV. "No toilet seat," he said.

"That's right, no toilet seat. No reason to be afraid. You've stayed in this room many times before. Do you feel comfortable?"

James stared at the TV.

"James, I asked if you felt comfortable here."

"Are we going to the airport in the morning?" James asked.

"Yes, we are, we're going to the Nantucket airport."

"Okay," James said.

"Okay. Mom is going to unpack and then go to sleep. Knock on my door if you need anything."

Andrea beckoned Mack into her room.

"Good night, James," Andrea said.

"Good night, James," Mack said.

"Good night," James said. "Good night."

Andrea shut the door and fell back onto the bed. "What an exhausting day. Every day with James is exhausting but travel really drains me." She unzipped her windbreaker. Underneath she wore a red T-shirt. "Do you notice a difference in him?" she asked.

"That's not fair," Mack said, plunging into the leather chair. "You know him much better than I do."

"I'm so close to him that I can't notice any changes. Tell me what's different from a year ago. Maybe I shouldn't ask you until tomorrow. He wasn't exactly the best version of himself tonight."

"Well," Mack said. He wasn't thinking of James, but of the lobby, which he had left open, and of the phone, which he left unattended. "Let me use your phone." Mack forwarded the hotel's calls to Andrea's room. Then he sat back down in the chair. "He's taller," Mack said. "He's getting a beard in, have you noticed that?"

"I've been ignoring it," Andrea said. She hugged her knees to her chest. "Really, as if it weren't difficult enough for me to raise a special-needs child on my own, now I have to raise a man? I have parents asking me questions all the time, about toilet training and school and what kinds of vitamins their kids should take, and I give them answers but I feel like such an impostor. Because meanwhile I'm watching James grow up and I don't know what to do about it. I don't know what to tell him about shaving, or about girls and sex. He loves to masturbate, and every time I find him doing it, I hide in my walk-in closet and cry. In a couple of years, I'm going to have to help him find a job and another place to live. There are hurdles in front of me and I can't even see how high they are."

"Do you hear from Raymond?" Mack asked.

"I heard his wife just had her third baby. He sends me large sums of money, really enormous sums that I'm simply socking away. But he won't see James, nothing's changed there. It's like the kid doesn't exist for Raymond, except as some kind of charity case to throw money at. Being rejected by your father is enough to break a normal kid. I don't know how it's affecting James."

"I can teach James to shave," Mack said. "Later in the week, once he's gotten used to me again."

Andrea flashed her green-grays at him and then she started to cry. "Thank you," she said. "I was hoping you'd offer. It's so horrible of me to depend on you, but you know what? I like having three weeks out of fifty-two when I know there's someone I can count on. It's nice to know I'm not completely alone."

"You're not alone," Mack said. He sat next to Andrea on the bed. He put his arms around her and she pressed her wet face into his chest. Mack closed his eyes and inhaled the scent of her hair. He loved Andrea's sadness. Her sadness was about the inscrutable mixed-up messages in her son's brain, and about being left to bring him up by herself, but Andrea's sadness was generous enough to encompass everything, including an eighteen-year-old Iowa farm boy losing both his parents in a single moment. And somehow she managed to make sadness, her own and everyone else's, seem necessary, right.

"I love you," Mack said.

She sniffled. "I know."

They had never made love. This was Andrea's rule from the beginning—it would make things too complicated, she said, and there was also the issue of logistics, because of James. There was always James—and long ago Mack suspected that after the ferocity with which Andrea loved James, there was little left over for anyone else. Andrea never told Mack she loved him—always she responded by saying "I know." She let him hug and kiss her and once or twice a summer when James was asleep in the other room they fell back on the bed groping for one another and Mack ground against her, sweating, crazy, aching. But she never gave in, she never let go.

The phone rang and Mack stood to answer it.

"Who could be calling me?" Andrea asked.

"It's Maribel," he said. He checked his watch. "It's almost midnight." He picked up the phone. "Nantucket Beach Club."

"Mack," Maribel said, "it's late."

"I know," he said. "I had a late check-in. I'll be home in a little while."

"I might be asleep."

"Okay," Mack said. He paused before he hung up, thinking about Maribel the night before as she lay asleep with the phone on her chest; he thought about the little kicks and twists she made in the night. He knew her so well. She was like another part of him. As Mack replaced the receiver he thought, *I love them both.* It happened, he supposed; he was just glad he didn't have to choose between them, not tonight, anyway.

"I should go," he said to Andrea.

"When are you going to marry her, Mack?"

"I don't know," Mack said. "I kind of wish people would quit asking me that."

Andrea smiled. "Would you like to come to the airport with James and me tomorrow? Normally we leave at six but since I'm on my much-needed vacation, we won't leave until seven. Want to join us for an hour?"

"Sure," Mack said. "I'll meet you in the parking lot, how's that?" He kissed Andrea, and stepped out onto the deck. "Good night."

Andrea closed the door behind him, and Mack walked over the

boardwalk into the sand. He looked at the stars and listened to the waves rushing onto the beach. He wondered if his parents could see him, and if they could see him, he wondered what they were thinking.

NOT ONLY WAS MARIBEL asleep when Mack got home, she was asleep when he rose at six-thirty the next morning. He considered waking her to let her know he was leaving early, but she looked peaceful, a strand of blond hair caught in the corner of her mouth, flutters underneath her eyelids.

"What are you dreaming about?" he whispered. But she didn't waken, and Mack got up to shower. Before he left the apartment, he picked a yellow zinnia from the flowerbed and put it on his pillow, where she would see it when she opened her eyes.

WHEN MACK GOT TO the hotel, Andrea was already behind the wheel of the Explorer with James in the passenger seat, reading his book. Mack hopped in the backseat.

"I hope I'm not late," he said.

Andrea smiled wearily. "Old habits die hard," she said. "We've been waiting since six."

"Since six," James said.

On the way to the airport, Andrea said, "James, the planes at this airport are going to be smaller than the ones we're used to seeing in Baltimore." She looked over the seat at Mack. "I don't want him to be disappointed."

"Maybe we'll get lucky and see a jet," Mack said.

"I see jets every day," James said. He paged through his book. "Boeing 747, 767, DC-10. Is there a tower at this airport?"

"I don't know," Mack said. "I can't remember."

James laughed. "*All* airports have a tower. It's where the air traffic controller sits so there are no crashes." James made an exploding noise and smacked his hands together.

Once they reached the airport, Andrea parked at the far edge of the field so they could watch the planes land. She turned off the ignition, leaned her head against the headrest, and closed her eyes. James, however, became extremely alert and animated; he was a different kid from the one Mack had seen the night before sitting in front of the TV.

"Here comes one!" James shouted. He riffled madly through the pages of his book.

Mack leaned over the front seat. He massaged Andrea's shoulder with one hand and looked through the windshield. "What kind is it?"

"I can't tell yet," James said. The sun was bright and James squinted. Mack offered James his sunglasses and James happily put them on.

"Mom, look!" James said.

Andrea opened her eyes for a second and smiled. "Very handsome," she said.

The plane landed, its wheels skidding and smoking on the runway. James clapped.

"Turboprop," he said. "Gets most of its thrust through the propellers."

"Have we seen those in Baltimore?" Andrea asked.

"Yes, Mom," James said. Something in James's tone of voice— ("*Yes, Mom, of course, Mom, don't be silly*")—sounded like a typical teenager. This was what made James so frustrating. He could be so normal—and at other times so impenetrable. Andrea once told Mack that the messages in James's brain were a code she could only crack randomly, with luck. A code without a key.

"Here comes one!" James said. The plane landed right in front of them, like an actor taking a bow, and James applauded. "Safe landing!"

They watched planes land and take off for forty minutes. James applauded for both occasions and during the lulls he paged through his book, reciting facts about planes for Mack.

"Planes are heavier than air," he said. "They need wings in order to fly. Planes have three kinds of motion: yaw, roll and pitch." He moved his hand through the air and made a noise with his lips.

"You sure know a lot about planes," Mack said.

"Yeah," James said. "I know it all."

Andrea was quiet, and finally she turned the key in the ignition.

James's spine stiffened. "Is it time?" he asked.

"It's time," she said.

James pointed to the blue numbers of the digital clock. "It's *not* time," he said. "We have until eight o'clock. This says seven-forty-five. Right here, Mom, see?"

"We have a visitor," Andrea said. "And Mack has to get the doughnuts so the rest of the people staying at the hotel will have their breakfast." She pulled away.

"Get the doughnuts," James said. "Getthedoughnutsgetthedoughnutsgetthedoughnuts." He rocked back and forth.

"James," Andrea said sternly, "we're coming back tomorrow. And tomorrow we'll stay until eight. Please don't get upset."

"Getthedoughnutsgetthedoughnutsgetthedoughnuts," James said.

Mack leaned forward. "Thank you for letting me come with you today."

"Getthedoughnuts," James said. "Airport, then shower."

"We have to get back to the hotel first, James," Andrea said. "There's no shower in the car."

"Airport, then shower," James said.

"That's right, James. When we get to the hotel, you can take a shower."

James rocked back and forth, saying under his breath, "Doughnuts, shower, doughnuts." Mack caught Andrea's face in the side-view mirror. She smiled weakly and shook her head.

When Andrea pulled into the Beach Club parking lot, she said, "Thank you, Mack, for coming with us. James, would you thank Mack?"

"Airport," James said. "Then shower. Thank you."

"Sounds like somebody wants to get in the shower," Mack said,

"How could you tell?" Andrea said. She got out of the car. James was already headed for his room. Mack looked up at Bill and Therese's house but saw no sign of stirrings and figured they were still in bed. Vance hadn't arrived yet, nor Love, nor the new beach boys. Mack followed Andrea to her room. Andrea unlocked James's door and James stripped his clothes on the way to the bathroom, including Mack's sunglasses, which fell to the floor.

"I thought you had to get the doughnuts," Andrea said. "Don't make a liar out of me. James, close the door, please!"

The door closed and the water came on.

"I do," Mack said. "But I feel bad for throwing off your routine."

"Flexibility isn't James's strong suit," Andrea said. "I should have thought of that before I invited you."

"And you were quiet in the car," Mack said. "Is everything all right?"

She picked up Mack's sunglasses and fingered them idly. "Going to the airport is good for James but it sure is lousy for me," she said. "I can't help thinking that James will never be able to just choose a place off the map and take a trip there. He's not safe in the world, Mack, and he's never going to be. I'm the only person who's going to love him enough."

Mack hugged her. "You don't know that."

"For a while taking care of him was getting easier," she said. "Now it's getting harder. And seeing you makes everything worse."

Mack held her at arm's length. "Worse? Why's that?"

"Because you make me remember that I'm not just a mother but a woman, with needs."

"You're not saying . . ."

"No," she said. "I haven't changed my mind about that." She sighed. "I'm having a hard time switching into my vacation mode. I promise I'm going to try and relax, okay? I'm going to sit under my cool blue beach umbrella and read my trashy novels and watch James as he decides if it's okay to go in the water. I'm going to order a couple of cheeseburgers from Joe's Broad Street Grill and have one of the darling college boys deliver them right to my umbrella. I'm going to try and have fun, dammit." She raised her face. "Do I say this every year?"

"Yes," Mack said. "And every year you succeed." He kissed her. If Maribel were a yellow zinnia, what would Andrea be? A red rose maybe, something a little more somber, a little more serious. "I'll see you later." He slipped from James's room out the back door and looked both ways. No one was around. It took him a split second to remember about the doughnuts, to remember that he had a hotel to run.

THE REASON MACK FORBADE his staff to date the guests was this: It was distracting. It was distracting to work in the same place that the object of your affection lay in the sun, swam, showered, ate breakfast, and slept. Because you wanted to join them, because you wanted to check on them every ten minutes, because you wanted to have fun with them—slip under their umbrella, join them for a nap, share a bagel. But you couldn't; you were at work. And so, Mack told his staff there would be No Dating the Guests. I'm making your life easier, he said. Trust me.

After all the years with Andrea, Mack had his distractions under control. She and James ate breakfast on their deck and Andrea, true to her word, rarely moved from her place on the beach, so Mack never wondered what she was up to. He did take a few more night shifts on the front desk from Tiny than usual, but he did this every June and Tiny never asked why.

Mack tried, most especially, to pay enough attention to Maribel. Nights he was home he took her out for dinner, he drove her down the beach to see the sunset, he made love to her with the windows open and the sounds of crickets floating around their dark bedroom. He tried not to think of Andrea while he was with Maribel, he tried not to think of Andrea's sad gray-green eyes, but it was impossible. He wondered if he were acting like someone with a guilty conscience.

One night as Mack and Maribel had dinner at Le Languedoc, Maribel reached over and took Mack's hand.

"I want to ask you something," she said.

Instantly, Mack started to sweat. "What's that?"

Maribel leaned in closer. "It's less than two weeks until the Fourth of July. The summer is flying by. And I want to know if you've thought any more about the profit sharing."

Mack blew out a stream of air. His body felt cool and tight. "Hmmmm." Under other circumstances, he might have been angry with Maribel for pushing this issue, but now there was Andrea. Mack had told Andrea about the phone call from David Pringle, and about the farm. He told her he might ask Bill to profit-share and Andrea said, "I'm surprised he hasn't offered it to you." Mack felt the same way: that Bill should *offer* him part of the profits.

"I haven't asked Bill yet," he said. "I'm still thinking it through."

"You have to give David an answer about the farm, Mack."

"I'm aware of that, Maribel," Mack said. "It's my farm. I have until fall anyway."

"Asking Bill about the profit sharing should make your decision clear. If he says yes, you sell the farm. If he says no, you run the farm."

"Nothing is clear," Mack said, although he realized it would seem that way to Maribel, or to anybody else for that matter. "I don't know if I want to run the farm. And I don't know if I want to sell it."

Maribel retracted her hand. "King of the I-don't-knows," she said.

She was baiting him, but Mack wouldn't argue. She was right. He didn't know a lot of things. For example, he didn't know how he could possibly be in love with two women. Had he felt this way last year? The year before that? Why was it hitting him so squarely in the jaw this year? Was it part of being thirty? Mack supposed he could confide in Bill, but for Bill, there had only been Therese, and no matter how much poetry Bill read, he wouldn't understand when Mack said, "I love them both."

AT THE END OF Andrea's first week, Mack had his usual Sunday night dinner with Lacey Gardner.

"What do you want to drink, dear?" Lacey asked him. "Dewar's or a Michelob?"

"I love them both," Mack said.

Lacey looked at him as though he'd just burped the alphabet. "Would you like me to pour you one of each, then, and you can drink them side by side?"

"I'm sorry," Mack said. "Michelob. Actually, better make that a Dewar's."

"Uh-oh," Lacey said. "Do we have a problem?"

"A couple of them," Mack said, taking a seat on the couch. The Sunday dinners weren't formal; Mack and Lacey each had about nine cocktails apiece and then if they remembered, they ate a sandwich, some cold meatloaf, or Lacey heated up a swordfish potpie.

"How big are these problems?" Lacey asked.

"The biggest," Mack said. "Love and work."

"Those aren't the biggest," Lacey said. "Health is the biggest. If we have our health, we're okay. Agreed?"

"Agreed," Mack said, thinking of James. "Agreed. But are love and money the second and third biggest?"

"Definitely top ten," Lacey said, bringing Mack his drink. She settled into her favorite leather armchair. She always dressed up for the Sunday dinners that weren't really dinners—tonight in a bright blue pantsuit with a gold Nantucket basket pin on her lapel. She'd been to the hairdresser and her white hair was fluffed and styled.

"You look great tonight, Gardner," Mack said. "Have I told you that already?"

Lacey waved at him. "You know why I invite you over here, don't you? Good for the ego. So, where shall we start?"

Mack sipped his drink. All Dewar's and no water. "I'm thinking of asking Bill to profit-share."

"You're speaking to the oldest of women," Lacey said. "What does that mean, profit-share? It sounds like one of those horrible terms from the 1980s."

"It just means that I get a portion of the bottom line. So my salary would depend on how well the hotel does. And we know the hotel does very well."

Lacey nodded. "What does Bill get in return for giving you his profits?"

"He keeps me happy," Mack said. "I stay."

"You're not happy?" Lacey asked. "That's news to me. And it'll be news to a lot of other people, I assure you."

"I'm happy and I'm not. I'm thirty years old, Lacey."

"And I'm eighty-eight," Lacey said. She pointed a manicured fingernail at him and smiled. "Gotcha there, didn't I?"

"Some things are happening back home," Mack said. "In Iowa. The boss on my father's farm is retiring and my lawyer wants me to sell the farm or go back and run it myself."

"I thought you were all finished with Iowa," Lacey said.

"There's five hundred acres with my name on it. I have to go back sometime."

"That's the argument for Iowa," Lacey said. "What's the argument for Nantucket?"

"I love it here."

"I concur. Where is better than Nantucket in the summer?" Lacey asked. "If there's a place more desirable than where you already are, Mack, do tell me about it."

"If I profit-share with Bill it would be easier to stay. I'd feel like the Beach Club is at least partially mine. I'll feel responsible for it."

"I thought you liked not feeling responsible for it," Lacey said.

"I have to grow up sometime."

"If you want to ask Bill for part of the hotel's profits, go ahead. Keep in mind that he'll have a reason for answering just as you have a reason for asking."

Mack had already given a lot of thought to what Bill might say. Bill might react as Mack hoped, and say, "Of course we can profit-share, I should have thought of that myself." Or he could simply say no. Or he could say, "Let me think it over. I'll run some numbers and get back to you." The worst thing would be if Bill said nothing, if he wrinkled his brow and retreated into himself, hurt that Mack had even asked for a piece of his business.

"We'll see," Mack said.

"Now, what about love?" Lacey asked. "But perhaps it's time for another drink?"

Mack spun the ice in his glass. "I'll make them," he said. He took the glasses to the kitchen and fixed two more drinks, adding a healthy dose of water to his own. "My problem is . . . Andrea's here."

"With James?" Lacey asked. "Is he any better?"

"A little bit," Mack said. That morning, Mack had helped James shave for the first time. Mack started the lesson by cutting his finger and letting the blood bloom to show James how sharp and dangerous the razor could be. Mack lathered up his face and then James's face. When James saw himself in the mirror, he giggled uncontrollably.

"Santa Claus," James said, touching his fingers to the shaving cream and tasting them. He grimaced and spat into the sink.

"That's right," Mack said. "When you lather up, you'll look like Santa Claus."

"Lather up, lather up!" James said.

Mack shaved a path from his own cheek down to his chin. Then he rinsed the razor. He put his arms around James from behind and said, "Now I'm going to do the same to you." But James raised his hands to his face and sidled away screaming, "Blood! Blood!"

"No," Mack said. Andrea was in the next room listening. "There isn't going to be any blood because I'm going to show you how to do it the right way." Mack knew that if he nicked James even a little bit, the lesson would be over. But Mack shaved smoothly and James giggled.

"It tickles," he said.

"Give me your hand." Mack guided James's hand with the razor along his face until he was completely shaved.

"No cuts this time," Mack said. "But sometimes there are cuts. And that's okay because they're little cuts." Mack finished shaving himself and then he showed James how to splash his face with water, and apply lotion.

"Some people use aftershave," Mack said. "But not me."

"Yeah," James said, "not me either."

"Look in the mirror, buddy, you're all shaved."

"All shaved," James repeated. He touched his face. His faint mustache was gone.

"We'll do it again in a couple days," Mack said. "Would you like that?"

James nodded.

"Do you want to show your mom?"

James burst out of the bathroom. "All shaved, Mom," he said. "No cuts this time."

Andrea, who had been sitting on the bed pretending to read a magazine, stood up. "You look so handsome," she said. She touched James's face. "Did Mack teach you how to shave?"

James nodded proudly, perhaps he was so proud that he lost language, because he said nothing. He let his mother hug him and then James turned and kissed Mack on the lips.

"HE'S BETTER," MACK SAID to Lacey. "And Andrea is great."

"So you're back to two women," Lacey said.

"I love them both," Mack said.

"Call me crazy, but I don't think you love either one," Lacey said.

"Of course I do," Mack said. "I definitely love Maribel. And with Andrea—well, Andrea is special. I love Andrea. There's no other word for it, although I feel differently about Andrea than I do about Maribel. But they both feel like love, Lacey."

"If you were going to marry Maribel you would have done it already. But you haven't. And who can blame you? You're already enjoying the party. Now, do I think you're going to marry Andrea? No! You've been fiddling around with her longer than Maribel."

"That's not fair," Mack said. He sometimes thought of showing up in Baltimore to live with Andrea, marry her, shoulder half her burden, and be like a father, or an uncle, to James. But wasn't Lacey right? Wasn't that just idle thinking on his part? Still, he couldn't imagine a life without Andrea, although if he married Maribel he would have to let Andrea go. "The reason it's a *problem*, Lacey, is that I don't know what to do."

"I stand by my word. You don't love either one," Lacey said. "When I spent time with Maximilian I knew I was with the only man for me. There was never another man, Mack, not even when Maximilian was away at the war."

Mack ran a hand through his hair. "I know," he said. Maximilian and Lacey had a storybook marriage, like his parents, like Bill and

Therese. Meant for each other, born to be together, holding hands every night before they went to sleep—it drove Mack nuts. Imagine being content every hour for forty-five years—surely Lacey was exaggerating. "Maybe you're right. Maybe I don't love either of them." When he said this, though, it sounded like a lie. He knew he loved them both.

THAT NIGHT WHEN MACK left Lacey's, he checked in at the front desk of the hotel with Tiny.

"Anything going on?" he asked.

Tiny looked up from her book, *One Hundred Years of Solitude*. This was the perfect title of a book for Tiny, who always seemed to be alone in her thoughts. She got her nickname because of her small voice, although her voice wasn't small so much as distant, as though she were talking to everyone from a faraway place, another dimension that she alone had reached.

"The couple in room four had a row and both room three and room five called to complain."

"What did you tell them?"

"What could I tell them?" Tiny said. "I can't be held accountable for other people's bad behavior."

"You must have told them something."

"I told them if it continued, I would call the manager and have him take care of it." She smiled a rare smile. "That would be you."

"Okay," Mack said. Vance poked his head out of the back office and made a face. "I'll check it out. Then I'm going home."

Mack tiptoed down the boardwalk with every intention of checking on room 4 but when he passed Andrea's room, the temptation was too great, and he knocked lightly on the door. A few seconds later, she let him in. The room was dark; Andrea had been asleep. She was wearing a white cotton T-shirt and white panties and her hair was loose around her shoulders.

"It's late," she said, putting her arms around his neck. She kissed him.

"Only ten o'clock," he said. He became aroused by the feel of her body through the T-shirt. She was still warm from bed. He sat on the bed and pulled her into his lap, and kissed her. Normally, this was when she pulled away, but tonight she responded with her tongue. She wiggled deliciously in his lap and ran her hands under his shirt. Mack rolled her onto the bed.

"I've been wanting this since the second you got here," he said.

Andrea ran her hand lightly over his erection. Mack groaned and sucked on her neck. He climbed on top of Andrea and rocked gently into her soft thigh. He was going crazy holding back, but he didn't want to scare her; he could feel himself sweating and he pulled off his shirt. He ran his hands under Andrea's T-shirt and caressed her full breasts. He lowered his mouth to her nipple and it hardened. Andrea pressed her hips into him.

"Will you let me inside you?" Mack asked. He cupped Andrea's ass inside her panties. "Will you?" If she said yes, he would go home and tell Maribel tonight, he swore it.

"No," Andrea said, breathing into his ear. "I can't."

"You can," Mack said. "Please?"

"I'm sorry, Mack," Andrea said. She pulled away and snapped on a light. "I got carried away. Sorry, sorry, sorry."

Mack squinted from the sudden brightness. He flopped onto his back, his erection pushing through his chinos. "Sorry?" he said, trying not to get angry. He lay there for a second, catching his breath. The room spun. Mack reached for Andrea's hand. "This actually hurts."

"Shame on you for showing up unannounced," she said.

Mack looked to the window and saw that Andrea's shades were up. A figure stopped at the window, then slunk away.

"Turn off the light," he said. He went to the window and dropped the shades, then he put his shirt back on. "I have to get out of here. I'll see you tomorrow."

"Give me a kiss good night," she said.

Mack kissed her. "I love you."

"I know," she said.

• • •

MACK STEPPED OFF ANDREA'S deck onto the boardwalk. He heard the sound of water rushing onto shore, and then, faintly, a woman crying. At first, he tried to convince himself it was a gull, but as he listened closer, he heard breathy sobs, definitely a woman crying. *Maribel.* Mack ran around the corner to the Gold Coast, trying to imagine what someone would have seen through the window: him lying on his back, shirtless, holding Andrea's hand, his erection straining through his pants. *Oh, God, Maribel.*

A blond woman sat on the deck of room 4. Mack cleared his throat and she looked up—it was difficult to see in the dark, but Mack knew instantly it wasn't Maribel. This woman's face was streaked with makeup; Mack recognized her from breakfast.

"Mrs. Fourchet?" Mack said. From Quebec, Mack recalled, where her husband owned a Porsche dealership.

"My husband hates me," she said in a defiant voice.

Another loud voice came from inside room 4. "I do not hate you, Meredith. Now will you please get inside?"

"We're paying to see the ocean, Jean-Marc," the woman squawked.

"It's too dark to see anything," the man said. "Now get in here."

"Folks, I'm going to have to ask you to pipe down," Mack said. He was so relieved that he smiled as he said this. "Could you please be a little quieter?"

The door to room 4 opened and Mr. Fourchet stepped onto the deck. "I paid six hundred bucks for this room. I'll have a brass band on this deck if I so choose."

Mack had to wipe the grin off his face. "A brass band?" Mack said. "Ask me in the morning and I'll see what I can do. Do you like the tuba?"

Mr. Fourchet looked at Mack strangely, then he shrugged and said in a softer voice to his wife, "Come in, Meredith, please?"

"I'm *not coming in!*" Mrs. Fourchet shrieked. "And if this fellow wants to call the police then so be it! The Nantucket Police Force can take me away. Ha! The Nantucket Police Force, I'm sure *that's* an intimidating group."

"Meredith, stop giving him a hard time," Mr. Fourchet said. "Will you come inside?"

"No!" Mrs. Fourchet said. "I'm not going anywhere until I see the Nantucket Police Force drive their dune buggy up the beach."

The door to room 3 opened: Janet Kava, wearing a pair of thick glasses, stepped onto her deck. Janet was a mathematics professor at the University of Pennsylvania. She and her partner, Eleanor, had brought along their new adopted baby.

"Mack," Janet said. "Thank God you're here. These people have been screaming at each other for half an hour."

Mrs. Fourchet shot Janet a withering look. "Dyke," she said.

"*Excuse* me?" Janet Kava said. She poked at the bridge of her glasses with a purposeful finger. "*What* did you say?"

"Your baby cries all night long, but that's okay, I suppose," Mrs. Fourchet said. "That's okay because she is the *love child* of you and your lesbian friend."

"That's right," Janet Kava said. "Eleanor and I love each other. We love each other emotionally and physically just like you and your brutish husband love each other. But we don't have squabbles for all the world to hear."

"I think I'm going to be sick," Mrs. Fourchet said.

"Meredith," Mr. Fourchet said.

"Ladies, please," Mack said.

"We are *women,* Mack," Janet Kava said. "Not ladies. Especially not one of us."

"I'll say," Mrs. Fourchet said. "The ladies I know like men."

"I'm ten seconds away from coming over there and demanding an apology," Janet said. "And it won't be very ladylike, I assure you."

Mrs. Fourchet wiped under her eyes. "I must look a mess," she said innocently. She stood up. "I think you're right, Jean-Marc, I think it's time to come in."

Janet Kava glared at Mrs. Fourchet until she disappeared, then she slammed her own screen door shut.

"Good night," Mack said.

Mack ran past the side deck rooms. He looked in Andrea's window but it was dark; she was probably already asleep. All of the lights on the side deck rooms were out and it was difficult to see as he made his way down the boardwalk toward the lobby. When he reached for the back door, he felt a strong hand on his shoulder. Mack swung around. Vance.

"How're you doing, man?" Mack asked. "I had a few words with the people in four. They seem to be settling down."

Vance's expression was strained, as though he were lifting a heavy weight.

"Are you all right?" Mack asked.

"I need to talk to you a minute," Vance said. His hand rested firmly on Mack's shoulder.

"Okay," Mack said. Vance was acting even stranger than normal, but this sometimes happened. Lots of little things bothered Vance and they built up once a summer to the point that he exploded and Mack had to placate him with an extra day off or a small cash bonus.

"I need to talk about you and room eighteen," Vance said. "I saw you in there just now, man. Pretty incriminating."

Mack's relief at finding Mrs. Fourchet instead of Maribel drained away. The four drinks he'd had at Lacey's kicked in; his head swam. "I know it probably looked bad, man, but it's not what you think."

"If it's not what I think, then what is it?"

"We're friends," Mack said. "I've known that lady a long time."

"I've known her just as long as you have, but you don't see me lying on her bed with my shirt off, now do you?" Vance asked. His fingertips dug into Mack's shoulder blade. "How do you explain holding this woman's hand and she's not wearing very many clothes herself?"

Mack took a deep breath. He tried to shrug Vance off. "I wish you'd just forget about it, okay? It's perfectly innocent."

Vance's nostrils flared. "You are so full of shit."

Then Vance raised his hand. He was holding a gun.

Mack's shoulders froze, except for the spot where Vance's hand rested, that spot was very hot and bright. "What are you doing?" Mack said.

Vance poked Mack in the chest with the gun. Mack couldn't move, his knees were locked. Mack was sweating; he felt the cold breeze coming off the water.

"You're going to tell Maribel," Vance said. His voice gurgled. "You're going to tell Maribel what you've been doing or I'll tell her for you."

"You don't know the first thing about it," Mack said.

"I know what I saw," Vance said. "I know what it looked like."

"I already told you, that's not how it is," Mack said.

"You're going to tell Maribel," Vance said. He pressed the gun deeper into Mack's chest. In the dim light, Vance's skin looked purplish. "You are such an idiot. You have a gorgeous, perfect woman like Maribel and you screw around on her. Total fucking idiot."

The nose of the gun stuck into Mack's chest. He thought about the hot, sharp pain of taking a bullet to his heart. His heart would explode and bits and pieces of Maribel and Andrea would splatter everywhere. He *was* an idiot, thinking idiot thoughts.

"I could fire you," Mack said.

"I could fire *you*," Vance said. "No dating the guests, remember? Not only breaking the rules, but showing yourself to be the hypocrite I always knew you were."

"But you have a gun," Mack said.

"That's right," Vance said. "I have a gun. And so I have a choice. I can fire you or I can kill you. Or I can hope you act smart and go home and tell Maribel that you've been in another woman's bed tonight."

Mack's mouth was dry. "Why are you threatening me? We work together. We've worked together since the beginning. We're, I don't know, buddies. Aren't we?"

Vance laughed, a sharp bark. "You have no idea how much I hate you. You really have no idea. Unbelievable. You step off the boat thirty fucking seconds sooner than I do and all of a sudden you're the white prince and you assume everyone loves you. Maribel loves you, room eighteen loves you, Bill and Therese and all the guests whose asses you kiss love you. No such luck, buddy. You push me right to the edge, Petersen, to where I can see myself doing something like this. I can see myself taking you out and saying it was an accident, saying I found the gun in a room and was fooling around and oops, it went off. So they send me to Walpole for a year or two. So what? It might be worth it, brother man."

"You're crazy," Mack whispered.

"Are you going to tell Maribel?" Vance asked. "That's all I'm really concerned about in the here and now. Are you going to tell her?"

Mack nodded. "Yes."

"Okay," Vance said. He took the gun away from Mack's chest and studied it. Mack exhaled and the muscles in his legs tingled. "This baby is fully loaded, ready to go. But if you tell a soul, I'm just going to say I was playing a joke on you."

"For Christ's sake, Vance."

"Hey," Vance said, pointing the gun in Mack's face. "I'm serious about Maribel. Either you tell her what's going on with you and room eighteen or I'll tell her what I saw. Which was you lying on that woman's bed, and the woman half-naked and you grabbing at her."

"I wasn't *grabbing* at her," Mack said.

"Tell Maribel," Vance said. He lowered the gun. "I *would* shoot you if I thought I could get away with it."

"Why do you hate me?" Mack asked. "I apologized for taking your job back when it happened. It had nothing to do with our skin color and you know it. Besides, Vance, that was another lifetime ago." Mack reached behind him for the doorknob to the lobby. He wanted to be in the warm, bright lobby with Tiny, although for all Mack knew she could be hiding around a corner waiting to club him with a tire iron.

Vance spat at the ground near Mack's feet. "Get out of here," he said.

BY THE TIME MACK pulled into the driveway, Maribel had finished drying the dishes and putting them away. She had changed out of her white shorts and soft beige half sweater and into a T-shirt and boxers. She had washed her face and her neck with Noxema. By the time Mack walked in the door at midnight—which was late even for a Lacey

Gardner night—Maribel was pretty sure she had eliminated all clues that Jem Crandall had been there for dinner.

Or *sinner*, which was what she started calling it as soon as they arranged the time and the place. Her sinner with Jem. A small, intimate sinner party.

Having Jem over had been the result of two things. The first was that Maribel kept thinking back to the day she spent with Jem at the beach. It felt like they were somehow *meant* to have run into each other in the parking lot of Stop & Shop. And Maribel instinctively took Jem to the nude beach in Miacomet. Why? They could just as easily have gone to Cisco. But Maribel had *wanted* to show herself to Jem. And show herself she did—all look and no touch—but the looks Maribel was unable to forget.

Secondly was the fact that, in the past week or so, Mack had pulled out his old Iowa church-social manners. He constantly asked how she was feeling, was she okay? Then at Le Languedoc, he balked when she asked about the profit sharing. Mack had no intention of asking Bill to profit-share, and no intention of marrying her, and this kindness was just a front, just a way of letting her down easy. More than anything, Mack hated when things actually *happened*—moments like the one when the sheriff told him his parents had been killed. And so he wouldn't ask Bill to profit-share but he wouldn't tell Maribel that. He would just keep on saying please and thank you and I don't know, sweetheart, I just don't know—forever.

The combination of these two things led Maribel to call Jem and invite him over.

"For Sunday," she said. She was in her quiet, safe, book-lined office at the Atheneum, with the door locked. "Dinner at my house. Seven-thirty?"

"Sunday?" Jem said. A twinge of uncertainty in his voice. "Sunday, you mean, while Mack's at Lacey's?"

"That's right," Maribel said.

Dead air. Maribel heard the soft murmur of library patrons' voices on the other side of her door.

"You're putting me in a bad place," Jem said. "You're asking me to lie to my boss."

"I'm asking you to dinner," Maribel said. "Mack won't be there. I won't tell him you're coming over unless you want me to. But really, Jem, it's no big deal. I frequently have people over, friends, you know. They . . . drop by."

"Yeah, well, this is more than me dropping by," Jem said. "This is you calling in advance. And the way my luck has been going, you'll tell Mack and I'll end up fired."

"I'll take that as a no, then," Maribel said. "Maybe another time."

"No," Jem said. "Not another time. Sunday's fine. I'll be there Sunday."

Maribel's hands were sweating; she rubbed her palm on the receiver and it made a squeaking noise. "Sunday," she said, "seven-thirty. For sinner, I mean, dinner. Dinner at seven-thirty. Do you know where I live?" It felt strange to say "I" instead of "we." "I live at ninety-five Pheasant Road, the basement apartment around back."

"I'll find it," Jem said.

WHEN MACK CAME HOME at five on Sunday evening before going to Lacey's, Maribel nearly confessed to her dinner plans. Mack was in the apartment for about an hour, and Maribel shadowed him from room to room. First, she lay next to him in bed while he napped. Mack was the kind of person who could fall asleep at will, like he was letting go the string of a kite, and this always amazed Maribel. Really, did he have no nagging thoughts? Was his mind such an easy friend that it just set him free? Apparently so. Maribel lay next to him, studying his sandy hair, his sunburned face and sun-cracked lips, her own eyes wide open, unblinking. Thinking, *I'll tell him when he wakes up. I'll tell him I'm being a good Samaritan, feeding a hungry kid. If he makes the slightest fuss, I'll call Jem and cancel.*

When Mack was in the shower, Maribel sat on the fuzzy toilet seat cover in the steam and thought, *I'll tell him when he gets out.* Mack turned off the water, pulled back the shower curtain and Maribel handed him a towel. He dried his face, and scruffed the towel over his head, he dried his chest, his arms, his balls, and stepped onto the bathmat, wrapped the towel around his waist. Mack never concerned himself with how he looked. He was perfectly comfortable in his own body, as though he knew he could drive Maribel absolutely mad by just existing.

Before he left the house, Mack popped open a beer, took a long swallow, kissed Maribel, and said, "Don't wait up tonight, I might be late," and he jogged out the door to his Jeep. It was obvious he trusted her implicitly. Maribel felt guilty for a second, but then she wondered if he were suffering from plain indifference. He hadn't asked what she was doing at all.

As soon as the rumble of the Jeep's engine faded, Maribel called her mother. Sundays her mother slept late, puttered in her tiny vegetable garden, and then sat on the screened-in porch with her friend Rita Ramone and drank vodka gimlets. Maribel knew Rita would be languishing on the chaise longue next to her mother, listening to every word, but Maribel called anyway.

"My little girl!" Tina cried out. "What a surprise! Do you have news for your mama?"

Maribel guessed Tina was on her third or fourth gimlet. "No," she said.

"Mack's off at Lacey's?" Tina asked. "Are you lonely, sweetie pie?"

"Not really," Maribel said. "I'm having someone for dinner."

"Well, I hope they taste good!" Tina said. She laughed with abandon and Maribel could hear Rita in the background asking, "What's so funny?"

"It's a guy I'm having over," Maribel said. "A cute guy."

Tina was still laughing. "How cute?"

"He was Mr. November in some calendar," Maribel said.

"Not the Christian calendar," Tina said. "Although a cute guy or two might boost sales."

"Mack doesn't know a thing about it, either," Maribel said.

Tina's voice sobered. "Oh, my." The phone was muffled: Tina relayed this news to Rita Ramone. Then she said, "Rita thinks the only way to get a man is to play hard to get. Is that what you're doing, sweetie? Playing hard to get?"

"I don't know what I'm doing," Maribel said.

"Well, that makes three of us," Tina said. "Here, now I'm going into the house so we can talk serious." In the background, a door closed. "Okay, tell me what you're thinking."

"I'm thinking Mack is a lost cause," Maribel said.

"You've thought that many times before," Tina said. "Is this time any different?"

"I suggested the profit sharing, but he hasn't said anything to Bill."

"Maybe he's waiting for the right time," Tina said.

"Maybe," Maribel said. "Or maybe he thinks it's okay to string me along forever. But it's not okay. There are other men in this world who find me attractive, and I just happened to invite one of them to dinner on a night when Mack's out. That's not a crime, is it?"

"You know I'm terrible at figuring out men," Tina said. "I wouldn't exactly call myself Queen of the Successful Relationship."

"Mama," Maribel said. Her mother's Sunday afternoons with Rita Ramone were half girl talk and half wallowing in self-pity. "Do you think it's okay that I invited this person for dinner?"

"Yes," Tina said definitively. "What's his name?"

"Jem," Love said. "Jem Crandall."

"Jem Crandall," Tina said. "God has blessed Jem Crandall. You know I love you?"

"Yes," Maribel said.

"Have fun and we'll talk on Wednesday. I have to get back to Rita before she burns the house down."

"Okay, Mama."

"Godspeed, Maribel."

AT EXACTLY SEVEN-THIRTY, JEM appeared at the door with a bottle of Chardonnay, looking as nervous as Maribel felt. His dark hair was wet and he was wearing a blue chambray shirt and navy shorts. Birkenstocks. He was so handsome. He was tall and broad-shouldered and strong and young and he had wavy dark hair and that beautiful smile and not an ounce of self-congratulation. It was perfectly normal to be attracted to people other than your partner, Maribel reasoned. She was indulging a crush. Flushing it out of her system.

"You brought wine," Maribel said, taking the bottle from Jem carefully, as though it were a baby. "That was very thoughtful."

"I know about wine," Jem said. "My father owns a bar." He put his hand on Maribel's arm and bent over and kissed her. The kiss was brief; Maribel was still holding the wine to her chest, but it threw the whole room into disarray.

"Oh," she said. They looked at each other. Jem had blue eyes that matched his shirt. He was ridiculously, absurdly handsome, and Maribel looked into his blue eyes until it was like too much chocolate cake, and she knew looking another second wouldn't be good for her. She shifted her gaze.

"I can give you the nickel tour of the place from right here," she said. "Kitchen, dining room, living room. The powder room is this door here and then the bedroom." Maribel paused after the word "bedroom."

"It's nice," Jem said. "I rent a room in some old house. I'd kill for my own kitchen."

"I made some munchies," Maribel said. "Let's sit down."

"Okay," Jem said. He bounced on the balls of his feet and rubbed his hands together. "Want to open the wine? I could use a drink. I have to tell you, I'm a little nervous."

"Nervous?" Maribel said. "About what?"

"Not about what you think," Jem said.

"What do I think?"

"I'm not worried that Mack is going to come home and find me here."

"Good," Maribel said. She knew Mack wouldn't show up before ten-thirty or eleven, even though right now a part of her wanted him to.

"I'm nervous just being around you," Jem said. "I want everything to go right. That day at the beach . . ."

"The day at the beach was lovely," Maribel said. She took the mushroom caps stuffed with Boursin cheese out of the oven and moved them onto a platter with a spatula.

"It was better than lovely," Jem said. "It changed my whole view of the island. Before that day, I hated it here. But after that day, things got a lot better. It was weird, the way that happened, like you have magic powers."

Maribel took the shrimp cocktail out of the fridge. "I wish," she said. She almost added, *If I did, I'd start by using them on Mack.* She handed the shrimp to Jem. "You can take these to the coffee table. We'll sit on the sofa."

They arranged the food on the coffee table and Jem poured the wine. Maribel lifted her glass.

"Cheers," she said. "Here's to being nervous."

They sipped their wine. "Really nervous," Jem said.

"Eat something," Maribel said. "You'll feel better."

Jem picked up a peachy pink shrimp and dragged it through the cocktail sauce. Maribel watched the muscles in his jaw working as he chewed.

"Delicious," he said. He sampled a few mushrooms.

"How old are you?" Maribel asked.

"Twenty-three," he said. "I'm basically still a work in progress."

"There's no better place to be a work in progress than Nantucket."

"I guess," Jem said, "but I feel like I'm just biding my time here. I feel like this is a resting point for me before my real life begins."

"Your real life?"

"California," Jem said. "I can't be your beach agent forever, you know." He drained his glass of wine and fell back into the cushions of the sofa. "I'm leaving for the West Coast in the fall. You should come with me." He picked up Maribel's hand and kissed her palm.

Maribel closed her eyes, thinking, *How refreshing, a man who's not afraid to admit he's nervous, not afraid of being a work in progress, not afraid to commit.*

"Thanks for the offer," she said.

"I'm serious," he said. "I want you to come with me."

Maribel gently reclaimed her hand. "I hardly even know you, Jem."

"We can fix that," he said. "I'll tell you everything. My father owns a bar, my mother stays at home, and my sister is a whacko with an eating disorder. I graduated from college with a three-point-one GPA, and I was Theta Chi. I played lacrosse in high school. I love going to the movies. And you know who you remind me of? Meg Ryan. I thought that the first time I saw you."

"Thanks," Maribel said. "I guess."

"When I was six years old, my parents belonged to a swim club. One day my sister and I were sitting on the edge of the pool while my parents did laps and when they were both at the other end of the pool, I pushed my sister in. She was only three or four at the time, and she sank to the bottom like a lead weight."

"Oh, God," Maribel said.

"A lifeguard noticed Gwennie and he saved her. Nobody ever knew I pushed her, they thought she fell. And Gwennie was too young to understand. Except when she went to therapy for her bulimia, she told the shrink I pushed her."

"But they don't think that caused her bulimia?" Maribel asked.

"It made me feel pretty bad anyway," he said. "But relieved, too, you know, because for a lot of years I was the only one who knew I almost drowned my sister. The worst thing I've ever done, by far. So now you know that about me. What's the worst thing you've ever done?"

Maribel frowned. She thought about getting drunk in high school, a white mouse she bought at a pet store and took to a slumber party to put in Ursula Cavanaugh's sleeping bag, cohabiting with Mack. This, her sinner with Jem.

"I guess the worst thing I've done isn't something I've done, it's something I've felt." She thought of Tina, who would be sacked out in front of *The X Files* by now. "There are times when I'm ashamed of my mother."

"Oh," Jem said. "Uh-oh."

"My mother was never married. She was a hippie, I guess, and she had sex with some guy she didn't know and never saw again and I was born."

"Wow," Jem said. His eyebrows shot up. "And she never remarried or anything?"

"She dated some, when I was younger, but there was no one serious and then she lost interest and gave up." Maribel sipped her wine. "She works in a calendar factory. A *Christian* calendar factory."

"Does she like it?" Jem asked.

"Yeah," Maribel said, "she does. She's in charge there. But it's not exactly the life she dreamed up for herself and it's not any kind of life I would want. She lives her life through me, she has all these hopes for me."

"That's nothing to be ashamed of," Jem said.

"I just wish she wanted something for herself," Maribel said. "But she doesn't. And that makes me angry, and even embarrassed. I feel like such a bad daughter, but I can't help it. Every once in a while, I think, *This woman cannot be my mother.*"

"I feel that way about my sister sometimes," Jem said. "My parents say my sister is giving us all lessons in love and acceptance."

"I need some of those lessons," Maribel said.

"We all do," Jem said. He kissed her hand again.

DINNER WAS GRILLED SALMON, cold herbed potato salad, some greens dressed with balsamic vinegar. They finished the bottle of wine and Maribel pulled out chocolate mousse, and one of Mack's beers for Jem. He was telling her stories about the Beach Club. For years, Maribel had been hearing stories about the Beach Club and never once had she enjoyed them. Mack took his job at the hotel so seriously that Maribel hadn't realized what a funny place it could be.

"There's one guest, Mr. Feeney," Jem said, "and he's staying at the hotel for a week. Every day Mr. Feeney calls the front desk to complain about his toilet."

Maribel giggled. "His toilet?"

Jem took a swallow of beer. "His toilet." He burped. "Excuse me. So anyway, Mr. Feeney calls up every day. The tank's not filling quickly enough, it's making noises that keep him and the missus up at night, every day something different. So each morning I check it out, jiggle the handle, not knowing what I'm doing, but Mr. Feeney doesn't realize that. He's crowding into the bathroom with me, just so damn pleased that someone is taking his toilet problems seriously. And I want to say to him, 'Mr. Feeney, you might enjoy your vacation more if you stopped worrying about your toilet and started sitting with your wife on the beach, dabble your feet into the ocean, enjoy the salt air.' But around the fourth day or so, I realize something very profound. You know what that is?"

"What?" Maribel said.

"Some people don't like being happy. They're much more comfortable when they have a problem. And such is the case with Mr. Feeney. The guy is on vacation with his wife, in a world-class hotel, but that's not good enough. He *likes* worrying about his toilet. It gives him pleasure. It's like a hobby for him."

"Mr. Feeney and his toilet hobby," Maribel said.

"Exactly. And I'm Mr. Feeney's toilet agent, as you might have guessed. So then, the last day of this guy's stay, he calls me. And I say, 'What's wrong with your toilet today, Mr. Feeney?' And he says, 'Well, Jem, it won't flush.' So I check it out and it's true—it won't flush. We jiggle the handle, we toy around with the floater, nothing. The toilet won't flush, it won't gurgle, nothing. I ask him, has he done anything special, anything out of the ordinary? He says no, and I can tell he's enjoying every second of this because now his toilet really is broken."

"So what do you do?" Maribel asked.

"Mack shows up and we try the plunger and it's clear something is clogging the john, something big, but the plunger isn't helping. So we lift the john right off the floor. Take it outside where we can maneuver it better and look inside and what do you think we find?"

"I don't know," Maribel said.

Jem motioned for Maribel to lean in close to him. She put her elbows on her knees and held her face in her hands and Jem did the same. Their noses were practically touching and Maribel could smell his tangy breath.

"What did you find?" she whispered.

"Cantaloupe rinds," he said. He scooted forward an inch and kissed Maribel once, very lightly. "We found cantaloupe rinds." He kissed Maribel again, he parted her lips and tasted her. He tasted her like a boy who had been living all summer without a kitchen, he tasted her like someone who wasn't just hungry but starving. Maribel thought, *This feels good, I feel good, I feel delicious. This boy is young, unfinished, he is so handsome and sweet.* She thought, *What would I do if Mack walked in right now, how would I explain this, Good Samaritan?* She thought, *Wasn't this what I was hoping for when I called him? But it's innocent, just kissing, a crush.* She thought, *How cantaloupe rinds? Why cantaloupe rinds?* She thought, *Is this the worst thing I've ever done or just the beginning of the worst thing?*

Finally, Jem separated from her and his eyes scanned the clock on the wall behind her. "I should go," he said. "I don't want to, but I should."

Maribel walked him to the door. She turned on the outside light and moths beat themselves against the screen.

"What does this mean?" Jem asked. "The whole time I was kissing you I was wondering what this could mean."

"I don't know," Maribel said, and at that moment she felt like Mack. Mack and his infuriating "I don't knows." But it was true; she didn't know what the kissing meant.

"Is this an affair?" he asked. He laughed sarcastically. "God, I'm having an affair with my boss's girlfriend. This is just great."

"Jem," Maribel said, "it isn't an affair. We just kissed. That's all we're talking about."

"We kissed," Jem said. "And I'd like to kiss you again sometime. In fact, I'd like to do more than kiss you. How about that?"

"Jem," Maribel said, "let's wait and see, okay? Let's play things by ear."

"I hope to God you're not a tease," Jem said. "I hope to God you didn't invite me for dinner and tell me all that stuff about your mother and kiss me for so long only to get Mack's goat. I hope you're not catching me up in the middle of something, Maribel. Because that would hurt my feelings. I do have feelings about you, you know."

Maribel nodded.

"Thanks for dinner," he said huskily. He opened the screen door and stepped out; his blue eyes and blue shirt disappeared into the dark night.

Maribel's lips felt stretched and blurred. "You're welcome," she said.

MARIBEL COVERED HER TRACKS in every way she could think of, but when Mack walked in the door of the apartment, he looked confused and uncomfortable. *He knows,* Maribel thought. She was curled up on the sofa, but when Mack came in, she sat up.

"What's wrong?" she said.

Mack sat next to Maribel and bent his head, ran his hands through his hair.

"Mari," he said.

"What is it?" She put her arms around his shoulders and kissed his cheek. "What's wrong?"

"I have to tell you something and I don't want you to get upset. Just hear me out."

"What is it?" she said.

"I mean it. I want you to let me say what I have to say."

"Okay," Maribel said. "I'll listen. You tell me."

Mack cleared his throat. "After Lacey's tonight I stopped by one of the rooms to see Andrea Krane. You remember Andrea? And her son James?"

"I remember Andrea," Maribel said. Andrea was a pretty older woman, and James, in the few times Maribel saw him, had tugged at her heart. A young boy with autism, whose whole life was a foggy day.

Mack said, "Well, I went to see Andrea and things happened."

"What kind of things?" Maribel asked. She thought of James flapping his arms and shrieking, she thought about his incessant rocking.

"I kissed her," Mack said. "I was in her room sitting on her bed and I kissed her."

Maribel was befuddled; this was some strange, cruel reversal. Was Mack telling her *he* kissed someone else? The back of her throat soured. He kissed Andrea, James's mother? Thoughts of Jem were suddenly crowded out of the room; Maribel's secret guilt and pleasure about Jem were spirited away, gone, replaced by horror, shock. Tears sprang to Maribel's eyes. *I'm a hypocrite,* she thought. *Mack did nothing worse than what I did tonight.* Nothing worse except to speak the truth out loud and that did make it seem a hundred times worse.

Mack stood up and came back with a box of Kleenex. He wiped at Maribel's face. "I'm sorry, Mari. I've known her a long time, longer than I've even known you. There's always been something between us. But this year, I don't know why, that something just got bigger. I think I love her."

"Love her?" Maribel repeated. She gathered her breath to speak, to match his brutal blow, but when she tried to find the words to tell him about Jem, she gagged. Maribel didn't love Jem. This wasn't a fair trade at all. *Oh, God,* she thought, *what is he doing to me?* Love *Andrea?* A guest? Six years later and it wasn't the farm or his job or Cecily at all, it was *Andrea Krane?* Maribel thought of Tina, and how this news would break her heart. It was over, a relationship over, just the way Mack had lost his parents. Boom. Over.

"You have to leave," Maribel said. "You have to move out, down to the hotel. I don't want you here."

"No," Mack said. "No, wait please, Mari. Maribel, hold on. I know you're upset. But please don't throw me out. I have to try and explain."

"You love Andrea," Maribel said. "What else is there to explain?"

"It's this summer, something is happening. The world wants me to grow up. You want me to grow up. And I don't want to grow up. I feel so childish. I love Andrea, but I love you, too, Maribel. You know I do. Andrea is vulnerable, and her life is difficult, much more difficult than you or I could ever imagine. I feel for that, Maribel. I feel for that and for the fact that she doesn't give up. I love her for that."

"Her life is difficult?" Maribel said. *"My* life is difficult! My life is very, very difficult. Have you forgotten that? Have you forgotten what I've gone through to get here, Mack?"

"That's different, Maribel. I'm not taking anything away from you. But you're not dealing with what Andrea is dealing with."

"Go to her then," Maribel said. Thinking, hatefully, *Go to her and her fucked-up son.* "Get out of here."

"But I love you, too," Mack said.

"Tough shit," Maribel said.

"I don't want to leave," Mack said.

"What *do* you want?" Maribel asked. "Do you have any idea? Do you want to sell the farm? Do you want to manage that blasted hotel your whole life? You don't know. Do you want to get married and have kids? You don't know. You don't know anything except that you love us both. You want me here at home and Andrea down at the hotel. I'm sorry, Mack. I am so, so sorry." Maribel was hysterical now, her breathing ragged, her tears hot and salty; her eyes stung. She plucked a Kleenex and tried to blow her nose but she was blocked up, stuck. She thought of the broken toilet. Her life was a toilet.

"I'm going to do something for you," Mack said.

"The only thing you can do for me is to get out of here," Maribel said. Her voice was small and nasal.

"I'm going to ask Bill to profit-share. I'm going to ask him right after the Fourth. I swear it, Maribel."

Maribel tried to snort, but her nose was stuffed up. Her snort sounded like a bleat. "Ha! Why now, Mack? So you can give James and Andrea a good life? So you can show them how important you are? Go ahead and ask Bill for the profits. I hope he turns you down. I hope he fires you and you leave this island."

"But I'm doing it for you, Maribel," Mack said. "I'm doing it because you want me to."

"I want you to *marry me!*" Maribel screamed. She couldn't believe how angry, how upset she was. Never in her life would she have predicted the relationship would crumble like this, so suddenly, in one night. "I want you to marry me! I thought the problem was with *you*. I thought you were just not *grown* yet, I thought you still had issues with your parents, the farm. And I thought if you asked Bill to profit-share you'd feel better about yourself, you'd feel established, you'd feel *ready*. What I didn't realize is that the problem isn't with you, Mack, it's with *me*. I'm not the woman you want."

"You are the woman I want," Mack said.

"Then *ask me to marry you*," Maribel said.

Mack reached for her again and she surrendered. She buried her face in his chest and cried even harder. His shirt, his smell, her Mack, she loved him so much. He was all she wanted, all she needed to fill the empty space where her father should have been. But she waited five minutes, ten minutes, and he said nothing. He was shushing into her hair, but he wasn't asking her to marry him. Suddenly her head was heavy, a sandbag, her mouth was dry and scratchy from the wine and the tears.

"You have to go," Maribel said. Unsteadily, she stood and pointed in the direction of the door. "I'm sorry."

"Mari, you don't mean that."

"I do," she said. She walked into the bedroom and fell onto the bed. Her eyes closed the second she heard Mack's Jeep pull away.

MACK SPENT THE REST of the night in the Jeep in the Beach Club parking lot. He considered sneaking into Lacey Gardner's cottage and crashing on her couch, but he didn't want to frighten her. And so, Mack wrapped himself in his Polar Fleece, put the seat back as far as it would go, and closed his eyes.

He woke to the sound of talking. He sat up and looked around—it was still dark. He didn't see anyone near the lobby or on the beach. Mack climbed out of the Jeep, quietly, and he made out the figure of Cecily sitting on the front step of her parents' house, talking on the portable phone. Mack checked his watch; it was three-thirty.

"I love you," she was saying. "I can't stand it here without you. I'm dying of love for you."

Please, Cecily, Mack thought. *Do not fall in love.* But from the sounds of it, it was too late. He climbed back into his car.

"I love you, Gabriel." Cecily's voice was sweet, pleading. "Can you hear me? I love you."

What seemed like only minutes later, Mack heard the sound of tapping on the window of the Jeep. He opened his eyes. It was Andrea and James. The sun was up. Mack checked his watch; it was six o'clock. He opened the door.

"Why do I get the feeling you're not here to go with us to the airport?" Andrea said.

"Is Mack coming to the airport?" James asked. "Are we shaving today, Mack?"

"How're you doing, buddy?" Mack asked. He looked at Andrea. "I told Maribel."

"Told her what?" Andrea asked. Her green-gray eyes widened. "About us? Why? Oh, Mack, what did you say?" She turned to James. "Get in the car, James. Mom will be there in five minutes."

"It's six-oh-three, Mom. We're late already."

"Five minutes," Andrea said.

"Five minutes." James tapped the face of his watch. "Mom will be there at six-oh-eight."

Andrea waited until James climbed into the Explorer, then she said, "What happened?"

"I had to tell her," Mack said. He thought of Vance, pointing the gun at him like it was some kind of toy. But when he got right down to it, Mack hadn't told Maribel because of Vance; he told her because it was time. He told her because he couldn't stand lying anymore. Vance was just a manifestation of Mack's own conscience, like something out of fucking Shakespeare. "I told her I loved you."

"No," Andrea said. She put her hand over her heart. "She must be devastated. The poor girl. Ouch."

"What about me?" Mack said. "She threw me out. I spent the

night here in the parking lot." His mouth felt as if it were lined with flannel, he stank with the four scotches he'd had at Lacey's, his head ached and his legs would cramp up as soon as he stepped out of the Jeep. He needed five more hours' sleep, a hot shower, some clean clothes.

"You're a man, Mack," Andrea said. "Men will always survive."

Mack touched Andrea's hair. "You might see me surviving this winter in Baltimore."

"Mack," Andrea said, shaking her head sadly.

"What?" Mack said. "I could help you with James. I could give you the help you need."

"Go home and take it all back," she said.

"You don't want me in Baltimore?"

"Just go home," she said. "I'm not coming between you and Maribel. She's much better for you than I am."

"But I love you," Mack said. "That's how I ended up here. I love you."

"Maybe," Andrea said. "Or maybe you feel sorry for me. The point is, you should be with Maribel. I'm just a friend, Mack, a summer friend. You have no idea what my life is like the rest of the year. You have no idea what happens once I return to America."

"I know I don't. What I'm saying is, I want to find out."

"I should stop coming here. I've depended on you too much, and I made you feel like you can help me. But you can't help me, Mack. Nobody can help me. James is my lot in life—he's my blessing, he's my albatross." She tried to smile. "Anyway, I hear the Vineyard is nice too. Maybe next year we'll go there."

"No," Mack said. This was too much: to lose them both in one night. "No way."

Andrea picked up Mack's wrist and checked his watch. "My five minutes is up," she said. "Go home." He listened to her footsteps crunch across the shells and the loose gravel. He heard the soft dinging of her open car door and James saying, "You're one minute late, Mom." Then Andrea started the car and drove away, but he didn't turn to watch her go.

Mack sat back in his seat and looked at the water. Maybe he should just drive into the sound. Then he heard a voice, a low thrumming voice. *Home.* He bowed his head. *Home.*

"I can't believe this," Mack said. He closed his eyes.

5

Independence Day

July 2

Dear Bill,

The answer to your question is yes, I am a parent. You do not need to know how many children I have, or if they are sons or daughters—it isn't relevant and it's too painful for me to discuss anyway, even in a letter. I know your daughter is quite young—seventeen? eighteen?—and I know she lives away from you a good part of the year. I wonder, Bill, if you have any idea what goes on in your daughter's heart and mind. Does she want what you want? Does she see herself continuing with the family business? Does she love the hotel the way you do, Bill? Have you ever asked her? Maybe before you turn my offer down, you should.

Sincerely,

S. B .T.

CECILY'S JOB THIS SUMMER was to watch the beach, keeping her eyes peeled for people who blatantly ignored the signs saying Nantucket Beach Club: Private Property. After four years at Middlesex—tens of thousands of dollars spent on her education—this was the job her parents gave her. Lookout. Policewoman. Head scout of the Nantucket Beach Club patrol.

Cecily sat on the steps of the pavilion with a clipboard and a computer generated list of the Beach Club members. If she saw people on the beach she didn't recognize, she had to ask their names. If their name appeared on the list, she smiled and repeated their name, "Why *hello*, Mrs. Papale!" as though she had recognized them all along. That was what a club was about: Being recognized, belonging.

If their names didn't appear on the list, she had to ask them, politely, to leave. Cecily's father was too chicken to do this job himself, although he claimed he wasn't afraid, but rather, too busy, doing financial things and reading from his volume of Robert Frost.

On one very hot and crowded day just before *the* major holiday of summer, Cecily encountered her first squatters. She was sitting with her legs stretched out in the sun when an unlikely couple wandered in from the right. What made them "unlikely" was exactly the thing that Cecily hated about her job: they looked poor. The price to sit on a swatch of her father's beach under one of the umbrellas her mother ordered from the south of France was five thousand dollars for the summer. It was too much money for almost anybody to afford—and definitely too much money for the couple spreading their towels (short white towels, the kind one might find in a Holiday Inn) under a royal blue umbrella.

The couple looked like Jack Sprat and wife. The man was skinny and pale, wearing a black T-shirt and cut-off jeans, and the woman wore an enormous turquoise muumuu. The woman carried a red Playmate cooler, which she plunked down at the foot of the towels.

Cecily heard a clicking noise behind her. She turned to see her father tapping with his pen on the window of his office. He pointed at the couple.

Reluctantly, Cecily stood up. She trudged through the hot sand, savoring the torturous burning on the soles of her feet. The man turned his head from left to right, checking, literally, to see if the coast were clear. The woman plucked a green bottle out of the cooler: a Heineken. The beer of choice at Middlesex. The man offered the woman a penknife from the front pocket of his jeans shorts and the woman flipped the top off the bottle and let it land in the sand.

"Excuse me," Cecily said. The man's head whipped around. He hadn't thought to look behind him. "I just need to check your name off our list."

The man stood up. The front of his T-shirt had a mandala on it. He had long dirty blonde hair and a mustache. He touched his mustache when Cecily spoke.

"The name's Cadillac," he said. "Joe Cadillac."

Joe Cadillac. It was a good try: maybe he thought it made him sound rich. Cecily checked her list. She could feel her father's eyes boring into her back. The burning of her feet became unbearable and she moved to stand in the shade of the royal blue umbrella.

"Cadillac, hmmmm. Like the car, Cadillac?"

The man cleared his throat. "That's right."

"I don't see it here," Cecily said. She didn't meet the man's eyes.

"Are you sure you're spelling it right?" he asked. "Cadillac, with a 'C?' With two 'C's?' "

"Yes," Cecily said, "I'm sure."

The man shoved his threadbare towel under one arm. "Okay," he said, "we'll go then."

The woman let out a long, shrill laugh, like a hand trickling down piano keys. "Heavens, *Joe*," she said. She had curly blond hair and wore red lipstick. "Would you please let us stay, sweetie?" she asked. "Just for today? I'm afraid in this sun I'll positively fry up." The woman had a stripe of bad sunburn already—across the tops of her round cheeks and the bridge of her nose.

"I can't let you stay," Cecily said. She felt horrible; she felt like a child or an angry neighbor saying "Get off of my property!"

The woman held out the beer. "Would you like a swig?" she asked. "It's ice cold."

Cecily eyed the sweating bottle. How she wanted to take it, and force her father to watch her making her own choices.

"Debra, let's go," the man said.

The woman beamed at Cecily. Mrs. Sprat, Mrs. Cadillac. Cecily tore her eyes away. She looked, instead, at Nantucket Sound, lapping lightly onto her father's beach.

"I'm sorry," she said.

CECILY WAS ALSO MAÎTRE D′ of the beach, the goodwill ambassador. She chatted with the Beach Club members, and made sure everyone was happy. Once she got to know the members by name and learn a little bit about them, the list would become unnecessary. Cecily hated chatting, she even hated the word *chatting.* She could never think of what to say that would sufficiently mask her real question. *Why are you spending your money this way? Haven't you heard of world hunger? Don't you have a conscience?* The Beach Club had existed since 1924. Back then, the club cost a quarter a day and was open to the public. Her father had sepia-tone pictures of men and women in old-fashioned bathing suits sitting under crazily striped and polka-dotted sunshades, drinking bottles of sarsaparilla. This was how Cecily preferred to think of it. She'd kept one of those pictures, framed, in her dorm room at school.

The number of people on the beach peaked on the Fourth of July, and this year, it was sunny and hot. On the south shore, Cecily knew there would be radios blaring, volleyball games, picnics, kegs, Frisbee, dogs. But here at the Beach Club, things were as much f un as a pile of wet bathing suits, as exciting as a handful of sand. Mr. Conroy, who had a glass eye and a pair of saggy old-man breasts, sported his star-spangled swim trunks. That was it in the way of excitement.

Cecily stood in her father's office. "Total hell," she said, looking out the window at the beach.

"Someday it's going to be yours," he said.

"What if I don't want it?" Cecily said.

"What's not to want?" Bill said. "Now get out there and show 'em who's boss."

"You're the boss," Cecily said. "*You* get out there."

Bill laughed, then his voice got serious. "Go," he said, "and don't forget to wish everyone a happy Fourth of July."

TO START HER ROUNDS, Cecily had to walk past Kevin and Bruce, the beach boys.

"Hey, sexy!" Bruce called out. Bruce was skinny with pimples and glasses, and he thought he was a hot shit because he was going to Yale in the fall.

Cecily gave him the finger. Kevin never said anything. He just sat next to Bruce and giggled. The beach boys were exactly that—boys. They set up the umbrellas in the morning and then plunked themselves in the sand like a couple of ugly frogs, and when a member needed help with chairs or towels, the boys reluctantly got to their feet. They had an even cushier job than her own.

Cecily walked by Mr. and Mrs. Spoonacre, Mr. and Mrs. Patterson, and stopped at the kelly green umbrella closest to the water where Major Crawley sat. Always the same spot closest to the water, always a kelly green umbrella, and always alone—because Mrs. Crawley was allergic to the beach. Major Crawley had retired from the army before Cecily was born, but he still looked like a major. He wore army green trunks, aviator sunglasses, and his gray-silver hair was clipped in a crew cut.

"Hello there, lady friend," the major said.

Cecily crouched in the sand next to the major's Sleepy Hollow chair. They had a short conversation every day. Cecily's father told her the major deserved extra attention. He'd been a Beach Club member for almost fifty years. "Hello, Major. Happy Fourth of July."

"Let me tell you a little something," the major said.

Major Crawley loved to tell Cecily stories about her grandfather. Sometimes, if Cecily was lucky, he would talk instead about his days on the last mounted cavalry in Germany, riding through the forest, looking for runaway Nazis.

"Your grandfather, Big Bill Elliott—and we all called him Big Bill— asked me for advice when he bought this Beach Club. You know what I told him?"

"Complimentary towels," Cecily said.

"That's right. Do you know why?"

"It's the small courtesies that make a place stand out," she said.

"Someday all this is going to be yours, and you're going to have to see that the place is run with integrity. I might not be around to prod you."

Cecily had heard the same speech dozens of times. She wanted to tell the major that she had no intention of running the Beach Club, because deeper, more exotic voices called her name. Other countries, other cultures. "Tell me about Germany again."

"Germany?" the major said. "My time in the hills, you mean? Riding Liebchen? That was a good horse. A mare. Mares don't frighten easily, and that's why we all rode mares. Because we were looking at some scary stuff there in the hills."

"Nazis," Cecily said. "The murderers."

"Had one of them Nazis hold a gun to my head," the major said. "Thought I was dead. Only eighteen years old. And do you know what I was thinking about, right at that second?"

"Mrs. Crawley?"

The major's aviator sunglasses slid to the end of his nose. "Hadn't met Mrs. Crawley yet. She came later."

"Your parents?"

"Nope." He poked at his sunglasses. "Thought about cigarettes and beer. Those were the two most important things in my life. All I wanted to do was smoke Luckies and drink Miller High-Life. And I thought how sad it was that all my smoking and drinking potential was about to fall facedown in the mud with a bullet shot through it."

"So then what happened?"

"The slimy German had the gun to my temple, pressed right into my brain and I could smell him. He stank like a pig. He had me on my knees and my eyes were level with his crotch and then I saw that the stinking bastard was wetting himself, he was so afraid. I knocked the gun out of his hand and that kid ran off. Someone in my company found him later and shot him dead." Major Crawley took off his sunglasses and lay back in his Sleepy Hollow chair. "I often wonder if maybe that weren't such a bad kid. Anyway, we killed him. Couldn't have mercy on someone who agreed to stand behind all that murdering of the Jews."

"There was a kid at my school who's a Nazi," Cecily said.

The major shook his head. "No, lady friend, not possible. We got them all." The major's words grew low and grumbly. "Today's the

Fourth of July and I'm happy to say you're in a safe place. No Nazis here." He nodded off to sleep in his chair. Cecily pulled his complimentary beach towel over his legs, so they wouldn't burn.

CECILY THREADED HER WAY between the umbrellas in the front row, past Mrs. Minella, the Papales, and the Hayeses, the only African American Beach Club members. She heard someone call to her.

"Miss! Miss!" A man under one of the canary yellow umbrellas gestured to her. Cecily walked slowly toward him and his wife, skimming her eyes over the list. These were new members this year—the Curtains? The Kershners? The man was balding but made up for it with a perfectly trimmed goatee. The woman had red hair like Cecily, only she had millions of freckles, whereas Cecily tanned.

Cecily smiled. "Hi, how can I help you?"

"We need you to settle an argument," the man said.

"Douglas!" the woman said. She folded her arms across the sheer top of her Chanel bathing suit.

Douglas and Mary Beth Kershner. Cecily found their names on the list.

"What you need to understand is that my wife is a *giving* person," Douglas Kershner said. "Charity woman *supreme*."

"Douglas," Mrs. Kershner snapped.

"And under the guise of the Church, she has planted a garden for the poor, so that the less fortunate citizens of Groton, Connecticut, can enjoy fresh produce," Douglas Kershner said.

There were tiny wrinkles in the corners of Mrs. Kershner's mouth.

"I didn't know there were any poor people in Groton," Cecily said. She'd only been to Groton once, for a field hockey game.

"There are poor people everywhere," Mrs. Kershner said.

"But now, in Groton, Connecticut, the poor can enjoy arugula, raddichio, and tarragon," Mr. Kershner said. "Tarragon for the poor!" He raised his hands above his head in a gesture of mock political triumph, giving Cecily a view of his hairy armpits. "Have you ever heard of anything so absurd?"

"Douglas!" Mrs. Kershner said.

"Why don't you plant corn?" Cecily asked. "Or tomatoes?"

"Or potatoes," Mr. Kershner added. "Something of substance."

Mrs. Kershner sniffled. Behind her black cat's-eye sunglasses, she was crying.

"You don't respect me, Douglas," she said. "You ridicule everything I even attempt. And you drag in complete strangers to throw rocks at my spirit."

Cecily took a step back. She hadn't meant to throw rocks at anyone's spirit. Gardens for the poor was a good idea. She thought about tending a plot of land, harvesting tomatoes and corn and shiny green peppers. Putting the produce in a basket and distributing it around Nantucket's public housing development, to the single mothers who drove a taxi or worked at the Stop & Shop. She wondered what her father would think about this. Cecily drifted away from the Kershners, but she couldn't help herself from turning around to look at them one last time. Mrs. Kershner packed her things to leave the beach, while Mr. Kershner continued speaking, waving his arms at the water.

AT THE VERY EDGE of the property Cecily found Maribel asleep face-down with the straps of her bathing suit untied. Her blond hair was caught up in a messy bun and her back was brown and slick with oil. Cecily sat carefully next to Maribel's towel and looked to her left at all the umbrellas neatly lined up in rows and columns. It was like an obstacle course she had to complete in order to get to this safe place, this good place, next to Maribel. With Maribel, Cecily could be herself; with Maribel, Cecily could talk about love.

Cecily had been in love for almost a year with Gabriel da Silva, a Brazilian who lived in the dorm across the quad from Cecily at school. Gabriel was a year older than the other boys, and taller, more muscular, more sophisticated. He spoke three languages—English, Spanish, and the beautiful Carioca Portuguese—and unlike the other boys, Gabriel had a soul. He told Cecily about the favelas in Rio, where children starved. Gabriel had adopted a family in the favelas—a mother and three sons. He gave them money and he watched the little boys while the mother, Magrite, sold coconut ice cream at a stand on Copacabana Beach. Gabriel would like the idea of a garden for the poor. Cecily pictured Gabriel without a shirt, standing under the brilliant Brazilian sun, his dark skin tanning to the color of tree bark, as he shoveled the rich, black earth—*a garden in the* favelas.

Thinking about Gabriel made Cecily impatient. She traced her pinky finger down Maribel's spine. If Cecily weren't in love with Gabriel, she would probably be in love with Maribel.

Maribel woke with a shiver and lifted her head. Her cheek was dusted with sand.

"Geez, Cecily," Maribel said. "You scared me."

"Sorry, lady friend," Cecily said. "I'm surprised to see you here. Have you talked to Mack?"

"I don't want to talk to Mack."

"You do so," Cecily said. "Otherwise you'd be at the beach somewhere else."

"It's the Fourth," Maribel said. "The other beaches are too crowded."

"Do you miss him?" Cecily asked.

"Of course I miss him," Maribel said.

"I miss Gabriel," Cecily said. They had made love exactly ten times the week before school let out, (discovered once, by the school's cleaning lady). By the time Cecily's parents showed up for graduation, the insides of her thighs were rubbed raw.

"It's not the same thing," Maribel said. "You and Gabriel are still together."

"I know," Cecily said. Cecily didn't know what was going on between Mack and Maribel. Some stupid, fucked-up *thing* that made them both miserable. "I have something to tell you."

"Tell me Andrea Krane has checked out," Maribel said. "Tell me she's *gone home*."

"Next week," Cecily said. "But don't worry, Mack is sleeping at Lacey's."

Maribel hid her face in her hands. "I don't even want to think about where Mack's sleeping. It makes me sick."

"What I have to tell you is . . ." Cecily waited until she had Maribel's full attention, or as much of her full attention as she could hope to get with Mack lurking around. "What I have to tell you is that I'm not going to college in September."

Maribel groaned. "Yes, you are, Cecily."

"No," Cecily said. "I'm not. I'm deferring a year. I've already signed the form saying I'm deferring. I'm eighteen, I can do that."

"And next you're going to tell me that you're flying to Brazil."

"And Argentina, and Ecuador and Venezuela. I'm traveling with Gabriel."

Maribel regathered her bun so that it stuck off the top of her head like a knob. "Everyone's lost their mind," she said. "Have you told your parents this?"

"No," Cecily said. "But I've been saving my money. It's ridiculous how much I make doing this stupid job." She knew she had to tell her parents soon, although she indulged a fantasy of boarding the plane for Charlottesville and simply continuing south, without telling them at all. If she called regularly, her parents might never know the difference. "They'll probably disown me. But that would be good for you. The club could go to Mack."

"What do I care now?" Maribel said. "It's over with Mack, I told you."

"You'll get back together," Cecily said. Then she heard someone calling her name.

"Miss Elliott." The voice was low and rich. "Excuse me, Miss Elliott."

Mrs. John Higgens stood on the pavilion with her cane out in front of her. She was wearing a blue one-piece bathing suit with a tissue tucked into her bosom. Cecily stood up, wiped off her hands, and jogged over.

"Can I help you, Mrs. Higgens?" Cecily asked. Sometimes older women needed an arm to hold on to in order to make it through the sand.

"Yes, my dear, I hope so." Mrs. Higgens was another person, like Major Crawley, who had belonged to the Beach Club for a hundred million years. "I certainly hope so. Stand with me here if you will and look at the beach. Do you see what's wrong?"

The edges of the umbrellas fluttered in the wind. Mr. Conroy, in his patriotic trunks, inched his way toward the water.

"No, Mrs. Higgens, I don't." It could be anything: children throwing sand, the return of Joe Cadillac, the wrong colored umbrella. "What's wrong?"

"There are two *black* people on the beach, my dear," Mrs. Higgens said. "That's what's wrong."

Cecily's bowels twisted. Not the wrong color umbrella, then, but the wrong color person. She watched Mr. Hayes step out of the ocean. Mrs. Hayes handed him a complimentary beach towel and he dried his face and arms.

"Yes, Mrs. Higgens. Those are the Hayeses," Cecily said. "They've been members since 1995." The Hayeses were quiet, normal people who respected one another. Mr. Hayes owned an office furniture business in New Jersey and Mrs. Hayes was an admissions officer at Princeton. They had three grown sons.

"I've seen the black young man who works here, what's his name? Vance? He puts up my umbrella, and that's fine. But working here and *belonging* here are two different things," Mrs. Higgens said. "Don't forget, young lady, I knew your grandfather. There were no *black members* when he was in charge."

Cecily wondered what would happen if she gave old Mrs. Higgens the shock of her lifetime. *For your information, Mrs. Higgens, my boyfriend is black. I make love with a black man and it is the kind of wonderful I'm sure you have never felt.*

"We want you to be happy, Mrs. Higgens," Cecily said. This was her father talking, the exact words he would say if she sent Mrs. Higgens into the office, which was what she should probably do: let *him* deal with it. But if she was going to start her life as an adult, she was going to have to be brave. "However, if you're not comfortable with people of other races on the beach, then I guess you'll have to find another beach club."

Cecily heard a pained gasp, as though she had stepped on Mrs. Higgens's foot with a heavy shoe, but Cecily didn't look back. She marched through the sand the way she imagined Major Crawley marched through Germany looking for Nazis—proudly, and with something to believe in. *We got them all.* She sat back down next to Maribel's towel.

"What did the old lady want?" Maribel asked.

"Nothing," Cecily said. She stared out at the cool blue water. Her face burned. "I'll tell my parents tonight. But right now, let's talk about love."

LOVE, IT WAS ALL so complicated. That was probably why you didn't get to the good kind of love until you were a teenager. Cecily's love for Maribel was the best shade of blue sky and blue water. Her love for Gabriel was a herd of wild horses galloping out of control. And her love for her parents was a nagging toothache, impossible to ignore and forget.

"YOU DID ABSOLUTELY THE right thing, sweetie," Therese said, her mouth full of tomato sandwich. "I hope we never see the woman again."

"It's five thousand dollars down the tubes," Bill said. He cleared his throat. "But of course when you get to my age, you understand that you can't put a price on human decency."

"The woman is a racist pig," Cecily said. "Who knows how many more of the members are like that deep down?"

"Hopefully none," Therese said. "But if we hear anyone else making comments like that, we'll set them straight."

Cecily looked at her dinner: a tomato sandwich on white bread, and some blue corn chips. A red, white, and blue dinner for the Fourth of

July, had her mother's idea of funny. Cecily couldn't bring herself to eat. She told her parents what happened with Mrs. Higgens, thinking they would be *angry* at the way she handled it. Then it would be easy for Cecily to be indignant, and to tell them she was leaving. But her parents, much to her dismay, were being supportive; they were being *cool*.

"You don't remember what this country went through in the sixties," Therese said. "But it was quite something. Mrs. Higgens is right about one thing, there weren't any black Beach Club members back then, were there, Bill?"

"I'm embarrassed to say, the Hayeses are the first black Beach Club members *ever*. Wait, that's not true. The Krupinskis, they were black."

"Well, *she* was black, he was Polish, remember?" Therese said. "They belonged to the club in, what, '83 and '84? They had that gorgeous café au lait child, the daughter."

"For God's sake," Cecily said. "Café au lait? You're talking about them like they're something exotic off the menu. You're as bad as Mrs. Higgens."

Therese gave her a strange look. "It's an expression, darling. Okay? My, you're touchy. And why aren't you eating?"

"This whole situation has got me really upset, okay?" Cecily said.

Bill frowned. "You're still so young," he said. "You have no idea how rotten people can be, but you'll learn."

"Bill, that's depressing," Therese said.

Cecily walked into the living room, to the bay window that overlooked the Beach Club. It was getting dark and the hotel guests emerged from their rooms to sit on the beach so they could watch the fireworks. Every year, Cecily and her parents watched the fireworks from the widow's walk. It was amazing to watch from that high up, with nothing separating you and the sky. Cecily turned around. Her parents were eating their sandwiches, munching on the chips.

"I have some news," Cecily said.

"More news?" Therese said. "More news aside from the Mrs. John Higgens news?"

"We're proud of the job you've been doing, by the way," Bill said, his voice getting dangerously sappy. "You handled this Mrs. Higgens situation with aplomb."

"Thanks," Cecily said flatly. Wishing her parents would stop being so nice. "Okay—here goes—bombs away. My news, you're ready?"

She was terrified: like jumping off the high dive at the indoor pool at school, like the first time Gabriel unwrapped a condom. She prayed to God, and to her dead brother, W.T., and to Gabriel. *Please let them understand.*

"I've decided to defer a year before I go to college, because I want to do some traveling. So I'm not going to UVA in September. I'm flying to Rio instead."

Cecily shifted her attention to the parking lot: two BMWs, one Rover, one Jag. Mack's Jeep. Lacey's Buick. The thousand scattered pieces of broken shell, the million grains of sand. When she felt confident enough to turn back around, her parents were both staring at her. Her mother had mayonnaise in the corner of her mouth. "Honey, I'm sorry, I don't understand what you're telling us."

"I've sent a slip to the admissions office at the University of Virginia, telling them I'm deferring a year. I'm traveling through South America with Gabriel instead. Which part don't you understand?"

Therese turned to Bill. "Bill?" Tears in her voice.

Bill took Therese's hand. "Cecily, wait a minute. Can you just wait a minute, please? Why are you telling us this? Are you trying to hurt us?"

"It's not about you guys," Cecily said. "It's about me. I need to break away."

"But you have college," Therese said. "That's what Middlesex was for. That's what prep school *means*—college preparatory."

"What about you, Mom? You never finished college." Cecily's mouth had an acidic tomato taste. "You never graduated from Hunter."

"I'm ashamed of that," Therese said. "I didn't have the smarts for school that you do."

"Don't pick on your mother, Cecily," Bill said. "That won't help you."

"Lots of people take a year off," Cecily said. "Why do you think UVA even has such a thing as a deferral form? Because it happens all the time. Everyone does it."

"Everyone does *not* do it," Bill said. "You know I hate hyperbole."

"Well, you know I hate it when you use words like hyperbole," Cecily said.

"If you want to go to South America, we can take you over Christmas break," Therese said. "It'll be fun!" She tittered. "I've always wanted to go to Iguazu Falls."

"I've always wanted to meet the girl from Ipanema," Bill said.

"I'm going with Gabriel," Cecily said. "He's a very nice person. You have no way of knowing that because he wasn't at graduation. He had to fly back early. But trust me, he's nice. We love each other. We've been in love for a while now."

"You can't go away with some boy, some *foreign* boy we've never met. You're a child, Cecily. So you can forget that idea right now," Therese said. She lifted her dinner plate, and Cecily's untouched plate of food. "I'm sorry."

"I'm counting on you taking over the hotel, Cecily," Bill said. "Your mother and I haven't told you everything that's been going on, but I need to retire soon. You can't just go running off to another continent. Being a part of this family comes with responsibility."

"I don't want the hotel," Cecily said. "I'm sorry to say it, Daddy, but I'm not interested."

"That's absurd. You can't be not interested. It was Grandpa Bill's, it's mine, it's going to be yours."

"Give it to Mack," Cecily said. "He wants it, I don't."

"It doesn't work like that. I can't give it to Mack."

"Why not?" Cecily asked. "He'd do a better job than me. Besides, when Grandpa Bill died, you *wanted* the club, you wanted to build hotel rooms. I don't want that. You can't make me want that."

Bill put his hand over his heart. "Oh, God."

Therese stood behind him. "Your father is sick, Cecily. We didn't want you to worry, but he's sick. You can't tell him things like this or he's going to have a heart attack."

Cecily rolled her eyes. "You guys are too much. Giving me a *guilt trip*, telling me Daddy's *sick*? You should have had more children. You should have had more than just me."

Therese winced. "How can you say that? You know about W.T.! For years we tried to have children, *for ten years*, and finally there was you. I'm sorry you don't like it, but some of us are not as fortunate as you, my dear, picking and choosing the way we'd like our lives to go. Most of us just have to take what life deals us, but I am *not* going to stand here and deal with you telling your father you don't want to be a part of the family tradition that has *sustained* you and given you a *good life*. I am not going to listen to you tell me where you are going with what strange boy." Therese wound her white streak of hair around her finger. A Mom trick, to make Cecily feel guilty. "Have you slept with this boy?"

Cecily laughed, looked back out the window. She remembered the startled expression on the cleaning lady's face. "Mother."

"Mother, what? Was I supposed to assume my fifteen-year-old was away at school having sex?"

"I'm eighteen, Mother, okay? Can we establish that fact?"

"You're not going to Brazil," Bill said.

Cecily held out her arms. "Put handcuffs on me, then," she said. "Put handcuffs on and lock me in the house, because that's what it's going to take to keep me here."

Therese started to cry. "I can't believe you're doing this to us," she said. "I can't believe that after what I had to endure before, I now have to endure this."

"It's not like I'm dying," Cecily said. She calculated in her head: if she had to leave tonight, could she do it? She'd cashed all her graduation checks plus two paychecks so far from her father. But it still wasn't enough. She'd have to stay a while longer. "I'm just going away for a year, okay. How about that? A year abroad. I'll be back next summer."

"You're not going anywhere," Bill said. "I'm sorry, honey."

Suddenly, there was a noise, a tremendous boom, so loud it rattled the window. Cecily looked outside in time to see the first fireworks, a brilliant spray of red and yellow and white. Then there was another boom—silver sparkles.

"Happy Independence Day," she said. She stomped down the stairs and left the house, slamming the door behind her.

JEM CRANDALL WATCHED THE fireworks from Jetties Beach with thousands of other people. Kids waved sparklers, parents nodded off to sleep in beach chairs, a group of college students sat in a circle singing the theme song from the Partridge Family. There was no reason for Jem to be amidst all this chaos when he could be down at the Beach Club enjoying peace and quiet, except that here, at Jetties, he was with Maribel. She sat beside him on a beach towel wearing a Nantucket red miniskirt, a white T-shirt, a navy blue cardigan sweater, her blond hair in a ponytail, her tan legs tucked neatly beneath her.

"Are you okay?" Jem asked her. She was quietly picking onions out of her sub sandwich, and tossing them into the sand. (When he called to suggest a picnic, he hoped she would cook, but she told him that now that Mack had left, she would never cook again, hence the sandwiches, and he ordered hers, stupidly, with onions.)

Maribel bit into her sandwich. He put his hand on her knee.

"What's wrong?" he asked. But, of course, he knew what was wrong: it had been a week since Mack moved out. At first, when Jem saw that Mack had moved into Lacey's, he thought Mack had found out about his date with Maribel. Jem asked Vance—carefully, casually—did he know what happened?

"Lover boy blew it with his babe," Vance said. "Screwed around with her on room eighteen."

Jem called Maribel immediately and she confirmed this. Mack was having some kind of relationship with Mrs. Krane, in room 18.

"I don't want to see you, Jem," Maribel said. "I'm a wreck. My life is a disaster area. I'm just sifting through the rubble."

She didn't want to see him but Jem called every day—sometimes she just cried into the phone and Jem held the receiver, helpless. Only with his sister, Gwennie, and her bulimia had he ever felt this helpless. But finally, Maribel agreed to see him—tonight, the Fourth of July, but only if they came to this beach and hid amongst all these people. She didn't want Mack to see them together.

Maribel turned to him. "The past six Fourth of Julys Mack kissed me when the fireworks started." Her eyes were glassy; she pulled a tissue from her skirt pocket. "I've lost a part of my life, Jem."

"I know," Jem said.

"Do you know?" she asked. "Have you ever been hurt like this? Have you ever experienced loss like this?"

"No," he admitted. He had never been in love. He'd never cared about someone more than himself. Jem did have real feelings for Maribel, though, scary feelings, lurking in a dark, unexplored place inside of him. He could feel them gathering strength. He wanted Maribel to be happy she was sitting with him this Fourth of July, but she treated him like the runner-up, the silver medallist, a stand-in.

A thunderclap, and the sky lit up with color. There was a collective "Oooooh, aaaaah!" Some clapping. A burning smell. The fireworks had begun. Jem looked at Maribel: even crying, she was still so pretty. He moved his face closer to hers. Her hand shot up, as if she might slap him.

"Don't," she said. "Please."

"I just want to hold your hand," he said. He wiped a tear from under her eye with his thumb. "Can I do that?"

Maribel surrendered. Jem held her hand all through the fireworks. Her lifeless, clammy hand that was clearly not excited about being held by Jem's hand. He was a mannequin, a crash-test dummy, a Band-Aid. But he didn't care.

LOVE GOT STUCK WORKING the front desk because Tiny wanted the night free. Free for what? Love wondered. Tiny didn't strike Love as a patriotic person.

"Are you going to watch the fireworks?" Love asked.

"No."

"What are you going to do?" Love said. She spent fifteen minutes every day with Tiny during their shift change, and yet Love knew absolutely nothing about her; nor, it seemed, did anyone else.

"That sounds like a personal question," Tiny said. "And I don't answer personal questions. But since you're so curious, I'll tell you that I'm avoiding the fireworks. I don't want anything to do with them."

By seven-thirty Love understood why. The fireworks were being set off from Jetties Beach down the way, but stragglers wandered into the lobby.

"Do you have a bathroom my daughter can use? She swears she's going to whiz herself. Hey . . . these are pretty quilts. This is a nice place. Where are we?"

At first Love was solicitous—she let fourteen people use the bathroom and then she locked not only the bathroom door but the door to the lobby as well. No one else was coming in! But then the Beach Club members arrived, knocking, waving, mouthing "It's me, it's me." They wanted their umbrellas set up, they wanted Sleepy Hollow chairs.

"I paid five thousand dollars for my membership," Mr. Cavendish said. "I will sit in comfort and watch the fireworks."

Mack materialized out of nowhere. That was one good thing about his breakup with Maribel—now he was always around.

"We can do chairs," Mack said. "I'll meet you out at the beach."

Love put Tchaikovsky's *1812 Overture* on the stereo for mood. Vance walked into the office.

"The fireworks are about to start," he said. "I came to show you how to get to the roof."

"The roof?"

"You want to see the fireworks, don't you?" Vance asked. "Come on, follow me."

"I can't leave the desk," Love said. "What if somebody needs something? What if somebody calls?"

Vance reached around Love and busied out the phones. His hand grazed Love's waist and she flinched.

"Relax," Vance said. He wheeled her through Mack's office and into the utility closet, his arm around her. The utility closet was dark and Vance reached for the string to the light, but he couldn't find it.

"What are we doing in the closet?" Love asked. She laughed nervously. This reminded her of stupid kissing games she had played at parties twenty-five years ago. Go into the closet with a boy and stay there until something happens.

"This is the way to get to the roof," Vance said. "There's an escape hatch, and I have a ladder. We climb up and pop out."

"Won't someone see us?" Love asked.

"I've been doing this for years," Vance said. "Do you trust me?" His voice was closer than Love expected.

"Yes," Love said.

"We just need to find the light is all," Vance said. He stumbled over something. "I should have brought my flashlight. Wait, here it is." Vance clicked on the light. They were standing among vacuum cleaners, mops, pails, extension cords, and huge boxes of toilet paper. "Before we go up, I want to show you something." Vance opened a toolbox and brought out some crinkled papers. "It's a short story I wrote that got published in *Slam!* Have you ever heard of *Slam!?*"

"No," Love said.

"I always see you reading so I thought you might want to take a look at it."

"Sure," Love said. The story was entitled "The Downward Spiral." Exactly the kind of gloomy title she expected from Vance. Still, she was touched he showed it to her. The paper was mildewed at the edges; it had obviously been sitting in that box a long time. "I'd be happy to read it. A published story! I'm impressed. I didn't know you were a writer."

Vance shrugged. "I thought since you used to work at a magazine . . . just read it and tell me what you think."

He set up the ladder. "You go first," he said. "I'll follow behind you."

Love climbed the ladder and Vance followed. She felt his breath on the backs of her knees, and she worried he could see up her skirt.

"Look above you," Vance said. "See the hatch?"

Planted in the dusty boards of the ceiling was a metal door, sealed with rubber like a refrigerator. It made a sucking noise as Love opened it to the night sky. She hoisted herself out onto the roof and Vance popped up beside her.

Love raised her arms to the cool air of the dark blue sky. "Much better than being stuck in the lobby." Below, hotel guests and Beach Club members arranged their chairs and blankets. Love could see all the way down to the mob of people at Jetties.

"Be careful," Vance said. He sat on the sloping roof. "Come here."

"But the ocean!" Love said. The water was a shimmering blue, one shade lighter than the sky. A ferry floated toward the island. "This is gorgeous. Thank you for bringing me here."

"I'd feel better if you sat down," Vance said.

"What's wrong, am I making you nervous?" She edged down to the lip of the sloping roof. It was just like skiing a double fault line.

"Love," Vance said. "Please come here."

She pretended she was at the Hadwen House, dancing under the stars. Love waltzed across the shingles to where Vance sat. He pulled her down so close to him that their shoulders brushed. And then, suddenly, Vance put his arm around her and kissed her cheek. Love stiffened. What was he doing? He kissed her mouth. Love wasn't sure what she expected from a kiss from Vance, but she certainly didn't expect it to be so soft, so warm, so tender.

There was a pop, like a giant balloon exploding, and then a shower of red, gold, white. Fireworks. Love closed her eyes and Vance kissed her again. Then she pulled away.

"Vance," she said. "What's going on?"

Vance's profile was cool as a coin.

"I like you," he said.

"You like me?" She stared across the roof of the hotel. There it was: a giant *L*, for Like.

"Yeah," he said. "I do. Is that some kind of crime?"

"No," Love said. "I'm just surprised." It was so odd—he was so odd, so sullen and grouchy, always lurking in the shadows, bad-mouthing Mack, peeling out of the parking lot in his Datsun. He seemed better suited for someone like . . . well, like Tiny. In fact, Love suspected from the beginning that Vance and Tiny were conducting a little romance. But no, Vance liked Love. She couldn't help but feel flattered.

"I'm much older than you," she said. "Do you know that?"

"Not that much older."

"Ten years older," she said. "You're thirty, right?"

Vance picked up her hand and held it. "I don't care how old you are. I think you look great," he said. "I think you look hot." He kissed her again.

He was a terrific kisser, that was for damn sure. He had a strong, fit body, and he might have a handsome face if he ever smiled. Love shuffled her expectations, rearranged her plans. Could this work? Could she have a fling with *Vance*?

"Let me ask you something," she said. "What do you think about children?"

Vance raised his eyebrows. "Children? What do you mean?"

"Do you want children?"

"Children?" Vance said. "Children? Hell, no. I just want to kiss you, Love."

Love felt if she walked to the edge of the roof she could pluck a star out of the sky and take a bite. Her dream getting closer: a child that would be hers, and hers alone.

"So kiss me," she said.

FOR MACK, THE FOURTH of July was the busiest day of the season. Still, each of the past six years, he sneaked away five minutes before the fireworks started to watch them with Maribel. Tonight, Maribel didn't show. It had been a week since he told her about Andrea. He'd returned to the basement apartment only once—in the middle of the day when he knew Maribel would be at work—to get some clothes and his toothbrush. Everything was where it belonged, and Mack didn't take too much. On his way back to the hotel he drove by the house on Sunset Hill, their Palace. They were so happy in the Palace. Mack idled his Jeep out front until another car pulled up behind him. He didn't know what to do.

THIS YEAR, FOR THE first time, he watched the fireworks with Andrea and James. They sat on the steps of their deck, Andrea drinking a glass of red wine.

"Mind if I join you?" Mack said. He sat between them. "How're you doing, James?"

"He has cotton in his ears," Andrea said. "The fireworks scare him. Too loud."

"Really?" Mack said.

"Of course, you'd have to be his mother to know that."

"Well, now I know and I'm not his mother," Mack said.

"You're not his father either," Andrea said.

Mack looked at her. He'd stopped by to help James shave again that morning, but Andrea was reading and barely looked up when he walked into the room. Now her honey-colored hair was wet and pulled severely into a bun. She slugged back her wine. "What do you mean by that?" he asked. "Are you angry with me?"

"I don't want to talk about it right now," Andrea said.

"Why not? James can't hear us."

"He'll intuit something is wrong."

"Is something wrong?"

"Oh, Mack," she said. "I don't know why you told Maribel."

"I had to tell her."

"You didn't have to tell her. The last six summers it wasn't a problem. You and I had our friendship and then you went home to Maribel. And James and I went home to Baltimore. But now it's ruined, my dear. The bubble's burst. The spell is broken. It's not fantasy anymore, it's reality, and someone got hurt. You're sleeping in an old woman's cottage, and I'm scared to death you're going to show up on our doorstep this winter."

"You made it clear you don't want that," Mack said.

"I don't want it and you don't want it either," Andrea said. She set down her wineglass and took his hand. "You're confused. You have to make a decision about your father's farm and your job here at the Beach Club, but you did *not* have to choose between me and Maribel. There was no decision to make."

"Because you don't love me," he said.

"It's not just me, it's you. You love Maribel. It's written all over you."

"I know," Mack said.

The sky crackled and caught on fire. James took Mack's other hand.

"Red," James said. "Silver. Purple. Green and purple."

"Here we go," Andrea said. "The Recitation of the Colors."

"Blue and gold. Silver only. Pink, purple, green."

Andrea sighed. "All I want is for him to grow up knowing I loved him. That I put him first. Do you think he'll ever know that?"

"Pink and gold. White squiggles."

Mack squeezed James's hand. "Of course he'll know you love him. He knows it now, he counts on it, he lives for it. I am *jealous* of James. He's cornered the market on your love. None left for anybody else."

"That's not fair," Andrea said.

"None left for me, then," Mack said.

"Silver and green," James said. "Blue and purple."

"Will you still help James shave?" Andrea asked. "Will you still wave good-bye to us when we pull out of the parking lot?"

"You know damn well I'll do whatever you ask me," Mack said.

"I want you to get back together with Maribel," Andrea said. "Please? I won't be able to leave until you patch this up."

"It's not that easy," Mack said. "I didn't leave Maribel, she kicked me out. I'm not sure she wants me back."

"Of course she wants you back," Andrea said. "You're Mack Petersen. Everybody wants a piece of you."

"Red and blue and white. Red, white, and blue, Mom!" James exclaimed.

"Everybody wants a piece of me except for you."

"Now you sound pitiful," Andrea said.

"When you leave, will that be the last time I ever see you?" Mack said. "Are you coming back next year?"

"I don't know," Andrea said. The fireworks lit up her face, and then it darkened again. "Are you?"

AT SEVEN-THIRTY THE NEXT morning, Mack knocked on the Elliotts' front door, something he'd never done before. If he had business at Bill and Therese's house, which was rare, he always just let himself in. But today, he knocked.

Therese opened the door. Her eyes were puffy. "Mack," she said. "What's wrong? I can't hear about a hotel emergency today. I just can't. I want to pretend the hotel doesn't exist. I was going to have Elizabeth check the rooms."

"Yeah?" Mack said. Something was wrong, but Therese was funny about telling other people her problems. "I came to talk to Bill."

Therese swung the door open. "He's upstairs. Go on up. He needs cheering."

"Okay," Mack said. His hands were numb. *I should leave,* he thought. *Now isn't the right time.* But Maribel would never take him back if he didn't at least *ask. This is going to go well,* he thought. *This is going to be the answer to the chaos in my head.*

He climbed the stairs and saw Bill sitting at the kitchen table with his book of Frost poems open in front of him. "Hey, boss," Mack said.

Bill looked up. "Mack," he said. "What's wrong?"

"Nothing's wrong. I need to talk to you about something. But if now's a bad time . . ."

"No, no, it's fine," Bill said. His face was pale and the translucent skin under his eyes was mapped with tiny red and blue lines. "Do you want coffee?"

"Maybe, yeah," Mack said. He took a mug of coffee from Bill and sat down at the table. He looked at the upside-down book of poems, and wondered if there were any clues in that book about how to live.

"What is it?" Bill said. "Is it about Maribel?"

"No," Mack said. "I want to explore a possibility with you."

Bill was quiet.

"You know, I've worked here twelve seasons, and I'd like to . . . well, I'd like to stay." Mack blew on his coffee but when he tasted it, it was lukewarm. "I was wondering if you'd be open to profit-sharing with me."

"Profit-sharing?"

Therese came into the kitchen. "You want what?"

Mack spun in his chair. "It was just an idea I had."

"What was?" Bill asked.

"Profit-sharing. You know, me getting paid based on how well the hotel does. Taking thirty percent or whatever."

"Thirty percent." Bill's face was expressionless.

"Does that sound outrageous?" Mack asked. "Maybe it is, but I do a fair amount of work around here. And you see, what's happened is my parents' lawyer has called and I have to make up my mind about the farm, do I want to live there, or do I want to sell it."

"So you're telling me you're leaving?" Bill said.

"No," Mack said. "I'm just exploring my options. It seems like this is a good time to discuss my future. And I'd like to profit-share."

Therese laughed, not happily. "Are we wearing bull's-eyes painted over our hearts, Bill? Is that what's happening? Everyone we love feels free to take a shot at us?"

"I'm not taking a shot at you," Mack said. "I just need to think about my future. You guys are like my . . . my family. You know Maribel and I are having problems. I need to *do* something to make her happy." He could feel Therese's instant disapproval. Why had he brought up Maribel? Was it easier to make it sound like this was *her* idea? "But it's for me, too. I have to decide about my family's farm. Either I sell it, which I don't want to do, or I go out there and run it, which I don't want to do. It's an impossible decision."

"Are you telling us that if we don't agree to profit-share, you'll leave?" Bill asked.

"I don't know," Mack said. "If you agree to profit-share, it'll be easier to decide."

Bill looked at his open book. "I see the difficulty of your position," he said. He traced his finger along the lines of the page, as though he were reading aloud. "You're a young man who has to make a choice. I can remember myself at your age. Should I take a risk and build the hotel rooms? But I was lucky. I had a wife who supported me."

"We can't profit-share," Therese said. She sat down at the table. Her orange hair hung in strings around her face and her white streak was tinged with gray, like dirty snow. "We can't profit-share, because of Cecily."

"I'm not asking to own a part of the hotel, Therese. I'm only asking for part of the profits."

Therese lowered her voice. "Cecily has threatened to leave," she said. "She informed us last night that she wants to travel through South America with the boyfriend."

Mack remembered Cecily on the phone in the middle of the night. *"I'm dying of love for you."* "Really?" he said.

"She *wants* us to give you the hotel," Therese said. "She said it herself. If we profit-share, she'll be *relieved*. She'll think, 'Okay, I'm free to go. Mack's in charge.' She'll think we've given up." Therese tapped the counter with her fingernail. "I'm *not* giving up. I already lost one child. I'm not about to lose number two. She might not go if she thinks we need her. I stayed up all night thinking it through. Cecily's weak spot is that she loves us. But if she knows we have some new, official arrangement with you, she'll leave."

"You don't know that," Mack said.

"Therese is right," Bill said. "I'm sorry, Mack. Under other circumstances I would consider it . . . but no, I'm sorry."

I'm sorry: Maribel was sorry but she had to kick him out; Andrea was sorry but she didn't love him; Bill and Therese were sorry but they wouldn't profit-share. *Sorry, Mack, but there's no room for you.* The summer was turning into a big cauldron of sorry stew.

Therese said, "You could always marry Cecily."

Mack was too angry and hurt for any words except the most mundane. "I have to get the doughnuts."

Bill dropped his elbows onto the table, folded his hands, and bowed his head. "Does this mean you're going to leave us, Mack?"

Mack shrugged. "We'll have to see."

6

The Boys of Summer

July 10

Dear S.B.T.,

If we are to continue in this strange correspondence, I want some answers. Who are you? What do you do for a living? Why do you want this hotel? What could it possibly mean to you? And, most crucially, what right do you have telling me what my own daughter wants or doesn't want? What do you know about me, really? You know only what I've told you in letters and what you might observe from the street. Isn't that right?

Or are you someone on the inside? Are you a Beach Club member, a hotel guest, someone who walks the property every day? Answer me!

Bill Elliott

MACK SPENT THE DAYS following the Fourth of July questioning his future. His sweat equity had turned out to be nothing but sweat—salty water—and at the Beach Club, there was more than enough of that to go around. He'd been threatened with a gun by one of his employees, his girlfriend had kicked him out, and the woman he loved didn't love him back. Running the farm in Iowa was looking better and better. It might not be so bad—climbing up into a combine again and knowing that as far as his eyes could see, the land belonged to him. He had half a mind to call David Pringle and tell him to hire a cleaning lady because Mack Petersen was moving back. He heard the eerie, haunting voice of Nantucket calling out *Home,* but Mack didn't know what that meant anymore. He always assumed it meant Nantucket was his home, but the other night it seemed just as feasible that the voice was telling him to go home to Iowa. It might feel good to return, Mack thought. It might feel as good as it had felt to leave.

But then, just as Mack had almost made up his mind, the Boys of Summer arrived.

"How-Baby" Comatis always made Mack feel better, because when Mack saw How-Baby, he thought about hot dogs and cold beer, dugouts, organ music, extra innings, home plate. He thought about baseball: the word that defined summertime for the rest of America. Howard Comatis was president of the Texas Rangers, and he stayed at the Beach Club every July during the all-star break. He came with his wife, Tonya, and his two baseball buddies—Roy Silverstein (VP of marketing for the California Angels) and Dominic Saint-Jean (president of the Montreal Expos) and their wives. How-Baby was in every way the group's leader—he was a tall, muscular Greek with a full head of black hair and a bushy mustache. His wife, Tonya, called everyone baby, and she always called Howard How-Baby, whether she was speaking to him or about him, and the name stuck. Mack had a hard time thinking of Howard Comatis as anything but How-Baby.

Mack first saw How-Baby when he opened the door of Lacey Gardner's cottage at seven-thirty in the morning. How-Baby was standing on Lacey's tiny porch.

"Howard," Mack said, startled. "Good morning. Welcome back."

How-Baby held out a Texas Rangers hat. "Put this on," he said. "We have fifty bucks riding on who could get you to wear their hat first. The other two bozos are waiting by the lobby. They have no detective skills whatsoever."

Mack took the hat. He had three like it at home from previous years, but he'd left them in the apartment with Maribel. He creased the brim, and tried it on: a good, snug fit. "All right," Mack said. "Thanks."

How-Baby put his arm around Mack's shoulder. "You're a good kid. Come with me. I want to show you off."

Sure enough, Roy Silverstein stood on the front porch of the lobby holding a California Angels cap and Dominic St. Jean was stationed out by the Nantucket Beach Club and Hotel sign, holding an Expos cap.

"Damn," Roy said, when Mack and How-Baby rounded the corner. "I thought for sure Dom was going to get Mack when he pulled in. Where'd you find him, How-Baby?"

"None of your business," How-Baby said. "Now pay up."

Roy was short, bald and skinny. He wore a pair of madras swim trunks cinched at the waist. He reached into his pocket and pulled out twenty-five dollars. "Hey, Dom," Roy said. "How-Baby got to Mack first. Don't ask me how."

Dominic crunched across the parking lot. Dominic was the most elegant of the three men. Because he was Canadian, he sometimes lapsed into speaking French, and he was the best dressed—this morning in creased navy slacks, a lemon yellow polo, and tasseled loafers.

"*Merde,*" Dominic said. He spun the cap around his index finger, then he tossed the cap to Mack. "Wear it tomorrow."

"No, wear mine tomorrow," Roy said.

"You stick with the front runner, Mack," How-Baby said. "Stick with the Rangers."

Tonya Comatis popped her head out the lobby door, her auburn beehive hair-do spun high like cotton candy. "Boys, get back to your rooms. I won't have you competing with each other all week." Her face brightened when she saw Mack. "Mack, baby," she said. She kissed his cheek, leaving, Mack was sure, a ruby red lipstick mark. "Why, you look ex-haus-taid!"

"It's early," Mack said.

"No, I mean, you look really *tired*. You look tired to your bones."

"Give the kid a break, Tonya," How-Baby said. "Now, Mack, can you find us the plastic bat and a few of those Wiffle balls for this afternoon? I'm going to teach these clowns a thing or two."

"You'd think they'd want to get away from baseball," Tonya said. "You'd think they'd want to forget all about it. But no. They love it. They absolutely love it."

"If baseball were a woman," How-Baby said, "I'd marry her."

"I'd marry her first," Roy said.

"She wouldn't marry either of you," Dominic said. "You're both too ugly."

• • •

THAT AFTERNOON AT FIVE o'clock when the beach boys took the umbrellas down for the day, the beach became a playing field. How-Baby and Roy marked the bases and the fair/foul line in the sand. Tonya and the other two wives—Dominic's wife was a quiet blonde named Genevieve, and Roy's wife this year wore ponytails and looked just about eighteen—pulled shorts on over their bikinis and brought out bottles of cold Evian. The teams were co-ed—usually How-Baby and the two wives versus Roy, Dominic, and Tonya, but sometimes it was How-Baby and Tonya against everyone else. One thing stayed the same: How-Baby's team always won. He clobbered the wiffle ball into the ocean every time he was up. The first two balls were lost out at sea. "That would have been a home run at Wrigley," How-Baby said, as he rounded the bases. "That would have been a homer at Candlestick." Then Tonya made a rule that hitting the ball into the water constituted an automatic home run.

"I know you, How-Baby," she said. "You'll try for the upper decks at Yankee Stadium next, and we'll lose the only ball we have left."

How-Baby was amazing in the field, too. He pitched so fast the ball was a white blur. He had Roy and Dominic and the ladies swinging at air, and if they did hit the ball it was usually a crazy-spinning pop-up that fell right into How-Baby's hands. There was a magic to the man, a magnetism that neither Bill nor Mack's father had taught him.

Nine innings with How-Baby took about an hour. Then, the players came in from the field, Roy wiping his bald head with a handkerchief.

"The bastard doesn't even cheat," Roy said to Mack. "If he cheated, at least I could hate him."

"I hate him anyway," Dominic said. He swatted How-Baby's behind.

"Join us for a cocktail," How-Baby said. He wasn't sweating or winded; he was as cool as the breeze off the water.

"Okay," Mack said. It was after six and he'd planned to spend the evening with Andrea—it was her final night on the island and he was supposed to help James shave. Then he hoped to walk with Andrea and James up the beach, but suddenly that seemed depressing. Mack might find a perfect scallop shell or a sand dollar and he would give it to Andrea as something to remember him by, knowing full well that by the time she reached Baltimore, it would be broken or lost. Better to spend time with people who made him feel good.

Mack followed How-Baby to room 1. (How-Baby always booked room 1—there was no question how the man felt about being first.) They sat in the deck chairs. Tonya appeared with two sweating beers, and How-Baby drank half of his in one long swallow. The man lived with gusto.

"So, Mack, tell me, how was your winter?"

"It was good," Mack said. A pale, unenthusiastic answer, but it was all he could muster—and it wasn't a lie. The winter *had* been good; it was only since May that things had started to spin out of his control. "Maribel and I lived on Sunset Hill again, next to the Oldest House."

How-Baby stroked his mustache. "I wanted to ask you about Maribel. I got worried when I heard you were living out in back of the hotel with an old lady. Because you know Tonya and I think you're a marquis player, but we like Maribel a whole bunch too."

"Everyone likes Maribel," Mack said.

Tonya stepped onto the deck. "So we'll see her, then?" she asked. "We'd like to take you kids out to dinner."

"I know you're busy," How-Baby said. "But there's something I want to ask you. Something big."

Tonya swatted How-Baby on the arm. "Now you're teasing," she said. "Just tell him what it is, How-Baby. Tell him right now."

"You don't have to tell me right now," Mack said. "Because, you see, with Maribel. . . ."

"Okay, I will tell him right now," How-Baby said. He finished his beer in a second swallow, then let out a strong, healthy belch. "I have a job for you."

"A job?"

"A job, working for me, working for the Rangers. When this job opened up, I thought to myself, 'I know exactly who I want this job to go to. Mack Petersen, that's who.' "

Mack laughed. "As you know, Howard, I already have a job."

How-Baby turned to Tonya and chuckled. "Didn't I tell you that's exactly what Mack was going to say?"

"You sure did, How-Baby. Now tell him the rest."

How-Baby leaned forward. "Son, I know you like your job here at the hotel. And the job I'm offering you is hotel-related. This job is you setting up travel plans for the team—flights, hotel rooms, restaurants. It means a lot of interaction with the players, it means seeing the rest of the country." He paused dramatically. "It means I will triple your salary. But you'll still have your winters off, just like you do here. You're free in the winter and in the summer you're traveling, fraternizing with the biggest names in the sport, and you're making money." How-Baby settled back in his chair. "How can you pass that up?"

The first word that popped into Mack's mind was *ridiculous*. The second word was *why? Why was it ridiculous?*

"It sounds tempting," Mack admitted.

"But you have doubts," How-Baby said. "You have doubts because I'm asking you to make a major league switcheroo here. I understand that. And so I want you to think it over. I want you to discuss it with your pretty Maribel and see what she has to say."

"We know she's going to love the idea," Tonya said.

"We know she's going to love the idea because that young lady has a good head on her shoulders. She knows a winner when she sees one. After all," How-Baby said, clapping Mack on the back, "she picked you, didn't she?"

"Sort of," Mack said. He felt stupid admitting the truth to How-Baby. How-Baby wasn't interested in what Mack had lost; he was interested in winning. "Maribel kicked me out of the apartment. I made a mistake."

Tonya tugged on her earlobe. "Another woman?" she whispered.

Mack's neck grew warm. "Something like that."

How-Baby slapped his leg. "I knew it," he said. He nudged Tonya.

"Didn't I tell you Mack was in the doghouse and that's why he was living out back? I knew it."

"It's worse than just the doghouse," Mack said. "It's complicated."

How-Baby put his hands behind his head and leaned back in his chair. "Of course it's complicated," he said. "It's love. Love is the greatest thing in the world. And you're talking to a man who's been married twenty-seven years."

"That's right," Tonya said. She kissed How-Baby's forehead, leaving two red lips behind. "But love is hard work too."

"Harder than pitching a no-hitter with four fingers," How-Baby said. "Harder than playing centerfield in a hundred-degree heat. It's damn hard."

"Yeah," Mack said.

"Let me ask you something," How-Baby said. "Do you love Maribel? Do you really love her?"

Mack nodded. "Yes."

"Well, then, let's hear you tell the world. Go on and say it."

"I love her," Mack said.

"Say it louder," How-Baby said.

"I love her," Mack said.

How-Baby scooted to the edge of his chair. "Say it louder."

Mack hesitated; this must be the way How-Baby motivated his players, by getting them to release their testosterone. "I love her!" Mack said.

"Say it louder," How-Baby said.

Tonya whispered. "Louder, Mack baby, louder."

"I love her!" Mack said.

How-Baby stood up. "Say it louder!" How-Baby screamed. "Say it as loud as you can. Stand up and say it from your guts."

Mack faced the water. There were still a few stragglers on the beach, but so what?

"I love her!!!" he shouted. "I . . . love . . . her!"

How-Baby applauded. "That's right," he said. "You love her. I believe you. I believe you love her."

Roy Silverstein came out onto the deck of room 2.

"I see How-Baby's doing his Baptist preacher routine again," he said.

Mack collapsed in his chair. For the first time in weeks, he really laughed. Was it crazy to even consider taking this job? He was so locked into his choice between Nantucket and Iowa, he had never even thought there might be a third option. He'd been sitting around waiting for Nantucket to speak to him—and maybe that's what had just happened. Maybe How-Baby was the voice he was waiting for. Mack wondered what the water looked like down in Texas. If he could get Maribel back, he would find out.

SOON THEREAFTER, MACK LEFT the deck, shaking hands with How-Baby, kissing Tonya on the cheek, and telling them he would consider their offer.

"Worry about the girl, first," How-Baby said. "That's what's important."

Mack rounded the corner to the side deck rooms. He knocked at room 18. Andrea opened the door. Behind her, Mack saw her half-packed suitcase, but he didn't feel as sad as he'd expected.

"I'm here to help James shave," he said. "I promised him."

She looked him over. "I *am* going to miss you, you know."

"Is James here?" Mack asked. He called into the room. "James, buddy, it's Mack. I'm here to help you shave."

"Hey," Andrea said. "I *said* I was going to miss you."

"You don't have to miss me," Mack said. "You're choosing to. Is James here?"

"Of course he's here. Where else would he be?" Andrea turned. "James, come here, please."

A few seconds later James skulked into the room.

"I'm here to help you shave," Mack said.

James spun on his heels and headed for the bathroom without a word. Mack followed him. James stood in front of the mirror, and Mack sat on the toilet.

"This is a graduation of sorts," Mack said. "Because you're leaving tomorrow." He wondered if Andrea had gone over all this with James already. He wondered if it would matter, if James had any concept, really, of what was going on around him.

"Time for shaving," James said.

"I'm going to watch you," Mack said. "You go ahead. Tell me what's first."

"I don't know," James said.

"Lather your face with shaving cream," Mack said. "Like Santa Claus, remember?"

James sprayed the foam onto his fingers and dabbed it onto his cheeks.

"And now what?" Mack said. "What comes next?"

James said nothing. How did How-Baby do it? How did he make people respond with exactly what he wanted to hear? "Pick up the razor," Mack said. "We've done this three times already. Now I want you to shave yourself, James."

"I don't know," James said.

"You don't know what?"

James stared into the mirror. Mack's heart deflated as he looked at the fifteen-year-old kid with a foamy white beard. He felt for Andrea, who would have to watch tomorrow, and next week, and maybe even next year, until James could get comfortable with the routine, until he could divide the task into steps. She was right, of course: nobody else would love James enough to have that kind of patience and that kind of stamina without losing their temper, without becoming frustrated enough to leave, as her husband had. Not even Mack.

Mack stood behind James and took the razor. He began to shave him gently.

"Do you like baseball, James?" Mack asked.

"Yes," James said, automatically.

"Do you hate baseball?" Mack asked.

"Yes," James said.

"You can't like it *and* hate it," Mack said. "You can't do both. Do you understand that, James? You can't like baseball and hate it."

"I like it in person," James said. "I hate it on TV."

Mack smiled as he shaved under the curve of James's chin. "Maybe I can get you some tickets to see the Orioles," he said. "How would you like that?"

"Yes," James said.

Mack shaved James's upper lip. "When you do this on your own, you have to be careful of your lip. You don't want to cut your lip or you'll bleed for hours. There, you're all done." Mack stepped back. "I want you to rinse your face," Mack said.

James turned on the water, splashed his face and dried it with a towel.

"What do we do after we rinse, James, can you remember?"

James stared into the mirror.

Mack picked up the lotion and squirted some into James's palm. "Rub this into your face. We don't use aftershave, do we, James?"

"No," James said.

"You're going to have to remind your mom of that. No aftershave, just lotion. And stand up for yourself. I'd hate to think of you walking around smelling funny."

James rubbed in the lotion. "All shaved," he said.

"All shaved. You're ready to go, then." Mack reached for the latch on the bathroom door, but then stopped short. "Do you like me, James?" he asked.

"No," James said. His green-gray eyes were a blank slate. "I love you."

BEFORE MACK LEFT THE room, he watched Andrea pack. "Your son's smooth faced again," he said. "But I don't think I taught him a thing. I'm sorry."

Andrea held a sweater under her chin and folded in the sleeves. "Don't worry about it," she said.

"Okay, then, I'm going," Mack said.

"I'm afraid I don't have the energy for a big emotional good-bye," she said.

"Me either," he said.

Andrea narrowed her eyes. "You aren't beholden to me or anyone else, Mack. You're your own person. A good person. But will you think about what I said, about Maribel?"

"I already have," Mack said.

Andrea slid one of James's flip-flops onto each of her hands. "I guess it's ridiculous to think I'll never see you again."

"I'm beginning to believe nothing is ridiculous," Mack said. "Let's just say so long for a while. You might see me again, but it won't be where you think."

"You're leaving here?"

"I promise I won't show up on your doorstep," he said.

"You're really leaving here?" Andrea said.

Mack gave her a squeeze. "Safe travels tomorrow." He inhaled the smell of her hair, but again, he wasn't as sad as he expected. He made a point of not saying "I love you," but Andrea seemed to hear it anyway.

"I know," she said.

MACK DROVE TO THE basement apartment. He knocked tentatively on the door, but heard nothing. Then, he knocked a little louder. After a second, Maribel swung the door open.

"Oh, God," she said. Her tan face went pale, as though she were going to be sick.

"Mari, I'm sorry, I have to talk to you."

"Talk?" she said.

"Can I come in?" Mack asked.

The skin above her eye twitched. "I guess," she said.

She pushed the screen door open for him and he stepped into the apartment. Jem Crandall was sitting at the dining table eating pizza from a box. He, too, looked sick when he saw Mack. He stood up.

"Jem," Mack said. "Hi."

"I'm going," Jem said. "I'm out of here."

Mack tried to hide his surprise. It was hard enough to see Maribel, but then to have one of his bellmen sitting at the dining table eating pizza?

"I don't get it," Mack said. "What are you doing here?"

"We're friends," Maribel said. "Get over your surprise. You don't know what my life is like anymore."

"No," Mack said. "Obviously I don't."

Jem moved toward the door, taking the piece of pizza he was eating with him. "I'll let you two hash this out," he said. Then he turned around. "But if you hurt her, Petersen, if you lay a hand on her or you make her cry with something you say, I'll kill you."

"Great," Mack said. Now both his bellmen wanted to kill him.

"I mean it," Jem said. "And I'm saying this despite the fact that you've been pretty cool to me. But you did a bad thing to Maribel, and if you do anything else, you're in trouble."

"Okay," Mack said. He repressed the urge to smile. "I'll keep that in mind."

Jem bit into his pizza. "Yeah," he said, his mouth full. "Do that."

After Jem left, Maribel sat at the dining table. "So, you've reclaimed your turf," she said. "Why don't you tell me what you want. You want closure? I figured as much, but I'd hoped you'd call first."

Mack looked around the apartment. He missed it. Even the shag carpet and the moldy, old-sponge smell. "I love you," he said.

"You don't cheat on someone you love. You don't perpetuate a lie for six years with someone you love. Okay, Mack? Do you see how your credibility has worn thin?"

"Yes," Mack said, "but I do love you."

"Ha."

"I asked Bill to profit-share," he said.

Maribel raised her eyebrows. "Really?"

"He turned me down," Mack said. "He and Therese both. They said . . . well, do you know what's going on with Cecily?"

"That she's deferring a year from school you mean? To be with the boyfriend?"

"It has them really upset. And they won't profit-share with me because they think if they do Cecily will be more likely to leave. They think she'll be glad I'm taking care of the hotel for them, and she'll feel free to go."

"They're absolutely right," Maribel said. "Cecily's said as much. So it sounds like you're out of luck."

Mack looked at his hands. "I did ask, though."

Maribel fidgeted with the corner of the pizza box. "You're too late, Mack."

"We only broke up two weeks ago. How can I be too late? And another thing I'd like to know is what Crandall was doing here."

"He likes me," Maribel said. "I could go out on a limb and say he's in love with me."

"Great," Mack said. "He's too young for you, you know."

Maribel snorted. "That isn't for you to decide."

"So you're an item, then? You've fallen for Mr. *November*?"

"I don't know what I'm doing, Mack," Maribel said. Her voice was sad now, not angry, not sarcastic. "I'm thinking of leaving the island."

"Why?" he said.

"Because I'm finished here. I gave it a shot and it didn't work. Six years ago, you and I had a summer romance and I decided to stay. But it was always a summer romance, wasn't it? The kind of romance that's so thrilling because you know it's going to end." She flashed her blue eyes at him. "And guess what? Our summer is finally over."

"I agree. Our summer is over."

"Plus, I think people who live on islands . . . well, I'm beginning to think there's something wrong with them. It's like they're *hiding* from something. It's like they're afraid of the rest of the world and so they *isolate* themselves, surrounded by all this water."

"What are we hiding from?" Mack asked. "What are we afraid of?"

Maribel tore the pizza box into tiny pieces. "I don't know," she said. "I'm afraid that you don't love me enough. You're afraid that I love you too much. Or maybe we're each just afraid of ourselves." She started to cry.

Mack reached across the table and took her hand. "I got a job offer today," he said. "And if you agree to come with me, I'm going to take it."

"What kind of offer?" she said.

"Working for How-Baby," Mack said. "For the Texas Rangers. Setting up hotel rooms, restaurants, flights. It would mean traveling around the States. It would mean the winters off. It would mean more money."

Maribel went to the sink, ripped a paper towel off the roll and blew her nose. "How-Baby," she said. "I always liked that man."

"He and Tonya want to see you," Mack said. "They can hardly wait. And How-Baby said he would triple my salary, Maribel. Triple it."

"What are you going to do about the farm?" Maribel asked.

Mack thought about that for a minute. He still didn't know what to do about the farm. "We'll figure it out," he said. "Maybe I'll wait a year to see how I like this job. I'll have Pringle hire someone for one harvest, and if the job works out, maybe I'll sell the farm. The thing is, we'll be able to do it, you and me, I know we will."

"You'll have to do it alone," Maribel said, bunching the paper towel in her hand. "I'm not going with you."

"You have to come with me."

Maribel paced the kitchen floor so that the soles of her running shoes squeaked against the linoleum. "You just don't *get it*, do you?"

Mack took a deep breath. He felt as though he were falling, in a dream. "You don't get it," he said. "I'm asking you to marry me."

For the first time in their relationship, he'd surprised her. Well, maybe the second time, because he knew finding out about Andrea had surprised her too. Just watching her gave Mack a rush. She was wearing a pale pink T-shirt, jean shorts, her running shoes. Her hair was in a bun held together by a pencil. At that moment, Mack wanted to *be* Maribel—she was getting something she'd wanted for so long.

"You're asking me to marry you?" Maribel said.

I should sink to one knee, he thought. It seemed silly, there in the dampness of their rented apartment, but Mack made himself do it. He knelt.

"Will you marry me? Will you be my wife?" The words came right out; it was easy. He would say them over and again; he would scream them out. "Will you please marry me?"

Maribel stared over the top of his head as though his thoughts were suspended in a balloon. *Answer me!* the balloon would say. And then for a second it occurred to him she might say no, and that was like peeking into a dark hole with no bottom.

"Maribel, will you marry me?" Mack asked a little louder.

She looked at his face as though she were surprised to find him there, on one knee, his eyes level with her tan legs.

"Of course," she said. "Of course I'll marry you."

LACEY GARDNER COULDN'T BELIEVE it. For twelve years she'd watched Mack grow up: She watched him run the hotel, graduate from the community college on the Cape, grieve for his parents; she watched him take girls on dates. And she watched him, especially carefully, with Maribel. But never in a million years would she have predicted this—and Lacey was old enough now to have very few things shock her. But this, yes. Mack brought her usual cup of coffee and the *Boston Globe* from the lobby, and before she even scanned the headlines, there was this news.

"I've asked Maribel to marry me and she said yes."

His tone of voice was barely repressed joy, pride, awe, and Lacey supposed that was as it should be. Lacey experienced first surprise and next, sadness. Mack, then, lost to her forever, in a way.

"And all this time, I thought you were saving yourself for me."

Mack hugged her across the shoulders so that she nearly spilled coffee in her lap. His energy astounded her—maybe he was in love with the girl after all. "You're the best, Gardner. The absolute best. You're the first person I've told."

"You'll be moving out, then?" Lacey said. She eyed the leather sofa where Mack had slept the last two weeks. Usually, he came in after she fell asleep and was up before she awoke, but for two weeks there was another human being under her roof, and that felt good. She sometimes heard Mack's footsteps or the toilet flush in the middle of the night, and once, when she couldn't sleep, she tiptoed out to the living room and saw his figure under the blankets and she wished he would never leave, that he would simply stay with her until she died.

"I'll be moving back to the apartment," he said. "But we'll still have our Sunday night dinners. I told Maribel that was part of the deal. Sunday nights are for you, Lacey."

"Well, good," she said.

Mack was getting married.

Lacey remembered back to September of 1941 when she and Maximilian drove Sam Archibald's dune buggy out to Madaket. Sam Archibald wasn't on Nantucket that summer because he'd enlisted in the army and was at training camp in Mississippi. Maximilian received a postcard from him that said, "*Half the gents here have never seen the Atlantic, much less played croquet in 'Sconset. Take the old girl around in the bug and have a good time for me.*" On September 16, that's what they were doing—driving to Madaket. The mood between Lacey and Maximilian was more serious than normal, because of the war. Everyone sat by their radios listening for word on Hitler. The military used Tom Nevers Field as a training ground for landing in the fog; the coast guard patrolled the beach, looking for U-boats. There were piles of sandbags in the streets of town and all around them, men enlisting in the service. Lacey supposed it wouldn't be long before Maximilian went away also. Then she would be left to drive the dune buggy to the beach alone.

When they reached Madaket, Lacey and Maximilian walked through the sand barefoot.

Maximilian said, "I brought you out here for a reason."

Lacey laughed, but it was so windy her laughter was carried away. "You brought me out here because Sam wrote and said you should. You men, always sticking together!"

Maximilian's necktie lifted in the breeze. "No, Lacey, that's not it."

And then, of course, she thought he was telling her that he was off for the war as well. *You men,* she thought, *always sticking together.* No wonder the armed forces worked. Men loved each other's company; they loved a group, the bigger the better. And she thought, *If Maximilian is going, I'll enlist too. I won't be left behind with the women, I just won't.*

But Maximilian said, "Lacey, I brought you here to ask for your hand in marriage, both hands, and the rest of you, for that matter, if you'll have me. I promise to provide you with a home, and to give you the life you're accustomed to as well as I possibly can—"

Lacey interrupted him by putting her fingers to his lips. She remembered that too, the way his warm lips felt under her fingertips. "Yes," she said. "The answer is yes."

She held tight to that memory, and to the flood of happiness it brought her, even though two months later Maximilian did join the service and was gone from her for three years. Those were days when love meant something because it stood side by side with life and death. Those who survived had a reason to be nostalgic, and she, Lacey, had survived.

Mack waited for her to speak. What could she say? Things were so different these days she could hardly understand them. "You're doing the right thing," she said finally.

Relief crossed his face like a ray of light.

"Thank you," he said. "I was hoping we'd have your blessing."

"You always have my blessing, Mack Petersen," Lacey said. And that much, at least, was the truth.

WHEN CECILY FOUND OUT Mack and Maribel were getting married, she experienced envy like a slap across the face. She heard the news from Maribel, over the phone.

"He's going to marry me! Mack and I are getting married! Can you believe it? Married, married, *married!*"

Cecily stared at herself in the mirror, a bad habit of her mother's. "You're so fucking lucky," she whispered. But Maribel blabbered something about a church and flowers, and didn't hear. Cecily quietly hung up the phone and took it off the hook. Then she fell facedown on her bed and cried. She should be *happy*; she had wanted this for both Mack and Maribel. But the truth was, she liked it better when Mack and Maribel were miserable. She liked it better when she was the one lucky in love. Now Mack and Maribel were beyond lucky; they'd hit the jackpot. *Married!* Cecily cried bitter, jealous tears. She knew Maribel would be trying to call back, but she didn't care. She couldn't talk to Maribel, and she couldn't face Mack. It was completely irrational—their good news didn't mean bad news for Cecily. Lots of people could fall in love and get married at one time. But that thought didn't make anything better, not with Gabriel thousands of miles away and Cecily stranded here, on this dinky, go-nowhere island.

Could it be she was so upset because *she* wanted to marry Mack? When Cecily was younger she'd had a terrible crush on him. Every day she wrote in her journal what Mack said to her: "Hey, there, Sunshine, whatcha up to?" "Cecily, babe, let's see you turn a cartwheel." She wrote down every time he pulled her curls or flung her over his shoulder like a sack of flour. Nights when he went on dates she stayed in her room without turning on the radio or TV, convinced that if she was having a miserable time, he was, too. Then the next day she pestered him for the name of the girl, what she looked like, what they did on their date. Dinner? Movie? Dancing? And then shyly, Cecily would ask, "Did you kiss her, Mack?" And Mack would either say, "Sure did, Sunshine," or "Nope, not that one, too ugly." Cecily always prayed for the latter answer. She prayed that all of Mack's dates had a faint mustache, or bad breath. She hoped he would realize no girl was as pretty as Cecily.

By the time Cecily was old enough to go on dates herself and Therese grabbed hold of the idea that Mack and Cecily should be together, Cecily was N.I.—Not Interested. By that time too, Maribel was in the picture, and Cecily fell for Maribel almost as hard as she'd fallen for Mack. Cecily imitated the way Maribel talked, the way she wore her hair, the way she dressed. From the beginning, Maribel treated Cecily like an equal, and it worked like magic. Cecily was hooked.

Was Cecily so upset because she was in love with Mack, or Maribel? She'd read Freud and other dead European males at Middlesex, and some would say she wanted to be married to both of them. Gobbledy-gook. She wanted to be married to Gabriel, that was all there was to it. But Mack and Maribel had separated themselves from her. *We're getting married. You're staying single.*

For the time being.

Cecily opened the drawer of her bedside table and counted her money. She was getting closer, but still not close enough. She snuffled, blew her nose, and went into the bathroom to splash water on her face. She was due on the beach in half an hour and as much as she wanted to stay hidden in her room, missing a day's work meant missing a day's salary, and money was the only thing keeping her from Gabriel.

She stomped upstairs to the living room and found her father staring out the bay window at the activity below. This was his quiet time, while Cecily's mother was busy with the chambermaids, and Cecily never interrupted. Plus, whenever Cecily talked to either of her parents now, they clung to her words as though she might never speak again. They must have thought if they paid her more attention, she wouldn't leave, but that was completely fucking erroneous on their part.

Cecily cleared her throat. Her father snapped to attention.

"Good morning," he said. "How are you this morning?"

"Mack and Maribel are getting married," Cecily said. The inside of her mouth was dry and chalky.

"I'm sorry?"

"They're getting married." Saying it aloud was the worst kind of pain—worse than menstrual cramps, worse than falling down and skinning her palms. "Maa—reed."

"They're getting married?" Bill said. "You know this for a fact?"

Cecily couldn't bring herself to say anything further. And if her father made a big, happy deal over it, she would leave immediately, tonight, today. But thankfully, he didn't. He took the news quietly and then seemed reflective, but not in a glad or happy way.

"Well," he said. "How about that?"

BILL ELLIOTT KNEW THE instant he heard the news about Mack and Maribel getting married that Mack was going to leave. Part of Bill cheered Mack on—*Good for you getting married, good for you return-*

ing to the land that's yours, good for you! But then the reality of the situation hit and Bill felt a familiar tightness in his chest. He left Cecily
banging cabinets, muttering, "There's never any fucking food in this
house," and went into his bedroom to lie down. Mack leaving spelled
disaster for the Beach Club. He was the manager and he managed like
nobody else. Kids loved him, adults loved him, the crotchety old
ladies of the Beach Club loved him. Most importantly, Bill loved him,
and if it weren't for the fact that he had a daughter of his own, Bill
would not only have profit-shared with Mack, he would have left the
hotel to him without a second thought. He lay on his bed, and
thought, *I have survived worse. I survived losing my son.* But thinking
about Mack leaving gave Bill an oddly similar feeling— empty, sad,
hopeless. He closed his eyes. Why not sell the hotel then? Cecily
didn't want it and how could Bill run it without Mack? S.B.T.'s face
appeared to him, a demon.

Later, his fears were confirmed. Mack was talking with a guest in
the lobby and Bill touched him on the elbow, and said, "When you get
a second."

Then Bill sat at his desk and looked out the window. The most
beautiful beach in the world—the blue water, the white sails in the distance, the brightly colored umbrellas in the sand. It was glorious here.

Mack knocked lightly, pushed open the door. "I guess you
heard?"

"Why don't you tell me yourself," Bill said.

Mack stuffed his hands in the pockets of his khaki shorts. "I'm
going to marry her."

"Getting married was the best thing I ever did," Bill said. "By far
the best thing."

Mack jingled his key ring. "I know you feel that way. You and
Therese have had a big influence on me. I really appreciate that.
You've been role models."

"That sounds like a good-bye," Bill said. "Is that a good-bye?"

"Did someone tell you I was leaving?"

"No one needed to," Bill said.

Mack looked out the window and Bill followed his gaze, willing him to see how beautiful it was, hoping he would understand that the rest of the world was not this beautiful.

"I'll stay through the season," Mack said. "I would never strand you midseason."

"But next year? . . ."

"Next year, no. This will be my last year. This is it."

The demon face of S.B.T. shimmered on the horizon. "I just can't picture you as a farmer," Bill said. "But I want you to know I understand why you're going back. In the end, you have to protect what belongs to you and your family."

Mack's lower lip dropped. "Oh . . . no. Whoops." He laughed. "Well, you got it half right anyway. I'm leaving, but I'm not going back to Iowa."

"You're not?" Bill said.

"No," Mack said. "I'm going to work for Howard Comatis. For the Texas Rangers. It's a baseball team."

"A baseball team?"

"Howard Comatis, room one. He's president of the Texas Rangers. He offered me a job yesterday. And I thought about what you said, about wanting to give the hotel to Cecily. So anyway, it just seemed right. And I'll still have winters off. So it's not as if I'll never see you again. We can visit you in Aspen. You can finally teach me to ski."

"Howard Comatis?" Bill said. "The big hairy guy? The loud obnoxious guy?"

"That's him."

"You're going to work for *him*?" Bill asked. This news affronted him. Mack working on his family farm was one thing, but a guest snatching him away was another. Guests had been trying to hire Mack away for years, but he'd always turned them down. "What will you be doing?"

"Hotel rooms, dinner reservations, travel plans. Getting the team from place to place, that kind of thing."

"How much is he paying you?" Bill asked.

"A lot," Mack said. "We haven't talked actual numbers but it'll be a lot."

Bill nodded. It must have been a lot for Mack to give up Nantucket.

"I'd do anything to keep you here, Mack," Bill said. "I'll give you a raise right now."

Mack put his keys back in his pocket. "Not this kind of raise. Besides, you made it clear that your first concern is Cecily, and that's okay." He knocked on Bill's desk. "Bill, that's okay."

Bill rubbed his forehead. "If Cecily weren't threatening to leave, if Therese and I hadn't already lost a child, all that, things would be different."

"But they aren't different," Mack said.

"I don't know what I'm going to do without you," Bill said.

"We don't have to say good-bye right now," Mack said. "It's only July. We still have lots of time."

Bill looked back out at the beach. Dutifully, Cecily started to circulate among the umbrellas; a ferry approached on the horizon.

"We have time," Bill said. "Okay, you're right. We have time." He stood up and stuck out his hand and when Mack shook it, Bill embraced him. "Congratulations," he said.

FOUR BRIDESMAIDS IN ROOM 19 destroyed the place. Therese put down her clipboard. Empty diet Coke bottles rolled around on the floor, potato chips were ground into powder in the carpet, three wet bikini bottoms sat in soggy clumps on the bathroom tile. The top bedsheet had been ripped in half, hair spray scum covered the mirror, a nail polish spill pooled like blood on the dresser. These girls had requested extra towels. Extra towels! They were lucky they were here in the name of love. Therese had half a mind to kick them out.

Elizabeth appeared in the doorway with her cleaning cart and her vacuum. "Gross."

"Gross, you're not kidding," Therese said. A pair of stockings fluttered over the brass reading lamp by the bed, a swollen tampon floated in the toilet. "This is the most disgusting room I have ever seen."

"Really?" Elizabeth asked. She seemed encouraged by this news. "This is the worst?"

"You don't have to clean this room," Therese said. "I'll do it."

"*You're* going to clean it?" Elizabeth said. She peered into the room. "They sure did drink a lot of diet Coke."

"Go on to eighteen," Therese said. "But leave me your vacuum."

Elizabeth left and Therese furiously unwound the cord for the vacuum. Mack appeared in the doorway. "Geez," he said. "What a mess. Here, let me help you." He started to pick up the bottles and put them in an empty Lion's Paw bag.

"Leave them be," Therese said. "Anyone who makes this much of a mess deserves to live with their own filth."

"But I want to help," Mack said. "What can I do to help?"

Therese looked him dead in the eye. "I'm not changing my mind about the profit sharing," she said. "You know I love you, Mack, but I can't do it. I have a teenage daughter to think of. When you have a teenager of your own, you'll understand. Boy, will you ever."

"It's not the profit sharing," he said. "I have something else to talk to you about."

Therese spied a bra dangling from the ceiling fan. She switched on the vacuum and swathed a path only where the floor was clear— around the cans, around the chips, around the clothes. It took her thirty seconds. She shut the vacuum off. "So what is it?" she said.

"I'm getting married."

Married. The word took her so by surprise that she closed her eyes. When she opened them again, she caught her reflection in the scummy mirror. She looked fuzzy, as if someone were trying to erase her. "You're getting *married*?"

"I asked Maribel and she said yes."

"I thought you two were on the rocks," Therese said. The room went out of focus. It looked like a wedding that had been through the blender. "I thought she threw you out."

"We've worked through that," Mack said. "I'm going to marry her, Therese."

"I don't believe it," she said. She didn't want to believe it. Her dream of Cecily marrying Mack, a dream for the trash. She stood on the bed and unhooked the bra from the fan and threw it on the floor with the rest of the girls' clothes, although what did it matter now? What did a messy room matter now that everything else was collapsing? Therese found a notepad. *"The proprietress has cleaned your room!"* she wrote. She left it amid the clutter on the nightstand and wondered if they would even see it, if they would even notice. Mack sat on the dresser, tapping his fingers on the top drawer.

I know what's best for you. Therese thought. *Nobody believes it, but I do.*

SHOTGUN WEDDING. HANDGUN WEDDING. However you phrased it, Vance had Influence. His stunt with the gun had brought about Mack and Maribel's breakup, and then Mack's proposal. Vance might have been jealous—Mack marrying someone as perfect as Maribel—but instead he felt a grand satisfaction. He snagged control from Mack's hands. He had made something happen. And oddly enough, it was something good.

It inspired Vance to go after Love. She was older than he was, but she was pretty and athletic and organized. He liked the way she spoke to guests; he liked the way she listened. He liked the way she didn't wear makeup or hairspray. She was a natural Colorado outdoor beauty. She smelled like a pine cone. A refreshing change from the girls Vance usually brought home from the bars. She made him want to lighten up. She made him want to laugh. So he would have his own summer romance for once. And who knew, maybe someday he'd be the one getting married. Vance. Vance Romance.

MARIBEL WONDERED IF SHE'D ever be this happy again. Hearing Mack finally propose was an answer to her daily prayers. Just when she'd given up hope, just when she thought she would have to somehow endeavor to move on, he asked. He asked and she said yes. More than anyone, Maribel wanted to tell her father. A man who didn't exist, except for in her mind. *See there, someone wants me. Someone wants to marry me!*

Maribel called Cecily, and then her mother, and after relaying the news to a teary, elated Tina ("God bless you, Maribel. God bless you and Mack"), Maribel called Jem. She called early in the morning—during the bracket of time when Mack had left for work but Jem would still be at home.

He answered sleepily. "Hello?"

"Jem, it's Maribel."

"Maribel?" He sounded confused, then alarmed. "Did Mack hurt you?"

Maribel felt a flurry of guilt. "He didn't hurt me," she said. "He proposed."

Silence. Then, quietly, "You're kidding."

Maribel winced. "No."

"Oh, God," Jem said. "Wow. He asked you to *marry* him? The nerve of that guy." More silence. "But you said no, right? I mean, this is a guy who left you in the dust for another woman. This is a guy who cheated on you."

"Jem . . ."

"You said no, didn't you?"

"I said yes."

"You said yes."

"It's complicated," Maribel said. "We've been together for six years. You understand that."

"Not really," Jem said. "Not really at all."

"Jem," Maribel said, "I'm sorry. You'll have to trust that I know I'm doing the right thing."

"Because you're in love?" Jem said.

"Yes," Maribel said.

"And what does being in love feel like?" Jem asked. "Does it feel like when you're with the person you're the best version of yourself and when you're not with the person your insides hurt?"

"I don't know, Jem," Maribel said gently. "It's different for everyone."

"And does that person become the only person who matters, and no matter what you can't stop thinking about her. Is that what it's like, Maribel?"

"Jem . . ."

"Is being in love finally realizing why we were put on this earth? Is it when everything starts to make sense?"

"Jem," Maribel said. What could she possibly say? He was right. "Yes, Jem."

"Yes," Jem said, "I thought so."

"You're not in love with me, Jem."

There was huff on the other end of the line. "I wish you were right," Jem said. "I really wish you were."

"Jem . . ."

"I have to go," Jem said. "I have to get to work." And with that, he hung up, and Maribel, who thought nothing could squelch her happiness, stared at the dead receiver. She closed her eyes and wished his pain away. She knew just how he felt.

THE NEXT EVENING, MACK and Maribel went to dinner with How-Baby and Tonya at Kendrick's, on Centre Street. How-Baby reserved the back room for just the four of them; a magnum of Dom Perignon chilled on the table. Mack had been very careful not to say anything to How-Baby about his engagement to Maribel or his decision about the job, but from the looks of things, How-Baby already knew. Or maybe this was just his superconfidence shining through: live as though everything was going to go your way. When Mack took his seat, though, he started to enjoy it: the private, candlelit room, the waiter pouring him a glass of Champagne. There was already the sense that things had changed.

How-Baby raised his glass. "I'd like to make a toast," he said. "To you charming young people. Maribel, you are positively glowing, and Mack, that makes you one lucky man." How-Baby winked.

They all clinked glasses and sipped the Champagne. Maribel *was* glowing—she hadn't stopped smiling since Mack proposed. When they were home alone, she talked about nothing but the wedding. Mack was tickled to see her so excited, although the idea of a wedding disheartened him. He had no family to speak of; he would invite Bill and Therese and Cecily and Lacey Gardner. He felt a pang of guilt. The people he loved best, the people he would soon be leaving. He looked across the table at How-Baby and Tonya. His future.

"I have a toast as well," he said. How-Baby raised his bushy eyebrows. The man knew, he just *knew*. "First of all, I'm proud to announce that Maribel and I are getting married."

Tonya squealed and grabbed How-Baby's arm. "You darlings!" Her beehive tipping dangerously close to the candle flame. "That is brilliant! We're so happy. Aren't we, How-Baby?"

How-Baby clapped his hands. "Congratulations! Maribel, my sources tell me you just landed the most eligible bachelor on the island."

"I sure did," Maribel said. "He's the answer to my prayers."

Mack laid his hands on either side of his dinner plate. "And I've thought about your proposition, Howard."

"Have you, now?" How-Baby said.

"I have," Mack said. He wondered what it would be like working for a guy who always sat on top of the world. Did the man ever falter, ever have a bad day? The Rangers had lost both halves of a doubleheader that very afternoon, but How-Baby was as smooth as ever.

"What did you decide?" How-Baby asked. "Did you decide to join the team? Or will you remain loyal to the Beach Club?"

"I've decided to join the team," Mack said.

Tonya squealed again. How-Baby rounded the table to shake Mack's hand.

"Good for you, Mack! I promise you won't be disappointed. You'll be our new travel and hospitality manager, answering directly to me. Tomorrow you show me your W-two from this year, and I will triple your salary." He grabbed a fistful of Mack's shoulder. "Welcome to the big league."

"It was a hard decision to make," Mack said, reaching for Maribel's hand under the table. "My job at the Beach Club is the only job I've ever had, unless you count some construction work or helping on my father's farm."

"That's right," How-Baby said. "I forgot about you coming from the heartland. Where is it? Indiana?"

"Iowa," Mack said.

"Do your parents still farm, Mack?" Tonya asked.

Mack paused. A new job meant starting over, explaining his circumstances, letting other people know him. He wished he could just say yes.

"My parents were killed in a car crash when I was eighteen," he said.

Silence. Always, when Mack told this part, there was silence. He longed for Bill and Therese, because with them there wasn't a need to explain.

How-Baby looked up from his menu. "Did you have a good relationship with your father?"

"I did," Mack said. "We had a very good relationship."

How-Baby nodded. "I can tell. Know why? Because you're a good kid. A team player. If I should be so fortunate as to meet your father someday in heaven, I'll tell him he raised a fine young man."

Mack looked at Maribel; her eyes were shining.

"Thanks," Mack said.

"Did you consider what your father would have thought about changing jobs?" How-Baby asked. "Did you maybe even have a conversation with him about it?"

"I figured he would tell me to do what was going to make me happy, and to go where I was wanted."

"You're wanted in Texas," How-Baby said. "We're going to take good care of you."

The Eight Weeks of August

August 1

Dear Bill,

Suffice it to say, I am someone who has made mistakes, and in buying the hotel, I am trying to remedy them. You may think I intend to raze the hotel and build trophy homes instead, or condominiums. Although that would be most lucrative, that's not what I propose. I want to keep the hotel as it is.

From what I gather of recent developments, you're going to have a real shake-up in personnel. I hate to capitalize on another man's misfortune, but in this case, I can't help myself. I raise my offer to 25 million, along with the promise that the Beach Club and Hotel will remain intact.

Don't be daft, Bill. Take the money.

S.B.T.

NOTE SCRIBBLED IN FRONT DESK NOTEBOOK (TINY'S HANDWRITING)
Beware the eight weeks of August!

LOVE AND VANCE LAY next to each other in Love's twin bed, naked. They had just made love for the eleventh time. Late last night, Love took her temperature and checked it against her temperature from earlier in the week. It had risen three degrees; she was ovulating. Now she propped her legs on the footboard of the bed. The conception books recommended fifteen minutes of repose to give the sperm a fighting chance.

Love and Vance had been dating for four weeks, ever since sitting on the roof of the hotel on the Fourth of July. Their first real date was a few days later. Vance borrowed Mack's Jeep and took Love to Eel Point to go clamming. Vance made his own clammer out of a piece of PVC pipe. It had handles and two holes punched into the sealed end. He chose a spot in the wet sand near the water's edge, and sank in the open end of the pipe. He put his thumbs over the holes and pulled up. When he released his thumbs, a column of sand fell from the pipe, along with four cherrystone clams. Love picked the clams up, rinsed them, and put them in the clamming bucket. She felt as if they'd struck gold.

"Can I try?" she asked.

"Sure," Vance said. They moved farther down the shore. It was the perfect Nantucket summer evening—light breeze, piping plovers and oystercatchers, the sinking sun.

Vance wrapped his arms around Love from behind and spoke softly into her ear. "Hold your hands like this and push down. There you go, push." His lips grazed her ear, sending a warm buzz through her body.

Love brought up six clams.

"Show me again," she said. She loved the feel of his arms around her.

They collected a bucket of clams, and then Vance laid a blanket out in the sand. He showed Love how to hold the clam knife, how to slide it between the tight halves of the clam to pry it open. *Unlock the clam.* They ate the sweet, salty clams right out of the shell, drank a bottle of wine, and watched the sunset.

The more Love discovered about Vance, the more he impressed her. Around work, he skulked and moped and bristled with negative energy. But away from work he was sincere, kind. He had interests: he clammed and fished, and scalloped in the fall; he could play rag tunes on the piano. He'd traveled all through Southeast Asia and he knew fifty Thai words. He taught Love to say hello, *sawadee kah!*

The first two weeks there was No Sex, because Love was ambivalent about entering a relationship. Vance told her he didn't want children, but Love had hoped for a complete and total stranger—someone like Arthur Beebe—who would impregnate her and be gone. Relationships could get sticky.

The night she gave in, they were sitting in the driveway of Love's house on Hooper Farm Road after an evening at Mitchell's Book Corner (Vance loved to read; he kept a list of books and checked them off when he finished, something Love did as well). Before Love got out of the car, Vance asked her to touch his head.

"You always look at my head like you're afraid of it. So I want you to touch it." He dipped his chin, and the bare, brown expanse of his skull pointed at her, a blank face. Love hesitated; Vance's head did scare her.

"You want me to touch your head?" she said.

"Yes."

She expected it to be cool and smooth, like a marble. But it was warm, and she felt the beginnings of stubble. She ran her hands over it the way one might rub a pregnant woman's belly: what was in there? Something mysterious, unknowable.

Love invited Vance inside.

NOW, TWO MORE WEEKS had passed and they'd made love eleven times. Vance frequently spent the night at Love's place; they developed a routine, a way of being together.

Love was lying with her feet on the headboard dreaming of a tiny brown baby when Vance asked her to read his published short story.

"Come on," he said. "I want to know what you think."

"Okay," Love said. "I'll read it." There was still time before they had to go to work, and the story had been on her nightstand since the Fourth of July. Love was wary, however. Her job at the magazine in Aspen taught her all about writers and their hypersensitivity to anything that might be construed as criticism.

"Thank you." Vance whipped the story off the nightstand and handed it to Love. A ring from her water glass marked the first page.

"Are you going to watch me while I read it?"

"I'm not going to *watch* you," Vance said. "I'll read, too." He picked an *Atlantic Monthly* off the floor.

"Fine," Love said.

"Fine," Vance said.

"The Downward Spiral" by Vance Robbins

There was little hope left for Jerome. His life was closing in on him like the walls of a cramped tunnel. Jerome needed to break out before the walls crushed him, but he knew that wouldn't happen. He was filled with hate.

Jerome's life of misery began when his mother, Lula, threw his father out of the house when Jerome was in kindergarten. His father had just lost his seventh job in a row. Lula herself had had the same job since before Jerome was born. She was a car mechanic. Fiats and MGs were her speciality.

Love looked up from the story. Vance flipped through the pages of the *Atlantic*. He caught her eye over the top of the magazine, like a spy at a bus stop.

"What do you think so far?" he asked.

"It's good," Love said. "I like how the mother is a car mechanic. Is *your* mother a car mechanic?" Here was one thing about their newly established routine that baffled Love: Vance never talked about his family or his home. He seemed to be without a past. When Love asked where he grew up, he said, "Here and there. The East mostly." He had majored in American literature at Fairleigh Dickinson University in New Jersey, which he called "Fairly Ridiculous." But there was no mention of parents, siblings, or a hometown; the one time she'd been over to his cottage, she saw a picture of two people she thought might be Vance's parents standing arm in arm in front of a split-level house with aluminum siding. When she asked him. "Are these your folks?" he didn't answer.

Vance didn't answer the question about his mother either. No surprise there.

"Keep going," Vance said. "A lot happens."

He went back to the *Atlantic* and Love continued reading.

Lula worked at Hal Duare's Garage until six in the evening, and then she stopped at JD's Lounge for a bloody Mary or two before she made her way home, smelling of motor oil and Tabasco sauce. Jerome was in charge of making dinner—bologna sandwiches mostly—and he fell asleep in front of the TV. Some mornings he woke up still in his clothes, his back stiff from the floorboards. Jerome always brought home A's from school, but Lula wasn't impressed. She glanced at his papers briefly before letting them waft into the trash can.

Love looked up. "I can't believe the way some people parent."

"Tell me about it," Vance said.

Love laid the pages over her bare breasts. "Parenting is such a daunting job," she said. She pictured her egg: a girl waiting for a date.

Vance closed his magazine. "I imagine it will be."

"Will be?" Love said. "But not for you. You don't want children."

"I never said that."

"Yes, you did," Love said. "I asked you when we were on the roof on the Fourth of July, did you want children, and you said no."

Vance maneuvered his arms around Love so he was holding her. He had muscular arms and nice hands with blossom pink palms. He kissed the corner of her eye. "You know I'm crazy about you."

Love's skin itched, as if she were about to break out in a rash. "I thought you definitely didn't want children. You hate all the children at the Beach Club."

"That's an act," Vance said. "My reputation as a grump must be upheld."

"So all this time I thought you hated children, you secretly wanted some of your own."

"I could see having a kid someday," he said.

"You've changed your mind, then. I can't believe this. Men aren't *allowed* to change their minds."

"I think it might be nice to have a kid someday."

"You think it might be *nice*," Love said. "Having children isn't *nice*, Vance. It's an enormous responsibility that lasts for the rest of your life."

"I know," Vance said. "Listen, I'm not saying I want to have a baby in nine months."

"You *don't* want to have a baby in nine months," Love said. "Of course not. Ridiculous thought." Her voice was reaching its upper registers, its screechy tones. She wondered if he thought this was a pleasant surprise, like the ragtime piano. *Surprise, I love children!*

"I said *someday*, Love. Someday is a word that women don't understand. It means, *possibly*, in the *future*. Women always want to know when, when, when. But all I'm saying here is someday. Someday I'd like to get married, someday I'd like to have children. Look at Mack. He told Maribel 'someday' for six years, and now they're going to tie the knot. So, you see, someday really exists."

"You want a child someday, but not anytime soon," Love said. She waited a beat. "And maybe not at all."

"I wouldn't go so far as to say not at all. I would like a child someday. And I just defined someday. Why are we having this conversation?"

"What conversation?" Love said. She was officially perspiring. She couldn't tell him what was happening in her body; he thought she was on the pill. She wanted a baby more than she wanted to tell the truth. "Back to the story," she said.

When Jerome grew older, he became attracted to women who reminded him of Lula. Women who worked hard and drank hard, women who mistreated him. First, there was Nan. Jerome met Nan when he was fourteen and she was twelve. She would tongue kiss him one minute and the next minute she would punch his thigh and call him a fag. It wasn't long before Jerome was in love with Nan.

After Nan came Delilah, who, like the biblical Delilah, insisted Jerome cut his hair. Jerome was so crazy for Delilah, he not only cut his hair, he shaved his head.

"Wait a minute," Love said. "Our hero just shaved his head for some woman named Delilah. Does any of this ring true? Did you shave your head for a woman?"

"I told you why I shaved my head," Vance said. "I like to feel the sun."

"Jerome shaves his head for a woman named Delilah."

"That's Jerome," Vance said. "He's a fic-tion-al character."

"Would you shave your head for me?" Love asked.

"I think the question is, would I grow my hair for you," Vance said. "And the answer is yes. I'd do anything for you."

"Anything?"

"Anything," Vance said. "In fact, I've been wanting to ask what you think about me coming out to Aspen this winter."

"Aspen?" Love said. This was getting out of hand. "What about going back to Thailand? I thought that was a definite."

"That was before I met you," he said.

"Okay, wait," Love said. "Wait, wait. This is all moving so fast."

"Don't you want to give this a fighting chance?" Vance said.

"I'm not coming back to Nantucket next summer," Love said. "*This* is a once-in-a-lifetime type of thing."

"I'm not stuck here either, you know," Vance said. "If Mack can leave, I can too."

"I thought you wanted to work here without Mack. I thought that was the goal of the last twelve years. You'll finally be in charge."

"Let me put it to you this way," Vance said. "I wouldn't be opposed to moving to Colorado."

Moving to Colorado? Love froze up with fear. *Moving to Colorado?*

"Let me finish your story," she said.

"I should shower," Vance said. "How are you getting to work?"

"Blading," Love said. Vance had to be at work earlier than Love so he could supervise the beach boys. As part of their routine, he'd been driving her home in the evenings, but as far as Love could tell, no one at the Beach Club knew she and Vance were seeing each other. Everyone was absorbed with the craziness of their own lives. Jem even caught Vance and Love standing in the utility closet—they were kissing when he opened the door looking for some bleach—and he didn't seem to think finding them in the dark closet together was strange. He just stood there and said glumly, "I need bleach," and after Love handed it to him, he closed the door.

While Vance was in the shower, Love tried to finish the story, but she found herself sucked back to those terrifying words, *moving to Colorado.* She closed her eyes and saw sperm shooting through her, racing for her waiting egg. She felt dizzy. *Wait! Stop!* she wanted to say. *He wants to move to Colorado! Stop!*

Love tried not to think about it. She read somewhere that 70 percent of conception was will, a positive attitude, and so she would fight her body with her mind. She would think negative thoughts, ugly, sad thoughts. She picked up Vance's story and skimmed through the pages to the end.

Jerome goes to college and gets a degree in hotel and restaurant management. He falls in love with an Italian girl named Mia, and marries her in a big, opulent wedding with lots of uncles and homemade gnocchi and finger kissing. Jerome and Mia open an Italian restaurant called Mamma Mia's. It's a very successful venture until some of the customers start getting sick and dying. Turns out Mia is putting poison in the red sauce.

Love reread that part. Could that be right? Mia, *poisoning* the red sauce?

Jerome gets sued and the business goes belly up. Mia is indicted and Jerome spends all the money he has left on her lawyer, a man (suspiciously) named Mark Paterson, with whom Mia falls immediately in love. She wants a divorce from Jerome so she can marry Mark when she gets out of jail. She's sentenced to thirty years.

Broke and without his wife, Jerome returns to his hometown and finds his mother sitting on a barstool at JD's Lounge drinking a bloody Mary, but when he approaches her she pretends she doesn't know who he is, and when he starts to repeat, "I'm your son. It's me, Mom, Jerome," she has the bouncer throw him out.

The story ends with Jerome buying a bottle of Courvoisier and setting out to drive his Datsun into the side of the Browning Elementary School. Without question, a downward spiral.

Love lowered her feet from the footboard and stood up. She jumped on the balls of her feet. A stream of warm semen trickled down the inside of her thigh. She was shaking from head to toe when Vance came out of the bathroom, a towel wrapped around his waist.

"What's wrong?" he asked.

I've conceived. We've conceived. How easily this too could become a downward spiral. Vance suing for custody and taking away the child that was meant to be hers alone. Stealing her dream.

"I read your story," Love said, and she burst into tears.

Vance put his arms around her. He kissed the top of her head. "It's just a piece of fiction." He ran his hands down her bare back, which, much to her dismay, aroused her.

She knocked his hands away. "You have to leave," she said.

"Come on," he said. "I can be a little late. The boys know what they're doing."

"You have to *leave!*" Love was so disappointed with herself, letting this get out of hand. First he wanted to visit Colorado, then move there, and the next thing she knew he would be asking her to marry him, he would be interested in fathering the child that was only minutes old inside of her. "Get out!" she said, pointing to the door.

"You hated the story," Vance said. "You thought it was trash."

"That's not it," Love said. "Your stupid story has nothing to do with it."

"It's not a stupid story," Vance said. "It is a published story. My only published story."

"Listen, I need some space, okay?" Love said. "I see you every day at work, and I see you every night. Can you give me some space for a couple of days? Please?"

Vance dropped his towel and angrily stepped into his boxer shorts. "You hated my story. And the irony is, I let you read it because I thought you would understand. Ha! I should have known that I, Vance Robbins, am utterly un-understandable. Story of my life." He slid on his red shorts and pulled a shirt over his head backward. When she touched his arm, he shrugged her off. "I'm leaving," he said, twisting the shirt around his body. "Enjoy your space."

AS IF THAT WEREN'T bad enough, it started to rain, which immediately presented the problem of how to get to work, because Love wouldn't be able to use Rollerblades, or ride her bike. She called a cab, and as she waited for it to show up, she imagined taking an EPT and having it turn out positive. Her stomach flippety-flopped. Damn Vance! He'd ruined it. Thinking about pregnancy was supposed to make her feel elated, not apprehensive.

Love's cab was thirteen minutes late. She huffed as she climbed into the backseat.

"I said eight-fifteen." She looked at the cab driver. The short black hair, the seven silver hoop earrings. It was Tracey, the girl who had picked Love up from the ferry her first day on the island.

"It's raining, lady," Tracey said. "You're not the only person on the island who wants a cab this morning."

"I know you," Love said, leaning forward. "You're Tracey. You gave me a ride in May, remember? I showed you the Hadwen House and the Old Mill."

Tracey blinked into the rearview. "Oh, yeah." She laughed. "You're the woman who wants a baby. So what happened? Did you get knocked up?"

"This morning, I think," Love said.

"Wow," Tracey said. "Congrats. You don't seem too happy about it. What's wrong, did you boink somebody ugly?"

The girl should write a book on how to be indelicate, Love thought. "No," she said. "Worse. I boinked someone who now claims he wants a child."

Tracey backed out of the driveway. "Okay, so what?"

"I want to be a single parent. I want the baby for myself."

Tracey turned down the radio. "You'll excuse me for saying so, but that's fucked up."

"I don't expect you to understand," Love said. "You're too young."

Tracey lifted her hands from the steering wheel and held them palm-up as if to say, *I am what I am.* "Are you going to tell the guy you're pregnant?"

"I might not be pregnant," Love said. "I just think I am."

"If you were thinking for the kid, you'd tell him," Tracey said. "Every kid should have a shot at two parents. To deny the kid that is wrong. That's my take on it. If you care."

"Well, I don't care," Love snapped. Immediately, she was embarrassed. First she yelled at Vance and now at Tracey, an innocent cab driver.

Tracey was quiet for the rest of the ride. When she reached the Beach Club, Love gave her a five-dollar tip, even though this was an ugly gesture in her book: act rude and then try to make up for it with money. But what else could she do?

"I'm sorry I was short," Love said. "Thanks for the ride."

"Tell him," Tracey said.

BECAUSE OF THE WEATHER, the lobby looked like a second grade classroom without a teacher. Guests were eating their muffins and bagels and doughnuts, leaving trails of powdered sugar and smears of cream cheese on everything they touched. Someone had spilled coffee on the green carpet, and sections of the newspaper were scattered about as though the whole pile had been dropped from the rafters. Kids ran around screaming, and the phone was ringing. Vance stood behind the desk, his lips puckered.

"You're late," he said.

"Vance, listen, I'm sorry," Love said.

He raised a hand. "I don't want to hear it."

"It wasn't about your story," Love said. "I liked your story."

"Love, the damage is done, okay? Don't insult me further by trying to backpedal."

The phone rang again. Vance made no move to answer it. Love hurried through the office, hanging her wet jacket on the handle of a vacuum. She popped out to the front desk and Vance disappeared. Vanishing Vance. The phone nagged at her like a crying baby.

"Nantucket Beach Club and Hotel," Love said.

"Do you have any rooms available for this weekend?" a woman asked. "The lady at Visitor Services told us you were located on the beach."

"We're fully booked, ma'am," Love said. "We've been fully booked since early spring."

"Can you check to see if someone has canceled?" the woman said.

"Just a moment, please." Love poked her head into the office. Vance sat at Mack's desk, staring out the window. Why did they have to work together today of all days? Why couldn't he be Jem? "Vance, do you know where Mack is? I have a reservation call."

Vance said nothing.

"Vance?" Love said.

Nothing.

"Okay, *fine*," she said. She picked up the phone. "No cancellations, ma'am. Sorry."

A man with horn-rimmed glasses stood at the desk. He had a muffin crumb in his mustache. "Do you know when the sky is going to clear?" he asked.

"Do I know when the sky is going to clear?" Love said. "No, sir, I don't. You have a TV in your room. You could check the weather channel."

The man wiped the crumb off his lip and Love relaxed a little. "My wife has forbidden me to turn on the TV," he said. "This is a no-TV vacation. Which is really going to be trying if the rain persists, you see what I mean?"

"I'm sorry," Love said.

A line formed at the front desk. This had never happened before—it was as though everyone thought of a question for Love at the same time.

An older woman with two children stepped up. "I'm Ruthie Soldier, room seven," she said. "What is there to do with kids when it rains?"

"There's the Whaling Museum," Love said. "That's only down the street. There's the Peter Folger Museum. There's the Hadwen House."

"Is there anything to do that will be fun for these kids?" Ruthie Soldier said. "I don't want to bore them with history."

"Thank you, Gramma," the older child, a girl wearing multicolored braces, said. "We have to go back to school in a few weeks anyway."

"You could go out for ice-cream sundaes," Love said.

"We just ate bagels," Mrs. Soldier said. "Is there a movie house with matinees?"

"No," Love said. The phone rang. She eyed the console's blinking red light.

"What about bowling?"

"No bowling."

"Do you have any board games?"

Love tried to block out the ringing phone. "Let me check," she said. She thought she'd seen an old, mildewed Parcheesi in one of the closets. In the office, Vance was still lounging at Mack's desk.

"Vance, do we have any board games?" Love asked. "These people want something to do with their kids."

Vance smiled meanly. He was his back-at-work creepy self. Someone whom Love would not date, not sleep with, and certainly never parent with.

The phone continued to ring. Love ran back to the desk to answer it. The people standing in line crossed their arms and shifted their weight. A man still in his pajamas tapped his bony, bare foot impatiently. Where was Mack?

"Nantucket Beach Club and Hotel," Love said.

"This is Mrs. Russo. I'm calling to see if the Beach Club is open today."

Love looked out the window. The peaked roof of the pavilion created a minifalls. "It's raining, Mrs. Russo. No Beach Club today."

"That's a shame," Mrs. Russo said. "We paid so much money."

Love hung up. The line of people swarmed and blurred in front of her hand and then she remembered Mrs. Soldier. "No games," Love said. "Would you like a VCR?"

"That would be lovely," Mrs. Soldier said.

Love went back to Vance. "Room seven wants a VCR."

"They're all signed out," he said.

Love returned to the desk. "The VCRs are all signed out," Love said. The man in the pajamas raised his hand. She was the second grade teacher.

"Yes?" Love said.

"You're out of coffee," he said.

"You're kidding," Love said. Several people in line sadly shook their heads. Normally, they didn't run out of coffee until midafternoon and by then things were quiet enough that Love could make more. She poked her head into the back office again. "Vance," she said, in her most pleasant, ass-kissing voice, "we're out of coffee. Could you be a doll and make some more?"

"That's your job," he said.

"I know," she said. "But I have a line of people out here who need help. Really, a line."

Vance smiled at her again. He hated her. "I wouldn't want to *infringe* on your *space*."

"Oh, God," Love said. "Please help me."

Vance had the crossword puzzle from the *Boston Globe* in front of him. Love thought she might cry. She stepped out to the desk. "The coffee is going to be a minute," she said.

The man in the pajamas pointed a bony finger at her. He was a health-class skeleton with skin. "We pay a lot of money for these rooms," he said. He looked to the person behind him in line, as though he wanted to organize some kind of group revolt. "I heard you say there are no more VCRs. Why not? Why doesn't every room have a VCR?"

"I don't know," Love said. "It's not my hotel."

The phone rang. Love's hand itched to answer it, but she was afraid that if she did, the guests would storm the desk. The rain had turned the normally well-heeled guests into a class of emotionally needy students, into a band of ruby red Communists. Where was Mack?

An elegant-looking gentleman in an Armani suit was next in line. Love remembered checking him in: Mr. Juarez, room 12. "I have a flight to New York at ten-thirty this morning. Would you be so kind as to call and see if it's going to be delayed?"

"I'd be happy to," Love said. This man, at least, was pleasant. She liked his tone of voice. She liked his calm demeanor. She wanted to shake his hand. Gold star student.

Love called the airport and found it was closed temporarily, due to lightning.

"I'm sorry, Mr. Juarez," she said. "The airport is closed. No one is flying."

"I have a lunch meeting at one o'clock that can't be missed," he said.

"The man at the airport said 'temporarily,' " Love said. "So perhaps they'll resume flying in a little while."

"Will you call again when you get a chance?" Mr. Juarez asked. He slid a fifty-dollar bill across the desk. Love hesitated. Everyone behind Mr. Juarez was watching.

"I'm sorry," she said softly. "I can't accept that."

Mr. Juarez slipped the bill into his coat pocket. "It's yours if you get me on a flight."

The honeymooners from room 20 stepped up; behind them, the room was a carnival. "We'd like lunch reservations," the wife said. "Somewhere in town. Where do you suggest?"

Sit in your room and feed each other grapes, Love thought. *There's a big bowl of them over there*—but when Love looked at the breakfast buffet, she saw the grapes were all gone.

"Why don't you go into town and try your luck?" Love said. "I can lend you an umbrella."

"Okay," the husband said.

"We'd like a reservation," the wife said. "We'd rather not waste our time."

The husband nodded along. "That's right."

"The Chanticleer serves lunch," Love said. "So does the Wauwinet. Which would you prefer?"

"I'd prefer coffee," the skeleton in the pajamas called out. "I'd really like a steaming mug of coffee to drink on this dreary day."

Back by the piano, two boys were yelling at each other. Love looked over in time to see them hit the floor. "Whose children are those?" she asked. No one answered. "Well, they must belong to somebody." Still no one. They pulled each other's hair and started slapping and punching. "Boys!" she said. "Stop it!" Her maternal instincts rose in her like a fever. "Boys!" No one in the line made a move to stop them. Love hoisted herself over the desk, and ran to where the boys were rolling around. They were stuck together, one had a death grip on the other's hair. Love physically wedged herself between the two boys. Then, perhaps realizing that there would be no more coffee or lunch reservations until this was taken care of, the honeymooners came to help Love hold the boys away from one another. The honeymooners smiled at each other, as if to say, *Isn't this cute, a fight?* One of the kids started to cry, and the other's nose bled all over the carpet. The husband took out a handkerchief and gave it to Mr. Bleeding.

"Are you two brothers?" Love asked.

Mr. Crying shook his head. He was pudgy and sweet looking, and now he had two raised red scratches under his eye. "No. We're not brothers. We're friends."

"I'm not your friend," Mr. Bleeding said. The handkerchief bloomed with red. "Not anymore."

Love herded both boys toward the office. She didn't make eye contact with anyone in line. At Mack's desk, Vance diligently counted squares on his crossword.

"You can help these two cowboys find their parents," Love said.

"Cowboys?" Mr. Bleeding said. "We are *not* cowboys."

"You're monsters," Vance said. He meant it to be derogatory, of course. Love had never heard Mr. I Want a Child Someday call children anything but monsters, but both boys brightened up.

"We're monsters," Mr. Crying said. He stopped crying, and nudged Mr. Bleeding.

"Yeah, we're monsters," Mr. Bleeding said. He gave Love a withering look. "But we're not cowboys."

"Whatever," Love said.

Reluctantly, Vance stood up. Love returned to the desk, and she heard Vance telling the boys a joke as they moved down the hallway.

Back at the desk, Love saw the skeleton in the pajamas shaking his head.

"What's your name, sir?" she asked him.

He straightened up and crossed his arms against his chest. "Michael Klutch."

Mr. Klutch! The man who had booked rooms 4, 5, and 6 all for himself. He was staying in room 5, and the other two rooms were "buffer rooms," so he didn't have to hear his neighbors shutting their dresser drawers or flushing their toilets.

"We're going to make a list," Love said. "Put your name on the list and I'll get to you as soon as I can. I am now going to make some coffee." Love walked back into Mack's office, and the phone rang. Love tried to walk past it, but the receiver was a magnet.

"Front desk," Love said.

"This is Audrey Cohn, room seventeen. My son just came in with blood all over his face! I'd like you to call an ambulance right away. There's blood everywhere."

"It's a bloody nose," Love said. "He was out here in the lobby unsupervised and he got into a fight. All he needs is a wet washcloth."

"*Please* call an ambulance," Audrey Cohn said.

Love was glad it had come to this—sirens and flashing lights—because maybe *that* would get Mack's attention. When Love stepped out into the hallway, she bumped into Mr. Juarez.

"I didn't sign the list," he said, "because you were helping me before." He removed the fifty-dollar bill from his pocket and wound it through his slender, tan fingers. "I was hoping you'd be so kind as to call the airport again."

"Mr. Juarez," Love said. "I have to make the coffee. Please sign the list." She hurried into the galley kitchen and closed the door. There, taped to the cabinets, was a piece of paper that had been ripped from the front desk notebook, and on it, a note in Tiny's handwriting. "Beware the eight weeks of August."

Love got the coffeemaker chugging and walked back into the lobby. The guests were still standing in a line. Love slowly made her way behind the desk.

"Now," she said. "Who's next?"

Before anyone could answer, Love heard the sirens and saw red lights whip around the lobby walls. A paramedic stormed in the lobby doors, black uniformed, self-important, his walkie-talkie alive with raspy static.

"Who's hurt?" he said.

Love called room 17. "Your ambulance is here."

Audrey Cohn laughed. "Jared is fine," she said. "We cleaned him up and it turns out it was just a bloody nose. No ambulance needed."

Love retreated into the office and sat in Mack's chair. The front of her dress was sticking to her. She heard a commotion in the lobby, everyone talking at once. Then, Vance walked in.

"What's with the ambulance?" he said.

"Room seventeen had me call it for the kid with the bloody nose. Now she doesn't want it. What should I tell the paramedic?"

"Tell him you're sorry," Vance said.

"I've told everybody I'm sorry this morning," Love said. "I'm sorry it's raining, I'm sorry the airport is closed. I'm sorry we don't have VCRs, nor do we have coffee. I am very sorry!"

"And don't forget you're sorry you asked me to leave this morning," Vance said. "You're sorry you hurt my feelings."

"Of course I am," Love said. She caught his eye. "Vance, I *am*."

"I won't come to Colorado this winter," he said. "Because you only want a summer romance, is that it? No strings attached?"

"Yes," Love said. Was her egg still waiting for a date? For a mate? "Is that okay?"

Vance rubbed the top of his head. Love knew what it felt like, warm and stubbly, alive, growing in. "Sure," he said. He gave her a hug; her feet weren't touching the ground when the paramedic stormed into the office.

"Is there a problem here or *not?*" he asked.

"No, bud, no problem here," Vance said.

The paramedic spun on his heels and left the office, slamming the door behind him. Love and Vance kissed a long making-up kiss, and then she returned to the desk—but the line had dispersed, all except for Mr. Juarez, who stood patiently with his hands folded in front of him.

Love called the airport and found it had opened. "You're all set," Love said. "Let me call you a cab." She thought uneasily of Tracey. *Tell him.*

Mr. Juarez gave Love the fifty, which she tucked into her pocket. Then she poured herself a cup of coffee. Outside, the rain slowed to a drizzle; the clouds were breaking up. Love heard piano music, bright and jangly, a rag tune. Across the lobby, Vance, her summer-romance man, played her a song.

JEM WAS GLAD WHEN August arrived because that meant he was one month closer to being finished with Nantucket. As soon as he heard Maribel and Mack were getting married, he wanted to pack his stuff, buy a ferry ticket, and leave. But Jem stayed. He needed the money, but more than that, he couldn't bring himself to leave the island because of Maribel. She came to the hotel almost every day now that she and Mack were engaged, and it was pure hell to see her. The last time, she showed off her diamond ring. It was a single round stone, simple and sparkling, like Maribel herself. It nearly killed Jem to look at the diamond. It was physical proof that she was Mack's. Time to start accepting it.

As painful as it was to see Maribel, Jem was certain that not seeing her would be much, much worse. And so, when she showed up around the hotel, he was both miserable and elated; he couldn't keep from talking to her. How's work at the library? How's your mother? How's the running? In turn, Maribel would ask, How's work going? Have you been to the beach much? Been out? Met anyone? She wanted him to find a girlfriend. But he wouldn't give her the satisfaction. If he made her feel guilty, so be it; at least he made her feel something.

"No," he answered. "Haven't been out. Haven't met anyone."

NEIL ROSENBLUM WAS THE first guest to snag Jem's interest in a long time. He looked like Stephen Spielberg. He had shoulder-length gray hair and tiny frameless glasses. He wore a Hawaiian shirt open at the neck, a pair of jeans, espadrilles. He was staying in room 5, alone, for three nights. He brought a knapsack and a garment bag, and when Jem tried to help him with these, he raised a hand, and said, "I never pack more than I can carry myself. But why don't you show me the way?"

Jem led Neil Rosenblum down the beach to his room, giving the usual spiel about the chambermaids, the ice machine, the Continental breakfast. Neil wasn't listening. He stared out over the beach, shaking his head. Jem climbed the three steps to the front deck of room 5 and unlocked the door.

"Here you go, sir," Jem said.

Neil Rosenblum walked past Jem into the room. Jem waited just a minute—the Tip Linger. Neil dropped his backpack and laid his garment bag across the leather chair.

"Let me know if you need anything," Jem said, backing up. The No-Tip Retreat.

Neil Rosenblum swung around. "Wait a minute," he said. "What's your name?"

"Jem Crandall."

Neil Rosenblum stuck out his hand. "I'm Neil," he said. "It's nice to meet you."

Jem shook his hand. "Likewise."

Neil Rosenblum looked around his room. "I have to tell you, Jem, this place is just what a guy like me needs. A place to let it dangle for a few days."

"Yes, sir, I know just what you mean."

"Call me Neil." Neil unzipped his backpack and took out a couple of folded shirts, a bathing suit, a pair of flip-flops, a disposable camera, a bottle of Ketel One vodka and a plastic baggie full of weed. He held the baggie up.

"Do you smoke, Jem?" Neil asked.

Jem tried not to show his surprise. "No, Neil, not really."

Neil opened the baggie and sniffed its contents. "Too bad." He held up the Ketel One. "Do you drink?"

Jem shifted his weight and looked at the room's digital clock radio. It was only 2:45. "I have to work until five o'clock."

"But you do drink?" Neil asked.

"Yes."

"I own Rosenblum Travel. Ever heard of it? Ever seen the commercials?"

"I don't think so."

"We're out of New York—Manhattan, New Jersey, Connecticut. It's a huge business. Huge! And it's killing me." Neil sat down on the bed. "Do you know why I'm here, Jem?"

"No," Jem said.

Neil kicked off his espadrilles. "I'm here to smoke dope, drink vodka cranberries, and sit in the sun. I'm here to dabble my feet at the ocean's edge. I'm here to do things I enjoy. I am not here to talk on the phone, read faxes, listen to voice mail, or send wealthy Mrs. Tolstoy or Mrs. Dostoevsky on a luxury cruise to Leningrad. I'm leaving Tuesday morning, at which time I'll take my suit out of this garment bag and put it on. But until then, I don't want any phone calls. No messages. If you knock on my door, it should be because you want to drink with Neil Rosenblum or help me smoke some of this weed."

"Okay," Jem said. "I understand."

"He understands, he says. I hope so. I really do." Neil pulled a bill out of his jeans and handed it to Jem. Tip Success. "Come back at five o'clock and we'll have a drink. See if you can round me up some tonic, a couple of limes, a little Ocean Spray. How does that sound?"

"Tonic, limes, Ocean Spray," Jem repeated. As he left Neil Rosenblum's room, he looked at the bill. It was a hundred dollars.

AT FIVE-TEN, JEM STEPPED onto the deck of room 5 with a paper bag containing two bottles of tonic, two of cranberry cocktail, and six limes. The door to room 5 was closed. Jem knocked, and waited. Neil opened the door. His hair was disheveled and he was wearing his Hawaiian shirt and his bathing suit but not his glasses. His eyes were red. He looked confused when he saw Jem. "Yes?" he said.

Jem held the bag out. "I brought you some tonic, the things you asked for. . . ."

"Oh, right, right. God, I fell asleep. Come on in, have a seat. I was on my way to the beach, but I guess I never made it." He picked up the baggie of dope. "The guy who gave this to me is a professional."

Jem sat on the edge of the bed. He couldn't help but notice the indented place where Neil had slept.

"Do I have glasses?" Neil asked.

"You were wearing some this afternoon," Jem said.

Neil rubbed his eyes and laughed. "My eyeglasses, yes. Thank you for reminding me. I meant do I have drinking glasses? Highballs? Martinis?"

"Glasses are on top of the fridge," Jem said.

Neil made the drinks. "Shall we go onto the deck?" he asked.

"Sure," Jem said. He felt awkward, as if this were a first date. Jem accepted one of the vodka cranberries from Neil and walked out onto the deck. Jem sank into one of the deck chairs. It had been a long time since he'd had a mixed drink; at the bars, he could only afford beer. Neil sat in the other deck chair, his eyeglasses in place. It was beautiful: the water, the sun, the cold cocktail, the surprisingly comfortable deck chair. A sliver of beautiful life.

"So, Jem, tell me," Neil said. "How did you find your way to this island?"

"I just picked it off the map," Jem said. "I knew kids in college whose families had homes here and I thought I could make money."

"Are you making money?" Neil asked.

"Well, yeah," Jem said. The hundred-dollar tip rested deep in his pocket. "I guess."

"And what are your plans after Nantucket?" Neil asked.

"I'm going to L.A.," Jem said. "I want to be an agent."

Neil Rosenblum threw his shaggy gray head back and laughed. "Oh, Christ," he said. "That's just gorgeous. He wants to be an agent. He's heading to L.A. You kill me, kid."

"Why?" Jem said. He didn't love being laughed at.

"Going to Hollywood to break into the business? I didn't think people did that anymore. Just like no one goes to Paris to become a writer; it's been done. Overdone. I can tell you what's going to happen. You're going to get to Cali and work at the Bel Air or Spago until you get fed up, and then you know what you're going to do?"

"What?" Jem asked.

"I don't know," Neil said. "I don't know what you're going to do. Come back East? Get hooked up with some pretty older lady like Nicole Simpson and have her jealous ex-husband hack you into tiny bits? Join a cult and participate in group suicide? I don't know."

Jem finished his drink. Neil said, "Do you want another?"

Jem shrugged. "Are you going to quit making fun of me?"

"Ooooh," Neil said. "I hurt his feelings. I'm sorry." He disappeared into the room, leaving Jem to stare at the water. Then he reappeared with fresh drinks. "You know what I was doing when I was your age? I was backpacking through Southeast Asia. Kathmandu, Bangkok, Koh Samui, Singapore, two months on Bali. I spent a penny a night in the teahouses in the Himalayas. Four bucks a night for a room in Thailand plus all the *paad thai* I could eat. I didn't shower for a month and when I finally saw a mirror I barely recognized myself. And guess what? I was the happiest I've ever been. Now look at me. I assume you know how much I'm paying for this room—more than I spent on my entire trip through Asia! And I'm no fucking happier than

I was watching the sun go down on Kuta Beach, drinking Bintang beer. That's the truth."

Jem chewed on a piece of ice. "I've worked hard for my money this summer," he said. "I'm not going to waste it traveling."

"Waste it!" Neil said. "You wouldn't be wasting it, my friend. You'd be giving yourself something you can take to the grave. And I'm not feeding you a sales pitch. You couldn't afford my tours and you wouldn't enjoy them. I'm saying you should go on your own, while you're young. See the Taj Mahal, the Nile River, the Raffles Hotel."

"My parents are going to be upset enough about California," Jem said. "Never mind Timbuktu."

Neil looked at Jem over his glasses. "Surely you don't still listen to your parents."

"I don't want to piss them off," Jem said. "Probably sounds childish to you, but that's how I feel." Jem watched the sun sink behind a bank of clouds. "I should go," he said.

"He should go, he says. Yes, by all means, go home. Get away from the old geezer who's putting ideas in your head."

THE NEXT MORNING, JEM was standing outside watering the roses when Maribel jogged over, her body glistening with sweat.

"Hit me with the hose," she said.

Jem sprayed a light mist in her direction.

"I'm hot, Jem," she said. "I mean it. Get me wet."

"Okay," Jem said. He pulled the trigger of the hose and the water hit her chest, her bare stomach, her legs. She turned around and he hosed off her shoulders, her back, her ass, until she was soaked and Jem had an erection.

"What if I wanted to take you on a trip through Southeast Asia?" he said. "Would you go with me? We could stay at the Raffles Hotel."

Water dripped off the end of Maribel's ponytail. "You're sweet," she said. "Thanks for the shower." She jogged away. Maribel probably didn't mean to tease him, but each time he saw her inspired hope, and then the hope was shot down. It was just like his sister, Gwennie. She ate a meal, and helped Jem's mother with the dishes, drying the plates with a tea towel and nesting them away. But then she retreated to the upstairs bathroom, turning on the noisy exhaust fan. "Putting on my makeup," she'd say. When she emerged, ten, fifteen minutes later, the bathroom smelled too piney, freshener fresh.

Jem gathered up the hose and went into the lobby. Love said, "You have a message. I can't believe this. There's finally a handsome, single man staying in the hotel alone, and he's after you." She handed Jem a pink message slip that said:"Happy hour? NR." "And since you're going over there, you might as well tell him he has two messages. I put his blinker on a long time ago but he hasn't responded."

"He doesn't want any messages," Jem said. "But, whatever, I'll take them."

Love handed two message slips to Jem, and he shoved them in his pants pocket. Then he popped out the side door and read them. It was like reading someone's mail, but Jem wanted to know a little more about the guy before he had drinks with him again. The first message said, "Your girlfriend called. 11:05 A.M." and the box that said "Please call" was checked. The second message was from a Dr. Kenton. Dr. Kenton was probably his psychiatrist. Since coming to Nantucket, Jem learned that everyone in New York saw a psychiatrist. Or Dr. Kenton could be a client who wanted Neil to set up a golf vacation in Tahiti. Jem crumpled both messages and put them back in his pocket.

After work, Jem knocked on the door of room 5. This time Neil was awake, smoking a joint.

"You wanna smoke?" Neil asked.

"Sure," Jem said. First, though, he sat in the leather chair. He'd stripped this room at least twenty times, and every time he wanted to sink into the chair. It felt like a giant hand. He pinched the joint between his thumb and index finger and inhaled. He held the smoke for as long as he could, and then he passed the joint back.

"Have you given any more thought to traveling?" Neil asked. "Because I was thinking about it after you left yesterday. If you're set on Cali, that's fine, but you should travel first."

"What do you care?" Jem said. "I mean, not to be rude, but what difference does it make to you if I go or not? You said I couldn't afford your tours and I'm sure you're right."

"I care as a fellow human being," Neil said. "When I look at you I see a young person with his whole life ahead of him, and I say to myself, 'Man, if I had it to do over, I'd go back. That trip is one thing I don't regret.' "

"So because you don't regret it, I have to go?" Jem said.

Neil smoked the joint down. "If you went, I promise you'd thank me. Guaranteed."

"Do you mind if I ask you a question?" Jem said. He went over to the dresser, which had become a makeshift bar, and poured himself a Ketel One.

"Go right ahead," Neil said.

"Why did you come on vacation alone? Obviously it's not to be by yourself otherwise you wouldn't keep inviting me here."

"Why did I come alone? Why do I keep inviting you here?" Neil threw his hands over his head, fell back onto the bed and addressed the rafters. "I have problems. A few small ones and a big one and I came here to think them through. Now, sometimes you want to think things through alone, but sometimes you want another input. An impartial input. You don't know me. I don't know you. You don't have to sit here and drink with me, but you've agreed to. Maybe that's because you want another hundred-dollar tip. Maybe you're doing this out of altruism. I don't know the reason why you're here. I asked you here because I need a disinterested third party. Do you know the difference between disinterested and uninterested?"

Jem shook his head. "Doesn't matter. I'm interested."

"He's interested, he says. Okay, fine. Do you think I'm married?"

"No," Jem said. He remembered the crumpled message slip in his pocket. *Your girlfriend.* Now would be the time to pull the message out and show it to Neil, but he didn't.

"Why not?"

"You don't strike me as the marrying type," Jem said. "You seem too free-wheeling."

"I'm not married," Neil said. "I live with a woman in New York. Her name is Desirée. Desirée, desire, that whole thing. If my life were a play, it'd be called 'A Girlfriend Named Desire.' Whoa!" He wobbled a little as he stood to fix himself a drink. "We have a baby together, a little girl."

"That's nice," Jem said. He laughed, although nothing was funny.

"Desirée isn't Jewish and she doesn't want to convert. This means my daughter, my only child, won't be raised Jewish."

"Is that the big problem?" Jem asked.

"That's a little problem," Neil said. "Another little problem is whether or not I should marry Desirée. I desire her, yes, but do I love her? Do I love her enough to make her my wife? Or, do I get married for my daughter's sake?"

Jem was receiving hazy messages, mixed-up messages that weren't making it from his brain to his tongue. He couldn't speak. He remembered Maribel that afternoon, *You're sweet*. And then he realized that she came into the parking lot and left without seeing Mack. "I love a woman named Maribel," Jem said. "I love her like crazy. But she's engaged to someone else. She's engaged to my fucking *boss*."

"You love her?" Neil said. "When you wake up she's the first thing on your mind?"

"She's before the first thing," Jem said. "I dated her for two weeks. I kissed her and held her hand, and I've seen her breasts." He leaned his head back against the chair. "This woman *infiltrated*."

"I'm going to roll another joint," Neil said. He found a station with jazz music on the clock radio. "The first thing on my mind when I wake up is an image of my favorite place—Pangboche, Nepal—in the Himalayas. That place defines peace, man. That's what I expect heaven to look like." Neil rolled the joint, licked it, lit it. Jem couldn't smoke anything else. He waved the joint away. Neil took a drag and talked in a pinched voice while he held his breath. "Second thing on my mind is my little girl, Zoe." He exhaled. "There's nothing better than having a woman-child. I'm forty-two years old and I've had my problems with women just like everybody else. And then I find myself the father of a woman-child. Finally, a woman who loves me unconditionally. It's a grand feeling." Neil took another hit off the joint; Jem's head reeled just watching him. "Third or fourth thing on my mind is maybe Desirée, if I'm lucky. If you've found a woman who's your first thing, man, you should go after her."

"I've tried," Jem said.

"Have you tried ignoring her?" Neil asked. "That works like a dream."

"I can't ignore her," Jem said. "It would be impossible."

"You must do it!" Neil said. "If you want her, you must shun her."

"She wants me to shun her," Jem said. "Because she's engaged to someone else. She has a diamond ring."

"Engagements get broken every day," Neil said. "Rings get returned."

"It'll never happen," Jem said.

"You have to ignore her," Neil said. "Starting right now." He gently pressed the joint into the sole of his flip-flop. "Let's go."

They walked the mile into town, and Neil devised a simple plan: they would start drinking at the bars closest to the harbor and work their way up Main Street. And so they went: a beer at Rope Walk, a goombay smash at Straight Wharf, a Cap'n Cooler at the Bamboo Bar, vodka cranberries at the Club Car. Neil brought his disposable camera, and at each bar, he took a picture of himself and Jem by holding the camera out and pushing the button. Jem wished he wasn't wearing his clownish uniform; he didn't exactly want to be remembered as looking like he worked on the Love Boat.

When they stepped out of the Club Car, it was dark. Jem had told Neil about his fuck-up with Mr. G and he told the Mr. Feeney toilet story. He was bone-dry on funny stories, except for the Mrs. Worley story, which only now, after five drinks, seemed even remotely funny. They walked over to the Boarding House for martinis and Jem told Neil about Mrs. Worley, about the moment of shock and horror when he opened the door and found her there, shorts sagging around her ankles, the desperate expression on her face as she reached for the door. They laughed until they were bent over on their barstools, hiccuping.

"We need food," Neil said.

At Languedoc, they ordered steaks, and by the time Jem's food arrived, he realized he'd barely thought of Maribel all night.

"Here's what I think you should do about Desirée," Jem said. He was so drunk he didn't know what he was going to say next. It sounded like he was about to give Neil Rosenblum advice about his woman problem, something he was ridiculously unqualified to do. "I think you should ask her to raise Zoe Jewish—ask her nicely—and if she refuses, then I think you should raise Zoe Jewish yourself."

"I can't do it," Neil said. "The mother has to be Jewish. That's how it works."

"Oh," Jem said. "That sucks."

"Yeah," Neil said. "I'd really like to resolve this. You want to know your kids are going to be okay." He got a serious look on his face, and Jem sensed the evening about to cave in, as though all the drinking and smoking might wash over them in an unpleasant way. But then Neil rebounded. He smiled. "Let's go dancing," he said.

They caught a cab on Water Street and went to the Muse, a dark, smoky club bar with live music. As soon as they stepped in the door, Jem spotted a group of women his age. Neil nudged him. "Here we go," he said. "*Good-bye, Maribel.*"

The girls were all looking at Jem. He picked out the prettiest one—a brunette who was wearing a baseball hat backward, a man's plain white T-shirt, jeans, and Birkenstocks. Jem approached her. "I need a glass of water," he said. "How about you? Can I buy you a glass of water?"

"I'm drinking Rolling Rock," she said, holding her bottle up.

"I need a glass of water," he said. "The inside of my mouth feels like a fur coat."

The girl smiled wanly, took a swig of her beer, and mouthed something to one of her girlfriends. Probably, *Help me!* Neil talked to two blondes, both wearing black dresses. Or maybe Jem was seeing double. Neil leaned across the bar waving a twenty, then he picked up three beers and handed one to each of the blondes. Definitely two girls there. Jem suddenly felt alone. He put his hand on the brunette's shoulder.

"What's your name?" he asked.

"Dee Dee."

"I'm Jem. Do you want to dance?"

"No, I want to sit and talk."

Jem stared at his shoes. They were covered with bar sludge. He wondered what people would think at work tomorrow.

Dee Dee put her beer down. "I'm only kidding," she said. "I want to dance."

They threaded their way through the crowd. The band was loud, funky—it was music without words. That was fine; Jem was suffering from sensory overload as it was. All these people! He wedged in close to Dee Dee and started to move his arms and legs. He was dancing, he thought. Soon Neil was dancing next to him with the blondes and he snapped a picture of Jem and Dee Dee with his disposable camera.

Good-bye, Maribel, Jem thought. He wanted worse than anything to be out of this bar and at Maribel's house. He just wanted to look at her.

He shouted into Dee Dee's ear, "I have to go." He stumbled off the dance floor and out into the parking lot, where throngs of people slouched and smoked, slurred their words. A police officer waited in a car across the street.

Don't do anything stupid, Jem told himself. He found ten bucks in the pocket of his Nantucket red shorts: another tip success. That would be enough to get him to Maribel's house or to his own, but not both.

A driver for Atlantic Cab idled in front of the bar, smoking a cigarette, reading the *Inquirer & Mirror.*

"I'm going to see her no matter what you say," Jem told the driver. "Ninety-five Pheasant."

"Hey, man, I won't stop you," the driver said. "Hop in." He nuzzled his radio. "I'm at the Muse, headed for Ninety-five Pheasant. One passenger."

"Two passengers."

Jem turned around. Neil was standing next to him.

"Two passengers," the driver said. "Let's go."

They climbed in and the cab pulled out of the parking lot.

"What was wrong with the young lady in the baseball hat?" Neil asked.

Jem slumped against the cab seat. "I'm going to see Maribel. I have to see her, man."

"No, you're not," Neil said. He handed some money to the cab driver. "Take us to the Nantucket Beach Club, please."

"We're going to see Maribel," Jem said. He was going to be sick. He raised his voice. "Driver, can you pull over?"

He must have had the sound of vomit in his voice, because the cab driver responded right away. "Pulling over."

Jem puked onto the side of the road. Gravel, a little grass, his chunky vomit.

"Are you okay, buddy?" Neil asked, patting him on the back.

"Happens every night," the cab driver said. "Believe me when I say, this is better than some. Had a chick last week blow chow into the back of my head."

Neil pulled Jem back into the cab. "You can't see Maribel tonight, my friend. You're a mess. I'm going to take you back to the Club. You need a swim. You need to cool off."

"Okay," Jem said. Sour mouth, pasty mouth. Water sounded good.

JEM STRIPPED TO HIS boxers and waded into the cool water of Nantucket Sound. Water he couldn't drink. What was that rhyme? Rub-a-dub-dub? He plunged all the way in, and the water lit up around him, a pale, glowing green. It was like magic; he had an aura, a body halo.

"Phosphorescence," Neil said. He waded in behind Jem and dove into the shallow water. The water lit up around him like a force field. Neil surfaced. "There are living organisms in the water, and when we disturb them, they glow. There's great phosphorescence off the coast of Puerto Rico. I send hundreds of people to see it every year."

Jem floated on his back and looked up at the sky, the stars, the moon. His stomach relaxed, his shoulders loosened. Everything was going to be okay, he told himself. He pictured himself pounding on

Maribel's door until he woke up both her and Mack. Jem would have said something stupid and sappy to Maribel and he would have punched Mack in the face, thereby losing his job. And for my finale, lady and gentleman—vomit all over the step.

Jem found his feet and stood on the sandy bottom. Neil was off about twenty yards, waving his hands through the water like fins, watching them glow.

"Thanks for bringing me back here," Jem said. "You kept me from embarrassing myself."

"I don't know about that," Neil said. He went under and surfaced closer to Jem. He looked like a different person with his hair wet, and without his glasses. "You stranded a pretty girl on the dance floor of the Muse, and you hurled all over Prospect Street."

"Yeah, but you didn't let me see Maribel. Thank you."

"You love her," Neil said. "Your dead-drunk behavior proves it. You love her. True love always wins. That sounds like total bullshit, but I happen to believe it. You'll get her."

"You've smoked too much dope," Jem said.

Neil kicked up his feet and floated on his back. "When I told you the man who gave me the weed is a professional, I meant it," he said. "He's a doctor."

"A doctor?" Jem said.

"I have pancreatic cancer," Neil said. "I'm dying." He said this the way one might announce he's a vegetarian, or a conscientious objector; he said it as though he wholeheartedly believed in it.

The water grew cold, and Jem started to shake. He swam to shore on one breath. He crawled onto the sand and cut his toe on something sharp. He flipped onto his ass and inspected the damage in the moonlight. There was a gash just below his toenail. He was bleeding.

"I cut myself," he said softly. Tears sprang to his eyes. He felt amazingly sad, and thirsty. He needed water. He wiped a drop of blood from his toe and tasted it—ringing, metallic, sweet. Was that disgusting, tasting your own blood? He gazed out at the water; Neil floated on his back. "Hey, fuck you!" Jem said. "Fuck you for messing with me like that." He was shouting but he didn't care. He didn't care if he woke up the whole hotel. "Fuck you for kidding around like that."

Jem heard a splash and seconds later, Neil was sitting next to him on the beach. He was kind of thin, now that Jem noticed, but he didn't look sick; he didn't look like a dying person.

"I'm not messing with you," Neil said. "I'm not kidding around."

Jem wiped at his tears angrily. Why the fuck was he crying? He'd only met Neil yesterday, for God's sake. He barely knew the guy. So he was dying, so what? They were all going to die, every single person, no one would escape it. Jem was going to die, Maribel, Mack, the girl Jem left at the Muse, the cab driver, Jem's parents, Gwennie, Mr. G, Mrs. Worley. Everyone. So why the tears? Maybe because life felt good—even though Jem was miserable about Maribel, it felt good to hurt, to yearn, to want. It felt good to drink twelve drinks in one night, it felt good to empty his stomach on the side of the road, it felt good to submerge his body in the cool water and watch it shine and sparkle around him.

"This is the big problem, then?" Jem asked. "It better be, because if you have one bigger than this, I don't want to hear about it."

"This is it."

"Okay," Jem said. He dug his wounded toe into the sand, and reached for his white shirt, pulled it over his head. It smelled like smoke. He looked around for his shorts, and when he found them, he said, "You had two messages, and I didn't give them to you because you said you didn't want them. But one was from Dr. Kenton. I should have told you."

"No, you obeyed my wishes. Dr. Kenton was calling to tell me I'm not getting better."

"You don't know that," Jem said.

"I do," Neil said. "Who was the other message from?"

"Desirée."

"My girlfriend full of desire. I guess she'll be the next one to find out."

"Man, don't tell me I'm the only person who knows."

"You and Dr. Kenton."

Jem needed a tall glass of water, with ice. "Why me?"

"Have you told anyone else how you feel about Maribel?"

"I told Maribel. But that's it," Jem said.

"Well, then, why me?" Neil asked.

"Because you were there," Jem said.

"Exactly," Neil said.

Jem sat quietly for a little while, watching the water lap onto the beach. He turned around; every light in the hotel was off. Tiny had gone home long ago. He tried to picture Neil dead, closed up in a box, buried in a hole in the ground, or burned into ashes. It was impossible. After Neil left the hotel, Jem would never see him again—but that was true of all the guests who stayed at the hotel. Jem knew them for a time, and then they left, and if and when they returned next summer, Jem would be gone. That was the depressing thing about working at a hotel. No one ever stayed. How did Mack and Vance do it year after year, getting to know people and then having them leave, sometimes never to be seen again?

"I think you should marry Desirée," Jem said. "For your daughter's sake. Maybe when she finds out you're . . . you know, sick, she'll convert to Judaism."

"Maybe it doesn't matter," Neil said. "I'll know soon enough."

Soon enough. Jem wondered what kind of time Neil was looking at. Months? Weeks? More tears fell, and Jem let them go.

"You really think I can get Maribel?" Jem asked.

"No," Neil said. "Yes. I don't know."

Jem fell back into the sand; he could go to sleep right there. "I should get home," he said. He felt bad abandoning Neil, but he had to make it back to his tiny rented room. He had to drink some water. He managed to stand up and Neil stood as well and they looked at each other through the darkness. Then, as though they were meeting for the first time, Neil stuck out his hand, and Jem shook it.

WALKING TO WORK THE next day, Jem thought, *I am alive.* He could move his feet, swing his arms, hear the sound of his own voice, *Hello.*

I'm alive. He'd put some Mycitracin and a Band-Aid on his toe, and it throbbed as he walked. *I'm alive.*

Jem half expected Neil to be gone when he got to the hotel. Or maybe that's what Jem hoped for—that Neil had disappeared in the night. Jem looked for him at breakfast, but he didn't show. Then Jem got caught up in his daily duties—stripping the rooms, sweeping up shells in the parking lot, trying to clean the bar sludge from his shoes. He bought two bottles of Gatorade from the soda machine and drank them straight down, thinking it would help his hangover. He ate a bagel with cream cheese left over from breakfast, and then he asked Love, "Has Neil Rosenblum checked out?"

"No," Love said. She consulted her notebook in that authoritative way she had, as though she were consulting the Bible. "He checks out tomorrow. You should know that, he's your friend. Did you two have fun last night?"

"Yeah," Jem said. "We did."

At noon, Jem knocked on Neil's door, but there was no answer. Jem scanned the beach: No Neil. Maybe he went to town, or maybe he was still asleep. Jem went back to the front desk.

"Are you *sure* Neil Rosenblum hasn't checked out?" he asked Love. "Did the chambermaids clean his room? Did they say his stuff was still there?"

"He's here," she said. "I just saw him out in the parking lot."

Jem hurried through the lobby and peered out the front doors. Sure enough, there was Neil standing between a Mercedes and a Range Rover, talking to a blonde. One of the girls from the Muse. Jem strolled over, and much to his horror realized the blonde was Maribel. Jem hesitated; he wanted to run away, but Maribel saw him and waved. Slowly, Jem approached. Neil could be telling Maribel any-thing—what did he care if he fiddled with Jem's relationship? He probably thought that dying gave him license to say or do whatever he pleased.

"Here's our boy now," Maribel said. Jem smiled weakly. "Mr. Rosenblum was just telling me how he was going to invest in your business in California. He says he's never seen anyone with more promise."

Neil fingered his glasses thoughtfully.

"I can't believe how lucky everyone is this summer," Maribel said. "First, Mack gets a job with the Texas Rangers, and now you're starting your own business in California. Aren't you excited, Jem?"

Neil pounded Jem on the back. "Of course he's excited. We're both excited. This is the kind of guy you run across once in a lifetime."

Maribel turned pink and nodded emphatically. "I agree."

"Whoever lands this fellow is lucky. Lucky!" Neil looked at Maribel. "You should have *seen* the women after him last night at the bars."

Jem glared at the pavement; he kicked a hermit crab shell into the tire of the Rover. "There weren't any women after me."

"I'll bet there were," Maribel said. Jem raised his eyes and let himself feast on her for just a few seconds. She was wearing crisp linen pants and a white tank sweater. Her toenails were painted silver; they glinted like chips of mica.

"Did you come from work?" he asked her.

"Actually," she said, "I came down to see if you wanted to go to lunch."

"Me?" Jem said. "What about Mack?"

"It's August," Maribel said. "He's busy. Do you want to go?"

"We already have lunch plans," Neil said. "Two of those women I was talking about are waiting for us in town."

Jem narrowed his eyes at Neil. *Shut up! She's asking me to lunch!* Maribel's smiled drooped. "You're meeting women for lunch?"

"No, we're not," Jem said. "At least, I'm not."

"You are," Neil said. "These women aren't interested in me. I'm old enough to be their grandfather. They're after you, buddy. They'll be crushed if you don't come."

"You'd better go then," Maribel said. She caught Jem's eye and he almost melted in a puddle on the pavement. *I love you, Maribel!* He called out silently. *I really love you!* Maribel turned to go. "See you later, Jem. It was nice meeting you, Mr. Rosenblum."

"It was nice meeting *you*, Maribel," Neil said. He put his arm around Jem and wheeled him toward the lobby. "I know this hurts, buddy, but it's for your own good. Did you see how crestfallen she was when she heard you already had a date? I know a jealous woman, and believe me, she was jealous."

"You're an ass," Jem said. "I could be at lunch with Maribel right now."

"But you're here with me," Neil said. "And your time with me is limited. You have the rest of your life to spend with Maribel."

"And what was that about you investing in my *business*," Jem said. "That was a lie."

"Absolutely," Neil said. "I was trying to help."

"Stop trying, please."

"Do you want to come to my room for a drink?" Neil asked.

Jem plucked his shirt away from his body. "I'm working, as you can see."

"Come on," Neil said. "Take a lunch break."

"I could've taken a lunch break with Maribel," Jem said. "But you ruined it."

"I hope I'm still alive when it's time for you to thank me," Neil said.

THAT EVENING, NEIL CALLED Desirée and proposed. He did it while Jem sat on the deck, and Jem could hear the happy screams coming all the way from New York City. Neil held the phone away from his ear. "She says yes," he whispered. Jem couldn't help but feel sorry for Desirée, for the moment when her joy became shock and horror. It seemed unfair that Jem should know what was in store for her, when she didn't even know herself.

Jem didn't have the heart to drink much, and neither did Neil. He smoked his joint. It turned his pain into background music. Without the dope, he said, the pain was like someone banging on the front door with a brick.

They ordered lobsters for dinner, and baked potatoes and corn and coleslaw and biscuits. It was Jem's first—and probably only—lobster of the summer, but he couldn't help thinking of death row and how a prisoner chose his last meal. They ate on Neil's deck and watched the sun go down. It was so nice out and so delicious, it seemed like just that, an ending.

"Tomorrow I get back into the suit," Neil said. "I'll get married, set up a trust fund for my daughter, fly to Nepal and die."

"Fly to Nepal?"

"Once things get really bad, I'm going to Pangboche. I'm going to stay in one of the teahouses until the end. The Nepalese will cremate me right away and scatter me in the mountains."

Jem tore the claws off his lobster. "You know what pisses me off?"

"What?" Neil poked a fork into his baked potato. "They didn't give us any sour cream."

"You're giving up. And that sucks. You don't care about anyone else, do you? You don't care about your daughter, or Desirée, or me. If you cared, you wouldn't give in."

Neil didn't look up from his dinner, but his voice was low and serious. "I have cancer, Jem. It's all through me. I don't have a choice here, buddy boy."

Jem stood suddenly, and drawn butter dripped down his leg. "You're not upset enough. You've accepted the fact that you're going to die and that's fine with you. But what if it's not fine with the rest of us?"

"Sit down and enjoy your lobster," Neil said. "And let's have another drink. I am getting married, you know. Let's have a toast."

Jem stormed into Neil's room. The garment bag had been opened and Neil's suit was laid neatly out on the bed. It was spooky almost, prescient, the empty suit. Jem picked up the bottle of vodka and drank from it straight. He gasped for air. Horrible burning, a big fat mistake. *I'm not giving up,* Jem thought. *I will fight for Maribel until the end.* He slumped in the leather chair.

After a while, Neil came in, pushed the suit aside, and sat on the bed. He removed his glasses, breathed on them, wiped them on his shirt, and put them back on. His face had changed; it was stripped of all confidence. It was a human face, a scared face.

"What would you have me do?" Neil asked.

"Stay alive," Jem said.

"Stay alive," Neil said, as though he had never considered it before. "Stay alive."

JEM ALMOST CALLED IN sick the next day. He woke up with his hand on his erection, thinking of Maribel. Then he remembered Neil, and his insides filled with a heavy sadness. He could barely get out of bed. Neil's flight left at nine, and Jem knew he had to get down to the hotel on time to say good-bye.

Jem put on his red shorts, his last clean white shirt, his messed-up shoes, and left the house. Normally he liked the walk down North Liberty Street—it was shady, the houses were kept-after, he passed blackberry bushes, and now that the berries were finally ripe, he picked a handful and ate them. He started down Cobblestone Road. Usually, this was where he considered his day: would anything interesting happen? What would be left after breakfast? Would he see Maribel? Today he thought about Neil, and how after only three days, Neil had become his friend.

Just before Jem turned onto North Beach Road and walked the last hundred yards to the Beach Club, he heard a car horn. Jem saw Neil, wearing a suit, sticking his whole torso out the window of a cab, but the cab didn't slow down. Neil was leaving.

"Hold on!" Jem said. "Wait!"

Neil cupped his hands around his mouth and called out, "I'm on my way, buddy!" Neil's tie waved good-bye in the breeze, and the cab disappeared around the bend. Just like that.

Jem stopped. He listened to the gulls. North Beach Road was sunny and still. *Okay,* Jem thought, *so it's over. He's gone.* Jem expected the devastation to hit him any second; he took tiny steps forward, waiting for it. He thought about taking a cab out to the airport, or even asking Mack if he could borrow the Jeep and drive out there himself to say good-bye. But the road was still and sunny, the gulls cried out. Neil was gone, and for a second, Jem felt something he thought might be peace.

THERE WAS AN ENVELOPE at the front desk with his name on it.

"That man was *so* handsome," Love said. "Especially in his suit. He was single, right?"

"Engaged," Jem said. He held the envelope up to the light of the window. Definitely not cash in there. It was probably a letter. Jem thought of Neil dressed in his suit, heading back to New York to get married and settle matters for his daughter—it made Jem happy. He didn't want to read any letter that might ruin this feeling.

Jem ate two mixed-berry muffins and a chocolate doughnut and then he threw the envelope into the trash and covered it with dirty napkins and banana peels and half-eaten pieces of wheat toast, just to be sure he wasn't tempted to pull it back out. It was a very manly thing to do, he decided, throwing the letter away. A woman would never throw away an envelope unopened.

JEM SAW MARIBEL RIGHT before quitting time. She was in her yellow bikini top and her jean shorts—the exact outfit she wore on their first date to Miacomet Beach. Jem watered Therese's plants on the lobby porch and Maribel slogged up the three steps in her flip-flops, her damp beach towel slung over her shoulder.

"Too much of a good thing today," she said. "The sun in August. How was your lunch date yesterday?"

Jem was on the verge of saying, "I didn't go. It was all made-up." But he didn't want to be disloyal to Neil. "It was fun," he said.

"Yeah?" Maribel said. Jem studied her. Did she seem jealous? "Mr. Rosenblum was so nice. Is he still around?"

"Left today."

"He really seemed to like you," Maribel said. "He seemed to believe in you."

Jem stopped watering and looked at Maribel. "He did like me. He did believe in me."

"Jem, what's wrong?"

"What do you mean?"

"You look strange," she said. "You look upset. Are you all right?"

"Now that you mention it," he said, "I'm not sure." He put down the watering can, walked past Maribel, through the lobby and into the galley kitchen. He held his breath and dug around in the trash until he pulled out the envelope. It was stained with coffee, smeared with strawberry jam.

Inside was a check for fifteen thousand dollars and two one-way tickets from Nantucket to Los Angeles, courtesy of Rosenblum Travel. The note attached said: "Get her. NR."

8

Heat Wave

August 14 (not sent)

Dear S.B.T.,

I have notified the authorities about your harassment by mail. Your letters—all of which I've saved—insinuate that you've been stalking me, spying on me, spying on the hotel. The police will uncover your identity and your pursuit of me and of the hotel will be put to an end. Leave me alone!

Bill Elliott

August 15 (sent)

Dear S.B.T.,

Do you read poetry?

Bill Elliott

IN THE MIDDLE OF August, a heat wave hit Nantucket like none Lacey Gardner could remember, and she had been on the island for close to a century of summers. In general, Nantucket was a place to escape the heat because of the sea breeze. It could be in the nineties in Boston and New York, and Nantucket would be a comfortable seventy-seven. Lacey had only noticed the heat once before—in 1975, on the day islanders called Hot Saturday, when the thermometer hit one hundred degrees. Lacey and Maximilian had stayed inside, running the fans at full blast, playing cards in the guest bedroom of their house on Cliff Road, because that room stayed dark most of the day. They drank three pitchers of lemonade and at four o'clock started with Mount Gay and tonics, heavy on the ice. Lacey felt as though she were on vacation—staying in the one room of the house she never used, sliding aces and queens across the quilted company bedspread. When it grew dark, she and Maximilian slipped into their bathing suits and walked to Steps Beach for an evening swim. They felt like teenagers, sneaking around in the night, although even in 1975, they were senior citizens, and had to grip the railing tightly as they descended the stairs to the sand.

When they arrived at the beach, it was as crowded as midday. A patchwork of towels and blankets covered the beach, citronella candles flickered, and in the moonlight, Lacey saw men with sideburns holding hands with topless girls. A radio played the Beatles' "The Long and Winding Road." Some of the kids brought picnics—summer sausages, cheese, chicken salad, and cold beer. Max and Lacey ate and drank and splashed around in the water as though they were forty years younger. Lacey watched Maximilian smoke marijuana for the first time with a man named Cedar. She studied all the young people as their lean bodies floated through the hot night, and she wished again for children. She decided to say something to Max walking home. It was almost midnight, Hot Saturday turning into Sultry Sunday. She said, "Maximilian do you ever wish we'd had children?"

Max didn't answer. Maybe it was the marijuana getting to his brain, or maybe it was his same old stubbornness on the topic. His determination never to admit he might have been wrong.

THIS AUGUST WAS THE worst heat of all. In the sun it was broiling, in the shade it was difficult to breathe. The flag out in front of the Beach Club drooped like an old nylon stocking. The first hot night, Lacey tossed in bed, kicked off the sheets, flipped her pillow. Finally she struggled for the lamp and made her way over to the air-conditioner and turned it up as high as it would go. That sufficed for the night, but when morning came and Lacey ventured into the hallway, she nearly gagged. The air was thick, syrupy, a steaming Turkish bath. She opened all of her windows and switched on her two ancient fans. She kept her bedroom door closed and cranked the air-conditioning, thinking that if worse came to worst, she could lie in bed and read her mystery novel all day, refusing to step out.

Mack appeared as usual. Instead of coffee, he brought her an icy Coca-Cola.

"Bless you, Mack Petersen," she said. It was eight-thirty, and already Mack's sandy hair was wet around his ears and he had the smell of a man who'd worked all day.

"It's eighty-two degrees right now," he said. "Radio said it would top ninety by ten o'clock."

Lacey took a sip of her cola. It was so cold and crisp, it stung the back of her throat and her eyes watered. She coughed.

"Be careful in this heat," Mack said. "I want you to promise me you won't exert yourself."

"Because this kind of weather kills old ladies, is that what you mean?" Lacey said. "Well, it won't kill me. I've lived through worse than this. But just to be safe, I'm going back to the bedroom where it's cool. Knock at the end of the day to see if I'm okay, would you, dear? But just knock. I have half a mind to sit in there naked."

Mack laughed. "You got it, Lacey."

He left with a wave, and Lacey took another swallow of cola and let out a healthy belch.

"What am I going to do when you're gone?" she said out loud. "Who will take care of me?" She sounded more plaintive than she meant to, but it was a fair question. What would she do when the handsome messenger that Maximilian sent, left her? She guessed either another boy would come, or her time with substitutes would finally be over, and she would join Maximilian in whatever came next. Dying wasn't quite as scary when she thought of it this way—as the place where Maximilian was waiting.

IT WAS SO HOT that Mack and Maribel slept nude under one thin sheet. Maribel made cool things for dinner—chilled cucumber soup, Caesar salad, melon balls. She recited cool words: silver, glass, mint, shade, green, blue, drink, flute, ice, a bed of ice, a world of ice. She pulled F. Scott Fitzgerald's "The Ice Palace" off the shelf at the library, and then "The Snows of Kilimanjaro," Ann Beattie's *Chilly Scenes of Winter*, David Guterson's *Snow Falling on Cedars,* and even Richard Russo's *The Risk Pool.* She stacked the books on her desk, looking at them every so often to repeat their cool titles in her head.

Maribel and Mack fought almost every night. Because of the heat, and the crazy things it did to the hotel staff and guests, Mack shut down. He came home, took off his clothes, ate what Maribel put in front of him, and sat in a sweaty heap in front of the TV until bedtime. If he and Maribel talked at all, they snapped at one another.

Mack never mentioned getting married anymore. They didn't talk about a wedding, they made no plans. Now Maribel feared she might end up one of these women who were engaged for fifteen years. One night, she asked Mack about it.

"Are we going to get married on the island this fall? Because if we are, we need to make plans."

"I don't know," he said, his eyes glued to the baseball scores. "I can't think."

"You can't think?" she said. "I'm asking you about our *wedding* and you can't think?"

"It's hot, Maribel," he said. "All day at work I have people complaining. The beach is hot, the sand is hot, the water is too warm. We had a beach boy get sunstroke today and off he goes to the hospital. I check on Lacey every two hours because I'm afraid she's going to wilt. I caught Jem with his ass in the ice machine. He was *sitting* in the ice machine. I don't have time to think about a wedding."

"Fine," Maribel said. "Maybe we won't get married then."

"Don't play games with me, Maribel," Mack said. "Because right now nothing is funny. Including that comment."

Maribel felt tears rising and she went into the bedroom where at least the fan was on. She lay across the bed and swept every strand of hair from her neck, tucked them into a bun. She moved so that the air from the fan hit her bare neck. She had never been able to enjoy happiness because she always wondered, *When will it end? When will something bad happen?* She wanted to call her mother, but the phone was in the other room. Besides, what would she tell Tina? That right now she hated Mack? That right now the thought of a whole life with him was dreary and depressing? That maybe, just maybe, she wanted to get married so badly that she made certain compromises. Compromises like the fact that she agreed to marry Mack when only weeks before he confessed he loved another woman. Maribel tried to forget about that, she decided to believe that when Andrea Krane left the island, Mack's feelings for her vanished as well. And since Mack planned on leaving his job at the hotel there was no danger of him seeing Andrea again. But did he still have feelings for her? Maribel was so thrilled, first with the proposal and then with the ring, that she hadn't allowed this question into her thoughts. But now, Maribel realized that of course Mack loved Andrea. You didn't stop loving someone in a matter of weeks. Mack had probably proposed to Andrea first, and when she said no, he came to Maribel. She was his second choice. No *wonder* Mack couldn't think about the wedding. He didn't want to marry her at all. That scene a few weeks ago with him all sincerity and sweet promises had been a lie.

Maribel marched out to the living room. Moths threw themselves against the screen door with reckless abandon.

"Do you still love Andrea?" Maribel asked.

"What?" Mack said. He wore only his boxer shorts. Twelve years ago he had left Iowa, but he still looked like a farmer: tan neck and arms, pasty white torso. "What did you just ask me?"

"Do you still love Andrea Krane? I want to know."

"You're ridiculous," Mack said. "I just spent a small fortune putting a diamond on your finger and you have the nerve to ask me that. What's gotten into you?"

"You're not answering my question," Maribel said.

"Your question is obnoxious," Mack said. "I asked you to marry me and you said yes. I gave you a ring. Now, why would I do that if I still loved Andrea?"

Maribel winced at the word "still" because it admitted one fact: he had loved her. "That sounds like an answer to my question, but it's not. You're not telling me you don't love her."

"What's wrong with you?" Mack was yelling now, standing up. Sweat dripped down his face. The temperature in the room rose; the room was boiling over. Maribel took a deep breath, trying to remember the stack of books on her desk, the chilly titles. What were they? All she could think of was *The Risk Pool*. A pool of risk, that's where she was right now, swimming in it. The moths batted themselves against the screen. If it weren't so abusively hot Maribel would have shut the door, to block out the horrible sound.

"Do you want to marry Andrea?" Maribel asked.

Mack's blue eyes were on fire. "I don't want to marry anybody," he said.

There was a split second of silence, enough time for only a single thought. *Oh, God.*

Mack said, "But you."

Except by then it was too late because in that speck of silence, Mack had told the truth. A silence so short, so small, an infinitesimal silence, exposed him. *I don't want to marry anybody.*

He came toward Maribel, cooling off, ticking like a car engine, and he put his arms around her gently so as not to smother her. "I don't want to marry anybody but you."

He could say whatever he wanted now, she supposed, because he'd told her the truth. For one glimmering instant, the truth was free, and Maribel recognized it. She had known it all along: Mack didn't want to marry anybody.

She bent her chin to her chest, and Mack kissed her forehead.

"Are you okay?" he asked.

She pulled away. "I'm just hot," she said. "I'm sorry."

She retreated into the bedroom, threw herself on the bed face down and cried. She didn't have the genius for love—if that was what love required—genius, like one had for painting, or the piano. Genius for love didn't run in her family. And so Maribel had relied on persistence, she gritted her teeth and dug in her heels and butted her head against the brick wall until it surrendered. Her tears cooled on her cheeks. Sore head, she thought, sore heart.

CECILY WAS IN THE office with her father when he discovered his big mistake. It was too hot for her to be out on the beach; walking on the sand would have blistered the soles of her feet. The heat freed her from chatting and schmoozing, thank God, but her father insisted she join him in the office so she could better understand how he ran the hotel. Because he wouldn't live forever, he said, and she might be in charge sooner than she thought.

Bill swiveled in his chair. "I can't believe it," he said. He shuffled some papers, ran his fingertips over one page, then another. He wiped his forehead with a handkerchief. "It must be this heat," he said. "In twenty years, I have never done this. Never!"

"Done what?" Cecily said. The mercury routinely rose to ninety-seven degrees in Rio. Soon, Cecily would be sweating next to Gabriel in bed. She only needed five hundred more dollars before she could escape. Her father had called UVA trying to reverse her deferral, but ha!—it was too late. Now her parents wanted her to come to Aspen, where they would ski with her, and teach her about the hotel. It was as if they were blind, deaf, stupid. "What'd you do?" she asked.

"I can't believe it," Bill repeated. He flipped through his book of Robert Frost poems. He did it again and again until Cecily realized he was having some kind of panic attack.

She sat up straight in her chair; in this heat, even that took effort. "Dad, what'd you do?"

"I double-booked a room," he said. "I have a confirmation letter here for a family of four, the Reeses, for room fourteen, August twenty-four through August twenty-seven. And I have a confirmation letter for a Mrs. Jane Hassiter for that same room for the same dates."

Cecily fell back in her chair. "Move somebody."

He opened the reservation book and Cecily peered at it. The whole month was highlighted in fluorescent green.

"We're full," he said.

• • •

THAT WAS HOW MRS. Jane Hassiter ended up staying in Cecily's house during the heat wave. First, though, Cecily and her father called every guest house and B and B in the phone book. No vacancy. There wasn't room on the island for even one more person, a lonely widow. That's how Cecily's mother described Mrs. Hassiter, a lonely widow. Cecily's father prayed for a cancellation, but none came. Her mother tried to calm him.

"Mrs. Hassiter can stay in our house," she said. "We have the extra room, don't forget."

"The extra room" was on the first floor in the front of the house, with a window looking over the parking lot at the beach. It even had its own bathroom. But in Cecily's eighteen years, no one had ever stayed in that room. It was meant to be the bedroom for Cecily's dead brother, W.T., but he'd never slept in it. W.T. didn't make it home from the hospital; he was born dead. Cecily's parents preserved the room, though, for the ghost baby, their dead son.

"I don't think that's a good idea," Bill said.

Cecily rolled her eyes. Her parents were outrageously predictable.

"*You* double-booked the room, Bill," Therese said. "Mrs. Hassiter is on her way. There isn't any space on the island. We don't have a choice. We made a mistake, we have to pay up."

"It'll be fine, Dad," Cecily said. Both her parents looked at her as if she'd spoken Portuguese. Those were the nicest words she'd said since the Fourth of July.

Bill exhaled; his shoulders loosened. "I hope you're right," he said.

CECILY WAS STANDING AT the front desk talking to Love when Jane Hassiter walked in. Hotel guests were a mixed bag, but they had one thing in common—they all looked rich. Their watches gave them away, their Italian shoes, their haircuts. Rarely did someone step into the lobby looking like Jane Hassiter.

It was terrible to say—horrendous, awful—but Mrs. Hassiter immediately reminded Cecily of the woman who cleaned her dormitory at Middlesex. Mrs. Hassiter walked into the lobby in the same way that woman skulked around the students' rooms—as though she didn't belong in a place so fancy and nice. And then, as Mrs. Hassiter got closer, Cecily zeroed in on her tight, steel gray pin curls, her watery blue eyes, and she filled with warm dread. Mrs. Hassiter *was* the woman who cleaned at Middlesex; she was the housekeeper, the custodian, right here in the lobby of the hotel. Jane—yes, her name was Jane. Cecily had said, "Good morning, Jane," when she swept the halls with her wide broom, and "Thank you, Jane," when she cleaned the bathroom and emptied the trash. The girls on Cecily's hall bought Jane a Christmas present every year—a silk flower wreath, a subscription to *Reader's Digest.*

Cecily shivered despite the heat. The last week of school, Jane unlocked the door to Cecily's room with her giant ring of keys, and walked in on Cecily and Gabriel making love. Cecily was sitting in Gabriel's lap, facing him, her legs wrapped around his back as he lifted her up and down on his beautiful penis. They were supposed to be at breakfast, but they had skipped so that they could make love yet again. Cecily heard the jangle of Jane's keys, and before she could move, Jane stepped in, ogled them. Cecily pulled Gabriel's face into her chest as though he were a child that needed protecting and she shrieked, "Get out! Get out of here, Jane!"

Jane, what could Jane have thought? She looked hurt, Cecily remembered. She said, softly, "I'm sorry. So sorry." And closed the door.

Cecily climbed off Gabriel and cried. She cried because Gabriel was leaving for Brazil and one of their last times making love had been ruined. She cried because now there was danger of being expelled, right before graduation. And she cried because she had yelled at Jane, frightened her, hurt her. Nobody yelled at Jane. No one except Cecily.

Jane didn't report them. Of course not, Gabriel said, who was she anyway? An old woman cleaning up after a bunch of teenagers. Cecily made herself forget about the incident; she concentrated instead on the vodka parties, graduation, making a scrapbook for Gabriel. Cecily cast her eyes down when she passed Jane in the hall.

It was the world's worst coincidence that Jane, the cleaning woman, whom Cecily hoped never to see again, was the only guest in the history of the hotel ever to stay in Cecily's house. Cecily had half a mind to hide in the back office. But this was the behavior of the old Cecily. The new Cecily, the one headed for South America, faced adversity when it walked in the door.

Jane wore a plaid blouse, a pair of men's denim overalls cuffed at the ankles, and shiny AirMax running shoes. Jane walked with her head down, every once in a while allowing herself to glimpse a quilt or a painting, when she gave a tiny gasp. She looked so painfully out of place that Cecily wanted to apologize a hundred times.

Vance came in the door behind Jane carrying two brown paper bags, like the kind they used at Stop & Shop. He set them down at the front desk, practically at Cecily's feet. *Those are her bags,* Cecily thought. *This is her luggage.* She wanted to weep. They occasionally saw people like Jane Hassiter over the years, but Cecily was too young then to care or understand: Men and women who saved up their whole lives to splurge like this, just once.

"I'm Jane Hassiter," she said to Love. "I have a reservation." It was Jane's voice. *I'm sorry. So sorry.*

"Indeed, Mrs. Hassiter," Love said. "You requested a side deck room, but I'm pleased to inform you we've upgraded your room, free of charge. You're going to be staying in the proprietor's suite."

"The proprietor's suite?" Jane said. She looked at her shoes. "That's wonderful."

"Vance will show you to your room," Love said.

"I'll do it," Cecily piped up.

"Okay," Love said. "Mrs. Hassiter, Cecily here, the owner's daughter, will show you to your room."

Jane raised her head and looked at Cecily. Cecily's cheeks burned. Jane smiled shyly. "It's nice to meet you, Cecily."

She was pretending. Cecily felt both relief and disappointment. In the last five minutes, Cecily's guilt swelled like a blister that needed to be popped with sharp words of accusation. *You little slut! You ungrateful, spoiled child!*

When Cecily found her voice, it was very small. "Welcome to Nantucket."

"Thank you," Jane said. "This place, it's yours? You lucky girl."

Cecily would gladly have signed the deed over to Jane that instant. *I don't want this place. I don't want it at all.* "It belongs to my parents," she said. She picked up the paper bags and allowed herself a peek at the contents. One bag held clothes and one held a second paper bag, twisted at the neck. Cecily made her way slowly through the lobby so Jane could enjoy it. The lobby was air-conditioned, but waves of heat rose from the asphalt out in the parking lot. It was a griddle. She let Jane through the lobby doors. "We're going to the big house over there."

"Forgive my asking," Jane said, "but what did I do to deserve this? The proprietor's suite, my God!"

"It's just the way things worked out," Cecily said. Her father was posted at the upstairs window, watching them swim through the waves of heat to the house. Earlier that day, he'd read Jane's confirmation letter out loud. " 'We look forward to having you stay with us.' Ha! Little did we know what we meant by that."

Cecily didn't enter the extra room very often. There was just a double bed, an empty dresser, a regular bathroom. When Cecily swung the door open, she saw her mother had fixed it up for Jane—a quilt on the bed, two of those idiotic miniature bicycles on the dresser, fresh flowers, and a box of chocolates from Sweet Inspirations, which were probably all melted together by now. A fluffy white robe hung in the empty closet.

Cecily closed the door in case her father should come wandering down. Now that they were alone, Cecily wanted to say something. She was about to burst.

"This is just lovely," Jane said. "So lovely. I can't believe my good fortune."

"Jane," Cecily said. "Mrs. Hassiter, Jane—"

Then there was a knock at the door and Therese stepped in.

"Hello, Mrs. Hassiter, welcome."

Jane shook hands with Therese. "Thank you. This room is so fine."

"I'm glad you like it," Therese said.

"It's my dead brother's room," Cecily said. Both her mother and Jane stared. Cecily wanted to kill herself. Why had she said that?

"Cecily," Therese said.

"Your dead brother?" Jane said. "I'm sorry to hear it."

Therese cleared her throat. "Go find your father," she said. "Go right now while I talk to Mrs. Hassiter."

Cecily stomped up the stairs to where her father was standing by the bay window watching Beach Club members pull up in their Range Rovers and unload beach bags, buckets and shovels, picnic lunches.

"I think we should let Mrs. Hassiter stay for free," Cecily said. "She's not even in the real hotel. Her room isn't on the beach."

"Has she complained?" Bill asked.

"No, she's happy. But you can't charge her. It wouldn't be fair." Cecily lowered her voice. "Besides, I don't think she has much money."

"We have fifty percent in a deposit," he said. "I'd be happy to leave it at that."

"No," Cecily said. "You should return it all."

"That's what you'd do if you were running the hotel?" Bill asked.

The obvious trap. Cecily sniffed. "I'm just saying what I think you should do, as a decent person."

"Decent person, huh?" her father said. He focused back out the window. "I can't believe this heat. It's like nothing I've ever seen."

"Dad?" Cecily said.

"Okay, we won't charge her," he said. "We'll just pretend like she's an old friend."

CECILY TRIED TO GET a minute alone with Jane—to apologize, and offer this up—her stay at the Beach Club free of charge. But Jane didn't emerge from her room, and Cecily was too timid to knock. Cecily spent an hour on the beach talking with Major Crawley, the Hayeses, and Mrs. Papale, who was turning herself into a human crouton. Cecily eyed the front door of her house for Jane, but Jane didn't materialize. Perhaps she hadn't brought a bathing suit. Cecily cursed guilt, the worst of all emotions, worse than hate and heartbreak put together. Cecily not only felt guilty about yelling at Jane and having sex with Gabriel when she should have been in the dining hall, but now she felt guilty about telling Jane she was staying in a dead boy's room. It wasn't even true, technically.

AT ELEVEN O'CLOCK THAT night, Cecily's usual hour to call Gabriel, she resisted picking up the phone. She had been lying on her bed for two hours, listening for any activity that might be going on in Jane's room. She heard the water (a shower), the water (teeth brushing) and two toilet flushes. Every fifteen minutes, Cecily checked down the hall to see if Jane's light was still on. If the light was on at midnight, Cecily was going down there. It would be impossible to sleep with this guilt hanging around her neck like a medieval shackle. Cecily replayed the awful moment in her room at Middlesex again and again in her mind, wishing she could somehow change the ending, change it so that it was not Jane who caught her *screwing* during breakfast, change it so that at the very least Cecily hadn't screamed *Get out of here!* and hadn't used Jane's name, *Get out of here, Jane!*

And then, at last, Cecily heard Jane's door open, she heard footsteps in the hallway. Cecily leaped from bed and opened her bedroom door. Jane stood in front of her in a high-collared nightgown.

"I think your brother is trying to contact me," Jane said.

"Excuse me?" Cecily said.

"He's trying to contact me. He's making noise."

Cecily followed Jane down the hall and into the extra room. Sure enough, there was a light tapping on the window.

"Turn off the light," Cecily said. She went to the window and peered out into the darkness to see if the wind was knocking a branch against the pane. But there was no wind; the American flag sagged in the spotlight, impotent. No one was outside, and yet Cecily heard the tapping, so light, so faint, it was all she could do to keep from imagining a baby's fist, the size of an egg, tapping the glass, demanding to be let in. "I need to get out of this place," she said.

"This room is haunted," Jane said.

Cecily sat on the edge of Jane's bed. "It could be. No one has ever slept in here before."

"Why me?"

"My father overbooked," Cecily admitted. She forgot about the ghostly tapping and became excited that at last she had gotten a chance to apologize to Jane. "Listen, I know you recognize me. Cecily Elliott, room two-seventeen, Darwin House. You saw me and my boyfriend . . . and I yelled when I shouldn't have. I feel terrible about it, but I love him so much. It's the kind of love that hurts whenever I breathe, practically, because he's living in South America, and I've been saving my money to go see him."

"I do know you," Jane said. "You're a hard person to forget. And your boyfriend, so handsome!"

"Yes," Cecily said. Longing for Gabriel rose in her throat, like a song she couldn't sing. "Anyway, I wanted you to know I was sorry. Also, I spoke with my father and he's not going to charge you for the room."

"Oh, please, dear," Jane said. "I want him to charge me."

"What?"

The tapping started again, and Cecily wondered if this were all just a very bizarre dream, caused by the unrelenting heat, a mirage.

"I want him to charge me," Jane said. "I have to get rid of my money." She opened the top drawer of the dresser and pulled out the paper bag that was twisted closed. She turned the bag upside down on the bed.

Money fell out of the bag, money the way it appeared in the movies, in neat stacks the size of bricks. Cecily gasped: hundreds and fifties and twenties.

"Where did you get that money?" Cecily asked. She almost asked Jane, *Did you steal it?* Jane, the cleaning woman, was filthy rich.

"It was my husband's money. He owned apartment buildings in

Lawrence, and this is twenty years of rent right here. It was supposed to go to my son but he refused to take it. My son thought Jerry was prejudiced because he wouldn't rent to blacks or Puerto Ricans."

"*Was* he prejudiced?" Cecily asked.

"Yes," Jane said, sadly. "Someone with dark skin, like your boyfriend, wouldn't have been able to rent from Jerry."

"That's really shitty," Cecily said. "I told off a woman this summer because she didn't want black people on our beach."

Jane wrung her wrinkly hands. "I can't excuse what Jerry did. But I don't want the money to go to waste."

"Why did you come here?" Cecily asked. "Why did you pick our hotel?"

"I found this," Jane said. She opened the second drawer where she had put her clothes. She pulled out a Nantucket Beach Club and Hotel brochure with the picture of the pavilion and the five blue Adirondack chairs, and handed it to Cecily. "I found it when I was doing the final clean at school."

"You found it in my room?" Cecily said.

"Must have been," Jane said. "I was pretty sure I'd recognize someone around here, but I didn't know it'd be you." Jane patted Cecily's hand. "I'm glad it was."

"Me too," Cecily said.

"How much money do you need to see your young man?" Jane asked.

"Five hundred dollars," Cecily said.

Jane counted out ten fifties and pressed them into Cecily's palm. "There you go," she said, "a little graduation present from old Jane."

Again, the tapping. Cecily closed her eyes and listened. Maybe it wasn't W.T. at all. Maybe it was Gabriel knocking, beckoning to her from far away.

"I can't take this," Cecily said. "I really want to but I can't."

Jane frowned. "You feel like my son, then? Won't take the money because it's tainted?"

"Sort of, yeah." Cecily thought of Mrs. John Higgens, and let the bills flutter to the bed.

Jane walked back to the dresser and pulled out her wallet. "I have four hundred and eighty-six dollars here from my last paycheck from Middlesex," she said. "Will you take this?"

Jane's paycheck, that she earned by cleaning up after Cecily and her classmates? It seemed strange to take that money, too, but at least it wouldn't be unethical. Cecily could fly to New York first thing in the morning, and she'd be on her way to Rio before her parents even realized she was gone. It was thrilling, and positively terrifying. Terrifying! She couldn't do it. But then Cecily thought of Gabriel, the way he cupped her face when he kissed her, the way his smile spread slowly across his face like a sunrise.

"Thank you, Jane," Cecily said.

"Where are you headed again?" Jane asked.

"Rio de Janeiro," Cecily said.

And with those words, she was free.

THERESE KNEW THE SECOND her baby boy died inside of her, and she knew as soon as her feet hit the ground in the morning that Cecily was gone. The house sounded hollow beneath her feet; it sounded like a house without children. She didn't let herself panic until she checked Cecily's bedroom, however, because in this heat, her instincts could be wrong. Therese tiptoed down the stairs so as not to wake their guest, Mrs. Hassiter. Knocking lightly on Cecily's door, Therese said, "Honey, are you in there?"

No answer, but that didn't mean anything. Cecily was probably still asleep; she didn't have to be on the beach until ten.

Therese was halfway up the stairs when she caught her reflection in the mirror. *Fooling yourself*, her reflection said. She marched back down to Cecily's room and opened the door.

Cecily's bed was made, the room neat and clean. It was a teenager's dream room: queen-size bed, TV, stereo, built-in bookshelves that held Cecily's schoolbooks and her field hockey trophies. There was a spartan desk—built to Cecily's specifications—an old hotel door sitting on two filing cabinets. A framed black-and-white photograph of the Beach Club circa 1928 hung over Cecily's bed. On the nightstand was a hotel envelope, the kind guests left tips in for the chambermaids. On the front, in Cecily's youthful hand, it said, "Mom and Dad."

Therese sat on Cecily's bed, picked up the envelope, and held it in her lap. Her hands trembled.

Therese knew all about running away. She'd practically done the same thing on her eighteenth birthday when she took the Long Island Railroad from Bilbo to Grand Central Station, her father's World War II army bag slung over her shoulder. She was only sixty miles from home, but it might as well have been another continent— her orderly, cookie-cutter neighborhood left behind for Manhattan. She would never admit it to Bill, but she understood why Cecily wanted more. Cecily was her mother's daughter. Forty years ago, Therese had gone searching for beauty, and found love. Cecily searched now for love—maybe she would be lucky enough to find beauty. Maybe: if she didn't get killed or end up in jail or contract some appalling disease.

Therese opened the envelope.

Dear Mom and Dad,

I'm sure you two are pissed like never before, and I'm sorry. You are great parents and I understand why you didn't want me to go. But I had to chase this feeling because it's the best feeling I've ever had. You two love each other, think of life without that and you'll under- stand why I left. I'll call to let you know I'm okay, but don't come after me because it will be an impossible search. I love you both and I'm sure you think leaving is easy for me, but trust me, it isn't.

Love, Cecily

Therese scanned Cecily's bookshelves for her yearbook, and when she brought it down, the book fell right open to Gabriel's picture.

Gabriel da Silva: He was filed under *S*. Therese studied his picture with a dissonant, high-pitched whine in her ears, like something caught in a vacuum cleaner. Gabriel was astonishingly handsome. Toasty brown skin, black hair, a diamond stud in his left ear. Perfect straight white teeth in the kind of smile that singed the page. He'd signed the yearbook next to his picture—something in another language, Portuguese?—and then: "I love every inch of you. Gabriel da Silva." Therese stared at the words. I love every inch of you. The words of a lover, forcing Therese to imagine the secret, soft inches of Cecily that Gabriel loved. But then, after that intimacy, he signed his full name. Therese held the book open and put the words and the picture together. *I love every inch of you. Gabriel da Silva.*

THERESE DIDN'T TELL BILL where she was going—he was in the kitchen eating his cereal. She left the house with a wave, and said, "I have to run a quick errand. Back soon." Mrs. Hassiter hadn't stirred and Therese was relieved; she didn't feel like explaining anything yet.

Outside, the air was thick as chowder. Therese cranked the air-conditioner in her car and opened all the windows on the way to the airport. She couldn't remember the last time she had left the property on a summer morning; always, her first concerns were the rooms, the chambermaids, and guests with problems more pressing than her own. But now Therese appreciated the morning, even though it was hot, and the lawns were turning brown and the hydrangeas had dried up into crisp little heads. It was nice to be off property. A lone jogger dripping with sweat plodded down North Beach Road. It was Maribel. Therese wanted to stop and ask, "Have you seen Cecily?"—but she flipped down the eye shade and accelerated.

At the airport, Therese searched for Cecily in the ladies' room, the gift shop, the restaurant. Not there. Then Therese surveyed the local carriers. When she asked at Colgan—Any young redheads on a plane to New York this morning?—the perky attendant bit as though Therese was holding out an apple. "You *must* be her mother, you two are, like, identical twins! I mean, gosh, you have the same hair. I guess people tell you that all the time."

"So she made her plane then?" Therese said. "Good. What time did it leave?"

The girl checked the board behind her. "She was on the first plane. The six-oh-five. It was early, I remember that!"

"And that was to New York?"

The girl bobbed her head. "La Guardia. I think she had a transfer to JFK, though."

"Thanks for your help," Therese said.

"Where was she headed, anyway?" the girl asked. "In the end, her final destination?"

Her final destination? Therese swallowed. "Brazil," she said.

Therese ordered breakfast in the restaurant. As she ate her eggs, she considered taking a poll of other mothers. *Do I get on a plane and go after her, or do I let her go?* Therese thought back to all the guests she had advised with their personal problems, guests like Leo Hearn. *No, Leo,* she thought, *there is no instruction manual for parents. I made it all up.* She bit off the corner of her toast and saw Cecily at a year and a half, toddling by herself through the sand, falling over onto her hands. Cecily at thirteen, the night of her first kiss, climbing into bed with Therese to tell her all about it. They were so close, identical twins, motherdaughter. And yet in only a couple of hours, so much distance between them. Where was Cecily? In another country, sleeping with the dark prince.

Out the window, a small propeller plane got ready for takeoff. The props spun, there was a lurch, and then the plane rolled forward, picked up speed, until just barely lifting its nose and soaring, soaring. There were a million metaphors for childhood, and here was one of them right outside the window. What could Therese do but hope that somewhere, Cecily was soaring?

"ARE YOU *KIDDING* ME?" Bill shouted. They were upstairs in the living room, and as far as Therese could tell, Mrs. Hassiter hadn't stirred.

Bill waved the letter in the air. His face was bright red and his hair glittered from silver to white; he was aging in front of her eyes.

"Your heart," Therese said. "Bill, please. I can't lose you, too."

"Why do you look so calm?" he said. Suspicion flickered across his face. "You knew, didn't you? She's your daughter, Therese. She's always been your daughter. She confided in you and you let her go."

"Not true," Therese said. But she did feel preternaturally calm, as though someone had drugged her. *I love every inch of you.* Therese never kept secrets from Bill, but she didn't show him the yearbook. "I had no idea! I just went to the airport to see if I could catch her."

Bill checked his watch. "We're going back right now. There's no way she's made it out of New York yet. International flights leave at night. We have all day to turn JFK upside down."

"You're thinking of west-east flights," Therese said. "Those leave in the evening. North-south flights leave in the morning." She had no idea if this were true; she didn't even know where the thought had come from.

"We'll go anyway," he said. "We're irresponsible parents if we don't. I'm sure she wants us to come after her."

"Bill, come here and sit down." Therese led him to the couch and he sat down despondently, his hands in his lap. Then, with a sudden burst of energy, he bounced up again.

"There isn't time to sit down," he said.

"We're not going to New York," Therese said.

"Cecily is *expecting* us," Bill said. "She's probably lingering at her gate, waiting for us to march down the concourse. This isn't the kind of thing you hope to get away with at the age of eighteen."

"There's only one person she wants to see," Therese said sadly. "And it's not you, and it's not me."

"I can't even *think* about that boy," Bill said. "If I think about that boy, I'm going to lose my mind."

"She's living her life, Bill."

"You're in cahoots with her," he said.

"No, it's just . . ." How to explain this feeling? Therese was worried, but seeing the picture of Gabriel da Silva excited her, too. And she hadn't expected to feel excited. Her daughter was alive and *living*. When Therese left home, wonderful things happened. She ended up here. "I thought Cecily leaving would kill me. But I feel okay. It's like anticipating her leaving was ten times worse than her actual leaving. She's *gone*, Bill. We're through worrying about how to keep her here. We're *liberated*, in a way."

"You're nuts," he said. "Cecily hasn't gone to overnight camp, my dear. She hasn't left for college, or another relatively safe place where we can get a hold of her. She has flown to *Brazil* to sleep with a boy we've never even met."

"I guess what I'm saying is that I know she's coming back," Therese said. "Unlike W.T., Cecily is coming back."

Bill collapsed on the sofa. "Oh, God," he said.

Therese heard soft footsteps on the stairs and Mrs. Hassiter popped into the living room. She looked at Therese expectantly.

"Breakfast is in the hotel lobby, Mrs. Hassiter," Therese said. "It's our compliments. Just go on over and help yourself."

"I already had breakfast," Mrs. Hassiter said. "I want to talk to you about something else."

So she'd overheard them. "We're having a bit of a family situation," Therese said. "Things might be rather hectic. I apologize."

"I understand," Mrs. Hassiter said. She looked at her hands. "I understand because I have a child of my own."

Therese got a funny twitching in her stomach. "Did you see my daughter this morning, Mrs. Hassiter? Did you see her last night?"

Mrs. Hassiter's pale blue eyes sought Therese's, then Bill's, helplessly. *Oh, dear God,* Therese thought. *She has some part in this.* But before Mrs. Hassiter could answer, Bill pointed his finger; his voice was tight and sharp.

"Do you know where our daughter is?" he asked. "Do you?"

Mrs. Hassiter nodded slowly. "I wasn't thinking as a parent last night. But these kids seem so grown-up. Much older than my own son at that age."

"What did you do?" Bill asked. Therese dug her fingernails into the buttery leather of the couch. "What did you do to Cecily?"

Mrs. Hassiter took a deep breath. "I gave her the money to go."

Therese felt all her previous calm fly from her, like her soul leaving her body. Gave Cecily the money! They let the woman into their home and she interfered with the delicate balance they had worked so hard to achieve. She tipped the scales in favor of Cecily and off Cecily went—with a stranger's money in her pocket—to Brazil.

Bill spoke first. "The nerve of you," he said. "You had no place doing that."

"I know," Mrs. Hassiter said. "I realized that this morning. I should have just let things be. But I was possessed by pride."

"By pride, Mrs. Hassiter?" Bill said. "What is *that* supposed to mean?"

Mrs. Hassiter looked at both of them, then her eyes took in the rest of the room: the leather couch, the Turkish rug. "I'm a janitor at your daughter's private school," she said. "At Middlesex. I clean the rooms. I've been doing it for twenty-one years."

"You know Cecily from Middlesex?" Therese asked.

"We didn't know each other well," Mrs. Hassiter said. "And I didn't know you folks owned this hotel. But when I saw your daughter here, I couldn't help myself. Those kids never thought much of me. They were always polite, but they thought of me as the cleaning woman. And they were all so young and beautiful and well-to-do. I wanted to prove I was good for something other than changing your daughter's linen and cleaning the toilets. So I gave her four hundred and eighty-six dollars. It was money I earned."

"Well, I hope you're *happy*!" Bill shouted. "Because here we sit without our daughter. We've been stripped of all our options, Mrs. Hassiter, thanks to you."

"I'm sorry," Mrs. Hassiter said.

"That doesn't fix a goddamned thing!" Bill said.

"Bill," Therese said. She squeezed his hand; she had never seen him this angry before. Therese looked at Mrs. Hassiter—her shoulders slumping, her feet bright and unlikely in a pair of fancy sneakers.

The thought that a woman this age felt she had to prove something to Cecily broke Therese's heart. She tried not to let herself soften toward Mrs. Hassiter, but she couldn't help it. The woman gave Cecily the money; in the end, she only expedited the inevitable. "There's nothing wrong with being a cleaning woman," Therese said. "I'm one myself. It's a job I respect."

Mrs. Hassiter looked at her hands again, as though she were ashamed of them. "It's not the same. You own this beautiful place."

"It is the same," Therese said. "In fact, you can do me a favor."

"What is it?" Mrs. Hassiter asked.

"I need you to supervise my chambermaids this morning while I take my husband out. Then you'll see how much our jobs are alike. And just so you know, I would only trust my job to a professional."

Mrs. Hassiter pushed up her sleeves. "I'd be glad to," she said. "I'll go right now."

THERESE SAID NOTHING TO Bill until they were both in the car and Mrs. Hassiter had safely reached the lobby. Therese turned the key in the ignition, set the air-conditioning, and adjusted the vents so that they blew directly onto herself and Bill. "I know you're mad at me," she said, backing out of the parking lot. "But I won't let myself blame that poor woman."

"I don't blame the woman," Bill said. "I blame myself for double-booking the room. There's a reason why we don't let strangers sleep in our home, Therese. They don't belong."

"Don't be angry with Mrs. Hassiter."

"She tells a sob story and that's all you need to hear. She's a saint now and a martyr."

"I feel for people, Bill," she said.

"If you're going to feel for people," Bill said, "how about starting with Cecily and me?"

"I have always put you first," Therese said. "Every day for thirty years I've put you first, and you know that." She turned onto Main Street, which was bustling with activity, and she was grateful for the distraction. "I can't remember the last time you and I were on Main Street on a summer day," she said. She pointed out the Bartlett Farm truck, its sectioned bed bursting with red and yellow tomatoes, zucchini and squash, string beans, lettuce, and a colorful array of flowers, which bloomed despite the heat. "Look over there. Bountiful summer."

"My summer hasn't been bountiful," Bill said. "First I lose Mack, then my only child."

Therese gripped the wheel with both hands as they rumbled over the cobblestones. "She's coming back."

"Where are we going?" Bill asked. "I see you're not driving to the airport."

"No," she said. "I'm not."

They reached the Somerset Road Cemetery and Therese wound her way through the sandy paths until they came to W.T.'s grave. Bill gave a little groan and smacked his head back against the seat. "You're trying to torture me."

"No," she said. "I just want to remind you what real loss feels like."

They stood together on the patch of dry grass in front of the headstone. Therese read the inscription aloud. "W.T. Elliott, beloved son, April seventh, 1970.' " Then, as if she had given them permission, they both started to cry. Bill pulled out his handkerchief and held it to his nose as his body wracked with sobs. Therese cried into the crook of Bill's arm. At one point, she gained a moment of clarity, enough to wonder what they must look like: two middle-aged people standing in the hottest Nantucket sun on record, crying for someone who died such a long time ago, someone they had never even known.

After a while, Therese let Bill go. She plucked her blouse away from her sweat-soaked body and flapped her arms as if she were a bird, as if she could fly. Then she took a tentative step toward the car. Sweat rolled down her back, and the edges of her mind were blurry with the tears, the grief, and from standing still for too long in the heat. Blurry from wondering—*would* Cecily be back? Or would they be left to cry in graveyards. Nobody's parents.

"You know what I want more than anything else?" Therese said.

"What?" Bill said.

"Rain," she said.

IT WAS SO HOT in Love's Hooper Farm Road house that she had to try the early pregnancy test three times. At dawn, she peed into a plastic cup, and then got ready to dunk the test strip to see if it changed color. The first strip stuck to her sweaty fingers like flypaper, and when she tried to unstick it, it ripped in half.

"Good thing they give you more than one chance," Love said. She'd been talking to herself since she woke up that morning. She treated her second test strip more delicately. It was supposed to turn pink (positive) or blue (negative) when she dipped it in the urine. But the second strip turned green as soon as she picked it up. Green! She dipped it gingerly into the urine, hoping the green would magically change, a frog turning into a prince. But no—it stayed a disappointing, sickly green.

Love hopped on her Cannondale and rode back to the Stop & Shop—the only place carrying early pregnancy tests that was open at six thirty in the morning—and she plucked another test off the shelf. Unfortunately, the sole cashier was the same young man Love went to an hour before, when she bought her first test.

"That's right," she said. "I need another one."

The cashier might have looked at her with understanding, or he might have made a gagging face, as if to say, *Too much information, ma'am;* Love couldn't meet his eyes to find out. *I could be pregnant!* she almost said. But, of course, he would realize that. Love managed to keep her mouth shut until she paid another eighteen dollars and hurried from the store.

BEFORE SHE DIPPED THE third strip, Love washed her hands and dried them thoroughly. Then she pinched the strip between her fingernails and dunked it like a doughnut. She laid it on the little resting pad provided. Now she had to wait—five minutes, the instructions said.

She had to wait.

Love walked out into the hallway, through the kitchen, to the small living room that faced the road. She sat on the dingy sofa and stared at the blank wall in front of her. Her roommates, Randy and Alison, were still asleep.

"I've never actually sat in this room before," Love whispered. "Probably a good thing." The room was perfect for waiting because of the innocuous rentedness of it—an ugly sofa with two rock-hard cushions, a braided rug, a TV with nonfunctional, rabbit-ear antenna. It was as sterile as a doctor's waiting room—nothing to excite or agitate, perfect for thinking.

Love had missed her last period. At first she thought she was just late, normal for her because she exercised so much. After a week, late became a miss. But Love wouldn't let herself get excited until she knew for sure. Her other symptoms could easily have been caused by the heat. She went to the bathroom more frequently—but she also drank water all day to keep from dehydrating. She felt dizzy and tired, but who wouldn't after skating in ninety-five-degree heat, 100 percent humidity? She vomited once—but that was after eating sushi, and in this heat the fish was probably spoiled. Love couldn't tell if she was pregnant, or just hot, like everyone else.

She checked her watch. Four minutes, twenty-six seconds. She made herself stand up.

"Good-bye living room," she said.

Then something caught her eye. On the wall behind the sofa was a picture the size of a baseball card. Love stepped closer to take a look, then recoiled. It was a photograph of an Indian swami, a brown-skinned man wearing a white turban, his hands in front of him in prayer, a mean-looking snake around his neck. Underneath the picture it said, *"Pray with Swami Jeff."*

Swami Jeff? Maybe Alison or Randy tacked the card to the wall as some sort of joke. The man's dark eyes penetrated Love and she shivered. He frightened her. She took the picture off the wall and held it in her hands. She wanted to throw it away. But instead Love raised the picture in front of her face and kissed Swami Jeff right on the lips. *You want me to pray with you, I will. I want a baby, Swami Jeff. Please, I want a baby!* She put the picture of Swami Jeff facedown in a kitchen drawer with the can opener and measuring spoons, and then bravely she walked into her room.

The strip was pink. *P* for pink, *P* for positive.

Love snatched up the resting pad. The strip was bright pink, lively pink, the pink of a healthy internal organ. There was no doubt about it. Love was *P* for pregnant.

She wanted to scream and shout and dance. She wanted to wake up Randy and Alison and tell them the good news. And what, *what* could be better news than this: another person coming into the world! A goal accomplished. A dream come true. She was pregnant!

Then, for just a second, Love experienced sheer terror. What made her think she was remotely qualified to be a mother? Or ready? So she was forty years old, so what? A person would have to be fifty or sixty to have the knowledge to raise another human being. It was an irrevocable thing she had just done. There was no going back.

She sat on her bed, and thought of Vance, who often slept with her there. Last night he'd declined because of the heat. What was she going to do about Vance? Love went back into the kitchen. She opened the drawer where she'd put the picture of Swami Jeff. Her knees buckled and she sucked in her breath. Through the holes of the cheese grater, Love saw Swami Jeff's intense black eyes; the picture was *face up* in the drawer. She nudged the cheese grater aside. Swami Jeff stared at her. Love shut the drawer. She was *positive* she'd put the picture in facedown. (*Positive,* she thought, *I'm positive.*) Love opened the drawer again and picked up the picture. She took Swami Jeff into the bedroom.

Okay, Swami, what am I going to do about Vance? Shall I tell him or not? She stared at Swami Jeff's face and tried to ignore the snake curled around his neck, baring fangs. She closed her eyes and pressed the picture to her forehead.

What was she expecting to see? A vision, maybe—a scene from the future, like a film clip—Love walking down Durant Street in Aspen pushing a stroller. Was Vance in the picture? That was what she wanted to know. But there was no scene, no vision at all. Love held the picture of Swami Jeff in front of her and neatly ripped the card down the middle, slicing him between the eyes.

Vance met Love in the parking lot of the Beach Club as she was locking up her bike.

"How was your night last night?" he asked. "I was thinking of you."

"Uneventful," Love said. "An absolute bore. A hot bore."

"I have some news," Vance said. "Big news."

"Big news?" Love asked. She hoped he wasn't about to propose coming to Colorado again. She hoped he wasn't about to propose anything. She shut her eyes, but saw nothing. "What is it?"

"Cecily's gone," Vance said. "She got on a plane and flew to Brazil without telling a soul. Bill said he and Therese woke up yesterday—and boom, Cecily was gone. She left them a note. The guy is really bumming."

"Poor Bill," Love said.

Vance shrugged. "I think it's only natural," he said. "You have kids and then at some point they leave the nest. What can you do?"

Instinctively, Love touched her abdomen. "You might feel differently if you had your own child," she said.

"My kids are going to be out of the house by eighteen," Vance said. He took out a navy bandanna and wiped his head. "But, listen, I don't want to talk about having kids right now."

I don't want to talk about having kids right now.

Love made a decision: She would tell Vance about the baby if she went home and found the picture of Swami Jeff restored to a whole.

"Me either," she said.

ON HER WAY TO the front desk, Love peeked into Bill's office. He sat at his desk with his eyes closed, his hands folded in front of him. The volume of Robert Frost was nowhere to be seen. *We are at the two ends of parenthood,* she thought. *I have just started to hold on, and Bill is letting go.* She wondered what that kind of pain must feel like. She couldn't imagine.

• • •

WHEN MACK HEARD CECILY was gone, his hand itched to call How-Baby and turn down his brand-new job. Bill was bereft, a man lost at sea, his heart floating on a refugee raft somewhere between Nantucket and Rio de Janeiro. Bill, his almost-father. Mack admired Cecily's courage for leaving. He'd run away once, twelve years before, but then Mack had run from emptiness. Cecily ran from a home where people loved her. When his turn came, Mack wondered, would he be brave enough to go?

JEM CALLED MARIBEL AT the library.
    "If you don't want to go to Southeast Asia, how about Brazil?"

THE FUNNY THING WAS, Maribel had just scoured the shelves for novels about Brazil, and finally found one by Jorge Amado called *Gabriela, Cinnamon and Cloves*. She hid in the stacks and read several passages, thinking, *This doesn't sound bad. This doesn't sound bad at all.*

"IT'S HOTTER IN BRAZIL than it is here!" Lacey exclaimed, when Mack told her of Cecily's escape. "What was the dear girl thinking?"
    Secretly, Lacey was elated. She was all for chasing a dream; she was all for chasing love.

BILL PUT HIS VOLUME of Robert Frost back on the shelf in his bedroom; it had done him no good. His daughter was gone, Mack was leaving, Bill's health was slipping away, and what did his wife want more than anything else? Rain. In the end, Bill decided, it was very Frost-like of Therese. To stare in the face of all this emotional anguish and want nothing more than a simple rain.

9

September

Dear Bill,

I am not one to say 'I told you so,' however, I do believe the abrupt departure of your daughter should send you a clear message. She isn't interested in the hotel, as I suspected. She has deserted it, and you. Your manager, Mack, is in line to leave next if you don't do something about it. The time has never been better for you to sell. What are you waiting for? A sign from God?

S.B.T.

SEPTEMBER: IT USED TO be Bill's favorite month of the year. After Labor Day weekend, the Beach Club closed and the property quieted down; it gained serenity. But Bill couldn't enjoy September without Cecily. He couldn't stomach listening to one more back-to-school-sale commercial on the radio, knowing that Cecily wasn't matriculating at the University of Virginia that fall. Bill didn't know where Cecily was or what she was doing. He had a horrible, recurring image: Cecily wandering through the streets of Rio, trailed by a gang of brown-skinned Brazilian boys wearing gray camouflage, carrying switchblades and razors, intent on raping and killing her.

He read and reread his latest letter from S.B.T. Who the hell was this guy, some kind of spy? That ass Comatis who had hired away Mack? Bill ran through the list of Beach Club members, but he came up empty. One thing was for sure: the letters from S.B.T. were eating at him. *What are you waiting for? A sign from God?* Yes, he thought. Exactly.

Bill had lost all his energy, and worse, his chest pain returned, a dull ache around his heart. He missed his daughter and he feared for the future of his hotel. The only thing he could do with ease was lie in bed with the remote control, flipping between channels to make sure there were no news stories about young American girls raped and killed abroad. It was far easier to watch TV than it was to read poetry. TV was colorful, silly, full of laughter and melodrama. TV made Robert Frost seem as exciting as a pile of dry twigs. Mornings after Cecily had left, Bill let himself get sucked into the TV.

That was how he first heard about Freida.

September 8, the Tuesday after Labor Day, Frieda was born in the West Indies. The National Hurricane Center in Miami posted a bulletin: She was a mean storm. The newscasters on the weather channel showed fancy graphics—Freida, a swirling, multicolored eye, 210 miles wide with sustained winds of 93 miles an hour, moving up the eastern seaboard. They expected her to make landfall around Cape Hatteras, but the following areas could expect trouble from Freida as well: the Chesapeake Bay, Long Island Sound, Nantucket. *Nantucket.* The newscaster said the name of the island and Bill felt a surge of recognition, as though his own name were being spoken aloud on national TV. He wondered if Cecily was listening.

"Nantucket?" Bill said.

"Of course the storm may miss Nantucket altogether and head northeast out to sea," the newscaster said.

BY THE TIME BILL made it down to the lobby, everyone was abuzz about Freida's arrival. Love talked to a couple about where the experts tracked Freida, and how she might move along, or might lose energy and scatter, dissipate. They discussed Freida as though she were a person. Was she organized? Did she have weak spots?

Mack waited in Bill's office, tensed, pumped up, ready to pounce. "Did you hear?" he said. "We're going to get creamed."

Out the window, it was the perfect September day, though still hot at eighty-five degrees. The sky was blue, the water flat. No clouds.

"We'll see. They said it might veer off into the North Atlantic. That's what they usually do. This island hasn't seen a bona fide hurricane since 1954."

"What's our plan of attack?" Mack asked.

A wave of exhaustion swept over Bill. It was ten-thirty and he wanted to put his head on the desk and sleep. "We're not going to do anything."

"What do you mean?" Mack said. "We have to board up. We have to bring everything inside. It's a hurricane, Bill."

Bill took a deep breath and closed his eyes. The Brazilian boys were gaining ground on Cecily, getting closer. They were after his daughter. Somehow, Bill had to flush that image.

"Bill?" Mack said. "Freida is going to hit the island from the west. She's two hundred miles wide. Do you realize how big that is?"

"It sounds like you *want* this hurricane to come," Bill said. "It sounds like maybe you want to watch the place get flooded. That would be fun for you, wouldn't it? Watch the place wash away and then take off for Fenway Park."

"You've got to be kidding me," Mack said. "I don't *want* the hurricane to come. But I'd like to be ready. There are people sitting in the rooms, facing the water."

"What do you care if the hotel gets wrecked? You're leaving at the end of the season." Bill was short of breath. "Tell me," he said. "I'd really like to know. What do you care?"

"I care," Mack said. "I've worked here for twelve years. Believe me, I care."

"Obviously not enough," Bill said. His chest was on fire. "Get out." He pointed to the door. "I don't want to talk about the storm. Now get out!"

Mack's eyes widened. He pressed his lips together and left the office.

Bill leaned back in his swivel chair and tried to take several deep breaths. In, out. In, out. His heart thrummed in his ears. He picked up the picture of Cecily that he kept on his desk. Cecily at fifteen, wearing her Middlesex Field Hockey T-shirt over her bathing suit, sitting in an

Adirondack chair, on the pavilion, her bare legs tucked underneath her (scab on one knee), her red hair crazy and curly around her face. An heiress sitting on her throne. *Where was she?*

By Thursday, Freida had wreaked havoc in the Bahamas, and she moved along the eastern coast of Florida where she hooked up with a local low-pressure system and increased in size and speed. Class four, 230 miles across, sustained winds of 101 miles per hour. The newscaster hadn't said "Nantucket" in twenty-four hours. Instead they showed clips of the Caribbean: palm trees with their heads ripped off, washed-out bridges, whole houses floating away. Every hour at fifty past, they flashed the international forecast. Rio was sunny, thirty-three degrees Centigrade.

Bill lugged his body out of bed and walked straight down to the beach. People lounged under the umbrellas, a man was swimming. No hurricane here. Then Bill heard someone coughing and he turned to see Clarissa Ford standing on the deck of room 7, smoking. She waved to him. He waved back. She waved *at* him, beckoning. Bill groaned inwardly. Clarissa was seventy years old, a widow, her very wealthy husband killed years ago by half a million cigarettes, and yet Clarissa continued to smoke. She stayed at the hotel for the whole month of September, spending over sixteen thousand dollars. A year's worth of the college tuition that Bill would not be paying to the University of Virginia. He slogged through the sand until he was a few feet from her deck.

"Bill," she said. Clarissa Ford's face was tan and wrinkled; she looked like dried tobacco. "Bill, how are you, my dear?"

"I'm okay, Clarissa, how are you?"

"Fine, dear, wonderful." She inhaled on her cigarette. "You see I've been obeying the little rule your wife set up for me this year. I've not smoked in the room once."

"I find that hard to believe, Clarissa," Bill said. Last year they had to air the room for three days after she left. And still room 7 had the faint smell of an ashtray.

"It's *true*," she said. "I've been out here morning, noon, and night."

"Thank you," Bill said. "We appreciate it."

Clarissa ashed into the sand just off the deck. There was a gray spot the size of a saucer already. "How's my darling Cecily?"

Bill looked out over the water. A ferry approached from Hyannis. "I don't know," Bill said. "She ran off to South America."

Clarissa's laugh sounded like wagon wheels rolling over gravel. It sounded like someone balling up a cellophane bag. "Tell her to come over and visit me when she gets a free second," Clarissa said. "I haven't seen her in eons. She must be all grown up! Is she ready for college?"

"I told you, Clarissa. She's run off to South America."

"Honestly, Bill. Will you send her over? I have some valuable wisdom to impart."

"Impart it to me," Bill said. "I could use it."

"You take yourself so seriously, Bill, dear," Clarissa said. She waved her cigarette like a magic wand. "Lighten up!"

"You know we're getting a hurricane?" Bill said. "The hotel could wash away."

Clarissa crushed her cigarette out on the railing of the deck. Bill winced. "Pshaw!" she said. "That's exactly what I mean by too seriously, Bill. It won't be a hurricane! It'll just be a little rain here in paradise."

ON FRIDAY, A PHONE call came to the house. It was Nantucket's fire chief, Anthony Mazzaco.

"We're going to get some weather here, Bill. It's not a pretty picture. You need me to send someone down to help ya? Mack tells me you haven't made a move. Now, you got people in those rooms, Bill, you have to make a move."

"Look outside, Tony," Bill said. "Do you see rain? Do you see a storm?"

"She's coming," Tony Mazzaco said. He, too, sounded excited. "She's coming."

• • •

ON SATURDAY, FREIDA MADE landfall in Norfolk, Virginia. The news-caster on the weather channel drew a yellow arrow off the coast of Long Island, heading out toward the North Atlantic. *Good*, Bill thought, *let Long Island take the hit*. But for some reason, the man said, "Nantucket is in a position to catch Freida's wrath. Nantucket is in her way." Nantucket again. Bill sat up, and saw how, as Freida moved for the chilly North Atlantic waters, she would sideswipe Nantucket. She was huge, two hundred plus miles wide. The island was thirteen by four. Freida could gobble them up.

Freida, the mean woman. Only in Bill's mind, Freida was a girl with crazy red hair—she was an angry teenager throwing a tantrum. The room blurred.

He sat in bed, trying to focus. He hadn't showered in two days. The bedsheets had a smell. Bill tried to care about the storm, about the hotel, about himself. He tried to care, but he couldn't. He would let her come.

IT WAS ALL OVER the TV and radio; everyone in town was talking about it. Tourists booked flights and hopped on the steamship. Stop & Shop's parking lot overflowed with people buying bottled water, bread, candles, Duraflame logs. Boats came out of the water, houses were shuttered, deck furniture stored. The Nantucket police and the fire station answered worried phone calls. There was a small-craft advisory and as of Sunday morning, the ferries were canceled. A hurricane watch and coastal flood warning were issued by the National Hurricane Center for the island of Nantucket. Hurricane watch became hurricane warning.

And Bill would do nothing about it. Mack had never seen him act like this. Since Cecily left, the guy had crumbled, caved in. He accused Mack of wanting this storm, *wanting* it! But nothing could be further from the truth. Mack loved the hotel and he would do whatever he could to protect it.

Even if it meant going over Bill's head.

Mack found Therese bringing her plants in from the front porch. A good sign—maybe she believed in Freida even if Bill didn't.

Mack kicked a hermit crab shell across the parking lot. "I'm going to gather Vance and Jem and start shuttering this place if that's all right with you."

Therese ran her hand through her pale orange hair. She looked tired, and sad. "What does Bill say?"

"He says don't do it. He doesn't seem to care what kind of hit we take."

"You're right," Therese said. "He doesn't care. Why should he care?"

"When Cecily comes back, Therese, it might be nice if there was a hotel left to pass on."

She touched the leaves of her geraniums. "I wish you'd asked her to marry you . . . just *asked* her, you know?"

"Therese," Mack said. "Can I please do my work?"

"Go ahead," she said. "Do what you have to do."

MACK BEGAN THE TIME-CONSUMING task of screwing wooden shutters over every window. It only took two or three minutes to put up a shutter—but there were so many windows. He raced to finish the lobby and office before it grew too dark to work. He hauled the wooden shutters out of storage, grabbed fistfuls of screws and kept two or three pinched between his lips as he worked. Just as he was finishing the windows of the lobby that faced the water, he smelled smoke. He looked around. Clarissa Ford stood behind him in the sand, the ubiquitous cigarette dangling between her fingers.

"You're not going to shutter my room, are you?" she asked.

"Tomorrow," he said. "Not tonight."

"Not tomorrow," Clarissa said.

"Yes, tomorrow. I'm sorry, but there's a storm coming."

"I don't want you to shutter my windows. And certainly not my door."

"I'll leave the back door alone," Mack said. "I don't want to trap you in there. But I'm sealing up the front. Especially your room, Mrs. Ford. Your room faces the water."

"I don't want you to do it. I'll sign whatever I have to, a release for my safety."

"Your safety's important to us, Mrs. Ford," Mack said. He wiggled his feet in his boots; talking to her was slowing him down. "But we're also concerned about the hotel room."

"I'll talk to Bill," Clarissa said. "He'll say to leave my room alone, I guarantee you."

Mack shrugged. "You're right," he said. He turned back to the shutter in his hand. "Fine, then. You'll go without."

AT DUSK, JEM AND Vance came off the beach, sweating. They'd put up snow fencing, and stored the deck furniture from every room. Mack finished with the lobby windows and called it a day. He looked over at Bill and Therese's house before he pulled out of the parking lot. It was dark and still, as though nobody lived there anymore.

AT HOME, MARIBEL COOKED a huge lasagna. "We can eat it for dinner over the next few days," she said.

"I may have to stay down at the hotel tomorrow night," Mack said.

"*Stay* at the hotel?" she said. "Are you kidding?"

"As it is, I left forty windows facing the water totally exposed. One of them could shatter. Someone could get hurt. I probably shouldn't have left tonight. I should have stayed down there."

"And worked in the *dark*?" Maribel said. She took a bite of lasagna. She'd been argumentative lately, like she didn't believe a word he said about anything anymore. "If you're staying at the club, I am, too."

"You'll be safer here," Mack said.

She stabbed a piece of lettuce. "I'm not staying here without you."

"Maribel, you'll be safer here. That's the only good thing about living mid-island. Away from the water you should be okay."

"Okay?" Maribel put her fork down with a clang and stared at him. "I should be *okay* here alone during the biggest storm this island has seen in forty years? What if a tree falls down? What if we lose power?"

"You probably will lose power," Mack said. "But you have candles and a flashlight."

"Great. So I spend three days in the dark by myself. We're *engaged,* Mack." She flashed her diamond in his face. "See this? It means we're part of a team. And I'm coming to the hotel with you."

"No, you're not."

"You don't want me around," she said. "You don't want anything to do with me."

"I'm thinking of your safety."

"You're thinking of yourself. As always."

"What's that supposed to mean?" he said.

"What do you *think* it means?" she asked. Her mouth twisted in an ugly way. "It means you only think about yourself and your stupid fucking job."

Mack tried to keep his voice steady. "You're not staying at the hotel, Maribel," he said. "Now stop acting like a five-year-old."

Maribel stood up. She pushed Mack's shoulders back, and then she moved to hit him. He raised his hands to shield his face. "What are you doing?" She clawed his arm so ferociously that he started to bleed. "What's *wrong* with you?" he asked. He went to the kitchen sink and washed his arm. Maribel collapsed in her chair, crying. Mack was afraid to look at her; he examined the marks on his arm. Then he heard a clatter, and he saw Maribel put her bare elbows in her food as she cried into her hands.

"Maribel, what's going on?"

She picked up her plate and threw it across the room. It crashed against the coffee table. The plate broke; lasagna and salad went everywhere. "What is wrong with you?" Mack said. "You scratched me. Do you see this? You made me bleed. Are you crazy?"

She nodded; her elbows were greasy with red sauce and salad dressing. "You don't love me," she said. "You've never loved me."

"I do love you," Mack said. "I asked you to marry me. That was what you wanted, wasn't it? I gave you what you wanted."

When Maribel stood up, she knocked her chair over. "I want *you* to want it!" she said. "I want you to want it as badly as I do. But you don't."

Mack tried to get a hold of her, but she smacked him out of the way. Her face was purple, she cried so hard he couldn't even see her eyes. "Maribel, people are different. I can't feel the way you do because I'm not you. I'm me. And I'm doing the best I can."

"It's not good enough!" she screamed. "You don't love me enough!" She hit herself in the face with her open palms. "There's something wrong with me! You don't love me enough. You don't! You don't love me enough."

Mack grabbed her arms, and she fought him. She snarled and cried in his face and he smelled her warm, garlicky breath. He held her by the wrists.

"I do love you enough," he said. A red mark surfaced where she'd hit herself. A red mark on her pretty face. How could he love her enough when she always wanted more?

"You're hurting me!" she said. Mack let go of her wrists. He'd gripped them so tightly, he left white marks. She darted into the bedroom, slamming the door behind her and locking it. Mack knocked on the door. "Maribel? Please open up. Mari, I don't know what's happening." He heard nothing from the other side of the door but her muffled crying. Her brokenhearted crying. Even with his best intentions, the best he could give, he'd somehow failed. Mack listened for a minute, and then he cleaned up the shattered plate and the thrown food, wrapped the tray of lasagna with foil, put it in the fridge. He washed his bloody scratch marks and held a clean dishtowel against them. He knocked on the door again. "Mari, please. Tell me what's wrong."

"You're what's wrong!" she screamed. "I'm what's wrong. This whole thing is wrong."

"Maribel, open the door, please. Please?"

"Leave me *alone!*" she shouted.

He tried the doorknob. Locked. He could jimmy it with something from the utensil drawer, but why? What was the point? *This whole thing is wrong.*

Mack went to the sofa to watch the weather channel.

Freida was off the Jersey Shore.

LACEY GARDNER COULDN'T CONCENTRATE on the storm because something else was bothering her. She had forgotten what Maximilian looked like. It was the oddest thing. She closed her eyes and concentrated on the things Max used to do—reading in his chair, making a tricky putt in golf. But she couldn't picture him at all. She couldn't imagine him in her mind.

She collected all her photographs of Maximilian and spread them out on the coffee table. Twenty-one pictures of Max—from the age of thirty-three in his military uniform to the photo of Max on the porch of the Cliff Road house during his last summer. Lacey studied each picture, and then she leaned back on the sofa and shut her eyes.

Nothing.

He had vanished. She could think his name, think of a hundred thousand moments with him, right up until the moment in bed the last night when he took her hand. But she couldn't see his face in her mind. She opened her eyes and there were twenty-one images of Maximilian smiling at her. Then she closed her eyes, and there was darkness.

Lacey started to weep. It might be a passing phase, brought on by all the stress, the heat, the impending storm. Or it might be that now, at age eighty-eight, she was slipping away. The best part of her—the part that remembered Maximilian and kept him alive—was gone.

There was a knock at the door. Lacey wiped her face quickly with her handkerchief, but not before Mack saw her.

"You're crying," he said.

"No, I'm not."

Mack waited a minute, then he said, "If something's bothering you,

you can tell me. You don't have to be everyone's pillar of strength and wisdom all the time."

"Nothing's bothering me," she said. She nodded at the coffee table. "I'm just looking at old pictures."

Mack surveyed the table. "Maximilian was a handsome man." He pointed to the picture of Max in uniform. "He looks like me in this picture, don't you think?"

"Yes," Lacey whispered. Her Max, her Mack. She took Mack's hand. "I love you. Do you know that? Have I ever told you that? I love you."

Mack knelt beside her. "Lacey, what's wrong?"

The tears started up again, out of her control. "I miss him," she said.

"I know, Lacey," Mack said. "I know you do."

She cried more tears, tears she thought had dried up long ago. Mack held her hand, saying nothing. After several minutes, she snuffled into her handkerchief, and blew her nose. "I'm okay now," she said. She noticed a bandage on Mack's arm. "What happened to you?"

"Rough night at home," he said. "Actually, I came to ask you a favor. I'd like to stay here tonight, if I could."

Relief flooded Lacey, replacing, almost, the emptiness, the blankness. "For Pete's sake, of course. Stay here, please."

Mack squeezed her hand. "Okay, I will. Thank you."

She wouldn't have to be alone, then. Maximilian was missing, but Mack would be here instead to help her fend off the horrible darkness. For one night more, at least.

MONDAY BEGAN AS A mild, sunny day, and Mack made headway on the remaining eighty shutters. Around noon, the wind shifted from southwest to due west and by the time the chambermaids finished cleaning the rooms at one o'clock, the sky was low and gunmetal gray.

Again, Bill didn't show up in the office. Therese fluttered around behind the chambermaids, but when they finished their work, she retreated to her house. Mack shuttered away. When the wind picked up, sand pelted the side of his face and the back of his neck, a thousand tiny needles. A gust lifted his Texas Rangers hat off his head. His hands were busy with shutter and drill gun, and all he could do was turn and watch his hat blow down the beach. It was eerie in a way; suddenly the beach was deserted. Bill and Therese had dropped the future of the hotel in Mack's hands.

By three o'clock, waves pounded the beach so that Mack felt the vibrations through the soles of his work boots as he rushed to finish shuttering. He skipped room 7, Clarissa Ford's room, and when he made it down to room 2, she stepped onto her deck with a lit cigarette. The wind plucked the cigarette from her fingers immediately; it was halfway to Jetties Beach before she even realized it was gone.

At 3:45, the first drops of rain fell. Mack screwed in the final shutters. The wind moaned; Mack's right ear filled with sand. Then the rain picked up. Sand blew in drifts halfway up the snow fence. Mack held his drill inside his jacket, raised his arm to shield his eyes, and ran for the back door of the lobby. By the time he reached the back door, he was soaked and his boots were filled with sand. He stood under the eaves and looked at the roiled, black sea. Mack thought of Maribel, at home on the sofa reading, her feet bundled in an afghan. She hadn't said a word to him when he left that morning. No apology, no explanation—nothing but the silent assurance that whatever he was doing, it wasn't enough. Mack watched the waves crest and crash. One came halfway up the beach. The next one even farther. He didn't understand her.

Inside, Vance and Love played gin rummy at the front desk. Jem was slumped in one of the wicker chairs, asleep.

"You can all go home," Mack said. "I'm staying at Lacey's tonight. I'll take care of things until this bitch passes." He shook Jem's shoulder. "You can leave, Jem. Why don't you take my Jeep? You can't walk home in this."

Jem opened his eyes. "The Jeep? What will you drive?"

"I'm not going home tonight." And then, before he could think better of it, he said, "Take the Jeep and check on Maribel. She's all by herself. I'm sure she wants company."

Jem sat upright in the chair. "Is that supposed to be some kind of joke?"

Mack's stomach prickled with jealousy, and with fear. He pictured Maribel crying, he pictured his fingers gripping her wrists, leaving behind white bracelets. "It's no joke, man. I can't get home tonight. You'd be doing me a favor if you checked on her."

"I'd be doing you a *favor*? Really?" Jem said.

"Just go," Mack said. He flipped Jem his keys.

Jem didn't hesitate. He took the keys and ran, following Vance and Love out the door. Because the windows were shuttered, Mack couldn't watch them drive away. And that kept him from yelling after Jem, and telling him it was all a mistake.

AS SOON AS THE rain started, Bill got out of bed and ran to the living room window. The ocean was huge, the waves bigger than any Bill could remember. The lobby was shuttered, and so were the rooms— Mack's doing. Bill couldn't bring himself to feel one way or another. He couldn't feel anything except this crazy longing, this crazy sadness.

Therese came up the stairs. "You're up," she said. She stood with him at the window. "Our kingdom. I hope it doesn't get washed away."

"What does it matter?" Bill said.

"Bill," Therese said, "she's coming back."

"She's not coming back!" Bill said. "Stop saying that, Therese. Cecily *isn't coming back!*"

Therese said quietly, "She is."

"She's not," Bill said. The Brazilian boys chased Cecily now. One boy—Gabriel—grabbed Cecily's bright red hair. He held a razor to her neck.

Bill went to the closet and put a slicker on over his pajamas. "I'm going up to the widow's walk."

"What?" Therese said. She collapsed on the leather sofa. "You've lost your mind."

"What does it matter?" Bill said. He marched through the bedroom and opened the door to the attic. In the attic was a flight of stairs leading to a hatch that popped up onto the widow's walk. Bill had trouble opening the hatch door; he pressed his hands flat against it and pushed with all his might. Then the door flipped open and the wind and the rain nearly knocked Bill down the stairs. He knelt on the stairs and clenched the railing. He would get up there, and sit on the widow's walk. It might kill him, but what did it matter? He was the father of two children: one dead, one missing.

Then he heard a voice, footsteps. Therese climbed up after him.

"I'm coming up there with you," she said. She was five or ten feet away, but it sounded as though she were calling to him from the end of a long tunnel. The wind lifted her pale orange hair; she looked like a ghost or a witch, but she looked beautiful, too—his bride, the woman he loved.

Bill gripped the railing with one hand and reached for her with the other. The wind was impossibly strong. Poetically strong—if they did manage to climb onto the widow's walk, maybe the wind would pick them up and carry them away, to their son, their daughter.

Rain drove through the hatch. Bill was soaked to the skin. He was in bare feet.

"Come on," he said. He raised his head through the opening. The sky screamed in his ears, the world rained down on him. All he could see was white. Bill tried to look around, but he couldn't find the sea, he couldn't find the hotel. The sky was blank, the color of wind. Wind filled his eyes, his ears, his nose—he was drowning in the wind. *What are you waiting for? A sign from God?* "You can have it!" Bill screamed to the sky. He was sure that somehow S.B.T. could hear him. "You . . . can . . . have . . . it!" He lost his balance and faltered in his footing, but Therese steadied him. He brought his head back inside. The stairs were wet and slippery; Therese's blouse stuck to her skin. Mascara ran down her face, her orange hair was wet, the color of a pumpkin.

"He can have it," Bill said. "I give up. He can have it."

Therese held on to him. "Who can have what?" she asked. "What are you talking about? Who are you screaming at?"

Bill had lost his hope. He didn't have the stuff in him; beneath his skin and bones and cartilage, he was dry, an empty gourd. He managed to close the hatch door, spurred on by what was now his hatred of this storm. Once the hatch was closed and locked, Bill followed Therese into the bathroom. He vomited into the toilet. He vomited up the Brazilian boys with their razor blades, and Cecily screaming with fear. He vomited up S.B.T. taking the Beach Club from him. He vomited up Dead and Missing. He vomited until it was all gone, and the inside of his mouth was puckered and sour.

Therese drew him a bath, and he gingerly lowered himself into the warm water. Therese sat next to him on the floor. He was the owner of a beach hotel waiting out a hurricane. Helpless. He was the father of a teenage daughter. Hopeless.

MARIBEL WAS ON THE phone with Tina when the power went out and the phone died in her hand. Maybe it was just as well. Tina had started to cry almost as soon as Maribel spoke.

"Mama, I'm going to break the engagement."

"What?"

"It's not meant to be, Mama. It's not going to work." Maribel had replayed the night before a hundred times in her mind. Something had broken inside her, and she lost control. She'd hurt Mack, she made him bleed. And he'd nearly snapped her hands off. They were finding new ways to hurt each other. It had to stop.

Tina hit full-blown snuffles, sobs. "You're just angry, Mari. You're angry at Mack now and you've been angry at him before. You'll get past it."

"I'm not angry anymore, Mama. I'm beyond angry. We don't make each other happy. We don't want the same things."

"Why are you giving up?" Tina said. "Why after so long?"

Maribel heard the desperate note in her mother's voice and she squeezed her eyes shut against it. *I want this for her,* Maribel thought. *I want to get married because I know it will make her happy. It will take away the demons of her loneliness, to know that I, at least, won't have to spend my life alone.*

"Will you love me anyway?" Maribel asked. "Will you love me even without Mack?"

More sobbing. "You know I love you best of anyone in the world. You know you're my number-one prize. If you made this decision, then it must be God's will."

"It's my will," Maribel said. "Mama, it's my will."

And then the power went out.

Maribel had candles and matches ready, and in seconds the apartment glowed with candlelight. She went into the bathroom and splashed water on her face, and then she opened a bottle of red wine.

Maribel toasted the air. "Fuck you, Freida," she said. She sipped her wine. She would get good and drunk.

There were headlights in her window. Maribel saw the Jeep swing into the driveway. Her heart stood up. Mack hadn't left her alone after all. He'd come home. Maribel's mind stumbled over words for an apology.

Oddly, there was a knock at the door. A knock? Maribel flung the door open, and there, standing in the rain, was Jem.

AS JEM DROVE THE Jeep to Maribel's apartment, he thought about the two words Neil Rosenblum had left him with: *Get her.* The wind was blowing so hard that Jem had to grip the steering wheel with both hands just to keep the Jeep on the road. The wipers flew back and forth, and at every low point, Jem drove through deep puddles that sloshed over the hood of the car. The rain was ridiculous, and Jem probably would have crashed if there had been other cars on the road. But from the look of things, Jem was the only one out. On his way to see Maribel, with Mack's permission.

Jem pulled into Maribel's driveway and switched off the ignition. The trees in Maribel's backyard bowed in the wind, and a carpet of fallen leaves covered the grass. A heavy branch crashed to the ground. Jem ran like hell down the sloping side yard to the apartment. The gas grill lay on its side. Jem knocked on the door. *Be home*, he thought. Maybe this was all a joke—maybe Maribel was off-island.

But then she opened the door. The apartment was lit by candles.

"Jem," she said. "I thought you were Mack."

Jem's heart sagged. Here he was standing out in the middle of a hurricane, and what did she say? *I thought you were Mack.*

"Mack's at the hotel," he said. "He sent me here to keep you company. Listen, can I come in?"

"He *sent* you here?" Maribel said. Her brow creased into lines that looked like an *M*. *M* for Maribel. Or more likely, an angry *M* for Mack. It occurred to Jem then that Maribel might not enjoy being handed off like a baton.

"Can I come in?" Jem pleaded. His shoes filled with water. The wind blew sideways. Another branch fell in the yard.

"For a minute," she said. She ushered him in and slammed the door behind him. "So Mack sent you here. He *sent* you here."

"Sort of." Jem was afraid to move anywhere in the room. He dripped onto the welcome mat. "Can I take my shoes off?"

"You're only staying as long as it takes you to tell me exactly what Mack said."

Jem looked around, stalling for time. "You lost power," he said. He needed to think. He felt hesitant to get Mack into trouble, since Mack was the one who gave him the okay to come. But that was the whole point. Mack was a creep. He was giving away his girlfriend.

"What did Mack say?" Maribel picked a glass of wine up off the coffee table.

"He said, uh . . . he said you'd be alone and that I should keep you company. And he gave me the keys to the Jeep."

Maribel slugged back some wine. "So he's pimping me out."

"Excuse me?" Jem didn't like the sound of that word anywhere near Maribel.

"He sent you over here because he wants us to have sex. That's his way out of the relationship." She finished her glass of wine and then she ripped her cardigan sweater right down the middle, so that the buttons popped off and disappeared into the shag carpet. Underneath the sweater, she wore a shiny blue bra, which she unhooked and flung onto the sofa. Jem was confused, but he couldn't keep from looking at her breasts. They seemed fuller than they had at the beach that day.

"What are you doing?" he asked.

She unbuttoned her jean shorts and let them fall to her ankles. She slid her hands inside her flowered panties and slipped these off as well. She stood before him, completely nude in the candlelight. Jem thought he might faint.

"You can take your shoes off," she said. "And the rest of your clothes, for that matter."

"What's going on?" he said. His body screamed out for her. Her ass, the curve under her chin, the backs of her knees. But something was wrong. She was steaming like a tea kettle, and it wasn't from desire for him.

"You're angry at Mack," he said.

"You're damn right I'm angry!" she said. "He set all this up. I'm sure he thinks he's doing us both a favor! But he's manipulating our feelings. And guess what? I don't care. He wants us to have sex, we'll have sex."

Just hearing Maribel say the words almost knocked Jem out. The front of his shorts was pitched like a tent. But this was wrong, everything about it was wrong.

"I love you, Maribel," Jem said. "And I've never been in love with anyone before, but I don't want you to sleep with me because you're angry with Mack. I'm going home." He opened the door, afraid to turn around and see what she was doing. He thought he heard her pour another glass of wine. He geared himself up to make a run for the Jeep, thinking if he timed it right he could run between gusts of wind.

Another branch fell, and Jem took that as his sign. He ran from Maribel's house as quickly as he could.

Once he was safely inside the Jeep, he thought it might be okay to cry, or yell, or do something to release all his haywire, fucked-up emotions. The rain pounded on the top of the Jeep; it was like sitting inside a tin can. He turned the key in the ignition, praying he hadn't ruined the engine by taking on those giant puddles. Fortunately, the engine started and Jem backed out of the driveway. He couldn't see where he was going, but that mattered very little. He pulled onto what looked like the road and hit the gas.

He made it about a hundred yards when he saw red and blue flashing lights—a police car blocked Bartlett Road, the road that led to everywhere else. A policeman in a fluorescent orange raincoat waved his arms at Jem. Jem rolled down the window.

"All the roads are closed," the policeman shouted. "You'll have to go back to wherever you came from."

"I can't," Jem said.

The officer shrugged. "I can't let you on the roads. You'll have to."

"I can't go back," Jem said. "I live on Liberty Street."

All Jem could see of the officer was his light blue eyes and his nose and his lips, which were scrunched together by his tightly drawn hood. "You can't go on the roads."

"Will you put me in jail if I try?" Jem asked. Jail was far preferable to returning to Maribel's.

"No, I won't put you in jail!" the officer said. "What I'm saying is, you can't pass. I'm sorry. Now turn around!"

Jem managed to turn the Jeep around and head back down Pheasant Road. He considered pulling into a random driveway and spending the night there. Spending the night in his wet clothes in a chilly, wet car without food or water when the woman he loved was a hundred yards away? Jem pictured Neil Rosenblum shouting at him. *Get her!*

Jem drove back to Maribel's and sat in the Jeep, thinking of what he might say. Then he raced to the house and knocked once again on the door.

Maribel had put her clothes back on, although her cardigan hung open.

"I love you," he said.

"Will you hold me?" she asked.

He nodded, and stepped inside.

• • •

MACK STAYED AT THE desk by himself. At seven o'clock, when the power went out, he ran along the back of the hotel, knocking on the rooms' back doors to make sure everyone was all right. Spirits were high. The guests lit candles, drank wine, ate sandwiches, read novels. When Mack was certain everyone was surviving, he returned to the desk. He sat by the light of three votive candles and listened. The wind was an opera—a baritone rumble and soprano whistle singing simultaneously. Mack heard sand hit the wall of the lobby, but not water. Not yet.

Mack wondered what was happening with Jem and Maribel. He wanted to race home and stop whatever was going on, but after the scene the night before, he knew he had no choice but to let Maribel go. *Let her go?* He gently removed the bandage from his arm and inspected his wound. He couldn't believe she'd scratched him like that, he couldn't believe he'd made her that unhappy. *This whole thing is wrong.* A six-year mistake.

By ten o'clock, Mack was tired of thinking. He stepped out the side door, and ran through a gust of sandy wind to Lacey's.

SHE WAS SITTING IN her armchair with ivory beeswax candles burning and a Dewar's on the table next to her. She wore her nightgown, a pink silk bathrobe, pink terry cloth slippers. The pictures of Maximilian had been collected into a neat pile.

"Max?" she said when he walked in. "Maximilian?"

Mack shook off water like a dog. "It's me, Lacey, Mack."

Lacey jumped. He wondered if he'd woken her. "Mack, dear, hello. How goes it?"

"Nothing's flooding. That's what's important. There's ankle-deep sand in the parking lot, but sand can be shoveled. Do you feel like talking?"

"Heavens, yes," Lacey said. "You know me, I always feel like talking."

Mack collapsed on the sofa. "What should we talk about?"

"Let's talk about your wedding," she said. "I want to buy a new dress. A bright red dress. I want people to call me a harlot!" She kicked her feet in their pink slippers. "You know, Maximilian and I actually got married twice. Have I told you that? We married the first time in November of '41, just before Max went off to the war. Judge Alcott performed the ceremony on Madaket Beach and Isabel and Ed Tolliver witnessed. After the ceremony, the four of us went to the Skipper for lunch. Max left for Maryland ten days later for basic training. Then, a few months later, Max was shipped to the Philippines. Those were gruesome times, because the Japanese had bombed Pearl Harbor, and there was Maximilian, practically in Japan himself. While Max was in the Philippines, our friend Sam Archibald died over in Europe, and I had to write to Max and tell him that." Lacey sipped her drink and stared into the candles. "Where was I headed with this story? Oh, yes, our two weddings. We had a church wedding when Maximilian returned. That was a waste of my father's money. We were already married!" Lacey finished her drink. "Let's talk about your wedding," she said. "I only want to talk about things that are in our future. I spend far too much time talking about the past. And I'm stopping, right here, right now. Here's to the future!" She raised her empty glass to him.

"I'm not going to marry Maribel," he said.

"You're not?" she said.

"No."

"Have you told Maribel this?" Lacey asked.

"Not in so many words," Mack said. Just thinking about Jem touching Maribel made him queasy. "But I think she has an idea. I don't know how to explain it. I just can't marry her."

"You don't have to explain it to me," Lacey said. "I have long lived by the expression, 'Nobody knows where it comes from, and nobody knows where it goes.' Love doesn't make sense most of the time and that's what's so wonderful about it."

They were both quiet. Freida calmed down, too, but only for a second.

Lacey pushed herself up from the chair and took a few steps toward Mack. "Some days I think I'm old and wise, and other days just old. I'm going to bed. You'll be in and out tonight, I suppose?"

"I'll try to be quiet."

"Don't worry about it. Just make sure you blow the candles out. We wouldn't want to burn down the cottage Big Bill left me."

Mack hugged Lacey around the shoulders. "So you don't think I'm crazy? Breaking my engagement?"

Lacey put her cool hands on his face. "What you must realize, Mack, dear, is that I will love you whatever you decide. That's the definition of love." She picked up a candle and teetered off down the dark hall. Mack stayed to make sure she reached her bedroom door safely. Before she opened it, she turned to him. The candle lit up her smile.

"You're my boy," she said.

WHEN MACK RETURNED TO the lobby, it was nearly eleven. Freida shook the hotel like a gambler shaking a cup of dice, as if she were trying to lift the hotel off its foundation. Mack pulled an extra pillow and blanket out of the utility closet and drifted to sleep lying on the floor behind the front desk. A loud crash woke him. He shined his flashlight around the walls of the lobby. Then he heard another crash. He walked out to the middle of the room and listened. Another crash, rhythmic crashing. Waves.

There was a knock on the back door of the lobby. Norris Williams, room 3.

"There's water on the decks," he said. He was wearing his white hotel robe; his hair was soaking wet, as though he'd just stepped out of the shower. "I can hear the waves crashing."

"Is there water coming into your room?" Mack asked. He didn't know what he was supposed to do. Where could the guests go? To Bill and Therese's? To Lacey's?

"Not yet," Mr. Williams said. He was the bookish type, with soft hands, an estate-planning lawyer. The type that wasn't good with emergencies of the physical kind. "My wife and I would like to come into the lobby, if you don't mind. We'd feel safer."

"That's fine," Mack said. No sooner had Mr. Williams left than there was another knock at the back door. Mrs. Frammer, from Denmark, room 6.

"The water's coming in. The carpet by the front door is wet," she said. "Are we supposed to stay on this ship until it goes down? I saw *Titanic*. We all did."

"You can come into the lobby," Mack said. He zipped up his jacket. Rain pelleted through the open door like machine-gun fire. Mrs. Frammer scooted past him inside and Mack dashed into the rain and pounded on back doors. "Come into the lobby!" he cried out.

The guests grabbed jackets and their flashlights and ran past Mack toward the lobby. Mack knocked on every door, and all the guests got ready to leave immediately, except for Clarissa Ford. She came to the back door, saw everyone running, and said, "God help us."

"I'm not kidding around this time, Clarissa. It's time to get out."

"I already told you, Mack, I'm not going anywhere."

Mack nudged past Clarissa into her room. A window was cracked. Mack grabbed the knob of the front door with both hands and yanked it open.

The waves crashed over the steps of the front decks. A wave ran right over Mack's feet onto the green carpet. But the carpet might be the least of their worries. The Gold Coast could break off and wash away altogether. Mack slammed the door shut and dead-bolted it. He jammed two bath towels into the crack at the bottom of the door.

He took Clarissa by the arm. "We have to get out of here," he said.

She pulled her arm away; Mack thought of Maribel. "I already said, I'm not going."

In the distance, over the screaming wind, Mack heard sirens.

"Fine," he said.

A fire engine and two vans pulled up on North Beach Road. The parking lot was so clogged with sand that they couldn't pull in. But it didn't matter; Mack was relieved to see help of any kind.

Four men in fluorescent orange coats entered the side door of the

lobby. "Someone called on a cell phone and said you needed evacua-
tion," one of the officers said. He was block shouldered and capable
looking, the type who flourished in physical emergencies. "So we're
here to take everybody to the high school. They have a generator running. They have food, water, and bedding."

"I was the one who called," Norris Williams said, brandishing his
phone as though it were a winning lottery ticket. He was still in his
bathrobe. "I'm ready to go. Lead the way."

Mack stationed himself at the side door and ushered the guests
outside, handed them off to the block-shouldered officer, who helped
them climb over the dunes to the vans. Mack counted heads. Mr.
Sikahama from Hawaii, room 14, said he wasn't paying six hundred
dollars to spend the night in the hallway outside of geometry class,
and he hoped he was getting a full refund. Mrs. Frammer kissed Mack
on the cheek, as though she expected never to see him again. After
everyone was delivered to the van, the officer came back to Mack. "Is
that everybody?"

"Just about," Mack said. "I'm staying here."

"And is there anyone else?"

Mack saw the beam of a flashlight coming from Bill and Therese's
doorway. "Wait a minute," he said. The beam bounced and jiggled,
and then Mack saw Therese, wearing Cecily's Middlesex Field
Hockey windbreaker over her nightgown. Bare feet.

"I'm going with those people," she said. "I think someone should
go with them, and Bill refuses to leave."

"Okay," he said. "Go."

"Lacey's already in the van?" Therese asked.

"Lacey," Mack said. He ran for Lacey's cottage, flung open the
door and charged down the hall to her bedroom. He knocked on her
door.

"Gardner?"

He heard a muffled noise, a grizzled breathing. He cracked the
door. Lacey was asleep, snoring softly. "Gardner," Mack said. "Wake
up."

Lacey's face was ghostly white in the beam of his flashlight. Mack toggled her shoulder. "Lacey, it's me."

Her eyelids fluttered. "Max?" She blinked.

"We're evacuating the hotel, Lacey," he said. "It's time to go."

"I knew it would be soon," she said. "But I'm not ready."

"Lacey, we're going to the high school. The firemen are here."

She opened her eyes. Blue eyes, sharply focused. "High school?"

"Water's hitting the decks. It's time to get everybody out."

"It'll take more than a little water to move me," Lacey said. "Are you going to the high school?"

"No," he said. "I'm staying here."

"Me, too," she said. "If we drown, we drown." She sank her head deeper into her feather pillow. "Wake me when it's morning, if you please. If you please."

THE SAND IN THE parking lot was sculpted into dunes, some of which held water. The wind thrummed and shrieked. Mack clambered over hills of sand to the lobby porch. He positioned himself behind one of the porch columns to keep out of the blowing sand. He shined his flashlight onto the beach.

The waves crashed over the pavilion as though it weren't there, and broke about ten feet shy of the lobby—ten feet, the length of a compact car. Mack was paralyzed, watching Nantucket Sound gone berserk. Attacking.

Mack heard someone call his name and he saw the beacon of a flashlight from Bill's doorway. Mack spotted Bill climbing over the sand dunes, around puddles the size of a child's swimming pool. He clenched a yellow slicker at the neck; underneath, he wore pajamas and a pair of galoshes.

"What's happening?" Bill yelled.

Mack couldn't speak; he was furious. *What's happening?* Mack pointed his flashlight at the beach. *What's happening is called a hurricane. A natural disaster. A state of fucking emergency.*

What Mack said was, "Everyone's out except for Clarissa and Lacey."

"How bad's the water?" Bill asked.

"It's pretty bad," Mack said. As angry as Mack was, he didn't want to have to break the news: water in the rooms, Bill's ship going down.

Bill switched off his flashlight and Mack did the same. They stood together in darkness. All Mack could see was the white foam getting closer and closer to the lobby.

Bill took Mack's hand and held it.

He's terrified, Mack thought. *First he loses me, then his daughter, then his hotel.* Mack wasn't sure what he'd do if Bill started to cry. Mack sneaked a sideways look at him. Bill was smiling. *The guy's lost his mind,* Mack thought. *He's gone insane.*

"I'm selling it," Bill said.

"What?" Mack said.

"I'm selling the hotel for twenty-five million dollars. I have a buyer, and I've decided to sell it."

Mack switched on his flashlight and aimed it at the water's edge. A wave crested and broke and the white foam danced up the beach.

"I don't believe you," Mack said.

"What's not to believe?" Bill said. "Cecily's gone, you're leaving, my baby son is dead. For me the hotel was never just the building, Mack. It was the people inside the building."

Mack kept his flashlight on the water, mentally marking the water line. He marked wave after wave after wave, until he fell into a kind of stupor. The waves kept rolling and crashing, Mack's eyelids drooped. In his standing dream-sleep, each wave that washed over him had a name. David Pringle, *If you're going to stick it out there in the East;* Vance and his snarling lip; Maribel in a sheen of sweat, begging, pleading, *Why did she always want?* Lacey wearing pink fuzzy slippers, *You're my boy.* Andrea and James, with their matching green-gray eyes. Therese, a dead-child white streak in her hair. Too-handsome Jem, Mr. November, running out the lobby door with his embarrassed happiness. Cecily crying into the phone, *I love you, Gabriel, I really love you.* Mack's parents, in Oblivion. As if none of this mattered. The waves lulled Mack back to May, to before May, before Andrea and How-Baby and David Pringle's phone call, back when things were normal, when things were easy. What had made him happy? The hotel—the front desk, the ringing phone, the beach. The guests, the staff. Bill, Therese, Cecily, Lacey. The Beach Club made him happy. Of course the hotel was more than just a building. For Mack it was a way of life. Even in the middle of a raging hurricane, this was where he wanted to be. Right here.

Mack snapped to attention; his legs were numb. The wind howled like a woman giving birth, but the water wasn't getting any closer. Mack looked to his right; he was surprised to see Bill still standing there, his lips moving. Reciting poetry. Praying.

"You can't sell the hotel," Mack said. "You've put your whole life into it."

"I can start a new life," Bill said. "Take Therese and move to Hawaii, or Saipan, wherever that is."

"Bill, you can't sell the hotel. I won't let you."

"You can't stop me," Bill said.

"I can stop you," Mack said.

"How?"

"I can stay."

Bill nodded slowly.

"Am I right?" Mack said. "Will that stop you?"

"Will you stay?"

"Will that stop you?"

Bill turned to him. "Is it you who's been writing me letters?" he asked. "Are *you* S.B.T.?"

"No," Mack said.

Bill shook his head. "No," he said. "I didn't think so."

"I'll stay," Mack said.

"Okay," Bill said. He shined his flashlight over the parking lot and Mack followed the beam—a Toyota 4-Runner was up to the tops of its tires in sand, and the bikes in the bicycle rack were buried to their handlebars. The wind wasn't letting up.

Then Mack heard a noise, a voice. The voice. *Home. Home.* It was the hum, loud and distinct over the scream of the wind. *Home.* Mack reached for Bill's arm. "Do you hear that?"

"What?" Bill said.

"That voice. The voice saying 'Home.' Do you hear it? Please tell me you hear it. Do you? There—there it is again. Home. Just tell me you hear it."

Bill climbed over a mound of sand, headed for the safety of his house. "I don't know what you're talking about," he said.

WHAT WOKE MACK UP first was the smell of coffee, and the promise of light. Mack feared opening his eyes; he didn't want to be disappointed. Then he heard whispers—giggles, laughing. Mack let himself rise to the surface of his sleep, enough to realize that his back ached, his arms ached, his feet ached. He opened his eyes. Vance and Love stood over him. Vance held two cartons of Hostess doughnuts and Love carried a cardboard tray of coffees.

Mack raised his head an inch. "Is it over?"

"It's over," Vance said. "But it's not pretty. Get up and see for yourself."

Mack managed to sit up on his own and with a hand from Vance, he stood. Light peeked in around the shutters all over the lobby.

"I can't believe it," Mack said. "That looks like sun."

"Maybe you'd better wait a while before you look outside," Vance said. "I'll give you a hint. I had to park the Datsun a quarter-mile up North Beach Road."

"We walked over the sand," Love said. "Thanks to my cross-country skiing experience, I got the coffee here without spilling a drop."

Vance threw his arm around Love's neck and kissed her. "That's my girl."

Mack thought of Maribel. Suddenly, more than his body ached. "Anybody seen Jem?" he asked hopefully. "Or my Jeep?"

Vance and Love shook their heads; Love looked at the ground.

"Have some coffee," Vance said. He handed Mack a cup. "Were you up all night?"

"Just about," Mack said. "Do we have power?"

"Not yet," Vance said.

"We evacuated all the guests," Mack said. "The fire trucks took everyone to the high school. I didn't want to leave the hotel."

"You're so loyal," Love said.

"He's crazy," Vance said. "You sure you're ready to go outside? Brace yourself, man. I'm warning you."

"I'm ready," Mack said. "It was pretty bad last night."

"Let's go," Vance said. "I want to see your face."

Mack and Vance walked out the side door. What struck Mack first was this: it was a beautiful day. The heat and humidity of the previous weeks were gone. It was crisp, and the sky was a brilliant, spectacular blue.

The Beach Club looked like the Sahara Desert. The sand in the parking lot was chest high in places. The front porch of the lobby where Bill and Mack stood the night before was buried—there were drifts of sand halfway up the lobby doors. The pavilion was entirely buried, with the exception of the peaked roof, which stuck out—a head with no body. The beach was strewn with seaweed, dead seagulls, rocks.

The hotel was still standing, although the decks were buried under sand. Mack and Vance walked around and entered the back door of each room. All the front deck rooms had saturated carpets—Mack's shoes squished as he walked. The bottoms of the bedskirts were wet, some of the dressers had water marks.

"If we take up all the carpets and cut a big hole in the floor, we might drain these rooms someday," Vance said.

"The carpet definitely has to be replaced," Mack said. "That'll be a big job."

"I'll bet you're glad you're leaving," Vance said. "You picked the right time to get out."

Mack didn't say anything.

He headed down to room 7. Clarissa Ford stood in the back doorway, smoking.

"You survived," Mack said. "How's your room?"

"Demolished," she said. She lowered her eyes. "I spent all night in the bathtub." Mack looked into room 7. Clarissa had piled all her clothes on top of the bed, but they were soaked. The lamps had shattered, the TV set was smashed, the leather chair ruined.

"Oh, God," Mack said. "It's amazing you lived."

Clarissa exhaled a stream of smoke. "I'll pay for it all, needless to say. I wonder if Therese will let me help her redecorate. Then when I come back next September it will really feel like home."

"Don't count on it," Mack said. "Anyway, what's important is that you're safe. It was quite a night."

"Oh, darling," Clarissa said. "I was part of it."

MACK NUDGED VANCE'S ELBOW before they reached the back door of the lobby. "Listen, will you call my house? If Jem's there, tell him to get his ass down here."

"I can't believe what you did yesterday," Vance said. "You gave her away, man. Why the hell did you do that?"

"I have my reasons," Mack said. He rubbed his hands over Vance's shaved head. "Will you call for me, man?"

Vance swatted Mack's hands away. "I'll call as long as you stop touching me. I don't love you, you know, Petersen."

"I know," Mack said. "Thanks."

WHEN MACK WALKED AROUND front, a school bus pulled up on North Beach Road and the hotel guests disembarked: Mrs. Frammer, Mr. Sikahama, Mr. Williams in his bathrobe. They climbed over the dunes toward the lobby. Therese, with Cecily's windbreaker zipped up to her throat, crawled toward Mack wearily, a soldier returning from war. She shielded her eyes from the sun.

"How was it?" Mack asked.

"Did Cecily call?" Therese said.

He hated the desperate note in her voice. She'd only been away eight hours. "Not that I know of. The phones were down all night."

"I was thinking if she watched the news or anything . . ." She dug her toe in the sand. "Our kingdom is destroyed. I thought maybe if she knew that, she'd call."

"Not destroyed, Therese. We were lucky. Only room seven is gone. The rest of the front deck rooms have carpet damage and some other minor stuff. Vance is going over them with the Shop Vac. They'll be okay for the guests by this afternoon."

Therese squinted. "Really?"

"Not great, but okay."

"Not ruined?"

"Not ruined."

"The guests can sit on the beach until then. We ate breakfast at the school. Have you seen Bill?"

"Not since last night," Mack said.

Therese glanced up at the bay window. "He's probably up there watching. If he hasn't keeled over from a heart attack. I don't even want to tell you what he went through last night."

"I saw him just before he went to bed," Mack said. "He looked all right."

Therese's eyes watered and she blinked tears. Mack couldn't remember ever seeing Therese cry. She looked like a child in her nightgown, the ill-fitting windbreaker, bare feet, her peach-colored hair tucked behind her tiny ears. He'd seen Cecily show an uncanny resemblance to Therese over the years, and now he witnessed the opposite: Therese slouched before him looking for all the world like her teenage daughter.

She sniffled and straightened up. "I'd better go see Bill," she said. "Let me know when Vance is finished and I'll send the chambermaids over."

"Will do," Mack said.

Therese turned back before she entered her house. "How's Lacey?" she asked.

MACK TOOK A CUP of coffee to Lacey's cottage. Her apartment was dim, light entered around the edges of the shutters, throwing stripes across the Oriental rug. "Gardner?" he called out. Mack tiptoed down to Lacey's bedroom and tapped on her door. "Lacey, it's safe to get up. The evil Freida has passed."

He listened, but heard nothing. She was still asleep. She'd asked him to wake her when morning came. *If you please.* Mack opened Lacey's bedroom door and peeked in.

Lacey's eyes were closed. One hand was clenched in a fist over her heart, and her other arm dangled off the edge of the bed. On the floor was a beeswax candle, broken in half. Had that been there last night? He couldn't remember.

"Lacey?" Mack said. He listened for her breath, for her soft snore. He listened, waiting for her eyes to snap open. Waiting for her to mistake him once again for Maximilian. He waited until he couldn't wait anymore, and then he touched her cheek—it was cold.

Lacey was dead.

MARIBEL KNEW THE POWER was back on when she heard the phone ring. She opened her eyes and was instantly aware of Jem's arm draped over her waist. She didn't rise to answer the phone. It was either Mack or Tina, and she didn't want to talk to either of them. The phone rang four times, but no message played—the tape must have been erased with the power outage.

Maribel rolled toward Jem. He lay facedown in Mack's pillow. His young, strong shoulders were bare, he had one arm folded under his head and one touching Maribel's side. Maribel felt a wave of desire. She lifted the covers. Jem wore only his boxer shorts.

She lay back, weighing her options. She could slip off Jem's boxers and make love to him, or she could let him be. Maribel looked out the tiny bedroom window. She saw actual sunlight, a good sign if ever there was one.

Before Maribel moved a muscle, she explained things to Mack in her mind. *I am not doing this because I'm angry. I'm not angry. I'm hurt and disappointed because I loved you in as many ways as I knew how and in the end, those weren't the right ways. So here I am now, about*

*to do this thing because I think it will help me to be happy, if only tem-
porarily. Although I'm coming to learn that all happiness is temporary.*

Maribel pressed her lips to Jem's shoulder. She moved her mouth
a fraction of an inch lower, and kissed him again. She waited, but he
didn't stir. She picked a spot on the curve that ran from the side of his
neck to his shoulder and she kissed him there, a ripe, wet kiss.

The phone rang again. Maribel counted the rings in her head. She
looked hopefully at Jem. He breathed heavily, oblivious. What was it
with men and their love affair with sleep? Maribel slid out of bed and
hurried into the living room for the ringing phone.

"Maribel?" It was a man's voice, but not Mack's.

"Yes?"

"It's me, Vance."

"Hi, Vance," Maribel said. "Mack's not here. I thought he was
down at the hotel."

"He's here," Vance said. "I'm, uh . . . I'm actually looking for Jem.
Is he there?"

Maribel dropped onto the sofa. "What makes you think he's
here?" she asked. Her heart thudded like heavy, scary footsteps. "Did
Mack say he was here?"

"Mack wanted Jem to check on you last night. But I'm glad he
didn't. He shouldn't have been out in the weather. I'll tell you what,
I'll try Jem at home."

"Don't bother," Maribel said. "He's here."

"He is?"

"Yes," Maribel said. "What do you need him for?"

"Uh . . ." There was a pause. "We need him to come down and
work."

"I'll tell him," Maribel said. "I'll send him down when he wakes
up."

"Okay," Vance said, though she could tell from the sound of his
voice that he thought it was anything but okay. "Thanks, Maribel."

"You bet," she said.

• • •

MARIBEL REPLACED THE PHONE and stepped outside to inspect the damage. The backyard was a disaster area. The trees were stripped of leaves and branches. The detritus was all over the yard—twigs the size of pencils, branches the size of a man's arm. A huge bough had fallen into Maribel's garden and crushed the zinnias and impatiens. There were standing puddles in the lawn, ankle deep. But the sun was shining and it felt good on Maribel's arms and bare legs.

She closed the door and went back into the bedroom. Jem was awake, sitting up. His dark hair was mussed and he had sleep marks on his face from the pillow. Maribel sat next to him on the edge of the bed.

"Who was on the phone?" he asked.

She placed a finger on his lips and chose a spot just below his collarbone, and kissed it. If there were going to be rumors, she thought, they might as well be true.

THE PHONE RANG FIVE more times while Maribel and Jem made love, although Jem didn't seem to notice. He concentrated on kissing her, caressing her. He was strong and young and sexy and he loved her. He said it over and over, "I love you, Maribel. I love you." When he came, he cried out. He was overwhelmed with love, and Maribel knew just how he felt. Here was a flower where all the petals said the same thing, *He loves me.*

Jem hugged her close and kissed her hair. "I want you to come to California with me."

"Oh, Jem."

"I do. I really do. I asked you before, when I came for dinner. Remember?"

"I remember," she said. The phone rang again—and again, Jem didn't seem to hear it. "I don't know what to say. I'm not sure I want to go to California."

"Where do you want to go?" Jem asked. "Tell me where and I'll take you."

Maribel smiled. "I want to go to Unadilla." She wanted to see her mother. She wanted to rock in Tina's arms.

"I'll go to Unadilla. I'll go, I swear it," he said.

It wasn't hard at all, to be loved this much. This was the kind of love Maribel needed—unconditional, blind, devoted; it was the love she had missed in a father.

Later, when Jem was in the shower, the phone rang again, and Maribel answered it. *I've made my decision,* she thought, *and whoever's on the other end is going to have to hear about it.*

"Hello?" she said.

"Mari?" It was Mack, but he sounded upset. It sounded like he was crying.

"What's wrong?" she said. He sobbed into the phone. Maribel narrowed her eyes. Had she done this to him? "Mack, what's wrong?"

"Lacey's dead," he said.

The words dropped in Maribel, like coins in a well. "Lacey's dead," she repeated. Lacey was dead. "Oh, God, Mack. I'm sorry. I'm so, so sorry."

He cried into the phone like a little boy. He cried, Maribel admitted, the way she wanted him to cry over her.

"She was my best friend," Mack said.

"I know," Maribel said, and she felt a stab of pain. Lacey Gardner had filled the role of best friend while Maribel had tried so desperately to fill the role of wife. Maribel had missed what was most important. She listened to Mack cry, shushing him every once in a while, marveling at how her love for him was like something she held underwater—as soon as she let go, it bobbed to the surface. She wanted to repeat over and over, "I'll be your friend, Mack, I'll be your friend," but she wondered if it was too late for that. Lacey was dead. The world as they knew it was ending.

BILL THANKED GOD FOR Therese. People in distress were her specialty, her domain. No sooner had she returned to the hotel with the guests than Mack pounded on the door to tell them the news about Lacey.

Therese brought Mack inside and gave him a glass of water, she sat next to him on the sofa and held his hand. She cried with him a little, and said, "Lacey's where she wants to be, Mack. She's with her husband, finally."

"But what if that's bullshit," Mack said. "What if there is no meeting place in the sky."

Bill waited to hear what Therese would say. He wondered this himself—every time he had chest pains, and last winter when the ambulance rushed him to the hospital—*what came next?* It was a question without an answer. Nobody knew, not even Robert Frost. Bill had always believed in something bigger; for twenty-eight years, since W.T. died, *something bigger* planted itself in Bill's mind. A reason. Lacey Gardner, here yesterday, gone today. Why?

Therese said to Mack, "We have to hope. When I'm dying and ready to go, you know what I'm going to do? I'm going to hope with all my heart. And then I'm going to let go. Hope I don't disappear. Hope I land somewhere safely."

The ends of Bill's fingers tingled. He loved his wife. When he was dying and ready to go, he would hope, too. He would hope that death did not separate them.

THERESE SENT FOR THE undertaker, and personally cleaned Lacey's cottage from top to bottom. It was Therese who found Lacey's will. Therese called the paper and put in the obituary. Therese contacted Father Eckerly at St. Mary's and arranged for the service, to be held on Friday.

That night as she and Bill lay in bed, Therese said, "I read Lacey's will before I sent it to her lawyer. She left Mack her cottage, you know."

"She did?"

"You didn't think she'd do otherwise?"

"I never gave it any thought at all," Bill said. That was the truth: Therese had fussed over Mack and the rest of the staff who were upset—Vance, Jem, Love—but no one asked Bill how he felt. And he had known Lacey Gardner longer than anyone. He met Lacey when he was eight years old, an ornery, sullen little boy. Lacey and her husband, Maximilian, were Beach Club members and they were on property every day of the summer after the war ended. Lacey used to shake Bill's hand like an adult, and say, "How do you do?" Bill would cross his arms across his chest and give her a withering look. Then Lacey promised she'd give him two pennies if he would smile. "Nope," he said. "I don't smile for money." Bill could remember what Lacey looked like as a young woman (blond hair in a chignon, dresses that cinched at the waist)—throwing her head back and laughing, wiping the corner of her eye with an embroidered handkerchief. She reminded him of that moment many times in the years that followed; it was their shared punch line. *I don't smile for money.* He supposed he meant his affections couldn't be bought; they had to be earned. And Lacey Gardner had earned them.

He never thought of Lacey dying—she seemed superhuman, the one member of his parents' generation who was going to live forever. But now she was dead. Not only was Bill deeply saddened by the loss but he knew what this meant: he was next.

"So she left her cottage to Mack," Bill said. He recalled his conversation with Mack during the storm. "He promised he'd stay." He took his wife in his arms and spoke into her sweet hair. "I just want someone to stay."

MACK MOVED HIS THINGS out of the basement apartment while Maribel was at work. He threw his clothes into garbage bags and sorted through the CDs. He packed his pay stubs and pictures of his parents. The TV was his, but he let Maribel keep it; the kitchen stuff was all hers, except for a bottle opener shaped like a whale that had belonged to Maximilian. Mack took that. They'd bought the gas grill together, but he let it be. He packed all his belongings into the back of the Jeep, and then he sat in the driveway. He considered leaving a note. A note saying what?

Back at the club, there was no shortage of work. Mack shoveled sand—it was like eating a giant plate of spaghetti—he couldn't seem to make any headway. It kept his body busy and hurting; he tried to concentrate on the physical pain and not his other pain. Lacey gone. Maribel gone.

After work, Mack carried his bags into Lacey's cottage. He dug out the whale bottle opener and popped the top off a Michelob. He settled down in Lacey's chair. He had two phone calls to make.

The first was to How-Baby.

A sugar-voiced, southern secretary answered the phone. "Is this *the* Mack Petersen, as in, our new vice president of travel and hospitality?"

"Yeah," Mack said weakly. "Can I speak to Howard, please?"

How-Baby came on the line, voice booming as though he were sitting three feet away. "I was worried about you!" he said. "We saw you take a real beating from Freida. Watched it on national news. How's the hotel?"

"She'll be okay," Mack said. "But there's a lot of work to be done."

"So it doesn't look like you'll be getting out of there easily," How-Baby said.

"I'm not getting out of here at all," Mack said. "That's why I called."

How-Baby was quiet.

"I'm calling to turn down your offer, Howard," Mack said. "I have to stay here. It's not personal and it has nothing to do with money. Believe me, everything you offered is top-notch. It's just what my gut is telling me."

Still How-Baby was quiet.

"Howard, are you there?"

How-Baby coughed; Mack tried to imagine him upset, agitated, thrown off guard. Caught unaware. It didn't seem possible.

"I'm here," How-Baby said. "You know, just last night Tonya asked what we were going to do next summer when we came to Nantucket and you weren't there. She said she couldn't imagine it."

"She won't have to imagine it," Mack said. *New job gone.*

"No," How-Baby said. "I guess she won't."

• • •

THE SECOND PHONE CALL was to David Pringle. Mack took a long swallow of his beer before dialing.

"David, it's Mack. Mack Petersen."

David chuckled. "It's only September, Mack. I was figuring you'd put off this phone call for at least another month."

"Nope!"

"What's happening?" David asked. "You had all summer to think about it. Come to any conclusions?"

"Has Wendell changed his mind?" Mack asked.

David whistled. Mack pictured him leaning back in his leather chair, shirt sleeves rolled up. "No, he hasn't changed his mind. He's rented a hall for his retirement party."

"Oh."

"You're going to sell, then?"

"No one else has shown any promise?" Mack asked. "This summer, no one . . ."

"Mack, I told you how things were. Nobody will put forth the effort on a farm that's not their own. Wendell did it out of love for your father, simple as that. There's no one else."

"Okay," Mack said. "Sell." *Farm gone.*

"I'll put it up first thing in the morning," David said. "We're not going to get rich from this, you know."

"I know."

"What should I do about the house?"

"Don't do anything," Mack said. "I'm coming back. I'll clean it out myself."

"You're coming back?"

"After the hotel closes, I'll drive out. Take a week or two."

"Call me when you get here," David said. "You can sign some papers. And, well . . . I'd like to see you, Mack. I'll bet you're all grown up."

"I am," he said.

• • •

THE NEXT DAY, MACK stood on the front steps of St. Mary's Church on Federal Street in gray pinstriped pants that belonged to a suit he never wore, greeting the people who came to Lacey's memorial service. This was no different from his job at the hotel, really—greeting people and making them feel welcome. Concierge of the funeral. Manager of grief. Vance and Love and Bill and Therese milled around the aisles of the church, seating people, but Mack didn't want to be inside any longer than he had to. He had "hired" Clarissa Ford to work at the front desk of the hotel and answer the phone. (She showed up wearing a bright blue suit, smelling like lilies of the valley. "There's no smoking in the lobby," he said. "It's okay," she said. "I'm quitting.")

Tiny arrived at the church, and with a man no less, a young man with a ponytail and a mustache.

"Mack," Tiny said, "this is Stephen Rook." She looked at Stephen. "This is Mack."

Mack shook Stephen Rook's hand. He wondered if this were Tiny's boyfriend.

Tiny said, "Stephen is my husband."

"Your husband?" Mack said. "I didn't know you were married, Tiny." He smiled apologetically at Stephen Rook. "She never tells us anything about her personal life."

Stephen Rook raised his hand as if to say, *Hey, that's cool,* and Tiny said, "Stephen is deaf, Mack."

"Whoops. I'm sorry. Tell him I'm sorry."

"He reads lips," she said.

"Thanks for coming," Mack said.

Stephen raised his hand again, and escorted Tiny into the church.

Many of the people at the service were elderly friends of Lacey from back in the day. They shook Mack's hand, explaining how they knew Lacey from Sankaty, or the Yacht Club, or how they used to shop in Lacey's hat store. Lacey's doctor and dentist came from Boston, and so did the Iranian doorman from her Boston apartment building, a slight, dark-skinned man named Rom. Rom whipped out a Polaroid of Lacey standing with his children in front of the Charles River. "She always said she loved Nantucket best," Rom said. "Now I'm here, I see why."

The current class president from Radcliffe arrived with a female friend—Meaghan and Meredith—Mack couldn't tell them apart once they introduced themselves. They called Lacey "Ms. Gardner" and said they were planning a fund-raising drive to start the Lacey Gardner Scholarship Fund for young women business owners. Mack was amazed. Here he was certain he knew Lacey better than anyone else, and yet he hadn't met half these people.

Then, just as Mack was about to head inside, Jem and Maribel walked up. Maribel wore a black linen dress, her blond hair pulled back in a clip, no makeup. She looked beautiful. Jem had on a navy blue double-breasted blazer, like something a sea captain would wear.

"Mack," Maribel said. She smiled sadly and hugged him, and Mack shut his eyes and squeezed her, thinking how if things were different, she might be coming to this church to marry him.

"I'm sorry," he whispered in her ear. "I'm sorry."

When they separated, her eyes were red; the crying had begun. "Me too," she said.

Mack shook Jem's hand. Mack wanted to thank him, and he wanted to toss him off the church steps. But before he could decide between the two, the church bells rang, and the three of them stepped into the sanctuary.

MACK HATED ORGAN MUSIC, he hated the cloying smell of funeral flowers. He hated coffins and pallbearers, although if Lacey had asked him, he would have carried her coffin on his back. Fortunately, though, Lacey had requested cremation, and Therese kept the urn of Lacey's ashes tucked under her arm next to her pocketbook. After the service, they were going to scatter the ashes at Altar Rock.

Mack sat in the front row of the church next to Bill and Therese. Behind him, he could hear people crying. The priest, Father Eckerly, spoke of Lacey's life: her years at Radcliffe, her tenure working for the

State Health Department, her marriage to Maximilian, her shop on Main Street. Her model life as a Catholic, and as a working woman who was also a devoted wife.

"Lacey provided us with many lessons about how to live," Father Eckerly said.

Mack shifted in his seat. He hated funerals because they all reminded him of the funeral service for his mother and father. His parents were rolled down the aisle of Swisher Presbyterian in matching coffins. Wendell gave the eulogy. He spoke of what a tragedy it was, how unfair, Mack, only eighteen, robbed of his parents. The church was packed with people—family, friends, neighbors, kids from school, farmers from as far away as Davenport and Katonah. They were there to pay their respects, but somehow the tragedy overshadowed his parents' simple, good-hearted natures. Somehow, his parents got lost in all the sadness.

After the ceremony, they buried Mack's parents in the cemetery behind the church. Mack watched stone-faced as they lowered his parents into the ground. When the minister threw a handful of dirt onto the coffins, Mack cut through the crowd and walked back to his house, which was over a mile away. He sat alone in his bedroom until his uncle came and fetched him. "They want to see you at the luncheon," his uncle said. "You're all that's left of this family and people want to see you." Mack went to his aunt's house, where everyone said it was the saddest thing they'd ever known to happen, it was the saddest funeral they'd ever attended.

The problem with funerals, Mack decided, was that they never did a person justice. Father Eckerly could drone all day about Lacey's balancing act of career and home—a woman before her time—but that didn't get at the real Lacey. The real Lacey drank Dewar's from the stroke of five o'clock until bedtime, she listened for hours without judging, she defended love and the strength of the human spirit.

Mack closed his eyes. He didn't know what he would do without her.

• • •

BY THE TIME THEY made it to Altar Rock, Mack felt better. He drove Love and Vance in his Jeep, Bill and Therese and Tiny and Stephen followed in the Cherokee, and Rom and the two Radcliffe women wanted to come along as well—so Mack suggested they take Lacey's Buick. The three cars twisted through the moors, which were just starting to turn red. Autumn was less than a week away. Mack ascended the steep hill to Altar Rock—the highest point on the island. He parked, picked the urn of Lacey's ashes off the front seat (Therese gave the urn to him after the ceremony, saying, "I think Lacey would want to ride with you"), and climbed out of the car.

When Mack first read Lacey's will, he wondered why she wanted her ashes scattered at Altar Rock—why not scatter them into the water at the Beach Club? But as soon as he stepped out of the car, he understood why. The panorama was spectacular—from here he could see Sankaty Lighthouse, Nantucket Harbor, and in the distance, Great Point Light. If they scattered Lacey's ashes at the Beach Club, the water might carry her away. But when they scattered her ashes here, she would become one with Nantucket.

Mack waited until the group gathered into a semicircle, then he opened the urn. He expected ashes, like from a cigarette—he thought fleetingly of Clarissa Ford—but these ashes were chunky and hard, like pieces of coral. He took a handful and passed the urn to his left, to Bill. Bill took a handful and passed the urn to Therese, and so on, until the urn reached Rom and Rom had to turn the urn upside down so that the last few pieces of Lacey's remains came loose in his palm.

Mack turned to Bill. "Do you want to recite a poem?" Mack whispered. "Or should we, I don't know . . . should we all say something?"

Therese leaned over. "Why don't we each pick a spot and say something privately before we scatter?"

Mack raised his voice. "Okay, uh . . . everyone can pick a spot and say something privately and then, I don't know . . . bombs away, I guess."

Love and Vance faced Sankaty Light, Bill and Therese faced south toward the airport, the Radcliffe women turned to the harbor. Tiny and Stephen Rook tossed their ashes out over the moors. Rom threw his into the air like a baseball.

Mack held his ashes. His hands were sweating and the ashes left a white, chalky residue. He stood next to the stone marker for Altar Rock, wondering what he could possibly say to Lacey, or to God. Lacey had no grandchildren, Bill and Therese had no son, Cecily had no brother, Maribel had no father, Andrea had no husband—and Mack had set himself down among these people like a piece in a jigsaw puzzle. He filled their gaps and they filled his. But now some of the pieces had disappeared, leaving Mack exposed. Lacey was gone. Whatever Mack held in his hand—the ashes of her bone, her heart, her brain—he wanted to keep, in a jar, or a sugar bowl somewhere. He wanted to keep this last little part of her with him.

Gradually he became aware that everyone else was finishing up, and while no one stared at him, he got the distinct feeling they were waiting. He couldn't shove Lacey's ashes in his pants pocket now.

He squeezed his eyes shut. *I love you, too, Gardner,* he said. *Thanks for being my friend.*

He let Lacey go.

THE GROUP STOOD AROUND Altar Rock a few moments longer in silence. Then Stephen Rook said something in sign language.

"It is a beautiful day," Tiny repeated.

Everyone nodded in agreement, and drifted toward their cars. They were going back to Lacey's cottage for some lunch. After everyone went home, Mack wanted to sit in Lacey's armchair, in Lacey's cottage—now his armchair in his cottage—and drink a stiff Dewar's.

He climbed into the Jeep and Love and Vance piled into the back, even though Lacey's ashes were no longer up front. The empty urn rolled around on the floor.

"I feel like your chauffeur," Mack said.

"We want to be together," Love said.

"Yeah," Vance said. In the rearview mirror, Mack watched him put his arm around Love's shoulders. Mack thought of Maribel, and he wondered if the feeling of being the stupidest person in the world would pass.

Mack led the caravan back down the hill into the thick of the moors. He was deep in thought—about Lacey, about his parents, and about Maribel—but he did notice when Love abruptly cleared her throat.

"I'm pregnant," she said.

10

Windshift

October 3

Dear S.B.T.,

I almost gave in to you. I almost let myself relinquish the hotel—not for the love of money—but out of frustration. My daughter is gone, that much is true. I don't know if or when she'll be back. Her disappearance has left me with a hole inside. After much thought, I realized that you, also, must have a hole inside—because what else drives one man's desire for what another man has? I hope that you find something to fill the void within yourself—but it will not be my hotel.

I have indulged this correspondence mostly for fun—it has been a piece of detective work, trying to discover your identity. I suspected everyone from Mack to Therese to my old, good friend Lacey Gardner, God rest her soul. I suspected hotel guests and Beach Club members. But now I would guess you are someone else entirely— someone on the outside looking in—possibly even a trickster without a penny to your name. It doesn't matter, S.B.T. I want to thank you for showing me how valuable the hotel is—worth much, much more than $25 million. You can't put a price on love.

And so, with this letter, I officially end our correspondence. I wish you luck in whatever else you pursue.

Yours truly,

Bill Elliott

NOW THAT AUTUMN HAD arrived, the front desk was a peaceful place to work. Love kept the woodstove fired throughout the day and a mug of warm herbal tea by the phone. She wore bulky sweaters and the fleeces she hadn't touched since early May. Normally, wearing winter clothes and lighting fires got Love excited for winter. Love had a plane ticket back to Aspen leaving after the hotel closed on Columbus Day, and although she was going to use it, she wasn't staying in Aspen. It was amazing, really, how her life had changed in less than six months. Not just the circumstances of her life but her way of thinking as well. Her whole life before coming to this island had been charted, graphed, strategized. What she realized now was that it was much more fun to let Life tell her how things were going to be.

Look at the way she announced her pregnancy. She'd resolved to keep it a secret, but then Lacey died, and although Love didn't know Lacey that well, she felt something up on Altar Rock, some sort of movement, a rush, what Vance would call a "gut feeling" that Lacey's death and her child's conception were not unrelated. They were part of a cycle, they were part of how the big picture worked. And descending into the moors—the breathtaking green-red-gold moors of Nantucket, Love blurted out the news.

She stunned Vance and Mack, that was for sure. Vance's expression remained unchanged for a split second, then his mouth opened and he laughed. Not a funny laugh, but a happy laugh. He hugged and kissed her and he laughed. He clapped Mack on the shoulder and Mack let go of the stick shift long enough to grab Vance's hand.

"That's terrific, you guys," Mack said. "Man, is that great. Congratulations."

"I'm going to be a dad," Vance said. His voice was filled with awe, Love supposed, and fear maybe too, but no hesitancy. "I'm going to be a father." The words didn't frighten her at all; driving down the bumpy, sandy road she knew she loved Vance. He was totally wrong for her—ten years too young, too sullen and moody and utterly mysterious—and yet she loved him. She wanted to be with him, she wanted to know him and she wanted him to father her child, in every sense. Standing on Altar Rock, she felt her heart open up to include other people; she felt her life grow beyond just herself. This was a gift she had never expected from pregnancy, or wanted, but here it was. She was forty years old and she was growing up.

Love and Vance talked about what they were going to do. First they considered Vance moving to Aspen. He could get a job at the Hotel Jerome, or the Little Nell. After the baby was born in May, they could return to Nantucket. This plan had its appeal, but when Love thought about it, she realized she didn't want to live in Aspen any longer. "Can we stay here?" she asked him. "Can we stay on Nantucket?"

He smiled. She wasn't used to this—him smiling all the time now. "Sure," he said.

Vance discovered that the house Mack and Maribel usually rented for the winter would be empty. So the house on Sunset Hill—the house Mack called the Palace—would be theirs. It was a house that fell out of the pages of Love's book, *Vintage Nantucket*. The uneven wooden floors might throw her pregnant body off-balance, but the ceilings and the doorways were low enough that she had plenty of places to brace herself.

And so, they would stay on Nantucket, and this seemed the final piece of Love's happiness. She was pregnant, she was in love with Vance, and over the past five months she had fallen in love with Nantucket. She was staying.

A COUPLE WEARING SWEATERS and gloves and hiking boots walked into the lobby, their cheeks bright with the cold. It was room 15, the Hendersons. They were young and laid back, the kind of couple Mack had promised would show up in the fall.

"We just walked the trails at Sanford Farm," Mrs. Henderson said. She had gray eyes and thick black eyelashes. "This place is so gorgeous. It's like make-believe. The houses in town, the shops, the restaurants. And then when you get out of town, the natural beauty is astounding."

"The island is magical," Love agreed.

Mr. Henderson approached the desk, one hand in his front jeans pocket, and one hand wrapped around a mug of coffee. "We're school-teachers in Vermont," he said. "And Vermont is beautiful. But not like this. It must have something to do with being on an island, all that water, you know." He looked at Love. "Do you live here?"

Here—Nantucket—the land of stars and clams, oxygen-rich air and romance?

"Yes," she said.

JEM CALLED HIS PARENTS from the phone in Maribel's apartment. He knew his family was waiting to hear from him. Waiting for him to come home.

His sister, Gwennie, answered the phone.

"It's me," he said. "Mom and Dad there?"

"That's just great," Gwennie said. "We don't hear from you in six months, and then you can't even say hello like a normal person? That's just great, Jem."

"Gwen, are Mom and Dad there, please? This is costing money."

"Don't you want to know how I am?"

"Sure," he said.

"I'm more blood than flesh," she said. "But I've gained six pounds."

"Excellent," he said. "No more puking?"

"Not as much. When are you coming home?"

"I need to talk to Mom or Dad," Jem said. "Put on whoever's in the vicinity."

Gwennie didn't bother to cover the receiver. "*Mom! Dad!*" she screamed. "*Jem's on the phone!*"

His mother got on. "Jem! Thank you for calling, honey."

"Hi, Mom."

"How are you?"

"I'm great. It's been quite a summer."

"It sounds like it. I photocopied your letters for my bridge club. You don't mind, do you? If it said something private, I blocked it out. But you really didn't say anything too private. Everyone wanted to know about the people you were meeting. It sounds like that island is really something."

"It is." He imagined his letters being passed around the bridge table like a cut-glass bowl of nuts.

"When are you coming home? Daddy and I want to pick you up at the airport."

Jem's father picked up the other phone. "Hey, boy! We miss you down here. Feels like you've been away forever."

"What's going on, Dad?"

"I'm watching the Redskins lose and your mother's making chili."

"Gwennie's just starting to get better," his mother whispered. "She's not purging nearly as often."

"She said she gained six pounds," Jem said. "That's great."

"I talked to Bob Beller about getting you an internship at Brookings," his father said. "How about that? The Brookings Institution—now, there's a high-powered place."

Jem took a deep breath. Hearing his parents' voices made him miss them—he pictured his house, the kitchen with the copper pots hanging, his bed and goose-down pillows, the den with the pool table and the organ that Gwennie hadn't touched since she was nine years old. He missed it—and he wondered if maybe that was what kept him from calling all summer. He didn't want to miss them too much.

"I'm not coming home," Jem said. "I'm going to New York State for a couple of weeks, and then I'm going to California." He coughed. "Actually, I'm moving to California."

Gwennie must have been listening on a third phone because she yelled out, "He's not coming home! I told you he wasn't coming home and I was right!"

"You're not moving anywhere," his father said.

"Paul," Jem's mother said. "We can't clip his wings." She sweetened her voice. "Why do you want to move to California, Jem? That's so far away."

"I want to be an agent," he said. "I want to open my own talent agency."

"You need capital to open a business," his father said. "Opening a business is not just something you do the year after you graduate from college."

"I know," Jem said. "I'll work for someone else first, and save my money." He thought about the fifteen thousand dollars sitting in Nantucket Bank with his name on it. He had *not* written home about that—his parents would think accepting Neil's money was wrong. They would wonder what he'd done to earn it. "Anyway, I have to be in California to break into the business."

"I was right!" Gwennie shouted. "I told you so!"

"What did you learn up there this summer?" his father asked. "That you don't need your family anymore?"

"Did you meet a girl?" his mother asked. "Did you . . . did you get some girl in trouble?"

With the exception of Gwennie's bulimia, his family was like something from the wrong decade. *Did you get some girl in trouble?* His mother couldn't even say the word *pregnant.*

"No," he said. "No one's in trouble."

"Except you," his father said. "If you don't get yourself home by the end of the month."

"I don't want to work at Brookings, Dad," Jem said. "And I don't want to tend bar at the Tower." The Locked Tower: now the very name of the place gave him the shivers.

"You're not going to California," his father said. "I forbid it."

"Paul!" Jem's mother said. "We talked about this. If Jem wants to go to California, what can we do to stop him? He's twenty-three years old."

"I am not pleased, Jeremy," his father said. "And I'm not sending you any money, so I hope you earned plenty up there. I'm going to call Bob and tell him to forget about the internship. Is that what you want me to do?"

"Yes," Jem said.

"Okay, then." His father hung up.

"Mom, are you still there?" Jem asked.

"Yes," she said.

"Her name is Maribel Cox," Jem said. "She's blond and pretty and nice and incredibly smart. She works at the library and she runs and she's a terrific cook. I love her, Mom."

"You love who?"

"Maribel Cox," he said. "You should be happy for me because this is, like, the best thing that's ever happened to me aside from being born." .

"You love Maribel Cox." His mother sighed. "It probably shouldn't surprise me, but it does. You've always been so levelheaded about girls."

"I'm being levelheaded now," Jem said. "I swear."

"Will you call us when you get to California? Will you tell us where you're living?"

"Do you think Dad will ever speak to me again?"

"He's disappointed, and I have to tell you, I'm disappointed, too, crushed, really. So when you hang up you tell Maribel Cox, whoever she is, that you hurt your mother's feelings."

"I'll call you and tell you where I am," he said. "I'm sorry about everything. I'm glad Gwennie's getting better, and—"

"That's enough, Jeremy," his mother said. "We love you."

She hung up.

"Whoa," Jem said. He punched off the portable phone and fell back into the sofa cushions. "Whoa." He thought back to what Lacey Gardner had told him, about how children should stop hoping for their parents' approval and just live their lives. This fortified him for a minute, but then he realized that just because Lacey was dead didn't mean she was right.

Maribel came into the living room. "How was it?" she asked softly.

"We're going," he said.

OF ALL THE GUESTS who stayed at the hotel, Cal West was Therese's favorite. She didn't know him particularly well; he wasn't what she would call a friend. He wasn't handsome or charming, and he didn't have any egregious personal problems for her to work out—no divorce, no untimely deaths, no emotional or psychological conditions. Nothing about Cal West stood out. He was boring.

Cal West came from Ohio, a place Therese imagined to be even more dull and orderly and monochromatic than the town she grew up in on Long Island. Ohio—the name of the state was deceptively rounded; what Therese pictured was a square of dun-colored carpeting, flat, unattractive. What did people do in Ohio? Cal West worked in the provost's office at Ohio State University. He processed papers having something to do with collegiate life.

Cal West had a triangular face—his forehead was wide and his chin narrow and the planes of his cheeks were straight edges. He had wispy brown hair which he combed down with water, a few faint acne scars, brown eyes. He stood five eight, wore sweater vests and loafers.

He'd started coming to the hotel six or seven years earlier for Columbus Day weekend. Therese might never have noticed him at all except the first year a strange thing happened. When she went in to clean Cal West's room, the place was immaculate. The bathroom sparkled, the bed was made with perfect corners. At first, Therese thought she'd entered a vacant room, but Cal West's suitcase was in the closet and his shirts and pants hung neatly on hangers. Therese checked the room the next day, and the next. His room was pristine. Therese could have gone through the motions of vacuuming the carpet and remaking the bed, but why? She had finally discovered a person as clean as she was.

Cal West spent hours reading in the lobby in front of the woodstove. One year he read the Bible, one year Shakespeare, one year every book that had won the Pulitzer Prize, in chronological order. In the evenings Cal removed his reading glasses, leaned back in the rocker, and listened to the music—Haydn, Schubert, Billie Holiday. Cal West seemed to have a quiet, contented life, and Therese envied that. She thought Cal West must be very wise. He'd done something right.

This year when Cal West walked into the lobby, he was as calm and unassuming as ever. He brought one plain black suitcase with a matching garment bag. He wore a maroon argyle sweater vest and a tweed jacket.

"Therese," Cal said. "Hello." He shook her hand. Always, with Cal, there was a warm handshake when he arrived and when he left. No more, no less.

"Hello, Cal," Therese said. "Welcome home."

Cal nodded; he took everything seriously. "Thank you," he said. "It's good to be home."

"How was your year?" Therese asked.

"Fine, just fine."

Just fine: The typical Cal West answer. But this year Therese wanted to know more. Surely there was something noisy, confusing, or messy in his life.

"How's work?" she asked.

"Fine," he said.

"What do you do again?" she asked. "You work for a university, but what do you *do*?"

"I work in the provost's office," he said. "I process complaints."

"Really?" Therese said. "What kind of complaints?"

"Professors complain about funding, and students complain about professors."

"Do you have a lot of student contact?" Therese asked.

"A little bit," Cal said. He shifted his weight; he was still holding both pieces of luggage. To put them down might anchor him permanently in this conversation with Therese—something he clearly didn't want. "I process written complaints only." He laughed. "My God, if I accepted verbal complaints, my job . . . well, it would be chaos."

Therese smiled at his sweater vest. "Any special women in your life, Cal?"

"No." The answer was taut and clipped. He nodded toward the front desk. "I think I'll check in now."

Cal moved for the front desk as though it were home base, a place where he'd be safe. Therese puttered around her plants, checking the leaves for waxiness, checking the soil for moisture. She looked at Cal West's back as he stood at the desk. What would it be like to be married to Cal West? To have life unfold evenly, without stumbling blocks, without unpleasant surprises like having a baby die inside you or waking up and finding your teenage daughter has disappeared? Therese would never know. She chose Nantucket, and the hotel, where things were always changing; she chose Bill. Bill, who climbed up on a widow's walk during the worst storm in forty years out of devotion to their daughter.

Before Cal headed down the hall and outside to his room, Therese called to him. "Cal!"

Cal turned around. The expression on his face was both fearful and annoyed.

"Let me walk you to your room," she said.

He stood, unmoving, until she was alongside him. She thought crazily, cruelly, of following Cal into his room and trying to seduce him. The idea of it was so completely out of the question that Therese laughed to keep from hating herself. She liked Cal West; what was her problem? Why did she have the urge to shake him up?

"You know," she said as they moved toward the back door of the lobby, "I have a complaint to file. Or maybe it's my daughter who's filed the complaint. She's run away."

"Really?" Cal said. "Run away?"

"She ran away to Brazil," Therese said. "After a very handsome boy." They stepped out onto the boardwalk. Cal West always rented room 20, which was only one room away from the lobby. As soon as they stepped outside, they were at his deck.

"I'm sorry to hear that," Cal said.

"Never mind," Therese said. Cal gripped his key tightly in his right hand; no doubt he wanted her to be on her merry way so that he could enjoy the hotel. "No, not never mind. I'm curious, Cal. I'm curious to know what you think about it. You work with young people. What do you think about an eighteen-year-old running away?"

"We don't get many kids running away from college," Cal said. "Especially not Ohio State. The kids love it. It's paradise for them."

"So you're saying no one runs away."

"No one I know of." He pointed his key at the door of his room.

"But I process complaints about grades and things. Bad food in the dining hall. Sorry I can't help."

"Okay. Look at it this way. What would you do if your daughter—your only child—ran away to another country for some boy?"

Cal licked his lips nervously and stared at his feet. She was torturing him by asking him such a question, by making him imagine such a thing could happen to him.

"I . . . I don't have any children. I really don't know what I would do."

"What if you did have children?" Therese asked.

"Well, then, I'd be quite a different person."

"Cal," Therese said—her voice was growing belligerent, she could hear it. She was verbally abusing her favorite guest, her fellow clean freak—but she yearned for an answer. "What do you think I should do?"

"I don't know, Therese. You're asking me a question that's impossible to answer."

Therese touched his shoulder. "You know, Cal," she said. "Sometimes I wish I could be you for a few days."

He nodded. "I feel the same way about you."

"You do?" Therese said.

"Of course," Cal said. He unlocked the door to room 20 and somehow managed to get himself and his bags inside and turn around so that he stood on the other side of the door, as though he were bidding her good-bye. "You took the risk."

"The risk?"

"The greatest risk there is. The risk of parenthood. You're a mother. And who am I? I'm a nobody."

"You're not a nobody, Cal. You're a man with a peaceful life."

He smiled wanly and closed the door, leaving Therese standing on the steps of his deck, thinking that maybe this was why Cal West was her favorite guest—not because he was the cleanest guest or the quietest, or even the last guest but because something about his calm, safe life made her feel loud and daring and brave. Like a mother.

• • •

VANCE CLEANED HIS HOUSE, literally and figuratively. He'd lived all summer in a rental cottage behind a giant house owned by Frank Purdue's chief financial officer. The house was called the Chicken and Vance's cottage was called the Egg. This fact alone had been enough to keep Vance from telling people where he lived. He didn't want to hear jokes about being an egghead or laying an egg or egg on his face, or which came first, the chicken or the egg—or any other stupid reference that people like Mack and Jem might come up with. Love had been to the cottage, but only a few times, and not for very long. It wasn't a good place to bring women. Vance didn't straighten often and so the cottage collected a jumble of CDs and books and tools.

That would all change now that Vance was going to be a father. Finally, after twelve years, Vance had two things that Mack didn't—a woman and a child-on-the-way. Finally, after twelve years, Vance was released from whatever evil spell Mack cast on him. He was set free with this new life, as a lover and a father.

Carefully, Vance went through everything in his cottage. He packed his books neatly in boxes, he folded his clean clothes and made a pile for laundry. He threw away his poster of Vanessa Williams, his car magazines, he threw away beer bottles and wrappers from frozen burritos. In two weeks, he and Love were moving into the house on Sunset Hill—it was a chance to start over with everything clean and in order.

It was while going through his kitchen cabinets—tossing out any dishes that had chips or hairline cracks—that Vance found Mr. Beebe's gun. The night after Vance pulled the gun on Mack, he brought it home and hid it inside a ceramic pitcher. As Vance lowered the pitcher from the shelf, he heard a rattling and instantly remembered the gun, a nickel-plated .38. Vance held it in his palm, marveling at himself. How had he ever summoned the guts to point this at someone? It was disgusting, and criminal, and Vance felt ashamed, stereotypical: a black guy with a gun. He'd held the gun to Mack's head, he poked it into his chest. What made Vance feel even worse was that Love had no idea he'd kept the gun; she thought he sent it back to that creep, Mr. Beebe.

Vance had to get rid of the gun.

It wasn't the kind of thing he could throw away in a plastic garbage bag with the flawed dishes. What if someone found it and traced the dishes back to him? No, it couldn't simply be *thrown away*; he had to dispose of it.

Vance wrapped the gun in a pair of his ratty old underwear and climbed into his Datsun. He drove to the beach known as Fat Ladies' Beach, which could only be reached by unpaved roads. Vance pulled up to the edge of the beach (the only problem with his Datsun was that he couldn't drive it in the sand). He picked up his underwear and got out of the car.

It was gray and foggy, and gray waves smacked the beach. Vance trudged through the sand to the water's edge. He looked to the left and the right to be sure no one was surf casting or digging for clams. When he was sure that he was all alone, he wiped the gun with his underwear to remove fingerprints and chucked the gun out into the water. He stuffed his dingy underwear into his jacket pocket and sat on the hood of his car for a minute to make sure the gun didn't wash up on shore.

OCTOBER WAS A GREAT month. He could sit on this strip of beach all day and not see another soul. Vance liked fog, he liked the cool, damp, drizzly weather, especially now that he had Love. This winter, he would bring her to see the ocean every day.

Vance climbed into his car and backed up. He turned to look at the water one last time—and he saw something shiny wash up on the beach. Vance squinted; he felt the beginnings of heartburn and he reached into the console for a Rolaid. Then he pulled his brake and ran out onto the beach. The gun lay there, shiny and wet.

He picked up the gun, wrapped it in his underwear, and ran to his car. He drove away from Fat Ladies' Beach, wondering what to do.

He drove to the dump.

The dump was crowded with end-of-the-season dumpers with

their end-of-the-season rubbish. People hauled bloated, shiny black bags of trash, milk crates of bottles and cans, and decrepit furniture to the dumpsters and recycling center. The gun wrapped in underwear lay on the passenger seat, an unwanted passenger. And now Vance wished he'd brought a bag of some kind to hide the gun instead of his underwear. A pair of white BVD's, with the telltale striped waistband. More gray than white.

Vance studied his choices for the gun. He could either toss it into a dumpster the size of a mobile home meant for household trash, or he could recycle the gun under metals. Vance decided immediately against household trash. A gun didn't qualify.

He recycled the gun.

Or tried to. Shoving the swaddled gun under his arm, he walked, head down, for the recycling shoot.

"Vance?"

Vance raised his eyes. Pale orange hair. The white streak. Like a skunk, Vance always thought.

"Hi, Therese."

She seemed upset, like maybe she'd been crying. Since Cecily had left, she cried a lot.

"I came to throw away some of Lacey's old things," she said. "Things nobody wanted."

"That's too bad," Vance said.

"A life lived fully and so much ends up here at the dump." Therese's billowing skirt was too exotic for the dump. For the disposal of life rubbish.

"Yeah," Vance said. "Well, see you."

But Therese had eyes like no one else. Dirt-seeking eyes.

She tugged at the crotch of the underwear that was sticking out from under his arm.

"What's this?" she asked.

"Old underwear."

"You came to throw away a pair of old underwear?"

"Yeah."

She smiled. "You men are so funny. I'll tell you what. Give your underwear to me. I'll use them as rags. That's what I do with Bill's underwear."

Vance tightened his crab claw on the gun. "Sorry. No can do."

Therese tugged at the crotch of his underwear. "Come on."

"Nope." Vance backed up until he felt the Datsun's hood against his legs. He opened the door and slid in, the gun pinched against him. Therese regarded him in a way he was used to—weirdo, oddity, freak. Little did she know he was trying to mend his ways.

VANCE DROVE INTO TOWN and parked at Steamship Wharf. The noon boat was barely visible on the horizon. The steamship workers took their lunch break. Vance walked behind the ticket office where a couple of benches overlooked the harbor, for tourists with enough ingenuity to find them. Some scallopers rigged their boats, but for the most part, the wharf and harbor were deserted. Vance stood on the very edge of the wharf and gazed down into the water. It looked deep, and still. Vance pulled out the underwear, wiped the gun and dropped it into the water. It made a satisfying plunk and disappeared.

Vance steadied his breathing. No cop approached to write him a ticket for littering, the steamship wasn't cruising into its slip holding seven hundred eyewitnesses to what he'd done. It was October, Vance was the father of a living being, and he was getting his house in order.

He waited a few minutes more to make certain the damn gun didn't come bobbing to the surface, and when he was confident the gun was gone forever, he walked back to his car.

Steamship Wharf: the place where twelve years before, he'd stepped off the boat thirty seconds behind Mack, thirty seconds too late. He'd spent a fair amount of time over those years bemoaning this fact. But now, he realized, it didn't matter. He was going to be a father. A father! Vance climbed into his car and drove off the wharf, and it was as close to a fresh start as he'd ever hoped to have.

• • •

DURING HER LAST WEEK on the island, Maribel ran. That was how she wanted to say good-bye—by running, fast and long. It was true autumn now, high autumn, the best season on Nantucket. Colors were vibrant—the dark reds of the bayberry in the moors, the red-orange of flaming bush, the ambers of the dune grass. Some days she was glad to be leaving Nantucket when it was most beautiful; she could always remember it like this. Other days she asked herself, *How can I possibly go?*

Maribel ran through the streets of town. Not only Main and Federal and Centre and the streets the tourists knew, but the narrow, twisting back streets as well—Fair and School and Darling and Farmer and Pine, South Mill, Angola. She studied the antique homes, the postage-stamp gardens and friendship stairs, the screened-in porches and widow's walks and transom windows. She loved the names of the houses—Fair Isle, Left Bank, A Separate Peace, Captain's Daughter, Beach Plum, Aloft, Nana-tucket, Molly's Folly, Hunky Dory, Independence Day, Life Savour. *Good-bye.*

Maribel ran to Surfside Beach and through the State Forest to the airport. She ran Polpis Road to Shimmo, Quaise, Quidnet. She ran out Cliff Road past the old golf course at Tupancy Links, down Eel Point Road by the truly huge summer homes on Dionis Beach. She ran to Madaket Harbor.

She ran to Miacomet on a perfect autumn morning—fifty degrees, bright sunshine, brilliant blue sky. She ran down Miacomet Road sheltered on both sides by pines, until the land opened up by the pond. Mallards paddled just off the banks, and three swans glided through the water. Three white swans like something out of a fairy tale, graciously curved necks, and white tufted feathers at their hind ends, fluffed like tulle. The swans looked like women in fancy dresses. They looked like women in wedding dresses.

At the end of Miacomet Pond, where she could see the ocean peeking over the dunes, Maribel stopped running. She sat down on the marshy bank of the pond and she cried. In the weeks since the hurricane, Maribel told herself that the turn of events was inevitable. Breaking up with Mack, getting together with Jem, leaving the island—all part of some larger plan for her life. But it wasn't easy. She remembered the rides she'd taken with Mack in the Jeep with the top down, all the walks through town in the winter, holding hands. Mack and Nantucket were interchangeable, one and the same, and that was why she had to leave.

She didn't want to chase love anymore, she didn't want to pursue a futile dream. She couldn't make Mack love her any more than she could make her father, whoever he was, wherever he was, love her. She wondered why God had created this kind of exquisite pain, a pain so awful and so complicated, it had its own word—unrequited. She was trading in unrequited for requited, for the opportunity to *be* loved, to be held and cherished the way she deserved. With Jem, she told herself, she would be loved more, she would hurt less.

And, too, Maribel felt the only way she might ever get Mack was to leave him. She didn't think he'd change his mind immediately—but maybe someday. Maybe someday when she was a school librarian in some Los Angeles suburb, a huge bouquet of yellow zinnias would arrive with a card from Mack. Or maybe she'd have to wait until she was as old as Lacey Gardner. She imagined sitting on a porch in rocking chairs and talking with Mack in fifty years—not about what went wrong with their relationship, because by then they would have forgotten what went wrong. No, they would remember happiness. Living in the Palace, seeing the seals at Cisco Beach, listening to Christmas carols from outside the Unitarian church. They would remember all the things that were good about being young and healthy and together on Nantucket. If Mack asked her to marry him when they were in their eighties, she would say yes. And the wait would be worth it.

THE DAY BEFORE SHE and Jem were scheduled to leave, Maribel found herself running down the familiar road to the hotel. She told herself she was headed down there to see Jem—he had to work right up until the very end, carrying bags for the last guest, stripping the last room. But she knew she was really running toward the Beach Club to see

Mack. Six years earlier, this was how they met. He waited for her every morning in the parking lot, pretending to sweep, and then one day he gathered the courage to offer her some water. She couldn't help but wonder, *What if I hadn't accepted it? What if I'd changed my course and never met Mack at all?* Her life would be a different shape, different colors. Many hours could be wasted this way: pondering the way things might have been.

Mack must have sensed her because he was out front by himself, taking down the Nantucket Beach Club and Hotel sign. He turned as soon as he heard footsteps, and when he saw her his face brightened, but only momentarily.

Maribel was terrified, her heart kept on its eight-minute-mile pace even after she stopped to talk to him. She was having difficulty catching her breath. This was ridiculous! she wanted to shout. How could they say good-bye?

Mack spoke first. "What boat are you on tomorrow?" he asked.

She swallowed. "Noon."

He held the unwieldy wooden sign out in front of him. "Another season almost over," he said. "Only Cal West is left."

"You're staying the winter?" she asked. "And next year?"

"Yeah," he said. "I called How-Baby and turned down the job. I think you were right about me. I think I'm stuck here."

She looked out across the beach at the water, at the ferry headed for Hyannis. Tomorrow, it would be her ferry. "You could be stuck worse places," she said.

"Do you want me to see you off tomorrow?" he asked.

"Would you?" she said.

He kicked a hermit crab shell across the road. "I'll be there."

Maribel bit her lip; she was going to cry, but he didn't have to know about it. She waved, turned toward home, and ran like hell.

BILL HAD SURVIVED ANOTHER season. Barely. And not without profound loss. His daughter was gone, and the hotel needed colossal amounts of work—the floors and carpets on the Gold Coast had to be relaid, sections of the roof had to be repaired, and Clarissa Ford's room—Lucky number 7—had to be totally renovated. Bill was leaving those projects until the spring, when he hoped he would feel more enthusiastic than he did now.

Bill couldn't run the hotel without Mack's help, that was for sure. Bill watched from his bay window as Mack walked into Lacey Gardner's. Mack would stay there over the winter—he'd already agreed to pay Bill for the cost of heating.

Bill went over to Lacey's. The cottage had a spare look to it inside, although the sign for Lacey's hat shop still hung, and her Radcliffe diploma. But the Spode was down and the flowery Nantucket prints. It looked less like an old lady's house and more like a monastery.

Mack came down the hallway carrying two empty boxes.

"You need some stuff for the walls," Bill said. "I'm sure Therese can spare a few things from the hotel."

"All the prints in our apartment were Maribel's," Mack said. "She's taking them. But that's okay. I'm going to bring some things from home."

"From home?" Bill said.

"I'm going back to Iowa at the end of the month," Mack said. "For Harvest."

"You're going to Iowa?"

"I'm selling the farm," Mack said. "I need to meet with my lawyer. I need to clean out my parents' house. So I figure I'll put a trailer on the back of the Jeep and haul it all back here."

"That's a big step," Bill said. "Selling your farm." Bill felt ashamed. With all the other excitement, he'd forgotten Mack had to make this decision about his farm. If he'd paid attention, there might have been a way he could have helped. But maybe not.

Mack threw the empty boxes down. "I haven't managed to make it back to Iowa in the last twelve years, I don't see myself moving back there in the next twelve. This is my home."

"Well, I've been rethinking your proposition about the profit sharing," Bill said.

"Forget about it," Mack said. "That was Maribel's idea, not mine."

"I want to give you something," Bill said. "I want to thank you for staying." An idea came to Bill then—an idea so crazy, so luminous that Bill flushed, his heart moved in his chest as though it were trying to escape. Where did the idea come from? From losing W.T., then Cecily, from Mack cleaning out his parent's house, from standing here in Lacey's cottage. It came from all of those places, and from the desert place inside of him. He should talk to Therese first, of course, they should think long and hard about this idea, they should have time to embrace it, shun it, and embrace it again. But Bill couldn't wait. Mack stood in front of him, sandy haired, ruddy faced, handsome, saying he would stay. The son Bill had always wanted.

Mack shoved his hands in his jeans pockets. "You don't have to give me anything," he said. "You've given me plenty already."

"I'd like to adopt you," Bill said.

"Adopt me?" Mack's brow folded and Bill felt like a fool. Just because he yearned for a son didn't mean Mack wanted parents. He'd had two perfectly good parents—that was obvious from who the boy grew up to be. "You want to adopt me?" Mack asked.

Bill nodded, and then he was overcome with the fear that Mack would say yes.

Mack smiled. "I'm flattered, Bill. I'm . . . I'm touched. But I don't know about that."

Bill exhaled; he hadn't realized he was holding his breath. "I don't know either," Bill said. "It was just an idea. You mean a lot to Therese and me. We want to do something for you."

"How about a raise?" Mack said. "I am saving to buy a piece of land."

"I'd be happy to give you a raise," Bill said. "A big raise."

"And full control next time there's a storm?"

"You got it," Bill said.

"And one afternoon off a week," Mack said. "If I ever get another girlfriend, I want to be able to spend some time with her."

"Agreed," Bill said. "Do you want this all in writing?"

"No," Mack said. "I trust you . . . Dad." Mack grinned, then laughed, then reached out to shake Bill's hand, and Bill embraced him. *Dad.* So it would be a joke between them from now on, that was fine. But Bill couldn't help wishing that sometime in the next twelve years Mack would take him up on his offer, and become his son.

When Bill returned to his house, Therese was on the phone with the realtor from Aspen, setting up arrangements for their winter house.

"We'll be there December fourth," Therese said.

After she hung up, Bill said, "Maybe we shouldn't go back to Aspen this year. After all, I can't ski anymore, really. Maybe we should go to . . . Hawaii."

Therese flashed him a disgusted look. "We can't go to Hawaii."

"Why not? It'll be warm. We'll get a condo with maid service and a cook. We can walk on the beach—"

Therese cut him off. "We can't go to Hawaii because Cecily won't know to look for us there. The only place she'll look for us is at the house in Aspen."

"Oh," Bill said. Two good ideas shot down in one day.

"Don't you see how it's going to work?" Therese said. "One morning we'll be sitting on the sofa drinking coffee and staring out at the back of the mountain, and we'll see a bright spot. Cecily's hair. She'll be trudging up the road from town with her backpack, and we'll see her beautiful hair. That's how it's going to work. That's how it's going to be."

Therese spoke adamantly. She was nuts, of course, as delusional as Bill had been during the storm. They were taking turns being crazy. *That's how it's going to be.* Bill admired her confidence. He closed his eyes and hazily saw the scenario she painted. The cool, sharp evergreens that bordered the road to Independence Pass, the snowdrifts three feet high—and sticking out so that they couldn't miss it, Cecily's red hair. He guessed it wasn't impossible. Maybe if they went through the motions of sitting on the sofa with their coffee every morning, God would recognize their pain, and more importantly, their devotion, the two of them sitting there like a kind of prayer, and He would let this wish come true. Okay, then, they would go to

Aspen and look out the window and wait for their daughter to come home.

Bill nodded to let Therese know that he agreed, and then he took her hand and led her into the bedroom. She was alive and warm and she was staying, had always stayed and always would. She was his wife of thirty years. Bill made love to Therese, even though it was three o'clock in the afternoon.

WHEN MACK WAS HALFWAY to Steamship Wharf, he wondered why he'd offered to see Maribel off. He supposed he owed it to her—you dated a woman for six years and lived with her for three and it felt suspiciously like a piece of you was getting on the boat and leaving. Mack wished he owned a dog; he could talk things over with a dog without worrying about a response. He needed someone to bounce ideas off; he was sick of himself. In Iowa, he would pick up a Labrador or a German shepherd from a large farm litter. A new best friend.

Mack occupied his mind with thoughts of his new dog until he reached the steamship parking lot. It was ten to twelve; Maribel's Jeep wasn't in the lot. He missed the statement she'd made, then, officially driving off Nantucket. Mack swung his Jeep into a space and hopped out. There were tourists dragging suitcases on wheels, and there were the usual stout Steamship Authority workers in their Day-Glo vests. But no Maribel. She probably decided to forgo the good-bye; she probably found it too difficult.

Then Mack felt a tap on his shoulder, and there she was.

"Jem drove the car on," she said. "I told him I was waiting for you."

"You've spent a lot of time waiting for me," he said.

She teared up immediately, and pulled a Kleenex out of her suede jacket. "I came prepared," she said, wiping her eyes.

"You'll be happier without me," Mack said. "That's why I did what I did."

"You gave up," she said.

"You deserve better."

"It doesn't help to hear you say that," she said. "Because I love you and I believe in you."

"I know," he said. He opened his arms and took her in. He'd seen enough movies to understand that there were two kinds of endings—the kind where Maribel decided at the last minute to stay with him despite everything, and the kind where she got on the boat and left. Mack didn't know which ending he was pulling for, a sign in and of itself. Maybe he had a warped sense of what love should be, but he thought that in love everything would be clear—instead of the muddy, confused, back-and-forths he'd had with Maribel. Still, as he held her, as she cried into his sweater, he thought, I will never watch her run in her sleep again. I will never see her jog toward me, ponytail swinging. I will never make her smile. It was his job now to play the uncaring ogre, so that she could leave and find happiness elsewhere. He owed her that much. But what about his own happiness? Where would he find that? Where would he even look if Maribel left?

Over the loudspeaker came the fuzzy announcement that the noon boat for Hyannis was ready to depart. Maribel lifted her face from his chest, her mascara ran and her upper lip quivered. But she said nothing. It was Mack's turn to speak.

"I can't believe this is happening," he said. "Will I ever see you again?"

"Does it matter?"

"Of course it matters," he said. "Maribel, I love you."

"You love me?" she said.

"Yes." He was sure that hearing this hurt worse than anything else he could have said, but what could he do? It was the truth.

Maribel blinked her blue eyes, more tears fell.

"I want you to stay," he said. "Please stay."

She smiled, and for a second Mack saw her as she was when it all began: Maribel standing in the stacks of the Nantucket Atheneum secretly reading a paperback romance. Six years younger and full of hope.

"I want you to stay," he said.

"You're lying," she said. "But thank you." Then, she turned and ran from him.

A Kleenex fell from her pocket and blew toward Mack. He picked it up—it was wet and stained with black splotches. He put it in his pocket and climbed into his Jeep. If he had a dog in the seat next to him, he might be able to watch the boat pull out of its slip and listen to its lonely moan of a horn. But he couldn't do it alone, so he drove away.

BACK AT THE HOTEL, things were quiet. The wind sang a bit, and Mack heard the thock of a gull dropping a hermit crab shell onto the asphalt. This was a taste of what the winter would be like—after Bill and Therese left for Aspen and it was just him, living alone in Lacey's cottage. He hoped he'd learn to appreciate his solitude. That was what Mack wanted—to hear this quiet and be able to call it peace.

A man jogged into the parking lot. He was in his early fifties, with thick blond hair, wearing a Nantucket sweatshirt and navy nylon shorts. His legs were red with the cold. He looked familiar and Mack ran through the summer's faces. Beach Club member? Hotel guest?

"You're Mack," the man said.

Mack smiled. Concierge to the very end. "That's right. Can I help you?"

The man trotted up to Mack. Sweat dripped down his temples. He had clear blue eyes. "I've been wanting to introduce myself for a long time," he said. "My name is Stephen Bigelow Tyler." He said the name in such a way that Mack felt he should recognize it. Stephen Bigelow Tyler? The guy looked familiar, but nothing clicked.

Mack stuck out his hand. "Pleasure."

Stephen Tyler glanced up at Bill and Therese's house. "I run down here all the time. Usually at dawn when it's quiet, but sometimes after dark."

"It's a beautiful spot," Mack said.

"I've been trying to buy the hotel from your boss for years," Tyler said, and he laughed, wiping his forehead against his shoulder. "Stubborn man you work for, he won't sell. Though I guess I should be glad. I offered him twenty-five million for it."

"You're the one who's been trying to buy the Beach Club?" Mack said.

"Quite unsuccessfully," Tyler said. "Which is too bad because I wanted to give it to you."

"Give what to me?"

"The hotel. I wanted to buy the hotel and give it to you."

"Give me the hotel?" Mack backed up a step. Any crazy person could come down here now that it was off-season. This guy didn't seem particularly dangerous—what seemed dangerous was that Mack felt he was telling the truth. Tyler wanted to give *him* the Beach Club? Mack thought of How-Baby, David Pringle, Vance pulling a gun on him in the middle of the night. Who was behind this?

"Who are you?" Mack said.

"I'm Maribel's father," he said.

A combination of fear and excitement spread through Mack as he stared at the man's ruddy legs, his neat white socks, his Nike AirMax running shoes, the same brand that Maribel wore. Maribel's father. Her *father*, for God's sake. Then Mack's eyes traveled back to the man's face. There was no doubt. The hair, the eyes, and something unnameable in his face that Mack had seen in another face every day for the past six years.

"Does she know you're here?" Mack asked. "Does she even know you exist?"

Tyler shook his head. "I found her years ago, by accident, when I spotted her with her mother at a shopping mall I was developing in upstate New York. I recognized her mother, and when I got a look at Maribel I had someone do a little research. I kept track of her all these years, although I never told her who I was. Because I have other children, and a wife, in Wellesley. I didn't want to complicate things for myself or for her or for her mother." He took a deep breath. "I just wanted to give her something wonderful, something huge, so that she would have a happy life."

"And you're telling me now because she's gone."

Tyler pushed up the sleeves of his sweatshirt, like he was getting ready to fight, but then his shoulders sagged. "I watched you two a few minutes ago, at the boat. I thought of introducing myself then, to give Maribel a reason to stay. But like I said, I didn't want to complicate her life, I wanted to make it easier. So now she's gone and she doesn't know. It's better that way."

Mack disliked the thought of someone watching his last minutes with Maribel. "Maybe," he said angrily. "Though I don't see how it could be. I know far too much about absent parents. If she ever calls me or comes back here, I'm going to tell her."

Tyler frowned. "I hate to say it, son, but I don't think she's coming back." He kicked at some gravel. "We both lost her. But hey, maybe I'm wrong. In any case, let me give you my card. I think I can help you sell your farm."

"My farm? You know about my farm? What are you, some kind of spy?"

Tyler shrugged. "I'm her father is all," he said. "I've been watching out for her." He took a business card from his shorts pocket, handed it to Mack, and before Mack could even read the scripted print: *S.B.T. Enterprises, Boston, Nevis, Nantucket*, Tyler jogged away.

Mack stood in the wind until Tyler disappeared down North Beach Road, taking Mack's dream with him. Owning the Beach Club, running it with Maribel. Now it was nothing more than a great story to tell.

But to whom?

MACK WALKED INTO THE office. A mistake, he realized, because out the window, he saw the ferry disappearing on the horizon.

The phone rang and it startled him, although it comforted him, too, the familiar sound, the reminder that summer's end was temporary, and not a true end. Someone always wanted to book for *next* July or August.

Mack picked it up. "Nantucket Beach Club and Hotel," he said.

"Mack?"

A female voice, distant-sounding, like someone calling from the other side of a long tunnel. Mack glanced back out the window, and fingered the Kleenex in his pocket. Maribel, calling from the ferry? It didn't sound like Maribel; it sounded more like a woman who expected him to be excited to hear from her. Andrea, in Baltimore?

"Yes," Mack said.

"Mack, it's me," the voice said. "Come on, I haven't been gone *that* long."

"Cecily?" Mack said. He plugged his other ear. "Cecily, where are you?"

"In Rio," she said. "At the airport."

"Are you coming home, kid? God, your parents are sick with worry."

"I'm coming home."

"What happened?" Mack asked. "Is everything all right?"

"It's over between Gabriel and me," Cecily said. "I feel like every bone in my body is broken, it hurts so bad."

"I know what you mean," Mack said.

"I'll tell you about it when I get home. In fact, I really need to talk to Maribel."

Mack could tell her about Maribel, and about Lacey, but they were subjects that required face time. Cecily thought she hurt now, and she was in for more.

"Listen, do you want me to put you through to your house? I know your parents are anxious to hear your voice."

"I'm leaving in a few hours," she said. "I should be back on the island tomorrow morning. I want to surprise them, Mack, okay? So don't tell."

"Okay," Mack said. "I won't tell." He remembered Bill's weak heart, but a heart wouldn't fail from too much good news, or relief.

"I missed you, Mack," Cecily said.

"I missed you too, kid."

"I'm not a kid," she said.

"Come home and prove it."

"Okay, fine, I will!" Mack heard her old spunk and he knew just how she was standing, with her hip thrown out like an attitude. The slouchy, bright-haired princess of the Beach Club kingdom was coming home.

"So I'll see you tomorrow, then?" she said.

What was home, really, but the place where a space just your shape and just your size waited for you. Here, on this island, at this Beach Club, a space for Mack, a space for Cecily.

"I'll be here," he said.

THE
AMERICAN
CENTURY

Also by Norman F. Cantor

The Sacred Chain
The Jewish Experience
The Medieval Reader
Medieval Lives
The Civilization of the Middle Ages
Inventing the Middle Ages
The English
Western Civilization: Its Genesis and Destiny
How to Study History (with R. I. Schneider)
Perspectives on the European Past

THE AMERICAN CENTURY

VARIETIES OF CULTURE IN
MODERN TIMES

Norman F. Cantor
Picture Essays by Mindy Cantor

HarperCollins*Publishers*

Picture credits follow page 591.

FIRST EDITION

Designed by Joseph Rutt
Inserts designed by Barbara D. Knowles, BDK Books, Inc.

Library of Congress Cataloging-in-Publication Data

Cantor, Norman F.
    The American century:varieties of culture in modern times/Norman
F. Cantor with Mindy Cantor. — 1st ed.
        p. cm.
    Rev. and expanded ed. of: Twentieth-century culture. 1988.
    Includes bibliographical references and index.
    ISBN 0-6-017451-x
        1. Civilization, Modern—20th century.   2. Modernism (Art)   3. Modernism
(Literature)   4. United States—Civilization—20th century.   I. Cantor, Mindy.
II. Cantor, Norman F.   Twentieth-century culture.   III. Title.
CB425.C28   1997
909.82—dc20   96-32186

---

97 98 99 00 01 ❖/RRD 10 9 8 7 6 5 4 3 2 1

To Judy, Howard, and Max

Contents

*Illustrations and essay on Modernism follow page 144;
Psychoanalysis, page 238; Postmodernism, page 396.*

PREFACE

This book is a revised and expanded version of *Twentieth Century Culture, Modernism to Deconstruction*, which was published in 1988 by Peter Lang, a small Swiss house. The original version of the book was selected by *Choice*, the review journal of the American Library Association, as "an outstanding academic book." While very pleased to receive this prestigious award, I had in fact addressed my book to the general public. I am grateful to my editor at HarperCollins, New York, Hugh Van Dusen, for the opportunity to reach a wide audience in this amended and updated version.

The origins of this book lie in my conviction that informed knowledge of our own and recent times is critical for good citizenship. The ancients thought so, as witness the works of the most persuasive of classical historians, Thucydides and Tacitus.

What has shaped this book is my further belief that it is especially intellectual and cultural development that should be highlighted, within a social and political context. Thereby readers will be equipped to understand the significance of what they read in the serious press and perceive in museums and in works of the performing arts, and be encouraged to study the critically important literary, philosophical, and scientific texts, both recent and contemporary.

Plenty of critics think it is bootless to attempt narrative history on the large scale attempted here. But I believe that it is helpful to the lay reader to present an intellectual road map of the twentieth century. A road map is only a diagram, an artificial construct, but you can't get far without it.

The main focus of this book is on Europe and the United States. This is not because of cultural chauvinism but because the dynamic ideas and artistic movements and scientific constructs of this century have lain, for better or worse, mostly in the West.

It is quite possible that the twenty-first century will see a shift in importance and leadership to East Asia, Latin America, and Africa, following on these societies' liberation from Western political and economic power, and that mankind will be better off for that shift. The twentieth century may be the last century of Western cultural and intellectual and scientific dominance. Certainly dark things as well as enlightened ones were the outcome of that now eroding hegemony.

But for now, looking back at the end of the twentieth century, it is the texture of thought and feeling in the West that demands close examination, if we are to perceive the roads well taken and forms of intellectual consciousness intensively pursued.

Mindy Cantor has not only selected and organized the illustrations for this book. I have discussed with her many times the issues and themes in it, and I have greatly benefited from her insights and learning, particularly on the art and music of the twentieth century.

I wish to express my thanks to my literary agent, Alexander Hoyt, for his advice and encouragement, and to my secretary, Eloise Jacobs-Brunner, for preparing the computer disk. Recognition is owed to Art Resources, Inc., for their cooperation with Mindy Cantor in her selection of the illustrations.

Dawn Marie Hayes has assisted in organizing the bibliography and checking each title against the listing in the Harvard University Library catalog.

INTRODUCTION: A.D. 2000

The end of the second Christian millennium and of the twentieth century is an especially appropriate time to look back over the past hundred years and make out the pattern of what has occurred, which may help us to assess where we are now and what the shape of the near future is likely to be.

The twentieth century has been marked by extremes of collective human behavior, both good and bad. It has been a century of unprecedented intellectual creativity and cultural advancement and an age whose terror and genocide were not anticipated by the optimistic pundits and visionaries of the nineteenth century.

From almost its very beginning to its end, the twentieth century has been characterized by the extremes of light and dark in its historical record. Historical writings alone cannot answer the question of the cause of this polarity—that would need insights provided by theology, anthropology, and psychology, among other disciplines. But a history of the twentieth century can at least show the pattern of thought and action that underlies the polarized outcomes of the past hundred years and, drawing on other disciplines, suggest why ours has been both the most accomplished and intellectually progressive and the most lethal and morally retrogressive one in recorded history.

Which ideas and social and material factors contributed to the variations in human attitudes and behavior that have characterized the twentieth century? How did these positive and negative factors interact with one another, and what is the future likely to hold for the human species that first appeared in East Africa two million years ago?

As we approach A.D. 2000 there are grounds for hoping that humankind has superseded the terror and violence that darkly disfigured the history of this century. Some writers think we are at the end of history, or at least violent and tempestuous history, and that we can look forward to a new age of enlighten-ment—of peace, rationality, and benign consensus. Others think that our problems are deep and systemic, and that we are living now in a brief interlude before renewed extremism, upheaval, and violence, and that indications of the latter dark forces indeed are already flashing on international and national horizons.

An understanding of what happened in the past hundred years has to be drawn upon in choosing between these contrasting scenarios and in enabling intelligent choices and heartfelt commitments at the turning of the century and the dawn of a new millennium.

In trying to discern a pattern in the cultural history of the West in the twenti-eth century, three themes stand out. The first is the rise, impact, and dissolu-tion of the cultural movement known as modernism, which profoundly affected the ethos and art of our century. Second, there was a continuing inter-action between ideas and art on one side and political movements and institu-tions of power on the other. There was a culture of the Left and also a culture of the Right. Whatever may have been the cultural conditions of previous cen-turies, the social and political shaping of ideas and art is readily apparent in the twentieth century.

The third theme in twentieth-century cultural history, more and more evi-dent with each passing decade, was the importance of the United States. Not only did the United States make major original contributions to philosophy, science, art, and literature, but the important facets of Western European cul-ture were absorbed into the American intellectual world and achieved their ultimate form and highest significance in the American context. It was the magnetic quality of American society and the determining force of American wealth and power that impelled intellectual movements that were heavily European in origin into their definitive historical forms.

THE
AMERICAN
CENTURY

1

THE CULTURAL WORLD OF 1900

The Four Cultural Revolutions There is some debate, as there always is when a new century begins, whether the starting point for the twenty-first century will be technically 2000 or 2001. No matter: As in 1900 (or 1901), a new century brings with it the widespread assumption among ruling groups that the cultural pattern of the previous decades will continue unchallenged, and among radical observers outside the power elite, the perception that intellectual and artistic life is threatened with a great upheaval.

One hundred years ago holders of political place and wielders of great wealth were indeed aware of some economic clouds on the horizon. From 1873 to 1896 there had been a long and debilitating economic depression, affecting Western Europe and the United States and inevitably also societies on the periphery. At the beginning of the new century, various kinds of socialist movements and workers' organizations threatened the monopoly of power in the hands of the old aristocracy and the advancing industrial and financial magnates. Even the world's greatest empire, that of Britain, showed itself vulnerable when faced with the stubborn independence movement of Dutch farmers in South Africa during the miserable Boer War (1899–1902). Suppressed by Imperial Britain with much effort, expense, and embarrassment, the war portended the colonial powers' ongoing difficulty in countervailing national liberation movements. In the end the British pacified the Boers only by acceding to their demand for a legally mandated racially segregated society in South Africa, in which the indigenous black majority totally lacked political power. This official recognition of legalized racism was another dark forecast for the twentieth century.

The stability and peace of Europe were also threatened in 1900 by the increasing competition for hegemony among the great powers, signaled by armament buildups, squabbles over overseas colonies, and aggressive international postures.

Along with these visible signs of fissures in the power systems of lords, militarists, and capitalists, established in the nineteenth century, the beginning of the twentieth was also marked by the slow emergence in great cities of the cultural upheaval of modernism, which challenged the consciousness, mindset, and artistic imagination of the eighteen hundreds.

In 1899 the Viennese psychiatrist and founder of psychoanalysis, Sigmund Freud, found a publisher for his book *The Interpretation of Dreams*. Although it was actually released before the New Year of the new century, Freud persuaded his publisher to put a 1900 copyright date on the book because he thought it heralded a new way of understanding human behavior and consciousness. He was right: Freud's was a major voice of the modernist cultural revolution.

If twentieth-century cultural history has a unifying theme, it is that of modernism: the emergence of modernism, its impact in multiple areas as diverse as painting, philosophy, science, and anthropology, and how it evolved. And the foundations of this cultural revolution consist of what was happening in Europe around 1900. So critical was this development that we call the period in which we live the age of postmodernism because we are not quite certain what it is—or what else to call it. What we do know is that it follows on the modernist era, and that we are its legatees.

Exhibitions of the work of the architect Ludwig Mies van der Rohe and the painter Henri Matisse are examples of our persistent concern with modernism. Hardly a month goes by without a showing in a major American city of some form of modernist art. Cultural weeklies and quarterlies as well as university humanities departments devote much time and attention to modernist literature and its influence. Modernism in fact remains dominant in the publishing world, more than it probably does in the culture as a whole, continuing to have a major and not always fortunate influence on what is published in poetry and fiction. The physics and microbiology that are central to natural scientists are rooted in the modernist view of the world, and are inconceivable without it. Psychoanalysis, sociological research, and anthropological theory as taught in our universities are alike products of modernism. Modernism is one of the four great cultural revolutions in Western civilization since 1500. By "cultural revolution" is meant a great upheaval in consciousness, perception, value systems, and ideology that has affected the way we think of ourselves and our world, and that has had a seminal impact in literature, philosophy, religion, political theory, and the visual and performing arts.

The first of these cultural revolutions was the Reformation of the sixteenth century, which not only generated Protestantism but involved the reshaping of the Catholic Church as well. It produced the Calvinist ethos and the great manifestations of baroque art and music.

The Protestant reformers taught that all is dung and dross in comparison with Christ. Each individual is driven back on one fundamental fact of human existence, his or her relationship to God. The "works," or institutions, of the church pale into insignificance when confronted with this existential fact. The only redemptive force in human life was ultimately God's love of human beings, his creature. And the only liberty or righteousness of which human beings are capable flowed from faith in God. This was Martin Luther's *Liberty of a Christian Man*: "No external thing, by whatever name it may be called, can in any way conduce to Christian righteousness or liberty." Thus the Protestant Reformation, at the same time as it declared the awesome majesty and omnipotence of God, taught the incomparable dignity and privilege of the individual human conscience. No other civilization has so prized individual liberty and conscience. And this message has not entirely vanished in the twentieth century, even in the most adverse environments, in the gulag or Auschwitz.

The second legacy of the Reformation was John Calvin's doctrine, deriving from Jewish, early Christian, and medieval eschatological traditions, of the holy community. State and society should be controlled by the godly, by those who have demonstrated their reception of God's grace. Nineteenth-century liberalism, which drew heavily on Calvinist tradition, softened this doctrine into the belief that if good and idealistic men could only take over the reins of government, the problems of industrial society would be resolved. This assumption endures in the program of the Democratic Party, and the pages of the *New York Times* and the *Washington Post*.

The third legacy of the cultural revolution of the Reformation was the distinctive attitude and style of life that are called the Puritan ethos or the Protestant work ethic: piety, frugality, long and intensive labor, postponed gratification, simplicity in dress and diet, a repressive sexual code, preservation of the nuclear family, and service to the local community. This ethos was particularly pronounced among English and American Calvinists, and its influence on the development of Britain and the United States before 1900 was profound.

Although the Reformation received its initial dynamic impetus from the

Protestant churches, the impact of this cultural revolution was sufficient also to reshape the Catholic Church and affect the way of life of millions of people in Catholic countries. There was a Catholic as well as a Protestant Reformation. (In several ways Catholic Ireland, just emerging from a time warp, is the country in the Western world that is still vestigially closest to the pristine attitudes and behavior patterns generated by this so-called Counter-Reformation.)

The second cultural revolution was the eighteenth-century Enlightenment, the liberal rationalism that eventually produced the American and French Revolutions and modern political liberalism, and that helped make the Constitution with which we in the United States are still trying to live by and sometimes to ignore.

The *philosophes* of the Enlightenment regarded John Locke's thesis that human understanding is the product of experience—the result of the impress of the environment on the mind—as a liberating doctrine. Men and women were not limited by a cast of mind or set of ideas they were born with, as claimed by Plato and Descartes. Human beings could know anything and be conditioned in any direction by the circumstances of environment, education, and experience. The future of humankind was unlimited—a comforting doctrine for the Tidewater planters who faced the uncoiled expanse of the American continent and the uncertain prospects of a new republic. The *philosophes* argued that Newton's discovery of the laws of the physical world had demonstrated the infinite capacity of the human mind, given us the key to the mastery of nature, and opened the possibility of solving social problems and creating a much better world for men and women to live in.

From these assumptions Jean-Jacques Rousseau extrapolated the principle that prevailing political institutions were merely artificial constructs that retained the sanctions neither of nature nor of ethics. They could and should be overturned: "It is plainly contrary to the laws of nature, however defined, that children should command old men, fools wise men, and the privileged few should gorge themselves with the superfluities while the starving multitude are in want of the bare necessities of life." Here is the voice and temperament of revolution, drawing hazardous sustenance from moral indignation.

Enlightenment intellectuals like Thomas Jefferson taught that life is an end in itself, and that all the resources of society and mind should be committed to the pursuit of human happiness. This doctrine has inspired modern liberal and radical political movements and the effort to apply science to technology in order to improve the circumstances of everyday life. Although the *philosophes* lived in a preindustrial, preponderantly aristocratic and landed society, their faith has deeply affected the modern industrial and democratic world.

The third cultural revolution was romanticism, which prevailed between 1790 and 1850. Romanticism produced an immense change in human consciousness and feeling and had a vast effect in philosophy and the arts. Indeed, it generated whole new art forms or transformed existing ones, such as lyric poetry and the opera. It made historical writing central rather than peripheral in literature.

The main idea of romanticism was transcendentalism; the enhancement of individual grandeur by uniting the individual with an irresistible force outside him- or herself, such as art, history, the nation, or the beloved. The shrinking of the individual and the diminution of individual freedom, threatened by the coming of industrial economy and the bureaucratic state, were resisted by romanticism's compensatory vision of the individual's symbiosis with some "Mighty Being" which was, in William Wordsworth's articulation, "awake/and doth with eternal motion make/a sound like thunder everlastingly." Thus romanticism sought to preserve the freedom and dignity of the individual that the two previous cultural revolutions, the Reformation and the Enlightenment, had posited, the former on religious and the latter on scientific grounds.

To affirm this continuing freedom, romanticism enunciated the philosophy of act. Ideals must be strenuously lived from day to day and freedom and redemption lie in the experience of the struggle itself. So we have Goethe's Faust: "He only earns his freedom and his life/Who takes them everyday by storm." And the Byronic hero: "To rise/I knew not whither." From the Faustian/Byronic ideal of life as act comes a long tradition that embraces "the man on horseback." The romantic novelist Stendhal said he respected a single man, Napoleon. This same tradition glorifies the uncompromising revolutionary storming of the barricades, the bohemian artist, the perpetually adolescent lover. These are types that permanently entered Western culture.

Finally there is modernism, the twentieth-century cultural revolution. As recently as 1980 it could be said that modernism was regarded as a marginal intellectual and artistic development within the general pattern of the twentieth century. Modernism was important in its way but was not viewed as driving the dynamic of early-twentieth-century history in the transatlantic world. It was much more important to art or literary critics than to historians, who placed the determining forces of this century's history in the economic and political realms. In recent decades this conventional view of modernism's significance has changed. It is now considered as more at the core and less on the periphery of this century's structural formations. There has been a vast outpouring of books on modernism, which has provided new insights along two lines. First, modernist art, literature, science, and philosophy have been examined more closely in their connections to pervasive social trends. The material and institutional bases of modernism have begun to be revealed. Second, strenuous biographical research has more clearly highlighted the motivations and behavior patterns of modernist masters. In spite of these advances in information and interpretation, however, historiographically modernism still does not quite rank with the Reformation, the Enlightenment, and romanticism as a cultural revolution that shaped a conventionally designated historical era.

Modernism's failure to develop a distinctive political ideology constitutes the main reason why it has not been fully and appropriately understood. The other cultural revolutions, such as the Reformation and the Enlightenment, eventually turned into political revolutions. In the case of the Reformation, modern statism, the centralized bureaucratic state, was rapidly entrenched. The Enlightenment fostered political liberalism. Romanticism's political outcome, on the other hand, was polarized. It produced a leftist ideology, Marxism, as well as a rightist one, a highly conscious and determined conservative nationalism. Romanticism thus generated coherent ideological, political, and social theories, to such an extent that we are either still living through their consequences or trying to extricate ourselves from them.

Modernism, on the other hand, never generated a clear political consequence. Strenuous efforts, which will be discussed in a later chapter, were made, particularly in the United States in the 1930s, to relate modernism to the Left. Although the attempt to conjoin Marxism and modernism has produced no obvious results, the issue still receives attention—in the pages, for instance, of *Partisan Review*, the *New York Review of Books*, and the *Village Voice*. In the Germany and Italy of the 1930s, there were also efforts to join modernism with the Right; and to some extent fascism was a consequence of linking right-wing traditions with modernism.

But modernism's political formation has never been elucidated. Modernism had its recognized impress in all other areas of human culture, in the visual and performing arts, literature, philosophy, and the natural and social sciences, but its political outcomes remained confused. Owing to the tendency among historians to make the political sphere their focal point, modernism has not been given its central place in twentieth-century history, for it never developed a clear political outcome. If the only way to write history is in political terms, then modernism becomes peripheral rather than a central focus.

It is perhaps the case in Western civilization that with each subsequent cultural revolution that the West undergoes, the cultural revolution's political effect becomes less lucid. The politics of the Reformation revealed its direction quickly. Almost from the very beginning it was clear that the Reformation was going to end medieval pluralism and establish state absolutism and centralization. It took about fifty years for the political consequence of the Enlightenment to become fully visible. The Enlightenment began in the areas of science, literature, and religion, and only slowly did it turn into an extremely powerful political movement. Romanticism ultimately produced strong bipolar political outcomes. Rather than a unified political consequence, it generated as strong a leftist stance as a rightist one.

Modernism never produced a clear political consequence. Interrupted by other concurrent upheavals in the socioeconomic and political spheres, such as the two world wars and the Great Depression, it produced a host of ambiguities and ambivalences. These had—as we shall see later—on the whole a negative effect on the articulation of modernism. Although World War I gave some impetus to modernism, the war also produced negative consequences for its development. The Great Depression and World War II further generated neo-Victorian tendencies and revivals of nineteenth-century attitudes, thereby impairing the road Western society had taken with modernism. That is why, even though we continue to extrapolate implications from modernism, we can nevertheless claim that as a coherent cultural movement it ended around 1940.

Still, despite modernism's lack of a distinct political stance, it was nevertheless a cultural revolution. It represents a transformation as profound as those of the Reformation, the Enlightenment, and romanticism, albeit more elusive and harder for us to encapsulate. It is easier to describe modernism's attributes than it is to define and establish its sociological model or cultural typology.

At this point we may use as a working definition of modernism that it was a cultural movement flourishing in the first four decades of this century, and that it emphasized ahistorical, nonnarrative, or "synchronic" ways of thinking: the microcosmic dimension; self-referentiality; and moral relativism. Above all, modernism was a revolt against Victorianism. These and other aspects of modernism will be explored in the next chapter. For the moment, however, this definition will be useful as we examine nineteenth-century background.

Foreshadowings of Modernism Modernism emerged around 1900 as a coherent movement. However, certain manifestations in the last two decades of the nineteenth century had signaled its emergence. In the 1940s, Helen and Robert Lynd, a husband-and-wife sociological team at Columbia University, in a pioneering study identified the 1880s as the major historical turning point in the modern world. To an extent this is true. In the 1880s there was a shift in consciousness and attitudes, particularly reflected in a new appreciation of sexuality and an involvement with new social concerns, which indicates that the pattern of nineteenth-century "Victorian" thought was in the course of erosion.

Although modernism does not distinctly begin until about 1900, the first signs of the change in values and attitudes become discernible in the 1880s. George Bernard Shaw, then an obscure Irish drama critic in his thirties, living in London, wrote that there were two things in the world that he hated: "My duty and my mother." (This even though—or perhaps because—his mother supported him until he was about forty years old.) Shaw's comments herald the beginning of a shift whose emergence he was one of the first to perceive. Though some of his critical writings were shallow and naive, and though he did not fully understand what was happening, between 1895 and 1910 Shaw wrote some of the earliest essays that identified a cultural change of great importance.

If we look back to the 1880s, we can see certain writers who are moving in a new direction that heralds modernism. Though not themselves what we might call modernist writers, still embedded in Victorian preconceptions, they display differences from Victorians proper. In Émile Zola's novel *Germinal*, dealing with miners in France, for example, we see an appreciation of the sensibility and circumstances of ordinary people that conflicts with the normal tendency of Victorian thought—that is, with the inclination to concentrate on the politically dominant and wealthy strata of society. Zola not only understands and appreciates the workings of life among the miserable, but also shows himself capable of genuine sensitivity toward working-class experiences.

The presence of a new consciousness is even stronger in the novels of Thomas Hardy, particularly in his most revolutionary and controversial novel, *Tess of the D'Urbervilles*, published in 1892. Outside the established English cultural world, trained as an architect's apprentice, Hardy lacked a university education. He lived in Dorset in the southwestern part of England and came from a lower-middle-class and peasant background. Although he usually kept his opinions private and gave vent to them only in his novels, he was extremely hostile to the comfortable world of the upper middle class. *Tess of the D'Urbervilles* is an assault on the fundamental assumptions of the Victorian world. Particularly Hardy's treatment of the theme of underprivileged women makes *Tess of the D'Urbervilles* a devastating account of the exploitation, misery, and abuse experienced by women who came from outside and below the middle class. Even more important for the future, there is a suggestion in Tess of psychosexual tension related to male domination that anticipates modernist psychoanalysis.

Another outsider writing in the late nineteenth century was the novelist Joseph Conrad. Born Józef Teodor Korzeniowski, from a Polish noble family. he left Poland on being charged with subversive activities against the Russian state, and became a merchant captain. He began to write novels about coastal society in Africa and the Orient, concentrating mainly on life within the British Empire. *Heart of Darkness,* one of his most famous and successful novels, as well as his shortest, has a dual message. One is that imperialism could not succeed because it tried to contend with cultures that were too vital, too old, too powerful, and too mysterious for the West; hence the West would not be able to maintain its foothold in Africa and Asia for long. Conrad articulated this view around 1890, and has been proved a visionary. Africa especially is a great Other, which cannot be understood by the Western mind.

The second emphasis in Conrad's novel exposes the terrible loneliness that we all experience when we try to establish a life based upon wealth and power. In so doing we engage in a slow process of self-destruction. The pursuit of wealth and power constitutes a process of dehumanization. The two ideas are presented in the novel as congenial: Imperialism is a massive dehumanization and desensitization of the West that will slowly erode Western morality. To some extent that has also been proved true.

Another writer who was active in the 1880s was Henrik Ibsen, regarded by many as the founder of modern drama, whatever that elusive term may mean. Ibsen came from a lower-middle-class family in Norway. He failed miserably as the director of a provincial theater; in fact, he failed twice. For seventeen years, in various places in Germany and Italy, particularly in Munich and Rome, he tried to turn himself into a successful dramatist before returning to Norway to spend the closing years of his life.

Ibsen did triumph. To the new literary generation of the eighties and nineties, he was an intellectual and artistic liberator. Around 1900 George Bernard Shaw published a book called *The Quintessence of Ibsenism.* For Shaw, Ibsen became the prophet of the modernist revolt against Victorian culture.

Even though Ibsen wrote some thirty plays, most of which are in prose and some early ones in verse, his best-known work today is *A Doll's House.* Ibsen intended *A Doll's House* to be not only a narrative of female liberation, which is the way it is interpreted today. It is a play that deconstructs the Victorian family, that questions values it finds to be against the needs, humanity, and desire for self-realization of a middle-class woman. But Ibsen understood this drama to portray the needs of everybody's humanity, male or female, and to show the antagonism to the individual expressed by the demands of social institutions.

There is a neoromantic strain in Ibsen, hence we are not altogether comfortable with him today. He is not a modernist, but a pre-modernist or, actually, a late romantic. He is a kind of Kierkegaardian and Nietzschean who pits a strong individual against society. But he heralds a shift in ideology and values that was fundamental and timely.

At the same time in the 1880s, it was recognized in vanguard scientific and literary circles that human sexuality is a complicated thing that can affect people's behavior in a variety of ways, including some that are not obvious and anticipated, and that sadomasochistic feelings are, if not normal, at least very common. This new understanding of sexuality and its place in human life was a significant departure from dominant Victorian opinions. It must be understood that although Freud drew on this new perception of sexuality and extended it greatly, he did not invent it. If this conception had not been gaining credence since the 1880s, Freud probably could not have produced his work. Early in his career, in 1885, Freud conducted postdoctoral work in Paris with the psychologist Jean-Martin Charcot, a pioneer in the use of hypnosis as a means to understand and probe the unconscious. From the work of Charcot as well as from that of several other psychiatrists in Paris and Vienna, Freud began to build his own conception of the structure and method of psychoanalysis.

Another important departure from Victorianism occurred in England in the 1880s, with the development of a new conception of history. As we shall shortly discuss, Victorianism depended deeply on historicism. If all phenomena (even natural ones) are seen in continuous temporal terms, and if in order to understand something, a full account of its nature is given and this history is seen as evolutionary, with each step in the process building on the preceding, the point of view is teleological, deterministic, and essentially Victorian. In the 1880s a professor of law at Cambridge University, Frederick William Maitland, began to take a very different approach to the understanding of history.

Maitland offered a new perspective for comprehending the history of English law that avoided historical continuity and rejected long-term teleological determinism. Maitland concentrated on the analysis of short-term phenomena. He looked at the intervention of will, and found that at a certain point in time the will of some people or group or even of an individual can change everything in ways that cannot be anticipated. What happens in history is unanticipated, according to Maitland. It is fortuitous, chancy, and not determined over a long term. It is accidental and immediate. There are breaks and discontinuities in history, rather than a seamless, inevitable flow.

To take an example from the twentieth century: One should not determine why Hitler arose in Germany in terms of events that occurred three hundred years before in German history, or even by incidents of fifty years before, but in terms of occurrences that took place perhaps three months or three days before Hitler came to power. Hitler's rise, therefore, was not predetermined by long-term circumstances, but by very immediate, discontinuous, accidental, even absurd happenings. That is the new approach Maitland adopted in his history of English law, which constituted a radical departure from Victorian thought. The importance of Maitland's work had not begun to be appreciated until about the time of his death in 1906, and this appreciation occurred mainly in the United States. But even though his writings were not fully understood for a long time (until the 1950s), they exemplify an intellectual change that emerged in the 1880s.

A number of other late-nineteenth-century figures are more familiar to us today. There is Friedrich Nietzsche, for example, who is nowadays often regarded as the prophet of the twentieth century. This is a controversial opinion. In some ways Nietzsche was the last of the great romantics rather than the first of the modernists. He was a German professor of philosophy who went mad at the age of forty-five, probably from syphilis, and although he did not die until 1900, he had written all he was going to by 1880. It took awhile for his work to begin to be read and appreciated, and his impact was not felt until the 1890s.

Nietzsche says some original things—although often in a confused and inconsistent manner—which, if taken seriously, represent a new direction in thought. First, he expressed a strongly relativistic view of ethics. He considered the prevailing system of Christian morality to be determined by the interests of certain groups and individuals and believed that, as such, this system bore no intrinsic legitimacy. He wanted new systems of ethics to emerge. He proclaimed the death of God—that is, the ending of the dominance of Christian values—and searched for a new value system in a changed world. This inclination toward ethical relativism is a theme that runs through twentieth-century thought. It had profound effects in the first twenty years of the twentieth century, and has undergone a great revival since about 1965.

Nietzsche's ethics had a supporting—although not causal—influence on modernism and in turn contributed to postmodernism, or what is termed the deconstructionist cultural movement of the 1970s. Particularly in France, Nietzsche has become very popular again.

Nietzsche also proposed a view of the "undiscovered country" far beyond contemporary Western civilization (a notion his sister, Elisabeth, and her husband, Bernhard Förster, twisted and took to excessive lengths by establishing Nueva Germania, a supposedly pure German colony in Paraguay). Western civilization, having exhausted itself, had to be transcended. Nietzsche proclaimed a going beyond everything that was imaginable in the nineteenth century, a penetration into undiscovered areas of the mind, a supersession and replacement of Victorian culture. His vision of the undiscovered country, of transcendence, and of a cultural revolution of momentous and unimaginable consequences is perhaps his greatest contribution to laying the background for modernism. Yet Nietzsche was not a modernist. He believed Richard Wagner's operas, the essence of Victorianism, to be the ultimate in art. His attitude toward women is extremely patronizing and sadistically cruel.

Other familiar late-nineteenth-century phenomena indicate the germination of cultural upheaval. One of these was the movement in French painting in the 1870s and 1880s called impressionism. Impressionism generated a new interest in color and its use, and by concentrating on the materials of painting as well as what is represented, it pointed the way toward the nonrepresentational art of the early twentieth century. Impressionism tried to improve representation by the careful use of color and of the materials of painting. When the representation of objects ceased to be a concern, and painting concentrated on its materials and their possible applications to the canvas, we can speak of modernist, nonrepresentational, abstract painting. Impressionism was therefore a transitional stage between Victorian painting, which focused on subject matter, and modernist painting, which emphasized the materials themselves.

We can also regard the late-nineteenth-century artistic (and poetic) movement of symbolism as a further herald of cultural transformation. Nineteenth-century art is full of symbolism, but its symbolism is largely drawn from classical mythology, Christianity, or from very familiar, traditional literary motifs. The symbolism of the 1880s and 1890s, on the other hand, creates new symbols that are divorced from traditional classical and Christian motifs. Thereby symbolism too is an artistic movement that is transitional between Victorianism and the new art of the twentieth century. It separates itself from Christian and classical symbolism in order to create new symbols, often the products of psychology or psychoneurosis, that show people in torture and torment. The feeling generated in the viewer by this contemporary, secular form of torment was more persuasive than the by now formalistic motifs of Christian hellfire. This was the beginning of something radically different in art.

Also in the 1880s, we find a new concern with the Orient and Oriental culture. This was not the first time the West felt such an interest. The Enlightenment, in the first half of the eighteenth century, had generated enthusiasm for Oriental style and culture. The interest was above all in Chinese art and style (especially interior decoration), or in what the eighteenth century thought was Chinese art—chinoiserie—and to a lesser extent, in Indian art. Historians of the Enlightenment find this to be the beginning of a break away from European parochialism, and the first time that Europe begins to appreciate another culture. The implications of this Enlightenment interest in the Orient were revolutionary. The appreciation of different artistic styles led to thinking about other political systems, and to the idea that, like culture, political systems too can be superseded. Once you have Chinese wallpaper, you may very well start thinking about the possibility of a different form of government.

In the 1880s and 1890s, there was a novel interest in Japanese and Buddhist art and culture, and to some extent in the Indian and Middle Eastern visual traditions. How accurate and professional a knowledge the late nineteenth century actually had of these cultures is beside the point. We know that Oriental studies were poorly developed in the West at the time. Hardly anybody knew the languages; translations were often inadequate. Nevertheless this new interest in Buddhism, and particularly in Japanese forms of Buddhism, emerged in the 1880s and became an important ingredient in modernist culture in the first twenty-five or thirty years of the next century. German expressionism, which runs through the period from about 1910 to 1930, reveals a deep fascination with these Oriental traditions.

Finally, in the 1890s, we come upon the movement called art nouveau, which is in a sense the first movement which we can properly call modernist. Art nouveau was concerned with detail. It displayed an aesthetic appreciation not for the grand and the large, but for the small. How to make a dramatic window or a better door, and specifically a more attractive stairway, were among its preoccupations. Just as the artists of the eighteenth century had spent a lot of time on doorways (Robert Adam), art nouveau occupied itself with the improvement of stairways (Victor Horta), wallpaper, and chairs. Originally called "the aesthetic movement," art nouveau was an effort to bring beauty, sensibility, and maximum utility to objects we experience most immediately at close range. A piece of household furniture, a decorative object, tableware, wallpaper, lithographs, were examined in detail, thereby articulating significant ingredients of modernism, Art nouveau (called *Jugendstil*—"youth style"—in Germany) was an important transition from the beginnings of cultural upheaval in the 1880s to the actual focusing of a movement that around 1900 became modernism.

Art nouveau, especially in England, can be viewed as an outgrowth of a desire to return to allegedly "pure," "folk" forms of art. This artistic puritanical populism was led in England by the utopian socialist William Morris and his disciples. In the United States a similar movement produced the "natural" breakfast food (Kellogg's Corn Flakes), anticipating the health food craze of our recent decades. It also encouraged a revival of furniture styles (Shaker, Pennsylvania Dutch) that were simpler and lighter than the heavy, fussy, and ornate objects Victorians had come to prefer. A related development in Germany was a novel organization of youth groups for camping and mountain climbing, which in turn paralleled the Anglo-American Boy Scout movement after 1900.

From William Morris and the folk art movement, the 1890s derived a marginal but significant aesthetic focus on the small beauties of everyday life. Although this was a departure from traditional Victorian attitudes, it was still characterized by the integration of aesthetics with ethics that was a fixation of the Victorian mind. Morris turned this obsession in a somewhat novel direction. He and his disciples on both sides of the Atlantic sought to recover a more spontaneous, preindustrial communal life whose art, it was believed, represented an authentic manifestation of the free human spirit. Perhaps this was not much more than an updated version of early-nineteenth-century transcendentalism, of Blake, Emerson, and Thoreau. The Morris dancers were late Walden.

At the same time there emerged a self-conscious aestheticism that separated beauty from ethics and made total concentration on art a positive lifestyle. In England this attitude was associated principally with Walter Pater and Oscar Wilde, and in Western Europe generally it was regarded as an expression of a fin-de-siècle decadence far removed on the cultural spectrum from Morris's folk art, fresh air movement. There was a lot of posturing involved in this art-for-art's-sake movement in the nineties, and in Pater's fruity essays on the Renaissance, art conjures up Edwardian drawing rooms with brocade wallpaper, port and cigars in an Oxford common room, and sodomy.

Yet there are other things in Pater's book on the Renaissance that *are* important for the future: His search for a distinctive language that would communicate his perceptions of Renaissance art with precision, and his ignoring of narrative history, that favorite Victorian genre, in favor of intensely close observation of particular objects and ideas. Here is a foreshadowing of the modernist temperament.

The aesthetic movement gave the new generation that emerged after 1900 confidence by allowing them to feel that their rebellion against Victorian triumphalism was not unprecedented. Wilde's aphorism that life imitates art more than art imitates life forecasts a principal theme in the modernist challenge to Victorian culture.

Characteristics of Victorian Culture Modernism was a revolt against Victorian culture. Therefore, in order to understand modernism, we first have to comprehend the dimensions, the characteristic attitudes, and the fundamental assumptions of the nineteenth century. As has already been pointed out, the first fundamental characteristic of Victorian culture was historicism—that is, the notion that the explanation of the nature of things is gained from the description of their histories. The nineteenth century applied this idea to everything from an individual to an entire society as well as to scientific phenomena. In each case, whether national constitutions or biological species, history would provide the explanation of the nature of the thing through its longitudinal evolution. What is *x*? Tell me its story so I can know it. That is the Victorian way of thinking.

This attitude advantageously triggered an unprecedented interest in biography. The biographies the nineteenth century produced were unprecedented for their voluminous detail, and they are still valuable even if they are rather tiresome for us to read. They are usually blind to psychological factors.

The interest in biography was accompanied by concentration on national history. For the purpose of understanding contemporary politics, it was deemed necessary to investigate political life in the Middle Ages or even earlier periods. Nineteenth-century Germany, the world of Bismarck, for example, could be understood by tracing the nation's teleological development from its existence in the forests under the barbarian chieftains. In order to understand

English politics in 1870, one began one's study by describing politics in 1270. This seems a trifle absurd and futile to us, since with respect to the study of history we have gone in a direction quite different from the Victorians. Between 1967 and 1982 the percentage of graduating B.A.'s majoring in history in the United States declined from 5.7 to 1.8 percent. We have not only gone beyond the Victorians in downgrading the value of historical explanation; we have gone twice beyond them, once in the early twentieth century, and again in the 1960s and 1970s.

It is difficult for us to comprehend the Victorian addiction to history. After the Bible the most popular book in Victorian England was Thomas Macaulay's *History of England*, in which the author—a liberal politician who had spent four years in the Indian civil service—gave lengthy descriptions of obscure political machinations by seventeenth-century aristocrats. He never got past 1695, but Victorian readers still thought the book was very relevant to contemporary events. When the French historian Jules Michelet lectured at the University of Paris in the 1830s, no theater could be found large enough for his audience. He was the rock star of his day. Hundreds of people lined up to hear Michelet talk about Joan of Arc, expecting that his account would somehow clarify events in modern France.

In light of the popularity of history, it is not surprising that Victorian art and literature exhibited a strong historicist tendency. Even when paintings, sculptures, novels, and poems were not treating subjects evoking the distant or recent past—and that occurred frequently—there was a dominant trend toward the depiction of a narrative. In Victorian literature and art, the conscious concern is with telling a story. Narrative is paramount over other considerations. The Victorian belief that truth and reality are found in temporal projections was what the audience wanted all writers and artists to address: Which narrative does the poem, novel, painting, or sculpture illustrate? What is the story? Victorian art was shaped by these questions.

This historicist mentality has made Victorian painting and sculpture of small interest to us today, despite recent valiant attempts by art historians to find qualities in them beyond the narrative line. Nineteenth-century poetry, between the exhaustion of romanticism in the 1830s and the symbolist anticipation of modernist poetry in the eighties and nineties, likewise has little appeal to us. Victorian poetry has a strong proclivity to historicism and dramatic narrative and is furthermore suffused with moral preaching. In spite of the academic effort in recent years to rehabilitate Tennyson, the cultural barrier between his poetry and our attitudes and taste is too great. "To strive, to seek, to find and not to yield." Even as history, this lacks conviction; Tennyson's Ulysses is a Protestant missionary. "Grow old along with me!/The best is yet to be": Browning's Rabbi Ben Ezra is a tedious schoolmaster on prize day.

Historicism does, however, perpetuate a function for Victorian novels— not normally to read them (because of their inordinate length and bewildering array of characters) but to adapt their story lines for transference to musical comedy, film, and especially TV series. Since the latter media are fixated primarily on narrative presentations, the Victorian novel maintains a half-life in that form, more readily than the modernist novel that succeeded it.

The counterpart of historicism in the sciences was organicism. The examination of long-term biological developments was the purpose of Darwin's *The Origin of Species.* Darwin explains biology through the organic evolution of biological species. He placed species in a sequential order and tried to account in temporal terms for existing biological features and for the capacity of certain species to survive. It turned out that chance and environmental adaptation ("natural selection") played the decisive roles. Darwin's is a biology very different from the vanguard biology of today.

Contrary to common belief, Darwinian biology did not shatter the Victorian frame of mind. On the contrary, Darwinist biology was expressed in the conventional historicist framework of Victorian thought. While the factor of chance rather than divine creation upset some people then and now, chance could be explained away as God's instrumental mechanism. With regard to the general theory he propounded, Darwin was not devastating Victorian thought. On the contrary, he was carrying out a value-salvage operation, protecting historicism from the impact of scientific data.

Darwin, a reclusive gentleman autodidact, had two historical theories to account for the evolution of all animate species over time. The first—the theory of common descent of all species from one source—was the one that aroused noisy controversy when he published it in 1859 because it deprivileged humanity, placing it, like apes and monkeys, in the general pattern of common descent of all species from some pristine animate matter. This theory was held by conservative people for awhile (and in some instances still is today) to be blasphemous and to deny the biblical view of man's creation in God's image.

The second theory propounded by Darwin is more interesting to us nowadays because of its decisive role in biological science: the theory of natural selection. In the evolution of species, including the human one, there is an infinite supply of genetic variation, the product of chance mutations. But which of these individual genetic variations become a species mutation depends on their suitability for adaption to environmental conditions. That one giraffe has a longer neck than others is a chance variation. But insofar as the idiosyncratic longer-necked giraffes are better suited to feed on trees and thereby survive, they participate in a process of natural selection and evolving modification of the species. By this theory Darwin's macrohistorical vision accounts for life forms.

Today biology does not give a high priority to speculating on what occurred in nature causing certain animals to disappear, or to pondering the fate of the extinct organisms that now exist only as fossils on South American islands. These kinds of historical speculation, now a marginal concern of biological science, were considered to be central in the nineteenth century. The fate of dinosaurs may still engage the attention of the popular press, but the big grants from foundations and contracts from corporations go to the molecular biologists, not the emulators of Darwin. The leaders of biological science, the Nobel laureates, are today in the labs, scrutinizing the screens on their electron microscopes, not in the boondocks collecting flora and fauna.

Nineteenth-century linguistics was historical philology. It posited that there had been an original "Indo-European" language that existed millennia ago somewhere between Turkey and Calcutta, and it was preoccupied with discovering how European languages evolved out of this allegedly pristine Indo-European language. Remote even from the linguistics studied in elementary school today, it has nothing whatsoever to do with current transformational grammar. There is in fact hardly anyone left today in the United States who knows about historical philology, except perhaps a few aged scholars. The study has completely disappeared from the university curriculum.

Historicism, then, was the first characteristic of Victorianism. The second was the tendency to macrocosm, for the big picture, for large-scale views. The Victorians thought that big is better. They believed not only in national history but in world history. When Georg Hegel produced a philosophy of history in which he presented a pattern of world history in four hundred pages, people took him seriously. One could make such claims in the nineteenth century; one could attempt to devise comprehensive systems.

Hegel tells us that "the history of the World has been a rational process." What distinguishes this process is the activity of "a World-Spirit . . . which unfolds this its one nature in the phenomena of the World's existence." What does this mean? It means that the triumph of reason and World-Spirit is represented by Protestant Christianity and the Prussian state. We may find this outcome anticlimactic, even a bit absurd, but there is no doubt that Hegel had a perception of the big historical picture.

In the sciences the macrolevel was likewise stressed by the Victorians. Science aimed at general biology, general physics, a general theory of chemistry. The purpose of physics was to propound universal laws. The purpose of chemistry was to discover all possible elements and map them on a "periodic" table, showing their relationships to one another. On the walls of some high school chemistry labs one can still see the faded periodic table, which was put together in 1890 by a Russian chemist. This tabulation of chemical elements has little to do with chemistry today; most chemists today would not even know the periodic table, nor would they have a use for it.

The proclivity of nineteenth-century science toward grand macrocosmic schemes of evolution in contrast to twentieth-century science's emphasis on the microcosmic level, or the smallest discernible unit, is demonstrated by the strange scientific career of Gregor Mendel. An Austrian monk teaching physics and other natural sciences in a provincial Catholic school after studying at the University of Vienna, Mendel did massive statistical studies of the growth and breeding of peas, and in 1866 published a revolutionary paper that established the basis of modern genetics. He was able to show the mathematical ratio (3:1) between dominant and recessive genes in each generation. This was a conceptual and methodological breakthrough of the greatest importance.

Only seven years after Darwin's *Origin of Species,* Mendel anticipated not only twentieth-century genetics but the essential microcosmic spirit of post-Victorian science: "The distinguishing characteristics of two plants can, after all, be caused only by differences in the composition and grouping of the elements existing in dynamic interaction in their primordial cells." The enunciation of scientific reality as lying in dynamic interaction in primordial cells was a trumpet call for modern science. Yet Mendel's work was entirely ignored until 1900, when geneticists thinking along similar lines rediscovered his paper and realized that Mendel had largely anticipated their work several decades earlier.

Mendel's failure to gain any recognition in his day, even though more than one hundred scientific libraries in Western Europe received published copies of his 1866 paper, reveals the dominance of macrohistoricism in Victorian science which blinded scientists to a novel way of thinking—micro and statistical—that would have taken them well beyond Darwin into the revolutions of twentieth-century science. Mendel's story is paradigmatic of the way in which the dominant mind-set conditions the course of scientific as well as other forms of theory.

The purpose of Victorian social science was the development of a universal theory of social evolution. The most prominent names under this heading were the Americans Lewis Morgan and William Graham Sumner and the prolific Englishman Herbert Spencer. Spencer tried to provide a general theory of sociology that could be applied to all peoples. At one end of the scientific spectrum was presumed to be the periodic table of chemical elements; at the other, the hierarchy of societies from the primitive to the advanced, from the simple to the most complex.

It is not difficult to imagine who occupied the lower end and who the higher positions. The theory according to which American Indians and the people of Africa constituted the simple peoples and occupied the lower end of the hierarchical ladder became known as Social Darwinism. Europeans were the more complicated peoples, it was held, and in the course of the universal process called "the struggle for existence" had built the more advanced societies. Obviously this Victorian effort to see the large sociological picture by positing a hierarchy of peoples was propaganda for imperialism. But Victorians believed it was social science.

When it came to social science, Victorian semiotics and iconology were not very subtle. Everyone knew what the "survival of the fittest" signified in the evolutionary struggle for existence. It meant lithe, handsome, preferably blond Englishmen playing cricket on the lawn of a Calcutta or Mombasa country club while quiescent natives in starched uniforms served gin-and-tonics to the chaste bosomy wives and daughters of the superior race. In the social macrocosm everyone had his or her designated place. The function of a general theory of society was to assure this rigidly structured situation.

Nineteenth-century painting also aimed at telling a story that would make the beholder macrocosmically recollect as many things as possible. Victorians painted huge, cluttered canvases in the 1850s and 1860s, presenting biblical stories or episodes from Virgil and Homer. The purpose was ultimately to stimulate in the viewer recollections of a cultural universe. Through viewing a detailed and dramatic scene from the Bible or classical mythology, the Victorian was supposed immediately to be reminded of the elaborate, tightly integrated cultural system he or she had imbibed from school and church. The function of art was principally to reinforce values and ideas. While an occasional critic like John Ruskin might struggle against this view that art was better the more it provided pedagogical and mnemonic services to the general ideas embedded in a cultural macrocosm, it remained a fixation of the Victorian mind and became a prime target of modernism.

In addition to historicism and macrocosm, the third Victorian characteristic was a rigid system of normative ethics. Nineteenth-century people could conceive of the good and of the bad, of the way to behave and not to behave, and they believed in the righteous imposition of their code by means of institutional power. There was authority in the world, represented usually by the father, the adult male, and the state, to enforce the system of ethics whose code derived from the Old and New Testaments, and from the churches as well as the behavioral pattern of a hierarchical family structure. The code, in other words, was set down by authority. What served the interests of pastors, fathers, lawyers, generals, and businessmen was given absolute moral sanction. In the twentieth century we see very little advantage in this inflexible system of ethics. Indeed, our century has spent much time undermining it.

Since the 1970s historians have expended much effort on researching Victorian sexual behavior. It has not been difficult to reveal that the Victorians normally had strong, human sexual urges and that males at least had no trouble satisfying them. Prostitution was blatantly prevalent in Victorian cities and tolerated by political and legal institutions. Victorian married couples of all social levels, with little or no mechanical protection against unwanted conception before the 1880s (and even then what they had was only marginal), engaged in regular acts of coitus. Among the industrial, working, and farming classes, the bride was pregnant at time of marriage perhaps a quarter or a third of the time. The difference between the later twentieth century and that of the Victorian world lies only moderately in sexual practice. Rather, it lies in the moral code and the socially imposed behavioral system in which sexual practice was immersed.

By the 1970s, there had been a tremendous erosion of this Victorian moral code, preceded by the enervating wave in the first three decades of the twentieth century. Currently, however, some people look back on it with nostalgia. They find that, although it may have done some harm, it nevertheless inculcated a powerful work ethic; unequivocally condemned street crime, alcoholism, and narcotic addiction; and allegedly did not require (or, more accurately, allow) as many abortions as we have today.

Above all, Victorian morality fostered the nuclear family. During the first four or five decades of the nineteenth century, society witnessed an alarming level of urban crime, alcoholism, and family dislocation, particularly among the industrial working class. All the moral resources of Western society transmitted by church, state, school, and the popular press were recruited to combat these indices of social pathology. The conventional family unit with two parents, dominance allocated to the father, and children in residence through adolescence was deemed the institutional realization of moral doctrine. Ethics meant family, with the middle-class model imposed on the working class as a norm that would make the latter respectable, secure, and prosperous.

This ethical legitimization of the nuclear family model was successful: There was a strong trend toward the stable family unit in the late nineteenth century. We—who have experienced a severe trend toward family disintegration and who might regard the Victorian situation with some envy—have to remember that the triumph of the Victorian family was not only the product of impersonal social and material forces. It was essentially made possible by strenuous moral teaching, which the modernist movement began to unravel after 1900. Today there is widespread concern about the decline of family stability and the increasing prominence of the one-parent family. Disagreement arises about the utility of restoring neo-Victorian ethics as the means to rebuilding family structure.

The fourth characteristic of Victorian thought was Western chauvinism and/or the justification of imperialism. The West was perceived as an advanced society while the people of Africa, for example, were regarded as primitives. The nineteenth century did not find much wrong in this respect with Chinese and Indian societies, for these were old cultures, but they were, in turn, regarded as effete and decadent. The West was the ideal social model, whereas other societies were either decadent or primitive. The West, neither too hot nor too cold, was just right, like Baby Bear's porridge in the story of Goldilocks. In the words of Rudyard Kipling's eponymous poem, written in honor of Teddy Roosevelt (who remarked to a friend that Kipling's encomium was bad poetry but good theory), it was not only the West's privilege but its moral duty to "take up the White Man's burden" and help the less fortunate (colored) races of mankind.

This patronizing imperialist doctrine gained overwhelming credence, especially in the second half of the nineteenth century. If there had not been pervasive faith in this doctrine, Western imperialism would not have existed. At most there would have been a few commercial stations here and there, to pursue business interests, but certainly no British domination of India, or American rule over "the little brown brothers" in the Philippines, or the European carving up of Africa.

Around 1850 the West still controlled little of Africa. But by 1900 its rule over the continent was complete. Only the concept of chauvinistic Western superiority justified this dominion, making it appear valuable and necessary.

The majority of these newly acquired European colonies in Africa were fiscally burdensome to the imperial powers, although a handful of entrepreneurs and corporations did well out of colonial exploitation. Without an imperialistic and racist mentality, European involvement in Africa would have been marginal.

Imperialism was profitable to only a handful of people—army officers, a few businessmen and administrators, and occasionally missionaries. By and large the balance sheet of imperialism was negative. Even though the Indian people were taxed to defray expenditure for government and defense, it cost the British more to rule India than they ever gained from it, with the result that, impoverished by World War II, they had to leave precipitously in 1947.

Over two long centuries of the British Raj, the British gained only two tangible as distinct from psychic advantages from the "jewel in the crown." India provided a large reservoir of military manpower, useful in the First World War and critically necessary in the Second. Furthermore, the Indian civil service, law courts, and army provided a steady pool of creative and challenging jobs for British men. In the words of an early-nineteenth-century anti-imperialist, the Empire and especially the Raj were "the great system of outdoor relief for the British upper classes." After 1947 such people had to become advertising executives, Oxbridge dons, BBC producers, or migrate to the United States to become Jaguar salesmen, newspaper editors, or Ivy League professors. Such was the menial denouement of the pith-helmet brigade. Indochina (Vietnam) was a fiscal sinkhole for the liberal French Third Republic; only for generals and Catholic missionaries was there an immediate advantage to be gained from the French-Vietnamese involvement. It had to be justified on grounds of disseminating French "civilization" among less fortunate people.

The notion that the West had a destiny and an obligation, and that it was at the right point of development between primitivism and decadence to shoulder the white man's burden, was believed in by educated people as well as the masses stirred up by the popular press. This attitude is difficult for us to conceive of today; there is very little of it left. But in the late nineteenth century, Western triumphalism was powerfully present, a fact to which much Victorian literature bears witness. Even generous liberals like Thomas Macaulay believed that it would be many decades, perhaps centuries, before the people of India would be ready to govern themselves. Self-government for Africans was not even a subject for speculation.

Rudyard Kipling, the poet laureate of the white man's burden, inserted a paradoxical note of pessimism into the imperialist doctrine. The non-Europeans, he cautioned, "half savage and half child," couldn't appreciate the fine things the English, Americans, and other colonial powers were doing in their empires: Imperialism would recede in coming decades. He was right.

The fifth characteristic of Victorian thought was philosophical idealism. The more abstract, general, and theoretical thought became, the more it could propound universal theorems, the closer it was to the truth. Truth did not reside in the particular, but in universal propositions. This was, in a way, the philosophical aspect of historicism and the macrocosm, but it can also be regarded as a distinct category. Professional philosophy in the nineteenth century—that is, what was taught by professors in the universities—was overwhelmingly idealist until about 1900.

The most influential philosopher of the nineteenth century was the German, Hegel, who believed in a kind of developmental Platonism. As we have seen, truth, according to Hegel, lay in general ideas that moved through time and history, evolving toward a grand finale (the Prussian state, he claimed). The purpose of thinking was to refine away all empirical data and attain pure abstraction, the most universal propositions ("the Absolute").

It may be hard for us to know what to make of such views, but they spelled truth itself for the nineteenth century. There were three reasons for the dominance of philosphical idealism in nineteenth-century thought. First, it drew on strong currents in the three previous cultural revolutions—the Reformation, the Enlightenment, and romanticism. Idealism was a reformulation of the most continuous philosophical movement in Western civilization, namely Platonism, and cheap and relatively accurate new translations into all the main European languages had recently made the Greek philosopher accessible to the Victorian educated public.

Second, philosophic idealism was in the Victorian mind a secularized substitute for Christianity. Idealism became a halfway house for middle-class intellectuals who had lost their faith in Christian revelation ("the long withdrawing roar" of the midcentury, in Matthew Arnold's words) but who wanted to preserve a certain way of looking at the world and human behavior compatible with the churches' teaching in many areas. Third, idealism was a philosophy for the sexually repressed. If Victorians in most (but not all) instances resisted coming to terms with sexual drives, idealism buttressed this severe repression, since truth lay only in general propositions (secularized Christian ethics) but not in empirical data (for example, dreams and neurotic behavior patterns).

Even in 1900 German universities were respectful of Hegelianism. Hegel preserved his importance in British universities too for a long time. In the United States, the philosophy department of Princeton University remained entirely Hegelian at the turn of the century. Still Hegelian in 1900 was Josiah Royce, a prominent professor of philosophy at Harvard. Hegelianism collapsed quite suddenly. Ten years later, at least outside Germany, it had almost disappeared. Overnight, as it were, Hegelian idealism had gone up in smoke. But at the end of the nineteenth century it was still dominant.

In the 1890s a radically modified, non-Hegelian form of philosophical idealism began to gain visibility in the heartland of idealism, the philosophy faculties of the German universities. Going back beyond Hegel to Immanuel Kant, neo-Kantian philosophy sustained the authenticity of intuitive general propositions about ethics and religion but also allowed the power of the human mind to derive empirically based models or types from the study of particular phenomena. Here was a middle ground between idealism and empiricism: the recognition of general propositions that were rationally created by human consciousness out of data. Using these neo-Kantian assumptions, Wilhelm Dilthey developed a cultural history that provided a high degree of patterning without the rigid, arbitrary, and unverifiable abstractions favored by Hegel and his disciples. Also in the 1890s Dilthey's colleague Max Weber set about fashioning his sociology of ideal types (based on accumulation and generalization from empirical data), such as the charismatic leader and bureaucratic government.

Nevertheless, while neo-Kantianism differed from Hegelianism, it remained a form of idealist philosophy: It found reality in the general forms that consciousness creates.

The sixth quality of Victorian thought was the concept of order, which was always regarded as preferable to disorder. The Enlightenment had a strong proclivity to system building; the romantic movement somewhat diminished the centrality of order. The mid-Victorians brought back systemic order to the foreground of cultural and social value. Coherence, organization, hierarchy, and systematization constituted the desiderata. In line with this penchant, one dealt with a problem by dividing it into the upper and the lower, the left and the right, thereby devising a system of order. The marginal, the disorderly, the particular, the uncontrolled, and the unpredictable were relegated to the realm of the negative. The determined and the predictable could be placed in sets of early and late, upper and lower, and were therefore good.

Some commentators see this penchant for order as a reaction to the

Industrial Revolution, which created upheaval and chaos, and such social and environmental change that in response to it, there was a desperate attempt to create order, an attempt that began with the family. From there, one hierarchically proceeded to build other invincible organizations and institutions.

In their pursuit of order the Victorians created the police force. There was very little in the way of a police organization anywhere in the West before the nineteenth century. The Victorian age established penitentiaries and the penal system. In some ways this was a reflection of all aspects of Victorian thought, that is, of a macrocosmic, idealist, historicist, and normative way of thinking, but it was also a reflection of fear of the disorder generated by the upheaval of the Industrial Revolution.

Thomas Mann's first novel, *Buddenbrooks*, is concerned primarily with this fascination with order and its debilitating consequences in the individual lives of an upper-middle-class North German family (much like his own). Writing in 1901, Mann claimed that middle-class families paid a harsh psychological price for the constant emphasis on social order. (What would he say after studying the activities of crack pushers, Valley girls, and porno video shops?)

Finally, the seventh feature of Victorianism was simplification and popularization. The nineteenth century believed that thought should not be esoteric, that it should not be the exclusive domain of professionals and scholars, just as it believed that poetry was not only for poets, or paintings for artists. Ideas should be communicated and made accessible to society as a whole, or at least to the educated middle class, which, due to the role of secondary education, either free or inexpensive, was very much on the increase in the second half of the nineteenth century.

To take complicated ideas and make them available to educated people, which in practice meant anyone with a high school education, was central to the Victorian cultural program. There was a tremendous urge to what the French call "high vulgarization," or to what we might call simplification and popularization. Whether novelists or philosophers, scientists or theologians, nineteenth-century intellectuals tried to address a broad, educated public and to express their ideas in ordinary, nontechnical language. Artists and poets used themes easily recognizable by the public. Culturally the Victorians tended towards democracy and away from elitism.

The very small proportion of Victorian men—and virtually no women— who attended university before the 1880s was a factor that contributed to this cultural populism. Even among intellectuals and professional people, only a minority were college graduates. To gain an audience, Victorian thinkers and writers had to use the language and conceptual level concomitant with secondary education (equivalent to the sophomore level in an American college today).

But there was more to the Victorian zeal for simplification and popularization than this social factor. They had a missionary calling to spread higher culture as far as possible in the middle class and among the more reliable and sober working class.

Victorians believed passionately in cultural accessibility. As a result, whether in poetry, fiction, literary criticism, or even scientific theory, anyone with a high school education could gain immediate access to the major works, for which there was consequently a substantial market. Victorian booksellers, like our own, sold a lot of trash, but they also sold major works of both fiction and nonfiction that could be purchased at a kiosk in a railway station. Consequently there exists the paradoxical situation that Heine, Stendhal, Arnold, Mill, and Darwin are much easier even for us to read than comparable classics of modernism and postmodernism. That is why in secondary school curricula, perhaps even in college curricula, there is today a disproportionate favoring of Victorian as against modernist and postmodernist writings.

This phenomenon, of intellectual accessibility in the nineteenth century, is admirable. It is, in fact, currently admired: The effort now being made to establish core curricula in American colleges is, in a way, a neo-Victorian statement. The attempt to reestablish a simplified base of knowledge available to everybody is certainly not something the modernist movement would have advocated. Modernism tended in an entirely different direction.

Causes of the Modernist Cultural Revolution Before establishing a model of modernism in the next chapter, it is necessary to discuss why the large-scale transformation occurred around 1900, what factors precipitated it, and why the modernist revolution came about specifically at the turn of the century. Why cultural revolutions occur, why there has been a Reformation, an Enlightenment, or romanticism, is something that historical science has not been able to explain persuasively. In the past four decades the fashion in academic historiography has been almost exclusive attention to durable structures and avoidance of even considering the causes of change. A few suggestions, however, may be offered explaining why modernism came about when and where it did.

First, there is the factor of entropy, or exhaustion. It is a fact of history that eventually a cultural movement or a worldview exhausts itself. It maintains its central position for a period of time. It is taught, believed in, but then, at a certain point, it seems to have solved its problems and said everything it could within the framework of its cardinal principles. No artist can achieve further visibility, no poet can attain a remarkable breakthrough, no philosopher can envision something new following the old assumptions. The assumptions lose their plasticity, and the cultural movement exhausts itself.

This is an old story. In 1600 Western Europeans had an insatiable taste for hearing about Christian doctrine. By 1680, however, people in Europe were no longer much interested in the dispute between Protestant and Catholic theology. By 1740 Voltaire could get a big laugh by simply listing the main themes of Reformation theology. Similarly, at a certain point (1790) the Enlightenment appeared tiresome, even shallow, and by the middle of the nineteenth century romanticism found itself exhausted. As early as the second decade of the century, Byron wrote: "So we'll go no more a-roving/So late into the night,/Though the heart be still as loving/And the moon be still as bright," expressing his weariness with romanticism.

Victorianism was such a rich culture, affirming its characteristics in such powerful ways, that by 1900, at least for artists and intellectuals, it had become tiresome and effete. There seemed nothing more to be obtained from it. Victorian culture lost its resiliency and its main assumptions appeared trivial and redundant. Intellectuals entered the way of rebellion, searched for new ways to express themselves, and developed points of view that ran counter to Victorian premises.

Therefore, the first cause of the emergence of modernism was the over-success of Victorianism and the corresponding entropy of Victorian culture. In the 1890s Victorian culture was broad and elaborate but thin—it increasingly lacked conviction, inspiration, and vitality. It appeared to the emerging generation of 1900 to be unimaginative and banal and indeed it was. It may be conceded that this explanation sounds like a tautology: Victorianism ended because it ended. But there is no better explanation for major cultural changes than the entropic model.

The celebrated explanation of the cause of scientific revolutions put forward by the MIT historian of science Thomas Kuhn—the old paradigm (like an overfilled bucket) can no longer absorb and reconcile new data—is essentially the same as the entropic explanation for cultural revolutions, and equally tautological.

The second explanation for the emergence of modernism was the demoralization that began to occur in the Victorian world for social reasons.

Victorians became conscious of the fact that they were having difficulties solving what they called the "social problem," a problem that still remains largely unsolved. Victorians faced the problems of the poor, the homeless, and—although there was much less in the late nineteenth century than what we have today—of crime. They felt pressed to resolve the prevalence of poverty and social pathology.

These concerns were exacerbated by the great depression the entire Western world underwent between 1873 and 1896. There was bankruptcy, unemployment, credit shortage—in short, every characteristic of a depression—duly accompanied by confusion as to how to resolve these difficulties. It took twenty years to get out of them. Historians are pretty sure as to the causes of the depression. For one thing, we know that nineteenth-century banking and credit institutions were deficient. But historians are uncertain as to how the Western world emerged from the depression. We can conjecture that with the discovery of gold mines in South Africa, the infusion into the Western world of gold advantageously increased the money supply.

At any rate the Victorians faced debilitating and apparently insoluble social problems and then a great depression that further undermined confidence in their doctrines. With so much concentrated social misery and poverty in the 1880s and early 1890s, belief in historicism, macrocosm, and traditional Christian ethics began to evaporate.

The third cause for the rise of modernism was that imperialism began to turn sour. The strangest facet of European imperialism is that it began its collapse at the moment it reached its zenith. Although it took until the 1920s for this fact to become fully manifest and to emerge in actual political movements for colonial liberation, we have seen that in 1897 Rudyard Kipling was already predicting the downfall of the white man's empire. The decline of imperialism was accompanied by the proliferation of ideologically anti-imperial sentiment in Europe. There was increasing feeling that imperialism was a hoax set up by soldiers and a few capitalists, particularly those engaged in mineral extraction like the "randlords" (mining billionaires) in South Africa, who were its only visible beneficiaries.

Two events of the 1880s demoralized many reflective people and inevitably raised questions about imperialism and Western chauvinism. One was the massacre of Zulus in South Africa by the British army, at the behest of white settlers who wanted the natives' land. Magnificent Zulu warriors were mercilessly mowed down by modern British machine guns. The other incident was the suppression of the French-Indian *métis*, or the "half-breeds" as the English called them, and the Indians in Saskatchewan, Canada. The French-Indians tried to establish an independent democratic republic in Saskatchewan; they, too, were crushed by a British army. The *métis* leader was tried and hanged for treason, becoming a perpetual martyr for French-speaking Canada.

These ugly events prompted rethinking about the purpose and utility of imperialism and signaled the diminution of imperialist enthusiasm. The Boer War, which began in South Africa in 1898, inflicted a mortal blow on imperialism. Strange as it may seem now, rebellious Afrikaner (Boer, Dutch) settlers trying (in the end, unsuccessfully) to throw off British rule were seen as heroes by the European Left. It was not noted that one reason they wanted independence was to be able to treat the black population more severely.

The guns had barely been stilled in South Africa when the myth of the natural superiority of the white man and effete quality of the Asian peoples was devastated by the Russo-Japanese War of 1904–5. After the Japanese had taken Russia's Far Eastern fortress of Port Arthur, the Russian Baltic Fleet, allegedly one of the more powerful in the world, sailed proudly more than halfway around the globe to confront the Japanese navy. The Russian fleet was sent to the bottom by the Japanese in an hour, anticipating the events of December 7, 1941. Drawing from the Russian naval catastrophe the lesson that the European empires in Asia were paper tigers, an obscure British-educated Indian lawyer, Mohandas K. Gandhi, soon emerged as the leading opponent of the Raj and began his four decades of persistent campaigning for Indian freedom.

With the decline of imperialism, the general unraveling of Victorian thought also accelerated. Since Victorianism and imperialism were intertwined, when imperialism began to collapse, it brought down with it other aspects of the surrounding culture.

This is essentially the theme of E. M. Forster's novel about imperialism, *A Passage to India.* Although published in 1924, it had been written several years earlier, and describes the Indian Raj of 1914. It is not only that imperialism, in Forster's view, is base, that it is terribly demoralizing and raises very grave questions about Western ethics. More fundamentally Forster believes that Indian civilization and the Indian middle class constitute a great Other, which even generous-minded Englishmen cannot comprehend. India is an endless dark cave that disorients and bewilders Westerners; they had best pack up and go home. This message is similar to that propounded by Conrad three decades earlier, but significantly it was now set forth in an acerbic manner, with very little sympathy for the imperial master class. They appear in Forster's novel not as tragic but as diminished, foolish, and petty.

In Forster's view imperialism is tattered and chintzy. Far from being grand, it is beginning to look sordid and soiled around the edges, even in its physical aspects. Although Forster's Indian novel was not written in modernist style, he himself was a close associate of modernist writers and artists, and in his mind was the idea that the decline of imperialism was related to the emergence of the new culture.

A third factor that helped generate the cultural revolution of modernism was the proliferation, to which we have already referred, of a large, educated middle class. Beginning in the 1870s throughout the Western world, first in Germany, then in France and the United States, and finally, rather late (1904), in England, virtually free secondary education became available, although of course it remained highly selective. From 1870 to 1900, the high school population rose from 2 to 10 percent of the male thirteen-to-seventeen age group, and in response to a voracious demand for office workers, women increasingly gained access to secondary education. (The Underwood typewriter did more for the liberation of women than all the feminist theory propounded before 1900). Although university populations remained small, compared to previous generations there was also a major expansion in higher education.

The educated middle class registered a quantum leap in one generation, which certainly led to concurrent changes in the arts, literature, and other intellectual pursuits. The conservative academies that had set the style and motifs for the visual arts in particular, and to some extent for the performing arts, could no longer exert the same control. The educated became so numerous, as did people with aesthetic taste and cultivation who could make discretionary expenditures on the arts and books, that a vanguard could emerge by 1900 eluding the authority of conservative institutions. That is, once a relatively large educated middle class came into being, it became impossible to control the socialization, education, and intellectual propensity of an entire rising generation or to sustain the hold of traditional cultural values.

There would henceforth be those at the social margin who would join the avant-garde. The Victorians believed very much in education, and made enormous strides in it. But they undermined their own system by producing a surplus of cultivated people, many more than their traditional intellectual and artistic institutions could control or absorb.

A host of additional social and material factors should also be mentioned that interactively played special roles in forging the new consciousness.

One of these was the end of the great depression in 1896. Between 1896 and

1906, the West witnessed great prosperity. The employment rate was high, inflation was low, and it was relatively cheap to live. Such periods of high employment and low inflation are infrequent in history, and they produce momentous cultural developments. A similar phenomenon recurred for a few years in the 1920s and in the 1960s. When a rising generation of educated people does not have to worry about securing its livelihood, about choice of profession, when it does not feel obliged to become accountants or lawyers, and can risk becoming artists or philosophers, or founding new theaters, or writing poetry, because it knows that it can always find a means for making a living, that period witnesses a cultural explosion. Such was the case between 1896 and 1906.

After 1906 the rapid rise of inflation was followed by the high unemployment that began three or four years before the first World War. Labor problems, strikes, layoffs, and cutbacks were features of the period leading up to World War I, which contrasted sharply with the fondly remembered Gay Nineties. Indeed, the epithet "Gay Nineties" is based on the social fact that in the decade after 1895 young people could easily find jobs as well as pursue the arts.

The second material factor that contributed to the modernist cultural revolution was inexpensive housing. Analogous to the principle of material determinism in history, one can cite a relationship between affordable living quarters in a period and cultural history. Extrapolating from this principle, we can easily claim that New York is now doomed as a cultural center. The future cultural vanguard of the United States will be located in places like Minneapolis; Burlington, Vermont; Tulsa, Oklahoma; Louisville, or Seattle.

The period of our concern was a time of unprecedented, phenomenally cheap housing in great metropolitan centers throughout the world. In the biography of Picasso, one finds out that around 1912, Picasso in Paris decided that he needed a new and larger studio, which he rented within a few hours for a trifling sum. Picasso was at the time still a relatively unknown artist. Nowadays a young artist could never afford a large studio in Montmartre, now a very attractive part of Paris, but then a low-rent district. This is the period that saw the emergence of New York's Greenwich Village as an artists' colony, and of Bloomsbury in London's West End as the habitat of intellectuals, writers, and philosophers. Virginia Woolf and her sister, Vanessa Bell, leased Bloomsbury houses that are today affordable only by stockbrokers or advertising executives, not by aspiring novelists and painters.

The availability of good housing around 1900 for artists, intellectuals, and academics was due to changes in metropolitan transportation. In the 1880s and 1890s the tram or trolley car systems were developed, electric railroads were introduced, and most important of all, the first subways were built. The early subways were so salubrious and safe that riding them was deemed a privilege rather than a burden. Entrance kiosks on the Vienna and Paris subways are still treasured as wonderful examples of art nouveau; ladies and gentlemen entered the New York IRT in evening dress to travel to the opera; London subways had special smoking cars. An enormous urban expansion inevitably followed the building of the new metropolitan transport lines around 1900. What enabled, for example, Columbia University to move from Manhattan's center to Morningside Heights in 1903 was the opening of the IRT subway line (the city's first, running up the West Side of Manhattan). When Columbia moved to its present location, the area was vacant land. In fact, someone suggested to Nicholas Murray Butler, then president of the university, that he buy the large meadow called Harlem that lay below Morningside Heights. He rejected the proposal on the grounds that no one would ever move and live up there "in the country."

In 1880 90 percent of New York's population lived below Central Park, and about 70 percent below Forty-second Street. In the 1890s the population density on Manhattan's Lower East Side was five hundred thousand people per square mile—what it is in Hong Kong today. This situation changed very rapidly in the later years of the nineteenth century and the beginning of the twentieth. The working class moved to Brooklyn, Queens, and the Bronx. There was nothing in the Bronx until the early years of the twentieth century except farmland. Queens, too, was largely unsettled. Similar transformations occurred in all the large cities of the Western world. Entire new areas emerged for the working class on the periphery of cities, which, as a result, expanded rapidly, vastly extending their territorial borders.

At the same time many in the middle class moved to the suburbs. This is the period of the musical comedy song "Forty-five Minutes to Broadway." It was Yonkers, the residential area for businessmen and the first bedroom community, that was forty-five minutes to Broadway, or more precisely, to Grand Central or Penn Station. These departures—by the working class to the periphery and the affluent class to the suburbs—left vacant and underutilized housing in the heart of the metropolitan areas, such as the West End of London, New York City below Fourteenth street, the area around the university in Munich, parts of Berlin, the Left Bank and Montmartre in Paris, central Vienna (now sought-after high-rent districts)—all of which provided superb opportunities for artists and intellectuals. They took over the housing abandoned by the working class, or, in some cases, by the middle class.

The new apartment blocks for the working class on the edge of old Vienna eased pressure on the housing stock in the central city, allowing young Dr. Freud and other impecunious intellectuals to rent comfortable homes or flats. Paradoxically, some of the new working class housing was so attractive that in the twenties it was much sought after by artists and writers. The Chelsea section of London experienced a similar history.

Not until decades later, after World War II, did these housing opportunities finally disappear. In the 1920s they were still there. An erosion of real estate opportunities for the avant-garde threatened in the thirties, but the depression dammed this trend. It was not until the 1950s that housing facilities for artists and intellectuals began their absolute decline. Since in the sixties and seventies in Paris and to a lesser extent elsewhere there was again some working-class movement to peripheral developments, the avant-garde real estate situation in European cities is not quite as bad as in New York, where it has become catastrophic.

Another factor in the emergence of modernism was the rise of fringe countries and provincial cities. The great centers of modernism were Berlin, London, Paris, Vienna, and New York, but there were other participating places: Dublin, the locale of the Irish Renaissance, was the city of Joyce and Yeats; Chicago and Glasgow were two of the important centers for modernist architecture; Oslo bred two great dramatists of the early twentieth century. Chicago was an important center in social science; Cambridge, Massachusetts, in philosophy and psychology.

Some scientists of the modernist era came from very distant places. Ernest Rutherford, who along with Einstein is one of the two most important physicists of the early twentieth century, came from New Zealand—and Einstein did his early, seminal work in Zurich, the home of Jung and final refuge of Joyce. Rutherford did most of his early research at McGill University in Montreal, which around 1910 was a lively place intellectually. Another important physicist, Niels Bohr, worked in Copenhagen. Marie Curie was a Pole who immigrated to Paris.

There was, in short, a major expansion in intellectual activity that drew on the Western population in a comprehensive way. Places that had once constituted the provinces became secondary metropolitan centers of Western culture. Newly founded or greatly expanded universities outside the old metropolitan centers—Johns Hopkins, Chicago, Manchester, Göttingen, and

Strasbourg—moved rapidly to the forefront of learning and research.

In the twenty years before World War I, Russia's contribution to Western culture, especially in music, attained not only an unprecedented level but a peak that it never regained under Communist rule. The cultural connection between St. Petersburg and Paris in the early modernist years was a close and productive one. Émigrés from the czarist empire dominated French ballet and were prominent in painting in both Paris and Berlin.

New media played a role in shaping the context of modernism. The revolution in the printing trades evolved into the late-nineteenth-century appearance of the paperback book, which meant fast and low-cost printing. People could now buy a softcover novel or a work in philosophy at a railway station kiosk before boarding their train. This novelty of the 1890s was made possible by new high-speed printing and cheap paper. With the technological revolution in the printing trades—the greatest since Gutenberg—hand presses became obsolete and were, in turn, bought by intellectuals who used them to turn out small magazines and vanguard books.

One of the great modernist scenes in the early 1920s is Virginia Woolf standing in the basement of her Bloomsbury house over such a hand press, which she and her husband, Leonard, had bought for a few pounds, setting type for the first edition of T. S. Eliot's *The Waste Land.* She and her husband founded their own press, the Hogarth, which is still in business although it does not use hand presses anymore.

The Woolfs were by no means the only writers and intellectuals to undertake such activity. The modernist era in literature was made possible by "little" magazines and small publishing houses. Joyce's *Ulysses* was originally published by an American bookstore proprietor in Paris, and the first edition of Proust's *Swann's Way* by a fledgling publishing house after being rejected by more prominent Parisian editors. Some of the most celebrated names among New York publishers became prominent and eventually affluent in the twenties and thirties as patrons of modernist fiction. Little magazines with paid circulation of less than a thousand each transformed literary and art criticism, and public taste.

Another novelty in the printing trade was color lithography, which became a major medium in modern art around 1900 and for a while was almost synonymous, along with stairways, with art nouveau. Some of the first manifestations of expressionist art appear in color lithographs that were produced around this time. Two of the pioneers of modernism, Edvard Munch, a Norwegian, in his first important work, and Gustav Klimt, an Austrian, in some of his early production, utilized this color lithography before they concentrated on painting. Some of Paul Klee's early work, too, was done in lithographs. This new medium played an important part in the formation of modernist art. Now one could actually hold an original work of art, bought for little money, in one's hands, not just a reproduction.

The role of photography in the emergence of modernism is not a simple story. First, photography was one of the ways in which secular symbolism expressed itself. Many of the early photographers of the 1880s and 1890s were artists. They looked on photography not so much as a way of depicting the real world, but as a method for representing a symbolic dimension. Photography was in its early decades the new medium for the creation and communication of original artistic forms and ideas. It was to take its place alongside paint and canvas, stone and metal, as an art form. This expectation has never entirely disappeared, and in recent years it has again become prominent.

Photography's second role in the making of modernist culture lay in precisely the opposite direction from this symbolic art photography. The effectiveness of the camera in reproducing images of the real or natural world made it seem superfluous for painting to pursue this task, as it had done through much of the nineteenth century as well as earlier. In 1914 art critic Clive Bell remarked: "Who doubts that one of those Daily Mirror photographers . . . can tell us far more about 'London by day' than any royal academician?" The painter or sculptor was no longer called on to illustrate scenes from life or the human face and body as they appeared to the eye: Photographs could do that well enough, and as the mobility of the camera improved and the chemistry of celluloid film became more sophisticated, it could do it better and far more cheaply and rapidly than the artist.

At the turn of the century, in London's Chelsea, Paris's Left Bank, or New York's Greenwich Village, the artist—unless he or she was a commercial illustrator—felt increasingly impelled to make a mark by depicting a nonrealistic world, the world seen by the inner imaginative but not physical eye; a nonrepresentational, abstract world. It is too simple to say that the Kodak camera made Picasso and Kandinsky inevitable, but there is a core of truth in this statement.

Finally photography and—although in 1900 it was still cumbersome and expensive—especially color photography revolutionized art education. In 1870 only the wealthy, or the beneficiaries of affluent patronage, could gain the rudiments of education in the visual arts because only they could afford to travel to galleries and museums. In 1900 people of modest means could, however, get some sense of what great painting and sculpure looked like by studying photographs. The new women's colleges that were founded at this time were the first institutions to realize clearly the educational possibilities that art photography represented and established basic courses in art history and criticism. Talented people in the provinces could now glimpse what was occurring in the metropolitan centers of avant-garde art and gain inspiration for joining the aesthetic vanguard.

Furthermore, they did not have to stay in the provinces. They could get on a train and for a reasonably priced ticket be on the Left Bank, in London's Bloomsbury, or in Greenwich Village in a matter of hours. Modernism emerged in that strange and ephemeral technological moment, the railroad era, which for practical purposes endured only from 1880 to 1955. It took until 1880 for the national railway networks to be built, and after 1955 the airplane for long journeys and automobile and bus service for shorter trips made the utility of the railroad marginal or even negligible.

Economic historians tell us that the railroad was never a technological necessity in Western Europe and the United States. If the magnificent canal system built in the eighteenth and early nineteenth centuries had been maintained and expanded, it could have distributed goods and people just as well (although not to precisely the same locations as the railroads) and could have done so more cheaply and with less ravaging of the countryside.

Railroads were built as speculative capitalist ventures or to suit the vanity of heads of government or facilitate the mobility of armies. From the beginning these fiscally leveraged, ruinously expensive enterprises made very little money as transportation systems: They survived out of land and mineral concessions or direct government subsidies. In some ways railroads were extravagant Potemkin villages (mere showpiece facades), like the bloated, unnecessary European empires that flourished at precisely the same time.

But the railways were built, and they made a difference. They brought to all areas outside metropolitan centers the possibility of rapid communication with these centers, and greatly expanded the market for information, educational materials, popular literature, and journalism. For centuries there had been one capital in each country in Europe as a whole, a small handful of central cities, while the majority of the population lived like medieval peasants, in darkness and ignorance, outside the circle of communication and learning. Provincial cities were dull, stifling, and vulgar enclaves.

The railways changed all that very rapidly in the last two decades of the nineteenth century. Through the information and communication network established by the railways, there was an overwhelming proliferation of ideas, knowledge, the performing arts, and popular culture just as there came about rapid tranportation of people. Steamships greatly reduced the time and discomfort of transatlantic travel and modified American intellectual isolation. In the new railroad and steamship era, Americans traveled to Europe in significant numbers to obtain M.D. and Ph.D. degrees.

Ordinary people—ordinary in terms of their means—could now move unprecedented distances. They could transport themselves to the metropolitan center in search of education and an artistic life. They could move rapidly and often across continents in large numbers. One of the reasons one should read Richard Ellmann's splendid biography of James Joyce is that Joyce's life demonstrates the impact of the railroad on modernism. He moved extensively over Europe—Ireland, England, Italy, France, and Switzerland, living in different cities, never hesitating to pack up and move on when it suited him, devastating as the moves were to his wife and children. It had become feasible even to try a city like Trieste. Living in Trieste in 1870 would have been completely alienating and stupefying. In 1910 Joyce did not feel cut off from the cultural and information network. He did some of his best writing in Trieste and supported himself by working in the tourist trade, teaching English in a Berlitz school.

If an intellectual in the railroad era came from an affluent family, he could become a Continental cosmopolite, moving easily from place to place in search of gurus and inspiration. Thus from 1906 to 1912 the young Viennese engineer and philosophy student, Ludwig Wittgenstein, moved back and forth between Berlin and Cambridge seeking guidance and testing his ideas. His face-to-face encounter with Bertrand Russell at Cambridge changed philosophy permanently.

The transportation network created by railways moved not only immigrants and workers, but also artists and intellectuals, and thereby made its own significant contribution to modernism. The speed and ease with which literary and artistic products could now be sent through the mails also helped to foster modernism as a trans-European and transatlantic phenomenon. The climactic moment in the early biography of modernist novelists and poets was the anxious dispatch of a manuscript through the railroad-carried mails to friend, patron, or publisher—and the expectation of prompt reply.

In the years after 1900 the railroad and steamship era made the literary and artistic expatriate a central figure in the modernist movement. Wassily Kandinsky and Paul Klee, a Russian and a Swiss German respectively, headed the Berlin expressionist movement in painting. Two Americans—Ezra Pound and Eliot—were the leaders of literary modernism in Britain. In Paris in the twenties, three American women, Gertrude Stein, Sylvia Beach, and Peggy Guggenheim played important roles in fostering literature and the arts. The Irishman Joyce, the Italian Amedeo Modigliani, the American Ernest Hemingway (fresh from working on a Toronto newspaper) and the Canadian Morley Callaghan, as well as the East European Jews Marc Chagall and Chaim Soutine, were prominent in the vibrant life of the Left Bank and Montmartre. Modernism was built on cheap metropolitan housing and steam transportation.

Railroads and railroad terminals by their nature gave psychological reinforcement to would-be expatriates or provincials heading for the cultural metropolis. In European and U.S. cities railroad depots were located in the city centers and had been built in the nineteenth century in the style of Greek temples, the Baths of Caracalla, or Gothic cathedrals. Entering a terminal to make the traumatic move to the bohemian sections of the metropolis, the undiscovered artist or writer from St. Louis, Toulouse, Wiesbaden, or Birmingham was making a public declaration of his or her new artistic commitment in an awesome structure. Such a traveler could not but feel that he or she had undertaken a sacred journey. Compare this with a similar artistic person heading for the metropolis by air in the 1960s: He or she would take a scruffy bus to a desolate airport terminal at the edge of the city. Embarking by air was—and remains—a plebeian, furtive, almost guilty act.

Taking a train to and from the likes of New York's old Pennsylvania Station, London's Victoria Station, or the Gare du Nord in Paris was, on the contrary, a celebratory, public, ego-boosting act. Thomas Wolfe's 1930s novel, *Look Homeward, Angel,* a bestseller in its day, evokes very well the epiphany of artists' and writers' journeys in the railroad/modernist era. So do the novels of an equally forgotten Canadian novelist of the 1920s, Frederick Philip Grove, who wrote about the vast, underpopulated Canadian West, traversed by steam trains.

Around 1900 the introduction of the automobile appeared to be bringing to a climax what electric light and steam transportation had started—the most profound changes in the circumstances of human life, especially in ever-expanding urban areas, that had occurred since Neolithic times. Shortly, educated people were aware that in universities the most important discoveries about the laws of the physical world were being made since the age of Newton. This technological and scientific transformation contributed to the reconstruction of art, literature, philosophy, and social theory so as to open to question received values and modes of expression.

A changed environment encouraged a cultural revolution that would provide a system of sensibility, reason, and learning for the new century. Perhaps even more radically, the culture of modernism eroded the restraining hold of traditional values and worldviews and allowed the new technology and science to shape social life in relatively emancipated fashion.

Modernism immediately affected vision. It impelled new ways of looking at the environment, and of conceiving physical lines. It propagated the beauty and morality of clean lines, sharply etched symbolic forms, and the intrinsic value of deep color fields. When you look at the new art deco furniture and interior design you know that something radical had occurred in human consciousness around 1900. The splendid art nouveau museum in Hamburg heralds a cultural revolution. The world looked different to the middle-class people who made and used these objects in the early years of this century.

Yet, just as each of the previous three cultural revolutions was related to the others, modernism was faced with choosing to break with attributes of the previous cultural movements or to reaffirm their focal message. The Reformation posited the freedom and dignity of individual conscience on theological grounds. The Enlightenment secularized this message, proclaiming the freedom and power of the rational mind shaped by a salubrious environment. Romanticism tried to protect this humanist tradition against materialism and power by transcendentalist projection.

Modernism addressed the question: Did modern society, technology, and learning demand a rupture with the humanist tradition, or a further reconstitution of this now venerable idea of freedom and dignity in the light of new experience and circumstances of living? This was the most difficult issue faced by modernism. It explored this issue intensively but never clearly resolved it. We have not definitively resolved it after passage of so many decades and such dramatic events.

Modernism never had a full opportunity to address this problem. By the 1930s and 1940s resurgent neo-Victorianism in the forms of Marxism and fascism, plus additional cultural trends during and after World War II, forestalled a definitive modernist response to the humanist traditions derived from previous cultural revolutions. The decline of the metropolis as a middle-class habitat after 1945 also undermined the modernist capacity to face critical questions.

Whether the generation of the early twenty-first century will benefit or suffer from the interruption of modernist speculation on individuality and freedom is a moot issue, suitable now only for the ever-expanding literature of science fiction.

The Victorian Achievement Cultural revolutions happen, and we ought to try to understand why and how in the specific instances, in this case the emergence of modernism. But we would be falling into the Victorian mode of historicism were we to celebrate the change as an unmitigated triumph and denigrate consistently what went before.

We are in some respects so distanced from the Victorian ambience that we are awed and mystified by aspects of their cultural system. We cannot refrain from a patronizing and contemptuous attitude to some dimensions of nineteenth-century culture. But it is necessary to stress the Victorian accomplishment within this cultural context.

The nineteenth century was the century of the long peace. There were no major wars in Europe between the Battle of Waterloo in 1815 and August 1914. The Crimean War in the 1850s was a squalid and miserable affair, but it did not last long and involved small armies. The Franco-Prussian War in 1870 was over in a few months and—although it had major poltical consequences—involved only one major battle. The only truly terrible conflict of the nineteenth century, in many ways a foreshadowing of the First and Second World Wars, was the American Civil War, an ideological struggle waged with remorseless savagery as a war of attrition. The nineteenth century knew no holocausts within Europe (the imperial scene was a different story, but not for long without censure). Again, apart from the American Civil War, civilian populations were treated with restraint and generosity.

Aside from spanning a century of peace, Victorian culture presided over the greatest technological and economic upheaval since the Neolithic era—the Industrial Revolution—with, after much initial confusion and misery (inspiring Marx and Engels), a high degree of rationality and humanity. There was during the nineteenth century an enormous growth in the size of the middle class, and a vast improvement in the welfare of the working class. The increase in the levels of education and literacy was unprecedented.

The Victorian era also was a time of increased political democracy and recognition of civil liberties—of course not consistently in each country—but on the whole there was political and legal progress almost everywhere. In 1900 the British (both in the United Kingdom and in their overseas dominions), the French, Germans, Scandinavians, and Italians enjoyed a very high degree of freedom, both intellectual and political. Even the evil empire of the nineteenth century, czarist Russia, looks relatively benign compared to what succeeded it in the same country in the 1930s. To compare the Berlin or Munich of 1900 with the same city four decades later is to move from an extremely beneficent and cultivated environment to the abyss of tyranny and barbarism.

One of the great questions in human history is why Western society—at the same time as it broke away from the confinements, and in enlightened fashion superseded the limitations, of Victorian culture—entered a dark age of iron and terror? How are these phenomena related?

In the late 1920s the Viennese novelist Robert Musil perceived the disturbing ambiguity of the modernist cultural upheaval. In *The Man Without Qualities* he wrote of a Europe rising in 1900 ambivalently and explosively to rebel against tradition.

This was an era in which both "the Superman was adored and the Subman was adored . . . one had faith and was skeptical, one was naturalistic and precious, robust and morbid." It was a time when "one dreamed . . . of vast horizons . . . the uprisings of slaves of toil, men and women in the primeval Garden and the destruction of society." No one evoked more dramatically the intellectual crisis at the beginning of the new century.

By 1938 Musil, one of the leading modernist writers, was fleeing with his Jewish wife from Vienna to Switzerland as the Nazis took over the old imperial city.

2

MODERNISM

A Model of Modernism In 1918 the British writer Lytton Strachey published *Eminent Victorians,* a biographical account of four prominent figures of Victorian England. Strachey came from a leading literary and political family and was a close friend of Virginia Woolf, her sister, the artist Vanessa Bell, as well as other members of the Bloomsbury group. Educator Thomas Arnold, health care administrator Florence Nightingale, military hero Gen. Charles George "Chinese" Gordon, and Henry Edward Cardinal Manning, head of the Roman Catholic Church in England during its great expansion in the late nineteenth century, were the personages portrayed in *Eminent Victorians.*

The book, which became an immediate bestseller, was a humorous and savage prostration of these Victorian icons. Thomas Arnold appears a snob and a bigot. Florence Nightingale is a busybody and a petty tyrant, General Gordon a racist and grotesque incompetent, and Cardinal Manning a vulgarian hypocrite. Most biographers today would question Strachey's characterizations, with the possible exception of that of General Gordon, who seems to have been a psychopath by all accounts. *Eminent Victorians* was tremendously popular and exemplified the reflexive anti-Victorianism that constituted a primary ingredient of modernism.

Rebellion against the Victorian world, hostility or contempt or at least a profound lack of sympathy for it, remained a hallmark throughout the modernist movement during the first half of the twentieth century. Just as we have posited, in our culture, that everything the American establishment did in the 1960s with respect to the Vietnam War was wrong, just as it once sufficed to mention names like Lyndon Johnson, McGeorge Bundy, or Richard Nixon to

43

elicit visceral negative reactions (justified or unjustified), so by the second decade of the twentieth century, one only had to name prominent Victorians, much admired in their own day, in order to get a similar unfavorable response.

In addition to this reflexive anti-Victorianism, which continued throughout the heyday of modernism and well into the 1950s, specific ideas and attitudes characteristic of modernism manifested themselves in fields ranging from literature and art to science and philosophy. By identifying these fundamentals, the modernist mentality can be reconstructed.

First of all, modernism was antihistoricist. It did not believe that truth lay in telling an evolutionary story. Modernism cared little for history; it was in fact hostile to it. Truth-finding became analytical rather than historical. As T. S. Eliot, a prime theoretician of modernism, wrote in 1923, the "narrative method" had been replaced by the "mythic method." The historical approach, in Eliot's view, was superseded by the very different program of concentrating on direct, inner, symbolic meaning, which was both completely external to history and irrelevant to considerations of temporality.

In the early 1930s Eliot wrote: "All time is unredeemable/What might have been and what has been point toward the same end,/Which is always the present." Reality is an ahistorical, unredeemable present. This negation of temporality was precisely opposed to the Victorian proclivity to place everything in sequential time.

Another way of stating this concept would be to say that modernist antihistoricism concentrated on immediate understanding, direct analysis, or on what is later termed "close reading," the intensive examination of the object removed from historical sequence. It will become apparent that this attitude had revolutionary consequences in many fields, but particularly in fiction, literary criticism, painting and the social sciences. The antihistoricism or the analytical, mythic method made a strong comeback in the 1970s, which removes us twice from nineteenth-century historicism: first through the modernist rebellion, and again through the upheaval witnessed in the last twenty-five years, which is sometimes referred to as the structuralist movement, or variously as deconstruction or postmodernism. Using the terminology of this later structuralism, modernism stressed the synchronic rather than the diachronic plane.

The second intellectual characteristic of modernism was its departure from the macrocosmic, universalist tendencies of nineteenth-century thought, and its focus instead on the microcosmic dimension. As has already been pointed out, the nineteenth century believed in the superior value of the big picture. Modernist thought adhered to the notion that the small was better—

and beautiful. The physics of the time, for example, has been called "particle physics," for it emphasized the subatomic particle, making it the prime subject of interest and research. Focus on a minute particle—of human experience or art as well as nature—conditioned all of modernist culture.

Throughout modernist culture it was held that the smallest segment would reveal an entire world when subjected to microcosmic, microscopic analysis; that it was investigation of the most minute conceivable or comprehensible unit that would establish the connection with reality rather than that on the generalized, macrocosmic level: The latter could yield nothing but empty words.

The emphasis here is on the precise and exact word, and on the concrete image, terms used by modernists themselves, along with the "particle" of science, the "datum" of social science, and the "microcosmic world" of the arts. This total shift in the level addressed by the mind—from the big to the small, from the general to the particular—made much of nineteenth-century thought—its philosophy, science, and social science—not only wrong but totally meaningless.

A third characteristic of modernism was the preoccupation with what is called self-referentiality or textuality, meaning that anything that is examined constitutes a self-enclosed world. To understand it it must be taken first of all, and often in the last analysis too, in terms of itself. The entity refers back to itself—it is self-referential. The text is simply what it is, and it is this self-enclosure of the text that should be studied. The painting does not represent something external to itself; the poem does not illustrate a story. Both exist in and for themselves, and are enclosed in and show a world that always refers back to itself. The text is finite rather than illustrative.

An American expatriate in Paris, Gertude Stein, saw with dramatic clarity in the early years of the century that self-referentiality was at the center of the whole modernist movement. Words, she said, "were not imitations either of sounds or colors or emotions," as the Victorians believed. She intended to write "as if the fact of writing were continually becoming true and completing itself, not as if it were leading to something." Six decades later the postmodernist critic Susan Sontag expressed the same idea about the essence of modernism in somewhat more elaborate form: "The idea that depths are obfuscating, demagogic, that no human essence stirs at the bottom of things, and that freedom lies in staying on the surface, the large glass on which desire circulates—this is the central argument of the modern aesthetic position."

A fourth quality of modernism was a penchant for the fragmented, the fractured, and the discordant. In opposition to the Victorians, who showed a predilection for the finished and the harmonious, modernism foregrounded the disharmonious and the unfinished, the splintered world, the piece that had broken off—the serendipitous—and pursued this preference to the point of making it an aesthetic principle.

The fifth feature of modernist culture was lack of predetermined pattern. Modernism favored random access. In attempting to understand something, one cannot presuppose either a spatial or temporal predetermined succession.. A sequence may be ultimately established, but this must be done empirically from within the object itself. Sequentiality cannot be imposed on it externally, nor can it be anticipated. There may not be a sequence involved at all in the object of study, for one may very well be face to face with discontinuity. And if there is in fact a continuity in the object, it is never one that can be presupposed in any predetermined program.

One of the weaknesses of Victorian thought certainly was this predisposition to continuity and to assuming prior knowledge of exact sequence. Among the problems this led to was to make much of Victorian social science hopeless or useless. Modernism began by questioning the assumption about continuity, whether it existed, and if it did, what its precise nature was.

Similarly, a sixth point in modernism's departure from Victorian thought was its rejection of philosophical idealism, especially Hegelian theory. The favorite philosophy of the nineteenth century was one that removed the empirical in order to arrive at the most general proposition, and at the purest concept that could be imagined by consciousness, or at what Hegel called "the absolute." This notion was discredited rapidly after 1900. Philosophical idealism was faulted and abandoned on two accounts: Insufficiently empirical, and impervious to concrete data, it dealt only with the realm of the conscious and ignored the unconscious. Ignorant of the empirical and the unconscious, nineteenth-century philosophy was perceived to be empty, and therefore invalid.

The seventh intellectual quality of modernism was functionalism. This term found particular application in the fields of architecture, where it is still in use (although not always in a laudatory way), and in sociology and anthropology. Once the object of analysis is understood as microcosmic, self-referential, and exterior to predetermined spatial and temporal sequentiality, what remains to be studied is how the object functions in and for itself. It can be concluded that functionalism was a product of other main characteristics of modernism. It can be viewed in another way, as expressing antihistoricism: External to history, the object exists in terms of its function.

Time and time again modernism asks how a thing works, and further, how it works in and for itself. From this functionalist point of view modern experimental physics was born, as well as field research in the social and behavioral sciences.

An eighth characteristic of modernism was its antipathy for, or rejection of, absolute polarities. Victorians assumed the polarity of male and female, object and subject, the higher and the lower, the early and the late, mass and energy, time and space. They were certain that the world and human life operated in terms of absolute, separable polarities. Modernism questioned this notion by claiming that these polarities were integrated with one another, that they were interactive and not absolute. It viewed them as convenient ways of talking about phenomena, which, when observed closely, revealed themselves to be related to one another, or, in other words, to be functions of one another.

The weakening or even abandonment of absolute polarities was central to modernism and had revolutionary consequences in many areas of thought and behavior. The Victorians reflexively separated things; the modernists felt compelled to integrate them. The interactive nature of apparent polarities and their possible symbiosis was a leading characteristic of both modernist art and science. Postmodernist thought since the 1960s has restored the importance of polarities, making a critical departure from modernism.

The ninth aspect of modernism, a particularly difficult and controversial one, was that in contrast to nineteenth-century culture, which tended strongly to vulgarization and popularization, it was elitist. Nineteenth-century scholars and writers believed that social science, philosophy and, above all, literature and art could be expressed in a way that was readily accessible by anyone with at least a high school education. Modernism, to the contrary, believed in complexity and difficulty. It addressed a narrow, highly selective, learned, and professional audience—the cultural vanguard.

This is a feature that runs through modernist culture in a fundamental way. From science to literature and art, modernism was a culture of the elite. It required sophistication, learning, intense application. In any given area, modernism was not accessible to the naive and unprepared person, to the "common man." Whether in art, philosophy, or science, modernist culture was only open to the specially prepared and specifically cultivated mind.

This particular quality of elitism presented important problems for modernism and constituted one of its fundamental tensions for the many modernists who also belonged to the political Left. They naturally had difficulty reconciling their elitism with their political democracy. This issue still churned away in the leftist weeklies and quarterlies into the 1960s.

A tenth characteristic of modernism was greater openness with regard to sexuality. Much research has been done recently about what the Victorians did in bed or around—or on—the kitchen table. Their practices appear not to have differed greatly from our own, but their way of talking about them was certainly different. Modernism produced a new frankness in the exchange about sexual relationships and, indeed, had a tendency toward the scatological, to what the Victorians would have regarded as "vulgar" and "dirty talk." At first the modernists were very self-conscious about this new sexual frankness. Virginia Woolf makes the use of the dread word "semen" at one of her early Bloomsbury parties an earth-shattering event. By the twenties intellectuals talked about sex as familiarly as Victorians conversed about God. Of course, Freud and psychoanalysis made a major difference.

Modernism also was sympathetic toward feminism and homosexuality and expressed an interest in the androgynous and the bisexual, another manifestation of the modernist tendency to break down polarities. Modernism was not committed to the separation of the male and the female on moral, biological, or psychological grounds, as the Victorians had been.

An eleventh quality of modernism was its attention to the outcomes of a technological culture. Modernism can be looked upon as an effort to address the cultural consequences of a new technological world and of a mass culture. The recognition that culture had changed as a result of the application of science to the needs of everyday life and particularly the revolution in transportation and communication systems, and the emergence of widespread, near universal literacy, marks modernism. Dealing with the implications of such transformations is something we are still very much engaged in. How the artist and philosopher should respond to a situation in which mechanization takes command and a revolutionary scientific paradigm has been attained was a continuing modernist concern.

On the one hand modernism was a product of the age of railroad and steamship and was fashioned by the rapid and easy means of transportation and commitment to the urban culture and the transatlantic metropolitan centers. On the other modernism was concerned with preservation of rationality, art, and learned intelligence in the age of mechanical reproduction and mass culture. The latter concern is reflected in modernism's elitist quality.

A twelfth characteristic of modernism can be located in the area of ethics. Although not shared by all modernists, there was a tendency in the movement toward moral relativism and departure from a normative code of ethics. It is conventional to say that modernism represented a relativistic rebellion against the puritanical normative ethics of the nineteenth century.

The issue, however, might be stated somewhat differently. Nineteenth-century ethics focused on the nuclear family and its value to society. Its entire ethical system was designed to maintain the nuclear family as the social norm. Modernism weakened this Victorian conception. On the one hand it gave a new authenticity to individualism and to individual search for values, and on the other, it valorized a unit larger than the family, namely culture as a whole. It sought for a moral theory and system that stemmed from the entire culture. While emphasizing the authenticity of individual ethics, it also stressed extended cultural solidarity.

Along with a deep but not universal tendency toward relativism, this perception undermined severely an ethic focused on the preservation of the family. The decline of the nuclear family began around 1900, owing to complex reasons, of which the emergence of modernism was probably the most critical.

In the nineteenth century, in the context of urbanization and salaried employment outside the home in an industrial economy, the family had become less of an economic agency and more of an affective, reproductive, and educational unit. The Victorian increase of sentiment in family relationships combined with the family ideology to bring the nuclear family to its zenith. By attacking patriarchal authority and questioning sexual repression, fostered by the Victorian family, as well as by stressing individualism and the demands of a cultural solidarity beyond the family, modernism precipitated a social and ethical revolution that is still unwinding. Its relativist frame of mind, which eroded legitimacy that had conventionally come to adhere to the nuclear family, has had profound social outcomes in our own day.

A thirteenth characteristic of modernism, which has had consequences for social policy as well as for aesthetics, was the conviction that humanity is in its most authentic, truly human condition when it is involved with the arts. In spite of monumental artistic achievements in the nineteenth century, the Victorians retained the Christian Augustinian conviction that humanity achieves its highest and purest nature in moral action. The modernists replaced the superiority of the ethical dimension with the primacy not only of artistic creation but also of common entitlement to participation in and consumption of art. This meant that the positive purpose of government and social institutions was not the fostering of a moral code but the provision of opportunities for the realization of entitlement to art.

Finally, modernism displayed a tendency toward cultural despair. Victorianism was by and large optimistic, or at least transcendental. It either believed that things were improving or, when this did not seem credible, it held that matters would improve eventually. Even Nietzsche, who found little to approve in his own times, felt certain about stepped-up future betterment. Modernism, however, tends toward pessimism and despair. The world in modernist imagery is often a bleak, devastated urban landscape. The world as a hospital, not a very hopeful one, where people are dying of terminal illness, or as a downscale tavern, or a brothel, or a cruel law court where there is no justice, are among its favorite social images and metaphors. Elias Canetti, the Viennese novelist and social philosopher, succinctly expressed modernism's harshly realistic and sad view of human nature: "Human beings ... accuse themselves by representing themselves as they are, and this is self-indictment, it does not come from someone else."

While Victorians were comforted by history, the modernists pessimistically considered it a nightmare from which we are trying to awaken, in James Joyce's phrase, and not successfully. "Force, hatred, history, all that," says Joyce's spokesman Leopold Bloom. "That's not life for men and women." Similarly, Marcel Proust advises us that the only paradise is the one we have lost.

It should be noted that this formulation of a model of modernism as integral to the culture of the early decades of the century is controversial. Some historians and critics believe in some such model, some do not. The skeptics, speaking in 1986 through the Irish critic Denis Donoghue, claim that "a motive supposedly held in common" by the writers, artists, and composers of the period 1910–25 "would have to be described in such general and abstract terms as to be virtually meaningless. We could designate it as modernism only if we were willing to ignore differences and to preserve at any cost a semblance of common purpose." This view we have shown to be mistaken, because a general model of modernist culture embraces specific ideas, motifs, and attitudes. Donoghue's skeptical view of modernism is itself inspired by a neo-Victorian mind-set that by denying that the writers and artists of the first thirty years of the century belong to a cohesive cultural movement seeks to postulate an unbroken continuity with Victorianism and late romanticism.

The fourteen characteristics of modernism that we have specified achieve validity not only as a general model that provides a persuasive order to complex phenomena. It is also a heuristic device for exploring particular aspects of literature and the arts and sciences. It teaches us what to look for. At the same time the discovery of modernist qualities in many diverse areas of culture inductively and empirically leads us back to confirmation of the model.

Of course, Donoghue and his followers have the option not to think along general lines, not to seek cultural patterns, and not to develop a historical model, but in a skeptical, nominalist way to list endless names of writers, artists, and composers without "a semblance of common purpose." This nominalist method precludes historical understanding and cultural analysis. The Donoghue approach prevents us from confronting the meaning of the complex intellectual, artistic, and scientific developments of the first four decades of the century, which are conditioned by a common mentality.

On the basis of the general model of modernism, particular manifestations of it can be examined in a variety of areas, in order to see how these characteristics were expressed. Modernism affected nearly every area of culture, and for us today, it is memorialized most dramatically in the novel and poem, architecture, in painting, philosophy, physics, and anthropology.

The Novel, Poetry, and Criticism There was a radical change in the novel around 1900 and in the following four decades in the entire Western world. The novel became a prime vehicle of modernist expression and the most readily accessible to educated people.

The Victorian novel, with its strong narrative and historicizing tendency, was for the most part popular literature. The modernist novel distinguishes itself radically from the Victorian in this respect. The novel becomes the literary form on which the modernist intellectual focuses. It is the genre around which much literary criticism develops and which soon occupies a central place in the university curriculum. The modernist novel is today still held up as the fictional ideal by critics and publishing houses.

The modernist novel met with initial strong resistance, but recognition did come quickly. By the mid-twenties, it was widely appreciated that a new form of novel had emerged that presented a distinct departure from the Victorian, and that this vanguard form of literature was extremely important and valuable. For educated people of refined tastes, the novel was consistently one of the most accessible forms of modernist culture.

Without doubt the Anglo-American Henry James in the last decade of the nineteenth century was the forerunner of the modernist novel. James readily recognized the writers after 1900 who were his disciples, particularly James Joyce and Marcel Proust, and understood the purpose and importance of their effort. Other prominent European novelists of the movement were Virginia Woolf and D. H. Lawrence in England; Franz Kafka in Prague, from whose large German Jewish population he emerged; and Robert Musil, Elias Canetti, and Hermann Broch in Vienna—these were the writers from the Austro-Hungarian Empire.

Leading modernist novelists in Germany were Heinrich Mann and his brother, Thomas, at least in the latter's middle period. Thomas Mann's first novel, *Buddenbrooks*, was Victorian in style and his later series on Joseph and his brothers is an early example of postmodernist fabulism. But *Death in Venice* and to a certain extent *The Magic Mountain* are novels from Mann's intermediary stage, which represent modernist efforts. Thomas Mann was like Picasso in that he could adopt any style and work in it, and for a while he was a modernist.

The leading American modernist novelists were Ernest Hemingway and William Faulkner. Hemingway was the most visible of the post-World War I generation of American expatriates in Paris and his novels also reflect a self-conscious midwestern muscularity. The technique of most of his fiction is centrally in the modernist tradition. Two methods distinguish all of Hemingway's novels. The action is moved forward mostly by dialogue and the reader is not clearly informed about key events that occur earlier or off-stage. Faulkner, writing mostly in the thirties and forties in Mississippi, consciously drew on the local color of the southern tradition. But he subtly altered it in the way Joyce exploited the British tradition of the provincial novel while pursuing intense examination of segments of universal experience.

The extremely talented F. Scott Fitzgerald could never quite decide where he stood between the Victorian and modernist traditions. Nevertheless *The Great Gatsby* is frequently called a major modernist novel. *The Day of the Locust*, by Nathaniel West, received little attention when it was published in 1939, but is now regarded as a quintessential modernist work. Thomas Wolfe is now largely neglected but was celebrated as a modernist exponent in the thirties.

Isak Dinesen (Baroness Karen Blixen), author of *Seven Gothic Tales* and *Out of Africa*, can be cited as the modernist fiction writer from Denmark. There are many others but these are the most prominent novelists of the movement.

Getting started was usually not easy for these novelists. Ellmann and other biographers describe the bizarre way in which Joyce had his first great modernist novel, *Ulysses*, published, with customers of Sylvia Beach's Paris bookstore assigned to make fair copy for the printers and editing Joyce's precious text in idiosyncratic and unauthorized ways, and French typesetters who knew no English. Proust was initially turned down by leading publishing houses in

Paris and found acceptance only from a newly established vanguard publisher; the last third of *Remembrance of Things Past* was still in manuscript when he died. Similarly, when Robert Musil died, in 1940, only half of his *The Man Without Qualities* had been published. Some of Kafka's novels were published posthumously. For many years in midcareer, D. H. Lawrence was anathema to publishers, who would not read his manuscripts.

But by and large these writers certainly received recognition by the late twenties. If they were not wealthy like Proust, or did not have a secure executive job like Kafka, or did not have an understanding spouse like Woolf, they found generous patrons, as did Joyce and Lawrence. Hemingway began as a journalist, and this experience affected his fiction. He provided terse bulletins from the front lines. Both Fitzgerald and Faulkner worked for a time as Hollywood film writers.

The fundamental characteristic of the modernist novel, particularly when compared with the Victorian, was stated by Marcel Proust in 1918. He said that the purpose of the novel was the discovery of what he called "a different self." The aim is not to tell a story, to expound a moral, or even to describe a social situation, although he certainly did the last. It is to achieve a breakthrough to a different self, through writing on the part of the author, and through reading on that of the reader. The self sought is different from the ordinary familial and social being known in everyday life.

The burden of the modernist novel is existential discovery of a deeper, mythic, more human self. The exploration of a sensibility replaces the Victorian purpose of telling a story. The modernist novel does contain a story, which may be by turns elaborate and minimal, but it serves only as a vehicle for the exploration of sensibility on the part of the author, which helps the reader to discover him- or herself. This feature continued down into the 1980s in what was known as "*The New Yorker* short story," which preserved the modernist value placed upon the exploration of sensibility.

It is also characteristic of the modernist novel that it supposes the possibility of a penetration or fragile transference from the conscious to the unconscious at any given time. A novel exists at the point of the meeting of the two, and is the exploration of their precarious interaction. The 1920s term "stream of consciousness" refers to this quality—but not accurately.

The modernist novel communicates not a programmed narrative but the confusion, hesitancies, and partial perception of fragmented individual experience. In the modernist novel we do not stand with the Victorian author on some distant Napoleonic height surveying the course of the action. We are close up, seeing and especially hearing—the action is often revealed through only partly coherent dialogue—what is happening from the limited point of view of one or two characters.

In the modernist novel we are immersed in the surface of things. We only slowly or never get the big picture or readily comprehend the general pattern of events. Indeed the major dramatic happenings will often occur somewhere offstage and we will be given only the impact on a particular consciousness. The Victorian novel was the fiction of sense, the modernist novel that of sensibility. If, after reading five pages, we do not comprehend what is happening but have a close perception of someone's consciousness, and/or glimpses into their unconscious, we are in a modernist novel.

Because of this focus on the surface confusion of experienced happenings and this enclosure within consciousness and unconsciousness, the modernist novel has deprivileged the author, who no longer stands outside the event as an imperial and omniscient manipulator of the action. The author is more a reporter than commander of events. Thereby the modernist novel to a significant degree liberated the reader from the author's authority and allowed him or her an autonomous condition, to shape the action and determine the meaning in his or her own mind.

George Eliot (Mary Ann Evans), the prominent Victorian novelist, and Virginia Woolf were women of similar character—very learned, extremely opinionated, masterful. Each, invited to a dinner party, would completely dominate the conversation, crushing male egos with a resounding crash. Yet the effect on the reader experiencing Eliot's *Adam Bede* compared with that of Woolf's *To the Lighthouse* is quite different. Eliot controls her novel to such an extent that she becomes something of a bore; we wish she would get out of the way. *Adam Bede* may be a more interesting and complex person than Eliot allows; we wish she would moderate her incessant historicizing and moralizing and let the novel play. Woolf gets us much closer to her characters, gives them much more autonomy, allows us to internalize them to a degree separately from her. That Woolf herself was an insufferable snob does not prevent us from discoursing directly with her middle-class characters.

The difference between the Victorian and modernist novels comes down to this: In the modernist novel we are seated in the third row of the theater, can hear and see everything, including the actors' perspiration, and can make our own judgment as to what is going on. In the Victorian novel we are seated in the eighth row of the balcony in a cavernous theater and have to strain to see and hear what is occurring onstage. Furthermore, a companion in the next seat keeps whispering in our ear what he thinks is happening onstage and freely interprets the action for us.

The modernist novel is a study in frustration and disappointment. It rarely presents an epiphany, but is an examination of the disappointments of modern life, of the difficulty of achieving ambitions, fulfilling love, and even of communicating, which becomes a frequent theme. A cognate theme is the tremendous exertion it takes to overcome these limitations, engage in a simple act of love or any other form of communication, and the terrible sense of loneliness, alienation, and defeat that often enervates the individual. If these impediments are overcome, the individual is still left exhausted, used up. If there is a moment of intense triumph, it is a very brief one indeed.

All fiction occurs in someone's memory. What was distinctive in the Victorian novel was the wide screen of memory and the steady pace of events projected on it. The narrator was omniscient or at least sufficiently well informed to recall in reportorial detail a broad front of events. Unless the novel was placed in a distant past, the events most frequently occurred about twenty to thirty years ago and from this starting point, clearly demarked, the narration moved steadily toward the present.

Memory in the modernist novel is much more narrowly focused. The time events usually appear to have occurred recently, although related to an earlier trauma, and the chronological time sequence is normally interrupted and distorted. Some physical act or a surge from the unconscious to the conscious mind activates images about an intensely visualized experience or set of connected experiences. Modernist memory gains in density and high luminosity for what it abandons in comprehensiveness and sequentiality. The focus of the modernist novel is on the memory of a compelling short-term experience (second, minute, day) and reflection on the implications of that experience.

Thus the mythic plane replaces the narrative projection. The modernist novel supersedes the Victorian assumption of sequential time with a microcosmic particle of remembered feeling. Stop-time substitutes for extended time. Memory summons up the Stop-time moment that can consist of an image of sitting in a deck chair on a beach (Woolf), biting into a *madeleine* (Proust), lying naked on a bed (Joyce), standing dry-mouthed before a judicial hearing (Kafka), or some gesture of sexual arousal, in a cabaret dressing room (H. Mann) or in the snow (Lawrence). Memory of taste and smell frequently accompanies the visual image. The coded image opens onto an infinite world of activated sensibility, concretely visualized happenings, and recurring symbols. The parallel with psychoanalysis is obvious.

These characteristics are present in all the cited novelists to a certain extent, despite the fact that they differ from one another in some other respects. A common pattern of what they are trying to achieve through the novel form is discernible in their works.

By the late 1920s it had become clear that there was a market for this kind of difficult and provocative literature, and the more established publishing houses began to show themselves receptive to it. With the development of professional literary criticism, and of college departments of English, the modernist novel also received the kind of defined public support that was important for its further development and dissemination.

It is significant, however, that the great era of the modernist novel was as brief as from about 1905 to 1930. The moment a certain degree of social triumph sets in—that is, when the established publishers welcome and support the genre, buying the publishing rights from the obscure vanguard houses or the literary executors—the size of the cadre of achieving modernist novelists begins to decrease precipitously. By 1940 very few of the literary giants were still at work.

The history of the modernist novel resembles that of another artistic phenomenon that has crucially affected Western culture—the painting of the High Renaissance. It, too, was the work of barely more than one phenomenal generation. The greatest writers of the movement, who are also among the literary giants of all time, emerged in one generation, between 1905 and 1930, and were soon monumentalized. They were appreciated in an endless series of commentaries and explications that continues unabated. But the giants themselves departed and were not replaced.

Modernism itself as a cultural movement was weakened in the 1930s, affected by the rise of Communism, fascism, the Great Depression, and various forms of neo-Victorianism. One discerns a failure of nerve as it were, in modernist culture, when it is faced with this revival of nineteenth-century modes of thinking, and the modernist novel particularly does not remain outside the disintegration.

The pattern of development in modernist poetry was similar to that of the novel. It forms a radical break from the nineteenth century, and presents a new poetic form. Modernist poetry, too, reached its peak around 1930, but it did not exhaust itself as rapidly as its novelistic counterpart, although it was certainly already past the zenith by 1940. The poets as well generated a canon, an authorized body of writing, which set the standard for subsequent twentieth-century poetry. After the modernist poets, in order to receive recognition as poet, it was necessary to write within the conventions of their canon.

Just as the modernist novel finds a forerunner in Henry James, modernist poetry has precursors in the 1880s with the work of the Frenchman Stéphane Mallarmé, and with that of Gerard Manley Hopkins in England in the 1890s. Mallarmé and Hopkins anticipate the poetry that will be written after 1900, whose most influential figures in the English-speaking world were the two American expatriates in England T. S. Eliot and Ezra Pound.

Tom Eliot came from a wealthy St. Louis family, studied at Harvard under the conservative classicist Irving Babbitt, and received a Ph.D. in philosophy. He migrated to England, and there married a genteel but unfortunately psychotic Englishwoman whom he eventually divorced and put in an insane asylum. (A play about this marriage was written and produced in the 1980s. Not very flattering to Eliot, *Tom and Viv* was filmed in 1994.) Eliot became the dominant transatlantic poet of the interwar years, not only through his poetic work, but also owing to his critical essays. Quite simply, it was Eliot who established, in essays as well as by his poetry, what poetry was henceforth supposed to be.

Eliot's colleague Ezra Pound, too, migrated, first to England and later to Italy, where he became a strong supporter of Mussolini, making broadcasts on his behalf during the Second World War. After the war, just before he was about to be tried and condemned for treason, his friends found a prominent psychiatrist in Washington, D.C., who certified him insane. Pound was released from St. Elizabeth's mental hospital in 1958; he died in 1972.

There is no doubt that Pound's reputation has steadily increased in recent decades, and now that he is evaluated in terms of his actual work—*The Cantos*—he has begun to be regarded as Eliot's equal if not even as his superior. The more Eliot's biography is explored—and this is not a very easy task since his widow has suppressed personal material and withheld it from the public— the more it becomes evident how much he learned and benefited from Pound. Ezra Pound was the editor of Eliot's early and perhaps most famous poem *The Waste Land* (1922). The original, before Pound worked on it, was considerably longer than the published version. Using modernist principles, which were not yet fully clear in Eliot's mind, Pound reduced the poem by about one-third and sharpened its effect.

A prominent modernist poet of the German language was the Austrian Hugo von Hofmannsthal, who was also the librettist for some of Richard Strauss's operas. The libretto of *The Woman Without Shadows*, for example, consists of a series of modernist poems by Hofmannsthal. The German Rainer Maria Rilke also stands alongside Eliot and Pound as one of the most accomplished of twentieth-century modernist poets. As with all modernist poets, his work is very difficult to translate.

Like Eliot and Pound, Rilke was very much aware of the poetic revolution he was carrying out. He had a broad view of the modernist movement, and published pioneering criticism on modernist art. For Rilke the modernist program was "to achieve the conviction and substantiality of things, a reality intensified and potentiated to the point of indestructibility by . . . experience of the object."

The Frenchman Paul Valéry also belongs in this group, as does the Irishman William Butler Yeats, whose contemporary and posthumous reputation has been extremely controversial because of his neo-Victorian proclivity to historicism and moralizing.

Two Americans, Robert Frost and Wallace Stevens, should be placed in the forefront of the modernist trend in poetry. Frost was an extremely ambitious man who assiduously promoted himself as an American visionary and poetic sage. His unpalatable personal qualities have retrospectively somewhat diminished his reputation as a poet, which deserves to be placed high.

Stevens's reputation has continued to grow. He now stands with Eliot, Pound, and Rilke as the most eminent of modernist poets. Stevens was a modest man who made a living as an insurance executive in Hartford, Connecticut. He did not promote himself much and was not very well known until the 1950s and 1960s. Stevens's conception of poetry is the same as Proust's view of the modernist novel. The self is bifurcated into the half that adheres to "common earth" and the half that reaches for "moonlit extensions" of reality. In the search for these moonlit extensions, Stevens believed, the poet attains a more creative and authentic identity.

In the opinion of many critics, the English poet W. H. Auden, who migrated to the United States in 1939, represents the late blossoming of modernism. His one-time associate Stephen Spender, who lived into the 1990s and was much venerated as a living memorial to the great modernists, already decidedly belongs in the epigone category.

One of the giants of modernist poetry is today almost unknown outside Israel. This is Chaim Nachman Bialik, whose earlier work was written mostly in Yiddish and later poems mostly in Hebrew. Bialik's huge output contains neoromantic work in the vein of Pushkin and Tennyson, but there is also a corpus of modernist poetry of the front rank, to which fragmentary English translations have not given access.

What exactly is this "modernist poetry" on which English, French, and

German literature departments today concentrate so intensely—and which it is nothing less than presumptuous on the one hand, and necessary on the other, to characterize in summary fashion? Modernist poetry is, first of all, not Victorian. It is not narrative and is usually very short. It is what is designated lyric poetry. Even longer modernist poems like Eliot's *The Waste Land* and *Four Quartets* are really cycles of short poems.

Modernist poetry propounds no moral, nor a popular message, and it is above all very difficult. An invariable quality of modernist poetry is that rather than admitting of easy reading, it calls for scrupulous and intensive study. Victorian poetry on the other hand was meant to be declaimed and easily read. Modernist poetry is extremely dense, contrived, and intellectual. Modernist poetry takes immense pains to be precisely accurate in communicating ideas and sensibility. This accuracy often requires difficult language because the ideas and sensibility are complex.

Under the modernist aegis the term "poetics" came to mean the theory of poetry. In view of the intense intellectualism of modernist poetry, the conjunction is an appropriate one.

Eliot never held an academic post, although he could have obtained one easily. He preferred to make his living first as a banker, and later as a publisher. But he did consent to giving public lectures at universities. Many of his lectures are devoted to defining what modernist poetry is. The definition he gave in lectures delivered in England and the United States in 1931 is characteristically concise and persuasive: "To find the word and give it the utmost meaning in its place; to mean as many things as possible; to make it [the word or the poem] both exact and comprehensive, and really to *unite* the disparate and the remote." The latter part of the definition contains the description of the modernist project in general, namely to unite the disparate and the remote. "To give them a fusion and a pattern with the word," that is to say, to bring together and contain them in the word—"surely this is the mastery at which the poet aims."

In other words modernist poetry is self-referential and textual. The poem is; it is a thing in and of itself, its meaning lies within it: It is not meant to illustrate, nor to refer to things, nor to propound a message or tell a story. It is a thick culture that stands by itself. The poem is something that is capable of absorbing, drawing into itself everything that it wants to express, and of containing it in concrete imagery. A poem is densely compacted experience and feeling.

Eliot as well as Valéry, Rilke, and Stevens aimed at exactitude, which, they

believed, could be achieved by an extremely dense imagery that was at the same
time concrete, and that would express deep feeling. Eliot hated Victorian
poets—and he even detested Milton, whom he denied the title of poet—on
the grounds that these writers were sloppy and imprecise, not concrete and
accurate. The Victorian poet, so Eliot said, expresses whatever comes to his
mind. His imagery falls apart under the slightest scrutiny precisely because it is
not exact and comprehensive, containing, as it does, ideas merely thrown
together. The Victorians—and Milton—failed to understand the principle of
the "objective correlative," which is that sensibility must be fully and intrinsically communicated in the language of the poem, not just vaguely described or
referred to. The poem does not declaim feeling, it *is* feeling.

Eliot's poet, pursuing the method of the objective correlative, is marked by
the complete mastery of imagery and by the ability to achieve density. The poem
is a thick presentation of sensibility. This conception still informs the perception of what twentieth-century poetry is and should be. The popular bardic
quality that was prominent in Victorian poetry was completely abandoned in
favor of a piercing intellectuality. Stevens saw contemporary culture as intrinsically unstable, "a postcard from the volcano," the new consuming the old. It is
the function of poetry to embody this transition. In the hands of the modernists,
poetry became a particularly exalted and sophisticated form of cultural criticism.

The rise of the modernist novel and poetry was closely connected to the
emergence of literary criticism. Every new form of literature needs a validating
system that legitimizes and authenticates it, that establishes the criteria of judgment by which the literary work can be evaluated aesthetically. It needs a critical system, that is, that is active in authorizing publications, convincing universities and media that the fictive or poetic work carries the stamp of
greatness, and in the awarding of prizes for literary achievement.

The nineteenth century had its own criteria, which were often based on
popularity, which, in turn, found their ready measure in the number of copies
a work sold. There were critical journals in the nineteenth century, too, which
praised or condemned literary works, as well as academies, often extremely
conservative, which handed out prizes. Now these institutional authorities
were superseded.

The rise of the modernist novel and poetry was accompanied between 1910
and 1930 by the rise of literary criticism as we know it. This is a kind of literary criticism very different from the one that had existed in the nineteenth century, not only in attitude but in vocation too, as criticism became increasingly
academic and technical.

It is rather difficult for us to imagine that there were no departments of English in 1900 except in a few American state universities and other vanguard institutions. Oxford and Cambridge did not have English departments at the turn of the century. The first important English departments began to take shape around 1910, and became really habilitated in the major universities in the early 1920s. English departments rose contemporaneously with the modernist novel and poetry, and they reinforced one another. The modernist novel and poetry became the particular province or subject in whose interpretation English departments specialized. The genres, in brief, found their authentication in these institutions' work, and acquired a legitimacy that would otherwise have been difficult to obtain.

The English departments acclaimed modernist novels and poems not only as real literature, but as literature of almost unprecedented quality as well. By 1930 one could not pretend to be an educated person or an intellectual unless one had read Joyce, Proust, Eliot, and Rilke—so said the academic literary critics.

Just as Henry James effected the transition to the modern novel, and Mallarmé and Hopkins to the corresponding poetry, so the Londoner Edmund Gosse was the first modernist critic. Gosse occupies the transition point between the Victorian "man of letters" and the twentieth-century critic. The man of letters had been a person of reading and breeding who expounded his views on literature, within the limits of his contemporaries' taste, and did so in a rather loose and unrigorous way. He provided literary appreciation rather than criticism. Close reading and evaluation were not his domain. He wrote short, pleasant essays that often had a strong historical flavor, to be published in magazines and journals. Gosse, too, began in this fashion, but became increasingly technical and analytical in his work, although he never fully achieved the thickness or rigor of modernist criticism. Therefore, by the 1920s, he was regarded as out-of-date and old-fashioned. Nevertheless, for his day, in 1910, he was a seminal figure who was leaving behind the easygoing Victorian man of letters and anticipating the close-reading, analytically oriented modern critic.

Furthermore Edmund Gosse was capable of appreciating the new trends. He was not in a position to grasp exactly what was going on, but he was generous in his evaluation of the new novels and poetry; and since he enjoyed tremendous prestige in his day, his judgment was influential and served as an early authentication of this literature.

Eliot himself is the first and most important of the modernist critics. He gained enormous influence and prestige, through his academic lectures and the journal of criticism he founded, the *Criterion*, which became an extremely important one. In addition Eliot was a force in the publishing world as a consultant to publishers and a partner in Faber & Faber, a leading house. What he determined to be publishable was published. He was a power broker, one might say, of modernist literature in the 1920s and 1930s.

After World War I, Cambridge University decided to constitute a faculty of English. A senior professor who already occupied a post at Cambridge, Hector Munro Chadwick, a remnant of the nineteenth-century literary historians but a scholar with a strong inclination toward anthropology, and who was a pioneer in comparative literature, recruited the new dons. Chadwick himself was a medievalist, but the people he invited to join the new English department of Cambridge were young critics interested in modern, and even contemporary, literature. Chadwick was a tough-minded person of great vision who could imagine new things and wider horizons.

He hired two remarkable people who arrived in Cambridge so newly demobilized that they were still wearing their army uniforms. The two men who were going to have powerful influence on the discipline of English literature and literary criticism between the two wars, and whose impact is still felt, were F. R. Leavis and I. A. Richards. They, along with Eliot, dominated literary criticism in the transatlantic world in the 1920s and 30s, and had much to do with the development of the new academic criticism which was hospitable to, and in many cases actively promoted, the new literature.

Frank Leavis, a complicated and still highly controversial figure, was actually part of a husband-and-wife team. His wife, Queenie Leavis, may have been the more brilliant of the two. Mrs. Leavis did not get much opportunity in her day. Contemporaneously with the German critic Walter Benjamin, she published the first studies of the impact of mass culture on literature. Yet Queenie Leavis—perhaps because she was a woman, and Jewish—was never offered an academic post at Cambridge except for an occasional invitation to teach an extension course. She did, however, play a major role in the development of the discipline. The couple edited a new journal entitled *Scrutiny*. Along with Eliot's *Criterion*, *Scrutiny* was the most important and influential English-language journal of literary criticism in the twenties and thirties in the United States as well as in England, and its back issues have again been put in print and are still studied.

Almost single-handedly Leavis created the reputation of D. H. Lawrence. He decided that Lawrence was an important novelist who belonged to the great nativist tradition of English novelists of which Jane Austen, Dickens, George Eliot and, to a certain extent, Henry James, were exclusive members. This occurred at a time when Lawrence lived in extreme isolation, and faced great difficulties in publishing his novels, occupying, as it were, the margins of both material and professional existence. Lawrence then found a patron, the eccentric American Mabel Dodge, who invited him and his aristocratic German wife to New Mexico, where the writer died in 1930. Without Leavis, Lawrence in his own lifetime would never have achieved much public recognition beyond his very first novel, the autobiographical *Sons and Lovers*.

I. A. Richards, a remarkable man of extraordinary talent and energy, was certainly one of the cultural heroes of the modernist world. Born in the 1880s, he lived almost a century, until 1979. He had three careers; the last, beginning in the late thirties, was devoted to the Basic English movement, bringing English literacy to China and the Third World. In his first career Richards became a Cambridge critic and the founder of the Cambridge School, which based itself on Eliot's poetic principles of density, concrete imagery, self-referentiality, and textuality. Richards brought the Eliot message into the university and became its spokesman. Then he moved to Harvard and revolutionized the Harvard English Department, which up to then had been largely historicist. He became the founder of the modernist American movement in criticism that was called New Criticism.

By no means did the modernist critics, also known as the New Critics, concentrate on or alter the understanding only of modernist literature, although that was their first consideration. They showed how masterpieces of the past could greatly benefit from close reading, the fussy screen of historicizing having been put aside. The more difficult and learned an old masterpiece was, the more attractive the New Critics found it. The works of Dante, Petrarch, and John Donne became popular texts among the New Critics. Old literature that was dense and learned particularly attracted them.

The achievement of the modernist critics is hard to demonstrate because they were so successful that their approach dominated the way literature was taught in all colleges, at least in the English-speaking world. What literature teaching was like before New Criticism is hard to recall. In 1910 a literature professor lecturing on the medieval German epic the *Nibelungenlied* would begin by telling his audience how many manuscripts survived (thirty-four) and into what recensions they were divided; then he would tell the students about the earlier poems on which the author of the *Nibelungenlied* may have drawn; then he would recount the history of the period in which the poem was written. By this time the semester was almost over, and all that was left was for the professor to utter a few vague bromides about the aesthetic quality of the poem.

The New Critic changed all that. He buoyantly came into class the first day, insisted that the students have their copies of the text in front of them, and without dipping into the murky river of scholarship and history, he simply proceeded to read the poem word by word, to try to understand what the poet was saying, and to ferret out the techniques the poet used. Or he analyzed the novel page by page, studying dense paragraphs scrupulously. Images and symbols were thoroughly scrutinized. Nor did the New Critic insist that everything in the novel or poem be articulated into common meaning. As self-referential literature, it was allowed to be, up to a point, opaque and mysterious.

The New Critic worked on the principle that literature had been created by a powerfully constructive mind, and that his or her job was to encounter that mind and reconstruct its conscious operation from the text of the poem or novel. Close reading and keen attention to the words and phrases of the work were what was needed, not the dumping of erudite libraries on the students' heads.

The New Critics carried out an educational as much as a critical revolution. At a time when college and university education was becoming more accessible, there was a pressing question concerning what the literature curriculum should concentrate on. What was to be the core of humanistic education? The New Critics said the literary work itself, and this approach fitted in neatly with the classroom situation. Very few colleges could in fact afford to stock their libraries with the background scholarship. But students could be told to go to the bookstore and buy a cheap edition of Eliot or a reasonably accurate translation of Dante. The New Critics, to the delight of parsimonious university presidents and the relief of college boards of trustees, said that expensive libraries were not necessary and in fact got in the way. What was necessary was to encounter the writer's mind directly, to read closely, to pore over the self-referential text. There was a good economic reason why Leavis was so popular with teachers in high schools and downscaled colleges: His kind of criticism was cheap; it required no library resources.

Furthermore Leavis and Eliot held that an ultimate purpose of humanistic studies in the university was to inculcate a common culture that would conserve social solidarity. The best way to do that was by universal study of a core of prescribed texts. In this way the debilitating consequences of mass culture could be countervailed.

So New Criticism satisfied at the same time the demands of literary study, cheap universal education, and the conservative fostering of cultural community. This was an unbeatable combination, and hence until the 1960s the heirs of Eliot, Leavis, and Richards overwhelmingly dominated English and other literature departments.

After 1940, as the modernist movement ran down and neo-Victorian historicism made a partial comeback, the radical self-confidence of the New Critics was slowly drained and close reading and textuality was somewhat softened by a partial reassertion of an historicist and ideological attitude to literature and humanistic education. Yet close reading remains the nucleus of literary study, around which everything else has been built.

New Criticism was the dominant force in the English departments, literary criticism, journals, and as time went on, inevitably also in the publishing houses of the twenties and the thirties. New Criticism propagated Eliot's message. Its proponents scorned the old-fashioned historical approach, which Leavis satirized as asking useless questions like "How many children had Lady Macbeth?" and turned to examining what the text itself contained. The New Critics could concentrate on two pages of Joyce, one of Proust, ten lines from Eliot, or six from Rilke, and could study them for days, if not for weeks or for a lifetime. By 1930 novels and poems were commonly studied in American as well as British colleges not for the story they told, the social ambience they reflected, or the traces of the author's biography they contained—for these, it was held, had nothing to do with criticism—but for the work in itself, submitting it to an intense close reading.

Nor did the legitimate line of modernist critics run out. In the war years of the forties the work of Cyril Connolly was deemed so important in Britain that his critical journal, *Horizon*, was granted special paper allocations by the government. The great tradition of modernist critics was perpetuated after the war by V. S. Pritchett, who at an advanced age in the 1980s was still writing in British journals and in *The New Yorker*.

The role of literary criticism in the development of French modernist literature was also dominant. In 1909 the critic and modernist novelist André Gide founded the *Nouvelle Revue Française*, which immediately acquired hegemonic influence in Parisian cultural circles. The *NRF* also established a publishing house, which acquired immense prestige; by 1914 to be published by the *NRF* and warmly praised in the pages of its journal was enough to make a literary career.

Ironically, Gide initially rejected *Swann's Way*, the first volume of Marcel

Proust's incomparable modernist series *Remembrance of Things Past.* Gide soon realized his potentially disastrous error, humbly begged Proust's pardon, and after painful negotiations obtained the publication rights to *Swann's Way* from the publishing house that had dared to undertake Proust's work—partly because the privately wealthy novelist had heavily subsidized his own novel.

The *NRF* continued to dominate French letters until World War II, during which its reputation became clouded because of its collaboration with the Nazi occupiers of Paris. The most prominent collaborationist editor committed suicide, and the journal was suppressed at the time of the liberation in 1944. But under the appropriate title of *Modern Times,* the modernist group of critics resumed their important, although no longer as dominant, role in French literary life.

One of the key ways in which the Nazis harmed German literature was by taking over or suspending the Berlin journals and publishing houses dedicated to modernism—either on racial or ideological grounds. The modernist tradition in German literature never recovered from the rupture.

In the United States, New Criticism spread out in the late twenties from Harvard to Yale and eventually through the entire country. Kenyon College, a small college in Ohio, became a center of New Criticism, and published a very influential journal, the *Kenyon Review,* which is still in existence. New Criticism spread among southern universities as well, and became particularly strong in the University of the South in Sewanee, Tennessee. It became associated with the renaissance of southern culture.

For white educated people in the southern United States in the 1930s, New Criticism came to represent an elitist, patrician culture, the intellectualized shield of revived southern humanism. While this attitude had conservative and racist overtones, the southern devotion to New Criticism and modernist literature was not a regional reactionary fantasy. Eliot, Pound, and Leavis held similar views. The southern commitment to New Criticism and modernism is still strong in literature departments in that part of the country.

When states in the southwest became temporarily flush with oil wealth in the sixties and seventies, both public and private universities in that region set about building monuments to modernist poets and novelists. Anyone today who wishes to do serious research on Joyce has to make his way to Tulsa, Oklahoma; the same holds for the manuscripts of Lawrence and many other writers at Austin, Texas. There is an authentic story about a poet of the Irish Renaissance who, in his geriatric years, sat down and copied out anew all his poems from published versions, selling these manuscripts to an eager southwestern library.

The prominent American names of New Criticism were Cleanth Brooks, a professor at Yale who exerted immense influence in the 1930s, John Crowe Ransom, Allen Tate, and Robert Penn Warren, who is better known today as a novelist and a poet than as a critic. In the late thirties Brooks and Warren published a textbook entitled *Understanding Poetry*, which was used for almost two generations in American colleges for the teaching of the methods and close-reading procedures of New Criticism. One other well-known American name of this school is R. P. Blackmur, who taught at Princeton in the 1940s and 1950s. Blackmur, a severe alcoholic who never received a bachelor's degree, is now considered one of the greatest American critics of the twentieth century.

The development of academic English, which had a very distinct perception of language, literature, and education, helps explain the rise of modernist novel and poetry. Certainly without men like Richards and Leavis, and in the United States, without Brooks and Blackmur, the penetration of these two modernist genres as canonic standards would have been much less prevalent.

Drama, Music, and Dance Modernist drama, however, cannot claim similar success. Particularly before 1940, it has no record of achievement comparable to that of the novel and poetry. If we are to examine modernist drama in strict accordance with modernist theory, we would have to focus on the period after the Second World War, and search for it in the works of Samuel Beckett, Harold Pinter, and more recently in those of Sam Shepard and David Mamet. Nevertheless there were some important efforts early in the century.

At the beginning of the century, theater was still the prime vehicle of popular entertainment—alongside drinking and prostitution. People attended the theater to have their prevailing assumptions about ethics and society reinforced in a diverting manner, not to be challenged and given new insights. They were easily shocked, and a great uproar could ensue. Thus Henrik Ibsen's dramas had aroused plenty of furious controversy in the nineties. And works that we now see as only marginally modernist, and more of historical than dramatic interest, were vehemently damned and also praised at their first performance.

This was the case with several new plays, products of the Irish Renaissance, put on at the avant-garde Abbey Theater in Dublin in the first decade of the century. This theater was founded and supported by a visionary wealthy woman of progressive attitudes, Lady Augusta Gregory. In 1907 Dublin was shaken and many professed themselves scandalized by John Millington Synge's *The Playboy of the Western World*, which was held to denigrate the noble Irish peasant and blaspheme the church. Nowadays there are more blasphemous and amoral things to be seen on any given evening on American TV. Synge's work now seems pretty tame stuff, but it was important in its day because it heralded a theater that would be critical rather than celebratory of contemporary values and institutions.

George Bernard Shaw wanted to become the great modernist dramatist. Many thought at the time that he succeeded, and he himself claimed to have been a cultural revolutionary. His dramas were published with long prefaces in which he announced himself as the great modernist playwright. Increasingly this appears not be the case. His dramas are infrequently produced today, and when they are, they are not very well received.

Shaw is a difficult transitional figure. His work is marked by historicism and is for the most part narrative. His plays are replete with a pastiche of trendy—but now sadly dated—ideas. He was still writing for a popular audience whose taste had been shaped by Victorian drama. Therefore he did not do what he probably could have done. The careful control and meticulously structured density that are the characteristics of modernist literature, are absent in his work. Shaw is much too sloppy by modernist standards: An occasional scene that is clearly in the modernist mode can be followed in his plays by one that looks like something from the Edwardian follies. Shaw could not decide whom he wanted in his audience.

Critics today think that the Swede August Strindberg, who was writing in the first decade of the twentieth century, stands out as the greatest of modernist playwrights. Strindberg acquires this title particularly because of his very direct approach to questions of sexuality and his explorations of the unconscious. His work has been regarded as the staged version of Freudian theory, even though there is no direct evidence that Strindberg ever read Freud. There is evidence, however, that Freud read Strindberg. Strindberg's plays appear to be enjoying a minirevival in the 1990s.

Bertolt Brecht is often regarded as a leading modernist dramatist. Brecht's problem was that he was a German Marxist ideologue, and Marxism remains a Victorian worldview that drew on Hegelian philosophy and historicism. These are features that do not mix well with modernism. Brecht was aware of, and sometimes tried to work around, this problem. There are examples of his work that are clearly in the modernist mode. Especially the opera *The Rise and Fall of the City of Mahagonny*, on which he collaborated with the composer Kurt Weill and which was produced once in Germany, in 1930, before it was banned by the Nazis, can be cited in this context. This opera was finally produced by New York's Metropolitan Opera in 1979. The production followed Brecht and

Weill's conception closely: Discordant, intense, pessimistic, violent, it was a marvelous example of German expressionism in drama and music.

Brecht and Weill had curious careers. Before *Mahagonny*, they had an immense success with the expressionist musical comedy *The Threepenny Opera*, which is still popular. When they were on the verge of a breakthrough in German expressionist opera and drama, they had to leave Germany. Brecht spent fifteen years in Hollywood, where he wrote screenplays which nobody produced. But he always got paid for them. On encountering political difficulties in the McCarthy era, he went to East Germany, where he became the director of the Berliner Ensemble, a state-supported theater. Only a small number of these later plays, which belong to the agitprop genre, have been translated and produced outside East Berlin. Immigrating to the United States with his wife, actress Lotte Lenya, Weill put aside the modernist style he had been developing, and took up the American musical comedy. Among his melodies, many of which are still popular today, is "September Song." In the 1990s Brecht's already controversial reputation was clouded by learned allegations that his plays were written in close collaboration with a series of mistresses and wives.

It is today widely recognized that Eugene O'Neill, an American, was one of the leading modernist dramatists. This is more valid with reference to his later work. Particularly plays written in the late thirties and early forties, such as *Long Day's Journey into Night* and *The Iceman Cometh*, through their intensity and pessimism, are works that partake of the modernist sensibility. O'Neill was a poor craftsman; his major dramas are long, tedious, and awkwardly stitched together, but his reputation as a leading modernist dramatist appears to be secure. Some twenty- or thirty-minute segments of O'Neill's two major works are hallmarks of modernist drama. The problem is that the plays run for four hours, as verbose and gloomy as the puritanical Irish-American culture in which they are set.

Confusion about reality is the theme of much of the work of Luigi Pirandello, an Italian dramatist whose plays were enthusiastically received in the 1920s. Pirandello's dramas were self-consciously experimental in format and his ideas in the vanguard of the time. Who is mad? Who is sane? Is not a private illogical universe a higher kind of rationality that offers escape and comfort from the ugly, corrupt world? These questions were provocative in the twenties, conventional nowadays. Pirandello's plays are rarely produced today. He is admired as a pioneer, but his place in the dramatic canon is a small one.

It cannot thus be claimed with as great certainty as in the case of the novel and poetry that drama in the first four decades of this century achieved a breakthrough that can be properly designated as modernist. In a sense drama was the first form of literature to signal a breakthrough to modernism on a grand scale, in the work of Henrik Ibsen in the 1880s and 1890s. Ibsen anticipates many of modernism's features. But aside from the work of Strindberg, and some of the work of Brecht and O'Neill, a comprehensive transformation of the genre did not occur. Because of the costs of production and the need to gain audiences, it was more difficult for dramatists than for novelists and poets to pursue the modernist style.

There is no doubt that the quintessential modernist dramatist is the Irishman Samuel Beckett, who built most of his career in Paris. He began writing in the 1930s but did not achieve much visibility until the fifties. Beckett's plays are minimalist, dense, difficult, self-referential, discordant, and gloomy—all key qualities of modernism. The work of the Englishman Harold Pinter in the fifties and early sixties also fully cultivates the modernist style.

The record of what can be termed modernist music is of an ambivalent nature, for a conscious effort was made in Europe and the United States along severely modernist lines, but with rather strange results. There is no doubt that there is a very strong and elaborate modernist tradition of dissonant and atonal music which can be described as disharmonious, fractured, intense, concrete, and thick. The technical term for this kind of modernist music is "serialism." The prominent composers of this music were Arnold Schoenberg, Paul Hindemith, Alban Berg, Anton Webern, and to some extent, the American Charles Ives. It is Alban Berg's opera *Lulu*, a product of the thirties, that, along with Brecht and Weill's *Mahagonny*, stands as the most remarkable achievement in dissonant modernist music.

The tradition of modernist serialist or atonal music has continued in the United States in the work of Roger Sessions, Milton Babbitt, and several other composers. The problem is that their work has not received much popular support even among educated audiences. It has been played infrequently and to limited audiences. The impact of atonal, discordant, disharmonious modernist music has been meager, and despite the efforts of a substantial number of composers to parallel the achievement of modernist novelists and poets, the mode continues to address itself to a narrow group of listeners. The educated public has not accepted this music in the way it has accepted modernist literature. Modernist music has not been able to receive the authenticating, legitimizing attention that the novel and poetry have obtained. Serialism has remained marginal.

& differences in impact of modernists poets & novelists to serialists.

An indicative phenomenon occurred in New York City in the early seventies, when the French vanguard composer and conductor Pierre Boulez, who was strongly committed to modernism, almost miraculously became the conductor of the New York Philharmonic and tried to involve the orchestra in performances of modernist music. The result was intense hostility: Subscriptions were cancelled, attendance fell, the critics of the popular press were cold, to say the least, and the orchestra itself rebelled. Boulez had to give up his project and was forced to resign, although he was easily the most distinguished conductor of the Philharmonic since Bruno Walter in the early fifties. Boulez retreated to run what might be called a museum of modernist music in Paris. This strange interlude is symbolic of the problem of modernist music.

There was programmatically no difference between the direction taken by the dissonant and atonalist composers and the modernist poets of the first four decades of the twentieth century. Even the idea of what we now call electronic music—then it was produced by electromechanical means—that would free composers from the limitations of traditional instruments appeared very early in the modernist era. The visionary Ferruccio Busoni, learning in 1907 that someone had invented a two-hundred-ton machine that allegedly could generate any kind of sound by electrical means, speculated: "In what direction does the next step lead? To abstract sound, to unhampered technique, to unlimited tonal material."

Busoni was clear-eyed about the modernist program in music. Not only should electronic music be pursued but its general dissonance was to replace Victorian "thematic" composition. Dissonance represented "nature." What Busoni acheived as a composer rather than as a critic and theorist is not as self-evident. Nonetheless, a British production in the 1980s of his opera *Dr. Faustus* was hailed in some quarters as masterly and intensely personal.

There was nothing shallow or timid about the modernist musical intention, and there was a lot of experimental effort. Then why did the modernist poets become the canonical force in poetry while the serialists remained at the margin of the musical world? It was much easier for the poets to publish than for the modernist composers to get their work performed frequently enough—and by major orchestras—so as to have a strong impact on public taste. By and large the modernist composers of thick, disharmonious, dense music failed to obtain an appropriate hearing—and still lack a forum.

Even more important, the modernist poets gained the overwhelming support of the major literary critics both within and outside the academic world.

Critical support for modernist dissonant music was again decidedly marginal. It never extended to the popular press and even in the cultural journals atonal music received only a moderate endorsement. The new serialist music lacked the support of opinion makers of the quality of Eliot and Brooks. This made a very substantial difference. But above all, even the more educated public found atonal music uninteresting and uninspiring. It appeared to be composed by intellectual formula and not created by musical feeling.

If atonal music had been performed enough, especially by prominent orchestras, it would perhaps have effected significant changes in taste. In the 1970s and 1980s there were still prominent conductors (like Sir Georg Solti) who very rarely performed anything later than Gustav Mahler, who was the last of the Victorian composers.

In spite of the intrinsic achievements of dissonant, atonal, and electronic music, a simple physical problem was and is an obstacle to its social acceptance. Difficult and thick as Joyce's novels or Pound's poetry are, the reader has the flexibility of pacing the required close reading over relatively short attention spans. Listening to serialist disharmony, particularly in a concert hall—and in the twenties, thirties, and forties it *was* principally in live performance—can be a test of endurance.

Aside from serialism, modernist music is marked by a shift from the elaborate symphonic form to short pieces designed to express intensely perceived themes—"tone poems." This became the dominant trend among composers between 1920 and 1940. The famous examples are Igor Stravinsky's *The Rite of Spring*, which was originally written for ballet, and the work of the prolific Richard Strauss, including *Don Juan*. (One of Strauss's tone poems, *Thus Spake Zarathustra*, later became popular when it was used in the soundtrack for the film *2001: A Space Odyssey*.)

Claude Debussy, Maurice Ravel, Ottorino Respighi, Jean Sibelius, Sergei Prokofiev, and Ralph Vaughan Williams followed the same method as these composers. Although they wrote the occasional formal symphony, they concentrated on the short piece designed to be the direct, concise expression of a particular theme. This kind of expressionist music was well received; its specimens were performed as soon as they were composed, became popular, and continue to enjoy a high degree of popularity.

There are close ties between this twenties musical expressionism and the Hollywood soundtracks of the late thirties and forties. Composers, usually good ones although not the most illustrious (such as Erich Korngold and Miklós Rozsa), who worked for the film companies brought elements of the expressionist school into their commercial work. Some of the soundtracks of the Hollywood films from these two decades are of high musical quality.

A change, therefore, did occur in music, wherein strenuous efforts were made to parallel modernist poetry and novels in atonal compositions. But whereas the efforts in serialist music did not receive much visibility and acceptance despite the considerable work that had been done (both quantitatively and qualitatively), the expressionist short piece, the tone poem, which emerged alongside the atonal compositions, by and large replaced the symphony as the favorite genre and gained a wide audience.

The pinnacle of what might be called modernist classical music was reached in the earlier work of Prokofiev in the 1920s and that of Béla Bartók in the thirties and forties. This comes very close to an effective combination of two strands of modernist music—blending experimental disharmony with expressionism or the programmatic tone poem. Some critics see the same achievement in the work of Ives, the American composer in the twenties (Ives, like the poet Stevens, was an insurance executive). Sergei Rachmaninoff was a successful continuer of nineteenth-century music, but Dmitri Shostakovich was certainly within the modernist tradition. He, along with Prokofiev, was concerned with the integration of music with other art forms: Both composed extensively for film, and one of Shostakovich's later symphonies uses symbolist poetry as a text. Nevertheless the commitment of Prokofiev and Shostakovich was restrained by the repressive Stalinist atmosphere in which they worked and the opposition of the Soviet authorities to modernist art forms.

Modernist music was also subject to an unfortunate historical circumstance in Germany. In 1930 and 1931, respectively, in Brecht and Weill's opera *The Rise and Fall of the City of Mahagonny* and in Alban Berg's *Lulu*, modernist music may have reached its peak and found its most suitable form in the expressionist opera. The exile of Brecht and Weill, the death of Berg, and Nazi hostility to modernist music cut short this promising development. Recently opera companies have shown small interest in these works. It is to the credit of the Metropolitan Opera that it has mounted productions, in some ways remarkable ones, of both. But the original productions of these modernist operas found no successors. These complicated works are difficult and expensive to stage. They require singers who are also unusually capable actors.

The above argument leads to the conclusion that the most successful forms of modernist music were neither atonal serialist nor the expressionist tone poem, although the latter became popular and is still frequently performed, but in fact two other forms occasioned by the modernist movement: the baroque revival and American jazz. Both of these forms are self-referential, textual, pure forms of music. Their prominence in the modernist era was not accidental.

The great baroque revival that began after the First World War was partly the result of a technical factor. Until the 1950s the low-fidelity phonograph record made it more possible than ever before to obtain a true impression of baroque music. Subsequent modes, such as the nineteenth-century symphony, required the high-fidelity stereo record of the 1960s in order to be heard with any degree of honesty. Baroque music was ideal for the phonograph, and Domenico Scarlatti and Antonio Vivaldi, whose music had hardly been played in two centuries, became immensely important and remained so. In a way, we can think of Vivaldi as the most performed modernist composer.

Simultaneously with this development came the upsurge of jazz, which achieved the unusual stature of being at once a popular art and one taken seriously by many intellectuals. The origins of jazz lie in African music that accompanied the black slaves to the New World. Out of this background came blues, black folk music recounting traumas in the lives of these repressed people after their legal emancipation during the Civil War. At the turn of the century, blues music was written down in musical notation. At the same time popular ragtime provided another source for jazz, which emerged in New Orleans among extraordinarily talented black musicians in the early years of the century.

Jazz migrated with black people to Chicago and other northern cities in the first two decades of the century, and with the help of nightclub and tavern owners, often Italian or Jewish, began to find a white audience. Phonograph records were also important in winning a general audience for black jazz. The first great jazz performer with a white following, Louis Armstrong, joined New Orleans jazz with swing, the emerging trend in popular music, and arranged jazz to accompany ballroom dancing in the twenties, further increasing its audience.

Yet this vulgarization or democratization of jazz did not detract from its fundamental modernist qualities, particularly in the work of the first great jazz composer, Ferdinand "Jelly Roll" Morton, and first prominent white jazz musician, Bix Beiderbecke. Jazz remained a highly self-referential, nonsequential, partly disharmonious, and above all intensely improvisatory and individualistic form of music. The driving beat of the best black jazz gave it a personal impact that was lost in the atonal music of the modernist era.

This self-referential, thickly textual kind of music experienced a further development in the 1940s and 1950s—bebop or progressive jazz, a more abstract variety with complicated harmonies that marks the work of Charlie Parker, Charlie Mingus, and John Coltrane. This later jazz, composed and played by well-trained and extremely sophisticated musicians, was the most original and creative product of the modernist era in music. The capacity of jazz to develop ever more complex and unique variants distinguished its intrinsic status as a major art form.

What endures in the work of the most celebrated American composer of the thirties, George Gershwin, is his partly successful efforts to blend blues and jazz motifs with the mainstream forms of popular music. He received lavish praise for this syncretic form in his day. In retrospect, his efforts appear idiosyncratic, because jazz itself has become mainstream, central to indigenous American culture as much as Hemingway or Jackson Pollock.

Aaron Copland's musical sources were similar to Gershwin's. He made use of blues, jazz, and folk songs, trying to express a native music. Copland has received more attention in recent years, his work of the 1940s receiving considerable appreciation.

George Gershwin's most memorable achievement was to provide the musical scores for popular songs to which his brother, Ira, wrote the lyrics. It is in this popular-song genre in the United States, closely tied to the Broadway stage as show tunes and then disseminated by radio and phonograph records, that Western music between 1920 and 1950, approximating the heyday of modernist culture, achieved its greatest impact. The singular achievement was not in the music but in the intricate poetic lyrics, mainly about heterosexual love.

The founders of this genre in the second decade of the century, drawing on European operetta, the nineteenth-century music hall, and jazz, but transcending them in a distinctive art form, were two New York City Jews of immigrant background, Irving Berlin and Jerome Kern. Along with the Gershwins, the masters of this popular music in the 1930s and 1940s were Richard Rodgers and his two lyricists Lorenz Hart and Oscar Hammerstein II. They were all Jews who from the vantage point of liberal metropolitan immigrant culture created a musical genre that equaled anything produced in European music and yet was perfectly related to the mass culture of America. The only one of these great music masters who was not Jewish was Cole Porter, an upper-class Episcopalian. He himself pointed out that his intense homosexuality made him, like his Jewish colleagues, a socially marginal artist able at the same time to stand outside the American mainstream and yet to epitomize it.

Around 1950 the great movement of American popular music began to deteriorate rapidly. The decline of mass literacy, the impact of crude early television, and the countervailing force of rock, along with mischievous commercialization of the industry by the music publishing industry, brought this high-profile cultural movement of the modernist era to a sudden close.

In the early years of the twentieth century in Paris, Sergey Diaghilev's Ballets Russes made its appearance, with its great performer and choreographer Vaslav Nijinsky. The company met with a remarkable reception, followed by equally profound impact. What the Diaghilev company showed was that a ballet did not necessarily have to follow traditional forms, that it could adjust to more recent departures in music, and especially that demands could be put on dancers to undertake body movements that did not exist in nineteenth-century ballet.

The Russian group in Paris also tried new work. In 1908 the Diaghilev company performed the *Polovtsian Dances,* a romantic piece from the late nineteenth century. This sentimental composition by Aleksandr Borodin appealed to the modernist temperament through its emphasis on folk music. Proust attended the premiere performance.

More radical in its modernist style was the Diaghilev ballet's production of *The Afternoon of a Faun* in 1910. The ballet, with choreography by Nijinsky, featured Debussy's setting of a poem by Mallarmé. Nijinsky aimed to fulfill Mallarmé's vision that "the ballerina is not a girl dancing. . . . She is not a girl but rather a metaphor. She does not dance but rather, writing with her body, she suggests things." Proust again attended *The Afternoon of a Faun* and noted that Nijinsky's choreography achieved a clarity that did not banish all mystery—a good description of modernist performance art. "My own inclinations are 'primitive,'" Nijinsky replied to a reporter's queries about his choreography. An extensive set of drawings and photographs of *The Afternoon* production has survived. They show an effort to create costumes that combine classical Greek style as seen on vases with a touch of the primitive. The dancers' poses are angular, intentionally abstracted.

Then, most important, in 1913 the Diaghilev group gave the first performance of *The Rite of Spring,* whose music was written by Stravinsky, and choreography executed by Nijinsky. The costumes used in this first production of *The Rite of Spring* were those of Ukrainian peasants—again the folk or William Morris motif—as can be ascertained from the photographs of the performance. Unfortunately we do not have a record of the choreography, but we do know that the production was found so shocking that it created an uproar bordering on a riot in the theater. The angular body movements, probably seen as sexually suggestive, were certainly not customary. The music, too, was provocative, although not exactly disharmonious, since Walt Disney incorporated Stravinsky's tone poem (with some editing) into his ambitious feature-length cartoon *Fantasia* in 1940. Nevertheless, to the ear of 1913, Stravinsky's music sounded original and disturbing.

In the early years of the century, it was customary for audiences to show their disapproval or appreciation by applauding, hooting, howling, and for the popular press to give vent to its outrage or approval in undisguised terms. People looked on the theater and the opera as places they went to to have their ideas confirmed. They attended performances for the reinforcement of their expectations, and they always knew what to expect. Nineteenth-century opera, for example, conformed to those expectations. Only a few operas from that period—Verdi's *Don Carlo* and a couple of the *Ring* operas of Wagner—have the capacity to tax their audience's minds.

Early in the twentieth century, therefore, when the major departures in the performing arts began to take place, audiences were far from being ready to grasp the new conceptions of the purpose of performance. They did not understand that they were there to explore, along with the artists, what Proust termed "the different self," that they were attending the performance to undergo the shock of recognition that led to an altered or more refined sensibility and not in order to have reinforced and reconfirmed what they already believed. Therefore a ballet so different from what they were accustomed to caused nothing less than outrage among these audiences.

Nevertheless, with the work of Nijinsky in particular, ballet did manage to turn in a new direction. The choreographer who succeeded Nijinsky in opening up the ballet as a creative art form was George Balanchine. He was a Russian who worked in the thirties first in Paris and then in New York, where in the late years of the decade he founded a major ballet company. He was fortunate enough to find a collaborator in Lincoln Kirstein, a patron of the arts who understood the new forms of ballet and who organized and managed the New York City Ballet, for which Balanchine did the modernist choreography.

Finally, the "modern dance" movement of the twenties and the thirties was consciously committed to modernism. The Americans Isadora Duncan, Ruth St. Denis, and Martha Graham played leading roles in the modern dance movement, which has been perpetuated in our day by Merce Cunningham, Paul Taylor, Alvin Ailey, and Twyla Tharp. Between 1920 and 1940 the manifestations of this movement seemed to be the quintessence of modernism in dance, and they were certainly intended to be so. They were free flowing in every respect, employed original sets and costumes, were set to expressionist music, intended to provoke, and had a strong sexual content.

In recent decades the modern dance movement has not been taken as seriously expressive of modernism as the ballet. The ballet has continued to develop as a creative art form, and incorporating some of the ideas of Martha Graham into its own field, it has become a combination of the traditional ballet and modern dance forms.

The modern dance movement, as presented by Duncan and Graham, has not achieved the recognition that its admirers in the forties expected. Whereas in the late forties, in order to see modernist dance, one still went to Jacob's Pillow in the Berkshires, where Ruth St. Denis and Ted Shawn, the teachers of Martha Graham, were performing, today it is to Lincoln Center, with its presentations of vanguard ballet, that one goes to in order to see the highest achievement in modernist dance. Nijinsky has triumphed over Isadora Duncan, a development not foreseen in the 1920s.

The modern dance movement resembles Ravel's *Bolero* and other prominent tone poems of the twenties. Its contrived and determined effort at modernism has not worn well. Just as the tone poem developed into the Hollywood music sound track, so did modern dance, beginning with Agnes de Mille's choreography for *Oklahoma!* in 1943, achieve popular adulation on the musical comedy stage. This represents a major social impact, but modernism was an elitist, vanguard movement, and it was, in the instance of modern dance as well as the tone poem, fragmented by popularization.

The Visual Arts While the record of modernism in music and dance is controversial and somewhat difficult to assess, its achievement in painting was seminal and overwhelming. The modernist movement in painting created the most important and productive era in terms of the application of color to canvas since the early sixteenth century—since, that is, the era of the High Renaissance that produced da Vinci, Michelangelo, Raphael, and El Greco. Since the Renaissance, there had not been as impressive a period of creation in the visual arts and such fundamental transformation as occurred in the first thirty years of the twentieth century. The Tate Gallery in London, several galleries in Paris, the Wallraf-Richartz/Ludwig Museum in Cologne, and New York museums such as the Museum of Modern Art, the Whitney and the Guggenheim are monuments to that effect, as is the current insatiable appetite of the art market for modernist work.

First among the social and material factors that contributed to the formation of the modernist era in painting came the proliferation of photography, and specifically its success in giving a realistic, or allegedly realistic, view of the world. Painting was pressed to take a different approach. Once the Kodak camera made its appearance, it became necessary for artists to move toward more nonrepresentational portrayals because the camera co-opted what had hitherto been the characteristic province of the painter—namely, to depict what the eye saw. Now the painter had to concentrate increasingly on what the inner eye saw.

Second, another contributing reason was the cheapness of painting materials, due in part to advances in chemistry. The most successful industry in the late nineteenth century was chemistry, and one by-product of this achievement was the production of inexpensive paint. Modern industrial processes also reduced the cost of canvas, thus it became more accessible for artists of modest means. Painting was no longer the exclusive domain of the academician or of artists in the carriage trade. Almost anybody could seriously attempt the artist's career.

Third, the opening of museums and art galleries to the public strongly affected modernist painting. These were supported by the state or, more frequently, by private benefactors and collectors who initially gathered art works for their own interest (for example, the Frick Collection) and then willed them to the public. What this meant above all—and here we have to take into account the aiding factor of affordable railroad transportation—was that artists could simply go and see the important work that had been and was being done in their field. That is, they now had immediate access not only to the work of their contemporaries but to the techniques developed by the old masters as well. The ways in which a painter handles the brushwork, how he or she solves the problems of perspective and color, are questions to be answered only through the close study of actual paintings in a museum. These features cannot be observed in photographs. And only in the early years of this century did the works of previous as well as contemporary artists become accessible to the public.

The importance of the availability of cheap housing and food in metropolitan centers in the first forty years of the century has been already mentioned as a factor in the development of modernist painting. The economic circumstances of the early decades of this century enabled a rather large group of artists to survive. Hundreds of painters were at work in Paris in the 1920s, many of whom never became well known but could nevertheless continue to paint because of the low cost of living.

Another reason for the modernist renaissance in painting was the development of an art market, owing first to the emergence of a large middle class whose taste was becoming increasingly more sympathetic to modernist forms, and second to the rise of the art dealer in the later years of the nineteenth century. Initially art dealers were interested only in the masters of the old school, mainly in the painters of the Renaissance. But increasingly, especially starting with the 1920s, they began to buy more recent work as well and became patrons to promising young artists. The modernist movement in painting rose along with the art market and the proliferation of commercial galleries.

A further factor that was intellectual as well as social was the increasing recognition that a technological civilization required a new kind of art. This view emerged particularly during and shortly after World War I, and was referred to at times as constructivism, and at others as futurism or surrealism. All these terms signified the recognition that the painter now had a new subject—the impact of technological civilization. He or she had to convey this awareness in ways different from those used by nineteenth-century artists, which had been, it was believed, expressive of a pretechnological civilization.

Before all else, however, the great artistic movement occurred because of a phenomenal generation of artists especially in France and the German-speaking countries. We cannot very well work around the fact that a remarkable number of artistic people appeared at a particular time in history. Historians cannot adequately explain such generational phenomena. It is no longer believed that this generation of modernist artists was confined to Europe. Increasingly, through major exhibitions and the efforts of art historians, the American modernist painters of the 1920s and 1930s, such as John Marin, Charles Demuth, Joseph Stella, and Georgia O'Keeffe, are recognized. In time it may be seen that what distinguished the Europeans of the modernist movement in painting in the decades betweeen the world wars was not so much intrinsic skill or superior conceptualization but better access to publicity and marketing. The Europeans may have outshone the American modernist painters before the 1940s because they were more integrated into an avant-garde cultural community that included novelists and poets. The Americans, on the other hand, were more on their own, less tied into a visible group or setting.

The principles of modernist painting are today common knowledge and self-evident to educated people. First, it is not the depicted subject but the craftsmanship that is paramount, particularly the use of color and the application of paint to canvas. What becomes central is the activity of the painter.

Regardless of whether he or she is painting a duchess, a Parisian back street, a fruit bowl, or six lines, the painter must concentrate on technique and the use of color. This is the modernist principle of textuality or self-referentiality.

Second, the artist is engaged in a symbolic representation of a world that borders consciousness and unconsciousness, oscillating between the two sides of the dividing line. Art is the product of the interaction of the conscious and unconscious domains. The realm of symbolism and fantasy is central to art. This, too, constitutes a fundamental modernist principle.

Third comes the principle that nonrepresentational or abstract art has a special claim to authenticity and aesthetic value. Despite the problems it met with in its beginnings, the recognition of nonrepresentational art, especially among younger intellectuals, as an important and authentic art form came very rapidly. In Paris, London, and Berlin, abstract art had gained wide recognition among young intellectuals even before World War I. Nonrepresentational art is entirely mythic or symbolic, and this is why it is pure art.

Finally, there was the tendency to exoticism. The appreciation of Oriental motifs and ideas appeared early in modernist art. In modernism a strong movement toward neoprimitivism was also discernible, at least in the shape of a recognition or even valorization of the primitive. Orientalism and primitivism are qualities that run through earlier modernist art.

It is the opinion of art historians that the forerunner of modernism in painting was Paul Cézanne, working from the late 1880s until 1906. Just as Henry James was a forerunner of the modernist novel, and Mallarmé and Hopkins forecast modernist poetry, Cézanne anticipated modernist painting, not only with respect to his work but also in terms of his statements on painting. Cézanne clearly articulated the modernist principles. He claimed that a picture, first of all, "should represent nothing but color." Further, "art is a harmony parallel to nature," which is to say that art does not imitate nature. It generates its own world parallel to nature. Art is a harmony, not derivative of nature, but one that exists in and for itself. Cézanne had a clear and revolutionary program for the painter.

Cézanne's work was carried on at the turn of the century by Vincent van Gogh and Paul Gauguin. In December 1910 there occurred in London an exhibition of the work of the Postimpressionist School, as Cézanne, van Gogh, and Gauguin—its principal exponents—came to be called. It had been organized by the art critic Clive Bell, brother-in-law of Virginia Woolf. Although the exhibition caused quite a furor, it found immediate acceptance among the younger generation, which had come to agree with Virginia Woolf that the world had changed fundamentally, that a new art and a new culture had come into being. Similarly in New York in 1913, the Armory Show introduced modernist painting to the general public. Marcel Duchamp's quasi-abstract *Nude Descending a Staircase* caused a media sensation.

Around the same time time Henri Matisse had begun his work in Paris. Throughout his sixty-year career as a painter, Matisse, who lived until 1954, played the important role of bridging the generations between van Gogh and the rise of American abstract expressionism. He began to paint as a near contemporary of van Gogh and died as a contemporary of Jackson Pollock and the New York School.

In the work of Gauguin, the efforts at Orientalism and primitivism are clearly observable. Gauguin lived in Tahiti for several years in order to find what he called "the grandeur, the profundity and the mystery of Tahiti"—that is, an abstract form for immediate truth, the mythic image of a primitive culture. At the same time, in Paris, Henri Rousseau achieved a different kind of primitivism, one that found its source in the artist's own mind. Rousseau, a genuine, self-taught primitive artist, explored the entirely private world of fantasy.

Van Gogh and Matisse were crucial for the early development of modernist painting because they showed the subject matter of art to be inconsequential. Van Gogh painted human subjects such as Belgian workers, then flowers and fields seen from his window in Arles, in the south of France. Matisse's favorite subjects were Parisian street scenes and coastal fishing villages. Both focused on the application of color to the painting surface; and the arbitrary, and wide, range of the subject matter helped place the subject in the background in favor of the technique and materials of painting. They took the stock subjects of Victorian art, such as flowers and street scenes, and transformed them by a radical technique that bespoke an altered sensibility.

At the same time, exploration of the unconscious, the world of dream and fantasy, had become a prime motif. The three artists who took the lead in the artistic meditation on the borders of the conscious and the unconscious were the Norwegian Edvard Munch, the Austrian Gustav Klimt and the French expressionist Odilon Redon. The work of these artists deals with what Redon termed "the coming of the unconscious." Their interest is in the dream, the fantasy, and the primal scream. Their work informs the background of the dadaism and surrealism of the 1920s, as well as much of later science-fiction imagery. In fact, elements of the iconography of contemporary science-fiction film can be traced back directly to the paintings of Munch,

Klimt, and Redon. "Nothing is small, nothing is great," wrote Munch. "Inside us are worlds."

Around 1910 Georges Braque and Pablo Picasso began to experiment with abstract forms in Paris, producing, for the first time since the Celtic art of the eighth century, wholly unrepresentational art. They were trying to get at what Picasso called "the abominable forms." This movement came to be called cubism because of a tendency to focus on rectangular lines and is now viewed as the seminal development in early twentieth-century painting. Out of simple lines and what were considered ugly patterns, out of rectangles, circles, and discordant traces, they generated the self-referential world of the canvas—painterly, or pure painting.

After World War I, Braque and Picasso were followed by a large group of painters who joined the abstract or nonrepresentational movement, among whom the most outstanding were Piet Mondrian and Jóan Miró. Just as this movement began to erode in Paris in the thirties, it emerged forcefully around 1940 in the United States in the work of Jackson Pollock and Willem de Kooning. From the Left Bank cafés, abstract art moved to Greenwich Village studios and to the Cedar Tavern, an unpretentious bar on University Place that became the clubhouse of the abstract expressionists. Later in the fifties Pollock and de Kooning moved to East Hampton, Long Island—because it was then considered cheap!

The modernist movement in sculpture was not as vast in productivity as in painting, primarily because of the great cost of working in sculpture. Whereas painterly materials were rather inexpensive in this period, materials for the latter, such as wood, stone, or metal, remained almost unaffordable. Sculpture is an art that entails difficult and slow work, and requires advance commissions. Picasso did some early work in sculpture and demonstrated his incredible talent in this medium as well. But he soon confined his work largely to canvas. Nevertheless, in the 1920s, in the work of Modigliani and Alberto Giacometti, the beginnings of sculptural abstract expressionism become discernible. Even more recognized was the work of the Englishman Henry Moore starting with the 1930s. Moore, who was greatly influenced by Gauguin as well as by Picasso, combined abstract expressionism with the worship of the primitive. Moore is now regarded as the leading modernist sculptor.

Again, around the same time, there was a very important movement in the Soviet Union, called constructivism. This was a movement parallel and related to the Paris School. Painters like Chagall and Soutine shuttled back and forth between Paris and Russia, participating in both movements. The most prominent names of the constructivist movement were Naum Gabo, both a painter and a sculptor, and Kasimir Malevich, a painter. Malevich's variety of constructivism was also called suprematism, after his statement that he aimed at "the supremacy of pure sensitivity in creative art." Only after the fall of Communism in the 1990s did many of Malevich's paintings, condemned by the Stalinist regime, come out of storage. Now it is known that he anticipated the work of the American abstract expressionists like Pollock and de Kooning. He is certainly one of the leading painters of this century. However, in 1922, modernism was declared to be a decadent bourgeois art by Lenin and Trotsky, and repressed by the Soviet government. In many cases the painters were imprisoned or exiled, thus bringing the great Russian constructivist movement to an end. Most of the constructivist works that were held by Soviet museums were not publicly exhibited until the 1990s.

A movement similar to constructivism, called futurism, can be seen in Italy during this period. Its leading exponent was Gino Severini. Both constructivism and futurism were dedicated not only to abstract art, but more specifically to abstract art that arose in response to contemporary events, technological culture, and to World War I. The most effective artistic responses to the war came from these two movements.

Although the futurist movement declined in the 1920s under Mussolini, Italian design—in furniture, clothes, and automobiles—was permanently influenced by it. The long-term success of Italian design from the 1920s to the present is the heritage of futurism.

The favorite typewriter of Allied war correspondents in the last two years of World War II was an Olivetti portable. Not only was it mechanically efficient and almost indestructible, but it was beautiful as well. Its simple, clean lines made the Olivetti portable—still in production—one of the finest examples of Italian design to come out of the futurist movement, and to outlast the neoromanticism of the fascist regime.

The influence of the Russian and Italian movements on the French surrealism of the 1920s, which attempted to present a very provocative nonrepresentational art and visceral anarchism, was powerful enough to enable us to designate the latter movement as a continuation of the traditions of constructivism and futurism. The leading surrealist figure in the 1920s was André Breton, not much of an artist per se, but a theorist and spokesman of considerable import. Breton is a prototype of the artistic pundit that anticipates the counterculture hero of the 1960s. He was certainly a very visible figure in his day.

Beginning around 1910 and continuing into the twenties, there was another great movement in painting—expressionism—this time in Germany. The two figures who predominate in this movement, Wassily Kandinsky and Paul Klee, stand, in the opinion of most critics, as the greatest of modernist painters along with Picasso and Braque. This German movement was originally known as the "Blue Rider" school, after a journal of art and social critique that its leaders published at this time. The German expressionist movement was influenced in its early years by the French painter Robert Delauney, whose reputation is currently on the rise.

Kandinsky, Klee, and some other members of the Blue Rider school joined the Bauhaus in the 1920s. The Bauhaus was an institute devoted to architecture, painting, and design, aiming at a revolutionary new era in the visual arts in conformity with modernist principles, new technology, and, to some extent, with socialism. Kandinsky and Klee taught painting in the Bauhaus. With the rise of Hitler to power, they went into exile, along with many other Bauhaus members and Brecht and Weill. Klee went to Switzerland and Kandinsky to Paris, where he died in 1944. Klee died in 1940 in Bern.

In his last years in Paris, Kandinsky had to struggle to find buyers and patrons. His paintings, along with those of van Gogh and some early Picasso work, now command the highest prices of any modernist artist. Kandinsky's influence on American abstract expressionism was more direct than that of any other European artist. Kandinsky humanized the abstract character of the Paris School. His nonrepresentational paintings are personal, emotional, and sometimes mystical and whimsical.

Klee was the theorist of the painterly modernism of the 1920s. Picasso wrote very little, perhaps because he was too occupied producing painting upon painting. Klee, however—who sold few paintings in his lifetime—wrote extensively about modernist art, and particularly about its abstract school. He maintained that his intention was to communicate "the primordial realm of psychic improvisation," which was necessary, he claimed, to release abstract structures which "transcend all schematic intent and to achieve a new naturalism." The abstract structures rose above all language and achieved a natural realm of their own. Klee was also very much influenced by Chinese and Indian art and philosophy, and to a degree, by Middle Eastern art as well. He made a trip to Tunisia before the First World War, where he acquired a taste for Middle Eastern art forms. His abstract art is highly symbolic, mythological, fantastic, and intensely personal.

By the 1920s, these artists, as well as many others less well known, had attained the status of celebrities. Yet some modernist paintings, which are sold today for between half a million and five million dollars, could still be bought in Paris in the late twenties for anywhere between two hundred and two thousand dollars. Painters made enough to live on, but substantial rewards were slow in coming. The situation was altered with the entry of the American buyers and art dealers into the market, the establishment of the Museum of Modern Art in 1937, and the compiling of the (Gertrude Vanderbilt) Whitney collection in the early 1930s, all of which were factors that contributed to the rise in the prices of modernist paintings. Henry Moore, for example, had become wealthy by the late thirties. Indeed, by the 1940s no metropolitan bank or corporate executive office felt secure without a primordial Moore figure reclining on its premises. Picasso by 1940 had become a mythic figure, like Einstein, and the embodiment in the popular imagination of what an artist should do and how he should live.

Obviously this market phenomenon was not altogether glorious, but it is indicative of the way modernist art achieved a central role in cultural life as well as popular support, and thereby changed people's aesthetic values. Today, what we wear, the colors we use, the furniture we sit on, the shape of our rooms, the imagery that appears nowadays in our stage sets and in our films have all been shaped through and by modernist painting. We see the world differently than did people before 1900. Not only are modernist painters themselves venerated, but they have actually transformed the visible world.

The modernist design style of the twenties and thirties, art deco, was a conscious and contrived reflection of modernist painting and its motifs and assumptions. Whereas a leading theme in art nouveau in the early years of the century reflected the folk art, fresh air movement of the 1890s, art deco sought a mode of interior design that reflected the lines and bold patterns—Picasso's "abominable forms"—of the Paris School. Instead of art nouveau's natural-grained wood and woven carpets, art deco favored lacquered wood furniture, parquet floors, and especially the use of burnished metallic objects indicative of a high-tech culture. Or it devised a few deeply colored pieces of furniture against an all-white background. The great monument to art deco is the foyer of Radio City Music Hall in New York. The Scandinavian design of the fifties represented a peculiar effort to combine elements of both art nouveau (natural-grained wood) and art deco (white walls, metal-and-glass tables), a kind of all-star modernist style.

Modernist art was helped by the emergence of critics and art historians.

Just as modernist poetry and novel achieved their penetration with the collaboration of critics and scholars, and just as serialist music, because it never quite achieved similar critical support, remained culturally marginal, so painting and sculpture benefited from the emergence of art criticism as a distinct intellectual force and profession. This emergence occurred principally in the twenties and thirties.

The first modern art critic and the prototype of the profession was Bernard Berenson, an immigrant Lithuanian Jew from the slums of Boston who won a scholarship to Harvard in the 1880s and became a self-taught, self-advertised expert on the Italian Renaissance. He collaborated with a rather flamboyant and unscrupulous art dealer named Lord Duveen from the 1890s until the twenties, and between them they dominated the market for Renaissance paintings. Duveen found Renaissance works in the back alleys of Siena and Florence, Berenson conveniently authenticated his colleague's finds, and the paintings skyrocketed in value. This showed what an art critic of competence, taste, learning, and a not-too-tender conscience could do. Although Berenson himself was never devoted to modernist art, and confined himself to the Renaissance, he created the prototype of the art critic who, as we well know by now, can be a very powerful figure in the art market.

Berenson had a disciple, a precocious Englishman named Kenneth Clark, who came from an extremely wealthy family. Clark studied with Berenson after leaving Oxford, and devoted himself, following his master, not only to the Renaissance, but also to modernist art. At the age of thirty-one, Clark became the director of the Tate Gallery in London, and proceeded to validate and popularize modernist art. In the early thirties, Clark purchased for the Tate van Gogh, Gauguin, Cézanne, and other modernist painters in large blocks at unimaginably low prices. The exhibitions he devised greatly enhanced the reputation of these works.

Clark single-handedly made a significant contribution to the inflation of the modernist art market and fostered the legitimacy of the Parisian school in gentry eyes. This is the same Sir Kenneth Clark who used to tell us the story of civilization on public television in the 1970s. At one point in his dealings, Clark came on a group of Matisse drawings for sale. Not having gallery funds to purchase them, he acquired them for a modest sum for his personal collection. These drawings alone by the 1960s made Sir Kenneth a multimillionaire.

Two influential and perceptive art critics appeared in the United States in the 1930s: Clement Greenberg and Meyer Schapiro. Greenberg, a largely self-educated person, wrote for the *Partisan Review* and other intellectual quarterlies.

Eventually, in the forties, he became an art critic for *The New Yorker*, and the primary spokesman for the American school of modernist painting and abstract expressionism. Greenberg made Pollock the way Leavis made Lawrence. Greenberg's essays are still readable. He found an illuminating way of encapsulating the modernist principle of self-referentiality. In modernist culture a "discipline criticizes itself by its own methods."

Still active in the 1980s, Meyer Schapiro was a colorful figure. Again mostly self-taught and with close personal ties to the New York painterly school, he got a Ph.D. at Columbia and became a medieval art historian, since entry into the academic art world was not possible in the 1930s unless one taught medieval or Renaissance art; he did some very fine work in that area. Schapiro gained a tenured professorship of art history at Columbia, where his lectures drew standing-room-only audiences. No one, in fact, has written more persuasively than the late Meyer Schapiro about Romanesque art, to which there is a protoexpressionist quality. But Schapiro's greatest interest was in modernism, and his essays on the subject, which go back to the thirties, are still very readable. From the influential vantage point of his Columbia professorship, Schapiro could foster a public critical acceptance for modernism. Only in the 1990s, when all of Schapiro's papers were finally collected and published in book form, was his stature as an art critic fully recognized.

With the opening of the Museum of Modern Art, modernism acquired in New York of the thirties an aura of elite orthodoxy. Only a quarter of century had elapsed since the media had heaped contempt on Marcel Duchamp and the pioneering Armory Show. Even the *New York Times* eventually surrendered to the modernist tide. The *Times* hired the astute and learned Harvard graduate Hilton Kramer, a disciple of Greenberg and Schapiro in his commitment to modernism, as its art critic because, so the editors told Kramer, the *Times* wanted to keep up with the aesthetic preferences of its readers.

That all three critics were Jewish was not accidental. New York Jewish intellectuals in the thirties and forties, having no investment in gentile—and genteel—Victorian art, could enthusiastically embrace modernist aesthetics for its intrinsic values of cultural liberation.

At the same time as the development of professional art criticism, the 1920s also saw the creation of another new field of scholarship, art history. This was largely a German creation—*Kunstgeschichte*—and owed some of its original conceptions to nineteenth-century philosophical idealism. But there was very much a modernist slant to the emergence of the field. Art history as we know it, as distinct from nineteenth-century connoisseurship or art appreciation, was a method of close analysis, and it was founded by two German scholars, Aby Warburg and Erwin Panofsky.

Warburg came from the prominent German Jewish banking family. He developed the method of art history that is called iconology or iconography, after the Greek word for "image." The purpose of the art historian, according to Warburg, is to carry out a close reading of a particular image as it appears in medieval manuscript illumination or in stained glass, say, in Chartres, as well as in all the other particular manifestations of the same icon. The art historian's task was to map out the entire field of the icon's meaning, use, and influence, including the literary motifs that helped generate the pictorial image, and everything that was entailed in the craftsmanship. Every image was ultimately related to a literary text.

Until Warburg the approach of the art historian had been devoid of a rigorous method. It had consisted mainly of learned but idiosyncratic connoisseurship—aesthetic appreciation of pretty pictures. Warburg displaced this with precepts for systematic and technical close reading, very much like those generated by the New Critics for the study of literature, and with special interest in iconological symbolism.

Warburg used his family's money to establish a great art historical library—which developed into a research institute—in Hamburg. In 1931, two years after Warburg died, some of his disciples, fearing the impending rise to power of the Nazis, moved the library and institute to London, where it became the graduate art history department of the University of London—one of the two finest such programs in the translatlantic world. The other—the Institute of Fine Arts—was for all practical purposes founded in the 1930s at NYU by another disciple of Warburg's, Erwin Panofsky. (It is now housed in the former Doris Duke mansion across the street from the Metropolitan Museum of Art, with which it conducts a joint program in conservation and preservation.)

Panofsky followed Warburg's method of close reading or iconographic study. In the forties he moved to the Institute for Advanced Study in Princeton, where he also helped create a distinguished department of art history at Princeton University.

Although art historians were initially interested in medieval and Renaissance art, eventually in the forties and fifties they came to incorporate the study of modernist art into their canon. The art history departments in such women's colleges as Barnard, Bennington, Wellesley, Smith, Sarah Lawrence, and Bryn Mawr were the first to make art history a discipline to be taught even to undergraduates, to release it from being a specialization for graduate students and researchers, and to make it central to the humanistic education of post-adolescents. They were also the first to give priority to the study of modernist art in their curricula. Bennington, which was founded in the late thirties, was a vehemently progressive college for affluent young women that placed its primary emphasis on the study of modernist dance, poetry, and art, and to some extent still does. When in the 1950s Oxford University finally established a chair in art history, the first appointment to its chair—Edgar Wind—was a German émigré Renaissance scholar who had taught at Smith College for many years.

From these colleges, art history departments spread first through the Ivy League schools and then through the state universities, and decisively contributed to the creation of a public taste. They generated a much larger market, consisting of knowledgeable people with a practiced eye and a sense of the scope of art history. The growth of art history as an academic subject was linked as closely to the profusion of galleries, museums, and the market for modernist art as the New Critics' activities were connected to the creation of a publishing market for modernist poetry and novel in the twenties and thirties.

Modernist architecture was often designated, especially in its first generation, as the functionalist style, and in the 1940s and 1950s as the international style. It was born in four different cities—Barcelona, Glasgow, Chicago, and Berlin— at about the same time but independently of one another.

The Barcelona architect was Antonio Gaudí, who was perhaps the most imaginative and creative art nouveau architect. He used flowing lines to create buildings whose strong decorative elements and sense of fantasy made them look like settings for science fiction films. Gaudi, who died in 1926, was not really appreciated until the 1960s.

The Glasgow architect was Charles Rennie Mackintosh, who had been locally trained (he was, in fact, an autodidact) but who had traveled widely on the Continent. He was a professor of architecture and design at the Glasgow School of Art. Mackintosh designed only a few buildings, most of which were local houses and schools. He has a single monumental public building, the Glasgow School of Art, which was built between 1910 and 1912. This is the first functionalist or modernist building in Britain, and it still is one of the most important and successful works of modernist architecture in terms of both its interior and exterior design.

Mackintosh was certainly very much a product of the art nouveau movement. He was influenced by William Morris and the folk art ethos of the late nineteenth century. His aims were to reduce a building to its essentials, to communicate a populist feeling, to use pure materials, such as local stone on the outside and almost entirely wood on the inside, and to create the building in which all elements were totally integrated. To this latter end, even the furniture and the entire decor of the building would be designed by the architect and his staff. The chief member of his staff was his wife, who was a prominent designer—she made her living for forty years designing wallpaper.

Mackintosh was an important, pioneering figure in the development of modernist architecture. Unfortunately he had difficulty getting commissions, and, whether out of disappointment or for another reason, he became a severe alcoholic, which eventually led to a breakdown. Although he did not die until the late 1930s, he produced very little work after World War I.

The first great name—and certainly the most versatile one—in the history of American architecture, was Louis Sullivan. One of Sullivan's important buildings in Chicago is the Auditorium. A great achievement of 1890s Victorian architecture, it is in the shape of a Roman basilica, emphasizing the horizontal, and holds three thousand people. The Auditorium Theatre was originally designed as an opera house, but is currently used—after complete restoration in the 1970s—as a concert hall. This marvelous work of architecture was also a pioneer in the use of electric illumination. The original electric bulbs were re-created at exorbitant cost as part of the restoration work.

In the early years of the century, Sullivan worked on his first modernist building, the first architectural artifact approaching a skyscraper in appearance, although it was only twelve stories. A vertical-functional edifice of what later came to be called the international style, this is the Carson Pirie Scott department store on State Street in Chicago. Sullivan was aware of the new possibilities for building relatively tall buildings opened up by the steel frame and the new pneumatic elevator that used compressed air. The Carson Pirie Scott building signaled the direction of twentieth-century architecture made possible by these technological advances.

Despite Sullivan's immense skill at decorating the facades of buildings, the relatively unadorned face of the Carson building also indicated a new trend. Nineteenth-century buildings were held up by their heavy stone walls, which the architect then adorned—this was called the beaux arts style. Thick walls became unnecessary in the engineering revolution of the early twentieth century, and the facades of buildings lost their decorative character to the sparse functionalist style. The Carson building still has some marvelously delicate ironwork. Nevertheless, in comparison with the beaux arts style, it inaugurated the transition to modernist minimalism.

Sullivan was fully conscious of what he was undertaking. His private papers reveal that Sullivan was very much influenced by Nietzsche. He certainly had a protomodernist, radical temperament. He was sensitive to the new ideas that were appearing in a variety of fields at the turn of the century. Sullivan had immense success with the Auditorium and other horizontally focused, heavily decorated buildings, but he realized that it was both possible and necessary to create a new style. The modernist style would have a relatively plain exterior and the building would simply demonstrate its function rather than memorialize some cultural heritage.

Sullivan's disciple was the midwestern native Frank Lloyd Wright, who received his education as an apprentice in Sullivan's firm and became his partner for a while before starting his own firm. Wright is one of the leading modernist architects even though he did not build skyscrapers and emphasize the vertical plane. To some extent, he was not entirely a functionalist. There is a highly decorative tone to Wright's work. In New York there is only one building of his design, the Guggenheim Museum, which was built in the early sixties and which reflects some of his main ideas: The emphasis is on integration and more on the horizontal than on the vertical; it highlights rounded forms rather than sharp corners.

But in order to understand Wright, one has to go to the Midwest, where his early work, and particularly his first houses, can be seen. Wright's major involvement was in domestic architecture—perhaps out of necessity, since he received very few public commissions. A flamboyant character and a utopian visionary, he had a rather stormy personal life. His first wife was killed under tragic circumstances, by an ax-murderer in Wisconsin, which became a media sensation and somehow cast a lurid light on him. In the 1920s Wright moved to Taos, New Mexico and created there a utopian art colony which is still in existence. His somewhat nonconformist life style may have discouraged patrons. Aside from the Guggenheim Museum, his major surviving public work in the United States consists of an office building for the Johnson Wax company in Wisconsin and a bank in a very small town in Minnesota.

Wright's most important and characteristic work, in domestic architecture, displays a substantial Japanese influence. Wright loved the Orient and designed a hotel in Tokyo that endured for three decades. Wright may also have been influenced by the Mayan architecture of Central America. His domestic buildings are dispersed from Pennsylvania through the Midwest.

Wright can be seen at his peak in the Johnson House in Racine, Wisconsin. Built in the 1920s for the family that owned Johnson's Wax, it is now used as a conference center. It incorporates all the ideas that are now found in expensive modern domestic architecture. The style Wright developed in this construct later became known first as the California style, and then as the Long Island style. He also designed the interior of the Johnson House, of which one innovative feature was the central fireplace and another the blond furniture.

Many of Wright's ideas, such as the central fireplace, have been so frequently used, particularly during the suburban development in the forties and fifties, that they now appear a trifle redundant. Aside from the Johnson House, among Wright's other well-known domestic work is the Robie House, which is on the campus of what is now the University of Chicago. Built before the university occupied the area, it is now open to the public.

The most admired and imitated of Wright's many private houses is Fallingwater (1936–37), built for the department-store-owning Kaufmann family in Bear Run, Pennsylvania. Here Wright's evocation of Mayan pyramidal temples and his efforts to integrate interior living space with outdoor terraces and a waterfall signal a neoromantic attitude that has been emphasized in the sixties and seventies in the works of Philip Johnson and John Burgee and the postmodernist architects. Like that of all of great artists, Wright's work transcends categories and embraces the whole architectural history of the century.

Wright's conception of architecture entails the idea of authenticity, and the notion that a house is a machine for living and therefore cannot be formidable and overpower its inhabitants; it is a humanistic machine. He emphasizes the use of local materials, the heavy use of wood, and the integration of the furniture with the design. The art nouveau influence on Wright, while not as pronounced as in the case of Mackintosh, was substantial, especially in his interior decoration.

It is, however, the German Bauhaus school that fully developed the modernist architecture that swept Europe and particularly the United States after World War II. It created Park Avenue in New York as we know it, as well as Third Avenue. Perhaps because of the overenthusiasm with which the Bauhaus style was received and applied, it produced a reaction, if not a rebellion, against itself, which was inaugurated by Philip Johnson in the late sixties and which still continues—although Frank Lloyd Wright's work can be seen as a modernist alternative to the Bauhaus skyscraper style.

Walter Gropius, Mies van der Rohe, and Marcel Breuer were the three remarkable originators of functional modernist skyscraper architecture. Gropius was the leading architect of the Bauhaus and Mies and Breuer were his disciples. After the Nazis came to power, Gropius became an architecture professor at Harvard. Mies and Breuer followed Gropius to the United States, where they had successful careers. In 1957 Mies built the Seagram Building on Park Avenue, which served as the prototype of the International Style in New York City. Breuer designed the Whitney Museum. He probably would not have objected to the later project of adding on to the top and sides of the existing building.

Gropius was a visionary and a socialist. He believed in a new architecture for the new day and the new technology that would use concrete, steel, and glass and be simple and direct. He built several factories around Berlin, most of which did not survive World War II. There are only about three left—small structures that do not look particularly imposing— but they constituted a significant breakthrough. They are memorable for the unprecedented expansion of glass and the use of glass bricks, a hallmark of art deco style, and a medium also favored by Frank Lloyd Wright. Gropius's factory buildings around 1910 unequivocally proclaim an architectural revolution.

According to Gropius—who designed the MetLife (formerly PanAm) Building behind New York City's Grand Central Station—a building was simply what it was. A factory building was a factory building, not a Roman temple, and what you saw, therefore also had to be precisely that: a factory building. The interior of the structure was to be predictable from the outside, and the building materials were to be cheap and accessible. Gropius's favorite project was working-class housing. His more comprehensive vision was the new technological city with rapid transportation and great concrete blocks of working-class housing. That such housing has become for us a symbol not of liberation but of misery demonstrates the downside of utopian expectations.

Mies, Gropius's prime disciple, aimed at elaborating on his teacher's project, and in 1921, he generated designs toward what he called the "city of the future." The design included vast circular towers forty to fifty stories high, which would house the working class of the future, pull them out of the slums, and literally elevate them above the city. Mies's plans presupposed the new metropolitan rapid transit systems. Had he been forced to ride the New York subway of the 1990s, he might have had second thoughts about the city of the future.

Mies received his opportunities not in Germany but in Chicago, where he went in 1937, four years after the Nazi dissolution of the Bauhaus. In Chicago he became a professor at the Illinois Institute of Technology, and eventually an associate of the largest American architectural firm, Skidmore, Owings & Merrill. On Lake Shore Drive in Chicago, one can see his series of four semicircular constructs, which were erected in the late fifties by the architect and his disciples, not, as it turned out, as working-class housing, but as Chicago's most expensive apartment complex. Mies remained loyal to his architectural principles, adapting them, however, to a different social environment—upper-middle-class America.

Mies's simple skyscraper effect, seen in the Seagram Building in New York, furnished the model for innumerable lesser buildings in the fifties and sixties. These buildings can be recognized by their emphasis on the steel frame, treating the brick, concrete, and glass as mere curtains that have no share in holding up the building. This style also emphasizes the high-speed elevator. And since the use of air-conditioning had become widespread in the fifties, these buildings easily accommodated air-conditioning ducts. The old horizontal, heavy block buildings were difficult to air-condition.

Gropius's and Mies's functional style envisions buildings that can harbor elements of modern technology while not occupying much space. It was ideal for New York City and it was also used extensively—although not exclusively—in rebuilding devastated Western Europe after 1945. On the skyline of West German cities the Bauhaus spirit has come home. Even in Paris the beaux arts ambience has been infiltrated by the Bauhaus heritage.

The phenomenal popularity of the Bauhaus in the fifties and sixties was the consequence of its compatibility with the technological capabilities and commercial interests of the period. The hundreds of corporate executives and commonplace architects who imitated the Seagram Building were motivated by other than aesthetic concerns—but this too was part of the functionalist ethos.

Breuer's prime accomplishment in Germany was not in architecture, although he was a major architect, but in furniture design. He was the developer of the Breuer or Bauhaus chair, which can be inexpensively purchased in any department store. With a curved tubular chrome or steel frame and a back and seat usually made of cane, it was the functional chair, and has, in the meantime, become the universal chair, whose imitations are used even in classrooms. Breuer became professor of architecture at Harvard, and supported by Harvard's prestige, he validated modernist architecture in the United States. He tried, however, in his later work to moderate the technological severity of the Bauhaus style. His Whitney Musuem is modernist architecture in its humanist form.

Another exponent of the effort to humanize Bauhaus functionalism was the work of the Swiss-French architect Le Corbusier (Charles-Édouard Jeanneret). His imaginative use of geometric forms other than rectangles and his bold use of poured concrete gave a sparkling vitality to functionalist principles. Le Corbusier worked in Brazil in the late thirties, fostering a renaissance in building and city planning that made the country a vanguard architectural center. The new interior capital of Brasília was created in the fifties by Le Corbusier's disciples. His most famous work in the large-scale urban mode was a provincial capital in Punjab, India, designed around a pool of water, begun in 1951. His own masterpiece was the Church of Nôtre-Dame-du-Haut in Ronchamp, France, completed in 1955, a decade before the end of his long life. This church combines stark but sloping and rounded concrete walls with a monumental flying concrete roof. The main structure closely resembles a nun's traditional headdress.

There is no doubt that in the Bauhaus, as there was in Sullivan and Mackintosh, there was a very strong ideological content. Bauhaus architects were idealistic and had social commitments. Yet the Bauhaus architects were commercially oriented, since it is not possible to work as an architect without such orientation. Frank Lloyd Wright, who subscribed least to commercial concerns, suffered for his nonconformist attitude. Regardless of how their achievement may be evaluated retroactively, the modernist architects conceived of themselves as creating an architecture for a new society and from Berlin to London to New York and Chicago their style now dominates the metropolitan skyline. If the harshness and repetitiveness of the result makes some long for the good old days of the beaux arts style, the fault does not lie with Gropius and his colleagues: Their urban vision was developed in the context of the earlier twentieth century, not its closing years. We have seen that Wright, Breuer, and Le Corbusier made strenuous efforts to avoid the redundancy and harshness of the international style.

Modernist culture generated a new art form, that of film. Technically speaking the development of film was largely the work of Americans and Frenchmen. Americans and the French developed film as a popular medium. Charlie Chaplin and Mack Sennett first attracted large audiences with one- and two-reeler slapstick comedies. Nowadays it is debatably held that Chaplin went much further, and drawing on his roots in British musical hall performance, created in his Tramp or Little Fellow a universal figure of sentimental pathos and indomitable courage who naively confronts the forces of power and technology. That

Chaplin intended this to be the message of his feature-length film *Modern Times* (1936) is evident, and it can also be inferred as the theme of *The Gold Rush* (1925).

Whatever Chaplin's place in the development of film, D. W. Griffith is now recognized as the first master of film for his extended narrations and the devising of many of the basic techniques of filmmaking. Griffith's *The Birth of a Nation* (1915) in its original form ran for more than three hours and signaled the emergence of a potential new medium of art and communication. This lachrymose celebration of the Old South and the Ku Klux Klan, rife with racism, reflected Griffith's southern background and his early experience in traveling theatrical companies devoted to popular melodrama. Griffith was a bizarre combination of vanguard technique and obsolete Victorian culture. Therefore he could not intellectually exploit, in spite of several later efforts, his pioneering mastery of technique. It was left to the German and Russian filmmakers to do so.

The expressionist art film was chiefly the achievement of Germans and Russians. It was the Germans in the 1920s who first tried to appropriate into film the techniques of expressionist painting as developed by Kandinsky, Klee, and their followers, as well as to adopt radical ideas from the modernist novel.

The two films that mark the great achievement of German expressionist film are Fritz Lang's *M* (1931), which is about a child murderer and involves sadomasochist motifs, and Josef von Sternberg's *The Blue Angel* (1930), which is based on Heinrich Mann's powerful modernist novel *Professor Unrath* and is about the savage humiliation and destruction of a repressed high school teacher (Emil Jannings) by a cruel cabaret girl (Marlene Dietrich). It is one of the great films of all time. A comparison of these films with the art of Klee and Kandinsky, and of fantasists like Klimt and Munch immediately demonstrates the influence of modernist painting on German expressionist film. The introduction of sound in 1930 provided further opportunity for the deployment of intellectual themes in film.

The Russian achievement in film was entirely the work of one man, Sergei Eisenstein. A devoted Bolshevik, in the twenties Eisenstein concentrated mostly on the propaganda film, although traces of expressionist technique are already visible in the two remarkable films he produced in this period to commemorate the revolution, *The Battleship Potemkin* (1925) and *Ten Days That Shook the World* (or *October*) (1928). The latter is a romanticized version of what really went on in the Winter Palace in 1917.

In the 1940s Eisenstein became more independent and boldly adopted German expressionist techniques in his two-part film *Ivan the Terrible* (1942–46), thereby falling out of favor with the Bolshevik authorities. Eisenstein is known today for his theory of montage, which he derived from close study of Griffith's technique. Eisenstein stresses that it is the material of film itself— that is, how the film is cut, how the scenes are put together, how they fade in and out of each other—that distinguishes film as an art form and renders it important. The notions of textuality, self-referentiality, and the ideas of modernist painting are evident in this theory of film.

It is this technical, microcosmic side of film that was Eisenstein's real interest, but he had to produce propagandistic narratives to satisfy his Bolshevik masters. *The Battleship Potemkin* tells a simple (and boring) story of a naval revolt against tyranny. Embedded in this post-Victorian narrative are immensely detailed studies of human visage and behavior. In one scene Eisenstein does a comparative study of the bad dental work of individuals in a mob. One can only imagine the films that Eisenstein would have made in a free environment.

As did their colleagues in other fields on the Nazi rise to power, many German filmmakersfled to the United States, and came to Hollywood. That the Hollywood film of the late thirties is the pinnacle of Hollywood creativity has diverse causes, but one of them was the arrival of the German expressionist filmmakers. Fritz Lang found a following there, as did the young Austrian Billy Wilder. The Hollywood genre of the late thirties and early forties, the "film noir," is so named for two reasons. Many of the scenes were shot at night to save on costs. But film noir is also a continuation of German expressionist film. Not only are the scenes sometimes very dark, but the topics are often very grim, with a heavy focus on the sadomasochistic. Many of the films noirs were directed by Lang and Wilder. Wilder's 1944 film *Double Indemnity* pursues the same theme of sadomasochistic sexuality as *The Blue Angel*. The German emigrants, applying their expressionist ideas, greatly raised the artistic level of the Hollywood film.

Orson Welles's *Citizen Kane* (1941), generally regarded as the greatest American film ever made, is deeply indebted for its narrative method and its brooding ambience to the film noir and the German expressionist tradition in filmmaking. The resurgence of neo-Victorian sensibility during World War II ruptured the expressionist heritage in Hollywood and resulted in a monumental artistic decline, as evidenced in the Hollywood film of the fifties.

Classical and Expressionist Modernism One fundamental polarity cuts across the literature, music, and visual and performing arts of the period of high modernism, which runs from 1905 to 1935. As central to the philosophy of the period as it is to the arts, this polarity resides in what one might call classical and expressionist modernism. One reason why historians do not find it easy to develop a clear perspective on modernism has been their failure to discern the presence of two tendencies within the movement. The two sides of the polarity do, however, share important assumptions. They are both microcosmic, discontinuous, antihistoricist, and self-referential. They both reject sequential temporality and emphasize immediacy of perception.

Classical modernism, which can also be called analytical or rationalist modernism, is found in Eliot, Pound, the New Critics, the American Southern Renaissance, the analytical philosophy of the period—which will be described below—as well as in the science and most of the social sciences of the period.

This vein of modernism holds emotions in check or represses them, and concentrates on the analysis of small phenomena brought under the scrutiny of the intellect. It acknowledges feeling but holds it in reserve. The emphasis is placed on the critical and analytic mind. The term "classical" is Eliot's own for his method and precepts. Eliot saw this type of modernism as recovering the rationalism of classical thought. Whether classical thought was really as rationalist as Eliot would have it, or what was the degree of selectiveness in his cultural appropriation, is largely beside the point.

Classical modernism envisaged a thick culture that was imparted through traditional institutions and that preserved social cohesion. You must never, warned Eliot, "neglect your shrines and churches"—not so much for their religion as for their ethical teaching and indoctrination of social solidarity. It is crucial to preserve "a certain uniformity of culture, expressed in education." There should be "a positive distinction . . . between the educated and the uneducated." Rationalist elitism was the hallmark of civilization and the preserver of social stability.

The term expressionist modernism was also used at the time. The German painters of the Blue Rider school, like Kandinsky and Klee, thought of themselves as expressionists. Heinrich Mann too designated his novels as expressionist. Hence, like "classical," "expressionist" is a contemporary term. The emphasis in expressionist modernism is on short bursts of intensive energy and feeling. The mind is not so much a detached observer and analyst of experience; rather it is imbued in it. The individual integrates him- or herself with a brief, intense burst of energy. Truth and art—and the perception of reality—lie in particles of energy that are permanently active in the world. The individual's salvation lies in integrating him- or herself with this intermittently disseminated universal force. Blood and sex are the most visible forms of this universal energy.

The expressionist ethos can also be called "vitalism" after the concept of *élan vital*, vital force, propounded by the French philosopher Henri Bergson around the time of the First World War. Regarded by his contemporaries as an important theorist, he was actually a cultural commentator who was trying to articulate what modern science meant to people of deep feeling. Very popular in his day, Bergson has become mostly unreadable. Yet some of the phrases he throws at the reader are eloquent in articulating expressionist concerns: "the thing we know most about in the world is ourself," "the creation of the self by the self," the "*élan vital*," all of which convey the vitalism, the energetic quality, and the sharply focused sentiment that mark the work of the German expressionists and are found also in the novels of Lawrence.

Lawrence is an interesting case in illustrating the problems that face historians when the duality in modernism is not recognized. Many professors of English today deny that Lawrence was a modernist on the basis of a comparison of his work with Eliot's. Lawrence was an expressionist, not a classical, modernist. He focuses on a vital force in the blood; surges of deep, unrestrained emotion; and specially on sexual drives. He perceives short, intense bursts of sexual energy as reflecting or perhaps comprising the structural, systematic forces that drive personal behavior. And he exults in revealing this blood-force and sexual energy rather than conducting cerebral, clinical analyses of sexuality. Lawrence's is a world of powerful homoerotic masculinity and also decisive earth-mother femininity that in the end androgynously blend together in the common, atavistic sexual drive of the human race. This is the theme of *Women in Love* (1920).

No wonder that even in the heyday of modernism, Lawrence's reputation was mixed, that he had a hard time finding publishers, and that he had to wait until the 1960s to gain an unchallenged reputation as one of the great novelists. The classical modernists thought him extreme, uncouth, unbalanced, not a little mad.

And certainly Lawrence's hard life and family pressures consumed him at the same time as they gave him the distinctive voice that he assumed. Lawrence's father was an alcoholic miner, his mother a lower-middle-class woman of genteel aspirations. His German wife—a distant cousin of the flying "Red Baron," Manfred von Richthofen, and with the same noble surname—never let Lawrence forget that she had abandoned an English middle-class professor husband and two children for an unstable bohemian life with him; also, she wouldn't do the dishes. Lawrence's vision of primordial reintegration of the folk blood through expression of sexual energy can be seen as his way of trying to transcend these domestic agonies. But he was also a reflective, learned, and very decent man.

As we have already seen, Frank Leavis chose to give legitimacy to Lawrence's work as a modernist, to move him from the margin to the cultural center. Leavis's criterion for including a novelist in the great tradition of the English novel was a writer's capability to communicate deep feeling, particularly a grave sensibility, a common moral seriousness, that Leavis thought always lurked just beneath the surface of working-class and middle-class life. On this criterion Lawrence was not only included in the great tradition; he marked its contemporary culmination.

Leavis spawned a large number of disciples who mostly became literature teachers in secondary schools. Sucking on their pipes, dressed in threadbare tweeds and baggy flannels, firmly reading from their paperback copies of the novels of the great tradition, never forgetting that Lawrence too had begun as a schoolteacher, the Leavisites were a small private army of expressionist advocates who had a major impact on English culture, not only through their role in education but also through the BBC, which they began to infiltrate in the thirties.

Leavis and his disciples believed in and advocated a primordial life force, a pure and authentic tradition of deep-rooted national culture, which had not changed in its essentials over time. Literature of the great tradition prepared people, and especially the young, to discover in their own hearts and minds this primordial life force and thereby to insulate themselves against the corrupting influence of a decadent, dehumanizing, technocratic environment.

The surrealists and dadaists of Paris in the 1920s also belong to the expressionist school of modernism. The dadaists claimed that the hegemonic culture and power system of the nineteenth century had been completely discredited. Like the hippies of the sixties, they fomented happenings to demonstrate the absurdity of the old culture and shock observers into a recognition of the new. The dadaists contended that the only starting point for a new culture was the aesthetic vitalism of individual artists.

The similar surrealist message was that the new technology had made all cultural forms obsolete. It was necessary to transcend the past with a new aesthetic vision that reflected the high-tech present but that allowed for the singularly authentic expression of personal feelings and private visions. Of course there was an element of Nietzschean philosophy in dadaism and surrealism, but they would have probably said the same things without Nietzsche.

In the Irish Renaissance, and particularly in the poetry and provocative essays of Yeats, there was another outlet for expressionist vitalism. This was tied to a murky but deep conviction that there was something especially valuable in the mentality of traditional Irish peasant culture. Yeats's professed devotion to Irish folk culture appears somewhat ironic in view of the fact that he did not know the Celtic language beyond a few convenient words, and until a patron gave him a country home in Eire, he lived most of the time as an expatriate in London.

Yeats is another figure who is not easily placed alongside Eliot, Pound, and Rilke, because in his poetry he is often more emotional than they, and because, especially in his essays, he stresses feeling and propounds what we have called vitalism. Yeats too expatiates on the folk blood, the primordial life force, that Lawrence and Leavis—and in a modified way also Paul Klee—talk about. "Justify all those renowned generations,/Justify all that have sunk in their blood . . . In every generation/Must Irishmen's blood be shed." Yeats's writings sound this threnody again and again. Klee ruminated on the "passionate movement toward transfiguration," as did the composer Richard Strauss.

Finally there was the cultural pundit who was prominent in Vienna from 1910 into the twenties, Karl Kraus, a satirist and critic who was very influential among the most prominent German figures of the time. Kraus's fundamental message is simply that the most important thing is art. Everything else is inauthentic, superficial, bourgeois. The only permanent value and beauty lie in art. This theme and other expressionist attitudes, as we shall see, affected leading German philosophers of the period 1910–30.

Strongly influenced by Kraus was the novelist—and later political philosopher—Elias Canetti. His *Auto-da-Fé* (1935) is a prime example of the expressionist novel, dealing with a case of paranoid obsession. Later Canetti summed up the thought and method of expressionist fiction: "One day, the thought came to me that the world should not be depicted . . . from one writer's standpoint, as it were; the world had *crumbled* and only if one had the courage to show it in its crumbled state could one possibly offer an authentic conception of it."

In both classical modernism and expressionist modernism there was a strong sense of individualism and a commitment to cultural solidarity. Both forms respected the capability of the individual mind to achieve truth-telling. For the classicals this was gained by a controlled rationality acting upon sensibility; for the expressionists, by some immediate charismatic vision. Adoration of the nuclear family, the stable force and dominant center in Victorian ethics, was abandoned by both the classicals and the expressionist modernists.

The possibility that powerful individualism could lead to social disintegration and cultural and moral anarchy the classicals and the expressionists were both anxious to avoid. For Eliot and the classicals, rationalized sensibility was to be placed in the service of traditional national institutions—the church, the university, and a social and cultural elite. The expressionists glimpsed an overpowering rebirth of national and group solidarity through a social experience characterized by the integrating impact of primordial vitality, which somehow imploded spontaneously within a common consciousness.

Historians have generally seen this expressionist attitude as a seedbed for fascism. But intrinsically it had no specific location on the political spectrum. If one can crudely specify the politics of the expressionists in the 1920s, many more were on the left than on the right. It was actually the rationalist classicists who were more inclined to the political right. Modernism eventually had political consequences; but it was a cultural revolution and an aesthetic and intellectual movement, not a political one.

Philosophy and Science At the beginning of this century, philosophy underwent a fundamental transformation, both in the United States and in Europe, which resulted in the repudiation and almost total elimination of idealism, the dominant nineteenth-century philosophical school. Three new schools of philosophy emerged: in Germany, the phenomenological school whose leading exponent was Martin Heidegger; second, Ludwig Wittgenstein's Anglo-Austrian school which was originally called logical positivism and which is now, since the forties, referred to as the analytic school; and third, the native American school of pragmatism whose most important names were William James and John Dewey.

The Heideggerian school is still dominant in departments of philosophy in Germany, and quite influential in France. Phenomenology has shown some influence on departments in the United States, but 80 percent of American philosophy professors, at least in the most prestigious departments, belong to the analytic school. In England the analytic school is universal. There is no English professor of philosophy who is not a logical positivist. The leading figure of the analytic school, Ludwig Wittgenstein, was an Anglo-Austrian visionary and a Cambridge professor. The third school, pragmatism, is American. Of its two greatest figures, William James was a professor at Harvard and the brother of the novelist Henry James. The other, John Dewey, was both a professor at Columbia University's Teachers College and a cultural guru in the 1930s, with a large following.

Nineteenth-century idealist philosophy had two main principles. One was that mind created and constituted everything. Nothing, no facet of reality, existed in the world that did not stem from the mind. The more the empirical was refined, the greater the departure from the material and the experiential, the more the purely intellectual was approached, the closer one came to truth, morality, existence, joy, or to what was referred to as the absolute. This was the Hegelian doctrine.

The second principle of idealism was that mind was active. It was a vital force that actually imposed itself on the world. It shaped the world. In the 1890s a new form of idealism, the neo-Kantian school, emerged in German universities, which tried to modify idealism as the nineteenth century had conceived of it by allowing room for the empirical. Neo-Kantians accepted that ideas had shaping power; yet they revised this premise to mean that the intellect and typologies (ideal types) controlled and molded the empirical. But to a neo-Kantian this did not mean that the empirical was dispensable to philosophy.

Neo-Kantianism realized that one could not study the fields of sociology and anthropology, which were becoming established in the universities at the time, by means of pure idealism, since these social sciences had to work with data. Removing the empirical was tantamount to removing data, and what would then remain was pure ideology, not social science. Neo-Kantians therefore generated room for data-based but idea-conditioned types. The greatest German sociologist, Max Weber, adhered to this neo-Kantian doctrine. The neo-Kantians retained the view, however, that the mind was a creative force. They preserved the conception of mind as capable of imposing itself on the world.

The new schools of philosophy after 1900 rebelled against this concept of mind. In the case of the analytic school, we find a total annihilation of every idealist precept. In the cases of phenomenology and pragmatism, the effort at elimination was not as blatant or comprehensive, but substantial nevertheless. They all rejected idealism and attempted to create new philosophies that generally cohered with modernist culture. In consequence philosophy as taught in universities today is as far removed from Victorian ways of thinking as are literature and science courses. It would have dismayed the Victorians to discover that in the 1990s the only visible disciples of Hegel are to be found among Marxists.

Just as modernist poetry found its forerunner in the 1880s in the works of Mallarmé, and the novel in those of James in the same decade, so twentieth-century philosophy had a precursor in the American Charles Sanders Peirce in the eighties. Unfortunately for him, Peirce never quite found an outlet for his ideas, which in many ways foreshadowed the new philosophy that was going to take shape after 1900. Many of Peirce's writings were unpublished in his lifetime, and in fact still remain so. Some of Peirce's important papers that did find their way into print saw publication only in *Popular Science* magazine in a vulgarized form to suit a general audience. Nor did Peirce ever receive a university professorship. However, he had considerable influence on the American pragmatists William James and John Dewey. To some extent he also anticipated the European philosophers of the early twentieth century, but the latter were not aware of the existence of this precursor. Peirce also foreshadowed the semiotic concerns of thinkers in the 1960s and 1970s.

Martin Heidegger is currently regarded as one of the two most influential philosophers of the twentieth century, and even though this is much more the case in Europe than in the United States, here too Heidegger is finding an increasing following. He obtained a professorship in the early 1920s and continued as a prolific writer until shortly before his death in 1979. His complete works, including previously unpublished material, are currently in preparation, and are allegedly going to comprise fifty-seven volumes.

Always difficult to read and virtually untranslatable into English, in the 1930s Heidegger was a prominent Nazi. He was the number one academic figure among the highest Nazi circles, and some of the speeches he gave during the thirties make for cruel reading today. Unsurprisingly, after the war he developed elaborate reinterpretations of what he had "actually" tried to say in those speeches. Regardless of what one thinks of them, there is no question that Heidegger had been a vehement supporter of the Nazi regime.

Heidegger had a strong following in Germany starting in the 1920s, and had important influences on an entire generation of German thinkers, many of whom became émigrés and a considerable number of whom were Jewish. Among them were his student and sometime mistress Hannah Arendt, the famous political theorist; Gershom Scholem, who later became the Israeli authority on Jewish mysticism; and the guru of the New Left of the late 1960s, Herbert Marcuse. All these diverse people had been students of Heidegger.

Heidegger had a long and complicated relationship with Hannah Arendt. The scion of a middle-class Jewish family, Arendt became Heidegger's mistress for several years in the late 1920s until, under pressure from his wife, Heidegger broke off the relationship and sent Arendt to complete her doctoral studies on another campus. In the late 1940s and 1950s Arendt was a prominent political philosopher and journalist in the United States. She resumed her friendship with Heidegger, and although she held no illusions about Heidegger's Nazi involvement, worked hard to resuscitate his reputation.

Heidegger is partly indebted for his ideas to his teacher Edmund Husserl, who claimed that the only source of knowledge is the intuitive action of individual consciousness. But putting Heidegger's debts aside, and concentrating on his phenomenological system in itself, it can be claimed that Heidegger has three propositions: The first concerns the principle of authenticity, which became widely used and strongly influenced French existentialism in the forties and fifties, and which has even entered into our own common language.

A person who has authenticity is one who is self-conscious of his wholeness and integrity as human being. Against the principle of authenticity are set alienation, artificiality, and decadence. There is no doubt that Heidegger had very specific images in mind when he talked of authenticity. His concept of the authentic focuses on the rural world. He thought that there was nothing more authentic than a German peasant, that fresh air and individual labor, physical as well as mental, contributed to authenticity. He also thought of the life in art, of the appreciation and particularly the creation of art, when he thought of authenticity. On the other side, comprising the inauthentic and artificial, were large cities, industrialization, a tendency toward depressing the individual into large groups so as to destroy individuality, and a philistinism that lacked in appreciation for the arts. If this sounds remarkably like the American counterculture of Woodstock of the late sixties, or of the Vermont woods in the 1980s, it is owing to a direct connection rather than to a fortuitous parallel. Heidegger's message of authenticity was preached by his disciples in this country, particularly by Herbert Marcuse, and was incorporated into the countercultural movement of the 1960s.

Behind this principle of authenticity is the metaphysical doctrine—later seized upon by the French existentialists—that being is not fixed, but rather that it is temporal and has to be seen in relation to its corollary—death. Being is "becoming"; it is existential activity. It is participation, a commitment. Again there is a long heritage descending from Heidegger's doctrine, including the interest in death studies in colleges today, predicated on the principle that death is as much part of our existence as being or life.

The second principle of Heideggerian thought is consciousness—that is, the idea that the only thing we really know is our own mind. This notion

Heidegger adopted from Husserl: There is nothing other than our capacity to think. The only certainty that we humans are capable of obtaining is achieved through our mental processes. This proposition bears certain resemblances to idealism, but also produces a high degree of relativism. Because if the only thing one can know is what one thinks, then the world comes to us only as we think it: The world consists of our perception of it.

Heidegger's third and most important principle distinguishes his thought from nineteenth-century idealism. It is the principle of phenomenology per se. There are things outside the mind. Outside the mind, the thing lives and exists for itself. The mind does not completely absorb everything in the world, which continues outside the mind. Furthermore, the mind cannot impose itself on things exterior to itself, since it is not sufficiently domineering, powerful, or creative to bring everything completely under its control. Instead, the fundamental act of the mind is to encounter, or to negotiate with, what lies exterior to itself. "That which shows itself should be seen from itself," claims Heidegger, meaning that we have to allow the authenticity of what exists outside the mind, whether it is the physical world or cultural and social processes, recognizing that we cannot dominate them.

What we can do is try to effect an interactive relationship with the world—an arbitrating, negotiating, encountering attitude. Phenomenology, as distinct from idealism, does not prescribe a fully active intellectuality. Its intellectuality is a more passive, less rigorous one, which encounters the world and, accepting it, attempts to live with it. Truth is a disclosure from the other. It is not something we control completely, as in idealism. The idealists had said, in the words of Schopenhauer, "the world is my idea." The phenomenologists say "the world is my experience," a much less aggressive, nonhegemonic, accommodating attitude.

Especially the latter principle of phenomenology played important transformative roles in various areas of twentieth-century thought ranging from the social sciences to literary studies. It has also influenced our culture in more pervasive ways that extend as far as affecting our worldview in the last twenty-five years. Translating Heideggerian principles into Californian language, we might articulate their message as "Go with the flow" and "Be laid back." Knowing that one cannot step outside one's consciousness, and that mind cannot dominate the world, one is justified in surrendering oneself to a life of aerobic exercises, jogging, communing in the Vermont woods or California mountains, and above all, to the cultivation of the arts.

Heidegger is indeed an up-to-date philosopher, and as time goes on his

intense flirtation with the Nazis is forgotten, or found to be relatively inconsequential, and his influence is constantly increasing. It is much greater today
than it was, say, in 1945. Analytical philosophers may scoff at Heidegger's
alleged murky neoidealism, but in fact, phenomenology departed measurably
from idealism. And we have to take seriously a philosophy that advocates
authenticity, commitment, and mellowness.

Whatever Heidegger's motives in his accommodation with the Nazis, this
behavior was fully in accordance with his philosophy. Phenomenology teaches
accommodation, encountering the thing, whatever it might be. After 1945
Heidegger repudiated his French disciples—Sartre and the existentialists—
not only because of their tendency to idealism but even more because in his
view they advocated neoromantic confrontation and conflict against evil: that
was not Heidegger's way. If only Lyndon Johnson had read Heidegger. If only
Reagan had. Nixon and Kissinger acted as if they had. Clinton is the most phenomenological American president.

The other influential philosopher of the twentieth century, and one of
modernism's personal gurus or culture heroes, was Ludwig Wittgenstein.
Beyond his influence as philosopher, Wittgenstein also commanded enormous
admiration among those who knew him. He has become something of a secular saint, a kind of Socrates of the twentieth century as it were, besides being
recognized as an important philosopher. He was Viennese. An enormously
wealthy iron and steel baron, his father was the Carnegie of Austria. The family were highly assimilated Jews, but Jews they were, and two of his close relatives, one sister and one aunt, perished in the Nazi death camps. Wittgenstein
probably would have too, had he been in Austria at the time of the Nazi
takeover.

Like Einstein, Wittgenstein was educated as an engineer, and already as an
engineer, he was sufficiently influenced by German physicists to begin to consider complicated mathematical and logical problems. In 1912 he went to
Cambridge University's Trinity College to seek out Bertrand Russell. A genuine aristocrat whose grandfather had been a prime minister of England,
Russell was even more a member of the social elite than Wittgenstein. Russell
himself was at the time an extremely important mathematician and philosopher who, with the assistance of another Englishman, Alfred North
Whitehead (who later became a professor at Harvard), was trying to construct
a new philosophy along the lines of mathematical analysis.

As Russell's version of the story goes, Wittgenstein turned up at Russell's
office, or "rooms," as they say in Cambridge, and told him that he had written

something and that he wanted to know whether he was a genius. Russell told him that he would read it that night and that he should come back tomorrow. When Wittgenstein returned the next day, Russell replied to him, "Yes, you are a genius, Wittgenstein."

During the two years before the First World War, Wittgenstein retreated to a hut on the coast of Norway and began to write his first and most influential philosophical treatise, *Tractatus Logico-Philosophicus.* (*Tractatus* is a Latin word that means "treatise.") He served in the Austrian army in the First World War. In 1918, his father died and left him several million dollars. Wittgenstein turned the entire sum over to a foundation that he established and which was committed to the support of artists and intellectuals. Among the first artists to receive a grant from the Wittgenstein foundation was the modernist German poet Rainer Maria Rilke.

Wittgenstein's *Tractatus* was published in 1921 and had immediate impact. He himself decided that he had terminated not only his own philosophy but all philosophy. Since there was nothing left to be said after the publication of the *Tractatus,* he became a schoolteacher in the backwoods of Austria for six years. Finally he heeded Russell's urging and accepted a position at Cambridge. Eventually he succeeded Russell as professor of philosophy. By the mid-thirties Wittgenstein held a monopoly over philosophy in Britain. No one who was not a Wittgenstein disciple could expect an appointment as professor of philosophy in the country. This is still the case.

After the Second World War, his influence made itself strongly felt in the United States, above all in the Ivy League schools. Even today, eighty percent of the philosophers in the top twenty-five universities in the United States are disciples of Wittgenstein. Outside Vienna, his influence on the Continent has not been very great. Strangely enough, however, in France interest in Wittgenstein has been increasing in the recent years. He has been the single most dominant name in philosophy in the English-speaking world. To a degree, this is unprecedented since the eighteenth-century ascendancy of John Locke and David Hume, with whom Wittgenstein has certain similarities.

The occupation of professor did not make Wittgenstein very happy. He claimed that it was easy to impress students and to be a good teacher, but that he wanted to get people to think rather than win teaching prizes. He probably greeted the Second World War with a certain amount of relief, for he left his professorship during the war and worked first as a farm laborer, greatly damaging his health; later, following a physical breakdown, he worked as an orderly in a hospital. He died in 1951.

Wittgenstein was gay and was sexually active. At Cambridge University in the 1930s he engaged in what would now be regarded as gross sexual exploitation of at least one of his graduate students. In the Cambridge ambience of that time such conduct was condoned. It does, however, raise questions about the personality behind Wittgenstein's philosophy. As described by his biographer, Wittgenstein comes through as someone ruthlessly engaged in the exploitation of vulnerable young men to satisfy his powerful homoerotic drive. (Thus, both Heidegger and Wittgenstein sexually exploited their graduate students.)

Wittgenstein's writings are oracular. They tend to consist of short paragraphs, often extremely opaque, and except for the *Tractatus* and a few short papers, he did not publish a book in his lifetime. His other four books were published posthumously, edited in some cases from fragments of drafts that he had written; in others, from students' notes. As with any other saintly guru, there is considerable dispute in the case of Wittgenstein as to what the master actually said. Consequently a vast body of commentary has grown out of the controversy over the content of his thought. The contemporary American philosopher Richard Rorty has remarked that Wittgenstein's impact on philosophy was very similar to that of Immanuel Kant in the early nineteenth century: His contemporaries knew that Kant had effected a philosophical revolution, but no one knew for certain what that revolution consisted of.

Nevertheless, what Wittgenstein has to say is fairly clear, especially in the *Tractatus.* He believes that the world as we see it is corrupt and run down. We are living in a period of moral and intellectual decline, a period that is hazardous. This he wrote in 1921, and it turned out to be true. The problem, according to Wittgenstein, is reflected in, and to a large degree created by, language, for we do not speak clearly and honestly. Our language consists of endless strings of falsehoods, doubtful propositions, and obscurities. It is the purpose of philosophy to clarify and verify the language of ordinary life—that is, the ordinary language we use to communicate with each other—in order that we may speak truth to each other. "The limits of my language mean the limits of my world."

The project of philosophy is, then, to redeem language from corruption. It is to purify it of slogans, myths, falsehoods and perversions. Philosophy is to undertake the analysis of ordinary language. Every other subject matter with which philosophy has dealt until now, particularly metaphysics, abstract concepts, are unverifiable, meaningless, even dangerous. In a sense Wittgenstein's message is the same as that of Voltaire, who had said in the eighteenth century, "Remove the infamous." Wittgenstein's infamous is the metaphysical idealism of the nineteenth century, which becomes, in Wittgenstein's thought, a mere cover for power, cruelty, and confusion. This particular Wittgensteinean theme has been developed at length by the recent French theorist Michel Foucault.

Wittgenstein's philosphical project of cleansing language can be seen as a repsonse to the cultural ambience of his era. He was the exact contemporary of Adolf Hitler, another Viennese, who was the great corrupter of the German language.

Since the propositions of ethics cannot be rationally verified, Wittgenstein claims that such propositions are philosophically not possible. Propositions cannot express, said Wittgenstein, anything pertaining to higher concepts. In his most famous and prophetic remark, he says, "Of all that matters in life, we must be silent." We cannot speak philosophically, rationally of momentous matters, including ethics and art. These fields are excluded from the domain of philosophy. Particularly to art Wittgenstein attributes the capacity to express the meaning of life, but art is exterior to philosophy.

Although Wittgenstein's analytic disciples generally regard Heidegger and the phenomenological school with contempt as bearers of Continental idealism and mysticism as compared to hardheaded Anglo-American empiricism, there is a way in which Wittgenstein agrees with a key doctrine in Heidegger's philosophy. For Wittgenstein as for Heidegger, there is something that exists outside ourselves that we cannot dominate, either metaphysically (Heidegger) or linguistically (Wittgenstein). "What expresses *itself* in language, *we* cannot express by means of language." This statement by Wittgenstein is quite phenomenological; indeed, it is reminiscent of Immanuel Kant.

Furthermore, that the world exists is a superrational fact: Wittgenstein maintains that we have to live with it as effectively as we can. "It is not how things are in the world that is mystical, but that it exists." Perhaps Wittgenstein has been perceived too much in the Vienna-Cambridge axis and not sufficiently within the context of historic German culture. The latter quotation recalls late medieval German mysticism.

The compatibility of extreme empiricism or skepticism with mysticism is a common theme in intellectual history, particularly in the later Middle Ages, and especially in England and Germany. When the writings of the great early-fourteenth-century Franciscan nominalists, Duns Scotus and William of Occam, began to be studied closely for the first time in the 1930s and 40s, it was discovered that these Oxford scholastics had in some respects anticipated Wittgenstein. This was no accident: These Franciscan friars were both mystics and empiricists. Was Wittgenstein conscious of this affinity? His biographers fail to deal with this issue.

Wittgenstein considered that philosophy deals not with the momentous, but with the marginalia of human communication, with the "limits of the world." But in our current corrupt situation, in a world in which vicious dictators and public monsters reign, purifying our language is critically important if we are to survive. With this in mind, Wittgenstein began to develop a new logic that deals with the analysis of ordinary language. In his later work Wittgenstein argued that, pragmatically, the meaning of words is settled through usage that reflects a "form of life." But this settlement is difficult and problematic because we "stretch" language beyond its limits. It is linguistic analysis that again can reduce this confusion and corruption and allow for authentic communication.

Wittgenstein did not complete this work of creating a new logic. He began it, and the project of completing it was continued by his most distinguished colleagues and disciples, one of whom was Rudolf Carnap, who left Vienna to become a professor at the University of Chicago. Others were the Englishmen John Austin and A. J. Ayer and yet another the Viennese émigré to Britain Karl Popper. In the younger generation of Wittgenstein's followers is the American Thomas Nagel, who teaches at New York University and continues to work on the project Wittgenstein left unfinished.

John Austin dominated the Wittgensteinian school of analytic philosophy at Oxford until his death in 1960. No statement—not even one expressed in mathematical language—is absolutely verifiable, Austin believed, because there is none whose meaning will not change meaning in altered circumstances. Everything depends on context. In a discussion of good or evil it is our varied usage of these concepts that is to be scrutinized—not any inherent meaning of the words. Austin's philosophy bears some resemblance to American pragmatism.

Wittgenstein's school was originally called "logical positivism" in the twenties and thirties. Since the fifties it has been known as "analytic philosophy," or as "philosophical analysis," or to use an even simpler term, "analysis." Wittgenstein's disciples have monopolized the term "analysis" for their own philosophical method.

Analytic philosophy is more temperament or a cast of mind than a precise set of doctrines—except that idealism is regarded as all wrong. The analytic philosopher examines a statement and asks: What are you really saying, if anything? What are the significations, if any, of this sentence? Analytic philosophy excludes metaphysics, ignores history, and concentrates closely on what can and cannot be said in an arguably meaningful manner. This analytic approach resembles a lawyer's close examination of a case, and one major impact of Wittgenstein, Austin, and their group has been in jurisprudence and legal philosophy, particularly in the writings of H. L. A. Hart and Ronald Dworkin. Hart was professor of jurisprudence at Oxford in the 1950s and 1960s. Dworkin, an American, holds the same distinguished chair today and also teaches at NYU Law School.

Of the two strands in modernism, the classical and the expressionist, Wittgenstein belongs to the classical school, which is one reason for the welcome he received in England. Under Eliot and his friends and disciples, this particular strand of modernism was achieving primacy in English culture, and Wittgenstein seemed to be a philosopher who cohered with the classical rationalism that the Eliot school propounded. A concern of Joyce, Pound, and other modernist writers was with an enclosed language world and Wittgenstein appeared to adhere remarkably well to this pursuit and indeed to justify it philosophically. Heidegger, on the other hand, is very much tied to the more intuitive, expressionist mode. In fact, he was inspired to a degree by German expressionist artists and writers, whom he, in turn, influenced as well.

The American school of pragmatism was famous in the twenties and thirties. In the American universities it was at least as important as phenomenology and logical positivism. One of the two leading pragmatist philosophers, John Dewey, was extremely visible in the 1930s. He was, in a way, the court philosopher of the New Deal. Writing articles for newspapers, making speeches on the radio, delivering commencement addresses throughout the country, he was difficult to avoid. After World War II, pragmatism entered a deep decline and was swept away, above all by the tide of Wittgensteinean analysis. In the last decade, pragmatism has begun to make a comeback. Richard Rorty, who is one of the most important American philosophers today, has taken lead in trying to revalidate pragmatism.

William James, the brother of Henry, came of a fiercely intellectual Boston family that was not a little eccentric. The father was a disciple of a Scandinavian mystic who had formed a religious-philosophical clique in this country. James held the first chair of psychology at Harvard, and wrote the first important textbook in that field. In addition he held a chair of philosophy and was also interested in religion. To the public at large, he was better known for a book he wrote called *Varieties of Religious Experience*, which celebrates, so to speak, precisely the compelling variousness and intensity of this experience, than he was for his philosophical and psychological work.

James has two main premises, the first of which is the presence of a strongly voluntarist element in thought. Thought does not come externally, but is worked out by the person in response to the environment in a way that is advantageous to him or her. We believe, in other words, what we want to believe, or what we think is to our advantage. What we think is what we feel we need to think. James postulates the existence of a will to believe, and given that the will is to think the advantageous, religion becomes a natural and even necessary component of human thought. He claims that issues of theology cannot be proved, for persons subscribe to religions for the comfort and integration afforded by them. And that is sufficient in itself. The useful is the true.

The second premise, this time a psychological one, that James propounded was that consciousness is not separate from the physical. Consciousness can, at times, affect or mold the physical, and yet the process is reversible. The physical can affect consciousness. The physical and consciousness are distinct from each other. However, by acting, doing something, we are capable of affecting our mental state. If we are depressed, for example, we can overcome this state by sheer activity. By some physical act of involvement, courage, or commitment, we can affect the mind. The mind is molded by the physical action and by the material environment, just as the mind at times affects physical action. A behavioral pattern can be established which will affect consciousness. Out of this Jamesean principle arose the American behaviorist school of psychology.

John Dewey was a midwesterner and a progressive liberal who first taught at the University of Chicago, and after establishing himself as a dominant thinker, became resident philosopher at the Teachers College at Columbia University. In an era when Americans and particularly New Yorkers still had faith in their public schools, the college gained overwhelming prestige, influence, and visibility in the twenties and thirties. It was a shaping force in American education for several decades.

Dewey's fundamental claim is that all thought is instrumental. A proposition is true if it can be used to attain a given end. Truth is not correspondence between our minds and the external world, nor is it harmony or consistency. It is an instrument in the shape of a proposition that serves to attain an end. This, in a nutshell, is the philosophy of pragmatism. Of course, James, and Peirce before him, made the same claim. What is distinctive about Dewey, however, is his concentration on social as well as individual instrumentalism. There are, he claims, clusters of ideas in society which are true because they achieve social reform and progress, the general happiness sought by all, and the desired degree of common welfare. The criterion of truth as something effective in achieving a desired end renders obsolete arguments from history as well as formal logic.

Dewey's extreme epistemological relativism fitted in very well with the new meliorism and progressivism of the New Deal. It collaborated with Keynesian economics, and cohered with the new winds that were blowing in the American law schools in the thirties. Dewey stood in the long American tradition of social improvement. He was a public-spirited figure who would sign any liberal petition, and who played an early role in the civil rights movement. He was concerned to create schools that would serve as miniworkshops for democracy, and he was immensely popular in his day. He profoundly influenced his generation.

Dewey found his disciples in the 1940s and 1950s not among philosophers but among a prominent group of American social scientists led by the historian Richard Hofstadter and the political scientists Louis Hartz and Robert Dahl. They identified American society as fundamentally different from European in that it was a pluralistic society made up of immigrants. In this perpetual condition of American exceptionalism, how could a consensus be achieved and maintained to bind together this pluralistic entity in a federal government? There were a variety of answers to this question; for instance, American history was claimed to have begun with the rejection of European feudalism and aristocracy. But the successful perpetuation of the exceptional pluralistic American consensus required the kind of democratic instrumental pragmatism that Dewey represented. His social instrumentalism was the kind of thinking that would maintain the American consensus and a democratic federalism within an intensely pluralistic society. For Hofstadter, Hartz, Dahl, and their many colleagues, Dewey's pragmatism was a central American social doctrine of crucial importance.

In spite of his close connection to the American political tradition of exceptionalism and pluralistic consensus, as a philosopher Dewey now makes for unpalatable reading. Wittgenstein is not readily accessible, even less so is Heidegger, but nevertheless, in these last two, there is a core that is immediately relevant to the reflective reader of today. To a degree the same can be claimed of James. Even though his style has much in common with evening musicales in the Cambridge, Massachusetts, of 1910, nevertheless James's ideas too strike one as relevant. But Dewey is out of date. Still, it is not possible to ignore contemporary philosophers like Richard Rorty and Alan Ryan, who claim that Dewey is a major thinker with much to say to the world in the 1990s.

While this tremendous change was occurring in philosophy, an at least equally significant transformation was taking place in science. Particularly the field of physics witnessed the greatest change since the Newtonian revolution of the early eighteenth century—the triumph of a new paradigm to explain physical phenomena.

The twentieth century has seen two scientific revolutions, the first of which generated the new physics of the period starting around 1905 and culminated in the late thirties or, more precisely, in August 1945 in Hiroshima. This period of physics and its culmination point have yielded not only new knowledge in physics but have also made it necessary to reconsider the aims and the organization of scientific research, as well as generally transforming our view of the natural world.

The second scientific revolution of the twentieth century, which began in the mid-sixties, was the biological revolution that rendered critically important the field of microbiology. It is an astonishing story that the laboratory that played the most important role in the first scientific revolution also played initially the greatest role in the second one. That was the Cavendish Laboratory at Cambridge University. It was there that Rutherford and his team were able to penetrate the inside of the atom and to discover subatomic particles, a field that is today referred to as high-energy physics. It was again in the same place that microbiology registered its great breakthrough to the discovery of the DNA molecule by Watson and Crick in 1953.

The Cavendish Laboratory came into existence in the 1880s in a peculiarly English way. There was at the time no physics laboratory at Cambridge, and it embarrassed the university that an institution as young as Manchester University had what they lacked. Cambridge officials turned to Lord Cavendish, who was a trustee of the university and himself a considerable scientist, and told him of the problem over sherry one day. Lord Cavendish took out his checkbook and wrote a check for the amount necessary to establish the laboratory. The check was the equivalent of five million dollars today—an instance of typical English amateurism.

As is well known, the great personage of the new physics was Albert Einstein, although it would certainly be correct to place Ernest Rutherford's name next to his. Rutherford was the second director of the Cavendish Laboratory, when the seminal experimental work in atomic physics was accomplished by Rutherford and his students. It was Einstein, however, who became the mythic figure, and certainly he was the prime theoretical leader.

There is enormous controversy about Einstein among his biographers. It is possible to read two biographies of him and wonder whether one is reading about the same man. The views of the man presented by physicists and non-physicists—and among the latter the work of Ronald Clark stands out—vary greatly.

The reason for this is that at a certain point in his life, in 1933 when he was driven from Germany and was justifiably confused and frightened, Einstein re-created his persona. An American department store magnate created the Institute for Advanced Study in Princeton as a place of refuge for Einstein. Although he held the town and its upper-middle-class ambience secretly in contempt, Einstein in public was friendly and accommodating to his new environment. He became a different public person than he had been in Berlin, transforming himself into an introverted guru, a Mahatma Gandhi, as it were, of science. Clad in tennis shoes and torn sweaters and puffing on his pipe, he became a man of peace and contentment, of gentility and joy. This is the way he wanted to be known to the world in his later years after he came to the United States, and this is the way scientists too now like to imagine him.

We know, however, that Einstein, from about 1910 to 1933, was a hell-raiser, a subscriber to almost every radical cause imaginable, a leftist, and probably something of an anarchist as well. It is not easy to define what his politics were but they were certainly far to the left of center. A dedicated Zionist, a moral relativist, a pacifist, and an extremely vehement critic of everything in the upper reaches of German society, he terrified the German establishment, and particularly the staid German academic world.

Typical of the reversal Einstein effected in his image is his statement, dating from the thirties, that his theory of physical relativity had no relationship to moral relativism. It was, he claimed, an accident that the same word was used in both cases, causing an unfortunate confusion. Scientist after scientist has echoed this statement by Einstein. Yet in the 1920s, Einstein clearly understood that he was a leader in a comprehensive intellectual revolution. "Today," he wrote in 1928, "faith in unbroken causality is threatened" by the new physics. Erosion of belief in causality removed the philosophical basis of normative ethics, making an extreme relativism the only possible moral theory. Although Einstein after coming to Princeton was almost universally revered as a saintly scientist, he never again achieved an intellectual breakthrough comparable in importance to the ideas of his earlier radical phase.

Einstein's early life has taken on a mythological quality that is familiar to most people today. The myth is substantially true. His family were middle-class German Jews. His father was an engineer who went into business and lost drastically. After this unsuccessful business attempt, the family moved to Italy, where the father hoped to recoup his fortunes. He abandoned Einstein when the latter was in high school. Unsurprisingly in these circumstances, Einstein finished high school with difficulty. He was not admitted to any university but only to an engineering school in Switzerland, where he received the only formal postsecondary education he was ever going to get. It is interesting that both Wittgenstein and Einstein received their formal education in engineering. These engineering schools were superior institutions, however.

Einstein then worked in the Swiss Patent Office in Bern, verifying, as an engineer would, proposals for patents. This job allowed him plenty of time to engage in intellectual and scientific work. There was one other person of some scientific background in the patent office with whom Einstein exchanged ideas. Unquestionably Einstein was an autodidact. At the time of the appearance of his first paper on the theory of relativity in 1905, he himself was ignorant of some other work in the field—particularly by the Dutch physicist Hendrik Lorentz—that had partly anticipated his own.

Contrary to the myth, however, Einstein was instantly recognized. Lorentz immediately acknowledged the importance of the work—which led to the slow, reluctant conversion of other German physicists—as did early on a leading physicist in Britain.

The problem with recognizing Einstein's theory was that it shattered the prevailing thought-world of physics. It made much of the theoretical work in contemporary physics obsolete. Physicists had to begin to think along radically novel lines. The pseudoautobiographical novel *Night Thoughts of a Physicist*, written by the American physicist Russell McCormmach, describes how a German physicist of the old school around 1918 would have reacted to Einstein and recounts the terrifying professional disaster Einstein's physics was likely to have meant for him: Einstein did nothing less than put scientists of the old school out of business.

The two important assumptions of Newtonian physics had been that mass and energy were distinct—in fact, that they constituted polarities—and, in addition, that the dimensions of space and time were absolutely distinct and separable. Perceiving the significance of the research of James Clerk Maxwell on electromagnetism, Einstein eliminated both assumptions. He propounded the interaction of mass and energy, and showed that they were ultimately interrelated and that each could transform into the other at a certain point in the interactive process. He also argued that space and time were ultimately not separable, that they too were interactive. Beyond space and time lie other dimensions that absorb both of them. This meant that Newtonian assumptions were henceforth fit only for high school physics laboratories and that the science of physics at the theoretical level had to begin anew.

Based on his theories and on the formulas derived from them, Einstein in 1915 predicted how the curvature of space bending starlight would be demonstrated in a total solar eclipse that would occur in the year 1919. Data from the eclipse viewed from the equator by a team of British scientists provided experimental verification for Einstein's theorizing. Einstein, who had held a research position in Berlin since 1913, became world famous overnight. Meanwhile Ernest (later Lord) Rutherford was effecting a similar upheaval in experimental physics.

Rutherford was a scholarship boy from New Zealand who knew hardly any advanced-level science when he arrived at the Cavendish Laboratory in the 1890s. He began his serious experimental work when he was a professor of physics at McGill University in Montreal, Canada, in 1902. He continued his work at Manchester, which was then a university as important as Cambridge in intellectual and scientific vigor, especially in the fields of physics and mathematics. Shortly before the war Rutherford became the director of the Cavendish Laboratory, a position he held until his death in 1937.

Rutherford, who eventually garnered every honor a scientist can attain to, was the prototype of the high-powered, politically well-connected scientist of the twentieth century. He was an experimentalist who built big laboratories and gathered around him large teams of brilliant young people. He did not much bother about their educational background, but based his recruitment on the interviews he held with candidates, and then put them immediately to work on complex experiments. This sink-or-swim approach is still characteristic of important scientific experimental work and doctoral training laboratories.

Rutherford worked with teams that built much of their own equipment, which is still frequent practice, and often achieved great results using the crudest equipment. The latter method, however, is no longer so fashionable. During a series of Rutherford's experiments it was important to count the number of flashes of light per minute. Rutherford's team had no feasible means of doing this except hiring shopgirls to keep count. Once, so the anecdote has it, one of the girls' missed count, which was realized after the results of the experiment had been made public. The papers had to be withdrawn.

The achievement of Rutherford and his group was nothing less than phenomenal. What they sought to discover, in Rutherford's words, was "the constitution of the atom . . . the great problem that lies at the base of all physics and chemistry. And if we know the constitution of atoms we ought to be able to predict everything that is happening in the universe." Rutherford's teacher, the first head of the Cavendish Laboratory, J. J. Thomson, had already discovered one subatomic particle, the electron, although it was not until Rutherford's work that the meaning of this discovery was fully perceived. Rutherford and his team discovered other subatomic particles, protons, and neutrons. Rutherford speculated that atomic structure was a kind of solar system with particles moving around an extremely dense nucleus. Rutherford's student, the Dane Niels Bohr (who later achieved an almost saintly reputation for his courageous resistance to the Nazis), in 1913 drew the map of particle orbits that became the standardized conception of atomic structure.

Rutherford experimentally implemented the artificial release of atomic energy, the transformation of the mass of the nuclear atom into energy. In 1917, working alone in the war-reduced Cavendish Laboratory with only one research assistant, Rutherford split the nitrogen atom, the first instance of controlled nuclear fission. Busy with war work, he did not announce this breakthrough, equivalent in importance to Einstein's, until 1919—that incredible year of modernist science—nor did he fully realize the implications of what he had achieved until the mid-twenties. Even then, Rutherford for several years insisted that his knowledge could not be used for military purposes. He said that if an atom bomb could actually be made, Cambridge would already have blown up. Finally, in the mid-thirties, shortly before his death, he was convinced by work done in Germany that it was indeed possible to make an atom bomb.

Rutherford is the prototype of the twentieth-century scientist in two further ways—first, in terms of the way in which he used data, namely according to the principle of quantified, aggregate data. The underlying conception of this principle is that the scientist never obtains an absolute, fully consistent set of data. The occurrence of anomalies—"outriders"—must always be acknowledged. This problem of inconsistency was to be circumvented by establishing a common aggregate pattern that reconciled most of the data, and that validated the verifiability of the experiment. The principle of aggregate quantification, which dispenses with the demand for total, complete consistency, has become a fundamental feature not only of natural science but also of quantified social science in the twentieth century.

The other feature that renders Rutherford the prototype of the twentieth-century scientist is his war work. In 1916 he was asked by the Royal Navy to devise a system by which British ships could locate German submarines, which were sinking vast tonnage of British shipping in the Atlantic. On this request, Rutherford and his group developed sonar, very quickly, even before the war was over. Sonar is used today to locate objects both of a military and nonmilitary nature far beneath the surface of the water—it works on the principle of echoing sound waves. However, it took Rutherford the rest of his life to convince the British Navy to use the system he had devised. Fortunately the mechanism was finally put to use just in time for the Second World War, and it did make an enormous difference. Britain would not have survived the early years of the war without it.

Rutherford was paradigmatic of the great scientific patron of the twentieth century, in his readiness to gather an international group of scientists around him. Hans Geiger, the inventor of the radiation counter that bears his name, was a German physicist who was one of Rutherford's students. One of the physicists who began his work in Rutherford's laboratory, Robert Watson-Watt, was the inventor of radar, without which Britain would not have won the air war in 1940, and without which commercial air travel would now be impossible. The prominent Soviet physicist Peter Kapitsa, who did the work on the Russian atom bomb, was also Rutherford's student. Rutherford loved to attend conferences, reading papers at venues from Australia to Paris, and he also traveled in order to recruit workers for his lab and to meet with other leading researchers. In Rutherford's conception "big science" was an international community.

Another team of experimental scientists, this time a husband and wife, were Pierre and Marie Curie. Madame Curie was a Pole who came to Paris to get a doctorate in physics, where she married another physicist, Pierre. The couple began their experimental work in the garage of their house under extremely difficult and hazardous conditions. They worked with radiation, discovered radium, and conducted many of the important early studies of uranium radiation and X-rays. Of course, in the end, this work killed Madame Curie, a fate that is by no means atypical for the early-twentieth-century physicist. They took risks with radiation that would now be considered suicidal. Many leading experimental physicists of this century died of radiation, including several of those who worked on the atom bomb during World War II. Marie Curie was one of the first to suffer.

In part because she was a woman, and in part because she was a Pole,

Madame Curie received very little recognition and support in France until she won the Nobel Prize in 1903 and again in 1911. But even so her work conditions improved but little, and doing science was a lifelong struggle. It is hard to believe that people could do major scientific work—indeed, win the Nobel Prize for it—and still continue working in a shack. (The physicists of the early twentieth century were heroic people—and to some extent thought of themselves in those terms, too.)

In the first three decades of the twentieth century, physics was the queen of the sciences in the German universities. In addition to Einstein there were several German physicists of great importance for theoretical work. Max Planck followed through on suggestions from Einstein himself, as well as from Bohr, in undertaking speculations that led to the quantum theory of the mid-twenties. In the refinement of the quantum theory, important contributions were made by the French scientist Prince Louis Victor de Broglie and the German mathemathical physicist Erwin Schrödinger.

Quantum mechanics, the basic theory of modernist physics, conceives that all energy (not just light) moves not continuously but in short bursts or waves called quanta. Schrödinger—who was to be the gentile German scientist most vociferous in opposing Hitler and who went into early exile—stated the essentials of the quantum theory in its definitive form in 1925. Particles are only "a group of waves of relatively small dimension in every direction." The quantum theory was developed further by Paul Dirac in the late twenties. In spite of his name, Dirac was British—his father was a Swiss immigrant. Dirac proposed the theory demonstrating the spin motion of an electron in an electromagnetic field, which constituted the inaugural basis of field theory.

Quantum field theory laid the foundation for the theoretical physics of the following three decades. The idea of an interactive region in which quantitative relations can be determined at any given point was to be central not only to physics but to the social sciences in the era of late modernism. Field theory was as important as relativity to the modernist vision of the world. Steven Weinberg, the 1979 Nobel laureate in physics, summed up the importance of the quantum field theory for his generation of quantum theoretical physicists: "Particles are bundles of energy and momentum . . . The particle is nothing else but a representation of its symmetry group [field]."

Thus, fully developed quantum field theory postulated two principles. The first was the principle of discontinuity, of brief, intense bursts of energy. The second was the principle of an interactive, definable field that could be quantitatively analyzed. Both discontinuity and field theory were conceptions central to modernist culture as a whole. They are represented in literature and art, and they were to play as great a role in social science as in physics. Strangely enough, once the quantum theory was developed, Einstein had second thoughts about it and, to the end of his life, never fully subscribed to it.

Even more celebrated than Schrödinger among German physicists was Werner Heisenberg, a conflicted, vain, extremely ambitious person who was a full professor at the age of twenty-four. Heisenberg carried his extensive knowledge of the humanities into his scientific work: "Through the surface of atomic phenomena, I was looking at a strangely beautiful interior." He also carried into his science his intense nationalism. He was a willing collaborator with the Nazis, and although originally a theoretician rather than an experimental physicist, he was in the early forties a member of the team of German physicists who worked on an atom bomb that, fortunately for mankind, was never constructed. The reasons, however, are still under dispute, one side claiming that the Germans "faked it," and only pretended to build an atom bomb for Hitler—that is, they sabotaged the project (obviously this is what Heisenberg and his collegues claimed after 1945). Or, a second explanation holds, the scientists working on the bomb simply had bad luck and took the wrong course in constructing it. A third view has it that the British and Americans, by means of commando raids and bombing, devastated the place in Norway from which the Germans were obtaining critical material for their atomic experiments.

Heisenberg's major contribution to theoretical physics was in completing the relativist trend inaugurated by Einstein and in expounding a phenomenological interpretation of physics compatible with Heidegger's philosophy. "Time and space," Heisenberg wrote in 1926, "are really only statistical concepts, something like, for instance, temperature, pressure and so on in a gas." No statement could more clearly articulate the modernist character of the new physics. Just as literature had become sensibility, and painting lines and materials, the physical world had become statistical categories.

Going on from this phenomenological assumption, Heisenberg developed his famous uncertainty or indeterminacy principle, which won him the Nobel Prize in 1932. Heisenberg's argument is that the scientist cannot obtain an entirely objective view of the world, primarily because the researcher cannot remove him- or herself absolutely from the scientific analysis or experiment. All scientific work is phenomenological—that is, it is to some degree conditioned by consciousness. The intrusion of the observer and his or her instruments prevents the measurement at the same time of both the position and momentum of an electron with complete accuracy. A minute but irreducible degree of uncertainty or indeterminacy intrudes.

The promulgation of Heisenberg's uncertainty principle in 1927 was hailed, in the words of another leading German physicist, as "the dawn of a new era." In actual scientific practice it did not have quite such a shattering impact. Experimental physicists generally ignored and still ignore the minute degree of indeterminacy in their work. Heisenberg's principle was, however, a theoretical contribution second only to Einstein's theory of relativity, of which it was an extension.

Indeterminacy and relativity were carried one step further in the thirties and forties by Bohr, in his principle of complementarity. He stated that the subatomic particle can appear as a wave and as a particle in different contexts. Complementarity not only set the scene for the next generation of research in physics after 1945, it superseded Einstein's comment that he could not believe that God "plays dice with the universe." Bohr was conscious of the extreme relativism of his theory if the same principle were applied in the social sciences. He speculated in the forties that societies are not hierarchically related, as the Social Darwinists had believed, but were related in a complementary way. We shall see that this kind of social relativism came to prevail in anthropology, where it is sometimes called the synchronic (comparative, complementary) approach, as opposed to the diachronic (historical) dimension of social categorization.

The uncertainty and complementarity principle thus spoke to the essentials of modernist culture and bridged the scientific world with philosophical, sociological, literary, and artistic trends. With the coming of relativity, uncertainty, and complementarity, the fixed, determinable macrocosmic Newtonian world had been displaced. A scientific revolution of unsurpassed magnitude had occurred, and—extending itself beyond physics into biology—this revolution is still playing itself out and deeply affecting our lives as well as our vision of the universe.

The media was for once quick to recognize the coming of a scientific revolution. REVOLUTION IN SCIENCE: NEW THEORY OF THE UNIVERSE. NEWTONIAN IDEAS OVERTHROWN, the *London Times* proclaimed in 1919. EINSTEIN THEORY TRIUMPHS echoed the *New York Times*. It is unfortunate that elementary and secondary education were so slow to respond, especially in the United States and Canada. In the forties most American and Canadian public schools were still teaching Newtonian physics and causing bored and confused students to memorize the laws of falling bodies.

The bovine inertia and parsimony of public school systems—new textbooks and informed physics teachers cost money—constituted a severe block for a generation in the dissemination of the new physics at the high school level—the only time most people ever take science courses. (At least Hiroshima had the beneficial effect of disturbing the American secondary school universe, the most impenetrable element in the world.)

Social and Behavioral Sciences Social and behavioral sciences were the creations of modernist culture. Except for some work in economics, there was nothing one would care to call, or recognize as, social science before the twentieth century. History was still entirely humanistic. Along with the novel approaches developed in other fields, with new courses of research, theories, and the new attitudes of professionalism, the social and behavioral sciences habilitated themselves in the universities for the first time during the modernist era.

There were three economists of stature before the twentieth century whose work remains significant. They were all British. Adam Smith was a Scottish professor of ethics, whose book *The Wealth of Nations,* published in 1776, created the theory of the market economy, and of the self-regulating invisible hand that is still central to the theory of market economy. This theory was fully developed by David Ricardo, a London Jewish banker, in the 1820s. He applied Adam Smith's precepts to labor, employment, and wages, expanding the former's simple market-oriented model to the whole of economic activity. Ricardo elaborated on issues such as unemployment as well as developing an elaborate theory of the workings of capital. Marx's knowledge of economics, for example, came almost entirely from David Ricardo.

The third great pre-twentieth-century economist was Alfred Marshall, who was a professor at Cambridge in the 1880s. Marshall's contribution was to introduce quantitative analysis to economics, to make, in other words, economic thought more analytic through quantitative projections.

John Maynard Keynes was a disciple of Marshall; he was a product of the Cambridge school of economics. Keynes came of one of the great Cambridge academic families, which achieved distinction in various fields and still continues to do so. Keynes was one of the Cambridge intellectuals of the closing years of the nineteenth century that in the 1920s came to be known as the Bloomsbury group in London. He was a friend of Virginia Woolf and her sister, Vanessa Bell, as well as of Lytton Strachey and the novelist E. M. Forster.

Like Strachey and Forster, Keynes was gay, or at least bisexual. He married a prominent Russian ballerina and was closely involved with the arts. He became the treasurer of his college, King's College at Cambridge, and, investing in the stock market for the college, greatly increased its income. Keynes first achieved prominence in 1919 as the British Treasury representative at the Versailles Peace Conference, when the British and the French imposed on the defeated Germans what Keynes called the Carthaginian peace. He published a book on the economic consequences of the peace in which he claimed that the heavy reparations being imposed on Germany would cause chaos and vast problems in Central Europe. Of course, he was absolutely right. Nonetheless, because of his public protest, Keynes was forced to resign from the Treasury.

For the next two decades, Keynes was an extremely influential professor at Cambridge. He reentered public service in 1939 and spent most of the war in Washington as economic liaison between the British and the Americans. After the war Keynes played the leading role in the establishment of a new international fiscal order. He died at the age of sixty-three in 1946. Keynes's contribution to economics was on par with Einstein's and Rutherford's to physics. Keynes was one of the culture heroes of modernism.

Keynes has three main ideas, two of which are commonly known, for his principles have become part of our culture and, particularly in the period between 1934 and 1974, were accepted as orthodoxy in the United States. As President Richard Nixon said in 1971, "We are all Keynesians now." Americans were nearly all Keynesians from the thirties through the early seventies. Beginning in the late seventies, there has been a fundamental reversal in economic doctrine and public policy, which is pointing once again in the direction of David Ricardo.

Keynes's first principle was that the market need not and should not be autonomous, that the state can intervene in order to make adjustments in the market. The argument of Smith, Ricardo, and Marshall had been that state intervention would consistently result in disasters and bad choices, and that in case of deflation, inflation, or unemployment, the market would have to be allowed, in spite of temporary mass suffering, to stabilize itself. They believed that eventually stability would reinstate itself, and that the state could and should not effect this result externally. Keynes interpreted this view as reflective of nineteenth-century historicism that did not meet modern standards, and claimed that the state could intervene in the economy through an act of will so as to reflate a depressed economy, actively reduce unemployment, and restore business confidence and activity.

Keynes designated the variety of ways in which this could be done: adjusting the money supply by printing more money; reducing taxes; making credit more accessible by lowering interest rates, thereby encouraging business resumption and expansion; and above all by directly providing work—undertaking public works programs and so providing employment. The essential solution was to stimulate aggregate demand by encouraging investment and dealing directly with unemployment through public works.

The state, then, according to Keynes, can and should undertake the regulation of the economy to the extent this is necessary to maintain economic equilibrium, and to prevent depression and breakdown. Keynes also pointed out the other end of the spectrum of possibilities, and stated that when the economy overheated, in the case of labor shortage, runaway speculation, overinvestment, and particularly in case of high inflation, the state ought to take restraining steps by, for example, increasing the price of credit. He never presented ways of dealing with inflation as clearly as he had set forth a program for dealing with deflation and depression. When he published his great treatise *The General Theory of Employment, Interest and Money* in 1936, the urgent problems were deflation and depression. When the Keynesians were in a position to deal with a booming economy in the sixties and seventies, a large-scale inflation occurred, and they did not have the means to contain it. Whether Keynes himself would have known how to deal with the inflationary crisis is an interesting question.

Keynes's ideas were taken up in American universities very quickly in the early thirties, with Harvard and Columbia universities in the lead. In the brain trust from the universities that Franklin Delano Roosevelt brought to Washington in 1933 to help restore the economy and restabilize the market were economists strongly committed to the Keynesian view of state intervention. The most prominent member of the Keynesian group at the time was the Harvard economist Seymour Harris, who became the chief Keynesian spokesman in the United States in the thirties and early forties. Another was Rexford G. Tugwell, a political scientist from Columbia University and a formidable and capable person. There were also a couple of young economists who went to work in Washington in the late thirties: John Kenneth Galbraith and Paul Samuelson. The former became a Harvard economist, and in the sixties a public official and vehement advocate of the welfare state. The latter became enormously famous as a Harvard economist and public commentator in the 1950s and 60s. Samuelson's textbook of economics, published in the early fifties, became the standard textbook used in American universities and indoctrinated a whole generation of college students in Keynesian economics.

Keynes's second, and enormously influential, proposition was that we are entitled to the good life. We are morally *entitled* to economic security, to health care, and above all, to enjoy the most important thing in the world, the arts. We have a right, in other words, to hear a symphony, to see a ballet, and nowadays, to watch public television. These do not constitute a privilege but a right in modern society. Accordingly, the economy and the government must operate so as to provide these entitlements. During and after World War II, this side of Keynesianism became increasingly more prominent. It became a dogma in Western Europe and informed the development of the welfare state in all European countries. It was a much more controversial proposition in the United States.

The first country to take up the Keynesian principle of entitlement on a grand scale was Sweden. The other Scandinavian countries followed suit, and have maintained the policy to this day, as did the new German Federal Republic, Britain, and France. A prime disciple of Keynes in this context, aside from the large group of continental economists and politicians, was the English economist William Beveridge, who in 1942 published the Beveridge Plan, which in turn became the blueprint for the British welfare state that was put into action between 1945 and 1951 under the socialist government.

In the United States, the Keynesian doctrine of entitlement became fully active in the 1960s under the Johnson administration, and—although this fact may conflict with leftist mythology—it was continued vehemently under the Nixon and Ford administrations. It was only with the Carter administration that the idea of entitlement began to weaken, and continued to do so until its partial reversal under Ronald Reagan. In the sixties and seventies, neo-Ricardian economists at the University of Chicago, led by Milton Friedman, attacked the idea of entitlement, and argued that persons were entitled only to what the market afforded them. Efforts to reduce student aid, Medicare, and federal support for the arts in the early eighties were part of the neo-Ricardian, anti-Keynesian movement that achieved power in the Reagan administration.

The final proposition Keynes advocated was that the international economic system could only function effectively as an international fiscal order. The organized integration of the world's currency and fiscal standard was necessary so as to achieve stability. Keynes believed very strongly that the disaster that had led to Nazism was the consequence of the breakdown of fiscal order in the twenties, and that nothing could be more likely to lead to totalitarianism, either of the Left or of the Right, than fiscal disorder, since this was above all likely to impoverish and demoralize the middle class. At the Bretton Woods Conference in New Hampshire in 1944, a world fiscal standard was achieved that related to the British pound and the American dollar. Eventually, by the mid-fifties, because of the impoverishment of England, the standard became simply a world-dollar currency, and every country's currency became fixed to the American dollar. In many cases the relationship was fixed artificially high in order to protect weaker economies. This was the reason why American tourists could go to Europe in the fifties and buy local lire and marks on the black market at favorable rates of exchange.

Keynes had argued that this uniform fiscal standard would stabilize world economy, and again he turned out to be right. The rapid development of European prosperity and the unprecedented industrial growth in Japan were made possible by the Bretton Woods agreement. In 1972 the United States rashly abandoned this agreement, and allowed the value of the dollar to float, resulting in fiscal volatitilty on the international scale. The floating American dollar has occasioned various kinds of dislocations of the world fiscal order since the United States abandoned the Keynesian agreement. The negative impact of this reversal on the Third World and Latin American countries has been particularly unfortunate. Once again Keynes has been shown to be an economic prophet.

It is agreed that the term "sociology" had been in existence before 1900. Looking at histories of sociological doctrine, one comes across nineteenth-century names like August Comte and Herbert Spencer, both of whom produced nothing more than garbled ideologies. The discipline of sociology truly finds its origins at the beginning of the twentieth century with the work of two great social thinkers, the German Max Weber and the French Émile Durkheim. They are the twin founders, the Romulus and Remus, of twentieth-century sociology. They were exact contemporaries and they died, respectively, in 1920 and 1917. Strangely enough they never met, and it is doubtful that they ever read each other's works. One reason why they may not have been familiar with each other's work was the deep political tension between Germany and France at the time.

Weber is a phenomenal figure whose influence began to be felt in the early years of the century, but has actually grown since the 1950s. He is only partly a modernist. He is idealist to a considerable degree; a more precise designation of his thought would be neo-Kantian. Weber's background in nineteenth-century thought also explains the growth of his importance since the fifties, for this was the time when neo-Victorian ideas again began to receive attention.

Weber is hard to read at times, and only about a quarter of his writings have been translated into English.

Weber came from a upper-middle-class Prussian family of civil servants. He was trained as a historian, and did important work in the economic history of Rome. Then he proceeded to create a new discipline, and occupied the first chair of sociology in Germany. He was universally admired and respected. Shortly before the First World War, he had a nervous breakdown, after which he did not return to teaching, although he continued to write. (It is a curious coincidence that the sister of D. H. Lawrence's aristocratic German wife was the mistress first of Max Weber and then of Weber's brother. Although the sisters occasionally corresponded, the novelist and sociologist had no contact with each other.)

Weber makes two fundamental propositions, the first of which is contained in his theory of ideal types. The occurrence of social change is shaped by the interaction of ideal forces that are cultural and moral, and that interact in order to create a new ethos. He applied this idea to the rise of capitalism in his most famous book *The Protestant Ethic and the Spirit of Capitalism.* Here Weber explains the emergence of capitalism by the new ethic propounded by Protestantism. This ethic Weber calls "the inner-worldly asceticism," that is, the asceticism of working in the world instead of in the monastery, as was allegedly done in the Middle Ages. Medieval asceticism was replaced by the new one that had been introduced by Protestantism into middle-class life.

This worldly asceticism, as it were, created a work ethic and fostered capital accumulation. It advocated the postponement of personal gratification, which translates into economic terms as savings. It was the Protestant ethic, advocating hard work and delayed satisfaction, that created capitalism. Without this work ethic neither capital accumulation nor the capitalist mentality would have come about. Weber was self-consciously anti-Marxist. It is ideas that shape social forces, he believed, not vice versa, as Marx advocated.

Weber's second theory, which still enjoys influence among political scientists, pertains to government. He identifies three types of government: the traditional or tribal, which is found in early, communal societies; the charismatic government of religious, mystical, dynamic leaders who assume a religious vocation of leadership on the force of their personality, and are taken as gods; and modern bureaucratic government. Weber was the first to identify that the modern tendency in what we now call both the public and the private sector is in the direction of bureaucracy and management. This phenomenon was referred to in the thirties as the "managerial revolution." Modern government and administration, at all levels of public and business life, is marked by the managerial and bureaucratic domination. People working in offices—that is the shape of the future according to Weber, and his prediction has been proved correct. He foresaw the world populated by M.B.A.'s.

What he did not foresee, however, was that there could be a union of the tribal, charismatic, and bureaucratic forms of government. This very explosive, terrible, and catastrophic union, which occurred in Germany in the 1930s, Weber did not anticipate. Essentially Weber was a neo-Kantian historicist who thought in terms of developmental stages over time. The possibility of a contraction of the past and the present into an explosive future was not discernible to him. Therein, he is very much a nineteenth-century mind who had visions of continuity. He explained how this continuity occurred through the interaction of ideal types. Because what happens in social change is the interaction of ideal types within consciousness, Weber was to a degree a phenomenologist. But he was concerned to plot the movement of value systems over time, making him a historicist.

Consequently, Weber did not get much of a hearing in the modernist era, that is, in the 1920s and 1930s, even though he was respected. It was only with the partial revival of historicism, after the Second World War, that Weber achieved his current prominence in sociology.

The seminal modernist mind in sociology was the French professor Émile Durkheim. Durkheim is the creator of sociology as we know it. Eighty percent of the topics studied in sociology departments of universities today are in line with Durkheim's constitution of the discipline. Durkheim is a leading modernist mind not only in terms of his thought, but also in terms of the way he behaved and conducted his professional life.

The characteristics of Durkheim's thought can be gathered around three essential principles. One is quantification. This principle, which, as we have seen, is also present in the work of Rutherford and the experimental physicists, prescribes the gathering of data for eventual quantification in an aggregate manner. It consists of establishing core data that will provide an observable pattern, and entails the rejection of anomalous outriders. In other words, it is not necessary according to this principle to have a 100 percent correlation in data. It suffices to record data sufficiently correlated in an aggregate manner for a social pattern to emerge.

The principle of quantification was applied in particular to population and health statistics, as well as to the undertaking of public opinion polls, or for what nowadays is called survey research. Graduate study in sociology today means above all training in conducting survey research for positions in political polling, market research, and advertising firms. Durkheim discerned this opportunity for applied social research.

The second idea Durkheim developed was that small marginal differences were significant. In evaluating social data, attention is to be paid to the differences at the margins, which constitute the most compelling information to be obtained from a particular body of data. To cite an example from Durkheim's own work: That the annual suicide rate in Sweden is higher by 2 or 3 percent than the one in France constitutes a significant factor. To a nineteenth-century mind this difference would have had no significance whatsoever. Nineteenth-century sociologists would first have sought a very large body of data, and then looked for substantial difference in order to attribute any value to the data. Durkheim, however, saw the importance of small differences. Having established the validity of the small difference, Durkheim proceeded to try to determine why the difference occurred. Durkheim's identification of the importance of marginal differences and extrapolation of meaning from this number was made possible by the expansion of statistical science in his day.

Durkheim's third idea was the theory of social operation, which has come to be referred to as functionalism. Durkheim believed that a given society is an enclosed field in which the various aspects of this society, such as the political, the economic, and the religious, interact with one another, that they are functions of one another. Therefore, one of the prime objects of sociological inquiry is to show the interaction of these enclosed social dimensions. How, in other words, religion is related to the political life in a given society, or what relationship exists between family structure and economic life, were questions the sociologist had to ask. To answer them was the main purpose of sociological thinking.

Furthermore, it was Durkheim's view that societies operate so as to sustain themselves. He believed that societies had strong self-preservative tendencies, and that when an anomaly or novelty appeared in one social domain, then all the other domains would operate on the newcomer in order to socialize it. Socialization means the integration of the novelty into the customary operative mode of the society in order that that society may continue to function without engaging in disharmony or dislocation. An obvious example of the preservative or socializing quality in recent American history would be that of the New Left of the late sixties. The tendency, strong and explicit, to socialize the Left, not only transformed many leftists into professors, but also enabled an agitator like Jane Fonda to make a fortune from exercise videos and to marry a conservative communications magnate. Her ex-husband, Tom Hayden, a one-time prominent radical leftist leader and a founder of the Students for a Democratic Society, became in the 1980s a moderate and liberal California state senator. This is a simple, obvious but telling example, which Durkheim would have found to his taste. He would have pointed out how society had once again found ways to assimilate and socialize the most radical rebels.

A further aspect of Durkheim's theory was the notion of anomie. Durkheim believed that a society can be threatened with disintegration when the value system becomes discrepant with the institutional system. If, that is, the ways in which people behave and organize themselves in a given society develop into directions that are discordant with the value system, we are face to face with an anomic situation that can bring about a breakdown and a revolution. He also, however, finds this anomic rupture to be an extremely rare occurrence, although it can and does happen, owing to conservation and socialization in society.

These conservatizing or socializing societal forces are so powerful that the threat of anomie almost always remains momentary, and is normally overcome by resolution of the conflict. Values bend a little, as do institutions, behavior is adapted, ideas adjusted, and society continues to function as an integrated system. The anomaly or discordancy has been absorbed into the prevailing order, which is slightly modified to achieve the accommodation.

Durkheim's ideas are still central in sociological thinking. Until the late sixties, aside from the doctrines of Max Weber, sociology had no other systematic theory than that provided by Durkheim. Whether sociologists have actually gone much beyond Durkheim today is a moot point.

Durkheim's impact on sociology is ascribed not only to his way of thinking, but as well to his way of behaving. Durkheim was the grand patron, to adopt a French expression, of social science. His role in French social science was identical to that of Rutherford in British physics. He was named to the Collège de France, which is the French equivalent of the Princeton Institute for Advanced Study, and used this position to amass extended patronage by which he could fund his students and the researchers sympathetic to his principles. He pioneered in making sociology an academic discipline, granting doctoral degrees, and finding research grants and employment for his students.

Durkheim also played an important role in the French educational system in the first quarter of this century, a role very similar to the one John Dewey played in the American educational world in the 1930s and 1940s. In fact, Durkheim began his teaching career as a professor of education and, even after establishing himself as sociologist, he continued to teach prospective high school teachers. To these, he propounded a doctrine of secular nationalism, in order to divest education of Catholic teaching, to drive religion out of the schools, and to spread a message of patriotism based on sociology. The twentieth-century French lycée, or public high school, was in many ways his monument.

Durkheim was a liberal Parisian Jew (he was, like another paragon of social theory, the anthropologist Claude Lévi-Strauss, from a rabbinical family) who was painfully conscious of the bitter conflicts over church-state relations in France during the early years of the century. He was aware that rightist Catholic intellectuals were not only combating efforts to secularize education but were also, in many instances, contributing to the growing anti-Semitism in the French press. Durkheim brought all his intellectual and professional resources to the support of the liberal, anticlerical majority in the Third Republic. For him sociology represented the party of rationality that ought to prevail over religious traditions and clerical institutions. This attitude gave his sociology a political relevance that attracted eager and capable young people from the liberal-Left spectrum. It also predisposed the discipline of sociology to a left-wing orientation from which it has, with a few distinguished exceptions, never departed and on account of which the scientific credibility of the discipline has been questioned.

In the thirties and forties Durkheim gained two important disciples in the United States, who shaped American sociology as it is practiced today. One of these was the American Talcott Parsons, who came from a fairly wealthy Boston family and was educated in Europe, became professor of sociology at Harvard in the mid-thirties, and dominated theoretical sociology in this country for the next forty years. Parsons's classic but largely unreadable book *The Structure of Social Action* (1937) is a lengthy presentation of Durkheim's functionalist theory. It remained unchallenged until the late 1960s.

The other disciple of Durkheim was a prolific scholar and academic entrepreneur who worked in the area of quantitative and survey research: Paul Lazarsfeld, an Austrian émigré who had come to the United States in the mid-thirties and become professor of sociology at Columbia. Lazarsfeld dominated applied research in sociology for the following three decades. He established the Bureau of Applied Social Research at Columbia, which was enormously influential and powerful through the sixties.

Lazarsfeld applied Durkheim's theories of quantitative survey research, organized vast numbers of graduate students and young researchers to undertake pioneering studies in political polling, and also entered into close collaboration with market research and advertising firms. Sociology was supported at Columbia, especially in the forties and fifties, by Lazarsfeld's contacts with polling and market research firms. Preferences shown for one political party or brand over another—the competition between Coca-Cola and Pepsi, for example—were domains to which Lazarsfeld applied Durkheim's theory. He demonstrated that 4 percent preferred one drink over another, and explained the marginal preference just as Durkheim had explained the suicide rate in Sweden in relationship to that in France by using his method of quantitative analysis. Through Lazarsfeld, Durkheim's sociology had a strong impact on American business.

Contemporaneous with the rise of sociology along the lines of modernist ideas was that of anthropology. Wherein lies the difference between the disciplines of soiology and anthropology, both products of modernist culture? By the 1930s these social sciences had developed distinctive methodologies that separated them in that respect. But it was in the early years of the twentieth century that the two began to be distinguished from each other simply by their subject matter. Sociology dealt with modern commercial and industrial societies; anthropology with early, premodern ones. Anthropology may be described as the modernist behavioral science in its purest form. There had indeed been anthropologists in the nineteenth century. But as we have noted, their work, primarily Social Darwinist or what would nowadays be called racist in orientation, is practically unreadable today. Today nineteenth-century anthropology has only historical value; it is prescientific.

The beginning of a transition to modernist anthropology occurred with the work of Sir James Frazer, a British ethnographer (student of early societies) who published in 1890 the first edition of his famous book *The Golden Bough*, which for many decades was esteemed as having primary importance in the field. Frazer pointed the way toward a departure from social Darwinism and nineteenth-century ideology in two respects. First, he was a functionalist— that is, he amassed a large body of data, about magic for instance, a topic he explored, without condemning it as superstitious or primitive, in order to discuss it in terms of how it operated in early societies. He treated magical practices as a form of social cohesion, and refrained from making moral judgments about them.

Frazer effected a transition to social relativism in his field, in that he was cautious about making distinctions between so-called advanced and primitive societies. He deliberately avoided using language that would evaluate societies in hierarchic terms.

Frazer lived until 1941. During his long lifetime, his *The Golden Bough,* which originally consisted of two volumes, grew into a gigantic thirteen-volume compendium of anthropological data. However, Frazer could not wholly break away from evolutionary ideas. There remained in his work traces of historicism. Nor is he what might properly be called a twentieth-century anthropologist, for he remained to the very end an armchair anthropologist. This is a typical feature of nineteenth-century social scientists, among whom Herbert Spencer could be cited. Frazer conducted his work in libraries, compiling data from reports written by missionaries and sea captains. He did not personally encounter the people he described; he assimilated information about them from the libraries of Oxford University. This research method, needless to say, has become thoroughly obsolete and prescientific in anthropology.

The creator of scientific anthropology was the German Jew Franz Boas, who received his original training in Germany as a geographer. He became interested in ethnography, the science that studies early peoples. He came to the United States, partly because he was sensitive to the anti-Semitism that prevailed in the German academic world in the first decades of the twentieth century, and began to work for the Marshall Field Museum in Chicago, one of the three great museums of ethnography in America, the other two being the Smithsonian, which became a government operation in the late nineteenth century, and the Museum of Natural History in New York. The Field Museum was founded by the liberal Chicago department store magnate.

The Field Museum undertook to support research among premodern peoples, sending out scientists to live among the peoples to be studied and to gather information and acquire artifacts. Boas was dispatched to Vancouver Island, on the west coast of Canada. Although the first research team Boas worked on was mainly sent out to collect totem poles (the Field Museum, like most anthropological museums of the time, was interested in acquiring these), he lived on Vancouver among the Indians, or "native Canadians," as they are called now, for several years and closely observed their way of life.

Among his discoveries on this field trip was that the Canadian government was destroying the social nexus of the Indians, who had devised their own monetary value, objects exchanged in a ceremony called "potlatch" by anthropologists, which the government arbitrarily declared to be useless. The native Indian currency was quickly devalued to point zero, with the result that families that had spent decades accumulating this distinctive wealth were pauperized overnight.

This led Boas to see that these societies presented very different qualities when considered from the inside, that they had their own systems, values, and ways of functioning, which to a Western Caucasian might appear primitive and crude, but which were in many cases very elaborate and sophisticated "thick cultures." He saw, in other words, the necessity of comprehending these cultures in their own terms and in self-referential contexts. This constitutes precisely the main principle of twentieth-century anthropology. The twentieth-century anthropologist, of whom Boas is the prototype, lives with the people he or she studies, eats their food, attends their meetings, learns their language, and tries to experience their family and value systems and understand behavior patterns from within the culture.

Boas became the founder and chairman of the Anthropology Department at Columbia University, which under his aegis, between 1910 and 1930, was the greatest anthropology department in the world. This is no longer the case, since the university administration has allowed it to run down shamefully, but the scientific tradition that Boas started has been continued in other universities, particularly at Chicago and Berkeley.

Aside from the necessity of doing field work, which undertakes the "close reading" of societies while assuming that the alien culture that is studied is as thick and complicated as the anthropologist's own, Boas propounded the view of total cultural relativism. This doctrine enunciates the impossibility of establishing a hierarchy of societies, since every society, claims Boas, is valuable and must be evaluated in its own terms. This assumption about cultural relativity is accompanied by the dismantling of the evolutionary view. Boas holds that societies are not evolving toward a supreme *telos* (ultimate end); they simply exist. Each consists of its own self-enclosed system of functional operations. Societies are not transforming themselves into one another. This is known as the synchronic (comparative), as opposed to the diachronic (historical), view of societies.

The diachronic was the nineteenth-century evolutionary view, which holds that societies are moving in a predetermined direction and, needless to say, that direction is the state of England in 1890 or the United States in 1950. The other view, the synchronic, is nonhistorical, nonevolutionary, nondevelopmental, and relativistic; it studies cultures in themselves. These are the fundamental principles, established by Boas, on which the discipline of social anthropology now operates.

Boas had many students. Perhaps the most memorable among them were two women, Ruth Benedict and Margaret Mead. Ruth Benedict came from a farming family in upstate New York. She went through a long struggle to obtain education. Eventually she became Boas's prime disciple and a professor at Barnard College, a position she held until she died at a young age in 1945.

In the forties it was possible to find copies of Ruth Benedict's *Patterns of Culture* not only in every bookstore, but practically in every drugstore in America. This book, of which hundreds of thousands of copies have been sold, is the all-time bestseller of anthropology. It is a study of various early societies in the American Southwest and the East Indies. It studies these cultures in terms of their own value systems from an entirely relativistic stance. Ruth Benedict was in addition a very fine writer. A compelling piece of work that is still very much worth reading, the book is, in fact, one of the great classics of modernist literature.

Margaret Mead was Benedict's student—and, for a short while, her lover. Although Benedict never married, Margaret Mead had three husbands and a child, who is also an anthropologist and a professor at Amherst. Although Columbia University often advertised her as a member of the faculty, in fact Margaret Mead never became more than an adjunct professor there. Through her long career she was a member of the staff of the Museum of Natural History.

Among her numerous books, the first and most famous is *Coming of Age in Samoa*, which she wrote on the basis of field research in Samoa in 1925. Although Mead's methods were not always controlled and systematic, *Coming of Age in Samoa* is still a fascinating book.

Margaret Mead's main interest was in comparative sexuality, and her aim was to show a complete alternative to repressive, puritanical, middle-class sexuality. She herself was a liberated woman who believed in open marriage. The purpose of *Samoa*, as well as many of her later books, was to remove what remained of Christian and Puritan standards of sexual behavior and marriage. Mead had very considerable influence in developing new sexual standards in this country. Her visibility revived during the countercultural movement of the sixties, which she espoused and helped to legitimize.

Along with sociology and anthropology, modernism manifests itself in the discipline of psychology as well. We shall see in the next chapter that early psychoanalysis and the work of Freud until 1920 fully cohere with modernism, although later developments in psychoanalysis point in a different direction.

Psychoanalysis, however, was not the only approach to the psyche that was developed in the modernist era. Behaviorism, which exhibits much of the radical, rationalist and microcosmic temperament that was so essential to modernist thought, constitutes a second direction taken by psychology. It has already been pointed out that the philosopher William James was the founder of behaviorist psychology.

James's great European disciple was the Russian physiologist Ivan Pavlov, who conducted the famous conditioning experiments with dogs. Pavlov exercised a dominant influence on Soviet psychology, which rejected psychoanalysis, just as nonrepresentational art was rejected in that country, as a product of decadent bourgeois culture. Behaviorist psychology was hailed in the 1920s as the psychology of the Soviet man and woman. The answer to the Soviet problem of breaking away from peasant forms of behavior was found in behaviorist psychology and in its tools of conditioning, which found wide application in Soviet society, including the gulag.

James's important American disciple was John Watson, founder of the American school of behaviorist psychology. In departments of psychology today, at least 60 percent of the work that is conducted is still along behavioral lines. This involves, above all, quantitative analysis—close scrutiny of minutiae, that is, very small segments of behavior, and the plotting of it quantitatively. To make this concrete: The quality of a behaviorist department of psychology can be recognized by the number of computers it owns.

Watson was a professor at Johns Hopkins University in Baltimore in the second and third decades of the century. After his sexual involvment with a woman graduate student became a public scandal, he was forced to resign by the university president. Watson moved to New York City and, applying his behaviorist psychology in the advertising business, became wealthy. It is a peculiar fact that another pioneer in American advertising in the 1930s was Edward Bernays, a Viennese Jewish émigré who was the uncle of Sigmund Freud's wife. Behavioral psychology and psychoanalysis met in the emerging manipulative advertising firms on Madison Avenue.

There was a utopian strain in American behaviorial psychology that is implicit in the work of Watson and his disciples in the twenties and thirties. It became explicit in Watson's most prominent disciple B. F. Skinner, who was, for three decades, a leading professor at Harvard. Skinner's book *Beyond Freedom and Dignity* presents the social and ethical theory of behavioral psychology. There is a strong modernist quality in his message.

Humanistic doctrines of freedom, Skinner claims, belong to the mystifications of nineteenth-century ethics. A good society is simply one in which people are appropriately conditioned to relate to their environment, and are adapted in their behavior patterns so as to be good citizens. Problems of crime are not solved by talking to and trying to persuade people; they are solved by conditioning environments from the time of a person's birth through their adolescence, as individuals are shaped to be the kind of people that are socially desired. Only this highly controlled environmental operation will preclude deviance and social pathology. Essentially Skinner's message is identical to Pavlov's and that of Soviet behaviorists. This view has been much more strongly resisted in this country than it was in the Soviet Union.

In the field of legal education and legal theory there was also a great upheaval through the application of modernist ideas in the first thirty years of this century. The first law school in the United States that is worthy of the name was Harvard Law School, from about 1890 on. Before that law schools were unintellectual places in which professors gave stereotyped lectures of either a rhetorical or a historical nature.

Two professors of law at Harvard University transformed the study of law between 1890 and 1920, and constituted law as an academic discipline. They also served as deans of the Harvard Law School. The first was the innovative educator Christopher Columbus Langdell, and the other and better-known one was Roscoe Pound, who was regarded in his day as the greatest legal mind in America—an esteem he did not really deserve. Nevertheless, he, like Langdell, was a great educator.

Instead of listening to lectures and memorizing textbooks, the students of Langdell and Pound did close readings of judicial decisions. Just as the modernist conception of the effective method of understanding poetry was to read the poem word by word in order to reconstruct its imaginative structure, so the way to learn law was understood as reading the decisions of the Federal Court of Appeals, and reconstructing the (allegedly) rational minds and course of reasoning of the federal judges. This is known as the case method.

Instead of lecturing, the professor of law now discussed case studies in class, analyzing the matter from printed texts—much the same method that Eliot, Richards, and Leavis used in literature. The close-reading method in law was similarly self-referential in its textuality. This modernist method is still used in law schools.

Because of his application of the American philosophy of pragmatism and the modernist doctrine of relativism to legal theory, Pound was also an influential theorist of law. Two prominent legal minds who advanced this doctrine further were Oliver Wendell Holmes, Jr., another product of Harvard Law School who became a Supreme Court justice, and Felix Frankfurter, who was a professor of law at Harvard before being appointed to the Court. The principles of legal pragmatism and relativism were most fully developed by Jerome

Frank, a federal judge, and Karl Llewellyn, an academic legal scholar at Columbia University.

The pragmatist-relativist approach to law, which became very prominent in the thirties and forties, was called legal realism, although "legal pragmatism" would have been a more accurate designation for the approach. Legal realism stands in contrast to legal formalism. The latter entailed the derivation of law from abstract principles such as natural law, or inversely, the evolving discovery of abstract principles in laws. Where formalism sought to discern the perpetuation of abstracted historical patterns and philosophical and ethical principles, legal realism regarded the law as thoroughly flexible and instrumental. Law was viewed as synchronic, contemporary, relativist, and instrumental in the pragmatist's sense of the term.

According to legal realism, law is the servant of social reform and the means of exercising power. In order to understand the present state of the law, one does not begin by studying Magna Carta or the intentions of the founders of the Constitution or the impact of natural law, but by investigating how legal decisions serve the interests of corporate or other groups that hold political power. Llewellyn's formulation of legal realism was particularly radical. He refused to give to lawmaking any special legitimacy or separation from other social acts. Whereas Pound, Holmes, Frankfurter, and Frank to varying degrees sought to preserve some autonomy and distinctiveness for legal determinations, Llewellyn conceded that legal realism cannot sustain this traditional valorization of law.

American legal realism, having eroded the legitimacy of prevailing legal doctrines associated with conservative economic and political groups, proceeded to envision new attitudes and principles that serve reforming and progressive interests and underprivileged groups.

This theory fitted in very well with the New Deal. When Franklin Roosevelt introduced the New Deal, along with new regulations for business and Social Security, he encountered a conservative Supreme Court that held that the changes proposed by Roosevelt conflicted with the Constitution. The legal realists replied to this by pointing out that the Constitution was not a fixed document, but that it always admitted of change in relation to social needs and the demands of those in power. From the realist point of view, to insist on the conservative faith in abstract constitutionality is to indulge in misguided nostalgia for Victorian formalism and historicism. The new approach did prevail, albeit after a lot of pressure from the White House.

In the late 1930s Roscoe Pound belatedly warned that the legal realists, by divorcing law from ethics, legitimized the Nazi terror state as well as the New Deal. The legal realists on law school faculties were not inclined to be concerned with Pound's warning because legal realism had served the New Deal and the Roosevelt administration well, and in turn the expansion of the regulatory and welfare state in the 1930s provided a large pool of new jobs for graduates of the better law schools. Armed with their legal realist doctrine, heedless of whether the new federal agencies that employed them operated within traditional constitutional boundaries, the young law school graduates enjoyed not only steady and respectable employment in Washington, D.C., but bureaucratic power. Young men (women law school graduates were still very scarce) who had never seen a cow or a plow close up found themselves drafting agricultural legislation that transformed American farming operations; some of these regulations are still federal law in the 1990s, a monument to the heyday of legal realism.

History and Theology There are two other areas to be discussed in which modernism manifested itself before 1940, namely history and theology. These are not domains that immediately lend themselves to modernist transformations because modernism is intrinsically anti-historical, and Western theology is by its very nature related to the Judaic and Christian views of the world, with their bias toward the traditional. It would be the measure of the power of modernism if it were indeed seen to have penetrated even these fields. And it did. The results of the penetration yielded new frontiers in historical thinking and revivified theology.

In order for historians to remain intellectually current, they had to adapt themselves to modernist ways of thinking. They encountered the formidable challenge of writing non-narrative history, a new mode of analytical history that reflected the method of close reading of a segment of past society and avoided the longitudinal projection of narrative histories that covered long-term developments, which was the fashionable mode of the nineteenth century.

A number of historians did rise to this challenge. The three most influential were the Dutchman Johan Huizinga, the Anglo-Polish Lewis Namier, and the American Frederick Jackson Turner. Huizinga was a graduate student at the University of Leiden when, in 1903, he organized the first exhibition of van Gogh's paintings in the painter's native country. Huizinga in fact proceeded to write a history that resembled van Gogh's paintings, at least the later van Gogh of sunflowers. Huizinga is an impressionist historian who takes a certain moment in time, such as the fifteenth century in his famous book *The Autumn of the Middle Ages,* and renders practically hundreds of detailed impressions of aspects of the culture, particularly stressing the arts and literature and what they communicate, as well as the behavioral patterns of the nobility. He attempts to construct an impressionistic model of fifteenth-century culture.

Lewis Namier came from the northeastern (Polish) stretches of the Austro-Hungarian Empire. His family were wealthy Jewish landowners. He was educated in England, where he spent most of his adult life. He taught first at the University of Manchester, then at the University of London. In the thirties and forties he was the dominant figure in British historiography.

Namier's approach can be described as radical positivism or realism. He focuses his attention on the eighteenth-century English constitution, and radically deconstructs it, eliminating the ideational content. Edmund Burke is dismissed as a mere propagandist as Namier assumes a severely functional approach to eighteenth-century Parliament. He asks how exactly Parliament operated in the eighteenth century and what the realities were within which the party system operated. He discards the ways in which people hoped the system functioned, or described it as functioning, and tries to uncover how it actually did function.

Namier too builds up a model from amassed data, the data being biographical for the most part. Namier set in motion the vast project of establishing the biography of every member of the eighteenth-century English Parliament. It took him and several associates twenty years to accomplish this, but they constructed a working model of the actual operations of the political system. Most relevant were patronage, corruption, and the actual reasons of "interest," for which people wind up in a particular political configuration as opposed to another. Namier dealt with the availability of jobs, wealth, influence, and gave no credence to ideology. Namier's is a highly functional, radical-positivistic approach, which aims primarily at political analysis without illusions or sentiments. Compared to the romanticization of the English past that had prevailed in the nineteenth and early twentieth centuries, Namier's work was revolutionary.

Not only because his middle name was Bernstein and because he was a fervent Zionist, but mainly because of his harsh modernist delegitimizing of ethical constructs in the English political system, Namier aroused deep resentment at Oxford and Cambridge and was persistently denied a chair in the old universities. But he was Britain's leading historian from the mid-thirties until the early sixties.

The third of the great triumvirate of analytic modernist historians was the

American Frederick Jackson Turner, a midwesterner who taught at the University of Wisconsin, and then at Harvard in the twenties and early thirties. Turner's approach was to find a reductionist or microcosmic factor in American history—some particle phenomenon, that is, that was not immediately visible but that lay underneath the surface of events, and had shaped the surface phenomena. Turner found this factor to be the frontier. It was the frontier, he claimed, that molded American culture and society and created its values and practices, at least down to the closing of the frontier in the 1890s.

Obviously one way of dealing with the modernist challenge to historical writing was to become more reductionist. The method was to find beneath the surface narrative a single factor that was driving the whole culture or society. Turner presented one model of how this method could be put to work in his frontier thesis. Thereby, he also opened the way to the popularity of Marxist reductionism.

Although there are some common elements in modern developments in Catholic, Protestant, and Jewish theology, each should be dealt with separately, with a view to its distinctive features. The greatest theologian of the twentieth century was the Swiss Calvinist Karl Barth, who published his work in the twenties. Barth was closely affected by modernist culture, and most immediately influenced by Heidegger and phenomenology. The catastrophe of the First World War is also among events to which he reacted very strongly.

Barthean theology owes a substantial debt to Saint Augustine. Barth is a neo-Augustinian, a school of which some aspects had been anticipated in the nineteenth century by the Danish theologian Søren Kierkegaard. In fact, Barth contributed significantly to the making of Kierkegaard's popularity in this century.

Barth's contention was that nineteenth-century liberal theology had been undermined by modernist culture and proved bankrupt by the moral catastrophe of World War I, which showed that human society was not getting better, that man was not improving, and that the advancement of Christian morality was not as visible as Victorians had anticipated. These were the starting assumptions of Barth's radical neo-Augustinianism.

Man does not change, according to Barth, and human nature is not affected by history. Man is still old Adam, he is still sinful, and as evil as he has always been. The fundamental fact of human nature is the microact of sin, which constitutes man's rebellion against God; and the fundamental fact of human life, in turn, is the evil that exists in the human heart, and that we are rescued from it only by the love of God, or actually by God's love of us.

1

2

3

4

5

7

8

9

10

11

12

13

14

15

16

17

18

19

20

21

22

23

24

25

26

27

28

29

30

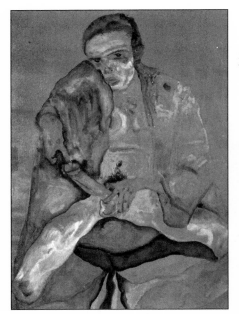

31

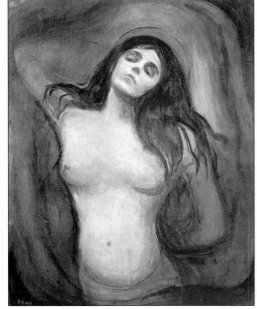

32

33

34

35

36

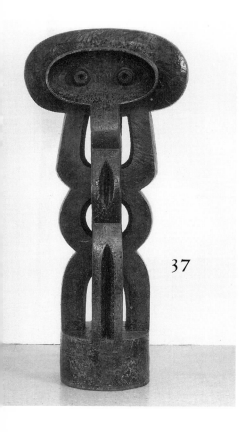

37

38

39

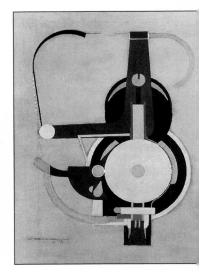

40

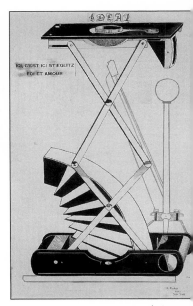

IGI, C'EST IGI STIEGLITZ
FOI ET AMOUR

41

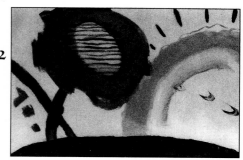

42

43

44

45

46

47

48

49

MODERNISM PICTURE ESSAY

Nineteenth-century artists in Paris documented the technological transformation of the city and its life. Monet painted the train station, the symbol of modernity, in his luminous and atmospheric impressionist style. Renoir portrayed an experience of light and color in an outdoor dance hall lit by gaslight. Manet, considered the first modernist painter, depicted the progressive writer Zola, with a Japanese landscape, and a Japanese warrior that refers to Manet. The flat, decorative surfaces of Japanese art had an important influence on the work of French artists. Degas's painting of a woman in a tub is a study of flattened forms, more abstract than real. Toulouse-Lautrec portrayed bourgeois nightlife in jarring color and Japanese perspective. Seurat's meticulously organized color system of patterned dots is coolly rational and abstract. Van Gogh's intense color and sweeping brushstrokes express his fluctuating emotional condition in the bloom and decay of sunflowers. Gauguin's Tahiti paintings portray symbolic patterns of bold color and line, embracing the exotic and primitive. Cézanne analyzed nature into geometric abstractions in his studies of bathers. Matisse's wild, exuberant color and decorative patterned compositions create a new kind of space in which his figures actively move. Heckel's German expressionist bathers reflect African influence. Inspired by Cézanne, Picasso's cubist analyses of women also show his interest in Iberian and African sculpture. Braque and Picasso together developed the analytical cubist style of flattening objects into planes of tonal color. Gris brought light and color to cubism while Gleizes expanded its range with expressive and lyrical curvilinear shapes. American modernists studied in Paris in the early 1900s. Weber, an American cubist, assimilated Parisian aesthetics and resembled Gris in his patterned planes yet demonstrated the energy of futurism. Duchamp's nude, causing a sensation at the New York Armory Show of 1913, exhibits a dynamism that relates more to futurism than to cubism. Delaunay painted a monument of technology against patterns of circular shapes that give a sense of rapid movement and fragmentation. The American modernist Marin focused on a technological monument in New York City that shows the influence of Parisian artists' spontaneous color and the dynamism of futurism. Kandinsky, working in Munich, was influenced by Delaunay, who developed a formula of colored circles and shapes that had no reference to nature, called orphism. Kandinsky based his theories on the harmony of line and color and their mystical communication of sensation from theosophy. Kupka's abstraction of color shapes, like Delaunay's, creates an abstract world of vibrating, rotating color circles. Macdonald-Wright, an American modernist, adopted cubism and the style of Delaunay and Kupka into a color movement called synchronism. Severini, working in Paris, and Balla formulated the movement of Italian futurism, which combined French cubist influence with a strong ideological message of the dynamism of modern technology. The Italian American Stella brought futurism to New York with an intense surface dynamism and the romantic ideal of a city exploding with energy. Lewis, leader of the British vorticists (similar to the futurists), stressed the machine and technology. The Russian constructivist Malevich took cubist geometry to pure abstraction, called suprematism; and Kandinsky, after returning to Russia during World War I and then working in Germany at the Bauhaus, changed to the geometric abstraction of the constructivists. Mondrian's utopian art sought to express universals through a dynamic balance of vertical and horizontal linear structure and harmonious color relationships. Léger's precision of machine forms and mechanical figures is a tribute to the machine age. Klimt, the leader of the anti-establishment Viennese Secession, was reacting against Victorian repressed sexuality, portraying the emotionally felt union of lovers with art nouveau flat patterned garments and background, while Beardsley attempted a more sardonic, English erotic art nouveau style. Munch blended the spiritual and sexual while Schiele explored his own sexuality with intentionally shocking explicitness. In sculpture Brancusi sought to communicate the universal essences of flight and birth in polished bronze; and in the 1920s, African-influenced Giacometti portrayed abstract figures as sexual symbols. Gabo, the Russian constructivist sculptor, explored a new reality of flattened solids and voids and brought industrial materials and processes into sculpture, while the Franco-American Lipchitz explored cubism in sculpture, and in later years created primitive totems with tremendous presence. Alfred Stieglitz, New York photographer and art dealer, was the first impresario of modernism in America. Schamberg, Dove, Demuth, Marin, Stella, and Stieglitz's wife, Georgia O'Keeffe, showed at his gallery. In 1915, through Stieglitz, Duchamp and Picabia founded the American counterpart of Dada. In *The Large Glass* Duchamp designated changes of a humanoid mechanical being energized by sexual passion, and Picabia portrayed Stieglitz as a camera. Schamberg was similar to Duchamp and Picabia. Demuth painted industrial landscapes, while O'Keeffe and Dove offered more mystical and spiritual works. O'Keeffe's flowers have the erotic quality of female sexuality. Modernist architecture was rooted in Gropius's industrial-based International Style. In the United States, Frank Lloyd Wright blended this technology with an organic feeling for nature. Le Corbusier first designed houses as "machines for living," later transformed into a more neospiritual expressionistic genre. Gaudí designed fanciful expressionistic architecture in Barcelona. In Glasgow, Mackintosh derived severe vertical linearity from art nouveau and the arts and crafts movement.

We are so embedded in our corruption that we cannot escape from it save by divine grace.

Barth's theology was a revival of Augustinian and Lutheran ideas, and represented a rebellion against the nineteenth-century view that man was changing in history, and that modern liberalism was elevating man out of his sinfulness. Barth denies this optimism. Of course, the Holocaust, which was to come only twenty years after Barth wrote, even more than World War I, was going to prove how right he had been.

Barth had numerous disciples, including leading Lutheran opponents of Hitler, such as Dietrich Bonhoeffer, who died at the hands of the Nazis. In the United States Barth had two main disciples: Reinhold Niebuhr, a professor at the Union Theological Seminary in New York City, who was extremely visible and influential in his day; and Paul Tillich, a student of Barth's who immigrated to America and also taught at the Union Theological Seminary and later at Harvard. Barth's theology became dominant at the Union Theological Seminary, and spread from there to other Protestant American institutions. In their later writing and preaching both Niebuhr and Tillich modified Barth's severely modernist theology with a revived historicism that was again, in the fifties, becoming fashionable.

In 1906 Albert Schweitzer had published a popular book entitled *The Quest for the Historical Jesus*. Schweitzer was a German theologian who subsequently became the famous saint of Africa through his missionary work as a doctor in French Equatorial Africa (Gabon). His book reviewed the vast body of nineteenth-century literature in which historians and theologians tried to reconstruct the historical Jesus.

In the late twenties and the thirties, the German theologian and biblical scholar Rudolf Bultmann announced that the quest, which had been futile from the very beginning, should now end, since the historical Jesus could never be discovered. Bultmann's close reading of New Testament literature, aided by his enormous learning in postexilic Judaism, that is, the Judaism of the time of Jesus, demonstrated that the lives of Jesus that had come down to us in the Gospels were really *Midrash*—that is to say, they were Jewish commentary and legend. Bultmann showed that the Gospels consisted of a pastiche of stories about holy men that existed in the Jewish literature of the time. There may have been a historical Jesus, Bultmann argued, but endeavoring to reconstruct him from the available material was bootless.

Bultmann's claim substantiated Barth's theology. The Christian approach to Jesus must base itself on an entirely theological, nonhistorical stance. Faith in Jesus cannot be achieved through history but solely by religious experience. Bultmann's work had tremendous impact in the period from 1930 to 1960.

The most important names in Jewish modernist thought belong to two disciples of Heidegger, Gershom Scholem and Martin Buber. Their thought was the product of an effort in the German Jewish community from about 1910 to 1930 to apply modern scholarship to Judaism, and to undertake the close reading of the Jewish past and tradition, using the instruments of academic scholarship. There had not been much work done in this critical vein before then. Judaism was full of history, but it was largely a mythological history—the sentimental kind that is still propagated from suburban synagogue pulpits on the Sabbath.

Scholem migrated to the newly founded Hebrew University in Jerusalem shortly after its establishment in 1926, and Buber followed him there in the mid-1930s. Gershom Scholem is the seminal twentieth-century scholar on the history of Judaism. It was his concern to undertake the phenomenological analysis of the Jewish past and to uncover the actual content of the Jewish consciousness, while asking what modern consciousness was capable of discovering in Jewish traditions.

Scholem established a very diverse Jewish heritage. Until his work, Judaism was founded on either a traditional Orthodox heritage, or a more secular liberal past. Scholem demonstrated that Jewish religious tradition was extremely varied. He showed that there was embedded within it a continuous strand of activist mysticism, as well as an equally strong apocalyptic messianic movement. These aspects of the Jewish past had been largely buried because neither activist mysticism nor messianism fitted in with twentieth-century Orthodox and liberal Judaism. Scholem showed that Judaism was an extremely complicated, rich, dynamic, and volatile religion, or rather, that it had been so for many centuries until about 1850.

His colleague Martin Buber was a philosopher and the visible embodiment of the mystical tradition. He reinterpreted Jewish mysticism in accordance with Heidegger's philosophy. Buber's famous vision of the relationship between the I and the Thou owed some of its inspiration to Kierkegaard and much of it to Heidegger. The relationship between consciousness and the external world in Heidegger's thought is transformed in Buber into the I-Thou relationship.

Buber spent much time and effort resurrecting stories about the mystical hasidic saints of late-eighteenth- and early-nineteenth-century Poland. He beleieved that hasidic men in their beards, boots, and long black coats dancing together in a circle communicated to the modern world the reality of religious experience. Through their enthusiastic communal engagement the hasidic saints were preaching the message that we first authentically discover truth and beauty in one another, and this interpersonal communication allows us eventually to communicate with God. But if we cannot first communicate authentically with and love one another, our hearts and minds will never know God. Buber intellectualized this phenomenological theology, heavily derived from Heidegger, in the theory of I and Thou. In the later decades of the century, it reverberated powerfully in New Age American religiosity.

At the beginning of this century, Catholicism was sunk in obscurantism and ignorance. These are harsh words, but nevertheless true. Nineteenth-century Catholicism, suffering a reaction against the French Revolution and the rise of secularism, tried to separate itself from modern thought. At the turn of the century, there was a movement in Catholicism called modernism, which tried to bring Catholic theology into contact with modern thinking in the comprehensive sense of the latter term. But in 1907 the Catholic modernist movement was suppressed by the papacy as being dangerous to the faith.

It was therefore the task, during the 1920s and 1930s, of Catholic thinkers who wished to modernize Catholic theology, to try to find a way around the disaster that had taken place in the early years of the century, a way around the papal condemnation. These thinkers were engaged in an activity that the overwhelming majority of the hierarchy, particularly of the Vatican, did not welcome. They were obliged to sneak, as it were, the modern world into Catholicism.

This movement found its two leaders in the Frenchmen Étienne Gilson and Jacques Maritain, who were the constituters of what came to be called the Neo-Thomist movement. Thomist here refers to the thirteenth-century philosopher and theologian Thomas Aquinas. Gilson and Maritain were devout Catholics, needless to say, and prestigious scholars, but they also operated in the secular world. They taught not in Catholic but in secular French universities. They were both educated at the University of Paris and in the thirties held chairs there. Gilson taught as well at the University of Toronto, and Maritain came to Princeton University in 1940 as a professor of philosophy. He stayed there and never returned to France.

Gilson and Maritain believed that the church had faced a comparable intellectual crisis earlier, in the thirteenth century, when it had to find the means of circumventing the problems posed by the vanguard science and philosophy of the time, which were Aristotelian. Thomas Aquinas, a Dominican friar who was teaching at the University of Paris, tried to achieve a reconciliation between Aristotelian science and traditional theology. It was because Thomas presented them with a precedent that Gilson and Maritain selected Thomism as their governing doctrine. They sought to use Thomas as a Trojan Horse for bringing the church into a more accommodating and mediating relationship with twentieth-century thought. Even with the base of their doctrine in Thomism, their task was not easy. They encountered stiff opposition, and if they had not been teaching in secular universities and had not both become very visible and celebrated in transatlantic academia, they would probably have been suppressed by the church hierarchy. But Gilson and Maritain had acquired such fame and importance that the Papacy was obliged to allow them their way.

Even though Gilson and Maritain strike the contemporary reader as all too tame, and their thirteenth-century Thomism as rigid and tiresome, they must be read with an eye on the circumstances in which they were writing. They were using Thomas Aquinas as an instrument in order to overcome the prohibition against modern thought that prevailed in the Catholic Church, and continued to prevail until the Second Vatican Council (1962).

A third Catholic thinker of the thirties was much more of a radical modernist than Gilson and Maritain. This was the English Benedictine monk David Knowles. He subsequently became famous in the forties and fifties as the leading Catholic historian in the world, and held the senior chair of history at Cambridge University. But that was the later Knowles. The Knowles of the 1920s and early 1930s was a young, intense Benedictine monk at Downside Abbey, the largest Catholic monastery in England. He was the editor of the *Downside Review*, which was the leading intellectual Catholic journal in England.

What Knowles advocated around 1930 was radical expressionism in Catholicism. Catholicism, he claimed, should aim toward a mystical, highly experimental recreation of medieval piety, not by emphasizing tradition and history but through the teaching of existential commitment to a fully Christian life. He proposed, in other words, a mode of Christian activism. This view incurred the wrath of his order and of the church, and Knowles was exiled to a backwater monastery where he had a nervous breakdown.

Fortunately, Knowles's path converged with that of a Scandinavian woman doctor in England who had converted to Catholicism and had become a mystic. For the next twenty-five years, they lived together, possibly in celibacy. She took care of him. During this period Knowles wrote his marvelous histories of medieval monasticism and Catholic culture, and eventually he became extremely influential and important. He is one of those innovative Catholic thinkers who contributed to the intellectual revolution of the Second Vatican Council.

Even in Knowles's mature and celebrated work as a historian of medieval church and culture, the most inspired and original sections are those concentrating on charismatic religious personalities who expressed in concentrated form the dynamic of Catholic religiosity. These intense exponents of Catholic experience are elevated above the normal flow of Knowles's historical narrative.

The Expansion of Modernist Culture We began this discussion of modernism in the first four decades of the twentieth century by designating its fundamental characteristics. Then we examined the manifestation of modernism in many areas of culture. In conclusion we shall now mention five areas of modernist culture that are perceptible but have not been specifically discussed. And finally we shall consider some general factors affecting modernism.

Modernist culture was manifested by a novel, intense interest in sport, as well as the professionalization of sport. In the modernist era, sport ceased to be a marginal, amateur activity and a gentleman's pastime. It became an object of full-time pursuit that deserved intense concentration. Sport thereby also became a self-referential field in itself, acquiring a thick culture of its own. It came to constitute a world of its own, a feature it was henceforth to share with, say, modernist painting, which is capable of absorbing everything around it and transforming it into its own terms. It developed its own microcosmic culture of intense density, which was sufficiently powerful to absorb and attract whatever approached its periphery.

This change occurred in the first quarter of the century. It is interesting to note that the particular sport in which this phenomenon first took place in the United States was baseball. In Europe it was soccer. Both became sports that could be intensively pursued, that allowed people to make a living in them and the masses to participate vicariously. Compared to American football or to European rugby, baseball and soccer are not sports in which serious injuries are common, and were therefore suitable for professional athletes. The development of these professional sports involves the establishing of patronage systems and exhibition stadia that closely parallel the role of art patrons and museums in the rise of modernist painting.

A phenomenon and an emergence similar to those of sports can be detected in the case of the radio in the twenties and thirties. Radio broadcasting technologically became possible by 1920. Commercial radio stations were already established in the early twenties in the United States, and state-controlled broadcasting emerged at the same time in Europe, but it was not until the early thirties that anyone knew what to do with radio broadcasting. Until then it was used mainly for providing information. In the early thirties, however, the radio came into being as a mass medium and developed a culture of its own. The principle of self-referentiality informs, in the case of radio too, the formation of a microcosmic culture within the wider context of modernism. Radio becomes a culture point that develops a distinctive form of drama and especially of comedy.

Radio drama did not survive the 1940s. The situation comedy that is still immensely popular originated in radio broadcasting in the 1930s and has not been significantly altered in its transition to television. Situation comedy is the distinctive genre of broadcasting. It is a thick point that draws everything to it. After about 1935 radio does not attempt to imitate the concert hall or the public platform, nor does it normally aspire to the lecture hall. It generates its own forms, as did modernist art. Jack Benny and Fibber McGee and Molly play the same role as Picasso and Klee in modernist painting. They create a self-enclosed world that draws others into it. The situation comedy exhibits a perpetual world within its thirty-minute frame—the same program that Cézanne identified for modernist art.

Another cultural phenomenon of the modernists has even now not yet been named. The term "folkish" is sometimes used to describe the ambience that manifests itself wherever movements for fresh air, clean bowels, long walks, mountain climbs, and corn flakes (the latter being a vanguard phenomenon in its day, believed to remake the individual) are found. The contiguous adoration of and devotion to youth must be added to this health list, perhaps as the most dynamic element on it. Through exercise and careful diet the middle-aged could preserve the physical exuberance and moral purity that were identified with youth.

Tied to this "folkishness" was theosophy, which blends together elements of Eastern philosophy, mostly derived from yoga, Zen Buddhism, and Islam or perhaps from misinterpretations thereof, with bits and pieces of Heideggerian phenomenology, into movements that operate on the margin, propounding the kind of religious philosophy that can be described as secularized mysticism. Again, this movement appears early in the century in all European countries and in the United States, and by the 1920s develops the prototype of the wise man, the guru, who is a conglomeration of the faith healer, the visionary, and the priest. The cultural phenomenon of the sophic guru, which almost disappears in the forties and fifties, comes back strong in the sixties.

The theosophical guru whose reputation is highest today is G. I. Gurdjieff. A Caucasian Russian, he became a theosophical leader first in Tashkent, then Moscow, Istanbul, and finally Fontainebleau, France (1922), where he established his Institute for the Harmonious Development of Man. His method of "self-observation" included sacred dance and components derived from the Sufi Muslim mystical sect. Since the 1960s recordings of Gurdjieff's music have been bestsellers. What Gurdjieff and other theosophical leaders preached was a puritanical cultivation of the self through contemplation, diet, and exercise, aiming for a disciplined inner harmony. This resulted in significant groups centering on strong leaders in the 1920s and has found a resounding echo in the 1980s and 1990s.

Another cultural phenomenon of the modernist era was feminism. Modernism was androgynous, and it represented a much greater acceptance of both feminism and homosexuality. The modernist movement begins in the early twentieth century at the same time as the first great wave of twentieth-century feminism emerges. Feminism is conditioned by the social fact that the new bureaucracies and administrations of government and business that Weber had talked about needed large armies of office workers and so liberated women from the home. Bureaucracy possibly liberated women from the home in order to imprison them in the office, as some upscale feminists would now claim, but it did liberate them from the home nevertheless, giving them a certain amount of independence.

Prominent in early twentieth-century feminism was the suffragette movement, which produced tremendous agitation in England and in the United States in the years before the First World War, in order to obtain for women the right to vote. The movement achieved its purpose shortly after the war as a reward for what women had done during the war in ammunition factories and hospitals and on farms. It is interesting that no sooner did women get the right to vote than by a clear margin they voted for conservative parties in both countries. No one has been able to explain why this should have been the case.

Feminism was articulated in an ideology, as represented by *A Room of One's Own*, a brief feminist treatise such as only Virgina Woolf could write, in which she advocated cultural and intellectual independence for women. Woolf spoke persuasively about the realization of women's artistic and intellectual possibilities and social benefits thereof. She herself was able to realize such possibilities because of a farseeing father and a very indulgent, or shall we say egalitarian, husband.

Another aspect of the period's feminism was the recognition that women were sexual beings, that their sexual drive was as powerful as men's, and that women had an equal right in sexual relations. The psychoanalytic movement contributed substantially to this recognition. It was immediately translated into a revolution in women's clothes—the abandonment of corsets, the raising of the hemline, and the advent of the brassiere.

By the late 1920s, the feminist movement had eroded. The trajectory of feminism is very similar to the trajectory of modernism: It reaches its peak in the early twenties, and it begins to run down in the late twenties. The job shortage in the Great Depression of the thirties fostered a return to the assumption that a woman's place is in the home. Feminism resurges in the prosperous, high-employment sixties.

The most compelling book of the early feminist movement was Vera Brittain's *Testament of Youth* (1933), which is an autobiographical account by an English journalist from the lower middle class, of her struggle to gain an education, her hospital work during the war, her love life, her experiences at Oxford after the war, and her hopes and disappointments. (Vera Brittain's daughter, Shirley Williams, was one of the three leaders of Britain's short-lived Social Democratic Party in the 1970s and early 1980s.) Brittain's *Testament* is one of the major modernist autobiographies. If it is less known now than Woolf's *A Room*, that is because Woolf's book is polemically concentrated while Brittain's work is one of complex humanity.

Finally there was the phenomenon of the rise of the university. Modernism arose in the same period as the one which witnessed the making of the modern university. By the 1930s, the university as we know it today had come into existence, and was teaching a significant portion of the college-age population. Though this was more true in the United States than in Europe, the number of young people attending universities was on the increase in Europe as well. In addition, the university had already become the center of science and research. Not all these features were entirely novel to this period, but only in the modernist era did the university become the vital center of intellectual life in the Western world.

This departure signified the professionalization of learning, the emergence of a social recognition and institutional base for research and analysis. The most important didactic minds, especially in philosophy, science, and the social sciences, were now university professors. This presents a very great difference from the situation in 1890. Between 1890 and 1930 the university had become the center of intellectual life and research.

Whereas in 1900 literary criticism was practiced almost entirely outside the university—by journalistic men of letters, poets, and novelists or combinations of these—by 1940 it had become a mostly (although not yet entirely) academic enterprise. The modernist transformation of literary criticism into a central academic endeavor was accentuated after World War II, culminating in today's situation, in which a respectable literary critic outside the university is as rare as one inside academe in 1900.

By 1930 the radical secular analysis, the microcosmic focus, the self-referentiality of learning that were central to modernist thought had become characteristics of the scholarship done at the universities. The rise of the modern university involved the quality of constituting learning as a self-enclosed universe and as a value in itself, irrespective of whatever popular support and acceptance it might achieve. This elitist attitude was a fundamental feature of modernist culture.

One of the most distinct features of modernism is the extent to which expatriates were involved in its making—that is, the degree to which modernism was a genuinely international movement. Expatriation played a prominent role in modernist culture long before artistic and intellectual refugees from Fascism had to migrate to the United States in the 1930s.

More than nineteenth-century culture certainly, and significantly more than the culture that has been in the making since World War II, modernism was carried forward by people who voluntarily left their own countries in order to make their mark as cultural leaders in a different environment. One might expect this internationalization process to be much more pronounced since the war, especially given the facility of inexpensive air travel at this time, but to the contrary. Expatriation has played a much smaller role in cultural development since 1945. Indeed, more and more people now study abroad—international education has become a big business in itself—but cultural leadership tends to remain, in our day, nativist and national.

The jet plane compared to earlier steam transportation has actually worked against cultural expatriation by making feasible short-term visits to foreign centers. Travel abroad in the jet plane era is easily accessible to artists and intellectuals, but compared to the 1920s, they do not stay abroad and become cultural leaders in a foreign country. (The exception to this pattern is the East European émigrés, whose expatriation before the 1990s was largely involuntary.)

Modernism was thus a movement in which expatriates played an important role, and in which there was a genuine internationalization of culture.

Although it is well known that there was a large expatriate community in Paris in the 1920s, the case of England was equally remarkable as a phenomenon of cultural expatriation and internationalization. In 1935 the leading philosopher in England was an Austrian Jew, Ludwig Wittgenstein. The leading historian was a Polish Jew from the Austro-Hungarian Empire, Lewis Namier, while the foremost literary critic and poet was the American, T. S. Eliot. The most important British novelist of the time, one who at least wrote in English and spent part of his time in Britain, was the Irishman, James Joyce. The most distinguished British scientist was the New Zealander, Ernest Rutherford. The situation was unprecedented in English culture, and has certainly not repeated itself since the war. Berlin's cultural life, in the 1920s, especially its painting, was also deeply affected by expatriates. The efflorescence of modernist culture in general was characterized by a tendency toward expatriation and internationalization.

It was the cosmopolitan champions of modernist culture who facilitated the relatively easy acceptance of academic and artistic refugees from fascism in the United States in the thirties and early forties. The migration across boundaries and oceans of artists, intellectuals, and academics had been made familiar and shown to be generally beneficial in the previous decade. The mostly involuntary expatriates from fascist-occupied countries in many instances struggled with underemployment and poverty in America, and professors especially were disadvantaged until they mastered spoken English. But the astonishing aspect of the cultured refugee migration in the thirties is the remarkably warm welcome and the rapid professional success the migrants enjoyed—and this during the Great Depression when academic and other intellectual jobs were hard to come by for the native-born.

It is true that many of the academic refugees were famous scholars and scientists who immediately magnified the quality of the university departments they joined. Princeton overnight became a world center for physics and mathematics, NYU gained celebrity in art history, and the New School for Social Research greatly enhanced its reputation in the social and behavioral sciences. Yale buttressed its standing in English literary criticism with giants in comparative and Continental literature. Berkeley gained distinction in medieval studies and Chicago in analytic philosophy as a result of the European migration. Yet it is astonishing that, at a time when American Ph.D.'s had to teach in the boondocks or take clerical jobs in Washington or work in Macy's, American universities were filling academic chairs and establishing new ones for refugee scholars whose European level of thought and thick foreign accents made them largely incomprehensible to the fresh-faced but naive young Ronald Reagan and Lucille Ball types in the classroom. Nor did the émigrés sufficiently realize the intrinsic quality of indigenous American scholarship, which they frequently crushed under their Teutonic tread. "That man," the chairman of the history department at Columbia said of his distinguished émigré colleague in classical studies, "is a fool in six languages."

It was the previous modernist expatriation and internalization of culture that made the thirties intellectual emigration from Europe to America possible. It could not occur today on anywhere near the same scale.

A second general quality of modernism was that it was carried out by urban groups—by groups of people, that is, living in the major cities of the Western world. It was in no sense a rural movement or a frontier movement, but entirely a metropolitan phenomenon whose leading centers were Paris, London, New York, Vienna, Berlin, as well as a number of subsidiary centers like Oslo and Dublin. Each of these centers harbored not a few intellectuals, but large groups of people active in numerous facets of the visual and performing arts, who interacted with the philosophers and scientists. The arts and sciences impinged on one another in these cities. Strong support groups in which artists and intellectuals assisted, encouraged, provoked, and inspired one other marked these urban cultures.

The famous Parisian scene in the 1920s was led by three remarkable American women who acted as patrons of literature and art. These were, first, Sylvia Beach, who worked for a living by running a very important bookstore, Shakespeare and Company. As is well known, she was the first publisher of James Joyce. Gertrude Stein, a graduate of Radcliffe, was a wealthy and somewhat eccentric American, a student of William James and herself a poet and a critic who sought a significant role as a patroness of culture. Although Stein never gained the public recognition she yearned for, her insights into the significance of modernism were among the earlier and sharper descriptions of the movement.

Peggy Guggenheim, the American millionaire heiress and patroness of the arts, is the third of this phenomenal triumvirate. A hell-raiser on two continents, Guggenheim claimed that during her long and stormy life she had slept with a thousand men. Among them were a goodly number of prominent artists including Max Ernst, to whom she was married for a short while. Forced to leave France during World War II, she established a thriving commercial gallery in New York that became the model for the postwar art trade. Guggenheim's fabulous collection of modernist painting—much of which, with visionary taste and on Ernst's recommendations, she bought for modest prices in the twenties, thirties and early forties,—is today in her former villa, now a museum in Venice, and in the Guggenheim Museum in New York, established by another member of her family. (The Guggenheims originally made their money in Colorado copper mining.)

In Paris, too, were the Frenchmen Paul Valéry and Marcel Proust, as well as James Joyce and the American Ernest Hemingway, and the Canadian Morley Callaghan, who was perhaps his country's leading novelist of the early twentieth century. Further there were the Spanish artist Picasso, the Russian Jewish painter Chagall, and the Italian painter-sculptor Modigliani. Henri Matisse and Georges Braque headed the legion of native French artists. These personalities knew, interacted with, and, most important, influenced one another.

The same can be said of London at that time. In London there were two such modernist groups. One was the cadre of poets and artists gathered around Eliot and Pound. Involved in this group were the Englishman Wyndham Lewis, a novelist and polemicist of modernism, and the novelist Ford Madox Ford. The other one was the Bloomsbury group, led by Virginia Woolf and her sister, Vanessa Bell. The group further consisted of Lytton Strachey, the novelist E. M. Forster, the economist John Maynard Keynes, the art critic Clive Bell, and the artist Duncan Grant, as well as numerous others.

These urban movements were made possible by cheap housing, cheap food, and steam transportation. The situation that prevailed as a result of these conditions no longer exists in the Western world.

A third characteristic of modernism is that Jews played a major role in it. Modernism was not a Jewish plot, not a chapter in the *Protocols of the Elders of Zion*, but Jews did make major contributions in its conception and perpetuation. This fact is especially remarkable when it is remembered that the entire Jewish population of Europe west of Poland was less than two million people. Franz Kafka was not only Jewish but so conscious of his Jewishness as to become a learned Jewish scholar and sympathetic to Zionism. He was descended, on his mother's side, from a long line of distinguished Prague rabbis and mystic visionaries. Had Kafka lived into the thirties, he would, along with his friend and literary executor, Max Brod, have immigrated to Palestine.

Marcel Proust was Jewish on his mother's side. His mother came of the famous Weil family, which produced a long line of distinguished businessmen, scholars, and professional and literary people in France. Proust felt himself to be Jewish, and when, in the late 1890s, the infamous Dreyfus case began, which maliciously charged a Jewish army captain with treason, Proust was one of the first to come to Dreyfus's aid and to organize a fund for his defense. The myth of Proust as a recluse has been overdone: One should not think of him entirely in terms of his later years, locked in a cork-lined room, allegedly removed from the world. As a matter of fact, Proust was very much engaged in the arts and was intensely interested in politics.

The role of Jews in social and behavioral sciences is phenomenal. We need mention only Durkheim, the founder of modern sociology; Franz Boas, the founder of anthropology; and of course, Sigmund Freud himself, the founder of psychoanalysis, as well as most of his early disciples.

Einstein's physics was denounced as "Jewish physics" in Nazi Germany. Einstein himself was extremely conscious of his Jewishness. A vehement Zionist, he was offered the first presidency of Israel in 1948 in recognition of his long support of Jewish nationalism. He turned it down, giving his age as the reason. The first president of Israel was another Jewish scientist, Chaim Weizmann, who had a distinguished career as a professor of chemistry at the University of Manchester.

Although traditional Jewish religion had been hostile to the visual arts, there was an important group of Jewish artists—expatriates from Eastern Europe—in Paris in the 1920s and 1930s, the most famous of whom were Chagall and Soutine. About thirty of these artists died in the Nazi death camps in the 1940s.

As we have noted, the philosopher Ludwig Wittgenstein was a scion of an assimilated millionaire Viennese-Jewish family. The leading European modernist historian, and in some ways the most radical historical modernist of the early thirties, Lewis Namier was, again, not only Jewish (his name was originally Namierowski), from the eastern frontier of the Austro-Hungarian Empire, but in the 1920s a vehement Zionist as well. It is interesting to note this recurrence of Zionism among Jewish modernists. Namier very much wanted to become the first president of Israel, but lost the leadership of the Zionist movement in England to Chaim Weizmann in 1930. It was only after he was eliminated from the top position of the Zionist organization that Namier turned all his attention to the writing of history.

The fact that Jews played an important role in the shaping of modernist culture has reasons intrinsic neither to the Jewish race—if such a thing indeed actually exists—nor to traditional Jewish culture, but rather to the time and place in the history of Jewish culture in which modernism appeared. Jewish modernists were the first generation of liberated Jews. They belonged to the first generation of Ashkenazic (Western) Jews, stretching from Poland to Britain and to New York, which had a reasonable opportunity to attend universities (although discrimination still continued against them) and to advance in the learned and university professions.

People who belong to traditional but highly literate cultures, when initially given the opportunity to break out of them, and to participate fully in secular and academic culture, undergo, in their own generation, intellectual explosion. The current situation of Asian-Americans in the United States is a comparable example. Asian-Americans are the rising intellectual group in this country today, just as Jews were in the generation of the twenties and thirties. It is said that if Columbia University had in the thirties accepted students entirely on the basis of their academic potential, 75 percent of the entering freshman class in 1935 would have been Jewish. (The Jewish quota was 15 percent). Today 30 percent of the entering class at Berkeley is Asian-American, a repetition of the pattern of Jewish achievement in modernist culture.

The prominent role played by Jews in the formation of modernist culture can therefore be explained as a sociological phenomenon typical of the first generation of a newly liberated and highly literate minority. A minority of this kind has to be one in which intellectual life is highly respected in the first place, even though its intellectual capacity has previously been devoted to sectarian religion or otherwise diverted.

The era of high modernism, which stretches from 1900 to 1940, is also the era of the rise of anti-Semitism in the West. Never before, and not afterward, since 1945, has an anti-Semitic explosion been seen that affected the Western world as strongly as the one that cuts through the decades between 1900 and the early 1940s. It came to an end only when General Eisenhower's armies reached some of the death camps in the spring of 1945 and revealed the Holocaust to the world.

The important relationship between modernism and anti-Semitism does not by any means cover the entire story of the phenomenon of anti-Semitism, which is one of the fundamental facts of twentieth-century culture and has many roots. Yet it is impossible to ignore the fact that in diverse ways modernism contributed to the rise of the anti-Semitic tide that overwhelmed the Jews.

The Jews were in a double bind. First, they played a very significant and visible role in modernism. They occupied, albeit not exclusively, a vanguard position in it. In response, traditionalists, who felt that radical, secular modernism was undermining—destructuring, as it were—traditional culture and

Christianity, that its internationalist bent was threatening national cultures and traditions, attributed the ills they perceived to the Jews and felt that the latter were serving Western culture poorly, and that they were effecting this through the vehicle of modernism. Jews had launched an assault, according to this view, on traditional, Christian, historical, and national cultures; and modernism, its secular internationalism, was their weapon. The traditionalists—especially Catholics—displaced their antimodernism into a fanatical hatred of Jews. Fervent nationalists often viewed Jewish intellectuals as cynical cosmopolites who were using modernist ideas to delegitimize patriotism.

French anti-Semitism was particularly affected by an ideological reaction against modernism. Right-wing French traditionalists were as strongly, and simultaneously, antimodernist as they were anti-Semitic. Yet the story is more complicated than that because in other places, particularly in England, it was the modernists who themselves were anti-Semites. The modernist movement in England, more specifically the circle of Eliot, Pound, and Lewis, was violently anti-Semitic. One could therefore be a leading modernist intellectual and nurse anti-Semitism at the same time.

The main reason why Eliot's widow has not allowed scholars general access to his papers is probably that when the archives are opened, it will be realized how extreme an anti-Semite her late husband Eliot was. We know for a fact that he was an anti-Semite particularly from a dreadful public lecture that he gave at the University of Virginia in 1931, which sounds like something that could have been written by Joseph Goebbels. Similar sentiments undoubtedly pervade his private papers. It is instructive and disturbing to discover how delicately Eliot's biographers have dealt with his virulent anti-Semitism.

Ezra Pound, who may have been the greatest modernist poet of the English language—one of three at any rate—became a paranoid fascist agitator, broadcasting from Rome during the war and denouncing Jews. Wyndham Lewis, a vanguard novelist, painter, and critic of major talent, produced several anti-Semitic pamphlets and articles in the thirties and lavished praise on Hitler. (Lewis's reputation in Britain became so clouded that he had to seek refuge as a professor at a small Catholic college in Canada.)

Anti-Semitism was present in German expressionism as well. Contempt for the Jewish businessman and the Jewish bourgeois and capitalist is a paradigmatic theme in the art and literature of this school. Though not an overwhelming expressionist theme, it is present nevertheless. Stereotyped depictions of the predatory, loathsome Jewish capitalist were popularized in the rightist French Catholic press at the time of the Dreyfus controversy. The leftist Berlin artist Georg Grosz replicated this stereotype of the bloated capitalist with great skill in the 1920s. He played down the anti-Semitic content and applied his socialist attitude to businessmen in general. But Nazi art in the early 1930s built upon Grosz's caricatures, reinserting the Jewish angle and recovering the early-twentieth-century French anti-Semitic motif. Thus did a prominent German expressionist come to serve Nazi propaganda. The lesson from this excursus into art history would be that anticapitalist imagery in the Eruopean context can readily be turned against Jews; it is a cultural toxic dump that ought not to be entered.

The question of why there should be an anti-Semitic strain in modernism is a difficult one but answerable. The Jews were seen as the archrepresentatives of the nineteenth-century culture against which modernism was rebelling. The Jews were historically and religiously minded. Particularly so were the Jewish immigrants from Eastern Europe, who had been coming to Western Europe in large numbers since 1900. The Jews, mostly Polish, who came into the West were traditionalist in their religious practices.

The Jews were a historical people. Their sense of identity was corporate and was expressed through historical consciousness—all of which were tendencies against which modernism rebelled. Also, the Jews were the visible beneficiaries of nineteenth-century liberalism. Nineteenth-century liberal historicism had advocated the liberation of the Jews, had protected them, had given them civil rights, and had argued for the right of Jews to participate fully in European society. For example, no British intellectual in the nineteenth century was more supportive of both the political and civil rights of Jews than Thomas Babington Macaulay—the leading Victorian historian. Therefore the Jews were seen as the archrepresentatives, but more important, as the archbeneficiaries of that liberal historicist culture so disliked by modernism.

The Jews were thus at the same time regarded as the archfiends of modernism, who were eroding traditional European Christian and national culture, and as the archbeneficiaries of everything that represented, to the radical modernist mind, superseded nineteenth-century culture. The way in which modernism developed contributed significantly to the rise of anti-Semitism between 1900 and 1940.

The final quality of modernism, and one that has proved most permanent in the popular mind, is what might be called the Greenwich Village and Bloomsbury phenomenon, or the Parisian Left Bank and Munich University sector phenomenon. Modernism revived something that had been very strong in the period ranging between 1820 and 1860 in romantic culture, namely, the bohemian—the middle-class artist who rebels against his own class, who retreats, not to the working-class district, but to the attics and fringes of middle-class living, and from there generates a vanguard artistic culture. In time the rebellious culture so generated is incorporated or socialized into middle-class life and culture. This is the pattern and fate of bohemia.

Modernism reenacted this pattern, advocating a bohemian culture, art as the authentic form of human expression, one it deemed far more important than politics, far more noble and pure than economics. Modernism was expressed through a bohemian life. Many of the modernists did live the bohemian life, and they certainly upheld the vanguard as the finest expression of European culture. This neobohemianism is central to the life of modernism.

Modernism and World War I The problematic relationship between World War I (1914–18) and modernism has received much attention. World War I was essentially the consequence of arrogance on the part of the ruling groups in European society. Bloated with military power, the political elites had structured huge armies and developed novel forms of armament like artillery and the long-range machine gun. They were beginning to experiment with the use of airplanes and armored cars. In the period from about 1880 to about 1910, they had engaged in a vast international imperialist race to carve up Africa and spheres of influence in Asia.

In the years leading up to 1914, Western countries began to envision a military confrontation for rule and hegemony within Europe as well as for world power. That is, they could no longer export their military competition, since they had already divided up the world, and were also finding that overseas empires were ruinously expensive. They began to turn their military competition back into Europe. The political elite also suffered from a deep misconception as to what a future war to determine world dominance (*Weltmacht*) would be like. They thought that such a war would be much like the Franco-Prussian War of 1870, which had featured one battle and was over in six weeks. They also thought that with the tremendous military capability that they had built up—a "star wars" capability it seemed to them—the war would be brief and everyone would be home for Christmas.

What the Western powers did not understand was that the prototype for the first great war of the twentieth century was not the Franco-Prussian War but the American Civil War of 1861–65—a war, that is, fought with masses of infantry, a war of attrition which would cause tremendous loss of life (six hundred thousand Americans were casualties in the Civil War, still the greatest war in American history in terms of loss of life), and a war that would eventually result in the impoverishment of the civilian population.

The exacerbation of the long-standing feud between Russia and Austria over which would dominate the Balkans was the immediate cause of the conflict in August 1914. But the German and British governments were most responsible for the war—the former for urging on their Austrian allies because the Berlin generals and politicians thought the moment was propitious for a German victory, the latter for not using its capability of interceding to prevent the outbreak.

The First World War was in fact one of unprecedented massacres in which ten million people died, nine million of them on the battlefield. One million consisted of civilians, mostly in Eastern Europe. After the long-planned German thrust to Paris failed, there was deadlock rather than triumph on the Western Front by Christmas 1914. Neither side was able to use its military power and advanced machinery to achieve the breakthrough it sought on the Western Front.

In the East the war fared differently. By 1917 the Russian army was shown to be a paper bear, there was a revolution in Russia and the new Bolshevik regime withdrew from the war. On the Western Front, military forces did not move more than a hundred miles in either direction during four incredibly horrible years, while vast numbers of young males were destroyed. Battles were fought in 1916 and 1917 in which each side suffered a quarter-million casualties in two days. The British had developed the tank, whose deployment could have broken the deadlock, but conservative British generals, still dreaming of cavalry charges, resisted its use. By 1916 the war was impacting on the civilian populations. The British were hungry, the Germans even more so. In 1917 massacre in the trenches and demoralization in Paris led to a huge mutiny in the French army, which was suppressed with great difficulty, and the French did little fighting in the next year.

The war came to an end for two reasons. First, by 1918 the Germans were suffering starvation, and a left-wing revolution was threatening in Berlin. As a matter of fact, a communist revolution did occur, but it was aborted. The second reason the war ended was U.S. entry into the war in 1917. In 1918, one million fresh, untrained, and inept American troops arrived in France, causing consternation among the Germans, who did not realize how unprepared the American army was for the war. When the Allies began to penetrate the German lines, the German generals panicked and advised the government in Berlin to seek an armistice, which meant surrender.

The war ended in a very peculiar way. It had never been fought on German soil. It took place entirely on Belgian and French (and in the East on Polish) soil, and the Germans surrendered before the battle reached Germany—in anticipation of what was going to happen now that the Yankees were over there.

There are two ways of interpreting the relationship between the coming of the War and modernism. One would be to claim that the First World War, the last gasp of the old order, had no relationship to modernism. The old order, which was one of militarism, historicism, hierarchy, nationalism, and militant Christianity, separately played out in the war its decadent manner, its tired ideology. On the other hand, it could be said that modernism had played an unconscious role in the cause of World War I. The old culture in 1914 was threatened by cultural revolution, which was very much under way in the first decade of the twentieth century, involving philosophy, the social sciences, the arts and literature, as much as the sciences themselves, developing in all fields new ways of perceiving the world that radically contradicted nineteenth-century modes of thinking.

World War I could be seen as a desperate, although largely unconscious, effort of the old order to save itself. The path of self-preservation for the old culture ran through war. For the war reasserted nationalism, historical traditions, male chauvinism, social hierarchy, and the old ideological Christianity. The war was the means used by the old culture to stave off the advent of the new. The effort proved to be suicidal, to a degree, but it was, nevertheless, an unconscious strategy for warding off the threat of the total transformation of Western culture.

There is a point to the latter interpretation, a visible one too, that is discernible in the way the war broke out in August 1914 amidst the joyous welcome of the military and landed classes and among the leadership groups in politics. The war meant a moral revival for these populations, restoring them to an importance they were losing.

Among the effects of the war on modernism, the one most frequently stressed is that the war strengthened the modernist movement because it discredited the old order. The old order had caused the death of ten million people, destroyed the czarist and Hapsburg empires, had impoverished France, crushed Germany, and in acts of unprecedented horror wiped out an entire generation of young men between the ages of eighteen and thirty. The old order, in other words, proved itself incredibly foolish and inept in its last effort to assert itself. By discrediting itself, the old order gave renewed valorization to modernism.

The literature of the postwar period stands as proof of this profound disillusion with the old order. The famous lines of William Butler Yeats: "Things fall apart, the center cannot hold;/Mere anarchy is loosed upon the world," written in 1919, reveal the new pessimism and despair. Paul Valéry's comment, "The mind has been cruelly wounded, it doubts itself profoundly," points toward a sense of loss that concerns more than the biological, namely, the psychological. To the extent modernism hated nationalism, militarism, historicism, and traditional Christianity, World War I presented solid justification for its hatred. The war demonstrated that the modernist hostile view of Victorian culture was well founded. Appropriately, Lytton Strachey's *Eminent Victorians* was published at the end of the war.

But modernism lost as well as gained from the war. The First World War also begins the revival of Victorian culture. That it began the recovery of historicism, nationalism, and traditional Christian ethics cannot be perceived very well during the years immediately following the end of the war, not clearly until the thirties. The vast military propaganda that had been possible in 1914 was again virulent in the thirties. The tremendous resurgence of Victorian historicism and national feeling that accompanied the war along with the assertion of male leadership and hierarchic order and the reaffirmation of traditional Christian ideals represented a powerful contradiction of modernism. By the 1930s the impact of this neo-Victorianism was evident and operative.

While in the short term, approximately from 1918 to 1928, modernism seemed to be given a new lease on life, a new vitality and validity, by World War I, by the later years of the twenties, the neo-Victorian cultural qualities stimulated by the war had begun to take hold and to threaten the new culture's vitality. Whereas some historians have seen World War I as only a positive force for modernism, its impact on modernism was, in fact, mixed.

The war's immediate consequence was to accelerate disillusion with Victorian ideals. Its longer-range outcome was to strengthen the reaction against modernism.

There is one way in which the consequences of World War I and modernism converge, and that is in a loss of conventional respect for human life. Modernism eroded traditional humanism. It allowed for the expression of moral relativism, the recognition of sadomasochistic feelings as a genuine and inevitable component of the human personality, while the Victorians, who certainly knew about such emotions, hid both the knowledge and its expression. Modernism acknowledged as central to the human personality those violent impulses that Victorianism repressed.

In German expressionism, French surrealism, and dadaism, and even in some tendencies of the English modernism, particularly as manifested in the writings of Pound and Lewis, modernism gave validity to cruelty, accepting it not as something to be simply resisted, but as a human act that was to be understood as an inseparable part of life. We shall see that psychoanalysis also recognized the centrality of sadomasochism in the human psyche.

The war's legacy desensitized popular feeling and everywhere taught the same message graphically. That the unprecedented destruction of human life in the First World War, and its horrifying traces, wounded people, physically as well as mentally, could be seen in every European city in the twenties. Cities were full of people with severed limbs. Since medicine did not emerge from the Dark Ages until the 1940s, post–World War I medicine knew only one way of dealing with severely wounded limbs—to cut them off. The amputees as well as the psychologically traumatized ("shell-shocked") remained a prominent fixture of the interwar period.

Europeans came to accept the brutal consequences of the war as a collective trauma: "In Flanders' fields the poppies blow/Between the crosses, row on row." The vast cemeteries became an accepted fact, a part of the regular landscape. Signs of death and destruction were internalized into European culture and thereby normalized. Human life was devaluated, and cruelty assumed a new legitimacy as a result of World War I.

This devaluation combined with the tendency in modernism to erode traditional Christian humanism and normative ethics, to validate relativism, to recognize sadomasochism and cruelty. Modernism coalesced with the catastrophic consequences of the war to produce a new streak in European mentality—the streak of unrestrained destruction, legitimized massacre, and socially acceptable holocaust. The roots of the Holocaust lie in several places, two of which are the First World War and modernism.

Only in the last three or four decades of the twentieth century have the cultural and moral consequences of the war been thoroughly explored. It was a catastrophe for European thought and feeling unprecedented in history since the later Middle Ages.

World War I was the shaping context of everything else in this century. Britain never recovered from the war. It was plunged into a long descent from its economic, imperial, and intellectual grandeur into mediocrity, confusion, and loss of confidence. The French have remained perpetually in conflict among themselves as to the meaning and locus of blame for the war. Russia was plunged into a nightmare of civil strife, terror, and poverty from which it may only be emerging in the 1990s. Germany alone of the great European nations at the close of this century has thrown off the morbid memory of the war and emerged serene, confident, and prosperous. Germany was only able to do so, however, by first undergoing the traumatic catharsis of the Nazi era and by the infinite devastation and mortality it caused (and endured) in World War II.

The society that benefited most from World War I was that of the United States. The process of the American rise to world hegemony was greatly advanced by World War II after 1941, but American centrality among world societies was already evident by 1918. This was not so much due to the American help to the desperate and exhausted English and French Allies in forcing Germany to surrender. Even more important, the war of 1914–18 brought the United States out of its relative cultural isolation, its intense concentration of its human resources on mastery of the Edenic continent, and to look outward toward Western Europe, and to absorb and consider the implications of European ideas.

The American expatriate writers and artists in Paris in the 1920s were more important in transformative effects in twentieth-century culture than the million doughboys who entered the front lines in 1918, convincing the Germans that the continuation of the war was hopeless, even though not a shot had been fired on German soil. The enhanced ambitions of the leading American universities—such as Columbia, Harvard, and Chicago—after the war, their determination to be global institutions in their intellectual reach, was the signal for a great westward shift in the primacy of thought and art in the later decades of the century.

3

PSYCHOANALYSIS

Psychoanalysis Today Psychoanalysis is experiencing difficult times in the 1990s. Its problems were already heralded in the mid-1980s in a series of articles in the *The New Yorker* by one of the magazine's prominent writers, Janet Malcolm. The articles were gathered into a book, *Psychoanalysis: The Impossible Profession*, whose title expresses its theme directly. What Ms. Malcolm did not fully anticipate, and certainly practicing psychoanalysts did not, was that a decade later the now dominant funding agencies for sick people, the big medical insurance companies like Aetna, and the health management organizations would regard with skepticism the clinical status of psychoanalysis. Looking around for ways to reduce the payout of escalating medical bills, the insurance companies and HMOs made psychoanalysis their favorite victim. Not only did they put a low ceiling on reimbursement by the hour to psychoanalytic therapists; they were reluctant to pay for an extended series of psychoanalytic sessions. After two or three such sessions, neurotic patients were supposed to be treated by drugs.

Even university administrations had by the 1990s often lost their respect for psychoanalysis, even if their departments of psychiatry and clinical psychology trained psychoanalytic therapists. For example, New York University was, in its faculty health plan, willing to pay only a third of the cost of psychoanalytic treatment. Psychoanalysis in the NYU health plan in any given year received less reimbursement than dental costs. Filling cavities was treated more seriously than treating neuroses. These humiliations were a far cry from the status that psychoanalysis had enjoyed around 1970. It was downhill from there.

It is quite possible that in the twenty-first century psychoanalysis will be regarded not as a branch of medicine but only as a cultural and humanistic movement—like romanticism and modernism. From various perspectives this is not an unjustified view, because psychoanalysis in its theory of the unconscious echoed themes in early-nineteenth-century romanticism. As articulated in the earlier writings of Sigmund Freud from 1900 to about 1925, psychoanalysis unquestionably lay at the core of the modernist movement. If modernism ever had a clear theoretical formulation, it was in early Freud.

The conflict that has existed in this country since the 1930s between psychoanalysts with medical degrees, and lay analysts, many of whom have Ph.D.'s in clinical psychology—and some even degrees in clinical social work—became exacerbated in the 1980s.

A primary question, in which psychoanalysis is currently entangled, is therefore whether psychoanalysis is a medical science or a cultural movement with a therapeutic branch. Does psychoanalysis have to be based on medical science? Sigmund Freud himself did not think so, even though in his case it was. He favored allowing lay analysis and training psychoanalysts who did not have a medical degree. His daughter Anna, who was also one of his prime disciples, was not an M.D. Nor was his last student, Erik Erikson, who had no degree at all.

The second and perhaps more important issue facing psychoanalysis is the rise of what is called psychopharmacology—that is, the use of drugs to alleviate mental illness that had hitherto been treated by psychoanalysis. This concerns particularly the illness of mood swings, or bipolarization, usually known as manic-depressive disorder. At least one-third and possibly one-half of the patients that psychoanalysts normally treat are people whose moods undergo swings from mania to depression, remaining for the most part in depression and occasionally breaking into euphoric hyperactivity, or mania. It became known in the fifties that Valium (diazepam) or similar substances can help many people in an anxious state. But for those in a severe arc of mood swing another treatment had to be found.

More than forty years ago, largely by the trial-and-error method of experimentation, it was discovered that a certain lithium compound had the effect of flattening out the mood swing, or at least of reducing its curve, thus alleviating the depression to a significant degree for 70 percent of manic-depressive patients. This lithium compound also almost eliminates the manic euphoria. Severe depression hurts work performance, impairs family relationships, and sometimes leads to suicide. The manic mood swing can lead to reckless behavior such as overspending and gambling. Lithium greatly reduces these dangerous behavior patterns for most patients.

While the immediate effects of lithium are known, the reasons why or how it produces them remain unknown. The impact on the individual's health of the long-term use of lithium are also uncertain, but after four decades of use no toxic consequences are yet evident. The use of lithium against mood swings may have another consequence. Many artists and other creative people are manic depressive. Their creativity comes predominantly in the manic phase, which lithium for the most part eliminates. Can society afford this threat to cultural creativity?

Valium is remarkably cheap. So are lithium compounds. They do not cost much more than Tylenol (acetaminophen) and therefore offer an attractive remedy in a variety of ways. Psychiatrists who are also psychoanalysts have in many instances abandoned treating manic-depressive mood swings by means of the slow and difficult analytic process, which takes on average three to four years, and do not hesitate to prescribe medication to these patients after very few sessions of therapy. In the majority of cases there are visibly positive results within three or four weeks. This situation poses a growing threat to psychoanalytic therapy. Why go through a long and expensive psychoanalysis when drugs can do the job quickly and cheaply?

In the 1990s new mood modification drugs, the best known of which was Prozac (fluoxetine hydrochloride), became extremely popular and seemed to be faster-acting than Valium and lithium. The subcultures that in previous centuries grew up around tobacco and liquor were now paralleled by the so-called Prozac generation. People who had been only marginally and momentarily affected by Valium and lithium now went around for weeks on end with happy looks on their faces. In a society in which selling half an ounce of heroin could result in long incarceration, pharmacists on the basis of hastily scribbled prescriptions by M.D.'s were dispensing Prozac (and other powerful drugs with similarly unknown side effects) by the bushel.

This situation was an immense threat to psychoanalysis as a form of medical therapy. Just as fluorides in drinking water greatly reduce cavities in children and eliminated at least half of the dentists' clientele, Prozac and other mind-bending drugs threatened the incomes and professional status of psychoanalysts. Looking back from the end of the twenty-first century, historians of science may very well remark that psychoanalysis had a much shorter run in intellectual history than did astrology, ending up in the same rubbish heap of fake science.

Paradoxically, the fathers of psychoanalysis, Freud and Jung, would probably have approved of the use of medication in the treatment of mental illness. Freud began his career as a neurologist, and he experimented with drugs in his earliest efforts to deal with neuroses. Even before the First World War, Jung foresaw that many mental illnesses including psychosis were the consequence of biochemical changes and hence might eventually be treated by pharmacology.

Another challenge to psychoanalysis comes from philosophers of science, particularly from the disciples of Ludwig Wittgenstein, and specifically from Karl Popper, a Wittgensteinian who was professor of philosophy at the University of London in the 1960s and 1970s, and his disciples. Having devoted his early career to proving that Plato was a fascist and not a philosopher to be taken seriously, Popper devoted the latter part to proving that from the standpoint of science Freud was nothing less than a charlatan. The claim contributed powerfully to Popper's being given a knighthood.

Popper and his colleagues argue that whatever else psychoanalysis may be, it is not a science, primarily because it lacks what is fundamental to science, which is in their view a principle of falsification. Psychoanalysis, they insist, is unable to posit a method by which a given proposition can be shown to be true or false. It is possible to regard psychoanalysis as a cultural theory, even as religion or poetry, they claim, but certainly not as science. This mode of anti-Freudianism has become popular, especially in English academic circles. Although psychoanalysts have long held that they are engaged in verifiable science, that their field does not consist simply of articles of faith, recent criticisms of both their theory and practice have obliged them to assume a defensive position and to begin to face this criticism. The first line of response to Popper is that his definition of science is a very narrow one. A second would be that psychoanalysis has helped millions of people, which constitutes verification. A third response points to research at Rockefeller University, which in the 1980s claimed significant experimental verification for Freud's theory of childhood development.

Despite the threats to the future of psychoanalysis, the field has had a remarkable history. It constitutes one of the great intellectual movements of the twentieth century. It has had a profound impact not only on individual self-image, but on our perception of the world as well. It has altered human sexual behavior in the Western world. It has recruited some of the leading minds of this century and influenced many other aspects of culture. Psychoanalysis, whatever its future, is a central cultural movement of this century, in some respects its leading intellectual accomplishment.

★　　★　　★

Nothing separates us more dramatically from the Victorians than our attitude to and practice of sexuality, and psychoanalysis has played the greatest role in the sexual transformation of this century's culture. What an eminent French medievalist said of the impact of Christianity on the culture of the fourth-century Roman Empire may also be said of the impact of psychoanalysis on twentieth-century culture: It is as if a dreamer on waking had seen a different constellation of stars in the heavens.

Psychoanalysis offered twentieth-century men and women a secular form of individual therapy to replace the therapeutic function that had traditionally been provided by religious organizations. Individuals suffer feelings of guilt, fear, depression, and mental agitation. To whom should they turn for help? Ecclesiastical systems traditionally affected people's lives more by their therapeutic responses than by their theologies, although theology conditioned the therapy a particular religious organization provided. The Catholic Church offered the comfort of good works—the sacraments, the moral priesthood, and the miraculous intervention of saints who were contemporaneously embodied in monks and nuns. The more conservative Protestant churches provided the therapeutic solace of belonging to the holy community, and the Jewish solution to personal distress was similar. The more evangelical Protestant sects offered the services of charismatic faith healers.

Toward the end of the nineteenth century the therapeutic functions of religious groups carried less conviction. A process of secularization and withdrawal from church and synagogue membership meant that many people, particularly among the educated middle class, turned to novel secular agencies for comfort, guidance, and help with psychological distress. The decline of the therapeutic popularity of the churches is one of the more significant turning points in the social history of the period. Many explanations have been given for this change: the impact of Darwinism and modern science; the result of the deracinating, materialist urban culture; the disturbing effect on confessional communities of long-distance immigration. One cause of the therapeutic change must be seen in the rise of public education at the secondary level in major Western countries in the late nineteenth century. In order to foster patriotism and avoid religious disputes among different groups, the new state-supported high schools taught a primarily secular culture, and this kind of instruction helped to shape the mentality of cohorts that looked beyond the churches and synagogues of their grandfathers and fathers to supportive agencies in the secular sector.

The religious organizations did not surrender a large segment of their therapeutic role without a struggle. In the twentieth century they undertook concerted measures to assert their traditional therapeutic dominance. The Catholic Church everywhere tightened its administration and invested heavily in parochial schools to countervail the state-supported secular high schools. The Protestant churches sharpened their theoretical formulations in the direction of a social gospel or Karl Barth's neo-Augustinianism or a combination of the two.. In Judaism there was a major expansion of the reform or liberal variety, designed to communicate easily with an educated, secularized clientele. Yet the churches and synagogues continued to experience a decline in their role of dealing with the emotional and psychological problems of an increasingly educated and secularized public.

Behavioral psychology could offer environmental conditioning as a therapeutic function to this population, but this was a limited service. It was psychoanalysis that could deal on an individual basis with guilt, fear, depression, and mental disturbance. It was psychoanalysis that in the vision of Sigmund Freud aimed to replace traditional Christianity as the therapeutic agency of twentieth-century people, and to a major degree succeeded in doing so.

The Origins of Psychoanalysis A remarkable scene in the early history of psychoanalysis took place at Clark University in Worcester, Massachusetts, in 1909. At that time the newly founded university conferred honorary degrees on Sigmund Freud and Carl Jung, in a ceremony that was the first moment of public recognition they received. It was Stanley Hall, the president of the university and a behavioral psychologist who was a disciple of William James, who invited Freud and Jung to Clark and celebrated them publicly. Included in the group of guests was the young British psychiatrist Ernest Jones, who later, in the 1950s, became Freud's official biographer. Following this public ceremony, one of the trustees of Clark University whisked Freud, Jung, and Jones away to his fishing lodge on the St. Lawrence River, where they spent some days in unaccustomed upscale luxury.

This was the first public display of appreciation for the work of psychoanalysis, and it is significant that it should have occurred in the United States, where psychoanalysis has had warmer reception and greater intellectual impact than anywhere else in the world.

Among the cultural foundations of Freudianism, the Vienna of Freud's time plays a major role. This was a Vienna that was experiencing the political decline of the Hapsburg Empire simultaneously with important developments in the arts. Viennese culture was at the time highly sensitive to the complexities and depth of human emotions, and displayed this affectivity in the rich variety of the arts, from music to painting, it was producing. The human possibility of being a monster as well as a saint is a perception that runs through the cultural output of turn-of-the-century Vienna.

Second, Freud's Jewish background ought to be taken into account in explaining the origins of psychoanalysis. He came from a middle-class Jewish family, and belonged to that first generation of liberated Jewish intellectuals that was described in the previous chapter. His realization of the discrepancy between appearance and reality, fundamental to psychoanalytic thought, can be traced to Freud's intimate experience of a formal religious culture that had lost its vitality, and was brewing, from its very core, motivations that were too deep-seated and novel to be immediately perceivable during occasional visits to the synagogue or the pleasantries exchanged around the Passover table. This is to say that amid the religious-ceremonial formality that was continuing to be observed, and that was crumbling and becoming increasingly hollow, individual Jews were breaking away from formalism and moving toward an expression of their personal, individual feelings. The Jewish culture of Freud's time is a dualistic one in which the formal structure cannot any longer contain and hold back individual experience. This polarized situation is paradigmatic of Freud's psychological theory.

Third, the advancements of nineteenth-century Darwinism must be considered as background element in the shaping of Freudian thought. The claim that human life is governed by biological drives, the struggle for existence and natural selection, once again determined by biological processes, in which not reason but chance plays the determining role, is the fundamental precept of Darwinism. This conception implements the replacement of the notions of reason, teleology, and divine purpose by the principles of chance and adaptation to a changing material environment. There is no doubt that Freud saw himself as the heir of Darwin. One of the more interesting books on Freud that have been published in recent decades is entitled *Freud, Biologist of the Mind*. It argues that Freud was a biological reductionist who continued Darwin's work, albeit on a microcosmic rather than on a macrocosmic scale .

Not only Darwinian biology but the contemporary advances in physics influenced Freud. Just as the appreciation of the particle, of the microcosm, and of descending beneath the surface become prominent in the domain of physics—that is, as physics develops around entities that are invisible not only to the human eye but even under the microscope—Freud similarly develops an approach to the psyche that seeks the secret, hidden, and mysterious element in human behavior.

At the time that physicists developed the argument of the convertibility of mass into energy, Freud was searching for the energy that drives the human psyche, which he discovered to be as dynamic as the energy conceived in physics. Freud repeats in psychology what Einstein and his colleagues were doing in the field of physics—and he did it consciously. He was cognizant of the intellectual revolution in physics. He wanted a similar revolution in psychology.

There is an element of Nietzscheanism in Freud. The Nietzschean search for the undiscovered country, and the movement toward a realm that is not immediately experienced but that will eventually be penetrated, inform Freud's concept of the unconscious.

A simpler, material factor that explains Freud's impact is the use of effective mechanical contraception. The rubber plantations in Malaya did not busy themselves in the late nineteenth century as much with the production of tires as with making rubber for contraceptives. The invention of the rubber condom, as the first viable, mass-produced method of contraception, brought into the foreground the role of sexuality in human life. Previously there was not much to be done about sexual desire except to repress it, unless one was willing to undergo unspeakable hazards. Before the invention of effective contraception, sexuality could not be separated from pregnancy and from its procreational function. Contraception opened up thinking about sexuality in ways that were divorced from its reproductive role. In a way contraception rendered Freudianism, or at least the questions Freud asked, necessary.

Some recent biographers of Freud have tried to depict unflattering aspects of his personality. He altered a major theory to stave off professional and popular criticism, it is claimed. He recklessly experimented with drug taking. He mistreated his family and is alleged to have conducted an affair with his sister-in-law. Generally he held women in lower esteem than men. He was harsh toward his disciples—so it is said. Despite the attacks and criticisms, however, Freud remains an imposing personality.

By nature a dualist, Freud engaged in polarities and—like some other leading twentieth-century figures—thought in terms of binary opposites. (Jung was another, as is Lévi-Strauss.) Freud posits the conscious against the unconscious as the primary duality of his system. Similarly sexuality is opposed to moral conscience, love to desire, the normal to the abnormal, and finally the illusion of Christianity to the truth of secular science.

It must be remembered that Freud was above all a therapist. He certainly did not start as one, but he became one nevertheless. Freud attended medical school even though he really wanted to be a research scientist—more specifically, a research biologist—in a field that was then referred to as neurology and today would be called microbiology. However, Freud could not pursue the career he wanted because he was a Jew without money. While he could enter the medical profession, the prospects of obtaining a professorship at the University of Vienna were, in that anti-Semitic era, very remote. His family enjoyed modest circumstances, and he could not take the risk of choosing a profession that did not guarantee him a living.

He got engaged when he was quite young (for that time and place). The engagement lasted five years, during which time he and his fiancée did not have sexual relations. (It is curious that Freud's uncle by marriage was the founder of modern American advertising, Edward Bernays.) The long engagement put additional fiscal—and psychological—pressures on the young Freud. In his milieu marriage did not usually occur until the groom could support a wife.

So Freud decided to become a psychiatrist because this was the branch of medicine that dealt with neuroses, and particularly with the hysteria of women, and he could practice as a therapist and earn a living. There was a tendency among middle-class women in those days to develop a variety of tics, physical disorders, anxieties, and delusions—collectively called hysteria—which guaranteed psychiatrists more than a modest income. After a brief period of post-doctoral work in Paris, conducted with two distinguished psychiatrists, Freud set up practice in a rather shabby neighborhood in Vienna. He did not leave this location until he had to flee the Nazis in 1938. On the ground floor of this modest building he set up his practice and began to treat neuroses, especially but not exclusively in women patients.

It is important to realize that Freud was a therapist and a clinician. He wanted to help his patients. All his early theories are based on his experience with patients and on ways of curing them. His theories grew out of his close observation of his patients.

Freud did not have grants to fund his work, nor was he sheltered by an institution such as a university. Even after he became famous, he did not rise at the University of Vienna to a position above that of adjunct associate professor. At the university he was no more than a shadow that flitted in to give an occasional lecture. Even in the 1930s, with all his fame, Freud's colleagues in the medical school were not friendly toward him.

Freud was a heroic character. He was thoroughly inner-directed, courageous, and bold enough to make pronouncements that were bound to be ill received and to make him unpopular. He continued in this manner to the end of his career. The occasions on which Freud tempered his statements were very few, if they existed at all. He changed his views, but he never became a conformist. He said unusual and uncomfortable, disconcerting things from the beginning to the end of his career. Someone who could insist publicly again and again that children exhibited strong sexual feelings and that Christianity was a dangerous illusion, and say this in Catholic Vienna, had to be someone of extraordinary courage. Freud was no more gentle to his fellow Jews. He argued that bibical Judiasm is founded in guilt arising from patricide. That Freud rapidly gained fame and success does not detract from the hard road he chose to follow.

Freud saw himself as a Moses, about whom he later wrote a book. That he suggested that Moses was by birth not a Jew indicated his view of himself as separate and lonely. He understood himself as the founder of a new dispensation, who was leading people toward a new promised land, a land of milk and honey where, at last, people could be free and happy. Beginning in his early days, when he was still a poor and obscure psychiatrist, Freud already saw himself as the founder of a school. Freud was the kind of person who, thoroughly rejected by the establishment, proceeds to create his own establishment. Such people are today usually regarded as highly neurotic and as badly in need of psychotherapy or Prozac.

Within a year after he began his practice as a psychiatrist, Freud was envisaging himself as the creator of a new method, theory, and school of psychology, even though he had no disciples and only three patients. He later said that he was an elder son, and that elder sons, especially in Jewish families, were smothered in maternal love and developed high opinions of themselves. Fortified with maternal love, they became, among other things, extraordinarily brave. So went Freud's analysis of himself, on which he spent a great deal of time. His self-analysis usually proceeded on self-flattering grounds, but nevertheless he had a rather acute sense of who he was.

Freud was a domineering personality, both in his family and toward his disciples. A typical German *paterfamilias,* he had six children and—after his eldest daughter died in her twenties—was interested only in his youngest, his daughter Anna, who, in turn, never married but became a distinguished child psychiatrist and his literary executor. His other surviving children, including his sons, he mostly ignored. His relationship with his wife, whom he thoroughly dominated, was quite conventional, almost formal. Although she seems to have been a highly intelligent and courageous woman, he never encouraged her to study, to develop her own mind, or to find a career. He was content that she raise their children and prepare the meals.

Freud may have had an affair with his wife's sister. He certainly had close feelings toward her, but whether they were acted upon is a matter of dispute among his biographers.

From his disciples Freud demanded absolute loyalty. He saw himself as Moses leading the Israelites, and those among his tribe who separated from him in order to worship foreign idols he metaphorically sent out into the desert to perish. Exhibiting extremely acrimonious attitudes toward any of his disciples who disagreed with him, Freud did not hesitate to expel them from his group at the first sign of dissent: One either agreed with him or one left.

Freud got along very well with women disciples. He was eager to train women as analysts, and several achieved distinction. The first was Lou Andreas Salomé, who had a long career as a courtesan, and had been the mistress of Nietzsche and many others. Becoming first Freud's patient and then his disciple, eventually Frau Lou emerged as a noted psychotherapist.

Another of his female disciples was Marie Bonaparte, of the aristocratic Bonaparte family. She became the founder of psychoanalysis in France and a renowned therapist. It was Marie Bonaparte's wealth and influence that were instrumental in saving Freud from the Nazis in 1938. A third woman disciple was Helene Deutsch, who was prominent in American psychiatric circles in the forties and fifties.

Further among his female disciples was a leading child psychiatrist, Melanie Klein. A German who had studied with Freud, Klein set up practice in England, where she became Anna Freud's chief competitor. A genuinely Freudian scenario of sibling rivalry and bitter psychosexual enmity ensued.

Most of Freud's male disciples, at least in his early years, were Jews. To the very end of Freud's life, psychoanalysis preserved its strong Jewish component, as it continued to do in the United States down into the 1990s. Freud spent a lot of time searching for gentile associates. Embarrassed by his prominently Jewish following, he wanted a number of blond disciples around him. His unfortunate relationship with Carl Jung was a consequence of this desire—as we shall see. It is not surprising that Freud chose a British gentile, Ernest Jones, as his official biographer. On the whole the choice was a fortunate one. Ironically, Jones's biography is known today principally not in its original three-volume version but in a skillful one-volume abridgement made by a New York Jewish literary critic.

Freud's intellectual history falls into two periods: The first lasts from 1895 until about 1920; the second, from 1920 until his death in 1939. Even though he had contracted cancer of the palate by the late twenties (probably because he chain-smoked cigars), and underwent several serious operations, none of which were successful, he continued to work and write with characteristic heroism until the end of his life. His last major book, *Civilization and Its Discontents*, was published in 1930.

The Early Freud and Depth Psychology In the first period of his career, Freud produced what might be called the classic Freudian theory, or the theory of depth psychology. In this period Freud is a reductionist, a microcosmicist, a behavioral scientist focusing on the particle of energy, a Darwinian—in brief a modernist. The later Freud, on the other hand, was to a degree a cultural theorist who comes close to following neo-Victorian precepts, and who modifies in significant ways the radical depth psychology of the early period.

The depth psychology of the early Freud comprises seven doctrines. The first is sexual reductionism—that is, the Freudian belief in the primacy of the libido, the sex drive, in motivating human behavior and more exactly, in making humans unhappy. It is the dysfunctioning of the sex drive that produces neuroses. Both the individual and society would be far more content, Freud maintains, if the primacy of human sexuality, that we are sexual beings first of all, were recognized.

Freud was very much aware of what he referred to as the ambiguities of everyday life. The ambiguity is owing to the fact that things are not what they seem. The formal, immediately visible level of behavior conceals actual deep meaning. Freud posits a line above which resides the formal level of psychic phenomena. Below the line of formal behavior operates that primary sexual desire that drives and determines the readily visible level.

Freud was not the only thinker in his time to have made this claim. His contemporary, the English journalist Havelock Ellis, published book after book on the primacy of the sex drive and the value of sexual liberation. But even though others among his contemporaries assumed approximately the same premise, Freud alone was able to give a systematic theoretical description of this perception of psychic structure and sustain this theory with case studies drawn from his therapeutic practice.

The second aspect of Freud's theory is the assumption that there is no distinction between a normal and a neurotic personality. Freud did not deal with psychosis (madness, such as schizophrenia), but with dysfunctions, the illusions of neurotics that prevent their full participation in normal life, making it impossible for them to work and play effectively. Anxieties, hysteria, phobias, manic-depressive disorder, impotence, compulsive behavior, and delusions of grandeur or of persecution are the anomalies that received Freud's attention. Freud said that we are all normal and we are all abnormal. We are all equally affected by our sexuality, and by the devious ways of the libido. Freud claimed that we never grow up; we can never escape from the libidinal impress upon us. We have no right to be arrogant, to make censorious judgments along sexual lines. We have no right to say that we compared to others have succeeded in repressing sexuality, because repressing sexuality would only make us neurotic and malfunctioning. Freud undresses people and makes them all into potential neurotics at the mercy of their sexuality. This proposition is what makes Freud so repulsive to many Roman Catholics and Orthodox Jews and all evangelical Protestants.

The early Freud's third and most distinctive doctrine is that sexuality begins in earliest childhood. There is no clear distinction, psychoanalytically speaking, between adulthood and childhood. From at least the age of two, there is a strong sexuality in children, which Freud finds himself able to identify. The only reason that the description of human sexuality begins with the age of two is that children cannot speak coherently before that age, thus making identification and proof problematic. If innocence means freedom from sexuality, children are not innocent.

Freud maintained that between the ages of two and four, children develop very strong sexual fixations toward the parent of the opposite sex. This he termed the oedipal feeling (after the Greek myth). According to this theory, the male child is attracted to the mother, as the female is to the father. One of the determinants of the process of growing up into a functioning human being is the capacity to socialize oedipal feelings—that is, consciously to come to terms with them, to become aware of them, and to learn to live with them. The oedipal feeling cannot be circumvented; it admits only of being compromised and controlled. When it is simply repressed, it becomes an insurmountable source of neurosis, and opens the way to a variety of disturbances centering on an inability to develop authentic relationships with the opposite sex. The repressed oedipal feeling, which is always still present, profoundly intervenes in the adult's efforts to establish relationships with a member of the opposite sex other than the parent.

It was Freud's doctrine of childhood sexuality that was most controversial among his propositions, both in his time and since. Even though others also claimed that sexuality constituted the main drive in human life, no one else had extended sexuality into the realm of childhood. The divestment of innocence from children, the view that children have strong sex drives, erotic fixations on their parents—these are the Freudian claims that particularly disturbed and disconcerted his contemporaries, including many psychiatrists.

Freud was fully aware of the controversial quality of his views on childhood sexuality—he could hardly fail to be when it brought down on him the contempt and wrath of the psychiatric faculty of the University of Vienna. But he developed his theory from data obtained from his patients, and after discussing the issues with an early associate, Wilhelm Fliess, Freud felt compelled, as a true scientist would, to publish his findings.

Childhood sexuality still remains the most controversial doctrine in Freudianism. As will be discussed below, most post-Freudians have departed from this doctrine to a greater or lesser degree while preserving other aspects of Freudian thought. With the exceptions of the child psychologist Melanie Klein and the radical psychoanalyst Wilhelm Reich, the leading post-Freudian psychoanalytic theorists have either modified or discarded his view on childhood sexuality.

The fourth Freudian doctrine, a familiar one, is the doctrine of the unconscious. One does not have to look long at the paintings of Freud's Viennese contemporaries, such as Gustav Klimt or Egon Schiele, or listen for more than a few minutes to a Richard Strauss–Hugo von Hofmannsthal opera to know that in Freud's Vienna the unconscious realm was widely recognized. Indeed, the idea of the unconscious had been a prime thesis of early-nineteenth-century romanticism. Freud can be viewed as the last of the great romantic thinkers. He did not discover the unconscious, he mapped it. He clinically defined the role of the unconscious in human behavior. And he associated the unconscious with sexuality.

Humans have conscious and unconscious lives that impinge drastically on each other, Freud claimed. The unconscious, massively driven by sexual feelings, is much stronger than the conscious. A sexual crisis is not at stake when one peruses a porno magazine like *Playboy*. The sexual trauma operates rather in the depths of the unconscious, when satisfaction is avoided and sexuality repressed. There are powerful repercussions in the unconscious that shape and possibly impair severely our conscious behavior.

The relationship between the unconscious and the conscious involves "the return of the repressed." Repressed sexuality constitutes the material of the unconscious, becoming unconscious memory and dominating the unconscious. From there it works its way back into consciousness in order to shape and determine conscious behavior. The unconscious, therefore, figures in conscious behavior, and impedes it, to the point of rendering the person visibly neurotic, unable to live, work, and function as a human being. The repression of sexuality, for the earlier Freud, is not a theological or even a moral issue. It is a health problem, a segment of psychobiology. Neurosis that is discernible in conscious behavior is the outcome of repression in the sphere of sexuality.

The repressed never fails to return into consciousness from unconsciousness, albeit always in altered form that needs be understood through analysis. While Freud's theories pertaining to childhood sexuality have met with resistance, and although they have been modified or rejected even by his disciples, his theory of the unconscious has not only been accepted by specialists, but has even entered into general knowledge and become part of the cultural assumptions of the twentieth century. Just as, before the late nineteenth century, most people believed, no matter how vaguely, in the existence of sin, so too in this century many educated people believe in the return of the repressed.

The fifth principle of early Freudian doctrine is the theory of dreams. Freud's first important book, the one that initially gained him attention, is *The Interpretation of Dreams*. This is one of the more important books of the twentieth century, and Freud expected it to become precisely that. The book was published in the latter part of the year 1899, but on Freud's request the publisher dated its publication as 1900. Freud knew that his book would have a profound effect on the coming century, and he was right.

In *The Interpretation of Dreams*, Freud argues that dreams reveal the imprint of sexual repression. Dreams constitute a screen on which the consequences of repression, of fantasies as well as sexually motivated wishes, are projected. Therefore, he claims, dreams are crucial in the therapy of neuroses. One of the two prime ways by which the therapist can look into the unconscious is provided by the analysis of dreams. In fact, according to the tradition that runs back to Freud, analysands are still frequently instructed to keep a notebook of their dreams, in order not to forget them and to be able to report them to the analyst.

The sixth principle of early Freud is the other entrée into the unconscious that is psychoanalysis per se. This is the method of free association, by which the patient talks freely under the questioning and guidance of the therapist, and eventually, so the expectation goes, reaches the point of catharsis when the disturbing contents of the unconscious make themselves conscious. The analysis is successful, in other words, when the repressions embedded in the unconscious are clearly articulated.

The process of free association and the interpretation of dreams are the two prime mechanisms by which psychoanalysis operates. Freud tried other means. Early in his career he tried drugs, particularly cocaine. Like many medical researchers who, unable to find patients who will accept the risk of trying a new method and use themselves as subjects, Freud experimented with cocaine on himself. He decided to quit when he began to develop an addiction to it. The other method he tried was hypnosis, in which he had been trained while studying with Charcot in Paris in 1885. He also abandoned the hypnotic method, first because it met with resistance from some subjets and was therefore unreliable, and second, posthypnotic suggestion posed problems, as did other possible side effects. He therefore replaced hypnosis with free association or psychoanalysis.

Psychoanalysis has two functions. One is to penetrate the unconscious, which requires highly trained, and gifted, therapists. The second function is to be the "talking cure." The psychoanalyst and the patient can bridge the unconscious and the conscious, releasing the repressed, which has decisive therapeutic effect.

The final principle of early or classic Freudianism is the principle of transference. Transference signifies that in the relationship between the therapist and the patient there has to take place a close emotional bonding, a symbiosis as it were, or else the analysis will not achieve its discovery and therapeutic goals. Therapist and patient must become bonded. The relationship can be a very stormy one; it can involve hatred as well as love, but it is necessary that there be the emotional involvement of transference for psychoanalysis to occur.

The psychotherapist him- or herself must undergo not only a very rigorous training, but complete psychoanalysis as well, which can last anywhere from five to twelve years, and which is absolutely necessary. This requirement, incidentally, is something that kept some candidates from becoming analysts. Not only the duration, but also the requirement that the analysis be complete, represented an obstacle to them. While it is possible to become a surgeon without ever having to undergo an operation, it is not possible to become a psychotherapist without subjecting oneself to the process of transference with another psychoanalyst. In this training period, a very close bond is established between the psychoanalyst in training and the training psychoanalyst. The transference then is extended from the trained analyst to his or her patients, so establishing a chain of transference.

In some ways the history of psychoanalysis is like the history of early

Christianity: The immediate apostles of Jesus were followed by the bishops, the shepherds of the flock, who had been the disciples of the Apostles, and so on through an infinite chain of laying on of hands. The history of psychoanalysis recapitulates, in a way, this history of the early church. Every psychoanalyst stands, at least in principle, in the pyramidic chain of analytic transference going back to Freud himself.

Freud's early life and career have undergone an enormous amount of inquiry and are still being intensely debated. The official biography of Freud by Ernest Jones, published in the 1950s under Anna Freud's scrutiny, soft pedaled some key issues. Not all of Freud's writings surviving from his early period have yet been made public. Freud's daughter Anna, who died in the mid–1980s in England, where she had emigrated with Freud in 1938, appointed herself the guardian of his writings. She and other aging disciples of the master suppressed some of the early material. Recently Freud's revealing correspondence with his early colleague and associate Fliess has finally been made public. But this does not exhaust the writings that still await publication. (The material that still remains inaccessible is mainly in the Library of Congress.)

Freud in the 1980s received some bold criticism from a young psychoanalyst and historian of psychoanalysis, Jeffrey Masson, who raised such a storm that he was expelled from the International Psychoanalytic Association. Nevertheless what Masson has to say is worth listening to, even though he has articulated it in a highly polemical way. And there have been other critics of the early Freud.

First of all, it is pointed out that Freud's use of cocaine can be seen as proof that he was quite a reckless man in his early years. Perhaps it was so, but then, the use of drugs was much more common and not socially censured at the beginning of this century. In fact, in the nineteenth century, opiate-based cough syrups and other home remedies were widely in use. The use of drugs was rather thinly disguised in the nineteenth century, even in fashionable circles. Therefore Freud's use of cocaine cannot be regarded from our contemporary perspective; it was not a highly controversial act in his day. As a matter of fact, the condemnation of hard drugs began only in the 1920s and was an offshoot of Prohibition against alcoholic drinks.

The second argument about the early Freud is the particular point that Masson has made. Masson claims that Freud began by believing that having been abused as a child was a common experience among his patients, and that many of their problems stemmed from these experiences of sexual abuse. Soon Freud abandoned the theory indicated by his data, Masson said. It was this claim of Masson's that caused nothing less than a tempest among psychoanalysts.

According to Masson, Freud backtracked and changed his theory to claim that patients had fantasies of being subjected to child abuse, and that actual abuses had usually not occurred. Masson accuses Freud of lacking the courage to continue to report on the actual experience of his patients. Insisting on the reality of child abuse as the source of neurosis, Freud concluded (says Masson) that widespread child abuse was not a socially acceptable proposition. Even today it would be immensely controversial. Most of the criminal trials of managers of day-care centers in the 1980s for allegedly abusing young children in their care resulted in exoneration sooner or later.

If Freud indeed backed off from the child abuse theory because of the opposition it would encounter, this was the only time in his life that Freud lacked the courage to report truthfully on his findings. However, we know from the recent controversies that have sprung up around child abuse that this is an area that does not admit of easy probing or persuasive proof. To accuse Freud of lacking courage is to accuse him of highly uncharacteristic behavior. Freud's revision of his earlier claim seems simply to have been the result of a change of diagnosis. It seems that he had decided, after talking further with patients, that the child abuse accounts were regressive fantasies rather than actual experiences.

A third critique of the early Freud is that he was a male chauvinist whose view of women was arrogant and excessively masculine, and that Freud could not, after all, break with nineteenth-century culture. Freud reported that many of his women patients had a sense of inferiority toward men. He reported on a phenomenon he termed "penis envy"—that in analysis his female patients exhibited a wish that they had been males, and that this was part of their problem. These women, he held, were not able to come to terms with their own sexuality, and saw and judged themselves only in relationship to male sexuality. Part of this problem came from very strong oedipal feelings (or an "Electra complex"—from Aeschylus's play *Electra*, in which Orestes' sister helps him kill their father) on the part of women who had had intense attachment to their fathers, which in turn rendered them incapable of having full sexual relationships with men or coming to orgasm.

As a consequence of this, beginning with the psychiatrist Karen Horney in the 1940s, and developing with the feminist movement of the 1970s, Freud has been severely criticized as being antifeminist. This is again a highly difficult and controversial matter. Freud was reporting what his patients told him, and these patients lived in a male-dominated world. They experienced a society in which even affluent women faced serious difficulties developing a self-image that did not take the male as its model. Freud was, to an extent, culture bound, and he did not explicitly condemn this situation. But neither did he condone it; he simply reported on the psychoanalytic situation of his women patients.

If Freud were working today, he would report this sense of inferiority on the part of women much less commonly, since the feeling of inferiority toward males has in the meantime often been replaced by different problems—which, however, are still frequently gender-specific. Freud was thus an observer and reporter of what the culture of his time produced in his female patients. It is difficult to see how he can be condemned for reporting the scientific truth that he found operating among his contemporaries.

Furthermore, no other twentieth-century thinker has contributed to the sexual liberation of women as much as Freud did. He had many women patients, but he also had many women disciples, whom he treated as equal to his male disciples. He accepted and encouraged them as psychotherapists. Among professional men of his day, he was far in advance of most in freely accepting women as colleagues.

Freud tried to help his women patients recover from mental illness, and from the terrible repressions of Victorian society. He helped them come to terms with their severe oedipal problems, and tried to show them that their so-called hysteria was a result of sexual repression, and that physically and morally there was nothing wrong with them. Although Freud has paradoxically become a bogeyman for feminists in recent years, in fact the psychoanalytic movement marked a major meliorative turning point in the cultural status of women. That Freud is not a radical feminist of the 1990s does not need to be reiterated, but then, he lived and worked in the male-dominated society of early-twentieth-century Vienna. A leading British feminist psychoanalyst, Juliet Mitchell, has in recent years come to Freud's defense against feminist censure.

The fourth accusation that is commonly directed against the early Freud is that he romanticized his autobiography by presenting himself as more of a hero than he really was. This is ultimately a matter of judgment and taste. In his own account, the early Freud was an isolated thinker rejected by the academic and medical worlds of his day and subject to intense professional as well as popular criticism. This self-view is somewhat exaggerated. But anyone who works against the stream, and must encounter as much antagonism on so many fronts as did Freud, is prone to such over-rationalization and dramatization.

It is true that as soon as Freud began to publish his work, he found disciples. He ceased to be alone. He found brilliant young people to support him not only in Vienna but in Switzerland, Germany, Hungary, Britain, Italy, and, after 1910, in the United States as well. He gained the attention and recognition of a very large segment of the more intelligent psychiatrists of the rising generation. Nevertheless it is also true that he became the butt of the press, that he was condemned from the pulpit, as it were, and, most important for Freud himself, he was rejected by the medical establishment, and particularly by the Department of Psychiatry of the University of Vienna.

Freud saw himself primarily as Viennese, and to be publicly condemned nearly every time he delivered a lecture or presented a paper at the University of Vienna, especially before World War I, was deeply disappointing for him. The Viennese scene became disagreeable, if not ugly, for him as he was pilloried by the leading professors of psychiatry. The feeling of rejection he experienced in Vienna and in his own university remained with him for the rest of his life. He may have exaggerated his sense of isolation, but it is understandable why he should have felt as heroic as he did.

Among the most significant products of his early career were Freud's clinical accounts of the actual processes of therapy he conducted with his patients. Two of the case histories he wrote in this period, *Dora* and *The Rat Man*, the names naturally being pseudonymous, rank not only among the great works of psychiatric literature but also among prominent literary works of the twentieth century. Stephen Marcus, a literary critic at Columbia University, has said that Freud's clinical accounts are among the great works of modernist literature, fully comparable to Joyce's writings.

In spite, or perhaps because, of Freud's literary capability, there is a problem involving the English translation of Freud. The standard edition in English was prepared in the 1920s and early 1930s by James Strachey (the brother of Lytton Strachey, the polemical modernist biographer), with the assistance of his wife, Alix. The Strachey translations do not entirely capture Freud's style, which becomes at times extremely facile and almost colloquial, instead rendering Freud's language and style more ceremonial, high, and pseudoscientific than they actually were. Freud is not easy to translate, partly because he frequently employs a simple and direct style. The Chicago psychiatrist Bruno Bettelheim claimed in the 1970s that Strachey's translation had engendered a rather stilted Freud that was at variance with the German Freud. Yet Strachey's service to Freud, producing twenty-four volumes of fundamental psychoanalytic literature in the heyday of modernism, was substantial.

The Later Freud and Cultural Theory As he grew older (1920–39), Freud became more of a guru, feeling compelled not only to develop means of psychotherapy and a theory to elucidate individual behavior, but to expand on these in order to comprise a theory of culture as well. The result of this Freudian enterprise, although always interesting, becomes at times rather unfortunate. His later theories are not infrequently vulnerable or at least problematic. Certainly Freud's is the case of a thinker becoming increasingly radical as he grows older—not radical in the sense of becoming more politically extreme, but in the sense of becoming bolder in theorizing and in speculation.

Freud was always conscious of and sensitive to competition, much of which came from his own disciples. In such cases the disciple would be expelled from the Freudian circle, as in the example of Carl Gustav Jung. Jung and Freud were both interested in the cultural implications of psychoanalysis. Freud, always competitive, always insisting that the first and last words in psychoanalytic matters be his, could not resist developing a psychoanalytic theory of culture himself when he saw that other analysts, some of them his former students, were developing this new field.

The radical modernism of Freud's early period became muted when he undertook the project of cultural theory, and he became idealistic in the philosophical sense of the term, as well as more historicist. A strain of neo-Victorianism began to develop in the thought of the later Freud, but certainly not as powerfully as it does in the work of most other psychoanalytic theorists of culture.

The trajectory of Freudian thought follows the trajectory of modernism. In the early twenties, when modernism reaches its climax, Freud the modernist thinker, too, reaches his high point. Then, in the later twenties and the thirties, when neo-Victorianism makes headway and modernism begins to lose ground, Freud moves with the times once again, modulating his radical modernism in the context of a cultural theory.

Nevertheless, Freud's ideas from the later period are extremely interesting, delightfully bold, and have certainly roused much interest in the last thirty years. The resurgence of interest in Freud in the last two decades has been mediated primarily by the field of literary criticism, as well as by social and political theory. This resurgence has drawn more on the later than on the early Freud.

The thoughts of the later Freud can be summarized in five principles. The first feature of later Freudianism is the viewing of life in terms of a dualistic conflict. On the one side, Freud posits "the pleasure principle," which is rooted in the libido or the sex drive. On the other, there is what he calls "the reality principle," which is generated by the family and social institutions. Life, according to this conception, is a struggle between the pleasure principle and the reality principle, between the sex drive and the social institutions that surround us.

In his later writings Freud develops new terms to describe this dualism, and articulates it as the struggle between *eros* and *thanatos*, two Greek words meaning "love" and "death." In Freud's view, the new terms were substantially expressing the same contention as the one expressed by the opposition between the reality and pleasure principles. The pleasure principle had become eros, and the reality principle thanatos. The identification between the two sets of terms is not unproblematic, for it is not easy to see how the family and other social institutions can be equated with death except in a vaguely metaphoric sense. In any case Freud understood himself as restating the same dualistic conflict the former pair of principles entailed.

Freud's dualistic conception introduces into the psyche a biological dimension, which is contained in eros and felt as pleasure. Thanatos, on the other hand, introduces a cultural and social principle, which represents reality. The concepts of eros and thanatos opened up new possibilities for literary theorists to pursue after 1970.

It is particularly in the context of this dualistic conflict that Freud undertakes the critique of religion in the Judeo-Christian tradition. He says that the Judeo-Christian tradition is an illusion that impedes us from achieving appropriate compromise or transference, or concordance or symbiosis, between the pleasure principle and the reality principle. Theistic, puritanical religion is an illusion that impedes our efforts to attain a harmonious, healthy, and functioning life, and repressively allows the sex drive to operate only within the limitations of the family and social institutions.

Therefore religion makes life dysfunctional and induces neuroses. It does not allow for a personally effected compromise between reality and pleasure, or between biology and society, eros and thanatos, and it overweights the scale, producing unhappiness. As he grew older Freud became increasingly severe in his treatment of Christianity. Doubtless the anti-Christian stance is not born suddenly with the later Freud. It is present in his earlier writings, too, but in the 1920s assumes a deliberateness and polemical edge that cannot be found in his earlier work. He devoted an entire book, entitled *The Future of an Illusion,* to the condemnation of Christianity and its restrictive impact on human life.

The second principle of later Freudian thought is the famous threefold division of the psyche into the id, the ego and the superego. The division caught on, so to speak, in the pop world, it entered the media, and became very well known in the 1930s. By this famous triad Freud tries to map out the psyche.

The id consists of sexual desire. It operates in the unconscious, but is at work as well in the preconscious, which is the borderline between the unconscious and the conscious, and to a certain extent, it inhabits the conscious, too. Insofar as the id operates in the preconscious, in that dimly known border area, it becomes conscious. The id is eros, the pleasure principle.

The superego consists of the moral principles, the constraining laws of the social world, which are internalized. It draws on parental authority as well as on the socialization we are subjected to in school, or by any other figure or institution construed as authority. The superego is therefore antithetical to the id. It is thanatos and the reality principle.

The third component of the psychic triad is the ego, which refers to the conscious personality, as it consciously acts in and experiences the world. It resides between the sexual drive of the id and the constraints of the superego, striving to work out an effective compromise between the two and so to shape itself. Neurosis is precisely the result of an inability to work out such a compromise, and occurs whenever there is an overpowerful internalization of external authority. It is the development of a strong superego, stifling the claims of the id, that makes for neurosis.

The third principle posited by the later Freud is not as well known as the concept of the triadic personality, and is propounded in the anthropological work *Totem and Taboo*. Freud's anthropology is more closely derived from anthropological myth rather than from empirically based anthropology proper. Freud certainly did not incline to extensive social research. He read only a few books—which were not always the most reliable ones— on the subjects he wrote about, but they sufficed at any rate to trigger his powerful imagination. So, too, with the anthropological myth, which was developed as part of his great competition with Jung. Jung was extremely involved in anthropology and actually took the trouble to gather a large body of anthropological materials.

In *Totem and Taboo* Freud conjectures a transitional phase between the state of nature and civil society. He takes up the old problem, in other words, that had preoccupied seventeenth- and eighteenth-century political thinkers such as Thomas Hobbes, introduces some anthropology into it, and reinterprets it in terms of the oedipal principle.

The beginning of organized society, Freud claims, was the result of the primordial killing of the father by his sexually excited and oedipally motivated sons. Instantly appalled by their deed, the sons organized themselves into civil society, the most distinct feature of which was the existence of the superego. In all taboos, according to all religious and moral precepts, the slaying of the father is prohibited. The horrible, primordial, oedipally motivated stain of patricide is thereby inhibited from recurring.

It is interesting to compare the Freudian myth with Hobbes's *Leviathan*. Hobbes claims that in the state of nature, all are at war against all, that man is fundamentally violent and brutish, and that the state of civil society and peace is attained only when power is handed over to the great Leviathan of the state. Only in the absolutist state is the human inclination to violence taken under control. Freud is rendering an updated, psychoanalytic version of Hobbes's theory, limiting to patricide the wider-ranging violence that Hobbes had ascribed to precivil society. In both theories violence is circumvented and organized society achieved by positing taboos, figured by Leviathan or by the superego. In Freud's account the establishment of the superego socializes the oedipal feeling. Social organization came into being in order to control oedipal feeling.

It is granted that the sexual life of civilized human beings is controlled and impaired, sometimes to such an extent that it causes neurosis. The function of psychotherapy is to provide a countervailing mechanism that enables one to deal with the limitations of sexuality that are necessary in civilized society. A terrible act in the distant past, a sadomasochistic one, that is endemic to human nature, has necessitated the development of a superego and attendent repressive social institutions. On the other hand, society must not go too far in the other direction. The same society that curbs the sexual drive must allow enough room for sexuality for the human race not to be become entirely neurotic. Psychotherapy helps find the balance between the two extremes.

The fourth principle of the later Freud, which is already implicit in Freud's anthropological myth, is that all existing social and cultural institutions, especially art and government, are the consequences of the sublimation of sexual desire. It is because of our need to control our sexual drive in civil society that we have mediating institutions. In this effort to control the forces of the psyche and to achieve a compromise between eros and thanatos, between pleasure and reality, between id and superego, we generate a cultural superstructure which expresses itself in various ways, of which art and government are perhaps the most significant.

The conception of social and cultural institutions as stemming from sublimation allowed Freud not only to write about Leonardo da Vinci and attempt other art criticism, but it also made his theory somewhat compatible with a particular brand of Marxism that flourished in the 1930s and in the 1960s and 1970s underwent a vigorous revival, a school of Marxist thought called "critical theory," which grew out of the Frankfurt school of sociology of the early thirties.

The neo-Marxists of the Frankfurt school and their disciples, who are very prominent today, believed in a cultural superstructure, but one that comes out of economic conflict. They believed that institutions were generated out of the material conflicts in society. Freud, on the other hand, thinks that the superstructure develops out of sexual conflicts. Because of this particular Freudian conception, some Marxists thought that they could achieve a Freudian Marxism (or a Marxist Freudianism). They could, that is, join together Marxism and Freudianism and develop a theory of the cultural mediation of sexuality as well as of class conflict. This constitutes an important strand in radical thought, especially since the 1960s.

The final principle to be found in the late Freud is implied by anthropological myth, and is presented in his last book, *Civilization and Its Discontents.* Long before the atom bomb, even before World War II (although by 1930 there were signs of imminent catastrophe) Freud, an anticipatory prophet of the nuclear age, was concerned that humanity was on the way to self-destruction. He argued for what might be called common sense or a middle way, saying that the repression of sexuality through social codes, the sense of guilt, and the bourgeois family are the price we have to pay for civilization.

Ultimately Freud favors neither license nor repression but opts for a middle path that will enable civilization to preserve itself, and at once to acknowledge and relax its terrible grip on inherent human tendencies. The violent, destructive, and sexual drives exist. This must be acknowledged. Sexuality cannot be repressed to the extent that we all become impaired. A balance must be struck between sexual repression on the one side and sadomasochistic license on the other. Civilization resides precisely in this balance.

Civilization requires a cultural mediation. Culture incorporates the sense of guilt, but the sense of guilt, in turn, must not suffocate the sexual drive. There has to be a freedom in personal life, which cannot, however, grant the freedom to destroy other people. That the primordial feelings of man tend toward the sadomasochistic, toward destruction and patricide, does not justify fascism. It does not justify delirious violence, mass destruction, or even unrestrained promiscuity. In the end Freud opts for control and for the reality principle, but the reality principle he recommends does not totally annihilate or suppress the sex drive.

Here too resides the importance of psychoanalysis. Psychoanalysis teaches the control of license, of patricide and primitivism, but at the same time it helps create the space within which the individual can live without being emotionally eviscerated. Freud knew very well that Western man stood on the brink of the volcano.

Jung Freud's psychology, particularly that of the earlier Freud, is referred to as depth psychology. Freud is here trying to deal with human behavior as it comes from the deep structures of biological drives. Subsequent development in psychoanalysis departs from Freud in two ways: first in developing what is called ego psychology, as a conception of psychology that is distinct from the Freudian depth psychology. It is sometimes also referred to as interpersonal psychology, and entails for the most part the study of adult psychology.

Ego psychology deemphasizes childhood and the sex drive, or at least substantially reduces their importance. This approach tries to consider adults in terms of their personality or ego in relation to their social and cultural context. Ego psychology begins from Freudian principles, but it all but eliminates the theory of childhood sexuality and determinism, and greatly reduces the central importance of the depth of the sex drive. Instead, it concentrates on the functioning adult ego in relation to the social environment.

The other significant departure from Freud in modern psychology is effected by what might be termed radical Freudianism. This approach rejects Freud's plea for compromise between the pleasure and the reality principles. It rejects social control and advocates the maximization of the pleasure principle and the unlimited achievement of sexual satisfaction. It condemns every social limitation that impedes the attainment of total gratification, and it attempts to envision a world in which society is organized so as to allow for maximum pleasure. Looking on Freud's compromise as a betrayal of his own premises, it interprets later Freudian theory as a conservative regression, and his compromise not as one aimed at self-preservation, but as one that yields to thanatos.

These two branches of post-Freudian psychology do not, of course, exhaust all the nuances of later psychoanalysis, but are large enough to outline the main tendencies. Freud had to encounter both veins of departure in his own lifetime, and dealt with either by means of denunciation. His great disappointment, however was with Carl Gustav Jung.

In 1909, when Clark University awarded Freud his first honorary degree, it awarded one to Jung as well. It was Freud himself who had brought Jung with him in order to introduce him as the crown prince of the psychoanalytical movement and his intellectual heir. On the way to the United States, Jung had a dream—which he related to Freud—in which he killed his mentor. Freud did not fully realize the significance of the dream until a couple of years later Jung began to publish papers that sharply conflicted with Freud.

Carl Gustav Jung lived until 1961. He graduated from medical school and began to study psychiatry in his native Switzerland in the year 1900. He was a very brilliant, precocious person and rapidly moved to the front rank of Swiss psychiatrists, who were already famous at the time for their clinical work. Jung worked for several years in a mental hospital. He read and was favorably impressed by Freud's *The Interpretation of Dreams*. Without entirely agreeing with him, he felt that Freud was a major figure who deserved respect.

Jung wrote to Freud, and so began the vigorous correspondence between the two psychoanalysts. Jung visited Vienna, and there were close contacts between them from 1908 until 1912. Freud was very conscious of the fact that most of his early disciples were Jews, and that the medical faculty at the University of Vienna was mocking Freud and his psychoanalysis for being a Judaic heresy. Freud was therefore eager to find gentile disciples, and certainly no one could be more gentile than Jung, who was descended from a long line of Calvinist ministers.

Jung was not only a gentile but a devout Protestant as well, in addition to being a brilliant psychiatrist who was already greatly respected in Switzerland. So Freud rashly proclaimed Jung his disciple and intellectual heir—a designation that, to be sure, Jung never sought. Jung never said that he fully agreed with Freud, nor did he ever see himself as the heir of Freudianism. He continued to do his own work and eventually published papers that made it clear that he fundamentally disagreed with Freud in a number of very important areas. The only two areas in which Jung agreed with Freud were the use of psychoanalysis and the importance of dream interpretation. When Jung began to publish his papers and the insurmountable differences between the two thinkers became evident, Freud denounced him as a traitor and expelled him from his circle.

Jung did not accept the theory of infant and child sexuality. He claimed that his clinical findings did not sustain the Freudian hypothesis. He rejected it, therefore, on clinical, scientific grounds.

Second, Jung rejected sexual reductionism. Even though he agreed that there was a strong sex drive at work through the libido, he nevertheless found that the libido was not a purely sexual force. It was, he said, a generalized psychic energy of which sexuality constitutes only a part. In Jung's own words: "Reality is not to be understood as a sexual function." No statement could articulate more clearly a fundamental divergence from the Freudian conception of psychic reality.

Third, whereas Freud never dealt with psychotics and treated only neurotics, Jung, whose earliest work took place in mental hospitals, was very interested in schizophrenics. Indeed, one of his later patients was James Joyce's schizophrenic daughter, whom Jung tried to help but could not, probably because her illness had already advanced too far. Jung propounded an innovative theory about schizophrenia, finding that in certain cases a genetic predisposition was at work. But in most instances, he claimed, schizophrenics had suffered a terrible trauma that had produced a biochemical reaction, "a toxin," in the brain.

Schizophrenia can totally remove a person from the world, making him or her unable to speak, eat—these catatonic schizophrenics are often fed intravenously—and enter into any form of interaction with the surrounding world. Or else it makes the patient hysterical, uncontrollably violent, so as to necessitate his or her physical restraint. Jung traced this mental state to a biochemical reaction in the brain, caused, in turn, by trauma. While Freud acknowledged that Jung's conception of schizophrenia as the result of a biochemical alteration in the brain was possibly correct, he himself insisted that there had to be some kind of link between schizophrenia—or any other form of psychosis, for that matter—and sexuality. Jung, however, did not find that the originating trauma necessarily had to be a sexual one. Indeed, he found that extremely unhappy family life could in itself constitute a trauma strong enough to cause psychosis. Unlike Freud, Jung could conceive of a variety of situations that could prove so painfully traumatic for a person as to produce a biochemical reaction.

Jung claimed that he had some success in treating schizophrenics, and especially in the first half of his career he devoted himself extensively to their care. He proposed that paying close individual attention to schizophrenics, placing them in novel, beneficial environments, and assigning them simple work tasks obtained positive results in some instances. The illness is not entirely hopeless, in other words, but requires careful, close work with the patients. Jung's method of working with schizophrenics was continued in the 1960s and 1970s by the British psychiatrist R. D. Laing. Jung's approach to schizophrenia thus anticipated later research undertaken by others.

That there is a biochemical problem involved in schizophrenia and that some melioration can occur through individualized treatment are only two of Jung's major contributions to psychology. Just about every precept in modern psychoanalysis and psychiatry that was not invented by Freud was suggested by Jung. His mind was almost as fertile as Freud's.

Jung also devoted attention in his early work to establishing personality types using nonsexual criteria. This attempt particularly annoyed Freud and his disciples, who claimed that Jung's nonsexual personality profiles were banal and useless, representing an absurd and unwelcome return to Victorianism.

It was Jung who invented the personality polarity of extrovert and introvert—a distinction that describes personality with respect to the individual's relationship to the environment—in terms, that is, of negative and positive responses to the world. On this basis Jung developed what he understood to be the entire spectrum of personality types.

This Jungian work is no longer considered very important, but from the 1930s through the 1950s, the extrovert/introvert dichotomy was very commonly pursued by therapists and psychologists. In the 1950s the Harvard sociologist David Riesman (with the assistance of Reuel Denney and Nathan Glazer), in *The Lonely Crowd*, developed Jung's personality polarities into the concept of inner-directed and outer-directed people. The social psychologist William Whyte, in *The Organization Man*, applied the Riesman model to white-collar workers in large organizations. The terms "inner-directed" and "other-directed," which are direct adaptations of the corresponding Jungian concepts, entered everyday language in the fifties and sixties. A cottage industry developed in sociology and the media to cultivate this personality model. The concept even found its way into a novel (subsequently filmed) by Sloan Wilson, entitled *The Man in the Grey Flannel Suit*, which focused on the other-directed person who was fit to work for large corporations and commute to the suburbs. The leftist wave of the sixties countercultural movement dismissed this notion from the rather central place it had come to occupy.

By the 1920s Jung had developed a very strong interest in mysticism and religion. He began to acquire data, mostly from libraries, and became an expert on Oriental religions, concentrating mostly on Buddhism, Zen, and yoga. If Freud had been the biologist of the mind, Jung, it could be claimed, was the anthropologist of the mind, who elaborated a complete anthropological theory of the psyche. This eventually developed into the Jungian model of the collective unconscious and the theory of archetypes—the doctrines for which he is best known and to which he devoted the last thirty years of his life. He published prolifically the results of his studies, which were always based on anthropological data.

In 1928, when he first enunciated the theory of archetypes, Jung said that the structure of the unconscious was independent of individuals. This, of course, once again implies a strong conflict with Freud. There exists, Jung claimed, a universal psychic realm, the collective unconscious, in which the individual unconscious participates. The universal unconscious exists in and for itself, discrete from the individual. The universal collective unconscious is composed of mythological archetypes that play an active role in our psychic development.

The archetypes are known to us partly through religion and partly through literature and art. They are also embedded in our unconscious. They have a developmental as well as a therapeutic value, providing the channels through which we develop as human beings. To understand the world, to constitute a symbolic reality, which is tantamount to making sense of the world, we use these archetypes, which we perceive with varying degrees of dimness and clarity. The archetypes can be described as the mythological guidelines that comprise the tracks of human behavior. The more we discover these tracks, the more secure we will feel about our development. The universal symbols point back toward infancy as well as forward to the yet-to-be-realized possibilities of human life.

In the last two or three decades of his life, Jung increasingly propounded this view in terms of what might be described as a structural, neoidealist historicism. He wrote that "the collective unconscious is an image of the world that takes aeons to form." Certain features have crystallized in the archetypes over the course of time, and these constitute "the powers" that rule the psyche. The development had already begun in the primitive world, and found its elaboration particularly in the great religions.

Archetypes are universal structures that allow us to develop personally, and to endow the world with meaning and order. Dreams are important because they reveal the workings of archetypes. In the symbolic implications of dreams, we can observe the connection between our individual unconscious and the universal. So, whereas for Freud, dreams constitute the screen that reveals the dysfunction of the individual sex drive, for Jung dreams represent the screen on which the associations between our individual psyche and the universal archetypes or collective unconscious are shown. Dreams are flashes on a screen that demonstrate the integration of the individual in the universal.

The theory of archetypes sounds mystical, and it is. It sounds neoreligious, which it also is. Further, it is historicist and idealistic. After about 1928 Jung turned away completely from modernism and classic Freudianism, to a religiously based idealistic and historicist stance. He anticipates Claude Lévi-Strauss by noting in the archetypal symbols the presence of a strong duality at work. Like Lévi-Strauss's structures, Jung's archetypes come in pairs. Paradoxically, although Lévi-Strauss acknowledges a debt to Freud, his 1955 intellectual autobiography never mentions Jung. Nevertheless the Jung of the 1930s resembles the Lévi-Strauss of the 1950s in some important ways.

In his later writings Jung becomes increasingly religious as well as increasingly defensive about religious revelation. While the later Freud denounces religion as an illusion that wrecks mankind and destroys the balance of culture, Jung advocates revelation as "unveiling the depths of the human soul." No wonder, then, that Freud could feel as obsessive as he did on the subject of Jung. Jung assumed the shape of Lucifer in Freud's mind, the fallen angel who committed the great betrayal.

Jung's influence in the English-speaking world was small until the 1960s. This owes primarily to the fact that little of his work had been translated. Jung is very difficult to translate because of the mystical and emotional qualities of his writing. Jung resembles the philosopher Martin Heidegger in terms of his career and impact outside of the German-speaking world. It has taken a long time, in the case of both thinkers, for their writings to be rendered into English.

In the 1950s a member of the American billionaire Mellon family became a devoted follower of Jung and established the multimillion-dollar Bollingen Foundation, whose principal function has been to translate into English and publish all of Jung's works, which comprise well over forty volumes. The series has been published by Princeton University Press. So it is only in the last three decades that Jung's writings have become extensively available in English. The Bollingen translations of Jung are skillfully executed and beautifully printed. Jung had to wait a long time for his English face, but he was more fortunate than Freud in the final result.

There is a further similarity between Heidegger and Jung in that the latter's reputation was also scorched by his affiliation with the Nazis. In 1933 the Nazis established an anti-Freudian, Jew-free psychiatric association. Jung allowed himself to be designated its president. He did not occupy the post for more than a year, but did deliver a speech in the capacity of president in which he was critical of Freudian depth psychology, making remarks that could be construed as racist. The remarks are ambiguous, but allow for racist interpretation, especially since they were made in 1933. A year later Jung resigned from the Nazi psychiatric association, and separated himself wholly from the Nazis long before Heidegger did. Of course, Jung was safely in Zurich, Switzerland, whereas Heidegger found himself in Freiburg, Germany.

Jung's short-lived flirtation with the Nazis seriously damaged his reputation outside Germany in the thirties and forties. It is only since the mid-sixties that this unfortunate association has been largely overlooked or forgotten. Furthermore, the rise of the counterculture in the 1960s, along with the accompanying interest in Oriental religions and the fascination with archetypes, certainly contributed to stimulating interest in Jung. Jung's reputation is very much on the rise, and it can be anticipated that his influence will continue to grow.

The rise of structuralism likewise in the sixties and seventies reinforced Jung, because Jung had anticipated in various ways the mind-set, if not always the precise formulations, found in Lévi-Strauss and French structuralist anthropology. Furthermore, as has already been mentioned, the results Jung obtained from his early work with schizophrenics, and his belief in the biochemical foundations of psychoses, have been confirmed by the recent trend in the direction of psychopharmacology.

It must be emphasized that the later Jung represents very much a departure from modernism. It assumes the prime form of neoidealism and neohistoricism, and partakes of the resurgence of Christianity.

The most severe criticism that can be made of Jung is that he was too much a reversion to the Victorian system builder in the Hegelian mold. He wanted to develop a world philosophy that would explain just about everything. We have seen that the later Freud, as distinct from the archmodernist early Freud, had some inclinations in this direction also, with not always fortunate results, and partly in competition with his designated rival. But Jung goes far beyond Freud in propounding a universal theory that incorporates all human experience. On the other hand, it is precisely this neo-Victorian macrocosmic kind of speculation that has contributed in a major way to Jung's enhanced reputation in recent years.

Jung's macrocosmic theory of archetypes was easily adaptable to artistic and literary criticism. He had a major impact on literary criticism, particularly in the work of the Canadian scholar Northrop Frye. In his *Anatomy of Criticism* (1957), which was regarded as a manifesto against modernist New Criticism, Frye contended that the major function of literary criticism was the identification and elaboration of archetypes that are embedded in literature, and particularly in poetry. Literature is made up of an "order of words," of structural archetypes derived from "the context of its Classical and Christian principles." When the poet writes, he or she "imposes mythical form on his [or her] content," making "adaptations" of the archetypes comprising "Christian symbolism." Criticism therefore becomes archetypal criticism, the analysis of the way the language forms or structures are elaborated in poetry and fiction. Frye's Jungian approach to literature was well received in the fifties, just at the point when modernist New Criticism appeared exhausted and its proponents to have lost their confidence and enthusiasm.

In 1965 the Yale critic Geoffrey Hartman praised Frye as, in Copernican fashion, the "virile man standing in the sun . . . overlooking the planets." A short while later Hartman became a leading exponent of the application of French structuralism to literary theory. Obviously, as New Criticism spent its force, the prominent critics had begun to look for a radically different approach, supplanting modernism with macrocosmic speculation. Frye's Jungianism was immediately attractive. For a few years his Christian typology was regarded as the last word in criticism.

In the 1970s Jungian theory was propagated in the United States by two intellectual centers, one in Chicago and the other principally in California. At the University of Chicago the dominant presence on the humanities faculty was Mircea Eliade, who produced a small library of learned volumes on archetypes in religious literature, especially in the Orient. Eliade thereby directly continued Jung's work of the thirties and forties with an overlay of the academic respectability of the now thriving field of comparative religion. Eliade advertised himself as Jung's disciple and personally consulted with the Swiss sage.

Eliade was originally a Romanian, and in the 1930s he was the leading intellectual in the main Romanian fascist and proto-Nazi organization, which eagerly welcomed the German occupation and the murder of Jews. (He spent the war as a diplomat in Lisbon and was not personally involved in the Holocaust.)

There was another unusual side to Eliade's biography: In the late 1920s he went to India to study with a Hindu sage, lived in the latter's house, and seduced his young daughter. In the early 1990s both Eliade and the Indian woman published not incompatible accounts of this great love affair. The academic world, not least the particularly staid University of Chicago, with its Baptist origin, has little room for colorful characters. However, Eliade was their favored strong personality, and his fascist origins were ignored.

That Jung should draw fascist disciples is not surprising. Throughtout Western Europe in the 1930s and 1940s—and not only in Romania but among conservative Catholics in France, for instance—Jung gained a following on the far right. His neoreligious perspectives were a source of appeal, but even more was the aura of romantic exaltation that runs through his writings.

In California in the 1960s, under the leadership of Carl Rogers, Jungian psychology influenced the development of a kind of popular psychoanalysis that stressed the goodness and redemptive qualities in individuals no matter how mean their circumstances or antisocial or violent their previous behavior. "It's all right now" was the theme, as the acrhetypes floated down and elevated individuals into harmonious loving communities. The same brand of quasi-Jungian "humanistic psychoanalysis" was taught at Brandeis University by Abraham Maslow in the 1960s. In the 1980s and 1990s this democratic senti-mental psychology gained enormous visibility on TV talk shows. Would Jung have recognized his progeny? Very likely he would have, and if he were around today would be presiding over a talk show with immense ratings.

The Radical Freudians Jung mixed psychoanalysis with Christian sentimen-tality. The radical Freudians combined Freud with various socialist and liberal Left ideas. Alfred Adler, the founder of the group of left-wing Freudians, was an early disciple of Freud. Adler was an Austrian psychiatrist who came to the United States in the 1930s. Although he died in 1937, he left a considerable her-itage in America, which became particularly powerful in the 1960s. Adler com-pletely desexualized Freud. He did not believe in childhood sexuality, nor did he find that sexual malfunctioning was the foundation of neurosis. Adler was a member of the strong Austrian Socialist Party, which was eliminated by the Nazis in 1938, and he wanted to achieve a just and neurosis-free society—something Freud did not believe to be possible. Freud thought that a sane, bal-anced society was attainable, and that neurosis could be individually alleviated, but he believed that the attempt to achieve a neurosis-free society was in itself a dangerous illusion.

The problem, according to Adler, is not related to the libido or to the sex drive. It is posed by the aggressive tendencies in the ego, which stem from a sense of inferiority. Adler was closely concerned with the rise of Nazism, which was of course originally born in Austria—let us recall that Hitler was born and raised in that country—and was as prevalent in the streets of Vienna as it was in the streets of Berlin. He was trying to find what it was that made people aggressive and violent, and to discover the source of what he called "the will to power." In other words, he investigated the dangerous type of neurosis that results in social harm, if not destruction.

The road to a just society ran for Adler through the identification and analysis of the causes of violence. In his view violent acts constituted overcompensation for a sense of inferiority. Someone who grows up with a physical or psychic disability, if he or she is financially deprived, for example, or feels ugly or is possibly handicapped in some way, or has a sense of some other kind of inferiority, will try to overcome the sense of deprivation by overcompensating in an aggressive manner. The way in which we can achieve this alleviation of the socially dangerous will to power, this aggressive bent for overcompensation, is to get individuals to recognize their problems without shame or guilt, and to enable them to live with their defects, to integrate their disabilities instead of going in the direction of overcompensation by harming others.

The biographies of Hitler and other Nazi leaders provide ample proof for the plausibility of Adler's theory. Many of the Nazi leaders suffered from a recognizable social or physical disability that—in Adler's theory—resulted in a paranoid eagerness to harm. In many cases Nazi leaders were extraordinarily brilliant and capable people but became extremely perverse, hateful, and socially dangerous out of an inability to deal with their sense of inferiority.

Adler's emphasis on adults, his deemphasis of sexuality, his highlighting that the bases of neurosis lie in the dysfunctioning relationship between the ego, or the adult person, and the environment, opened the way to an important school of left-wing psychoanalysis. It also influenced a more moderate liberal American school of ego psychology, whose leading spokesman was Harry Stack Sullivan. This school continues to play an important role in American psychiatry to the present day. Sullivan and the liberal American school of ego psychology, as well as some of the more radical left-wing Freudians, find their start in the theories of Adler. Therefore, even though Adler is not very well known today, his heritage in the development of psychoanalysis is an important one.

The approach of the remaining three leaders of the group of left-wing Freudians, Wilhelm Reich, Norman O. Brown, and Herbert Marcuse, differs from the theory of Alfred Adler, and is indeed much more radical than Adler's. Reich, Brown, and Marcuse believe in the total liberation of the pleasure principle and in the attainment of the full satisfaction of the erotic drive. Thanatos, or the reality principle, is indeed death, according to this group of analysts, and represents the suicidal wish for personal dehumanization and social destruction. In their view authentic humanity can be only achieved by the removal of the social barriers to erotic fulfillment.

This branch of left-wing Freudianism emphasizes the pleasure principle and speaks in the name of the complete triumph of the id. In the view of its proponents, the later Freud compromised with his own theory, betraying his own early radical doctrines and departing from his biologically reductive theory, particularly in his last book, *Civilization and Its Discontents,* in which he proposed a compromise between sexuality and society. This, in the view of Reich, Brown, and Marcuse, was the wrong way to go. We will never achieve either social justice or personal happiness, they claim, by compromising between the reality principle and the pleasure principle. And Freud's mediative doctrine of culture, as a middle point between sexual freedom and sexual repression, can only lead to personal neurosis and to social oppression. This, in a nutshell, constitutes their fundamental message, which became a very popular message in the late 1960s and permeated the culture of the New Left. It was proclaimed prominently among the generation that filled the universities at the time, and generally by the rock and drug culture of the late sixties and early seventies.

Wilhelm Reich was an Austrian from Vienna, and a student and disciple of Freud, whom Freud regarded initially as an extremely brilliant theorist and one of his prime disciples. Then Reich became involved with Austrian socialism of a particularly militant brand, which was in the 1930s engaged in street battles against the Austrian fascists. Freud increasingly believed that Reich was becoming too radical and dogmatic, and he finally decided that Reich was mentally ill. He said that Reich was clearly paranoid.

Reich came to the United States in 1938 and became a very successful psychotherapist. Charismatic, he built up a large following both of patients and disciples. In the mid-forties he moved to rural Maine and established an institute there, a successful one that gathered around him highly capable people. Among the latter was a brilliant young Harvard psychologist who later became Reich's biographer.

Reich upholds, quite vehemently, Freud's doctrine of childhood sexuality, but what he himself was most interested in was the sexual liberation of the adult. Reich increasingly encountered difficulties. He emphasized the special therapeutic value of orgasm, a view that does not constitute a departure from Freud. But he claimed that he could stimulate psychic energy and prepare for orgasm by placing people in an "orgone box." Reich seems to have appropriated some of the theosophic ideas of the 1920s and 1930s. He believed in the existence of powerful energy forces in the universe. The subject placed in the orgone box could apply these energy forces to his or her unconscious in order to stimulate and liberate it. This was a kind of kinetic chiropractic. Reich's orgone box would have been much less controversial today than it was in the fifties. Reich's belief that the energy system that exists in the individual's psyche and body could be activated and stimulated to improve well-being would be readily welcomed in the 1990s.

Reich was warned by federal officials that selling this orgone box would be fraudulent. The first trouble he encountered was with the United States Postal Service, and later with the FBI. When he persisted in his sales of the orgone box, he was indicted and convicted of fraud, and sentenced to five years in a federal penitentiary, where he died. His disciples, then and since, claim that Reich was railroaded during the McCarthy era for his radical ideas, and that he was the victim of an FBI conspiracy. That there was a valid legal case against him is probable. That he was treated mercilessly is also true. But Reich was a bit ahead of his time; in the California of the seventies there would have been nothing extreme or reprehensible about his orgone box.

Like Adler, Reich in his younger and calmer days sought for a psychoanalytic explanation of fascism. Reich's seminal book, published in 1934, *The Mass Psychology of Fascism,* is still one of the more interesting and original works on Nazi culture. He argued that the same attitudes and behavioral mechanisms that are at work in sexual repression constitute the phenomenon of fascism. Fascism is the generalized death wish, the thanatos, of humanity. Reich claims that individual sexual repression translates into societal terms as the repression of sexual freedom. Therefore whatever contributes to sexual liberation undercuts fascism, and whatever in society favors sexual repression encourages and develops fascism. Fascism signifies for Reich the crystallization of an aggravated and violent form of traditional repression in Western society.

Reich argues that sexually repressed persons are potential fascists. They harbor strong oedipal feelings and engage in behavior patterns that are repressive of their sexual feelings and their authentic humanity. The roots of fascism, therefore, lie deep in the Victorian family and the repressive policies of Victorian church and society. Reich's is a plausible, albeit partial, explanation of German fascist culture.

Reich also presents the brilliant insight that fascists in general, and the Nazis in particular, were aware of their connection to antisexuality. Their sadomasochistic institutions, their violent and destructive behavior, constitute a persuasive and fatally attractive alternative to sexual freedom. He locates the root of Nazi violence in the sadomasochistic displacement of sexuality. The members of the Nazi movement compensated for their sexual repression through sadomasochism and violence. This insight was later used by the Italian director Lina Wertmüller in her remarkable film *Seven Beauties*—a film recognizably based on Reich's theory.

The second of the sexual liberationists was Norman O. Brown, who has lived an interesting life, and certainly a much happier one than Wilhelm Reich. Brown is still alive and leading the existence of a guru in the Carmel Peninsula in California. "Nobby" Brown began his career as a classics professor at Wesleyan University, and he continued in the same capacity at the University of Rochester. He was a distinguished scholar before, perhaps for personal reasons, he began to read Freud, and applied to Freud's text the same close reading he had to the classics. In 1954 he published his most famous book, *Life Against Death*, which was rejected by many commercial publishers and was finally brought out by the Wesleyan University Press. The book met at first with silence and was almost totally ignored, only to become immensely popular in the sixties among the New Left as a bible of the counterculture.

Brown published another seminal book in the late sixties, *Love's Body*. In the same period he became professor at the new campus of the University of California at Santa Cruz, which became the college of the flower children and of the counterculture. (The students on the Santa Cruz campus of the University of California were reputed to spend more time cultivating gardens than reading books in the library.)

Brown became very prominent and has continued to write and publish. A saintly, impressive person in every way, he essentially follows the views of Wilhelm Reich but borrows from Nietzsche as well. He is more interested in cultural liberation than in political upheaval. In his view sexuality in its fullest cultivation wipes away both individual repression and social oppression. Through intense, unremitting, and unending copulation, one can attain Nietzsche's "undiscovered country." Nietzsche had presented the concept of the undiscovered country as an image transcending nineteenth-century culture. Brown specifies the method of realizing this cultural goal.

Through copulation, unrestrained promiscuity, we reach a new cultural plateau. Of course, this message was very much welcomed by the Woodstock generation. However, Brown's greatest contribution is as a cultural theorist, and his influence is mainly in literary and historical scholarship. It must be remembered that Brown never practiced as a psychotherapist, although his knowledge of Freud is deep and professional.

Brown argues that cultural structures can be read as psychoanalytic texts, that the culture of a society becomes a hypostatized, or mediated or raised, substance that can be read and studied as a text. So his aim is in a sense to combine the reductionist radicalism of the early Freud with the cultural theorizing of the later Freud, and introduce into this mixture the Nietzschean concept of the undiscovered country or a new transcendental culture, along with modernist analytical scholarship. In his second book, *Love's Body*, Brown reads political and social theory as psychoanalytic text—that is, discourse on the "body politic" becomes, in Brown's reading, literally the sexual body politic. He tries to show the psychoanalytic and sexual underpinnings of this familiar concept of political theory.

Brown's work opened up the way for a large group of psychoanalytic cultural theorists and historians of the 1970s and 1980s. Among the most prominent of these are Peter Gay, holder of a distinguished humanities chair at Yale University; Stephen Marcus, sometime chairman of Columbia University's Department of English; and John Demos, who has a history chair at Yale University. These highly visible scholars have followed the path opened by Brown in the late fifties and sixties, in one way or another studying culture as a psychoanalytic text.

The third member of the group of left-wing Freudians, the one perhaps best known through the media because he became a pop figure for a while in the late sixties and early seventies, was Herbert Marcuse. There were times between 1968 and 1971 when Marcuse must have been seen on the TV news once a week, haranguing college crowds from San Diego to Berlin in his thick and largely impenetrable German accent.

Herbert Marcuse started out as a member of the Marxist Frankfurt school of critical theory, but later came to the United States, where he struggled abysmally for many years, teaching in marginal institutions like the New School for Social Research, or working as an adjunct professor at Columbia University. He published at this time one of the best books in English on Hegel, *Reason and Revolution*. In the late forties, when Brandeis University was founded, Marcuse was made professor of philosophy there.

In the 1950s and early 1960s, Marcuse spoke softly about Marxism and presented himself for the most part as a radical Freudian. In the early sixties, he published what might be termed his best book, *Eros and Civilization*, a radical Freudian tract containing as well elements of a subdued Marxism. Marcuse freely owns his debt to Reich, even though he does not entirely agree with him. In the late sixties and early seventies, perhaps overtaken by his new popularity among the flower children and the New Left, Marcuse began to shift more toward attempting a direct synthesis of Marxism and Freudianism. His later work, of which the most important is *One-Dimensional Man*, tries to achieve this synthesis.

The early Marcuse, that is, the Marcuse of the fifties and the sixties who produced *Eros and Civilization*, claims the need to achieve the fullest sexual liberation possible and the cultivation of the pleasure principle. He does note that Reich's interpretation of fascism is important, but nevertheless he thinks that Reich's model is oversimplified because it ignores economic factors. Yet like Reich, Marcuse himself is a utopian with respect to what he expects a movement of sexual liberation to achieve. He believes that the intense cultivation of sexuality will unleash and magnify human energy, providing that extraordinary capability by which humanity will build the just society.

Through unlimited sexual practice, in other words, we will become not only full but also superhuman beings, which will enable us to ascend to a new social plane and achieve a just society. The sexual superman and superwoman will shake off their chains to work like so much dew, and so create a new society that is both erotic and just. Unsurprisingly Marcuse's message became immensely popular in the counterculture of the sixties, and to a lesser extent his doctrine shaped the counterculture's ideological expression. Thanks to the reception he found in this culture, Marcuse, after being totally ignored for nearly twenty years, became a guru almost overnight, and was lavished with invitations to address adoring multitudes from California to Germany. And, once in a while, somebody in the audience actually understood what he was saying. Marcuse was not a very charismatic person, and his heavy accent and opaque Hegelian terminology usually disappointed his audience.

The president of Brandeis was frightened by the discovery that he had a popular radical cultural hero on his faculty, and he refused to keep Marcuse on past retirement. But Marcuse found a ready welcome at the University of California at San Diego. Marcuse was a stimulating and learned thinker, and despite his appropriation by sixties movements, he is well worth reading even outside that context.

The American School of Ego Psychology

Far more moderate than Reich and his disciples was the mainstream American school of Freudian therapy from the thirties on. The American school of ego psychology is also referred to as the school of developmental or interpersonal psychology. The school is an immensely influential one. The average New York psychotherapist today is likely to be the product of an ego-psychological training. The leading names of the school in its founding period were Abraham Cardner, Harry Stack Sullivan, Erich Fromm, and Karen Horney, all of whom were well-known and important intellectual figures in the forties and fifties in the United States.

The American school emphasized the role of social conditioning in the formation of the psyche. It was the spokesman of the reasonable, moderate, and liberal life. It deemphasized sexual reductionism, and although it sought a happy sexual life for people, it did not nurse utopian expectations. The "undiscovered country," as well as magnified human energy through copulation and boxes and uncontaminated social justice, were, in the eyes of this school, remote fantasies. While sexuality was central to life, it had to be practiced in the context of social and familial framework.

The school of ego psychology presented a sensible, middle-of-the-road approach. It greatly admired John Dewey, and certainly could be seen, particularly as manifest in the work of Cardner and Sullivan, as an offshoot of the American philosophical school of pragmatism. Cardner was prominent in the late thirties and forties, at which time he was a passionate advocate of the New Deal and a great admirer of John Dewey. He believed that personality is to a very large degree culturally conditioned, and that it is related to the needs of social institutions.

The American school of liberal ego psychology rose to immense prominence and prosperity in the quarter of a century after the Second World War not only for intellectual reasons—their skillful adaptation of Freud to the needs and attitudes of the American upper middle class, especially in New York City; the cultivation of Adler's ideas; and their professed devotion to John Dewey's nativist brand of pragmatism—but also for fortunate professional reasons.

During the war, in the early 1940s, mainline psychiatrists very sympathetic to Freudian or modified Freudian psychoanalysis gained the leaderhip in the American armed forces psychiatric and mental health services. Among them were Karl and William Menninger, who ran a famous mental hospital in the improbable location of Topeka, Kansas. Consequently psychoanalysis became legitimated in the medical profession to a much greater extent than ever before. If therapy was good enough for American heroes overseas, or recovering in hospitals back home, it was good enough for middle-class Americans. The media, including the then influential weekly newsmagazines, endorsed psychoanalysis with unrestrained enthusiasm. Furthermore the medical profession in the 1950s accepted the orthodoxy of the theory of psychosomatic illness—that many physical ailments, including asthma and gastrointestinal disorders, were the consequence of psychological stress or repression. For the first time, M.D.'s with psychoanalytic training enjoyed the legitimacy—and sometimes even the income—of cardiologists and surgeons. This was the benign world in which Cardner and Stack Sullivan, Fromm, and Horney functioned and prospered.

The superego, according to Cardner, is *not* the product of menacing repression caused by parental dictates, clerical traditions, and social constraint. It is rather a category that society creates over time. The superego simply constitutes the sensible, moral substratum of a democratic society. In a progressive democratic society like the United States of Franklin Delano Roosevelt and Harry Truman, we need not take a negative view of the superego, and instead recognize that the superego contains mostly liberal and progressive sense. We must, therefore, control our desires and direct our personality along the lines of these progressive ideals. The superego is culturally conditioned, which means that it changes with time and, at least in a democratic society, can be looked on as a positive force in life. This view represents a conservative departure from Freud, especially the younger Freud.

In sum Cardner believes that the New Deal is a good superego. Of course, problems arise when one attempts to practice therapy according to this theory in a fascist or otherwise totalitarian country, but then Freudian psychotherapists do not usually last very long in those countries in any case.

The dominant personality in the American school, and perhaps the single most influential figure after Freud himself in the history of American psychotherapy, was Harry Stack Sullivan. Sullivan, who died in 1949, was particularly influential in the thirties and forties. He began his work in Chicago, developed a large practice in Washington, and later became the most visible psychotherapist in New York. Not only was he the psychotherapist for the carriage trade, but he exercised enormous influence on the training of the new generation of New York psychotherapists, many of whom are still practicing. One reason for Sullivan's influence and power is that he became the hegemonic figure in the New York Psychoanalytic Institute, which accredits about 70 percent of the psychotherapists in the metropolis.

Furthermore Sullivan was the prime training analyst of the William Alanson White Foundation. The training analyst is the one who analyzes the candidate who wants to become an analyst, and supervises the candidate's early clinical work. Every candidate has to undergo analysis for a number of years before he or she can become a psychoanalyst himself. Therefore a significant number of an entire generation of analysts in New York City were strongly under Sullivan's influence and, in many cases, personally psychoanalyzed by him. Sullivan's enormous impact is still felt through his host of disciples and disciples of disciples.

It transpires, however, that Sullivan was a medical fraud. He always signed himself as Harry Stack Sullivan, M.D., yet his medical degree was inferior even to those from quack offshore medical schools with which "Doonesbury" amuses itself. In the early years of this century, down to the time of World War I, there were many phony medical schools in the United States that dispensed paper degrees. These were eventually closed down by the American Medical Association, but Sullivan managed to become an M.D. just before the last of these paper mills was eliminated.

Sullivan concentrates on the adult individual and on the need of the adult to "conform"—this is a word dear to Sullivan—to the social environment. Neurosis, in his view, is largely the result of a disconformity or of a conflict between the adult individual and the social environment. While this does not exhaust the matter for Sullivan, it does constitute the key problem. The function of the psychotherapist is to get the patient to adapt and conform to social norms. These social norms, in turn, prevail over personal feelings. Needless to say this view presents a major departure from Freudian theory.

Society is right, according to Sullivan; individual rebellion is nearly always wrong. It was Sullivan who devised the psychoanalytic strategy that is still used by most psychotherapists in New York. He insisted that the first thing that the psychotherapist must do is to dismantle "the delusion of unique individuality" in the patient. No patient should believe that he or she is a special person with special problems. The therapist must persuade the patient that he is ordinary, with common, universal problems. The initial period of therapy is devoted to convincing the patient of the ordinariness of his problems and the common quality of his identity. Suppose the patient were actually an Einstein or a Joyce: Would Sullivan still advocate this approach? Presumably yes, unless the patient were already world famous.

In the 1930s and 1940s, Sullivan's theory had liberal connotations. That is, the people who were in conflict with the social order of the time were often reactionary misfits. The prevailing code was that of the liberal New Deal and of liberal secularism, and people who were in conflict with it were those of a traditional or evangelical religious persuasion, and/or believed in runaway capitalism, and generally held retrograde cultural or political opinions. In the thirties and forties Sullivan could therefore be viewed as advocating adaptation to a set of social norms that had progressive and secular content. However, by the

1950s, during the Eisenhower era, those social norms had been replaced by conservative ones that upheld the "togetherness" of the suburban family and the more competitive mode of capitalism. They were the norms of the "man in the gray flannel suit," and Sullivan's teachings from being progressive were transformed into conservative ones. Now they were used to brand people who were leftists and socialists, or otherwise critics of the establishment, as neurotics. This reflexive conformism remains central in the New York psychiatric profession.

Sullivan made an enduring contribution to psychiatry through his work with schizophrenics. Like Jung, he believed that the therapist could work advantageously with psychotics, and he applied his doctrine of environmental conditioning to schizophrenics. He did not think that the "mad"—the inhabitants of mental hospitals who were entirely dysfunctional, catatonic, or violent—were hopeless. He thought that their problem was one of extreme disassociation from the environment, and he believed that placement in an appropriate environment would benefit many psychotic patients. The approach had been suggested by Jung; Sullivan worked at its application.

Sullivan's greatest critic in the American school was Erich Fromm, who immigrated to the United States from Austria, where he had been a student and disciple of Freud. The ego psychology Fromm developed had a strong existential flavor. It bore distinct parallels to the existentialist philosophies of Jean-Paul Sartre and Albert Camus, who were prominent in France in the forties and fifties.

Fromm began as a Marxist trying to reconcile the principles of the American ego-developmental school of psychology with Marxism. His Marxism became more muted with time, even though he always remained a leftist thinker. Ultimately his approach can be identified as existential psychoanalysis.

Fromm claims that members of capitalist societies suffer from loneliness and alienation in an environment that is dehumanizing. This, of course, is a classic Marxist doctrine. Therefore mental health problems stem from the loneliness of the individual in capitalist society. Unlike Cardner and Sullivan, Fromm does not whistle in the dark, claiming that all is right with the world. He acknowledges that the majority is still suffering from adverse social and cultural conditions. On the other hand, he does not agree with Marcuse either, that capitalist society is totally dehumanizing and that freedom cannot be attained unless capitalist society is abolished as a totality.

Fromm believes that capitalism will yet continue for a while, and the main occupation of the psychotherapist is to teach people how to live in this society—thereby accepting the adaptationist assumption of the American school. And the way to live in it is to make rational choices. We have to learn to live with our loneliness, to prepare to live alone, to recognize that in our daily lives we are going to be in conflict with society. We have to be able to carve out a place for ourselves in a social and cultural environment that is inhospitable. The wrong thing to do is to "escape from freedom," to use the title of Fromm's most famous book, which was very popular in the forties and the fifties. The escape from freedom is the work of false consciousness—here Fromm uses another Marxist idea—by which we persuade ourselves that this society is good when it is not, and so try to conform to it. Sullivan was wrong: We have to recognize that society is not good, and that the individual *is*.

The individual, by making rational choices, stays within him- or herself, often living a life of psychological and physical loneliness, and yet preserves his or her dignity, knowing that the culture is dehumanizing, and struggling against this dehumanization. This view is the translation, as it were, into psychoanalytic terms of the teachings of Camus. Camus, who was writing at the same time, says that the world is absurd, the individual alone is good, and we must live with the absurd, knowing that the only good thing in the world is a good individual. Fromm is teaching essentially the same doctrine, expressed in psychoanalytic terms. Fromm's writings were very popular in the fifties and early sixties, and they are still worth reading. There is a tough-minded dignity to his doctrine.

The final leading member of the American school was Karen Horney. Although Horney was influenced by Fromm, she was not as political as he was. She was further influenced by the anthropologists Ruth Benedict and Margaret Mead. Of Danish-German descent, Karen Horney studied with Freud, came to the United States in the mid-thirties, practiced mainly in Chicago, and died in 1952. Late in her career she was expelled from the American Psychoanalytic Association, because she wrote severe criticisms of Freud and because of her vehement, pioneering feminism.

As a psychoanalytic feminist, Horney was largely ignored in her day and had only a small following. She specialized in treating women patients. Her reputation was marginal until the feminist movement of the seventies rediscovered her. She is now very well known, and her writings have become bestsellers in feminist circles.

Horney criticized Freud severely for what she regarded as his excessive male chauvinism. She believed that Freud had mistakenly applied his biological determinism to gender. She argued that gender differences were determined not biologically but culturally. It is a moot point whether she was reading Freud right. Freud had discovered that his women patients were often conscious of a feeling of powerlessness because they were not males, a perception he formulated in the theory of penis envy. It is not clear, however, whether he thought that this gender-sensitivity was a trait his patients had picked up from their cultural and familial environment or whether he thought it an inevitable, inherent feeling. In any case he did not clearly say that it was culturally determined. Freud probably believed that it was both biologically and culturally determined, whereas Horney argued against any supposition of a real emotional difference between men and women except as the culture makes them different.

One can imagine, Horney claimed, an androgynous culture that could be achieved by transforming the codes and institutions of society. This would remove not only repression from women, but also their consciousness of gender differences. At the same time male consciousness of gender differences would undergo transformation. This doctrine has become one of the leading tenets of feminist thought, and, although not all feminists subscribe to it, it has a perpetual place in the mainstream of feminist theory.

Psychoanalytic Structuralism Jean Piaget, Erik Erikson, and Jacques Lacan are the three most prominent psychologists of more recent times. They may be described as comprising the school of psychoanalytic structuralism, and since structuralism became very important in the sixties and seventies, this form of psychoanalysis fitted in with the dominant cultural movement, which will be discussed in a later chapter.

The three masters of psychoanalytic structuralism possibly had a forerunner in Otto Rank, who died quite young in 1939 and has only in recent years begun to receive much attention. Erich Fromm denounced Rank in the thirties as a fascist, and Freud, with whom Rank had once been very close, also repudiated him. The basic principle of Rank's "will therapy" is that we must learn to live with our illusions. Truth does not lie behind these illusions; truth lies in the actual structure of the illusions. "This constantly effective process of self-deceiving, pretending and blundering . . . is the essence of reality." The task of the therapist is not to wean the subject away from his illusions but to get him to "learn to live with his split, his conflict, his ambivalence, which no therapy can take away." Freud saw this doctrine as another great betrayal of his message. It is only after the ideas of Piaget, Erikson, and Lacan gained currency that what Rank was trying to say in his rather crude and unreflective manner has become clearer. We cannot break out of this structure; we have to learn to live with it and confront it.

Of all the leading post-Freudian psychiatrists, Piaget appears to be the least influenced by Freud. In fact, he created his own system. One can plausibly claim that along with Freud and Jung, Piaget is one of the three most original minds of psychoanalytic thinking.

Piaget had a very long career, which began around 1921 and spanned half a century. The greatest influence on Piaget was the eighteenth-century Swiss-French philosopher Jean-Jacques Rousseau, who argued in *Émile,* his book on child development, that a child will develop spontaneously and advantageously through innate structures of the mind. He advised leaving the child alone, not intervening in the natural development of the innate mental structures. Rousseau further advocated that a pleasant environment be created for the child, within which he or she can pursue his or her own development. These psychological precepts were of course in accordance with Rousseau's idealist doctrine that society is fundamentally bad, and the individual good: "Man is born free and is everywhere in chains."

In Piaget's native Switzerland, in Rousseau's hometown of Geneva, there was an institute of child psychology devoted to studying and implementing Rousseau's theory. Piaget was trained principally there, and in 1921, at the age of twenty-five, became its research director. Shortly after, he was made the head of the Rousseau Institute, over which he presided for close to half a century.

In addition to the influence of Rousseau, Piaget acknowledges debts to Bergson and Durkheim. How much anyone can owe to Bergson remains a matter of doubt. But Piaget's debt to Durkheim is a real one, as we shall see. There are also considerable resemblances between Piaget and some of the ideas of James and Dewey. There is a certain overlap in Piaget's ideas with the American philosophy of pragmatism.

Piaget's initial assertion concerns a stage theory in the mental growth of the child. He says that, from early days through adolescence, the child undergoes distinct developmental stages that Piaget finds himself on the basis of clinical evidence able to map out and describe year by year. He finds that each stage is marked by very distinct and visible changes that represent the gradual growth in the child's symbolic capability—the capability, that is, of symbolizing the world and manipulating it mentally and internally. The process, Piaget says, is slow and strictly programmed: A child of four cannot do what a child of six is capable of achieving; and at six, a child cannot accomplish what he will easily manage at the age of eight, and so on. A child is only capable of achieving a certain level of symbolic rationality at a particular age. The child cannot and should not be asked to go beyond what Piaget terms "structures" or the mental systems and capabilities suitable for his age.

The human psyche matures slowly. It cannot be rushed. Although a good environment is conducive to growth, nevertheless even the best environment cannot make a child of six do what he or she will not have the capacity for doing until the age of eight. Piaget thus enunciates a principle that has become very widely accepted in children's education as well as in many other fields, including athletics. Athletes can often be heard these days speaking of "staying within themselves," meaning that an athlete can achieve only what he or she can achieve— that is to say, go only so far as his or her structural capacity allows. This is Piaget applied to athletics.

Even though the stages of childhood development cannot be significantly advanced, even under the most favorable conditions, they can be held back. The child can be inhibited by a negative, impoverished, fearful environment. Such environments can disturb the child's mental growth. Therefore, Piaget stands halfway between the idealism of Rousseau and the behaviorism of William James or Harry Stack Sullivan.

The second theory that Piaget develops, something we have already touched on, is that the most important part of mental development, which is fulfilled in late adolescence, is the attainment of a capacity to transform physical actions into mental operations. This capacity represents symbolic perception, that is, being able to perform a physical action as mental operation. It is the capability to see in the mind, to imagine oneself doing something without actually carrying out the action. And the development of this capacity is important not only with respect to performing mature mental operations, but also, most significantly, it enables one to understand oneself as a person, to grasp one's own identity. But if there has not been appropriate childhood development, if a child has grown up in a negative environment and therefore not lived fully through each developmental stage, he or she will undergo an identity crisis around the age of fifteen or sixteen. The child will not be able to imagine and comprehend his or her identity and so develop an appropriate consciousness of self—which is to say not fully achieve the capacity for human symbolic operation.

This conception of Piaget approximates Durkheim's notion of *anomie*. A society is anomic, according to Durkheim, when the value system of that society, which signifies its symbolic understanding of itself, is out of phase with the institutional behavior. Similarly, if a child has not been allowed to develop appropriately, there is an imbalance between his or her external behavior and symbolic consciousness. This, in turn, produces a poor sense of self, which leads to terrible frustration, crime, and violence. Piaget would say that if one grows up in a pathological familial and educational environment, the result can be an underdeveloped sense of self. The only available means of self-expression that remains to such persons is socially dysfunctional behavior and ultimately violence, whose cost to society is likely to be formidable.

Piaget was not an armchair theorist. His clinical output was impressive. His theories are always based on clinical, experimental work with children as well as with adults. One eminent child psychiatrist who was influenced by Piaget was the Chicago psychoanalyst Bruno Bettelheim. Bettelheim, an Austrian émigré, for forty years headed an institute at the University of Chicago for autistic, that is, schizophrenic, children. Working with autistic children along the lines of Piaget's findings, Bettelheim had more success in his work with preadolescent schizophrenics than anyone else. Piaget's principles pervade Bettelheim's writings. He advocated above all that children have their own distinct culture, and reminded readers that children are not adults, and that this simple but important fact should not be forgotten when environments and programs for children are designed.

The most interesting extension, however, of Piaget's theory, is to be found in the work of Erikson, who became a national guru in the late sixties and seventies, competing on public platforms with Brown and Marcuse.

If Sullivan had a phony degree, Erikson, refreshingly honest, had none except honorary ones. In spite of his Scandinavian name and Viking visage (which probably contributed to his guru image in the sixties) Erikson was a north German; he got his name from a Danish stepfather. Erikson was Freud's last student in Vienna and came to the United States in 1938 at the age of twenty-one, starting work in a mental hospital near Boston. He was trained as a lay therapist and began to publish papers as well as books, which rapidly became influential. He ended up as professor of psychiatry at Harvard University. In the late sixties and seventies, he became world famous.

Erikson essentially has three important ideas. The first of these consists of an application of Piaget's theory of the stages of childhood development to adults. Erikson combined Piaget with Sullivan and the American developmental school. Not only adolescents, but adults as well, Erikson found, go through distinct stages of development, and undergo identity crises approximately once every ten years. In the late seventies, the New York journalist Gail Sheehy wrote a popular book based on this Eriksonian theory, *Passages*, which became a bestseller.

Erikson believes that the development of adulthood is affected both by an internal core and by the environment. Personality is significantly shaped by the period and society we live in, acting on our innate personality. Identity, he says, "is located both in the core of the individual and in the core of communal culture." The innate capability and personality of the individual moves forward in a developmental way, and undergoes periodic crises and adjusts, effectively or ineffectively, to the cultural environment.

The second principle, already implicit in the first, that Erikson propounds is that neuroses have a strong cultural component. They are not fixed as in Freud's view, by the repression of the sex drive, but have a wider range according to period and culture. Erikson claims that different eras generate different neuroses. The form of neurosis dear to Freud's patients was hysteria, Erikson notes, and he agrees that this hysteria was indeed induced by sexual repression. But Erikson identified the emergence, in the 1960s, of a new kind of neurosis, which he called narcissism. Erikson's view of narcissism as a dominant modern form of neurosis was immediately taken up and popularized by a number of writers. The American historian Christopher Lasch tried to develop Erikson's idea of narcissism into a theory of modern social history.

Narcissism is the mental disease of late modern culture. It consists of "an inner uncertainty," Erikson writes, "and purposelessness concerning undefined avenues of life." In late modern culture, people have lost their bearings, their ideals, they have poor identity and lack purpose, which results in the situation that currently constitutes one of the biggest problems preoccupying psychoanalysts: well-educated, affluent people who have no moral purpose and low self-esteem.

Erikson's third contribution to modern psychoanalysis was his development of psychobiography. Freud published provocative studies of Moses and Leonardo da Vinci, but they were too abstract and formulaic to be regarded as biographies. His study of Woodrow Wilson, written in collaboration with the American ambassador to France William Bullitt, is more of a circumstantial psychobiography, although highly polemical. It was withheld from publication for several decades because it was possibly libelous. In the 1920s, certain writers, most of whom were popular journalists, tried to apply Freudian analysis to circumstantial accounts of personalities of the past. Among them was the German journalist Emil Ludwig, who psychoanalyzed a number of historical people. Ludwig's psychobiographies sold very well, despite the strictures of professional historians against the practice of psychoanalyzing people from the past.

It was Erikson who legitimized psychobiography in the academic world. He claimed that it was possible, and intellectually profitable, to psychoanalyze historical personalities, granted that enough material could be found about the personality to be analyzed. He strongly advocated the writing of psychobiographies of great personalities, and he himself demonstrated how to pursue this genre with his book on *Young Man Luther*. He explained Luther's development in terms of an identity crisis the reformer had undergone in late adolescence. Erikson, to be sure, did not do original research to write Luther's psychobiography. He relied on standard biographical works, particularly on the work of the prominent German historian Heinrich Böhmer, whose study of the young Luther he subjected to psychoanalytic reinterpretation.

Erikson's other psychobiographical work was on Gandhi. In order to write this, however, he actually traveled to India in order to interview people who had known the Mahatma. The latter book is not as successful as the one on Luther. It presents a Gandhi who is too good, too much a latter-day Buddha, whereas the real Gandhi was a more complicated, problematic figure, perhaps more Machiavellian than angelic. Nevertheless the book became very influential, opening the way to a new psychoanalytic mode of writing.

Erikson outflanked the historical profession, which had denied the legitimacy of psychobiography for half a century. With his formidable academic authority as well as popularity, Erikson forced the reluctant historical profession to accept the validity of psychobiography. By the early seventies this genre was at least grudgingly approved by the academic cadre of historians, with the proviso that such work had to be done not by intuition but by scholars whose mastery of psychoanalytic theory as well as historical method was professionally respectable. Such novel historian–lay psychoanalysts as Carol Berkin and Peter Gay soon appeared in university history departments. Erikson had legitimized them as psychohistorians.

Rudolf Binion at Brandeis University was perhaps the most skillful practitioner of psychobiography. Binion does voluminous original research for his psychobiographies. He is also an orthodox Freudian. *Frau Lou*, his psychobiography of Lou Andreas Salomé, the courtesan and mistress of Nietzsche become Freudian disciple become psychotherapist, is methodologically superior to Erikson's work. Binion's psychoanalytic biography of Hitler, *Hitler and the Germans*, offers a convincing oedipal account of why Hitler became a psychopathic anti-Semite. Peter Gay at Yale wrote a three-volume psychoanalytic history of Victorian sexuality as well as a biography of Freud.

The third of the structuralist psychoanalysts is Jacques Lacan, who died in

1981. He was considered the most eminent French psychoanalyst of his day even though he was expelled in 1964 from the French Psychoanalytic Association. His expulsion appears to be mainly due to an allegation that he was abusing his therapeutic practice. Lacan decided that a psychotherapeutic session either brought about transference, an emotional action between the analyst and the analysand, or it did not; and, Lacan thought, if it did not give rise to transference, there was simply no point in holding a forty-five- or fifty-minute session. Therefore he would tell the patient when there was no transference to leave after five or ten minutes. On the other hand, if transference did occur early in the therapy session, Lacan sometimes also dismissed the patient, in this instance apparently feeling that no more could be accomplished at that session. These idiosyncratic choices on Lacan's part qualified as bad professional practice in the eyes of French therapists and led to his expulsion.

Lacan was a Freudian, and he identified himself as such. He wanted to improve on Freud, to build upon Freud's theory without ever essentially leaving the orthodox line of the early Freud. By the 1930s Lacan had already developed the rudiments of his own theory, and he published a small book in which he propounded his views. The book went unnoticed at the time, and it was not until the late sixties that Lacan gained wide attention and became the idol of the Left Bank. Not only did he gain a large practice but intellectuals flocked to study with him. He began to hold seminars at the University of Paris. No theater could be found that was big enough to contain the audiences for his public lectures. He became so eminent a guru that students began to write autobiographical accounts of the privileged seminars they attended with him. Lacan was now frequently interviewed by the media. Every fragment of a word that dripped from the mouth of the master found its way into print.

Lacan was influenced by Ferdinand de Saussure, a Swiss-French professor at the University of Geneva from 1891 to 1913. Saussure was a pioneer in the science of linguistics. Lacan made use of Saussure's theory and nomenclature to reinterpret the Freudian system as psychoanalytic linguistics. Saussure's treatise on linguistics itself had oracular qualities. Put together from Saussure's lectures and published posthumously, it is an opaque, difficult work.

Lacan begins by abolishing the ego, claiming that the invention of the ego was a mistake Freud made. Contrary to the superego and the id, which were real, Lacan found that the ego was a fictive construct. What is experienced as the ego is nothing but the balance struck between the superego and the id. The focal point of psychoanalysis, Lacan claimed, must be the interaction of the id and the superego in the unconscious.

Lacan tries to carry on Freud's work of mapping the unconscious, and he thinks that by applying Saussure's linguistics, he can develop a closer map of the unconscious. He says that "the unconscious is structured as a language." The structure of language is the key to understanding the unconscious. Language shapes the unconscious, and an indispensable means of penetration into the unconscious is through the structure of language. The libido is submitted to linguistic order. There is no structure except through and in language. It is the order of words that constitutes the order of things.

Many Freudians found Lacan's pronouncements to be nonsensical, claiming that the Lacanian theory constitutes neoidealist ravings under the influence of an arcane treatise on linguistics. But, particularly in the sixties, seventies, and eighties Lacan was taken very seriously, first in France and then in the United States, although his following in this country has been much more among literary and linguistic theorists than among psychoanalysts.

The world of words, the world of language, says Lacan, consists of "the signifier." The signifier is the creative force that operates in the unconscious and generates and shapes everything else. By everything else is meant the signified. Words and the structure of language constitute the creative signifier operating in the unconscious that shape and order the signified perceptions that make their way into the unconscious. From this, Lacan derives the formula S/s, in which S stands for the signifier, and s for the signified. The signifier S is the ordering principle at work in the unconscious, by which the experiential material s is organized so as to generate meaning.

Lacan's view is certainly idealistic. It seeks to apply an idealistic theory to Freud—to combine Freudian modernistic, sexualist reductionism with neoidealistic structuralism. But the merit of Lacanian theory does not reside as much in the elimination of the ego, nor in the formula of S/s—even though there is a genuine insight in the statement that linguistic structures play an important role in the workings of the unconscious—as it does in the Lacanian theory of the Other.

The theory of the Other can also be described as the theory of the divided self. This is really a Freudian concept—and the title of a book by R. D. Laing—but Lacan develops it elaborately. Freud had introduced the notion of above the line and below the line. There is always a shadow personality that accompanies us, an Other that moves with the formal, social person. The Other lives in the unconscious. The idea of the shadow, of the Other, the secret sharer of our lives, the alternative person, is a Freudian theme that cuts across twentieth-century literature.

Lacan says that the Other is "man's radical extraneousness to himself." Humankind projects and becomes conscious of an Other that is always with us. "Man's desire finds its meaning in the desire of the Other." The Other, the unconscious or alternative self, is a more authentic person that is capable of expressing true desire. "The discourse of the unconscious is the discourse of the Other from which the subject receives his own forgotten message." The message is retrieved from the unconscious in the process of psychoanalysis.

Lacan claims that this Other is oedipally generated, constituted in the struggle between the subject and the oedipal object. The Other is the product of the primordial estrangement, that is, the estrangement that derives from the subject's struggle against his Oedipal feelings. "The Other is the Name-of-the-Father." Lacan's re-articulation of Freudian theory accommodates Freudianism to literary theory. And that is why, aside from his direct interest in linguistics, Lacan has had such strong impact in the literary field.

Lacan was certainly influenced by French surrealism. Among other things the jokes and puns that pervade his writings verify this. Lacan thinks that jokes and the use of paradox in language are the means of attaining the truth of the unconscious, since these discrepancies reflect the discourse of the unconscious. Freud in a famous essay had shown that "Freudian slips" and sometimes jokes gave out messages from the unconscious. Lacan extends this observation. The unconscious "always says an-other thing." Every act of speech says something that is an Other. Every discourse has a hidden meaning, the other meaning, from which the unconscious can be elucidated. Similarly a surrealist like André Breton had said in 1920 that the way to truth lay in thinking in terms of opposites and paradoxes.

This aspect of Lacan is one of the foundation stones of what is called deconstruction. Deconstruction is the view in literary criticism and philosophy propounded by Jacques Derrida, who will be discussed in a later chapter. Deconstructionists hold that every statement deconstructs itself, that behind every statement is a hidden meaning which is very different from the statement's surface meaning. This view is fully compatible with, and in many respects inspired by, Lacan's theory of the Other.

The Other, then, is a concept that is valid not only with respect to the psyche, but can be applied to any statement or discourse. Every utterance contains an alternative meaning that contradicts the surface truth, regardless of the context in which it is spoken. Lacan is therefore not only a structuralist through his foregrounding of the structure of language as shaping the unconscious; he is also a father, so to speak, of deconstruction. His view that every discourse contradicts itself and harbors another meaning that is not immediately graspable is the foundation of deconstruction.

Thereby Lacan joins Piaget and Erikson not only in developing psychoanalytic theory but also in making a more general contribution to cultural theory.

Radical British Theorists Two radical British theorists of psychoanalysis influential after the war were R. D. Laing and Melanie Klein. Laing was from Scotland, a native British psychotherapist, and the head of the London psychoanalytic Tavistock Institute, which is devoted to the treatment of schizophrenics. Laing spent twenty years of his career working with schizophrenics. From this work evolved Laing's theories of madness. He increasingly became a general theorist. For a while in the sixties and early seventies, he was very popular among the counterculture and the New left.

His clinical work with schizophrenics convinced Laing of the destructive role of the family. Jung and Sullivan had already perceived this. But Laing extended their views into a provocative doctrine. In many ways, he found, the schizophrenics were rational personalities. They lived in such terrible familial environments that the only solution and exit out of the situation was to become either catatonic or violent. These people were not mad, said Laing. They resorted to the only approach to survival in horrifying situations. To "go mad" under such dire circumstances as his patients had been subjected to, Laing claimed, is a perfectly rational response.

Laing organized a mental hospital like a commune, providing schizophrenics with a supportive, friendly environment in which they could communicate and work. He persisted in maintaining the semblance of a normal life in the clinic, and he frequently elicited positive therapeutic responses from his patients. Laing acquired the reputation of being more successful in the treatment of schizophrenics than anyone else practicing in Britain in his time.

From this therapeutic base Laing began to propound generally radical doctrines. He asked the simple but interesting question of who, after all, could be called mad and who sane. He went to the extent of suspecting that perhaps those we call mad were after all the truly sane, and those that are held to be sane, the mad. The "normal," repressed people, it could turn out, were the really mad. Rational society is really mad society, and the more extreme the form of that which we call madness, the more one approaches genuine sanity. Pirandello in the 1920s anticipated Laing's relativism.

This conception of Laing's began to be used in the sixties as justification for a heavy intake of drugs to induce artificial schizophrenia, in order to be able to reach toward a true sanity and to escape from the mad world. It is a matter of controversy whether Laing himself ever preached this pursuit or whether it was read into his work. He himself claimed in the 1980s never to have advocated drug taking, and that this was a misinterpretation of his work.

There is an extreme relativism in Laing, characteristic of the sixties and early seventies. If he does not eliminate he certainly erodes the distinctions between sanity and insanity, and claims that we live in a world in which the insane may be the truly rational people. In the days of the counterculture and the Vietnam War, when Richard Nixon was in the White House, Laing had a compelling argument. Whatever his merits as a cultural theorist, it must be stressed that Laing was a formidable psychiatrist and a compassionate human being who helped many abandoned and desperate people.

Melanie Klein was a German, a disciple of Freud, who moved to England in the thirties after a very colorful career in Berlin. (She was famous for nonstop all-night dancing.) She became a very prominent and successful child psychologist in England and died in 1960. When Freud's daughter Anna arrived in England in 1938 to practice child psychology, the two women became great rivals.

If Sullivan can be called Doctor Feelgood, Klein can be called Doctor Feelbad. An interesting feature of her thought is that she is really a neo-Augustinian. She believed in a secularized version of the old-fashioned Christian view of sin. If we were to go back and read the Puritan writers, we would find that they were convinced that children were full of sin, for which they had to be bound, whipped, and checked in every possible way in order to be saved. The Puritan writers conceived of children as monsters. Strangely enough, Melanie Klein came to the same conclusion after decades of work with children.

Children were monsters, Klein found. They were full of aggressive and vicious fantasies, and of fantasies of fear and oppression. Klein does not find that it is so much infantile sexuality that is at work in the child's psyche as infantile monstrousness. Children had to be controlled and subjected to environmental conditioning in order to be brought into balance with the reality principle of social codes, lest they remain monsters. In her view, the violent and crime-prone adolescent is not so much somebody who has undergone improper structural development as a child, as is the view of Piaget, but rather is someone whose innate aggressive fantasy has not been acculturated and socialized. That Klein was a radical thinker is obvious, but her theory appears more supportive of a rightist than a leftist ideology. A couple of weeks' reading in the New York tabloids about the mayhem inflicted by adolescents, from mugging to carjackings, makes Klein's theory highly plausible.

The other important theory Klein proposed was the principle of object relations. The growth of the child's personality centrally involves an attachment to an external object. This can be, for example, a mother's breast, a teddy bear, father's pipe and glasses, or—as in Orson Welles's *Citizen Kane*—a sled called Rosebud. The attachment to an object is an inevitable part of childhood psychology. But protracted or overly intense fixation on the object can produce severe neurosis, and prevent adequate socialization. One of the key things that the psychoanalyst has to discover is the pattern of object relationship in his patient's unconscious. Klein's theory, which is quite compatible with both Freud and Jung, has been well received in the psychoanalytic profession, and a whole Anglo-American school has developed around its exploration. Klein was an extraordinarily insightful psychoanalyst whose innovative theories have gained high recognition several decades after her death.

The Psychoanalytic Heritage Psychoanalysis was the theory of the most sexualized culture since the Roman Empire. The Rome of the second and third centuries was given to highly free sexuality, as can be gathered from the accounts of contemporaries. There were no real limitations on the variety of sexual practices. This came to an end around A.D. 350, through fear generated by the spread of plague and venereal diseases and the impact of Christian ethics. Along with Christianity arose the repression of both heterosexuality and of homosexual practices.

Psychoanalysis both contributed to renewed sexual freedom and was the consequence of the rising sexual tide. Yet the twentieth century may still turn out to be an intermediary sexual time in history. This may not be the end of the history of sexuality but—as AIDS continues to wind its way, like the bubonic plague that befell the Roman Empire and the medieval world—just a flashpoint. Beyond a doubt AIDS has conduced a withdrawal from sexual freedom toward discretion and control.

We have previously witnessed a cyclic pattern in the history of sexuality. In the twelfth century, there was a partial departure, at least among the aristocracy, from repressive Christian attitudes that had prevailed since approximately A.D. 350. Then, in the late sixteenth century, there was a return to repression with the age of puritanism. The eighteenth century saw a liberation, and if we were to investigate the sexual lives of some of the fathers of this country, like Benjamin Franklin and Thomas Jefferson, we would find major disparities with the ethic of sexual control and family values. When Franklin was

American ambassador in Paris no upper-class Frenchwoman was safe; Jefferson slept with his female slaves.

The nineteenth century marks a return to repression, but after 1900 only in order to yield to sexual liberation, aided by innovations in contraceptive methods and the theory of psychoanalysis. We may now once again be approaching a restrictive era in terms of sexual practices.

Putting aside whatever it may be that the future holds, and returning to the past, it is seen that of all the countries in the world, psychoanalysis had its greatest reception in the United States, with the single exception of Argentina. The two cities that harbor the largest number of psychoanalysts per capita are New York City and Buenos Aires. The case of the latter can be partly explained by the fact that there are many Germans and Jews living in that city.

The question is: Why the United States? How to account for the phenomenal impact of psychoanalysis in New York, Chicago, and Los Angeles? One explanation is that between 1910 and 1940, when psychoanalysis developed in this country, the United States was very weak in its infrastructure, that is, in its social institutions. This was the period of the disintegration of the American family due to tremendous mobility, industrialization, and the decline of the churches as well as of public schools. The weakness of the societal infrastructure drove people back into themselves, and they needed a theory and a behavioral method that provided them with the means of functioning as individuals in a society with eroded and collapsing institutions. Psychotherapy, and in particular psychoanalysis in various Freudian derivatives, posed the solution or the alternative. If it had been possible to maintain the churches of the nineteenth century, psychotherapy would or could not have effected this penetration.

A second factor that has rendered the United States so receptive to psychotherapy is the peculiar history here of the medical profession. As has been mentioned with respect to the phoniness of Harry Stack Sullivan, the medical profession took hold in the United States suddenly, severely, and arrogantly around 1910, just as psychoanalysis made its appearance. The state of the medical art between 1910 and 1940 was such that there was not much for medical doctors to do except surgery. It was not until the discovery of antibiotics in 1940 that the medical profession found means of treatment besides amputation and prescribing aspirin. Therefore, when psychoanalysis appeared on the scene, it presented doctors with a welcome alternative, with something to do as it were.

Psychoanalysis gave them an entire new branch of medicine to explore and to practice. The field had some basis in science, was socially valuable, had a market, and was financially rewarding. Therefore the American medical profession eagerly embraced and legitimized psychoanalysis. In the dark ages of twentieth-century medicine, before antibiotics, since doctors usually could not cure patients, they devoted themselves to primary care. They made house calls. They offered psychotherapy.

Psychoanalysis also fitted in comfortably with current literary ideas, with the classicist literary modernism of Eliot as well as with the continental expressionist branch of modernism. It fitted in with the prominent literary theme of the *Doppelgänger* (the double, the Other, the shadow), and with the microcosmic, word-centered, language-based approach to literary creativity and criticism. Psychoanalysis was a psychological theory that was immensely compatible with, and stimulative of, the literary trends of the first forty years of this century.

Psychoanalysis began as definitely a prime bastion of modernism. If there is a single theorist of modernism, it is the younger Sigmund Freud. Psychoanalysis began as modernist, but increasingly, especially as witnessed in the writings of the later Freud and in the work of Jung, Piaget, Erikson, and Lacan, it moves more and more into structuralist or neo-idealist directions. It found ways to reintroduce ideas such as that of macrocosmic forms operating within the individual as well as in culture, and to look at the individual in the context of structural forms. While marking a radical departure from the doctrine established by the early Freud, this trend actually strengthened the cultural hold of psychoanalysis, as after the 1940s, there was a movement away from modernism. A neoidealist, neo-Victorian movement expressed itself in structuralist anthropology as well as in other fields.

Psychoanalysis, by departing from its early radical, microcosmic, biological reductionism, and by moving toward affirmation of various kinds of psychocultural systems and structures, remained compatible with the cultural history of the later twentieth century. Psychoanalysis demonstrated its historical resiliency and subtle adaptability to shifting intellectual trends. This later psychoanalysis, however, paid the price for adaptability by losing its radical edge and its creative leadership in twentieth-century culture. Somewhere in the forties, fifties, and sixties psychoanalysis begins to be more concerned with keeping up with intellectual trends that originate elsewhere than with setting the trend in humanistic theory.

The therapeutic value of psychoanalysis must ultimately be stressed in judging its role in twentieth-century culture. Sexual and familial relationships lie at the root of a great deal of human misery in advanced industrial societies. At any given time in the United States in the 1980s there were five million people undergoing psychotherapy—less in the 1990s—that was closely or loosely based on psychoanalytic theory, that in turn follows from the Freudian heritage. The life of a sizable share of these people was made happier and more stable and productive as a result of this psychotherapy. The psychoanalytic achievement as a therapeutic force in modern society was assuredly not less than the care offered by religious groups in earlier times, and, one could surmise, it was probably more effective and more compassionate. Psychoanalysis had its problems and its vociferous enemies, but it was a major positive dimension in twentieth-century culture. It was a hallmark of the advance of civilization. It reflected the application of reason and science to intimate human relationships. If life is in some ways more humane and beneficent in the later twentieth century as compared with society of a hundred years ago, psychoanalysis merits a substantial share of the credit.

It is difficult to predict the fate and course of psychoanalysis in the early twenty-first century. As a form of medical therapy it is in sharp decline. The medical profession, and the public at large, have turned to drugs to alleviate most of the neurotic symptoms, especially mood swing and depression, that psychoanalysis had previously combated. There developed an impatience with the slow and lengthy treatment that psychoanalysis provided. Lithium, Prozac, and other drugs seemed to offer instant help, although with what long-term side effects, no one knows. The medical schools in the 1980s and nineties became disillusioned with the theory of psychosomatic medicine they had readily embraced and taught in the 1950s and sixties. Vast research funds provided to prove that asthma and gastrointestinal illnesses were psychologically generated led to no certain results. The drastic change in health insurance and the power of HMOs, with their eye on the bottom line, placed psychoanalytic therapy in a perilous position. A situation in which psychoanalysis is regarded mostly as a humanistic theory with powerful impact on academic criticism of literature and art has its positive sides, but is far from the therapeutic vision of psychoanalysis held and practiced by Freud, Jung, and their disciples. It is just possible that the inveterate enemies of psychoanalysis will prevail and will marginalize the Freudian heritage to humanities departments. If that happens, the vigorous capacity of psychoanalysis to generate new theory is bound to suffer severely, even leaving aside the virtual elimination of its place in the health care profession.

4

MARXISM AND THE LEFT

American Marxism Today There are two contextual factors conducive to the strength of the Marxist Left on the American campus today, particularly in the top three or four dozen universities. The first is that the collapse of Communism in Central and Eastern Europe and especially the ending of the Soviet Union in 1991 has lifted a dead weight that the American Left has had to carry like an albatross since the late 1920s. Countries that hailed Karl Marx as their intellectual forefather were also authoritarian societies where crimes against millions of people, including professed socialists, were savagely carried out. Now American leftists feel they don't have to worry about the ugly Bolshevik face in the mirror when they ask who is the most moral and just of all. They heaved a sigh of relief and set about their task of transforming the humanities and social sciences and even the history and philosophy of science into integral parts of a socialist culture—bridging campus discourse with the ethos of the *New York Review of Books.*

The second contextual factor is the failure of the Right when in political power, as in the cases of Britain in the Thatcher years and the United States in the Reagan-Bush era, to make significant progress toward the professed rightist aim of dismantling the welfare state that emerged in the Western world in the three decades after 1945. The fundamental achievement of the Left in Western Europe and the Americas in the twentieth century has been the creation of the regulatory and welfare state. No freely elected conservative regime, no matter how committed to the doctrine of free market economy, has been able to undo this condition. The welfare state must be seen not as a temporal instrument but as a phase of history like feudalism and commercial and industrial capitalism. It cannot be mitigated by conservative regimes and will take centuries to play itself out.

In these two favorable contexts the academic Left in the 1990s is busily at work solidifying and enriching campus socialist culture, and making great strides toward this goal.

Marxism has emerged as a major intellectual movement in the American university and in Western culture in general, and there is every sign that it will become ever more so in the decades to come.

One, and perhaps the most important, reason why Marxism has become so important in American academe is that the commitment to Marxism continues the trends of the sixties: Academic Marxism is the grand heritage of the disorderly sixties. This can be understood in very concrete terms. A generation of graduate students in the humanities and social sciences, who were in the universities in the sixties and early seventies during the height of the public agitation over the Vietnam War, developed strong left-wing commitments that continued through their academic careers. In the meantime this generation of scholars has become senior faculty and department chairmen, holding powerful positions. Many of them are distinguished professors indeed, occupying prominent places among the scholars of their generation.

Furthermore, in the 1970s and 1980s, the academic profession underwent severe impoverishment. In the seventies academic salaries declined 20 percent in real dollars, which embittered many academics. This situation encouraged a left-wing orientation. If the power and money elite of this country does not want the university faculties to have a strongly leftist, anticapitalist orientation, the way to achieve this is certainly not by reducing faculty salaries, particularly at a time when the income of other learned professions, such as law and medicine, was skyrocketing.

In 1966 there was only a 30 percent discrepancy between the salary for a new Ph.D. in the humanities starting to teach at an Ivy League college and that of a new lawyer starting his or her career as an associate in a major New York law firm. Currently the salary differential is 300 percent. Under these conditions resentment and radicalization are to be expected, which in turn encourage a left-wing orientation.

A third factor in the strengthening of Marxism is that in the 1970s, American universities suffered a failure of nerve, in the sense that they became increasingly dependent on ideas generated and developed in Europe, particularly those coming out of France and England. Between the two world wars, American universities had developed strong intellectual autonomy and native intellectual traditions. The reliance on native production continued for a while in the fifties, but began to erode around the mid-sixties, when American scholars began to regard Paris and Oxbridge as the source of truth in many fields. At the time the University of Paris was particularly dominated by Marxism in all its faculties, and for those who were already favorably disposed toward French ideas, importing and assimilating Marxism from France appeared salutary.

The same phenomenon can be observed in American academic relations with Oxford, Cambridge, and the other British universities. Indeed, though Marxism was not dominant in British universities, it had achieved a strong penetration there by the mid-sixties. Turning to Paris or Oxbridge for intellectual leadership and for imitation was therefore inevitably to result in the importation of Marxist ideas into American universities.

Finally, there has always been a strong Emersonian strain in the American academic world. Most prominent American academics do not settle simply for teaching and engaging in research; they want nothing less than to change the world. From time to time the Emersonian tradition becomes quite vibrant. It had been there in the thirties, returned in the sixties, and is still in the foreground. There is a characteristic restlessness in the American academic world. The self-image of the American academic is that of a would-be guru and social improver, and not merely of someone who is conveying information and sponsoring research. The United States, not having been able to develop a powerful right-wing doctrine since John Calhoun in the 1840s and William Graham Sumner in the 1880s, is bound to express utopian reformism in terms of a left-wing ideology.

Foundations of Socialism Marxism and all brands of socialism were originally nineteenth-century creations. There was a variety of left-wing currents of thought in the nineteenth century. All these socialist currents were conditioned by a rebellion against capitalism, market economics, and the dominion of the bourgeoisie, in other words, the upper middle class.

Especially after 1850 there was a persistent feeling in intellectual circles—a minority view but a determined one—that the achievements of capitalism were lacking in moral quality. Capitalism offended moral sensibilities, it was held, and bourgeois culture was philistine—that is, it assaulted aesthetic and artistic sensibility. Granted, capitalism had altered the face of the world, a fact Marx himself was the first to recognize, but it had not necessarily changed the world for the better. Capitalism had perhaps been an inevitable stage in history, but it had to be transcended in the name of a better world. Capitalism and bourgeois rule were therefore not the end of history, but only an intermediate stage that was deficient in moral and aesthetic qualities: This is a fundamental dogma of socialism.

Marxism was only one strand in nineteenth-century socialism. One group of socialists felt very strongly that capitalism had ravaged the environment, that the beautiful world of preindustrial society had been ruthlessly pillaged by the railroad and the steel age. They objected that the atmosphere had been polluted, the world drenched in smoke and carbon deposits, and held that a socialist community would be able to remedy these conditions, saving and purifying the environment. This point of view was held by a talented group of artists and art critics in England, headed by John Ruskin and William Morris. They were particularly influential in the period between 1870 and 1900, although Ruskin had advocated this point of view since the 1850s.

This group can be described as aesthetic socialists, who nursed the vision of a soulful community that would create a beautiful world. What they wanted was very much what environmental groups demand today. They wanted to control the ravages of capitalist materialism and to place an emphasis on an attractive and healthy environment. The aesthetic socialists found that precapitalist societies, such as the medieval, were better than modern ones. While medieval people in fact did not respect the environment any more than modern ones do, they lacked the technology to ravage it as severely as the Industrial Revolution made possible. Ruskin and Morris, however, persuaded themselves that medieval men and women were more finely in tune with their environment than those of the nineteenth century.

In contrast with the beneficent medieval world, Francis Bacon's early-seventeenth-century doctrine that knowledge is power, and Daniel Defoe's Robinson Crusoe as the prototype of the asocial individual entrepreneur—so socialist critics claimed—signified a new market ideology that meant disaster for beauty and refinement.

There was another group in the nineteenth century, which it is possible to describe as "welfare liberals," although they called themselves the New Liberals. They had a vision that became in effect the welfare state of the twentieth century. This group thought it had a mandate for its vision in the philosophy of Plato. Their political bible was Plato's *Republic,* which presented them with a model for a strong communal organization and for the rule of the "philosopher kings." This elite would achieve a harmonious society whose citizens received their necessary rewards not on the basis of how well they competed economically, but in terms of what was best for society as a whole and according to what was beneficial for the individual in order to develop his or her intellectual and artistic qualities.

The New Liberals claimed that this social model could be achieved by the establishment of a strong central government that would severely regulate capitalist industry, expropriate some of it, engage in heavy taxation of capitalists and landlords, and redistribute income as well as provide for excellent educational and health services. A society would follow, it was claimed, in which every individual could develop his or her potential.

This view was enunciated most eloquently by Thomas Hill Green, who was a professor of philosophy at Balliol College, Oxford, in the 1880s, and Bernard Bosanquet, who was an innovative social and moral theorist working among the London poor in the 1890s. Bosanquet and Green gathered around them a group of influential disciples, particularly Graham Wallas. They exercised a strong influence on the British Liberal Party, which in the late nineteenth century transformed itself from being the party of capitalists, merchants, and industrialists to being the party of the lower middle class as well as, so they hoped, of the working class.

In 1906 this reconstituted Liberal Party won a landslide victory in the British general election. Three-quarters of their membership in Parliament were either schoolteachers or Protestant ministers, which makes it quite clear who it was that believed in the uses of legislation for moral purposes and common benefits. The party introduced heavier taxation, particularly on landownership; old-age pensions; and the first health insurance. Thus the reconstituted Liberal Party began to take the first steps in Britain toward the welfare state, representing a radical departure from the market ideals of nineteenth-century liberalism.

Behind the new welfare liberalism of the late nineteenth century was a pessimism about the capability of capitalism to grow far enough to eliminate poverty. The stubborn persistence of harsh poverty in British society was demonstrated by pioneering social work inquiries funded by Quaker philanthropists. The argument the New Liberals were making at the turn of the century was that economic growth in itself would not eliminate poverty, and that positive state action was therefore necessary.

It is under the heritage of the philosophy of Green and Bosanquet that the word "liberal" came to connote someone who believes in the welfare state—a meaning the word still holds—as opposed to designating one who believes in unlimited capitalist competition, which was the previous nineteenth-century meaning of the word. The opinionated British couple Beatrice and Sidney

Webb were the prototypes for the new breed of welfare liberals. They believed that in the welfare state the wasteful habits of the poor that offended their elitist sensibilities would be eroded, while appropriate positions of power would be assured to enlightened social activists like themselves. Indeed, the clearest outcome of the welfare state has been more and better administrative jobs for the middle class.

Beatrice and Sidney Webb and Graham Wallas were the prime movers in the founding of the London School of Economics in the early years of the century. Its original purpose was to train social researchers, civil servants, and academics who would advance the cause of welfare liberalism and state-supported socialist arrangements. By becoming part of the University of London, the school received full academic legitimacy.

In the United States the critical shift in liberalism began before the First World War in the presidency of Woodrow Wilson, when the welfare liberals were called Progressives. It was fully achieved in the New Deal of the 1930s.

The American Progressives of the second decade of the century, such as Herbert Croly and other writers and academics who congregated around the political weekly the *New Republic*, were from one point of view simply an American offshoot of the English welfare liberals. But there were other ingredients in the Progressives' intellectual makeup. There was a vein of Emersonian nationalism in their outlook—a conviction that the "promise of American life," based on the exploitation of an Edenic continent, meant that there were sufficient material and human resources in America to eradicate poverty and mitigate social misery.

Yet another ingredient was a fear of the huge wave of Central, Eastern, and Southern European immigrants that poured into the country under its very liberal immigration policies from 1880 until American entry into World War I in 1917. Progressivism was from one perspective an effort to maintain white Anglo-Saxon Protestant leadership in American society by attributing to the WASPs a special capacity for rational planning and social engineering, as compared to that of, say, Jews and Italians.

Given the distinct and somewhat conflicting tributaries of the Progressive movement, it is not surprising that it disintegrated when Wilson, feeling impelled to rescue the failing English and French Allies and prevent a German victory, abruptly led America into the war. Although the political and economic atmosphere in the United States shifted sharply to the right in the 1920s, elements of progressivism reasserted themselves in the New Deal of the 1930s, and still echo in the liberal Left of the 1990s.

Another group of socialists, a loud and radical one, called themselves anarchists in the nineteenth century. In the beginning of the twentieth century, particularly in France, they began to call themselves syndicalists, which derives from *syndicat*, the French word for "labor union." The movement can therefore be referred to as anarchosyndicalism. The intellectual leader of nineteenth-century anarchism in Western Europe was the Russian émigré Pyotr Kropotkin. The movement found its twentieth-century theorist in the French philosopher Georges Sorel. One of the leaders of this movement in the United States was Joe Hill, who is memorialized in the once-well-known folk song "The Ballad of Joe Hill." Joe Hill was a member of the IWW, the Industrial Workers of the World (also known as the Wobblies), an anarchosyndicalist union that was active primarily among the miners of Nevada. Convicted (some say on trumped-up charges) of murder by the state of Utah, Hill was executed by firing squad in 1915.

What the anarchists believed in was the destruction of the prevailing economic and political system by confrontation, and if necessary, by violent confrontation. They advocated a general strike, in mobilizing all the workers so that in one ineffable moment, when all factories and industries had ceased functioning, capitalism and the state alike would grind to a halt, and the workers would take over. This was in fact attempted from time to time, but it never worked. It was certainly tried on a large scale in England in 1926. Closer to home, one such strike was attempted in Canada in 1919, and others in the mining districts of the West in 1906 and 1916. The results were always negative. Nevertheless the general strike was a revolutionary method dear to anarchists.

Anarchists believed in terrorism as well, and particularly in the assassination of political leaders. One successful such attempt was directed at President William McKinley in the United States. The idea was to force the prevailing establishment to be repressive, to force it to take counterterrorist tactics and so discredit itself morally. This idea became very popular among the New Left in the 1960s, and is still occasionally propounded today.

Anarchosyndicalists were essentially Rousseauists: Men and women are by nature good; it is the state and capitalism that corrupt them. Once the state and capitalism have been overthrown by the general strike, terrorism, and revolution, men and women will spontaneously form communes and cultivate their initial goodness. The New Left of the sixties spent a lot of time and energy trying to implement these anarchist principles, beginning with participatory democracy, a cardinal Rousseauist doctrine.

Anarchosyndicalism found support in areas of Europe and the United

₋₋₋ates where the Industrial Revolution had been delayed, where it was coming in slowly at the turn of the century, and where, therefore, its ravages were particularly severe. Industrial revolutions treat workers worst in their initial phases, only later improving the conditions of their existence. Therefore places that remained marginal to the Industrial Revolution for a long while, like southern France, Spain, Sicily, the Rocky Mountain area, and Arizona, and agricultural and mining regions therein, were areas where anarchosyndicalism found support in the early 1900s.

Karl Marx loathed anarchists almost as much as he contended with capitalists. He found them "adventurous," hyper-romantic, and irrational, and claimed that they would discredit the socialist movement. Marx vehemently disagreed with the anarchist view that the state was intrinsically evil.

Finally, the nineteenth century produced the doctrines of Marx and his associate Friedrich Engels, and the Marxist movement in the First and Second Internationales. Marxist theory has become so familiar that it can be summarized quite succinctly. Of primary importance to Marxist doctrine is the labor theory of value, which holds that it is the contribution of the actual manual or blue-collar worker that creates economic value. There is no value in management—in any aspect of economic activity, in fact—other than the actual product of the worker's labor. Nor does the capitalist have any social or moral rights to a return on his or her investment.

Marx did not originate the labor theory of economic value. What is critical, however, is the central importance he gave it. His theory is an extremely narrow and constricted one, and it is the foundation of everything else in his system.

Second, Marxism holds the view that capital is a substance—that is, it is a tremendous economic force that follows specific, idiosyncratic patterns of development and takes on an independence, a life of its own. This notion will become central to the theory of the Frankfurt school of the 1920s and 1930s. There is such a thing, an entity, as capital, which is capable of becoming a living force. Once it achieves a certain degree of accumulation of capital, capitalism enters a course of development that is irresistible. Eventually, of course, it runs its course and breaks down, but on the upswing, as capital reaches a certain level of vitality, it will inevitably continue to evolve.

There is a close parallel here between Marxism and Darwinism. Marx acknowledged his admiration for Darwin. Once a certain species has developed, said Darwin, by a process of natural selection and adaptation to the environment, it will have been irreversibly constituted and prepared for a long course of endurance and further development, albeit one that, as in the case of the Marxian concept of capital, will not last forever. Marxism is founded on Victorian organicism.

(Third,) Marxist doctrine speaks of alienation or dehumanization. This concept was particularly propounded, and quite eloquently too, by the younger Marx in the 1840s in the collection of essays now referred to as *The 1844 Manuscripts.* These writings—not published in Marx's lifetime and in fact not widely known until the 1930s—present the doctrine of alienation most elaborately among Marx's works. Yet it appears in his other writings, too, particularly in *The German Ideology.* It is also referred to in his major work *Capital,* but not fully developed there.

The doctrine of alienation describes the process of the dehumanization of the worker as he engages in industrial capitalist production. Laboring on the assembly line, workers become appendages to and extensions of the machine, which dehumanizes by subjecting them to the fragmented labor required by the modern industrial mode of production, and by separating them from their authentic nature.

Under the conditions of industrial capitalism the workers have become proletarians. They have been subjected to "naked, shameless, direct, brutal exploitation" by the bourgeoisie. "The work of the proletarians has lost all individual character and consequently all charm for the workman." The life of the worker in industrial capitalism is characterized by "accumulation of misery, agony of toil, slavery, ignorance, brutality, moral degradation." Nor can the intellectuals, artists, and learned professionals among the middle class themselves escape the dehumanizing effects of the capitalist Moloch. The bourgeoisie "has resolved personal worth into exchange value [and] . . . converted the physician, the lawyer, the priest, the poet, the man of science into its paid wage laborers. . . . [Capitalism] has reduced the family relation to a mere money relation."

Marx and Engels were themselves products of the German middle class in the later years of the romantic era. When they encountered the Industrial Revolution in England, where they migrated before and after the abortive revolutions of 1848, their sensibility was shocked by the material and social changes they encountered. Unquestionably some truly adverse consequences of industrialization were witnessed by them and found to be repulsive. Many men and women of sensibility in England, such as William Wordsworth, Elizabeth Gaskell, George Eliot, Charles Dickens, and Thomas Carlyle, were also repelled by the social and environmental brutalities of the earlier phase of industrialization. The strange thing about Marx and Engels is that well before Marx's death in 1884 (and Engels's some years later), much more beneficent consequences of industrial capitalism were evident, and a significant proportion of the working class was relatively prosperous and contented. The professional middle class, and to a substantial degree intellectuals and artists, were much better off under the industrial and financial capitalism of the later nineteenth century than under the ancien régime. Yet Marx and Engels did not modify their judgment of capitalism, although they had ample opportunity to do so.

There is no stranger phenomenon in twentieth-century culture than that of many thousands of left-wing intellectuals assenting to an assessment of capitalism that was based on conditions in the 1840s and 1850s that were rapidly superseded in advanced industrial countries. Clearly the Marxist doctrine of alienation has appeared convincing to so many in this century for other than objective economic and social conditions. An obvious explanation is that *any* social system that subjects human beings to control and regimentation in the interests of productivity is regarded as reprehensible by Marxists. At bottom there is a deep affinity between Marxism and aesthetic socialism.

This also explains why latter-day Marxists are so deeply concerned about the welfare of the masses in the less developed countries, the so-called Third World, a sentiment that was notably lacking in Marx and Engels. In the Third World, with its involvement in the incipient phase of the Industrial Revolution, the Marxist vision of the unrelieved misery of the working class still is plausibly circumstantial. By the end of Marx's own lifetime his view of capitalism was incompatible with actual conditions in Britain, Germany, and some parts of the United States.

The purpose of socialism in Marxist doctrine is precisely to rehumanize the industrial worker. It is under socialism, and particularly in the Communist society, which is the final stage of historical development, that the industrial worker will be restored to full humanity.

Marx spent the last thirty years of his life trying to prove that the capitalist system would undergo a series of crises and disintegrate from within. In this final critical phase of capitalism a proletarian revolution would inaugurate "the Communist society," which in its "higher phase" would eliminate "the enslaving subordination of the individual to the division of labor . . . and with it the antagonisms between intellectual and manual labor." Then will come "the development of the individual in every sense . . . and all the springs of collective wealth will flow with abundance."

There is no essential difference between this view of the world and that of the radical romantic poet Percy Bysshe Shelley in the early 1820s: "Rise like lions after slumber/In unvanquishable number/Shake your chains to earth like dew/Which in sleep had fallen on you." Marx—this learned, idealistic, pathetic son of a lawyer from the Rhineland, grinding away at statistical materials in the Reading Room of the British Museum year after year, beset by family and fiscal problems, living on handouts from his junior collaborator Engels, the rich son of a German textile magnate—it is all a poignant story. Marx's doctrines reflect his projection of his personal problems onto a society he held responsible and came to loathe.

Marxism also has a distinctive doctrine of history, which consists of the materialist version of the Hegelian theory of history, and which is based on the concept of class struggle. Marx, who studied with Hegel in Germany, can be described as a left-wing Hegelian.

The Marxian theory of history, or the doctrine of dialectical materialism, teaches that around 1500 feudalism—the social structure based on the rule of landlords over peasants—began to yield to the capitalist modes of production, which did not, however, receive their fullest form before the Industrial Revolution of the eighteenth and early nineteenth centuries. This structure, in turn, Marx holds, will be replaced by the historical stage of development that will be dominated by proletarian rule. The late stage of capitalism is marked by periodic crisis and increasingly aggravated confrontation between the narrow stratum of capitalists on the one side and the ever larger mass of increasingly impoverished workers on the other. So goes, according to Marx, the dialectical movement of history. It is a model of history that describes the entire development of human societies and is applicable to every society. Marxist historiography obviously constitutes a secularized version of the old Christian apocalyptic vision.

A key ingredient in the Marxian theory of history is the doctrine of false consciousness. This doctrine, which has been critically important for all of the more radical and activist socialists in this century, explains the inability of the proletarian to know and realize his or her own advantage. The worker's consciousness has been falsified and misguided by explicit propaganda as well as by subtler forms of ideological manipulation. This is why the Communist Party, even without the majority support of the proletariat, is justified in undertaking the revolution against capitalism. That the Communist movement may momentarily not receive strong support from the proletariat is explained by the fact that the working class is entrapped by false consciousness, which prevents its members from perceiving the sordid operations of capitalism and the conditions of their victimization in a full and clear light. This subtle paradox has enabled generations of Marxists to be democrats and oligarchs at the same time—or, as Communists said in the 1930s, to be adherents of "democratic centralism."

The doctrine of false consciousness finds an extended elaboration in the work of Lenin, who uses it to justify the revolutionary role of the Bolshevik Party in the revolution of 1917, although it began as decidedly a minority party, even among Russian socialists. Those who remained outside the Bolshevik circle, Lenin believed, did so because of false consciousness. It never bothered Lenin to find himself and his cadre in a minority, even a very small one. On the contrary, a minority role gave Lenin added confidence that he was right, that he was in tune with the forces of justice and history, while his opponents wallowed in evil and false consciousness.

Was this nineteenth-century socialist heritage at all compatible with modernism, or was the former a theory discrepant with main currents of the cultural revolution the early twentieth century witnessed? There are three ways in which the socialist legacy could be regarded as compatible with modernism, the first of which is the aesthetic condemnation of the prevailing social system. The modernists posited entitlement to participation in the arts as the highest social value—indeed, perhaps as the only social value. The sole instance in which modernists approach anything resembling a social theory is in the context of arguing for the universal right to cultivate the arts. This modernist argument can be construed as compatible with the Marxist and socialist condemnation of capitalism on aesthetic grounds. Both modernism and socialist thought find that the prevailing social system deprives people of access to the arts as well as of full entitlement to artistic development. That modernism and Marxism differ absolutely on the role of the state in control over the arts does not preclude a short-term alliance against alleged bourgeois philistinism.

Anarchosyndicalism has some compatibility with the expressionist tradition of modernism. The latter believes in the possibility of capturing a glorious moment when humanity attains its highest degree of fulfillment. This expressionist conception of the moment of truth, and of unlimited fulfillment of the deepest instincts of humanity, parallels the anarchosyndicalist doctrine of the general strike and terrorism, the ineffable moment of social truth. Certainly Sorel's way of thinking lay within the expressionist tradition in modernism.

50

51

52

53

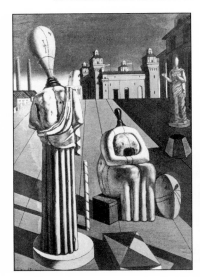

54

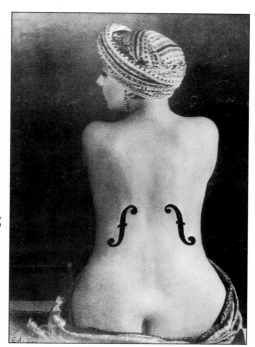

55

56

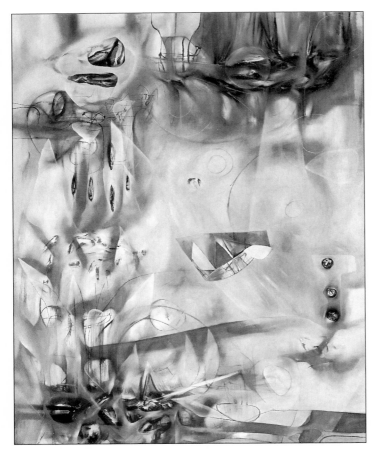

57

58

59

60

61

62

63

64

65

66

67

68

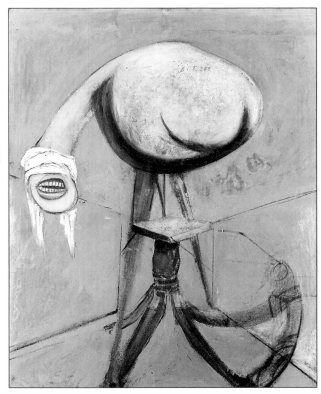

69

70

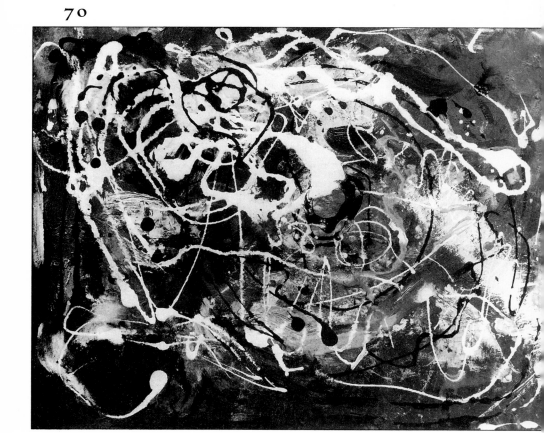

71

72

73

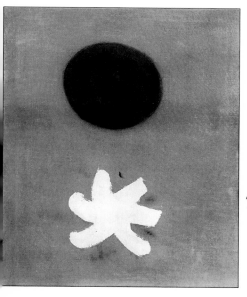

74

75

76

77

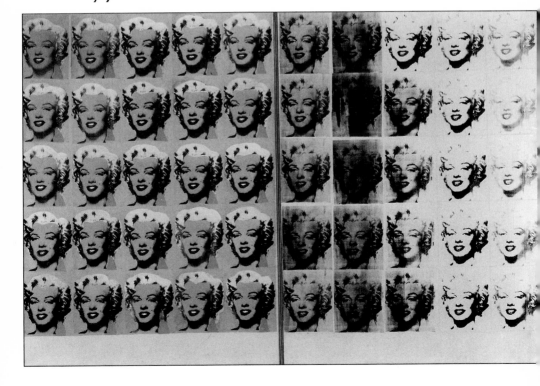

78

79

80

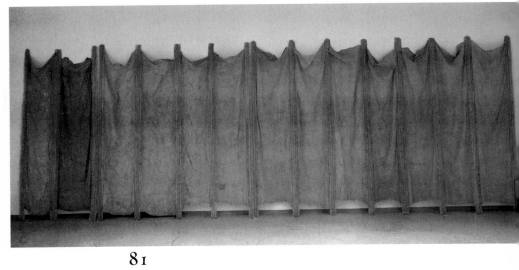

81

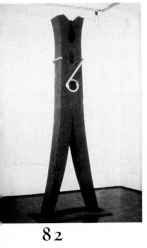

82

83

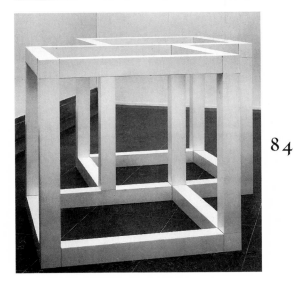

84

PSYCHOANALYSIS PICTURE ESSAY

The surrealists followed Freud in stressing the importance of dreams and the unconscious. Their intention was to explore the world of psychic experience through chance, randomness, and automatism: The paintings came about without control of the medium in response to unconscious feelings. Ernst, instrumental in formulating surrealism, created dream landscapes of mystical symbols. More Jungian than the surrealists, Klee posited the necessity of psychic union of male and female or conscious and unconscious in his art. De Chirico was a precursor of surrealism with his dreamlike, mysterious architectural settings and ghostlike figures. Moore showed his affiliation with the surrealists; his reclining figures of void and mass are abstract and other-worldly. Man Ray, a leader of American surrealism and dadaism, mocked Ingres's classical rationalism in his playfully elegant photograph. Delvaux presented a dreamlike scene of nude women, phases of the female moon, contrasted with academic men engaged in scientific examination. Beckmann's magical realism, indicating the political situation in Germany, agreed with Freud's concerns about war. Similarly, in a detail from a triptych panel, the British painter Bacon employed an open-mouthed, blindfolded birdlike creature to indicate the horrors of war. Dubuffet combined macabre figures on a thick ground of sand, soot, earth, and pigment to suggest the art of the insane and create a primordial mysterious effect. The surrealists' impact on the New York School of artists who became known as the abstract expressionists was extensive. The organic or bimorphic surrealism of Miró and Matta was especially influential. Matta's organic abstractions are lyrical space fantasies, while Miró's organic shapes make for an unreal world filled with delight and humor. Like Miró's work, Calder's mobiles are playfully humorous and fanciful. Gorky's landscapes of organic shapes and fantasies show the link between the European surrealists and the American abstract expressionists. Another influence on American painters, particularly Pollock, were the Mexican muralists Orozco and Siqueiros. Their social protest combined with the Jungian emphasis on the primitive, and shared archetypes appear in Pollock's early work as totemic and ritualistic qualities. After World War II, as New York became the center of the art world, American painters sought an abstract art divorced from European tradition that would express individual identity. Originality, immediacy and spontaneity would be revealed in their marks and gestures on the canvas. Pollock and de Kooning, the leaders of abstract expressionism, were concerned with the gestures and action of the paintbrush and the texture of their paint. De Kooning, though, always retained to some extent his European origins, and his series of monumental women, powerful and menacing, are reminiscent of Picasso's. Considered to epitomize American originality, Pollock—with his action painting of jumping in and out of his canvas on the floor in rhythmic movements that were both conscious and unconscious gestures of paint flung, dripped, and poured—achieved a spontaneity and immediacy of flat, meandering lines of color. Krasner, Pollock's wife, academically trained in art, influenced and was influenced by her husband. Hoffman, who had contacts with the Paris avant-garde before World War I and who headed an important art school in Munich between the wars, taught the abstract expressionists in his Greenwich Village school about color and pictorial structure. Newman, Rothko, and Gottlieb represented another branch of abstract expressionism, color-field painting. Their intense color fields have a mystical quality that invites the viewer into the changing dynamics of color to discover a Jungian spiritual awareness. The Japanese American sculptor Noguchi combined Eastern and Western concepts that render the mythic rituals and rhythms of nature in Jungian fashion. Lichtenstein and Warhol, leaders of pop art, take elements from the industrialized and commercial world to make a depersonalized art of mass-produced objects. The artist no longer seeks self but the communality brought about by mass communication and media that identifies American life. Rauschenberg combines the Renaissance world with mass media through collage, silkscreen, and painterly brush. John's flag series communicates an ambiguity that makes the viewer rethink what is being seen. Frank Stella's pure formal paintings are unambiguous objects of seeing; as he said, "What you see is what you see." The minimalist sculptors Andre and LeWitt advocate simplicity, seriality, and systems and work with solid materials. The viewer can relate to the object as a whole, to its parts, and to the environment around it. Hesse's sculptures in materials that look shabby, soft, and vulnerable emphasize the process of making. Oldenburg takes everyday objects and re-creates and transforms them with unique inventiveness into monumental exaggeration, recalling Jungian archetypes.

Finally the Marxist doctrine of alienation bears a resemblance to Heidegger's doctrine of authenticity. Heidegger belonged to the right wing and was vehemently anti-Communist, but nevertheless the Heideggerian concept of authenticity and the Marxian concept of alienation both aim at the achievement and realization of the full humanity of the individual. Both assert that the purpose of life is to reach that moment of the deepest realization of one's authentic human quality, and Heidegger was indeed aware of this particular parallel between his philosophy and Marxism.

In spite of their fragmentary affinities, however, the socialist tradition, particularly in its Marxist form, was essentially incompatible and in conflict with modernism. Marxism was moralistic, historicist—being entirely and inextricably based on a philosophy of history—and macrocosmic. Modernism strived to depart from Victorian moralism, whereas socialism is based precisely on Victorian moralism. Modernists wanted to remove history from the field of attention. They were ahistorical or antihistorical. According to the socialists, particularly to Marxists, every phenomenon is to be studied in the context of history, which is also very much a Victorian idea.

Where modernism was microcosmic, socialism remained macrocosmic, once again complying with assumptions of Victorian culture. Socialism, in all its forms, believes in universal theories.

There are additional incompatibilities between modernism and Marxism, which became immediately evident whenever a Communist or Soviet regime gains power. Modernism was elitist and was concerned with a highly sophisticated intellectual and academic culture. Socialism had to believe that culture must serve the masses and that, for example, art and literature must be expressed in a style that the masses can comprehend. Hence the Soviet emphasis on "socialist realism" and proscription of abstract art and experimental, nonnarrative literature.

The bitterest conflict between Marxism and modernism always comes over the question of whether art and literature are self-referential and whether artists and writers are independent of the state. Communist regimes always insist just the opposite: Art, literature, and all forms of thought (even physics and biology) are to be developed in the context of the needs of the proletariat (in practice, according to state policy) and artists, writers, philosophers, and scientists are state functionaries as much as farmers and engineers.

The issue comes down to freedom: Modernism assumes the highest degree of autonomy for the arts, letters, and sciences. Marxism finds this anathema and treason to the revolution and the socialist state. In the later stages of the ancien régime, Communist revolutionaries and modernist artists appear momentarily to be allies. The former conspires against the dying order; the latter criticizes and satirizes it. Once the Marxists have come to power, however, modernism suffers an early condemnation. This story has been repeated wherever Communists have gained power in the twentieth century. The story is different where social democrats like the British Labour Party have held sway, only because in such political systems the socialists are subject to democratic processes and the rule of law and lack the mechanisms of state oppression, and because mixed in among the social democrats are welfare liberals who are only marginally Marxists.

One of the greatest problems for Marxist thinkers in the twentieth century consisted of the stresses and strains between Marxism, stemming from its Victorian legacy, and modernism. Since Western Marxists saw themselves as the progressives in every social and cultural dimension, they could not bring themselves, in many instances, to reject the artistic and intellectual avant-garde of modernism. The problem remained how to bridge the gap between Marxism and modernism. This posed a particularly important problem for American modernists, which was investigated in the New York journal *Partisan Review* of the 1930s and 1940s. *Partisan Review* solved the problem by abandoning Marxism in the 1950s.

In cultural history logic does not always prevail. The incompatible is sometimes made compatible and the union of very different modes of thinking in the end can prevail against very long odds. The task of bridging Marxism and modernism represented almost insuperable difficulties, since they stood at such polar opposites from each other in the spectrum of cultural theory. Yet attempts made by left-wing intellectuals to affect a symbiosis of Marxism and modernism were not without some interesting and partially fruitful results.

The understanding of twentieth-century cultural history requires attention to this fundamental issue: Socialism, especially in its Marxist form, represented a powerful manifestation of neo-Victorianism, contradicting modernism in fundamental ways. The more Marxism gained credibility among intellectuals, the more this situation detracted from triumph of the modernist cultural revolution.

Lenin and his Bolshevik colleagues saw this clearly in 1922 when they condemned constructivism as reactionary bourgeois art, terminated a modernist movement in Leningrad and Moscow that was of major consequence, and formulated the dogma that modernist principles were anti-Bolshevik. The liberating efforts of luminaries among three generations of Soviet artists and intellectuals before 1940 were not able to reverse this Bolshevik condemnation of modernism, nor did Lenin err in his assessment of the ideological relationship of modernism and Bolshevism. Stalin considered modernists, whether in literature, painting, or music, to be enemies of the people. It was significant that whenever a new Soviet leader came along before 1990, and Kremlinologists sought to discover his policy, they looked for an easing of the proscriptions on modernism as a prime indicator. Gorbachev in the late 1980s was held to be taking a softer line on Leninism because he allowed occasional exhibitions of abstract art. Yeltsin did not care one way or another. The history of modernism in other Soviet regimes or in Red China has not been different than it was in Soviet Russia.

At most a Communist state can tolerate some marginal modernist activity in the arts but the Marxists-Leninists can never allow modernist culture to take hold in the media and in education if they wish to retain their hold on the minds of the population. A strong, highly visible modernist movement will always delegitimize Marxism as assuredly as twentieth-century culture departs from the nineteenth. It is only because Western Marxists have never exercised total power that they have the paradoxical luxury of denying this cardinal fact.

Because of the rooted conflict between Marxism and modernism, the Communist triumph in Russia and the way in which the Soviet Union and its admirers became highly influential in Western socialism in the twenties, followed by the leftist advance during the Great Depression and the New Deal in the thirties, represented an adverse set of circumstances for the continued flourishing of high modernist culture. The advance of Marxism and the Left in Europe and the United States was a prime factor in the erosion of the modernist consciousness in the thirties.

The Prewar Era Between 1900 and the First World War there was a strong increase of support for socialism in Europe. By 1914 the Social Democratic Party, which was more or less Marxist, was the largest political party in Germany. This did not mean that it held political power, as Germany did not have a democratic system at the time. But the largest group in the German parliament was Social Democrats, most of whom were socialists and some even vehement Marxists, and if Germany had had a democratic political system then, the government would have been in the hands of the socialists.

Indeed, the socialists became so strong politically in the late nineteenth century that the country's government under Chancellor Otto von Bismarck had to introduce the welfare state into Germany in the 1880s. Germany was the

first European country to have the welfare state, features of which were introduced as a way to pacify the German voter, to keep him from consistently voting for the Social Democrats. This political ploy could be glamorized as a
harking back to the paternalism of the now-superseded mercantilist state, but
the method did not fulfill its aim, and the Germans continued to vote for the
socialists.

In England from 1906 to World War I, a strong group of welfare liberals
was in power. The same period saw the beginnings of the British Labour Party,
which first formed a government in England in 1924, but which held a significant minority in the House of Commons by 1914. The French socialists were
already highly visible by 1914, under the leadership of Jean Jaurès, who was
assassinated shortly before World War I broke out. In the United States in
1912 and 1920, the socialists, under the leadership of Eugene V. Debs, received
one million votes, which is the most that any socialist party has ever gained in
an American presidential election.

The socialist political advance in the prewar period was accompanied by
significant development in Marxist theory. In Germany the two leading
Marxist intellectuals were Eduard Bernstein and Rosa Luxemburg. Bernstein
argued that socialism could come to power in Germany by the ballot.
Revolution, he claimed, was not necessary. Eventually, as long as the German
workers continued to vote for the Social Democrats, the kaiser would have to
give in and form a government of socialists. Bernstein may very well have been
right. The war, however, intervened, followed by the kaiser's abdication in 1918.

Rosa Luxemburg, on the other hand, believed that socialist victory by
democratic means was not likely to happen, and that revolution was necessary.
In 1918–19, she was one of the two leaders of a Communist revolution in Berlin,
which took place during the confusion that followed the collapse of Germany
at the end of the War. Munich, too, was the site of a Communist revolution in
the winter of 1918. The Munich revolution was momentarily successful and for
three months a Communist government held power in Bavaria. The Berlin revolution failed, and Rosa Luxemburg was murdered by a group of rightist naval
officers. Luxemburg, a Polish Jew with a marginal anarchist penchant, is now
revered by Marxist feminists.

In England in 1902 the Labour Party theorist, J. A. Hobson, made a major
contribution to Marxist theory. Marx himself had never vehemently condemned imperialism. Although he suggested that imperialism was tied in with
capitalism, on the other hand he was very much a Western chauvinist who had
a very low opinion of what has recently been referred to as the Third World.

He thought that imperialism was good for the Third World, that it was a necessary stage that brought about industrialization in those countries, which they themselves could never have achieved. He did not see any intrinsic value in Oriental culture, and thought that imperialism was an inevitable stage these societies had to go through in order to be modernized.

Hobson produced a study of imperialism that condemned imperialism as the final stage of capitalism. According to Hobson imperialism developed as capitalism deteriorated, exhausted its markets, and had to go in search of both new markets and new sources of cheap raw materials. Imperialism is the way in which capitalism tries to stave off its terminal illness. Imperialism is the product of the crises of late capitalism which force the bourgeoisie to find new markets to deliver itself of the product of surplus manufacture. The colonial countries are also forced by the imperialists to surrender their raw material cheaply and assure the capitalists of continual profits.

Hobson's theory of imperialism was taken up by Lenin. Lenin was a leader of a far-left-wing revolutionary fringe in the Russian socialist movement, the Bolsheviks, who lived in exile in Zurich, Switzerland, until the 1917 revolution began. Lenin agreed with Rosa Luxemburg that revolution was the only means by which Communism could ever be brought about. He too was convinced that the overthrow of capitalism could not come about democratically, and that it required revolution under the leadership of the vanguard cadre of the Communist Party at the appropriate time. Lenin remained in Zurich, read and wrote books, awaiting his moment. Lenin also took Hobson's theory of imperialism and inserted it into Communist theory, where it has remained a dominant segment of Marxist-Leninist doctrine.

The period before the First World War also witnessed the beginnings of Marxist historical scholarship. Of all the academic or protoacademic scholarship, history is the easiest for Marxism, since Marxism is a historicist philosophy. The theoretical foundations of Marxism facilitate the writing of history, and the beginnings of a learned Marxist tradition of history occur in the ten years preceding the First World War, during which time four Marxist historians rose to eminence.

The first of these was Karl Kautsky, who was a colleague of Bernstein and Luxemburg in the German Marxist movement. His own views lie somewhere between the moderation of Bernstein and the radical authoritarianism of Luxemburg. Kautsky's contribution lay in his undertaking of a Marxist analysis of sixteenth- and seventeenth-century history in order to show in detail the emergence of capitalism out of medieval European society. Kautsky was not really in possession of the necessary scholarly equipment, but he did make the first efforts in this vein. It was Kautsky, too, who first suggested that the English Civil War or Puritan revolution of the 1640s was fundamentally a capitalist insurgence against feudalism, and he drew attention to democratic and protosocialist ideas on the left wing of the Puritan revolution.

Kautsky saw the revolution of the 1640s as the great turning point that marked the beginning of the modern era. This idea was taken up by the great historian Richard Henry Tawney, who became professor of economic history at the London School of Economics around 1910. Tawney was the intellectual founder of the British Labor Party. It is his book *The Acquisitive Society* that became the theoretical bible of the British Labor Party until the 1930s. Tawney also was a prime founder of the adult education movement in England. He taught adult education classes for London workers in socialist theory, economics, and history. This was the first substantial adult education program in England.

Tawney also produced seminal historical works in the course of a long career (he died in 1962). He became the dominant spokesman for Marxist historiography not only in England, but perhaps in the entire English-speaking world. Tawney envisaged the Middle Ages as having had strong communal structures. He believed that before 1500 the workers were taken care of by the church, and that this relatively beneficent society was overthrown by the intrusion of capitalist agriculture into sixteenth-century England. The 1640s Puritan revolution was conducted in the name of the rise of the capitalist gentry. The rural middle class, not satisfied with what they had gained in the way of economic advancement in the sixteenth century, wanted to introduce the free market into England, and to eliminate the last vestiges of medieval regulation of the market by the Crown. The purpose of the Puritan revolution was, in his view, to annihilate the remnants of medieval paternalism and institute unlimited capitalism.

Tawney advanced this argument in a series of eloquent books of which the most famous was *Religion and the Rise of Capitalism*, published in the early 1920s. Here Tawney disputed Max Weber on the meaning of the Reformation. Weber said that the Protestant Reformation had made capitalism possible by introducing a work ethic and by valorizing capital accumulation. Tawney found that Weber had reversed the matter. He claimed that the causality ran in the opposite direction, namely that capitalism advanced in the sixteenth century and used Protestantism as its ideology. Capitalism manipulates and assimilates Protestantism in order to endow itself with a moral ideology suitable to its interests. Protestantism is, then, the instrument of the sixteenth-century capitalist revolution, rather than the Weberian shift in values that generated capitalism.

Tawney's *Religion and the Rise of Capitalism* is one of the all-time bestsellers of historical writing. Tawney was a master of English prose, and his book had enormous influence for a very long time. Through a host of Tawney's admirers and disciples, his grand Marxist interpretation of the Reformation endures as a legitimated model for the history of sixteenth and seventeenth centuries.

The third great historian on the radical Left was Charles Beard, an American and a professor of political science at Columbia University until the United States entered World War I in 1917. Beard vociferously opposed the entry into the war and was fired by the Columbia Board of Trustees. He never sought to regain his professorship. Having discovered that he could write bestselling history books, he retired to the Berkshires, where he became known as the sage of New Milford, Connecticut, and devoted himself to highly controversial historical writing well into the 1950s.

Beard's first and most famous book, which was published in 1913, was *An Economic Interpretation of the Constitution*, wherein he argued that the Constitution was created by a group of speculators, frontier developers, and prominent merchants and their lawyers, who wanted a strong federal government in order to protect their interests as creditors and to allow them to gain entry into the western lands, "western lands" then meaning western Pennsylvania, and the old Northwest Territory—Ohio, Indiana, Michigan, and Illinois. There is of course some truth to Beard's argument, since George Washington was the leading investor in the Susquehanna Company, which controlled a third of New York State and what is now western Pennsylvania. The examples can be easily multiplied. Beard claimed provocatively that the Constitution was the document of a capitalist counterrevolution designed to protect the interests of the capitalist landlord and merchant class in the new nation, to deprive the proletariat and the small farmers of the benefits of the American Revolution, and to establish a market economy. His book had enormous impact and caused controversy both in and outside the academic world for several decades.

Finally, the last of the great quartet of pre-1914 Marxist historians was Albert Mathiez, who became professor of the history of the French Revolution at the University of Paris, the first Marxist historian to be appointed a professor in Paris. Around 1910 the University of Paris was the site of a bitter controversy about the interpretation of the French Revolution. The contention was primarily between the socialists and the conservatives, particularly those of the Catholic persuasion. The argument was finally settled by creating two chairs of history, one for the conservative interpretation of the Revolution, the other for the socialist—a tradition that still continues at the University of Paris.

Mathiez argued that the Jacobins, led by Robespierre, were left-wingers who wanted to establish a strong central government in order to limit unregulated capitalism and protect the interests of the common people. Even further to the left of Robespierre was Gracchus Babeuf, a doctrinaire socialist. The democratic and prospective socialist revolutions were aborted by the Thermidorian reaction—that is, by counterrevolution—but Robespierre and a few less celebrated personages even further to the left of him, were unquestionably on the road to socialism, said Mathiez. Thus the beginnings of the socialist tradition in France are found in the French Republic itself. The vision of Jean Jaurès is firmly rooted in the traditions of Robespierre and Jacobinism. This view of the French Revolution is still regarded as gospel by all leftists in France, including the late François Mitterrand.

Leninist and Western Marxism Marx and Engels did not conceive of the Communist revolution first occurring in Russia. They, and many others in Europe, thought that Germany would precede all other countries in the road to socialism, since the German Empire was the most advanced industrial society, with the largest Socialist Party. What happened in Russia in 1917 was that there was first a liberal revolution, which prevailed after terrible losses suffered by the Russian army in the First World War. It was this situation, combined with food shortages and rioting in Petrograd and Moscow, that caused the czar's government to collapse. The breakdown of the Russian economy and near starvation in the large cities enabled the liberal government, whose second chairman was the lawyer Aleksandr Kerensky, to come to power in February 1917. The czar abdicated in favor of another member of the royal family, who forthwith also abdicated, suddenly leaving Russia a republic.

Kerensky was begged by the Western Allies to continue the Russian war against Germany, for the Allies were terrified that if the German army did not have to fight the Russians in the East any longer, then it would have enough power to achieve a breakthrough on the western front. This in fact did not happen, but it was what motivated the Allies to urge Russia to remain in the war. Kerensky tried to continue the war, and the result was increasing chaos and disorder. At this point the German government provided a special train to carry Lenin from Zurich to the Finland Station in Petrograd (renamed

Leningrad after the revolution) because they felt that if Lenin appeared on the scene, he might be able to engender sufficient chaos so as to render the war effort of the Russians negligible. It is highly unlikely that it had ever occurred to the Germans that Lenin would gain complete power.

Even though Lenin's Bolshevik Party constituted a minority among the Russian Marxists, Lenin perceived that the organization of collectives (Soviets) of workers and soldiers in the major cities raised the possibility of a Communist takeover of power from the increasingly discredited liberal regime headed by Kerensky.

Lenin was assisted by Leon Trotsky (a Russian Jew whose real name was Bronstein), who rushed back to Russia from Brooklyn, where he had been doing nothing but waiting for the revolution. Another East European Jew living in New York at the same time, Sholem Rabinowitz, also adopted a pseudonym: Sholem Aleichem. He was the famous writer of the stories about the shtetl in Eastern Europe that half a century later were drawn upon for the musical comedy and film, *Fiddler on the Roof.* While Trotsky was writing turgid Bolshevik pamphlets that few wanted to read, Sholem Aleichem was gaining a vast reputation as a humorist in the Jewish press. The two writers—who may have passed each other in Ratner's Dairy Restaurant on the Lower East Side— represented two aspects of Jewish destiny in the twentieth century; the successful and prosperous immigrant to America from the shtetl and the Jewish Bolshevik leader who created a terror state that was to be worse for the millions of East European Jews than the rotten anti-Semitic czarist regime it replaced.

Great credit must be given to Lenin in that even though most of his own party did not believe that a successful coup d'état was possible, he insisted that there was sufficient support in the Russian armed forces, particularly in the navy, for the Bolsheviks, the radical Communists, whom he led, to seize the Winter Palace, where Kerensky's government was located. In November 1917 (October according to the old Russian calendar), with about two hundred sailors, the Bolsheviks seized the government which was housed in the czar's Winter Palace. By this time, according to recent Marxist historians, the Bolshevik worker and military soviets, or cadres, had 250,000 members. Even if this figure is accurate, which is doubtful, this would represent only an insignificant minority of the Russian population.

Red October was not a mass revolution but a coup d'état, conducted by a very small group of brave and determined revolutionaries with the help of a handful of sailors and soldiers. The result was four years of civil war. The real decision in Russia was not made until 1921. In the meantime the Bolsheviks were not only fighting the Whites, that is, the supporters of the czar, the counterrevolutionaries. The Bolsheviks murdered the czar and his family in the summer of 1918 in order to discourage the White army. Between 1918 and 1921 Lenin's government also had to fight against Allied armies that were sent into northern Russia as well as into Siberia to fight the Bolsheviks.

If the Bolshevik government later exhibited perpetual paranoia toward the West, it has to be remembered that it was partly because the English and the Americans tried to overthrow the Bolshevik government between 1918 and 1921. The Allied attempt failed because the Western governments would not commit to the enterprise armies that were large enough—a prototype for later failure against Communism in East Asia.

Trotsky, until then known mainly as a pamphlet writer, proved himself a military genius, and organized the Red Army. Of course, he received help from former czarist officers who had gone over to the Bolshevik regime. Trotsky defeated the Whites in southern Russia and in the Ukraine, and fought the Allied armies to a standstill. The latter had to withdraw ignominiously from the Russian front in 1921. Meanwhile, in order to get a free hand, the Bolsheviks had signed a peace treaty with the Germans in 1918, before the war ended on the western front. The Treaty of Brest-Litovsk, which was signed in the spring of 1918, gave away enormous territory from the czar's empire. Poland, Latvia, Lithuania, and Estonia were given up by Lenin and Trotsky, to be regained in 1939 and 1945.

What happened in Russia was in one way a great triumph for Western Marxism, and in another an irrevocable disaster. The fact that the Russian Revolution had occurred meant that Marxism now had a power base in one of the leading countries in the world. Marxism was here to stay. Soviet Russia preserved high status in the international socialist community even though it had emerged impoverished from the war and the revolution. Russia did not regain the productive capacity that it had enjoyed in 1913 until the early 1960s.

On the other hand, the most left-wing and almost idiosyncratic form of Marxism had come to power. It believed in the use of violence to gain power and in the mechanism of oligarchic dictatorship and the secret police to retain it. The Russian Revolution gave to the authoritarian view of communism, as had been held by Rosa Luxemburg and Lenin, a tremendous and hitherto unprecedented prestige. This presented Western Marxism with a constant challenge as well as a complicated intellectual problem. Western Marxists henceforth had to develop their doctrine in face of the prestige and influence held by the Soviet Union in the socialist world and the effort at manipulation of Western Communist parties engaged in by the Soviet Union well into the second half of the century.

Nevertheless, in the 1920s and 1930s, there was a very important intellectual development in Western Marxism out of which arose some learned and subtle thinkers who were quite influential in their day, and who have become much more so since the 1950s. It is this non-Leninist group of Western Marxist thinkers of the 1920s and 1930s who are worth the closest attention among socialists of the period. They made the most original contributions to twentieth-century Marxist theory. In spite of the enormous prestige that Soviet Communism now enjoyed in the West, this group of Western Marxist thinkers developed a cultural theory that contrasted sharply with Marxist-Leninism. If it was in the mainstream of the Marxist tradition, it was also closer to the younger, more idealist Marx of *The 1844 Manuscripts,* rather than the later, more materialist Marx of *Capital.*

The Hungarian Georg Lukács had a background in Hegelian philosophy and became a brilliant and original literary critic. For Lukács the advent of socialism implied primarily the triumph of a cultural rather than a political liberation. He advocated the development of a society that would be devoted to the cultivation of the arts and literature, which he believed to be attainable only through socialism. Lukács also carried out pioneering Marxist interpretations of literary history, and particularly the history of the novel.

Lukács is most remembered for his theory of reification, which remains a central concept in Marxist theory. Reification means the controlled domination of the cultural, intellectual, and artistic aspects of life by capitalism. Capitalism objectifies, or reifies, all human relationships, including culture and art. It enslaves all aspects of cultural production, transforming all such products into its instruments. Capitalism is a strong substance, a great machinery, as it were, that runs through everything, from human relationships to artistic activity, subjecting all to its power and using them to perpetuate its own wealth. All art and literature that is so generated becomes, therefore, ideologically imprisoned in the service of capitalism. This is the fundamental Lukácsian theory of reification. Just as industrial capitalism dehumanizes and alienates the individual, so capitalism dehumanizes, by reification or objectification, all culture. This culture is not free, since it is the instrument of capitalism.

Lukács was required in the twenties by the Hungarian Communist Party, to which he belonged, to avow his loyalty to Leninism. He became a Stalinist after Stalinism came to dominate the Hungarian Communist Party in the

1930s. His own point of view, however, as ascertained in his early and creative work, is not in fact Stalinist, and his writings constitute the beginnings of a Western Marxism that departs from Leninist and Stalinist authoritarianism.

The second prominent Western Marxist thinker was Antonio Gramsci, who was the founder in 1921 of the Italian Communist Party. He spent most of his adult life in fascist jails, and his main writings are entitled *The Prison Notebooks.* This material, was not published until after World War II and the end of the fascist period in Italy. *The Prison Notebooks* produced immediate impact upon publication, and continued to exert influence until in the 1960s Gramsci became a revered theorist of the New Left. His reputation continues to grow, and Marxist intellectual journals today constantly devote critical studies to him.

Gramsci can be said to be founder of the characteristic Western Marxist doctrine of base and superstructure. The foundation of every society consists in an economic base. It is out of this economic base that the cultural and institutional superstructure rises. The base is formed of the material aspects of existence, and the superstructure consists of the political and legal system, literature and the arts. Even though the superstructure arises from the base, it nevertheless assumes a life of its own. It is not entirely, immediately determined by the material base. To a significant degree, the superstructural aspects of a society assume a vitality, a development, and a history of their own.

The superstructure is part of what Gramsci calls the hegemony in society. That is to say, the ruling capitalists dominate not simply through economic control, but also through the hegemonic superstructure. Their hegemony or power is effected through institutions, law, art, and literature. This superstructure is therefore the means by which capitalist hegemony or rule consolidates itself. But, Gramsci continues, since the superstructure has a degree of autonomy, it can be used by the socialists to undercut capitalist rule. It is not necessary to wait for the moment of total transformation of the capitalist economic and social system. The superstructure itself can be used to confront and overthrow the capitalist hegemony. The arts and literature can occupy the vanguard of the revolution. The socialist revolution can be a cultural revolution.

Since capitalists rule through the hegemony of cultural superstructure, alterations in the superstructure can work back to erode the power of the capitalists and prepare for a socialist revolution. A cultural revolution can therefore anticipate and prepare the way for a social and economic one. This theory understandably became very popular in the 1960s in the United States as well as in France. It supported the view that if radical students could take over the university and if the counterculture could become dominant in society, capitalist hegemony would be eroded. Student radicals leading sit-ins, and folk-rock singers, were in the vanguard of the revolution—so Gramsci was interpreted.

Gramsci's theory has remained a very controversial and much debated reinterpretation of Marxism. The English Marxist Raymond Williams, for example, who was a professor of literature at Cambridge University in the 1960s, found Gramsci's theory to be attractive, but held that it ignores the fact that the culture of capitalism is too thick, rich, and complicated to admit of significant change. The counterculture can therefore only succeed in making very small inroads into the superstructural fabric of capitalist society. Gramsci, in Williams's view, underestimates the strength, and, in a sense, the creativity of the capitalist superstructure. The popularity of radical songs and the production of profound, rigorous Marxist literary theories do not necessarily signify substantial transformation of the capitalist superstructure.

On the other hand, there is the view of Jürgen Habermas, the German philosopher and sociologist, writing in the 1970s, who thought valid Gramsci's view that the strength of capitalism depended on its moral visage and justification, and that capitalism would be delegitimized if it lost its moral presence and rationale. This, Habermas believed, could cause a severe breakdown in the entire bourgeois system. In other words, a cultural revolution focusing on the moral foundations of capitalism can in fact be effective. The debate in Marxist circles over Gramsci's theory still continues.

One characteristic of Gramsci's thought is clear: It is rooted in idealist philosophy. The leading school of Italian philosophy in the early twentieth century was the neo-Hegelian doctrine of Benedetto Croce. Gramsci's theory comes right out of this background.

There is similarly an idealist vein in the work of the dominant German Marxist non-Leninist group of the interwar period, the Frankfurt school of critical theory. The ideas of the Frankfurt school, whose organizer was Max Horkheimer and whose main intellectual luminaries were Walter Benjamin and Theodor W. Adorno, gained enormous prestige and attention in the transatlantic Marxist world in the sixties. Their work has now become habilitated in the academic world, first in Germany, and since the early seventies in the United States under the leadership of Martin Jay and a group of disciples at the University of California.

In the eighties and nineties there has been an incessant stream of monographs and scholarly articles on the thought of the Frankfurt school. Benjamin has come to be recognized as one of the more important literary critics of the twentieth century, even though his major work in the field was turned down by his university when in the twenties he offered it in support of his abortive effort to obtain a professorship. Adorno has come to be regarded in sociology departments and sometimes in philosophy departments as one of the leading theorists of the twentieth century, and he has been placed alongside and perhaps even above Gramsci in the Marxist pantheon of great thinkers. As time goes on and his collected works, comprising some twenty-two volumes, are published and translated into English, Adorno will gain recognition in academe generally as one of the half dozen most influential thinkers of this century—and perhaps of the twenty-first century.

As is the case with Heidegger and Jung, Adorno's writings require great effort and skill to translate into English, full as they are of Marxist and metaphysical jargon compounded with subtle paradoxes and asides that sometimes seem to be questioning the main argument. The best translated of Adorno's books and easiest introduction to his thought is *Prisms,* a collection of critical and expository essays. Of the torrent of recent monographs on Adorno, the most valuable and knowledgeable is by the British scholar Gillian Rose.

In the late 1920s a group of socialist thinkers in the industrial city of Frankfurt, which also had a large university, founded the Institute for Social Research. At the time the institute was not part of the University of Frankfurt. It was founded as a counter- or free school, designed to develop socialist ideas and a Marxist sociology outside the university. It raised funds from private sources and was particularly funded by the sociologist who became its second director, Max Horkheimer. Not much had been done when Horkheimer took over the institute in 1930. He became, in a way, its real founder as well as funder.

The three leaders of the Frankfurt school were Horkheimer, Benjamin, and Adorno. A younger member of the School was Herbert Marcuse, who has also been discussed above in his connection to Freudianism. As prominent left-wing intellectuals and as Jews or half-Jews, the leaders of the Frankfurt school, which the Nazis closed down, could not stay in Hitler's Germany. They had to seek refuge and resumption of their careers elsewhere. Horkheimer found his way to the United States, and with the help of Paul Lazarsfeld, the disciple of Durkheim, he reestablished the Institute for Social Research at Columbia University in 1938. Although Lazarsfeld was no Marxist, he was very protective of the Frankfurt school in exile and did much to help its members in their unfamiliar environment.

Adorno for a short while remained in Germany and went into hiding. His father was a German-Jewish wine merchant; his mother was an Italian Catholic who was devoted to music, and from whom Adorno inherited his lifelong interest in music. When the Nazis came to power, Adorno exchanged his father's German-Jewish name for his mother's Italian one, which did not for long fool the Gestapo. Adorno had to leave the country. He too eventually made his way to Morningside Heights.

Walter Benjamin had a tragic end. Benjamin first decided he would go to Israel (then Palestine), and he asked his friend Gershom Scholem, the Jewish scholar of mysticism who had become a professor at the Hebrew University in Jerusalem, to obtain him a professorship there. Scholem did so, but Benjamin turned down the offer, only to change his mind and write Scholem once again, asking him to revive the offer. This time Scholem did not reply. (This account is from a book by Scholem himself, written in the 1970s.)

Benjamin then fled to Paris, where he lived under impoverished circumstances, mainly on handouts from a Jewish refugee organization. The woman who ran the organization was herself a German émigrée named Hannah Arendt, the former student and mistress of Martin Heidegger and later a famous political theorist. Benjamin turning up once every two weeks to receive a handout from Hannah Arendt—there may be material here for an interesting drama.

Finally, when the war broke out, Benjamin, unable to make up his mind about what course to take, remained in Paris. In 1940, however, when the German tanks rolled into Paris, he and a group of left-wing intellectuals obtained American visas and fled to the Spanish border, intending to go from Spain, which was neutral, to the United States. When they reached the Spanish border, they were stopped by the guards who refused them passage into Spain. They were told to come back the next day. Benjamin decided that the Spaniards would never admit him and that he would end up in Nazi hands. He returned to his hotel and killed himself. He was still in his late forties. It turned out that the problem on the Spanish border had been merely one of bureaucracy, and the next morning, his companions were admitted to Spain. Benjamin's fate constitutes a great loss to literary criticism as well as a personal tragedy.

Adorno was an extremely resilient person whose career in the United States was complicated and successful. Upon arrival, he went to work for Lazarsfeld on the new science of radio polling. Adorno's job, which he enjoyed, involved telephoning people to ask which radio stations they preferred. Following this employment he received a large grant from the American Jewish Congress to preside over an elaborate study of the authoritarian personality, which resulted in a famous work in social psychology that was published in the late forties. Although Adorno became known while in the United States as a social psychologist, this field was not his real interest. In fact, he believed that the foundations of fascism were sociological rather than psychological. He did not really believe in the authoritarian personality type that—to make a living—he expounded so persuasively during his American exile.

In 1950 Horkheimer and Adorno returned in triumph to West Germany. Horkheimer became rector of Frankfurt University, while Adorno held a senior chair of sociology and philosophy. Both were lionized by the students. They remained influential until the mid-sixties—until, that is, the rise of the radical New Left among the students in Berlin. Increasingly in his later years Adorno devoted himself to music criticism, which had always been his great passion, and became increasingly moderate, almost apolitical. In his last years Adorno came under severe criticism from the militant Marxist university students in Berlin. In the last year of his life, in 1969, his classes were disrupted by these radicals.

There are striking similarities within the Frankfurt school between the theories of Adorno and Benjamin. There are also similarities between the theories of the two Frankfurt thinkers and Lukács's and Gramsci's ideas, even though Benjamin and Adorno probably did not know about Gramsci's theory, since the latter's work was not published until the fifties.

Benjamin made a significant contribution to literary criticism by highlighting the importance of the change that had occurred in literature with the coming of the market, of mechanical reproduction, and of mass culture. This change Benjamin located in the eighteenth century. At about the same time, in 1932, Queenie Leavis, the Cambridge critic and F. E. Leavis's spouse, published a book making the same point, not from the Marxist point of view but still arguing much the same theme. (Leavis and Benjamin did not know each other's work.)

Further, Benjamin developed a social and cultural theory. He said that out of literary and philosophical texts there develops "an active figuration of constellated images." In other words, a cultural superstructure is generated out of a social context through the medium of words and concepts. The key word in the theory is "active." These constellated images take on a life of their own. While it is ultimately embedded in the social context, culture nevertheless has a high degree of autonomy, and operates its own world of symbols and dialectical images. Benjamin's theory is thus very similar to Gramsci's concept of the hegemonic superstructure.

Similarly Adorno finds that in capitalist society a process of reification occurs in culture, which constitutes a kind of "fetishism." Capitalist cultural reification is "structural mystification." Capitalist society generates a system of symbols, literary and other artistic forms, a cultural superstructure, which has to be understood anthropologically. Just as in the study of primitive cultures, one realizes and takes into account that there are systems of magic, religion, kinship—an entire culture—which arise out of the economic base of that society, so too in studying capitalist society, the existence of a complicated fetishistic cultural mystification must be perceived.

In Adorno's theory the generation of fetishism is a process of mediation— that is to say, the culture, the superstructural fetishism that inevitably emerges, is very thick. It is not simply an economic instrument to which one can readily refer as capitalist ideology. It becomes a form of mediation; it undertakes a life of its own, developing its own strengths and impact on the world. It is active and creative. Capitalism engenders a system of literature, the arts, and other symbolic forms that are structures of mediation.

As an example, jazz emerges out of American capitalist society, deeply conditioned by the exploitation of black people, but jazz nevertheless constitutes an art form of its own, which has characteristics that cannot simply be attributed to the social and economic status of blacks. One cannot understand and fully describe what constitutes jazz as such by only describing the economic and social conditions of which it is a product. Jazz is a mediated culture that has to be understood on its own terms and not just as a social derivative.

The theory of structural mystification and cultural mediation represents a significant departure from the mature Marx of *Capital*, although it has some affinities with the younger Marx of the *1844 Manuscripts*. This should occasion no surprise, because the younger Marx was still something of a philosophical idealist, still under the influence of his teacher Hegel. The mature Marx stands Hegel on his head—instead of ideas creating the world, the material world determines ideas. Adorno has now gone part way in turning Marx on his head because of the creative force and relative autonomy that he gives to culture.

Adorno's theory not only represents a partial resurgence of idealism in Marxism. His theory of cultural mediation bears a strong parallel to Freud's theory of mediation as propounded in *Civilization and Its Discontents*. In Freud culture is a consequence of the interaction of the pleasure and reality principles. In Adorno culture is the anthropological entity that arises out of economic practice. In both instances culture is a mediated structure.

It is not surprising, then, that Marcuse, a younger colleague of Adorno in the Frankfurt school, thought that a synthesis of Marxism and Freudianism was possible. Adorno's theory of structural mystification also to a degree anticipates Lévi-Strauss and the structuralism of the sixties and seventies. While there is no evidence from Lévi-Strauss's intellectual biography that he was influenced by Adorno, the affinity between their doctrines made possible efforts, still ongoing on the intellectual Left, to achieve a synthesis of structuralism and Frankfurt school critical theory.

Adorno's theory of cultural mediation is accompanied in his work by a doctrine of absolute relativism. Every "authentic" work of art and "true" philosophy, Adorno tells us, has "always stood in relation to the actual life-process of society." The mind cannot escape from marketability and acts of exchange even when it consciously wants to. "Rather [the mind] grows to resemble ever more closely the status quo even where it subjectively refrains from making a commodity of itself." This statement can be construed as articulating in Marxist terminology Durkheim's principle of society's conservative capacity for functional socialization.

Adorno thus propounds a doctrine of false *unconsciousness* as well as consciousness, and a doctrine of total, unavoidable reification. Even when the mind seeks to free itself from socialization and the dictates of market and commodity, it cannot do so, he claims. Here Adorno advances a theory of absolute cultural relativism that in the sixties was developed into the deconstructivist theory of Foucault. The obvious question to be addressed is whether Adorno sees his own theory as exempt from unconscious relationship to the social network. And if not, what is its philosophical or scientific authority?

At times Adorno vigorously upholds an idealist humanism. "The reification of life results not from too much enlightenment but from too little. . . . Few things have contributed so greatly to dehumanization as has the universal belief that the products of the mind are justified only in so far as they exist for men." The latter statements make one think of Jung and Heidegger, or Jacques Maritain, but they are in fact Adorno's.

It is characteristic of the ambivalence of Adorno's thought that his proclivity to idealist humanism did not lead him toward utopianism, toward an affirmation of a social solution in which all contradictions are overcome and all problems resolved. He specifically rejected utopianism and advocated instead the principle of "negative dialectics." This concept, which got him into trouble with the New Left utopian-minded students in the late sixties, essentially means that even in socialist thought there are no final answers. There is a negative dialectic or intrinsic weakness within any theoretical proposition, including a Marxist one.

The historical dialectic never comes to a conclusion, not in Hegel's Prussian state or even in Lenin's Communist one. There are always contradictions to be resolved, social issues to be addressed, novel factors to be integrated. Socialist perfection is an ongoing, endless process, according to Adorno. The actual problems of society are always greater than even the best-intentioned and most skillful socialist thinking to resolve them. We "must . . . reject the illusions . . . that the power of thought is sufficient to grasp the totality of the real." In Adorno's view Marxism had an open-ended intellectual quality; it was a never-ending story.

In his voluminous musical criticism Adorno frequently disarms us. One would assume that as an eminent Marxist critic he would unreservedly praise black jazz and condemn Arnold Schoenberg's modernism as bourgeois decadence. The reverse is true: He finds jazz lacking in developmental qualities—a view that would nowadays be regarded on the Left as conservative or even racist (he is in fact wrong about jazz). On the other hand, Adorno thinks Schoenberg is wonderful, one of the truly great composers. Adorno's inconsistency and idiosyncrasy is refreshing and intriguing.

It is evident that Adorno wished to develop a sociology of culture along generally Marxist lines, but he also wanted to preserve the independent character of critical judgment from ideological and political dictates. His temperament is very far from Leninism. Stalin would have sent him to the gulag. Adorno remained a German philosopher in the idealist tradition. He was an immensely learned and creative sociologist whose ideas shifted from time to time, and he appears inconsistent in his theoretical exposition—facts that make Adorno's writings all the more seminal as a bubbling spring of Marxist theory.

Consistency, in any case, has not been a characteristic of twentieth-century Marxist thought. Marxist theorists have in general sought to perpetuate the main doctrines developed by Marx and Engels. They had to take account of the authoritarian system built by Lenin and Stalin, either finding some way to defend it as a necessary transition or dismiss it as an aberration from true socialist principles. In the 1990s Marxist thinkers in the West were challenged to explain the sudden collapse of the Soviet system around 1990 and to assess the kind of government and society developing in Russia after Gorbachev—a task whose difficulty is compounded by the instability characteristic of the

Yeltsin era. They have had a penchant for the revival of Victorian idealism from which Marx started and then for its repudiation and reinsertion back into Marxist theory. And there has also been among many Marxist theorists a wish somehow to affiliate with the cultural avant-garde, which has meant some kind of positive relationship to modernism. Out of these diverse strands it has not been easy to fashion a consistent and comprehensive theory. Indeed, it can be claimed that it is impossible to do so. But in cultural theory, the impossible sometimes bends to will and circumstance.

Because Adorno's thought is paradigmatic of the general intellectual agenda of Western Marxism from 1930 to the present day, and because of the intrinsic quality of this work, his influence and reputation is higher today in leftist circles than in his own lifetime. He has become the most seminal and admired of Marxist thinkers.

The Left in the Great Depression and World War II The background of the socialist movement in the 1930s lies first of all in the Great Depression. The depression—which did not make itself felt everywhere at the same time— began between 1929 and 1931, and it produced unprecedented economic disasters in the Western world, particularly deflation, decline in productivity, and massive unemployment. Not that the business cycle had not suffered crises before, for the West had lived through a serious depression in the 1870s and 1880s, which nevertheless did not come anywhere near the decisiveness of the one of the thirties. The level of unemployment in the United States had reached 25 percent by the time Franklin Roosevelt became president in 1932. It was indeed bold of Roosevelt to declare under those circumstances that the nation had "nothing to fear but fear itself." Even in 1940 the level of unemployment in America continued to remain over ten percent. There were industrial cities in northern England where unemployment approximated 50 percent—a record England once again approached under Mrs. Thatcher. By 1931 the situation in Germany was as bad as in England and the United States.

Among the causes of the Great Depression was first of all the crisis in banking, which Keynes had predicted as the probable result of the unwise Carthaginian peace settlement that had been imposed on Germany at the end of World War I, largely at the insistence of the French. The democratic Weimar Republic, which had succeeded the empire in 1918, was saddled with enormous reparations, helping to perpetuate the chaotic state of the German economy until the mid-twenties. Under these adverse conditions, the Germans did not have the money to pay their reparations, and they borrowed from U.S.

financial institutions, until, in 1928, they repudiated their debt to American banks, producing tremendous fiscal instability and a credit crisis first in the United States and then worldwide.

Therefore the first cause of the depression was a banking collapse followed by a credit crisis. The implication of a credit crisis is that businesses cannot rely on credit to sustain their loans and so preserve their current condition and remain in business, let alone have any prospect of expansion and growth. This will result in bankruptcy, not to mention the fear and panic any such adverse, wide-ranging phenomenon can produce.

Second among the causes of the depression was excessive speculation on an unregulated Wall Street, which brought about all manner of suspicions about the business world and the withdrawal of public support, to the extent of causing the stock market collapse of October 1929.

Third, in the 1920s, there had been an agricultural depression that cut across the Western world. The farming communities of the West had not been much affected by the First World War, and they were tremendously productive in the 1920s, with the result that there was an extensive overproduction along with the accompanying agricultural depression which made itself fully felt around 1926–27. The decline in rural consumption, in turn, eventually stimulated or at least exacerbated the depression in the industrial sector.

A fourth cause of the depression that historians have favored was the imposition of high tariffs on imports in the late twenties and early thirties, particularly by the United States. This rash protectionism disturbed international trade and encouraged a reversion to economic "autarchy," or self-subsistence. It is questionable, however, whether protectionism was a basic cause of the depression or more a response to the onset of bad times that exacerbated a deteriorating situation.

Finally the depression was worsened in its impact and assured of a long life by the unfortunate efforts of the governments in the Western world, in the critical period between 1929 and 1932, to deal with it. Their approach to the imminent collapse was sharply to reduce government spending; to do, in other words, the opposite of what Keynes advocated. They cut back in public works, laid off thousands of civil servants, and reduced the accessibility of government credit.

The advance of the Great Depression—WALL STREET LAYS AN EGG, the entertainment newspaper *Variety* headlined it at the time—generated a massive shift to the left in public opinion, particularly among educated people, in the thirties. Within a few months, and certainly within three or four years, very significant numbers of university students and faculty throughout the Western world had shifted to democratic socialism, and in many cases, to support for Soviet Communism. In 1932 Norman Thomas, running for president on the socialist ticket, gathered nine hundred thousand votes, the second highest a socialist presidential candidate has ever gained. (Debs had received a slightly higher number of votes in 1912 and 1920.)

The more important effect, however, of the advance of the depression was on the opinion or the mind-set of a generation of people who were graduating from college without any prospect of jobs. A tremendous bitterness and massive withdrawal of faith in capitalism inevitably brought about the fundamental leftward ideological shift of an entire generation, which was not significantly altered until the late 1940s.

The second factor that occurred in the 1930s was Stalinism. In 1927, after Lenin's death and a bitter feud within the Communist Party, Lenin's chief colleague, Trotsky, was defeated and exiled, and Joseph Stalin became the secretary of the Party and, in effect, the dictator of the Soviet Union. Stalin believed that Lenin and Trotsky had been far too soft on the Russian peasantry. He believed, and he was probably right, that if one was to achieve industrialization in the Soviet Union, the government had to break up the small farms of the kulaks, the wealthy peasants, which had come into being in the late nineteenth century, after the emancipation of the serfs. The way to achieve modernization of the Russian economy was, according to Stalin, to destroy the conservative and entrenched peasantry.

Stalin had the lessons of history on his side. The Industrial Revolution had occurred in England only after the elimination of the old medieval peasantry, along with their smallholdings, between 1500 and 1800. Similarly, the rise of German industrial power in the late nineteenth century had occurred after the peasantry had been devastated in northern Germany. But what happened in the Soviet Union was deeply tragic in that Stalin moved too fast, and utilized the repressive engines of a police state, which had already been constructed by Lenin. Applying a far more oppressive system than the one the czars had had at their command, Stalin engineered the slaughter of one to two million peasants, particularly in the Ukraine, in the early thirties. The exact number we do not know—and probably will never know—but it was a devastating massacre that even so did not produce the intended effect. Russian agricultural productivity fell behind rather than increased under the forced collectivization scheme.

Stalin then became paranoid, believing that his colleagues in the Politburo, the executive body of the Party, were going to turn against him, and that they, in collaboration with the army, were going to remove him from power. This may very well have been the case; Stalin's fears may not have been groundless. In any event—although historians have not discovered any significant evidence that a coup against Stalin was in the making—he acted against his colleagues before they could undertake to act against him. The result was the infamous purge trials of the "old Bolsheviks" between 1934 and 1936. These were show trials in which the Bolshevik leaders confessed to elaborate treason plots, probably on the promise that they or their families would be freed, which, of course, usually did not occur. They were shot and their families either murdered or deported to Siberia. The huge secret police mechanism that Stalin had elaborated then got completely out of control and decimated not only the Bolshevik leaders but the rank and file of the Communist Party.

These strange events presented a great problem for Western Communism. Were these trials genuine? Were the old Bolsheviks actually conspiring with Trotsky and the Nazis to surrender the Soviet Union and/or to overthrow the Soviet regime (as the purge trials contended)? It was difficult for Western Communists to make decisions about these matters. Consequently, most of them in the thirties decided that the trials were genuine. Even Western journalists, including a reporter from the *New York Times*, observing the trials, decided in most instances that they were genuine. Even the American ambassador to Moscow agreed. These purge trials produced a moral crisis for Western Communism and for Marxism in general, which reverberates to the present day.

In 1938 Stalin carried out a second wave of purges, staging trials of the senior ranks of the army, including the commander in chief, with the result that the vast Soviet army, which was larger and probably better equipped than the German army, became incapable of withstanding the initial phase of the German invasion in 1941. Contrary to common belief at the time, which accorded the Wehrmacht a specious invincibility, this is the main reason why the Germans succeeded in Russia for some twelve to fourteen months, penetrating to the gates of Moscow and Leningrad. Almost the whole senior echelon of the Soviet army had been purged by Stalin in 1938 because he feared they were going to overthrow him.

For Western Marxists the second crisis after Stalinism in the 1930s was the rise of fascism. The crisis went along the following lines: Was fascism a new phenomenon? Or was it simply a particularly vicious form of bourgeois capitalism in its final phase? Were the fascists a threat to everybody, to bourgeois liberals and Communists and democratic socialists alike? Should all these ranks therefore combine against fascism, or was fascism simply representative of the death throes of the decadent bourgeoisie? It took Communists, and even Western Marxists, the better part of a decade to come to a decision about the nature of fascism.

One reason why Hitler was able to gain and consolidate power in 1931–33 was the belief of German Communists, whose number was a critical factor, that he did not pose a great threat but was merely an extreme extension of the bourgeoisie. This accorded with the advice given German Communists by Moscow. Consequently they would not cooperate with the Social Democrats, the moderate socialists, and the liberals—"Social Fascists," they called them— against the Nazis. Because of this initial Communist view of Hitler, a united front against the Nazi advance to power was impossible.

Between 1936 and 1938 the international Communist organization under Soviet leadership, the Comintern, pursued an alternative policy and created the international Popular Front against fascism. This action was very well received by Western Marxists as well as by many liberals, and made Stalin popular. It cast a favorable image for him and helped cover up the significance of the purge trials which were reaching their height at the same time. Stalin presented himself as the patron and leader of the united crusade against fascism.

In 1939 the Soviets changed their policy again, producing yet another crisis for Western Communists and Marxists, and signed the Hitler-Stalin pact of September 1939. The pact was based on the agreement of Hitler and Stalin to divide Poland and not to undertake war against each other. Stalin gave Hitler a free mandate to invade and conquer about 60 percent of Poland, retaining 40 percent of the country for himself. Also he promised to send valuable war matériel, including oil and steel, to help the Nazis in their war against the decadent bourgeois Allies in France and England—something he continued to do until the very day in June 1941 when Hitler invaded the Soviet Union.

The apologists for Stalin claim that he believed, rightly or wrongly, that he was about to be betrayed by the Allies. He believed that the British, under prime minister Neville Chamberlain, who had already made a pact with Hitler in 1938 at Munich, and the French were going to join in a crusade against the Soviet Union. Stalin acted, so the apologetic argument runs, to forestall them and therefore signed his pact with Hitler. This is a controversial issue which diplomatic historians have not been able to untangle.

Whatever the reasons and justification for Stalin's act, it nevertheless presented one more crisis for the West. The Popular Front had of course been repudiated by this time, and during the first year and a half of the Second World War, from September 1939 until Hitler invaded the Soviet Union in June of 1941, Western Communists opposed the Allied war effort. It was not easy to be a Communist in Britain, France, or the United States in the late 1930s, trying to understand and deal with the unending series of crises and reversals of Soviet policy. "Their line has changed again" went the refrain of an anti-Communist leftist song of the thirties.

By the mid-thirties the long tradition of Marxist thought in Germany had been interrupted, not to resume again until the 1950s. While some German socialist thinkers, such as members of the Frankfurt school, continued their work in exile, all that remained of the large and diverse socialist movement within Nazi Germany was a small Communist underground. Until World War II began to go badly for Germany in 1943, this Communist underground was the only organized resistance movement to Hitler, irrespective of later self-serving mythmaking. Similarly in German-occupied France from June 1940 until the Allied invasion became imminent early in 1944, the organized resistance to the Wehrmacht and Gestapo came mostly from the Communist underground, although there was also a smaller and less effective non-Communist underground lavishly supported and stimulated from London.

After the liberation of Paris in the summer of 1944, a glorious myth of extensive resistance to the Nazi occupiers was disseminated. While there had been certain instances of exemplary heroism on the part of the non-Communist underground, many postwar French resistance heroes and heroines had actually done their service in Left Bank cafés.

The Communist Party in the United States during the thirties flourished as never before or since. Its total membership remained insignificant, but it did manage to enroll temporarily in its membership a noticeable number of young intellectuals and media people, as well as gain momentarily representation in the executives of some labor unions. But the American Communist Party was poorly led, faction ridden, and periodically disturbed by changes in the Moscow line. The Popular Front motif of 1936–38 was highly beneficial to it, as it could thereby sponsor well-attended congresses of writers and intellectuals. The purge trials produced some unease among Communist Party members and fellow travelers. The Hitler-Stalin pact of 1939 was, however, the death knell of Communism as a significant movement in the United States.

The most important development by far on the American Left of the 1930s was the advancing tide of New Deal welfare liberalism. It absorbed the preponderance of progressive sentiment and assured that the Communist Party and other socialist groups would remain small and politically impotent factions, although not without some influence in academe, the media, and labor unions. Thus the patrician liberal FDR was indeed the savior of American capitalism; New Deal liberalism became the prime focus for the American Left, not a variety of Marxism. The immediate access to power promised by the New Deal contributed to its attractiveness.

From the conservative public policy of the 1920s, the country went over to welfare liberalism in the 1930s. It is true that the New Deal was not as successful as Arthur Schlesinger and other historians of the New Deal claimed. Nevertheless there was under its aegis considerable economic improvement, restoration of confidence and renewed vitality in business, and decline in unemployment between 1934 and 1938. However, the year 1938 brought another crash, which continued until Americans began to build war matériel for England in 1940. It was the coming of the Second World War, and not the New Deal, that ended the depression in America. The war, and the new needs and markets it provided, followed by the drafting of millions into the armed forces, totally ended unemployment and created unprecedented prosperity and power for American industry.

The defenders of the New Deal can plausibly claim that a conservative Supreme Court fought a bitter rear-guard action for a long time, and that some of the bolder and more imaginative ventures of the New Deal were rendered ineffective by the Court between 1933 and 1936. Whatever the New Deal's intrinsic capability in controlling the depression, the historical consensus remains that the New Deal changed American life. It brought about the federal regulation of commerce and industry, and governmental supervision of Wall Street and banking. The deployment of the Federal Reserve System to control credit supply was perhaps the single most important and effective New Deal enterprise. The establishment of the Social Security system and federally funded public works were also consequential. The former brought the USA closer to Europe in providing for the elderly. The latter improved environmental conditions such as good roads and electric power dams and made a dent in the appalling unemployment rate.

What the New Deal program lacked was the establishment of a national health scheme, which the United States still needs, and a rigorous plan of federal aid to education, which by and large did not commence until the 1960s. Nor did the New Deal do anything substantial by way of helping racial minorities, except to undertake some laudatory and ceremonial ventures such as an invitation for a black opera star to the White House, which caused nothing less than a sensation in 1937. Black people felt good about this novelty, but the first step in the liberation of blacks in this country came only during the War when there were some marginal efforts to integrate the armed forces. Yet, Roosevelt never showed the boldness and courage actually to effect the integration. It was not until Harry Truman held the presidential office that, in 1947, the U.S. army was integrated by presidential order. This event marks the real beginning of the civil rights movement in this country.

Whatever the actual accomplishments of the New Deal—still a moot issue—intellectuals, academics, and media people lined up behind Roosevelt and the New Deal enthusiastically and in overwhelming numbers. Most American university professors in the 1920s probably voted Republican. The Ivy League faculties were then certainly overwhelmingly Republican and conservative. Even after the depression began, many were still preaching Social Darwinism and unregulated market economy in their classes. With Roosevelt's charismatic leadership and the New Deal's political success, there was a radical change. Even in the early 1950s, 90 percent of the History Department at Princeton University were voting the straight Democratic ticket, just the opposite of what they had been doing in the late 1920s.

The political transformation brought about in the New Deal era was profound and long lasting. It moved the mass of American academics and intelligentsia to the left of center where it remains, although there were some significant neoconservative defections among prominent scholars in the 1970s.

The paradigmatic New Deal intellectual was Lionel Trilling, the literary critic at Columbia University who became a leader of the New York intellectual world and gained enormous devotion and international prestige. He was the first Jew to become a professor of English at Columbia—and the last one until the 1950s. Another brilliant young Jewish literary scholar, Clifton Fadiman, applied for a job in the Columbia English Department shortly after Trilling, only to be told that the Jewish quota, which was precisely one, was full. Fadiman had to find consolation in becoming rich and famous running a radio quiz program and the Book-of-the-Month Club.

What was there in Trilling that drew so much devotion and attention? He was able to associate the New Deal with the liberal traditions of the nineteenth century. Trilling was an authority on Matthew Arnold, the English humanist poet and critic of the mid-nineteenth century, and by very skillful intellectual sleight-of-hand, he convinced his audience that the New Deal was in line with the best traditions of Victorian liberal humanism. It was not an infeasible argument; it was certainly not nonsense.

Trilling was thus an historicist. He placed the New Deal and the liberal-Left in the grand tradition of Western Civilization. With his colleagues, he elaborated a core curriculum at Columbia College, which is still in use today, called "Introduction to Contemporary Civilization in the West." In the sixties the program was still using the canon that Trilling and his colleagues had prepared in the thirties. Every prominent name in the course, from Plato through Aquinas, Machiavelli, Descartes, Kant—with the possible exception of Thomas Hobbes—belonged to Trilling's canon of the grand Western tradition, which came to a crashing climax with FDR, Keynes, and the New Deal. Many other American colleges closely imitated the Columbia core curriculum. Two of Trilling's colleagues in the Columbia History Department, Henry Steele Commager and Allan Nevins, rewrote American history to make the New Deal the triumphant culmination of national destiny. FDR was the heir of Jefferson, Jackson, and Lincoln.

The Trilling group developed a philosophy of history, and an educational theory and curriculum, which came to occupy a central place in academe and molded the mentality of two generations of American students. Trilling's historicizing of the liberal tradition and his placement of the New Deal within it effectively brought about the persuasion of public opinion. The media, led by the *New York Times* and the *Washington Post*, disseminated the Trilling model through its news and editorial columns (they still do). By the late thirties the identification of FDR and the New Deal with the liberal tradition and humanist canons of Western Civilization encountered no effective dissent within either the media or academe. Under these cultural conditions Roosevelt continued to win elections, and the Democrats, with the exception of the Eisenhower interlude (1952–60), which did not weaken the their dominance of college faculties, continued to hold power from 1932 until 1968.

Trilling's collection of critical essays *The Liberal Imagination* became a monument to his generation's efforts to combine New Deal politics with English humanism. His greatest accomplishment was actually as a novelist, not as a critic. In *The Middle of the Journey*, a work of the fifties, Trilling portrayed unflinchingly and honestly the Communist fellow traveling of his New York friends in the thirties and forties. This is one of the more important political novels of the century. But this more pessimistic side of Trilling was ignored.

Among the vanguard intellectuals in New York in the 1930s and 1940s were a number of instructors at the Washington Square College of New York University. Shortly before the First World War, Washington Square College—which goes back to the 1840s—was, for all practical purposes, closed down and became a night school run to make money. The trustees of NYU hated Jews and immigrants of all kinds. They established a new residential campus on University Heights in the Bronx, with very strict quotas against Jewish students. Washington Square College continued its existence as a mere milch cow night school for immigrants.

However, in the 1920s, so many people, mostly Jews as well as some Italians and Irish, wanted to attend NYU that Washington Square College reopened as a day school. It was run on the cheap side, and most of the instructors were adjuncts, some of whom were extraordinarily brilliant people. These included William Phillips, Sidney Hook, and Delmore Schwartz, who belonged to the *Partisan Review* group, as well as the novelist Tom Wolfe. These formed New York's group of socialist intellectuals. They were mostly Trotskyites—that is, Communists who had decided already then against Stalin. Soon the group dispensed with Trotsky, too. Trotsky was by this time vegetating in his Mexican exile until he was assassinated in 1940 by a Stalin agent using an icepick.

It was a remarkable group of free-floating intellectuals who produced the quarterly journal called *Partisan Review,* which became the leading left-wing intellectual publication in the United States. It is still in existence and is now published at Boston University. Its two founding editors were Philip Rahv and William Phillips, both of whom originally had very foreign Jewish names, which they changed. Phillips, now over eighty years old, still edits the journal. In 1939 *Partisan Review* had a paid circulation of five thousand, which even today would be considered a good circulation for a literary quarterly. Each issue of the journal must have been read by thirty or forty thousand intellectuals and academics.

Partisan Review exercised an enormous influence on the entire generation of the thirties and forties. Those who worked for it comprised many of the leading literary minds of that generation: Dwight McDonald, the political theorist; Edmund Wilson, the literary critic who is regarded by many as one of the three or four greatest literary critics this country has ever produced; the nobel laureate novelist Saul Bellow and the poet Delmore Schwartz; Harold Rosenberg, the modernist art critic; Irving Howe, who for many decades before his death in 1993 was a university professor at City College and who gained additional fame in the sixties by writing about the Jewish immigrant culture, alongside his many publications about socialism; Mary McCarthy, the well-known novelist; Sidney Hook, chairman for thirty years of the philosophy department at Washington Square College; Daniel Bell, the Columbia and later Harvard sociologist; and Irving Kristol, now a neoconservative theorist. The review's list of names and achievements is long and highly distinguished.

The New York intelligentsia of the thirties and early forties, about 85 percent Jewish, began its formation for the most part in the Brooklyn ghetto and ended life in upscale apartments on Riverside Drive. The title of the autobiography—*Making It*—of a younger member of this group, Norman Podhoretz, later editor of *Commentary,* speaks for this destiny. Quite a few members of this group have written their autobiographies in recent years, describing life in those days. They all portray themselves as poor, idealist genuises whose lives bear a touch of sadness because their deep and somewhat simple socialist, and in some cases Communist, commitments could not always be maintained. The world changed and some of them became mere liberals in the fifties and sixties, and even conservatives in the seventies.

The common theme in all their writing is that they were intellectual and literary giants who saved American culture, that America would have been immensely impoverished without them. The *New Yorker* cartoon depicting America according to New York intellectuals as consisting 90 percent of Manhattan and 10 percent of of the rest of the country particularly communicates the perspective of these intellectuals on the United States (although the attitude was meant to be that of New Yorkers in general). Hardly any of them went west of the Hudson except to go on lecture and book-signing tours.

The *Partisan Review* group and their affiliates—"the New York intellectuals" as they are now called—have developed their own mythology. There are several graphic accounts, for example, of occurrences in the City College cafeteria in 1933–36, of heated conversations in Alcove I and Alcove II, where the young Jewish intellectuals, arrived by subway from Brooklyn, would sit and debate endlessly the Moscow purge trials or some new critical essay written by Edmund Wilson or some new pseudoproletarian novel. They caricatured themselves in their memoirs. Their total achievement as theorists and writers is not anywhere as impressive as they themselves claim. Yet some of them gained a place in twentieth-century thought.

Sidney Hook in the 1980s was a fellow of the Hoover Institute in Palo Alto, California, where he turned out brilliant right-wing pro-Reaganite treatises. In the 1930s he was the leading authority on Marxist theory in this country. His book on the intellectual and particularly Hegelian origins of Marxism, *From Hegel to Marx,* is an astonishingly brilliant work, still the best on the subject. Hook was a very fine historian of ideas.

Edmund Wilson began as a critic of modernism in the early thirties, when he wrote important essays on modernist literature. He was very much taken by the left-wing trend of the thirties, and in 1939, published a book on the history of Marxism entitled *To the Finland Station*, which became a bestseller. Even though it is now out-of-date and superseded by later scholarship, if one were asked to pick a book to be read on the history of Marxism as an intellectual movement down to the Russian Revolution, Wilson's fine, readable work would still be the consensus choice.

Wilson's greatest achievement, however, is *Patriotic Gore*, which was published in 1962. Unquestionably the most exciting work written on the culture of the American Civil War era, it is a study of the ideas prevailing in both South and North. Wilson is particularly brilliant and insightful on the South, and when he describes the process wherein two cultures slowly separate and come into conflict. Wilson also wrote a pioneering study on the Dead Sea Scrolls, for which he taught himself Semitic languages. One can add to the list of his achievements that he wrote the first significant book on Canadian literature, and perhaps also the last interesting study of that remote topic. Wilson was an astonishing, brilliant, and diverse man, an American original. One more reason to admire him was his refusal to pay income tax, peculiarly anticipating the hostility toward the federal government exhibited by the right-wing militias in the 1990s.

Harold Rosenberg was an important New York art critic from the late thirties to the sixties. He worked to achieve a symbiosis of Marxism and modernism, starting from the principle that modernism was a cultural vanguard while Marxism constituted the social and political vanguard, claiming, therefore, that they must be compatible, existing as two sides of the same coin. He did not find it easy to forge this argument, which necessitated twists such as claiming that Eliot was not a modernist. To sustain his argument, Rosenberg had to purge modernism of its rightist, conservative wing. To claim that Eliot is not a modernist is tantamount to arguing that the pope is not a Catholic. (There have indeed been people who have claimed both.)

American socialists, while highly visible in the intellectual and literary world of the thirties, achieved only a small penetration of academe. This was a time when the university faculties were contracting. Because of the depression, professors had been fired, and consequently, even though there was a generation of radical graduate students, few of them could get jobs in universities, since, regardless of the applicant's political stance, jobs were simply not available. Nevertheless there were three important Marxist humanists in American academe by 1940. One of these was Sidney Hook, who used his chairmanship of the philosophy department at Washington Square to appoint his friends, such as William Barrett. A second was F. O. Matthiessen, who came from a prominent New England family, wrote a brilliant Marxist interpretation of the New England renaissance of the 1830s and 1840s, and rehabilitated the reputation of Melville as a novelist. Matthiessen, who was a professor at Harvard University, committed suicide in 1941.

Finally, and perhaps most important, was Kenneth Burke, who became professor of English literature at Bennington College and later taught at many other institutions. He was still alive and publishing in the late 1980s, having produced a vast corpus of idiosyncratic Marxist or quasi-Marxist theory on literature. Because Burke's most important work appeared in the 1950s, when there was a movement away from Marxism, he was not appreciated as much as he ought to have been. He has been rediscovered, however, by the recent Marxist cadre in the universities and generally febrile interest in literary theory. He is now receiving a great deal of attention, not only in Marxist publications but also in mainstream journals of literary criticism. Burke and Edmund Wilson will be recognized as the two leading left-wing literary critics that the United States produced before the sixties. There is an attractive nativist asperity about them. They worked things out for themselves and did not take orders from Paris or London.

In the Britain of the thirties and early forties, there was a left-wing group that was comparable to the one that had gathered around *Partisan Review* in the United States. Here too was a group that assumed a mythological aura, which they likewise later skillfully promoted. This was primarily a group of poets at Oxford and Cambridge Universities. The most distinguished among them was W. H. Auden, who came to the United States in 1939, and is still regarded as a major modernist poet. Another was Stephen Spender, who until his death in 1995 undertook lecture tours and published memoirs in which he assiduously cultivated reminiscences of the heroic thirties. The group also included Julian Bell, the nephew of Virginia Woolf, who gained reverential martyrdom in the Spanish Civil War.

Among this generational cohort of British leftists were a group of students at Cambridge University who became Soviet moles. Writers, civil servants, and art historians were recruited by Soviet agents to enter the British intelligence services, where they spent twenty years causing havoc by selling state secrets to the Russians and, what was worse, betraying British and Allied agents. Homosexuality as well as ideology bound their group together; its leader was Kim Philby.

As regards the more academic and theoretically oriented representatives of British Marxism, two thirties anthropologists stand out because they presented Marxist or quasi-Marxist interpretations of anthropology that gained credibility among the social scientists and the educated public at large. The first of these was the Polish émigré Bronislaw Malinowski, who began his field work during the First World War in the Trobriand Islands, and in the 1920s became professor of anthropology at the London School of Economics. Malinowski was a materialist who believed that all institutions in early society are outcomes of food-gathering activity and the satisfaction of other material wants. He was a good trainer of field workers, which enabled him to acquire many disciples. Malinowski trained many of the following generation of British anthropologists.

More theoretical as well as more dogmatically Marxist was V. Gordon Childe, who became professor of anthropology at the University of London. Originally an Australian, Childe was an historian of early societies. In 1942 he published the first edition of his *What Happened in History?* which, along with Ruth Benedict's *Patterns of Culture,* remains the all-time bestselling anthropological book of the twentieth century. Childe raises the question of how civilization emerged in the Ancient Near East, and he describes it in terms of a class struggle, and more particularly, in terms of the emergence of a bourgeoisie in the cities of the ancient Near East, which gained control over the resources of their society and organized the technology of the society in their interest. Childe provides an early chapter to the Marxist historical theory of dialectical materialism by showing the beginnings of history in terms of class struggle.

Childe concludes his book by suggesting that the persistent class struggle continues into civilized societies of later eras. He comforted Marxists of his generation with the thought that the Marxist historical model was firmly grounded in archaeological and anthropological data from the Ancient Near East. Until the work of the Chicago anthropologist Robert Braidwood in the sixties, Childe's Marxist construct seemed credible.

Another Marxist working in Britain was Karl Polyani, a Hungarian who became a professor of economic history at the University of London, and later, in the 1950s, at Columbia, until he and his wife found disfavor with the American immigration officers of the McCarthy era. Polyani published what is still the classic Marxist work on the Industrial Revolution, entitled *The Great Transformation,* which is a work of exceptional subtlety, and fully in line with the ideas of the Frankfurt school. Applying the Frankfurt school's ideas to history, Polyani attempts to show how the circumstances of the Industrial Revolution bring about the transformation from the old paternalistic view of economy and mercantilism to the development of market ideas in the service of industrial capitalism.

Finally there was Harold Laski, famous in the 1930s and 1940s. Everybody knew about Laski in Britain just as everybody knew of John Dewey in the United States. Every progressive petition would bear his name; at every mass meeting and leftist conference Laski would either appear in person or would send a telegram. He came of a wealthy Jewish Manchester family, taught for a while at Harvard, and became professor of political science at the London School of Economics.

Laski provided opportunity, in the thirties and forties, for young people of Marxist views to get Ph.D.'s in political science and social theory. There were hardly any Marxists in that period who were political scientists, and Laski provided them the access route. He was also a prolific writer of books committed to pop-Marxist historiography, for example his account of economic individualism. Laski's books make painful reading today. Although he was both learned and insightful, Laski's books from the thirties and early forties are dominated by heavy-handed ideological advocacy in response to the economic and political crises of the time. Nevertheless, through his teaching he exercised a powerful influence on the academic Left of the emerging generation.

In retrospect two of the more original Marxist scholars in Britain in the late 1930s and 1940s were art historians. In the German-speaking world in the late twenties, there were two centers of art history: the one in Berlin produced the modernist school of iconology, which has been previously discussed, in the work of Warburg and Panofsky. In Vienna, on the other hand, there was a group of left-wing art historians who tried to develop a social history of art, establishing the connection of the development of artistic schools and styles to social and economic history. Needless to say, this school was devastated by the rise of fascism in Austria and by the union of Austria with Germany in 1938.

Two members of the Viennese school, however, managed to make their way to England: Arnold Hauser and Frederick Anthal. These two certainly did not get their due in England. Neither of them ever found a real academic post, and both ended up teaching adult education classes, never receiving a professorship. They met with difficulties in large part because England did not have a penchant for art history, not only of the Marxist but of any bent. Outside the Warburg Institute in London, which had a private endowment, there were no art history departments in England.

Anthal produced a very interesting Marxist interpretation of Florentine

Renaissance art. Even though it was scathingly rejected by the iconological school, it is nevertheless a work worth looking at. Arnold Hauser, on the other hand, acquired fame with his four-volume *A Social History of Art,* which has become in paperback an all-time bestseller. Paradoxically, a very large number of people have received their introduction to the field of art history from Hauser's work. The book is a grab bag of information some of which can become quite silly, establishing vulgar correspondences between the economic life of a society and its artistic products. Nevertheless, Hauser was a man of deep learning and is indeed capable of fertile insights. Doubtlessly, there is an economic and political side to art, and Hauser has a valid point.

Anthal and Hauser started a Marxist school of art history in Britain, which remained largely subterranean for several decades. But a product of this school, Timothy J. Clarke, a British scholar and disciple of Hauser and Anthal, became in the 1980s a senior professor and the leading influence in the art history department at Harvard University and then at Berkeley. In a way Hauser and Anthal have triumphed in the end, and their Marxist ideas, carried from Vienna to the unwelcoming ground of England, have been eventually transplanted to American academia, where they are now flourishing.

A new era of left-wing thought in France begins in 1936, when a leftist coalition, the Popular Front, was established under Léon Blum, the disciple of the socialist leader Jean Jaurès. Blum's doctrinal position within the Left was rather vague. He was a mild socialist who can also be described as a welfare liberal. A left-winger nevertheless, he headed the first leftist government of France, which lasted for only two years. Blum's government did not accomplish much, but it was a great rallying cry for socialists in France and provided a starting point for a French leftist intellectual tradition that persisted into the 1960s and beyond. François Mitterrand was a disciple of Blum and his ultimate successor.

The prime fields of intellectual accomplishment among the French Left in the late thirties and forties were history and philosophy. Two historians, Lucien Febvre and Marc Bloch, were the founders of the seminal French school of social history called the *Annales,* named after the journal they had founded in the early thirties. Febvre and Bloch were first professors of history at the University of Strasbourg, which was at the time a vanguard institution. Until 1919 the University of Strasbourg had been a German university, and was reconstituted as a French university after the reconquest of Lorraine at the end the First World War, and endowed with a new, young faculty.

Febvre's interest was in the sixteenth and seventeenth centuries, while

Bloch—who was killed by the Nazis in 1944 while he was in the resistance—was the most prominent French medievalist of his generation. Both Febvre and Bloch moved to the University of Paris in the 1930s, where they began to exert enormous influence on French historiography. Since the 1950s their *Annales* school has gained strong influence in the United States as well.

Febvre was very much interested in geography and environmental history—in the effect of climate and topography, of material forces, that is, on social institutions such as religion. He applied the concepts and methods of early-twentieth-century French geography to the era of the Protestant Reformation, which he examined in terms of the influence of environmental and physical factors on religious values. Bloch attempted an understanding of feudalism in terms not only of its social structures, but also with reference to its cultural values. He examined feudal cultural values and ideology as generated by social structures.

Febvre and Bloch were committed to a program they termed "total history," which implies a combination of Durkheim's functionalist sociology with environmental determinism. Total history investigates how a social and cultural system is shaped by a variety of material factors and how a social "mentality" is conditioned by diverse forces, especially material ones. Neither Febvre nor Bloch was ideologically dogmatic, nor were they Marxists in the strict sense of the term. They can rather be described as left-wing functionalists, and as radical followers of Durkheim, who were interested in the ways in which a total social system operates in terms of the physical environment. They are concerned with values but of an impersonal, collective kind that comprise the mentality of social groups. What they really started was a school of historical sociology, which was to become widely popular in the fifties and sixties and to dominate the historical imagination of the late decades of the century throughout the Western world.

In the late forties, partly in response to Bloch's heroism, the *Annales* school became a well-endowed, state-supported Parisian institute and almost totally monopolized French historiography of the next generation. The deep learning and careful analyses that had distinguished the work of Febvre and Bloch were relaxed in the postwar era. The *Annales* school's commitment to total history and social mentalities became a convenient cover for a young, ambitious, and energetic group of historians who were more ideologically committed to Marxism and to the political Left than the two founding fathers.

The second area in which French leftists were productive was philosophy, in which the leading personalities were Maurice Merleau-Ponty, Jean-Paul

Sartre, Simone de Beauvoir, and Albert Camus. The philosophy they produced can be described as a left-wing phenomenology that drew on Hegel as well as on Heidegger, but transformed the ideas of the two German thinkers into a distinctly French philosophy. Out of the teaching of Merleau-Ponty, who was a professor of Hegelian philosophy at the University of Paris in the thirties and forties, and out of the elegant writings of Sartre, de Beauvoir, and Camus, emerged the highly visible French school of left-wing existentialism of the forties and fifties.

French existentialism holds that the individual, committed to moral principles, stands against an unfavorable social environment as well as against a cruel physical surrounding. The only thing that the individual knows that is good in the world, says Camus, is his or her own mind. Everything else, for Camus, is absurd. The only way the individual can secure his or existence, and achieve any degree of authenticity and integrity, is to continue struggling against the unfavorable environment, despite the knowledge that he or she cannot make much headway.

Camus uses the Greek myth of Sisyphus in order to describe life as tantamount to rolling uphill, with great effort, a rock that will roll back down the moment it has reached the top. Nevertheless, despite the fact that one knows the fate of the rock that one is rolling uphill, one continues to work at it. There is no alternative. An individual's only means to maintain his or her humanity consists of shouldering the struggle, knowing well that it is futile. "The absurd is born of this confrontation between the human need [for commitment] and the unreasonable silence of the world. This must not be forgotten. This must be clung to because the whole consequence of life can depend on it."

While Camus was fond of quoting Nietzsche and Kierkegaard, essentially his exentialism was an idealized version of Heidegger's phenomenological doctrine of authenticity. Camus—who died in an automobile accident in 1960—was a French colonial, a native of the French Algerian empire and the only philosopher of consequence to emerge out of the vast array of European overseas imperialism. It is also possible to see in his writings some of the fatalism, the wistful romantic idealism, that characterizes much of Muslim thought, particularly the Sufism that was popular in North Africa for centuries.

Yet existentialism was above all a response to the Second World War, the humiliating French defeat and surrender to Hitler in 1940, and the determination of de Gaulle and the Free French and the resistance at home to maintain the struggle against the Nazi occupation under circumstances that initially appeared hopeless. Camus was an active writer and theorist in the Resistance, and *The Myth of Sisyphus* was originally published by the underground press in 1942.

In the face of a dark situation that for a while seemed to promise neither survival nor deliverance from the Nazis, the existentialists showed a way to continue to affirm one's humanity and moral integrity. We must, they said, resist the Nazis, not give in; any other mode of action would destroy our humanity. Existentialism became the philosophy of the Resistance and then, for the early years after the liberation in 1944, of the revived French republic.

It increased the popularity of Camus and his two famous colleagues, Sartre and de Beauvoir, in the existentialist movement that they were not academics but made their living as professional writers and editors, that they were masters of French prose, and that what they said was easily understood. In spite of their leftist orientation (although Camus denounced Soviet Communism) the existentialists became popular figures even in the American media.

Jean-Paul Sartre and Simone de Beauvoir were middle-class philosophy students who took seminars in Hegelianism in the late thirties with Merleau-Ponty at the University of Paris and visited the Left Bank cafés, where they read Heidegger, and, according to de Beauvoir's memoirs, ignored the world around them. Even when the Nazis were attacking France, she writes, they did not pay much attention. Finally, partly as a result of Sartre's experiences as a prisoner of war in Germany in 1941, they became converted to a doctrine of left-wing existentialism and to the principles of the Resistance. Though their actual activities in the Resistance did not entail anything of note, they were part of it nevertheless, at least intellectually.

Sartre became a Communist. He tried to combine the existentialism of Merleau-Ponty and Camus with Marxism—not an immediately intelligible project since existentialism is a highly individualistic philosophy, which would render it incompatible with Marxism. But Sartre's argument, stripped of jargon, runs as follows: Granted we find ourselves in a rotten world in which the only good is the individual. But Communism will create a new and better world, and the revolution will no longer have to be confined to individual members of the underground; no longer will they be in conflict with the absurd environment. The existentialist will be reconciled to both the environment and society. Society will be changed, so making possible the process of the reunification of the individual with society.

Sartre contrasts existence with essence, and existentialism with essentialism. Essentialism is held to be the despicable bourgeois attitude that believes in the fixed character of personality within the social and natural order. The rich are essentially rational and good, the poor shiftless and irrational. Existentialism, according to Sartre, believes in the freedom of human existence, the freedom to grow and develop and become what the individual wants to and can become: It is the absolute freedom of existence, which precedes or over-rules essence.

Yet in subscribing to Communism Sartre was committing himself to a neo-Victorian doctrine that rigidly defined the essence not only of individuals but of groups and classes. Marxism held to the mechanistic psychological theory that the essence of a bourgeois person was prescribed by class, which predetermines behavior. This seems to be far from Sartre's existentialist freedom and radical individualism. Not only bourgeois ideology was essentialist; Marxism was as much or more so.

Sartre's was the dilemma of the leftist intellectual of the first half of the twentieth century, who subscribed to a radical individualism and yet was politically committed to Marxism, which was an enemy of such individualism. Sartre repeated the problem of the *Partisan Review* intellectuals of the thirties, who wanted to combine modernism and Marxism. No wonder he was strongly admired in the same circles after the War. Camus was a clearer and more honest, if less philosophically capable, thinker than Sartre. Sensing the incompatibility between existentialism and Marxism, Camus realized that existentialists could be vaguely on the Left but not Communists and/or subscribers to Marxist doctrine. Truth to tell, existentialism was more compatible with anarchism than with Marxism—an insight that was indeed occasionally glimpsed in New Left circles in America and France in the late sixties.

Simone de Beauvoir agreed with Sartre's existentialist philosophy, as she did regarding almost everything else. Her own main interest, however, was in feminism. Her book *The Second Sex,* published in France in 1949 and in the United States four years later, is the first great work in the feminist movement of the recent times. Her argument starts from the existentialist principle that the individual—male or female—can achieve authenticity and dignity against a rotten environment. Women have as much right to this freedom, dignity, and authenticity as do men.

Simone de Beauvoir lived the life of freedom of choice she advocated for all women, in spite of her decades-long personal devotion to Sartre, his career, and his ideas. It was characteristic of her that when *The Second Sex* became an American bestseller, she appeared abruptly at her New York publisher's door, demanded her royalties in cash, bought a car, and with a woman companion toured the United States for several weeks. Although it was fashionable among

Parisian intellectuals in the fifties to dismiss the United States as a land of crude capitalism, racism, and Coca-Cola (especially bad compared to French wine), de Beauvoir explored the vast and diverse country and had a generally positive response to it. It was very sad that before Sartre died in 1980, he took a new, young mistress to whom he left all his papers in his will, including the letters that de Beauvoir had written him over many decades. A bitter and complicated lawsuit finally returned to her the right to edit and publish this intriguing correspondence.

When Heidegger discovered, after World War I, what his now famous disciples in France were saying, he repudiated them, claiming that his French students had misunderstood phenomenology. Heidegger rejected the idea that the individual had to fight the environment, and claimed that instead one had to negotiate with it. One has to encounter the world, Heidegger thought, but also to respect it, and so arrive at a solution and a compromise. He termed the French philosophers neoromantics rather than phenomenologists. Whereas he was teaching accommodation and integration, he found that the French were romantic revolutionaries.

The last of the prominent French left-wing intellectuals of the War era was André Malraux, who gained notoriety in the twenties for unsuccessfully trying to smuggle antiquities out of Cambodia, and who was famous in the 1930s as a left-wing novelist. He wrote revolutionary romantic novels—*Man's Fate, Man's Hope*—and then became known in the fifties and sixties as an art critic—*The Voices of Silence*. He also served as minister of culture in the Gaullist government of the 1960s. In that capacity he did much useful work, refurbishing museums and becoming the greatest governmental patron of the arts since Louis XIV. In the interest of gaining a share of political power in which he could advance the artistic creation and entitlement that had become his major concern, Malraux in his later years was willing to make a political pilgrimage from Left to center (there had always been something of the buccaneer about him).

After the German victory in 1940, Malraux fled to the Riviera, where for three years he lived in his mistress's villa and consumed the entire wine cellar. In January 1944, when it became evident that the Allies were going to invade France and the Germans were going to be driven out, Malraux dashed back to Paris and became an officer in the Resistance. He arrived just in time for the liberation and became a hero and a leading member of the Gaullist entourage.

Malraux's association with Gaullist centrism was a rarity in the political orientation of postwar French intellectuals. French academics by 1960—whether philosophers, anthropologists, sociologists, historians, or literary critics—could not resist the leftist orbit of French intellectual life. If for no other reason than to maintain their credibility in the journals and cafés and among their students, they were compelled to do their work within the leftist context. In view of the Francophilia of American academe in the late sixties and seventies, this development had momentous consequences for American universities that sought a strong presence in the intellectual and disciplinary vanguard.

Simone de Beauvoir's novel of the mid-fifties, *The Mandarins,* subtly describes the elite leftist culture that emerged in postwar France and whose first wave was existential Marxism. The German conquest, the collaboration of many on the intellectual right with the Nazi occupiers, or their participation in the now discredited Vichy regime devastated the intellectual right and disrupted the French conservative tradition. This right, with its intense nationalism, fervent anti-Communism, and ties—either cultural or religious or both—to the Catholic Church has not yet recovered from the events of the early forties.

In the three decades following the war, Parisian vanguard culture—its journals, publishing houses, its art and literature, and its vibrant academic wing—was completely dominated by the Left, as never before in French history since the early 1790s. The Left was not homogeneous and was deeply split over Soviet Communism, but there was a persistent leftist orientation in French intellectual life, a strong role for Marxism, and a reflexive hostility to American capitalism that only began to alleviate in the mid-seventies. For the French intellectual mandarins of the decades following the liberation in 1944, one began with a set of predisposed leftist assumptions and worked out one's cultural theory in that context.

There is a vast literature on the American, British, and French intellectual Left of the 1930s. There has evolved an elaborate mythology about those heroic days, part of which is grounded in reality and part of which consists of highly romanticized versions of real occurrences. The charismatic event for the American and European Left in the thirties was the Spanish Civil War of 1936–39. It began as a coup d'état undertaken by a group of right-wing military officers, led by General Franco, in alliance with a native fascist movement, against the constitutionally elected socialist coalition government, which was dominated by anarchists. The war turned into the critical moment of truth for the international Left. To the surprise of Franco and the militarists, the "Loyalists" in the legitimate republican government resisted the coup and managed to fight on for two years against the overwhelming numbers of the Spanish armed forces, which were battling to bring down their own government. As is the case in many Third World countries—for example in Argentina in recent times—the Spanish army was far to the right of the republican government. Spain was experiencing the agonizing impact of the early stages of industrialization. The country had become deeply divided between the traditional Catholic majority and the large minority of diverse leftists and secularists who were thoroughly hostile to the church.

What actually happened during the Spanish Civil War still remains something of an enigma, despite the innumerable books that have been produced on the topic. Atrocities were committed on both sides. Aided by German and Italian planes, Franco and the fascists bombed Spanish cities in Loyalist hands and inflicted terror on the civilian population. On the other side the Loyalists—and particularly the anarchists—sacked monasteries and killed monks and nuns.

The civil war was an agonizing struggle for the soul of Spain, and it is perhaps only in recent years, following the demise of the Franco regime, that the Spaniards' moral and cultural wounds have begun to heal. In addition the Basques in northern Spain, an ethnically separate group that has been resisting unification with Spain for about seven hundred years, conducted its own civil war against every other party involved in the larger battle—and still does.

The chief external support for the Loyalists, that is, for the legitimate socialist government, was provided by the Soviets. This meant that the Communists assumed an increasingly dominant role in the left-wing coalition. A significant number of British, French, and Americans, all young leftists, formed volunteer brigades, such as the famous Abraham Lincoln Brigade from New York City, and went to Spain to fight on the Loyalist side. In the view of the Left, the Spanish Civil War was the rehearsal for a conflict between the Left and the Right, which eventually became the Second World War.

The God That Failed Some of the non-Spanish intellectuals who joined the Loyalist cause in the Civil War became disillusioned by the heavy-handed Soviet involvement and the way in which the Soviets were attempting to expropriate the loyalist cause. Among these disillusioned participants from abroad was a celebrated left-wing journalist, Eric Blair, whom we know by his pen name George Orwell. Orwell's second book, *Homage to Catalonia*, published in 1938, displays a visceral hatred of the fascists, but it also shows a deep disillusionment with the Soviets and with Communism. Orwell came from a solidly middle-class British family.

Orwell was one of the early and leading participants in an intellectual movement that began shortly before the Second World War, around 1938–39, and continued into the mid-sixties—a movement that might be called "The God That Failed," after an eponymous book of essays, edited by Authur Koestler, of the early fifties, setting forth individual pilgrimages to anti-Communism. Such writers had been active Communists or fellow travelers in the thirties before the massive disillusionment set in; some remained on the democratic Left, while others moved further to the right. All believed the Soviet goal was to dismantle the democratic movement of Western Marxism, that the Soviet system was a ruthless tyranny, and that the Stalinist regime was a disaster for the Russian people and a threat to others.

The God-that-failed group was naturally greeted with enthusiasm by European and especially American centrists and conservatives, and often became heroes and heroines in the media. This group of disillusioned leftists provided the principal editors of and many contributors to a marvelous intellectual monthly, *Encounter*, coedited for a long time by the distinguished poet Stephen Spender. By a circuitous route *Encounter* was secretly funded for the first twenty of the thirty years of its existence by the CIA, which saw a splendid opportunity to campaign against Communism and the Soviet Union by supporting sundry intellectual and artistic efforts of the democratic Left. *Encounter*'s political commitment was clearly on the Left and sympathetic to democratic socialism and the welfare state. (In retrospect it is hard to see what damage the CIA inflicted by its covert support for the best journal of cultural criticism of the sixties and seventies. Now that *Encounter* has vanished because of fiscal difficulties after CIA funding was withdrawn, is anyone better off?)

Orwell set the course that many intellectuals, especially in Britain and the United States, were to follow. He was a writer admired by many on the Left, which made for the powerful impact of his critique and hatred of the Soviets. Toward the end of World War II he published *Animal Farm*, an acidulous parable of life in a commune, where everybody is equal but some more so than others, and whose leaders are selfish and cynical. Orwell's novel reflects the growing belief at the time that the purges of the 1930s were fraudulent and manipulative, and that Stalin was an oppressive dictator. It is a matter of dispute whether Orwell was any longer a socialist in his later years. His last and most famous book, *1984*, was a chilly and convincing vision of what the world would be like under a totalitarian regime. Orwell's vision of totalitarianism was constructed as much out of the Nazi as of the Soviet experience, but in the early fifties the book was construed as an anti-Communist polemic.

Orwell participated in the Cold War reaction of the fifties against the

Soviet system, which made him, during these years when he accommodated himself to the conservative forces in the media, the darling of rightist *Time* magazine. In fact, Orwell's later career and what he then really believed have engendered a cottage industry of Talmudic interpretation. When he wrote *1984* and even *Animal Farm*, it is a fact that he was anti-Soviet. To what extent he was by then also antisocialist is an open question. Possibly Orwell himself did not know. It was revealed in 1996 that in the last years of his life, Orwell supplied lists of alleged Communist fellow travelers to a friend who worked for British intelligence.

The other pioneer of the God-that-failed movement, an ex-Communist who became a most severe and damaging critic of the Soviet regime, was Arthur Koestler. He has now somewhat faded from view, but from the forties through the early sixties, he was one of the most influential writers in the Western world. He exerted his influence particularly as a skillful political novelist. Originally a Hungarian Jew with Zionist sympathies, Koestler in the early thirties was not only a Communist but a Soviet agent in Berlin. He belonged to the secret organization that later came to be called "the Red Orchestra," a Soviet spy ring in Berlin. Koestler moved to Paris in the late thirties, and this was the time of the crystallization of his deep disillusionment with the Soviet regime.

On the basis of his insider's knowledge of the Soviet system, acquired during the time he worked for the Soviet intelligence service, Koestler arrived at the decision that the great purge trials of the thirties had been thoroughly fraudulent and were instruments of monstrous tyranny. The result of this inference was his first novel, *Darkness at Noon*, which he originally wrote in Paris in 1939. But he lost the manuscript in 1940, while fleeing through Spain to Britain, and had to rewrite the book, this time in English. It was published in 1941. At the time the novel presented a devastating exposé of the Soviets, a quality it still preserves, and it is still the most subtle explanation of what happened in the Soviet Union of the thirties.

Perhaps Koestler's novel is somewhat too subtle, since the book is the story of the elaborate brainwashing of former Bolshevik leaders, and of the processes whereby they become convinced of their guilt. The actual story of why they confessed, based on circumstantial historical accounts, is simpler than Koestler's reconstruction. They were beaten into submission and/or deceitfully promised that their families would be unharmed if they were to confess. Brainwashing played a relatively minor role. In any case Koestler's novel will endure. It is one of the most influential anti-Soviet works of literature.

Koestler's later career was varied and successful. In addition to political novels, including a harshly critical view of life on an Israeli kibbutz, he wrote books about the history of science, and became closely involved in parapsychology and funded research in the field. When he committed suicide with his wife in 1980, Koestler left his substantial inheritance to support research in parapsychology.

Another outstanding figure of the God-that-failed movement was Hannah Arendt. The brilliant and ambitious daughter of a cultivated Berlin Jewish family, Arendt commenced her remarkable career as a student and mistress of Heidegger. (There still survives a series of letters between them, to which Arendt's skillful, authorized biographer did not have access.) Arendt in her early years was a strong Zionist and she worked for a Zionist organization in France in the thirties dispensing aid to other German Jewish refugees, including the hapless Walter Benjamin. But she had married a gentile Communist, and so the couple immigrated to the United States.

In America, Arendt acquired an impressive reputation first as a political journalist—eventually with *The New Yorker*—and then as an academic. She was offered a chair in political theory at the University of Chicago. She also taught for a while at Princeton University.

Hannah Arendt's major work in political theory is a study of totalitarianism, in which she argues that there is essentially no fundamental difference between Stalinism and Hitlerism. They are both movements of political autocracy and are terrorist states designed to perpetuate the power of a small oligarchy. Their instruments are terror and the manipulation of public opinion.

Arendt's study of totalitarianism was very influential in the fifties and sixties. It was well received not only in moderate and conservative circles, where Soviet Communism had always been a fearful anathema. Her thesis on totalitarianism provided learned and academically authoritative justification for the many intellectuals, especially in the United States, who were making the rightward journey to avowal that the Soviet system betrayed democracy and liberal humanity. The resurgent Left of the late sixties and thereafter was less enthusiastic about Arendt's thesis. Today she is a controversial figure in left-wing circles and regarded by some leftist critics as a rightist thinker.

Arendt's other famous book, in which she reverted to her Zionist interest, is *Eichmann in Jerusalem*. The book elicited powerful reactions in the American Jewish community and in Israel when it appeared in the mid-sixties. It begins as an account of the trial, held in Jerusalem, of the Nazi mass murderer Adolf Eichmann, and continues as a discussion of the "banality of evil," the commonplace bureaucracy involved in the Holocaust, and of the occurrences in the Jewish communities in eastern Europe, particularly in Hungary, in 1943 and 1944. Her thesis is that the ordinary Jews were betrayed, in many cases, by the wealthier Jews, who were also the leaders of their communities. The thesis is not implausible, and there is supporting evidence for it, particularly provided by events in Hungary, where Eichmann had been in charge of the deportation of Jews. Arendt, who was extraordinarily courageous and self-assured, effectively defended herself against her Jewish critics. Subsequent research on the Holocaust by the American historian Raul Hilberg has firmly supported Arendt's view of Jewish community collaboration with the Nazi genocide program, particularly though not exclusively in Hungary. Like all great political journalists, Arendt had the knack of drawing the right conclusions from even sketchy evidence.

Another member of the group of ex-Communist intellectuals who did not spare the Soviets the criticism that was their due was Karl Wittfogel, a German Marxist theoretician in the early thirties. Wittfogel came to the United States and pursued his career as professor of East Asian history at the University of Washington in Seattle. He published a big book in the late fifties in which he argued that the Soviet system was merely a perpetuation of conventional Oriental despotism. It was a manifestation of what he called a "hydraulic society," by which term he understands a society whose technological organization requires that a peasant society be ruthlessly controlled by a ruling oligarchy. This narrow political elite enslaves the people in order to be able to control the material and technological means and to keep itself in power. Such hydraulic tyrannies were endemic to the ancient Near East and East Asia, Wittfogel claimed.

Wittfogel's theory does not constitute a significant departure from Karl Marx's view of Eastern societies. Assuming that Marx would not have approved of the Soviet system, he might very well have said something similar to Wittfogel's perception of Stalinist Russia, for the thesis of Oriental despotism was originally suggested by Marx himself. Wittfogel contributed to it the additional focus on the massive technological developments, of which Marx could not have known much.

After World War II, and even more in the fifties, all sorts of circumstantial accounts appeared as to what had happened in Russia in the thirties, and about the continued existence of mass forced labor in the gulags of Siberia. These revelations caused increasing doubt and confusion in Western socialist circles. Nevertheless, there were still many on the Left who resisted accepting the evidence which came from Russian defectors and émigrés. As a matter of fact, in 1946 a Ukrainian cipher clerk in the Soviet Embassy in Ottawa, Canada, defected with a host of documentary evidence about Soviet tyranny. But many Western leftists continued to claim that the documentation had been forged by the CIA.

In 1968 an English expert on the Soviet Union named Robert Conquest published *The Great Terror,* which elaborated in detail what had really happened in the Soviet Union in the thirties. The book included a mass of circumstantial and statistical information. In this case, too, there were American leftists who insisted that Conquest's research had been funded by the CIA, which was possibly true but irrelevant. It was claimed that Conquest relied too heavily on accounts by Soviet émigrés and other opponents of the Stalinist regime; presumably official Soviet documents were more reliable.

Finally, in the early seventies the last vestiges of Stalinist credibility appeared to be demolished by the publication of novels and other accounts by Soviet émigrés, the best known being Alexander Solzhenitsyn, and especially by an authoritative, lengthy historical work by the Soviet Marxist scholar Roy Medvedev, whose *Let History Judge* was published in America in 1973. In 1958 the Soviet leader Nikita Khrushchev had denounced Stalin at the Communist Party Congress. Khrushchev's speech was kept secret, but a copy was obtained by Israeli intelligence and leaked to the CIA. In the Khrushchev "thaw," the short-lived relatively liberal period of the early sixties in Moscow, Medvedev gained access to Soviet archives and probably worked under Khrushchev's protection. Medvedev's book, which may have been completed several years before it was published in the United States (it did not appear in the former Soviet Union until the late 1990s), provided a detailed and devastating account of the dark period of Soviet history.

Substantially *Let History Judge* confirms all the claims that had been made by Conquest in 1968: The nefarious CIA was right after all in its assessment of the Stalinist regime. The Stalinist system competed with the Nazi regime for being the worst terrorist system of all time. Under Stalin possibly twenty million people lost their lives at the hands of the Soviet state, millions more were enslaved, millions on millions of Russian families were made wretched, and the violence reached the point at which inevitably it became uncontrollable. Taking into account the research of Medvedev and others, as well as his own investigation, Conquest concluded in 1986 that in the Stalinist terror half of the Soviet Communist Party perished and "about a tenth or twelfth of the remaining adult population." Only the Nazi Holocaust of the Jews and other peoples

1940–45 was a crime of comparable magnitude in human history. By the late thirties Stalin himself probably became unable to control and halt the terror system he had himself created. The mechanism of the police state that Stalin used was set in place by Lenin himself.

By 1980, shortly before his death, even Jean-Paul Sartre decided that the Stalinist system had been—shall we say—unfortunate. Sartre was probably the last prominent left-wing intellectual in the Western world to admit doubt about the morality and propriety of the Stalinist regime.

That it took so many years after the purge trials, and after ample information on the details of the Stalinist terror system was available, for Western leftists to turn overwhelmingly against the Soviet regime demonstrates the intensely religious character of the socialist faith. Stalinist terror having been finally acknowledged, a new question had to be addressed. Was the Soviet misfortune a grotesque aberration in the history of Marxism or reflective of an inbuilt structural defect in Marxism?

The disintegration of the Soviet Union in 1991 and the loss of power by the Communist Party could be used to support the former contention. The Stalinist era was a nightmare for socialists, but one they now could awake from. It was an aberration, just as the Nazi era and its devastation and criminality were an interlude in German history. So went the leftist argument.

The ending of the Communist regime opened up hitherto inaccessible archives in Moscow. But since only some of the higher echelons' archives were available to researchers while others remained closed, and information in many instances was released by privileged Russian historians—often transformed former military and intelligence officials—the reliability of released documents and new historical accounts was uncertain. American intelligence intercepts of Soviet expionage communications in the 1940s were also made available in 1995. If the new information can be believed, the Russians ran a vast atomic spy network in the 1940s that penetrated even more deeply into the ranks of American scientists than previously imagined and the American Communist Party was an espionage mechanism and was lavishly funded by Moscow.

On the other hand, some American academics in the 1990s were using new material from the Stalinist era to mitigate the picture of tyranny and mass murder presented by Conquest and Medvedev. Estimates of the number of Stalin's victims differed widely.

Resurgence of the Intellectual Left In the sixties, and increasingly in the seventies, eighties, and early nineties, a new wave of intellectual Marxism appeared and was systematically habilitated in the universities. Marxist theory was legitimized in the academic humanities and social sciences. The motivations that triggered this renewed Marxist intellectual movement have been discussed at the beginning of the present chapter, where the Marxist academic advent of the seventies and eighties was shown to have emerged in association with the New Left upheaval of the sixties.

Following the disillusionment of the fifties, Marxism resurged as a stronger and more credible theory. Unburdening itself of the Soviets and of the obligation to justify and come to terms with Stalinism, Western Marxism came into its own. Henceforth, Western Marxists did not have to devote their time and attention to defending the Soviet system, and were free to develop their own point of view.

Georges Lefebvre was a role model for this new brand of Western Marxist thinkers and scholars. He succeeded Albert Mathiez in the Marxist chair of the history of the French Revolution at the University of Paris. As early as the thirties, Lefebvre was working on a learned Marxist explanation of the origins of the French Revolution as grounded in class struggle. His argument was that the eighteenth-century aristocracy undertook a militant, reactionary attack on the French monarchical state, and the confusion that resulted from the struggle between the reactionary aristocracy and the monarchy provided the opportune moment for a bourgeois revolution.

Lefebvre commanded a host of admirers and disciples, and by the 1950s the dominant point of view in the historical faculty of the University of Paris was clearly along Marxist lines. Academic history moved consciously to unite with the leftist sentiment that prevailed in the cafés and literary journals. This was the cultural context in which the thought and career of Ferdinand Braudel developed. Braudel was the dominant figure in French historiography in the postwar era down to the eighties and the single most esteemed and influential historian in the Western World. As the disciple of Lucien Febvre and Marc Bloch, he assumed the directorship of their journal, *Annales*, the prime outlet for radical historical writing, and what was more important, of the government-funded institute of social history that had been founded after the war.

This situation allowed Braudel to become the most powerful patron in French academic life since Durkheim. By the sixties, through the funding of student research and the placement of his disciples in professorships in the expanded French university system, the "Annalists" had become the overwhelmingly dominant group in French historiography. Catholic, liberal, and conservative historians were in danger of being blown away by the Braudelian surge; the media lavished attention on Braudel and his disciples and ignored other points of view; American universities fell over themselves to invite Braudel and his colleagues to come and give public lectures (even though, being French academicians, few of them could speak comprehensible English); and it was rare for a new French academic post in history to go to anyone except a Braudel nominee.

In postwar Paris Lucien Febvre noticed a golden funding opportunity for the leftist Annales school, and Braudel, who took over leadership from Febvre in 1952, fully capitalized on it. The Annales historians were on the Left but they were not Communists. This was the basis for highly successful solicitation from the French government and from American foundations, the latter also serving as a conduit for CIA funding, under the gambit of supporting "cultural freedom." This allowed the physical embodiment of the Annales school in a handsome building, the Museum of the Sciences of Man, and lavish funding to support publications, research, and graduate students. While the old center-right in French historiography, encamped in its crumbling bastion in the Sorbonne, looked on passively, Braudel captured for his movement the best brains of a new generation of French historians, and set them to work on aspects of social history, material environment, and class struggle in all periods of French history. Braudel was also in the fifties the chief adviser on the history curriculum in French schools and thereby prepared a generation of young French people for his brand of leftist history even before they got to the university. Braudel's achievement as a historian are debatable, as is the work of all historians. But as an academic politician and entrepreneur he was unsurpassed. He grounded the historiography of the Left in the fiscal and political resources of the Right. His prominent disciples in the United States in the 1960s and 1970s—Lawrence Stone of Princeton, Immanuel Wallerstein at Binghamton University—artfully imitated Braudel's strategy.

Braudel's first book, *The Mediterranean and the Mediterranean World in the Reign of Philip II*, was based on the dissertation he had completed under Febvre's direction while teaching during the war and shortly thereafter in Algeria. It is not only the greatest single accomplishment of the Annales school, being a more finished work than Bloch's famous study of feudal society, but also stands out among the leading works of historical science in this century. Not since Maitland's history of English law in the 1890s had there appeared such a historical tour de force.

Braudel takes the entire Mediterranean world in the sixteenth century, both Christian and Muslim, as a regional unit and tries to discuss every aspect of life, particularly material life, in terms of climate, food, trade, industry. He shows how, in spite of the religious and political divisions, the Mediterranean remained an economic and social unit. Among Braudel's accomplishments in this book was his impressive capacity to do statistical or quantitative analysis, using very complicated and somewhat arcane materials from the sixteenth century. He showed that it was possible to use the quantitative methods to investigate the premodern period as well as the modern era. Braudel's model generated a vast tradition of quantitative history that dealt with the medieval and the early modern world. The social history of premodern societies was thoroughly transformed from dependency on anecdotal information to grounding in statistical structures.

Braudel's later work, the three-volume *Capitalism and Material Life,* adheres much more closely than the former work to Marxist dialectical lines. Braudel was obviously influenced by the Marxist atmosphere at the University of Paris in the sixties and the seventies. The work is a grand analysis of what might be called the cultural superstructure of capitalism between 1500 and 1800. What exactly the cultural value system was in the emerging capitalist world during these three centuries is the question Braudel seeks to answer in three volumes.

Capitalism and Material Life is conditioned by two principles. The first is the doctrine of "the long duration." The world changes very slowly, ephemeral political crises having been shunted to an allegedly minor, almost invisible role. Society continues to be governed by the same material forces and to exhibit the same class and group structures and behavior patterns over long periods. In writing about the period from 1400 to 1800, Braudel felt he was writing about the same enduring society. Marx would enthusiastically have agreed.

The second principle in Braudel's work was that capitalism existed as a structural entity; it was the force driving everything else. The historian's task was to show by a mass of anecdotal and statistical data the capitalist impact in operation. Braudel did not establish sociologically the existence of the capitalist structure; he assumed its existence and demonstrated its detailed impact. Braudel's work is the show and tell of capitalism.

As befits a French mandarin, Braudel is especially fascinating and amusing when he talks about diet. He tells the wonderful story—on the whole, true—of how the German invaders terrorized the inhabitants of the Mediterranean world in the early Middle Ages simply by their unusual proclivity for consuming barbecued steaks, in violent contrast to the largely grain- and cereal-based diet of Mediterranean (and of Asian) peoples.

The other leftist luminary in Parisian historical circles was Emmanuel Le

Roy Ladurie, whose father had been a fascist collaborator. Ladurie became for a while a Communist and then a student and disciple of Braudel. A handsome and eloquent man, Ladurie became an internationally popular figure as a lecturer and the darling of the French television and other media, as well as the holder of high academic preferment. Under President Mittérrand he became the director of the National Library in Paris.

Ladurie's early work consists of orthodox quantitative Marxist social history. His study of the peasantry of Languedoc over four hundred years is an example of strict class history that seeks evidence in statistics. More interesting is his output since the early 1970s, which has been along the lines of an attempt at historical anthropology. The later Ladurie argues that there is no substantial difference in personal behavior between the medieval world and ours. The long duration appears to be infinite. The way a peasant living in an obscure village in the Pyrenees in 1380 behaved, and the values he or she held, do not differ substantially from the behavior and values of a member of the modern world, particularly from those of a modern French peasant. Employment, sex, and piety dominate the mentality of the fourteenth-century peasant, as they would today. There is a constant in social history, according to Ladurie.

It could be argued that Ladurie's categories of mentality are at such a general, macrocosmic level as to make discrimination of fine but real differences over time imperceptible. Ladurie like the later Braudel follows the Marxist, antimodernist, neo-Victorian propensity to grossly large-scale generalities. Viewed at that general level, social mentalities are bound to be durable. It is like looking at the planet Earth from a thousand miles away. Nothing seems to change over time; the continents and oceans remain.

In England a group of voluble Marxist scholars emerged in the early sixties. The vibrance of intellectual and academic Marxism was bound to follow the election returns. From 1945 to 1951 the first Labour Party government with an effective parliamentary majority fully introduced the welfare state in Britain, and in spite of some marginal countervailing efforts by Margaret Thatcher and John Major's Conservatives since 1978, this anxious public commitment to welfare benefits for the population has not been reversed. The welfare state Beveridge plan of 1944 was realized and then some.

Whether it was wise for Britain, economically drained and physically exhausted by the war, to reduce sharply the pool of capital available for business investment and recovery of the private sector by the extremely high rates of taxation needed to finance the welfare state has been questioned more sharply in recent years than it was in the late forties. In the postwar period the concern was that the miserable conditions the working and lower middle classes had experienced in the Great Depression should not be repeated, and the priorities were public spending and governmental regulation and outright control of industry to sustain this popular welfare. Even the Empire had to give way to the needs of the welfare state. The Labour government, lacking the resources to maintain the British presence in India, abandoned it suddenly in 1947, leaving Hindus and Muslims to massacre each other. The dismantling of the rest of the Empire followed steadily in the next two decades. Billions of pounds of Victorian investment were simply abandoned.

It was not widely recognized at the time that Britain's industry had been in an almost steady decline since the beginning of the century, that even before the war British investment capital had fled overseas, and that British human and technical resources for industrial productivity were at a low ebb, in spite of superhuman efforts in the early forties at arms production.

British higher education, in terms of both numbers of students and curricula, was all wrong for an advanced industrial society. Britain was so weak in business enterprise and applied engineering that two marvelous British inventions of the period 1938–40—radar and penicillin—could not be put into large-scale production in the United Kingdom and were effectively developed in the United States. Nor could Britain capitalize on its early lead in nuclear weapons research and again had to give way to vastly superior American technology and resources.

In 1945 Britain still had the world's largest automobile industry, next to Detroit. Nowadays the only British cars built for export are upscale luxury items, and in Britain itself the largest-selling car is the Nissan. By 1985 Britain's industrial capacity was not only far behind Japan's; it was—a member of Thatcher's cabinet admitted—inferior to South Korea's. Socialism had made the British people healthier and happier. It had also made them technologically and fiscally a Third World country.

British socialist theorists from Green to Tawney to Harold Laski had assumed that the social agenda was to redistribute the wealth of a fundamentally prosperous society. They had never considered that the wealth of Britain was itself fragile and temporary. They had not faced the issue that the commitment to the welfare state would be in itself a contributing factor in Britain's economic decline.

The Labour Party therefore never considered the possible consequences of heavy commitment to the welfare state in conditions of technological obsolescence, educational weakness, and investment shortage—a one-way ticket to economic decline of massive proportions. But the Conservatives who alternated in power with the Labour Government throughout the sixties and seventies—before the advent of the neo-Ricardian Mrs. Thatcher in 1979—were not much better in perceiving fiscal and industrial realities. The almost unanimous admiration among university faculties for the welfare state and unlimited public spending provided a cultural and intellectual context and constant inspiration for hazardous public policy.

When Britain, following on the watershed Butler Education Act of 1944, quadrupled its postsecondary educational system in the three decades after the war, it still severely shortchanged the engineering schools, created no American style business schools, and retained the late-nineteenth-century Oxbridge humanist curriculum as the dominant educational mode for college students. Nearly always the British civil servant of the postwar period was steeped in the humanities, wrote beautifully, and understood little economics and no science. The civil servant came out of his college years with a dogmatic faith in the utility of the welfare state, and with an acerbic contempt for capitalist enterprise and a horror of an untrammeled market economy.

The long shadow of Ruskin, Morris, Green, and Tawney prevailed. Laski was the chief theoretician of the Labour Party during its first creative period of power after 1945. Not only did he get the world he wanted, but the assumptions about public policy and human welfare that were central to his Marxist vision impinged themselves very deeply onto British academic culture. Only since the mid-seventies has there been a modest alleviation of this socialist faith in British academic circles. The visceral anti-Americanism that surged during the war has also scarcely been moderated.

In the socialist era an array of publicly acclaimed and well-rewarded academic British Marxists came to the fore, especially in the sixties and early seventies. Perhaps the most far-ranging and subtle mind among them was Raymond Williams, who was a prominent professor of literature at Cambridge in the sixties and seventies. In the late fifties Williams founded the journal the *Universities and Left Review,* which is still in existence as the leading neo-Marxist intellectual publication in Britain. Williams's first major book, published in 1962, was a history of English literature since 1800 in relation to social and economic conditions. In it Williams investigates the effects of the Industrial Revolution on the English novel, and how the novel, in turn, illuminates the Industrial Revolution. The influence here of Walter Benjamin and of the Frankfurt school is strong, but the indigenous influence of Queenie Leavis, the academically neglected wife of F. R. Leavis, too, must be taken into account. Williams is an able writer, delightfully amusing and clever. Among his many other books is a consistently interesting history of twentieth-century drama.

Another pioneering English Marxist was Edward P. Thompson, who in the seventies became the leader of the unilateral nuclear disarmament movement in Britain. Edward Thompson came from a wealthy family and never had to teach. For a while he did hold a chair at the University of Warwick, which he did not find very rewarding, for he resigned quickly and continued to live from his private sources and the income of his books. He was in the great tradition of idiosyncratic leftist thinkers and personalities like Ruskin and Morris, partaking of the same evangelical, puritanical English tradition.

Thompson's book, *The Making of the English Working Class*, published in the early sixties, was a vehement attack on Namier, the conservative modernist historian of the 1930s. Thompson claims that Namier's had been a narrow, conservative history that viewed the world from the perspective of the elite, and was interested more in the mechanisms by which they maintained their power than in the more significant phenomenon, around 1800, of the emergence of class consciousness and a democratic movement among the new industrial working class. Almost everything of substance in Thompson's book had been said many years before by an obscure scholar named S. Maccoby. Yet Thompson set forth the Marxist reinterpretation in a colorful and polemical fashion. He was hailed immediately on both sides of the Atlantic as the leftist and historicist liberator from Namier's modernism and conservatism. From Cambridge, England, to Cambridge, Massachusetts, droves of radical graduate students during the sixties clutched Thompson's book as a talisman.

There are four other important historical scholars who subscribed to Marxism, one of whom was Christopher Hill. Hill became very prominent as an Oxford professor and the Master of Balliol College, holding one of the half dozen most elite academic positions in England. He presented an orthodox Marxist interpretation of the English Civil War, which differs greatly, to say the least, from the royalist BBC version of this critical segment of British history, which was broadcast during Mrs. Thatcher's tenure. Hill continued the tradition established by Kautsky and R. H. Tawney early in the century, seeing the civil war as a bourgeois revolution and also the setting for the emergence of radical, proto-socialist ideology.

Eric Hobsbawm was professor of history at the University of London and then later at the New School for Social Research in New York. He has presented skillful Marxist interpretations of various historical periods and phenomena, particularly of nineteenth-century English and twentieth-century world history.

Lawrence Stone, another of the leading group of British Marxist historians, became a distinguished professor and director of an institute at Princeton University after a controversial career at Oxford. Stone, too, has presented an elaborate analysis of the English Civil War. The deferential culture that sustained the power of the aristocracy was eroded, and this aristocratic decline made way for the rising gentry. Stone's work on the English Civil War is very similar to Georges Lefebvre's interpretation of the origins of the French Revolution. Both analyses revolve around the perception of an ailing aristocracy that loses power and is overtaken by a bourgeois revolution. Stone was a direct disciple of Tawney, whose interpretation of the Civil War, he said in 1985, was "largely true." As director of a well-endowed institute at Princeton—funded by a very conservative oil magnate–alumnus—Stone had the patronage power to advance his leftist views of social history, as did Braudel in France. The influence of Adorno and the Frankfurt school on Stone is also obvious.

More interesting than the conventional Western Marxists like Stone and Hill is Perry Anderson, a self-educated freewheeling dogmatic Leninist who acquired a special celebrity by marrying a prominent Romanian film actress. Anderson's multivolume history of European society from medieval feudalism to modern capitalism is curiously illuminative, not only because of its learning and clear presentation, but because of its commitment to an orthodox, pre-Frankfurt-school Leninist view of the world. It was on precisely this difference between Western and Soviet Marxism that Thompson and Anderson engaged in a noisy public dispute in the late seventies. Anderson now teaches at UCLA.

The efflorescence of Marxist historiography and literary criticism in the sixties and seventies in Britain represents a polar opposition to, and rejection of, the modernists Eliot and Namier. Why did not only the provincial and new universities but also the Oxbridge citadel of the establishment welcome and foster the advance of academic Marxism? We have suggested one reason for this mainline cultural trend, the political triumphs of the Labour Party and the entrenchment of the welfare state. However, there is another, longer-range factor at work.

The triumph of British academic Marxism represents the revenge of landed Toryism on modern industrial society. The rise of the industrial capitalists and the steam-engine entrepreneurial mentality in the nineteenth century had never sat well with the traditional gentry leaders of British society and their landed antitechnocratic patrician culture. They had no alternative, however, but to make way for the institutional power of the new entrepreneurial families, most of which originated in the Midlands and the north rather than in the vested centers of inherited dominance in the south. What gentry culture did was to try to socialize the scions of the new industrial families through perpetuation of the old humanistic and gentlemanly curricula in the great preparatory schools and Oxbridge. But gentry culture was always on the lookout for additional ways to delegitimize and repudiate the capitalist entrepreneurial mind they intrinsically condemned and feared.

The rise of a generation of Tawney disciples after the war was therefore welcomed in conservative academic circles. Eliot and Namier were, after all, outsiders, the one an American Anglo-Catholic, the other an Austrian Polish Jew; and their modernist critique could be construed as hazardous to cherished traditions of gentry culture. Marxist literary criticism and historiography were directed at capitalist entrepreneurship and the consequences of the Industrial Revolution. These departures had raised Britain to unprecedented world power and enriched the gentry as well as the manufacturers and merchants. But this was not enough for the gentry heirs in the twentieth century. They sought a restoration of a pre-Ricardian culture, one based on deference and sentiment rather than the pound sterling.

The mythmaking and moralizing of the Marxist scholars was useful in this gaining of the cultural restitution of precapitalist Britain. That in so doing the establishment risked shooting itself in the foot, divesting Britain of its entrepreneurial mentality and economic power, was not a matter of crucial concern. So Williams and Hill gained high preferment.

Marxist historiography emerged in the United States in the sixties and early seventies, and focused particularly on the American Civil War and on the Old South, studying the pre–Civil War South and its slave system. The two names that stand out among those of American Marxist historians are Eugene Genovese, who became chairman of the history department at the University of Rochester and now holds a chair in Atlanta, and Eric Foner, who teaches at Columbia University.

Genovese is a colorful character. He began his career as historian at Rutgers University, and was an early opponent of the Vietnam War. His opposition was unwelcome, to the extent of depriving him of his academic post at Rutgers and necessitating flight to Canada. He taught in Canada for some years until he published work that earned him great distinction. Eventually he became department chairman at the University of Rochester.

Genovese's work is Marxist in the tradition of the Frankfurt school. He has published elaborate studies of slave society in the early South, in which the superstructure of the plantation aristocracy assumes partial cultural independence and takes on a mediating vitality of its own.

Like Leavis, Genovese is part of a husband-and-wife team, and again it is possibly the wife who has the better brains of the tandem. Elizabeth Fox-Genovese teaches feminist history and theory at Emory University. She is the daughter of the respected Cornell scholar Edward Fox, is deeply learned, and brings a humanistic elegance to her writing. In the 1990s Fox-Genovese's espousal of feminist theory moved several notches to the right, occasionally sounding a neoconservative note.

Eric Foner is the nephew of Philip Foner, a leading American Communist historian and theorist of the 1930s and 1940s who could be heard delivering speeches in New York City's Union Square almost every Sunday afternoon. Foner is a widely admired authority on the Civil War era. He was a student of the New Deal liberal historian Richard Hofstadter, and his work subtly combines the intellectual strands represented by his uncle's circle and by Hofstadter.

With the rise of the New Left in the late sixties, Marcuse, the younger colleague in the Frankfurt school of Adorno and Benjamin, who was then a professor of philosophy at Brandeis University, reverted from radical Freudianism, which he had increasingly propounded since his arrival in the United States, to a Freudian Marxism, which had been his original position. The result of this transformation was his most celebrated book, published in the late sixties, *One Dimensional Man*, which contains an argument for simultaneous revolution in the sexual and social realms. Certainly present in Marcuse's early work too, the notion is never as pronounced as in this later effort to synthesize Marxism and Freudianism.

In this and subsequent books, Marcuse condemned the capitalist system with unsurpassed vigor. There is nothing that capitalism can undertake that will ensure the desired freedom. Even freedom of speech and the relative tolerance of capitalist democracy are "repressive"—treacherously and insincerely manipulative. Capitalists can never do right, even when they offer civil liberties. These so-called freedoms are subtle repressive mechanisms by which the bourgeoisie seeks to pacify and so undermine opposition—a line of argument that continues to inform the columns of leftist publications such as the *Village Voice* or *The Nation*. Marcuse's doctrine of repressive tolerance remains a popular theory among many Marxist social scientists. Thereby Marxist academics can personally benefit from American capitalism and condemn it at the same time.

Marcuse was almost as critical of the Soviet system as he was of the capitalist. His position in his later work is actually closer to anarchism than to Marxism. He seeks to transcend the old industrial society, be it capitalist or Soviet, into a world of environmental bliss and libidinal freedom. It is not surprising that this message found a warm welcome from the countercultural movement of the 1960s—indeed, Marcuse helped to articulate its doctrine. Among his disciples was the Yippie leader Abbie Hoffman. There could not have been anyone farther removed in personal style from a sixties flower child than Marcuse—a buttoned-up, sober 1930s German professor. But his message certainly cohered with that of the counterculture, as we have seen.

At the same time, in the social sciences an important group of left-wing and Marxist scholars had emerged. Especially in the anthropology and sociology departments at Columbia University, a movement, which gathered a number of remarkably brilliant scholars, became clearly discernible in the 1960s. One of the members of this group was the anthropologist Marvin Harris, for many years the chairman of the anthropology department at Columbia, who now lives in Florida. Harris continues to publish, becoming increasingly radical with age.

Harris is arguing for a strictly materialist interpretation in anthropological theory. He takes the Marxist approach of Malinowski and Childe and drives it home even harder. Harris's *The Rise of Anthropological Theory*, which appeared in the late sixties, is the best history of anthropology, one can easily claim, that has ever been written. In his book Harris runs through the entire history of anthropology, evaluating the workers in the field according to a Marxist scale, which does not, however, divest his work of credibility and insight. Margaret Mead is among those who suffer particularly from Harris's lucid and clever appraisal. He is the leading Marxist anthropological theorist in the United States.

Another distinguished Marxist spokesman among anthropologists is Eric Wolfe of the City University of New York. He is best known for his sympathetic and facile account *Peasant Wars of the Twentieth Century.* The peasants, of course, are always seeking what justly belongs to them; the landlords are inevitably the embodiment of evil.

By the late fifties, metropolitan sociology departments in the United States had taken on the aura of bastions of moderation and conformity. They were heavily involved in political polling and market research, and following Talcott Parsons, they interpreted Durkheim's functionalist theory so as to cast grave doubts on the feasibility of radical movements. Ever eager to ride the crest of the trend, Daniel Bell proclaimed "the end of ideology." The strong exception to this conservative trend among sociologists was the dramatic figure on the Columbia campus of C. Wright Mills. Arriving on Morningside Heights in a leather jacket on his motorcycle (which soon killed him) from his home in Rockland County, Mills became the forerunner and role model for the large and influential group of Marxist sociologists that emerged later, in the closing years of the sixties. There is little to Mills's most celebrated book *The Power Elite* beyond the confrontational title. Mills discovered a power elite in society and he didn't like them. Nor was he satisfied with Parsons's, Durkheim's, or Bell's eagerness to sound the retreat from sociological radicalism.

The other herald of a new day was Alvin Gouldner, who taught first at Buffalo and then became Max Weber Professor of Sociology at Washington University in St. Louis. A group of radical graduate students migrated from Buffalo to St. Louis with Gouldner. Led by Paul Piccone, they established *Telos*, still the most interesting Marxist intellectual journal in the United States. (*Telos* is now published in Greenwich Village.)

Gouldner's polemical study of the sociological profession, *The Coming Crisis of Western Sociology*, was intended to be a leftist call to militancy and activism. Durkheim and Parsons—especially the latter—were condemned as political conservatives, and "functionalism" in Gouldner's use became a dirty word, a synonym for conformity and surrender. How well Gouldner actually understood Durkheim and Parsons is questionable. The sociological profession was scathingly criticized in Gouldner's book for its involvements with governmental agencies and business corporations—its only sources of income outside of teaching. Gouldner overrated the opposition: There was no crisis of sociology. But his view easily prevailed. In the late sixties, as a younger generation of social scientists came forward, there was a strongly sympathetic response to the student radicals and New Left of the era and a shift several degrees to the left on the part of the sociological profession in the United States. A similar trajectory occurred in France and West Germany. Marxism rapidly became—for the first time—the central theory in Western sociology.

Two young Columbia sociologists, Immanuel Wallerstein and Terence Hopkins, were the most vehement supporters of the student revolution at Columbia in 1968. Since both had tenure, they could not be fired for the support they lent the rebellious students, but they did fall into disfavor. They went into exile: Wallerstein to Canada, to the same city, Montreal, to which Genovese had been obliged to withdraw, and Hopkins to the West Indies for a couple of years. They returned and in the early seventies found their way to

Binghamton University, where they took over the sociology department and founded the Ferdinand Braudel Center, an institute of historical sociology along Marxist lines. Braudel came for the official opening of the institute, which took place in 1976. Under a huge marquee pitched on the campus, Braudel cut the red ribbon himself.

The Braudel Center has become an important and influential agency in the field of Marxist sociology. No one asked the long-suffering taxpayers of New York State whether they wished to support a distinguished Marxist institute, especially respected by anti-American groups in the Third World.

What Wallerstein and Hopkins are pursuing is a universal historical science of sociology structured along the lines of what is called "dependency theory." This theory finds its origins in the theory of imperialism propounded by Hobson, the English socialist at the beginning of this century, and later by Lenin, and its elaboration in the work of Hopkins and Wallerstein. It was delineated by the Latin American Marxist theorist André Gunder Franck, who claims that the economy of Third World countries is thoroughly controlled and exploited by American capitalism. Wallerstein and Hopkins put this thesis on a historical projection, called world systems theory. They claimed that since the beginning of the sixteenth century, Western capitalism has organized the entire world economy so as to support itself and make non-Western economies dependent on Western capitalism. The phenomenon of Western imperialism's economic programs does not originate in the nineteenth century, with enterprises such as the United Fruit Company in Guatemala, say, but in the sixteenth century.

An early case of this phenomenon is the famous enserfment of the peasantry in Eastern Europe around 1500. At the same time as most of the peasantry were enfranchised or liberated from serfdom in Western Europe, they were forced into serfdom in Poland and the Ukraine, for in the capitalist world system these regions were assigned the task of producing grain in order to support the Western economy. To ensure the availability of labor for the production of grain and in order to maintain production on the needed level, the Polish and Ukrainian peasantry had to be enserfed. This phenomenon, according to the dependency theorists, became the prototype of the global workings of Western capitalism. The role of the Spaniards in Mexico and Peru, the Dutch in Indonesia, the Belgians in the Congo, and the British in India offered dramatic case studies to support Wallerstein's thesis.

Wallerstein's treatise on the capitalist world system was crowned by the highest prize of the American Sociological Association. Latin American intellectuals consider that he stands shoulder to shoulder with Marx, Lenin, Castro, and Che Guevara in the pantheon of heroes. Unfortunately, the dependency theory that Western capitalism, and especially the United States, made itself rich at the expense of the rest of the world, including Latin America and Africa, is vulnerable. Lawrence E. Harrison, in a persuasive critique of the dependency theory in 1986, pointed out that in the nineteenth century the United States, Canada, and Australia were exporters of primary materials and recipients of foreign investments—the same allegedly victimized role occupied by Third World countries.

In spite of the Franck-Wallerstein-Hopkins vision of the bloated American capitalist octopus squeezing the interlocked world economy, the American economy since the early twentieth century has been largely self-sufficient. As far as American trade is concerned, it is today largely with developed countries of Western Europe, Japan, and Canada rather than with Latin America. The United States trades with and invests more in Canada than it does all of Central and South America. Harrison points out that "the total effective demand of the five Central American countries for U.S. products approximates that of Springfield, Mass."

Developments in the American and world economies during the past fifteen years have severely damaged Wallerstein's world systems thesis. With the decline of the U.S. steel and automobile industries, the greater value of American exports has come to reside, as it did a hundred years ago, again in grain, lumber, and other primary materials. It is the peripheral and Third World countries, not the center of the capitalist world system, according to Wallerstein's vision, that should be providing the primary materials. If the Wallerstein thesis made sense, the current center of the capitalist world system would lie in Japan and Germany, not the United States. But this would not suit the wish of Wallerstein and his Third World Marxist friends to blame the problems of Latin America and Africa on American capitalism. What Wallerstein wanted to do was to provide a historical thesis to disparage the United States (which succeeded nineteenth-century Britain as the center of capitalist world hegemony) and make the Third World feel and look good. In the sixties, when he developed his thesis with assistance from Franck and Hopkins, Wallerstein seemed momentarily to have some persuasive arguments. Yet, economic history has moved into another era, involving the decline of American heavy industry, and the probabilities in support of his thesis have diminished.

The British economist, P. T. Bauer, has argued the point very effectively that the Third World's problems are principally generated by its own weaknesses, especially in the political realm. As a case in point, in 1945 Argentina's gross national product was equal to Canada's; now it is much smaller. This has been due not to American interference but to the calamitous rule of crackpot dictators and greedy militarists.

A similar situation prevails in many other Latin American and African countries. Even the lavish U.S. (and, in some instances, Soviet) aid to these Third World countries has been grossly misused and has worked against making their economies self-sustaining. Bauer has pointed out that the greatest error the postcolonial states, especially in Africa, have made is to try to develop heavy industry long before their economies and cultures were ready for this departure. These countries lacked the educational infrastructure, technology, political stability, and capital necessary for industrial revolutions. At the same time they neglected the fine agricultural legacies they inherited from the colonial era, leading to catastrophic poverty unknown in the 1950s. A 1986 conference at the UN reached the same conclusion.

Following Wallerstein's view of economic history, it is easy to see how liberated Third World governments would make such grievous errors. While Wallerstein was collecting scholarly honors and endowed chairs, his Third World disciples implemented his theory in state policies of industrialization and embarked on a one-way trip to economic oblivion.

For earlier centuries Wallerstein can point to some dramatic anecdotal instances to support his world systems theory. Since statistical data are fragmentary, it is hard either to prove or disprove his longitudinal thesis. Yet a close survey of the European overseas empires reveals a mixed balance sheet. Sometimes the imperialist states made big profits from their colonial empires. Sometimes the governments lost money and only individuals profited. Sometimes nearly everybody lost in imperial ventures. If a generalization about the history of imperialism is needed, the facts appear to support the conservative view of Nathan Rosenberg and L. E. Birdsell, Jr. Western "economic growth seem[s] more a cause of imperialism . . . than its result." It is systematic cultural and economic factors intrinsic to the West, not its alleged domination of the Third World, that accounts for the rise of Western Europe and the United States. Wallerstein's elaborate and brilliant effort to foist a meta-historical guilt on the West is not convincing.

At the same time as Wallerstein and Hopkins developed their dependency theory, another approach—anarchosyndicalist in spirit—was being propounded to elucidate the relations between Western capitalism and the Third

World. This theory, formulated by Franz Fanon, became, at least momentarily in the sixties, very visible. A West Indian physician who had been educated in France, where he came under the influence of Sartre and the existential Marxism of the fifties, Fanon became the theorist of African liberation in the sixties. His theory also had considerable influence on the black movement in the United States in the sixties and early seventies. There is no question that Fanon was also strongly influenced by Sorel and French anarchosyndicalism.

Only the revolution against Western imperialism itself will create a new kind of human being in Africa, Fanon argues. Whatever the problems of lack of education and other facets of underdevelopment, however insurmountable they may seem, the actual act of revolution will not fail to liberate the mentality of the African people, providing the basis for a new society. The question, therefore, of whether the Africans are ready for freedom is meaningless. Only the reality of freedom itself will reconstruct African culture.

This romantic doctrine—influential in the Third World in the sixties and early seventies—was embraced by the more radical wing of the Black Liberation movement in the United States. The marginal destiny of African liberation and the unfortunate history of many of the new African states—their decline into poverty—has raised questions about its validity. Nigeria, Ghana, and Zaire, for example, were in fact much more productive under white rule. The end of imperial rule in the countries lying between the Sahara and South Africa inaugurated an era of political ineptitude and corruption that adversely affected productivity and economic stability. Of course Third World advocates and Fanon disciples can respond that the political failures of the liberated African countries are the consequences of the devastating imperialist legacy. Colonial rule, it is said, destroyed the traditional political infrastructure in African societies and did not train a native elite to replace the European governors. Precisely when black Africans can assume responsibility for their own shortcomings is unclear.

Alongside Fanon and Wallerstein in speaking for non-Western peoples who feel themselves exploited and mistreated by Western colonialism is the elegant figure of Edward Said. An upper- middle-class Christian Arab, born in Jerusalem, raised in Egypt, and further educated in Britain and the United States, Said occupies the senior chair in the humanities at Columbia University. Although Said was renowned as literary theorist, it was his polemical work on the East-West problem, *Orientalism*, published in 1978, that made him a powerful presence on the world leftist spectrum and got him elected to the board of the PLO.

Orientalism is an effort at historiograpical criticism. Said presents a picture of how Western historians, beginning with German and Austrian Arabists who were mostly Jews, and embodied in the current generation in Bernard Lewis, a Jew from London and a Zionist, who taught first at the University of London and then at Princeton, created an adverse view of Arabs as backward, ignorant, and fanatical. A special entity called Orientalism was created to serve colonialist purposes. This subservient picture of Arabs and the Muslim world, served to justify Middle Eastern colonialism and Zionist mistreatment of the Arabs and the Israelis' criminal exclusion of the Arabs (including Said's family) from their anscestral homeland. Written with wit and passion, *Orientalism* is one of the half dozen most influential books of the last quarter of the twentieth century. It became the holy writ of the Departments of Near Eastern Studies established on many American campuses, with Arab oil money, and heavily (except at Princeton, where three Jews including Lewis held on as teachers of Arabic and Muslim history) staffed by anti-Israeli Arab scholars. Said was bitterly opposed to the acquiescence of the PLO leadership in peace efforts with the Israelis in 1991 and subsequently. Embedded in *Orientalism* and a similar later book is an unquenchable hatred for Israel and for Jewish scholars, who in Said's eyes should be banned from studying the Arabic world because of their innate bias. Bernard Lewis became for Said and his legion of militant Arab and leftist followers a symbol for Jewish colonialist ideology. Lewis understood full well the implications of Said's position and tried to respond, with no help from the Israelis or from rich American Jews. The arrrogant and naive Israeli academics, in awe of Said as a literary theorist, never marshaled their formidable intellectual resources against him, nor did the rich Jews who endowed Columbia University in recent decades bring their influence to bear to stop Said's constant advancement to the highest level of the Columbia faculty. As long as the state of Israel exists, Said will never withdraw his allegations about the nefarious consequences of Jewish-fronted imperialist, Western chauvinist orientalism.

Recent Marxist Theory The most important Marxist theorists of the sixties, seventies, and eighties were Lucien Goldmann, Louis Althusser, both Parisian professors, and Jürgen Habermas, professor of sociology and philosophy at the Free University of Berlin. Habermas is probably the most interesting and original Marxist theorist of the last thirty years.

Lucien Goldmann was a Marxist structuralist. His fundamental project consisted of the attempt to join the thought of Marx and Piaget. He argues that societies undergo specific stages characterized by cultural structures. Each social stage generates its cultural structures as well, such as, for example, Enlightenment culture and the culture of romanticism. Cultural structures are then reflected in particular texts. The sequence is then as follows: Social change produces cultural value systems or cultural superstructures, which are in turn reiterated, or represented, in specific textual formulations.

Goldmann's method is designed to write Marxist intellectual history, focusing on the culture and on the value systems as well as upon social and economic systems. It can be described as the academic outcome of the theories of Adorno, Benjamin, and Gramsci, with help from Piaget. It comprises a Marxist theory conducive to writing cultural history. Hayden White, of the University of California at Santa Cruz, who currently enjoys a high degree of visibility, is an important disciple of Goldmann in the United States.

Althusser was a Stalinist idealist—an unusual combination indeed. He was one of the few left-wing intellectuals in France who remained loyal to Stalinism, and justified it on the grounds that the world of ideology and the empirical world are not connected. One cannot, in other words, establish the two discrete systems of ideology and socioeconomics as complementary and interrelated. They operate in disconnected realms, and therefore one is free to believe whatever one wants. The empirical data about the gulag do not necessarily have to lead opinion to turn against Stalin or the Soviet Union. The world of ideology is not informed by the empirical world of data. Althusser is a twentieth-century Averroist or Occamist. He has resurrected the medieval double-faith theory.

Basing belief on the empirical can lead only to false consciousness, Althusser claims. Given this, belief is and must be radically divorced from data, and operates according to its own laws which leave the individual free to choose his ideological course. If one wants to believe in Stalinism, there is no empirical evidence that is capable of preventing one from doing so. This recalls William James's "will to believe."

Another way of arriving at this conclusion runs through the principle of overdetermination, which is a clever historical theory of skepticism. Any given historical event is overdetermined—that is, there are so many factors, ranging from the social and economic through the political to the cultural that contribute to phenomena, that it is impossible to specify and exhaust the causes. There is, in other words, no such thing as a capability of determining the cause of a historical event. Therefore one can decide for oneself what is at work in history, which decision then constitutes one's ideology. Just as economic determinism cannot be proved, it cannot be disproved either. The theory of history is something the individual works out for himself; necessarily so, since it does not admit of empirical and rational demonstration.

Althusser's theory can obtain the sympathy of historians who are familiar with the ambivalences of their discipline. His theory was immensely popular for a while with Parisian students who acknowledged at last the truth about the gulag but did not want to stop being Communists. Althusser's theory can also be used by conservatives. Whatever the sleazebag qualities of the Nixon and Reagan administrations, there is no empirical need to give up rightist conservatism.

In 1980 Althusser murdered his wife and was found to be unfit to stand trial. These events adversely affected his reputation on the Left Bank.

Jürgen Habermas is Adorno's principal disciple and the most celebrated German thinker of the last three decades. His work is not easy to read, but the effort is rewarding. Habermas has three theories, of which two are not particularly original, but the third one is extremely interesting and rather original.

The first theory strictly continues and revives the Frankfurt school. Following Adorno and Benjamin and their assertion that cultural superstructures assume independence from base structures, Habermas claims that "social systems are life-worlds that are symbolically structured."

Second, there is the theory of displacement, which teaches that capitalist society is very tightly integrated and that a crisis in one segment of society will bring about a displacement effect on another. The breakdown of capitalism will not necessarily occur in the domain of technology or in the system of banking or in the economy, but it can occur anywhere. The principle of displacement will work, running through the entire system, regardless of the original domain of the crisis. This supports Gramsci.

Habermas's third theory is the seminal one of legitimation crisis, in which he tries to deal with the cultural and moral issues in late capitalism, a specific problem of recent times. He proposes that late capitalism is threatened by a cultural crisis or a crisis of legitimation, owing to the fact that it has generated expectations and anxieties in important segments of the population, including the bourgeoisie itself, that the system cannot satisfy. Late capitalism is an ever-expanding balloon, as it were, that is bound to explode. The cultural values, the ethics, which have been generated by capitalism itself, demand so much from the capitalist system, they are so inflated, that they will inevitably render the system incapable of functioning.

There is an anomic split, according to Habermas, in late capitalism

between values and social institutions. The anomie that Durkheim had identified as the possibility of a social crisis that heretofore remained hypothetical,
Habermas finds to be in fact occurring. The recuperative, functionalizing,
socializing capabilities of late capitalism are under unprecedented challenge.
Why? What is happening at this stage of the development of capitalism is that
grandiose expectations are being built up through the spread of education. The
middle class expects a reward from its university education and professional
training, to which the market society cannot respond. "The market is losing its
credibility as a mechanism for the allocation of chances of life. . . . Market success is being replaced by professional success resulting from formal education."
The rise of narcissism is a reflection of this novel situation, representing the
critical decline of the bourgeois work ethic as well as increasing disappointment and frustration among the professional middle class. Capitalism cannot
always satisfy the yuppies and generation X, with their "instrumental attitude
to work." Their loyalty to the market system is fragile. Their narcissistic loyalties to themselves, which capitalism has enormously fed and affirmed
through its educational system, are incomparably stronger. The inevitable consequence of this is progressive demoralization among professionals. A momentous "erosion of bourgeois traditions" is occurring, accompanied by the emergence of "normative structures" that threaten the viability of capitalist culture.

At the same time, the scientific and technocratic culture of late capitalism
has established a constant stream of information and legitimized criticism,
which it, once again, cannot control. It has created a scientific, technocratic
mechanism, which has become a modern Frankenstein monster that has
assumed autonomy and is progressively becoming more critical of its parent
system, feeding on the vast flow of information about the defects of society.
The informational and scientific mechanisms that capitalism has created are
undermining the system that spawned them. Habermas also sees modern art as
the site on which a counterculture is being generated that provides one more
important avenue of criticism and erosion of capitalist values. "Modern art is
the cocoon in which the transformation of bourgeois art into counter-culture
is bred."

Above all, there is emerging an unrestrained, universalistic morality in late
capitalism. The civil rights movement for minorities, affirmative action, the
women's liberation movement, (we might now add multiculturalism and
demands for diversity)—in the last three decades capitalism has been unceas-
ingly bombarded by universalitic ethical demands which, while it finds them
intrinsically and serially justified, it now struggles anomically to satisfy. The

values of capitalist society have exceeded "the dogma of mere tradition." Capitalism is constantly asked to fulfill absolute values, which it cannot easily do, and when it does, this effort sends shock waves through the whole system. Capitalism is being eroded from within by its own ethical values.

Western society is deluding itself if it thinks it can integrate devastating egalitarianism without major outcomes. Until recently capitalism discriminated between the public sphere of activity, which is conditioned only marginally by ethical considerations, and family and private life, wherein absolute values play a much larger role. Now the barriers between the public and private spheres are being demolished. "Competitive capitalism has for the first time given binding force to strictly universal value systems." As a result late capitalism is in a condition of growing crisis. The traditional model of legitimation "is breaking down, while at the same time new and increased demands for legitimation are arising."

Habermas's theory of legitimation crisis is the most original and illuminating sociological doctrine since Durkheim. He is the only sociologist to deal realistically with the massive impact of the egalitarian changes of the past thirty years upon Western society. He identified the upheavals that Western society experienced in the seventies, eighties, and nineties as a result of civil rights extension, feminism, affirmative action, and multiculturalism. He broke the conspiracy of silence that social scientists have engaged in so as not to disturb the unimpeded advances of these radical departures that their leftist ideology advocates so vehemently. Habermas has in abundance the first quality of a great social scientist: honesty. Habermas's arguments can serve the conservative point of view as well as they can serve the Left. There are Burkean overtones to the theory of legitimation crisis. If Reaganite conservatives had read and understood Habermas, which is unthinkable, they would have found a social theory to support their efforts to slow down the civil rights movements and women's liberation.

Lenin had said that capitalists are so greedy that they will sell the rope that will hang them. Habermas suggests that capitalists have become so driven by abstract moral principles that they will overextend and functionally impair the culture that has bred and sustained them. In the end capitalism will find itself unable to justify its own continued existence and to maintain a stable institutional framework that will satisfy incessant demands and criticisms. The perpetual flow of information and the resultant criticism this occasions, as well as abstract moralizing, becomes even harder to respond to. Of course, a system such as the Soviets' would never have to encounter such a problem. That is why the Soviet government was so fanatical in restricting information. Legitimation is now a problem that is intrinsic to capitalism. It is also one facet of the new liberal regimes in Eastern Europe.

In recent years there has been a fusion of Marxist literary and art criticism. We will here only mention the most outstanding Anglo-American workers in this field, without lingering on the details of their thought. The most prominent Englishman in this respect is Terry Eagleton, whose *Literary Theory* has become a bestseller and is both a valuable source of information and very subtle Marxist polemics. At the end of the 1980s Eagleton was elected to the senior chair of English literature at Oxford University, a dramatic legitimization of Marxist literary theory in the academic world.

Students and the educated public at large in the eighties, as in the thirties, were anxious to acquire a basic knowledge of philosophy and cultural theory. In the 1930s a New Deal liberal who held marginal teaching jobs in New York colleges, Will Durant, satisfied the urge to gain this basic knowledge of Plato, Descartes, and Kant in his *The Story of Philosophy,* one of the all-time nonfiction bestsellers. In the eighties Eagleton achieved the same measure of success with his *Literary Theory.* This book could be seen stacked in huge piles at bookstores on or near college campuses all over the country.

It is highly significant that Eagleton's orientation was aggressively Marxist, as Durant's had been blatantly New Deal liberal. The success of Eagleton's book represented the unquestioned habilitation of scholarly Marxism in the Anglo-American college world. For thousands of postadolescents, and also more mature students in the eighties, their introduction to the history of twentieth-century literary criticism was accompanied by a thick coating of Marxist interpretation. The traces of these discourses in the readers' mentality would not soon or easily be eroded.

In the United States the leading Marxist critics of the new generation are Frederic Jameson and Frank Lentricchia. Lentricchia is a capable historian of literary theory, while Jameson is a theorist. He applies the doctrines of Adorno and the Frankfurt school to the study of literary texts. Here is a passage that renders well the Marxist flavor of Jameson's style and thought: "Even hegemonic or ruling class culture and ideology are utopian, not in spite of their instrumental function to secure and perpetuate class privilege and power, but rather precisely because their function is also in and of itself the affirmation of collective solidarity." (Translation: Bourgeois culture ideally seeks class power sustained by group feeling.) Further: "The text liberates us from the empirical object, whether institution, event or individual work." The literary text, according to Jameson, becomes a cultural superstructure, taking on a life of its own, and is separated from the empirical world. This is Adorno-Benjamin with a flavoring of Althusser.

Several leading universities in the eighties vigorously competed for Jameson's services, and he now occupies an endowed chair in the humanities at Duke. Why is Jameson so much in demand? He only presents cumbersome restatements of Adorno, Benjamin, and the Frankfurt school. The Berkeley critic Frederick Crews has called Jameson "the Spruce Goose" of the academic world, after Howard Hughes's monstrous wooden plane that flew only once, just a few yards off the ground. What Jameson has to offer is what the transatlantic academic world keenly wanted in the late eighties and nineties. Quentin Skinner, the Oxford political philosopher, has, not facetiously, called this trend "the return of grand theory in the human sciences"—in other words, variants of Marxism applied to the humanities.

It is of great moment for the culture of the twentieth fin-de-siècle that writing authoritatively, as Jameson does, along the lines of the Frankfurt school is now the most valued commodity in the humanistic marketplace. Poor, poor Walter Benjamin, failing to get his seminal monograph accepted by his university, and later dying alone and by his own hand in 1940 in a bleak hotel on the Spanish border. Now he could have his pick of endowed chairs, visiting lectures, and honorary degrees in American universities. Nothing could more dramatically signify the alteration in the academic legitimacy of Marxism than comparing the destinies of Benjamin and his intellectual heir Jameson.

By the early 1990s, literary and artistic criticism had become mainline in prominent American universities. It was often called "cultural studies," with NYU, Berkeley and Columbia among its centers. But Marxism had also gained a strong foothold in the law faculties of some prominent universities, particularly Harvard, Stanford, and Georgetown, which would rank on anyone's list of the country's top ten law schools. The Marxist legal scholars advertised that they were pursuing "critical legal studies," indicating their empathy with the Frankfurt school of critical theory. At Harvard Law School the leading historian Morton Horwitz was prominent in the critical legal studies movement, while two judicial theorists, Duncan Kennedy and Roberto Unger, were also "crits." In the mid-eighties acrimony between the Marxist and anti-Marxist faculty in Harvard Law School became so heated that one of the prominent conservative professors departed abruptly for University of Chicago Law School, the bastion of judicial conservatism. In response to concern expressed by law school alumni, the Harvard University president appointed a moderate as the new dean of the law school, and a more placid ambience had developed by the mid-nineties. Nevertheless, the rise of critical legal studies was an important development on the American academic scene. Hitherto moderate or conservative professional schools now provided forums for outspoken leftists. There had been a bit of this in the 1930s, but never to such a significant degree.

The importance of critical legal studies is that it represents the penetration of Marxism into the intellectual bastions of the business corporations, the elite law schools. When the graduates of classes taught by CLS professors assume partnerships in corporate law firms during the next decade, its impact can be determined.

Finally the formation of a Marxist-feminist group has occurred in recent years. Feminism will be discussed at greater length in a later chapter. There is in existence a very important group of Marxist feminist theorists, who use as their starting point a suggestion made by Engels, to the effect that the subjection of women historically came about simultaneously with the introduction of private property.

Taking their cue from Engels, Marxist-feminists claim that it is industrial capitalism that has played a particularly grievous part in the subjection of women. They hold that the removal of women from rural society, from the family farm, in which there had been a certain degree of equality between the husband and wife who worked side by side, and their transfer to the city have led to the reduction of equality, and the change of the role model for women, thus bringing about the deterioration of their position. The path to the liberation of women, so runs their conclusion, leads through a socialist society—not a Soviet one, which evidently did not release women from their former mode of existence, but through a genuinely socialistic society.

Among leading Marxist feminist theorists are Mary Nolan, who is in the history department of New York University, and Barbara Ehrenreich, who is prominent in New York feminist circles and frequently writes for the *New York Times.*

The Sixties and the New Left The novelist Harold Brodkey, writing in the *New York Times Book Review* in 1986, disparaged the sixties by remarking: "Sixties culture changed everything and accomplished nothing." But the sixties did accomplish many things. First it produced the movements for civil rights and for black liberation. It advanced the Third World, as it did the feminist movement. All these movements, even though their origins can be traced further back, do come out of the sixties. It was the sixties that placed them in the front of social action.

Second, the sixties produced a new popular culture—the rock culture—by taking an aspect of black culture and universalizing it. It commercialized rock, one could possibly claim, and corrupted it, but it did transform popular culture.

Third, the sixties legitimated television. In the fifties, it was fashionable for intellectuals and many professionals to declare that one did not own a television set, and that even if one did, one hated it. The sixties altered this, making television an acceptable cultural element. Furthermore the social impact of new forms of electronic communication was now a prominent concern of intellectuals and academics.

Fourth, the sixties introduced Marxism into the universities, creating a large generation of young scholars who came from among the radical students.

Fifth, the sixties validated sects and subcultures within American life. Although many of the particular sects and subcultures of the sixties have died out, others have appeared to take their place. The new tolerance for nonorthodox and adversary groups that the sixties imparted appears to have become a permanent part of the American heritage, and a productive and worthy one, on the whole.

Finally the sixties created the tradition of hating America as the bastion of capitalism and imperialism. It is true that there was a countertradition at work in the Reagan era of the 1980s. But the residual odium felt for "Amerika" was a prominent sixties sentiment, according to which everything that came out of America had to become the object of protest, since this was also the country that produced every world evil, from acid rain and Vietnam to trashy movies. While there has been a reaction, an intensely cultivated one, too, against this feeling, nevertheless the sixties' trend has left behind a powerful trail of pervasive, reflexive hatred against America, not least in the United States itself.

What factors contributed to laying the foundations of the sixties' phenomena described above? What forces triggered the upheaval that led to May 1968, when radical students took control of Columbia University, and when in Paris revolutionaries held not only the university but the streets as well, to cite a few among numerous other dramatic incidents?

The most prominent factor is the demographic one, for a population tidal wave had begun after the Second World War. By the late fifties all demographers—that is, population experts—were agreeing that a population cohort of unprecedented size would reach maturity, or at least postadolescence, in the mid-sixties, and that social institutions would not be able to cope with them.

Indeed, their predictions proved valid. That is precisely what happened in the sixties. One thing about which we can be absolutely certain as regards history is that population cohorts advance because, quite simply, people are born. The institutions of society, particularly the educational institutions, could not absorb in the sixties this vast generation of unprecedented size. No matter how many new state colleges were formed, regardless of how quickly faculties were expanded, educational institutions could not effectively absorb the tide of incoming students. Between 1960 and 1972 the number of college students increased from 3 to 7.5 million. But they were poorly socialized and deeply discontented.

After the May 1968 upheaval at Columbia University was over, the university administration appointed a commission led by Archibald Cox, the old New Dealer and civil rights professor of law from Harvard, to investigate why the May events had taken place. His conclusion was that the greatest problem had been that the dormitories and the meals provided by the university had not been satisfactory. No wonder, was Cox's amazing conclusion, that students were discontented. This is a realistic appraisal of the events, despite the humor it contains, and responsible for the severe deterioration of living conditions at the university was the demographic tidal wave. The proximity of Harlem, the accessibility of East Village radicals to the campus, and the Vietnam War also contributed to the Columbia upheaval.

The numbers of college students increased so rapidly in the sixties that the normal socializing processes were rendered ineffective. The members of this vast generation taught one another, rather than being taught by adults. Youth culture became a thing unto itself. The fifties, on the other hand, had produced a very conservative and conformist generation. Because there had been a very low birth rate during the Great Depression, the population that reached maturity around 1950 was abnormally small. This facilitated their easy control and socialization by adults. The sixties, however, saw the opposite of what had happened in the fifties.

The period between 1958 and 1968 was also one of unprecedented prosperity, featuring full employment. In periods when every college graduate, and even the literate high school graduate, can easily secure employment, and livelihood itself does not pose problems, large segments of the population can devote themselves to the intellectual and artistic life and to radical political action. They are not frightened or anxious. They can become cultural and political radicals. This had been the case in the first decade of the twentieth century and again in the early 1920s; it occurred as well in the 1960s. To compound the favorable economic situation, there was a welfare liberal government in Washington, which generated even more jobs than the system of market economy could have done by itself. The federal government under the welfare state liberals in the Kennedy and Johnson administrations vastly expanded during this period. It poured money into education as well as into social services. Particularly the Johnson government generated jobs artificially.

One factor operating in the formation of the sixties is what might be called the heritage of moral absolutism. Beginning with World War II, "the last good war," as it has been called, the United States found itself drenched in ethics. Americans were saints, they were good people, who had first fought the evil Nazis, and then, in the fifties, had held back the malevolent Soviet Communists. Then, beginning with John F. Kennedy, they launched the crusade to improve society. The United States was provided with twenty years of unceasing ideological motivation toward rigorous ethical standards.

Eventually this crusading mentality began to have its effect on the behavior and outlook of people at large, particularly on those of the younger generation. They began to look for ways in which to be even more ethical. The civil rights movement was one such channel. If America was striving to become the heavenly city, the problems that were plaguing the South could no longer be endured. So white students joined the blacks of the South in "freedom rides" to end segregation. The questioning of the war in Vietnam also took place in this context. A pure and moral society could not engage in the evils of imperialism, which this war was held to be.

The ethical shortcomings of the Vietnam conflict became especially evident after middle-class college students became eligible for the draft and after the Vietcong appeared to gain a big victory in the 1968 Tet Offensive (it was actually a Vietcong defeat, but the leftist-inspired media claimed otherwise).

The establishment of this country allowed itself to slip into a situation in which it preached ethics for two decades, and, unsurprisingly, it soon found itself face to face with a generation that cashed in the moral blank checks it had been issued. A new generation sought ever new areas for the application of ethical standards. Of course, the establishment was found wanting. This is precisely what Habermas points to in his argument about legitimation crises in late capitalism. The ruling groups of the United States, particularly when they got involved in the Vietnam War, could not defend their position in terms of abstract moral claims.

McGeorge Bundy had preached high standards of public ethics to students while he was dean at Harvard. He preached ethics to the American people while he was national security adviser to President Johnson. Then he advocated involvement in Vietnam. He soon found himself drowning in the moral cauldron he had prepared so assiduously. Bundy and the rest of "the best and the brightest" liberal Democrats lost their legitimacy. Unable to articulate a defense of their foreign and military policies as ethically determined, the Ivy League academics serving Johnson, like Bundy and W. W. Rostow, went down with a resounding crash.

Another way in which social change in the late forties and throughout the fifties prepared the way for the upheavals of the sixties was the very rapid suburban development outside major cities. The coming of the automobile age in the second and third decades of the century had actually had a much greater impact on rural and small-town America—except for Southern California, where expansion anticipated what happened in all metropolitan centers in the late forties and fifties—than on its major cities. The Ford and other cheap cars broke down the isolation of farming and village life in the 1920s but did not greatly affect the lifestyle in the large cities. This changed rapidly after the war, abetted by improvements in the home construction industry and the availability of cheap mortgages for veterans, but above all by the building of networks of highways radiating out from the major cities, especially under the interstate highway program launched by the federal government under President Dwight Eisenhower. No federal program ever had a more immediate and profound effect on American life. Now the automobile and suburban highways, along with little or no restriction on land use, resulted in almost incredibly rapid suburban development. But the suburbs were dull places, inducing alienation and hostility in the first generation that grew up in them, which became the radical generation of the sixties.

The sixties culture was in revolt against the fifties—the time of conformist suburbia, of middle-class communality, and of boredom. How long could a culture be sustained in which people sat in Levittown and watched extremely primitive black-and-white television? It is hard to imagine how rudimentary television was a few decades ago. It was not enough to sustain suburban life at a time when restaurants, clubs, adequate movies, and the like scarcely existed there. Suburban life had little to offer the new, postmodern generation. The shopping malls could not distract them for long. College students in the fifties were called "the Silent Generation." They were putatively docile and conformist, supposed to be satisfied with studies and job searches and Doris Day movies. They could not be silent forever.

The rebellion against suburban conformity was first expressed by young men who wore pegged pants and shiny, duck-billed hair and who adulated the actor James Dean and the rock singer Elvis Presley. These nonconformists were denounced as "juvenile delinquents," a catchall fifties phrase for young rebels.

The rebellion was further articulated by the Beat movement of the late fifties. Jack Kerouac, his novel *On the Road*, and his Beat friends moving restlessly from San Francisco to New York—these reflected postadolescent protest against the boredom of suburban life. It was bound to happen because the dullness of the fifties stood in contrast to the exuberance of the American tradition of living; the twenties and the thirties provided a sharp comparison. Kerouac wrote most of *On the Road* on his mother's kitchen table in Lowell, Massachusetts, and the vision he presented of vanguard North Beach San Francisco culture was really a revived image of the twenties culture.

Rock music in the 1950s initially represented a form of revolt by American adolescents against conformist postwar middle-class culture and a vehicle for legitimating their desire for a more liberated kind of sexual behavior. Rock-and-roll also took advantage of the new availability of cheap electric guitars. Through Buddy Holly and Elvis Presley and Jerry Lee Lewis, all from a poor southern white background, pre-existing African American rhythm-and-blues, as this genre was called among black people, was somewhat sanitized and made available to eager white adolescents. In the early 1960s the Beatles and then the Rolling Stones further elaborated rock music and incorporated into it overtones of British working-class cultural autonomy. Rock's immense popularity was partly attributable to the skill and resources with which it was presented by commercial producers, record companies, and AM radio stations. By the early 1960s rock music was not simply reflective of adolescent American culture; it was shaping it and validating the new sexual permissiveness. This made rock culture attractive to a postadolescent generation as well, and in modified dance beat form, rock became integrated into that middle-class world against which, from the American South and in the streets of Liverpool and London, it initially signaled rebellion.

The Haight-Ashbury section of San Francisco, the eastern part of Greenwich Village in Manhattan, and the Near North Side of Chicago became the centers of the sixties folk-rock counterculture, which played an indispensable role in the development of leftist influence and radical expression. The sources for this distinctive American subculture, which spread not only to most major American cities but to the metropolises of Western Europe as well, were rock music and black culture, the Beat movement, and the leftist folk-song brigades of the thirties. At summer camps, Marxist-oriented Black Mountain College, Bennington College, and the New School and Union Square in New York City and other places in the thirties the vehicle of the traditional Anglo-American folk song was transformed into consciously created ballads of political opinion. The fascists and the Nazis had done the same thing in the twenties and thirties—for example, the marching song of the Italian blackshirts was a snappy folk-type song significantly called "Giovinezza [youth]."

It took a poet and musician of genius, Bob Dylan (formerly Robert Zimmerman, a Jewish boy improbably from the agricultural town of Hibbing, Minnesota), to merge these disparate elements into anthems for his generation. Carrying an acoustic guitar, Zimmerman appeared eagerly in folk-song taverns in Greenwich Village and was generously well instructed by a veteran of the leftist folk-song movement, Dave van Ronk. Dylan surpassed van Ronk and all his predecessors, even those thirties paragons of leftist folk songs, Woody Guthrie and Pete Seeger, although Seeger remained popular into the seventies.

Dylan, in powerful musical lines that initially—to the dismay of the Left—took on more and more of a rock beat, found the words to express the hearts and minds of a generation: "Come mothers and fathers throughout the land./Don't criticize what you can't understand./Your sons and daughters are beyond your command./The old world is rapidly changing/Please get out of the new one if you can't lend a hand./The first now will later be last./The times they are a'changing."

This is the best the sixties radical culture had to offer. Another Bob Dylan song became the anthem of the civil rights and antiwar movements: "How many roads must a man walk down/Before they call him a man?/How many seas must a white dove sail/Before she sleeps in the sand?/. . . The answer my friend is blowing in the wind. . . ." Dylan and the radical folk-rock singers were admired by their generation and given maximum attention by the sympathetic media. They both reflected and stimulated rebellion and protest. "You don't need a weatherman to know which way the wind is blowing," sang Dylan again. He was sure it was blowing toward a revolution of some kind.

At the heart of the folk-rock subculture was the idea of formation of communities by choice. Whether in Haight-Ashbury, Greenwich Village, or in northern Vermont, groups of middle-class students, artists, and political activists chose to live together affectively, pool their intellectual and fiscal resources, and devote themselves to a vanguard cause. In the worst-case scenarios, these communes became infected by drug taking and power struggles, and disintegrated after a few years or months. But in the best situations, they developed over many years and made enormous demands on their members, who lived predominantly puritanical lives and engaged in some form of socially valuable work.

A prime example of the latter was the Bread and Puppet Theater. It was founded by a scion of German expressionist theater, Peter Schumann, in Greenwich Village in the late sixties and devoted itself to political theater involving giant puppets accompanied by music, dance, and circus effects. The Bread and Puppet Theater soon migrated to a commune in the depths of rural northern Vermont, became famous throughout the transatlantic world, and was still going strong in the mid-nineties. It made strenuous demands on its talented members that no commercial theater could claim. Each summer all its alumni and friends still gather for a two-day puppet and circus festival in Vermont and celebrate an affective festival in the manner of the sixties. The Bread and Puppet Theater even has its own museum, in which retired giant puppets from past years are reverently preserved as totems of political theater.

Among the subcultures of the sixties were hippies who wanted to focus on communal and improved individual behavior, not political and economic slogans. This movement toward creating new subgroups did not want to clash with government so much as to be ignored by it. They were often in conflict with the political radicals that Bob Dylan represented, whom they saw as driven by psychological needs they would not face. The rock group the Grateful Dead were spokesmen for the hippie philosophy. And the Beatles sang: "If you're talking about destruction, brother you can count me out" and "with your pictures of Chairman Mao, ain't gonna make it with me anyhow."

Yet another factor in the shaping of the sixties was the reassertion of the Old Left. The fifties were an artificially reactionary period that featured the Cold War red scare, and the repressive McCarthy time, frequently referred to as an "era" even though it lasted no longer than four years. Left-wing intellectuals, particularly in academia and in the media, temporarily withdrew and kept a low profile. At most, they spoke about the purge trials and condemned Stalinism. But they did not abandon their socialist ideals and the old thirties traditions. When the heat was off, which was largely the case by 1958, and was completely true the day liberal Democrat John F. Kennedy was sworn in as president in January 1961, these intellectuals began to reemerge. There is a strong continuity between the Left of the thirties and early forties and the Left of the sixties. The aging generation of leftists provided a strong support for the "red diaper babies"—their children in the emerging radical generation.

The American New Left differed from the Old Left in only two ways. The New Left was the program of a new generation, more populous and affluent, bolder and more self-confident. Second, the New Left was much more sympathetic to anarchosyndicalism than the old Left had been.

How did the Students for a Democratic Society (SDS), the most important organization of New Left student radicals, get started? It began as the youth division of an organization called the League for Industrial Democracy, an old Marxist organization of the 1930s. In its early years the SDS was supported by the league.

Elaborate sociological studies of the New Left student activists pointed to two clusters of data. A significant number of these young leftists were children of Old Left parents; an even larger number were Jewish. The discontents and ambitions of postwar suburbia extended the impact of inherited radical traditions from the thirties.

Another factor was a shift in Marxist theory due to the rise of Maoism. The sixties was the great age of Mao Tse-tung, not his age of greatest accomplishment, but the period when he was most visible. He was leading the Chinese cultural revolution at the time, and issuing a stream of theoretical pronouncements. The Chinese Communists came to power in 1949 in a society that was very far from an industrial revolution, even further removed, that is, than Russia had been in 1917. In the First World War, Russia was in the early stages of industrialization. China, however, was still, in 1949, a rural peasant society. Therefore, to justify the revolution in terms of Marxist theory, Mao developed the view that the revolution could be carried out by cadres other than the industrial proletariat. The revolution could be carried out by peasants as well as by students; there could even be a peasant-student front. Mao in the mid-sixties called on the students to purify the revolution. The revolution would be initiated by the peasants, and purified and solidified by the students.

Maoist theory presented a revision of Marxist theory that also supported developments in the United States, where the left-wing penetration among industrial workers was extremely meager. In the sixties American blue-collar workers were opposed to student radicalism. For the most part the unions remained removed from the Left. By and large this was also true in France and West Germany at the time. It was therefore necessary for the New Left to hold that students could be the vanguard of the revolution, and this was essentially a Maoist position.

An additional factor that went into the making of the sixties was the rise of subcultures, primarily black and Hispanic ones, that were in many ways hostile or contradictory to the white Protestant culture of America. In the sixties the dominant culture was confronted by the emergence and legitimization of subcultures, which were very different from itself. Even if the subculture was Protestant in origin, then it was—among the blacks—evangelical Protestant. In the case of the Hispanic Americans, the culture was Catholic, but this, in turn, was a Catholicism that had derived from Latin America rather than from Ireland or Italy.

The final factor is the electronic revolution that gave rise to the so-called plugged-in generation. The cultural revolution produced by television and the electronic media was identified by Marshall McLuhan in the mid-sixties. McLuhan had begun as a professor of English at the University of Toronto, where he had been an expert on Tennyson. However, he had a colleague in the Economics Department in the forties and the early fifties, an extraordinarily brilliant man named Harold Innes, of whom few Americans have ever heard, who taught McLuhan that the phenomena that transform culture are caused by changes in communication systems and methods, and in transportation. Changes in communication and transportation networks produce cultural revolutions. While Innes's great interest was the Canadian fishing and fur-trading industries, McLuhan applied this idea to the cases of television, stereophonic sound, rock music, and instantaneous forms of world communication.

The results of McLuhan's study can be distilled into two arguments. The first is the thesis of the "global village." We have been compacted into a world culture, he finds. Boundaries that hitherto isolated cultures have been broken down as a result of the development of television and film. Increasingly the world is being assimilated into a homogeneous culture. There was much truth to McLuhan's argument when he first began to develop it, and it has assumed much greater truth since then, for in the meantime, satellites were introduced, further transforming communication and hence culture. Faxes and computers, with the World Wide Web and the Internet, have astronomically increased this. It must be remembered that McLuhan was writing at a time when, in order for an American network to bring to the television screen something that was happening in France, the company had to fly film or tape across the Atlantic—a method that now seems almost medieval.

The other argument McLuhan presented was that television was a cool medium. The television viewer establishes an acutely personal, one-to-one relationship to the screen. The "hot" orator of the pretelevision era used to address great crowds, which necessitated a specific form of loud address. That,

McLuhan held, would not work anymore. Hubert Humphrey's and Walter Mondale's formal and complicated rhetoric, for example, were wrong for television, which needs another rhetorical "cool" mode in order to be effective: a simple, sincere mode of address, as found in Reagan's style, by which he acted the old friend and fellow citizen talking to the viewer person to person. McLuhan's theory has been proved right. In a sense, he predicted what the politician of the future would be like. Bill Clinton is that future.

McLuhan's theory is that television culture is on the one hand macrocosmic, instantaneously universalizing everything that happens, generating a world culture, but it is at the same time microscosmic and intimate, its focus being intensely individualistic and personal. With television, we have entered, McLuhan claimed, the greatest cultural revolution since the invention of printing. The medium is the message and the massage, McLuhan said. With electronic communication the rationalist, linear, print culture, "the Gutenberg Galaxy" that emerged around A.D. 1500, is finally being transcended.

It was the young radicals who first perceived McLuhan as a cultural prophet. The people who were in charge in the sixties of political and educational life and of the media did not themselves clearly understand the nature of the transformation of the domains they commanded. They did not understand that a substantial transformation was taking place in the culture as a whole, even though they knew, of course, that they were dealing with a new communications technology. The transformation, however, was working not only in communications systems but also in interpersonal relations and in social mentality.

It was the younger generation, the students and the radicals, who more clearly sensed the meaning of what was happening. They were the first to understand why the seven o'clock news was important, to realize that it made a difference to watch it rather than wait for the following day's *New York Times*. More significant, it was the SDS who grasped the meaning of, and put to use, the seven o'clock news. The student Left would plan and schedule its demonstrations and other events so that they could be filmed and be part of the early evening news. The radicals understood the importance of doing this long before the politicians of this country did. Reagan, Clinton, and other politicians of the eighties and nineties certainly understood it very well, but the SDS were the pioneers. The slowness of the older generation to react to a cultural revolution that was in the making provided opportunity for the radicals, who knew how to utilize what the new system offered.

The dramatic scenes at Columbia in May 1968, wherein New Left student radicals held a half dozen buildings for two weeks, brought the university to a halt, were dispersed only by violent police intervention, and achieved the resignation of the president and provost—similar scenes were repeated on dozens of campuses, including Harvard. At Harvard the dean of the faculty was sacrificed to leftist agitation. New Left demonstrators precipitated a confrontation with Chicago police during the Democratic Convention in August 1968, discrediting the Democratic nominee, the welfare liberal Hubert Humphrey. Their constant verbal attacks on Humphrey brought about his defeat and the election of Richard Nixon, the Republican candidate.

The principle on which the New Left was operating was the same as the Communists in Germany between 1930 and 1933: The most important enemy was not the Right but the "social fascist" liberals. The election of Nixon would, they believed, bring about the ultimate confrontation between a conservative government and the radical movement, raising consciousness everywhere and attaining the revolution.

This scenario appeared to be playing itself out in May 1970. American intervention in Cambodia led to a new wave of campus demonstrations. During one of these, at Kent State University in Ohio, a poorly led National Guard contingent panicked and fired on student demonstrators, killing four of them. This was the climax of the New Left movement. Demonstrations and strikes erupted on hundreds of campuses. The middle class, the image of its sons and daughters slaughtered by the National Guard projected incessantly by the media, appeared momentarily to be on the verge of radicalization. Final exams were cancelled on hundreds of campuses.

The country, however, returned from the brink. The Nixon administration, which, contrary to expectations, had done very little to retreat from the welfare state measures of the Johnson administration, finally pulled itself together and also turned down the Vietnamese War. In the end 1968 did not inaugurate the age of revolution. But the year was what the historian G. M. Trevelyan had called 1848—"a turning-point in history that failed to turn." Ineptitude and corruption in the Nixon administration combined with media pressure and leftist agitation to bring down the president in the summer of 1974, but the succeeding Ford administration rapidly restored the dignity of the White House and the federal government. The resiliency of centrist and conservative forces in the country weathered this unprecedented crisis easily. By the time Gerald Ford acceded to the presidency, the revolutionary tide had receded beyond the horizon. Campuses had returned to peaceful routine. Most of the New Left leaders sought private careers, some highly lucrative ones in media, entertainment, and academe.

The New Left revolution failed for three reasons. First, the so-called establishment learned to adjust to, appease, and avoid radical confrontation. They negotiated; they made piecemeal concessions; they shamefully abandoned the Vietnamese people to their iron Stalinist fate. McGeorge Bundy fled Washington and became president of the Ford Foundation, which he used to fund radical causes and appease militants on the Left.

It was the lawyer Edward Levi, as President of the University of Chicago, who demonstrated how the tide of campus sit-ins and occupation of buildings could be stemmed. The presidents of Columbia and Harvard summoned the police, thereby discrediting themselves and playing exactly the confrontational and delegitimizing role that anarchist theory prescribed. Levi did exactly nothing. He engaged in polite, desultory, and token negotiations with the SDS occupiers of campus buildings. He made sure that university life continued as normally as possible around those buildings. After a time the bored and bewildered radicals quietly abandoned their citadels of confrontation. Levi showed hundreds of other college presidents how to deal with the student militants.

The New Left revolution failed in the early 70s because the radicals could not maintain a united front. By 1970 they were split into a variety of factions. One of these, the Weathermen, engaged in terrorism and helped to discredit the movement in general among the middle classes.

At first the Weathermen were content to lead street demonstrations and "off the pigs" (fight with policemen). Then they made bombs in upscale apartments and town houses or suburban "safe" houses, and used them against government installations and war industries, sometimes killing themselves in the process. Then, led by the daughter of a prominent Old Left family, Kathy Boudin, a Bryn Mawr alumna, they went deeply into the underground, joined up with black revolutionaries and just plain black criminals and took to robbing banks and armored cars in order to finance the revolution. The Weathermen justified all the critical remarks that Marx and Lenin had made about anarchist adventurists.

Economic conditions began to worsen in the early seventies, and under Republican government federal funding stopped expanding. The boom and boondoggle days when any college graduate could get a good job were over. The Big Chill set in. Anxiety about personal futures weakened the courage of the younger generation and eroded solidarity and activism. By the mid–seventies the behavioral mode of the postadolescent generation was again shifting from socialist activism to Social Darwinist privatism.

Both the New Left and the yuppiedom that succeeded it were sociologically the outcome of the greatly expanded suburban middle class of the fifties and sixties. The children of this middle class, often programmed by their over-worked and frustrated parents, sought a share of national power. Their first avenue was radical politics in the shape of the New Left and the SDS and cam-pus upheavals. When that possibility no longer looked feasible, the new mid-dle class turned to private means of satisfying their ambition through advance-ment in the corporate world. The celebrated paradox is only a superficial one that contrasts the bearded, disheveled radical or hippie of the sixties with the three-piece-suited, finely coiffed executive of the eighties. There is a sociolog-ical—and in many instances personal—continuity here. The suburban middle class was struggling for a place in the sun, one way or another. Yet, while the New Left failed to sustain the mass support of the college population, its impact lived on in the academic and media worlds.

The student radicals and activists of the sixties have assumed diverse, interest-ing, and in some cases leading roles in American life in the eighties and nineties. Tom Hayden, one of the key founders of the SDS, is a liberal Democratic state senator in California. He was married to the film actress and exercise impresario Jane Fonda (now married to Ted Turner), who was the Vietcong queen in the sixties, condemning "Amerika" vociferously from Hanoi. Fonda is now very quiet about subsequent events in Vietnam. Bernardine Dohrn, the leader for several years of the underground Weathermen, is a graduate of law school, works in an attorney's office, and regularly petitions the American Bar Association for admission to the bar, claiming that she has the requisite good character. She is married to another militant of the sixties, whose father was a utilities magnate in Chicago. Eldridge Cleaver, the black activist, is a spokesman for the conservative Moral Majority. Staughton Lynd, once the highly visible Yale faculty radical, quietly practices labor law. Gary Hart became the familiar senator from Colorado and self-destructing presidential candidate from the "neo-liberal" wing of the Democratic Party. Jerry Rubin, the one-time hippie militant, sells bonds on Wall Street and engages in other business enterprises.

David Stockman's dramatic career is paradigmatic of his generation. It has taken him from Marxism at Michigan State and antiwar activism at Harvard Divinity School to Republican congressman from Michigan, to director of the Office of Management and Budget and self-proclaimed theoretican of the Reagan rightist revolution, to his current preferment on Wall Street.

Some biographies of sixties radicals ended in tragedy rather than prosperity. Sam Melville died in 1972 in the Attica prison riots, of which he was a leader. Two SDS leaders died in a town house on West Eleventh Street in New York City in 1971, when it blew up while it was being used as a bomb factory. Kathy Boudin, the daughter of an old Left activist of the thirties, is serving a long prison sentence for murdering a policeman during an armored-car holdup in Rockland County in 1981. This was the last of some twenty robberies of banks and armored cars by a gang of Weathermen and black revolutionaries.

These are classic American stories, products of the anxieties and ironies, paradoxes and tragedies of the sixties and since. These are the destinies of the American Left in the late twentieth century. It is apparently a never-ending story.

A century after the death of Karl Marx, his intellectual progeny, in various shades of red and pink, are entrenched as never before in the academic, intellectual, and media circles of the Western world. As a quintessential Victorian form of thought, with emphasis on historicism, macrocosm, referentiality, and moral absolutism—all attitudes hateful and contemptible to high modernism—the prosperity of Marxism and the triumph of leftist political culture signifies a continuing ebbing in the spirit of the modernist cultural revolution.

Marxists, in their perpetually learned and informed manner, realizing that modernism was the cutting edge of cultural inquiry and artistic form in this century, and wanting to identify with this intellectual vanguard and appropriate its prestige for their putative social and moral forces of progress, persist in attempting to claim that Marxism is no threat to modernism, but on the contrary can be combined theoretically with modernism in a popular front against alleged conservatism and reaction.

Perusal of the *New York Review of Books* and the *Village Voice* and other prominent leftist weeklies and study of the leading Marxist cultural journals, such as *Telos* and *October*, reveals that the political Left still dreams of a coordinated and comprehensive "adversary culture" to combat capitalism and the bourgeois ethos as currently personified by Newt Gingrich. The Left passionately believes in the doctrine of Gramsci and the Frankfurt school that literature, the visual arts, and painting can be a hegemonic battlefield on which the Left will triumph, no matter how decisively repudiated at the polls and the barricades.

The only problem for Marxists and the Left in the articulation of this adversary culture is the precise ingredient of literature and the arts that should be expropriated in the interest of putative progress. The residual devotion to modernism as the joint force with leftist ideology in a comprehensive adversary culture still prevails. There is, however, a minority opinion, expressed by

Jameson among others, that raises the difficult question as to whether or not modernism is not obsolete for political purposes. Is it not too much identified with allegedly specious bourgeois individualism? A French Marxist critic, Serge Guilbaut, went so far as to suggest in the early eighties that American modernist painting during the Cold War became an instrument of the CIA. Tom Bender, of NYU's History Department, endorsed this thesis.

Where will the Marxists find the aesthetic balance of adversary culture? In the late 1980s Jameson hailed postmodernism as the ascending culture to be joined with Marxism in the adversary culture. A decade later the binding of Marxism and postmodernist thought is the most vital trend in the academic humanities. It tends to take leftist theory away from social and toward cultural analysis, away from the travails of the working class toward the discourse of the comfortable elite. Now this is where the intellectual academic Left is voyaging in the closing years of the century. With little in the political world to latch onto, with an ostensibly liberal Democratic president announcing that the days of big government are over and endorsing rightist legislation to dismantle key New Deal welfare programs, there is perhaps nowhere for leftist thinkers to go, save into an interior world of complex humanistic theory.

Even the most skillful politcal and legal theorists on the Left seem content to retreat into a world of intellectual gamesmanship. There was the clever deployment in the political and juristic philosophies propounded by John Rawls of Harvard and Ronald Dworkin of Oxford and NYU, of the forensic style of analytic philosophy. Rawls updated John Locke's social contract theory (1690). In the transition from the state of nature to civil society, the overwhelming majority of people are "screened" from knowing whether in the civil society they will be one of the few rich or the many and miserable poor. They play it safe by opting for egalitarian institutions and welfare policies to be written into the social contract. Dworkin's theory was suggested by Sir William Blackstone (1760). While rights are not founded in nature, they still determine laws because when wise "herculean" judges have to decide determinative hard cases, they rely on principles derived from communal morality, which will have an egalitarian or at least generous cast to them. Rawls and Dworkin allowed an adhesion to leftist goals achieved by other than Marxist argumentation. In eclectic postmodernist culture this was regarded as intellectual liberation and moral illumination.

The habilitation in university literature departments of leftist theory and the dominance of leftist jurisprudence in at least five of the six top law schools in the United States demonstrates the continued fecundity and capacity to recreate itself of Marxist and cognate leftist theory. This was the most important fact in the culture of the United States and Western Europe in the closing decades of the twentieth century. Although the right gained some important political victories in the 1980s and early 1990s, it failed to transform the opportunities opened up by this position of state power into dislodging the Left from its dominance of university humanities and social science departments and the more intellectual side of journalism, film, and broadcasting. In terms of richness and innovative quality of cultural theory and impact on the educated middle class, the story of the Left since the mid-1960s has been one of broad and persistent success.

Even the commercial theater has done much to communicate the leftist view of history and society. One of the most successful stage presentations, on Broadway, in London's West End, and worldwide in the last two decades of the twentieth century has been the musical version of Victor Hugo's *Les Miserables*, which is set in France at the time of the July Revolution of 1830. Its theme, even more coarsely set out than in the original novel, is the righteousness of the common man against the malevolent bastions of state power and wealth. The climactic set scene in the musical is a mounting of the barricades by workers waving a red flag. Every week in a dozen cities around the world, this image is stamped on the minds of thousands of spectators who have paid gladly for expensive tickets to a festival of blatant leftist propaganda to the accompaniment of mediocre and derivative music. Against such an impact, the Right in the 1990s has nothing to offer. Of all rightist groups in this century only the Nazis and fascists could have produced a similar extravaganza.

A special place in the cultural history of the American Left has been taken since the late 1960s by the weekly journal the *New York Review of Books*, whose chief editor for three decades has been Robert Silvers. Not an academic himself but a fervent admirer of Oxbridge dons and Harvard and Princeton professors on the leftist side of the political spectrum, Silvers has achieved a remarkable symbiosis of New York, mainly Jewish, leftist culture with its subtly altering foci over time, and 90 percent of the academic elite in the top fifty universities in the country.

Silvers once told one of his ace reviewers, NYU's Denis Donoghue, that the typical subscriber to the *New York Review of Books* was an associate professor of history at the University of Iowa. The journal has one hundred thousand subscribers, and it can be assumed that it is read each week by at least three times that number. Its influence is therefore a weighty one in American culture in the closing years of the twentieth century.

Silvers and his founding coeditor of the *Review*, Barbara Epstein, got rich when after a quarter of a century they sold the journal to a southern millionaire wanting to make a splash in New York. Silvers's careful guidance of the magazine and the kind of cultural setup he singlehandedly created merits his fiscal and even more his public success. The *New York Review* cleverly draws on its favored stable of academic reviewers to validate specific points of view within the leftist camp. In the 1990s it is circumspectly within the liberal wing of the Democratic Party. It tells the associate professor at Iowa and elsewhere what is currently the modish line. But at the same time, by its approval or condemning of particular academic writing, it decides on membership in the academic peer group. Silvers has more influence in shaping the development of American academic culture than any fifty university presidents put together.

5

TRADITIONS ON THE RIGHT

The American Right Today A major threat to the visibility and durability of Western Marxism was the Stalinist terror that threatened the moral credibility of the left-wing spectrum from the mid-thirties to the late fifties. Yet Western Marxism survived triumphantly the threat of ethical and emotional association with the discredited Stalinist legacy, achieved a popular revival in the sixties, and in the late seventies and eighties attained an unprecedented penetration of the more respectable academic circles.

The destiny of the Right in the twentieth-century Western world contrasts sharply with this beneficent course of Marxist development. The Right suffered a devastating and near-mortal blow in the forties due to the militarist and genocidal conduct of the German Nazi dictatorship and similar terrorist behavior by other fascist countries. The Holocaust placed an irrevocable human stigma and divine damnation onto the fascist movements of the thirties and forties and dispatched into social and cultural oblivion a large part of the rightist program of the twenties and thirties.

The millions who died or suffered terribly at the hands of the Stalinist regime presented only momentarily an uncomfortable issue for Western Marxism—these devastations were, after all, it was claimed and widely accepted, the product of an Eastern aberration for which Western Marxists were in no way responsible. On the other hand, the fifty million people, about half of them civilians, who died in the Second World War, were universally seen as the victims of fascism, whose seedbed was held to be the rightist ideology of the early twentieth century. Hitler in reference to the Right was seen by many people not as an aberration like Stalin on the Left but as a polar extrapolation for whom rightist culture was responsible.

Hence a large part of the rightist program of the first four decades of the twentieth century was condemned to death with Hitler in the ashes of his bunker in the devastated Berlin of April 1945. The expiation and penance that rightist culture had to undertake in the five following decades in consequence of its association with and responsibility for fascist terror and the Holocaust obliterated several cardinal tenets of right-wing doctrine and fundamentally modified others. These were: racism and biological hierarchy among peoples, expiated by unprecedented social and political egalitarianism and negation of white and Western superiority; the end of Western colonialism and the independence of the Third World; a major diminution of anti-Semitism, the social and economic advancement of the Jews, and the creation and rise of the State of Israel; the proliferation of social democracy, Keynesianism, and the welfare state; and in the Catholic Church, the decrease of papal power, the decentralization and democratization of authority, and the belated doctrinal and cultural modernization of the church. By 1970 rightist culture as it had existed in the mid-thirties appeared to have all but vanished.

In the fifties and sixties the only alternative to the drift of leftist politics and ideology in the West appeared to be a kind of stodgy, inarticulate centrism represented by avuncular vestiges of the thirties: Alcide de Gasperi in Italy, Charles de Gaulle in France, Konrad Adenauer in West Germany, and Dwight Eisenhower in the United States. The vehemently anti-Communist movement in the United States identified retrospectively although not quite accurately as McCarthyism, was very short-lived. Although Republican Richard Nixon had first gained political visibility in the vanguard of anti-Communism, his presidency from 1969–74 perpetuated and even expanded on the aggressive welfare liberal program of his immediate predecessor, the left-wing Democrat Lyndon Johnson.

Nixon's presidency involved Keynesian economics; no reduction of the welfare state; enhancement of affirmative-action support for minorities and women; termination of the Vietnam War in an ignominious and chaotic manner, betraying the Vietnamese people into Stalinist hands; and rapprochement with Red China. If welfare liberal Hubert Humphrey or New Leftist George McGovern, Nixon's Democratic Party opponents, had been elected in 1968 and 1972, respectively, and if they had followed the policies that Nixon actually implemented with the prime assistance of his secretary of state, Henry Kissinger, the former Harvard professor, their presidencies would have been acceptable to most leftist circles.

Even Nixon's accommodation to leftist policies did not save him from destruction by the media, continuing into compulsive vendetta against the Right—"Tricky Dick" had to be punished for his vehement anti-Communism of the early fifties. It is true that the Nixon White House exhibited marginally corrupt and illegal practices, but not more so than the Kennedy and Johnson administrations, which were held safe harmless by the compliant, Left-oriented media. Nixon arbitrarily and unconstitutionally made use of the IRS, FBI, and the CIA, but so did Kennedy and Johnson. Nor did Nixon, like Kennedy, bring upscale prostitution into the White House for his personal delectation or conduct an exploitive clandestine affair with a movie queen. What made Nixon vulnerable to his enemies was his arrogance, a sense of impregnability, and a self-destructive personality trait.

Nixon's error was to neglect the media luminaries from the *Washington Post* and the *New York Times* and the TV anchormen, and not to court assiduously prominent Ivy League professors in the social sciences. These two groups had become the dominant opinion makers in the United States during the sixties.

In the mid-seventies the political Right in the Western world stirred from its three decades of somnolence. In the United States in 1980 and Israel in 1978, Britain in 1979, Western Germany in 1982, France and Canada in 1985, an array of conservative parties gained power. There were four reasons for this change. First, in the early seventies leftist regimes showed their incapacity to use Keynesian strategies to stem escalating inflation that threatened middle-class security, and the incessant bloating of the welfare state stagnated capital investment in economic expansion. Second, the conservative political revival was helped by the articulation of neorightist doctrine in academic and intellectual circles against the rising tide of the cultural Left.

Third, the mass of respectable, conscientious middle- and working-class people became concerned with the unrestrained egalitarianism that leftist governments endorsed and stimulated. They viscerally came to the same conclusion as Habermas, that a legitimation crisis of Western capitalism was being precipitated. Finally, conservative political parties found effective popular leaders, especially in Ronald Reagan, Margaret Thatcher, Menachem Begin, and Kurt Waldheim.

Four ideologies comprise the intellectual American Right today. Reaganism—perpetuated in the mid-nineties by Newt Gingrich—is the first of these, and it has solid intellectual foundations that originated principally in the neo-Ricardian free market and monetarist economic theories of Milton Friedman at the University of Chicago. At Chicago Friedman spawned a group of true believers, such as George Gilder, and he gained many disciples in economics departments and business schools elsewhere. Friedman in turn was a follower of two central European émigré conservative theorists at Chicago in the forties, the political theorist Leo Strauss and the economic theorist and antisocialist polemicist Friedrich von Hayek.

In Friedman's view the welfare state has become a burden on society. Even at the time when it had not yet become corrupt, the welfare state occasioned overspending and excessive government regulation of the economy. It withdrew capital from the private sector and produced dysfunction in the economy.

Friedman offered the solution of adjustment in the monetary supply along with a cutback in the size of the government and reduction of taxation. In a relatively unregulated economy, conditioned only by changes in the money supply, economic expansion would be ensured. Unrestrained market forces could in a relatively short time bring more capital into the market and induce business recovery. Inflation would be reduced by the classic method of layoff of redundant workers, union-busting, and wage restraint. The ills of the American economy in the seventies, which resulted in high inflation and unemployment rates following from business stagnation, could then be remedied by these neo-Ricardian methods.

A more extreme statement of the Chicago school came from Friedman's disciple George Gilder. He argued that capitalism is the true altruism, socialism a form of vicious selfishness serving only the needs and interests of a small oligarchy. "The heroes of capitalism are not arrogant producers of goods immaculately conceived in their own minds; capitalists imaginatively serve the minds and needs of others." A favorite theme of Gilder and the Chicago school is that the welfare state is the opposite of generous and humanitarian. It is in fact "a cheap charity that all too often spends the earnings of others in ways that degrade and demoralize the alleged beneficiaries." For example, the erosion of black families was the consequence of federal aid to single-parent families. Gilder's views were endorsed by Newt Gingrich and his followers in the mid-1990s.

From the late 1980s through the mid-1990s, two conservative polemicists gained high visibility and put their books on the bestseller lists. The liberal Left media and leftist academics assigned to review their books in newspapers and political and cultural weeklies canonized the two—Charles Murray and Robert Bork—as the authentic and despicable voices of the American Right. In reality Murray and Bork developed well-worn concepts of the conservative tradition clustered in sundry academic writings of one or the other University of Chicago professor into neat packages for polemical dissemination that at least momentarily captured public attention. Murray began by denouncing welfare dependency of poor people who relied on federal aid, which in his view, following Gilder's, corrupted these vulnerable people into helpless incapacity. Then, in 1993, Murray again captured public attention with *The Bell Curve*, written in collaboration with a Harvard professor, that in straight-line neo-Darwinian fashion established a hierarchy of group intelligence—descendants of European Jews at the top, Chinese just below them, and African Americans dragging along at the bottom. Robert Bork was a former Yale Law School Professor and federal judge whose nomination to the Supreme Court by Ronald Reagan in 1987 was blocked by liberal Democrats and feminists because of his conservative opinions. Bork then emerged as a bestselling author with *The Tempting of America* (1988), which claimed that liberal lawmaking by the Supreme Court had elevated the judiciary into an illegitimate supremacist position above the popular will embodied in Congress. In 1996 another widely discussed book by Bork advocated a constitutional amendment that would allow congressional legislation to cancel a liberal Left Supreme Court decision. This was populist democracy turned to the instrumental service of the Right.

Why should the University of Chicago have become in the seventies and eighties the intellectual center of the American Right? Not only did its business school and economics department revive neo-Ricardianism, and indeed go beyond that conservative philosophy, but its law school also took a strongly rightist position. One of its former law professors, Antonin Scalia, was designated by Reagan for the Supreme Court. Scalia was famous not only for neo-Ricardianism but for hostility to affirmative action. In 1986 a prominent Harvard Law School professor fled to Chicago from the critical legal studies Marxists, who increasingly dominated the Harvard institution.

The rightist coloration of the University of Chicago was partly happenstance—the heritage of the dynamic two Central European émigré rightists Strauss and Hayek. It was partly the result of the physical location of the university in the midwestern citadel of capitalism, and even more important, in its location on the South Side of Chicago, in the middle of a huge black ghetto, a location that had the effect of stimulating the largely white academy. It forced the university inward, surrounding itself completely with walls and expensive real estate buffers (one of the faculty apartment houses had both a wall and a moat). Thereby the university was cut off from the city of Chicago and had to stress abstract theory.

But the most important reason for UC's rightism is that the intellectual opening in the American academic world was on the Right, the Ivy League and Berkeley having previously joined forces with the Left. When Princeton was the stamping ground of Lawrence Stone, and other academic Marxists and adherents of the Frankfurt school of critical theory held sway at the University of California, the only place on the spectrum of political culture where the University of Chicago could distinguish itself in the seventies and eighties was on the Right.

Founded by the Rockefeller family in the early years of the century, the University of Chicago gained prominence between the wars in the social, behaviorial, and physical sciences. In the forties and fifties it experienced an intellectual decline under the unfortunate leadership of President Robert Maynard Hutchins and his immediate successors, who stressed the undergraduate college and neo-Victorian core curriculum. Emerging from the doldrums in the late sixties under the shrewd lawyer and conqueror of the student Left, Edward Levi, UC in the seventies, under a judicious president, Hannah Holborn Gray, became again a thriving center of research and scholarly inquiry. With a heavy infusion of new local money, it greatly improved its facilities and faculty, and Milton Friedman showed the university the intellectual road it could follow to regain the front-rank intellectual stature it had enjoyed in the halcyon pre-Hutchins era.

Gilder's rightist leaning was so extreme that he found highly laudatory things to say about Ayn Rand, an eccentric popular novelist of the forties who wrote bestselling stories about heroic, utterly selfish, rugged individualists. Gilder called one of Rand's works "the most important novel of ideas" since Tolstoy. Ayn Rand had heretofore been a laughingstock in the academic world. Nothing demonstrates more dramatically the intellectual revolution that the Friedmanite school sought to achieve. With the Republican majority in both Houses of Congress after the 1994 elections, the Friedmanite doctrines became a political agenda as well.

Friedman's program had considerable success under the aegis of the Reagan government. Inflation was greatly reduced and business recovery generated. Taxation was held in check and reduced for upper-middle-class families, whose entrepreneurial ambition and investment capabilities were encouraged. With the help of the Reagan administration, the power of the labor unions was severely reduced. Unfortunately high defense spending produced a sizable deficit, but Reagan was no more inhibited by deficits than FDR had been.

A remarkable example of the effectiveness of Reaganism was to be found in the solution of the oil and gasoline problems. Twice in the seventies, first during the Nixon and later during the Carter administration, there were consumer gasoline shortages that reached critical dimensions. The Friedmanite economists advised at the time that if the government would simply stop regulating oil and gasoline, the market would adjust itself and the shortage cease. They were proved right.

The other intellectual source of Reaganism was in the scientific theory of sociobiology, which was propounded principally by E. O. Wilson, a Harvard zoologist. If Friedmanist economic theory is neo-Ricardian, Wilson's social biology is neo–Social Darwinist and entails belief in competition in every sphere of life, including the human. Wilson's research work was on insects and he applied the patterns he discovered in insect life, which were regulated by competitive principles, to human existence. The same reassertion of the competitive model among humanity can be found in Reaganism. Wilson did not rule out the occasional intrusion of altruism in sociobiology, but his world is essentially a modified version of the Social Darwinist struggle for existence.

Wilson does not agree with Austrian ethologist Konrad Lorenz that constant aggression is prevalent in social groups. Wilson argues that the message of sociobiology is a reciprocal altruism, a social cooperation based on individual calculation and exchange of interest. He argues a paradoxical message of "true altruism" and "true selfishness" as distinct from the romantic leftist beliefs in an altruism that transcends personal selfishness. "Human beings appear to be sufficiently selfish and calculating to be capable of infinitely greater harmony. . . . True selfishness, if obedient to the other constraints of mammalian biology, is the key to a more nearly perfect social contract." In practical terms it is hard to see that this is in any way different from Friedman's and Gilder's neo-Ricardianism. It is a variant of the old social contract theory. In the nineteenth century there was a close collaboration between market economists and biological theorists like Darwin and Spencer. This seems to have happened again in the age of Reagan.

While New Leftists of the sixties and seventies had talked incessantly about participating in democracy and communal bonds, in fact they had aggressively sought power and preferment as much as any capitalist entrepreneur. Yet in the academic world and the leftist media it became the fashion to denigrate not only racism, imperialism, and capitalism but competitive strategies and judgmental structures of any kind. Leftist critics like Allen Chase and Stephen Jay Gould lumped IQ testing in the same category with nineteenth-century craniology (measuring brain cavities speciously to show that white people had bigger brains) and early-twentieth-century eugenics (selective breeding to foster a vigorous white race). SAT tests were denounced as socially biased and discriminatory against blacks, Hispanics, women— whomever.

In the Carter administration, leading members of the federal Civil Rights Commission, such as Eleanor Holmes Norton and Mary Berry, aimed to remove all competitive structure and standards as an obstacle to affirmative action and the perpetually egalitarian society. Quotas, euphemistically called goals, were enforced by federal agencies, since the new quotas were designed to assist minorities and the underprivileged to get ahead.

Against leftist egalitarianism Reaganism both reflected and fostered a resurgence of legitimate competitiveness, the last glimmer of Social Darwinism. Harvard psychologist Arthur Jenson argued anew for the scientific validity of IQ tests as measuring an inheritable, biologically based intelligence and not just environmental impacts—nature as against nurture. The elite law schools fiercely held on to their LSAT tests as the most important criteria for admission, claiming a high correlation between the LSAT scores (combined with grade-point averages) and law school performances. The yuppie genera- tion, not marching to the barricades any more, but preferring to drive there in their BMWs, were comfortable with competitive standards in professional schools and the business world, which assured them of high salaries, power, and interesting jobs. Because the egalitarian trumpeters of the Left in their moment of power had in most instances not refrained from personal advan- tage, this minimalist new Social Darwinism of the eighties exuded a refresh- ingly honest tone of cynical reality.

The second ideological strand on the American Right, after the free mar- ket economy, was evangelical Christianity, whose most visible spokesmen, if not always its most skillful ones, were Rev. Jerry Falwell and Rev. Pat Robertson. In this country, not only in the South, but also in the Midwest and on the West Coast, albeit less so in the Northeast, there has been an upsurge of evangelical, Baptist, Seventh-day Adventist, Mormon, and other more expe- riential forms of Christianity in the last forty years. Access to television has greatly increased the reach and wealth of the evangelical churches. This impor- tant development, although it involves fifty million people, has been underex- amined. The attention it has received from the media is inadequate, and it has received only modest attention in the academic world. Evangelical Christianity constitutes a very important movement.

Evangelical Christianity has registered striking gains in some parts of this

country, and it is a major right-wing phenomenon. Like evangelical and mil-
lenary Christians throughout history, the current group draws its support from
the upwardly mobile lower middle class—or people not more than one generation removed from that class—who customarily feel lacking in power in proportion to their numbers and sobriety.

The evangelicals ("born-again Christians"), who might be described as
neopuritanical and neo-Victorian, supported Reaganism and in the 1990s
found a new idol in Newt Gingrich, the former state college history professor
from Georgia who became Speaker of the House after the election of 1994.
Evangelical Christians are hostile to high taxation, welfare payments, abortion,
the teaching of contraception in schools, federal regulation of the environment, gun control, convenient divorce laws, sexual permissiveness and pornography, and the teaching of Darwinian evolution. In general they dislike secular
liiberal culture. Although there is a background of anti-Semitism among evangelical groups, some of them have also become vehement supporters of Israel
because this fits in with their apocalyptic model of history and because—
before 1991—of Soviet hostility to Israel. In the 1994 congressional elections
the Christian Coalition, an evangelical Christian funding and lobbying group,
showed strong political muscle. It played a significant role in the election of a
nucleus of far-right congressmen, mainly from the South and the mountain
states.

The third ideological stream in the American Right today is constituted
by a group of mainly New York neoconservative, rightist intellectuals who
have their leading outlet in the monthly journals *Commentary* and the *New
Criterion.* This group has emerged as the New York intellectual crowd and
their successors, which were focused on *Partisan Review* in the forties, has split
asunder.

Commentary was originally funded by the American Jewish Committee,
which is indicative of a partial right-wing shift in upper-middle-class Jewish
circles that has come about in the last twenty-five years. The *New Criterion* was
supported by a group of conservative foundations, headed by the John M. Olin
Foundation.

Both journals were edited by former Jewish liberals and modernist critics—*Commentary* by Norman Podhoretz, until his retirement in 1996.
Podhoretz was a disciple of Leavis and of Trilling, the prominent modernist
critic of Columbia University in the thirties and forties. Podhoretz and his
wife, Midge Decter, who also writes frequently in *Commentary,* are committed
to Enlightenment traditions and preserving the manifestations of modernist

culture. They are also enthusiastic about Israel and Zionism. They support the right-wing Likud Party in Israel. The consistency of their views is created by loyalty to New York Jewish middle-class culture of the forties and fifties.

Theirs is the politics of liberal nostalgia. In their view it is not they who have moved to the right. Their position has remained constant in their own eyes. It is the political fulcrum that since the mid-sixties has moved sharply to the left, they claim. They view themselves as loyal to the political and cultural ideals of forties liberalism. Meanwhile the New Left serpent—with its extreme egalitarianism, erosion of American patriotism, advocacy of Third World production, support for allegedly Communist movements like the Sandinistas in Nicaragua, and hostility to Israel and Zionism and sympathy for the Palestinians and the formerly terrorist PLO—has allegedly intruded into the Edenic garden of forties liberalism. Eternal vigilance must be exercised, according to *Commentary,* to challenge prospective anti-Semitic resurgence on the Left and socialism everywhere.

The editor of the *New Criterion,* Hilton Kramer, is a modernist art critic of substantial reputation, who left his prominent and influential position at the *New York Times* to establish a monthly journal of critical opinion in the spirit of Eliot's culturally modernist and politically conservative *The Criterion* of the twenties and thirties. It is obviously not Eliot the genteel anti-Semite whom Kramer has in mind to emulate. It is Eliot the modernist, the rationalist, the classicist, the visionary for a transatlantic community dedicated to a closely held and well-read elite culture, stretching from Dante to Joyce, who is recalled. For Kramer the West reached its cultural zenith in the late forties, with Eliot flourishing in London and the Museum of Modern Art in New York. Kramer sees modernism as apolitical. The efforts of the Left to politicize high culture and co-opt modernism is a special heresy he contends against.

The *New Criterion* rapidly exhibited itself as an important critical voice and anguished the Left precisely because of its learning and sophistication, qualities that since the mid-sixties the American Left has monopolistically claimed for itself as an exclusive privilege. The *New Criterion* challenged the leftist caricature of the Right as a motley array of Neanderthals and ignoramuses. This stereotype would not have been possible in the twenties, and Kramer has vindicated his dedication to Eliot by severely eroding it. He has made the Right a respectable intellectual force in America and thereby aroused the frightened fury of the *New Republic, The Nation,* the *Village Voice,* and the *Radical History Review.*

The *New Criterion* is also significant because its pages have served as an outlet for publication of critical essays of varying quality by young people whom

Kramer has discovered, such as his managing editors, Erich Eichman and Roger Kimball, as Eliot and Leavis did in their own journals in the twenties and thirties. It is encouraging for American intellectual vitality in general, and not just for the Right, to see this group emerge, precisely because most of them are not academics yet are learned and perceptive. In 1986 the London *Times Literary Supplement* hailed the *New Criterion* as "probably more consistently worth reading than any other monthly magazine in English." Eliot would have been pleased.

Kramer and his colleagues act as cultural whistle-blowers from a neo-modernist and rationalist position. They perform the salutary service of point-ing to the more vulnerable and hysterical cultural and artistic activities of the Left that since the mid-sixties have been legitimized in the more prestigious leftist journals such as the *New York Review of Books*. Kramer sees the modernist heritage as the best that twentieth-century culture has to offer and finds it threatened and betrayed by a leftist cultural movement that is not devoted to the arts per se but mainly wants—in his view—to misuse the arts and manip-ulate the modernist aura in the interests of premodernist socialism.

The neoconservative interpretation of the recent American past is gener-ally that in the sixties, seventies and eighties, there was an excessive left-wing shift in the political views of Americans, which affected the universities, the media, and the entire intellectual world, and which undermined traditions of rationality, liberal discourse, and civility. The rising tide of Marxism, neocon-servatives maintain, was accompanied by an excessive commitment to unre-strained egalitarianism expressed through affirmative action, which is in turn eroding and destabilizing professional and academic groups in the United States.

This view is not confined to the pages of the *New Criterion* and *Commentary*. It has gained powerful, if decidedly minority, support in the academic world. The neoconservative interpretation of the sixties was argued in the seventies by academicians William O'Neill (Rutgers), Ronald Berman (California–San Diego), and William Bennett (Boston University). Berman became director of the National Endowment for the Humanities under Nixon, and Bennett held the same position (he was subsequently secretary of education) under Reagan.

In 1985 Allan Matusow of Rice University published an extremely learned and convincing account of the sixties, *The Unraveling of America*. As the title implies, it takes a neoconservative view, although expressed in a careful and mostly nonpolemical manner. What is doubly significant is that Matusow's volume appears in *The New American Nation*, a high-establishment, multivolume history of the United States edited by two venerable New Deal liberal historians, Henry Steele Commager and Richard B. Morris.

In the early 1990s academic conservatives coalesced into the National Academy of Scholars, a somewhat desultory and shy group whose main activity is the publication of a good journal, *Academic Quest*. The keynote speaker at the first national NAS convention in 1991 was Decter, who not only railed against leftists on the campus, but also expressed her contempt for academics in general, to the discomfort of many professors in the audience. When some rose to protest, the microphones were cut off.

In the opinion of some informed observers, the key figure in the New York Jewish neoconservative group has been Irving Kristol. He is certainly among the most visible. The holder of the John Olin Chair of Social Theory in the NYU Business School (although his academic credentials are negligible), he edits his own dry journal of rightist opinion, the *National Interest*, and, more important, he is a regular columnist in the American paper with the largest circulation, the *Wall Street Journal*. Kristol's spouse is Gertude Himmelfarb, a historian at the City University of New York, who has turned out a stream of books arguing how much better things were in mid-Victorian times before the Left liberals and socialists took over. Charles Dickens would have had a wonderful time satirizing this neo-Scrooge fantasy.

The son of Kristol and Himmelfarb is a prominent figure in Washington. After serving as a speechwriter in the Bush administration, William Kristol got the rightist Australian-American press lord, Rupert Murdoch, to fund yet another rightist journal, the *Weekly Standard*. It has nothing particularly new to say.

None of the neoconservative publications in the mid-nineties edited by New York Jews and their spouses and scions is up to the quality of the *Washington Times*, a vastly money-losing daily newspaper. It is funded by Rev. Sung Myung Moon, the Korean religious leader. The *Washington Times* consistently publishes thought-provoking reviews of serious books in the humanities and policy studies.

One may look at the intellectual Right in the United States in the mid-1990s as a very small group—maybe fifty, maybe less—of highly articulate people sitting on huge funding resources. Remove the support of the John M. Olin Foundation especially, together with support from Rupert Murdoch and the Reverend Moon, and all these impressive, well-informed, and insightful publications in New York and Washington would grind to a halt in a few days. There is a bit of a Wizard of Oz effect going on in rightist intellectual circles. If these publications in the East disappeared, along with their lavish subsidies, the only significant right-wing national publication still in business would be *Chronicles*, a monthly published in Davenport, Iowa, that harks back to the nativist classical conservatism of colleges in Tennessee and Virginia in the 1940s.

From the point of view of cultural theory, what is most intriguing about Kramer-Podhoretz-Kristol neoconservatism is the unusual effort to combine modernism with right-wing political theory. This is, however, by no means an unheard-of attempt. As will be seen below, there were several points of coincidence between modernism and fascism in the twenties and thirties. Although the Jewish neoconservatives in New York and the genteel and gentile Christians in Iowa hate one another, they all adore Eliot.

The neoconservatives are small in number, but because of their journals, and because of their representation in university circles, however limited, they manage to procure serious attention. They and the evangelical Christians might not be thought to make very good allies, although Kristol has made strenuous efforts to establish a feasible alliance between them. Kramer lectured at evangelical colleges and was well received there. Still, it is unlikely that anything will come of these maneuvers.

There was certainly a connection between the neoconservatives and the Reaganites. The former spilled over into think tanks in Washington, D.C., such as the Heritage Foundation, and from their ranks came a considerable number of subcabinet personnel in the Reagan and Bush administrations. The son-in-law of Norman Podhoretz, for example, was a highly controversial assistant secretary in the State Department in the mid-eighties.

A fourth ideological strand in the American Right in the late eighties was libertarianism, which has a substantial following but has not yet found a convincing intellectual statement unless it be in the novels of Ayn Rand. Libertarianism was a kind of underground movement on the Right.

Libertarianism seems at first merely an extreme extension of the views of Milton Friedman and the Chicago school of market theorists. But there is quite a different ingredient in libertarianism. It is an anarchism of the Right. It despairs of any moral or positive quality in the state and wishes to disassemble all political structure as far as possible. But it is unclear how far is possible. There is a prominent strain of deep despair in libertarianism, a total rejection of the political road the federal government began to take, not just in the administration of FDR but even in that of Woodrow Wilson.

There appears to be a latent revolutionary consciousness in libertarianism, a Rousseauist yearning for a return to pristine nature and a rejection of social constraints. It is a peculiar kind of American fascism. On its activist wing, libertariansm became the ideology of the militias that organized in farming villages in the South and Midwest in the 1990s. In most cases these demotic military groups were harmless, but in some instances—the bombing of a federal office building in Oklahoma City in 1995, possibly the burning of African-American churches all over the South—they became terrorist organizations.

Consider from the point of view of cultural theory the fact that American conservatism is marked by two contradictory spectrums. One is spread between extreme libertarianism on the one side—the wish to keep the state out of people's lives—and a yearning for control on the other, such as public monitoring of art galleries to prevent exhibition of allegedly pornographic art. The other spectrum involves at the one extreme a commitment to the untrammeled mechanism of a market economy, and the other pole a hankering after paternalist and communitarian caring for people. These tensions remain unresolved and possibly they will always be unresolved among people who think of themselves as conservatives who live in the American democracy.

Fundamentals of Rightist Culture The Right in the United States today, or at any time and place in the Western world in this century, whether France in 1910, Germany in 1930, or Britain in 1950, drew on a common pool of ideas and traditions that comprise the spectrum of rightist theory. At any given time and place, what constitutes rightist thinking will make use of a majority of this spectrum of traditions, and frequently it will try to embrace all of them. The ideas and traditions are not all readily reconcilable with one another. It is the specific selection of traditions and ideas that will be made—frequently one or two from the total spectrum, such as anti-Semitism, being rejected—and the precise way in which the ideas and traditions are fitted together—that will shape the direction and determine the polemical tone of a particular rightist doctrine.

Let us negate at the outset the claim that all this is a specious and futile undertaking, a false perception, that there is no such thing as a rightist culture in the way we have perceived it and now intend to explain it. It might be said that a point of view that places Churchill, Herbert Hoover, and Kramer within a common spectrum of rightist thought and culture is heuristically useless—no more so than an interpretation that places Beard, Benjamin, and Stalin within a spectrum of leftist thought and culture, as was done in the previous chapter. As a matter of fact, neither of these perceptions and interpretations is wrong or absurd. They are both intellectually and heuristically viable.

These are two dominant political cultures or traditions in the twentieth-century West—the leftist and the rightist. Each culture is composed of a spectrum of ideas. The shape and direction of leftist and rightist thought is fashioned out of how these ideas and traditions are drawn upon and fitted together. This is central to the shape of culture in our century.

If a substantial majority of the ideas and traditions in the full spectrum of one of the political cultures is reflected in someone's writings, Kramer, Churchill, and Hoover do all belong to the Right's tradition. It does not mean that they agree on all issues. Similarly Beard and Benjamin were not personally responsible for Stalin, and if they had lived in a Soviet country, they would have probably been liquidated by the Stalinists.

The fundamental fact remains that there is a leftist and a rightist political culture, with distinctive sets of traditions and ideas in each case, and Kramer, Churchill, and Hoover should be perceived—and can only be fully understood—in the context of the rightist tradition.

The spectrum of ideas on which right-wing theories have drawn in this century—which again is not to say that every rightist thinker has embraced all of them—consists of eight traditions. The first of these is inequality.

All right-wing thought is discriminatory, hierarchically judgmental, and exclusive, in some way. It believes in better and worse, upper and lower, whether it is considering a nation, an ethnic group, or a work of art. Marxist thought may point pejoratively to current inequalities but these are deemed only transient and will be obliterated in the egalitarian Communist society of the future when all class, national, and ethnic barriers will vanish in a Communist system, and when all art will be equally devoted to the service of the proletariat. In practice this may be unattainable—"some are more equal than others"—and if attainable it will be in a totalitarian gulag nightmare, but that is what Marxism advocates and envisions—ultimate total equality, complete social and cultural homogeneity.

The rightist philosophy is fundamentally different. It believes in a necessary and salutary degree of inequality. The degree and form may vary momentously but the fundamental issue that separates Left from Right is the belief in equality versus inequality. The extreme and aggressive forms of inequality that some rightists adhere to—slavery, genocide, apartheid—will be condemned by other rightists in the strongest possible terms. Some rightists believe in inequality among groups. Others only in inequality of performance capability, and hence of gained social reward (status and income), among individuals. What binds all to the Right is the conviction that some measure or criterion of differentiation and effective hierarchy is inevitable in nature and beneficial in human nurture.

This need not be the belief in the legitimacy of Western colonialism by the Aryan master race over so-called degenerate people. More often, especially since 1945, the rightist doctrine of inequality simply means some paintings are more beneficial than others; some works of literature more compelling and evocative—that a particular work is closer to true art than another. From Matthew Arnold in the 1860s to Hilton Kramer in the 1990s, conservative art and literary criticism have advocated a "touchstone" of superiority, differentiating the quality of one work from another, and therefore of the social value of the artist or writer who created it. The right of an individual to special rewards for superior performance is the controversial issue.

The rightist doctrine of inequality means minimally that some individuals are more or less intelligent or talented than the mean and this claimed fact implies that the superior intelligences or talents have a social and moral right to admission to elite college and professional schools in preference to the less capable. Adolescents of allegedly inferior intelligence should be satisfied with starting their postsecondary education at a community college rather than a top university.

The rightist doctrine can also mean that when a specific nation or social group at a particular time shows itself more enterprising, whether in making war or making automobiles, it has the prescriptive right to enjoy the fruits of that superiority, whether through Israeli control of the West Bank in the 1980s or Toyota dealerships and plants in the United States in the 1990s.

The bitterest and most protracted debates in this country in the past three decades have been over the issue of affirmative action, and this is because affirmative action strategies and policies speak directly to the issue of equality/inequality that separates the Left from the Right. It is to this question that the Left's more subtle and learned intellects have addressed themselves, making very fine distinctions between "quotas" and "goals."

Rawls at Harvard and Dworkin of NYU Law School have developed elaborate philosophical arguments justifying the more aggressive efforts to provide compensatory mechanisms for overcoming inequality. This means not just eradicating inequality of opportunity but obliterating measurable differences of intelligence and rational capability. Ethics demands, says Rawls, and the Constitution dictates, says Dworkin, that admission to elite schools and colleges and the giving of financial aid should nearly always favor the black applicant from Harlem rather than the Jewish applicant from Great Neck (assuming the black candidate has a high school diploma and has met the minimal conceivable qualifications for admission). Rawls's and Dworkin's sophisticated and much applauded treatises come down to advocating the prescriptive right of leveling equality over existential inequality.

Another celebrated scholar of the Left, Harvard biologist and historian of science Stephen Jay Gould, zealously takes out after Lewis Terman, the Stanford behavioral psychologist of the interwar period, and the father of school IQ tests and college admission SAT tests. All "hereditarian" views of intelligence lack scientific validity as well as ethical legitimacy, according to Gould's *The Mismeasure of Man.* In his view biologically determinative differentiations among social groups, (as in nineteenth-century craniology and Social Darwinism and current sociobiology) are without merit of any kind. It is also impossible, says Gould, to make such differentiation among individuals because personal intelligence is an immeasurable function. Against Terman and the Educational Testing Service, Gould opts for total "flexibility [as] the hallmark of evolution" and in assessing individual potential.

What this means in practice is that ethical and social considerations demand admission to Princeton with a full scholarship for the marginal applicant from Harlem in preference to the readily qualified middle-class white applicant from Great Neck. You cannot compare their intelligence or rationally estimate their established potential, Gould believes. So political and ethical standards are the only criteria left. Gould would support the leftist view of affirmative action advocated by Rawls and Dworkin. It is indicative of the penetration of the Left into the media and publishing world that Gould's polemic won the National Book Critics' Circle award—the premier prize for nonfiction—in 1981.

It is the leftist doctrine of equality and its application to affirmative action that makes the Right recoil in anger and frustration. The Right has looked to the Supreme Court for succor, but even the Reagan administration gained little help from that direction. Indeed the Supreme Court affirmed the constitutionality of quotas as long as they compensate for previous racial discrimination. Thus the struggle between believers in the validity and legitimacy of a residual degree of inequality and the partisans of total equality—the first criterion separating the Right from the Left in this century—is infinitely perpetuated. The Right's last resort to legitimating inequality was represented in the California statewide referendum against affirmative action in 1996.

The dispute between the advocate of equality and inequality is directly related to the tension between modernism and the preceding culture. Equality was a romantic ideal—that Marx elaborated in gargantuan fashion—not a modernist one. Modernism had a penchant for small-scale differentiation and fine discrimination. While rejecting facile nineteenth-century assumptions about macrocosmic social hierarchies, modernism enthusiastically preserved distinctions at the microsocial and individual levels. It is precisely this particular kind of differentiation that affirmative action and its subtler advocates like Rawls, Dworkin, and Gould sought to expunge. Thus the struggle between inequality and equality in the context of twentieth-century cultural history involves competition between the modernist heritage and neo-Victorianism.

The second tradition that distinguished the Right in the twentieth century is anti-Communism. Since 1917, be it Churchillian British conservatism or American McCarthyism, Reaganism, or Nazism, the Right has consistently identified itself as anti-Communist. Next to inequality anti-Communism is the most persistent and pervasive rightist belief.

The threat of the "red menace," that of the "evil empire," particularly of Communism in its Soviet form, of the persistent attack on the middle class by the Left, and particularly by Marxists, has lent a solidarity to right-wing movements. If the Right means anything in the twentieth century, it means anti-Communism and anti-Marxism. If the Russian Revolution had not taken place, if Russia had gone on being ruled by czars and grand dukes, the history of the Right in this century, as well as of the Left, would have been very different.

The split between Left and Right in political culture in this century is along the seismic fault that separates on one side those who believe that the Bolshevik October Revolution, however unfortunate the Stalinist aberration and disappointing some of the other outcomes, signified a universal, irresistible summons to a better world. On the other side there are those who claim the October Revolution spawned a series of widespread tyrannies of the worst kind and treacherously exploited the moral traditions of the West in the interest of the Soviet thrust for world power.

The Left thinks the October Revolution should in one way or another be emulated; the Right believes it must be contained. The question is: What does the policy of containing Communism mean? Its original propounder, George F. Kennan, then a State Department official and later a distinguished diplomatic historian, argued that he had advocated a short-term, pragmatic, flexible policy of containment. Others held that containment was a long-term effort permanently to restrain and thereby damage the "evil empire," as Reagan called it. So, was containment short-term and tactical or long-term and strategic? Similarly, should Communist and Marxist fellow travelers be excluded from positions of social responsibility and political influence in the civil service and education or should they have the full rights of citizenship, including free speech and employment anywhere, in the expectation that in the free trade of ideas the anti-Communists will prevail by the intrinsic merit of their case? Is there such a theory as an anti-Communist Marxism, a liberal or Western Marxism, or is there no real difference among the shades of red?

These are issues that have divided the Right. But about the fundamental persistence of anti-Communism as a distinguishing tradition of the Right there is no doubt. In any cocktail party in Cambridge, Massachusetts; Berkeley, California; or Greenwich Village, New York, this is the issue, sometimes spoken, often unspoken, that divides the associated academics and other intellectuals and professionals. In the words of the 1930s leftist folk song, "Which side are you on?/ . . . There are no neutrals there."

The third tradition on which the Right has drawn is theistic religion, central to Christianity and Judaism, that can be generally represented by the term *magisterium*. This is the doctrinal term espoused by the conservative majority of the Roman Catholic Church in recent decades. In the Catholic context, the term has a twofold significance. It stands for its literal meaning of magistracy or authority and signifies those Catholics in Rome and elsewhere who uphold papal infallibility, the autocratic reserved power of the papal administration, and the plenary power of the hierarchy in faith and morals.

Magisterium also refers to those Catholics who perpetuate the Augustinian tradition of stressing the majesty and goodness of God in comparison with the weakness and corruption of humankind. Without God human beings are nothing good, and therefore the Christian ministry, the carrier of God's word in the world, is the focal point for the reformation and transformation of the world. To believe that a fiercely secular force, whether the Roman State in the time of Saint Augustine or the Communist or Democratic parties nowadays, can function as that focal point is blasphemy and anathema. Take away justice that comes into the world only from the church, says Augustine, "and what is the state but a band of robbers?"

The Augustinian doctrine of God's majesty was espoused by the Protestant Reformation in the teachings of Luther and Calvin, again foregrounded in the early twentieth century by Barth, and stressed in our time by the more conservative Protestant groups, especially the American evangelical churches. Along with the conservative majority in the Catholic Church that holds fast to papal authority, the Protestant evangelicals are the largest group on the Right drawing on Christian tradition. Of course, these two groups, comprising together more than one hundred million people in the United States alone, have no agreement nor probably a future capacity for accommodation on the subject of papal authority. But conservative Catholics and Protestant evangelicals coincide on an Augustinian theology of *magisterium*— divine majesty and human weakness without God's gift of his love (grace). They do agree on the so-called social issues of abortion, contraception, and pornography and they have a common enemy in the Christian Left.

In Catholicism this means determined opposition to those who interpret Vatican Council II of 1962–64 as sanctioning the democratization and decentralization of the Catholic Church, the dismantling of papal authority, and a social activism in alliance with Marxists and other leftist activists—the "liberation theology."

The evangelicals on their part challenge a Protestant social gospel that believes in human freedom to change the world for the better through the secular means of the welfare state. The Protestant Left over the past fifty years has come to acknowledge the anti-Augustinian principle that we live in the secular city—in the term of Harvard theologian Harvey Cox—and that the Protestant calling is an individual and internal matter, a source of personal inspiration, while in the public and communal sphere, it is the movement and ideology of the Left that perpetuates Christian action. The good Christian today, this leftist gospel specifies, votes for Bill Clinton, subscribes to *The Nation,* and studies with Wallerstein or some other Marxist totem.

Where does Rev. Jesse Jackson stand between the Right and Left Christian tradition as currently formulated? He walks a very fine line, aiming to conflate the theism of the Christian Right with the policies of the Christian Left.

Jackson's balancing act points to the political and social ambivalence that has always lain at the heart of the Augustinian tradition and still characterizes it. It is possible to begin with Augustinian theology and convince oneself to move in either a conservative or revolutionary political direction. The Catholic upholders of the *magisterium,* such as Cardinal O'Connor of New York, and the evangelical activists, like Rev. Jerry Falwell, have taken the rightist orientation. But they are not blind to the attraction of the other road in the political fork. If the papacy and the Catholic majority would interpret Vatican II in a radical way, if the bishops would espouse liberation theology, there would be a worldwide upheaval. Catholicism could threaten to take over the world. But this victory by a leftist Catholicism would likely be short-lived. The Catholic Church would in the midst of this turmoil fragment into pieces to a degree greater than it did in the sixteenth century.

Similarly, if the dynamism of the American evangelicals were committed to the Left rather than to the Right, the radical crusades momentarily threatening in the period from 1895–1910, in the form of southern and midwestern populism that in the days of William Jennings Bryan embraced the left wing of the Democratic party, would revive. Early-twentieth-century populists could never decide whether they belonged on the Left or the Right—their program embraced both welfare liberalism and a kind of visceral, grass-roots fascism and anti-Semitism. Nowadays evangelical Protestants, in response to the urbanization and partial industrialization and enrichment of the South, have chosen to stress the rightist implications of their theology of theistic majesty, but they are the heirs of populist dynamism.

In Judaism there is also a theological base for a rightist group. The most important religious development in the Jewish world since 1945 has been the revival, in both the United States and Israel, of Orthodoxy, or traditional Judaism. In the first four decades of the century Orthodox Judaism, devoted to the *Halacha* (traditional doctrine and ritual, including twice-daily prayer, the Kashrut laws, and gender segregation), was relatively weak and politically of low visibility. In Palestine/Israel the dominant Jewish group were the East European socialist and secularist kibbutzniks, who founded the Labor Party and controlled the Israeli government for three decades after Israeli independence in 1948.

In the United States from the 1890s to 1924 (the closing of mass immigration) a vast and chaotic Jewish immigration from the eastern European shtetls pulverized traditional communal institutions, eviscerated the leadership of the Orthodox rabbinate, and by absorbing Jews atomistically into secular life, compelled them defensively into leftist political groups. Since the fifties there has been a renaissance of Orthodox Judaism, channeled largely through synagogues and parochial schools. Multiparty Israeli politics has given a disproportionately large share of power to the "religious parties." Similarly, in the United States, there has been not only a significant proportionate increase in number of Halacha-observant Jews (partly by persuasion and partly demography—that is, larger-size Orthodox families as well as due to the assimilation of secular Jews into the gentile world). Orthodoxy has gained in visibility and influences as Conservative Judaism, the largest Jewish denomination, has become stodgy and hesitant and Reform Judaism lost its vitality and became uncertain of its mission.

What the Orthodox renaissance has done—drawing on the scholarship of Scholem and Buber—is to reestablish contact with the spirituality and mysticism of the Jewish reformation of the seventeenth and eighteenth centuries. In this respect Orthodox Judaism runs parallel to the Catholic majority holding fast to the papal *magisterium* and to evangelical Protestantism.

Orthodox Judaism also resembles Catholicism in containing within it a coiled spring of homiletic dynamism that can potentially explode in any political direction. A key Jewish figure is Rabbi Irving Greenberg, a Ph.D. in American history from Harvard, for several years the venerated rabbi of an upscale Orthodox synagogue in the Riverdale section of the Bronx, New York, and now the organizer and leader of his own sectarian group, ostensibly committed to "religious educational research" but actually to a charismatic revolution in Judaism. His wife, Blu, is the leader of Orthodox feminism.

The volatility of the Judeo-Christian tradition of prophesy makes political categorization of the future course hazardous. "He shall decide for many peoples" and "My kingdom is not of this world" can be read in a variety of ways—and have been through the centuries. But in this theistic religion there is a venerable, complex, and dynamic tradition for the Right to draw on and in turn to be conditioned by. As long as Marxism with its intense secularism dominates leftist thought, the continued affiliation of the Right with the tradition of theistic religion is the more likely prospect.

The message of Augustine's *City of God*, written about A.D. 425, remains central to the Christian Right: "The heavenly city . . . while in its state of pilgrimage, avails itself of the peace of earth, and so far as it can without injuring faith and godliness . . . makes this earthly peace bear upon the peace of heaven." Such is the plasticity and volatility of the Judeo-Christian gospel that the Augustinian teaching can conceivably be incorporated into a Marxist Christianity, a liberation theology, but the more obvious and easiest accommodation is on the political Right.

The fourth intellectual tradition that the Right can draw on is formalism. By formalism is meant a body of ideas and symbols or a cultural structure which conditions behavior along preconceived lines. Formalism allows a greater or lesser degree of individual choice. But it sets up a conditioning or confining program that strongly influences or predetermines the ultimate choice that the individual will make.

Formalism accords intrinsic legitimacy to this conditioning structure of individual and group behavior. This is formalism's most distinctive characteristic as compared with relativism, which may acknowledge the powerful influence of a conditioning structure, but divests this structure of intrinsic legitimacy. The formalist view of the world grants a positive, prescriptive quality to cultural structures that control behavior. It not only perceives behavior as actually shaped by a body of ideas and symbols. It wants it to be conditioned in this manner, for the outcome will be deemed advantageous and as perpetuating beneficial and durable forces. Nor is this pragmatic justification sufficient; formalism believes in the intrinsic value of the system, program, or law itself.

Formalism believes in extended cultural and intellectual systems and that the discipline of conforming to those systems makes the individual or group involved embrace civilization and affirm truth.

Several familiar manifestations of twentieth-century rightist thought and action are actually aspects of formalist tradition. Among these are rationalism and classicism, semiotics and iconology, and legalism.

Rationalism and classicism cultivate refined intellectuality and humanist learning expressed in elaborate formulations of precise language. Rationalism and classicism reject emotional affects and mass culture and demotic privilege. Truth and civilization are disclosed by and essentially integral with language patterns. Durable patterns of thought and expression that were for the most part established in ancient Greece and Rome, Renaissance Italy, and baroque France form the core of rationalism and classicism.

Recondite imagery, complicated rhetoric, and allusions to venerable and esoteric motifs make rationalism and classicism an elite code. This formalist structuralism is normally accessible only through expensive education in highly selective schools, followed by long apprenticeship.

Rationalism and classicism disdain leftist ideology without having to engage in polemics against it. From the point of view of the rationalist and the classicist, the Left is automatically excluded from genuine intellectual concerns because its language, fraught with vague neo-Victorianisms, is alien to the elite code and its mode of experience is generally vulgar and hysterical.

The Left characteristically lays claim to moral traditions in Western civilization in order to capitalize on middle-class guilt. Rationalism and classicism, which indeed endorse a narrow and conventional ethic for the social and cultural elite, have moved the standards of legitimized intellectualizing and of authentic discourse to an alternative dimension, that of language and learning.

Obviously a substantial segment of the Right will always find in rationalism and classicism immediate inspiration and comfort. They comprise a subset of formalism that is immediately accessible to the Right, provided that they are willing to be associated with elitism and intellectual privilege.

Similarly with semiotics and iconology. Semiotics is the study of signs built into language, literature, art, and social gestures. Iconology is the study of themes and images in art history particularly as related to literary motifs. These scholarly pursuits extensively overlap, iconology being a vanguard discipline of the twenties and thirties, and semiotics playing the same role in the seventies and eighties.

Semiotics and iconology have indeed attracted leftist scholars who are eager to show how literary symbols and artistic images have been employed as ideological signification by the bourgeoisie in its allegedly hegemonic culture. Yet the formalist quality of these disciplines is essentially remote from Marxist interpretation. They speak of a world of symbol, metaphor, allusion, and illusion that constitutes continuing imaging of the prebourgeois aristocratic culture that Huizinga the modernist historian revealed as emerging in the late Middle Ages in Burgundian court culture. While a semiotics and iconology of bourgeois culture is feasible, such as in a study of advertising imagery or imperialist totems, the original and more substantial subject matter of these disciplines lies in the folio volumes and vast artworks of the baroque and earlier aristocratic worlds. Here there was a very thick formal culture of elaborate signification—to take relatively plebeian examples, the iconology of seventeenth-century wax and lead seals is itself a demanding and complex subject, as is numismatics. This former culture can be summoned up and cultivated to fix the Right in a venerable and durable structure infinitely distinct from the meretricious persiflage of leftist polemics.

The study of common law in the Anglo-American tradition is a third manifestation of formalism, to go along with rationalism and classicism, semiotics and iconology as sources for a rightist culture. The common law is by its nature formalist, since its only substantial quality is what has been called since the mid-fourteenth century the due process of the law found in writs, adversarial court procedure, judicial review, and lawyering. Legalism is the congealing of procedural and normative rationality—much more important than precedent—through the making of this miscellany into a social and cultural system.

The hallmark of the common law is not in legislative statutes, which are only an extraneous given—reflecting the frivolities of courtiers, the wiles of bureaucrats, and the scurvy ambitions of politicians—to be massaged and incorporated into the deployment of selectively accessible and coded language and in the signifying gestures of lawyering. Anglo-American legalism is as ritualized and rigidly formulary as the puberty rites of New Guinea natives.

Fully elaborated by the mid-fourteenth century in a culture that Cambridge historical anthropologist Alan Macfarlane has called "English individualism" but that might more properly be termed common law formalism, the psychology of legalism has undergone little change between a justice of common pleas in the reign of Edward III and Lord Denning, the distinguished chief judge of civil appeal in the 1970s. In the United States, in reaction against New Deal legal realism and Marxist critical legal studies, the University of Chicago Law School has become the center of legal formalism (joining up on the Right there with the Friedman, neo-Ricardian group of economists—indeed, they set up a joint program in law and economics).

We have seen that a product of this school, Justice Scalia, was appointed by President Reagan to the Supreme Court. Another brilliant spokesman for legal formalism was former University of Pennsylvania Law School professor Morris Arnold; he is now on the federal district court in Arkansas. He is an excellent medieval scholar as well as a distinguished jurist (and was also chairman of the Reagan reelection campaign in Arkansas). Arnold is able to bring a historical as well as theoretical understanding to his formulation of rightist legalism which stands prominently alongside other varieties of formalism as prospective foundations of rightist culture. Additional formalists appointed to the federal circuit court were Richard Posner, from Chicago, and Robert Bork, from Yale. Following Congress's rejection of Bork's elevation to the U.S. Supreme Court, he pursued a new career as a bestselling author.

The fifth intellectual tradition the Right can draw on is ethnic and national solidarity. Contemporary German sociologist Ernst Nolte terms this feeling "anti-transcendentalism," that is, an antileveling reaction against leftist practices that transcendentally supersede and break down group, ethnic, and national loyalties. Whether in Germany in the twenties or the United States in the nineties, there was a widespread feeling that the Left, welfare liberalism, and the circumstances of life in late-industrial society were leveling or transcending ethnic distinctions and community boundaries and undermining national traditions.

The consequences of this erosion were pervasive feelings of insecurity, a sense of being abandoned without a community to which a person can belong and from which to take sustenance. A process of atomization was taking place, driven by leftist ideology as well as by cultural changes derived from developments in technology and communications. It was feared that these ideological challenges and social changes, if undeflected, would destroy the vestiges of community life. That this leveling of community, which could destroy all roots as well as all ethnic and national communal identity, should be resisted is a pervasive and deeply felt conviction the Right can draw on. In the 1920s the German rightists were exclaiming that the *Gemeinschaft* (community) had to be protected from the *Gesellschaft* (society) and *Kultur* from *Zivilisation*. These were code words for an ethos protective of ethnic and national feeling. A similar sense of ethnic solidarity inspired the railings against affirmative action by Podhoretz in *Commentary* magazine. Kramer envisages modernism as an intellectual community threatened with dispersion by leftist activism in the cultural realm.

The phenomenal success of *Gone With the Wind*, both Margaret Mitchell's 1936 novel and the 1939 film made from it, must in large part be attributed to an "antitranscendental," antileveling nostalgia for cultural solidarity that decadent late capitalism and leftist ideology and politics alike seek to devastate. *Gone With the Wind* not uncritically celebrated an aristocratic Southern culture that becomes a representative sign for all the subcultures that have flourished and declined on the soil of the United States, leaving behind a sense of regretful and irreplaceable loss in younger generations deprived of this thick sustenance.

Those who are not privileged to be among the handful of actual descendants of the antebellum gentry of Georgia or South Carolina, the dreamed flower of the doomed Confederacy, can project through the novel and film their own vicarious participation in *Gone With the Wind*'s imaging of this superior if fragile culture, even if their own lost worlds were much less romantic and memorable—Irish peat-bog country, illiterate Sicilian villages, impoverished shtetls. The latter subcultures have also fallen victim to demotic and homogeneous leveling that the Left for its own purposes has foisted on us (with the help of later-twentieth-century communications and information technology) since the New Deal cultural earthquake of the late thirties, which was effected under the principal aegis of the metropolitan academic and intellectual crowd, the Trillings and their later epigones.

A sixth aspect of possible rightist tradition is the leadership principle, which does not appear in every right-wing movement, but when it does emerge, it does not fail to prove explosive. This principle derives from the belief that it is necessary to find a strong, charismatic leader on whom the lonely crowd of modern society can rely. A paternalistic figure that tends to his or her subjects, the leader will be the focal point of the communal feelings of society and he or she will demand and gain fervent loyalty. Not that there have not been strong leaders on the Left, who could assume, as in the case of Stalin, the shape of a cult of leadership, but by and large it has been the Right that has involved the führer principle, or the Il Duce figure, or the Churchillian savior of a democratic nation.

Sometimes this principle has served as a substitute for thought, in the absence of a coherent and elaborated rightist doctrine—just give absolute loyalty to the leader and forget about everybody else. The leadership principle can give emotional and unifying force to a broad array—and a perhaps not entirely reconcilable set—of rightist traditions. It can demand a personal commitment that is so overpowering that it either slowly or immediately overrides and all but eliminates other doctrines on the Right. The leadership principle is a stimulant, but it can also be a dangerous intoxicant.

Intoxication with the personal charisma of the führer is what happened in Germany in the thirties and early forties, and the absolutely horrendous consequences show the hazard of primary reliance on the leadership principle, unrestrained by other rightist traditions.

The British story under Winston Churchill from 1940 to 1945 is a very different one. By the summer of 1940 the British people were so fearfully desperate and so immediately inspired by Churchill's rhetoric and visage that in their condition of isolation and military weakness, they would have probably been willing to surrender all power to him and abandon their democratic institutions. Yet Churchill did not seek to create a dictatorial position for himself. He continued to practice democracy, which he once called the worst form of government until all others are considered. Churchill maintained legalistic formalism in war-torn Britain. He continued to respond traditionally to questions and criticism in the House of Commons—even in peacetime a lengthy and wearisome task for a British prime minister. And he took great pains to frame his call for national salvation in the language of rationalism and classicism, of which none was a greater master than he.

Churchill was very much a man of the Right. All through the thirties and forties he remained a vociferous opponent of colonial independence and the dismemberment of the British Empire. He favored welfare measures—indeed, he had been a pioneer in this area before World War I—but he was strongly opposed to socialist nationalization of industry. Churchill was a nephew of the then duke of Marlborough, in whose Blenheim Palace he was born. He professed unbounded admiration for the first duke of Marlborough of the early eighteenth century, whose biography he wrote. Yet that military hero, too, had remained loyal and subservient to elected civilian governments. And this was also Winston Churchill's political ideal, although he was personally arrogant and possessed dynamic qualities of leadership comparable to Hitler's.

Adolf Hitler took a very different road and led himself and the German people to damnation. Hitler's version of the leadership principle was totalitarian in that he required his military officers to swear absolute personal loyalty to him, superseding their loyalty to the German state. This significantly postponed—as Hitler foresaw—to mid-1944 the effort of some senior officers to assassinate him, with terrible consequences for Germans as well as others, even when the war had been irreparably lost by the summer of 1943. Hitler made the law courts just another personal element of tyranny and he polluted the German language, perhaps irretrievably, with his own coarse melodrama and hysteria. His leadership was such a personal one that the splendid German bureaucracy and brilliant general staff of the army could not function effectively, since all major and many minor decisions had to be carried back to him.

The leadership principle is a valuable tradition for the Right, and it is not easy to conceive of an effective rightist movement without its prominent display. But when deployed in virtual isolation, or even when it dwarfs other traditions we have discussed, the leadership principle becomes a dangerous one and one that is self-defeating for the best interests and higher purposes of the Right. On a modest scale this effect was exhibited in the presidency of Ronald Reagan. His personal leadership was exercised so effectively and popularly that the long-range ideological and political structures for the Right were not as well developed during his time in the White House as they could and should have been. If Churchill finally came to put too much stock in his own charisma, his humiliating repudiation by the British electorate in 1945 and his replacement as prime minister by socialist Clement Attlee ("a modest man," said Churchill, "and he has much to be modest about") taught him a salutary lesson, which he applied effectively when he returned to power in 1951. He worked to rebuild the Conservative Party for the long haul.

The seventh tradition of the Right has been militarism. In the Western world of the twentieth century, beginning in Germany, France, and England before the First World War and continuing in the United States into the 1980s and 1990s, the military has been on the Right. This has by no means always been the case in Western civilization.

In the eighteenth century the military in the Western world was often on the Left. After all, George Washington, who led the American Revolution, was a military man. In France the royal officer class went over in large numbers to join the French revolutionary state and give it almost incomparable military power, much to the astonishment and chagrin of monarchical regimes.

Napoleon Bonaparte, a Corsican aristocrat, and typical product of French military training under the auspices of the crown, was a member of this new officer class in the revolutionary state, who were sufficiently radical to give their loyalty to what appeared to be the wave of the future. Thus in the Age of Enlightenment the officer class did not necessarily support the Right; it had a reputation in fact for abandoning the old regime in the interest of government reform, and, if necessary, of revolution.

The military, in its pursuit of battlefield victory, could not afford to be sentimental about the disorders and incompetence of the old regime. In eighteenth-century Western society, the military—whether fighting on the American frontier or standing watch on the Rhine—was one professional group that had to be committed to the radical standards of rationality and efficiency. Decadent monarchy and privileged and effete aristocracy often stood in the way of military reform and maximal capability in war. Hence the younger and more ambitious of the officer class could be persuaded to join the forces of the revolutionary state. This also happened in Russia in 1917–21, when Trotsky formed the Red Army and, with the help of former czarist officers, overcame the enemies of the Soviet regime.

Yet, in the twentieth century, the tendency of the military in the transatlantic world has always been on the Right, to be associated with the privileged classes and rightist forces, to be hostile to the Left and socialist movements. This was true of England and France in World War I; of the German general staff—possibly the finest set of generals since Napoleon's marshals—in the Nazi era; of the French military during the Algerian revolution in the 1950s, when some refused to accept the French withdrawal from empire and rebelled against even their mentor Charles de Gaulle; and of the graduates of West Point, Annapolis, and the Air Force Academy in the Vietnam War and since.

Why are the military and military traditions associated with the Right? There appear to be two reasons for this phenomenon. First, the Right unequivocally accords legitimacy to war as a necessary expedient at critical moments, and accords to participation in war a superior moral quality when that war is pursued in a good cause. This tradition on the Right has a long history—dating back to Saint Augustine and the medieval church's preaching of a just war against its enemies. The Right has not believed in pacifism; it has unambiguously embraced military force as a moral necessity.

The second reason why the military have been in the transatlantic world almost unananimously on the Right is that the Left has, since the early years of the century, not only denounced the military as myrmidons of reaction and enemies of justice and the workers. It has also flirted with pacificism and denial of the legitimacy of military solutions. This intrinsic leftist hostility to war certainly gave an edge to agitation against the Vietnam War. This pacificism is enshrined for us in Francis Coppola's 1974 film *Apocalypse Now*, in which military iconology and semiotics are themselves depicted as evil. It is reflected in the ruthless vendetta in which the leftist media group pursued Gen. William Westmoreland and disgracefully denounced him as a liar and traitor in a notorious pseudodocumentary about the Vietnam War. It is reflected strongly in the way the transatlantic Left turned against Israel after its entirely merited military victories over the Arab world in 1967.

The Soviets took great advantage of the reflexive antimilitarism of the Left and in the sixties and seventies launched successive waves of disinformation "peace" campaigns against Western military preparedness while maintaining the largest army in the world. This military force was furthermore directed against efforts to liberalize the Soviet regimes, whether in Hungary in 1956, Czechoslovakia in 1968, or Poland in 1981. Only the Right from 1945 to 1990 was consistently clear-headed about the implications of Soviet military power. All the more reason why the military in the Western world is reflexively on the Right.

The eighth and final ingredient in the rightist tradition has been anti-Semitism. Like the leadership principle, this factor is not present in every rightist movement, but it is nevertheless common in right-wing thought. Anti-Semitism is not a universal but a frequent characteristic of the Right.

While Soviet Communism also drew on anti-Semitic traditions, and other leftist groups in the West have not entirely been free of anti-Semitism—for example, the British Labor Party and American populism—it is true that anti-Semitism has been mainly, while not exclusively, a rightist phenomenon in the twentieth century. The Holocaust and the universal recoil in horror in 1944–45 when the genocide of the Jews was fully revealed was therefore severely damaging to the Right. Nowadays, when Catholicism no longer denounces the Jews as Christ killers, when evangelical Protestants bask in the glow of Israeli triumphs as signals of the Second Coming, when wealthy American Jews contribute millions to the coffers of the Republican as well as the Democratic Party, and after Reagan was the most pro-Zionist president since the incomparable Truman (who as much as any other single person created the State of Israel in 1948), the long and dreadfully consequential embrace of anti-Semitism by the Right has begun to fade from history. Among intellectuals and writers in the transatlantic world, anti-Semitism has become more a function of the Left than the Right.

Modern anti-Semitism in the Western world dates from the 1880s. Aside from residual and waning Christian Judeophobia, there was very little of it in the nineteenth century before the last two decades. Indeed, the Victorian record on the Jewish question was a noble one. Then the Jews in the Western world made greater strides toward political and economic emancipation and cultural assimilation than at any previous time in the second Christian millennium. There were, however, only tiny minorities of Jews in the Western countries, and, as in the case of Italy and France, these minute minorities had in many instances lived there since the time of the Caesars, scarcely qualifying as recent immigrants. Furthermore the Jews were a learned, generally affluent, economically enterprising group with important contributions to make in professional, intellectual, and artistic life when they were given half a chance, and by the 1870s they were certainly given that.

In the 1870s Britain had a prime minister, Benjamin Disraeli, who, while converted as a child to the Church of England, went out of his way to remind everyone that he was not only a Jew ethnically but proud of it. In Disraeli's bestselling novels, written in the 1830s and 1840s before his entry into political life, the blond Christian hero and heroine are often saved by a swarthy, mysterious, immensely rich, and learned Jewish sage. Disraeli never repudiated this view of the role of the Jews in European life. Indeed, he acted upon it and applied it to himself. Not only did he take care that his dress and haircut would remind everyone that he was descended from Italian Sephardim who migrated to England in the eighteenth century (Disraeli's father was a distinguished literary critic and antiquary). When Disraeli as a prime minister needed funds to help Britain buy a controlling share in the Suez Canal, he borrowed the money from the most famous private Jewish bank in Europe, that of the Parisian Rothschilds. This act of chutzpah aroused little indignation about an international Jewish capitalist conspiracy, as would such an action thirty years later— or today. Indeed, Queen Victoria, the British aristocracy, and usually the majority of the British electorate alike found Disrali to be reliable and admirable.

The situation for Jews in the Western world changed radically in the period between the mid-eighties and the First World War. Anti-Semitism became endemic in European life and raged uncontrolled until pictures of Belsen and other death camps appeared in newspapers and newsreels in the summer of 1945 (since 1967 anti-Semitism has been on the rise again). There are five reasons for the rise of anti-Semitism at the turn of the century: the demographic, the cultural, the economic, the political, and the psychological.

Beginning in the 1880s millions of Jews poured westward out of the ghettos and shtetls of the czarist and Austro-Hungarian empires, especially from Russia, Poland, the Ukraine, and Austrian Galicia, impelled by discrimination, pogroms (in the case of Russia, state-supported), and economic distress. It is well known and frequently sentimentally celebrated that 3 million Jews went to the United States before a racist-influenced new immigration law in 1924 practically closed the doors. But at least a million Jews also went into Western Europe, particularly Germany, Austria proper, France, and Britain. While still remaining a small minority of the population, by the 1930s (there was another wave of Jewish westward immigration after World War I and the Bolshevik Revolution) there were some 450,000 Jews in Germany, 300,000 each in France and Britain, 190,000 in Austria, 40,000 in Italy, and 75,000 in Greece. The figures today inspire reflection: 30,000 in Western Germany, 15,000 in Austria, 10,000 in Greece. Britain's Jewish population is about the same as in 1930, France's Jewish population has risen to half a million because of the Algerian Jewish expulsion in the sixties. In 1939 there were 140,000 Jews in Holland, many of them from families that had been there since the seventeenth century. The Nazis killed 75 percent of the Dutch Jews. Of the 350,000 Jews in prewar Czechoslovakia, only 25,000 survived the war. Thus, in the majority of Western and Central European countries, the Final Solution appears to have been precisely that.

Of course, the Polish experience is most thought provoking: A onetime Jewish population of 3.3 million is now about 25,000 (3 million were killed by Nazi and Polish anti-Semitism in 1941–44, with a further emigration of most of the remaining Jews in the fifties to escape renewed anti-Semitism). There are now far more Hungarian and Romanian Jews in Israel than in their home countries. As far as can be statistically established, some 5.8 million Jews perished under Nazi rule.

It was not just the number of Jewish immigrants between 1885 and 1920 that raised the Jewish question. While the great majority of immigrant Jews were hardworking people with some minimal literacy, that they were often pointed to as disease- and crime-ridden was just what could have been—and often *was*—said of any group of slum dwellers.

The immensely popular American musical comedy *Fiddler on the Roof* and the general romanticization of their history in which American Jews indulge have cast a golden glow over life in the East European shtetl. But even the stories of Sholem Aleichem reflect the poverty and ignorance of Jewish life in the Russian empire. Far worse is the bitter picture in the realistic novels of the writer who used the pseudonym Mendele the Bookseller. Here, in a Zola-like vein, are accounts of a sordid world of unrelieved misery and superstition. That immigrants from such a society would arouse loathing and fear in Western society is only to be expected. What is amazing is how quickly the Jews successfully adapted to their new environment. A prime reason is that the great emigration from Eastern Europe came at a low ebb in the organizational capacity of the Jewish communities, unable to withstand the intrusions of the industrial revolution. The further shock of emigration devastated rabbinical leadership and communal institutions and allowed Jewish immigrants to assimilate in a generation or two to different ambient cultures.

Unfortunately for the Jews, social and behavioral science at the turn of the century were still so steeped in Victorian prejudices and rigidities that these simple sociological facts were not understood. Given the racist and Social Darwinist doctrine of the late nineteenth century, characteristics that were common to any impoverished and oppressed group were hypostasized into the belief that in evolutionary terms they were a degenerate, perpetually downscale race. An American psychologist around 1920, after examining hundreds of Jewish immigrants at Ellis Island, pronounced them genetically deficient in intelligence.

When, however, the new Jewish settlers proved themselves industrious and commercially skillful and provided tough economic competition for the European middle and working classes, this racist contempt was inflamed by economic jealousy. The members of this scurvy race, while of course degenerate, were also, it transpired, unfair competitors for jobs and wealth. Of course these prejudices were inconsistent—degenerate races should not be tough economic competition. But anti-Semitism was a set of irrational and inconsistent doctrines.

The position of the Jews deteriorated at the turn of the century, when European politicians facing democratic electorates sought to capitalize on exploiting the hatred and fear of the Jews. It is regrettable that Winston Churchill in his early political career was one of these—as home secretary (minister of the interior), he personally led police in a tumultuous raid on the alleged headquarters of alleged Jewish anarchists and gangsters in London (little was found).

It was in Germany, Austria, and France, however, that political anti-Semitism became an elaborate art. Long before Hitler's regime, anti-Semitism was a central theme in Viennese politics. In Vienna, which critic Karl Kraus prophetically called "the proving ground of the world's destruction," Mayor

Karl Lüger was elected on a mainly anti-Semitic platform in the 1890s. (In 1985, at a historical exhibition in Vienna, there was a celebratory display on Lüger, that didn't once mention that he was a prominent anti-Semite). In the years before World War I, young Adolf Hitler learned his anti-Semitic trade from the Viennese politicians. The final factor conducive to anti-Semitism was psychological. Jews played the role that demons and witches had in the seventeenth century. They were the scapegoats for the troubles that racked the Western world in the first half of the twentieth century. In an example of demonization and reification on a grand scale, Jews were held responsible for all the troubles that plagued war-torn and depression-ridden Europe.

Jewish capitalists, it was claimed in the popular press, manipulated stock markets and caused banks to fail. Jewish Communists conspired against governments and betrayed their countries to the Bolsheviks. The Jewish proletariat took jobs away from Christian workers. Middle-class Jews thronged and destabilized the learned professions. Jewish intellectuals were modernists who eroded traditional values. On the other hand, Jews maintained faith in a theistic religion that reason and science had long discredited intellectually. Jews were wanderers who had no country and therefore no patriotic soul. On the other hand, the Zionists were displacing the Arabs in Palestine from what was rightfully theirs. Jews were too ignorant and backward to be admitted to universities. If they had placed near the top in entrance exams, their admission had to be limited by narrow quotas lest they overrun academies and the learned professions. The Jews could do no good.

With these endemic and near universal feelings of hatred and resentment against Jews, it was not hard for Hitler to gain assent for removing "the Jewish bacillus infecting the life of people." "The annihilation of Jews," he said as early as 1922, "will be my first and foremost task." He kept his word.

When Hitler and his colleagues and followers began their persecution and then genocide, there was little intervention from anyone else, because gentile society as a whole was implicated in the Holocaust. Sixty years of anti-Semitism had made the Holocaust possible. If universal hatred is vented on a defenseless minority, persistently and consistently, nothing short of divine intervention will avoid holocaust. Some group of thugs and gangsters will sooner or later carry out the murders that are in everyone's mind to do. Capitalist and proletarian, rabbi and professor, elderly and children: The Jews all perished in unimaginable numbers in the Hitlerian gas chambers.

It was the greatest crime in human history, for which twentieth-century culture as a whole was responsible. It is to the eternal discredit of the Western

Right that it succumbed so easily to anti-Semitism—in some cases passionately and sincerely, in others cynically, in most simply recklessly and reflexively.

What is most amazing is how hardhearted Western people were in the early forties toward the pitiable Jewish victims of Nazism, even to children. The British under Churchill interned Jewish refugees as enemy aliens and potential spies and deported them to internment camps in the Quebec icefields. The American government persistently refused to admit Jewish refugees in significant numbers—not more than a handful were admitted during the early forties. One group was held in a prison camp in Oswego, New York. Although Canada was basically an empty country that desperately needed immigrants (Germans were intensively recruited after 1945), the title of a recent book—quoting a Canadian government official—aptly states Canadian immigration policy toward Jewish refugees: "None is too many."

To placate the Arabs, Palestine under British rule remained sealed to Jewish refugees above a paltry annual number. Incredibly, three overloaded ships of desperate Jewish refugees from Nazi Europe in 1942–44 were turned back by the British navy from landing their desperate cargo on Palestinian shores. One of these—the *Sturma*—sank off the coast of Turkey with five hundred dead and only two survivors. British and American military officials also refused to use planes to destroy railroads bringing Jewish victims to the Eastern European death camps. Until 1944 British and American government officials refused to authenticate fully reliable information on the Holocaust that was being smuggled out of Germany through Switzerland.

Such was the intensity of popular anti-Semitism in the United States in the early forties that not only was FDR afraid to help the Jewish victims of the Nazis, but even the top leaders of the Jewish community in the United States, Rabbi Stephen Wise of New York and Rabbi Abba Hillel Silver of Cleveland, were reluctant to protest American policy, especially immigration quotas, too loudly, lest anti-Semitism be stimulated. Wise and Silver and other establishment Jewish leaders made an occasional speech and delivered a few petitions to Washington. But they held no hunger strikes and conducted no sit-ins. It never entered their minds to chain themselves to the White House gate until President Roosevelt did something tangible to help their European brethren perishing daily in vast numbers in the death camps.

Wise and Silver were gentlemen who knew full well that in the Departments of State and Justice were droves of anti-Semitic graduates of Ivy

League colleges. The only noise about saving Jews was made by a right-wing Zionist agent (Hillel Cook, the nephew of a famous Israeli rabbi) who operated outside established American Jewish communal institutions. Cook stimulated the popular dramatist Ben Hecht to write a play about how the Jews were dying while the world looked on passively. (Hecht's play was considered in more refined Jewish circles to be melodramatic and in bad taste.)

The fact is that not even Zionists liked ghetto and shtetl Jews very much. The East European socialist Zionists who created Israel in the first half of the twentieth century were committed to the principle of creating a new Jew—secular, rational, close to the land, devoid of the unpalatable characteristics that anti-Semites in Europe had condemned. The philosopher of Labor Zionism was A. D. Gordon, who settled in Palestine in a large northern kibbutz in Galilee, around 1903. Gordon, a self-proclaimed disciple of Tolstoy, collected flora and fauna that have been reverentially preserved at Kibbutz Degania for inspection by today's puzzled American tourists (the Gordon natural history collection looks exactly like something from a bad American junior high school lab of the early twentieth century).

Working the land with their own hands in a socialist kibbutz, declared Gordon, would redeem Jews from centuries of putrid ghetto life and make them as healthy and powerful as in ancient times. Abandoning Yiddish, that accursed German medieval ghetto patois, for Hebrew, the clean language, patriarchal and prophetic, would also have a redeeming effect. King David and Bar Kochba would live again. This indeed happened, but lounging in the Tel Aviv Hilton today and watching Israeli capitalists and politicians dash by to make their deals brings one light-years away from the world of Gordon. In the early eighties the big thrust in kibbutzism was to install closed-circuit cable TV and VCRs to play films nightly for the bored kibbutzniks. Collecting flora and fauna as Gordon had was no longer enough for Jewish redemption.

The right-wing Zionists of the interwar era went so far from ghetto and shtetl culture as to develop an affinity for fascism. This group was led by the Polish intellectual Ze'ev Jabotinsky and became well known as the Revisionists. Menachem Begin came out of the Revisionist movement in Poland. He was a leader of the paramilitary Revisionist auxiliary, Betar, modeled consciously on the German storm troopers and Mussolini's fascist Blackshirts. (Revisionists are now called the Herut Party, the main component of the Likud coalition).

Jabotinsky and Begin welcomed the Nazis, who, they thought, would drive the Jews out of Europe to Palestine. They also admired the Nazis' militant and

terrorist tactics. The future belonged, they concluded, to fascist parties and terrorist groups, and they formed their own. This was useful during the worst
days of British rule, in 1943–47. The Irgun Zvi Leumi (Begin) and Stern Gang
(Yitzhak Shamir), underground terrorist organizations, grew out of the
Revisionist movement and its Betar military organization. They specialized in
taking reprisals against the callous British colonialists, who were still restricting Jewish immigration by hanging British army sergeants, assassinating diplomats, blowing up the British headquarters in the King David Hotel in
Jerusalem, and massacring Arab peasants.

One thing is clear about this Zionist world: Whether socialist or rightist,
the Zionists didn't like European Jews as they had been any more than gentile
anti-Semites did. Not genocide but redemption was their solution. Through
collective agriculture or terrorist movements new Jews would be created—as
they were. The Zionists agreed with anti-Semites that the European Jews were
indeed parasitical degenerates. But instead of exterminating them, the Zionists
believed that the European Jews could be thoroughly transformed.

An apologist for Hitler would say that this outcome was indeed along the
lines of one of Hitler's earlier proposals for solving the Jewish problem. He
wanted, like the Zionists, or at least rightist Zionists, to expel all Jews from
Europe. Only the uncooperative stance of the British in not opening the immigration doors to Palestine forced the Nazis to use a more violent solution. The
apologist would point out that Eichmann, the head Nazi exterminator in
Hungary, was still talking in 1944 about exchanging Jews for trucks and other
war matériel the Germans needed.

How sincere Hitler and Eichmann were in their migratory rather than
mortal proposals for solving the Jewish problem we shall never know; not even
Hitler and Eichmann themselves probably knew. It may have been just part of
the endless stream of manic Nazi chatter. It is true, however, that Roosevelt
and Churchill made no real effort to find out. They could not offend their
electorates by proposing to transport Jews from occupied Europe to the
United States or Palestine. To suggest that, the British felt, would have so
inflamed anti-Semitic sentiment as to damage the war effort. Hard as it is now
to believe it, there was a kernel of truth in this apology.

In addition to revulsion at the Holocaust, another reason for the decline
of anti-Semitism on the Right is that the old Jewish stereotype was eroded by
mid-century. Jews were either killed by the Nazis or transformed into muscular, bronzed, secular, victorious Israeli soldiers or into clean-visaged American
Jewish businesspeople and philanthropists. One way or another the old Jews

were gone. This was one of the least controversial changes of the twentieth century.

Rightist National Heritages The national variations in rightist political culture in the West are greater than the national differences on the Left. Drawing on the eight basic ingredients of rightist thought, characteristic rightist doctrines and movements have developed in the major countries of the West. While there is much in common among the rightist doctrines across national lines, each country has developed a distinctive blend of doctrines derived from the basic traditions. Because a sense of national community is itself central to rightist culture, the way in which each country has evolved its rightist traditions offers a significant degree of distinctiveness.

A second characteristic of rightist thought is that, like leftist thought, it has been subject to temporal variance—that is, it has flourished and waned at different periods. Rightist thought reached a peak of influence around 1939–40, and greatly declined, with the collapse of fascism, in 1944–45. In the late seventies a partial revival in the strength of rightist thinking occurred, although within a more limited set of ideas than in the thirties, and this rightist renaissance continued in the late eighties and nineties. In the academic and media worlds, rightist thought is not as powerful or influential as leftist ideology today, but it has shown renewed vigor and creativity in recent years.

In discussing modernism we pointed to the rightist intellectual group in Britain—centered on Eliot, Pound, and Wyndham Lewis—that constituted England's most astute rightist theorists of the interwar period. Their outlook was characterized by four main attitudes. The first of these was rationalism and classicism. The second was a desire to preserve not so much Christian tradition as the sense of hierarchy and stability that they derived from Christian culture. The third aspect of their rightist outlook was an outspoken anti-Semitism. Finally they were fervent anti-Communists aiming at the sustenance of group solidarity.

As high modernists they were not historicists, but they wished to fashion in education and elite culture a mythic content that contained ingredients recruited from the past, among which Augustinian theology and Dante's synthetic Christian humanism predominated. They saw themselves as defending the traditions of a timeless Western civilization against what they feared witnessing—namely a deracinated, overly technocratic, atomizing culture. We have noted the profound influence of this group on literature, criticism, the arts, and education.

Great efforts were made, especially in the United States, to sustain and propagate the essential messages of this group while disguising its more polemical rightist political teaching, and particularly its blatant anti-Semitism, which became sufficiently subliminal that the message of the Eliot group could be enunciated even by American Jewish humanists, who were fortunate enough to penetrate discriminatory screening and obtain posts in humanities departments.

This kind of refined intellectual rightism, the heritage of Eliot and Lewis and the others, is still strong at Oxbridge. While the anti-Semitic component was muted after the revelation of the Holocaust, it slowly revived after the Israeli victory in 1967 and has now become again quite blatant, thinly disguised as anti-Zionism. The austere pages of the *Times Literary Supplement* and the *London Review of Books* are replete with this humanistic neo-anti-Semitism. Eliot, Pound, and Lewis would have been delighted at the revival of this interwar era tradition.

A second rightist group in Britain consisted of Roman Catholics and their sympathizers. The most polemical members of this group were G. K. Chesterton and Hilaire Belloc, two very prolific journalists and historians writing in the first forty years of the twentieth century. Both lived long and productive lives. Chesterton and Belloc had two things to say, namely that the Middle Ages were the best time the world had ever known, since it was during that period when people were living under the happy guidance and rule of the Catholic Church; and that Jews were no good.

A more sophisticated member of the Catholic group was the novelist Evelyn Waugh, who was anti-Semitic as well, and very much committed to traditional Catholicism. But he was at the same time a novelist of extraordinary ingenuity. His most ambitious work, *Brideshead Revisited*, was published in 1945 and constitutes a lament for, and a panegyric upon, an old aristocratic Catholic family of the kind that had ruled England for centuries, but had become provincial, eccentric, and powerless after the Reformation as a result of its marginalization within English society and culture. Nevertheless, according to Waugh, these were the people who knew how to provide disinterested leadership, a decent ethic, and a fine balance in English life. Had old England only survived—this is the longing of *Brideshead Revisited*, which is one of the major political novels in the English language.

The phenomenal popularity of the skillful TV version of *Brideshead Revisited* in 1982 was not accidental. *Brideshead Revisited* is a passionate but rightist polemic from start to finish. Note who are the bad guys in Waugh's view of the world:

businessmen, Jews, Americans, and academics. These are the traitors to the venerable and decent Roman Catholic hierarchical heritage.

Another important English Catholic thinker was the historian Christopher Dawson, a prolific writer who published several books about the medieval church. He never received much attention in England and held only an adjunct position at a small university. To the surprise of Englishmen, however, his books gained many admirers in the United States. In 1952 he was appointed to a chair at Harvard University. Nathan Pusey, who was then the president of Harvard and a right-wing Christian, created a chair for Dawson, enabling him to spend the latter part of his career teaching college students in Cambridge, Massachusetts.

The central theme in Dawson's work is that the medieval world had achieved a synthesis between faith and reason under the beneficent rule of the Roman Catholic Church, which the modern world has lost. Modern culture polarizes faith and reason, which makes for confusion and alienation, and for which the solution lies in a return to Catholic existence and church rule. In a series of polemical, clever, and often very learned books, Dawson propounded this thesis—essentially the same as Chesterton's and Belloc's but stated in a much more refined and learned manner.

Dawson had another argument, however, which held that the future of Catholicism lay in what is now referred to as the Third World, namely, in Africa and Asia. It would be Asia and Africa that would bring about the revival of Catholic leadership in the world. As the twentieth century draws to a close, Dawson's estimate of the best prospects for the Roman church become ever more persuasive and sound.

A fringe member of this group, who, although not a Catholic, nevertheless thought in line with Catholicism, was Arnold Toynbee, the famous author of *A Study of History*. In the fifties, his six-volume work entered half the literate homes in America in the one-volume abridged edition promoted by the Book-of-the-Month Club. Toynbee was honored at just about every major American university, and his portrait graced the cover of *Time* magazine. (Henry Luce, the publisher of *Time*, had a devout Catholic wife, Clare Boothe Luce, the actress, dramatist, and congresswoman.)

One of Toynbee's numerous theses fitted in with the views of the British Catholic group. This was also the idea that remained most permanent and ubiquitous in his thought. The outcome of a civilization, Toynbee claimed, was to produce a religion. Identifying exactly thirty-one civilizations in history, he delineated their progressional pattern of rise and fall, and argued that in the course of their inevitable decline, civilizations did not fail to produce religion. Out of the dying civilization emerges a universal religion, which is the "chrysalis" of a new civilization. On the verge of its demise, the caterpillar transforms itself into a butterfly. In the course of its decline, the Roman Empire gave birth to Christianity. Toynbee, an authority on classical civilization, began with this example and found, he claimed, many other examples to fit this distinctive pattern of historical change.

In *Civilization on Trial*, which he published in 1953, Toynbee argued that such was the intrinsic quality of Christianity that this religion may be able to save Western civilization. Even though every civilization that the world has known hitherto has not been able to resist inevitable decline, Christianity, owing to its intrinsic superiority, will buttress and save Western civilization. This is a thesis in which Evelyn Waugh believed, and it is one in which also Christopher Dawson believed. It is also expressed by William Bennett, the conservative Republican spokesperson on values.

Toynbee incorporated a vigorous streak of anti-Semitism into his rightist opinion. As director of the prestigious Royal Institute for International Affairs in the twenties and thirties, he advocated the pro-Arab and anti-Zionist policy that was adopted—with fateful consequences for millions of European Jews— by the British government. Toynbee's Arabism could be seen as characteristic of his generation of Englishmen (it revived in the seventies and eighties.) It was not merely strategic, however, in the interests of British power and oil in the Middle East. It reflected a romantic attachment to the allegedly clean-limbed people of the desert, most romantically expressed in the idiosyncratic exploits of T. E. Lawrence in the region in World War I and the subsequent heading of the Transjordanian army by the white-mustached Englishman Sir John Bagot Glubb, known as Glubb Pasha. But Toynbee genuinely held Jews in contempt as well. In his *Study of History*, he dismisses Judaism as a "fossilized" religion, a synonym for the condition of degeneracy that European anti-Semites of his generation universally attributed to Jews. Catholic and rightist Christian thinkers of the interwar years summarily hated Jews both for religious and racial reasons. Toynbee belonged to this group.

Why was Catholic or proto-Catholic thought so vigorous on the British Right during the interwar years? The answer would seem to lie in basic demographics. Between the mid-nineteenth century and the First World War the proportion of Catholics almost doubled within the British population due to Irish immigration, large families, and conversions. Catholic thought reflected this new prominence of Roman Church members in the British population. A second factor was that Catholics, like Jews, only entered into British academia, the learned professions, journalism, and publishing in significant numbers at the turn of the century. The inevitable effort to construct a social and political theory that was partial to traditional Catholicism followed. More reflective Catholics, like David Knowles, who aimed at a more subtle doctrine and one more self-critical and sensitive to varying traditions within Catholicism, were ignored or suppressed.

Fascism was never a prominent doctrine in England, which had suffered too much in the First World War to become enthusiastic over militarism. The British were also not eager to embrace the leadership principle. Yet fascism did make some inroads. We have noted the doctrine of expressive blood trumpeted by D. H. Lawrence and Yeats. A tiny fascist movement per se emerged in the midst of the Great Depression of the thirties under the leadership of Sir Oswald Mosley, who led street demonstrations against Jewish shopkeepers and declared Hitler the savior of civilization. Mosley was related to the English aristocracy through marriage, and began his political career on the radical wing of the Labour Party, but soon found that the party was not sufficiently charismatic and that it lacked a leader. He declared himself to be the führer who would save England and ended up in prison. The English can be trusted not to have the boldness to produce serious fascism.

In the forties Neville Chamberlain, conservative prime minister from 1937 to 1940, was pilloried by the Left as a sympathizer with fascism. In fact Labour intellectuals even formed a book club, the Left Book Club, to darken Chamberlain's reputation. They published a new book every month in order to condemn Chamberlain as the one responsible for the crime of Munich, for the Second World War, the depression, and for the terrible appeasement of Hitler.

Neville Chamberlain actually had inclinations toward welfare liberalism. He came from Birmingham, where his father had been a radical mayor. Even though his father later became a prominent imperialist, Chamberlain remained loyal to his radical heritage from Birmingham. He became minister of health in the twenties, and made important contributions to the government system of health insurance. He was a man of peace who believed that the First World War had been the most futile and disastrous war of all time. He did not approve of Hitler even in the beginning, but he felt that Hitler would not last long, and that if he were appeased, by sacrificing, for example, a distant "little known" country like Czechoslovakia, he could be kept under control. Chamberlain expected that Hitler would shortly demonstrate he was a toothless tiger or would be overthrown by the German generals, and so the cataclysm of war would be prevented. Chamberlain foresaw that a Second World War would produce unprecedented massacre, and he tried to avoid it. He failed, but he was right about the portending catastrophe.

Chamberlain's policy was wrong. If England and France had gone to war in 1938 over Hitler's expansionist designs on Czechoslovakia, the German military, who at that time considered themselves unready to fight the Allies, might well have overthrown Hitler. At least Hitler, faced with internal opposition in the army and a determined Allied resistance, would have had to back down and thereby suffer a serious defeat. Chamberlain played the wrong card at Munich and capitulated to most of Hitler's demands, a move he almost immediately regretted when it became evident that not even a major concession could contain Hitler's expansionism.

Yet Chamberlain was withal a decent man. He was not as much of a rightist as Churchill, being unenthusiastic about the Empire and willing to give India a substantial measure of self-government, a change that Churchill adamantly—and for the moment successfully—opposed.

The darkening of Chamberlain's reputation by denigrating him as a fascist sympathizer; the repudiation of his successor Churchill by the British electorate in 1945; and the Labour government of 1945–51 and its introduction of a full-fledged welfare state with many socialist trimmings followed by the dismemberment of the Empire, were severe blows for the English Right. Even more crippling were the heavy income and inheritance taxes that the socialists imposed, fiscally ruining many gentry families that had for centuries been the backbone of British conservatism. Aristocrats could always survive—they could make advertisements or appear in commercials, join the diplomatic corps, or sell ice cream to tourists visiting their ancestral homes for two shillings a head. But it was tougher for the gentry.

Notwithstanding these setbacks and the fact that Jews now had occasionally to be admitted to clubs and universities, a revived rightist doctrine was slowly constituted in the late forties and fifties. In spite of the triumph of the Labour Party in 1945 and several socialist governments in the sixties and early seventies, this British right-wing movement remained steadfast and gained renewed political power in 1979 with Margaret Thatcher's election to office, followed by John Major in 1991.

First among the intellectual generators of the reinstated British rightist tradition was the philosopher R. G. Collingwood, who taught at Oxford University for thirty years. He was unique for his time in that he was the only holder of a professorship in philosophy in England who was not a disciple of Wittgenstein. He was in fact an idealist, who held that history was a perception. History does not consist of mundane facts, he claimed; it does not exist objectively. It is what we imagine our past to be. And we have the right to create an image of the past that is non-Marxist. No view of history can legitimately claim exclusive objectivity, and neither can Marxism. If history is a mental image of the past, then an image can be created that suits mainstream conservatism.

Collingwood, too, was a neomedievalist. He agreed with the Catholic group that the medieval world had achieved a fine integration and balance as well as a moral and religious structure, which prevented alienation and lent people a means for self-understanding. He advocated the return to this religion-centered order.

The second member of the conservative intellectual tradition in England was Herbert Butterfield, professor of modern history at Cambridge University in the forties and fifties. Largely forgotten now, in the fifties he was well known, and popular enough to go on lecture tours in the United States. Butterfield argues that there are legitimate points of view other than the liberal. The historian can find a sanction and a legitimacy for the Conservatives, the gentry, the Anglican Church (this, even though he was himself a Methodist)—in other words, for people other than the secular liberals. History is not a field that lends itself only to elaboration from the secular liberal perspective.

Second, Butterfield was a neo-Augustinian. His famous book, *Christianity and History,* based on a BBC lecture series, argued against applying absolute moral standards to history. What happens in history is not a struggle between the saints and the sinners, but rather a struggle among a lot of sinners. A conservative interpretation of history is one that recognizes that the City of God, as Augustine termed it, is inward, and that history consists of variants of the Earthly City—variants, that is, of partial people, of fallible people with partial ideas. It is a great mistake to write history as New Dealers like Arthur Schlesinger, Jr., or Henry Steele Commager did, interpreting it as the development of one righteous party. No one party and its history can represent justice in the past, since there is only a private morality that does not admit of such generalized, public representation. There is no public morality that can be accorded a historical triumph.

Among the more subtle and finely tuned statements of the rightist position in the bureaucratic, technological, and Keynesian world of postwar Britain were the novels of C. P. Snow. Originally a physicist and a Cambridge don, Charles Snow (later Lord Snow) became a leading manpower expert in the civil service during the war, and afterward one of the top corporate executives in Britain. His own experience thereby bridged the academic, bureaucratic, and corporate worlds. Snow's eleven-volume series of novels, entitled *Strangers and Brothers,* is concerned primarily with—to cite the titles of two of his novels—"the corridors of powers" and "the masters."

Writing in the nineteenth-century premodernist realist style, Snow reports through the eyes of his narrator, a prominent lawyer, how men and women in the circles of power react to the pressures of ambitions, crises, and moral concerns. Snow, perhaps under the influence of his wife, the accomplished novelist Pamela Hansford Johnson, was memorably effective at depicting the wives of powerful men, a special breed.

The message that Snow imparts is first that those in leadership positions and the learned professions are essentially decent and well-meaning people doing difficult and necessary jobs under great pressure. Some are able to function better than others; some deteriorate under the strain; a small minority become crooks of one sort or another. Later-twentieth-century society demands proportionately more from these men and women in the corridors of power than it can possibly provide in compensation of whatever kind.

The second theme, an especially conservative one, is that the pragmatists, the compromising bureaucrats, are not only necessary for an establishment (the term became popular in Britain around 1950) to function, but they are the most reliable types to entrust with power and wealth. The idealists, the romantics, and the rebels are interesting personalities (here again Snow is adept at portraying them, especially academic radicals), but in the end they are untrustworthy. They either crack under the strain or become dangerous and oppressive fanatics who ruin other people's lives.

The third message that Snow wishes to impart—and which he also propounded in expository fashion in a famous little book whose title, *The Two Cultures,* entered the language—is that to benefit from the new science and advanced technology there has to be an interactive and mutually understanding dialogue between science and traditional humanism. It is the humanists who are more at fault, Snow believes, for the chasm between the two cultures of the later twentieth century.

There are insightful subsidiary themes in Snow's novels: his ambiguous feelings about Cambridge, which appears as a mixture of the brilliant, the foolish, and the senile, adding up to a not-very-flattering composite picture; a prominent and very wealthy London Jewish family that comes close to serving the same function of saving the gentiles that Disraeli accorded to Jewish millionaire sages; and as a work of fiction his best effort—a study in the destruction of a marriage by the wife's schizophrenia, a highly convincing portrayal of extended psychological pain, yet hardly noticed by the critics.

Generally Snow's rightist fiction about the world of power was well received by critics in the late forties and fifties, but without enthusiasm after the sixties had imposed its leftist critique on the cultural world. He receives almost no critical attention nowadays, although the series continues to sell well.

An effort by the BBC in the early eighties to turn Snow's novels into a TV miniseries was an uncharacteristic disaster, failing by a large margin to capture the ambience and indeed obvious message of the novels. The TV characters came through as boring, tiresome, petty, and distinctly unpleasant people jabbering away at each other in overdecorated upper-middle-class rooms. That is just the opposite of the point Snow was making. He believed that the masters who inhabit the corridors of power are critically important because their decisions shape our lives in the current world of a bureaucratic, technological, Keynesian state. Superficially they may seem dull, even appear as stuffed shirts at a distance, but they are distinct personalities. They have deep passions both about power and love (which Snow recognizes as interrelated—the Freudian heritage is delicately prevalent in his work), and on the whole they are doing very difficult jobs in a socially beneficial manner. Their feelings run deep, and you cannot judge them by their public occasions. Whatever rewards they receive are relatively modest compared to the constant responsibilities and pressures that eat away at them. This conservative doctrine seemed to be beyond the comprehension of the TV producers. Indeed, it is a rightist rather than a leftist vision, and one more fashionable in the twenty years after the war (when Snow was writing) than since.

The heavyweight theorist on the Right in postwar Britain was Michael Oakeshott. Oakeshott became professor of political science at the London School of Economics in 1951, when he took over the chair of the pop-Marxist Harold Laski, the spokesman of the Labour Party. Much to everyone's surprise and to the annoyance of the leftist students, on Laski's retirement, the LSE trustees judiciously appointed a Conservative in his place. Oakeshott held this important chair of political theory from 1951 until 1969.

Oakeshott found that there are two kinds of political systems: *societas* (society) and *universitas* (the corporation). He is opposed to the corporate state, which tells people what to believe and how to behave. He contends that the good society is one in which there is as great a degree of personal freedom as possible. The state cannot provide the important things in life. It cannot, for example, endow a person with moral goodness or make him or her see the truth. It has to allow people to work out the processes of their lives by private negotiations and exchange. The state should be as noninterventionist as possible, and should allow for the greatest opportunity for small group institutions like the family and local government. This Augustinian message had already been sounded by Butterfield, but Oakeshott elaborated it in a particularly persuasive manner, stressing secular rather than theological arguments.

There is a strong Burkean tone to Oakeshott—that is, in many ways he can be considered a disciple of the late-eighteenth-century conservative thinker Edmund Burke. Oakeshott argues that law is of fundamental importance, not ethics. The state cannot impose a specific morality on people. What it can do is provide due process, a legal continuum, by which the rules of the game will be enforced. The rest is a personal matter, which must be effected in a legal framework. Oakeshott draws on the view of English law propounded in the 1890s by the great modernist pioneer Maitland, whose thought has been discussed in the first chapter. He had described the rise of due process in English law as the result of thousands upon thousands of individual choices rather than of a mandate imposed by the state.

Oakeshott favored a deregulated economy. The practices of the Labour Party were anathema to him. The welfare state, he concluded, took more than it gave: It destroyed people's lives, and eroded small group institutions. It deprived people of the opportunity of choice, and it overburdened the economy. Ever since the 1820s, leftist England had dreamed about the socialist state. The future had finally arrived, Oakeshott contended, and it didn't work.

A group of British political intellectuals who emerged in the late sixties and seventies were very much influenced by Oakeshott. One member of this group was Margaret Thatcher. Along with many other officers in her government, she was a disciple of Oakeshott, who, with some help from Butterfield and Collingwood, had reconstructed a distinctive rightist political theory.

The fact is, however, that another ingredient entered into Thatcherism beside Oakeshott's theory, namely a very strong neo-Ricardian component. Indeed, while Thatcherism put into practice to the greatest degree Oakeshott's political theory, the influences of Friedman and of American Reaganism were also very much present in the policies followed by Thatcher's government. This included a certain delight felt in humiliating people, particularly the unemployed of the old industrial towns of the north and people who are affiliated with the universities and with the more militant unions. This vengefulness directed at the poor, at university faculty and students, and at unions was a rightist revanche against welfare liberals.

A recent leader of the English rightist tradition was Maurice Cowling, a history professor and philosopher at Cambridge University. In the 1980s Cowling published two volumes advocating a return to what he called the "confessional state," by which he meant a state based on religious principles. According to Cowling the worst years in English history were 1828 and 1829. These were the two years during which the Anglican Church lost its monopoly, when civil rights were granted to Catholics and the more radical Protestants, and shortly after, to the Jews. Thereby the Church of England lost the monopoly it had enjoyed within the political system since the 1670s.

In textbooks of English history, the granting of civil rights to Catholics, Protestant dissenters, and Jews is conventionally regarded as one of the finest moments of English history, not, as Cowling assumes, its darkest. But for Cowling this was the period when the opportunity to achieve the union of church and state was lost. Cowling was trying to revive the ideas of the Oxford movement of the 1820s and 1830s, particularly those of John Henry (later Cardinal) Newman: a view of the state as joined together with the church in trying to attain a moral framework in society; a consistency of culture, morality and politics, merged in subjection to the Church of England. The influence of Eliot and Leavis is evident.

Understandably Cowling does not yet enjoy a large following, but nevertheless he and his colleagues at Peterhouse College in Cambridge effectively made known their point of view, which is very much an extreme rightist doctrine. This view lies far to the right of Thatcherism, and while Cowling professed that he had great admiration for Oakeshott, what he was arguing is a point of view that is closer to Continental fascism, particularly in the forms it assumed in Vichy France, Franco's Spain, and Mussolini's Italy, than to anything that belonged in the English tradition. Nor is Cowling's thought free of anti-Semitism. He has a very ambivalent attitude toward Chesterton and Belloc, and to their anti-Semitic diatribes.

Along with Cowling, the most original rightist theorist in Britain of the eighties was Roger Scruton, philosophy professor at the University of London, who belonged to a group of conservative philosophers advising Prime Minister Thatcher on public policy. Scruton does not hesitate to address leftist theorists in polemical fashion. He rejects *The Communist Manifesto* as "schoolboy history."

But his original contribution consists of arguing for the moral necessity of sexual restraint or "decency" in opposition to the sexual liberation of the sixties. Indeed, says Scruton, it is standards of decency and restraint that make sexual activity desirable. One is a function of the other. "There could be neither arousal, nor desire, nor the pleasures that pertain to them, without the presence, in the very heart of these responses, of the moral scruples which limit them." And these standards of restraint, this ethic of decency, are not bourgeois; they are classical, they are universal. They are propounded by the leading philosophers and the best writers in the history of Western culture. The so-called bourgeois standards of sexuality and the family are the universal moral standards essential to civilization, Scruton claims.

Historians of fascism frequently claim that the purest strain of fascist theory emerged in France. In Germany, Italy, and Spain, numerous idiosyncratic politics shaped fascism, but it was in France in the 1930s and early 1940s that a strong and genuine theoretical formulation of fascism occurred. The French Right and French fascism grew out of, or at least found their generative occasion in, the Dreyfus case which occurred at the beginning of the century. Dreyfus was a Jewish army captain who was railroaded by a group of anti-Semitic army officers, falsely convicted of treason, and sent to Devil's Island. Various liberals and Jews, including Marcel Proust and Émile Zola, came to his support, and eventually another trial showed that he had been the victim of false evidence, and he was eventually pardoned. The real traitor, a rightist officer, fled to England, and one of his accomplices committed suicide.

The Dreyfus controversy, which continued for a decade, produced an enormous public conflict, and the anti-Dreyfusards—those who felt that Dreyfus was guilty, and that even if he were shown to be innocent, he *should* have been guilty—marked the inception of pervasive right-wing sentiments in France. The opponents of Dreyfus were those who were deeply concerned about the advancement of secularism, the deconfessionalization of French education, the progress of the Left, the economic and social success of Jews, and the decline of church influence and clerical traditions.

Durkheim was their bogeyman. They found their spokesman in Charles Maurras, who remained the leading right-wing intellectual in France in the twenties and the thirties.

Maurras and his colleagues formed a hypernationalist movement called L'Action Française, which was to constitute the base of the French fascism of the thirties and forties. Maurras and his followers believed that French national honor was being betrayed by socialists, liberals, secularists, atheists, and Jews. They found that France had achieved glory under a strong centralized government, as well as a powerful elite, a vigorous war policy, and a homogeneous educational system that taught traditional Catholic values. The world was closing in on these native French traditions, corrupting France from within and weakening its military power. The "degenerate" Jews were taking over in political and academic life. France was losing its moral fiber and its family structure, and its native traditions were being eroded.

Essentially what Maurras and his followers wanted was a medieval revival. They envisaged a society bound together by a code that upheld Christian values if not clericalism, a code that emphasized the corporate community of citizens working harmoniously for the common good. When they looked at the Cathedral of Notre Dame they thought of the medieval guildsmen harmoniously working together, a hymn allegedly on their lips, to build what was a monument to Christian communal solidarity as much as it was a church dedicated to the Virgin Mary. Why could not this communal solidarity live again in France? Maurras and his followers were not antibusiness, but they expected capitalists to devote themselves to the public interest and only marginally to entrepreneurial profit taking. They wanted to recover the Victorian commitment to the nuclear family, and they wanted an educational system and curriculum that provided training in values, tradition, and citizenship rather than refinement of critical faculties. They disliked the party system in democracy, which in their view inculcated corruption and petty deals. They wanted political parties to stand for comprehensive sets of ideals, not subtle combinations of interests.

They saw Jews as the enemies of all aspects of this program: The Jews were anti-Christian, cosmopolites, profit takers, Communists, and political tricksters. Because of the fierce anti-Semitism of Maurras and his followers, and because they increasingly became sympathetic to Hitler as an alternative to the socialist leader Léon Blum, it is easy in retrospect to dismiss their program as inherently wrong and them as evil. Yet Maurras was propounding a program that was central to rightist traditions in this century and was intellectually the most persuasive form of fascism.

The Action Française group fought back vehemently against the Left through newspapers and journals, all of which were unmistakably and consistently anti-Semitic. They also employed militant action, not only holding huge public meetings but also forming paramilitary groups which undertook such activities as breaking up the meetings of leftists and attacking the offices of Left-wing newspapers. In spite of the sympathy L'Action Française felt toward the Roman Catholic Church, and despite the reciprocated sympathy of French bishops in the twenties and the thirties, the papacy condemned the organization in 1930 as excessively militant and violent. But, then, formal papal condemnation did not mean much in the French context. It was, in fact, a cover for clerical support of Maurras and his followers on the local level.

While the leftist Popular Front of Léon Blum took shape in 1936–38, and while the Spanish Civil War was going on, French intellectuals and politicians became more and more polarized. There was a growing feeling among the Right wing that it would be better to collaborate with the Germans and allow a German victory over France than to let the decadent, secular, leftist Third Republic win. In other words, many Frenchmen felt that the Third Republic was not worth saving, and that a German victory would at least prepare the way for a new kind of neo-Catholic French republic. This view prevailed in spite of the obvious fact that the Nazis were heathens and Hitler was no friend of the church. With this sentiment—strong in intellectual circles, among the youth, in the media, and in the French Catholic Church—it was not surprising that France's efforts to withstand the Germans in 1939 and 1940 present a feeble record.

The French army was at the outbreak of war in 1939 larger than the German. It was better armed, and had more tanks and more airplanes. The French army was, however, abysmally led. The generals who were responsible for stopping the German attack in May 1940 had been mostly trained in the empire. They were mostly used to fighting defenseless people in Algeria and Morocco and Vietnam, and in spite of their technological superiority, military technology was not put to full use. Some French officers were outright traitors, who agreed with L'Action Française in wishing for German victory.

Others were simply defeatist and exaggerated the power of the Germans. The media in English-speaking countries also at the time characteristically exaggerated German strength and accorded an aura of invincibility to the Nazi blitzkrieg ("lightning war"). Among French officers, a defeatist attitude was especially prominent. As a matter of fact, if the French had been able to hold and throw back the German attack in the spring of 1940, it is possible that the Germans would have had to sue for peace. Although the German army was very well trained and superbly led, it was a relatively small one and Hitler had no reserves in June 1940.

Still other Frenchmen in 1940 were simply foolish. The head of the French army locked himself up in a château in a Parisian suburb, to which there was not even a telephone connection. Messages had to be taken there by motorcycle. Why? He was an obtuse person who had learned military tactics in the empire in the twenties and stuck to them.

In any case the Germans won an easy victory. The French in the interwar years had built at huge expense an impressive string of fortifications, the Maginot Line, to defend against a German attack through Belgium, as in World War I. The German army simply moved at unprecedented speed around both ends of the Maginot Line, on one side along the coastline, and on the other through the Ardennes Forest. The French generals had convinced themselves that the German armored brigade could not move through the Ardennes. It is hard to see how the French came to this conclusion, because the French government had built an excellent paved road right through the forest. The German tanks rolled along as if on Sunday parade.

In spite of these disasters, however, the French army was not conclusively defeated. Still, it surrendered before it lost Paris. While in August and September 1914 the French had thrown back the Germans thirty miles from Paris, this time, in May and June 1940, when the Germans were not quite as close, the French republican government disintegrated and a new government, defeatist and to some extent pro-German in composition, surrendered on miserable terms. The desperate new British prime minister, Winston Churchill, flew to France and offered the French generals and politicians attractive terms for a political union with Britain if they would only keep fighting. The French navy, second in Europe only to the British, was completely intact and there were still French armies in the colonies—but to no avail.

Had it not been for Hitler's Aryan cast of mind, the war on the western front would have ended then and there in a complete Nazi triumph and the extinction of Western civilization. The British expeditionary force in France, which numbered a quarter of a million, was cut off and surrounded in the French port of Dunkirk. But Hitler convinced himself that if he were generous, the fellow-Saxon British would negotiate peace with him. He allowed most of the British army, although without their arms, to escape across the channel. This was the famous "miracle of Dunkirk."

After the humiliating defeat and harsh peace, France was broken into two parts. The northern part was ruled directly by the occupying Germans out of Paris, whereas the new rightist government ruled the south from the old spa town of Vichy, whose mineral water export—among many others—we still consume. The government was presided over by Marshal Henri Pétain (the hero of Verdun in World War I), and the prime minister was Pierre Laval. In Paris a group of very active collaborators readily appeared. They consisted of a large and vocal group of French Nazis basking under German protection and rule in 1941–44. The leading intellectual of the group was Pierre Drieu de la Rochelle, who was a disciple of Maurras, and a prominent critic and journalist. He advocated for the French a variant of German Nazism.

A leading novelist of the time was Louis-Fernand Céline, who specialized in foul-mouthed anti-Semitic diatribes. He immediately became the literary darling of the collaboration era. La Rochelle and Céline advocated a resurgence of French corporatist and clerical traditions under strong leadership, and above all they called not only for anti-Semitic legislation but for the extermination of Jews. In fact, they elaborated extensively on a vision of a possible holocaust.

Céline, whose novels are still read in French literature courses, is regarded by many critics today as one of the great French writers of the twentieth century. In such 1930s novels as *Death on the Installment Plan*, he was the first French novelist to write in the authentic voice of the working class and to exhibit their mind-set, which included militant anti-Semitism. Céline worked for two decades as a physician in an underfunded clinic in working-class sections of Paris. His evocation of the common man's discourse has a ring of authenticity. He is forerunner of the scatological rhetoric of later-twentieth-century fiction and film. Yet from a legal and ideological viewpoint he was a Jew persecutor and a Nazi collaborationist. At the end of the war he took refuge in Denmark, where he had hidden the proceeds of his bestselling novels in a secret bank account. He returned peacefully to Paris after a year.

The head of the Vichy government, Marshal Pétain, had been a great hero of the First World War, saving the French army in 1917 when it had mutinied. Widely respected, Pétain claimed that France was being punished by God because it had surrendered its noble and venerable religious, aristocratic, familial and work traditions. The Vichy government would restore the genuinely French way of life. Léon Blum and his colleagues were tried for treason and sent to concentration camps.

Since Pétain was old and feeble, the government was mostly run by Pierre Laval, who not only collaborated with the Nazis but sometimes even exceeded their demands. When the Germans ordered him to round up Jews, for example, he rounded up not only the adults but the children as well, even when he was not required to do so. Laval tried very hard to keep France staunchly on the German side. He was convinced that a permanent new European order had been created by Hitler and aimed to gain for France a prominent place in this order.

Vichy was opposed by the Free French, a group of French officials and soldiers who had fled overseas. These gathered around Charles De Gaulle in London. Only a colonel in 1940, de Gaulle had already achieved some celebrity by advocating a highly mobilized war strategy, a fast-moving war conducted mainly by tanks. It was mainly the German generals who had read his treatise. De Gaulle can be regarded as a centrist, a moderate conservative. He believed in strong government but was not clerical or anti-Semitic. He was intensely nationalist, was hostile to French fascists, and believed in restoring an effective republican order under a strong presidency. Above all he found it particularly important to create a France that was powerful on the international stage. De Gaulle's political vision was essentially Napoleonic.

After the Allied Liberation, in 1944, La Rochelle committed suicide, Laval was shot as a traitor, along with several hundred collaborators, Pétain was sent to prison for life, where he died, and Céline, after being held briefly by the Danish authorities, managed to continue his illustrious literary career. De Gaulle became the first president of the Fourth Republic, which office he soon gave up because he felt that the restored government, specifically the executive, was too weak. He returned to power, however, in the late fifties and created a new Fifth Republic, with a strong presidency and a constitution that France has preserved to this day.

By and large the French rightist tradition—Catholic, corporatist, anti-Semitic—died in August 1944, when de Gaulle and the Allies liberated Paris. The remnants of the prewar French rightist tradition are barely in existence today. The Gaullists have recently again regained power in France, but this is a group that is centrist and technocratic, and believe in a modernized France. While they advocate an aggressive, strong foreign policy, they are not rightists. The real French rightist tradition ended with the Second World War. The only rightist movement currently in existence belongs to the petit bourgeoisie, and goes back to the old clerical ideology that cherishes the family and the church and that is opposed to modernity, the Parisians, the intellectuals, and the Jews. This group is, however, now a relatively small one that managed to obtain only 8 percent of the votes in the last French elections.

In the 1930s, during the depression, there were two strong figures on the American Right. The first of these was Father Charles Coughlin, an eloquent, obstreperous priest in Detroit, who gave political sermons on the radio every Sunday. His sermons were fervently antisocialist, anti–New Deal, and anti-Semitic. He was particularly popular in Boston, as well as in some parts of Brooklyn. His point of view was very similar to that of the French fascists. Coughlin was eventually silenced by the Catholic hierarchy, not because the latter disagreed with his opinions but because he was gaining too much popular support.

The other right-wing figure was Huey Long, who emerged out of Louisiana populism and became the governor of that state. He was probably the only politician in the thirties who truly worried Franklin Roosevelt. Long appealed to the poor whites and, to some degree, also to the poor blacks of the South. There is a right-wing populist tradition in the United States that goes back to groups within the Democratic Party in the early years of the century, which had sought to forestall the modern world, find a way to redistribute wealth, and to provide for a right-wing welfare state, paradoxical as this may sound. Huey Long drew on this tradition, which contains fascist overtones. He was a brilliant orator and gained wide support. He was assassinated in a private quarrel in 1936.

The other allegedly right-wing figure in twentieth-century American history, one who has become extremely celebrated, was Senator Joseph McCarthy of Wisconsin. He has entered particularly into leftist demonology. The McCarthy "era" of the early fifties was a rather dark period, but it was not all that important, either in duration or in practice.

McCarthy was a cynical demagogue. When he was first elected to office in Wisconsin, it was actually as a left-winger and a populist. The year was 1950. He appraised the political tenor of the country. It was the period of the Cold War and the Communist takeover in China, which aroused fear and loathing. There was an increasing concern in this country about loyalty among the government staff, particularly in the State Department. McCarthy detected an opportunity there. He claimed that he had a list of more than three hundred traitors in the State Department. He never produced the list, of course, but he did make his political rounds generating extravagant accusations against people in the government as well as in the universities and the media. He ruined the public careers of some worthy government officials, again concentrating mostly on the State Department, but contrary to subsequent leftist mythology, his influence in the universities was relatively trivial. Only about a dozen faculty in the whole country lost their jobs owing to McCarthyite accusations. Of course McCarthy and his supporters fostered a repressively conservative atmosphere. Faculty leftists hunkered down and kept quiet until the storm passed. The most prominent refugee from McCarthyite accusation was the scholar of ancient history Moses Finley, who found refuge in Cambridge, England.

McCarthy's greatest influence was on Hollywood, where his followers succeeded in getting a group of actors, writers, and directors in film and TV blacklisted because they had allegedly belonged to Communist and other left-wing organizations in the 1930s. Among those who were blacklisted was the prolific screenwriter Dalton Trumbo. Trumbo was certainly on the far Left. In one of his films U.S. capitalism is symbolized by a truckload of toilet paper. Another McCarthy victim was the director Joseph Losey, who left the United States and continued his distinguished career in Britain and France. The president of the Screen Actors Guild, Ronald Reagan, soon welcomed the McCarthyite intervention in Hollywood.

McCarthy came along at the same time as television, and he received high visibility from this new technological dimension in U.S. life as well as constant attention from the press. But his actual period of flourishing was brief, certainly not more than the period between 1950 and 1955. In the summer of 1955, McCarthy was publicly disgraced when he accused the army of harboring Communists. His claims were shown in televised hearings to be fraudulent. The army hired Joseph N. Welch, a very skillful Boston attorney from one of the top law firms in the country, who publicly demolished the senator. McCarthy was censured by the Senate; two years later he was dead of cirrhosis.

There is no question that after the army hearings, the Republican Party establishment turned against McCarthy. Even though President Eisenhower never clearly denounced him, he had been working behind the scenes to undermine McCarthy. McCarthy was a Republican Huey Long. In both cases the wrong style had been adopted for the viability of the party system. Like Long, McCarthy was charismatic and uncontrollable. He would not heed the party, which made him a dangerous man, and he had to be brought down. The only respect in which McCarthy was clearly right-wing was that he was an anti-Communist. He was an opportunist who used some rightist rhetoric.

One of McCarthy's three chief assistants was Roy Cohn, who went on to have a controversial career as an attorney, culminating in his disbarment. Another was Robert Kennedy, who later achieved a considerable reputation on the Left and became attorney general and a candidate for the presidency, until he was assassinated by a PLO lunatic. The third was another young man named G. David Schine, who became a hotel executive in Florida and was never again heard from.

Senator McCarthy did do damage in American public life, but not so much by his coarse violation of civil rights and his actual ruination of the careers of government officials, academics, and media types. The long-range damage caused by his depredations lay in his becoming the scapegoat demon of the Left. Subsequently, in the late seventies and eighties, any effort to point to the hazardous penetration of Marxists into university departments and to the pop-Left ambience prevalent in much of the media was immediately denounced as McCarthyism, which was ipso facto undiscussably evil.

There is much controversy and discussion about Gen. Dwight Eisenhower and what it was that he actually believed in, but even after reading the vast corpus on the issue, one cannot be very certain. It is likely that Eisenhower was a moderate conservative, a centrist. There are many similarities between Eisenhower and De Gaulle, except that de Gaulle produced a larger and more glamorous show, as well as more noise, than Eisenhower. The latter was an easygoing man, who as president seemed to spend an inordinate amount of time on the golf course. Subsequently it has been claimed that he had a penetrating mind as well as phenomenal managerial skill, and that he always knew how to interpret events correctly as he played the fourteenth hole. His facility in government surpassed even his skill at his favorite sport, it is alleged.

As president from 1953 to 1961, Eisenhower was a centrist in domestic matters. He did not expand the welfare state or civil rights. On the other end, he did not shrink them either. He was very concerned about the American presence abroad. Yet he was a man of peace and refused to let the British and French return to imperialism and gunboat diplomacy during the Suez Crisis in 1956. He had a right-wing activist secretary of state, John Foster Dulles, and an equally activist and conspiratorial head of the CIA, Allen Dulles (his brother), another member of the same peculiar, devout Protestant family. It now appears likely that Eisenhower was using these people as foils, as lightning rods to satisfy right-wing sentiments, while actually controlling them, keeping them on a very short leash.

The Reagan administration was the long-range successor to the Eisenhower administration, and is in many ways similar to its predecessor. It pursued an incomparably more negative policy than Eisenhower's toward the institutions of the welfare state, but then, there was much more of a welfare state in the 1980s than there was in Eisenhower's time. The welfare state doubled, even tripled, during the Lyndon Johnson administration in the late sixties. Reagan cut it back by 10 or 20 percent—less than the 50 percent that had been the plan. The project of reducing the welfare state program by 50 percent may very well have been largely a matter of show, something the Reagan administration knew to be impossible to put into effect.

Both the Eisenhower and the Reagan administrations were moderately rightist-center in domestic matters, strongly nationalistic in foreign matters. In between on the conservative spectrum was the Nixon-Ford administration, which did nothing against the welfare state. The welfare state continued pretty well along the lines established under Lyndon Johnson, and, as a matter of fact, affirmative action was significantly expanded under Nixon and Ford. If affirmative action on behalf of women and minorities is a left-of-center policy, then the Nixon-Ford administration had its opportunistic strain.

Their foreign policy was nationalist. Kissinger, the opinionated former Harvard professor, taught and pursued an elaborate system of international power politics, envisioning himself a combination of Machiavelli and Talleyrand. Nevertheless, the Nixon government did withdraw from Vietnam, although under public pressure. Nixon and Kissinger may have withdrawn because public agitation over the matter was reaching uncontrollable intensity, but the fact is that it was this administration that terminated the divisive war.

The Nixon-Ford administration was ideologically on the Right, but pragmatic in its policy. The Reagan administration was both ideologically and practically more on the Right. It did little, however, to establish a permanent intellectual bastion on the Right. Reaganism drew more from academia than it supported and shaped a rightist following in universities. The crucial test for the Reagan and Bush administrations in the 1980s and early 1990s with respect to the cultural realm lay in the operation of the National Endowment for the Humanities, first under William Bennett and then Lynn Cheney. They held, respectively, Ph.D.'s in philosophy and literature, and their personal ideological stance was staunchly conservative. Both expressed criticism of university faculties overwhelmingly on the left.

During this long Republican tenure of the chairmanship of the NEH, representatives of the small minority of academic conservatives were summoned to Washington and given an unaccustomed role on the consultative commitees of academics that made final decisions on federal grants for research and education, an advantageous role these academics had been accorded neither before nor since. But otherwise there was no significant change in NEH policy. Federal support for academics of liberal Left or Marxist orientation, especially when they were on the faculties of Ivy League or other prestigious universities, continued as before. Toward the end of her tenure, Cheney appointed as the chairman of a national commission on a school history curriculum a strongly leftist scholar from a West Coast university, and later complained loudly when the commission's report was decidely leftist in orientation. What did she expect?

★   ★   ★

Four intellectuals in the Italian and Spanish world in the twenties and early thirties contributed to a right-wing philosophy. The first of these was the Spaniard José Ortega y Gasset, a philosopher whose most influential book was the 1928 *The Revolt of the Masses*. Ortega argues that civilization is a matter of and for the elite, and as Western civilization is absorbed by the masses—Ortega assumes that such an absorption on the part of the masses takes place—and as democracy takes over, civilization, that elitist flower, will be vulgarized, resulting in the establishment of popular dictatorships. A similar argument was used at the same time by Michael Rostovtzeff, an émigré anti-Communist classical scholar of great distinction who taught at Wisconsin and Yale, to explain the decline of the Roman Empire. Ortega y Gasset did not advocate popular dictatorship. To the contrary, he favored the preservation of the traditional elite culture as the great bulwark against the rule of the masses.

Another conservative believer in elites was Ortega's somewhat older contemporary Vilfredo Pareto. He died in 1923, one year after the fascist takeover in Italy. Pareto was an Italian aristocrat who spent the latter part of his long life teaching and writing in Switzerland. Originally a free-market liberal and a democrat, he came to believe in the falsity of liberal theory and sensed the grave danger to European civilization in the rise of Marxism. Although Pareto's style is far removed from Mussolini and the fascists, his is a strongly right-wing doctrine that could be and was used to justify the fascist takeover of Rome.

Pareto began as a civil engineer, and the engineering principle of equilibrium is highly visible in his sociological theory. Essentially Pareto's theory represents the views of Edmund Burke, the English conservative of the eighteenth century, reinterpreted and expressed through the medium of Durkheim's functionalist sociology.

Pareto has two main ideas: All societies, whatever their political form, are ruled by a small minority or elite, and social processes operate so that over time one elite is replaced by another. Liberal democracy is merely a facade for one kind of elite that dominates by guile and artifice (Class I elite). Other ruling groups dominate by force and bureaucratic mechanisms (Class II elite). The former is a more innovative elite; it is also more materialistic. There is obviously a flash of plausibility in Pareto's elite theory. The second leading idea in Pareto's writing won favor in the 1980s among rightist economic theorists in the United States. This is the view that whereas some human activities are rational or logical and some irrational, there is a tendency to logicalize irrational activity and make it seem logical. We must not fall into the dogma of the market economists, however, and overrationalize human activity. We must recognize the value and influence of irrationalism—emotional belief systems, for example—in politics and economics. The social utility of a belief or theory is not coincident with its scientific, demonstrable truth.

Whether this austere aristocrat and Mussolini the street hustler would have got on is doubtful but unquestionably Pareto's rightist sociology could be used to justify fascism, arguing that society is ruled in any case by an elite and democracy is a sham, and the highly emotional side of the fascist program— its symbolism and political mysticism—accorded with social reality and human nature. It is thoroughly human to be a fascist.

The Italian Benedetto Croce was an idealist philosopher arguing for historical Hegelianism against Marxism. With respect to politics itself Croce was centrist. Mussolini repeatedly tried to decorate him, and Croce consistently did not attend the ceremonies scheduled on his behalf. But Croce did argue against Marxism.

Finally, among the right-wing intellectuals of the Mediterranean world, there was Giovanni Gentile, who did attend Mussolini's ceremonies in order to receive his medals. Gentile argues for a corporatist Catholic state, which follows the lines of the precepts of French Fascists like Maurras and La Rochelle.

The Spanish general Francisco Franco was a right-wing Catholic militarist. There was indeed a fascist movement in Spain called Falange, a radical, militant organization that was everything a rightist organization could be, including anti-Semitism in its program in a country that could not boast of a significant Jewish population. (The Jews had been exiled from Spain in 1492.) The Falange supported Franco and his rightist military coup. Franco was a capable and clever man, whose aim was to disarm the anarchists as well as the Communists, to centralize the government and the economy, to recover the church's social influence in Spain and to regain the cultural life of the seventeenth century. Franco achieved everything he wanted. He was smart enough to keep Spain out of the war, in spite of Hitler's entreaties, so that the country could continue its political and cultural existence on more or less stable grounds.

Franco had two important problems. First, he could not figure out a means for industrializing Spain in a major way. Taking Spain culturally back to the age of the Bourbons did not provide a very efficient context for industrialization. Spaniards were praying and producing large families—none of which encouraged Franco's penchant for economic progress. Second, like most military dictators, Franco could not devise the means to perpetuate his regime. Eventually he gave in to the expedient of calling back the monarchy. After his death the monarchy reinstituted the liberal constitution Franco had sought to demolish.

In short, Spain went through tremendous turmoil between 1936 and the 1970s, and emerged from it approximately at the same point from which it had started. Now it is involved in the difficult tasks of modernizing industrially and absorbing twentieth-century culture, while trying to hold on to political unity.

The authoritative biography of Mussolini has been written by an Englishman, Dennis Mack Smith, which may say something about the dictator's reputation in his native country. Mack Smith, an Oxford professor, worked for thirty years on this book, which finally appeared in 1985. According to Mack Smith, Mussolini was a fraud and a nihilist.

Mussolini actually began his political career as an effective socialist editor. He faced stiff opposition for leadership of the socialist party and above all Mussolini wanted to be *Il Duce*, the leader. He was also impressed with the following gained by the rightist activist poet Gabriele D'Annunzio. So in 1918 Mussolini switched over to a rightist, extreme nationalist position, dedicated to saving Italy from Communism and Marxism, ending the rule of inept liberal democratic governments, and above all giving glory in the world to the long-suffering and depressed Italian people. The Italians fought on the Allied side in the First World War. They endured heavy losses at the hands of the Austrians, and the rich compensation of reallocated Austrian territory they anticipated at the Versailles Peace Conference was only modestly granted. The Italian people were very disappointed that all those lives had been lost for so little, and they were therefore susceptible to Mussolini's chauvinist rhetoric.

Mussolini gathered a group of discontented, demobilized veterans around him at a time when Italy was undergoing a deep depression. Under conditions of economic depression and national disappointment, Mussolini found it easy to gather a few thousand toughs and criminals, to clad them in black shirts, announce they were fascists, put on a Roman symbol, get on a train to Rome, and make a coup d'état. It is indicative of the nature of Italian fascism that the fascists arrived in Rome by train for their famous 1922 "March on Rome."

Mussolini was acceptable to the monarchy as well as to the church and to many industrialists. The Vatican, especially, welcomed him because he offered an alternative to the Left. There was a disorganized but rather strong leftist movement in Italy, against which Mussolini offered comfort. He talked grandly about the corporatist state but did very little to improve the Italian economy. His philosopher companions like Gentile, who read and drew on

French newspapers and journals to put together some ideas about what the aims of the new government would be, provided material for his eloquence. Aside from making long speeches from Roman balconies, Mussolini spent most of his time attending sporting events and indulging his insatiable appetite for women, food, and drink, and talked confusedly about the military glory and the Communist danger. His career was one big fraud from beginning to end.

Mussolini's worst flaw was that he began to believe his own propaganda. He actually persuaded himself that Italy was a rising industrial power, that it had one of the greatest armies in Europe. Then, he witnessed, in anguish, the rise of Hitler. If Hitler had not come along, it is just as possible that Mussolini would have remained a bizarre interlude in Italian history, and would eventually have died of overeating and syphilis. The episode would have passed as comic opera, had it not been for the advent of Hitler, with the kind of substance that had eluded Mussolini.

In 1938 Mussolini established the "pact of steel" with Hitler. Although his generals warned Mussolini that they had had a hard time fighting even the Ethiopians, let alone taking on the Allies, Mussolini did not heed them and blundered into war in 1940. The result was catastrophic. The Italian army could not even defeat the Greeks and the Yugoslavs. Mussolini was only kept in power by Hitler's support. Finally, in 1943, after the Allies had invaded Italy, even those closest to him forced his resignation. He was held in confinement in a winter resort, from which he was rescued by the German army, which established him in a puppet regime in Northern Italy. Finally, in the spring of 1945, the Italian Communist partisans found Mussolini, shot him and his current mistress, and strung them up by their heels in Milan.

Mussolini was a megalomaniacal poseur who left his country about as poor as he found it. During his regime there was some industrial advance in the north, which would have occurred in any case, and Italian design—given impetus by futurist art—moved to the front rank, where it has stayed. Aside from a few bombastic buildings in Rome, there was no other legacy of his regime. Italian economic growth began in the fifties, with critical assistance from the United States.

Finally, there was Juan Perón, the right-wing dictator of Argentina in the forties and early fifties, who returned to power for a year and a half in the seventies. In 1945 the gross national product of Argentina was equal to that of Canada. By 1980 it had about 50 percent of the GNP of Canada. Perón was largely responsible for that.

Perón was an army colonel who belonged to a group of officers who carried out a military coup and then did not know what to do with the government they had seized. Perón was a populist, and appropriately found support in the labor unions and the peasantry. It was his idea to redistribute wealth; his government created innumerable artificial jobs. Merely a bulwark against the Left, Perón was an extremely incompetent ruler. The only difference between him and Mussolini was that the Argentinian dictator had a very capable and determined wife—a former radio soap opera actress—who created a great image for herself among the people before she died of cancer. Eva Perón provided for much of the charismatic leadership during the early part of Perón's rule. Perón himself ruined the Argentinian economy and demoralized the people, from which neither has yet recovered.

Nazism and the Second World War The literature on Nazism is vast and, as may be expected, a substantial part of the output is in German. In the mid-sixties the Germans began to publish furiously on this subject, which they still continue to do. Among the conclusions drawn from this research on Nazism is that there was such a thing as an intellectual component of Nazism. There were intellectuals and academics, scholars as well as serious writers, who generated views that were incorporated into Nazism. More than simply producing ideas for Nazism, many of these intellectuals also took active part in Nazi operations, either in an official capacity or privately.

Among the most important intellectual contributors to the rise of Nazism was Oswald Spengler, a flamboyant critic and writer who was famous in the 1920s as the author of *The Decline of the West*, a nine-hundred-page volume published shortly after the First World War. The book became a bestseller not only in Germany, but in the 1930s in the English-speaking world as well. Spengler's name is not visible today, but between the two wars it was prominent. All civilizations go through an organic cycle, Spengler tells us, and Western civilization has fallen into its winter of discontent; only charismatic leadership can save it.

Ernst Jünger was probably the most reflective and thoughtful among Nazi theorists, and the most comprehensive. He became the court intellectual. During the Nazi occupation of Paris, he was the designated intermediary between the occupying powers and the French right-wing intellectuals. Jünger is assumed to have played a key role in persuading Gen. Dietrich von Choltitz, the German commander of Paris in 1944, not to burn the city as the Allies were approaching. This was Jünger's main contribution to culture. He was a good European. Jünger's theory runs along the line of cultural order that appealed to Eliot.

Stefan George, the prominent German poet of the twenties, was the center of a right-wing intellectual circle. He is still regarded as a major lyric poet, albeit with a strong political bent in the direction of fascism.

One of George's prime disciples was the flamboyant medievalist Ernst Kantorowicz, who enjoyed a wonderful career. His family, multimillionaire Prussian Jews, dominated the whiskey business. Kantorowicz was close to Hermann Göring, the number two Nazi, although, being a Jew, he had to withdraw from professorial duties in 1934—the Nuremberg Laws of 1935 put an end to the scholarly careers of Jews. However, he continued to live in Berlin until 1938 and to draw a salary. Finally he was persuaded by a prominent English academic who was visiting Berlin that his good fortune would not be long-lived and that he ought to leave Germany. He first went to Oxford, and, just as war broke out, to Berkeley.

Among Kantorowicz's many learned and imaginative volumes on medieval culture was a biography of the Hohenstaufen emperor Frederick II; indeed, this was his first book, and it created such a storm that it gained him a chair at a relatively young age. Young Kantorowicz's associations and opinions were extremely rightist; the book on Emperor Frederick has a swastika on the cover; it ends with a hysterical call for a new great leader to save Germany.

In 1951 Kantorowicz was forced to resign his professorship at Berkeley during the famous "loyalty oath" controversy. In the fifties the California legislature required that all professors in the state university system swear an oath to show their innocence of Communism. Kantorowicz refused to swear the oath, finding that it violated academic freedom. He said that he had shot many Communists in Berlin in 1918 and 1919, which was true, and that he did not feel obliged to prove his loyalty. But he was nevertheless forced to resign. He then became professor at the Institute of Advanced Study at Princeton, as well as the recipient of numerous academic honors. Beyond doubt Kantorowicz was a Nazi, as those who knew him personally could readily ascertain. Only the accident of his Jewish birth prevented Kantorowicz from ascending to the highest circles of the Nazi regime.

Percy Ernst Schramm, another important German medievalist, and probably the greatest medieval historian of the twentieth century, came from an old mercantile Hamburg family. He became an authority on medieval symbols of statecraft. He was certainly very closely involved with the Nazis, and was the official keeper of the war diaries of the German general staff. After the war, in 1952, he also published an edition of Hitler's table talk, a volume consisting of remarks Hitler made at dinner, presented with a rather laudatory introduction. One thing that must be admitted of Schramm is that he was unrepentant.

Another intellectual contributor to Nazism was Elisabeth Förster, Nietzche's sister and his literary executor. She illicitly made Nietzsche the prophet of Nazism, interpreting his work so as to make him an advocate of a race of Aryan supermen who transcended moral standards and were free to push everyone else around. She even corrupted the text of Nietzsche's writings to make this fascist message more unequivocal. The best scholarly opinion today is that while Nietzsche obviously had a repressive attitude toward women, and while he was sometimes careless in what he said, he was thinking of a transcendental group of intellectual, not physical or military supermen. Certainly Nietzsche was not a racist and he condemned his one-time colleague Richard Wagner for his anti-Semitic proclivity.

The philosopher Heidegger, who was a Nazi collaborator for many years, has been discussed in a previous chapter, as has the psychoanalyst Jung, who had a short-lived flirtation with the Nazis.

What was there in Nazism that attracted these intellectuals? First among the factors historians enumerate is that of cultural despair. The cited intellectuals felt, in other words, that the traditions of Western civilization, the *Kultur*—a German word which may be rendered as "culture" but nevertheless remains untranslatable for its implications—were being destroyed by the rise of the masses, by technology, and by Communism and socialism. The culture was on the ramparts, fighting for survival. Desperate times require desperate measures. They necessitated, so it seemed, the use of military force and the violent instruments of the state in order to repress the masses and bar the Communist tide. The intellectuals who joined the Nazis shared this desperate vision of the future of Western culture.

Second, the intellectuals were antidemocratic. They believed that liberal democratic republics at best produced mediocrity, as in the case of England and the United States, and at worst chaos and disgrace, as in the case of the Weimar Republic of the 1920s, which they saw as epitomizing the betrayal of German national interest. Democratic politics were corrupt politics. It consisted of mean little men selling public interest for personal gain. Against such ills the rule of an elite was needed, of learned, cultured people who were also physically superior, who were, in short, putative Nietzschean *overmen*, able to withstand the corruptions of democracy.

Thirdly, the Nazi intellectuals also shared the belief in the *führer Prinzip*, the leadership principle. In one way or another, each harbored visions of the great powerful leader who would be as charismatic and capable of controlling the masses as he would be able to activate the forces of the state in the interests of Western culture and national destiny. They shared a romantic faith in the advent of a leader in the great tradition of Charlemagne and Friedrich Barbarossa, the medieval German emperor. In his person, in his heart, mind, and body, this leader would be an expression of all that was best in Western culture and in the *Deutsches Volk*, the German people.

The fourth principle Nazi intellectuals commonly subscribed to was that of community and reintegration. They longed for an event that would reunite the German people, instead of being divisive, which was what democracy and socialism had been. Unification, reintegration, and community were the desiderata that were pitted against the concept of atomizing society. The latter was conceived of as disorienting, disunited, selfish, whereas the former would bring altruism, communality, unity, and join the people together in an endless chorus singing "Deutschland über Alles."

The intellectuals thought they saw these qualities in the Nazi movement in the late twenties and early thirties. But they were not naive; they did not believe that the Nazi party represented these ideas without qualification or without certain imperfections. Nevertheless they did think that Nazism, the National Socialist Party, could develop a program disseminating and putting to work the ideas described above, and, to varying degrees, they committed themselves to the rising movement of National Socialism.

These are the ideas that led intellectuals and scholars to support Nazism. What of the German people as a whole? Why did they in the elections of 1932 make Hitler the leader of the largest party in the German parliament? The extensive research on this issue shows that while Nazism appeared to have special strengths among lower-middle-class people and among Protestants rather than Catholics, support for Hitler was not class or group oriented. In roughly equal proportions Nazism gained adherents among all groups in German society. Support for Hitler in the early thirties appears to have been more a psychological than a sociological phenomenon.

Hitler and the Nazi movement capitalized, to be sure, on the economic miseries of the Weimar Republic, but, far more important, they exploited the frustrated yearning for respect and dignity of all those who believed that in politics and society they were held in contemptuous disregard. The German soldier who returned from the front in World War I and had difficulty obtain-

ing a job and keeping his head above water economically bore deep resent-
ments. What impressed him above all was the ingratitude of the government.
This experience accounts for the whining note that recurs constantly in these
accounts of postwar personal struggles.

The German people, who were accustomed to regarding themselves as the
salt of the earth who were supposed to dominate the twentieth century, found
that the material and moral basis for their lives seemed to have vanished. Their
indictment began to transcend purely political issues, and the suspicion grew
that something was corrupt and rotten throughout German society, that a
worm was not only eating away savings in the bank but also threatening to
undermine family life, religious convictions, and moral standards. Many of the
men who became activists in the Hitler movement were people who in normal
times would have left politics and public life strictly alone, asking nothing
more than to be allowed to rear their families and pursue their careers in tranquillity.

The inability of the liberal Weimar government to arouse confidence had
many causes, which are recited in all historical accounts of Nazism. There was
the onerous burden of its "responsibility" for accepting the excessively severe
terms of the Versailles Treaty, a myth that the republicans should have
attacked at every opportunity—instead they allowed it to work its slow poison. There was also the inability to deal effectively with the Communist-led
revolutions and strikes that plagued the government's early years. There were
inflation and the painful question of reparations to the Allies.

But above all there was a critical psychological factor: The Weimar government was completely unable to establish any mystique. Republicanism in
Germany had no roots, no traditions to which it could appeal. There were no
republican barricades in German history to which the government could hark
back: no republican songs, no slogans like Liberty, Equality, Fraternity. Indeed
all the German traditions ran counter to republicanism; the German Republic's
constitution was drafted at Weimar, but its capital was Prussian Berlin. The
proliferation of postwar political parties and the resulting practice of political
horse trading made the Weimar parliamentarians seem to be sordid political
hustlers performing continual sleight-of-hand tricks to stay in office, apparently striving for no higher goal than that of simply hanging on.

The frustrated idealism of the generation that had swallowed the exalted
shibboleths of wartime propaganda could not endure this spectacle. The
German bourgeois, who felt acutely their own insignificance, their own precarious hold on a livelihood, their own inadequacy at coping with defeat and the

depression, had no wish to see their own miserable struggles mirrored among the men who ruled Germany. The scorn that fell on the Weimar officials was an elaborate form of displaced self-hatred. The German people craved strong and confident leadership.

In contrast to the tired, confused men of the Weimar government, the stress on youth in Germany of the 1920s became an ideology in itself, something of a fetish in fact, which Hitler was to incorporate as part of the fascist image. German students, after the war as before it, sang paeans of praise to the *Volk*, the great German people, pure and simple in heart. Before the war the quest for the unspoiled *Volk* had produced activity of the sort that goes on anywhere when a people is in compulsive pursuit of its roots. Many folk songs had been resurrected for performance around campfires. Students had organized long hikes to explore the verdant beauties of pastoral Germany. Sports and gymnasiums were in fashion, and ancient pagan holidays like the feast of the summer solstice had been self-consciously celebrated. These quasi-mystical celebrations of the *Volk* all looked toward the great "spiritual revolution" that the students and young people were supposed to be preparing. The myth of a great German, or Aryan, race was already blossoming.

Anti-Semitism was the perfect foil for the neoromantic kind of political and social thought which characterized the youth groups. Before the war they had conducted soul-searching debates on whether or not Jews were themselves a *Volk*, and whether or not they could ever be sufficiently assimilated to become part of the German *Volk.* The verdict had been various, though in the main negative. Around the turn of the century a fierce debate had taken place on whether or not Jews could participate in the time-honored university practice of joining dueling societies, the question revolving around whether or not Jews had any honor to defend. Jews were excluded from most fraternities, and in some universities the creation of Jewish fraternities was looked upon as a provocative act. Periodically petitions would circulate in the classrooms, asking that Jews be excluded from government jobs and the professions.

But it was during the Weimar period that "the Jewish question" came to assume a kind of absolute prominence. The regeneration of the *Volk* had once been the main motivation of the "youth movement"; a number of its leaders had regarded the wrangle over Jews as merely an annoying distraction from the main task. They had wanted the self-consciousness of the German *Volk* to develop not merely negatively—that is, in opposition to Jews—but positively, through a rediscovery of roots, customs, and traditions.

During the Weimar period the old groups that had insisted on the importance of the folk dances, idyllic rambles in the countryside, and celebrations of festivals came to be regarded as naive and obsolete. They lost members to the more strident activist organizations. Anti-Semitism was no longer a subject for debate; it had become axiomatic, part of the dogma. The anti-Semitic obsession was exacerbated by general disrespect for the government, which was supposed to be riddled with Jews. Anti-Semitic riots became frequent in German universities in the 1920s.

The Nazis were infinitely rich and imaginative in symbolism, mythology, and pageantry. They had insignia, songs, slogans, salutes, and uniforms, the function of which was not so much to convince as to bewitch. The most famous symbol, the swastika, came from the Free Corps, a gang of terrorist army and navy officers who in 1918–19 assassinated Communists in Berlin, including Rosa Luxemburg. (Ernst Kantorowicz was a member of the Free Corps.) The red color of the Nazi flag came from socialism and the blood of soldiers. The salute came from Italian fascism and, according to legend at least, from ancient Rome. The fervent *Heil* came from beer halls and ancient public gatherings. When Hitler spoke on public stages—at the annual Nuremberg rallies, for example—the production trappings assaulted the senses as if they were part of a Hollywood extravaganza. The Nazi rallies were carefully choreographed and in the 1930s filmed by a woman director of genius, Leni Riefenstahl, nowadays much admired by feminists and filmmakers. Thousands of torches held aloft by devout youngsters from the Hitler Youth groups lined the routes of march, and Wagnerian music preceded the speeches.

Despite the essential paganism of Nazi philosophy, traditional religion was pressed into service, and Nazi speakers in small towns regularly found priests and Lutheran ministers sharing their platforms. The whole panoply of bourgeois fetishes was brought onto the political platform. The family, the sanctity of the home, and motherhood were invoked. (Hitler once promised an audience that under National Socialism every German girl would find a husband.) Politicians of other parties talked politics, but the Nazis talked about the whole man—his family, his fireside, his pocketbook, his vague aspirations to status and glory, his inchoate religious sentiments, his latent sense of decency.

Above all, Nazi speakers skillfully played on the deepest fears of German families: their fears of drowning in a Red bloodbath, of being unmanned, castrated by French imperialists, of losing golden-haired daughters to inferior races. (Julius Streicher, a fanatical early Hitler supporter, made his career as a journalist by "exposing" Jewish sexual crimes.) The Nazis tapped them all.

85

86

87

88

89

90

92

91

93

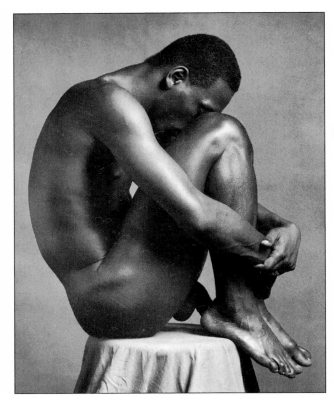

94

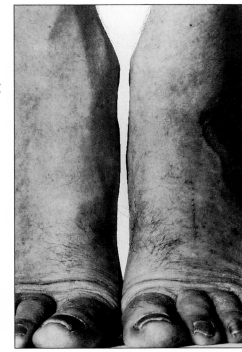

95

96

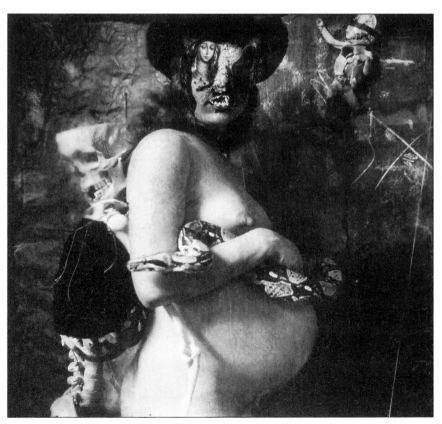

97

98

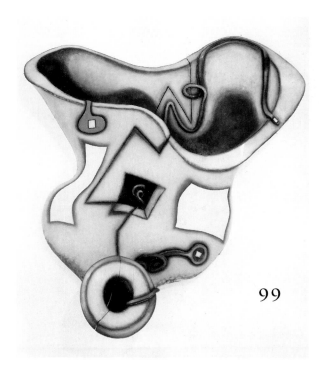

99

100

101

102

103

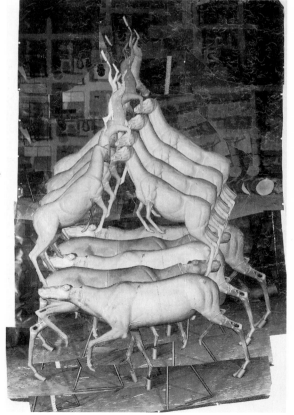

104

105

106

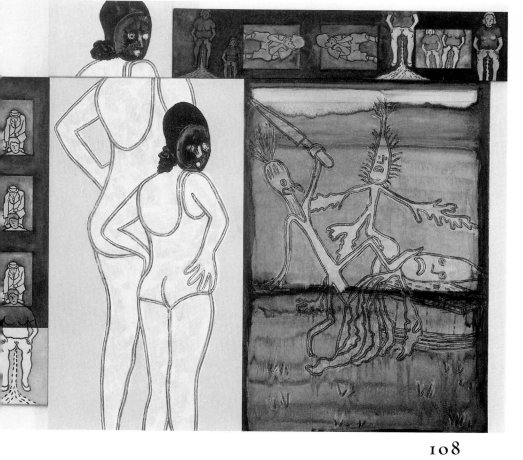

109

110

III

112

113

POSTMODERNISM PICTURE ESSAY

Postmodernism may be seen as a critique of the modernist notion of originality and spontaneity, as imitation and ridicule of modernist style, as a critique of historical narrative, as feminist theory, and as a reflection of multicultural diversity. Postmodernism began to emerge in the late sixties, with conceptual and performance art. Baldessari uses photographs to communicate relationship to the world through the media. He scrambles or spells words backwards to form new words. *Ashputtle*, the title for a series of photos on movies, is a wordplay. Performance artist Acconci has rubber balls thrown to him one at a time. He anticipates responding to the balls' impact and both shields himself and attempts to catch them, thereby positing a general adaptive situation of stress. Cindy Sherman is both the photographer and the actress-model in her series of femmes fatales. Here she poses and demonstrates the representations of women: in this case the housewife, who is both submissive and provocative. Prince appropriates images from magazine advertisements, here the Marlboro man, and reshoots them as his own. By making images again he makes them new. Graffiti art and cartoons became the expression for a young group of Americans who had used the subways and city walls as their canvas. Haitian-American Basquiat, basically untrained, quickly reached star status through the market-oriented establishment and through his own ability to express new ideas and images with bold gestures. German and Italian neo-expressionists broke the monopoly American artists had since World War II by exhibiting their monumental paintings of myths, allegory, and imagination. The Germans dealt with their past. Baselitz's heavily impastoed canvas with the figure hanging upside-down is a deconstructive process of healing for the artist. In the eighties Kiefer used elements of scorching and burning in his paintings to demonstrate the horrors of war and new beginnings. The Italian neoexpressionist Clemente, more lyrical and fanciful, explored Eastern and Western religions. Schnabel, an American, gained attention by using such unconventional textures as velvet for canvas, juxtaposed with broken plates and found objects such as antlers. Coplans's feet have a quality of the primordial and the primitive, of life's evolutionary processes and universal experience. Mapplethorpe's seated black male nude, more like the Greek classical idea of beauty, glorifies the male body. This homoerotic quality made him a highly controversial photographer. The video artist Viola explores regeneration and views of death and its meaning in his triptych. Witkin's photographs use actual models, often with physical abnormalities, and carnival freaks to explore sex, violence, and death. The body in Kiki Smith's work is always in process. Smith wants to represent the female body in a way that will take it out of female-male tradition and make it neutral and universal. Murray fragments her canvases with vibrant colors and forms. In the torso-shaped canvas, a navel with umbilical cord going down into the vagina is an image of unwanted pregnancy and the right to abortion. *The Bed* is a tribute Pepon makes to a black woman he considered his second mother, and to the spiritual richness she gave him. The lavish bedspread is made of hundreds of stitched souvenirs given in Puerto Rico at special celebrations. Trained in African carpentry, Puryear depicted a retreat or holy place, reflecting his desire for the primitive and spiritual. In *Public Opinion* Torres uses seven hundred pounds of cellophane-wrapped black-rod licorice candy of various sizes and invites the viewer to partake of the pile. Hirst shocks in a carnival-like installation with tanks of cows in sawed sections and pigs in formaldehyde solutions. One bisected pig is dragged back and forth by a mechanized track. More poignant than shocking is Nauman's animal pyramid, which was a model for an installation of a carousel going round and round with casts of dead animals. The infinite drone of Nauman's mechanism accentuates the finiteness of the dead animals. Beuys's *Terremoto* (earthquake) aims to recall early-twentieth-century Italian revolutionary politics. Whether mental or physical, an eruption would be followed by renewal. Holzer and Kruger use the consumer messages of the street—billboards, museum walls, neon signs—to address the connection between gender and marketplace. Holzer's installation created a "verbal sensorium" with texts appearing in columns of moving colored digitalized lights juxtaposed with texts carved into the tops of sarcophagi. Kruger's crucified nude and text aggressively attack the viewer. Applebroog's feminist work is more playful and spontaneous. In the postmodern era architecture and sculpture share many qualities. Sculptors may use the building materials of architecture and take on the problems of engineering their structures; architecture can be sculptural. Buildings create an environment, and site-specific sculpture, such as works by di Suvero and Serra, can complement the environment or be anti-environment, as Serra believes it should be. Both the technological process of the building and its sculptural qualities are evident in I. M. Pei's Rock and Roll Museum. Johnson's sculptural Gate House makes reference to German expressionist fantasy architecture. Graves uses quotations from historical styles and color to give levels of meaning to his buildings.

While other parties spoke of interest and expediency, the Nazis spoke of blood and race and thus summoned up what Joseph Conrad once called "fierce mouthings from prehistoric ages." The mysterious and formidable powers of ancient and other rituals, of "blood" and "soil," were constantly evoked by the Nazis.

This kind of appeal served the purpose of making National Socialism seem very much more than a mere political party. Hitler never liked the word "party." He led, he said, a "movement" that was in fact nothing less than the efflorescence of the ancient Aryan soul. He was no scurvy politician. He did not *represent* any group or individual, he claimed; rather he *embodied* the essence of German man. That was the secret of the Nazi leadership principle. It enabled Hitler to boast, years after he had come to power, that he was like a tree rooted in the people, deriving his existence and his sustenance from them. According to this formulation, Hitler was nothing less than Barbarossa, the German King Arthur, the once and future king who wakes now and then in the course of history and rouses his slumbering people, summoning them to their destiny and glory. During the Weimar years the Nazis appropriated all the best German myths.

Millions of Germans echoed Joseph Goebbels, Hitler's propaganda minister, who wrote in his diary, "Adolf Hitler, I love you because you are both great and simple." In the 1870s the historian Jacob Burckhardt, a friend of Nietzsche, had warned against the coming of the terrible simplifiers of the twentieth century. The warning was prophetic. Hitler was the most terrible simplifier of all. Hitler promised the German people that under National Socialism, Germany would again enjoy wealth and power. The irreconcilable antagonisms between bankers and ditchdiggers would be reconciled. When economists or generals produced blueprints of insurmountable obstacles, Hitler said to hell with them all. Versailles had produced maps of Germany's borders, but they had only to be torn up. Hitler recognized no borders. All obstacles could be effaced through struggle, through a determined effort of the will. The Nazi ascent to power was "the triumph of the will." Any obstacle could be surmounted by will. The German army could invade Russia in June of 1941 without a supply of winter clothing and be in Moscow before the snow fell. All it took was a supreme act of will.

This philosophy conformed exactly to Hitler's own experience. From a penniless derelict at the Vienna Home for Men he had risen to be chancellor of Germany. Struggle, effort, and willpower were at the center of Hitler's political creed. He impressed the exaltation of struggle on his followers and disciples. His was a philosophy of self-reliance applied collectively to the German people, the supposed Aryan race. It declared directly and brutally that there were no barriers, no anonymous and transcendent powers to limit and curb human potential. To still any final doubts, Hitler confided to his followers that they were part of a Nietzschean super-race, that their triumph was preordained. German man was Prometheus unbound, and conquest was the test of virtue.

"That man for chancellor? I'll make him a postmaster and he can lick stamps with my head on them," old President Hindenburg is reputed to have said after his first meeting with Hitler in August 1932. But within two years Hitler and the Nazis had carried out a *Gleichschaltung* ("coordination"), a euphemism for state terrorism that eliminated all effective opposition. The only limits on the power of the Nazi dictatorship were internal to the regime itself—the constant struggles for power and privilege among party factions, the army, and the civil service.

At 8:00 P.M. on August 31, 1939, the German army faked a Polish attack on a German radio station. At dawn on September 1, German guns began to fire on Poland. Britain's Chamberlain government characteristically delayed sending an ultimatum to Berlin until the morning of September 3. The ultimatum expired that day at 11:00 A.M., and Britain at once declared war on Germany. France declared war on Germany at 5:00 in the afternoon.

The military struggle that began with Germany's Polish campaign was to reach a magnitude undreamed of by the diplomats of the interwar era or even generals of World War I. Tens of millions of men were to be engaged in campaigns in Europe, on the Asian mainland, on scores of Pacific islands, in North Africa, on the oceans, and in the air over much of the world. The amount of strategic materials produced and expended and the number of civilian and military casualties suffered would have seemed absolutely beyond the powers of the nations of the 1930s to survive.

Yet if the taking of human life can ever be justified, the Second World War was a just one—it prevented Europe, and perhaps the world, from falling under Nazi control. It must be remembered that in 1940 Hitler's triumph seemed highly likely. If Britain, like France, had betrayed its heritage and made peace with Hitler, the end of Western civilization might have been the result. It is to the eternal credit of the British that, rallied by a conservative from one of the first families of the British aristocracy, they chose to fight on, alone and against seemingly hopeless odds. As Churchill said, this was his country's "finest hour." What Churchill said of the RAF fighter pilots in the Battle of

Britain can be said of Great Britain's role in World War II: Never have so many owed so much to so few.

The main consequence of the Second World War was that it brought to a climax the trend that had begun in the First: Western Europe's power and influence in the world declined, and global leadership passed to the Soviet Union and the United States. In 1945, Germany was in ashes, Japan thoroughly beaten, Britain exhausted and impoverished, France and Italy confused and demoralized. Victory lay with the United States and the Soviet Union. They were to be the superpowers of the postwar world.

The Second World War was called by Arthur Koestler, the ex-Communist novelist, a struggle "between a lie and a half-lie." More accurately, it has been called the last good war, the last war in which the West, and particularly the British and the Americans, had no doubt who was in the right. Italy entered the war in May of 1940 to participate in the spoils of Europe that were accruing to Hitler. Japan, which had come under the rule of an expansionist military clique in the 1930s, entered the war with the bombing of Pearl Harbor, "the day of infamy," on December 7, 1941.

Japan entered the war for two reasons. First, their German allies urged them to do so, so as to distract the Americans, who had been giving extensive aid to Britain since 1939 and were thought by Hitler to be certain to come into the war sooner or later. Secondly, Japan's military expansion in China as well as Japan's intention to dominate the East Asian economy were opposed by the Roosevelt government. In retrospect Roosevelt's judgment was laughable: By preventing Japan from taking control of China, he prepared the way for the Maoist Communists to do so in 1948. And Japan now dominates much more than the East Asian economy—good chunks of the U.S. economy as well. The Japanese did not seriously believe that they could defeat the Americans and the British. They aimed at getting spectacular early victories, which they did, and then holding on while Hitler won at least a negotiated peace in Europe. The Japanese were wrong about the German military capability, and they underrated the Americans. At the Battle of Midway in May of 1942, the Americans—helped by phenomenal good luck—so badly crippled the Japanese fleet that the Japanese were immediately put on the defensive and slowly forced to yield their conquests in a half-forgotten war of incredible savagery.

The European war was the greatest military struggle in history. After the surrender of France in June 1940, Hitler ruled a united Europe from Warsaw to the Channel Islands. While there were pockets of bitter resistance, especially in Holland and Denmark, the great majority of European people readily accommodated themselves to Hitler's New Order. Hitler offered a generous peace to the British, allowing their defeated army to escape from Dunkirk, France, and then promising Churchill that Britain could retain its Empire (and even get pieces of French overseas territory) if Britain would make peace and allow Hitler unimpeded to start his crusade against Bolshevik Russia. Although Churchill's advisers informed him explicitly that Britain's economic position would be ruined by a protracted war, Churchill told the Parliament and people he would never surrender and the British should never make peace with Hitler.

Frustrated in his plan to divide the world among the two Saxon races, Hitler turned his attention to Stalinist Russia, and his armored divisions plunged into the Soviet heartland in June of 1941. Having purged and murdered his generals in 1938, Stalin was in no shape to fight the German army. Even puny Finland had been a formidable foe for the Red Army in a war during 1939–40. Stalin, much more appeasing of Hitler than Chamberlain had ever been, desperately sought to forestall war by shipping immense quantities of oil and metal to Germany. Even when war began, Stalin was indecisive for several weeks.

The Germans were within sight of Moscow and already fighting in the suburbs of Leningrad when the Russian winter descended unusually early in late October 1941, and the advance came to a halt. The Germans had expected an early blitzkrieg victory as in France; they were not prepared for a winter conflict.

Initially many Soviet minorities, especially the Ukrainian peasants who had suffered so terribly at Stalin's hands, welcomed the German army, but Nazi rule turned out to be even more savage and bloody than Communist rule, and the Soviet peoples rallied behind Stalin in what is known in Russia as the Great Patriotic War. Under the leadership of General (later Marshal) Andrei Zhukov and other young generals who had learned their trade on the field of battle, the Russians fought back, although suffering incredible losses—so many, in fact, that neither the Soviet nor the subsequent Russian government ever revealed how many soldiers it lost in World War II: The figure is assuredly in excess of ten million. With tremendous national zeal and aid from the United States, the Soviet army slowly gained the upper hand. In the winter 1942–43, an army of six hundrd thousand Germans was wiped out at Stalingrad on the Volga. In July of 1943, the Battle of Kursk, the largest tank battle in history (until the Battle of the Golan Heights in 1973), fought on the central plains near Minsk, was a draw but the Germans could not replace the devastating losses to their vaunted armored brigade. Germany was now a crippled giant, and it was only a matter of time before German resistance would collapse.

Western Allied victories in North Africa and Italy were of modest consequence compared to the Soviet triumph. Finally the Allies invaded Normandy, France, on June 6, 1944, liberated Paris by August and pushed on to the Rhine. The Allied leaders and Stalin had agreed to accept only unconditional surrender, so Hitler and the Nazis fought on, hoping some miracle would save them. (As a matter of fact, if the development of the ballistic missile—the V-2—and jet fighter by the Germans had come a year earlier and German physicists had made an atom bomb, the outcome might have been different.) German cities were leveled, ten million Germans were killed—eight million on the battlefield or in Soviet prison camps (the Germans on their side also let Soviet prisoners starve to death) and two million civilians—before Hitler perished in his bunker under the Berlin Chancellery in April 1945.

The German defeat was by no means inevitable. Not only did Hitler come close to getting operative a ballistic missile (intra- if not intercontinental) with a possible atomic warhead. If he had not waited until 1943 to mobilize fully German industry and manpower, the war might have ended in his favor or at least in a forced negotiated peace. But Hitler had promised the German people in 1939 that the war would not be hard on them, and until the middle of 1943— when he turned over industrial production to a brilliant engineer and manager, the architect Albert Speer—he pretended that the war was not interfering with German consumption of Volkswagens and sauerbraten. This was his great error. Exterminating millions of Jewish skilled workers whom Speer badly needed in his slave labor factories was also severely damaging to the German war effort.

One thing Hitler had in abundance—a marvelous collection of superior generals, such as Erwin Rommel, who fought the Allies in North Africa to a standstill for two years with inferior armaments and personnel, and Heinz Guderian, perhaps the best tank commander in history, who rolled up the French defenses in May 1940. The British lacked a first-rate general in the war (Bernard Montgomery was largely a PR stunt); the Americans had only one, George S. Patton, who was unfortunately something of a psychotic paranoiac; and the Russians, three or four. The Japanese had a naval commander of genius, Admiral Yamamoto, who planned and executed the Pearl Harbor attack, as well as some very good generals.

What the Allies had was the inexhaustible supply of Russian manpower and the incomparable dynamism of U.S. industrial production. Even great generals could not overcome these long odds—Hitler, Mussolini, and the Japanese leaders all greatly underrated American military potential because they could not extrapolate from a depressed American industry to its full potential, and because in any case they believed that Americans were too soft and peaceful a people to maximize their military capacity. By the end of 1942 it was evident the fascist powers had made a fatal error.

Fascism and Modernism As historians look back at the wild events and carnage in Germany, Italy, France, Spain, and also Japan in the thirties and forties, a historiographical debate has raged for three decades as to what was the general pattern that occurred in that time and place: What exactly was fascism?

The term fascism is derived from *fasces,* the double-headed ax that was a symbol of state power in the Roman Empire and that Mussolini took as the symbol of his movement. A skeptical nominalist point of view on fascism holds that the term is applicable only to Mussolini and his black-shirted followers. There are too many differences, it is said, from what was going on in other countries to use the term "fascism" generically. Hitler and his followers, for instance, called themselves National Socialists (abbreviated as Nazis); fascism had no official standing as a term in Germany. A second view of fascism holds that there never was a genuine ideology of that name anywhere. In various countries in the thirties and forties particular groups of militarists, gangsters, and terrorists sought power. These criminal gangs grasped pragmatically at any array of hysterical pronouncements to screen and justify their dreadful terror activities, but there were no fascist movements, only individual dictators and gangster followers.

A third view, to which we subscribe, holds that there was indeed a sociological phenomenon called fascism and as such the phenomenon in appropriate circumstances endures. Granted that the word originated in Italy and that not all fascist movements liked to use the term applied to themselves; granted that criminal activities were frequently involved and that ideology was often used cynically as a screen. Fascism was nevertheless a general phenomenon applicable to, and an ideology determining, political movements in various places and even in other times than the thirties and forties.

Fascism was a subset of rightist political culture, just as Stalinism was a political subset of the Left. Fascism embraced all the eight rightist traditions we have spoken of, although its use of rationalism and classicism, and of formalism, was distinctive and highly manipulative. Fascism stressed inequality, militarism, the leadership principle, and anti-Semitism. When these traditions are joined with a particularly ruthless and violent kind of behavior, fascism is in place, whether in Europe in the 1930s or Latin America in the 1980s. All systems of power provide an opportunity for corruption and looting of public resources; fascism's proclivity in this regard is especially pronounced, but not unique. Nor is mass murder unique to fascism; we have seen it also occur in Stalinism.

To say that fascism is a subset of rightist culture, and that it is founded on rightist doctrines, does not make others on the Right responsible for fascism any more than others on the Left are responsible for Stalinism. Winston Churchill and Hilton Kramer are no more responsible for Auschwitz or recent rightist terrorism in Argentina than Walter Benjamin, Harold Laski, and Jürgen Habermas for the gulag.

Fascism emerged in the era of high modernism in the 1920s. What was the relationship between the two movements? How did these two cultural phenomena positively or negatively affect each other?

There are clear points of contact between fascism and modernism. First, both had deep respect for twentieth-century technology as well as for the novel technocratic, advanced industrial society. Fascism is a peculiar combination of efforts to restore nineteenth-century mentalities, such as romanticism and Social Darwinism, within the framework of the modern technocratic state, which makes for an explosive fusion. Whereas the details of this view can be debated, modernism and fascism clearly share a fascination with technocracy. This appreciation manifests itself in two special ways in fascism.

It was in the period of Italian fascism that the country's important contribution to modern design was inaugurated. Probably the only legacy of Mussolini's Italy is the design industry in clothing, furniture, and automobiles, which developed in Milan under fascist rule.

Similarly, the medium favored by the Nazis was film. The great propaganda films produced by Leni Riefenstahl—among which *Triumph of the Will*, a documentation of a grand Nazi meeting, deserves special mention—were in the vanguard of their day and are paradigmatic not only for modern political art but as well in terms of motifs that are still at work in advertising today. The lighting techniques were especially subtle in Nazi films. The Nazis were not interested in books, except to burn them. Their interest rested with media developed by modern technology. The German film industry flourished greatly under Nazi rule.

The second way in which modernism and fascism may be deemed compatible is their adherence to moral relativism. Although it did not entirely eliminate it, modernism certainly eroded nineteenth-century normative ethics, whose standards, right or wrong, were deconstructed in modernist thought. Much more radical than modernism in this respect, Nazism had no faith whatsoever in normative ethics. Insofar as the Nazis subscribed to a moral system, it was that of power, violence and of a master race. Traditional moral standards, which prohibited violence, murder and genocide, went, needless to say, unrecognized by them. The moral relativism of modernism does overlap, it must be admitted, with the moral nihilism of fascism.

Third, particularly in its psychoanalytic mode, modernism recognizes the reality of sadomasochism in human nature. It admits that every individual has such tendencies, undeniably, and this constitutes one more trait that Nazism cultivates and shares with modernism. Nor did Nazism only cultivate sadomasochistic tendencies: It exhibited them; it was proud of them. The Nazis built on the sadomasochistic reality in human nature, which psychoanalysis had revealed, in order to legitimize the violence that was typical of them.

Fourth, the expressionist stream in modernism valorized the beautiful moment, the climactic moment, one of whose streaks was violence. Also, it stressed blood, both as a visual figure which was a frequent motif in Expressionist art, and as a theme of reflection. The blood philosophy, the conception of blood as capable of spurting forth an ineffable moment of creativity, which existed in the expressionist movement of the 1920s, and which was particularly strong in the writings of Lawrence and Yeats, recurs in fascism.

Another common element fascism and modernism share is nonsense, or irrationalism. The rejection of traditional rational modes of thinking and representation, which is the basis of the dadaist and surrealist streams in modernism, the fascination with chaos and the dominion of nonsense, are fundamental to fascist culture. The rule of unreason and of nonsense, therefore, is another priority fascism and modernism, at least in its expressionist branch, have in common. Mussolini's career itself, from the time he marched on Rome in 1922 to the time he was hanged by partisans in 1945, exemplifies dadaism to its fullest. His career contained nothing sincere or planned. It was spontaneous as well as phony, one big rule of unreason from beginning to end.

Finally fascism and modernism had a proclivity for the "thick point," that again returns to the notion of the ineffable moment, in which the great personality and creativity meet at the right time, making for beauty, vitality, and joy. The result is one terrible moment of construction, destruction, and violence.

Here one can recognize that notion, equally dear to modernism, of the thick, microcosmic, reductionist, and therefore significant, moment. This modernist conception is imitated in fascism, albeit in caricature form, but it is the same notion nevertheless. The moment of the emergence of Hitler, of the führer who embodied, so to speak, one thousand years of German history, and who promised glory to Germans as he promised the destruction of the world, paradoxically foretelling liberation through violence, and the achievement of truth and beauty in the very act of destroying—for so Nazi ideology described it—finds a corresponding articulation in modernism's concept of the microcosmic thick point.

However, it could be claimed with equal validity that on the other hand many features of fascism are in conflict with those of modernism. For fascism was historical, and further, retold history in mythological terms. All fascist movements, whether French, Italian, or German, were historicist, and this kind of history was mythic rather than academic. Fascist thought was neo-Victorian. It believed in telling stories and in narrative art. It was opposed to nonrepresentational modernist art, which it regarded as decadent.

In its approach to culture fascism was populist, whereas modernism was elitist. Even though fascism believed in the rule of a political elite, the culture it propounded was that of ordinary, middle-class folk. The music, art, and literature it favored were predominantly neo-Victorian. Therefore, while on the one hand fascism gained from and capitalized on modernism, and to a degree it became a terrible, deadly caricature of modernism, on the other hand, in its historicism, neo-Victorianism, subscription to the narrative in art and to populism in cultural policy, it was antithetical to modernism. It thereby helped to dam the advancing tide of modernism in the 1930s.

Since Hitlerian Berlin was reduced to rubble in 1945, very little is now visible in Germany that is a legacy of Nazi culture. The best example, and one that shows the ambivalent relationship to modernism, is Carl Orff's oratorio *Carmina Burana*, first performed before an appreciative Nazi audience in 1937. Orff's music, if not atonal, is certainly in the expressionist, tone-poem mood, and there is a threnody of violence running through the work. The text, however, is a cycle of medieval student poems. Yet this historicism is artificial and in conflict with the music, which could scarcely be less medieval. Its pulsating rhythms make us think of storm troopers and tanks, not medieval clerics and students. The words are essentially meaningless in this context, a mere mythic pretext; the burden of Orff's work lies in the remarkable music, which sounds modernist and like a military band at the same time.

Not only in Russia was the Second World War the Great Patriotic War. It was that too in Britain, the United States, and beginning in the summer of 1944, in France as well. For those not in the front lines or under Nazi rule, the war was in many respects a salutary event. The bitterness, poverty, and divisiveness of the thirties was replaced by national solidarity, good feelings about vicariously participating in a just war for freedom and human dignity, and in the case of the United States at least, full employment and unprecedented prosperity. The historicist, macrocosmic, and rigidly moralistic ambience of the war years ran directly counter to the modernist mentality. Joined with central ingredients in Marxism and fascism, revived neo-Victorian mentality during the war weakened and dispersed the modernist movement.

Modernism persisted as a mentality and style of importance in the arts and humanities. It by no means disappeared—in architecture and painting for example, modernism had a long way to go and analytic philosophy only reached its peak of influence in the postwar academic world. But modernism as a broad-fronted cultural revolution was enervated in the thirties by Marxism and fascism and was all but halted by the wartime ambience of historicism, patriotism, and nationalism.

The Emergence of Colossal Science The Japanese continued to fight on after the end of the war against Germany in April 1945. The Pacific conflict ended only after the U.S. Air Force dropped atomic bombs on Hiroshima and Nagasaki in August of 1945. Although almost universally applauded at the time, the atomic bombing of Japan has been a matter of great controversy since the mid-sixties. It was then revealed that some of the most distinguished physicists who had worked on the bomb, including Niels Bohr and Hans Bethe, later a Nobel laureate at Cornell, had after the German surrender urged that the atomic bomb project not be carried through to its terrible fruition, or at most, that a public demonstration of this unprecedented weapon be made and that the Japanese, after such a demonstration, be given the chance to surrender before it was used against them. (It was also disclosed that Nagasaki was the most Christian city in Japan and that it had been only marginally a military target; Nagasaki was in fact only a fallback secondary target when the first choice was obscured by cloud cover).

The American government under its new president Harry Truman—who knew nothing of the atom bomb project until Roosevelt died in April 1945, a few days before Hitler—refused to listen to the dissident minority of physicists. When Bohr tried to appeal to Churchill, he was almost arrested. The official American view then and since has been that the Pacific war had been an extremely costly one in American lives, that the Japanese had fought with incomparable ferocity, that the Japanese had been given ample opportunity to surrender but that the fanatical militarist clique in power since the early thirties was unmoved, and that not even the savage fire-bombing of Tokyo had brought about a Japanese collapse, that although the Japanese navy was virtually eliminated by 1945, Japan had many millions of experienced soldiers still under arms, and that the projected invasion of the imperial homeland would cost a million American lives. There was no alternative except the dropping of the bomb on Japan. A demonstration project on some uninhabited Pacific island would solve nothing: the Japanese fanatical militarists would not be impressed and no one knew whether the bomb would actually detonate. The bomb had to be dropped on a Japanese city for the dawning of a new era of military terror to be proved.

The contrary point of view laments the catastrophic impact on civilians in the two Japanese cities, and raises the question of whether a racist contempt for Asians was involved. It contends that the Japanese would have surrendered in at most a few weeks, possibly a few days, that the nuclear explosions were militarily unnecessary to end the Pacific war, and that the real purpose of Hiroshima and Nagasaki was to impress and frighten the Russians, whose aggressive behavior in Central Europe in the spring of 1945 had angered the Allies in what was the opening phase of what became the Cold War. Since nobody knows whether or not the Japanese would have surrendered without the atomic detonations—not even Emperor Hirohito (who died in 1989) knew, as he was before Hiroshima unsuccessfully trying to persuade the militarists to agree to surrender—there is no way to resolve this interminable dispute.

Hiroshima not only inaugurated a new era in warfare that has threatened the future of the human race on this planet (the Russians had their own atom bomb within a half dozen years under the leadership of Rutherford's disciple Peter Kapitsa, and with the help of captured German physicists). Not only were the bombs used against the Japanese dwarfed by the hydrogen bomb developed by the United States by 1952 (and almost as quickly by the Soviets). The coming of age of nuclear war had the paradoxical effect of impeding the two superpowers from going to war against each other in the following decades at such moments of bitter conflict as the Cuban missile crisis of 1962, when errors in judgment on the part of both the Russian leader Nikita Khrushchev and U.S. President Kennedy brought the two countries into a position of direct confrontation, Khrushchev backing down and ruining his own political career.

Nuclear armaments meant that a U.S.–Soviet war would be the end of civilization as we know it, or worse; therefore the two countries could not bring themselves to press the nuclear button, and the Cold War never became a shooting war. Without the atom bomb, relying on so-called conventional weapons, it is likely that a Soviet-American armed conflict, such as in 1962, would have occurred. Here is an instance of the altruism of reciprocal selfishness.

The atom bomb also signaled the inauguration of a new age of colossal science. The labs in which British and German physicists had achieved nuclear fission in the twenties and thirties and made atomic warfare possible were incredibly puny affairs by later standards: They would not pass muster today at a good American college or even an affluent suburban high school. The monstrous Manhattan Project that made the atom bomb (beginning indeed in Manhattan at Columbia, migrating to a lab under an abandoned football stadium in Chicago; then to specially created, secret international colonies of physicists and their families in Oak Ridge, Tennessee, and Los Alamos, New Mexico, with a subsidiary operation in Hanford, Washington) completely changed the way applied scientific research was done.

Now it was to involve vast establishments, usually but not exclusively on or contiguous to university campuses, and billions of dollars of annual government expenditure. It was to involve so-called peer review, which meant in practice that a handful of established scientists decided how the government support for research should be distributed. And it was to involve close association between scientists on the one side and military and corporate worlds on the other.

As early as ten years after the war, the most powerful person on a university campus was certainly not the harrassed and overworked prexy, not even the football coach, but the Nobel laureate physicist. Colossal science had become as important as a Rose Bowl football championship in establishing a university's national prestige. When the faculty of the University of California at Berkeley—which had been founded in a vegetable field at the turn of the century—was revealed around 1960 to have as many Nobel laureates as the whole of Britain, its stature equivalent to Harvard, Princeton, and MIT was confirmed.

The Manhattan Project taught scientists how to organize their collective endeavors. It is salutary to compare the making of the atom bomb with the one previous effort at colossal science in the United States—the making of the first cyclotron atom-smasher by Ernest Lawrence at Berkeley in 1937–38. He raised a million dollars (more than ten million in 1990 dollars) and recruited a large team. But Lawrence based his machine on a diagram of a model built by a German physicist. Unfortunately Lawrence could not read German, and he did not realize that in the text accompanying the diagram, the German physicist admitted that his model was not operational. Neither did Lawrence's cyclotron work.

The Manhattan Project's success was due to the scientific and/or managerial genius of four tempestuous personalities: Robert Oppenheimer, Leslie Grove, Enrico Fermi, and Edward Teller, although many others, including some British scientists transported to the United States (one was a Soviet spy, it later transpired) were involved. Oppenheimer was a brooding megalomaniacal genius, an American trained in Germany and a professor at Berkeley, who had never up to that point fulfilled the high expectations held of him. He was the intellectual leader of the project, but he also exhibited superb leadership capacity and surprising managerial skill. Leslie Grove was an army engineer who was the managerial head of the project. Without his patience, tact, humor, and wisdom, nothing much would have happened. He chose Oppenheimer to head the scientific research in spite of hysterical warnings from the FBI that Oppenheimer's extremely neurotic wife was an ex-Communist and his brother was a Communist. Fermi made the most important scientific discoveries establishing the immediate feasibility of the bomb. He left Italy, where he was the premiere physicist because Mussolini, after his ill-fated pact with Hitler in 1938, was pressured by the Nazis into anti-Semitic legislation, and Fermi's wife was Jewish. Teller was a mercurial Hungarian Jewish refugee and an applied researcher of unsurpassed capability. The relations between him and Oppenheimer were always tense. After the war Teller wanted to press on to make a hydrogen bomb, while Oppenheimer demurred. Teller denounced Oppenheimer, by that time director of Einstein's Institute for Advanced Study in Princeton, to the authorities, and after a lengthy and highly controversial investigation, Oppenheimer lost his security clearance, which meant he no longer could work for his country.

After the expenditure of billions of dollars (Truman perhaps had no choice but to conclude the Manhattan Project at Hiroshima since this unprecedented secret expenditure eventually had to be justified to Congress) and the most intense labor by a small army of physicists and engineers, these four leaders of the project were successful. What Oppenheimer called the Day of Trinity occurred in the New Mexican desert in July 1945, when an experimental bomb was detonated before a group of stunned scientists and military, followed three weeks later by the dropping of "Fat Man" on Japan.

Along with nuclear physicists, the pressure and opportunities of the wartime ambience also transformed medicine and biochemistry with the deployment of penicillin, the first effective antibiotic, to save the lives of hundreds of thousands of wounded men. Penicillin was discovered in a mold in the laboratory of a London biochemist, Alexander Fleming, as early as 1928. Fleming had an unusual approach to research; he believed in serendipity—that is, he never cleaned his lab, hoping that in the mess, something important would spontaneously be generated. After severe and rapid changes in temperature in London while Fleming was on summer vacation, he returned to find this peculiar mold with unprecedented germ-killing capacity. The problem was to synthesize penicillin—that is, to make it artificially and in such quantities that it could be used in medical practice. This was accomplished by Ernest Chain and a team of researchers at Oxford in 1938. Chain offered his discovery to the British pharmaceutical industry; they were unwilling to take the risk of the huge investment involved in setting up new factories to manufacture penicillin. Realizing the potential for his new discovery among the wounded of the fast-approaching war (in World War I, wounded soldiers died almost as miserably as their predecessors had in the Napoleonic Wars), Chain turned to the United States and found there the entrepreneurial attitude, risk capital, and the engineering skill required to make penicillin the miracle drug of World War II.

The coming of antibiotics revolutionized medical practice. Since the emergence of anesthesia and antiseptic surgery in the 1870s and psychoanalysis, there had been no major medical advance until the 1940s. In the thirties doctors still spent most of their time comforting dying patients they could not cure. Bedside manner, not science, characterized the medical profession. Antibiotics, headed by penicillin, changed all that. Medicine entered its modern golden age. Doctors could actually fight disease and save patients. Medicine was henceforth built on extensive, often government-supported, and—like nuclear physics—very costly research.

In terms of applied science and technology, the success of the Manhattan Project and the discovery of synthesized penicillin seemed to mean that Sir Francis Bacon's seventeenth-century vision of man's rational power over nature had been realized. It now appeared, in the postwar years, that with sufficient resources, scientists could put together teams of researchers that could do anything: build the hydrogen bomb, discover a vaccine for the dread disease of polio or an oral contraceptive that would alter sexual and family life for billions of people, or carry out heart and organ transplants. It remains to be seen whether AIDS is similarly susceptible to massive scientific research.

These breakthroughs incomparably elevated the position of scientists not only on university campuses but on national horizons. In 1930 humanists still seemed to be in the same league as their colleagues in physics and biology departments. By 1970 scientists were operating in a separate dimension of intellect, power, and wealth. This was one of the major cultural consequences of the Second World War, one of the unforeseen legacies of the fascist era.

Expiation and the Revival of the Right The Left in the Western world took no responsibility for Stalinism, and except for the United States during the Cold War in the 1950s, lost no ground therefrom. The Right, on the contrary, was severely damaged by fascism, the Holocaust, and the Second World War that fascism was reasonably held to have engendered. The two decades after the war were a period of expiation and penance for the Right, and to some extent for Western Europe as a whole.

This expiation occurred in four directions: the ending of European militarism; the dissolution of the European empires; the creation and rise of the State of Israel; and the modernization and democratization of the Roman Catholic Church.

The great European wars had disturbed the human universe in the first half of the twentieth century. Amid the ashes of European and especially German cities in 1945, the determination arose: Never again! At least not in our lifetime. The Europeans henceforth devoted themselves to the arts of peace, not the expertise of war. In the 1950s the Western Europeans formed an economic community to facilitate trade and business recovery and as a stepping-stone to political union that is yet to occur. With generous assistance from the Americans, the Europeans rebuilt their cities and, in the case of West Germany (the former Federal Republic), France, and Italy, had by the 1960s reached an unprecedented level of industrial productivity and national prosperity. For really the first time, at least the northern half of Italy became a modern country economically. France resumed its aborted industrial revolution, which had ground to a halt before World War I, and became by 1970 an advanced technological society. The greatest achievement was in West Germany, one of the two countries into which Hitler's Germany had been split between 1945 and

1948 because the Allies and the Russians could not agree on the political future of their fallen enemy (Berlin itself was divided into eastern and western zones).

German cities lay devastated in 1945, and ten million people, 80 percent of them young men, had been lost. But the German road system (the most advanced in the world, due to Nazi building of autobahns) and rail network were largely intact. Within three years German agriculture had recovered. And most important of all, German technological skill, scientific knowledge, and entrepreneurial ambitions and work discipline had not been eroded under the Nazi regime. With American aid and investment, new cities rose on the ruins of the old, so that German cities by the seventies were the most modern, cleanest, best organized in the Western world. Although West Germany's population had a Catholic majority (even after a large migration of Protestants from East Germany), all the traditions of the Protestant work ethic in Weber's model were exhibited in the new Germany. Munich today glistens with a cleanliness that is undreamed of in the United States. Not only affluent Americans but upper-middle-class Japanese want to buy German cars. The hands that made the blitzkrieg soon made German industry even more technologically and fiscally powerful and creative than it had been in 1914.

Whether the collapse of the German Democratic Republic in 1990 and the reunification of West and East Germany meant more of the same, with the American army no longer needed, or whether this dramatic event would in the future be seen as the prologue to the resumption of the rise of German power in Western and Central Europe, was a major question of the 1990s. The very presence of this large, reunited political entity was bound to have an impact. It was seen immediately in the case of Yugoslavia. Germany's immediate recognition of the seceding Croat and Bosnian entities (which had been Nazi Germany's fervent allies in World War II) decisively destabilized the Yugoslavian state and brought on civil conflict. It may also be that the costly and slow economic and technological revamping of East Germany, when it is concluded somewhere in the early twenty-first century, will give Germany such fiscal power as to make it superior to any other economic unit in the world, and a variety of problems will flow from this exalted ststaus—which Germany would have gained by 1920 if it had not foolishly entered into the military gamble of 1914.

The most critical issue is whether Germany will at some time in the future resume its military and imperialist stance, a constant threat to its neighbors and a meddlesome participant in diplomatic crises anywhere, as was the case in the old imperial Germany. Perish the thought, German businessmen, politicians, and professors will insist; those aggressive days are as much in the past as the age of Charlemagne. And, indeed, the German elite is now an extraordinarily discreet, polite, and soft-spoken group. What the German leadership cohort will be like two descades into the next century is unpredictable. Possibly the immersion of Germany in a European Union will have a moderating impact. That is the French hope.

How long the European empires would have lasted in Asia and Africa without World War II is unfathomable. They would not have lasted forever, but patches of empire would still be around today. As it happened, within two decades of World War II most of the European colonies had gained independence, within three decades virtually all. It took three hundred years for the Roman Empire to fall; it took thirty years for the British Empire and the other European empires to fade away. But the Romans to the bitter end of the Gothic Wars were proud of their empire and made it a literal synonym for civilization. The Europeans had deep doubts in the interwar years. By the mid-fifties they could only speak of imperialism with shame and regret.

Japan showed that the European empires in East Asia were paper tigers. In the four months after December 7, 1941, Japan conquered four hundred years of European empire in East Asia—one of the more formidable military accomplishments in history. Within a week after Pearl Harbor, Japanese carrier-based planes sent Britain's two best battleships to the bottom of the sea off the Malaysian Peninsula. In February 1942, in what Churchill called the worst defeat in British history, the commander of Singapore surrendered 130,000 troops to a Japanese army that was less than half that size. It had landed two hundred miles up the coast and advanced untouched on Singapore (whose big guns only pointed out to sea) on bicycles. The Americans had a large air fleet in Manila; the Japanese destroyed it by bombing while it was still on the ground, as General Douglas MacArthur looked on in bewildered disgust.

The European empires never recovered from these incredible humiliations. Franklin Roosevelt, a fanatical anti-imperialist and consequently a man of the radical Left on this issue, would not allow the Dutch to resume their rule in Indonesia, which they had governed quietly for two hundred years. The French adamantly held on to Vietnam until they suffered a military disaster in 1954. Within a half dozen years they had also abandoned Algeria, forcing hundreds of thousands of French families and Jews to flee before Arab rule.

The key decision that unhinged imperialism was Britain's abrupt withdrawal in 1947 from the Indian subcontinent, leaving behind the new republics of India and Pakistan as well as unspeakable atrocities by contending religious and ethnic groups. Attlee's Labour government scuttled the Raj, sending a member of the royal family, the rash Lord Mountbatten, to do its dirty work. Lord and Lady Mountbatten made a formidable team. As an admiral in the war, he had established a record in the British navy for getting more ships shot out from underneath him than any other commanding officer. Then, as a senior officer with the Commandos, he became famous for designing unintended suicide missions. Lady Mountbatten, a famous millionaire debutante in her day, conducted an affair with the Indian leader Jawaharlal Nehru while her husband was negotiating with him; Lord Mountbatten appears not to have been offended by this.

Mountbatten died in 1972, while fishing on a lake in Ireland, at the hands of Irish Republican Army terrorists. There is thus an uncanny and ironic connection between the revolt against British imperial rule in Ireland from its insurrection in 1916 to its mostly successful conclusion in 1922, with the establishment of the Irish Free State (Eire) in all but the heavily Protestant-populated northeastern enclave. The Irish rebels showed—not by their initial, futile Easter rebellion in Dublin in 1916, which was brutally suppressed by the British, but by their long guerrilla war against Britain from 1918 to 1922—that the deconstruction of (in this case four centuries of) British rule was far from impossible. The British had no heart—they were too liberal—for extended repression of national liberation movements, and British governments in London were increasingly wary of spending resources to crush colonial rebellions. What had begun in Ireland reached a climax in India in 1947—the unraveling of the British Empire.

A plausible argument can be made that British rule in India was benefcial to the indigenous upper classes, whether Hindu or Muslim. The British brought peace and political stability. They built railroads and highways. They introduced Western medicine and the rudiments of colleges as well as good secondary schools—all to the advantage of wealthy and well-established Indians. Aside from enjoying the generally peaceful conditions imposed by the British Raj, the argument would go, the Indian masses gained little and lost much under British rule. The native textile industry was largely destroyed by the colonial government because it competed with British cotton manufacture. Western medicine generated a population boom and urban misery. Taxation fell heavily on the mass of the population, not on the wealthy. Vaunted English law deprived millions of small landowners of their family property.

Between 1900 and 1941, two developments prepared the way for a national liberation movement that coalesced around the charismatic figure of

Mohandas K. Gandhi, a British-educated middle-class lawyer who transformed himself into a holy man. The expanding Indian middle class, produced by British-founded schools and colleges, were increasingly dissatisfied with positions in the lower echelons of the colonial civil service. They wanted to ascend to higher governmental levels but these were traditionally reserved for Brtish graduates of Oxford and Cambridge Universities. The other problem was that officials of the Raj, who had been energetic and at times progressive in the nineteenth century, had become defensive and conservative by the 1920s. They were overwhelmed and immobilized by vast economic and social problems of the subcointinent. In this sitation, confrontation between Indian political leaders and the imperial administration was inevitable. In the 1930s, fomented by Gandhi and his ambitious colleagues, it had reached a critical if still nonviolent stage.

There were several reasons why the British made the sudden, critical withdrawal from India, which doomed the vestige of the imperialist cause: British postwar poverty is such that Britain is the only European country worse off economically today than it was in 1939. This meant that the country lacked the military and fiscal resources to combat determined independence movements led by Nehru and Gandhi (Hindu) and Mohammed Ali Jinnah (Muslim). British guilt about imperialism was involved. In 1947 Churchill, no longer in power, was the only prominent political leader even on the Right to insist that the "jewel in the crown" should be held on to at all costs. Since 1914 India's main value to Britain had been as a source of military manpower during the two world wars. It was impossible to frame an argument to hold on to India for this reason (which was not publicized in any case). The disgrace and loss of Singapore and Hong Kong to the Japanese, and the severe losses in the defense of Burma, had made the British appear puny and used up in Asian eyes. There was a long-standing Labour Party commitment to give India its independence. Attlee felt this personally, since in 1937 he had spent several months in India as a member of one of an endless number of investigating commissions and decided that the British cause was hopeless.

The dismantling of the Raj set the stage for the abandonment of the British Empire in Africa, beginning with the Gold Coast (Ghana) in 1957, and another ten colonies by the early seventies. The British believed around 1955 that they should hold fast in Africa for another twenty years. Thus they repressed the Mau Mau rebellion in Kenya with unaccustomed determination and skill. But it soon transpired that the whole African native leadership was already in rebellion against them and could not be trained to take over responsible leadership. The only thing to do was get out and hand over the keys to the governor's mansion, for better or worse, to the rebels. Insurgents in British jails on life sentences were a week or two later putting on snappy uniforms and becoming presidents of new republics. The British Colonial Office, always assiduous in paperwork, developed a special ceremony for running down the Union Jack for the last time.

Underlying the British withdrawal was a pervasive and thoroughly justified sense of guilt at not having done enough for the African people (the British did much more for India) and for allowing the numerous white settlers in South Africa, Kenya, and Southern Rhodesia to exploit and mistreat the indigenous popuation. This guilt was exacerbated by the egalitarian heritage of World War II.

The end of empire and the death of imperialism were encapsulated in fragmented memorials. One of these was South Africa itself, where the ruling Afrikaners (the Calvinist Dutch Boers), who were the heroes of the European Left in the Boer War of 1899–1902, fought the last rearguard action for white hegemony of the continent until the 1990s.

A second memorial to vanished empire was the Commonwealth (in 1945 called the British Commonwealth of Nations), the collective organization of all the states that once were under the British flag and on whom British, Canadian, and Australian schoolchildren were once proudly taught the sun never sets. The Commonwealth heads of state solemnly meet each year and do absolutely nothing; at most this meeting is an act of piety.

A third memorial to what existed before the imperialist collapse of the forties and fifties are the Rhodes scholars at Oxford. In the early years of the century, billionaire South African politician Cecil Rhodes was so proud of the Empire that he Left his vast fortune (he was a bachelor) in trust to train its future leaders at Oxford until the end of time. This is how the Rhodes scholarships were founded. Rhodes seems to have forgotten about the American Revolution, because he also provided for U.S. Rhodes scholars. Rhodes's bones still lie under a monster rock on a hill in Zimbabwe (formerly Southern Rhodesia). But little else of his dream remains. Every year at Rhodes House in Oxford, a hundred or so of his Rhodes scholars in residence and about to leave the old university (they now include women and even an occasional black), rise while wearing evening clothes and toast "the Founder," who looks down on them from a bigger-than-life-size portrait. Rhodes in this painting is appropriately wearing riding clothes and bears a remarkable resemblance to Hitler. Then the Rhodes scholars go off, not to rule the Punjab or Zambesi but—in the case of the Americans—to attend Harvard Law School or take jobs on Wall Street, whose firms assiduously recruit this reputed elite each year, or to occupy the White House.

Anti-Zionists in Britain and in the Arab world today are fond of saying that Hitler created the State of Israel. There is truth in this, as in many other sick jokes. Without the sympathy for the Jewish refugees in 1945–48 and revulsion against the implications of the Holocaust, Israel most likely would not have come into existence. The second creator of Israel was President Truman, who, given his Southern Baptist background (unless it was just a bid for Jewish money and votes), doggedly supported Israel against the hysterical opposition of his own State Department. The third supporter was, strangely, the Soviets. It was widely anticipated that the Russians at the UN in 1947 would vote against the creation of Israel. But although the Soviets before this had been anti-Zionist and continued to be fiercely so thereafter, until the Soviet Union disintegrated in 1990, Russia endorsed the Zionist state.

Even more important for the survival of the new state was Czechoslovakia, and especially its military industry, which was a legacy of Nazi rule in Prague. In 1947–48 Israel had to fight for existence against six invading Arab armies, one of which, the Jordanian, was well trained and equipped and led by British officers. The Israelis had to fight for survival while the United States and Western Europe had imposed an embargo on arms shipments to the Middle East. The Czechs provided the Israelis with armaments, especially the critical airplanes (basically Messerschmitts) bought with cash from U.S. Jews. Why did the Czechs do this? Perhaps the Russians, who wanted a long-term war in the Middle East and did not anticipate a relatively quick Israeli victory, told them to. Perhaps it was because the head of the Czech government, Rudolf Slansky, and some of his colleagues, were Jewish. In 1952 the Soviets purged and hanged Slansky and most of his colleagues.

In 1967 General Nasser of Egypt blockaded the Israeli port of Eilat and the Gulf of Aqaba—an act of war. Syria and Jordan joined the war at Egypt's side. Using tactics of lightning armored attacks and coordination of air force and ground armies developed in World War II, first by the Germans and Japanese, then by the Allied forces, the Israelis in the Six-Day War of June 1967 made a preemptive strike against the Egyptian air force and destroyed most of it on the ground. Israeli armored columns raced across the Sinai Desert and after destroying much of Egypt's tank corps, reached the Suez Canal. The Israeli army fought a hard battle with the capable Syrian forces to take the Golan Heights on the northern border between the two countries. East Jerusalem, which the Israelis had failed to take in 1948, was now captured from Jordan. Israeli conquest of the West Bank and Gaza brought two million Palestinians under Israeli rule, in addition to the three-quarters of a million who were Israeli citizens. The Sinai Peninsula, with its valuable oil reserves, was returned to Egypt in 1980 in exchange for a peace treaty. Gaza and part of the West Bank were given to a Palestinian political entity in the 1990s as part of a peace settlement. The future of East Jerusalem and the Golan Heights remains a matter of contention among Israelis, as well as between Israel and Syria and Jordan.

The Israeli victory in 1967 was generally applauded in the Western world—somehow it squared accounts with the Holocaust. But as Israel became an American client state in the 1970s and the Israelis maintained their control over large Arab populations, anti-Zionism, merging into anti-Semitism, returned to Western Europe. The ill-fated Israeli invasion of Lebanon in 1982 wiped away Holocaust guilt in Western Europe, though not in the United States. Whether this is because Americans better remember the Holocaust or politicians of both parties remember how important Jewish money is in their campaigns, or Jewish votes in certain cities, is moot. Soviet hostility to Israel in the seventies and eighties and evangelical Protestant belief that Israel fulfilled biblical prophecy also helped the Israeli cause in the United States. By the mid-eighties the American Left was deeply divided on the Israeli question. The leftist weekly *The Nation* published in 1986 an anti-Zionist and anti-Semitic diatribe that would have won a medal from Hitler. The American Right is largely and sometimes fervently pro-Zionist.

Degania is the largest Israeli kibbutz. It is located in the Galilee on the shores of Lake Kinneret, some forty miles south of the Golan Heights and the current frontier with Syria. In 1948 it was twenty miles closer to the border. In the middle of the kibbutz, a few yards from the children's house, there stands today a peculiar monument, a rusting Syrian tank, which in the War of Independence in 1948 broke into the kibbutz and was immobilized at that point, which became the limit of Arab advance against the newborn state. Its survival was a close thing.

That little Israel with a Jewish population of three million, by 1970 the same number as in New York City, should emerge as the fourth military power in the world with an air force and tank brigade that even in 1973 turned back the Soviet-armed and trained armies after a surprise attack and have inflicted defeat after defeat on hundreds of millions of Arabs—that Israel should have become the Prussia of the Middle East—is partly explained by that salvage monument in Degania. Sheer desperation and the memory of the Holocaust forced the Israelis to become one of the great military powers on earth, demonstrating a military capability that only the Germans and Japanese in the early forties and perhaps the Russians in 1943–44 have matched.

Yet this necessary fact altered the character of Israel that its founders, headed by David Ben-Gurion, and nearly all the Eastern European socialists of the generation of the Second Aliyah (socialist wave of immigration around 1910) had envisaged.

By the mid-1990s—due mainly to immigration from Russia in the eighties and early nineties—Israel's Jewish population had risen to about five million, roughly equal to the Jewish population of the United States. The country was now heavily urbanized; less than 3 percent of its population lived on the old socialist agricultural settlements. The country's future—it was widely agreed among leaders of nearly all parties—lay in the building of high-technology industry and close trading relations with East Asia and black Africa, and, it was hoped, with Jordan, whose own future prosperity depended on a close connection between its economy and Israel's. In order to attract heavy capital investment from abroad, it was necessary to work out peace treaties with the neighboring Arab states as well as keeping the one million Palestinians who were now Israeli citizens contented and loyal. How far concession of territories captured in 1967 should go in order to gain this general peace was the contentious issue in Israeli politics.

Nor is Israel thoroughly secular, as the socialist pioneers had expected: The religious parties are politically influential and are part of every government whether of the Left or Right. Orthodox and even ultra-Orthodox (messianic fanatics) from the large section of the population displaced from Arab countries or immigrants from Brooklyn have given a religious coloration to the country. The Israeli airlines and the bus lines do not run on the Sabbath. The government subsidizes Orthodox schools at an extravagant rate while charging heavy tuition for the secular high schools.

Nor is Israel socialist. Whoever is in power, it is a capitalist society with strong welfare components. Its economy and social system are therefore similar to those of most countries in Western Europe. The Israeli elite consists of wily politicians; ambitious army officers and speculative entrepreneurs; and scientists and scholars who spend a lot of time abroad. The ambience of Tel Aviv is very close to that of the more affluent American cities of similar size. In addition Israel is a garrison state. It requires three years' military service of its sons and daughters and a month's annual reserve duty of every male (except the ultra-Orthodox) until the age of fifty-five. It has mild-looking professors of archaeology and medieval history who are trained commandos and para-troopers of professional caliber.

Israel has shown that white colonies could have been made viable in the Afro-Asian world if enough settlers had immigrated, if they were fanatically determined and inspired by a great cause and were not social parasites, and if enough capital investment had been made. Imperialism failed, the case of Israel demonstrates, because it was too half-hearted, the investment of human and material resources was simply not great enough. So it was easy to wipe out the results of one to two centuries of colonial history.

In the first two decades of the twentieth century the advocates of European and American imperialism persistently oversold their cause. They claimed that Western colonalism in East Asia, Africa, and the Middle East, and even in Latin America, would provide profits that could sustain the incip-ient welfare state at home. This "social imperialism" contravened the actual balance sheet of imperialism, as was already evident by the 1920s. Western imperialism brought immense wealth to a handful of entrepreneurs and corpo-rations. But on the whole the balance sheet was negative. It cost more in mate-rial and human resources to sustain the Western colonial entities than Western societies and governments received in return. The case of Israel indicates that a Western enclave in a non-Western environment could gain permanent status over time, but only with immense effort and personal sacrifice, and with stu-pendous and continuing fiscal investment. The advocates of imperialism were not prepared to make their case in these terms. They contended early in the century that the colonies would be self-sustaining or even provide profits that could be used back home. When this argument could no longer be made, Western imperialism was doomed. Israel's durability represents an alternative outcome to the colonial story in the Afro-Asian world.

It was the Jewish question as much as any other factor that led to the upheaval in the Catholic Church in the early sixties, the biggest transformation for Rome since the sixteenth, possibly the twelfth, century. Pius XII, pope dur-ing World War II, disgraced the papacy by failing to come to the help of the dying Jews (outside Rome itself) and allowing the Holocaust to occur without significant public demur, let alone strong opposition from the church. If there was ever a time when the church had to confront the world in order to prove true to its confession, when the risk of martyrdom had to be broached, this was the moment. But Pius XII, a conservative diplomat who had been papal ambas-sador to Germany in the twenties and early thirties and was a Germanophile, remained steadfastly neutral. His silence gave no comfort at all to German

Catholics wanting to oppose Hitler. His silence doomed the Jews.

In the fifties there was a huge controversy about the pope's role in World War II. Both Jewish and German sources condemned him. Of course the church vigorously defended Pius XII. A subtle argument was presented. It would have been all too easy to play the self-indulgent martyr and confront the Nazis; Pius saved millions of Catholic lives by his neutrality, it was claimed. This casuistry convinced no one. The *magisterium* had been disgraced and expiation for papal cowardice—or worse—collaboration—had to be made. It took the form of the Holy Spirit directing the electing cardinals to choose as an "interim pope" an elderly, obscure Venetian archbishop of unknown views who became John XXIII, the greatest reforming pope since the thirteenth century.

John called the Vatican Council II of 1962–64, during whose later stages he died. It unequivocally condemned anti-Semitism; henceforth to denounce Jews as Christ killers was wrong. It allowed, indeed demanded, that most of the liturgy be conducted in vernacular languages, rather than Latin, which laymen rarely understood. At last billions of Catholics knew what they were saying in church. It freed Catholic scholarship and theology from its narrow bonds of censorship and repression and liberated the friars and nuns and other church intellectuals to follow reason and learning. It made the church much more of a consensual, democratic, and decentralized institution—how much was left undecided. It entered into a greater spirit of cooperation with other faiths.

The spirit and theory of Vatican II was stated with unsurpassable clarity by Father Hans Küng, then a young Swiss theologian who attended the council as an adviser to the German archbishops: "Faith in . . . the Church . . . being maintained in truth . . . is related to the whole Church as believing community. It is not primarily related to certain ecclesiastical institutions or authorities, which for the most part did not exist at all or did not exist in this form from the beginning and will not exist or need not exist in this form forever." The core of the church was community and not *magisterium.*

By the early seventies, a Benedictine monastery on the St. Lawrence was not only using a guitar and folk songs in its liturgy. It was using a Quaker-style speaking with tongues (spontaneous preaching by laypeople) in its service. By this time, too, most American nuns had abandoned wearing their traditional habits (not ordained in fact by Christ but only modeled on widows' robes from seventeenth-century France). By this time Catholic schools of theology were carrying out a modernization of doctrine and synthesis with secular thought, as Thomas Aquinas had done in 1250, but which had been prohibited by the papacy for modern times in 1907. By this time the proportion of

Catholics using artificial contraception was almost as large as among Protestants and Jews. By this time Jesuits in South America in some instances had turned Marxist, were cooperating with Communists and were preaching a liberation theology. The *magisterium* was losing its hold on the church.

In recent years, under the Polish pope John Paul II, a reaction has set in; strenuous efforts to restore the *magisterium* have been partly successful. Father Hans Küng was evicted from his chair of Catholic theology at Marburg. Liberation theology has been condemned. Efforts were made to restore discipline over priests, friars, and nuns. Contraception as well as abortion has been condemned unequivocally by Rome—although Catholics continue, with surreptitious assent from many priests, to practice both. John Paul II makes pilgrimages to the Catholic population all over the world, preaches personally to hundreds of thousands, tries to make the papacy a missionary force on the Right. His style is a long way from Pius XII, the austere aristocrat who never left the Vatican. The colossal iceberg of the Church, however, having started to move toward reform and democratization, is hard to reverse. The leading churchmen in Germany and Holland and many in Latin American countries clearly remain on the Left. The late archbishop of Chicago was a well-known liberal. In the United States it is hard to discipline priests when there is a terrible shortage of clergy due to the monumental decline of new professions. It is hard to control what nuns and friars teach when the Catholic schools are entirely dependent on this highly skilled, low-paid work force.

A Catholic scene from the eighties: The bishop of Brooklyn, an elderly liberal, is apparently mortally ill. The nuns who run a college in Brooklyn gather to pray vehemently for his recovery, especially because should the bishop die, his replacement made by Rome might be a neoconservative, Cardinal O'Connor type with whom the radical nuns will be in instant conflict. A miracle: The old bishop recovers for a few years (and is then replaced by a conservative).

How long can the Catholic Church endure such internal strains without a schism comparable in magnitude to the one that occurred in the Reformation era? God only knows. Whom will the Holy Spirit, acting through the cardinals, choose as the next pope? Having given up the Italian succession, possibly a Latin American or African bishop will be the next pope and he will heal the divisions in the church. Possibly the church will split apart at the next papal election into its Left and Right polarities.

Having expiated its putative sins of association with fascism and consequent responsibility for World War II, the Right since the mid-seventies has begun to re-create a political culture. It is no longer willing to allow the Left to occupy the dominant ground in the universe of discourse prevailing in the academic and media worlds. As of the mid-nineties, there was no question but that the Left's position was still the hegemonic one; the playing field between the two camps of political culture was not level: It still favored the Left by a significant interval. Serious weeklies, monthlies, and quarterlies with a leftist tilt or blatant leftist orientation still greatly outnumbered the outlets of rightist opinion, and surpassed the latter too with very few exceptions, in terms of quality. From every TV network, upscale newspaper, and a host of university chairs, leftist culture is disseminated on a very wide variety of topics. When threatened or confronted, the Left never hesitates to use *ad hominem* arguments and concentrate firepower until the public credibility of their audacious opponent is shattered. Thus one problem for the Right was a practical one—commanding its resources so as to gain as great a visibility as the Left in the academic and media worlds. In this application of resources to the cultural needs of the Right, a handful of conservative foundations play the critical role. Unless the evangelical Christians exercise political power on the federal scene, the future of the American Right is probably in the hands of these foundations.

The problem of the Right was also intellectual—its theory was still anemic. From the eight traditions of the Right came three formulations of rightist theory in the nineties. These were: Friedmanite-Reagan-Thatcher neo-Ricardian economics; E. O. Wilson's sociobiological neo-Darwinism; the more conservative forms of Christianity in the Catholic Church and evangelical Protestantism.

None of the theoretical expressions of rightist culture has gained overwhelming allegiance of intellectuals, although these theories have become much more popular since the mid-seventies in the transatlantic world. It seems safe to conclude, however, that the Right has still much more intellectual homework to do, and that the rightist theory of the early twenty-first century has not yet been clearly articulated. There are places to look for activity: among Cowling and his colleagues at Peterhouse, Cambridge; among the *New Criterion* group; at the University of Chicago's law and business schools; among evangelical Protestants in the southeastern United States; in a Jesuit order over which the papacy reasserted its control in recent years. But all this is guesswork based on past performance. The provenance as well as the specific contents of the message of the New Right remain obscure.

What is most intriguing about the rightist theoretical revival is that the more vigorous it becomes, with the exception of the *New Criterion* group, the less conscious it appears to be about the modernist cultural revolution and the involvement of rightist thinkers and writers with the modernist mentality. In recently reinvigorated rightism, there appears to be an absence of mind about twentieth-century intellectual history and particularly the modernist heritage. The Right nowadays seems inclined to let the Left try to appropriate modernism and thereby increase its legitimacy. The Right nowadays appears for the most part to write off the modernist era and hark back directly to Victorian modes and concepts.

As the new century and millennium beckon, the Right in the United States increasingly builds its discourse by looking backward to the time before 1900. This nostalgia for the old economy and interpersonal value system has very little appeal to the professional, academic, and scientific elite of the rising American generation. The latter's intellectual horizons stretch toward a future of high technology, global information systems, high consumption, sexual freedom, and personal autonomy. There is hopeful talk on the cultural Right of a conservative advance borne on the shoulders of evangelical Protestantism and conservative Catholicism. It is evident that large blocs of population exist that are committed to these causes, but no significant body of thought or art has emerged from these groups, or is likely to. The evangelical Protestants stir fear and resentment among educated groups and distaste generally among the upper middle class. Reassertion of old traditions in the Catholic Church stimulates conflict, dissension, and possibly secession within that institution itself. In retrospect it appears more and more evident that the time for cultural breakthrough by the American Right—the years of the Reagan and Bush administrations—has come and gone. With the approach of the end of the century, in spite of of vast fiscal and human resources, the support of billionaires and of large masses of society, the cultural Right is incapable of specifying its goals clearly—of defining the kind of society it wants to achieve—let alone building consensus and gaining power to arrive at such goals.

6

POSTMODERNISM

The Coming of a New Age In the 1970s a new age emerged, without fanfare and almost imperceptibly. By the beginning of the eighties its manifestations were in place. The coming of a new age was not announced by dramatic events like a war or a depression, although the ending of the Vietnam War was a salutary and necessary preparation. After the dramatic events of the sixties, a new era whose characteristics were soft rather than hard news was bound not to be much celebrated by the media. But by the mid-eighties it was obvious to more intelligent journalistic commentators and to cultural critics that a new time was rapidly developing.

Three technological innovations comprised a material and scientific infrastructure for the new era: biotechnology, computer applications, and instantaneous world information distribution through communications satellites.

Biotechnology was the outgrowth of the discovery of the double-helix structure of the DNA molecule in 1953 at the Cavendish Laboratory in Cambridge, England (which Rutherford had once directed), by the joint efforts of the English biophysicist Francis Crick and the young American molecular biologist James Watson. For more than a decade DNA (deoxyribonucleic acid) had already been identified as the template of animate life. The issue was to identify its structure so that it could be controlled and manipulated by laboratory science. It was this possibility that Crick and Watson's discovery made possible, and for which they were awarded the Nobel Prize (although two other teams of scientists, one in London and one at CalTech, were on the verge of the same discovery.)

This was a scientific breakthrough in biology comparable to the work of

425

Darwin and Mendel in the nineteenth century. It meant that the new physics of Einstein, Rutherford, Bohr, and Heisenberg would now be applied in molecular biology and be committed to the analysis and shaping of life forms. By the mid-seventies advanced work in molecular biology had spawned vast new areas of biological engineering. A technology devoted to the artificial, lab-centered creation of life constituents emerged. By 1986 vaccines made of genetic mutants were introduced.

Biotechnology opened up unlimited horizons of accomplishment in science and engineering. It meant that humankind was beginning to control not just the physical environment—this reached a zenith when a man first walked on the moon on July 20, 1969—but its own nature, the biochemistry of life itself. In some respects molecular biology and DNA marked the ultimate fulfillment of the modernist program that had begun with the century. The aim of finding the smallest particle had resulted in knowledge of the double-helix structure of DNA—the chemical basis of animate matter.

The extended application of computers to research knowledge, industry, and government was the second material constituent of the infrastructure of a new age. The idea of a computer is not an invention of this century. Charles Babbage, a contemporary and friend of mathematician Charles Lutwidge Dodgson (as Lewis Carroll, the author of *Alice in Wonderland*), had stipulated the main mathematical principle of automated computing (using the age-old binary theorem—that is, a system whose only digits are 1 and 0 and all numbers are combinations of them) in the 1860s. In the 1930s Alan Turing, a young British mathematician, had developed an elaborate project for a mathematical machine and something like it appears to have been built and put into use by British intelligence during World War II in the breaking of the German codes using the Enigma machine (a cipher machine that a Polish agent had sneaked out of Germany).

In the period 1943–46, first at Iowa State University, then at the University of Pennsylvania, the first publicly known and commercially feasible computers were built. They used easily breakable vacuum tubes, needed intensive artificial cooling, and occupied enormous space. The computer power now provided by hardware about the size of a typewriter then required a machine larger than a basketball court. Further refinements were made in the postwar period by IBM, Sperry, and other corporations. The turning point came, however, in the late sixties, with the introduction of readily manufactured microchips to replace the large and cumbersome vacuum tubes. The microchip was developed simultaneously by engineers in Texas and Illinois.

By the early seventies businesses and universities with pretensions to status and grandeur each had their computer center. A further major breakthrough in the late seventies, made possible by further miniaturization of the transistor and cheaper production—in which first the Japanese and then the South Koreans excelled—fostered the proliferation of "personal" desktop and even portable minicomputers. This breakthrough revolutionized many age-old processes, including banking and book production, and carried further the revolution in the storage and retrieval and massaging of data that had begun in the sixties with the first still relatively large and awkward computers.

Both the biotech and the computer revolutions used the same key words—code and program—to describe their basic functions. In both instances a structure of design and information drove processes that predetermined formulations: in the case of biotech and DNA, genetic histories; in the case of computers, knowledge for business and research, humanities or science, peace and war. Even the great achievements of the first three decades of the century in the application of science and technology were significantly transcended. A new interval in the evolution of the power of the human intellect had occurred.

Yet, at the same time, since the biotech code and the computer program operated integrally for long stretches without human intervention, shaping life or crunching number sequences, a certain diminution of individual stature was also thought to have occurred. The biotech and computer breakthroughs both enhanced and diminished the power and value of the individual. They enhanced human mentality as a whole but made less necessary and valuable the mental capacity of any one individual. Such at least was the feeling.

It was the molecular biologists who especially articulated a theory of impersonal code overriding personal choices. Evolution, said Crick, has a creative "perfection of design" that operates outside the values of humanistic culture. "Scientific revelation," of which DNA is the highest dogma, takes the place of the nonsensical "modes of yesterday," he alleged. Life on earth started with a spaceship from a doomed civilization on another planet landing on earth; after that the genetic code functioned autonomously. Similarly Jacques Monod, another Nobel laureate in microbiology, spoke with contempt of those who continue to believe in "anthropocentric illusion." The discovery of life codes forces us to recognize at last that man "is alone in the universe's unfeeling immensity, out of which he emerged only by chance. His destiny is nowhere spelled out, nor is his duty." The Nazis would have applauded Monod's nihilist thesis.

Similarly, a group of computer scientists centering on Herbert Simon, working at MIT, aimed to divest the human mentality of that distinctiveness that philosophers since Aristotle have accorded it. They believe that computers can function as artificial intelligence and think like humans as well as compute and remember in ways that exceed human capacity. Only a technological failure to get computers to equal human intelligence has impeded the full formulation of this mechanistic philosophy from the computer side to go along with microbiologists' proclamation of a scientific revolution in which the genetic code functions outside personal human intervention.

The placing of communications satellites in the heavens was an innovation of the mid-seventies. It realized McLuhan's prophetic vision of a global village. Now everyone around the globe in front of a TV set could see and hear the same event "live." This was a major advance in communications technology, and it contributed not only to sports and entertainment but also to the growth and proliferation of the multinational corporation, which through phone, satellite, fax, TV, and computer linkups could now instantaneously straddle the earth. The citizenship of the world that eighteenth-century philosophers had dreamed about (when it took six weeks—with good weather—for a letter to cross the Atlantic) and the universalization of capitalist power against which Marx and Lenin had fulminated were now indeed realized.

As in the case of computers, satellite communications seemed at the same time to increase human capability and efficiency and diminish human stature. The individual, any individual, now seemed small and feeble in comparison with the world communications network and the global corporations it made operative.

Satellite communications were the main practical outcome of the American space program that began in the early sixties, when it was feared that the Soviets would conquer space before the United States. The American space program combined German rocketry science carried over from World War II, in the person of Wernher von Braun, with American engineering and capital. The idea behind the moon landing project of 1969 was that somehow the attainment of this centuries-old dream would result in colonization of other planets. It turned out that the moon was several million square miles of useless rock and rubble, and the other planets in the solar system were also lifeless and essentially uninhabitable except at prohibitive expense. The manned space program in the seventies then tried to make itself remunerative by serving as the means for launching communications satellites, and this program continued at a steady and largely successful pace until the disastrous explosion of the

Challenger space vehicle in January 1986. It was resumed in the 1990s in cooperation with the Russians and focused on the collection of scientific data. At the same time, unmanned probes of the planets Jupiter and Mars greatly increased knowledge of the solar system and its constituents.

The second great change ushering in a new age in the late seventies was the rise of the Pacific Rim, involving not only Japan (whose success was most visible and celebrated), but other East Asian countries such as South Korea, Singapore, and Malaysia. Western Europe continued the course of technological and economic progress it had started in the fifties, although dreams of political union, in spite of the creation of a largely powerless European parliament, were a long way from realization. It was the United States that felt the crunch of competition from the Pacific Rim and declined rapidly as an industrial power, losing large sections of its automobile, steel, and electronics as well as textile manufacturing capability to the Japanese and other Asian producers.

Fluctuations in oil supply and gas prices in the seventies seemed momentarily to play a key role in this development. But Japan had no oil while the United States produced the greater part of its own supply. The oil glut of the mid-eighties showed that oil and gas were not factors in this novel economic equation. The major factor was cultural: The decline of the work ethic in the United States, the deterioration of its educational system, the loosening of family bonds, and the weakening of socialization in disciplined behavior—these were the key factors.

Two other causes were involved in the rise of the Asian rim. The East Asian peoples were only one or two generations removed from feudalism, the historical moment of greatest industrial work capacity and social discipline for modern productivity. They were where Britain had been in 1780–1820 and Germany from 1870 to 1910. Beyond that, there was the factor of the Buddhist, Shinto, and other highly austere religious traditions of East Asia, inculcating self-control and group solidarity.

A peculiar revelation of American loss of self-confidence occurred when General Motors and Toyota began to produce jointly Toyota Corollas in a new plant in California and agreed to have them marketed by GM as Chevrolet Novas. In 1986 these Novas were a glut on the market while American consumers were willing to pay several hundred dollars more for exactly the same car with a Toyota nameplate on it. In the early forties American industry was the master of the world. Four decades later American industry became a dirty word.

In the late eighties it appeared that the Americans had been infected by the

British economic disease. Financial instruments became ever more subtle and complicated, what with a rash of unproductive takeovers of corporations by other corporations, and the devising of clever and expensive means to preclude this fiscal warfare, while industrial productivity stagnated, research and development of new products deteriorated, and family farmers were driven to ruin. The madcap dance of financiers surrounded by the gloom of industrial decline, agricultural insolvency, unemployment and underemployment, and the deterioration of applied research: This distinguished the British economy and it now threatened to become America's fate as well. Soon every American boy and girl born would be fated to become an investment banker, a corporate lawyer, or a hamburger chef or a supermarket checkout clerk.

By the mid-1990s American business corporations had made a comeback. They downsized their payrolls, especially at the middle management level. They imitated the Japanese in introducing a greater degree of teamwork in production lines. They massively made use of computerization, both for information systems and for automated production facilities. They exported large segments of their factory production to Latin America and East Asia to make use of much cheaper labor. They also took advantage of lax American immigration laws and the inability of the federal Immigration and Naturalization Service to stem the tide of illegal immigration to employ cheap and eager immigrant labor—as they had done in the early twentieth century. Cutting down on the generous benefits and pension plans that had proliferated in the 1960s and 1970s also increased the profit levels of the large corporations, and these profits were reflected in higher returns to ever-more-demanding stockholders and in the remuneration of the top-level executives. The fiscal rewards to American executives were much greater than those in Japan and substantially more than managers received in Europe.

The real income of American workers did not increase in the fifteen years after 1980, and in the estimate of some economists slightly declined. The white-collar middle class, with downsizing layoffs by large corporations, experienced insecurity it had not known since the Great Depression of the 1930s. But American corporations by the mid-nineties were the envy of leadership in Europe, there weighed down by generous wages and benefits and commitments to heavily unionized workers. The Japanese now had to recognize that the technological and organizational edge that Japanese industry had appeared to enjoy over American business in the mid-eighties had mostly vanished a decade later.

Once again American capitalists had demonstrated their resourcefulness and meanness. They were helped by federal and state governments, whether Republican or Democratic, that gave priority to the profit margins of big corporations at the expense of middle-class security and working-class incomes.

If government would not make this obeisance to big business, the latter's multinational organization, welcome in cheap-labor areas in- or outside the United States, and then the global communications and transportation networks made these American corporations' mobility to propitious environments quick and easy.

The gloomy prospects for American business in the 1980s was paralleled by the decline of the American university. But institutional recovery in higher education did not run alongside the resurgent success of American business in the 1990s.

From about 1910 until the late 1930s, the American university had developed its own distinctive forms and largely native talent. It borrowed what it needed from Europe but it was proud of its own emerging traditions and accomplishments. The advent of academic refugees from Hitler in the 1930s began to open fissures in the self-confidence of U.S. academics. In the postwar era these fissures widened into chasms as American faculties were shaken, first by McCarthyite questioning of their loyalty in the fifties, then by the onslaught of New Left students in the sixties, then by the decline in real salaries and massive academic unemployment in the seventies.

The latter factor was probably the most important. The academic profession, except for law, medicine, and business schools, did not participate in the American economic boom after about 1965, and its fiscal status deteriorated. The professional devastation was worst in the humanities and soft social sciences excepting economics, which enjoyed affiliation with business schools. In 1996 the American Historical Association admitted that only one in four new Ph.D.'s in modern American history would obtain a regular, full-time teaching job. The academic market in most other fields of the humanities was similarly dismal. It was in these arrays of humanistic disciplines that efforts to create an indigenous American academic culture were abandoned and there was a rush to adopt European intellectual models, especially from France. This development shaped the rise of postmodernist theory, although some other dimensions of the new era also contributed to it.

Whether we call the new age postindustrial or postmodern or eventually find a new term is not important. It had a distinctive set of characteristics, in addition to ones we have already delineated.

The visibility of psychoanalysis as a form of therapy was under attack after

1980 and being eroded by the rise of psychopharmacology. Perhaps more important, the leading position of psychoanalysis in cultural theory has softened. Psychoanalysis in the mid-nineties seems more prone to absorb cultural theory into its canon than to go out front and shape it in an innovative manner. Psychoanalysis as vanguard theory has declined, becoming more reactive than creative.

The welfare state has lost the internal impetus it had from the early years of the century until the mid-seventies. While the welfare state is likely to be around for a long time, probably forever, it has dissipated the capacity to stimulate the imagination and elevate hopes. It has proved a costly burden on federal, state, and municipal budgets, as conservatives had predicted. The faith that somehow if only social security, state-generated employment, and health insurance would be expanded all other problems would fall into place has greatly weakened. We have social pathology such as drug traffic and one-parent families that the welfare state seems to exacerbate, not alleviate. It is not completely clear why the welfare state had fallen so far short of optimistic expectations as the solution to social problems. But by the 1980s it was clearly a failure in several respects.

On the other hand, if the Left has no social panacea, the rightist claim that neo-Ricardian free-market economics without compassion will solve all economic problems has likewise been proven vain. Neither ballooning nor shrinking the welfare state makes as great a difference as Left and Right polemicists believed in the early seventies. We appear to have reached a point at which debate about the welfare state is obsolete. We have to formulate a social doctrine and cultural theory along some other spectrum, such as group solidarity and personal discipline. Social progress seems unlikely without another cultural change.

There is a growing discordance, as there was not in the three decades after World War II, between the media and academic cultures. The latter have propounded theories that the media have difficulty comprehending or at least integrating into their work and are left either to ignore or satirize in vulgar fashion. As an example, in 1985 the *New York Times Magazine* set out to publish an article on deconstruction at Yale. The result was a miserable insult to common intelligence. The author failed to explain what deconstruction was, and clearly could not understand its social significance. He fell back on the bankrupt motifs of the dreamy professor and cloistered academic lifestyles.

The *Times* did not write about Einstein and relativity in 1919 in this futile, vulgar vein, nor would it today write about Wall Street brokers and investment practices in this cavalier manner. Another instructive example: In 1986 the *New Criterion* devoted a whole issue to a symposium on New York in the eighties. Not one of the eighteen contributors (they complained a lot about the real estate situation) was a professor from the two leading New York City universities, Columbia and NYU. Would this have been possible in a similar symposium in 1936 or 1966? Absolutely not.

There is an unprecedented amount of learning available today, abetted by storage, sample analysis, retrieval, and dissemination by computers and communications satellites. There is a lack, however, of fresh cultural and social theories to make sense and meaning out of all this information.

The way in which modernism developed its revolutionary theories in challenge to Victorianism is no longer operational or feasible. There is no longer extant a systematic Victorian culture to push against and grow strong in conflict with. The wall off which modernism played for four decades has dissolved into a nostalgic persiflage of artistic bricks and intellectual mortars. Furthermore the resurgence of neo-Victorianism that began in the thirties and continues with vigor today has generated a nostalgic neo-Victorianism that makes the anti-Victorian modernist program additionally obsolete.

The effort in the sixties to create a leftist culture adversary to capitalism and the putative bourgeois ethos—an effort that is still pursued in some quarters, especially university humanities departments—has produced a narrow band of thought that perpetuates partisan polemic rather than confronts the complex and novel circumstances of the new age.

Perhaps in desperation at the exhaustion of the modernist program and the futility of New Left doctrine, the culture of the developing age exhibits a propensity to arbitrary and random appropriation and imitation of particular old themes and nostalgic traditions rather than comprehensive and original theorizing about contemporary culture. This quality of arbitrariness, random impetuosity, and pastiche characterizes postmodernist culture as much as anything. Central to postmodernism is the propensity to unresolved syncretism of diverse cultural strains, learned traditions, and diverse theories. Much is effortlessly imitated and distinctive cultures are blended together.

The new age has seen a reversal of the antiurban ethos of the postwar era of the fifties and sixties. Then there was a flight to the suburbs and a pseudo-agricultural ethos that marginally harmed the continued progress of modernist culture stemming from metropolitan life of the early decades of the century. Now there is a renewed appreciation for the civilities and sophistication of urbanism, and particularly of urban centers. But the real estate situation has made New York and to a lesser extent London and Paris inaccessible to the avant-garde—the young artists and intellectuals who carry the aesthetic and cultural theory of the future.

We have seen a reversion to the metropolis as a fiscal and managerial center, but we cannot find the means to regenerate it as a center of cultural revolution. We build bigger and more elaborate metropolitan museums, and at the same time drive the painters and sculptors who will replenish these elegant galleries to the urban fringes, provincial towns, and boondocks. Here is a remarkable contrast between the infrastructure of the age of modernism and the new era of postmodernism.

Perhaps a hundred or even fifty years from now, historians will see that the most important development in the new age was none of the above. Rather, it was the triumph of feminism and women's liberation from domesticity. For the first time middle-class women in large numbers are entering academia, the learned professions, and at least the middle ranks of business management. The historical profession itself, if current trends maintain themselves, by 2010 will be—like nursing a century before—overwhelmingly a female one. When betwen 49 and 51 percent of the entering class of NYU Law School, one of the top ten in the country, is women, what does this portend for the future not only of the legal profession but corporate management and the criminal justice system? We are possibly at the beginning of a matriarchical revolution that will reverse five thousand years of social history. Psychoanalytic and cultural theory has barely begun to address this portending upheaval, whose psychological scars could run deep and painful. The impact on men will be as great as the significance for women. Child rearing and with it the delicate socialization of oedipal feelings is changing.

The historian some decades from now may see the main difference between the era of modernism and the age of postmodernism to lie along a polarity of integration and fragmentation. Modernist culture of the first four decades of this century was characterized by a comprehensive cultural and aesthetic theory and by political and social fragmentation of a world rent by nationalism and fratricidal conflict within the human race, and was still hampered by the relatively primitive steam and electromechanical means of transport and communication.

Postmodernist culture comprises a world integrated by identification and manipulation of the universal genetic code, computer programs, communications satellites and multinational corporations, and the absence of major wars. It is, however, a world fragmented culturally and aesthetically, a world of subcultures, small-group choices on aesthetic principles and idiosyncratic, nostalgic recapitulations of the past, but one in which a comprehensive, integrating cultural theory is lacking.

The modernist era—to its great loss—allowed dysfunctional political and economic decisions. The postmodernist era—to what loss?—allowed random, privatist cultural decisions and the composition of arbitrary cultural pastiches.

Structuralism The leading cultural theory that developed in the two decades after World War II was structuralism. It initially loomed large on the French intellectual horizon in 1955, with the publication of Claude Lévi-Strauss's intellectual autobiography and testament, *Tristes Tropiques.* This book ranks with Joyce's *Ulysses,* Proust's *Swann's Way,* and Freud's *The Interpretation of Dreams* as one of the enduring classics of the century.

By the early seventies structuralism was the leading cultural theory in France. It had come to dominate French anthropology and social sciences. It also deeply affected transatlantic literary theory and criticism, eventually penetrating into the entire field of the humanities—"the human sciences," as the Parisians called them. In the late sixties, more specifically in 1969 with a special issue of *Yale French Studies,* structuralism migrated to the United States, beginning its penetration with the literary humanities, principally through the faculties of the English, French, and Comparative Literature departments of Yale University. From there, it spread to several other universities, including Johns Hopkins, Columbia, Cornell, and Chicago.

Since the mid-seventies, structuralism in its original form has been in decline in France, having been superseded by deconstruction as the main cultural theory. It has been challenged in the United States as well. Nevertheless it does remain an important movement in the humanities in this country, as well as in England and Germany. Therefore, even though it lost its initial thrust somewhere around 1975, structuralism is the single most important intellectual movement of the last forty years. It could be claimed that had structuralism not come into being, there would have been no deconstruction either, since deconstruction developed as a movement responding to, growing out of, and criticizing structuralism. Deconstruction can be seen as a subset and late variation of the intellectual movement called structuralism.

The reason for the emergence of structuralism can be located first of all in the exhaustion of existentialism, which had been the leading intellectual movement in France in the postwar period. We have seen that existentialism was a system of romantic phenomenology emphasizing the good individual against the absurd and hostile environment. It was a dramatic philosophy that had been valuable and meaningful in the early forties during the period of Nazi rule. It had become the philosophy of resistance, as will be remembered from an earlier chapter. But existentialism was not a sophisticated philosophy, and it exhausted itself once the political conditions that rendered it important had disappeared—how long can someone continue to shake his or her fist against the world before one begins to look juvenile and naive?

Lévi-Strauss realized the weakness of existentialism, he tells us, even when it was in its formative stage in the thirties. It was partly because of his antipathy to the then emerging existentialism that he abandoned his doctoral studies in philosophy at Paris, switched over to anthropology, and although a novice in this social science discipline, got a teaching job in Brazil. The position was obtained through his mentor Marcel Mauss, Durkheim's nephew and professional heir. In the late 1940s, when Lévi-Strauss was starting to teach in Paris after a period of wartime exile in the United States, he found existentialism the rage of the cafés and the boulevards as well as the university. Nevertheless he boldly declared not only his independence from Sartre and Camus, but his direct opposition to existentialism.

Structuralism moves the focus of reality and the center of attention from the individual to the system. It makes the structured system, rather than the individual, into the locus of the real and the meaningful. Structuralism signifies a transference of meaning and authenticity from the individual to the system, which makes structuralism a theory that rebels against the anthropomorphism of existentialism.

The second point of origin of the structuralist movement lay in the failure of the New Left and of the student upheaval in 1968. Existentialism was the mode of the 1968 rebellion, in that the uprising was primarily individualistic, conducted by a small group of highly self-conscious personalities who stood against the world at large. After a series of dramatic successes, the leftist heroes and heroines failed, and therefore a reconsideration of the whole situation on the Left became inevitable. The heroic individual or the heroic vanguard, consisting of a handful of radicals who sought to dismantle the establishment, had obviously suffered defeat, rendering necessary a revision of the entire system of belief. This caused a shift, rechanneling attention from the individual to the system.

Thus structuralism arose out of a reconsideration of what may be called the radical program, in view of the failure of the radical heroism of the late sixties. Instead of calling for people to mount the barricades, structuralism proposed to incorporate the barricades into a larger social system. Structuralism proposed to transcend the conflict between the individual and society by giving priority to universal structures in which both were subsumed.

Structuralism can lend itself to rightist interpretation, but in the hands of Lévi-Strauss and his French disciples it was intended to be a doctrine of the Left. It was an effort to create a post-Marxist as well as postexistential leftist cultural theory, based on behavioral data and with impeccable intellectual credentials. The rise of structuralism is therefore a postscript to the tumult and defeat of 1968.

A third basis of structuralism lies in the economic and technological developments that were occurring in the late sixties and early seventies, one of which was the growing recognition of the central role of multinational corporations. Increasing attention was being paid for the first time to the elaborateness of economic institutions which extended over many countries. In a sense such multinational corporations had been in existence for quite a while, at least since the late nineteenth century, when they were called cartels.

Unlike its parent institution, which had received frequent moral condemnation, the multinational corporation received good press, to the extent that universities developed programs for the dispensation of special degrees—MBAs—for admission into the work force of these international companies. During the 1970s, multinational corporations began to receive attention as complex computer-based economic and social systems, providing a springboard for general reflection on the elaborate, systemic quality of other institutional structures.

What now counted economically was not so much individual entrepreneurship or national distinctiveness but global corporate institutions with homogeneous behavior and universal fiscal instruments and databases.

It was discovered that the modern world was increasingly tending toward rigorously defined system building, and structuralism became the articulation of this insight in the domain of the humanities and the soft social sciences. The extension of computer applications and satellite communications in the seventies not only made the multinational corporation much more functional. It increased the attractiveness of a theory that gave prominence to codes and programs: This was structuralism.

A fourth general source of structuralism lay in formalism, which we identified as one of the foundations of rightist thinking. It usually finds its political place on the Right, but Lévi-Strauss was not prepared to let the matter lie there. He sensed from his study of early peoples how much their lives were conditioned by behavioral codes, language structures, and symbols. He did not think that at bottom it was any different for people in more advanced societies, although the formalistic conditioning of behavior may be harder to trace in complex societies.

Lévi-Strauss and his disciples were not prepared to allow the Right to appropriate formalism exclusively for their conservative programs. Lévi-Strauss, whose political sympathies lay on the Left—he was a vehement anti-imperialist—wanted the Left not to rely on simple-minded empiricism, vulnerable existentialism, and—in his eyes—discredited historicism. He wanted the best intellectual foundation for the leftist program, and that meant formalism.

A Soviet theorist named Mikhail Bakhtin had already perceived this point in the thirties, but formalism stood perpetually condemned in the Soviet Union as bourgeois, counterrevolutionary reaction. Hence Bakhtin never exercised much influence in Russia (he was rediscovered in the eighties by American critics). Lévi-Strauss aimed to do what Bakhtin could not—namely create a highly visible leftist theory based on formalism. This was certainly an audacious and largely successful move.

Historically structuralism goes back to Lévi-Strauss's work in the 1930s and 1940s, and particularly to the early forties when he was a refugee teacher at the "University in Exile" in New York, a branch of the New School for Social Research. Claude Lévi-Strauss was the son of a Belgian rabbi, which lends him a certain affinity with Émile Durkheim, who was also a rabbi's son.

When Lévi-Strauss began his behavioral studies under Marcel Mauss, there was no major distinction at the University of Paris between sociology and anthropology. After Mauss found Lévi-Strauss a teaching position in São Paulo, Brazil, in 1934, Lévi-Strauss encountered the Third World. In 1938, shortly before the outbreak of World War II, he made an extensive trip up the Amazon, where he conducted fieldwork. It was during this trip that he began to study the social codes, languages, and the diet of primitive peoples of the Amazon region. Anglo-American anthropologists find his fieldwork somewhat brief and also careless (he did not know the natives' languages and thus used interpreters). Nevertheless Lévi-Strauss's Amazon trip was a turning point in his intellectual development.

A couple of years after Lévi-Strauss returned to France from Brazil (1938), he had to flee—along with many other Jewish professors—to refuge in the United States, as the German army entered Paris. In New York during and shortly after the war Lévi-Strauss taught at the New School for Social

Research in Greenwich Village, where a unit was created for refugee professors. He also taught uptown at Barnard College, in the summer of 1945 teaching freshman anthropology to young women there. (In New York he took to
calling himself Mr. Strauss because students asked him if he belonged to the
family that made blue jeans.)

By 1949 Lévi-Strauss's publications were sufficiently recognized that a
position in social anthropology was created for him at the Collège de France—
a kind of institute for advanced study. It has only professors, no students (the
height of academic prestige), and the professors are limited to forty at a time,
embracing all disciplines. Lévi-Strauss's ascension to this exalted group made
him highly visible in French intellectual life and put a stamp of legitimacy on
his theorizing.

At the New School in New York during the war, Lévi-Strauss had
encountered a remarkable polymath, Roman Jakobson, who was a product of
the East European (mainly Russian and Czech) school of linguistic formalism.
Jakobson's field is difficult to specify, given the wide range of work he produced, but his greatest interest was in the science of linguistics. He tried to
develop a formalist theory of linguistics that would include the description of
a code that underlay all language.

Jakobson's formalistic approach to linguistics drew on the one hand on
Wittgenstein and the logical positivist school, which had been very strong in
Prague. It was also indebted to early-twentieth-century Russian literary theo-
rists. There was a long East European ancestry in the tradition, viewing all lan-
guages as having been generated by the one essential code. After the war
Jakobson became professor of linguistics and Russian and comparative
Literature at Harvard University. He died in 1982 at the age of eighty-five, hav-
ing remained to the end a zealot and an advocate of formalist linguistic theory.

In his intellectual autobiography Lévi-Strauss almost certainly underesti-
mated the reality of his debt to Jakobson in the development of his structuralist theory. Instead he stressed the influence of the Swiss pioneer in linguistics
of the second decade of the century, Saussure, who also influenced Lacan. Yet
at the time that Lévi-Strauss encountered Jakobson and his formalist system of
linguistics in wartime New York, he could not have known very much of
Saussure's similar linguistics theory, since the latter never published a book in
his lifetime. Saussure's treatise only appeared in the fifties, put together out of
lecture notes by his students. Nor does Lévi-Strauss in *Tristes Tropiques*
acknowledge a debt to Lacan, although they propounded some similar doctrines. Yet it is possible that Lévi-Strauss did not encounter Lacan's ideas until

his own had been formed. Lacan practiced as a private psychoanalyst and did not gain academic attention until the 1960s.

Why Lévi-Strauss does not mention Jung among his forebears is puzzling, however, since Jung's theory of archetypes contained some strong resemblances to Lévi-Strauss's structuralist anthropology. In his intellectual biography, Lévi-Strauss does express his debt to Marx, Freud, and Jean-Jacques Rousseau. While structuralist elements can be pointed out in the work of these three thinkers, beyond question this appears to be mainly an act of formal piety on Lévi-Strauss's part, a typological bow to the masters that would please the Parisian Left Bank cafés and his students. Lévi-Strauss always exhibited superior skill in public relations. (His theory is certainly closer to Piaget than to Rousseau.)

Lévi-Strauss was a very prolific writer. *Tristes Tropiques* (1955), one of the great testaments of the twentieth century, is highly commendable as an introduction to his thought. It was splendidly translated into English by John Weightman in 1983. Another of his books, *The Savage Mind*, is a more didactic introduction to his thinking, although unfortunately it was poorly translated. A four-volume collection of studies, whose first volume is titled *The Raw and the Cooked*, is very much worth reading as well.

Lévi-Strauss believes in an objective, universal social-mental code. What constitutes a society and a culture is a universal code that runs through the culture and the institutional and behavioral forms of that society. The code is objective—that is, it is not ideational, only a mental image, but it exists independently of individuals and individual minds, and governs both human behavior and ways of thought. This universal cultural system exists objectively, structuring mental processes as well as social institutions. As humans we are involved in this code. It shapes our lives, our capacity to communicate, and how we function—but it is independent of us.

Second, Lévi-Strauss holds that this code exists in language and in myth. In order to discover the code and reduce it to its basic grid, one would have to look both at the findings of the science of linguistics and at mythology. To do the former suggests Jakobson's and Saussure's influence (Lacan said the same thing), whereas opting for the latter points toward Jung. Furthermore the code operates in the unconscious—not for nothing does Lévi-Strauss claim that he learned from Freud.

We have the hope, says Lévi-Strauss, "of overcoming the opposition between the collective nature of culture and its manifestation in the individual" because the collective unconscious is "no more than the expression, on the level of individual thought and behavior, of certain time and space modalities of the universal laws which make up the unconscious activity of the mind." (Jung would agree.) Thus Lévi-Strauss is not satisfied merely to eliminate the authenticity of existential heroism. He even eliminates meaningful individual thought, integrating it with universal laws that operate in the unconscious. Lévi-Strauss sounds the first great trumpet call for the project that has run through French thought since the late sixties—the project that is often called "the death of the subject"—that is, the elimination of the value and significance of individual consciousness.

Lévi-Strauss's structuralism further claims that the savage, or primitive, mind and that of the savant, or learned mind of complex societies, have the same deep structure. Just as Freud said that there was no fundamental difference between the neurotic and the normal, so Lévi-Strauss argues that there is no fundamental difference between the savage and the savant mind in terms of the way in which they operate and create mythological structures in order to explain reality. The same human mind, the same mental structures, are at work in either case. Where the savage may create an elaborate mythology about the gods, the savant may produce a theory of physics, but at stake in both cases is the recourse to a structure of reality to explain ourselves, how we behave, and how we exist.

The savant and the savage mind differ in this respect. The former is the mind of the engineer and is "adapted to perception and imagination." The primitive thinker is like a *bricoleur*, or handyman. He is "adept at executing a great number of diversified tasks. . . . His instrumental universe is closed, and the rule of his game is always to make do with the means at hand." Thereby a special dignity and authenticity accrues to the primitive *bricoleur*. He or she remains close to his sources and does not, like oversophisticated modern humans, continually generate new concepts but constantly manipulates and refines preexisting ones.

Lévi-Strauss the Parisian academic and Left Bank intellectual identifies the Amazon primitives with those weatherbeaten, canny, diversely knowledgeable *bricoleurs* he finds in the French countryside when he goes for his long summer vacation. They possess a special intellectual power, they reflect an earlier thick French culture that cannot be matched in the halls of the Sorbonne or the upscale apartment houses on the Right Bank. There is something Rousseauesque in Lévi-Strauss's identification of the savage mind with the *bricoleur* temperament.

Lévi-Strauss is very sympathetic to primitive peoples. One of the main themes of *Tristes Tropiques*, aside from propounding his structuralist theory, is a dirge for primitive society and a regret about the transformations being undergone by the Third World. In primitive society, so Lévi-Strauss claims, people live on more intimate terms with fundamental structures. In primitive culture there is no host of complicated and decadent interventions and corrupting obscurities to separate people from their basic structure of mind and society. Therefore, by implication, advanced society is repressive, confused, corrupt, decadent, and inauthentic. Primitive society, on the other hand, is more humanly authentic for its proximity to basic structures. There is a parallel here with Heidegger's belief in the superior authenticity of the German farmer.

Lévi-Strauss sees in the primitive peoples of the Amazon Basin a beauty, a simplicity and a closeness to nature that we have lost. They have been able to combine their institutions, way of government, economy, mythology, religion, music, art, and food in a systemic whole. All facets of their life are closely integrated, while we, advanced peoples, have confused and disoriented all the above. We are so burdened by the inhibitions, oversophistication, and discordancies of advanced culture that we have lost this authentic integration.

But Lévi-Strauss is a realist. He examines the present rather than laments for the past. As he returns to the Amazon after a period of absence there, as he travels through India, he discerns how the dislocating, disorienting aspects of modern culture are affecting primitive peoples. He sees that we have done these cultures a disservice, that the greatest crime of imperialism is that of cultural disintegration.

In addition Lévi-Strauss writes that as he searches for the universal code, he finds that it is always binary. The code exists and operates in terms of binary oppositions: space and time; the male and the female; the raw and the cooked. Complementary, reciprocal sets of oppositions, he proposes, cut through all areas of primitive life and thought. The kinship system of primitive peoples, which is the basis of their social organization, is based on a binary system, which constitutes a form of the underlying code. He finds as well that the same code is at work in their diets. As might be expected of a French mandarin, he finds it easiest to extrapolate a universal code in diet along with language.

Finally Lévi-Strauss emphasizes the synchronic rather than the diachronic plane—that is, the comparative, the universal, the mythic, the immediate rather than the historical and the temporal. He has rather severe observations about history, one of which is that it is an impossibility, and even if it were possible to write history, it would be largely a waste of time. Gathering data, collecting information about the past, does not guarantee that the information can be submitted to meaning. The heap of information is bound to remain precisely that—a heap of information, a bundle of nonsense.

Further, the accumulation of extensive information does not necessarily guarantee that one can obtain the needed information. It is just as likely that one will end up with misappropriated, misdirected information. History will not teach anything. Truth comes through a synchronic analysis of universal social codes in the present. The most fruitful activity is the analysis of what exists simultaneously in the present. To ask questions about the past and the origin of present phenomena is futile, and—even if there were such a thing as history—in any case it could not be recovered. History is a waste and a foolishness. Lévi-Strauss's position is therefore strongly antihistorical and exclusively considers the synchronic.

Lévi-Strauss's powerful impact can be judged by the fact that, along with the historian Ferdinand Braudel, he was one of the two great intellectuals in the French-speaking world in the sixties and the seventies. Braudel indeed did much to accommodate himself to Lévi-Strauss. He agreed with Lévi-Strauss that the writing of fact-centered "eventual" history is an insignificant activity, and that what is needed is the delineation of broad historical structures. Lévi-Strauss was the darling of the French intellectual world in the sixties and the seventies, and in the seventies and eighties became almost as influential in the United States.

In the dissemination of his influence, in France as well as abroad (particularly in the United States), Lévi-Strauss was assisted by Roland Barthes, the central figure of the Parisian literary intelligentsia in the the sixties and seventies. Barthes began as a modernist and an existentialist after the Second World War, but when Lévi-Strauss gained in importance, he became a structuralist. A highly skilled popularizer, or public communicator, of structuralist ideas, Barthes did eventually, near the end of his life, become a professor, but most of his career was spent as an intellectual journalist, like Albert Camus before him.

Editor of the prestigious journal *Tel Quel*, the leading intellectual journal in France in the fifties and sixties, which it still is, Barthes cleverly propagated the structuralist gospel. Before he died in a 1980 accident (crossing the street, he was run over by a truck), he became a deconstructionist. Barthes's career reiterates the development of French theory and intellectual fashion since the war. His views were disseminated in the United States by the prolific critic Susan Sontag.

In a 1966 essay that was extremely influential in the United States as well as in France, Barthes demonstrated how Lévi-Strauss's theories could be applied to literary criticism, indeed had to be applied if literary criticism was to remain intellectually respectable. Barthes advocated the creation of a science of narrative structure. "Either a narrative is merely a rambling collection of events . . . or else it shares with other narratives a common structure which is open to analysis." Structuralism's "constant aim," said Barthes, is "to master the infinity of utterances by describing the language [code] of which they are the products. . . . From the point of view of narrative, what we call time does not exist, or at least only exists functionally, as an element of a semiotic system." These propositions by Barthes set the direction of vanguard literary criticism in France and the United States, and to some extent also in West Germany and Britain, for the next two decades. Barthes's most remarkable tour de force was a little aphoristic work called *Barthes by Barthes,* published in 1975 (English translation in 1977). It combined autobiography, literary criticism, and expositions in postcard form of the messages of structuralism and deconstruction.

How can we account for Lévi-Strauss's popularity and influence, aside from his good fortune in having Roland Barthes as his press agent? First of all, the intellectual world of the time demanded emphasis upon system. It wanted some vehicle to approach the systemic level rather than the individual level, and this demand could be found in a wide range of disciplines. Secondly, there is a certain quality of honesty about Lévi-Strauss, who strikes one as a man without illusions. He seems to be a wise man, well-traveled and well-informed. He is one of the cultural gurus of this century.

He is, in brief, an eloquent writer who is able to draw on a wealth of experience, reading, and observation. *Tristes Tropiques* has already become one of the great classics of French literature and has been read variously as an anthropological treatise, an autobiography, and as a *Bildungsroman,* the story of one individual's development. One simple reason for his popularity, but a true one, given the typical French love for beautiful, elegant books, may be the simple fact that Lévi-Strauss could and often did write remarkable French prose.

At the time Lévi-Strauss was beginning his work, linguistics was making its appearance as the paradigm of human sciences. It became very popular at the University of Paris in the fifties and sixties, and Lévi-Strauss was showing why this difficult science was important, demonstrating that it was the basis of social science as well as of philosophy. His work fitted in with the rise of the central role of linguistics. It is interesting to note that in French films of the sixties and seventies, characters that are supposed to be university students frequently claim to be studying linguistics. In an American film this would strike one as nothing less than ridiculous.

Lévi-Strauss not only benefited from the connection of his theory with linguistics, but also with the emerging science of semiotics. We have seen that this variant of formalism is the study of signs within language, the visual arts, and other cultural expressions. As in the case of Barthes and literary criticism, Lévi-Strauss was fortunate in the appearance of another follower stimulated by his structuralist doctrine to develop a theory of semiotics. This was the Italian medievalist, literary critic, and bestselling novelist Umberto Eco. Following Lévi-Strauss's anthropology, Eco propounded the view that "every act of communication to or between human beings . . . presupposes a signification system as its necessary condition." Signs bounce off one another in an endless series of significations: "Signs are the provisional result of coding rules which establish *transitory* correlations of elements, each of these elements being entitled to enter—under coded circumstances—into another correlation and thus to form a new sign."

Since signs are cultural units interacting infinitely, and since semiotics embraces all forms of communication—not only language but also involving art history, film, and advertising—it is obvious that semiotics has much material to explore, and it is fun to pursue this enterprise as well. Hence its burgeoning popularity in the seventies and its academic respectability thereafter.

Semiotics was a wonderful subject for subliterate American college students. They didn't have to struggle with Milton or Keats; they could write essays on Coca-Cola ads. Since, according to Eco, signs are infinitely referential, it is possible plausibly to say anything about them. (Appropriately enough, perhaps, a Brown University student in 1986 who was indicted for prostitution turned out to be a semiotics major.)

Eco's theory of semiotics owes something to the philosophy of Charles Saunders Peirce, who propounded a theory of semiotics as early as the 1880s (hardly noticed except by William James and *Popular Science* magazine). It owes a good deal to the developers of linguistics like Saussure and Jakobson. But above all it was inspired by Lévi-Strauss's structuralism. The emergence of semiotics as an academic discipline, and its popularity with students on both sides of the Atlantic, contributed further to Lévi-Strauss's fame and reputation.

Structuralism received another boost from the transformational grammar theory of the American Noam Chomsky, which achieved very high visibility in the sixties and early seventies. Chomsky as a theorist of linguistics was, as he acknowledged, saying essentially the same thing as Roman Jakobson. His celebrity owed not a little to his role as a spokesman against the Vietnam War and his superior skills as a controversialist and polemicist. There is a universal structure to language, says Chomsky, which we humans can discover because we are genetically endowed (a bow to microbiology) with a "language faculty." The transformations of language constructions are "invariably structure-dependent." Again: "Language is generated by a system of rules and principles [which] . . . are in large measure unconscious and beyond the reach of potential consciousness." This is pure Lévi-Strauss (and Lacan). Chomsky's fame contributed to Lévi-Strauss's guru status in the Western world by the early seventies.

In the sixties the discovery of DNA and therein of the deep biological structure, along with the introduction of computers and their coded programs, posed seeming confirmations and proofs of the validity of Lévi-Strauss's approach. Even Lévi-Strauss's binary reductionism was confirmed by computer science. His structural anthropology fitted in with psychoanalysis as well, particularly the Jungian variant, which was very much on the rise in the sixties.

Therefore Lévi-Strauss's seemed to be a philosophy that cohered with developments in most other fields of learning, ranging from the hard sciences to the social. And structuralism opened up attractive new opportunities for literary and art criticism. It became a channel for a new cultural wave, both stimulating and reflecting this new wave. Like all hegemonic cultural movements, structuralism articulated widespread wants and feelings.

It could be claimed that Lévi-Strauss's theory was idealistic, since it subscribed to the notion of a universal code that runs through all areas of life. Lévi-Strauss himself would deny that his thought is idealist, replying that it is objective not subjective, meaning that his is not a system that foresees the self-imposition of the mind upon the world, but rather that it is a system that is exterior even to the mind and locatable in everything, including the nonmental. The mind, according to Lévi-Strauss, does not create structure, it partakes of it.

This contention could lead into a long philosophical debate. Wittgenstein's student, the English logical positivist A. J. Ayer, claimed in his history of twentieth-century philosophy that structuralism is either idealism or it is rubbish. This is not to say that Ayer's judgment is right, but only to point out how a disciple of Wittgenstein, an exponent of high modernist philosophy, responded to structuralism. Ayer's judgment indicated that structuralism could be perceived as tending toward idealism and therefore politically it could be construed as non-Marxist, not even politically radical, and susceptible to a conservative interpretation. If the world as it exists is an objective system, then the world must be accepted for what it is: This is the rightist implication of idealist philosophy in all times and places.

Lévi-Strauss did not see himself as a rightist idealist. Far from it. He thought of himself as a leftist, regarding his theory as a post-Marxist radicalism. And he was explicitly pro–Third World and critical of Western imperialism. In the fifties and sixties colonialism was still an issue, and his views qualified Lévi-Strauss, in his own eyes, and in the eyes of the Left, as staunchly leftist. But the Yale critics, who, stimulated by Barthes, hailed Lévi-Strauss as an intellectual savior around 1969 (a time when American anthropologists were not very enthusiastic about him), overlooked his views on the Third World or deemed them politically inconsequential. Considering structuralism as a whole, they found it readily adaptable for exegesis without menacing political implications. It seemed indeed to mesh well with traditional New Deal academic liberalism.

Lévi-Strauss did not get a warm reception from American anthropologists before 1970 because his approach to anthropology did not conjoin with either of the dominant modes of ethnographic thinking on the American scene in the sixties. It was left for the humanists and literary critics initially to imbibe and propagate structuralism—after which, by the late seventies, the anthropologists fell into line and became more respectful of the Parisian master. The Marxists could not stomach Lévi-Strauss because whether or not he was a philosophical idealist, he was certainly not a materialist in the sense of Malinowski or Marvin Harris. The dominant group of ethnographic functionalists, intellectual descendants of Franz Boas, and admirers of Ruth Benedict and Margaret Mead, noticed the sharp distinction between Boas's and Lévi-Strauss's methodological argument, even though with respect to judgment on the Third World, they came in the end to approximately the same conclusion. As an anthropological thinker Lévi-Strauss was antimodernist and anti-Boasian, even though their political views were close together.

Boas had to challenge Social Darwinism, the universalist theory that claimed that the Third World was primitive, backward, or decadent, and that it was located lower on the hierarchical classification of cultures than the white West. The primitive people were culturally retarded and would never attain the level of civilization and high morality that the whites had achieved. The old cultures of East Asia were effete and exhausted. Therefore the whites deserved to rule the world.

Boas opposed this view, proposing that each culture be taken as a closed system in itself. Cultures cannot be compared, they cannot be classified in hierarchical terms. The primitive cannot be opposed to the advanced, or described as decadent over against what is arbitrarily selected as morally superior. Each cultural system must be taken in and for itself. Each has its own needs, values, and the features of each, their functions exist in order to respond to these needs and articulate those values. This view may have satisfied Mauss, Lévi-Strauss's early teacher, but it did not at all coincide with structuralism.

Lévi-Strauss reached the same egalitarian conclusion as Boas, but arrived there through different means. That is, he too vehemently opposed Social Darwinism and imperialism, but not by means of the modernist route. He did not claim that each culture is distinct, self-enclosed, self-referential, and does not admit of comparison with others, but, quite to the contrary, he found that all cultures operated within the same system. Not only therefore is the Third World the same as the so-called civilized world, operating according to the same structural paradigm, but it is better than the latter, its cultural procedures being more immediately informed by the universal code.

Lévi-Strauss thus arrived at a beautiful conclusion that comes close to Heidegger's ultimate message. In the end, he stressed the theme of authenticity that is found in phenomenology, except that Lévi-Strauss applied this superior quality to societies, to behavioral groups, whereas Heidegger was more inclined to speak of the authentic individual.

Deconstruction Andy Warhol, the postmodernist painter and cultural critic, remarked that someday everyone would be famous for fifteen minutes. Intellectual systems and their gurus wore out almost as fast in the seventies and eighties as celebrities in the gossip columns. And partly at least for the same reason: overexposure. After being delineated in the classroom in a major university, expounded in several books that appeared in rapid succession, explicated further in interviews with radical-chic journals, taken on a road show of public lectures in American universities, and popularized in a spate of paperbacks, any new intellectual system began to look tired after a decade of such intensive exploitation.

Structuralism became so famous and got so much exposure that even though many academics and all but a handful of students still did not understand what it was, it began to face the challenge of a cognate but still distinctive alternative theory during the late seventies. This was deconstruction and its leading spokesmen were the Parisian masters Derrida and Foucault, although Lacan had been saying and applying in therapy many of its key ideas for many years. Until his untimely death Barthes was again a highly skillful popularizer of the new movement. He has had a host of successors, including Christopher Norris in Britain (the author of the best short treatment of deconstruction) and Jonathan Culler in the United States.

It may be wondered why French culture produced so many influential mandarins in the postwar period and especially in the seventies and eighties. There appear to be three reasons, all quite mundane. First, France retained its superb elitist secondary school system, in which everyone received a rigorous training in traditional philosophy. Second, the top echelon of French professors, particularly but not exclusively those in the Collège de France, a sort of institute for advanced study, had little or no teaching to do and were free to speculate and write major books. Third, French academics had an unequalled support system in the form of droves of admiring students, intellectual journals that propounded their more imaginative ideas, cafés where they were lionized, and a press and TV that took their ideas seriously.

While some of this exists in and around any major university, nowhere did it function with the intensity and rich stimulation as on the Left Bank of the Seine. Parisian professors asserted important ideas because a whole infrastructure existed to demand that they ought to expound important ideas, and when they did say something interesting, there was unbounded adulation and reward.

Deconstruction's formation took place in the context of the then dominant intellectual mode of structuralism. In fact, to realize that deconstruction emerges from within structuralism as defined by Lévi-Strauss is imperative for a thorough appraisal of the movement.

Deconstruction is therefore a radical variant of structuralism. It can be seen as a culturally and, to some extent, politically left-wing offshoot of structuralism. Or it can be understood too as a further development within structuralism, wherefore it is sometimes referred to as poststructuralism. The latter term is synonymous with deconstruction.

Deconstruction shares three fundamental doctrines with Lévi-Strauss's structuralism. The first of these is that authenticity, or reality, is given to the system rather than to the individual. By assuming that it is the system that has validity, deconstruction shares with structuralism a philosophical opposition to existentialism and traditional humanism, which hold that authenticity and meaning reside with the individual.

The second structuralist doctrine deconstruction shares is the attribution to language systems of the function of fundamental mental structures, thereby endowing the sciences of linguistics and semiotics with the property of constituting the interpretive code. "Mentality" consists of a systematic code of signification to which linguistics and semiotics hold the key. French deconstructionists share enthusiasm for the linguistics of Saussure. It is not so easy to ascertain whether Saussure's status arises from the intrinsic quality of his work or the fact that he was French.

The third doctrine that deconstruction and structuralism have in common is the assumption that the mental system or deep structure operates in the unconscious as well as in the conscious realm. Deconstruction accepts this psychoanalytic doctrine, fundamental to structuralism, of the continuity between the unconscious and the conscious.

How then does deconstruction differ from Lévi-Strauss's structuralism, rendering it a radical variant of the latter? Deconstruction begins with a concern that in Lévi-Strauss at any rate, structuralism is philosophically idealistic. From the doctrine that a common universal structure runs through all mind and all societies, which can be stated in terms of a general code, structuralism can be readily converted, deconstruction believes, into a conservative philosophy. Although personally he was on the Left and passionately committed to the Third World, the political implications of Lévi-Strauss's system are nevertheless ambivalent, in the view of deconstruction. Structuralism *per se* can be interpreted as a theory which accepts the world as it is and looks for ideal deep structures within the world as it is.

Deconstruction, on the other hand, seeks to avoid precisely this potential in structuralism, which can be used to legitimize a conservative neoidealism. It wants to save, as it were, structuralism from being put to work in a conservative way. Deconstruction wants to continue the radical leftist program of 1968, but it undertakes this by basing itself on structuralism rather than on existentialism.

In the 1960s it was a Marxist brand of existentialism, as expressed by Sartre, which was the inspiring doctrine of the student Left in France, and which was eventually repudiated, just as its American counterpart was discredited. The strong individualism and anarchism of the New Left lost vigor and value as a result of the failure of the revolution in 1968. Deconstruction, then, wants to fulfill the radical intent, but to do so by abandoning humanism and existentialism, and by building its radical philosophy on the new reigning doctrine of structuralism. For this purpose the revised structuralism of deconstruction is necessary. So runs, in brief, the intellectual history of the late sixties and early seventies.

Lacan was certainly the forerunner of deconstruction. For there are ideas in Lacan, which he was propounding as early as the thirties, and certainly publishing in the fifties, that can be understood as being in the deconstructionist mode. The two masters, however, who emerged in the sixties as the deconstructionist spokesmen were, first, Derrida, who is still very much alive, being sixty-six years old in 1996. He holds a chair in Paris but has taught frequently in the United States, first at Yale University and more recently at New York University. The second master of deconstruction was Foucault, who held a chair in the College de France in Paris until he died in 1984 at the age of sixty-two.

Barthes, who began his intellectual career as an existentialist and a modernist in the late forties, and continued as a structuralist in the fifties and sixties, was in his later years a popularizer of deconstruction. Barthes was thus the intellectual bellwether of his generation in France.

The prime missionaries of deconstruction in the United States have been a group of eminent critics at Yale, to which group a Chicago critic must be added. The Yale group consisted of Paul de Man, who died in 1985; J. Hillis Miller, who now teaches at the University of California at Irvine; and Geoffrey Hartman, who remains at Yale. The fourth member of the Yale group is Harold Bloom, who also teaches at New York University. Bloom's stance within or vis-à-vis deconstruction remains in dispute. He thinks of himself as unique. Bloom sees himself as heir to very old intellectual traditions associated with Gnosticism, a theosophy that goes back to ancient Persia and posits the world as the scene of a struggle between the god of light and the god of darkness. Gnosticism had a strong influence on medieval Jewish cabala, and Bloom places himself within this venerable cultural strain. Paul Ricoeur was another deconstructionist who, like Lacan, pursued a strongly psychoanalytic orientation. He taught at Chicago and frequently at Paris as well.

An impressive group of disciples has emerged after these masters, including some in England. Among the prominent ones in this country are Culler at Cornell University, as well as two scholars who are deeply engaged in trying to arrive at a synthesis of Marxism and deconstruction, Michael Ryan of the University of California and Fredric Jameson of Duke University.

There is not much doubt that the overwhelming elite of the younger generation of literary critics or scholars who received their doctoral degrees in a field of literature in the United States in the 1980s and 1990s were deconstructionists. It has in fact become difficult for a recent recipient of a Ph.D. in literature to find appointment at one of the top one hundred American institutions without demonstrating strong familiarity with deconstructionist theory.

The triumph of deconstructionism in American literature departments in the 1980s was reflected in—and at the same time abetted by—the acquisition policy of the leading university presses. They all gave preference to manuscripts submitted by deconstructionist academic critics, partly for intellectual and partly for market reasons. Given that no one could get tenure in a literature department in the top one hundred American universities without having a book published, and that access to commercial (nonuniversity) presses was rare, the devotion of the university presses to deconstructionist work forced literary scholars, at least the younger ones, to adopt this approach, whatever their private feelings about it. Certain editors at the leading university presses who specialized in the acquisition of deconstructionist criticism therefore came to exercise a powerful influence on the course of academic literary theory in the 1990s. They meant as much or more to younger professors of literature in terms of shaping their careers than did their senior colleagues still plugging away at literary biographies or—even more rare—pursuing now-old-line modernist criticism.

Derrida's major book is entitled *Of Grammatology.* Even though he may be accused of not being quite intelligible in this and other books, it is a fact that deconstruction is not easy to present in writing—paradoxically for a theory that so valorizes the written text. A good introduction to Derrida's thought can be found in the concise volume *Positions,* which consists of interviews with Derrida and presents his theory in a fully comprehensible manner.

Derrida's biography is unusual. He is an Algerian Jew. It is indeed difficult to be more of an outsider in French society than by coming from this doubly alien background. In late-nineteenth-century Algeria, which had become part of the French empire in the 1830s, a very substantial Jewish community had emerged. The nucleus of this community went as far back as the Middle Ages, but it grew with waves of immigration through the centuries. It was a thriving and highly literate, though not particularly wealthy, middle-class community.

In the Vichy period during the early forties, Algerian Jews were stripped of their French citizenship by Marshal Pétain and the Vichy government, only to be restored to citizenship in 1944, under the aegis of General Eisenhower. Against the bitter opposition of the French government in Algeria, he insisted that the citizenship of Algerian Jews be reconfirmed. The Algerian Jews were squeezed out during the independence movement of the late fifties—something that is ignored in Gillo Pontecorvo's famous film *The Battle Of Algiers*— and they had to flee. Some 20 percent of the three hundred thousand Jewish population left Algeria for Israel, while 80 percent, including the poorer segments, went to France, with the result that France, which had until then one of the smaller Jewish populations in Europe, became the country with the largest Jewish community on the continent, west of Russia. The Algerian Jews are mainly congregated in Marseille and other Mediterranean cities, and they remain marginal and poor in French society. This is the background from which Derrida emerged, and if he occasionally sounds like someone with a chip on his shoulder, then he comes by this condition honestly.

Derrida expresses his debt to Nietzsche, Freud, and Heidegger. Although his greatest influence has been on literary criticism, he in fact holds a chair of philosophy. He spent the early years of his career lecturing on Heidegger and philosophy. Derrida never mentions Lacan as having exerted a real influence on him, for reasons that are not evident, but he does express a debt to Mallarmé, the late-nineteenth-century French protomodernist poet and critic. Derrida sees his deconstructionist stance as going back to the French culture of Mallarmé's time and to the modernist movement in general. And it can indeed be claimed that deconstruction, as defined by Derrida, is a kind of neomodernism—let us here emphasize the words "a kind of"—for there are also incompatibilities between Derridean deconstruction and modernism.

Modernist thought and deconstruction overlap in three ways, the first and most important of which is the notion of the self-referentiality of the text as an *épistémè*, which is one of the central concepts in deconstruction. *Épistémè* describes the self-enclosed structure of a system of knowledge. In other words, what modernism referred to as the self-referentiality of the text is subsumed in deconstruction under the rubric of the *épistémè*, according to which the text is a self-enclosed, structural world of knowledge.

Second, Derrida and the modernists both display preference for *écriture*, the written text, as opposed to oral texts. This doctrine, which demonstrates one more similarity between deconstruction and modernism, points as well at a major difference between Derrida and Lévi-Strauss. As a cultural anthropologist, Lévi-Strauss has a natural liking for oral evidence, whereas Derrida's emphasis, an unmistakably modernist inclination, falls entirely on the written text. Modernist critics of the first two decades of the twentieth century fastened their theory on the written as deliberately opposed to the oral text.

The third compatibility between deconstruction and modernism resides in the emphasis on close reading, or what the deconstructionists call *hermeneutics*, a term that has become a code-word for deconstructionists. Originally used in biblical criticism and familiarly by Talmudic scholars, the word "hermeneutics," given that it figures so prominently in deconstruction, has interesting bearings on Derrida's thought and is telling in terms of the cultural and ethnic background he comes from. In its modern deconstructionist usage, "hermeneutics" means the close reading and interpretation of texts so as to yield the structure of knowledge and the signification contained therein. In a sense this is precisely what Eliot, Richards, Brooks, and Blackmur had in mind when they valorized the close reading of the text.

There is, therefore, a propensity in deconstruction to do as the modernists: to assume the self-referentiality of the text, to emphasize the written text, and to engage in close reading. Except that now the process of reading and interpretation is described as the pursuit of the *epistémè* through a study of the *écriture* by the method of hermeneutics. This is essentially the same as the modernist program.

This is a prime reason why Derrida has found such favorable reception at Yale University. In the forties and fifties Yale had been the capital of modernism in the United States. The modernist movement in criticism in this country began at Harvard, but its center moved to Yale in the late thirties and forties, where critics like Brooks and Ransom were teaching. And Derrida, because his deconstruction carries some strong affinities to modernism, was particularly welcomed at this institution.

At the same time, after four decades, modernism appeared exhausted and redundant. The Yale critics in the mid-sixties looked around for something new. Hartman momentarily hailed the Jungian Northrop Frye as an intellectual savior. This prepared the way for the reception of structuralism at the end of the sixties. But structuralism was diametrically opposed to modernism, and this forced the Yale critics toward an intellectual crisis they did not want to encounter. Derrida was a perfect solution for them. He emerged out of the structuralist tradition, maintained some of structuralism's cardinal principles, but also reasserted modernist traditions that Yale could not bring itself, after four decades, to surrender. Furthermore Derrida was a philosophy professor at Paris and eminently respectable, and he knew a lot about Heidegger and Nietzsche. Made to order, he became Yale's main man.

The key concept in Derrida's thought is *différance*, not to be reduced to the word "difference," which is nevertheless contained in the Derridean concept. *Différance* is, and means, a combination of differences. He defines the concept as "the idea of conflictuality," which is the best translation in English of *différance*. It can also be described as intrinsic oppositions.

In each signifying text, in each text that holds meaning, there are by its nature oppositions or internal conflicts at work, by which the text deconstructs itself. This is the condition of *différance* or conflictuality. The process takes the surface signification, or the surface meaning, and breaks it down, disintegrates it, because of the oppositional and conflictual nature of language. The text, through a self-generating mechanism that is inscribed in the very being of language, breaks itself down into several simultaneous layers of meaning.

There is not one canonical signification to a text, as humanists have (allegedly) thought all along, but rather, there lies, beyond the surface meaning, one more meaning, and then additional layers of meaning. There are, in fact, infinite meanings in the text, moving from the immediate, conscious layer toward the unconscious, until finally one approaches the strata of meaning that border on the unconscious. Deconstruction is theoretically an objective, involuntary process because of the intrinsically fragmenting nature of the signifier.

This notion of the instability of signification is based on the oppositional, conflictual structures built into language. That this is the nature of language is not an assumption that admits of proof. Nor does one get the impression, having read Derrida's *Of Grammatology*, that he himself has succeeded in proving it. But building on Saussure, from whom comes the notion of the arbitrariness of the sign, he claims an essential instability in language. The nature of language is such that it conceals meaning but does not do so fully, leaving traces on the surface that yield to pursuit.

There is certainly an element of common sense in Derrida's theory of *différance*. We frequently observe in didactic theory of humanistic exposition fragmentary indices that do not fit the main thrust of the argument. Derrida is saying that this implies the return of the repressed opposition from the unconscious. Again this is not implausible.

Anomalies exist on the surface of the text. A text emits a message on the surface, but on the same surface it harbors as well, albeit sporadically, anomalies or gaps, which, when taken into account, are found to conflict and call into question what is signified. Derrida stresses these gaps—between words, in meaning—which exist on the virtual margins of the text. As one focuses on these gaps, the text begins to deconstruct itself. The gaps spread, get bigger. The margins fall into the body of the text. It is not, however, the critic who is procuring that this happens, but the text itself, the signifier, systematically deconstructing itself before the reader's expectant eyes.

In the master's own words: "The play of *différance* ... prevents any word, any concept, any major enunciation from coming to summarize, and to govern ... the movement and textual spacing of differences." Because of the *différance* (conflictuality) at work in language, no single meaning can claim absolute authority over a given text, nor can the critic control, despite all effort, this movement of the text. Language is characterized by "the structural impossibility of limiting this [conceptual] network, of putting an edge on its weave," of "tracing a margin that would not be a new mark." There is, in other words, a structural impossibility of imposing a finity and a fixity, or a conclusion, to textual signification. When the humanist professor reads a text in order to find there a single, consecrated meaning, the text explodes in his face.

Derrida confronts Lévi-Strauss as a dangerous intellectual conservative, or at least, potentially so. Derrida advocates "a general strategy of deconstruction," writing that the latter is to avoid both "*neutralizing* the binary oppositions of metaphysics [that is, idealism], and simply *residing* within the closed field of these oppositions, thereby confirming it [that is, conservatism]." The problem with Lévi-Strauss's structuralism as seen by Derrida is that it acknowledges the binary oppositions in mental and language codes, but it also tries to control and neutralize them, thereby attempting to keep them residual, rather than unbounding the text and the binary oppositions to the free play that is the aim of radical deconstruction. In Derrida's view Lévi-Strauss wants to systematize and control binary conflicts while Derrida wants to liberate them into intellectual revolutions.

Derrida speaks of "the necessity of an interminable analysis." We all have heard of the never-ending story. Here is its counterpart, never-ending criticism. He sounds the call for radical thinking: "The time for overturning is never a dead letter." That which is overturned are conventional meaning, traditional significations, surface readings. The perpetual overturning of meaning is in the nature of language, as is the interpenetration of layers of significations, reaching into the unconscious.

Derrida is aware of the radical social implications of his theory. His statement that "to deconstruct the opposition, first of all, is to overturn the hierarchy of a given moment" is tantamount to a call for an intellectual revolution which has broad cultural and social implications. Further, he claims that "'thought' means nothing." "Thought" means, in this context, humanistic thought—that is, what the humanist tradition has hypothesized as thought, a canonical system or Western civilization itself. Derrida is putting into question consecrated, unquestioned entities such as "the humanities," "the classical tradition," "the medieval heritage" or "the liberal doctrine," all of which he regards as unstable and untenable concepts that mean, quite simply, nothing. The liberal humanists, in Derrida's view, are at best pathetically obsolete. At worst they are the enemy who must be mercilessly overthrown.

The obvious implication of all this is that Derrida is an antihumanist, since, first of all, he believes that there is no fixed meaning, canon, or tradition. There is only an infinity of meaning. The humanists struggled over the centuries to create a canon, a received sacred tradition of valid texts that extended from Plato through Hegel. Derrida, by deconstructing the texts and by presumably pointing at significations in these texts which undercut both the continuity among and the meaning in them, demonstrates that the fixity of the humanist tradition is based on naught. All canons may be scrambled, all texts are subject to reevaluation, and their meanings are open to perpetual reconsideration. Derrida offers unlimited horizons for busy literary critics; no wonder they love him.

Derrida's position becomes clearer when he is compared with Lionel Trilling, who was the idol of literary criticism in the United States in the forties and fifties. Trilling and his colleagues at Columbia University, as will be remembered from a previous chapter, devoted much time to determining the essential texts of Western civilization which every student in Columbia College should have to read and reread, not only for what might be understood as their intrinsic worth, but as a tradition which culminates and finds its ulterior fulfillment in New Deal liberalism. Derrida's response to this project would be to point out that the number of canons are as numerous as the possible readings and combinations of texts, which is but to say that the number is practically infinite. What Trilling was doing was impossible and meretricious in its implications.

In the 1930s and 1940s Trilling tried mightily to construct and valorize a canon of texts for Western civilization. In the sixties and seventies Derrida tried just as hard to deconstruct and devalue the same canon. This comparison illuminates the contrasting status of the Jewish intellectual in the Western world between 1940 and 1970. He moved from the defensive, from trying to show that he belonged within the humanist liberal Christian tradition, to flaunting his opposition, his expression of conflictuality, his disdain for that tradition. Eliot the anti-Semite would have had some interesting comments to make on this contrast.

Another reason why Derrida can be considered antihumanistic is his disbelief in the notion of the controlling mind. As the text deconstructs itself and generates its own multiplicity of meaning, the critic, or the reader, is a mere witness to the text's self-unraveling. There is of course some speciousness involved here, for when Derrida himself spends two hours deconstructing a brief philosophical or literary fragment (which he was prone to do from the lecture platform for a high fee), his mind is very much at work, not to say in control. Rather than the text working itself, it appears to be clever Derrida at work on the text. But he claims that he is himself acting as a *conduit*, transferring from the text into critical language the multiplicity of significations that comprise the text. He is rendering, in other words, what the text renders to him.

At this point it becomes clear that Derrida's main departure from the modernists of the twenties and the thirties is that the latter were committed humanists. Richards, Eliot, and Brooks believed first of all that there was very much a canonical tradition, and second that the canon in fact admitted of interpretation. Derrida, while also engaging in close reading, denies the real existence of both the canon and the canonical interpretation. In this sense he is posthumanist and post-modernist.

Derrida's published writings are concerned with philosophy, language studies, and literary and semiotic criticism. The radical political implications are present and are meant to be present, but in implicit rather than explicit form. Yet the leftist orientation is sufficient for Marxists to make a strenuous effort to bridge Marxism and Derrida's deconstruction. Jameson, Rosalind Krauss, and Michael Ryan, among others, are hard at work on his project, producing reams of dense literary and art criticism.

The enthusiasm of leftist theorists like Jameson, Krauss, and Ryan for Derrida derives from his appearing to be the long-sought fulfiller of the Frankfurt school. He was attacking the bourgeoisie at its hegemonic cultural center, its canonical texts embodying its faith in the Western consciousness. And Derrida was attaining the holy grail of the Left with the blessing of a good part of the academic world. Whether it was from the English Department at Yale, the French Department at NYU, or the Humanities Institute at Cornell, Derrida was the recipient of lavish praise and public honor. Through Derrida the Left believed it was having its cultural epiphany at last.

A final reason for Derrida's popularity and influence is his familiarity with the language and concept formation of German phenomenology. Derrida first gained attention in Paris as a persuasive teacher of Heidegger's philosophy, and his deconstructive theory can be viewed as having a certain compatibility with phenomenology. The text, in Derrida's interpretation, is an active Other, with its own rules of conflictual *différance* separated from consciousness. The deconstructive process involves coming to terms, engaging interactively, with this autonomous text. This view readily parallels the key ingredient in Heidegger's philosophy. Derrida's theory could be regarded as a skillful effort to blend

French structuralism and German phenomenology. This intellectual bridging of the Rhine was unusual in the postwar era and contributed to Derrida's visibility and influence.

At the beginning of the 1990s an unusual problem faced the literary deconstructionists in the United States and France, that of political and personal scandal. Revelations were made about the early life of Paul de Man, who stood at the center of the Yale deconstructionists in the 1970s and 1980s. As a young man in Belgium during World War II de Man (who was related to a prominent collaborator with the Nazi occupiers) had worked for a collaborationist newspaper, during which he wrote a couple of relatively mild anti-Semitic columns. After the war he abandoned his wife and child and created a new life in the United States, eventually emerging as a distinguished professor at Yale. The intellectual and political enemies of deconstruction made much of the information to disparage de Man, who had recently died, and to tar Derrida and the deconstructionist movement as unethical. Derrida responded that these matters were irrelevant to the philosophical and literary program he had fostered with de Man's assistance.

Deconstruction has been customarily affiliated with leftist opposition to the political and academic establishment. But as a doctrine that undermines all prevailing and traditional systems, it could just as easily be tied to rightist radicalism, and indeed to volatile fascist hostility to liberal ethics and generalizing propositions. It could be argued that this is where de Man started, in a kind of Nietzschean fascist contempt for received liberal-Jewish culture. But the evidence for this intellectual profile is weak. Young de Man was just a desperate, confused person living in bad times and trying to survive by trimming his ideas to the wind. His postwar personal and family history have nothing to do with deconstruction—an academic mistreating his wife and child is a common story in every faculty club in the world. Derrida was right to dismiss the de Man scandal as having no intellectual significance.

The other leading deconstructionist thinker, Michel Foucault, was a social theorist and cultural historian. His radical critique of culture and society was therefore entirely explicit, and he therefore gained extravagant adulation on the left in the seventies and eighties. On the whole this leftist enthusiasm for Foucault is justified, although not quite in the unqualified form that it often takes, because there is a problem for the Left in his doctrine.

It can be said that Marx and Nietzsche were Foucault's main inspiration with the influence of Durkheim, the *Annales* school, and Lacan also prevalent.

With regard to Marx, Foucault frankly said that "it is impossible at the present time to write history without using a whole series of concepts directly or indirectly related to Marx's thought and situating itself within a horizon of thought which has been defined and described by Marx." Nietzsche was important because he was concerned with "power relation," which Foucault also wanted to explore. Indeed, he said that like Nietzsche, he was engaged in a study of the "genealogy of morals." Like Lacan, he thought that human beings are always accompanied by "an element of darkness . . . the unthought . . . the Other." Like Durkheim and Braudel and the *Annales* school, Foucault saw society as an integrated, functioning whole. "Power comes from below; that is, there is no binary and all-encompassing opposition between rulers and ruled and the root of all power relations." Adorno's theory of cultural mediation is also reflected in Foucault's theory.

Obviously Foucault was a very learned scholar. The purpose of all this learning was to develop a theory of power. "The rules of right, the mechanisms of power, the effects of truth or if you like, the rules of power and the power of true discourses . . . formed the general terrain of my concern."

Foucault was the son of a prominent provincial doctor. His late teens and early twenties were devoted to escaping from his upper-middle-class family and his father's oppressive mien by excelling in secondary and university studies in the humanities in Paris. Not without much frustration and struggle, he eventually succeeded, but Foucault was always something of an outsider and a loner in Parisian academic circles. His academic field was cultural and sociological history. When, after several major publications that made him celebrated in intellectual circles, he was elected to a chair at the prestigious Collège de France, not one historian on its faculty voted for him.

It was Foucault's active homosexuality that—even in tolerant Paris—especially set him apart. In the decade before his death in 1985 he discovered the gay community in San Francisco while visiting at Berkeley. This provided personal happiness but also killed him at the age of sixty-one from AIDS he contracted in a San Francisco bathhouse. Foucault's biographers leave unsettled the accusations made after his death that he continued to practice unsafe sex even though he knew he was HIV positive. Foucault comes through in his books as a rather fierce personality, although in person he was quiet and extremely civil.

Foucault became known in the mid-fifties from his first book, translated in English as *Madness and Civilization*. It reflected the year in his early career when he worked in mental hospitals. It showed how doctors in seventeenth-century

France connived with political and social authorities to categorize certain behavior as madness, which justified segregation in institutions. The book can be construed as a blow against his father, the physician. Foucault intensely disliked the learned professions. *Discipline and Punish*, a later work, pours scorn on lawyers.

Those who read Foucault for the first time in the late fifties and early sixties agreed that he was a clever and first-rate historian of ideas. It was realized only later that the book on madness was part of an entire new program.

In the sixties Foucault represented himself as a structuralist, and in the seventies, as a deconstructionist. As will be seen, some aspects of his thought are strongly deconstructionist, while others remain as strongly structuralist. Of course, his deconstruction is a radical form of structuralism, and generates no problematic contradiction between the two movements. Above all it should be pointed out that ultimately Foucault did not like to describe himself in terms of any label but that of the human scientist.

There are three basic concepts in Foucault's work. The first of these is the archaeology of knowledge. Foucault tried to write nonhistorical, or discontinuous, history. What are important are the *épistémés*, the deep structures of knowledge, that exist in society in particular eras. Although officially he was a professor of the history of ideas, Foucault did not call himself a historian. He preferred the title "archaeologist of knowledge." Like an archaeologist, he sinks shafts down into the culture of a particular period and excavates its *épistémé* or the structure of knowledge at work in that society. In that sense, his work is deeply structural, for, in the last analysis, Foucault, like Braudel, is writing history that might be acceptable to Lévi-Strauss. Braudel presents the deep structures of society, and Foucault those of culture or systems of knowledge. His is the cultural or intellectual equivalent of Braudel's work in social history.

Foucault does not believe that the paths of change can be extrapolated. The study of the past comprises a series of discrete, discontinuous archaeological digs into culture and mentality.

The second Foucaultian doctrine that becomes increasingly pronounced in his work is ethical theory. Foucault is entirely, thoroughly, a moral relativist. He writes that all the institutions of a society, as well as all its ethical principles and cultural forms, are instruments of power. It is the will to power that perpetually plays itself out in history. No matter how brilliant and how admired, aesthetically or otherwise, cultural forms have as their fundamental function this instrumentality for power, and serve or seek the interests of a ruling body.

This theory obviously draws on a Nietzschean notion, as well as extrapolating a Marxian conception.

It was the Marxists who had held that the bourgeoisie used culture—residually, viscerally, and fundamentally—in order to sustain their power. Foucault uses this idea, but unlike Marxists, who limit this cultural practice to the bourgeoisie, he includes all ruling groups—the aristocracy and monarchy and democratic adversary groups—as much as the bourgeoisie, in the scheme. The hegemonic struggle for power is not terminated by the triumph of Communists, feminists, or Third World liberators. It is endemic, secular, and perpetual. Of course, this assumption begs the question whether Foucault's books are then designed to achieve *his* power. (The answer is affirmative.)

Foucault wrote a series of provocative books demonstrating power at work in manipulating culture. He is especially interested in showing that the progressive ideas in a culture are archetypal of this search for power. It is not merely the decadent or reactionary forces that partake of power structures, but the progressive ones, the innovators, the reputed great instruments of human progress that are in fact designed to enhance power.

Foucault considers first of all the insane asylum, which was the invention of the seventeenth century. Instead of letting the mad wander around the streets, as in the Middle Ages, or in any large American city today, the seventeenth century incarcerated them in asylums. Whereas the Middle Ages had marginalized lepers, and appointed them for exclusion from society, the seventeenth century selected people it called "the mad" for incarceration. Who were these "mad"? They were mystics, nonconformists, misfits, and the unhappy—people, in other words, who in one way or another were torn apart by social institutions such as the family and local government and were expressing their discontent and resistance, and who thereby attracted attention within either the family or other small social groups. "'Dangerous' people had to be isolated . . . so that they could not act as a spearhead for popular resistance."

It may momentarily, and superficially, seem that the seventeenth-century introduction of insane asylums constituted an instance of human progress, since these, it could be construed, were shelters that protected the mad from abuse. But the same institution can be also regarded as segregatory, says Foucault, excluding from the world the nonconformists, as lepers had been isolated in the Middle Ages.

In *Discipline and Punish* Foucault takes up the late-eighteenth early-nineteenth-century invention of the penitentiary, which marked the switch from the practice of either executing criminals or transporting them to Australia or other colonies. Now the criminal was locked up in the local penitentiary, where he or she was supposed to be restrained but also reeducated and so transformed into a good citizen. In this way, criminals were not only to pay their "debt to society," but they were to be disciplined into mental transformation as well.

Once again Foucault claims the use of discipline and segregation to remove nonconformists from social life, since criminals too, like the mad, were people who were in conflict with the social order. Their criminality was very often inherited. They came, for the most part, from the vast ghettos of the late-eighteenth- and early-nineteenth-century city, whose dark panorama is so well drawn in the novels of Charles Dickens. The penitentiary, whose original rationale was that it would rediscipline and reform the criminal for reintegration into society, became one more means of segregating and removing threats to social order. This novel institution was much talked about, or talked up, as it were, and praised by the progressives of the day, and above all by Quaker reformers and liberal idealists, who were in fact instruments in the repression and segregation of dissenting and adversary people.

It must be realized that the issues Foucault has taken up were crucial for many developments in French culture in the post–World War II period. In the late forties and fifties, Frenchmen were fascinated by criminality, by what constituted the criminal, and whether the criminal was different from other, normal people. Foucault's book on punishment and the penitentiary draws on this proclivity in the French culture of the postwar period, which took a relativistic stance on criminality, an idea that was perhaps made possible by experiencing the Gestapo at work in the streets of Paris, and its repression of the Resistance—an effective way of driving home the idea that the determination of what is criminal is a relative enterprise.

Another source of relativist attitude to criminality came from gays, who still experienced social marginality. As a gay, Foucault imbibed their radically ambivalent view of criminality.

In his later years Foucault embarked on a multivolume history of sexuality, and he died having completed three volumes, all of which are now available in English. This is a brilliant piece of work, very different from what we might expect from a work of that title. Another one of Foucault's demonstrations of the will to power, *The History of Sexuality*, volume 1, shows that the sexual liberation movement that began at the beginning of this century and went through successive phases, especially influential ones in the sixties and the seventies, has been once again the power play of those seeking hegemony in society. He asks us to remember that while the sexual liberation movement did indeed increase human happiness, the people who were leading it were also engaged in manipulation. For them it was another forum for achieving their desired place in the world. It was an instrument, a mechanism, for advancing their situation within the power structure.

It is also Foucault the gay who is talking here, taking an acerbic and critical view of women's liberation as a form of instrumentation and assertion of power by one social group. Given Foucault's position on the sexual liberation movement, it becomes amusing to find publications such as the *Village Voice* hailing him as the champion of sexual liberation. He is, of course, that in some ways, but reading *The History of Sexuality,* one discovers that he does not exempt that movement from the same kind of moral and institutional ambivalence that he ascribes to all forms of progressive emancipation.

The deconstructive side of Foucault is much in evidence here. Just as for Derrida, all texts and concepts spontaneously fragment into their intrinsically conflictual segments, so for Foucault all moral affirmations disintegrate into thrusts for power and manipulative domination. There is no ethical system that rises above the corrosive force of total moral relativism.

The third important idea of Foucault is his proclamation of the "end of man"—the passing of bourgeois and humanistic man. Man as he has been perceived in bourgeois liberal humanism is being dismantled, deconstructed, and cannot withstand the cold light of moral relativism that is cast on him. The self-satisfied, self-congratulatory liberal humanism is disintegrating as it reveals itself as the instrument of class power and of the socially and educationally privileged. The individual subject with his or her conscience and reason—which was the product of the cultural revolutions of the Reformation, the Enlightenment, and romanticism—is dying just as, according to Nietzsche, the idea of a transcendent, theistic God died in the nineteenth century.

Thus Derrida announces that humanist thought is nothing, and Foucault proclaims the end of bourgeois man. Both are heralds of the decease of humanist bourgeois rationalism.

In the case of Derrida, the deconstruction movement has generated a theory of literary criticism, an extremely influential one. In the case of Foucault, on the other hand, it has led to a post-Marxist relativism. If Derrida spells literary or linguistic deconstruction, Foucault stands for social and moral deconstruction. In both cases there is found an instrument of radical theorizing against humanistic values and particularly against the liberal values of the 1940s and 1950s. Therefore both Derrida and Foucault have strongly appealed to the younger generation of Marxist scholars and theorists. Their deconstructive theories contain instruments for the further critique of bourgeois traditions and capitalist culture. They point at ways that step beyond Adorno and the Frankfurt school, and using deconstructionist theory, it is possible to propagate an additional erosion of contemporary culture.

There are three journals, lively ones and very much worthy of perusal—*Telos,* which began publication in St. Louis but is now being published in the East Village in New York; *October,* edited by Rosalind Krauss of the City University of New York; and *Social Text,* edited by Andrew Ross of New York University, who are involved in the program of developing a new post-Marxist critique of capitalist culture using deconstruction.

Marx would see Derrida and Foucault as more within the anarchist tradition than as his own followers. That in part accounts for the immense popularity and prestige Derrida and Foucault gained in American universities in the late seventies and eighties. There had been a strong anarchist vein in the New Left. Now that the New Left was no longer marching to the barricades and offing the pigs, but had withdrawn into its academic citadel, studying and applying Derrida and Foucault offered a vicarious thrill of anarchist-type radicalism.

By 1990 Derrida and Foucault had become established figures in the graduate schools of the humanities throughout the Western world. They were no longer at the radical margin but at the cultural and academic center. Academic conferences devoted to literature, whether modern or medieval, featured many sessions based on their ideas. The field of art history, hitherto embedded in the intellectual world of early-twentieth-century modernism, felt their impact. Historians talked about the need to pursue "the linguistic turn" with Derrida and made Foucault an icon in the discipline's intellectual pantheon.

Academic Vicissitudes The culture of the postwar Western world was heavily focused on the expansion of universities and their enhanced role in intellectual life and national well-being. While this was particularly the case in the United States, where the campus came to play a major role even in the performing and visual arts, it was also true of Western society as a whole. By 1960 the importance of scientist and scholar to society was endorsed by government officials and corporate leaders alike and the need to provide the best possible college teaching and training facilities to the emerging generation was not questioned.

With the demographic tidal wave of the sixties, universities in the

Western world experienced an unprecedented student demand and enjoyed a new level of prosperity and expansionary capacity. This high tide of social appreciation and fiscal affluence for universities turned out, however, to be relatively short-lived. Once again the American university was the bellwether institution, and its destiny was shared, although again not as critically, by European universities.

One of the intriguing untold stories of the late sixties and early seventies was how the radical turmoil of the period particularly unsettled those white ethnic professors—particularly Jews, Italians, and Slavs—who had finally broken their way into the departments and even some administrations of the old, established American universities. What they had wanted to conquer were the shining heights of the academic establishment. They had their sights on the pinnacle for half a century, and by the mid-sixties they had finally succeeded in scaling these heights. But open admissions and campus activism were threatening to change the nature of the American university overnight into a very different kind of democratizing, politically conditioned institution. It was not for this that they had struggled through City College in the forties and suffered privation and insults at Harvard, Columbia, or Princeton in the fifties. They had not painfully internalized the tenuous, complex heritage of European aristocratic culture now to be publicly abused by black activists and SDS ideologues, or to devote themselves to teaching the rudiments of English composition to the semiliterate.

All the turmoil and disorder, which 1968 symbolized and in many instances directly caused, as well as the resurgence of conservatism on the campus and in society at large, led in the seventies to the downgrading of the experimental and more individualized curricula that had begun to appear fitfully in the sixties—and rarely as yet with any clear advance in learning. Instead in the late seventies there was a return toward the mandated distribution of course requirements and basic skills courses of the 1950s. Since the Eisenhower era was deemed to have been a happy one in U.S. history, by the late seventies many colleges were taking a bold, innovative step forward into the curriculum of the 1950s.

The reintroduction, with much fanfare, of distribution requirements at Harvard, under the leadership of Dean Henry Rosovsky, encouraged many other campuses, such as Stanford, NYU, and Brooklyn College, to do the same. Rosovsky advertised his program as a "core curriculum." It was really a smorgasbord of allegedly tasty items from a stale menu culled out of Western civilization.

There were some very fine institutions—the colleges at Columbia, at the University of Chicago, St. John's College in Maryland—that had never departed from the intellectually demanding, highly structured "great books" core curricula in the humanities that they had established in the 1920s and 1930s. A highly structured core curriculum adapted to the intellectual and social milieu of the eighties could be an interesting and beneficial experiment, especially if it involved the natural and social sciences as well as literature and philosophy. But the resurgence of mandatory distribution and basic skill requirements in a host of institutions in the eighties can scarcely be categorized as innovative and experimental. It was more a reflection of the cautious attitudes that affected the administrations and faculties at that time, and of the failure of the American university to stem the decline of the American high school.

The widely felt need in the late seventies to establish in the first year of college basic skill courses in English composition and mathematical computation, and distribution requirements aiming to instruct freshmen and sophomores in the rudiments of history, literature, philosophy, and natural and social scientific thinking, was a recognition that even high-prestige and very selective colleges found that students were emerging from high school in effect unprepared for university-level education. Instead of using its then rich available resources in the sixties to upgrade secondary education, the American higher education establishment now felt obligated in the more austere seventies to instruct the products of lamentably inadequate high schools in the kind of basic cognition that students in Europe gained at the secondary education level.

The American university had itself contributed to the decline in the quality of secondary education by developing schools of "professional education" and by getting state and municipal boards to require this kind of marginal training for certification to teach in public schools. It was the ineffective teaching in the high schools by the graduates of these schools of education that now required even highly selective colleges like Harvard and Stanford to compensate for the low quality of instruction and standardization in the high schools.

The 1960s, extending into the early years of the 1970s, was an era of intellectual ferment and cognitive advancement in the American university. Through the latter part of the seventies and into the late eighties, there was a slowing down of intellectual advancement, a retreat from pedagogical experimentation, and a general conservatizing trend.

In the sciences, outside of biology and computer science, the American universities were no longer secure in their worldwide performance and in many disciplines their intellectual leadership was fast eroding. A 1980 study showed the severe decline in the quality of scientific research instrumentation on the major American campuses in the 1970s.

During the 1970s the most important discoveries in the physics of elementary particles were made at the laboratory of CERN (Conseil Européen pour Récherche Nucléaire) in Geneva—a European consortium center for advanced work in physics. No laboratory in the United States could equal CERN's experimental facilities. While federal sponsorship of basic research increased in the mid-eighties, the extra margin of support was narrowly focused on five high-speed computer centers and the Strategic Defense Initiative (SDI).

In the humanities almost entirely, and in the social sciences outside of economics, the American university was looking for intellectual leadership to Western Europe, particularly to France and to some extent England and West Germany. Paris was again the intellectual capital of the West. As in the first three decades of this century, university professors were significantly better paid in West Germany and some of the other Continental European countries than in the United States, with long-term consequences for the quality of research on campus.

The reduction of federal support for research, the aftershocks of the political upheavals of the late sixties, and the return of a great depression in the academic world, producing miserable job prospects for Ph.D.'s in the humanities and the soft social sciences who poured out of both the old and new graduate schools in the seventies, were disincentives for the best minds to enter these professionally unrewarding fields in the eighties. The loss of real income by faculty in the late seventies, as salaries did not keep pace with inflation by a significant margin, the retrenchment of university budgets effected by state governments, and the fiscal difficulties of many private universities, even some of the more distinguished—all had a severely depressing effect on the intellectual vitality and cognitive ambience of American campuses. The adverse labor market in the eighties drove the college students so powerfully toward career-oriented undergraduate programs that professors in physics, philosophy, literature, and history faced shrinking classes at both undergraduate and graduate levels.

In these adverse circumstances, arts and science faculty increasingly lost confidence in the value of what they were doing, or retreated into privatism and the pursuit of research that won the plaudits of a few colleagues in other institutions but could receive little recognition and no tangible reward in society at large.

Just as the tone and mode of American academic life changed rapidly in the early sixties as the upward swing of demographic revolution became visible, so the sharp decline in college-age population in the eighties produced a widespread sense of futility and foreboding of defeat on the American campus. The talk was now all retrenchment, cost-cutting, and the "management of decline."

One of the positive advances on the American campus in the seventies had indeed been improved planning and more effective management: Would that the expansion of campuses and the creation of whole new universities in the sixties had been carried out with similar care and skillful control as was exhibited by a number of campus administrators in the following decade.

The American academic world made some bad mistakes during the era of prosperity in the sixties and early seventies. Why was it so shortsighted, reckless, and profligate? The 1950s had been a time of low risk-taking and relative rigidity on the campuses, both institutionally and intellectually. There was a constant fear in the 1950s that after the World War II and Korean War veterans on the GI Bill were gone, the depressed condition of the thirties on the campus would return. This caution served as an unfavorable background for the expansionary and rapidly changing situation to be encountered in the 1960s, which required highly imaginative and novel strategies. Leadership was poor in the academic world, good planning and careful management virtually nonexistent.

Unanticipated by the reckless expansionary campus policies of the sixties and seventies, the downside of the demographic revolution in the 1980s became a terrifying reality. The traditional college-age population declined nationally by 20 to 25 percent in at least three-quarters of the states. An optimistic view presented by some higher-education analysts that the shrinkage of the national college-age population would be balanced by an increased percentage of this group going to college—that is, the demographic base would shrink, but more of this cohort would attend college—did not occur. On the contrary, from 1973 to 1978 the proportion of the college-age population going to college actually declined by a significant margin.

For those in the higher-education establishment who could see nothing to do except manage decline and plan and implement retrenchment, history offered a certain sanction and authority. There have, after all, been only two short periods of creativity and affluence in the history of the American university. These eras—before World War II and the sixties and the very early seventies—were, it could be claimed, moments of exception. Now, with the late seventies and eighties, the American university was returning to the norm, to the shrinkage of the higher educational delivery system. It was said in the mid-eighties that the United States could not now avoid the impoverishment of faculties, of a severe level of academic unemployment, of little or no pedagogical experimentation, and of research capacity lagging behind more prosperous countries such as the World War II vanquished foes, West Germany and Japan, whom America did the favor of proscribing from heavy defense investment so they could invest more of their internal resources in scientific and technological research.

It is not only in cars and electronic equipment that the United Stetes was overtaken by other countries. In the humanities and human sciences, there was in the eighties a shrinking campus intellectual base that could not compete with the venerable, deep, and ever-resilient aristocratic cultures of France and England. Incredible as it might have seemed in 1965, the United States in the mid-eighties was witness to the replaying of the Jamesian scenario in which the United States took the role of the intellectual colonial, the academic dependent of Europe.

David Riesman and Christopher Jencks, in their celebrated book *The Academic Revolution,* published in 1968, thought that they had portrayed the shape of higher education in this country—dominated by the imperial research universities and their affluent elite faculty—for a long time to come. They had actually described a very ephemeral moment in American higher education.

Not only this optimistic view of the American campus from the perspective of Harvard Square but just about everyone's perception of the American college and university in the late sixties and early seventies—NYU Chancellor Alan Carter's was a lonely Cassandra voice on the future of the American college and university—was based on assumptions about an expanding American economy and affluent society that by 1980 appeared very doubtful. A situation prevailed at both the federal and state levels in which higher education had to compete desperately and often disadvantageously for public support against other priorities within a stagnant or declining tax base.

By 1986 the downward spiral in the condition of the American university seemed to have leveled out. There appeared to be a renewed interest in humanities courses in the upscale colleges and a modest improvement in the academic job market for Ph.D.'s. But this meliorating situation was mostly illusory. For a dozen years wave after wave of adverse circumstances had hit the campuses. By the mid-eighties the prosperity and expansion of the sixties had been so much forgotten, and there had developed such desensitivity to growth and improvement, that even a hiatus in exploding disaster looked like a good thing.

The decline of the American university in the seventies and eighties was by no means the consequence only of the external factors involving deterioration of fiscal resources, loss of public support, and the decline of the demographic curve. Weak leadership and defects in governance—internal structural problems—also affected the universities severely. While there are remarkable exceptions, the kinds of people that rose to the top level of university administration—presidents, provosts, and deans—were politicians, compromisers, apparatchiks, devoid of strong beliefs and lacking in visions of progress and reform.

The hegemony of these kinds of neutral people in university administration is partly a consequence of the upheavals of the sixties. Then it was discovered that university administrators with strongly held beliefs fared less well in dealing with student radicals than easier-going negotiator types who could bend to the wind and were spared the brittleness that often characterized the idealists among university leaders.

A second factor leading to the rise of the apparatchiks in university administration was the large increase in consensual instruments of university governance during the seventies. Faculty senates, student councils, or combined faculty-student assemblies gained much greater visibility and frequently held a significant measure of reserved decision-making power. With this politicization of the university, it became necessary, it was thought, for the president and other senior officials to be people who were not distinguished by educational convictions or scholarly accomplishment but someone who was a skilled politician, able to manipulate assemblies. Thus the same qualifications for university leadership were inscribed as were valued in the political world at large.

Sometimes prominent politicians were simply appointed as university presidents. Terry Sanford, the former Democratic governor of North Carolina, became president of Duke. John Brademas, a liberal Democratic leader for twenty years, ascended to the presidency of New York University after as vehement a campaign as he ever waged in his Indiana congressional district. Familar party machine politicians became presidents of the state universities of Oklahoma and Massachusetts in 1995. More often, however, academia grew its politicians at home.

The kind of faculty who shone in university senates were professors who had lost interest in teaching and whose career in research and scholarship were on a downward trajectory. University politics became a viable and interesting substitute, with the immediate rewards of power and influence, and the longer-term possibility of gaining a top position in university administration.

Emerging out of this consensual governance structure, and with the aim of bringing cohesion and peace to the campus, the politician-type university administrator did succeed in healing the wounds and covering up the fissures inherited from the tumultuous sixties. This accomplishment was not without value. The price paid was, however, severe. It instilled in the eighties and early nineties a mood of pliancy and caution in the university presidencies, an absence of strong and imaginative leadership either on the campus or in representing the university to society at large, and university administrations in the late eighties and nineties were devoid of specific programs to improve education and advance the life of the mind. There was not one new programmatic idea in American education in the two decades after 1975. Everything done on the campus was the cultivation of concepts and programs that had emerged in the previous half century. Perhaps after the turmoil of the sixties a decade of stocktaking and reaffirmation was in order, but by the late eighties the American campus had become a quiescent and stultifying place. No wonder the brighter and more ambitious students chose programs and embarked on life careers on mostly material and selfish grounds. There was very little on campus to fire their imaginations or inculcate high ideals.

The last innovation in American higher education was the introduction of what in the parlance of the nineties was called multiculturalism or diversity. These were programs focusing on the cultures of disadvantaged groups, beginning with African-Americans and going on to Hispanics, Native Americans, and women. By the 1980s the trend to multicultural programs also led to the proliferation of Jewish Studies and Holocaust programs. While the multicultural campus trend was not fully elaborated until around 1990, its contours were clearly set down in the first Black Studies programs established—often after controversy and turmoil—in the late sixties. The features of these programs were all the same, whether the subject was African Americans, Hispanics, Native Americans, women, or Jews. The programs were interdisciplinary, and the faculty were usually habilitated in traditional departments. The content of courses was more ideological than normal, and the manner of teaching often pastoral and therapeutic. The students who enrolled—and there was often a disappointing dearth of them—were mostly members of the same group that was being studied. The quality of faculty in these programs was uneven, sometimes marginal to start with, but improved sharply as time went on and more Ph.D.'s were specifically trained to participate in this kind of work.

There had been an exciting moment on the campus in the 1960s, when an interactive engagement was in process between scholarly ideals and capacity on the one hand and education and pedagogy on the other. Professors talked meaningfully to students and tried to relate their learning and thought worlds to the classroom and the seminar, and to involve students in their concept formation. What characterized the campus of the late eighties and nineties was the polar opposite of this situation. Almost never now did a scientist of distinction teach a basic freshman-sophomore class in his discipline—that was left to the novice and the lame mediocrity. The leading social scientists devoted themselves to their separate research institutes, grant development, and consulting outside the campus. The humanists had become like medieval scholastics, talking to one another in the arcane rarefied codes of analytic philosophy and deconstructionist criticism, which only a few invited acolytes could fully comprehend and to which only partisans cared to listen closely.

The quiescence of the American campus in the late eighties and the dominance of its governance by neutral apparatchiks explains why the Marxists—who by now had advanced to being a cadre of senior professors—were able to have such a renewed impact on the campuses. They were the only substantial group with strong convictions, ready to convert undergraduates, indoctrinate graduate students, and use financial aid to bring the recalcitrant ones into line, and adept at taking advantage of every vacancy and recruitment in the humanities and social sciences to add to their numbers. University administrators, in the interest of preserving campus peace and in the name of academic freedom, were willing to allow this creeping politicization of the campus to occur, as long as it stopped short of the presidential suite or the provost's office.

The accommodation between the leftist-dominated American faculty and the apparatchik-type administrator had the salutary effect of producing by the mid-nineties a renewed degree of calm and stability on the American campus. It was possible to pursue unimpeded and without distraction the faculty's craft of teaching and research. As the dynamic quality of French thought slowed down, it also became possible for American academics to work on indigenous development in their disciplines. The mid-nineties was not a flourishing era of innovation on the American campus, but the basis was being laid—by serious attention to teaching and research—for a new era of intellectual advancement on the campus. In that way the nineties resembled the 1950s on the American academic scene.

The problems of decreases in funding in many of the American state university systems, especially in New York and California, remained a source of aggravation and confusion. The academic job market remained fragile. This affected even the natural sciences. A single tenure-track position in physics in the early nineties at upscale Amherst College generated eight hundred applicants. Even though the undergraduate population resumed significant growth in the mid-nineties, the bulge was taken up by using adjunct (part-time) faculty and graduate teaching assistants. About a third of all classes in American colleges—in metropolitan areas close to half—were taught by adjuncts. Though highly qualified people, they had only marginal situations on the campuses. They were harassed by money problems and demoralized by their insecure and subservient positions. This was a poor context for innovative or even conventionally excellent pedagogy.

The most interesting development on the transatlantic academic scene occurred in Britain in the late 1980s and early 1990s. There the Thatcher and post-Thatcher Conservative government promoted the "polytechnics," state colleges of marginal quality and reputation, to full university status, hoping that this would generate a competitive academic marketplace, bringing many beneficial outcomes. It was a bold move and a highly successful one. Freed to develop programs and seek nonstate funding, many of the new universities rapidly transformed themselves into vibrant educational and intellectual centers. Ironically, in the humanities they became the sites of interdisciplinary "cultural studies" that were greatly influenced by the Marxists of the Frankfurt school, and the postmodernists Derrida and Foucault. The most visible outcome of the Conservative government's efforts to create a free market in higher education was to therefore strengthen immeasurably the leftist cultural centers in British higher education.

The tremendous expansion of universities in the transatlantic world in the 1960s and the enhanced visibility and prosperity of their faculties at the time had engendered the impression that universities were tough and well-nigh impregnable institutions—proud towers of learning and teaching. This was a false conclusion. Universities are rather fragile institutions, and they can go into decline and even fall apart under the blows of political conflict and sharp funding decline. This was the situation in the late seventies and eighties. Although universities were still mired in fiscal difficulties in the nineties, the relative calm and stability on the campuses in that decade allowed healing to set in, and campus recovery of confidence and attention to academic tasks. But the universities' future and intellectual and cultural force was still uncertain.

Feminism Since the mid-sixties we have been living through the second wave of feminism in the twentieth century, the first of which occurred in the first two decades of the twentieth century and concentrated ultimately on the question of suffrage. The first phase was inspired by the movement of women out of domestic work and their absorption into the bureaucratic and business workplace and to an unprecedented degree. The invention of the Underwood typewriter in the 1880s had great impact on the employment opportunities for women. It was secretarial work that withdrew women from domestic labor (inside or outside the family), which, along with factory labor, had hitherto constituted their main occupation. Women now had the opportunity to work in offices.

Then, during the First World War, because of the labor shortage, women were employed in greater numbers in factories, frequently engaging in hard physical labor in ammunition production. At this time too they became responsible for farm labor to an unprecedented degree. These social and economic situations, and their necessary results in terms of the use of women's labor, gave a validity or a compelling argument to the suffragette cause, resulting in the gaining of the vote by women at the end of the First World War in most Western countries.

The socialist movement favored the equality of women, and while middle-class liberals were split on the matter, they too eventually converted to the pro-women position. Then, with the Great Depression, there was a reversal in the advancement of women's liberation, which is a movement that always does poorly in times of high unemployment, since the economic crisis, whose solution inevitably lies in decreasing the competition on the job market, collaborates with those who prefer to see women at home.

There was a hiatus in the attempt to drive women back into the home during the Second World War, when women were once again needed in war work for four or five years. But then, in the late forties and the fifties, there emerged the motif of "togetherness," the reconstruction of the holy, middle-class family, comfortably settled in the suburban ranch house. Women were once again expected to stay at home, rear children, mix martinis, and prepare extravagant meals for their spouses. During the early forties it was feared that once the war ended, there would once again be massive unemployment. The prosperity that would become evident by the mid-fifties was not anticipated, hence the recurrence of the outcry to segregate women in the home in the years immediately following the war.

Since the late fifties and particularly since the mid-sixties, the women's liberation movement has been pursued with unprecedented strength, taking the movement far beyond the demand for suffrage—which, it should be noted, women have never used to a significant degree. Historians have always been rather taken by the fact that when women began to vote, in England and the United States, around 1920, they voted conservatively, for the most part following their husbands and fathers. They more rarely voted for the liberal Left or socialists—not that is, for those parties that had assiduously sought their rights. Their direct participation in political life was negligible.

The factors that have produced, and continue to produce, the current wave of the women's liberation movement, or feminism, include the great economic expansion that began in the late fifties and was recognized by the mid-sixties, which produced again a demand, particularly for educated women in nonfactory labor, including various kinds of professional as well as clerical positions. The first cause of the massive expansion of feminism was, then, the favorable labor market.

Second, the equally great educational expansion of the fifties and sixties, from which millions of women benefited—51 percent of students in the sixties when the state universities were expanding were women—is another factor and collaborates with the expansion of the labor market. By 1970 millions of well-educated women were active on the labor market, which could not but alter the situation irreversibly. Many of these women would decline returning to the former domestic mode of female life.

Third, the egalitarian ideology of the sixties, which had produced the civil rights movement along with the movement for the liberation of the blacks and the New Left, presented an example for women. There is no doubt that the women's liberation movement was initially modeled on that of black liberation, and in its early stages, in the late sixties, it was not entirely welcomed by the black leaders who thought that it would erode the thrust of their campaign. To some extent this did indeed happen.

The fourth factor fostering women's liberation was the federal affirmative action program. It is well known that federal affirmative action was never legislated. It was decreed by presidential order of President Johnson, and the Supreme Court is still debating whether Johnson and the succeeding presidents' affirmative action directives were in fact constitutional. It should be noted that the affirmative action program, though begun under President Johnson, expanded first under the Nixon administration and later under President Carter. Under Nixon and Carter, one a crook and the other a wimp, there was a very substantially expanded affirmative action program, particularly in ways that were helpful to women. That women began extensively to obtain academic posts outside women's colleges in the 1970s was almost entirely due to federal affirmative action impositions on university administrations.

The final impact was that of the private foundations, among which the role of the Ford Foundation under McGeorge Bundy was particularly important. Ford and other foundations poured vast amounts of money into the causes of civil rights, not only of blacks and Hispanics, but women's programs as well. All major universities, beginning with Northeastern University in Boston, developed women's "reentry" programs, which were designed to help women, especially college-educated and middle-aged ones, make the transition from home into professional careers. These programs, the first of which was started in 1964, were among those that received extensive help from private foundations. They also gained, needless to say, efficient sources of income for the universities.

The main question, of course, centers on what it is that has actually changed. What does "women's liberation" mean? In 1939 the average women's wage in the United States was 63 percent of men's. In 1986 it was 64 percent. Women's wages, in other words, as compared to men's, rose on average by 1 percent in the forty-seven years. For some women, indeed, there was also a deterioration in their general situation during the sixties and seventies, because one-parent families, which usually implies that the one parent is a woman, became much more common. The reason for this was the easing of the divorce laws. In a rather unimaginative and reckless moment, radical advocates began to deconstruct divorce laws and, in so doing, albeit unintentionally, they made it very difficult to enforce alimony and child-support regulations on most men, abandoning women to very difficult situations.

A study done in California in 1985 by a Stanford University sociologist argued that for middle-class women divorce means a deterioration in their income and their general economic well-being, whereas for their divorced spouse, it means an increase in income.

Nevertheless, the women's liberation movement has effected immense changes, the most positive among which have benefited professional women. A social revolution is occurring in this country, whose effects will be fully perceived in the early twenty-first century. This is the case for professional women—academics, lawyers, physicians, accountants, economists, and engineers. These women are advancing to the highest levels of the learned professions, which means that women will come to play an increasingly important role on the highest corporate levels. The leadership in the United States, the professional elite, has been undergoing the most radical change since the early nineteenth century.

The situation in the legal profession in the 1990s is particularly important in view of the important role played by lawyers in the corporate, business, and political worlds. In the mid-1960s women played a minor role both in terms of numbers and prominence in the American legal profession. Women students at Harvard and other elite law schools comprised less than 5 percent of each entering class. Judith Kaye was admitted to NYU Law School but shunted off to its (now defunct) evening division. By 1995 half of the entering class at Harvard and other elite law schools were women, and Judith Kaye was the chief administrative judge and chief judge of the Court of Appeals in New York State—the top position on the state bench. One-third of the legal profession are now women. Extrapolated outward a few years in terms of the impact on corporations and the political sphere, the result will be a gender revolution.

The decline of fertility in middle-class women, one cannot help but surmise, is a consequence of the liberation and professional advancement of women as well as the availability of greatly improved forms of contraception. Women who engage in professional careers either do not marry, or they marry and do not bear children—and even if they do, the number of children they produce rarely exceeds the replacement level of two, and often remains at one. In fact, it is frequently the case that a professional married woman will bear one child when in her mid- or late thirties. The result of this is of course a decline in aggregate fertility.

An unknown but possibly major consequence of the new status of women concerns the mind-set of a generation—hundreds of thousands, indeed millions—of children brought up in various child-care and surrogate facilities but without the daytime presence of their mothers, who by choice or necessity are employed outside the home. Of course this was not unheard-of in previous decades, but now its operation is found on a much larger scale, and among middle-class families as well as less privileged ones. Of American children under three, more than half have mothers that work. Eight million mothers of preschool children are in the work force outside the home.

How will this affect socialization of Freud's oedipal process? How will it impact, if at all, on Piaget's stages of childhood? Will such children become disassociated from Klein's object relations? Will personalities be changed by the absence of the nurturing mother? For the worse? For the better? Psychologists cannot tell us the answers to these questions, or rather their estimates now vary sharply. It is only when a generation has grown to maturity under the new familial regime of the working and absent mother that the outcomes will begin to become clear.

The impact of women's liberation on men is very significant too. Nor is this the case only in terms of a decline of opportunity for men in the learned professions, owing to the competition presented by women. Men who rank below a certain point of intelligence and capability, who previously would, for example, have been guaranteed a good position in a corporate law firm, now have to go to work for legal aid or in the real estate or criminal defense bar. They are, in brief, being pushed out of the better jobs—where in many instances thay didn't deserve to be in the first place—by women. The increasing spread of male homosexuality merits consideration in this context too, as do the possible implications of women's changing situation for other aspects of male personality. Inevitably the workplace pressures on men and the deterioration of their privileged employment status has encouraged assumption of male defensive postures. The forming of male support groups and the popularity of retreats for men in remote areas, where they engage camping and other forms of playful bonding are examples of this reaction. So too are the reappearance of that Victorian phenomenon, the smoking club, where men can relax and partake of long cigars and enjoy one another's company in a symbolically phallic ambience.

Along with the social fact of the women's liberation movement, there has developed feminist theory, which by 1990 had taken a central place in university curricula. Actually it is more correct to speak of feminist theories in the plural, since it is possible to group them under three doctrinal headings.

One of them is the egalitarian or liberal theory, which can also be described as the androgynous theory. This approach holds that there is no difference between men and women, claiming that the biological differences are insignificant and the psychological ones nonexistent. Gender-specific cultural characteristics, further, are totally unitary and homogeneous. Therefore women are not different from men. Gender is cultural, not biological. Karen Horney, the psychoanalyst whose views were discussed in a previous chapter, was making these claims as early as the forties, on pain of getting expelled from the New York Psychoanalytic Society. Currently, however, this school of feminism constitutes the more moderate branch. Among its leading exponents are Carol Berkin of the City University of New York and Mary Beth Norton of Cornell.

Berkin and Norton have widely disseminated their androgynous theory through school and college textbooks in U.S. history that they have published from the feminist egalitarian point of view. Berkin's school text has been adopted by the whole state of Texas. Norton's college text has also been immensely successful. A generation of school children and college students is thereby imbibing the androgynous egalitarian theory of the sexes.

Second, there is the Marxist-feminist theory, which, drawing on Engels, claims that the subjection of women was instituted at the same time as the concept of private property. Therefore women will not achieve full freedom until the demise of capitalism. Reductionist as this argument is, the Marxist branch of feminism has a strong hold in the universities. Alice Kessler-Harris, who teaches at Hofstra University, is one of the outstanding examples of this school. Another is Mary Nolan of NYU.

The third category in feminism is the separatist theory, which is the entire opposite of the egalitarian theory. This holds that there are major differences between men and women and, further, that women are superior. The separatist theory is inspired by the views of the American psychologists Carol Gilligan and Nancy Rule Goldberger and the French theorist Hélène Cixous: that women's way of knowing and moral reasoning is different from that of men— it is more communal, nonlinear, and is more emotionally conditioned. The separatist theory was articulated in polemical form by the acerbic Australian-British feminist scholar Germaine Greer in *The Female Eunuch* (1971). "Women have very little idea how much men hate them. . . . Is it too much to ask that women be spared the daily struggle for superhuman beauty in order to offer it to the caresses of a subhumanly ugly mate?" The separatist theory was developed further in the United States in a lengthy and learned 1986 book, which received high visibility, by Gerda Lerner, who was then the leading feminist historian in this country. She taught at the University of Wisconsin.

Lerner's theory is based on an anthropological myth, which is by no means to accuse it of falseness, for Freud as well as Lévi-Strauss used myths as the starting point of their theories. Starting from anthropological data and historical evidence from early societies, Lerner maintained that societies in their original state were naturally matriarchal. She proposed that the natural, original state of society be taken into account and that matriarchal power be restored.

By 1990 there were many varieties of feminism. At the radical pole stood Catherine Mackinnon, a legal scholar who argued for many years, against bitter opposition, that a hostile work environment along gender lines constituted sexual harassment and had to be compensated by heavy fiscal awards against companies and corporate executives. Mackinnon's juristic theory of an uncomfortable environment as sexual harassment even though there is no overtly aggressive physical act involved, came by the early 1990s to be universally accepted in court decisions and legislation. This victory had a major impact on gender relations in the American workplace. For long pilloried in the press as an extremist, Mackinnon was accepted into the academic and legal establishment and was appointed to a tenured professorship at the University of Michigan Law School, one of the country's leading law centers.

At the other pole were feminists who cautioned that the feminist movement had lost touch with the needs of working-class women and the realities of family life. It needed to be more cautious, caring, cooperative with men, and less ideological. The distinguished historian Elizabeth Fox-Genovese, who headed the women's study program at Emory University, took this moderate view. The economist Sylvia Hewlett (at Barnard College) stressed the need for adequate child-care centers as serving the genuine interests of working-class women, a need long recognized and acted upon in the strong welfare states of Western and Northern Europe.

In humanities departments in the 1990s, feminist readings of literature, history, and art had become mainline. If some of the mature male professors had reservations about this feminist interpretation, they learned to keep quiet. Every academic conference in the humanities could expect to see at least a quarter of its sessions devoted to feminist papers, which drew the largest audiences. The private foundations and the national endowments invested heavily in feminist research. The chairs of departments at major universities were often now held by women—English at Princeton, Anthropology and History at New York University.

In the early 1990s a woman for the first time was dean of an elite law school—at Columbia University. Next to blacks of either gender, Caucasian women dominated the tenure-track hiring rolls of the major universities in the 1990s—a development that was likely to reshape the character of the academic profession in the twenty-first century.

Postmodernism In the Arts and Literature
Postmodernist culture is indeed postmodernist. It comes after the great achievements of modernism. It

draws on modernism to some degree and also departs from it and partially reverts to Victorianism.

We are not in the midst of a great moment in the arts and literature. We are in a period "after the fall," a period of fragmentation and reconsideration, perhaps of the beginning of a comprehensive new movement in literature and the arts, but it is still too early to tell what the coalescing shape of this new movement will be. On the other hand, we may be in a time of frustration, doubling back, of essentially standing still.

There are three characteristics of postmodernist culture in literature and the arts: partial perpetuation of modernism; a tendency toward fabulism and fantasy; and arbitrary appropriation and imitation of the past.

There has been a strong neomodernist movement in drama. The dominant figure here is Samuel Beckett, the Irishman who spent his whole working life in Paris. A bridge between the thirties and the seventies, in the latter decade he continued to write and produce his highly self-referential, enclosed, depressing, intensively thick, and relatively short plays. *Rockababy* is the quintessence of modernist minimalism and despair: a one-character play in which a very old woman sits in a rocking chair and unhappily but convincingly recollects her drab life.

Three dramatists of the new generation who worked in the Beckett tradition were the Englishman Harold Pinter and the Americans Sam Shepard and David Mamet. Pinter gained recognition in the late fifties with *The Caretaker,* a three-character drama about poor, angry, and miserable people speaking in a fragmentary manner. He became actively involved in film writing, and the result was first the drama and then the film of *Betrayal,* an astonishingly successful effort to combine upscale domestic drama with structuralist perception. The depersonalization of personalities is done very skillfully here; individual wills are involved, but the objective system at the same time closes in and prevails.

Shepard is more in the expressionist tradition, touched up with 1980s deconstruction, which in *True West* takes place among lower-middle-class characters over the kitchen sink. His is the theater of rage. David Mamet's *Glengarry Glen Ross* is a perfect neomodernist drama: a self-contained wretched little world in Chicago, of lower-middle-class shabby salesmen whose humanity does come through—all too painfully.

The traditions of modernism light up the film of the postmodernist era. A gargantuan figure was the French director François Truffaut who as a critic first advocated a New Wave postbourgeois French film and then showed everyone how to do it. *Jules and Jim* is an incomparable evocation of the second and third decades of the century in Paris. His later film *Day for Night* shows the strong influence of Roland Barthes and structuralism. In all of Truffaut's films, there is a sharp struggle between a modernist and a neoromantic sensibility.

The American director Martin Scorsese is usually free of such tension. His is usually a straightforward, piercing neomodernist evocation of a lower-middle-class world, not passive but strenuous, desperate, and angry. This appears in three imposing films, *Mean Streets, Taxi Driver,* and *Raging Bull.* The latter was a conscious effort, both in cinematography and story, to evoke the late, high-modernist world of the early forties. Scorsese's one effort at neoromanticism, *New York, New York,* is held to be unsuccessful.

The modernist music tradition was perpetuated in the highly improvisatory jazz compositions of John Coltrane and the abstract, almost baroque sound produced by trumpeter Wynton Marsalis.

The modernist tradition in music is also perpetuated in the work of Steve Reich and Philip Glass, minimalists who use complex and repeated rhythms in complex, orchestrated frameworks. Glass is involved in a series of operatic productions on grandiose subjects, while Reich works with large-scale orchestras. Their generally accessible, not difficult, although at times boring, music attempts to use the incantatory power of repetition to achieve a sparse, sonic structuralism.

In painting, modernism came to late fruition in Britain and the United States. Francis Bacon, who began his work in the late thirties, but is mostly known for his art of the fifties and sixties, must be regarded as one of the great later masters of modernism. There is not only a strong element of distortion but also a sense of sadomasochism in his work.

The American school of abstract expressionism began in the late thirties with Jackson Pollock and reached its peak in the sixties and late seventies in his work and that of Willem de Kooning, Barnett Newman, Robert Rauschenberg (who is still active), Franz Kline, Robert Motherwell, and Mark Rothko. The direct influence of the German expressionism of Klee and Kandinsky, brought directly to America by Max Ernst and other refugee artists during the war, is readily apparent. Nevertheless the work of the New York School, as it is called, should be seen not as derivative but as a distinctive late chapter in the history of modernism, and especially of postimpressionist and nonrepresentational art.

The group was particularly effective in the use of color and in the case of

Pollock and de Kooning, in "action painting," the dripping of paint on canvas or throwing it on. With the help of astute New York gallery owners, the group became immensely popular and wealthy. Modernist painting, particularly that of the New York School, became integral to interior design for affluent people.

Two American sculptors in the sixties and seventies who represented the postmodernist continuation and cultivation of the modernist tradition in art were Louise Nevelson and Claes Oldenburg. Nevelson, born in Russia, constructed a display wall (*Royal Tide IV*) of thirty-five ordinary wooden boxes, painted gold. In each box were standard pieces of finished wood objects, such as finials, shaped newel posts, cones, and the like. The result is to communicate a distinctive world of shape and signs through the arrangement of common objects. Oldenburg, born in Sweden, experimented in the late sixties with a series of larger-than-life sculptures in soft vinyl, such as a washbasin and *The Great Swedish Soft Light Switch*. The purpose appears to be to force recognition through contrasting the soft shape of objects with the familiar hard ones. Thus Oldenburg sought to realize Salvador Dalí's proclaimed "era of the soft."

A leading neomodernist sculptor of the postwar era was David Smith, whose stark, abstract, welded images perpetuated the work of Giacometti and other modernists of the interwar period. An innovative sculptor of the seventies was George Segal, whose life-size white plaster figures are a late and persuasive form of expressionism.

In poetry a leading late modernist writer was an American resident in Britain, Sylvia Plath. Her early death by suicide ended a major talent. From her college studies, she learned the lessons of modernist lyrical intensity and applied them well. A bad marriage to a prominent English poet and critic, and the harshness of English urban life contributed to the sense of disorientation between the self and the immediate word that is characteristic of Plath and of postmodernist potry in general. This is a culture of dissociation, polarity, and misfortune. Plath's near-contemporary, the Welsh poet Dylan Thomas, also played a significant role in expanding the prewar modernist tradition. A raging alcoholic and frenetic personality, Thomas also acted out on college campuses and in the bars of two continents the popular conception of the existential poet raging against the world.

There is a similarity in theme between the poetry of Plath and her contemporary, the Chicago novelist Saul Bellow, who published *Dangling Man* in 1944, *The Adventures of Augie March* in 1953, and *Henderson the Rain King* in 1959. These and later works comprise a body of writing that gained Bellow the Nobel Prize in literature. The theme again and again is discordance between an idealistic if somewhat unstable self and an unsympathetic environment, which is inescapable. "The world comes after you," the protagonist of *Dangling Man* asserts, and this is the theme of all Bellow's novels. The sense of frustration, loss, incapacity, and misfortune prevalent in Plath's writing is also asserted by Bellow. In spite of the prosperity and power of postwar America, these two writers communicate a deep distress about the relationship between self and society.

The leading neomodernist American novelist of the sixties was Vladimir Nabokov, who followed in the tradition of the Mann brothers, particularly of Heinrich. Nabokov's account of the life of a Cornell professor, *Pnin*, is a softened version of Mann's Professor Unrath. His account of the infatuation of a middle-aged man for a pubescent child, *Lolita*, is entirely in the sadomasochist, German expressionist tradition. The leading neomodernist novelist of the seventies was the Czech Milan Kundera. His stories of lives circumscribed by bureaucracy and technology are again a softened, more whimsical version of Kafkaesque themes.

In postwar France, and continuing into the seventies, there occurred an extremely self-conscious and doctrinaire flowering of the minimalist, nonnarrative modernist novel. Nathalie Sarraute, who began publishing in the thirties, served as a bridge from the era of modernism to the new age of post-modernism. The leading figure of this neo-modernist movement in French fiction, called *le nouveau roman* (the new novel, although it was really not very new) was Alain Robbe-Grillet, a close collaborator in vanguard intellectual circles with Roland Barthes. His most influential work was *Les Gommes* (Erasers), which was a minimalist work devoid of of a single discernible plot. It was a radicalized, more extreme version of Joyce and Woolf.

The second current in postmodernist art and literature was fabulism and fantasy, a world of imaginative invention, whimsy, and exotic referentiality that was far removed from the austerity of modernism. Along with the outpouring of science fiction and Arthurian retellings, the leading exponents of this post-modernist genre included the two Latin American writers Gabriel García-Márquez and Jorge Luis Borges. Fantasy and fabulism were a way of absorbing the pain of the terror and failures of their societies and the irresponsibility of the educated middle class from which they came. It was also a way of bridging the gap between the austere European, mainly French or English, culture in which they were educated and the native Hispanic-Indian village life they knew about in their home countries—that is, a way of preserving their European cultural identities.

Somewhat similar is the fabulist inspiration of Isaac Bashevis Singer in his cycle of stories about his father's rabbinical court in the romanticized shtetl world of Eastern Europe. Singer was capable of writing graphically modernist, quite Freudian stories of the sex life of pressured immigrants in New York in the thirties. But when he came to write about Eastern Europe he felt compelled to screen the events with a romantic hasidic overlay to soften the pain of recollection. Two other prominent American novelists in the fabulist and fantastic tradition were John Gardner and Thomas Pynchon.

Thomas Mann's series of novels on Joseph and his brothers published in the thirties and forties had been a forecast of the fabulist stream in postmodernism. A novelist of past years who now came to prominence was the prolific German writer, both novelist and poet, Hermann Hesse. Actually of the generation of high modernism; he died in 1962 at the age of eighty-five. His many novels dealt with stories of mythological and moral fabulism. One of these, *Steppenwolf*, originally published in 1927 and focusing on the theme of the struggle between man's animal instincts and bourgeois respectability, became a bestseller in the 1970s. Hesse's style is that of the neomedieval moral and miracle story.

The most widely read European postmodernist novelist of the late seventies and eighties was Umberto Eco, a professor of linguistics and medieval literature at the University of Milan. He takes a poignant theme or issue from the medieval world or an arcane principle from linguistics and uses it as the context of a quasi-fabulist story. The most prominent British novelist of the late eighties and nineties, Salman Rushdie, builds his fabulist world out of the ingredients of postcolonial societies, either back home in Muslim countries or in the streets of London.

The arcane postmodernist fabulism of the late sixties and seventies in the United States, in the writings of Thomas Pynchon and John Barth, among others, preserves modernist obscurity within a fabulist genre. Much more straightforward and easily readable and immensely popular is the most prominent postmodern American novelist of the eighties and nineties, Anne Rice. From hoary vampire stories or fables about Jewish mystics, she builds fabulistic accounts that are nonetheless rooted in suburban culture and easily accessible by the middle-class reader—hence the Hollywood producers who offer her fortunes for the screen rights to her fictions.

The most skillful American novelist of the sixties and seventies from a technical point of view was Raymond Carver, who by the 1990s had come to exercise a powerful influence on the new generation of American and British novelists and short-story writers (often the fiction volumes were, as in Carver's case, collections of short stories). In their simple style and careful rootedness in precise locations and historical movements, there was a shift in these writers of the nineties, such as Nicholson Baker and Jonathan Franzen, back toward a kind of early-twentieth-century realism, but filtered through the restraining prism of modernism with an occasional hint of postmodern fabulism. The tone is one of recollection in tranquillity by depressed and disappointed temperaments. The consequence of the many writing schools in American and British colleges is evident in the technical skill and discipline of this work.

The fabulism and fantasy that comprise a central theme in the postmodernist novel also condition the historical writing of the period. The leading exponent of this interest is Natalie Zemon Davis, the highly visible Princeton historian, although Le Roy Ladurie and another French scholar, Jacques Le Goff, have also been active in this area.

Zemon Davis writes about carnivals, street theater, riots, adolescent and male-bonded high jinks in sixteenth-century France. Her work follows a principle proposed by the Soviet theorist Mikhail Bakhtin that such mini-explosions in society are an expression of adversary culture against authority in premodern societies. Aside from this Marxist influence, Zemon Davis' work on activist fabulism in premodern society reflects the doctrines of French structuralism and deconstruction. The marginal activities are part of the systemic structure of preindustrial society, and they also show the deconstructive operation of the social text. Following Zemon Davis, whose work has achieved such celebrity that she was elected president of the American Historical Association, there has been a rush of disciples to describe marginal activist fantasies in social history.

The influence of Lévi-Strauss's anthropology on Zemon Davis comes to her directly through the work of the American symbolic anthropologists Victor Turner and Clifford Geertz. They were concerned to identify the ritual symbols in early society that represent the dominant cultural forms expressing the thick culture revealed by ethnography. Transferring this to historical research, Zemon Davis is attempting the symbolic anthropology of thick culture of sixteenth-century peasant society. Applying Bakhtinian doctrines, she believes that this symbolic structure is readily perceived in fabulist and fantastic activity.

Another manifestation of postmodernist fantasy and fabulism was science fiction films, making bold and ingenious use of computer graphics, which were Hollywood's prime achievement in the late seventies and early eighties. It is salutary to compare these science fiction films with the two previous genres in which Hollywood excelled. These were the film noir of the thirties and the musical comedy films of the forties and fifties. The latter, borrowing Broadway talent and techniques, went beyond anything Broadway could do in view of the elaborate sets, concentration of remarkable and expensive talents, and innovative camerawork. Metro-Goldwyn-Mayer studios excelled and specialized in musical comedy and the genre reached its high point in *Singin' in the Rain* (1952). Changing public taste and the extreme expense of these films led to their decline in the sixties, and the period of the sixties and early seventies were distinguished by the neomodernist New Wave French films. In the late seventies and early eighties Hollywood made a comeback with the incomparable special effects of science fiction films such as *Star Wars* and *E.T.* The creative people were Steven Spielberg and George Lucas, but the key to success was the skillful adaptation of computer graphics developed at the University of Illinois and other research centers. The science fiction film was a distinctive and novel subculture of postmodernism. It is perhaps the most accomplished and skillful expression of postmodernist fabulism and fantasy.

The third stream in postmodernist culture—and one that became more prominent over the years—was the random appropriation of the past. This constituted a highly personal and idiosyncratic reaching back nostalgically for themes and motifs, especially but not exclusively to the Victorian past. There was a heavy neo-Victorian flavor to this historicizing at all times.

There is a random and arbitrary quality to the iconography and semiotics of these themes. The writers and artists of our day have a vast heritage behind them, not only as painterly and literary productions but a heritage that has produced, and finds support in, an equally extensive scholarly and theoretical output. The accessibility to all the materials of Western civilization is easy. Books, libraries and museums make everything available. In spite of this or perhaps because of this, postmodern culture is fragmented and has a random and arbitrary quality to it. Its producers are arbitrarily picking up fragments of the past, which are found supremely appealing by postmodern culture, and seek to revive them, but always in and as fragments. Every new year, in fact, reaches for different aspects of the past. This imitative quality of postmodernist culture frequently gives it a pastiche character.

This historicizing and random appropriation of the past was very pronounced in architecture in the work of Philip Johnson's associate John Burgee and also in the work of Robert Venturi. They were determined to break away from the international Bauhaus style (even though Johnson had begun his career as a junior associate of Mies van der Rohe), and they did this with the help of cornices, pediments, and other pieces rescued from the past. The prime example is the neo-Edwardian top of the Johnson and Burgee AT&T building in New York. Another blatant piece of historicizing and random nostalgia-tripping by Johnson was his Bobst Library for New York University. Recalling Foucault, it is modeled on a Victorian penitentiary.

In a remarkaable autobiography published in 1995, Johnson revealed that he had been a fervent supporter of German Nazism in the late 1930s, when he was a young man. The pastiche and historicizing quality of Nazi architecture, and its shapeless grandiosity, were resurrected in Johnson's much later work, after being put through the cleansing screen of 1950s modernism. THE BAUHAUS GOES NEO-NAZI might be the tabloid description.

Neo-Victorian qualifications are well represented in music, poetry, and painting. In music a major talent, David Del Tredici, departed from discordant serialism and composed lyrical works with a strong neoromantic flavor. Perhaps the most popular of these is his rendering of *Alice in Wonderland, Child Alice,* to which the late Danish choreographer Erik Bruhn articulated an original ballet for the Canadian national company, combining modernist and nostalgic ingredients. Del Tredici's work was enthusiastically received by critics and the concert public alike. In poetry Philip Larkin, the British poet laureate, tried to bring back the age of Tennyson and Kipling and was widely applauded.

In painting the American Susan Rothenberg composed large representational canvases featuring horses—a random nostalgic icon—that resemble those on the walls of neolithic caves. She described them as "charged images." The Victorian ambience was consciously recreated by the immensely popular American painter Andrew Wyeth. His canvases could easily be products of the 1860s, and there is in his work a distinct resemblance to British painters of that era. Wyeth is a neo-Victorian not only in his photographically representational style, but in his subjects, of which mysterious women of great beauty are the favorite.

The leading artist of postmodernism was Frank Stella, and he also stands as one of the cultural heroes of the closing years of the century. A brilliant history major at Princeton, he forsook a promising scholarly career to take up painting in the abstract expressionist mode. His geometric patterns were consciously done according to the modernist theory of Cézanne, Klee, and Picasso, and Stella's skill, use of color and whimsical powers of invention made him immensely popular and wealthy. But Stella was not just a neomodernist. He incorporated the other two strands of postmodernism as well. He saw himself as recovering the ideals and techniques of baroque art, on which theme he wrote a lengthy paper at Princeton. He was especially interested in Caravaggio and gave a remarkable series of lectures on this baroque artist at Harvard in 1984, combining criticism of unusual insight with deep learning.

In Stella's later work there is a strong element of fantasy, constant experimentation with random objects, and an effort to combine painting and sculpture (including welding)—a neo-Victorian avocation. One wonders what Stella could have accomplished if he had not become a multimillionaire so young, if collectors did not simply swoop down and stockpile whatever he produces, if there were a little bit of pressure and personal anxiety placed on him. That he is one of the half dozen most accomplished and resourceful artists of the century is unquestionable.

In the sixties and early seventies, pop art painting was in the forefront of postmodernist painting. Andy Warhol, Jasper Johns, and Roy Lichtenstein constructed large canvases replicating soup can labels, panels from comic strips, U.S. flags, or publicity stills of movie queens. Not only did museums and critics take these paintings seriously as vanguard art, but private collectors paid large sums for them (they were indeed effective against the blank white walls of the newly fashionable loft apartments). Although the popularity of pop art waned in the late seventies, it has come to be recognized as a canonical constituent of postmodernism.

Three obvious principles inspired pop art; indeed, its theory was more convincing than its aesthetic results. First, since modernism had legislated that it was the painterly constituents, not the subject matter, that counted, why not take as subject matter any random object from popular culture? Pop art could thus be regarded as the *reductio ad absurdum* of modernism. Second, pop art accommodated to the new interest in semiotics and the Eco principle that all signs were infinitely referential. Anything was meaningful and ultimately related to everything else, so what difference did it make where one started? The Mona Lisa was in the total semiotic scheme not much more signworthy than a soup can label. Third, pop art reflected the postmodernist tendency to arbitrariness, random appropriation, and pastiche.

One of the finest examples of pop art as a meaningful art form was Robert Rauschenberg's *Axle*. It was a vast silk-screen collage of various semiotic totems of the sixties (for example, JFK, space travel) put together in a way that suggested cultural patterns and communal feeling. It was pop art, but it was persuasively symbolic and not decadent.

The quintessence of postmodernist pastiche of art forms was performance art, whose most visible exponent was Laurie Anderson. Combining music, the visual arts, and dance with theater and the use of elaborate lighting effects, performance art evoked the world of New York SoHo lofts and the special effects of science fiction films. At a time when each art form was cultivating its past and not breaking through to anything particularly new, blending traditionally distinct genres seemed an attractive program.

An art form that resembles performance art in its combination of several distinct genres is British soft-rock musical comedy. Its most creative people are Andrew Lloyd Webber and Trevor Nunn. It adapts the American musical comedy of the forties and fifties, rock music, and elaborate technical effects that are normally only seen on film. Leading examples of their works are *Evita* (the life of Evita and Juan Perón), *Cats* (based loosely on a series of whimsical poems by Eliot), and *Starlight Express.* The latter is performed at breakneck speed entirely on roller skates. This stage spectacle appears to be among postmodernism's ultimate achievements in the performing arts.

A prime trend in the painting of the later eighties was the renewed internationalization of art and the blending of cultural motifs. A common figure is the German, Italian, or Israeli artist who has homes on two or three continents, always including a studio in Greenwich Village or Brooklyn Heights. New York remains the art capital of the world and the center of the art market, but along with the decline of American academic leadership is the coming to the fore of European painters. The outstanding figure is Francesco Clemente, an Italian who lives and works in his native country but also in India and New York. Clemente has gained high visibility in the New York art market. His expressionist-style canvases are much in demand. He offers a kaleidoscopic blending of ideas, motifs, and cultural traces. "I like art that has no scale," he says, perhaps meaning art that is arbitrary in its iconography and is open to a variety of influences.

It is significant that the finely educated Clemente is drawn to the baroque-type literature of the Roman Empire. *The Golden Ass* of Apuleius is one of his favorite books. And there is a similarity between late Roman culture and Clemente's work: "Eclectic," "pastiche," "exotic," "arbitrary," and "decadent" are terms that can describe this postmodernist genre as it characterizes late Roman literature. In the 1990s sculpture was a highly prolific and much admired field of postmodernist art. The qualities of pastiche, eclecticism, and exoticism that marked Clemente's work was seen in the scupture of Damien Hurst, Bruce Nauman, Richard Serra, and Mark di Suvero.

The most important aspects of the American art scene in the 1990s did not lie in the work of particular painters and sculptors but in the social aspects of art. Modernist painters gained immense popular attention, and a major exhibit of a modernist painter's work—especially if he or she was French or Dutch—generated vast crowds paying admission, as well as media coverage. At the same time galleries showing the work of contemporary painters proliferated in New York, Los Angeles, and other cities. In upscale summer resorts on eastern Long Island, the gallery opening became the connecting thread of the social scene, as it featured in the upper-middle-class social whirl in Manhattan in the autumn. The art world generated more ideological attention in the late 1990s than did the theater. An opening at the Museum of Modern Art or the Whitney was bound to produce critical broadsides from the Left and Right, the latter always led by Hilton Kramer, the former by Rosalind Krauss and an array of her colleagues. Benjamin and Adorno had prophesied the commodification of art under late capitalism, but these developments were far more complex and variable in their social impact than the Frankfurt school could ever have imagined. With all the visibility of the art scene, politicians inevitably joined the fray. Any exhibition of photographs—such as those by Robert Mapplethorpe—or other work that could be claimed to be sexually suggestive was heatedly condemned by demagogic congressmen, and the National Endowment for the Arts had its modest budget sharply reduced as punishment for its token support of this putatively dangerous art.

Of all the art forms, the one that most readily combined the three currents in postmodernism—neomodernism, fabulism, and random nostalgia—was rock music. In the sixties this was brilliantly accomplished in the work of the Beatles, Jefferson Airplane. and the Rolling Stones. These rock groups also achieved what the visionary modernists of the early years of the century had foreseen: electronic music. It was rock musicians, not John Cage and other serialists, who created an electronic music joined to voice that attained a central cultural role.

The later development of rock music was somewhat disappointing. It came under the sway of commercial entrepreneurs who controlled the recording studios and concert tours and pushed rock music to the lowest adolescent denominator.

The innovative aspects of rock music in the 1990s was exhibited in "grunge" and "rap" forms. Grunge was a kind of dadaist version of rock—ugly and nonsensical, carrying a message of rejection and alienation. Rap represented the adaptation into rock of African American traditions of truth-telling in churches and at political meetings. There was a strong vein of scatological communication in grunge and rap.

The turning of rock into these radical and controversial forms, while appealing to millions of adolescents, separated it from the sensibility of the older generation of Americans. Instead of combining rock with the traditions of the musical comedy to generate a compelling new musical form, the older generation turned nostalgically back to the commercial Broadway musical comedy of the period 1935–65. Revivals of the Broadway musicals of that period were lavishly mounted. The most successful composer and producer of new musicals in the eighties and nineties, Andrew Lloyd Webber, avoided hard-core rock in favor of the conservative direction of the old Broadway musical comedy.

The melding of diverse cultural traditions characterized the commercially successful painting and musical comedy of the postmodernist era. The same tendency toward blending may be found in social theory.

One of the characteristics of postmodernism is the use of modernist analysis and concepts to sustain essentially leftist, prosocialist arguments. We have seen in the last chapter that John Rawls and Ronald Dworkin used Wittgensteinian analysis and the mode of argument characteristic of analytic philosophy to sustain radical arguments on behalf of affirmative action. A similar use of modernism against itself features the work of the Nobel laureate and Harvard economist Kenneth Arrow. On the surface Arrow appears to be working in the tradition of classical economics and to be using the traditions of Keynes. But Arrow's argument wends its way, by subtle dialectics, toward policies favored on the contemporary Left. Arrow's close analysis of market operations leads him to affirmation of the intrinsic weakness of classical market economics. Its self-contradictions, inefficiency, and irrationality necessitate the ingredients of a welfare-state socialist system: "The logic and uncertainty of ideal competitive behavior . . . force us to recognize the incomplete description of reality supplied by the impersonal price system." Marx would cheer this conclusion.

Rawls and Dworkin use modernist, Wittgensteinian philosophy to support radical Left social policies. Arrow uses the language of and concepts from the modernist tradition but reasons toward welfare economics as the rational solution. Private individuals lack the information to make rational self-interested choices in an open market. Some kind of collective, statist intervention is therefore in the end frequently necessary.

Among the aspects of the culture in which we live is big science, which began with Rutherford and Einstein in the modernist era, and now continues, drawing on vast resources and the close affiliations between science, government, and the corporate world. There are those that darkly predict that this spells the end of humanity, as well as those who claim that it will lead to unprecedented health and prosperity. It is hard to know which is the sounder prediction, but it is a fact that the resources are available to science to develop new technologies—military, health, and otherwise—and to allow the scientists themselves to make decisions that are crucial for humanity. This process began before the First World War but has reached a climax in our day.

A characteristic of the postmodernist age is the Americanization of Europe and the beginnings of this process in Japan and the Pacific Rim. Middle-class Europeans dress like Americans—including the extensive use of jeans as dress in the home and, away from business, in the street. All night long radio stations throughout Europe fill the airwaves with American popular music, making these stations almost indistinguishable from the American Forces Network broadcasting alongside them. Upper-class Europeans decorate their homes according to the standards of the upscale American magazine *Architectural Digest*. American TV programs, films, and musical comedies are popular favorites. A similar cultural Americanization has set in among affluent Japanese, South Koreans, and Filipinos.

This process has occurred because of the admiration for the United States among ruling and wealthy groups in Western Europe and the Pacific Rim. The United States rescued them from fascism and then protected them against Communism for four decades. American culture has triumphed on several continents among the affluent groups, the way the peoples of Spain and North Africa in the Roman Empire wore togas and taught their children Cicero and Virgil. To be an American in dress and manner is to be a citizen of a free world.

The United States is also the preferred place of investment for the rich of all countries that are free to export their capital. Japanese investment alone in U.S. real estate in 1986 totaled five billion dollars. The United States is the safest place for investing capital. The economy is held to be stable. Taxes are moderate. Socialism will never prevail to expropriate capital. So it is believed. To West Germans and Japanese, the deep fissures and critical problems of American society do not appear significant.

To be a European or citizen of the Pacific Rim in the postmodernist era is to imitate American culture and exploit the American economy. This is at the center of their being. While on visits to the United States they lounge at posh, upscale hotels in New York and rush to Broadway shows. The homeless in the streets of Manhattan, the unemployed steel worker in Pittsburgh, the landless farmer in Minnesota mean nothing to them.

A fundamental characteristic of postmodern culture is therefore the American homogenization of the lifestyle and taste of affluent people, whether in Greenwich, Connecticut; London; Hamburg; Tokyo; or Buenos Aires. Since they are the same people who are patrons of painting, opera, and the more expensive kinds of theater, their attitudes determine the greater part of the market for the visual and performing arts. Whereas it was a prominent feature of modernism to establish a separate radical culture, this is largely lacking in the postmodernist era. Adversary culture is mostly left by default to leftist polemicists. Postmodernism tends to be the culture of the Americanized international bourgeoisie and the artist, writer, and performer who serve them, along with their usual entourage of domestic servants, chauffeurs, and bodyguards.

Another quality of contemporary culture is the decline of American public service, which may be the reverse side of political nihilism. One of the glories of the United States in the late thirties and forties was the high prestige and quality of public service. This was true to a degree also in Britain. Certainly the United States would not have survived the Second World War if it had not been for the high quality of the public service sector. To serve in the public domain, either as a civilian or in the military, was conceived of not as a way of dominating others, or as a way of gaining money, but in terms of citizenship, as dedication to the public need.

This country has never been blessed with more dedicated and wiser public servants than George C. Marshall, secretary of defense during World War II (and secretary of state after it), and General Eisenhower, head of the Allied armies and later president. Whether Eisenhower was a good president or not may be a matter of dispute, but that he was a skillful and wise military organizer and leader is a fact. These public servants did not acquire riches. They retired from service relatively poor men, with only their pensions. This was characteristic of numerous people in the forties. To serve in Washington was desirable at the time, and continued to be so until the early sixties. Now it is understood as either undesirable, or dangerous, or as a road to personal gain and corruption.

The decline of the public service of the republic is a fundamental fact of postmodern culture. In the forties and fifties public service was regarded as a life for rich men like Averell Harriman and Nelson Rockefeller. In the post-modernist era, it is viewed as a way to become rich.

The Clinton administration was supposed to reverse the trend away from public service that had marked the 1980s and early 1990s. Bill Clinton himself knew almost no other career than public service. First Lady Hillary Clinton was ideologically committed to the ideas of the liberal Left and the operations of the welfare state. The Clintons gathered around them in Washington a group of relatively young people dedicated to public service. After failing to get the Clintons' plan for comprehensive national health care adopted, things fell apart. The media was savage in attacking their private lives and revealing small mistakes in their public tactics. One of the most dedicated of the Clinton group committed suicide, leaving behind a note decrying the way in which Washington destroys people's reputations. This augurs poorly for the future of public service in the United States.

The media are as much to blame as the politicians. High-paid media figures destroy the careers of modestly remunerated public servants over peccadilloes. No ambitious and intelligent person would want to enter the limelight in Washington in these circumstances. The decline of enthusiasm for public service is a hallmark of postmodernist culture, tied to a cognate public cynicism about people who hold government jobs at all levels.

Along with the decline of public service, postmodernist culture features the disappearance of the text in the traditional form of the printed page, which was the instrument of communication and the means of linear rationality since the sixteenth century. It is not just the nonlinear medium of television that is at work. Now books are written on a screen and compressed into and published from a computer disk, and read on CD-ROMs and distributed on the Internet through cyberspace. On the one side, there is much greater facility of informational organization, storage, and retrieval. On the other, the intensive thought, quiet reflection, and rational order that went into the old way of writing with pen and on the typewriter, slow typesetting, and storage in and retrieval from a printed book is eroding. The quality of sensibility, the peace of insight, the perception offered by slow literary production is challenged by the new ways.

In the 1960s McLuhan predicted that the "cool medium" of television would generate a different consciousness, an altered way of thinking, than the hot medium of print. Combined with rock music, TV has produced a distinctive subliterate adolescent culture. But literature and expository writing have not been changed by TV. Not even educational delivery, the most obvious application of TV to traditional culture, has been much amended. In 90 percent of the college classrooms in the United States what goes on in the way of communicating in 1996 is the same as in 1956. The impact of the newer information technology may similarly be marginal. But an intellectual as well as a communications revolution could be on the horizon. McLuhan's apocalyptic prophecies, applied to the next wave, may come true.

What is the most positive characteristic of the postmodern culture in which we are living? It does give freedom to some remarkable people like Frank Stella, Martin Scorsese, and David Del Tredici to cultivate a complex heritage to an unprecedented degree. This rich, intense historicizing, this versatile command of past heritages, makes postmodernism similar to seventeenth-century baroque culture.

But the culture of postmodernism is reminiscent of the baroque era of the seventeenth century in a more negative way. Both periods display astounding capability in detailed technique, in the mastery of technology, whether it be the technology of science or art and language. Yet these capabilities are accompanied in both periods by the same redundancy and sterility of ideas. Seventeenth-century culture could not decide what it believed in or where it wanted to go, and above all, it could not decide on a political theory. It merely recirculated the ideologies of the past and devoted much time to trying to determine whether the medieval theory of representation or the Renaissance theory of absolutism was more suitable, and it did not go anywhere. The only outlet for this ideological frustration lay in civil wars and abortive rebellions.

Baroque culture was, in other words, socially and politically built on an ancien régime that is a culture of great literary, intellectual, and technological capacity, but of political redundancy and ideological feebleness. Postmodern culture exhibited this feature, and that is also why the iconology and themes of its art and literature of today were so much random recycling, consisting of nostalgic appropriations and pastiches of segments of the past, without, however, any clear attendant theory of culture or philosophy of humanity. Only a new paradigm and a new vision will enable a breakout from the enclosure into which we seem to have drifted since the mid-seventies.

The Neobaroque The first four decades of the twentieth century were characterized and shaped by a cultural revolution called modernism. A self-conscious, broad-based rebellion against the main dimensions of Victorian mentality, it is represented in all major aspects of the humanities. the arts, and the physical and behavioral sciences.

This age of high modernism was the creative age of the twentieth century. Everything enduring and creative since then in the cultural and intellectual realms is largely the playing out and elaboration of the modernist revolution. We are still spending the intellectual capital of modernism.

The erosion of the modernist revolution in the thirties and forties was the consequence of neo-Victorian modes of thinking arising from the two world wars, the Great Depression, and Marxism and fascism. Although Marxism sought an affiliation with modernism in a common adversary culture against the bourgeois ethos, it could on the whole not sustain this symbiosis because of the intrinsic oppositions between Marxism as a neo-Victorian mode of thought and modernism. There was a closer affiliation between fascism and modernism, but the two also had strongly conflicting ingredients. In any case fascism was for the most part eliminated (or at least discredited) by the policies of Nazism, and by its resultant demise.

Modernism was a release from the entropic quality of Victorian culture. It opened new vistas in the arts and architecture; it created social and behavioral science as we know them; it became modern science in physics and biology. It shaped a way of philosophical thinking that superseded nineteenth-century ideologies. It contributed to the advent of a revised economic doctrine and the welfare state. It enshrined the faith that all—rich or poor, young or old—are entitled to access to the arts, to the refreshment and illumination of the soul. But it could not overcome the persistence of Victorian ways of government and macrocosmic ways of thinking about war and peace, and of acting on these Victorian theories. It could not withstand the revival of historical nationalism, the impact of class consciousness, the dictates of group feelings, the flaunting of macrocosmic proportions. Out of the romantic revolution, the two world wars, the Great Depression, the New Deal, the movements on the Left and the Right, neo-Victorianism reasserted itself, and the modernist cultural revolution was dissipated as a cohesive cultural force although it continued to have a strong impact in some specific areas.

Our current baroque condition is not as pathetic as Victorian fin-de-siècle entropy, since we can still profitably cultivate the culture of this century. But we are far from the blissful dawn that the intellectuals and artists of the first quarter of this century enjoyed.

One of the most intriguing questions with respect to the prospective cultural revolution is what its political mien will be. Modernism's essentially apolitical character made it vulnerable to the Left and the Right, which tried to co-opt it for their own purposes.

A possible projection is that the next cultural revolution will expound a new politics, an ideology that will transcend the conflicts between the Left and the Right that have disadvantageously dominated the twentieth century.

The twentieth century began with a cultural revolution that promised the liberation of the human spirit. And it did achieve as much in the arts and the realm of science and intellect as any of the great cultural movements of the past, perhaps more so. After all the destruction, death, and disappointment of this century, we have only a few more years in the nineteen hundreds to make good on the promise of modernism.

We cannot recover the modernist ambience. We can only hope to fulfill its promise of intellectual progress and cultural revolution. But this will have to be within a new paradigm, a new cultural theory, which may pick up ingredients from both modernism and neo-Victorianism but which transcends them both in a new vision of humanity.

The Left constantly promises fresh insights, but as long as it remains essentially loyal to Marxism it will not be able, at bottom, to transcend nineteenth-century modes of thinking, no matter how vehemently it claims to be an adversary culture. The Right—only recently awakened from the long somnolence it fell into while expiating the crimes of fascism—has reflexively resorted to neo-Victorian modes of thought and policy proposals that neither resolve the many problems that we face nor even quicken the imagination.

We are at the baroque outer wall of a cultural ancien régime, arrogantly and expensively devouring the past and demonstrating our learning and technical skills, but we have not begun to find a new idea. Perhaps reflection on the complex history of twentieth-century culture will free us to begin dreaming of a different culture for the twenty-first. It is now a hundred years since the first indications of what became the modernist cultural revolution flashed on the transatlantic horizon. Perhaps similar indices of the new culture of the twenty-first century are already with us, their significance not yet clearly perceived. This observer can perceive in postmodernism only continuations of modernism, fabulism, and random nostalgia. But perhaps there is more here than meets the eye.

We have sent our last postcard from the volcano, in Wallace Stevens's phrase. We want to go home at last. As Herman Hesse wrote in his neomedieval fable *Steppenwolf,* "We have to stumble through so much dirt and humbug before we reach home. And we have no one to guide us. Our only guide is homesickness."

Modernism is paradise lost. We cannot return to it as a cultural entity, as

theory for today. As deeply as we still drink from the bottomless well of modernist culture, it is essentially a thing of the past. Its capability as a determining
cultural revolution has played itself out at last. It has become an objectified historical entity like the Reformation, the Enlightenment, and romanticism. Of
course it is much more vibrant and meaningful to us than the three previous
cultural revolutions, but it has already entered into past heritage. It is something we draw upon, not something we seek to create. Modernism is our past,
not our future.

Although neo-Victorianism is a prime ingredient of current postmodernist culture, it neither can nor should be the cultural trend of the future.
Neo-Victorianism cannot prevail because it was too decisively discredited by
modernism. The confusion characteristic of current postmodernism, with its
neo-Victorian ingredients, reflect modernism's persistent countervailing of
neo-Victorian culture. Nor should a full-fledged neo-Victorianism be the culture of the coming decades, because this would bring back the historicism,
philosophic idealism, macrocosmic thinking, and perhaps too the racism and
imperialism of the nineteenth century. After all the travails of this century, we
do not want to experience again all that to which we and our parents' generation have wisely chosen to say good-bye.

We stand therefore at a baroque interval between cultural waves, knowing
that modernism has spent its force but not knowing the content of the next
wave. Deconstruction presently amuses because it scrapes away some of the
cant and unreflective arrogance that has been prominent in academic culture
since World War II.

The current baroque interval gives momentary plausibility to the program
of the academic and intellectual Left to declare the death of the subject, the end
of bourgeois man, and—in the manner of Derrida and Foucault—to post the
death notice of Western culture's individual consciousness.

Yet the elaborate funeral arrangements for Western culture appear prema-
ture. It may be granted that the culture of the future is likely to place a greater
emphasis on communal responsibility and group solidarity. We are socially in
need of this shift, which structuralism emphasized. There is much talk today
about a new comunalism from politicians like Hillary and Bill Clinton and
from academic theorists like Amitai Etzioni. It is not at all clear what it signifies in detailed application. But it does not seem likely that self-consciousness
and subjectivity—which all the cultural revolutions, from the the Reformation
to modernism, fostered in one way or another—are going to pass away.
Derrida and Foucault themselves as sentient beings, whatever their theoretical

pronouncements, are very much within the Western tradition of individual consciousness and personal affirmation. They may have been prophetic, but they are not exemplars of a new, objective impersonal dispensation.

The new communications and information technology binds together a global network in one sense, but at the same time it makes possible a greater degree of individuality and a more intense and protracted withdrawal form society. Fifty years ago to do bibliographical research in the Harvard University Library catalog, I had to get on a train to Boston and for a few days immerse myself in the society of Cambridge, Massachusetts. Now I can do this research by on-line computer hookup; I do not have to stir from my room. Communalism in another sense may be deteriorating in consequence of the new technology. Fifty years ago as a Yankee fan, I had to go to the Bronx; now I can watch the game on cable in my home one hundred miles away. "Where have you gone, Joe DiMaggio?" indeed.

The inexorable trend of Western civilization will continue to work in its creatively ferocious manner as it has in the past: It will again generate a cultural revolution. If the history of the twentieth century teaches one lesson, it is that of the capacity of the human spirit over time to overcome seemingly impossible odds, a capacity that makes predictions of the future hazardous. This fact is represented by a tale of two cities—Tel Aviv, Israel, and Hamburg, Germany.

In 1939 Tel Aviv was a new city of two hundred thousand eager to welcome Jewish refugees from Europe but prevented from doing so by the British government's policy of appeasing the Arabs by blocking Jewish immigration. Tel Aviv was then an impoverished, weak, marginal city. Now it is the marketplace of Israel, with a population of 1.2 million, and eclipses its sister Arab city of Jaffa on which it steadily encroaches. It is a wealthy, self-confident Mediterranean metropolis that can welcome Jews or anyone it wants to a powerful, self-confident, and democratic state, the ultimate apotheosis of the medieval Crusader kingdom centered on Jerusalem and Acre.

In 1945 Hamburg lay 60 percent destroyed by Allied bombing raids. The core of the city was burned out; most of its historic buildings lay in ashes. Forty thousand of its population died in the war; the rest faced starvation and homelessness. Today, only five decades later, there is only one sign of the ashes of 1945—an old church that has intentionally been left in ruins as a memorial to the Nazi and wartime era. Hamburg's streets, buildings, parks, and canals are rebuilt well beyond the aesthetic level that existed before. It houses comfortably, often elegantly, 1.6 million people. It is a city exhibiting the remark-

able work ethic of social discipline, efficiency, and innovation that characterizes Germany. It is a prosperous, gleaming, and democratic metropolis of the
north, as Tel Aviv is of the south.

This tale of two cities demonstrates at once the astonishing resiliency of
Western culture in the face of highly adverse material circumstances—and
how hard it is to predict the future, even half a century on.

7

A MILLENNIUM AND A CENTURY END: A NEW ERA BEGINS

Historians writing in the mid-twentieth century looked back on the 1880s and saw that decade as the time of cultural and social stirrings that generated modernism and laid the intellectual and artistic foundations of the twentieth century. Historians writing in the mid-twenty-first century will look back on the decade 1985–95 and perceive in those ten years the critical developments that generated the contexts for the advent of the new millennium. The structural ingredients of change, the patterns of alteration and anticipation, were the driving forces toward the world of the new century and the third millennium of the common era that began to emerge at that time.

The first ingredient involved a negative condition, the failure of 1980s conservatism of the Reagan-Thatcher era to develop a coherent philosophy and a decisive program that could durably shape society and culture. At the heart of political conservatism in its heyday of power in the late 1980s was a fatal contradiction. Reagan-Thatcher conservatism embraced the doctrine of the free market economy, but the harsh application of market preferences conflicted with the principles of traditional conservatism, its giving of primary value to family, community, nation, and church. Neoconservatism of the 1980s and early 1990s tried to ride the twin horses of mechanical materialism—the hegemony of unbridled market and technological forces—and the romantic sentiment of group and spiritual values that were idealistic rather than materialistic, sentimental rather than mechanical. (Britain's leading conservative theorist of the 1980s, the Oxford political philosopher John Gray, perhaps saw this tension more clearly than anyone, eventually leading him to move from a strongly rightist to a more centrist position.)

The two horses could not be yoked together, and hence the conservative movement of the 1980s disintegrated. The neoconservative free marketeers and the conservative-romantic value advocates fell to quarreling among themselves, and they fumbled the opportunity to establish a stronghold on political power.

The free market economic materialists took special aim at the welfare state and its alleged blocking of the maximization of profits. They wanted total fiscal rationalization and application of technological innovation irrespective of human consequences. The more traditional conservatives could not bear to see family, community, and middle-class values ground up in the maw of market economy and therefore could not endorse elimination of the welfare state. The two wings of the conservative movement could never even agree on the issue of abortion. Faced with conflict within their ranks, Anglo-American conservatives largely wasted their decade of political power and changed very little in the application of domestic policy.

The conservative high tide of the mid-1980s also receded within a decade because the rightists had built so much of their ideological program on Manichean conflict with world Communism, especially in the Soviet Union and other eastern and central European countries. Between 1989 and 1991, Communist parties in the European Soviet countries fell apart and lost control. Poland, the Czech Republic, and Hungary became democratic states. The Soviet Union broke apart and Russia moved unsteadily towards political democracy and privatization of important segments of its economy.

The failure of Communism was due mainly to an incapacity to maintain a high degree of military capability and centralized bureaucracy in face of the structural failure of demand economics to stimulate technological advances and offer a reasonably high standard of living to their citizens.

Without the bogeyman of Reagan's "evil empire" and vision of the security threat of world Communism, the political force of Reaganite conservatism lost its vigor and much of its ideological and moral persuasiveness. The Cold War seemed in retrospect as wasteful on the Western as it had been calamitous on the Soviet side.

Even more, much of the political history of the twentieth century and the limitless expenditure of blood and money now seemed questionable. Germany after reunification of the Federal Republic and the German Democratic Republic in 1991 was closely on the way back to what it had been territorially and economically in the early twentieth century. Suppose that Neville

Chamberlain's appeasement of Hitler had worked, or that the German generals had removed Hitler before 1939, what would have been the historical destiny of Germany at the end of the twentieth century? Germany would have been the dominant economic force in Western Europe—the political arbiter of Central Europe—picking and choosing allies and satellites like Bosnia and Croatia among the small Balkan states—and Germany would have been ruled by a conservative clique of bureaucrats, bankers, and industrialists, while pacifying the comatose masses with an elaborate array of welfare benefits. That is what Germany was, however, by 1995, making the whole Hitlerian interlude and the six million Germans, six million Jews and thirty million Russians (not to speak of millions of other victims) who died in World War II a nightmare whose real happening it was now even harder to contemplate and justify.

A prime aim of Hitler and his Nazi government was a new world order, which involved minimally the economic union of Europe under the German aegis. That is precisely what the European Union is now turning out to be. What began in the 1950s with French and Belgian as well as German initiatives had a half century later turned into a monetary as well as commercial union under German domination. Given the size, wealth, and capability of the German people, it appeared around 1910 that their economic domination of Europe was going to be a condition of the twentieth century. The two world wars had been aberrations and Germany's defeats impediments, but as the twenty-first century loomed, the German economic hegemony in Europe was after all being realized. Perhaps the only special consequence of World War II was to make anti-Semitism politically and morally unacceptable in Germany and in Western Europe generally.

The failure of Anglo-American conservatism (perhaps symbolized by the almost total destruction of the long-regnant Canadian Conservative Party in 1992); the end of the Cold war and the revelation of its uselessness to the well-being of both sides; and the resurgence of Germany to a point resembling its situation in 1938, perhaps even 1914—this radical remapping of the political situation in the European and Western world—was a major departure from the mid-1980s and a foundation of the new millennium and the new century.

The second set of changes and anticipations peeking over the horizon of the new millennium and the lip of the next century may be characterized as social rather than political—how people experience their daily lives rather than the ephemeral power systems that govern and control them. This dimension may be called universalization and homogenization. This means that with a modicum of peace and stable educational contexts everyone can and will pursue the same patterns of employment and lifestyle, wherever in the world they live, and whatever ethnic, national, linguistic, or religious groups they are born into. This was a novel condition.

The most stubborn dogma of the nineteenth century was that of conservative Social Darwinism, or a belief in the hierarchy of peoples. This signified that even if the Western empires were driven out by national liberation movements and independent states set up in the Middle East, black Africa, or East Asia (or wherever), these postcolonial (in postmodernist jargon "subaltern") societies would be underdeveloped, impoverished, backward, and lagging far behind the West in technology. An Iraqi-fired missile crashing into Tel Aviv in 1991 or TV satellites hanging over Hong Kong and Riyadh in 1994, or computers effortlessly run in New Delhi or Singapore in 1996, have disproved all that, the last vestige of Western self-congratulating cultural chauvinism.

Those who roam the open-air markets of the Middle East, black Africa, or East Asia—they or at least their progeny, with a modicum of schooling and training—can run computers, build and dispatch missiles, participate in international fiscal transactions, or manage the automated production lines to turn out high-quality clothing, autos, and TV sets. They don't have to descend anymore on the West as legal or illegal immigrants; they can stay home and do their modern thing, and—given modest requirements of government and educational institutions and appropriate investment levels and social peace—they will.

There are no longer Kipling's "lesser breeds without the law"—or, rather, given a modicum of law, they are no longer lesser breeds, downscale on educational, business, or technological ladders. The ladders, the intellectual hierarchies, are vanishing rapidly, as the new millennium rushes toward us. By the second decade of the twenty-first century, if not by 2000 itself, they will be gone. By a revolutionary, irresistible process of universalization and homogenization, everyone, wherever he or she is born and lives, can and probably will have substantially the same schooling, the same job opportunities, the same middle-class-ambitious lifestyle .

Let us reserve a margin of difference for religious and ethnic family traditions, but 80 percent of things mankind wants and does will be the same, wherever they are. The old ladders are being replaced by the common global grid of lifestyle, job experience, information technology, English language, and TV watching. The world is moving from a vertical to a lateral plane.

The rich in the West will adapt, are adapting, and will get richer from investing in the further technological transformation of the East and South. Their billionaires are already raising satellites over East Asia and the Middle

East or, in the pinstriped suits of bankers and diplomats, working out nexuses of government and capital. They will be all right, even if they have to surrender much of the hegemonic status they enjoyed during and immediately after the Cold War. It is the white middle class and working classes in the United States and other Western countries who will suffer as they find themselves in direct, pitiless competition with Koreans and Iranians, all passion spent, all privileges of race and history expiring before their eyes. White man's burden gone, white man's privilege no longer even remembered by 2050—this will be the theme of some neo-Kipling of 2020. International terror will no longer be delivered in bomb casings but in the form of pink slips in the already shrunken pay envelopes of the white middle class, as they are made redundant by the clever, now schooled and eager masses of the Orient and the South.

When adjustment for inflation is taken into account, the income of the American working class and lower middle class has actually decreased slightly since the early 1970s. The steady increase in productivity of American workers from the early 1940s to the early 1970s ceased, and with it their salary increases. Job insecurity is an even greater threat to them as downsizing occurs on a broad scale, partly in response to automation in industry, partly because cheap labor in Latin America and overseas is easily usable by American corporations or their affiliates. With diminished American tariff barriers, the good-quality overseas products are readily imported. The American blue-collar worker and lower echelons of the white-collar workers are caught in an alliance between the large multinational corporations, under pressure from their stockholders to maximize profits and ready to set up shop abroad, and the unlimited pool of easily trained workers available there.

Eighty percent of life's motions will take place on the universal and homogeneous grid of commonality committed to industrial productivity. The other 20 percent will be given over to religious and ethnic identity, which will be held all the more passionately as everyday life assumes a common pattern everywhere. The twenty-first century globally threatens to be like the Age of the Reformation, the sixteenth century in Western Europe, when there was a common lifestyle, an identical pattern of greed and power, a similar cultural and educational pattern on both sides of the barrier, among the warring Catholic and Protestant groups. But the religious polarity became all the more intense because other polarities had all but disappeared. Catholic and Protestant groups fought each other with sectarian intensity and cruelty even as they experienced a common employment and lifestyle.

It is hard to estimate if that will in fact be the world pattern of the twenty-first century. Possibly religious and ethnic identities will assume a greater and greater importance as other distinctions are obliterated. The outcome is left to leadership and luck to determine.

The vision of a peaceful and harmonious global "end of history" can be legitimated as a hoped-for outcome. But the horrendous vision of a worldwide civil war fought by sectarian groups of equal technical and military capacity, venting their religious and ethnic hatreds on humankind with unprecedented fury and damage, cannot be excluded from the looming horizon of the millennium.

If population booms and the frenetic pace of urbanization continues without significant abatement in Latin America, black Africa, the Middle East, and some parts of East Asia, an additional pressure of social impoverishment will pit the East and South against the West and North for a share of world resources, reinforcing religious and ethnic hatreds. Social Darwinism as an excuse for and projection of European hegemony long ago crashed, but ironically the Social Darwinist nightmare of a struggle for existence by the deprived against the comfortable societies may return to threaten the future and the peace and well-being of mankind.

In this situation postmodernist theory is of marginal value. Its most acute thinker, Claude Lévi-Strauss, takes as his major theme a universalism against Western claims to hegemony and superiority. In his best book, *Tristes Tropiques* (1955), he holds up the decadent and greedy West against the more pristine and authentic societies of what was then called the Third World. These ideas reflect the era in which they were written: the closing era of Western colonialism and the early stages of the formulation of a global communications network. Levi-Strauss's sensibility and sense are in retrospect admirable. But they provide no succor in the context of a global nightmare of the underprivileged against the advanced societies.

Derrida and Foucault are even less helpful. They are concerned with toppling the West's confidence and eroding its solidarity and legitimacy by language theory or radical sociology. Conditioned by academic propensity to the endless recycling of established ideas, the liberal Left intelligentsia reflexively and now uselessly fights old battles and wins phantom victories. The time may be close at hand when the West needs moral boosting, solidifying, and encouragement rather than another layer of disparagement.

The possibility of impending social crisis and war on a global scale is thus not alleviated by the cultural situation at the end of the 1990s. Educational systems atrophy. Middle-class fiscal support for the visual arts is on the decline as new generations come forward. The impact of television, sporting events, and rock music blocks off canonical literary and artistic traditions and works sharply against linear rationality. Literary and artistic studies assume more and more the shape of preservation; they are backward-looking and unable to address the contours of present dangers.

The hope for humankind's welfare in the coming decades is that the universalizing and homogenizing grid will amicably transform the South and East and that a world system of technology, industry, and information will fasten itself into place. Whatever tensions remain between the old Western core and the non-Western periphery will be resolved pragmatically by political leadership and economic advantaging. Neither the religious and ethnic passions of the East and South, nor the barbarous pressures flowing from population bulge and poverty will impede the binding of regions and nations together. Looking to intellectuals and academicians, writers and artists, for leadership and healing will hopefully stimulate new cultural theory that will aid in the process of global unification and pacification.

At the end of the twentieth century there are two cultural conditions that are especially important and whose problems remain unresolved.

The first of these is the continued bifurcation between the old linear, rational, learned culture centered in the universities, the book-publishing industry, and the intellectually upscale weeklies and monthlies on the one side; and popular culture situated in film, television, and rock music on the other. There is some overlap and interaction between the two cultures—mostly in the work of a handful of filmmakers—but it is marginal in coverage and fragmentary in impact. The optimistic forecast in the 1960s that a new synthetic culture would emerge out of the confluence of these two polarities has not been realized.

There is plenty of blame to go around in accounting for this cultural condition of bifurcation and polarity: the intellectual conservatism of academics, fed by fearful reaction against the upheaval of the sixties and by the economic depression visited on academia by shortsighted politicians in the eighties and nineties, sapping the spirit of innovation from the academic world; the narrow horizons and the greed of the media moguls, whether of TV, Hollywood, or print, who are increasingly the same people and megacorporations; the secluded world of the more intellectual among book editors in New York, sunk in their Ivy League reveries; the domination of the intellectual and literary weeklies and monthlies by the tired and redundant liberal Left intelligensia, whose agenda is much more political than intellectual or artistic (so different from the first four decades of the century in the heyday of modernism); the paranoid mentality of a small number of rightist intellectual publications and their vulgar rejection of postmodernist theory; and the manipulative consequences of the important funding in cultural life that comes from a handful of big foundations and endowments, each with rigid programs and mischievous tactics (for example, the Macarthur Foundation funds not just "geniuses" but specifically leftist geniuses; the John M. Olin Foundation supports only individuals and enterprises approved by a very small clique of New York–Jewish rightist publicists).

Whatever the reason for the split between high and popular culture, it has been a major cause of the intellectual stagnation that set in during the early nineties, after the creative wave of postmodernism, and the fructifying impact of French theory, had passed. The way is open for new cultural visions, new intellectual and artistic pursuits, and especially for the stimulating synthesis of the intellectual and popular culture. Film and cable TV are the most likely media for this purpose.

The other problematic cultural condition visible at the turn of the century is that of religious revival. Whatever the faith—Catholic, Protestant, Jewish, Muslim, Buddhist, and Confucian—there is no doubt that many people embrace these faiths who are intense in cultivating the spiritual and personal implication of their beliefs. The religions mean much to people who are believers in greater degree now than in 1970.

That much is clear. What is unclear is whether the faiths are being more intensely cultivated by small visible core groups of believers or whether they are gaining more adherents aside from special populations who are in familiar fashion using religion as a way of expressing identity and solidarity—Muslims among the least fortunate in the impoverished Middle East and North African societies; evangelical and Pentecostal Christians among some of the upwardly mobile middle class in the American South and pockets of suburbia elsewhere.

If the Roman Catholic Church would under a new pope turn liberal, tolerant, and modern, or if Muslim groups similarly come under the leadership of liberal and tolerant mullahs, Catholicism and Islam would have the capability of major gains in adherents as well as greater acceptance by middle-class intellectuals.

Whether such a renaissance of Roman Catholicism and Islam would be a good thing for humankind is a difficult question from a secular point of view.

A nightmare projection for the twenty-first century would be expanded and exuberant Catholic and Muslim faiths in increased world competition for global dominance—a perilous vision of historical recycling back to the future of the Middle Ages.

The defining moment of the second half of the century, considered in retrospect, was the time between 1945 and 1948 when the Cold War began. The two sides were about equally to blame—the Americans by cutting off aid to the Soviet Union at a time when the USSR, having sustained the loss of thirty million people, staggered exhausted and hungry from the ruins of war; the Soviet leadership by pressing to gain the elevation of power of Communist parties everywhere.

The Cold War set the scene for the last decade of the century when the Soviet economy collapsed because of overcentralization and undercapitalization, as well as technological backwardness, but above all because of the cost of military preparedness. At the same time the American economy also experienced difficulties because of a lack of discipline and leadership in its work force. The Cold War meant huge defense and intelligence expenditures for the United States, which had to be paid for by severe cuts in elementary and secondary education. This contributed mightily to the decline of American schools: The United States, with the crumbling of public education, could not prepare enough students to meet the demands of the work force.

Both the Soviet Union and the United States had poured incalculable amounts of human and fiscal resources into building up other countries as their allies and dependents. What all this meant by the last decade of the century was the crumbling of both American and Russian wealth and power and the rise of non-Western peoples. From the perspective of the later twenty-first century, the Cold War will seem much like the Peloponnesian Wars that ruined ancient Greece. Just as Athens and Sparta fought to the death for hegemony in Greece, so the Americans and Soviets struggled in many ways and varied locales against each other. They stopped short of a direct military conflict, but the initiatives and response each side committed to this conflict damaged both of the giants of the postwar era severely. The conflict was unnecessary. Just as the Peloponnesian Wars' important outcome was the opportunity for the rise of Rome, so the meaningful result of the Cold War may be the rise of China to fiscal and perhaps military power early in the next century.

The West's nightmare projection for the twenty-first century and the start of the third Christian millennium is aggressive political and military stance by

China combined with a renewed Muslim onslaught on the Western world. It is impossible either to predict or deny the possibility of this doomsday scenario. Even taking the most benign view of the future, the belief by Marx and Weber alike, along with generations of colonialists and imperialists, that the East was structurally different from the West—perhaps attributable to a different kind of bourgeoisie or more pacific kind of religion—is no longer credible. Not just Japan but all the countries of East Asia have demonstrated their capacity to master the ingredients of fiscal and industrial capitalism.

Whether Western superiority was ever founded on structural differences or was simply a fortuitous and transitory phase, that era has gone. The best hope for the West is the strengthening of lateral, universal, technological, and political structures. This will make life good and secure for the elites in the West, but place the Western working and lower middle class on par with the masses of East Asia, Latin America, and in time Africa as well. For those who are not well educated, wealthy, or resourceful in the West, this is an unhappy prospect. In spite of all the devastation and mortality of the twentieth century, fifty years from now our century may in retrospect look like a golden age of the common man in the West before absorption into the universal underclass.

This renewal of social polarization on a global scale, which Karl Marx foresaw, will not, at least in the early decades of the new millennium and the new century, diminish the enterprise and intellectual force of the American economic and intellectual elite. Grounded in the strength of their universities and professional schools, in their fiscal institutions and their capacity to work effectively in the most diverse contexts, Americans will dominate learning, science, technology, enterprise, and the arts for many years to come. Fortunate are they who are raised to be members of this dominant group, who have made the cultural development of the twentieth century their social instrument of creativity and power. Thus, in spite of structural flaws in the current status of the United States in relation to other societies, and the country's significant decline from its former position in the years after World War II, the condition of the American elite remains a fortunate one. Thre are too many variables for anyone to predict how long it is likely to remain at such a level of felicity.

APPENDIX
CULTURAL ANALYSIS THROUGH FILM

Film—along with TV—is a highly effective medium for the expression of cultural history. In some respects the narrative and analytic qualities of film exceed the capability of expository prose to evoke complex and subtle aspects of twentieth-century culture.

The following film and TV list includes works that are representative of cultural motifs at a particular moment as well as consciously contrived historical re-creations of past cultural themes. While the list is far from exhaustive, a viewing of all these films offers a substantial education in the main currents of twentieth-century culture from 1900 to the present.

The Cultural World of 1900

Gunga Din (1937) This Hollywood film, from the Rudyard Kipling poem of the same name, is not just a sentimental story about the nineteenth-century British Raj. In itself it represents the ethos of imperialism and makes one wonder about American or at least Hollywood culture in the age of Franklin D. Roosevelt. So patronizingly racist that it has to be seen to be believed, this film demonstrates that, on the issues of imperialism and racism, the 1930s mentality is much closer to that of the Victorians than it is to ours.

Great Expectations (1947) David Lean directed this film from Dickens's novel and if anything, improved on it. The film subtly shows the meaning of getting ahead in Victorian society, and the tensions and anxieties involved.

The Charge of the Light Brigade (1968) Tony Richardson wanted his film to be a definitive critique of Victorian militarism and imperialism. He tried so hard that the film was unsuccessful commercially and exhibits a hesitant, uncertain quality that was bound to confuse and annoy the mass audience (they much preferred the simpler-minded Hollywood version of the same incident, a companion piece to *Gunga Din*). What remains valuable in Richardson's film is the effort to get inside the minds of Victorian soldiers and show that behind their splendid uniforms, they were individuals—by no means all alike.

Burn! (1969) The leftist Italian director Gillo Pontecorvo, with the help of Marlon Brando as a duplicitous British agent, unsympathetically scrutinizes imperialism in the nineteenth-century West Indies. The first half of the film, on the transition from Spanish to British rule, is persuasive.

The Organizer (1963) Marcello Mastroianni in a slow-moving but depressingly accurate account of a lonely and desperate labor union organizer during the earlier stages of industrialization in nineteenth-century Italy. The film exposes eloquently the roots of Italian anarchism.

Tess (1979) Roman Polanski's faithful and convincing version of Thomas Hardy's controversial and bitter novel that reprimands Victorian culture, and particularly its treatment of underprivileged women.

The Bostonians (1984) James Ivory's exubrant version of Henry James's early novel; to be seen for Vanessa Redgrave's stunning portrayal of a frenetic, dominating, lesbian late-nineteenth-century feminist.

Buddenbrooks (1983) A marvelous spare-no-expense German TV series closely derived from Thomas Mann's first great novel, about the rise and decline of a wealthy North German mercantile family (based on his own). Dubbed skillfully into English, this is the best depiction of the nineteenth-century bourgeoisie ever done on film or TV.

Hester Street (1975) Jewish immigrant life on the Lower East Side of Manhattan at the end of the nineteenth century, directed with compassion and care by Joan Micklin Silver.

The Godfather Part II (1974) Francis Ford Coppola's reverent yet convincing account of the rise of a Sicilian immigrant on Mulberry Street in Lower Manhattan in and through organized crime at the turn of the century.

The Go-Between (1971) Joseph Losey's film from L. P. Hartley's novel subtly examines hierarchy and sensibility, passion and power, in an Edwardian country house. A convincing evocation, at the same time nostalgic and critical, of a vanished world: "The past is a foreign country; they do things differently there."

A Passage to India (1984) E. M. Forster's novel described the British in India and their incapacity to communicate with the restless Indian middle class or to comprehend ancient, deep Indian culture. The novel was published in 1924 but may have been written earlier, and the world depicted is that of the Raj in 1914. David Lean's film, which greatly accentuates the pomp and circumstance, elaborately shows the prewar sahib ambience. Not fully faithful to the novel, because Forster depicts the Raj as tired and defensive, almost tattered and defeated, while Lean's nostalgic grandeur comes close to making the Raj attractive again. This is still one of the best films about imperialism and its decadence.

Heat and Dust (1983) Similar in theme to *A Passage to India* if less grand in ambience, this film is more direct in exploring the intense sexuality involved in imperial power and racial tensions. Director James Ivory has a deep feeling for the complexities of the colonial world, perhaps more so than Lean did.

A Room with a View (1986) James Ivory's elegant and hilarious film of E. M. Forster's novel shows the Edwardians cracking under the strain of sexual repression in contact with more liberated Italian culture. The novel is again somewhat different in tone: Forster glossed his comedy with a distant, critical view of the Edwardians that has almost disappeared from the nostalgic, delightful film.

Howard's End (1992) James Ivory's commercially successful film of Forster's subtle, acerbic novel about class divisions and cultural differences in early-twentieth-century England has a splendid cast and elaborate sets and costumes and much to recommend it. But Ivory and his collaborators have fundamentally softened the main social point of Forster's novel. The book involves the marriage of an intellectual woman, whose genteel family is slowly becoming poorer, to an aggressive, uneducated businessman. The point is lost because in the film the latter is played with great charm by Anthony Hopkins, his uncouth qualities downplayed and only slightly visible. Nevertheless this is the best film ever made about Edwardian England.

Modernism

The Blue Angel (1930) The classic by Joseph von Sternberg, with Marlene Dietrich and Emil Jannings, based on Heinrich Mann's expressionist novel about a schoolteacher's self-destructive infatuation for a music hall girl. The film is a study in sadomasochism. This film, one of the seminal works of cinema, is both an exemplar of and memorial to German modernism at its zenith.

Ulysses (1967) A bold but only modestly successful 1967 effort by Joseph Strick to illustrate parts of Joyce's novel; the film for the most part fails to capture Joyce's style, but its Dublin scenes are helpful in memoralizing the novel's environment. Molly Bloom's soliloquy is well done. Joyce would probably have admired this film more than the critics did.

Swann in Love (1984) This ambitious film by the German director Volker Schlöndorff attempted to depict part of Proust's *Swann's Way*. It was savaged by both literary and film critics. The film fails to capture Proust's style and is quite dull. But it does faithfully illustrate the houses, clothes, and faces of Proust's world, and that is not insignificant.

Jules and Jim (1961) François Truffaut's monumental effort to recreate the art nouveau world of early-twentieth-century France and in modernist vein to examine intensively human relationships in that world does not always stay in historical focus. Truffaut's innate neoromanticism intervenes, but nevertheless this is one of the great films of cultural history, a piercing, incomparable evocation of a very important time and place. Pauline Kael has said that Truffaut's film is the best portrayal of the F. Scott Fitzgerald era—a valid assessment. The film is regarded by many as the one in which Jeanne Moreau gives her finest performance.

Raging Bull (1982) Martin Scorsese's incredibly ambitious postmodernist effort to make a film in the modernist style about professional boxing in the early forties. This black-and-white film recovers the ambience of the era in a hundred subtle ways. The film is an entirely enclosed, self-referential, dirty, violent but somehow attractive little world. Since Scorsese's temperament leans to the modernist mold, there are no disconcerting cultural crosscurrents in it. It might be said that Scorsese made the film that Hemingway tried in his novels to communicate, but never in as consistent and direct a manner as here (perhaps because Scorsese has more confidence in himself and feels less need than Hemingway to please the limousine liberals in media and academe.) The film was praised by most critics, however, who often didn't understand what Scorsese was trying to do. The film was a disappointment commercially, not because the American audience does not want to see films about boxing. It loves them—as witness the Rocky series, a license to print money—as long as the theme is presented in neoromantic vein. The harsh modernism of Scorsese's film disturbed and offended the popular audience and confused some of the critics. Until someone makes a good film of a Hemingway or Faulkner novel—the results have been close to zero thus far—Scorsese's boxing film will stand as the American cinematic effort at recreating the modernist ethos, parallelling Truffaut's work in *Jules and Jim*.

The Day of the Locust (1975) The plot of Nathaniel West's modernist novel is preserved, but John Schlesinger's film does not communicate the same harsh ambience and theme. The film is an exercise in nostalgia for the old Hollywood of pre–World War II.

Death in Venice (1971) Luchino Visconti's earnest but only partly successful effort to illustrate Thomas Mann's modernist novella, the film is instructive, if not inspiring. Dirk Bogarde as a character modeled on Gustav Mahler.

Orlando (1993) Sally Porter's beautifully composed adaptation of Virginia Woolf's historical novel about androgyny, written as a valentine to Woolf's lesbian lover, in every way captures the sexual excitment of the 1920s and early 1930s and at the same time provides a remarkable short course in English cultural history and interior design.

Carrington (1995); *Dorothy Parker and the Vicious Circle* (1995) Intellectuals in the 1920s, British and American. In *Carrington* Lytton Strachey and some of the London Bloomsbury Group are featured. In *Dorothy Parker* it is the *New Yorker* writers and their hangout, the Algonquin Hotel roundtable, that are depicted. Jonathan Pryce is brilliantly convincing and sympathetic as Strachey; he comes through as more thoughtful, subtle, and kind than Strachey's books would indicate. Jennifer Jason Leigh is riveting and scary as Dorothy Parker. Strachey's and Parker's worlds are somewhat remote from ours. Both the Americans and Brits smoke constantly and drink heavily, the Americans to a near suicidal level. While the Bloomsbury group is named after a section of London's West End, in this film (as in life) their heart is really in the British countryside but safely within commuting distance of London. The Americans are entirely urban people (New York and later, in 1930s Hollywood). Both film stories are concerned with famous unrequited loves; the painter Dora Carrington for Strachey; Dorothy Parker for the writer Robert Benchley. Both films (which failed commercially) are elaborate and expensive efforts (by Christopher Hampton in *Carrington* and Alan Rudolph in *Parker*) to re-create the metropolitan writers' world of the 1920s and the ambience in which they worked. The writers' astonishing courage and independence look now simply like fortunate naïveté sharpened by volatile reaction to World War I.

Women in Love (1969) One of the great films, with two explosive sensibilities at work: Ken Russell on D. H. Lawrence. There has been much controversy as to whether Russell was faithful to Lawrence or went off on his own. This depends on what one thinks Lawrence was trying to do in the novel. Whatever the ultimate critical judgment, Russell does communicate Lawrence's masochistic fascination with intelligent and powerful women and strong but flawed men (that is, his wife, Frieda, and himself) and his vitalist vision. Glenda Jackson plays the character based on Frieda Lawrence.

Long Day's Journey into Night (1962) Jason Robards, Jr., endlessly chews the scenery as Eugene O'Neill's Irish American, alcoholic, self-pitying actor-father. For those who think O'Neill was a great modernist writer—which includes the drama critics of the *New York Times* and some other people.

Double Indemnity (1944) In this high point of Hollywood film noir, the Austrian émigre director Billy Wilder presents a sadomasochistic theme similar in tone to *The Blue Angel*, and laced with violence derived from Wilder's mentor Fritz Lang and the German expressionist tradition as well as from the American detective novel of the thirties.

Madame Curie (1982) Not the 1940s Hollywood weepie but the British TV series, which accurately and depressingly depicts the poverty, misery, and sacrificial courage in the life of Marie and Pierre Curie. The series captures the fanatical devotion and unlimited, foolish expectations of the new physicists of the early twentieth century.

The Horse's Mouth (1958) Although painting is one of the glories of twentieth century culture, this British film of the fifties, based on the Joyce Cary novel, is one of the few good films ever made about a modernist artist. Alec Guinness's painter is exclusively devoted to his avant-garde art and destructively treats everyone and everything else with contempt.

Vincent and Theo (1990) This ambitious, thoughtful, well-acted film by Robert Altman (from a French TV miniseries) depicts the later years of Vincent van Gogh, during which his loyal and loving brother tried unsuccessfully to sell his pictures and the painter descends slowly into madness and suicide. The scenes in the brilliant Arles sunshine that inspired van Gogh's most famous paintings—which nobody bought in his lifetime but which are now almost priceless—are particularly well done. Yet van Gogh's personality in the film remains a puzzle.

Psychoanalysis

Fanny and Alexander (1983) Ingmar Bergman's passionate and powerful recreation of the family and sexual life of a middle-class, turn-of-the-century Swedish family (his own). The oedipal and sexual rebellion against Christian patriarchialism and puritanism is better portrayed here than in any other film and it is precisely in this ambience that Freudianism emerged. Freud would have loved this film.

Freud (1962) An enthusiastic but not altogether accurate Hollywood portrayal of Freud's early career, directed by John Huston. Nevertheless Montgomery Clift's depiction of an intense, groping Freud is a possible and certainly absorbing interpretation. A better film than critics have allowed.

Diary of a Country Priest (1950) Based on a 1930s novel, this classic work by Robert Bresson depicts in shattering fashion the struggle between traditional Catholicism and modern sexuality. Again this is the cultural context in which Freud began his work. Not Cardinal O'Connor's version of the Catholic church, but not incompatible with Vatican II.

Spellbound (1945) This 1945 Hollywood view of psychiatry, directed by Alfred Hitchcock, is alternately interesting and silly, but it is a curious and valuable historical document, showing what psychiatry had come to mean in the popular American mind. Salvador Dalí designed the dream sequence.

My Night at Maud's (1969); *Claire's Knee* (1971); *Pauline at the Beach* (1983) Eric Rohmer's brilliant and delightful trilogy about all facets of sexuality in the life of the younger French generation of the late sixties, seventies, and early eighties. The films fall under the category of comedy, but they deal analytically with the ways in which sexuality affects the lives and thought of affluent, sophisticated middle-class people. Rohmer was focusing on yuppiedom and narcissism before these terms had entered into common parlance. The vibrancy and originality of French culture as well as the technique of the "new wave" of French filmmaking are reflected in these masterful films. The films furthermore are studies in the facets of the new West European culture of prosperity that followed from the tremendous postwar recovery. Rohmer doesn't miss a beat: His young people, when they attend university, take courses in linguistics, and we can assume they have been analyzed by Jacques Lacan.

Scenes from a Marriage (1973) Bergman's view of modern marriage illustrates both the doctrines of Freud and his disciples and how these ideas, entering into middle-class culture, have become as influential in human behavior as was Christianity in earlier centuries. If Freud could have seen this film early in his career, he might have had second thoughts about what he was trying to do.

Marxism and the Left

Ten Days that Shook the World (October) (1928) Eisenstein's official propaganda version of the Russian Revolution, or how the Leninists wanted themselves to be memorialized. Everyone else will, or should be, depressed by this film.

Reds (1981) The first half of Warren Beatty's film convincingly portrays leftist intellectuals in Greenwich Village c. 1914, with a bravura cameo by Jack Nicholson as Eugene O'Neill. The film is about the pristine Communist John Reed (who wrote the original book *Ten Days that Shook the World*). The second half, after the revolution, is confused, but does convincingly portray the betrayal of noble ideals both in Moscow and New York. The uneven quality of this film offended the critics, but it is withal a superior, undervalued historical work.

Dr. Zhivago (1965) David Lean's film from the celebrated autobiographical novel by Boris Pasternak depicts the Russian revolution from the point of view of the liberal middle class. The harshness and sterility of Bolshevik rule and the relative well-being of life under the czarist regime is strongly portrayed.

1900 (1977) How the Italian Marxist Bernardo Bertolucci visualizes the conflict of the rich and poor in his country since 1900. The first half is interesting and persuasive; the second half is dull Communist propaganda.

Dodsworth (1936) This Hollywood film by William Wyler, from the novel by Sinclair Lewis, illustrates two aspects of the New Deal liberal mentality. First, successful business entrepreneurs, especially if they are self-made billionaire industrial magnates, are intrinsically creative and fascinating people. Secondly, there is no problem in American society that goodwill on the part of someone in power cannot solve (anticipating the existential philosophy of the wartime and postwar eras). This film also commemorates a now vanished time when entrepreneurs were admired for making something (in this instance, automobiles) rather than for financial manipulation or real estate speculation.

Mr. Smith Goes to Washington (1939) Frank Capra's film reveals how New Deal liberals wanted to see themselves. James Stewart is an idealistic senator struggling against conformity and corruption on the floor of the Senate. There are some thought-provoking touches. The heroic senator needs the advice and help of a sophisticated woman journalist. The senator triumphs through use of the filibuster, which later became a favorite technique of southern conservative senators battling against civil rights laws. The purity of the boondocks vs. the cynical corruption of Washington theme that New Dealer Capra emphasizes was used three decades later very effectively in the campaigns of Carter and Reagan. What is disturbing in this monument to New Deal virtue is its sentimentality and self-righteousness.

The Grand Illusion (1937) Jean Renoir's work is the most powerful pacifist film ever made. It is about a group of French officers and soldiers interned in a World War I German prison camp and the common humanity that emerges between captors and prisoners. The film is profoundly moving but had no effect; three years later the German army was marching triumphantly through the streets of Paris.

Citizen Kane (1941) Orson Welles's masterpiece is a narrative account, using the techniques of German expressionist film as transmuted through Hollywood film noir, of the life of the right-wing newspaper magnate William Randolph Hearst. Welles shows the New Deal liberal mentality in its most effective and attractive form: as a critique of bloated and irresponsible capitalism, but still fascinated by capitalist power.

Yankee Doodle Dandy (1942) James Cagney's charismatic performance as George M. Cohan, the flag-waving Irish American songwriter and music hall performer. This film by Michael Curtiz portrays in concentrated form the thick national patriotism and self-congratulatory ethic that the war, coming on the heels of the similarly oriented New Deal, generated. This thick public ethic and patriotism were to shape powerfully postwar American policy and ultimately to inspire the Vietnam disaster. This film unsurprisingly received a lot of TV play in the Reagan era. What is not often noted is Cagney's careful, authentic depiction of Irish American cultural traits, including the stiff-legged dancing style derived from the Irish jig.

From Here to Eternity (1953) Fred Zinnemann's film from the James Jones novel ostensibly depicts army life in Hawaii on the eve of World War II. The film is intellectually a hymn to New Deal liberal values and postwar existentialism.

Bound for Glory (1977) This resounding commercial failure by Hal Ashby depicting the earlier life of Woody Guthrie, the folk singer, presents a wonderfully graphic account of the Great Depression and the heroic early days of union organization among agricultural workers in California, subjects that the American public now does not want to hear about. This film captures the spirit of the New Deal era and its leftist protagonists better than any other.

Daniel (1983) Sidney Lumet's version of the Rosenberg case, seen, as in the E. L. Doctorow novel on which it is based, from the point of view of the devastated children. This has got to be one of the most depressing films ever made, but its account is quite plausible.

Rebel Without a Cause (1955) Nicholas Ray, an old leftist from the thirties, directed James Dean in this 1955 story about the rebellion of a "juvenile delinquent" against conformist society. The film was hortatory as well as expository. Dean became a symbol of teenage rebellion.

Easy Rider (1969) Dennis Hopper's film about two hippie motorcyclists and drug dealers in the Southwest who are destroyed by corrupt and conformist society played a cultural role identical to *Rebel Without a Cause*. It not only depicted rebellion; it advocated it. *Easy Rider* is the essential anti-establishment film of the sixties. It was a box-office smash.

Odd Man Out (1949) Carol Reed's film, with a subtle performance by a young James Mason as a fallen resistance hero on the run, deals with the Time of Troubles (1920–22) in Ireland, the period of independence of most of the island from British rule and the civil war among factions of the Irish liberation movement. It is instructive that in view of the time it was made, Reed's film is much more honest in showing conflicts and betrayals within the revolutionary movement than later, more polemical and one-sided accounts of colonial liberation (compare *The Battle of Algiers* and *Gandhi*). It was still possible in 1949—as it was much more difficult a dozen years later—to show that the colonials were not all saints and heroes.

The Battle of Algiers (1965) Gillo Pontecorvo's pseudodocumentary reconstructing the Algerian revolution against French rule in the 1950s, told entirely from the Arab revolutionaries' point of view. The French are cruel villains. The perspective is dogmatically that of the European left of the sixties, and it more accurately reflects the Maoist revolutionary ideology of the period than the subtleties (the Jews, many of whose families had lived in Algeria for hundreds of years, were summarily driven out) of the Algerian war of liberation. Yet Pontecorvo's mise-en scène is compelling: The black and white photography captures the North African sun-drenched, dessicated environment very well.

If . . . (1968) The 1960s spawned a host of films about student revolution, all of them forgettable except this one by the British director Lindsay Anderson, which depicts a revolution in a British boys' school. The point of view is sympathetic to the students but the savage, nihilistic conclusion raises very disturbing—and appropriate—questions about 1960s radicalism.

The Confession (1970) How the Communist dream became a nightmare of state terror. Costa-Gavras pulls no punches in depicting the show trials in Prague in the 1950s and how the party turned (as in Moscow in the 1930s) against many of its idealistic leaders and against human decency. The film is based on the autobiographical account by one of the victims—one of the few to survive the terror—and is fully accurate.

Apocalypse Now (1979) Francis Ford Coppola's film about the Vietnam War, loosely based on Conrad's *Heart of Darkness,* is valuable not as an account of the war, but for the way in which the leftist discrediting of the war became firmly, probably eternally fixed in the popular mind as a very bad show in which the military acted discreditably and worse. Poor General Westmoreland—he never had a chance.

All the President's Men (1991) The fall of Richard Nixon as perceived and engineered by the *Washington Post.* A liberal morality tale, possibly about 60 percent true.

JFK (1991) Oliver Stone's 1991 film was lambasted by historians and many film critics alike for its fantastic attribution of Kennedy's assassination to an incredibly complex conspiracy among just about every agency of the American establishment and its elevation of a raunchy New Orleans D.A. into a hero. Yet the film is fascinating not only for Stone's immense technical skill at popular filmmaking but for his demonstration that the 1960s paranoid vision of the American Left still has capacity to gain visceral acclamation among millions of the American filmgoing public.

Traditions on the Right

Brideshead Revisited (1981) This British TV series powerfully and eloquently expounded Evelyn Waugh's sympathetic portrayal of a patrician English Catholic family between the wars. Their lavish lifestyle and conservative values come through clearly, although Waugh's conviction that these are the kind of people who deserve to rule and prosper is somewhat muted and his anti-Semitism is ignored. The type of aristocratic family that Waugh portrayed was easy prey for fascism throughout Western Europe as a counterweight to Communism and democracy.

Remains of the Day (1993) Fascist and pro-German sentiment among the British upper class in the 1930s as seen through the eyes of a loyal and at times troubled butler (Anthony Hopkins again), as well as the rigidity of the British class system, is what this subtle, brilliantly acted film has to offer. What is remarkable is that the pro-Nazi lord of the country mansion comes through as a complex, almost sympathetic character.

The Garden of the Finzi-Continis (1971) Vittorio de Sica's masterpiece, based on Giorgio Bassani's autobiographical Italian novel, delicately depicts the slow strangulation of a wealthy and aristocratic Jewish family in the fascist era—although Mussolini's fascism was initially and for many years not anti-Semitic. The troubles of the Italian Jews really began in 1938 after Mussolini's alliance with Hitler. The family depicted in this film represents hundreds of cultivated, wealthy, very old Jewish families throughout Continental Europe who perished in the Nazi era, a unique, effete cultural and social group that can never be re-created.

The Sorrow and the Pity (1970) Interviews with survivors of the Vichy era persuasively and not entirely unsympathetically explain what happened in France under Pétain and the Nazi occupation. Marcel Ophuls's searching, intelligent indictment of rightist France and how the Jews became the victims.

Shoah (1985) Claude Lanzmann's very lengthy series of interviews with survivors—victims, perpetrators, and not-so-innocent bystanders—of the Holocaust establishes the purpose and unspeakable horror of the greatest crime in the twentieth century. The film shows convincingly that East European ethnics—such as Poles—were almost as much involved as the Germans. This unpopular message has not gained sufficient public attention up to now, and its clear communication in this film has inevitably aroused resentment, especially in Poland. It is a wonder that this film, which took a decade to make, could have been made and that the participants were willing to speak so freely; this in itself is a disturbing message.

Mephisto (1981) If you are going to see only one film on the Nazi era, this is the one to see. Through a study of a leading German actor and director of the period—from Klaus Mann's novel based on a true story—István Szabó's film depicts the deceit, ambitions, and fears that made possible the rise of Hitler and the willing surrender of educated Germans to the Nazis. A persuasive account of why relatively decent people became Nazis.

Seven Beauties (1976) Lina Wertmüller's candid portrayal of the sexual sado-masochistic feelings that contributed to fascism and the Holocaust. The message appears to be the Augustinian one that fascist terror is rooted in the universal evil in human nature.

Europa, Europa (1991) A German Jewish boy on the lam from Nazis in German-occupied Poland and how he transforms his identity into that of an Aryan youth and survives the war is what this subtle rendering of a purportedly true story is about.

Schindler's List (1993) Steven Spielberg depicts the Holocaust and makes everyone feel good by depicting a good German businessman—again a true story—who saves Jewish lives. The hysterical enthusiasm with which this film was greeted tells a lot about the 1990s if not the 1940s.

The Bridge on the River Kwai (1957) David Lean directs a thoroughly convincing portrayal by Alec Guinness of the authoritarian personality exhibited by a British officer in a Japanese prison camp. Fascism as a universal category.

Lawrence of Arabia (1962) Another study by David Lean in the social psychology of fascism. What is remarkably suggested in Peter O'Toole's portrayal of the British leader of Arab nationalism is the hero's sadomasochism, homosexuality, and self-destructive qualities. A textbook example of Adler's psychoanalytic explanation of fascism as rooted in a sense of inferiority.

Patton (1970) George C. Scott's over-the-top portrayal of an authoritarian, charismatic, half-mad American general in World War II captures a key ingredient in twentieth-century militarism.

The Third Man (1949) Carol Reed's film, from a script by Graham Greene, depicts the malaise and corruption of postwar Europe, in this instance Vienna. The film also has the effect of contrasting a Nietzschean fascist (Orson Welles) with a good-hearted mid-American (Joseph Cotten). It also shows the Russians as heavies, reflecting the coming of the Cold War.

Oppenheimer (1982) This lengthy British TV series depicts Robert Oppenheimer and an international group of dedicated, brilliant, and ultimately agonized and divided group of physicists and engineers making the atom bomb in Los Alamos, New Mexico, 1943–45. The wives are not ignored, particularly Mrs. Oppenheimer, here truthfully portrayed as a brooding, difficult ex-Communist. The lookalike American actor Sam Waterston plays Oppenheimer in a thor-

526 ★ CULTURAL ANALYSIS THROUGH FILM

oughly convincing manner—except that he smiles too much—getting across the complex, Faustian character of this tormented, unique personality. The mise-en-scène is done very accurately: The claustrophobic quality of the environment in which the scientists worked comes through clearly. (There is also an American documentary film, *Day After Trinity*, about Oppenheimer and the making of the atom bomb that is powerful and instructive.) What is special about *Oppenheimer* are the nuanced explorations of the temperament and ideals of physicists in the age of colossal science, including their authoritarianism and arrogance. It is easy to envisage Oppenheimer, if he had occupied Werner Heisenberg's position, eagerly trying to make the atom bomb for Hitler and saying later he was sorry, as he accepts a chair at MIT. The British are fascinated with this theme of science in the service of government and destruction (compare the fifties film of exceptional value, *Breaking the Sound Barrier,* and the novels of C. P. Snow).

Judgment at Nuremberg (1961) Stanley Kramer's sober, careful docudrama about the trial of the leading Nazi war criminals in 1946 not only gets inside the minds of the monster-defendants but describes how the onset of the Cold War mitigated criminal justice and denazification in postwar Germany. The film was intended to make American as well as German audiences feel uncomfortable; perhaps that is why it was commercially not very successful and was unavailable for several decades.

Z (1969) Neofascism in Greece in the fifties. Costa-Gavras's film is left-wing propaganda, but he does get an important point across: fascism is nothing special; it is rooted in militarism and bureaucracy. Cf. Arendt's "banality of evil."

The Official Story (1985) A subtle and complex account of the motivation and expectations involved in the rightist terror that produced the "disappeared" under the militarist regime in Argentina in the 1970s. This is a very good film because it is not leftist propaganda; it is not entirely unsympathetic to the businessmen who collaborated with the neofascist regime, and it grasps some of the subtle and complex motives that drive relatively decent people to the far right in times of stress.

Gandhi (1982) An elaborate, very long epic of the Indian independence movement and its hero, and the end of the British Raj, told in wooden fashion by Richard Attenborough, and filmed in India at infinite expense. The film was a huge commercial success possibly because it carefully avoids subtlety and controversy. Except for a handful of British officers, who, after abusing the natives, slink off to drink gin-and-tonics and curse the darkness, everybody looks good. Gandhi is presented almost entirely in the conventional form of anti-colonialism's heroic saint. Yet the film is worth seeing because, with almost no help from the script, Ben Kingsley as Gandhi suggests some of the immense complexity of the Mahatma. As is customary in liberation epics, the early scenes under colonial rule are much more interesting—and historically accurate—than the later moments of triumph.

Nixon (1995) Oliver Stone's 1995 biography of Nixon is very different in theme from *All the President's Men*, and in tone from his own *JFK*. Although Anthony Hopkins is miscast as Nixon (coming across as a British prime minister from Wales rather than an American president from California), this film presents a careful and complex portrait and suggests that Nixon was mostly a decent man and a very capable administrator and innovative policy maker who was undone by his family and cultural background and by bad luck. Since the film conflicted with the liberal prejudices of the critics and the negative iconic image built into the American popular consciousness, it was a miserable failure at the box office. Decades from now it will be seen as the classic study of American conservatism in its better guise, and Oliver Stone will receive appropriate recognition as America's greatest maker of political films after Orson Welles.

Postmodernism

The Red Desert (1964) Michelangelo Antonioni's classic of nihilist boredom. What happened in economically recovered Europe when existential heroism was no longer believed in. Watching this film is like watching paint dry, but the rise of the structural system over the individual is evident.

A Clockwork Orange (1971) The Anthony Burgess–Stanley Kubrick evocation of a near future of punk rock fascist terror. The Nietzschean deconstruction of middle-class values turned into nightmare. Heavy metal.

Day for Night (1973) Truffaut as Roland Barthes: signifier, signified, referents, and the whole semiotical structure subtly (and not paradoxically) inserted into filmmaking.

The Deer Hunter (1978) Michael Cimino's film about the Vietnam War disturbed the American Left because of his postmodernist, or at least post-sixties, ambivalences about the whole mess and his sympathy for the American servicemen involved, particularly those of white ethnic background. Cimino's vigorous appropriation of patriotic traditions and his faith in the integrity and decency of the silent majority were remarkably prophetic of the age of Reagan.

Betrayal (1983) Harold Pinter's structuralist love story; this is the best evocation on film of structuralist dehumanization of personality. Effectively directed by David Jones and brilliantly acted. An important and underrated film, that quintessentially represents postmodernism as *The Blue Angel* reflected modernist culture.

The Big Chill (1983) This Hollywood film by Lawrence Kasdan doesn't stand up too well compared to Truffaut's and Pinter's versions of structuralism and postmodernism. Its theme of eighties cultural forms imposing themselves on nostalgia for the sixties doesn't quite come off, but it's fun.

The Return of Martin Guerre (1982) This film is based on a historical work by the Princeton postmodernist historian Natalie Zemon Davis and she also acted as a consultant for the film. Based on court records, it describes unusual crises in a peasant family in sixteenth-century France. The structuralism of Fernand Braudel and Claude Lévi-Strauss looms large in this film. The peasants are not only quite affluent but are highly articulate. Was that the way it was? Zemon Davis thinks so, audaciously citing a court record drawn up by a Protestant judge.

True West (1982) Domestic wrangles among the lower middle class, in which Sam Shepard deconstructs Western civilization—and particularly American mass culture—over the kitchen sink.

Stranger than Paradise (1984) Jim Jarmusch, a graduate of the NYU film school, pursues much of the same deconstructive, nihilist theme, but with delicacy and humor and in the end suggests that, contrary to Foucault, man is not dead. There is also a nostalgic subtext of immigrant survival in the New World—a neo-Victorianism if there ever was one.

Chariots of Fire (1981) This immensely popular British film illustrates the way in which the postmodernist culture of the eighties arbitrarily appropriates in nostalgic vein segments of the past that modernist culture considered anathema. The heroes are two young Brits in 1924 who win races at the Olympics: a priggish, ambitious London Jew and an evangelical Bible-thumping Scot from a missionary family. On seeing this film, T. S. Eliot would have ruminated darkly on the decline of civilization; Joyce would have thought it hilarious. While the historicist sentimentality is laid on thick, what makes this a post-modernist film is that the two heroes come through as yuppies more than as imperial idols. The early twenties ambience is constructed with infinite care by director Hugh Hudson, yet the heroes are readily identifiable as eighties people.

The Falcon and the Snowman (1985) John Schlesinger's film about the actual case of two alienated California postadolescents who sold government secrets to the Russians was not a commercial success. It is a discomfiting portrayal of the nihilism and sullen hostility affecting many young people in the eighties. Habermas's legitimation crisis brought to life in an unusual way.

The Man Who Fell to Earth (1976) This science fiction film by Nicolas Roeg had only modest commercial success but, more than the famous *Star Wars* trilogy and without the blizzard of special effects and computer graphics, it was the finest achievement of science fiction moviemaking of the seventies. It tells of a pilgrim from a dry, dying planet—played appropriately by the rock star David Bowie—who comes to earth in search of water. Of course this is an eschatalogical vision of the end of planet Earth itself.

Kramer vs. Kramer (1979) Seventies liberal feminism. Meryl Streep abandons her decent, hardworking husband and her son in order to find herself. Several years later she returns, and a protracted lawsuit justifies her behavior while not denigrating her husband. Nicey-nicey.

Thelma and Louise (1991) Hard-core late 1980s militant feminism. In order to gain their psychic freedom it is okay for two young women to rob, kill, and cost the taxpayers many thousands of dollars in police actions. Their suicide is epiphanic. The wildly positive response to this calculated commercial film directed by Ridley Scott speaks volumes about the social acceptance of ideological feminism.

The Right Stuff (1983) This detailed, historically careful account of the U.S. space program was a commercial disappointment. Its postmodernist 1983 ambience mystified the mass audience who came to cheer a patriotic triumph that deconstructed before their eyes into nontriumphal, dismaying, acerbic levels of signification. The enormous cost of this film by Philip Kaufman indicates that it was intended for a mass audience, but the public at large is not prepared for the emotional downer of deconstruction.

Brazil (1985) Terry Gilliam's brilliant, original vision of retromedievalism as postmodernism. This visionary British film was much more favorably received by the Los Angeles film critics than by the New York ones, which suggests that in California they have seen the future and they know it doesn't work.

Pulp Fiction (1994) Quentin Tarantino's provocative film is an intriguing exercise in American postmodernism. It is about a day in the life of a handful of violent and constantly foulmouthed California criminals, and the deconstructive level of universal humanist values underneath the brutal behavior and talk.

SELECT BIBLIOGRAPHY
The Cultural World of 1900

Andersen, Wayne V. *Gauguin's Paradise Lost.* New York: Viking, 1971.

Anderson, Linda R. *Bennett, Wells, and Conrad: Narrative in Transition.* London: Macmillan, 1988.

Architectural Heritage Society of Scotland. *The Age of Mackintosh.* Edinburgh: University Press, 1992.

Bellamy, Richard, ed. *Victorian Liberalism: Nineteenth-Century Political Thought and Practice.* London, New York: Routledge, 1990.

Bloom, Clive, ed. *Literature and Culture in Modern Britain.* London; New York: Longman, 1993–.

Boos, Florence S., ed. *History and Community: Essays in Victorian Medievalism.* New York: Garland, 1992.

Bowman, Frank Paul. *French Romanticism: Intertextual and Interdisciplinary Readings.* Baltimore: Johns Hopkins University Press, 1990.

Callow, Philip. *Lost Earth: A Life of Cézanne.* Chicago: Ivan R. Dee, 1995.

Chadwick, Owen. *The Secularization of the European Mind in the Nineteenth Century.* Cambridge, England; New York: Cambridge University Press, 1990.

Coontz, Stephanie. *The Social Origins of Private Life: A History of American Families, 1600–1900.* London, New York: Verso, 1988.

Dassow, Laura. *Henry David Thoreau and Nineteenth-Century Natural Science.* Madison: University of Wisconsin Press, 1995.

Dellheim, Charles. *The Face of the Past: The Preservation of the Medieval Inheritance in Victorian England.* Cambridge, England; New York: Cambridge University Press, 1982.

Drabble, Margaret. *Arnold Bennett: A Biography.* Boston: G. K. Hall, 1986.

Duncan, Alistair. *Art Nouveau.* London: Thames & Hudson, 1994.

Edel, Leon. *Henry James: A Life.* London: Collins, 1987. This single-volume life is derived from the five-volume biography written between 1950 and 1971.

Eisenman, Stephen F. *Nineteenth-Century Art: A Critical History.* London, New York: Thames & Hudson, 1994.

Elazar, Daniel J., ed. *Covenant in the Nineteenth Century: The Decline of an American Political Tradition.* Lanham, Md.: Rowman & Littlefield, 1994.

Felski, Rita. *The Gender of Modernity.* Cambridge, Mass.: Harvard University Press, 1995.

Gibson, James. *Thomas Hardy: A Literary Life.* Basingstoke, England: Macmillan, 1996.

Gilmour, Robin. *The Victorian Period: The Intellectual and Cultural Context of English Literature, 1830–1890.* London; New York: Longman, 1993.

Goldwater, Robert John. *Symbolism.* London: Allen Lane; New York: Harper & Row, 1979.

Graham, Kenneth. *Henry James: A Literary Life.* Basingstoke, England: Macmillan; New York: St. Martin's Press, 1995.

Greiff, Constance M. *Art Nouveau.* New York: Abbeville Press, 1995.

Hall, Catherine. *White, Male, and Middle-Class: Explorations in Feminism and History.* New York: Routledge, 1992.

Harrison, Antony H. *Swinburne's Medievalism: A Study in Victorian Love Poetry.* Baton Rouge, La.: Louisiana State University Press, 1988.

Hayman, Ronald. *Nietzsche, A Critical Life.* Harmondsworth, England; New York: Penguin Books, 1982.

Henderson, Heather. *The Victorian Self: Autobiography and Biblical Narrative.* Ithaca, N.Y.: Cornell University Press, 1989.

Hofstatter, Hans Hellmut, with contributions by W. Jaworska and S. Hofstatter. *Art Nouveau: Prints, Illustrations and Posters.* New York: Greenwich House, 1984.

Holub, Robert C. *Friedrich Nietzsche.* New York: Twayne, 1995.

Hoover, Arlie J. *Friedrich Nietzsche: His Life and Thought.* Westport, Conn.: Praeger, 1994.

Houghton, Walter Edwards. *The Victorian Frame of Mind, 1830–1870.* New Haven, Conn.: Published for Wellesley College by Yale University Press, 1957.

Hynes, Samuel Lynn. *The Edwardian Turn of Mind.* London: Pimlico, 1991.

———. *A War Imagined: The First World War and English Culture.* New York: Atheneum; Maxwell Macmillan International, 1991.

Judson, Pieter M. *Inventing Germanness: Class, Ethnicity, and Colonial Fantasy at the Margins of the Habsburg Monarchy.* Minneapolis: Center for Austrian Studies, University of Minnesota, 1993.

Karl, Frederick Robert. *Joseph Conrad: The Three Lives.* New York: Farrar, Straus, & Giroux, 1979.

Kern, Stephen. *The Culture of Love: Victorians to Moderns.* Cambridge, Mass.: Harvard University Press, 1992.

———. *The Culture of Time and Space, 1880–1918.* London: Weidenfeld & Nicolson; Cambridge, Mass.: Harvard University Press, 1983.

Kloppenberg, James T. *Uncertain Victory: Social Democracy and Progressivism in European and American Thought, 1870–1920.* Oxford, England; New York: Oxford University Press, 1988.

Lagercrantz, Olof Gustaf Hugo. *August Strindberg.* Translated by Anselm Hollo. London; Boston: Faber & Faber, 1984.

Lears, T. J. Jackson. *No Place of Grace: Antimodernism and the Transformation of American Culture, 1880–1920.* London; Chicago: University of Chicago Press, 1994.

Ledger, Sally, and Scott McCracken, eds. *Cultural Politics at the Fin de Siècle.* Cambridge, England; New York: Cambridge University Press, 1995.

Lynd, Helen Merrell, with a new introduction by Gerald M. Pomper. *England in the Eighteen-Eighties: Toward a Social Basis for Freedom.* 1945. Reprint, New Brunswick, N.J.: Transaction Books, 1984.

MacCarthy, Fiona. *William Morris: A Life for Our Time.* New York: Alfred A. Knopf, 1995.

Macleod, Robert. *Charles Rennie Mackintosh.* Feltham, England: For Country Life Books by Hamlyn Publishing Group, 1968.

Masur, Gerhard. *Prophets of Yesterday: Studies in European Culture, 1890–1914.* New York: Harper & Row, 1966.

Matsuda, Matt K. *The Memory of the Modern.* Oxford, England; New York: Oxford University Press, 1996.

McCarthy, Michael H. *The Crisis of Philosophy.* Albany: State University of New York Press, 1990.

Medina, Joyce. *Cézanne and Modernism: The Poetics of Painting.* Albany: State University of New York Press, 1995.

Meyer, Michael Leverson. *Ibsen.* London: Cardinal Books, 1992.

———. *Strindberg.* New York: Random House, 1985.

Meyers, Jeffrey. *Joseph Conrad: A Biography.* New York: Charles Scribner's Sons, 1991.

Millgate, Michael. *Thomas Hardy: A Biography.* Oxford, England; Toronto; New York: Oxford University Press, 1985.

Mills, Patricia Jagentowicz, ed. *Feminist Interpretations of G. W. F. Hegel.* University Park: Pennsylvania State University Press, 1996.

Mitterauer, Michael, and Reinhard Sieder. *The European Family: Patriarchy to Partnership from the Middle Ages to the Present.* Translated by Karla Oosterveen and Manfred Horzinger. Oxford, England: Blackwell; Chicago: University of Chicago Press, 1982.

Monneret, Sophie. *Renoir.* Translated by Emily Read. London: Barrie & Jenkins, 1990.

Pemble, John. *The Mediterranean Passion: Victorians and Edwardians in the South.* Oxford, England; New York: Oxford University Press, 1988.

Perkin, Harold James. *The Rise of Professional Society: England since 1880.* London; New York: Routledge, 1989.

Pinion, F. B. *Thomas Hardy: His Life and Friends,* corrected ed. Basingstoke, England: Macmillan, 1994.

Ray, Martin, ed. *Joseph Conrad: Interviews and Recollections.* Basingstoke, England: Macmillan, 1990.

Renoir, Auguste. *Renoir by Renoir.* Edited by Rachel Barnes. Exeter, England: Webb & Bower, 1990.

Robertson, Ritchie, and Edward Timms, eds. *The Habsburg Legacy: National Identity in Historical Perspective.* Edinburgh: Edinburgh University Press, 1994.

Rodmell, Graham E. *French Drama of the Revolutionary Years.* London, New York: Routledge, 1990.

Roper, Jon. *Democracy and its Critics: Anglo-American Democratic Thought in the Nineteenth Century.* London, Boston: Unwin Hyman, 1989.

Schorske, Carl E. *Fin-de-siècle Vienna: Politics and Culture.* New York: Vintage Books, 1981.

Sealts, Merton M., Jr. *Emerson on the Scholar.* Columbia, Mo.: University of Missouri Press, 1992.

Seigel, Jerrold E. *Bohemian Paris: Culture, Politics, and the Boundaries of Bourgeois Life, 1830–1930.* New York: Penguin Books, 1987.

Shafer, Yvonne. *Henrik Ibsen: Life, Work, and Criticism.* Fredericton, Canada: York Press, 1985.

Shattuck, Roger. *The Banquet Years: The Origins of the Avant-Garde in France, 1885 to World War I.* Rev. ed. Salem, N.H.: Ayer, 1984.

Shiff, Richard. *Cézanne and the End of Impressionism: A Study of the Theory, Technique, and Critical Evaluation of Modern Art.* Chicago: University of Chicago Press, 1986.

Sigsworth, Eric M. *In Search of Victorian Values: Aspects of Nineteenth-Century Thought and Society.* Manchester, England; New York: Manchester University Press; New York: St. Martin's Press, 1988.

Spitzer, Alan Barrie. *The French Generation of 1820.* Princeton: Princeton University Press, 1987.

Stansky, Peter. *Redesigning the World: William Morris, the 1880s, and the Arts and Crafts.* Palo Alto, Calif.: Society for the Promotion of Science and Scholarship, 1996.

Steele, James. *Charles Rennie Mackintosh: Synthesis in Form.* London: Academy Editions; New York: St. Martin's Press, 1994.

Sussman, Henry. *The Hegelian Aftermath: Readings in Hegel, Kierkegaard, Freud, Proust, and James.* Baltimore: Johns Hopkins University Press, 1982.

Sweetman, David. *Paul Gauguin, A Complete Life.* London: Hodder & Stoughton, 1995.

Thwaite, Ann. *Edmund Gosse: A Literary Landscape, 1849–1928.* Oxford, England; New York: Oxford University Press, 1985 [1984].

Waal, Carla. *Harriet Bosse: Strindberg's Muse and Interpreter.* Carbondale: Southern Illinois University Press, 1990.

Walvin, James. *Victorian Values.* Athens: University of Georgia Press, 1988.

Wank, Solomon. *The Nationalities Question in the Habsburg Monarchy: Reflections on the Historical Record.* Minneapolis: Center for Austrian Studies, University of Minnesota, 1993.

Watts, Cedric Thomas. *Joseph Conrad: A Literary Life.* Basingstoke, England: Macmillan, 1989.

Weber, Eugen Joseph. *France, Fin de Siècle.* Cambridge, Mass.: Belknap Press, 1986.

West, Shearer. *Fin de Siècle.* Woodstock, N.Y.: Overlook Press, 1994.

White, Barbara Ehrlich. *Renoir, His Life, Art, and Letters.* New York: Abrams, 1984.

Modernism

Ackroyd, Peter. *T. S. Eliot.* London: Hamish Hamilton; New York: Simon & Schuster, 1984.

Adams, Hazard. *The Book of Yeats's Vision: Romantic Modernism and Antithetical Tradition.* Ann Arbor, Mich.: University of Michigan Press, 1995.

Adelson, Leslie A. *Making Bodies, Making History: Feminism & German Identity.* Lincoln: University of Nebraska Press, 1993.

Amann, Per. *Edvard Munch.* Translated by Jennifer Barnes. Thornbury, England: Artline
    Editions, 1987.

Ayer, Alfred Jules. *Wittgenstein.* London: Weidenfeld & Nicolson, 1985.

————. *Philosophy in the Twentieth Century.* New York: Random House, 1982.

Badash, Lawrence. *Kapitza, Rutherford, and the Kremlin.* New Haven: Yale University Press,
    1985.

Balakian, Anna Elizabeth. *André Breton, Magus of Surrealism.* New York: Oxford University
    Press, 1971.

Bangerter, Lowell A. *Robert Musil.* New York: Continuum, 1989.

Barraclough, Geoffrey. *Main Trends in History.* Expanded and updated by Michael Burns.
    New York: Holmes & Meier, 1991.

Bates, Milton J. *Wallace Stevens: A Mythology of Self.* Berkeley: University of California Press,
    1985.

Beckson, Karl E. *London in the 1890s: A Cultural History.* New York: Norton, 1992.

Behr, Shulamith. *Women Expressionists.* New York: Rizzoli, 1988.

Behr, Shulamith, David Fanning, and Douglas Jarman, eds. *Expressionism Reassessed.*
    Manchester, England; Manchester University Press; New York: St. Martin's Press,
    1993.

Beja, Morris. *James Joyce: A Literary Life.* Columbus, Ohio: Ohio State University Press,
    1992.

Bell, Quentin. *Virginia Woolf: A Biography.* Rev. ed. London: London, 1996.

Berger, Maurice, ed. *Modern Art and Society: An Anthology of Social and Multicultural Readings.*
    New York: Icon Editions, 1994.

Berman, Art. *Preface to Modernism.* Urbana: University of Illinois Press, 1994.

Bernheimer, Charles, ed. *Comparative Literature in the Age of Multiculturalism.* Baltimore: Johns
    Hopkins University Press, 1995.

Bernstein, Jeremy. *Einstein.* 2d ed. Fontana Press, 1991.

Bersani, Leo, and Ulysse Dutoit. *Arts of Impoverishment: Beckett, Rothko, Resnais.* Cambridge,
    Mass.: Harvard University Press, 1993.

Bethe, Hans Albrecht. *The Road from Los Alamos.* New York: American Institute of Physics,
    1991.

Bevan, David, ed. *Literature and War.* Amsterdam; Atlanta, Ga.: Rodopi, 1990.

Blaser, Werner. *Mies van der Rohe: The Art of Structure.* New York: Whitney Library of
    Design, 1994.

Boe, Alf. *Edvard Munch.* Translated by Robert Ferguson. New York: Rizzoli, 1989.

Boggs, Carl. *Intellectuals and the Crisis of Modernity.* Albany: State University of New York
    Press, 1993.

Bonnefoy, Yves. *Alberto Giacometti: A Biography of His Work.* Translated by Jean Stewart.
    Paris: Flammarion, 1991.

Boone, Daniele. *Picasso.* Rev. ed. Translated by John Greaves. London: Studio Editions,
    1993.

Bouveresse, Jacques. with a foreword by Vincent Descombes. *Wittgenstein Reads Freud: The Myth of the Unconscious.* Translated by Carol Cosman. Princeton: Princeton University Press, 1995.

Brée, Germaine. *The World of Marcel Proust.* Boston: Houghton Mifflin, 1966.

Bronner, Stephen Eric and Douglas Kellner, eds. *Passion and Rebellion: The Expressionist Heritage.* New York: Columbia University Press, 1988 [1983].

Brooker, Peter. *Bertolt Brecht: Dialectics, Poetry, Politics.* London; New York: Croom Helm, 1988.

Brooker, Peter, ed. *Modernism/Postmodernism.* London; New York: Longman, 1992.

Brown, JoAnne, and David K. van Keuren, eds. *The Estate of Social Knowledge.* Baltimore: Johns Hopkins University Press, 1991.

Brown, Laurie M., Abraham Paris, and Brian Pippard. *Twentieth-Century Physics.* 3 vols. Philadelphia: Institute of Physics, 1995.

Bucky, Peter A., in collaboration with Allen G. Weakland. *The Private Albert Einstein.* Kansas City: Andrews & McMeel, 1992.

Buhle, Mari Jo, Paul Buhle, and Harvey J. Kaye, eds., with a foreword by Eric Foner. *The American Radical.* New York: Routledge, 1994.

Burdick, Charles, Hans-Adolf Jacobsen, and Winfried Kudszus, eds. *Contemporary Germany: Politics and Culture.* Boulder, Co.: Westview Press, 1984.

Burger, Peter. *The Decline of Modernism.* Translated by Nicholas Walker. Cambridge, England: Polity Press; University Park: Pennsylvania State University Press, 1992.

Burgess, Anthony. *Flame into Being: The Life and Work of D. H. Lawrence.* London: Heinemann; New York: Arbor House, 1985.

Bush, Clive. *Halfway to Revolution: Investigation and Crisis in the Work of Henry Adams, William James, and Gertrude Stein.* New Haven, Conn.: Yale University Press, 1991.

Bush, Ronald. *T. S. Eliot: A Study in Character and Style.* New York: Oxford University Press, 1983.

Byles, Joan Montgomery. *War, Women, and Poetry, 1914–1945: British and German Writers and Activists.* London: Associated University Presses; Newark: University of Delaware Press, 1995.

Byrne, Janet. *A Genius for Living: The Life of Frieda Lawrence.* New York: HarperCollins, 1995.

Caffrey, Margaret Mary. *Ruth Benedict: Stranger in this Land.* Austin, Tex.: University of Texas Press, 1989.

Calinescu, Matei. *Five Faces of Modernity: Modernism, Avant-Garde, Decadence, Kitsch, Postmodernism.* Durham, N.C.: Duke University Press, 1987.

Carey, John. *The Intellectuals and the Masses: Pride and Prejudice among the Literary Intelligentsia, 1880–1939.* London, Boston: Faber & Faber, 1992.

Caws, Mary Ann. *Women of Bloomsbury: Virginia, Vanessa, and Carrington.* New York: Routledge, 1990.

Chernaik, Warren, Warwick Gould, and Ian R. Willison, eds. *Modernist Writers and the Marketplace.* London: Macmillan, 1995.

Clark, Ronald William. *Einstein, the Life and Times: An Illustrated Biography.* New York: H. N. Abrams, 1984.

Clark, Suzanne. *Sentimental Modernism: Women Writers and the Revolution of the Word.* Bloomington: Indiana University Press, 1991.

Clifford, James. *The Predicament of Culture: Twentieth-Century Ethnography, Literature, and Art.* Cambridge, Mass.: Harvard University Press, 1988.

Comens, Bruce. *Apocalypse and After: Modern Strategy and Postmodern Tactics in Pound, Williams, and Zukofsky.* Tuscaloosa: University of Alabama Press, 1995.

Comte, Philippe. *Paul Klee.* Translated by Carol Marshall. Woodstock, N.Y.: Overlook Press, 1991.

Connolly, Cyril. *100 Key Books of the Modern Movement from England, France & America, 1880–1950.* London: Allison & Busby, 1986.

Connolly, William E. *Political Theory and Modernity.* 2d ed., with a new epilogue. Ithaca, N.Y.: Cornell University Press, 1993.

Cottom, Daniel. *Abyss of Reason: Cultural Movements, Revelations, and Betrayals.* New York: Oxford University Press, 1991.

Cottrell, Allin F., and Michael S. Lawlor, eds. *New Perspectives on Keynes.* Durham, N.C.: Duke University Press, 1995.

Crawford, John C., and Dorothy L. Crawford. *Expressionism in Twentieth-Century Music.* Bloomington: Indiana University Press, 1993.

Da Silva, N. Takei. *Modernism and Virginia Woolf.* Windsor, England: Windsor Publications, 1990.

Daix, Pierre. *Picasso, Life and Art.* Translated by Olivia Emmet. New York: Icon Editions, 1993.

Danchev, Alex, ed. *Fin de Siècle: The Meaning of the Twentieth Century.* London: Tauris Academic Studies; New York: St. Martin's Press, 1995.

D'Aquila, Ulysses L. *Bloomsbury and Modernism.* New York: P. Lang, 1989.

Dassow, Laura. *Henry David Thoreau and Nineteenth-Century Natural Science.* Madison: University of Wisconsin Press, 1995.

DeKoven, Marianne. *Rich and Strange: Gender, History, and Modernism.* Princeton: Princeton University Press, 1991.

Delany, Paul. *D. H. Lawrence's Nightmare: The Writer and His Circle in the Years of the Great War.* New York: Basic Books, 1978.

Denham, Scott D. *Visions of War: Ideologies and Images of War in German Literature before and after the Great War.* Bern; New York: P. Lang, 1992.

Donoghue, Denis. *The Old Moderns: Essays on Literature and Theory.* New York: Alfred A. Knopf, 1994.

———. *We Irish.* Brighton, England: Harvester, 1986.

———, with an introduction by Ronald Schuchard. *Being Modern Together.* Atlanta, Ga.: Scholars Press, 1991.

Dortch, Virginia M., ed. *Peggy Guggenheim and her Friends.* Milan: Berenice, 1994.

Downing, David B., and Susan Bazargan, eds. *Image and Ideology in Modern/Postmodern Discourse.* Albany: State University of New York Press, 1991.

Eberle, Matthias. *World War I and the Weimar Artists: Dix, Grosz, Beckmann, Schlemmer.* Translated by John Gabriel. New Haven, Conn.: Yale University Press, 1985.

Edel, Leon. *Bloomsbury: A House of Lions.* London: Hogarth; Philadelphia: Lippincott, 1979.

Ehrlich, Doreen. *The Bauhaus.* Winston, England: Magna Books, 1991.

Eigler, Friederike, and Peter C. Pfeiffer, eds. *Cultural Transformations in the New Germany: American and German Perspectives.* Columbia, S.C.: Camden House, 1993.

Elliott, Bridget, and Jo-Ann Wallace. *Women Artists and Writers: Modernist (Im)Positionings.* London, New York: Routledge, 1994.

Ellmann, Richard. *James Joyce.* New and rev. ed. Oxford, England; New York: Oxford University Press, 1983.

Emig, Rainer. *Modernism in Poetry: Motivation, Structures, and Limits.* London, New York: Longman, 1996.

Erickson, Victoria Lee. *Where Silence Speaks: Feminism, Social Theory, and Religion.* Minneapolis: Fortress Press, 1993.

Esslin, Martin. *Brecht, A Choice of Evils: A Critical Study of the Man, His Work, and His Opinions.* 4th rev. ed. London, New York: Methuen, 1984.

Feinstein, Howard M. *Becoming William James.* Ithaca, N.Y.: Cornell University Press, 1984.

Feuer, Lewis Samuel. *Einstein and the Generations of Science.* 2d ed. New Brunswick, N.J.: Transaction Books, 1982.

Field, Frank. *British and French Writers of the First World War: Comparative Studies in Cultural History.* Cambridge, England; New York: Cambridge University Press, 1991.

Filreis, Alan. *Modernism from Right to Left: Wallace Stevens, the Thirties, & Literary Radicalism.* Cambridge, England; New York: Cambridge University Press, 1994.

Finch, Henry Le Roy. *Wittgenstein.* Rockport, Mass.: Element, 1995.

Findlay, John Niermeyer. *Wittgenstein, A Critique.* London; Boston: Routledge & Kegan Paul, 1984.

Fineberg, Jonathan David. *Art since 1940: Strategies of Being.* London: Laurence King; New York: H.N. Abrams, 1995.

Flavell, Mary Kay. *George Grosz, A Biography.* New Haven, Conn.: Yale University Press, 1988.

Fleming, Bruce Edward. *Modernism and its Discontents: Philosophical Problems of Twentieth-Century Literary Theory.* New York: P. Lang, 1995.

Forgacs, Eva. *The Bauhaus Idea and Bauhaus Politics.* Translated by John Bakti. Budapest, New York: Central European University Press, 1995.

Franciscono, Marcel. *Paul Klee: His Work and Thought.* Chicago: University of Chicago Press, 1991.

Frascina, Francis, and Jonathan Harris, eds. *Art in Modern Culture: An Anthology of Critical Texts.* New York: HarperCollins, 1992.

Frascina, Francis, and Charles Harrison, eds. *Modern Art and Modernism: A Critical Anthology.*

London, New York: Harper & Row in association with the Open University, 1982.

Frazier, Nancy. *Louis Sullivan and the Chicago School.* New York: Crescent Books, 1991.

Freedman, Ralph. *Life of a Poet: A Biography of Rainer Maria Rilke.* New York: Farrar, Straus & Giroux, 1995.

Fuegi, John. *Brecht and Company: Sex, Politics, and the Making of the Modern Drama.* New York: Grove Press, 1994.

Fussell, Paul. *The Great War and Modern Memory.* London, New York: Oxford University Press, 1975.

Gabbard, Ken, ed. *Representing Jazz.* Durham, N.C.: Duke University Press, 1995.

Gelpi, Albert, ed. *Wallace Stevens, the Poetics of Modernism.* Cambridge, England; New York: Cambridge University Press, 1985.

Genova, Judith. *Wittgenstein: A Way of Seeing.* New York: Routledge, 1995.

Gibson, Mary Ellis. *Epic Reinvented: Ezra Pound and the Victorians.* Ithaca, N.Y.: Cornell University Press, 1995.

Gilpin, George H. *The Art of Contemporary English Culture.* Basingstoke, England: Macmillan; New York: St. Martin's Press, 1991.

Glynn, Sean, and Alan Booth. *Modern Britain: An Economic and Social History.* London, New York: Routledge, 1996.

Golding, John. *Visions of the Modern.* Berkeley: University of California Press, 1994.

Goldschmidt, Bertrand. *Atomic Rivals.* Translated by Georges M. Temmer. New Brunswick, N.J.: Rutgers University Press, 1990.

Gordon, Donald E. *Expressionism: Art and Idea.* New Haven, Conn.: Yale University Press, 1987.

Gran, Peter. *Beyond Eurocentrism: A New View of Modern World History.* Syracuse, N.Y.: Syracuse University Press, 1996.

Graver, David. *The Aesthetics of Disturbance: Anti-Art in Avant-Garde Drama.* Ann Arbor: University of Michigan Press, 1995.

Green, Martin Burgess. *The Von Richthofen Sisters: The Triumphant and the Tragic Modes of Love: Else and Frieda von Richthofen, Otto Gross, Max Weber, and D. H. Lawrence in the Years 1870-1970.* Albuquerque: University of New Mexico Press, 1988 [1974].

Greenberg, Allan Carl. *Artists and Revolution: Dada and the Bauhaus, 1917–1925.* Ann Arbor, Mich.: UMI Research Press, 1979.

Grenville, Anthony. *Cockpit of Ideologies: The Literature and Political History of the Weimar Republic.* Bern, New York: P. Lang, 1995.

Griffin, Gabriele, ed. *Difference in View: Women and Modernism.* London; Bristol, Pa.: Taylor & Francis, 1994.

Griffiths, Paul. *Modern Music and After.* Rev. ed. of *Modern Music: The Avant-Garde since 1945.* Oxford, England; New York: Oxford University Press, 1995.

Grimm, Reinhold, and Jost Hermand, eds. *High and Low Cultures: German Attempts at Mediation.* Madison: Published for Monatshefte by University of Wisconsin Press, 1994.

Gunning, Tom. *D. W. Griffith and the Origins of American Film Narrative: The Early Years at Biograph.* Urbana: University of Illinois Press, 1991.

Hahl-Koch, Jelena. *Kandinsky.* Translated by Karen Brown, Ralph Harratz, and Katharine Harrison. New York: Rizzoli, 1993.

Halsey, A. H. *Change in British Society.* 4th ed. Oxford, England; New York: Oxford University Press, 1995.

Hamilton, George Heard, with a revised bibliography by Richard Cork. *Painting and Sculpture in Europe, 1880–1940.* 6th ed. New Haven, Conn.: Yale University Press, 1993.

Hamilton, Nigel. *The Brothers Mann: The Lives of Heinrich and Thomas Mann.* London: Secker & Warburg; New Haven, Conn.: Yale University Press, 1978.

Hardison, O. B., Jr. *Disappearing through the Skylight: Culture and Technology in the Twentieth Century.* New York: Viking, 1989.

Harris, Marvin. *The Rise of Anthropological Theory: A History of Theories of Culture.* New York: Crowell, 1968.

Harrison, Charles. *English Art and Modernism, 1900–1939.* London: Allen Lane; Bloomington: Indiana University Press, 1981.

Harrod, Roy Forbes. *The Life of John Maynard Keynes.* 1951. Reprint, New York: A. M. Kelley, 1969.

Harwood, John. *Eliot to Derrida: The Poverty of Interpretation.* Basingstoke, England: Macmillan, 1995.

Hayman, Ronald. *Proust: A Biography.* London: Minerva, 1991.

————. *Thomas Mann: A Biography.* New York: Scribner, 1995.

Hays, Peter L. *Ernest Hemingway.* New York: Continuum, 1990.

Hedges, Inez. *Languages of Revolt: Dada and Surrealist Literature and Film.* Durham, N.C.: Duke University Press, 1983.

Heilbron, Johan. *The Rise of Social Theory.* Translated by Sheila Gogol. Minneapolis: University of Minnesota Press, 1995.

Heilbut, Anthony. *Thomas Mann: A Biography.* New York: Alfred A. Knopf, 1995.

Heller, Reinhold. *Munch: His Life and Work.* London: J. Murray; Chicago: University of Chicago Press, 1984.

Herrera, Hayden. *Matisse: A Portrait.* New York: Harcourt Brace, 1993.

Hickman, Hannah. *Robert Musil & the Culture of Vienna.* London: Croom Helm; La Salle, Ill.: Open Court Publishing, 1984.

Highfield, Roger, and Paul Carter. *The Private Lives of Albert Einstein.* New York: St. Martin's Press, 1994.

Hight, Eleanor M. *Picturing Modernism: Moholy-Nagy and Photography in Weimar Germany.* Cambridge, Mass.: MIT Press, 1995.

Hobhouse, Janet. *Everybody Who Was Anybody: A Biography of Gertrude Stein.* New York: Doubleday, 1989.

Hofstadter, Richard, with a new introduction by Eric Foner. *Social Darwinism in American Thought.* 1944. Reprint, Boston: Beacon Press, 1992.

Holton, Gerald, and Yehuda Elkana, eds. *Albert Einstein, Historical and Cultural Perspectives: The Centennial Symposium in Jerusalem.* Princeton: Princeton University Press, 1982.

Horowitz, Irving Louis. *The Decomposition of Sociology.* New York: Oxford University Press, 1993.

Hughes, John A., Peter J. Martin, and W. W. Sharrock. *Understanding Classical Sociology: Marx, Weber, Durkheim.* London; Thousand Oaks, Calif.: Sage, 1995.

Hynes, Samuel Lynn. *A War Imagined: The First World War and English Culture.* New York: Atheneum; Maxwell Macmillan International, 1991.

Jackson, Tony E. *The Subject of Modernism: Narrative Alterations in the Fiction of Eliot, Conrad, Woolf, and Joyce.* Ann Arbor: University of Michigan Press, 1994.

Janik, Allan, and Stephen Toulmin. *Wittgenstein's Vienna.* New York: Simon & Schuster, 1973.

Jardi, Enric. *Paul Klee.* Translated by Jennifer Jackson and Kerstin Engstrom. New York: Rizzoli, 1991.

Jay, Martin. *Force Fields: Between Intellectual History and Cultural Critique.* New York: Routledge, 1993.

Jensen, Robert. *Marketing Modernism in Fin de Siècle Europe.* Princeton: Princeton University Press, 1994.

Johnson, Paul. *Modern Times: A History of the World from the 1920s to the 1990s.* Rev. ed. New York: HarperPerennial, 1992.

Johnson, Robert David, ed. *On Cultural Ground: Essays in International History.* Chicago: Imprint Publications, 1994.

Jones, Robert Alun. *Emile Durkheim: An Introduction to Four Major Works.* Beverly Hills, Calif.: Sage Publications, 1986.

Judson, Pieter M. *Inventing Germanness: Class, Ethnicity, and Colonial Fantasy at the Margins of the Habsburg Monarchy.* Minneapolis: Center for Austrian Studies, University of Minnesota, 1993.

Jump, Harriet Devine, ed., with a foreword by Julia Briggs. *Diverse Voices: Essays on Twentieth-Century Women Writers in English.* New York: St. Martin's Press, 1991.

Karcher, Eva. *Dix.* Translated by John Ormrod. New York: Crown Publishers, 1987.

Karl, Frederick Robert. *Franz Kafka, Representative Man.* New York: Ticknor & Fields, 1991.

————. *Modern and Modernism: The Sovereignty of the Artist, 1885–1925.* New York: Atheneum, 1985.

Kaufmann, Michael. *Textual Bodies: Modernism, Postmodernism, and Print.* London: Associated University Presses; Lewisburg, Pa.: Bucknell University Press, 1994.

Kavanaugh, Gaynor. *Museums and the First World War: A Social History.* London: Leicester University Press; New York: St. Martin's Press, 1994.

Kearney, Richard. *Modern Movements in European Philosophy.* 2d ed. Manchester, England; New York: Manchester University Press, 1994.

Kenner, Hugh. *A Colder Eye: The Modern Irish Writers.* Baltimore: Johns Hopkins University Press, 1989 [1983].

————. *The Pound Era.* Berkeley: University of California Press, 1971.

Kenny, Anthony. *Wittgenstein.* London: Allen Lane; Cambridge, Mass.: Harvard University Press, 1973.

Keppel, Ben. *The Work of Democracy: Ralph Bunche, Kenneth B. Clark, Lorraine Hansberry, and the Cultural Politics of Race.* Cambridge, Mass.: Harvard University Press, 1995.

Kiely, Robert, ed. *Modernism Reconsidered.* Cambridge, Mass.: Harvard University Press, 1983.

King, James. *Virginia Woolf.* New York: Norton, 1995.

Kivisto, Peter, and William H. Swatos, Jr. *Max Weber, A Bio-Bibliography.* New York: Greenwood Press, 1988.

Knapp, Bettina Liebowitz. *Gertrude Stein.* New York: Continuum, 1990.

Kniesche, Thomas W., and Stephen Brockmann, eds. *Dancing on the Volcano: Essays on the Culture of the Weimar Republic.* Columbia, S.C.: Camden House, 1994.

Kuenzli, Rudolf E., ed. *Dada and Surrealist Film.* New York: Willis, Locker & Owens, 1987.

Langslet, Lars Roar. *Henrik Ibsen, Edvard Munch: To Genier Motes [Two Geniuses Meet].* Oslo: J.W. Cappelen, 1994.

Lefebvre, Henri. *Introduction to Modernity: Twelve Preludes, September 1959-May 1961.* Translated by John Moore. London, New York: Verso, 1995.

Lehmann, Jennifer M. *Durkheim and Women.* Lincoln: University of Nebraska Press, 1994.

Lentricchia, Frank. *Modernist Quartet.* Cambridge, England; New York: Cambridge University Press, 1994.

Leondopoulos, Jordan. *Still the Moving World: Intolerance, Modernism, and Heart of Darkness.* New York: P. Lang, 1991.

Leppmann, Wolfgang. *Rilke: A Life.* Translated by Russell M. Stockman. Verse translations by Richard Exner. New York: Fromm International, 1984.

Levenson, Michael Harry. *A Genealogy of Modernism: A Study of English Literary Doctrine, 1908–1922.* Cambridge, England; New York: Cambridge University Press, 1984.

Levin, Harry. *Memories of the Moderns.* New York: New Directions, 1980.

Levine, Donald Nathan. *Visions of the Sociological Tradition.* Chicago: University of Chicago Press, 1995.

Lloyd, Jill. *German Expressionism: Primitivism and Modernity.* New Haven, Conn.: Yale University Press, 1991.

Lord, James. *Giacometti, A Biography.* New York: Farrar, Straus, & Giroux, 1985.

Lucie Smith, Edward. *Movements in Art since 1945: Issues and Concepts.* 3d rev. and expanded ed. New York: Thames & Hudson, 1995.

Lukacs, John. *The End of the Twentieth Century and the End of the Modern Age.* New York: Ticknor & Fields, 1993.

Lukes, Steven. *Emile Durkheim, His Life and Work: A Historical and Critical Study.* Stanford, Calif.: Stanford University Press, 1985 [1972].

Lyndall, Gordon. *Eliot's New Life.* Oxford, England; New York: Oxford University Press, 1988.

Mac Liammoir, Micheal, and Eavan Boland. *W. B. Yeats and His World.* London: Thames & Hudson; New York: Viking, 1971.

MacKillop, Ian Duncan. *F. R. Leavis: A Life in Criticism.* London: Allen Lane, 1995.

MacPherson, Malcolm. *Time Bomb: Fermi, Heisenberg, and the Race for the Atomic Bomb.* New York: Dutton, 1986.

Macrae, Alisdair D. F. *W. B. Yeats: A Literary Life.* New York: St. Martin's Press, 1995.

Maddox, Brenda. *D. H. Lawrence, the Story of a Marriage.* New York: Simon & Schuster, 1994.

Maddox, Robert James. *Weapons for Victory: The Hiroshima Decision Fifty Years Later.* Columbia: University of Missouri Press, 1995.

Malins, Edward Greenway. *A Preface to Yeats.* 2d ed. Revisions and additional material by John Purkis. London; New York: Longman, 1994.

Marcus, Greil. *The Dustbin of History.* Cambridge, Mass.: Harvard University Press, 1995.

Marwick, Arthur. *The Deluge: British Society and the First World War.* New York: Norton, 1970.

McCormmach, Russell. *Night Thoughts of a Classical Physicist.* New York: Avon, 1983.

McGann, Jerome J. *Black Riders: The Visible Language of Modernism.* Princeton: Princeton University Press, 1993.

Megill, Donald D. and Richard S. Demory. *Introduction to Jazz History.* 4th ed. Upper Saddle River, N.J.: Prentice Hall, 1996.

Mellow, James R. *Hemingway: A Life Without Consequences.* Boston: Houghton Mifflin, 1992.

————. *Charmed Circle: Gertrude Stein and Company.* London: Phaidon Press; New York: Praeger, 1974.

Melzer, Annabelle Henkin. *Dada and Surrealist Performance.* Baltimore: Johns Hopkins University Press, 1994.

Mercier, Vivian. *Modern Irish Literature: Sources and Founders.* Edited by Eilis Dillon. Oxford, England; New York: Oxford University Press, 1994.

Mestrovic, Stjepan Gabriel. *Durkheim and Postmodern Culture.* New York: A. de Gruyter, 1992.

Metzidakis, Stamos. *Difference Unbound: The Rise of Pluralism in Literature and Criticism.* Amsterdam; Atlanta, Ga.: Rodopi, 1995.

Meyer, Leonard B. *Music, the Arts, and Ideas: Patterns and Predictions in Twentieth-Century Culture.* Chicago: University of Chicago Press, 1994 [1967].

Meyers, Jeffrey. *D. H. Lawrence: A Biography.* New York: Alfred A. Knopf, 1990.

————. *Hemingway, A Biography.* New York: Harper & Row, 1985.

Middleton, Peter. *The Inward Gaze: Masculinity and Subjectivity in Modern Culture.* London, New York: Routledge, 1992.

Miller, Simon, ed. *The Last Post: Music after Modernism.* Manchester, England: Manchester University Press; New York: St. Martin's Press, 1993.

Mini, Piero V. *Keynes, Bloomsbury, and The General Theory.* Basingstoke, England: Macmillan, 1991.

Mitchell, Donald, with an introduction by Edward W. Said. *The Language of Modern Music.* New ed. Philadelphia: University of Pennsylvania Press, 1994.

Modell, Judith Schachter. *Ruth Benedict, Patterns of a Life.* Philadelphia: University of Pennsylvania Press, 1983.

Moggridge, Donald Edward. *Maynard Keynes: An Economist's Biography.* London, New York: Routledge, 1992.

Morrison, Roy Dennis. *Science, Theology, and the Transcendental Horizon: Einstein, Kant, and Tillich.* Atlanta, Ga.: Scholars Press, 1994.

Mulhern, Francis. *The Moment of "Scrutiny."* London: NLB, 1979.

Munch, Richard. *Understanding Modernity: Toward a New Perspective Going Beyond Durkheim and Weber.* London, New York: Routledge, 1988.

Murphy, William Michael. *Family Secrets: William Butler Yeats and His Relatives.* Syracuse, N.Y.: Syracuse University Press, 1995.

Nalbantian, Suzanne. *Aesthetic Autobiography: From Life to Art in Marcel Proust, James Joyce, Virginia Woolf, and Anaïs Nin.* Basingstoke, England: Macmillan, 1994.

Naylor, Gillian, ed. *Bloomsbury: Its Artists, Authors, and Designers.* Boston: Little, Brown, 1990.

Needle, Jan, and Peter Thompson. *Brecht.* Oxford: Blackwell, 1981.

Neuman, Shirley, and Ira B. Nadel. *Gertrude Stein and the Making of Literature.* Boston: Northeastern University Press, 1988.

Neville, Robert Cummings. *The High Road Around Modernism.* Albany: State University of New York Press, 1992.

Niebylski, Dianna C. *The Poem on the Edge of the Word: The Limits of Language and the Uses of Silence in the Poetry of Mallarmé, Rilke, and Vallejo.* New York: P. Lang, 1993.

Noel, Bernard. *Matisse.* New York: Universe Books, 1987.

North, Michael. *The Dialectic of Modernism: Race, Language, and Twentieth-Century Literature.* New York: Oxford University Press, 1994.

Northey, Anthony. *Kafka's Relative's: Their Lives and his Writing.* New Haven, Conn.: Yale University Press, 1991.

O'Connor, Kathleen. *Robert Musil and the Tradition of the German Novelle.* Riverside, Calif.: Ariadne Press, 1991.

O'Gorman, James F. *Three American Architects: Richardson, Sullivan, and Wright, 1865–1915.* Chicago: University of Chicago Press, 1991.

Painter, George Duncan. *Marcel Proust: A Biography.* Rev. and enl. ed. 2 vols. London: Chatto & Windus, 1989.

Paret, Peter. *The Berlin Succession: Modernism and its Enemies in Imperial Germany.* Cambridge, Mass.: Belknap Press of Harvard University Press, 1980.

Parkin, Frank. *Durkheim.* Oxford, England; New York: Oxford University Press, 1992.

Pawel, Ernst. *The Nightmare of Reason: A Life of Franz Kafka.* New York: Farrar, Straus, & Giroux, 1984.

Pearce, Richard. *The Politics of Narration: James Joyce, William Faulkner, and Virginia Woolf.* New Brunswick, N.J.: Rutgers University Press, 1991.

Penrose, Roland. *Picasso, His Life and Work.* 3d ed. Berkeley: University of California Press, 1981 [1958].

Perelman, Bob. *The Trouble with Genius: Reading Pound, Joyce, Stein, and Zukofsky.* Berkeley: University of California Press, 1994.

Perl, Jeffrey M. *The Tradition of Return: The Implicit History of Modern Literature.* Princeton: Princeton University Press, 1984.

Pierce, David. *Yeats's Worlds: Ireland, England and the Poetic Imagination.* New Haven, Conn.: Yale University Press, 1995.

Poggioli, Renato. *The Theory of the Avant-Garde.* Translated by Gerald Fitzgerald. Cambridge, Mass.: Belknap Press of Harvard University Press, 1982.

Polizzotti, Mark. *Revolution of the Mind: The Life of André Breton.* New York: Farrar, Strauss, & Giroux, 1995.

Poole, Roger. *The Unknown Virginia Woolf.* 4th ed. Cambridge, England; New York: Cambridge University Press, 1996.

Posnock, Ross. *The Trial of Curiosity: Henry James, William James, and the Challenge of Modernity.* New York: Oxford University Press, 1991.

Prater, Donald A. *Thomas Mann: A Life.* Oxford, England; New York: Oxford University Press, 1995.

Pratt, William. *Singing the Chaos: Madness and Wisdom in Modern Poetry.* Columbia: University of Missouri Press, 1996.

Purcell, Edward A. Jr. *The Crisis of Democratic Theory: Scientific Naturalism and the Problem of Value.* Lexington: University Press of Kentucky, 1973.

Quinones, Ricardo J. *Mapping Literary Modernism: Time and Development.* Princeton: Princeton University Press, 1985.

Raabe, Paul, ed. *The Era of German Expressionism.* Translated by J. M. Ritchie. Woodstock, N.Y.: Overlook Press, 1974.

Reich-Ranicki, Marcel. *Thomas Mann and his Family.* Translated by Ralph Manheim. London: Collins, 1989.

———. *The King and His Rival: The Expanded New Edition of the Correspondence between Thomas and Heinrich Mann.* Translated by Timothy Nevill. Bonn: Inter Nationes, 1985.

Reynolds, Dee. *Symbolist Aesthetics and Early Abstract Art: Sites of Imaginary Space.* Cambridge, England; New York: Cambridge University Press, 1995.

Rhodes, Richard. *The Making of the Atomic Bomb.* New York: Simon & Schuster, 1986.

Richardson, Elizabeth P. *A Bloomsbury Iconography.* Winchester, England: St. Paul's Bibliographies, 1989.

Richardson, John. *A Life of Picasso.* With the collaboration of Marilyn McCully. New York: Random House, 1991–.

Richter, Melvin. *The History of Political and Social Concepts: A Critical Introduction.* New York: Oxford University Press, 1995.

Robert, Marthe. *As Lonely as Franz Kafka.* Translated by Ralph Manheim. New York: Schocken Books, 1986.

Roberts, John, ed. *Art Has No History!: The Making and Unmaking of Modern Art.* London; New York: Verso, 1994.

Rogoff, Irit, ed. *The Divided Heritage: Themes and Problems in German Modernism.* Cambridge, England; New York: Cambridge University Press, 1991.

Rogowski, Christian. *Distinguished Outsider: Robert Musil and His Critics.* Columbia, S.C.: Camden House, 1994.

Rorty, Richard. *Consequences of Pragmatism: Essays, 1972–1980.* Minneapolis: University of Minnesota Press, 1982.

Rosenbaum, Stanford Patrick. *Edwardian Bloomsbury.* Basingstoke, England: Macmillan, 1994.

Roskill, Mark W. *Klee, Kandinsky, and the Thought of their Time: A Critical Perspective.* Urbana, Ill.: University of Illinois Press, 1992.

Ross, Dorothy, ed. *Modernist Impulses in the Human Sciences, 1870-1930.* Baltimore: Johns Hopkins University Press, 1994.

———. *The Origins of American Social Science.* Cambridge, England; New York: Cambridge University Press, 1991.

Roters, Eberhard. *Berlin, 1910–1933.* Translated by Marguerite Mounier. New York: Rizzoli, 1982.

San Lazzaro, Gualtieri di, ed. *Homage to Wassily Kandinsky.* Translated by Wade Stevenson. New York: L. Amiel, 1975.

Sartiliot, Claudette. *Citation and Modernity: Derrida, Joyce, and Brecht.* Norman: University of Oklahoma Press, 1993.

Sass, Louis Aronson. *Madness and Modernism: Insanity in the Light of Modern Art, Literature and Thought.* New York: Basic Books, 1992.

Sayen, Jamie. *Einstein in America: The Scientist's Conscience in the Age of Hitler and Hiroshima.* New York: Crown, 1985.

Schapiro, Meyer. *Modern Art, 19th and 20th Centuries: Selected Papers.* New York: G. Braziller, 1982.

Schickel, Richard. *D. W. Griffith: An American Life.* London: Pavilion; New York: Simon & Schuster, 1984.

Schneidau, Herbert N. *Waking Giants: The Presence of the Past in Modernism.* New York: Oxford University Press, 1991.

Schneider, Pierre. *Matisse.* Translated by Michael Taylor and Bridget Strevens Romer. New York: Rizzoli, 1984.

Schrader, Barbel and Jurgen Schebera. *The "Golden" Twenties: Art and Literature in the Weimar Republic.* New Haven, Conn.: Yale University Press, 1988.

Schuller, Gunther. *Early Jazz: Its Roots and Musical Development.* New York: Oxford University Press, 1986 [1968].

Schulze, Franz. *Mies van der Rohe: A Critical Biography.* London; Chicago: University of Chicago Press, 1985.

Schulze, Franz, ed. *Mies van der Rohe: Critical Essays.* New York: Museum of Modern Art; Cambridge, Mass.: MIT Press, 1989.

Schwartz, Sanford. *The Matrix of Modernism: Pound, Eliot, and Early Twentieth-Century Thought.* Princeton: Princeton University Press, 1985.

Scott, Bonnie Kime. *Refiguring Modernism.* Bloomington: Indiana University Press, 1995.

Secrest, Meryle. *Kenneth Clark: A Biography.* New York: Holt, Rinehart, & Winston, 1985.

Selz, Peter. *German Expressionist Painting.* London; Berkeley; Los Angeles: University of California Press, 1974 [1957].

Shaffer, Brian W. *The Blinding Torch: Modern British Fiction and the Discourse of Civilization.* Amherst: University of Massachusetts Press, 1993.

Shannon, Christopher. *Conspicuous Criticism: Tradition, the Individual, and Culture in American Social Thought, from Veblen to Mills.* Baltimore: Johns Hopkins University Press, 1996.

Shapiro, Theda. *Painters and Politics: The European Avant-Garde and Society, 1900–1925.* New York: Elsevier, 1976.

Sharpe, Tony. *T. S. Eliot: A Literary Life.* New York: St. Martin's Press, 1991.

Shattuck, Roger. *The Innocent Eye: On Modern Literature and the Arts.* New York: Farrar, Straus, & Giroux, 1984.

———. *Marcel Proust.* New York: Viking, 1974.

Sherry, Vincent. *Ezra Pound, Wyndham Lewis, and Radical Modernism.* New York: Oxford University Press, 1993.

Shils, Edward Albert. *The Calling of Sociology and Other Essays on the Pursuit of Learning.* Chicago: University of Chicago Press, 1980.

Short, Robert. *Dada & Surrealism.* London: Laurence King, 1994 [1980].

Siegfried, Charlene Haddock. *Pragmatism and Feminism: Reweaving the Social Fabric.* Chicago: University of Chicago Press, 1996.

Simon, Linda. *Gertrude Stein Remembered.* Lincoln, Neb.: University of Nebraska Press, 1994.

Skidelsky, Robert Jacob Alexander. *Keynes.* Oxford, England; New York: Oxford University Press, 1995.

———. *John Maynard Keynes: A Biography.* 2 vols. New York: Viking, 1986 [1983].

Snow, Charles Percy. *The Physicists.* Introduction by William Cooper. London: Macmillan; Boston: Little, Brown, 1981.

Solomon, Neale E. *The Problem of Modernity.* Oakland, Ca.: Academic Ventures Press, 1993.

Sontag, Frederick. *Wittgenstein and the Mystical: Philosophy as an Ascetic Practice.* Atlanta, Ga.: Scholars Press, 1995.

Speirs, Ronald. *Bertolt Brecht.* Basingstoke, England: Macmillan, 1987.

Stevenson, Randall. *Modernist Fiction: An Introduction.* New York: Harvester Wheatsheaf, 1992.

Stock, Noel. *The Life of Ezra Pound,* expanded ed. San Francisco: North Point Press, 1982.

Surette, Leon. *The Birth of Modernism: Ezra Pound, T. S. Eliot, W. B. Yeats, and the Occult.* Montreal; Buffalo, N.Y.: McGill–Queen's University Press, 1993.

Sylvester, David. *Looking at Giacometti.* Photographs by Patricia Matisse. London: Chatto & Windus, 1994.

Terdiman, Richard. *Present Past: Modernity and the Memory Crisis.* Ithaca, N.Y.: Cornell University Press, 1993.

Thompson, Paul Richard. *The Edwardians: The Remaking of British Society.* 2d ed. London; New York: Routledge, 1992 [1st ed., 1985].

Tirro, Frank. *Jazz: A History.* 2d ed. New York: Norton, 1993 [1st ed., 1977].

Tomlin, Eric Walter Frederick. *T. S. Eliot, A Friendship.* London: Routledge, 1988.

Torjusen, Bente. *Words and Images of Edvard Munch.* Chelsea, Vt.: Chelsea Green, 1986.

Tratner, Michael. *Modernism and Mass Politics: Joyce, Woolf, Eliot, Yeats.* Stanford: Stanford University Press, 1995.

Trigg, George L. *Landmark Experiments in Twentieth-Century Physics.* New York: Dover, 1995.

Twitchell, James B. *Dreadful Pleasures: An Anatomy of Modern Horror.* New York: Oxford University Press, 1985.

Twombly, Robert C. *Louis Sullivan, His Life and Work.* New York: Viking, 1986.

Tylee, Claire M. *The Great War and Women's Consciousness: Images of Militarism and Womanhood in Women's Writings, 1914–1964.* Basingstoke, England: Macmillan; Iowa City: University of Iowa Press, 1990.

Veisland, Jorgen S. *Kierkegaard and the Dialectics of Modernism.* New York: P. Lang, 1985.

Verdi, Richard. *Klee and Nature.* New York: Rizzoli, 1985.

Wagner-Martin, Linda. *Favored Strangers: Gertrude Stein and her Family.* New Brunswick, N.J.: Rutgers University Press, 1995.

Walter, Maila L. *Science and Cultural Crisis: An Intellectual Biography of Percy Williams Bridgman (1882–1961).* Stanford: Stanford University Press, 1990.

Weekes, Ann Owens. *Irish Women Writers: An Unchartered Tradition.* Lexington.: University Press of Kentucky, 1990.

Weld, Jacqueline Bograd. *Peggy, the Wayward Guggenheim.* New York: Dutton, 1986.

Werner, Otto. *The Origin and Development of Jazz.* 3d ed. Dubuque, Iowa: Kendall/Hunt, 1994.

Westphal, Uwe. *The Bauhaus.* Translated by John Harrison. London: Studio Editions, 1991.

White, Michael, and John Gribbin. *Einstein: A Life in Science.* London, New York: Simon & Schuster, 1993; New York: Dutton, 1994.

Wilhelm, James J. *Ezra Pound: The Tragic Years, 1925–1972.* University Park, Pa.: Pennsylvania State University Press, 1994.

Willett, John. *Art and Politics in the Weimar Period: The New Sobriety, 1917–1933.* London: Thames & Hudson; New York: Pantheon Books, 1978.

———. *Expressionism.* London: Weidenfeld & Nicolson; New York: McGraw-Hill, 1970.

Williams, Linda. *Figures of Desire: A Theory and Analysis of Surrealist Film.* Berkeley: University of California Press, 1992.

Williams, Raymond. *Drama from Ibsen to Brecht.* London: Chatto & Windus, 1968.

Wilson, David. *Rutherford, Simple Genius.* London: Hodder & Stoughton, 1983.

Wilson, Jane S., and Charlotte Serber, eds. *Standing By and Making Do: Women of Wartime Los Alamos.* Los Alamos, N.M.: Los Alamos Historical Society, 1988.

Wohl, Robert. *The Generation of 1914.* Cambridge, Mass.: Harvard University Press, 1979.

Worthen, John. *D. H. Lawrence.* Cambridge; New York: Cambridge University Press, 1991–.

Wright, Georg Henrik von. *Wittgenstein.* Oxford: Blackwell, 1982.

Zukowsky, John. *Mies Reconsidered: His Career, Legacy, and Disciples.* Chicago: Art Institute of Chicago; New York: Rizzoli, 1986.

Psychoanalysis

Apollon, Willy, and Richard Feldstein, eds. *Lacan, Politics, Aesthetics.* Albany: State University of New York Press, 1996.

Barratt, Barnaby B. *Psychoanalysis and the Postmodern Impulse: Knowing and Being since Freud's Psychology.* Baltimore: Johns Hopkins University Press, 1993.

Bowie, Malcolm. *Psychoanalysis and the Future of Theory.* Oxford, England; Cambridge, Mass.: Blackwell, 1994.

Bracher, Mark. *Lacan, Discourse, and Social Change: A Psychoanalytic Cultural Criticism.* Ithaca, N.Y.: Cornell University Press, 1993.

Brunner, José. *Freud and the Politics of Psychoanalysis.* Oxford, England; Cambridge, Mass.: Blackwell, 1995.

Chodorow, Nancy. *Femininities, Masculinities, Sexualities: Freud and Beyond.* Lexington: University Press of Kentucky, 1994.

Clark, Ronald W. *Freud: The Man and the Cause.* London: Paladin Grafton, 1982.

Clement, Catherine. *The Lives and Legends of Jacques Lacan.* Translated by Arthur Goldhammer. New York: Columbia University Press, 1983.

Cooper, Arnold M., Otto F. Kernberg, and Ethel Spector Person. *Psychoanalysis: Toward the Second Century.* New Haven, Conn.: Yale University Press, 1989.

Donald, James, ed. *Psychoanalysis and Cultural Theory: Thresholds.* Basingstoke, England: Macmillan; London: ICA, 1991.

Donnelly, Margaret E., ed. *Reinterpreting the Legacy of William James.* Washington, D.C.: American Psychological Association, 1992.

Dufresne, Todd, ed. *Returns of the "French Freud."* New York: Routledge, 1996.

Ellenberger, Henri Frederic. *The Discovery of the Unconscious: The History and Evolution of Dynamic Psychiatry.* New York: Basic Books, 1970.

Elliott, Anthony, and Stephen Frosh, eds. *Psychoanalysis in Contexts: Paths between Theory and Modern Culture.* London; New York: Routledge, 1995.

Endleman, Robert. *Relativism under Fire: The Psychoanalytic Challenge.* New York: Psyche Press, 1995.

Fine, Reuben. *The History of Psychoanalysis.* New expanded ed. New York: Continuum, 1990.

Fisher, David James. *Cultural Theory and Psychoanalytic Tradition.* New Brunswick, N.J.: Transaction, 1991.

Fordham, Michael. *Freud, Jung, Klein—The Fenceless Field: Essays on Psychoanalysis and Analytical Psychology.* Edited by Roger Hobdell. London; New York: Routledge, 1995.

Freud, Ernst, Lucie Freud, and Ilse Grubrich-Simitis, eds., with a biographical sketch by K. R. Eissler. *Sigmund Freud: His Life in Pictures and Words.* Translated by Christine Trollope. New York: Harcourt Brace Jovanovich, 1978.

Frosh, Stephen. *Identity Crisis: Modernity, Psychoanalysis, and the Self.* London: Macmillan; New York: Routledge, 1991.

Gay, Peter. *Freud: A Life for Our Times.* London: J. M. Dent; New York: Norton, 1988.

———. *Freud, Jews, and Other Germans: Masters and Victims in Modernist Culture.* New York: Oxford University Press, 1978.

Gliserman, Martin J. *Psychoanalysis, Language, and the Body of the Text.* Gainesville: University Press of Florida, 1996.

Greenberg, Jay R., and Stephen A. Mitchell. *Object Relations in Psychoanalytic Theory.* Cambridge, Mass.: Harvard University Press, 1983.

Grosskurth, Phyllis. *The Secret Ring: Freud's Inner Circle and the Politics of Psychoanalysis.* London: J. Cape, 1991.

———. *Melanie Klein: Her World and Her Work.* Cambridge, Mass.: Harvard University Press, 1987 [1986].

Grunbaum, Adolf. *The Foundations of Psychoanalysis: A Philosophical Critique.* Berkeley: University of California Press, 1984.

Hale, Nathan G., Jr. *The Rise and Crisis of Psychoanalysis in America: Freud and the Americans, 1917–1985.* New York: Oxford University Press, 1995.

Hogenson, George B. *Jung's Struggle with Freud.* Rev. ed. Wilmette, Ill.: Chiron, 1994 [1983].

Homans, Peter. *Jung in Context: Modernity and the Making of a Psychology.* 2d ed. Chicago: University of Chicago Press, 1995.

———. *The Ability to Mourn: Disillusionment and the Social Origins of Psychoanalysis.* Chicago: University of Chicago Press, 1989.

Isbister, J. N. *Freud, An Introduction to His Life and Work.* Cambridge, England: Polity Press; Oxford, England; New York: Blackwell, 1985.

Jacoby, Russell. *Social Amnesia: A Critique of Conformist Psychology.* With a new introduction. New Brunswick, N.J.: Transaction, 1996 [1975].

Jasnow, Alexander. *Freud and Cézanne: Psychotherapy as Modern Art.* Norwood, N.J.: Ablex, 1993.

Jones, Ernest. *The Life and Work of Sigmund Freud.* Edited and abridged by Lionel Trilling and Steven Marcus. Introduction by Lionel Trilling. Garden City, N.Y.: Doubleday, 1963 [condensed from the 3-volume 1953 edition].

Julien, Philippe. *Jacques Lacan's Return to Freud: The Real, the Symbolic, and the Imaginary.* Translated by Devra Beck Simiu. New York: New York University Press, 1994.

Jung, Carl Gustav. *The Essential Jung.* Selected and introduced by Anthony Storr. Princeton: Princeton University Press, 1983.

Karier, Clarence J. *Scientists of the Mind: Intellectual Founders of Modern Psychology.* Urbana: University of Illinois Press, 1986.

Kirschner, Suzanne R. *The Religious and Romantic Origins of Psychoanalysis: Individuation and Integration in Post-Freudian Theory.* Cambridge, England; New York: Cambridge University Press, 1996.

Kurzweil, Edith. *Freudians and Feminists.* Boulder, Colo.: Westview Press, 1995.

Lieberman, E. James. *Acts of the Will: The Life and Work of Otto Rank.* With a new preface. Amherst: University of Massachusetts Press, 1993.

Lunbeck, Elizabeth. *The Psychiatric Persuasion: Knowledge, Gender, and Power in Modern America.* Princeton: Princeton University Press, 1994.

Macey, David. *Lacan in Contexts.* London, New York: Verso, 1988.

Maidenbaum, Aryeh, and Stephen A. Martin, eds. *Lingering Shadows: Jungians, Freudians, and Anti-Semitism.* Boston, Mass.: Shambhala, 1991.

Malcolm, Janet. *Psychoanalysis, the Impossible Profession.* New York: Vintage Books, 1982 [1981].

Marcus, Steven. *Freud and the Culture of Psychoanalysis: Studies in the Transition from Victorian Humanism to Modernity.* Boston: Allen & Unwin, 1984.

Marini, Marcelle. *Jacques Lacan: The French Context.* Translated by Anne Tomiche. New Brunswick, N.J.: Rutgers University Press, 1992.

McGrath, William J. *Freud's Discovery of Psychoanalysis: The Politics of Hysteria.* Ithaca, N.Y.: Cornell University Press, 1986.

Mitchell, Stephen A., and Margaret J. Black. *Freud and Beyond: A History of Modern Psychoanalytic Thought.* New York: Basic Books, 1995.

Ragland-Sullivan, Ellie. *Jacques Lacan and the Philosophy of Psychoanalysis.* Urbana: University of Illinois Press, 1986.

Rank, Otto. *A Psychology of Difference: The American Lectures.* Selected, edited, and introduced by Robert Kramer. With a foreword by Rollo May. Princeton: Princeton University Press, 1996.

Richards, Barry. *Disciplines of Delight: The Psychoanalysis of Popular Culture.* London: Free Association Books, 1994.

Ricoeur, Paul. *Freud and Philosophy: An Essay on Interpretation.* Translated by Denis Savage. New Haven, Conn.: Yale University Press, 1970.

Rieff, Philip. *The Triumph of the Therapeutic: Uses of Faith after Freud.* With a new preface. Chicago: University of Chicago Press, 1987.

Roazen, Paul. *Helene Deutsch: A Psychoanalyst's Life.* With a new introduction. New Brunswick, N.J.: Transaction Books, 1992.

———. *Freud and His Followers.* New York: New York University Press, 1984 [1974].

Rose, Jacqueline. *Why War—Psychoanalysis, Politics, and the Return to Melanie Klein.* Oxford, England; Cambridge, Mass.: Blackwell, 1993.

Rosenzweig, Saul. *The Historic Expedition to America (1909): Freud, Jung, and Hall the King-Maker, with G. Stanley Hall as Host and William James as Guest.* 2d rev. ed. St. Louis: Rana House, 1994.

Royle, Nicholas. *After Derrida.* Manchester, England: Manchester University Press; New York: St. Martin's Press, 1995.

Rudnytsky, Peter L. *The Psychoanalytic Vocation: Rank, Winnicott, and the Legacy of Freud.* New Haven, Conn.: Yale University Press, 1991.

Rustin, Michael. *The Good Society and the Inner World: Psychoanalysis, Politics, and Culture.* London; New York: Verso, 1991.

Samuels, Andrew. *Jung and the Post-Jungians.* London, Boston: Routledge & Kegan Paul, 1985.

Samuels, Robert. *Between Philosophy and Psychoanalysis: Lacan's Reconstruction of Freud.* New York: Routledge, 1993.

Sarup, Madan. *Jacques Lacan.* Toronto; Buffalo, N.Y.: University of Toronto Press, 1992.

Sayers, Janet. *Mothers of Psychoanalysis: Helene Deutsch, Karen Horney, Anna Freud, Melanie Klein.* New York: Norton, 1991.

Schur, Max. *Freud: Living and Dying.* London: Hogarth Press and the Institute of Psycho-Analysis; New York: International Universities Press, 1972.

Segal, Julia. *Melanie Klein.* London; Newbury Park, Calif.: Sage, 1992.

Shamdasani, Sonu, and Michael Munchow, eds. *Speculations after Freud: Psychoanalysis, Philosophy, and Culture.* London; New York: Routledge, 1994.

Sharaf, Myron R. *Fury on Earth: A Biography of Wilhelm Reich.* New York: St. Martin's Press/Marek, 1983.

Slipp, Samuel. *The Freudian Mystique: Freud, Women, and Feminism.* New York: New York University Press, 1993.

Smith, Joseph H. and William Kerrigan, eds. *Taking Chances: Derrida, Psychoanalysis, and Literature.* Baltimore: Johns Hopkins University Press, 1984.

Steele, Robert S. *Freud and Jung, Conflicts of Interpretation.* London, Boston: Routledge & Kegan Paul, 1982.

Stein, Murray, ed. *Jungian Analysis.* 2d ed. Chicago: Open Court, 1995.

Stevens, Anthony. *Jung.* Oxford, England; New York: Oxford University Press, 1994.

Sulloway, Frank J. *Freud, Biologist of the Mind: Beyond the Psychoanalytic Legend.* New York: Basic Books, 1979.

Taylor, Benjamin. *Into the Open: Reflections on Genius and Modernity.* New York: New York University Press, 1995.

Turkle, Sherry. *Psychoanalytic Politics: Jacques Lacan and Freud's French Revolution.* London: Free Association Books; New York: Guilford Press, 1992.

Weatherill, Rob. *Cultural Collapse.* London: Free Association Books, 1994.

Weber, Samuel. *The Legend of Freud.* Minneapolis: University of Minnesota Press, 1982.

Weininger, Otto, with a foreword by James S. Grotstein. *Melanie Klein: From Theory to Reality.* London: Karnac, 1992.

Wilson, Stephen Robert. *The Cradle of Violence: Essays on Psychiatry, Psychoanalysis, and Literature.* London; Bristol, Pa.: J. Kingsley, 1995.

Zizek, Slavoj. *Looking Awry: An Introduction to Jacques Lacan through Popular Culture.* Cambridge, Mass.: MIT Press, 1991.

Marxism and the Left

Abrahams, Edward. *The Lyrical Left: Randolph Bourne, Alfred Stieglitz, and the Origins of Cultural Radicalism in America.* Charlottesville: University Press of Virginia, 1986.

Adamson, Walter L. *Marx and the Disillusionment of Marxism.* Berkeley: University of California Press, 1985.

Alway, Joan. *Critical Theory and Political Possibilities: Conceptions of Emancipatory Politics in the Works of Horkheimer, Adorno, Marcuse, and Habermas.* Westport, Conn.: Greenwood Press, 1995.

Bailey, Leon. *Critical Theory and the Sociology of Knowledge: A Comparative Study in the Theory of Ideology.* New York: P. Lang, 1994.

Bauer, Peter Tamas. *Equality, the Third World, and Economic Delusion.* Cambridge, Mass.: Harvard University Press, 1981.

Beaud, Michel. *Socialism in the Crucible of History.* Translated and introduced by Thomas Dickman. Atlantic Highlands, N.J.: Humanities Press, 1993.

Benhabib, Seyla, Wolfgang Bonss, and John McCole, eds. *On Max Horkheimer: New Perspectives.* Cambridge, Mass.: MIT Press, 1993.

Benjamin, Andrew, ed. *The Problems of Modernity: Adorno and Benjamin.* London; New York: Routledge, 1989.

Benstock, Shari. *Women of the Left Bank: Paris, 1900–1940.* Austin: University of Texas Press, 1986.

Berlin, Isaiah. *Karl Marx: His Life and Environment,* 4th ed. New York: Oxford University Press, 1996 [1st ed., 1939].

Bernard-Donals, Michael F. *Mikhail Bakhtin: Between Phenomenology and Marxism.* Cambridge, England; New York: Cambridge University Press, 1994.

Bernstein, J. M. *Recovering Ethical Life: Jürgen Habermas and the Future of Critical Theory.* London, New York: Routledge, 1995.

Birnbaum, Norman. *Searching for the Light: Essays on Thought and Culture.* New York: Oxford University Press, 1993.

Black, Allida M. *Casting her Own Shadow: Eleanor Roosevelt and the Shaping of Postwar Liberalism.* New York: Columbia University Press, 1996.

Blamires, Harry. *A History of Literary Criticism.* Basingstoke, England: Macmillan Education, 1991.

Bloom, Alexander. *Prodigal Sons: The New York Intellectuals and their World.* New York: Oxford University Press, 1986.

Bloom, Alexander, ed. *"Takin' It to the Streets": A Sixties Reader.* New York: Oxford University Press, 1995.

Bolz, Norbert and Willem van Reijen. *Walter Benjamin.* Atlantic Highlands, N.J.: Humanities Press, 1995.

Bronner, Stephen Eric. *Of Critical Theory and its Theorists.* Oxford, England; Cambridge, Mass.: Blackwell, 1994.

———. *Moments of Decision: Political History and the Crises of Radicalism.* New York: Routledge, 1992.

———. *Socialism Unbound.* New York: Routledge, 1990.

Buck-Morss, Susan. *The Origin of Negative Dialectics: Theodor W. Adorno, Walter Benjamin, and the Frankfurt Institute.* Hassocks, England: Harvester Press; New York: Free Press, 1977.

Burger, Peter. *Theory of the Avant-Garde.* Translated by Michael Shaw. Foreword by Jochen Schulte-Sasse. Minneapolis: University of Minnesota Press, 1984.

Calhoun, Craig J. *Critical Social Theory: Culture, History, and the Challenge of Difference.* Oxford, England; Cambridge, Mass.: Blackwell, 1995.

Callinicos, Alex. *Marxism and Philosophy.* Oxford, England: Clarendon Press; New York: Oxford University Press, 1983.

Castellucci, John. *The Big Dance: The Untold Story of Kathy Boudin and the Terrorist Family that Committed the Brink's Robbery Murders.* New York: Dodd, Mead, 1986.

Castronovo, David. *Edmund Wilson.* New York: F. Ungar, 1984.

Clark, Henry Balsley. *Serenity, Courage, and Wisdom: The Enduring Legacy of Reinhold Niebuhr.* Cleveland, Ohio: Pilgrim Press, 1994.

Clark, Katerina, and Michael Holquist. *Mikhail Bakhtin.* Cambridge, Mass.: Belknap Press of Harvard University Press, 1984.

Clecak, Peter. *Radical Paradoxes; Dilemmas of the American Left: 1945–1970.* New York: Harper & Row, 1973.

Colombo, Joseph A. *An Essay on Theology and History: Studies in Pannenberg, Metz, and the Frankfurt School.* Atlanta, Ga.: Scholars Press, 1990.

Colton, Joel G., with a new introduction and supplementary bibliography. *Leon Blum: Humanist in Politics.* Durham, N.C.: Duke University Press, 1987 [1966].

Conquest, Robert. *The Great Terror: A Reassessment.* London: Hutchinson; New York: Oxford University Press, 1990.

Crick, Bernard. *George Orwell, A Life.* Rev. ed. London: Secker & Warburg, 1981.

Dallmayr, Fred Reinhard. *Between Freiburg and Frankfurt: Toward a Critical Ontology.* Amherst: University of Massachusetts Press, 1991.

Davis, Robert Con, and Ronald Schleifer. *Contemporary Literary Criticism: Literary and Cultural Studies,* 3d ed. New York: Longman, 1994 [1st ed., 1986].

Davison, Peter Hobley. *George Orwell: A Literary Life.* Basingstoke, England: Macmillan, 1995.

Dietrich, Julia. *The Old Left in History and Literature.* London: Prentice Hall International; New York: Twayne, 1996.

Dubiel, Helmut. *Theory and Politics: Studies in the Development of Critical Theory.* Translated by Benjamin Gregg, with an introduction by Martin Jay. Cambridge, Mass.: MIT Press, 1985.

Dunayevskaya, Raya. *Rosa Luxemburg, Women's Liberation, and Marx's Philosophy of Revolution,* 2d ed. With a foreword by Adrienne Rich. Urbana: University of Illinois Press, 1991 [1st ed., 1982].

Dussel, Enrique D. *The Underside of Modernity: Apel, Ricoeur, Rorty, Taylor, and the Philosophy of Liberation.* Translated and edited by Eduardo Mendieta. Atlantic Highlands, N.J.: Humanities Press, 1996.

Elster, Jon. *Making Sense of Marx.* Paris: Editions de la Maison des Sciences de l'Homme; Cambridge, England; New York: Cambridge University Press, 1985.

Erickson, John. *The Road to Berlin.* London: Weidenfeld & Nicolson, 1983.

Ford, R. A. D. *A Moscow Literary Memoir: Among the Great Artists of Russia from 1946 to 1980.* Edited by Carole Jerome. Toronto; Buffalo, N.Y.: University of Toronto Press, 1995.

Fox, Richard Wightman. *Reinhold Niebuhr: A Biography.* New York: Pantheon Books, 1985.

Friedman, George. *The Political Philosophy of the Frankfurt School.* Ithaca, N.Y.: Cornell University Press, 1981.

Gluck, Mary. *Georg Lukacs and His Generation, 1900–1918.* Cambridge, Mass.: Harvard University Press, 1985.

Gorman, Paul R. *Left Intellectuals and Popular Culture in Twentieth-Century America.* Chapel Hill: University of North Carolina Press, 1996.

Gottlieb, Roger S. *Marxism, 1844–1990: Origins, Betrayal, Rebirth.* New York: Routledge, 1992.

Gottlieb, Roger S., ed. *An Anthology of Western Marxism: From Lukacs and Gramsci to Socialist-Feminism.* New York: Oxford University Press, 1989.

Heilbut, Anthony. *Exiled in Paradise: German Refugee Artists and Intellectuals in America, from the 1930s to the Present.* New York: Viking, 1983.

Held, David. *Introduction to Critical Theory: Horkheimer to Habermas.* Berkeley: University of California Press, 1980.

Hohendahl, Peter Uwe. *Prismatic Thought: Theodor W. Adorno.* Lincoln: University of Nebraska Press, 1995.

———. *The Institution of Criticism.* Ithaca, N.Y.: Cornell University Press, 1982.

Hook, Sidney. *From Hegel to Marx: Studies in the Intellectual Development of Karl Marx,* Columbia University Press Morningside ed. New York: Columbia University Press, 1994.

Hudelson, Richard. *Marxism and Philosophy in the Twentieth Century: A Defense of Vulgar Marxism.* New York: Praeger, 1990.

Hughes, Henry Stuart, with a new introduction. *Between Committment and Disillusion: The Obstructed Path and the Sea Change, 1930–1965,* 2 vols. Middletown, Conn.: Wesleyan University Press, 1987.

Jacoby, Russell. *Dialectic of Defeat: Contours of Western Marxism.* Cambridge, England; New York: Cambridge University Press, 1981.

Jay, Martin. *The Dialectical Imagination: A History of the Frankfurt School and the Institute of Social Research, 1923-1950.* Berkeley: University of California Press, 1996 [1973].

———. *Marxism and Totality: The Adventures of a Concept from Lukacs to Habermas.* Berkeley: University of California Press, 1984.

Jordan, Nicole. *The Popular Front and Central Europe: The Dilemmas of French Impotence, 1918–1940.* Cambridge, England; New York: Cambridge University Press, 1992.

Kardakay, Arpad. *Georg Lukacs: Life, Thought, and Politics.* Cambridge, Mass.: Blackwell, 1991.

Kellner, Douglas. *Herbert Marcuse and the Crisis of Marxism.* London: Macmillan; Berkeley: University of California Press, 1984.

Kolakowski, Leszek. *Main Currents of Marxism: Its Origins, Growth, and Dissolution.* 3 vols. Translated by P. S. Falla. Oxford, England; New York: Oxford University Press, 1981 [1978].

Krupnick, Mark. *Lionel Trilling and the Fate of Cultural Criticism.* Evanston, Ill.: Northwestern University Press, 1986.

Laing, Dave. *The Marxist Theory of Art.* Hassocks, England: Harvester Press; Atlantic Highlands, N.J.: Humanities Press, 1978.

Langer, Elinor. *Josephine Herbst.* Boston: Little, Brown, 1984.

Lapping, Brian. *End of Empire.* London: Granada in association with Channel Four Television Company and Granada Television, 1985.

Le Tissier, Tony. *Zhukov at the Oder: The Decisive Battle for Berlin.* Westport, Conn.: Praeger, 1996.

Lottman, Herbert R. *The Left Bank: Writers, Artists, and Politics from the Popular Front to the Cold War.* Boston: Houghton Mifflin, 1982.

Lunn, Eugene. *Marxism and Modernism: An Historical Study of Lukacs, Brecht, Benjamin, and Adorno.* Berkeley: University of California Press, 1982.

Marwick, Arthur. *British Society since 1945,* 2d rev. ed. Harmondsworth, England; New York: Penguin, 1995 [1st ed., 1982].

Matusow, Allen J. *The Unraveling of America: A History of Liberalism in the 1960s.* New York: Harper & Row, 1984.

McCarthy, Thomas A. *The Critical Theory of Jürgen Habermas.* Cambridge, Mass.: MIT Press, 1978.

McLellan, David. *The Thought of Karl Marx: An Introduction,* 3d ed. London: Papermac, 1995.

Medvedev, Roy Aleksandrovich. *Let History Judge: The Origins and Consequences of Stalinism.* Rev. and expanded ed. Edited and translated by George Shriver. Oxford, England: Oxford University Press; New York: Columbia University Press, 1989.

Meyers, Jeffrey. *Edmund Wilson: A Biography.* Boston: Houghton Mifflin, 1995.

Miller, Jim. *Democracy in the Streets: From Port Huron to the Siege of Chicago.* With a new preface. Cambridge, Mass.: Harvard University Press, 1994.

Morgan, Ted. *FDR: A Biography.* New York: Simon & Schuster, 1985.

Nelson, Cary, and Lawrence Grossberg, eds. *Marxism and the Interpretation of Culture.* Basingstoke, England: Macmillan Education; Urbana: University of Illinois Press, 1988.

Nettl, J. P., with an inroduction by Hannah Arendt. *Rosa Luxemburg.* Abridged ed. . New York: Schocken Books, 1989.

O'Hara, Daniel T. *Lionel Trilling: The Work of Liberation.* Madison: University of Wisconsin Press, 1988.

O'Neill, William L., with a new introduction by the author. *A Better World: Stalinism and the American Intellectuals.* New Brunswick, N.J.: Transaction Books, 1990.

Patsouras, Louis, ed. *Debating Marx.* Lewiston, N.Y.: EmText, 1994.

Peck, Abraham J., ed. *The German-Jewish Legacy in America, 1938-1988: From Bildung to the Bill of Rights.* Detroit: Wayne State University Press, 1989.

Post, Ken. *Regaining Marxism.* Basingstoke, England: Macmillan Press; New York: St. Martin's Press, 1996.

Poster, Mark. *Existential Marxism in Postwar France: From Sartre to Althusser.* Princeton: Princeton University Press, 1975.

Pugh, Martin. *The Making of Modern British Politics, 1867–1939,* 2d ed. Oxford, England; Cambridge, Mass.: Blackwell, 1993.

Resch, Robert Paul. *Althusser and the Renewal of Marxist Social Theory.* Berkeley: University of California Press, 1992.

Roberts, Nora Ruth. *Three Radical Women Writers: Class and Gender in Meridel Le Sueur, Tillie Olsen, and Josephine Herbst.* New York: Garland, 1996.

Rose, Gillian. *The Melancholy Science: An Introduction to the Thought of Theodor W. Adorno.* London: Macmillan; New York: Columbia University Press, 1978.

Ross, Andrew. *No Respect: Intellectuals and Popular Culture.* New York: Routledge, 1989.

Sale, Kirkpatrick. *SDS.* New York: Vintage, 1974.

Sayres, Sohnya, et al., eds. *The 60s without Apology.* Minneapolis: University of Minnesota Press in cooperation with Social Text, 1984.

Schlesinger, Arthur Meier. *The Age of Roosevelt.* 3 vols. 1957–60. Reprint, Boston: Houghton Mifflin, 1988.

Sheehan, Helena. *Marxism and the Philosophy of Science: A Critical History: The First Hundred Years.* Atlantic Highlands, N.J.: Humanities Press, 1993.

Shelton, Robert. *No Direction Home: The Life and Music of Bob Dylan.* New York: Morrow, 1986.

Sim, Stuart. *Georg Lukacs.* New York: Harvester Wheatsheaf, 1994.

Smith, Steven. *Reading Althusser: An Essay on Structural Marxism.* Ithaca, N.Y.: Cornell University Press, 1984.

Stam, Robert. *Subversive Pleasures: Bakhtin, Cultural Criticism, and Film.* Baltimore: Johns Hopkins University Press, 1992.

Teres, Harvey M. *Renewing the Left: Politics, Imagination, and the New York Intellectuals.* New York: Oxford University Press, 1996.

Terrill, Ross. *R. H. Tawney and His Times; Socialism as Fellowship*. Cambridge, Mass.: Harvard University Press, 1973.

Thurston, Robert W. *Life and Terror in Stalin's Russia, 1934–1941*. New Haven, Conn.: Yale University Press, 1996.

Ulam, Adam Bruno. *Ideologies and Illusions: Revolutionary Thought from Herzen to Solzhenitsyn*. Cambridge, Mass.: Harvard University Press, 1976.

Wald, Alan M. *Writing from the Left: New Essays on Radical Culture and Politics*. London; New York: Verso, 1994.

Wiggershaus, Rolf. *The Frankfurt School: Its History, Theories, and Political Significance*. Translated by Michael Robertson. Cambridge, Mass.: MIT Press, 1994.

Williams, Raymond. *Marxism and Literature*. Oxford, England: Oxford University Press, 1996.

Wolin, Richard, with a new introduction by the author. *Walter Benjamin, An Aesthetic of Redemption*. Berkeley: University of California Press, 1994 [1982].

Wright, Anthony. *R. H. Tawney*. Manchester, England: Manchester University Press, 1987.

Young-Bruehl, Elisabeth. *Hannah Arendt, For Love of the World*. New Haven, Conn.: Yale University Press, 1982.

Traditions on the Right

Adam, Peter. *Art of the Third Reich*. New York: H. N. Abrams, 1992.

Ambrose, Stephen E. *Eisenhower: Soldier and President*. New York: Simon & Schuster, 1990 [condensed version of a two-volume work originally published as *Eisenhower* (1983–84)].

Arendt, Hannah. *Eichmann in Jerusalem: A Report on the Banality of Evil*. Rev. and enlarged ed. New York: Penguin Books, 1994.

Arnal, Oscar L. *Ambivalent Alliance: The Catholic Church and the Action Française, 1899–1939*. Pittsburgh: University of Pittsburgh Press, 1985.

Aycoberry, Pierre. *The Nazi Question: An Essay on the Interpretations of National Socialism (1922–1975)*. Translated by Robert Hurley. London: Routledge & Kegan Paul; New York: Pantheon Books, 1981.

Barnouw, Dagmar. *Weimar Intellectuals and the Threat of Modernity*. Bloomington: Indiana University Press, 1988.

Berghahn, Volker Rolf. *Modern Germany: Society, Economy, and Politics in the Twentieth Century*. 2d ed. Cambridge, England; New York: Cambridge University Press, 1987.

Betts, Raymond F. *Uncertain Dimensions: Western Overseas Empires in the Twentieth Century*. Minneapolis: University of Minnesota Press, 1985.

Beyerchen, Alan D. *Scientists under Hitler: Politics and the Physics Community in the Third Reich*. New Haven: Yale University Press, 1977.

Binion, Rudolph. *Hitler Among the Germans*. DeKalb, Ill.: Northern Illinois University Press, 1984 [1976].

Bracher, Karl Dietrich, with a foreword by Abbott Gleason. *Turning Points in Modern Times: Essays on German and European History.* Translated by Thomas Dunlap. Cambridge, Mass.: Harvard University Press, 1995.

―――. *The German Dictatorship; The Origins, Structure, and Effects of National Socialism.* Translated by Jean Steinberg, with an introduction by Peter Gay. New York: Praeger, 1970.

Breitman, Richard. *The Architect of Genocide: Himmler and the Final Solution.* Hanover, N.H.: University Press of New England, 1992.

Brinkley, Alan. *Voices of Protest: Huey Long, Father Coughlin, and the Great Depression.* New York: Vintage Books, 1983.

Bullock, Alan. *Hitler: A Study in Tyranny.* Abridged ed. New York: HarperPerennial, 1991.

Burns, Rob, ed. *German Cultural Studies: An Introduction.* Oxford, England: Clarendon Press, 1995.

Burrin, Philippe. *Hitler and the Jews: The Genesis of the Holocaust.* Translated by Patsy Southgate, with an introduction by Saul Friedländer. London; New York: Arnold, 1994.

Cain, P. J. *British Imperialism: Crisis and Deconstruction, 1914-1990.* London, New York: Longman, 1993.

Calleo, David P. *The German Problem Reconsidered: Germany and the World Order, 1870 to the Present.* Cambridge, England; New York: Cambridge University Press, 1978.

Chafets, Ze'ev. *Heroes and Hustlers, Hard Hats and Holy Men: Inside the New Israel.* New York: Morrow, 1986.

Clark, Alan. *Barbarossa; The Russian-German Conflict, 1941–45.* New York: Morrow, 1965.

Clark, Ronald William. *The Greatest Power on Earth: The International Race for Nuclear Supremacy.* New York: Harper & Row, 1981.

Coser, Lewis A. *Refugee Scholars in America: Their Impact and their Experiences.* New Haven, Conn.: Yale University Press, 1984.

Costello, John. *The Pacific War.* London: Collins; New York: Rawson, Wade, 1981.

Covell, Charles. *The Redefinition of Conservatism: Politics and Doctrine.* Houndmills, England: Macmillan, 1986.

Cowling, Maurice. *Religion and Public Doctrine in Modern England.* Cambridge, England; New York: Cambridge University Press, 1980.

Craig, Cairns. *Yeats, Eliot, Pound, and the Politics of Poetry: Richest to the Richest.* London: Croom Helm, 1982.

Craig, Gordon Alexander. *The Germans.* New York: Meridian, 1991.

Dawidowicz, Lucy S. *The War Against the Jews, 1933–1945.* 10th anniversary ed. Toronto, New York: Bantam Books, 1986.

De Grand, Alexander J. *Fascist Italy and Nazi Germany: The 'Fascist' Style of Rule.* London; New York: Routledge, 1995.

Doering, Bernard E. *Jacques Maritain and the French Catholic Intellectuals.* Notre Dame, Ind.: University of Notre Dame Press, 1983.

Dower, John W. *War without Mercy: Race and Power in the Pacific War.* New York: Pantheon Books, 1986.

Dulffer, Jost. *Nazi Germany 1933–1945: Faith and Annihilation.* Translated by Dean S. McMurry. London; New York: Arnold, 1996.

Esenwein, George Richard, and Adrian Schubert. *Spain at War: The Spanish Civil War in Context, 1931–1939.* London, New York: Longman, 1995.

Fekete, John. *The Critical Twilight: Explorations in the Ideology of Anglo-American Literary Theory from Eliot to McLuhan.* London, Boston: Routledge & Kegan Paul, 1977.

Ferry, Luc, and Alain Renaut. *Heidegger and Modernity.* Translated by Franklin Philip. Chicago: University of Chicago Press, 1990.

Fest, Joachim C. *The Face of the Third Reich.* Translated by Michael Bullock. London: Weidenfeld & Nicolson, 1970.

Fischer, Klaus P. *Nazi Germany: A New History.* New York: Continuum, 1995.

Friedlander, Henry. *The Origins of Nazi Genocide: From Euthanasia to the Final Solution.* Chapel Hill: University of North Carolina Press, 1995.

Friedlander, Saul. *Pius XII and the Third Reich: A Documentation.* Translated by Charles Fullman. New York: Knopf, 1966.

Furedi, Frank. *Colonial Wars and the Politics of Third World Nationalism.* London: I. B. Tauris; New York: St. Martin's Press, 1994.

Gadamer, Hans Georg. *Philosophical Apprenticeships.* Translated by Robert R. Sullivan. Cambridge, Mass.: MIT Press, 1985.

Gilbert, Martin. *Auschwitz and the Allies.* New York: Holt, Rinehart & Winston, 1981.

Glantz, David M., and Jonathan M. House, eds. *When Titans Clashed: How the Red Army Stopped Hitler.* Lawrence: University Press of Kansas, 1995.

Goldschmidt, Bertrand. *Atomic Rivals.* Translated by Georges M. Temmer. New Brunswick, N.J.: Rutgers University Press, 1990.

Gould, Stephen Jay. *The Mismeasure of Man.* New York: Norton, 1981.

Graml, Hermann. *Antisemitism in the Third Reich.* Translated by Tim Kirk. Oxford, England; Cambridge, Mass.: Blackwell, 1992.

Guinness, Jonathan. *The House of Mitford.* New York: Viking, 1985.

Halls, W. D. *Politics, Society and Christianity in Vichy France.* Oxford, England; Providence: Berg, 1995.

Hamilton, Neil W. *Zealotry and Academic Freedom: A Legal and Historical Perspective.* New Brunswick, N.J.: Transaction, 1995.

Harrison, John Raymond, with a preface by William Empson. *The Reactionaries.* London: Gollancz, 1966.

Hastings, Selina. *Evelyn Waugh: A Biography.* 2d rev. ed. London: Minerva, 1995.

Helmreich, Ernst Christian. *The German Churches under Hitler: Background, Struggle, and Epilogue.* Detroit, Mich.: Wayne State University Press, 1979.

Herf, Jeffrey. *Reactionary Modernism: Technology, Culture, and Politics in Weimar and the Third Reich.* Cambridge, England; New York: Cambridge University Press, 1984.

Hilberg, Raul. *The Destruction of the European Jews.* Rev. and definitive ed. 3 vols. New York: Holmes & Meier, 1985.

Hildebrand, Klaus. *The Third Reich.* Translated by P. S. Falla. London; Boston: Allen & Unwin, 1984.

Holmes, Colin. *Anti-Semitism in British Society, 1876–1939.* London: E. Arnold; New York: Holmes & Meier, 1979.

Holmes, J. Derek, with a foreword by John Tracy Ellis. *The Papacy in the Modern World, 1914–1978.* New York: Crossroad, 1981.

Horsley, Lee. *Fictions of Power in English Literature, 1900–1950.* London; New York: Longman, 1995.

James, Lawrence. *The Rise and Fall of the British Empire.* New York: St. Martin's Press, 1996.

Jay, Martin. *Permanent Exiles: Essays on the Intellectual Migration from Germany to America.* New York: Columbia University Press, 1986.

Jedin, Hubert. *The Church in the Modern World.* Abridged ed. English translation edited by John Dolan. Abridged by D. Larrimore Holland. New York: Crossroad, 1993.

Kedward, Roderick, and Roger Austin, eds. *Vichy France and the Resistance: Culture & Ideology.* London: Croom Helm; Totowa, N.J.: Barnes & Noble, 1985.

Kevles, Daniel J. *In the Name of Eugenics: Genetics and the Uses of Human Heredity.* Berkeley: University of California Press, 1986.

Kline, Benjamin, and Stephen Payne, eds. *Imperialism and its Legacy: Issues and Perspectives.* Lanham, Md.: University Press of America, 1990.

Kritzman, Lawrence D., ed. *Auschwitz and After: Race, Culture, and "The Jewish Question" in France.* New York: Routledge, 1995.

Kushner, Tony Antony Robin Jeremy. *The Holocaust and the Liberal Imagination: A Social and Cultural History.* Cambridge, Mass.: Blackwell, 1994.

_____. *The Persistence of Prejudice: Antisemitism in British Society during the Second World War.* Manchester, England; New York: Manchester University Press; New York: Distributed in the USA and Canada by St. Martin's Press, 1989.

Lewis, David Stephen. *Illusions of Grandeur: Mosley, Fascism, and British Society, 1931–1981.* Manchester, England; Wolfeboro, N.H.: Manchester University Press, 1987.

Lewy, Guenter. *The Catholic Church and Nazi Germany.* New York: McGraw-Hill, 1964.

Lottman, Herbert R. *The Purge.* New York: Morrow, 1986.

Macann, Christopher, ed. *Martin Heidegger: Critical Assessments.* 4 vols. New York: Routledge, 1992.

Mack Smith, Denis. *Mussolini.* New York: Alfred A. Knopf, 1982.

Malino, Frances, and Bernard Wasserstein, eds. *The Jews in Modern France.* Hanover, N.H.: Published for Brandeis University Press by University Press of New England, 1985.

Marrus, Michael Robert, and Robert O. Paxton, eds., with a new foreword by Stanley Hoffman. *Vichy France and the Jews.* New ed. Stanford, Calif.: Stanford University Press; New York: Basic Books, 1995.

Meyers, Jeffrey. *The Enemy: A Biography of Wyndham Lewis.* London: Routledge & Kegan Paul, 1980.

Morris, James. *Farewell the Trumpets: An Imperial Retreat.* London; Boston: Faber & Faber; New York: Harcourt Brace Jovanovich, 1978.

Morrison, Paul A. *The Poetics of Fascism: Ezra Pound, T.S. Eliot, Paul de Man.* New York: Oxford University Press, 1996.

Mosse, George Lachmann. *The Crisis of German Ideology: Intellectual Origins of the Third Reich.* New York: Schocken Books, 1981.

Mosse, George Lachmann, ed. *Nazi Culture: Intellectual, Cultural, and Social Life in the Third Reich.* Translated by Salvator Attanasio et al. New York: Grosset & Dunlap, 1966.

Müller, Klaus-Jürgen. *The Army, Politics, and Society in Germany, 1933–1945: Studies in the Army's Relation to Nazism.* Manchester, England: Manchester University Press, 1987.

Nicholas, Lynn H. *The Rape of Europa: The Fate of Europe's Treasures in the Third Reich.* New York: Alfred A. Knopf, 1994.

Nolte, Ernst. *Three Faces of Fascism; Action Française, Italian Fascism, National Socialism.* Translated by Leila Vennewitz. New York: Holt, Rinehart & Winston, 1966.

Normand, Tom. *Wyndham Lewis the Artist: Holding the Mirror up to Politics.* Cambridge, England; New York: Cambridge University Press, 1992.

Pakenham, Valerie. *Out in the Noonday Sun: Edwardians in the Tropics.* New York: Random House, 1985.

Paul, Diane B. *Controlling Human Heredity, 1865 to the Present.* Atlantic Highlands, N.J.: Humanities Press, 1995.

Paxton, Robert O. *Vichy France: Old Guard and New Order, 1940–1944.* New York: Columbia University Press, 1982.

Payne, Stanley G. *A History of Fascism, 1914–1945.* Madison: University of Wisconsin Press, 1995.

Pells, Richard H. *The Liberal Mind in a Conservative Age: American Intellectuals in the 1940s and 1950s,* 2d ed. With a new introduction. Middletown, Conn.: Wesleyan University Press, 1989 [1st ed., 1985].

Petropoulos, Jonathan. *Art as Politics in the Third Reich.* Chapel Hill, N.C.: University of North Carolina Press, 1996.

Phelan, Anthony, ed. *The Weimar Dilemma: Intellectuals in the Weimar Republic.* Manchester, England; Dover, N.H.: Manchester University Press, 1985.

Power, M. Susan. *Jacques Maritain (1882–1973), Christian Democrat, and the Quest for a New Commonwealth.* Lewiston, N.Y.: E. Mellen Press, 1992.

Pulzer, Peter G. J. *The Rise of Political Anti-Semitism in Germany and Austria.* Rev. ed. London: P. Halban; Cambridge, Mass.: Harvard University Press, 1988.

Reich, Simon. *The Fruits of Fascism: Postwar Prosperity in Historical Perspective.* Ithaca, N.Y.: Cornell University Press, 1990.

Rhodes, Anthony Richard Ewart. *The Vatican in the Age of Dictators: 1922–1945.* London: Hodder & Stoughton, 1973.

Rousso, Henry. *The Vichy Syndrome: History and Memory in France since 1944.* Translated by Arthur Goldhammer. Cambridge, Mass.: Harvard University Press, 1991.

Sanders, David. *Losing an Empire, Finding a Role: An Introduction to British Foreign Policy since 1945.* Basingstoke, England: Macmillan, 1990.

Schiff, Ze'ev, and Ehud Ya'ari. *Israel's Lebanon War.* Edited and translated by Ina Friedman. New York: Simon & Schuster, 1984.

Schrecker, Ellen. *No Ivory Tower: McCarthyism and the Universities.* New York: Oxford University Press, 1986.

Scott, Christina, with a postscript by Christopher Dawson and a new introduction by Russell Kirk. *A Historian and His World: A Life of Christopher Dawson.* New Brunswick, N.J.: Transaction Books, 1992.

Seaton, Albert. *The German Army, 1933–45.* New York: St. Martin's Press, 1982.

Shook, Laurence K. *Etienne Gilson.* Toronto: Pontifical Institute of Mediaeval Studies, 1984.

Singer, Barnett. *Modern France: Mind, Politics, Society.* Montreal: Harvest House; Seattle: University of Washington Press, 1980.

Skidelsky, Robert Jacob Alexander. *Oswald Mosley.* 3d ed. London: Papermac, 1990.

Smith, Woodruff D. *The Ideological Origins of Nazi Imperialism.* New York: Oxford University Press, 1986.

Spielvogel, Jackson J. *Hitler and Nazi Germany: A History.* 3d ed. Englewood Cliffs, N.J.: Prentice Hall, 1996.

Stein, George H. *The Waffen SS: Hitler's Elite Guard at War, 1939-1945.* Ithaca, N.Y.: Cornell University Press, 1966.

Struve, Walter. *Elites Against Democracy: Leadership Ideals in Bourgeois Political Thought in Germany, 1890–1933.* Princeton: Princeton University Press, 1973.

Sykes, Christopher. *Evelyn Waugh: A Biography,* rev. ed. Harmondsworth, England; New York: Penguin, 1977.

Taylor, Brandon, and Wilfried van der Will, eds. *The Nazification of Art: Art, Design, Music, Architecture, and Film in the Third Reich.* Winchester, England: Winchester Press, Winchester School of Art, 1990.

Thomas, Hugh, with a new preface by the author. *The Spanish Civil War.* 3d ed. . London: Hamish Hamilton, 1986.

Toland, John. *The Rising Sun: The Decline and Fall of the Japanese Empire, 1936–1945.* New York: Bantam Books, 1971.

Turner, Henry Ashby, Jr. *German Big Business and the Rise of Hitler.* New York: Oxford University Press, 1985.

Turner, Stephen P., and Dirk Kasler, eds. *Sociology Responds to Fascism.* New York: Routledge, 1992.

Waterhouse, Roger. *A Heidegger Critique: A Critical Examination of the Existential Phenomenology of Martin Heidegger.* Brighton, England: Harvester Press; Atlantic Highlands, N.J.: Humanities Press, 1981.

Weber, Eugen. *Action Française: Royalism and Reaction in Twentieth-Century France.* Stanford, Calif.: Stanford University Press, 1962.

Weisberg, Richard H. *Vichy Law and the Holocaust in France.* New York: New York University Press, 1995.

Weisbord, Robert G., and Wallace P. Sillanpoa. *The Chief Rabbi, the Pope, and the Holocaust: An Era in Vatican-Jewish Relations.* New Brunswick, N.J.: Transaction, 1992.

Weiss, John. *Ideology of Death: Why the Holocaust Happened in Germany.* Chicago: I. R. Dee, 1996.

Whittam, John. *Fascist Italy.* Manchester, England; New York: Manchester University Press, 1995.

Williamson, D. G. *The Third Reich.* 2d ed. London; New York: Longman, 1995.

Williamson, Gordon. *The SS: Hitler's Instrument of Terror.* London: Sidgwick & Jackson, 1994.

Wilson, A. N. *Hilaire Belloc.* London: Hamish Hamilton; New York: Atheneum, 1984.

Wistrich, Robert S. *Hitler's Apocalypse: Jews and the Nazi Legacy.* London: Weidenfeld & Nicolson, 1985.

Wistrich, Robert S. and David Ohana, eds. *The Shaping of Israeli Identity: Myth, Memory, and Trauma.* London; Portland, Ore.: F. Cass, 1995.

Wyman, David S. *The Abandonment of the Jews: America and the Holocaust, 1941–1945.* New York: Pantheon Books, 1985 [1984].

Ziegler, Philip. *Mountbatten.* New York: Alfred A. Knopf, 1985.

Zuccotti, Susan. *The Holocaust, the French, and the Jews.* New York: Basic Books, 1993.

Postmodernism

Ades, Dawn, and Andrew Forge, with a note on technique by Andrew Durham. *Francis Bacon.* London: Thames & Hudson, in association with the Tate Gallery; New York: H. N. Abrams, 1985.

Agger, Ben. *Cultural Studies as Critical Theory.* London; Washington, D.C.: Falmer Press, 1992.
———. *A Critical Theory of Public Life: Knowledge, Discourse, and Politics in an Age of Decline.* London; New York: Falmer Press, 1991.

Allen, James Sloan. *The Romance of Commerce and Culture: Capitalism, Modernism, and the Chicago-Aspen Crusade for Cultural Reform.* Chicago: University of Chicago Press, 1983.

Amiran, Eyal, and John Unsworth, eds. *Essays in Postmodern Culture.* New York: Oxford University Press, 1994.

Andrew, James Dudley. *Concepts in Film Theory.* Oxford, England; New York: Oxford University Press, 1984.

Arac, Jonathan, Wlad Godzich, and Wallace Martin, eds. *The Yale Critics: Deconstruction in America.* Minneapolis: University of Minnesota Press, 1983.

Ashton, Dore. *The New York School: A Cultural Reckoning.* Harmondsworth, England; New York: Penguin, 1979 [1972].

Assiter, Alison. *Enlightened Women: Modernist Feminism in a Postmodern Age.* London, New York: Routledge, 1996.

Becker, Howard Saul. *Art Worlds.* Berkeley: University of California Press, 1982.

Behler, Ernst. *Confrontations: Derrida, Heidegger, Nietzsche.* Translated, with an afterword, by Steven Taubeneck. Stanford, Calif.: Stanford University Press, 1991.

Bloom, Allan David, with a foreword by Saul Bellow. *The Closing of the American Mind: How Higher Education Has Failed Democracy and Impoverished the Souls of Today's Students.* New York: Simon & Schuster, 1988 [1987].

Bridges, Thomas. *The Culture of Citizenship: Inventing Postmodern Civic Culture.* Albany: State University of New York Press, 1994.

Brill, Susan B. *Wittgenstein and Critical Theory: Beyond Postmodern Criticism and Toward Descriptive Investigations.* Athens, Ohio: Ohio University Press, 1995.

Brockman, John. *Einstein, Gertrude Stein, Wittgenstein & Frankenstein: Reinventing the Universe.* London: Century; New York: Viking, 1986.

Brunette, Peter, and David Wills, eds. *Deconstruction and the Visual Arts: Art, Media, Architecture.* Cambridge, England; New York: Cambridge University Press, 1994.

Buckley, William K. and James Seaton, eds. *Beyond Cheering and Bashing: New Perspectives on the Closing of the American Mind.* Bowling Green, Ohio: Bowling Green State University Popular Press, 1992.

Butler, Christopher. *Interpretation, Deconstruction, and Ideology: An Introduction to Some Current Issues in Literary Theory.* Oxford, England: Clarendon Press; New York: Oxford University Press, 1984.

Cain, William E. *The Crisis in Criticism: Theory, Literature, and Reform in English Studies.* Baltimore: Johns Hopkins University Press, 1984.

Callari, Antonio, and David Ruccio, eds. *Postmodern Materialism and the Future of Marxist Theory: Essays in the Althusserian Tradition.* Hanover, N.H.: University Press of New England, 1996.

Callinicos, Alex. *Against Postmodernism: A Marxist Critique.* New York: St. Martin's Press, 1990.

Carroll, David. *The Subject in Question: The Languages of Theory and the Strategies of Fiction.* Chicago: University of Chicago Press, 1982.

Champagne, Roland A. *Jacques Derrida.* Canada: Maxwell Macmillan; New York: Twayne Publishers, 1995.

Clarke, Simon. *The Foundations of Structuralism: A Critique of Lévi-Strauss and the Structuralist Movement.* Brighton, England: Harvester Press; Totowa, N.J.: Barnes & Noble, 1981.

Constantinidis, Stratos E. *Theatre Under Deconstruction?: A Question of Approach.* New York: Garland, 1993.

Crease, Robert P. and Charles C. Mann. *The Second Creation: Makers of the Revolution in Twentieth-Century Physics.* New Brunswick, N.J.: Rutgers University Press, 1996.

Culler, Jonathan D. *On Deconstruction: Theory and Criticism after Structuralism.* Ithaca, N.Y.: Cornell University Press, 1982.

————. *The Pursuit of Signs: Semiotics, Literature, Deconstruction.* Ithaca, N.Y.: Cornell University Press, 1981.

————. *Structuralist Poetics: Structuralism, Linguistics, and the Study of Literature.* London: Routledge & Kegan Paul; Ithaca, N.Y.: Cornell University Press, 1975.

Davis, Robert Con, and Ronald Schleifer, eds. *Rhetoric and Form: Deconstruction at Yale.* Norman: University of Oklahoma Press, 1985.

Denisoff, R. Serge. *Solid Gold: The Popular Record Industry.* New Brunswick, N.J.: Transaction Books, 1975.

Descombes, Vincent. *Modern French Philosophy.* Translated by L. Scott-Fox and J.M. Harding. Cambridge, England; New York: Cambridge University Press, 1980.

Dillon, Martin C. *Semiological Reductionism: A Critique of the Deconstructionist Movement in Postmodern Thought.* Albany: State University of New York Press, 1995.

Donoghue, Denis. *Ferocious Alphabets.* Boston: Little, Brown, 1981.

Dreyfus, Hubert L. and Paul Rabinow. *Michel Foucault, Beyond Structuralism and Hermeneutics,* 2d ed. With an afterword by and an interview with Michel Foucault. Chicago: University of Chicago Press, 1983 [1st ed., 1982].

Dyson, Freeman J. *Disturbing the Universe.* New York: Harper & Row, 1981 [1979].

Eagleton, Terry. *Literary Theory: An Introduction.* Oxford, England: Blackwell; Minneapolis: University of Minnesota Press, 1983.

Eco, Umberto, Richard Rorty, Johnathan Culler, and Christine Brooke-Rose. *Interpretation and Overinterpretation.* Edited by Stefan Collini. Cambridge, England; New York: Cambridge University Press, 1992.

Eisenstein, Hester. *Contemporary Feminist Thought.* London: Allen & Unwin; Boston: G.K. Hall, 1984 [1983].

Fekete, John, ed. *The Structural Allegory: Reconstructive Encounters with the New French Thought.* Minneapolis: University of Minnesota Press, 1984.

Felperin, Howard. *Beyond Deconstruction: The Uses and Abuses of Literary Theory.* Oxford, England: Clarendon Press; New York: Oxford University Press, 1986.

Ferguson, Russell, et al., eds., with a foreword by Marcia Tucker. *Discourses: Conversations in Postmodern Art and Culture.* New York: New Museum of Contemporary Art; Cambridge, Mass.: MIT Press, 1990.

Foster, Hal, ed. *The Anti-Aesthetic: Essays on Postmodern Culture.* Port Townsend, Wash.: Bay Press, 1983.

Freedman, Ralph. *Herman Hesse: Pilgrim of Crisis: A Biography.* New York: Pantheon Books, 1978.

Fullbrook, Kate and Edward Fullbrook. *Simone de Beauvoir and Jean-Paul Sartre: The Remaking of a Twentieth-Century Legend.* Brighton, England: Harvester Wheatsheaf, 1994.

Gablik, Suzi. *Has Modernism Failed?* New York: Thames & Hudson, 1984.

Gardner, Howard. *The Mind's New Science: A History of the Cognitive Revolution.* New York: Basic Books, 1985.

_____. *The Quest for Mind: Piaget, Levi-Strauss, and the Structuralist Movement*, 2d ed. Chicago: University of Chicago Press, 1981 [1st ed., 1972].

Garver, Newton, and Seung-Chong Lee. *Derrida & Wittgenstein*. Philadelphia: Temple University Press, 1994.

Genette, Gerard. *Figures of Literary Discourse*. Translated by Alan Sheridan. Introduction by Marie-Rose Logan. New York: Columbia University Press, 1982.

Giddens, Anthony. *The Consequences of Modernity*. Cambridge, England: Polity Press in association with Basil Blackwell; Oxford, England; Stanford, Calif.: Stanford University Press, 1990.

Gillett, Charlie. *The Sound of the City: The Rise of Rock and Roll*. Rev. ed. London: Souvenir, 1984.

Glucksmann, Miriam. *Structuralist Analysis in Contemporary Social Thought; A Comparison of the Theories of Claude Lévi-Strauss and Louis Althusser*. London; Boston: Routledge & Kegan Paul, 1974.

Graff, Gerald. *Literature against Itself: Literary Ideas in Modern Society*. With a new preface. Chicago: I. R. Dee, 1995..

Graham, Loren R. *Between Science and Values*. New York: Columbia University Press, 1981.

Greer, Germaine. *The Female Eunuch*. With a new foreword. London: Paladin, 1991.

Guilbaut, Serge. *How New York Stole the Idea of Modern Art: Abstract Expressionism, Freedom, and the Cold War*. Translated by Arthur Goldhammer. Chicago: University of Chicago Press, 1983.

Gutting, Gary, ed. *The Cambridge Companion to Foucault*. Cambridge, England; New York: Cambridge University Press, 1994.

Hagberg, Garry. *Art as Language: Wittgenstein, Meaning, and Aesthetic Theory*. Ithaca, N.Y.: Cornell University Press, 1995.

Harari, Josue V., ed. *Textual Strategies: Perspectives in Post-Structuralist Criticism*. Ithaca, N.Y.: Cornell University Press, 1979.

Harris, Wendell V., ed. *Beyond Poststructuralism: The Speculations of Theory and the Experience of Reading*. University Park: Pennsylvania State University Press, 1996.

Hartrich, Edwin. *The Fourth and Richest Reich*. New York: Macmillan, 1980.

Hassan, Ihab, and Sally Hassan, eds. *Innovation/Renovation: New Perspectives on the Humanities*. Madison: University of Wisconsin Press, 1983.

Hawkes, Terence. *Structuralism & Semiotics*. Berkeley: University of California Press, 1977.

Held, Barbara S. *Back to Reality: A Critique of Postmodern Theory in Psychotherapy*. New York: Norton, 1995.

Hernadi, Paul, ed. *The Horizon of Literature*. Lincoln: University of Nebraska Press, 1982.

Hollinger, Robert and David Depew, eds. *Pragmatism: From Progressivism to Postmodernism*. Westport, Conn.: Praeger, 1995.

Howells, Christina, ed. *Sartre*. London, New York: Longman, 1995.

Humm, Maggie, ed. *Practicing Feminist Criticism: An Introduction*. Brighton, England: Harvester Wheatsheaf, 1995.

Hunter, Sam, with sections on architecture by John Hacobus. *American Art of the Twentieth Century: Painting, Sculpture, Architecture.* New York: H. N. Abrams, 1973.

Jacoby, Russell. *Dogmatic Wisdom: How the Cultural Wars Divert Education and Distract America.* New York: Doubleday, 1994.

Jameson, Fredric. *The Political Unconscious: Narrative as a Socially Symbolic Act.* Ithaca, N.Y.: Cornell University Press, 1981.

Johnson, Barbara. *The Wake of Deconstruction.* Oxford, England; Cambridge, Mass.: Blackwell, 1994.

Judson, Horace Freeland. *The Eighth Day of Creation: Makers of the Revolution in Biology.* New York: Simon & Schuster, 1980.

Kaye, Howard L. *The Social Meaning of Modern Biology: From Social Darwinism to Sociobiology.* New Haven: Yale University Press, 1986.

Keohane, Nannerl O., Michelle Z. Rosaldo and Barbara C. Gelpi, eds. *Feminist Theory: A Critique of Ideology.* Chicago: University of Chicago Press, 1982.

Kramer, Hilton. *The Revenge of the Philistines: Art and Culture, 1972–1984.* London: Secker & Warburg, 1986.

Kramer, Lawrence. *Classical Music and Postmodern Knowledge.* Berkeley: University of California Press, 1995.

Kramer, Matthew H. *Legal Theory, Political Theory, and Deconstruction: Against Rhadamanthus.* Bloomington: Indiana University Press, 1991.

Krauss, Rosalind E. *The Originality of the Avant-Garde and Other Modernist Myths.* Cambridge, Mass.: MIT Press, 1986 [1985].

Kurzweil, Edith. *The Age of Structuralism: Levi-Strauss to Foucault.* New Brunswick, N.J.: Transaction, 1996 [1980].

LaCapra, Dominick. *A Preface to Sartre.* Ithaca, N.Y.: Cornell University Press, 1978.

Lavers, Annette. *Roland Barthes, Structuralism and After.* London: Methuen; Cambridge, Mass.: Harvard University Press, 1982.

Leach, Edmund Ronald. *Claude Lévi-Strauss.* Rev. ed. Chicago: University of Chicago Press, 1989.

Leitch, Vincent B. *Cultural Criticism, Literary Theory, Poststructuralism.* New York: Columbia University Press, 1992.

———. *Deconstructive Criticism: An Advanced Introduction.* New York: Columbia University Press, 1983.

Lemert, Charles C. and Garth Gillan. *Michel Foucault: Social Theory as Transgression.* New York: Columbia University Press, 1982.

Lentricchia, Frank. *Criticism and Social Change.* Chicago: University of Chicago Press, 1983.

———. *After the New Criticism.* London: Athlone; Chicago: University of Chicago Press, 1980.

Lévi-Strauss, Claude, and Didier Eribon. *Conversations with Claude Lévi-Strauss.* Translated by Paula Wissing. Chicago: University of Chicago Press, 1991.

Lipsitz, George. *Dangerous Crossroads: Popular Music, Postmodernism, and the Poetics of Place.* London, New York: Verso, 1994.

Lodge, David. *Working with Structuralism: Essays and Reviews of Nineteenth- and Twentieth-Century Literature.* Boston: Routledge & Kegan Paul, 1981.

Lovell, Terry, ed. *Feminist Cultural Studies.* 2 vols. Aldershot, England; Brookfield, Vt.: E. Elgar, 1995.

Lowe, Donald M. *History of Bourgeois Perception.* Chicago: University of Chicago Press, 1982.

Lyons, John. *Noam Chomsky.* Rev. ed. Harmondsworth, England; New York: Penguin, 1978.

Lyotard, Jean-François. *The Postmodern Condition: A Report on Knowledge.* Translated by Geoff Bennington and Brian Massumi, with a foreword by Fredric Jameson. Minneapolis: University of Minnesota Press, 1984.

Macey, David. *The Lives of Michel Foucault: A Biography.* New York: Pantheon, 1993.

Major-Poetzl, Pamela. *Michel Foucault's Archaeology of Western Culture: Toward a New Science of History.* Chapel Hill: University of North Carolina Press, 1983.

Martin, Bill. *Humanism and its Aftermath: The Shared Fate of Deconstruction and Politics.* Atlantic Highlands, N.J.: Humanities Press, 1995.

Matthews, Eric. *Twentieth-Century French Philosophy.* Oxford, England; New York: Oxford University Press, 1996.

Mayr, Ernst. *The Growth of Biological Thought: Diversity, Evolution, and Inheritance.* Cambridge, Mass.: Belknap Press of Harvard University Press, 1982.

Megill, Allan. *Prophets of Extremity: Nietzsche, Heidegger, Foucault, Derrida.* Berkeley: University of California Press, 1985.

Mileur, Jean-Pierre. *Literary Revisionism and the Burden of Modernity.* Berkeley: University of California Press, 1985.

Mirzoeff, Nicholas. *Bodyscape: Art, Modernity, and the Ideal Figure.* London; New York: Routledge, 1995.

Mitchell, W. J. Thomas, ed. *The Politics of Interpretation.* Chicago: University of Chicago Press, 1983.

Moxey, Keith P. F. *The Practice of Theory: Poststructuralism, Cultural Politics, and Art History.* Ithaca, N.Y.: Cornell University Press, 1994.

Norris, Christopher. *Deconstruction, Theory and Practice.* Rev. ed. London, New York: Routledge & Kegan Paul, 1991 [1982].

———. *The Deconstructive Turn: Essays in the Rhetoric of Philosophy.* London; New York: Methuen, 1984 [1983].

Norris, Christopher and Andrew Benjamin. *What is Deconstruction?* London: Academy Editions; New York: St. Martin's Press, 1988.

Otero, Carlos P., ed. *Noam Chomsky: Critical Assessments.* 2 vols. London; New York: Routledge, 1994.

Pace, David. *Claude Levi-Strauss, the Bearer of Ashes.* Boston: Routledge & Kegan Paul, 1983.

Poster, Mark. *Critical Theory and Poststructuralism: In Search of a Context.* Ithaca, N.Y.: Cornell University Press, 1989.

Rajchman, John. *Michel Foucault: The Freedom of Philosophy.* New York: Columbia University Press, 1985.

Ray, William. *Literary Meaning: From Phenomenology to Deconstruction.* Oxford, England: Blackwell, 1984.

Rifflet-Lemaire, Anika. *Jacques Lacan.* Translated by David Macey. London; New York: Routledge & Kegan Paul, 1979.

Rockwell, John. *All American Music: Composition in the Late Twentieth Century.* New York: Alfred A. Knopf, 1983.

Rosecrance, Richard N. *The Rise of the Trading State: Commerce and Conquest in the Modern World.* New York: Basic Books, 1986.

Royle, Nicholas. *After Derrida.* Manchester, England; New York: Manchester University Press, 1995.

Ryan, Michael. *Marxism and Deconstruction: A Critical Articulation.* Baltimore: Johns Hopkins University Press, 1982.

Sallis, John. *Double Truth.* Albany: State University of New York Press, 1995.

Scholes, Robert E. *Semiotics and Interpretation.* New Haven: Yale University Press, 1982.

————. *Structuralism in Literature; An Introduction.* New Haven: Yale University Press, 1974.

Selz, Peter Howard. *Art in Our Times: A Pictorial History, 1890-1980.* New York: H.N. Abrams, 1981.

Shapiro, Gary, ed. *After the Future: Postmodern Times and Places.* Albany: State University of New York Press, 1990.

Sheridan, Alan. *Michel Foucault: The Will to Truth.* London; New York: Tavistock, 1980.

Silverman, Hugh J. *Textualities: Between Hermeneutics and Deconstruction.* New York: Routledge, 1994.

Sim, Stuart. *Beyond Aesthetics: Confrontations with Poststructuralism and Postmodernism.* London, New York: Harvester Wheatsheaf, 1992.

Sinclair, Andrew. *Francis Bacon: His Life and Violent Times.* New York: Crown, 1993.

Skinner, Quentin, ed. *The Return of Grand Theory in the Human Sciences.* Cambridge, England; New York: Cambridge University Press, 1990.

Smith, Barry, ed. *European Philosophy and the American Academy.* La Salle, Ill.: Hegeler Institute, 1994.

Smith, Gregory Bruce. *Nietzsche, Heidegger, and the Transition to Postmodernity.* Chicago: University of Chicago Press, 1996.

Staten, Henry. *Wittgenstein and Derrida.* Oxford, England: Blackwell, 1985.

Stelzig, Eugene L. *Hermann Hesse's Fictions of the Self: Autobiography and the Confessional Imagination.* Princeton: Princeton University Press, 1988.

Sturrock, John, ed. *Structuralism and Since: From Lévi-Strauss to Derrida.* Oxford, England; New York: Oxford University Press, 1979.

Szondi, Peter. *Introduction to Literary Hermeneutics.* Translated by Martha Woodmansee. Cambridge, England; New York: Cambridge University Press, 1995.

Thiher, Allen. *Words in Reflection: Modern Language Theory and Postmodern Fiction.* Chicago: University of Chicago Press, 1984.

Tredell, Nicolas. *The Critical Decade: Culture in Crisis.* Manchester, England: Carcanet, 1993.

Turkle, Sherry. *The Second Self: Computers and the Human Spirit.* New York: Simon & Schuster, 1984.

Wallis, Brian, ed., with a foreword by Marcia Tucker. *Art after Modernism: Rethinking Representation.* Boston: D.R. Godine; New York: New Museum of Contemporary Art, 1984.

Weinstein, Michael A. *Culture/Flesh: Explorations of Postcivilized Modernity.* Lanham, Md.: Rowman & Littlefield, 1995.

Williams, Jeffrey, ed. *PC Wars: Politics and Theory in the Academy.* New York: Routledge, 1995.

Zavarzadeh, Masud, and Donald Morton. *Theory as Resistance: Politics and Culture after (Post)Structuralism.* New York: Guilford Press, 1994.

A Millennium and a Century End: A New Era Begins

Aruri, Naseer Hasan. *The Obstruction of Peace: The United States, Israel, and the Palestinians.* Monroe, Me.: Common Courage Press, 1995.

Barner-Barry, Carol, and Cynthia A. Hody. *The Politics of Change: The Transformation of the Former Soviet Union.* New York: St. Martin's Press, 1995.

Ben-Artzi Pelssof, Noa. *In the Name of Sorrow and Hope.* New York: Alfred A. Knopf, 1996.

Benvenisti, Meron, with a foreword by Thomas Friedman. *Intimate Enemies: Jews and Arabs in a Shared Land.* Berkeley: University of California Press, 1995.

Bowker, Mike, and Robin Brown, eds. *From Cold War to Collapse: Theory and World Politics in the 1980s.* Cambridge, England; New York: Cambridge University Press, 1993.

Boyer, Paul S. *When Time Shall Be No More: Prophecy Belief in Modern American Culture.* Cambridge, Mass.: Belknap Press of Harvard University Press, 1992.

Cimbala, Stephen J., and Sidney R. Waldman, eds. *Controlling and Ending Conflict: Issues before and after the Cold War.* New York: Greenwood Press, 1992.

Collins, Gail, and Dan Collins. *The Millennium Book: Your Essential All-Purpose Guide to the Year 2000.* New York: Doubleday, 1991.

Crotty, William. *Post–Cold War Policy: The International Context.* Chicago: Nelson-Hall, 1995.

Dunbabin, J. P. D. *International Relations Since 1945: A History in Two Volumes.* Vol. 2: *The Post-Imperial Age: The Great Powers and the Wider World.* London; New York: Longman, 1994.

Enloe, Cynthia H. *The Morning After: Sexual Politics at the End of the Cold War.* Berkeley: University of California Press, 1993.

Flamhaft, Ziva. *Israel on the Road to Peace: Accepting the Unacceptable.* Boulder, Colo.: Westview Press, 1996.

Fritsch-Bournazel, Renata. *Europe and German Unification.* New York: Berg, 1992.

Garthoff, Raymond L. *The Great Transition: American-Soviet Relations and the End of the Cold War.* Washington, D.C.: Brookings Institution, 1994.

Garton Ash, Timothy. *In Europe's Name: Germany and the Divided Continent.* New York: Vintage Books, 1994.

Gill, Graeme J. *The Collapse of a Single Party System: The Disintegration of the Communist Party of the Soviet Union.* Cambridge, England; New York: Cambridge University Press, 1994.

Glynn, Patrick. *Closing Pandora's Box: Arms Races, Arms Control, and the History of the Cold War.* New York: Basic Books, 1992.

Goscilo, Helena. *Dehexing Sex: Russian Womanhood During and after Glasnost.* Ann Arbor: University of Michigan Press, 1996.

Hamalainen, Pekka Kalevi. *Uniting Germany: Actions and Reactions.* Aldershot, England; Brookfield, Vt.: Dartmouth, 1994.

Hareven, Shulamith. *The Vocabulary of Peace: Life, Culture, and Politics in the Middle East.* San Francisco: Mercury House, 1995.

Hogan, Michael J. *The End of the Cold War: Its Meaning and Implications.* Cambridge, England; New York: Cambridge University Press, 1992.

James, Harold, and Marla Stone, eds. *When the Wall Came Down: Reactions to German Unification.* New York: Routledge, 1992.

Jones, Alun. *The New Germany: A Human Geography.* Chichester, England; New York: J. Wiley & Sons, 1994.

Kakonen, Jyrki, ed. *Changes in the Northern Hemisphere in the 1990s.* Tampere, Finland: Tampere Peace Research Institute, 1993.

Katz, David S., and Jonathan I. Israel, eds. *Sceptics, Millenarians, and Jews.* Leiden, the Netherlands; New York: E. J. Brill, 1990.

Kumar, Krishan and Stephen Bann, eds. *Utopias and the Millennium.* London: Reaktion Books, 1993.

Lebow, Richard Ned and Janice Gross Stein. *We All Lost the Cold War.* Princeton: Princeton University Press, 1994.

Lings, Martin. *The Eleventh Hour: The Spiritual Crisis of the Modern World in the Light of Tradition and Prophecy.* Cambridge, England: Quinta Essentia, 1987.

Meissner, William W. *Thy Kingdom Come: Psychoanalytic Perspectives on the Messiah and the Millennium.* Kansas City, Mo.: Sheed & Ward, 1995.

Menges, Constantine C., ed. *Transitions from Communism in Russia and Eastern Europe: Analysis and Perspectives.* Washington, D.C.: George Washington University, Program on Transitions to Democracy; Lanham, Md.: University Press of America, 1994.

Naylor, Thomas H. *The Cold War Legacy.* Lexington, Mass.: Lexington Books, 1991.

North, Gary. *Millennialism and Social Theory.* Tyler, Tex.: Institute for Christian Economics, 1990.

O'Brien, Conor Cruise. *On the Eve of the Millennium: The Future of Democracy Through an Age of Unreason.* New York: Free Press, 1995.

Perry, Mark. *A Fire in Zion: The Israeli-Palestinian Search for Peace.* New York: Morrow, 1994.

Redhead, Steve. *The End of the Century Party: Youth and Pop towards 2000.* With photographs by Kevin Cummins. Manchester, England; New York: Manchester University Press, 1990.

Robinson, Jeffrey. *The End of the American Century: Hidden Agendas of the Cold War.* London: Hutchinson, 1992.

Robinson, Neil. *Ideology and the Collapse of the Soviet System: A Critical History of Soviet Ideological Discourse.* Aldershot, England; Brookfield, Vt.: E. Elgar, 1995.

Rubin, Barry, Joseph Ginat, and Moshe Ma'oz, eds., with an introductory chapter by Ezer Weizman. *From War to Peace: Arab-Israeli Relations, 1973–1993.* New York: New York University Press, 1994.

Said, Edward W., with a preface by Christopher Hitchens. *Peace and its Discontents: Essays on Palestine in the Middle East Process.* New York: Vintage Books, 1996.

———. *The Politics of Dispossession: The Struggle for Palestinian Self-Determination, 1969–1994.* New York: Pantheon Books, 1994.

Schwartz, Hillel. *Century's End: A Cultural History of the Fin de Siècle—from the 990s through the 1990s.* New York: Doubleday, 1990.

Shane, Scott. *Dismantling Utopia: How Information Ended the Soviet Union.* Chicago: Ivan R. Dee, 1994.

Snow, Donald M. *The Shape of the Future: The Post-Cold War World.* 2d ed. Armonk, N.Y.: M. E. Sharpe, 1995.

St. Clair, Michael. *Millennarian Movements in Historical Context.* New York: Garland, 1992.

Steele, Jonathan. *Eternal Russia: Yeltsin, Gorbachev, and the Mirage of Democracy,* rev. and updated ed. London: Faber, 1995 [1994].

Stone, Jon R. *A Guide to the End of the World: Popular Eschatology in America.* New York: Garland, 1993.

Tolz, Vera, and Iain Elliot. *The Demise of the USSR: From Communism to Independence.* Basingstoke, England: Macmillan, 1995.

Turpin, Jennifer E. *Reinventing the Soviet Self: Media and Social Change in the Former Soviet Union.* Westport, Conn.: Praeger, 1995.

Verheyen, Dirk. *The German Question: A Cultural, Historical, and Geopolitical Exploration.* Boulder, Colo.: Westview Press, 1991.

Walker, Martin. *The Cold War: A History.* New York: H. Holt, 1995.

Watson, Alan. *The Germans: Who are they Now?,* 2d rev. ed. and updated. London: Mandarin, 1995.

INDEX

1. Monet, Claude. French. *La Gare Saint-Lazare*, 1877. Musée d'Orsay, Paris, France. *(Art Resource, N.Y.)*
2. Manet, Édouard. French. *Portrait d'Émile Zola*, 1868. Musée d'Orsay, Paris, France. *(Giraudon/Art Resource, N.Y.)*
3. Toulouse-Lautrec, Henri de. French. *Jardin De Paris, Jane Avril*, 1893. Musée Toulouse-Lautrec, Albi, France. *(Giraudon/Art Resource, N.Y.)*
4. Seurat, Georges. French. *The Circus*, 1891. Musée d'Orsay, Paris, France. *(Giraudon/Art Resource, N.Y.)*
5. Renoir, Auguste. French. *Le Moulin de la Galette*, 1876. Louvre, Paris, France. *(Giraudon/Art Resource, N.Y.)*
6. Gauguin, Paul. French. *Maternity*, c. 1899. Collection C. Vogel, New York. *(Giraudon/Art Resource, N.Y.)*
7. Gogh, Vincent van. Dutch. *Sunflowers*, 1888. National Gallery, London. *(Foto Marburg/Art Resource, N.Y.)*
8. Degas, Edgar. French. *The Tub*, 1886. Musée d'Orsay, Paris, France. *(Giraudon/Art Resource, N.Y.)*
9. Cézanne, Paul. French. *The Bathers*, 1879–82. Musée du Petit Palais, Paris, France. *(Giraudon/Art Resource, N.Y.)*
10. Matisse, Henri. French. *Nasturtiums with Dance II*, 1912. Pushkin Museum of Fine Arts, Moscow, Russia. *(Art Resource, N.Y.)*
11. Heckel, Erich. German. *Bathers at the Sea*, c. 1910. (Copyright ARS, N.Y.) Fundacion Coleccion. *(Scala/Art Resource, N.Y.)*
12. Picasso, Pablo. French. *The Three Women*, 1908. Pushkin Museum of Fine Arts, Moscow, Russia. *(Foto Marburg/Art Resource, N.Y.)*
13. Duchamp, Marcel. French. *Nude Descending the Stairs, number 2*, 1912. Philadelphia Museum of Art, Louise and Walter Arenberg Collection. *(Photographer: Graydon Wood)*
14. Braque, Georges. French. *Man with a Guitar*, 1911–12. Museum of Modern Art, N.Y. Acquired through the Lillie P. Bliss Bequest. *(Photograph © 1997 Museum of Modern Art, N.Y.)*
15. Gris, Juan. Spanish. *Composition on a Table*, 1916. Collection Gerard Bonnier, Stockholm, Sweden. *(Giraudon/Art Resource, N.Y.)*
16. Gleizes, Albert. French. *Portrait of Stravinsky*, 1914. Collection Fregerico, Paris, France. *(Art Resource, N.Y.)*
17. Weber, Max. American. *Chinese Restaurant*, 1915. Collection of Whitney Museum of American Art, N.Y.
18. Delaunay, Robert. French. *The Eiffel Tower*, 1910–12. Kunstmuseum, Basel, Switzerland. *(Giraudon/Art Resource, N.Y.)*
19. Kandinsky, Wassily. Russian. *Black Lines*, December 1913. Solomon R. Guggenheim Museum, N.Y. *(Photograph: Robert E. Mates © Solomon R. Guggenheim Foundation, N.Y.)*
20. Marin, John. American. *Lower Manhattan (Composition Derived from Top of Woolworth Building)*, 1922. Museum of Modern Art, N.Y. Acquired through the Lillie P. Bliss Bequest. *(Photograph © 1997 Museum of Modern Art, N.Y.)*
21. Kupka, Frank. French. *Disks of Newton*, Study for Fugue, 1912. Philadelphia Museum of Art: Louise and Walter Arensberg Collection. *(Photograph by Graydon Wood)*
22. MacDonald-Wright, Stanton. American. *"Conception" Synchromy*, 1915. Collection of Whitney Museum of American Art, N.Y. Gift of George F. Of.
23. Severini, Gino. Italian. *Bicycle in the Sun*. Paris, France. *(Giraudon/Art Resource, N.Y.)*

24. Stella, Joseph. American. *Battle of Lights*, Coney Island, Mardi Gras, 1922. Yale University Art Gallery. Dorothea Dreier from the artist; gift of her estate to the Société Anonyme.

25. Lewis, Percy Wyndham. English. *Workshop*, c. 1914–15. *(Tate Gallery, London/Art Resource, N.Y.)*

26. Balla, Giacomo. Italian. *Abstrat Speed—The Car Has Passed*, 1913. *(Tate Gallery, London/Art Resource, N.Y.)*

27. Kandinsky, Wassily. Russian. *Orange*, 1923. Museum of Modern Art, N.Y. Abby Aldrich Rockefeller Fund. *(Photograph © 1997 Museum of Modern Art, N.Y.)*

28. Mondrian, Piet. Dutch. *Tableau II*, 1921–1925. *(Giraudon/Art Resource, N.Y.; © Mondrian Estate/Holtzman Trust)*

29. Malevich, Kasimir. Russian. *Dynamic Suprematism*, 1915 or 1916. *(Tate Gallery, London/Art Resource, N.Y.).*

30. Léger, Fernand. French. *Woman in an Interior*, 1922. Musée National d'Art Moderne, Paris, France. *(Giraudon/Art Resource, N.Y.)*

31. Schiele, Egon. Austrian. *Self-Portrait Masturbating*, 1911. Private collection. *(Bridgemann/Art Resource, N.Y.)*

32. Munch, Edvard. Norwegian. *Madonna*, 1893–94. National Gallery, Oslo, Norway. *(Scala/Art Resource, N.Y.)*

33. Beardsley, Aubrey. English. *"The Climax," llustration for Oscar Wilde's Salome*, 1893. Victoria and Albert Museum, London, England. *(Victoria & Albert Museum, London/Art Resource, N.Y.)*

34. Klimt, Gustav. Austrian. *The Kiss*, 1907–8. *(Courtesy Galerie St. Etienne, N.Y./Österreichische Galerie, Vienna)*

35. Brancusi, Constantin. French-Romanian. *Young Bird*, 1928. Museum of Modern Art, N.Y. Gift of Mr. and Mrs. William A. M. Burden. *(Photograph © 1997 Museum of Modern Art, N.Y.)*

36. Gabo, Naum. Russian. *Head No. 2*, 1916 (enlarged version, 1964). *(Tate Gallery, London/Art Resource, N.Y.)*

37. Lipchitz, Jacques. French-American. *Figure*, 1926–30. Museum of Modern Art, N.Y. Van Gogh Purchase Fund. *(Photograph © 1997 Museum of Modern Art, N.Y.)*

38. Giacometti, Alberto. Swiss. *The Couple*, 1926–27. Foundation A. Giacometti, Basel, Switzerland. *(Giraudon/Art Resource, N.Y.)*

39. Duchamp, Marcel. French. *The Large Glass: Bride Stripped Bare by Her Bachelors*, c. 1915–23. Philadelphia Museum of Art. Bequest of Katherine S. Dreier.

40. Schamberg, Morton Livingston. American. *Machine*, 1916. Yale University Art Gallery. Gift of Collection Société Anonyme.

41. Picabia, Francis. French. *Içi, Ç'est Içi Stieglitz*, 1915. Metropolitan Museum of Art, Alfred Stieglitz Collection, 1949.

42. Dove, Arthur. American. *Distraction*, 1929. Collection of Whitney Museum of American Art, N.Y. Gift of an anonymous donor.

43. Demuth, Charles. American. *My Egypt*, 1927. Collection of Whitney Museum of American Art, N.Y. Purchased with funds from Gertrude Vanderbilt Whitney.

44. O'Keeffe, Georgia. American. *Black Iris*, 1929. Metropolitan Museum of Art, Alfred Stieglitz Collection, 1949.

45. Gropius, Walter. German. Bauhaus, Dessau, Germany, 1925–26. *(Giraudon/Art Resource, N.Y.)*

46. Gaudí, Antoní. Spanish. View of Sagrada Familia Church, Barcelona, Spain (detail of a wall), 1883–1926. *(Foto Marburg/Art Resource, N.Y.)*

47. Wright, Frank Lloyd. American. Fallingwater, Bear Run, Pennsylvania, Western Pennsylvania Conservancy, 1936. *(Art Resource, N.Y.)*

48. Le Corbusier, French. Chapelle Nôtre-Dame-du-Haut (view from northeast), 1955. Ronchamp, France. *(Copyright ARS; Foto Marburg/Art Resource, N.Y.)*
49. Mackintosh, Charles Rennie. Scots. Wall in a Scottish Interior, 1890–1910. *(Foto Marburg/Art Resource, N.Y.)*
50. Klee, Paul. Swiss. *Der Verliebte*, 1923. *(Foto Marburg/Art Resource, N.Y.)*
51. Ernst, Max. German. *Men Shall Know Nothing of This*, 1923. *(Tate Gallery, London/Art Resource, N.Y.)*
52. Beckmann, Max. German. *Departure*, 1923–33. Museum of Modern Art, N.Y. Given anonymously. *(Photograph © 1997 Museum of Modern Art, N.Y.)*
53. DeChirico, Giorgio. Italian. *The Disquieting Muse*, 1925. Private collection, Milan, Italy. *(Art Resource, N.Y.)*
54. Delvaux, Paul. French. *Phases of the Moon (Les Phases de la lune)*, 1939. Museum of Modern Art, New York. Purchase. *(Photograph © 1997 Museum of Modern Art, N.Y.)*
55. Man Ray. American. *The Violin of Ingres*, 1924. Private collection, Paris, France. *(Photograph © copyright ARS, N.Y.; Giraudon/Art Resource, N.Y.)*
56. Moore, Henry. English. *Recumbent Figure*, 1938. *(Tate Gallery, London/Art Resource, N.Y.; reproduced by permission of the Henry Moore Foundation)*
57. Matta-Echaurren, Roberto. Chilean. *Here, Sir. Fire, Eat!* 1942. Museum of Modern Art, N.Y. James Thrall Soby Bequest. *(Photograph © 1997, Museum of Modern Art, N.Y.)*
58. Gorky, Arshile. American. *Diary of a Seducer*, 1945. Museum of Modern Art, N.Y. Gift of Mr. and Mrs. William A. M. Burden. *(Photograph © 1997 Museum of Modern Art, N.Y.)*
59. Miró, Juan. Spanish. *Composition*, 1933. National Gallery, Prague, Czech Republic. *(Giraudon/Art Resource, N.Y.; © Artist Rights Society [ARS], N.Y./ADAGP, Paris)*
60. Calder, Alexander. American. *Mobile*, 1936(?). Solomon R. Guggenheim Museum, New York. Collection Mary Reynolds, gift of her brother, 1954. *(Photograph by Robert E. Mates © Solomon R. Guggenheim Foundation, N.Y.)*
61. Pollock, Jackson. American. *Birth*, 1938–41. *(Tate Gallery, London/Art Resource, N.Y.; © 1997 Pollock-Krasner Foundation/Artist Rights Society [ARS], N.Y.)*
62. Lam, Wilfredo. Cuban. *The Jungle*, 1943. Museum of Modern Art, N.Y. Inter-American fund. *(Photograph © 1997 Museum of Modern Art, N.Y.)*
63. Orozco, Jose Clemente. Mexican. *The Phantoms of Religions in Alliance with Militarism*, 1937. Palacio de Gobierno, Guadalajara, Jalisco, Mexico. *(Schalkwijk/Art Resource, N.Y.)*
64. Siqueiros, David Alfaro. Mexican. *The Echo of a Scream*, 1937. Museum of Modern Art, N.Y. Gift of Edward M. M. Warburg. *(Photograph © 1997 Museum of Modern Art, N.Y.)*
65. de Kooning, Willem. American. *Woman I*, 1950–52. Museum of Modern Art, N.Y. Purchase. *(Photograph © 1997 Museum of Modern Art, New York)*
66. Dubuffet, Jean. French. *Woman with Folded Arms*, 1946. Museum of Modern Art, N.Y. Helen Acheson Bequest. *(Photograph © 1997 Museum of Modern Art, N.Y.)*
67. Picasso, Pablo. Spanish. *Weeping Woman*, 1937. *(Tate Gallery, London/Art Resource, N.Y.; © 1997 Estate of Pablo Picasso/Artist Rights Society [ARS], N.Y.)*
68. Bacon, Francis. English. *Three Studies for Figures at the Base of a Crucifixion* (detail), 1944. *(Tate Gallery, London/Art Resource, N.Y.)*
69. Krasner, Lee. American. *Gothic Landscape*, 1961. *(Tate Gallery, London/Art Resource, N.Y.; © 1997 Pollock-Krasner Foundation/Artist Rights Society [ARS], N.Y.)*
70. Hoffman, Hans. German. *Spring*, 1944–45, dated 1940. Museum of Modern Art, N.Y. Gift of Mr. & Mrs. Peter Rubel. *(Photograph © 1997 Museum of Modern Art, N.Y.)*
71. Pollock, Jackson. American. *One Number 31*, 1950. Museum of Modern Art, N.Y. Sidney and Harriet Janis Collection Fund (by exchange). (Photograph © 1996 Museum of Modern Art, N.Y.)

72. Newman, Barnett. American. *Onement III*, 1949. Museum of Modern Art, N.Y. Gift of Mr. & Mrs. Joseph Slifka.

73. Rothko, Mark. American. *Untitled*, 1951–55. *(Tate Gallery, London/Art Resource, N.Y.; © 1997 Kate Rothko-Prizel & Christopher Rothko/Artist Rights Society [ARS], N.Y)*

74. Gottlieb, Adolph. American. *Orange on Red*, 1965. *(Art Resource, N.Y.; © 1997 Adolph and Esther Gottlieb Foundation/licensed by VAGA, New York, N.Y.)*

75. Noguchi, Isamu. Japanese-American. *The Stone of Spiritual Understanding*, 1962. Museum of Modern Art, New York, gift of the artist. *(Photograph © 1997 Museum of Modern Art, N.Y.)*

76. Lichtenstein, Roy. American. *Whaam!* *(© Roy Lichtenstein; Tate Gallery, London/Art Resource, N.Y.)*

77. Warhol, Andy. American. *Marilyn Diptych*, 1962. *(Tate Gallery, London/Art Resource, N.Y. © 1997 Andy Warhol Foundation for the Visual Arts/Artist Rights Society [ARS], N.Y.)*

78. Rauschenberg, Robert. American. *Tracer*, 1964. Private collection, Altoona, Pa. *(Giraudon/Art Resource, N.Y.; licensed by VAGA, N.Y.)*

79. Johns, Jasper. American. *Flag on Orange Field*, 1957. Cologne, Germany, Museum Wallraf-Richartz/Ludwig. *(Giraudon/Art Resource, N.Y.; licensed by VAGA, N.Y.)*

80. Stella, Frank. American. *Empress of India I, V series*, 1968. Private collection. *(Art Resource, N.Y.; © 1997 Frank Stella/Artist Rights Society [ARS], N.Y.)*

81. Hesse, Eva. American. *Expanded Expansion*, 1969. Solomon R. Guggenheim Museum, New York, Gift, Family of Eva Hesse, 1975. *(Photograph by David Heald © Solomon R. Guggenheim Foundation, New York)*

82. Claes Oldenburg. American. *The Clothespin*, Philadelphia, Pennsylvania, 1976. *(Scala/Art Resource, N.Y.)*

83. Andre, Carl. American. *144 Lead Square*, 1969. Museum of Modern Art, N.Y. Advisory Committee Fund. *(Photograph © 1997 Museum of Modern Art, N.Y.)*

84. LeWitt, Sol. American. *Two Open Modular Cubes, Half-Off*, 1972. *(Tate Gallery, London/Art Resource, N.Y.; © 1997 Sol LeWitt/Artist Rights Society [ARS], N.Y.)*

85. Baldessari, John. American. *Ashputtle*, 1982. Whitney Museum of American Art, N.Y. Purchase with funds from the Painting and Sculpture Committee. *(Photograph by Geoffrey Clements; copyright © 1996 Whitney Museum of American Art, N.Y.)*

86. Sherman, Cindy. American. *Untitled*, 1979. *(Courtesy of the artist and Metro Pictures)*

87. Acconci, Vito. American. *Blindfolded Catching*, 1970. *(Courtesy Barbara Gladstone Gallery)*

88. Prince, Richard. American. *Untitled (Cowboys)*, 1987. *(Courtesy Barbara Gladstone Gallery)*

89. Basquiat, Jean-Michel. American. *In the Cipher*, 1982. *(Courtesy Tony Shafrazi Gallery)*

90. Schnabel, Julian. American. *Exile*, 1980. *(Photograph courtesy PaceWildenstein Gallery)*

91. Baselitz, Georg. German. *Beautiful Portrait #5*, 1988. *(Courtesy Michael Werner Gallery, New York and Cologne)*

92. Clemente, Francesco. Italian. *The Black Paintings*, 1993. *(Courtesy Gagosian Gallery)*

93. Kiefer, Anselm. German. *Sternhimmel*, 1995. *(Photograph by Ann and Tom Abbott; courtesy Marian Goodman Gallery, N.Y.)*

94. Mapplethorpe, Robert. America. *Ajitto*, 1981. *(Copyright © 1981 Estate of Robert Mapplethorpe/A & C Anthology)*

95. Coplans, John. American. *Self-Portrait: Feet Frontal*, 1984. *(Tate Gallery, London/Art Resource, N.Y.)*

96. Viola, Bill. American. *Nantes Triptych*, 1992. *(Tate Gallery, London/Art Resource, N.Y.)*

97. Witkin, Joel-Peter. American. *The Wife of Cain*, 1981. *(Courtesy of the artist and Pace/MacGill Gallery)*

98. Smith, Kiki. American. *Lilith*, 1994. Collection of Metropolitan Museum of Art. *(Photograph courtesy of PaceWildenstein Gallery)*

99. Murray, Elizabeth. American. *Careless Love*, 1995–96. *(Photograph by Ellen Page Wilson; courtesy of PaceWildenstein Gallery)*

100. Osorio, Pepon. Puerto Rican. *La Cama (The Bed)*, 1987. El Museo del Barrio, N.Y.

101. Puryear, Martin. American. *Sanctum*, 1985. Whitney Museum of American Art, N.Y. Purchased with Funds from the Painting and Sculpture Committee. *(Photograph by Geoffrey Clements; copyright © 1996 Whitney Museum of American Art, N.Y.)*

102. Gonzalez-Torres, Felix. Cuban-American. *Public Opinion*, 1991. Solomon R. Guggenheim Museum, N.Y. *(Photograph by Lee B. Ewing © Solomon R. Guggenheim Foundation, N.Y.)*

103. Hirst, Damien. British. *No Sense of Absolute Corruption*, 1996. *(Courtesy Gagosian Gallery)*

104. Nauman, Bruce. American. *Model for Animal Pyramid II*, 1989. Museum of Modern Art, N.Y. Gift of Agnes Gund and Ronald S. Lauder. *(Photograph © 1997 The Museum of Modern Art, N.Y.)*

105. Beuys, Joseph. German. *Terremoto*, 1981. Solomon R. Guggenheim Museum, N.Y. *(Photograph by David Heald; © Solomon R. Guggenheim Foundation, N.Y.)*

106. Holzer, Jenny. American. *Laments* (installation at Dia Art Foundation), 1989–90. *(Photograph by Bill Jacobson Studio, N.Y.; courtesy Dia Art Foundation)*

107. Kruger, Barbara. American. *"Untitled" (It's Our Pleasure to Disgust You)*, 1991. *(Courtesy Mary Boone Gallery)*

108. Appelbroog, Ida. American. *Baby, Baby, Suck Your Thumb*, 1994. *(Photograph by Dennis Cowley; courtesy Ronald Feldman Fine Arts, N.Y.)*

109. Sculpture group *(clockwise)*: Richard Serra, Robert Rauschenberg, Chris Burden, Walter De Maria. American. 1995. *(Courtesy Gagosian Gallery)*

110. Mark di Suvero. American. *New Sculpture*, 1995. *(Courtesy Gagosian Gallery)*

111. Pei, I. M. American. Rock and Roll Hall of Fame and Museum, 1994, Cleveland, Ohio. *(Photograph by Timothy Hursley; courtesy Pei, Cobb, Freed, and Partners)*

112. Johnson, Philip. American. Gate House, New Canaan, Connecticut. (entrance to Philip Johnson's estate), 1996. *(Photograph: Michael Moran; courtesy Philip Johnson)*

113. Graves, Michael. American. Humana Building, Louisville, Kentucky (view from Main Street), 1985. *(Photograph: Taylor Photographics; courtesy Michael Graves)*